SOMETHING NASTY

I reached over and curled my fingers around the sword. I touched the door, spreading the fingers of my right hand against smooth iron. My rings rang and vacillated, reading the flow of whatever was behind the door.

Oh, gods above and below, I thought. *Whatever it is, it's big.*

I unlocked the door and stepped back, my sword half-drawn. The door creaked slowly open.

Standing on my front step was a tall, spare, golden-skinned man dressed in black jeans and a long, black, Chinese-collared coat. The bright silver gun he held level to my chest was only slightly less disconcerting than the fact that his aura was cloaked in twisting black-diamond flames. He had dark hair cut short and laser-green eyes.

Great. A demon on my doorstep, I thought, and didn't move. I barely even *breathed.*

"Danny Valentine?" he asked.

Praise for *Dante Valentine*

"She's a brave, charismatic protagonist with a smart mouth and a suicidal streak. What's not to love? Fans of Laurell K. Hamilton should warm to Saintcrow's dark evocative debut."

— *Publishers Weekly*

"Saintcrow's amazing protagonist is gutsy, stubborn to a fault and vaguely suicidal, meaning there's never a dull moment... This is the ultimate in urban fantasy!"

— *Romantic Times* (Top Pick)

"The characters are rich in detail and the story line continues on its own unique path of magical death and destruction."

— http://darquereviews.blogspot.com

"Hands down, one of the best series I have ever read."

— blogcritics.org

"This hard-hitting urban fantasy will keep you on the edge of your seat and the conclusion delivers a shocker that will both stun and please."

— Freshfiction.com

"Without a doubt, Lilith Saintcrow has penned a fabulous, unforgettable story that will have readers lining up to buy her previous releases and waiting with bated breath for her next book in this outstanding new series."

— Curledup.com

"Dark, gritty, urban fantasy at its best."

— blogcritics.org

Books by Lilith Saintcrow

Dante Valentine (Omnibus)

Jill Kismet Novels

Night Shift
Hunter's Prayer
Redemption Alley
Flesh Circus
Heaven's Spite
Angel Town

Dark Watcher
Storm Watcher
Fire Watcher
Cloud Watcher
The Society
Hunter, Healer
Mindhealer

Steelflower

DANTE VALENTINE

THE COMPLETE SERIES

LILITH SAINTCROW

www.orbitbooks.net

Compilation Copyright © 2011 by Lilith Saintcrow
Working for the Devil Copyright © 2005 by Lilith Saintcrow
Dead Man Rising Copyright © 2006 by Lilith Saintcrow
The Devil's Right Hand Copyright © 2007 by Lilith Saintcrow
Saint City Sinners Copyright © 2007 by Lilith Saintcrow
To Hell and Back Copyright © 2008 by Lilith Saintcrow
Excerpt from *Night Shift* Copyright © 2008 by Lilith Saintcrow

Orbit
Hachette Book Group
237 Park Avenue, New York, NY 10017
www.HachetteBookGroup.com

First Compilation Edition: March 2011

Orbit is an imprint of Hachette Book Group, Inc.
The Orbit name and logo are trademarks of Little, Brown Book Group Limited.

The publisher is not responsible for websites (or their content) that are not owned by the publisher.

Library of Congress Control Number: 2010937413
ISBN 978-0-316-10196-7

10 9 8 7 6 5 4 3 2 1

Printed in the United States of America

To Miriam and Devi, because they believed.

Contents

Book 1

Working for the Devil

To L.I.
I keep my bargains.

Nel mezzo del cammin di nostra vita
    mi ritrovai per una selva oscura,
    che la diritta via era smarrita.
    —Dante

    Hell hath no limits, nor is circumscribed
    In one self place, for where we are is hell,
    And where hell is must we ever be.
    —Mephistopheles, by way of Marlowe

CHAPTER 1

My working relationship with Lucifer began on a rainy Monday. I'd just settled down to a long afternoon of watching the holovid soaps and doing a little divination, spreading the cards and runes out on the hank of blue silk I'd laid out, when there was a bashing on my door that shook the walls.

I turned over a card, my lacquered fingernails scraping. The amber ring on my left middle finger sparked. The Devil card pulsed, landing atop a pile of flat runestones. I hadn't touched it. The card I turned over was blank.

"Interesting," I said, gooseflesh rippling up my back. Then I hauled myself up off the red threadbare carpet and padded barefoot out into the hallway. My rings flashed, a drift of green sparks snapping and popping down my fingers. I shook them off, frowning.

The lines of Power wedded to my front door twirled uneasily. Something nasty was on my front step. I hitched up my jeans, then reached over and curled my fingers around the sword hanging on the wall. I lifted it down, chucked the blade free with my thumb against the guard.

The peephole in the middle of the door was black, no light spilling through. I didn't bother looking. Instead, I touched the door, spreading the fingers of my right hand against smooth iron. My rings rang and vacillated, reading the flow of whatever was behind the door.

Oh, gods above and below, I thought. *Whatever it is, it's big.*

Bracing myself for murder or a new job, I unlocked the door and stepped back, my sword half-drawn. The blue glow from Power-drenched steel lit up my front hall, glimmering against the white paint and the full-length mirror hung next to my coatrack. I waited.

The door creaked slowly open. *Let's have some mood music for effect,* I thought sardonically, and prepared to sell myself dear if it was murder.

I can draw my sword in a little under a second and a half. Thankfully, there was no need to. I blinked.

Standing on my front step was a tall, spare, golden-skinned man dressed in black jeans and a long, black, Chinese-collared coat. The bright silver gun he held level to my chest was only slightly less disconcerting than the fact that his aura was cloaked in twisting black-diamond flames. He had dark hair cut short and laser-green eyes, a forgettable face and dreamy wide shoulders.

Great. A demon on my doorstep, I thought, and didn't move. I barely even *breathed.*

"Danny Valentine?" he asked. Well, demanded, actually.

"Who wants to know?" I shot back, automatically. The silvery gun didn't look like a plasgun, it looked like an old-fashioned 9mm.

"I wish to speak with Danny Valentine," the demon enunciated clearly, "or I will kill you."

"Come on in," I said. "And put that thing away. Didn't your mother ever teach you it was bad manners to wave a gun at a woman?"

"Who knows what a Necromance has guarding his door?" the demon replied. "Where is Danny Valentine?"

I heaved a mental sigh. "Come on in off my front porch," I said. "*I'm* Danny Valentine, and you're being really rude. If you're going to try to kill me, get it over with. If you want to hire me, this is *so* the wrong way to go about it."

I don't think I've ever seen a demon look nonplussed before. He holstered his gun and stepped into my front hall, peeling through the layers of my warding, which parted obediently to let him through. When he stood in front of me, kicking the door shut with one booted foot, I had him calculated down to the last erg of Power.

This is not going to be fun, I thought. *What is a Lord of Hell doing on my doorstep?*

Well, no time like the present to ask. "What's a Lord of Hell doing on my doorstep?" I asked.

"I have come to offer you a contract," he said. "Or more precisely, to invite you to audience with the Prince, where he will present you with a contract. Fulfill this contract successfully, and you will be allowed to live with riches beyond your wildest dreams." It didn't sound like a rote speech.

I nodded. "And if I said I wasn't interested?" I asked. "You know, I'm a busy girl. Raising the dead for a living is a high-demand skill nowadays."

The demon regarded me for maybe twenty seconds before he grinned, and a cold sweat broke out all over my body. My nape prickled and my fingers twitched. The three wide scars on my back twitched uneasily.

"Okay," I said. "Let me get my things, and I'll be happy to attend His Gracious Princeship, yadda-yadda, bing-bong. Capice?"

He looked only slightly less amused, his thin grim face lit with a murderous smile. "Of course. You have twenty minutes."

If I'd known what I was getting into, I would have asked for a few days. Like maybe the rest of my life.

CHAPTER 2

The demon spent those twenty minutes in my living room, examining my bookshelves. At least, he appeared to be looking at the books when I came downstairs, shrugging my coat on. Abracadabra once called me "the Indiana Jones of the necromantic world," high praise from the Spider of Saint City—if she meant it kindly. I liked to dress for just about any occasion.

So my working outfit consists of: a Trade Bargains microfiber shirt, dries quickly and sheds dirt with a simple brush-off; a pair of butter-soft broken-in jeans; scuffed engineer boots with worn heels; my messenger bag strapped diagonally across my torso; and an old explorer coat made for photojournalists in war zones, with plenty of pockets and Kevlar panels sewn in. I finished braiding my hair and tied it off with an elastic band as I stepped into the living room, now full of the smell of man and cologne as well as the entirely nonphysical smell of demon—a cross between burning cinnamon and heavy amber musk. "My literary collection seems to please you," I said, maybe a little sardonically. My palms were sweating. My teeth wanted to chatter. "I don't suppose you could give me any idea of what your Prince wants with me."

He turned away from my bookshelves and shrugged. Demons shrug a lot. I suppose they think a lot of what humans do deserves nothing more than a shrug. "Great," I muttered, and scooped up my athame and the little jar of blessed water from my fieldstone altar. My back prickled with fresh waves of gooseflesh. *There's a demon in my living room. He's behind me. I have a demon behind me. Dammit, Danny, focus!*

"It's a little rude to bring blessed items before the Prince," the demon told me.

I snorted. "It's a little rude to point a gun in my face if you want me to work for you." I passed my hand over my altar—no, nothing else. I crossed to the big oak armoire and started flipping through the drawers. *I wish my hands would stop shaking.*

"The Prince specifically requested you, and sent me to collect you. He said nothing about the finer points of *human* etiquette." The demon regarded me with laser-green eyes. "There is some urgency attached to this situation."

"Mmmh." I waved a sweating, shaking hand over my shoulder. "Yeah. And if I walk out that door half-prepared I'm not going to do your Prince any good, am I?"

"You reek of fear," he said quietly.

"Well, I just had a gun shoved in my face by a Lord of Hell. I don't think you're the average imp-class demon that I very rarely deal with, boyo. And you're telling me that the Devil wants my company." I dug in the third drawer down and extracted my turquoise necklace, slipped it over my head, and dropped it down my shirt. *At least I sound good,* I thought, the lunatic urge to laugh rising up under my breastbone. *I don't sound like I'm shitting my pants with fright. Goody for me.*

"The Prince wishes you for an audience," he said.

I guess the Prince of Hell doesn't like to be called the Devil. On any other day I might have found that funny. "So what do I call you?" I asked, casually enough.

"You may address me as Jaf," he answered after a long crackling pause.

Shit, I thought. If he'd given me his Name I could have maybe used it. "Jaf," however, might have been a joke or a nickname. Demons were tricky. "Nice to meet you, Jaf," I said. "So how did you get stuck with messenger duty?"

"This is a sensitive situation." He sounded just like a politician. I slipped the stiletto up my sleeve into its sheath, and turned to find him watching me. "Discretion would be wise."

"I'm good at discretion," I told him, settling my bag so that it hung right.

"You should practice more," he replied, straight-faced.

I shrugged. "I suppose we're not stopping for drinks on the way."

"You are already late."

It was like talking to a robot. I wished I'd studied more about demons at the Academy. It wasn't like them to carry guns. I racked my brains, trying to think of any armed demon I'd heard of.

None sprang to mind. Of course, I was no Magi, I had no truck with demons. Only the dead.

I carried my sword into the front hall and waited for him. "You go out first," I said. "I've got to close up the house."

He nodded and brushed past me. The smell of demon washed over me—it would start to dye the air in a confined space, the psychic equivalent of static. I followed him out my front door, snapping my house shields closed out of long habit, the Power shifting and closing like an airlock in an old B movie. Rain flashed and jittered down, smashed into the porch roof and the paved walk. The garden bowed and nodded under the water.

I followed the demon down my front walk. The rain didn't touch him—then again, how would I have noticed, his hair was so dark it looked wet anyway. And his long, dark, high-collared coat, too. My boots made a wet shushing sound against the pavement. I thought about dashing back for the dubious safety of my house.

The demon glanced over his shoulder, a flash of green eyes in the rain. "Follow me," he said.

"Like I have another option?" I spread my hands a little, indicating the rain. "If you don't mind, it's awful wet out here. I'd hate to catch pneumonia and sneeze all over His Majesty."

He set off down my street. I glanced around. No visible car. Was I expected to walk to Hell?

The demon walked up to the end of the block and turned left, letting me trot behind him. Apparently I *was* expected to hoof it.

Great.

CHAPTER 3

Carrying a sword on the subway does tend to give you a certain amount of space, even on crowded hovertrains. I'm an accredited and tattooed Necromance, capable of carrying anything short of an assault rifle on the streets and allowed edged metal in transports. Spending the thirty thousand credits for testing and accreditation at the Academy had been the best step I'd ever taken for personal safety.

Although passing the final Test had turned a few of my hairs white. There weren't many accredited Necromances around.

The demon also granted me a fair amount of space. Although none of the normals could really tell what he was, they still gave him a wide berth. Normals can't see psychic power and energy shifts, but they *feel* it if it's strong enough, like a cold draft.

As soon as we started down the steps into the underground, Jaf dropped back until he was walking right next to me, indicating which stile to walk through and dropping two old-fashioned tokens in. I suppressed the shiver that caused—demons didn't usually pay for anything. What the bloody blue blazes was going on?

We got on the southbound train, the press of the crowd soft and choking against my mental borders. My knuckles were white, my fingers rigid around the scabbard. The demon stood slightly behind me, my back prickling with the thought—*he could slip a knife between my ribs and leave me here, gods protect me.* The whine of antigrav settled into my back teeth as the retrofitted train slid forward on its reactive-greased rails, the antigrav giving every bump a queer floating sensation.

Whispers and mutters filled the car. One little blonde girl in a school uniform stared at my face. She was probably examining the tattoo on my left cheek, a twisted caduceus with a flashing emerald set at the top. An emerald was the mark of a Necromance—as if anyone could have missed the sword. I smiled at her and she smiled back, her blue eyes twinkling. Her whey-faced mother, loaded down with shopping bags, saw this and gasped, hugging her child into her side a little harder than was absolutely necessary.

The smile dropped from my face.

The demon bumped me as the train bulleted around a bend. I jumped nervously, would have sidled away if the crowd had allowed. As it was, I accidentally elbowed an older woman with a crackling plastic bag, who let out an undignified squeak.

This is why I never take public transportation, I thought, and smiled an apology. The woman turned pale under her gray coif, coughed, and looked away.

I sighed, the smile again falling from my face. *I don't know why I even try. They don't see anything but my tat anyway.*

Normals feared psions regardless—there was an atavistic fear that we were all reading normal minds and laughing at them, preparing some nefarious plot to make them our mental slaves. The tats and accreditation were supposed to defray that by making psions visible and instituting tight controls over who could charge for psychic services—but all it did was make us more vulnerable to hatred. Normals didn't understand that for us, dipping into their brains was like taking a bath in a sewer. It took a serious emergency before a psi would read a normal's mind. The Parapsychic Act had stopped psions from being bought and sold like cattle, but it did nothing to stop the hate. And the fear, which fed the hate. And so on.

Six stops later I was heartily tired of people jamming into the subway car, seeing me, and beating a hasty retreat. Another three stops after that the car was mostly empty, since we had passed rapidly out of downtown. The little girl held her mother's hand and still stared at me, and there was a group of young toughs on the other end of the car, sallow and muttering in the fluorescent lights. I stood, my right arm wrapped around a pole to keep my hand free to draw if I had to. I hated sitting down in germ-laden subway seats.

"The next stop," Jaf-the-demon said. I nodded. He still stood very close to me, the smell of demon overpowering the canned air and effluvia of the subways. I glanced down at the end of the car and saw that the young men were elbowing each other and whispering.

Oh, great. It looked like another street tough was going to find out whether or not my blade was just for show. I'd never understood Necromances who carry only ceremonial steel to use during apparitions. If you're allowed to carry steel, you should know how to use it. Then again, most Necromances didn't do mercenary work, they just lived in shitty little apartments until they paid off their accreditation fees and *then* started trying to buy a house. Me? I decided to take the quicker way. As usual.

One of them got to his feet and stamped down the central aisle. The little girl's mother, a statuesque brunette in nurse's scrubs and Nikesi sneakers, her three plastic bags rustling, pulled the little girl into her side again as he passed.

The pimpled young man jolted to a stop right in front of me. He didn't smell like Chill or hash, which was a good thing; a street tough hyped on Chill would make the situation rapidly unbearable. On the other hand, if he was stone-cold sober and still this stupid—"Hey, pretty baby," he said, his eyes skittering from my feet to my breasts to my cheek and then back to my breasts, "Wassup?"

"Nothing," I replied, pitching my voice low and neutral.

"You got a blade," he said. "You licensed to carry that, sugar?"

I tilted my head slightly, presenting my cheek. The emerald would be glinting and winking under the harsh lights. "You bet I am," I said. "And I even know how to use it. So go trundle back to your friends, Popsicle."

His wet fishmouth worked a little, stunned. Then he reached for his waistband.

I had a split second to decide if he was armed or just trying to start some trouble. I never got to make the decision, though, because the demon stepped past me, bumping me aside, and smacked the youngster. It was an open-handed backhand strike, not meaning to do any real damage, but it still tossed the kid to the other end of the subway car, back into the clutch of teen toughs.

I sighed. "Fuck." I let go of the pole as soon as I regained my balance. "You didn't have to do that."

Then one of the punk's friends pulled out a Transom 987 projectile gun, and I crouched for nonexistent cover. The demon moved, stepping past me, and I watched events come to their foregone conclusion.

The kids boiled up from their seats, one of them yanking their injured, pimply-faced friend to his feet. They were all wearing black denim jackets and green bandannas—yet another minigang.

The demon blinked across intervening space and slapped the illegal (if you weren't accredited or a police officer) gun out of the boy's hand, sent it skittering against the floor. The nurse covered her daughter's ear with her hand, staring, her mouth agape. I moved forward, coming to my feet, my sword singing free of the sheath, and slid myself in between them and the gang, where the demon had broken one boy's arm and was now in the process of holding the gunner up by his throat, shaking him as negligently as a cat might shake a mouse.

"You want to get off at the next stop," I told the mother, who stared at me. "Trust me."

She nodded. Her eyes were wide and wet with terror. The little girl stared at me.

I turned back to find the demon standing in the center of a ring of limp bodies. "Hello!" I shouted, holding the sword in my right hand with the blade level across my body, the reinforced scabbard reversed along my left forearm to act as a shield. It was a highly unorthodox way to hold a katana, but Jado-sensei always cared less about orthodox than keeping alive, and I found I agreed with him. If the demon came for me, I could buy some time with the steel and a little more time with Power. He'd eat me alive, of course, but I had a chance—

He turned, brushing his hands together as if wiping away dust. One of the boys groaned. "Yes?" Same level, robotic voice.

"You didn't kill anyone, did you?" I asked.

Bright green eyes scorched the air. He shrugged. "That would create trouble," he said.

"Is that a yes or a no?" I firmed my grip on the hilt. "Did you kill any of them?" I didn't want to do the paperwork even if it was a legitimate kill in response to an assault.

"No, they'll live," he said, glancing down. Then he stepped mincingly free of the ring of bodies.

"Anubis et'her ka," I breathed. *Anubis, protect me.*

The demon's lips compressed into a thin line. The train slowed, deceleration rocking me back on my heels. If he was going to attack, this would be a great time. "The Prince requested you delivered unharmed," he said, and sidled to the door, not turning his back to my blade.

"Remind me to thank him," I shot back, swallowing against the sudden dust in my mouth. I wondered what other "requests" the Prince had made.

CHAPTER 4

We ended up on the platform, me sliding my sword reluctantly back into the sheath, the demon watching as the nurse hurried her little girl up the steps. The stop was deserted, sound echoing off ceramic tiles as the train slid along its reactive-greased tracks. I took a deep breath, tried to calm my racing heart.

When the last footstep had faded, the demon turned on his heel and leapt down onto the tracks.

"Oh, no," I said. "No way. Negatory." I actually backed up two steps. "Look, I'm *human*. I can't go running around on subway tracks." For a moment the station seemed to shrink, the earth behind the walls pressing in, and I snapped a longing glance at the stairs.

He looked up at me, his long thin golden hands shoved deep in his coat pockets. "There is nothing to fear," he said finally.

"Says *you*," I snapped. "You're not the one who could die here. Come on. No way."

"This is the quickest way," he said, but his mouth thinned even more once he stopped speaking. I could tell he was losing patience with my stupid human self. "I promise you, there is no danger. However, if you keep balking I will have no choice but to drag you."

I just saw him blast six neopunks without even breaking a sweat. And he's a demon. Who knows what he'll do?

"Give me your Name," I said, "and I will."

As soon as it escaped my mouth, I backed up another two steps, wishing I hadn't said it. It was too late. The demon made a sound that might have been a laugh.

"Don't make me drag you, Necromance," he said, finally. "The Prince would be most displeased."

"That isn't my problem," I pointed out. "No way. I can't trust you."

"You have left the safety of your abode and followed me here." His eyes narrowed. "Unwise of you, to cavil now."

"So I'm too curious for my own good," I said. "Give me your Name, and I'll follow you."

He shrugged, spreading his hands. I waited. If the Prince truly wanted me delivered unharmed, the demon would give me his Name. It barely mattered—I was no Magi, able to force a minor demon into working my will or able to negotiate a bargain with a greater demon for years of service in exchange for blood, sex, or publicity. I rarely ever dealt with demons. He was right, that I'd come this far and it wasn't exactly wise to start backing down now, but better to back down now while I still had a running chance at reaching the surface than have the demon drag me into a subway tunnel. At least with his Name I might be able to stop him from killing me.

"Tierce Japhrimel," he said, finally.

I blinked, amazed he'd given in, and did some rapid mental calculations. "Do you swear on the Prince of Hell and the waters of Lethe that your true, full Name truly is Tierce Japhrimel?"

He shrugged. "I swear," he said after a long tense sweating second of silence.

I hopped down into the dark well of the tracks, jolting my knees. *I'm too old for this shit,* I thought. *I was too old for this shit ten years ago.* "Good deal," I mumbled. "Fine, lead the way, then. I'm warning you, though, any tricks and I'll haunt you, demon or not."

"That would indeed be a feat," he said. I think he meant to say it quietly, but the entire station echoed.

With that said, my sword ready, and no more excuses handy, I followed the demon into darkness.

CHAPTER 5

If I had to say with any certainty where the demon opened the door that led into a red glare, I would be at somewhat of a loss. I lose a lot of my sense of direction underground. The demon's tearing at the fabric of reality to split the walls of the worlds...well, it's complex, and takes an inhuman amount of Power, and I've never seen anyone but a demon do it. Magi sometimes tried unsuccessfully to force doors between this reality and the world of demons lying cheek-by-jowl with it instead of pleading for a demon to come through and make an appearance, but I was a Necromance. The only alternate reality I knew or cared about was the world of Death.

Some of the Magi said that the higher forms of Power were a result of the leaching of substance between this world and the world of the demons. I had never seen that—humans and the earth's own well of natural Power were all I'd ever noticed. Even though Magi training techniques were used as the basis for teaching psions how to control Power, every Magi had his or her own kind of trade secrets passed on from teacher to student and written in code, if not memorized. It was like Skinlin with their plant DNA maps or a Necromance's psychopomp, personal information.

There was an access hatch, I remember that much, that the demon opened as if it had been deliberately left unlocked. Then again, who would be running around down here? A long concrete-floored corridor lit faintly by buzzing fluorescents, and a door at the end of it — but this door was ironbound wood with a spiked, fluid glyph carved deeply into the surface of the wood. The glyph smoked and twisted; I felt reality tearing and shifting around us until the demon was the only solid thing.

I was seriously nauseated by now, swallowing bile and nearly choking. *This isn't built for humans,* I thought, vicious little mouths nipping at my skin. It was akin to freefall, this walking between the worlds; that was why you were only supposed to do it astrally. The physical structure of my body was being stressed, the very building blocks of my cellular structure taking loads they weren't designed to handle. Not to mention the fact that the twisting of visual and auditory input screwed up my perceptions, and the *alienness* of the Power here made my aura compress close to my skin and shiver. When the demon opened up the door and red light spilled out, I almost lost the chicken soup I'd bolted for lunch. The demon grabbed my arm and hauled me through, and I understood why he'd been standing so close to me. As soon as the smell of demon washed over me, I felt a little better. The demon's aura stretched to cover me, and when the door closed behind us with a thud I found myself with a demon holding my elbow, volcanic heat lapping at my skin, and a gigantic hall with what appeared to be an obsidian floor and long narrow windows. Red light from spitting, ever-burning torches ran wetly over the floor and the ceiling, which I only glanced at and then back at the floor, shutting my eyes.

I heard, dimly, the demon saying something. The sense of sudden freefall stopped with a thump, as if normal gravity had reasserted itself. Nausea retreated — mostly. I choked, and tried to stop myself from spewing.

The demon pressed the fingers of his free hand against my sweating forehead and said something else, in a sliding harsh language that hurt my ears. Warm blood dripped down from my nose. I kept my fingers around my sword.

It took a few minutes for the spinning to stop and my stomach to decide it wouldn't turn itself inside-out. "I'm okay," I said finally, feeling sweat trickle down my spine. "Just a little...whoa. That's... oh, *shit* —"

"It's a common reaction," he replied. "Just breathe."

I forced myself to stand upright, swallowed sour heat and copper blood. "I'm okay," I repeated. "The sooner I get this over with, the sooner I can go home, right?"

He nodded. His lips were turned down at the corners now, and I saw that his long black coat was now in the same geometric scheme as the rest of the world. That was part of the problem — the angles of the floor and walls were just a little wrong, just a crucial millimeter off. My brain kept trying to make it fit and failing, and that made my stomach resemble a Tilt-A-Whirl, only without the fun part.

"Fine," I said. "Let's go."

He kept his hand closed around my elbow as we negotiated the vast expanse of the ballroom. *Is this the antechamber to Hell?* I thought, and had a difficult time not giggling. *I think I'm doing well with this. Really well.*

Then we reached the end of the hall, and the demon pushed open another large ironbound door, and all thoughts of dealing really well went right out the window. I even dropped my sword. The demon made a quick movement, and had my blade...I never dropped my sword. *Never.*

"A *human*," the Thing sitting behind the massive desk said. It had three spiraling horns sprouting from its head and wide, lidless, cat-slit yellow eyes that fastened on me. Its body was a shapeless mass of yellow blubber, festooned with long bristling black hairs in a few random places. Three nipples clustered on its chest, and the skin looked wrong, and greasy. The worst part was the hinged mouth and razor-sharp teeth — but even worse than that were the long spidery fingers that looked like maggots crawling among the papers on its desk. My brain went merrily rambling on — *a demonic bureaucrat, even Hell has its paperwork...*

"Not for you, Trikornus," the green-eyed demon said. "She's for the Prince."

"What a lovely present. Finally back in the good graces, assassin?" It was still staring at me. A dripping, purple-red tongue slid out, caressed its chin with a sound like screaming sandpaper. "Ooooh, give us a taste. Just a little taste?"

"She is *for the Prince*, Baron," Jaf enunciated clearly. I was too busy suddenly studying my boot-toes. *How did I get here?* I wondered. *If I'd known, I would never have been a Necromance. But jeez, they never told me dealing with dead people would get me here, I thought only Magi dealt with demons —*

"Very well, you greedy spoilsport," the horror behind the desk said. I had a vivid mental image of those sharp teeth clamping in my upper thigh while blood squirted out, and barely suppressed a shudder. I felt cold under the sick fiery heat coating my skin. The thing gave a snorting, hitching laugh. "The Prince is in his study, waiting for you. Second door on the left."

I felt more than saw Jaf's nod. *Who ever would have thought that he'd seem like the lesser of two evils?* I thought, then felt a chill finger touch the back of my sweating neck. That this Japhrimel looked a little more human didn't mean that he was any less of an alien being.

He guided me past the desk, and I was grateful that he was between me and the four-eyed demon. What would I have done if *that* thing had been sent to come fetch me? And what the hell would a demon need a Necromance for?

The world grew very dim for a few moments, but the demon half-dragged me through another ironbound door. "Keep breathing, human," he said, and stopped moving for a few seconds. "The Baron likes to dress in a different skin for each visitor," he continued. "It's normal. Just breathe."

If this is normal, don't let me see weird. "You mean you do this to other people, too?" I gasped out.

He made a brief snorting sound. "Not me. Sometimes people come without their flesh, Magi and the like. Very few are sent for. Only the desperate come here."

"I can believe that." I took a deep whooping breath. Felt bile burn the back of my throat. "Thanks," I said, finally, and he started off again. This hall was narrow but high, and there were paintings hanging on the wall that I didn't want to look at after catching a glimpse of the first one. Instead I stared at my feet moving under me, and had a brief flash of unreality—my feet didn't look like mine.

Jaf's fingers closed around my nape and I took in a deep breath. I'd stumbled and half-fallen. "Not long now," he said, releasing my neck, pulling me along by my arm. "Just hold on."

I was in bad shape, shivering and trying not to retch, when he opened another door and pulled me through a subliminal *snap*. My feet took on their normal dimensions, and I slumped gratefully into the demon's grasp. The only thing holding me up was his fingers.

Then I felt something in my hand. He closed his free hand around mine, the sword held by both of us now. "Here," he said. "Hold on to your blade, Necromance."

"Indeed, it wouldn't do to drop it." This voice was smooth as silk, persuasive, filtering into my ears. "She survived the Hall. Very impressive."

Japhrimel said nothing. I was actually kind of starting to like him.

Not really.

I opened my eyes. The demon's chest was right in front of me. I tilted my head back, looked up into his face. His eyes scorched mine. "Thanks," I told him, my voice trembling slightly. "That first step's a lulu."

He didn't say anything, but his lips thinned out. Then he stepped aside.

I found myself confronted with a perfectly reasonable neo-Victorian study, carpeted in plush crimson. Leather-clad books lined up on bookcases against the dark-paneled wooden walls, three red velvet chairs in front of a roaring fireplace, red tasseled drapes drawn over what might have been a window. A large mahogany desk sat obediently to one side.

A slim dark shape stood next to the fireplace. The air was drunk and dizzy with the scent of demons. I tightened my fingers on my sword, fisted my other hand, felt my lacquered nails dig into my palm.

The man—at least, it had a manlike shape—had an amazing corona of golden hair standing out from his head. A plain black T-shirt and jeans, bare golden-brown feet. I took a deep rasping breath.

"What though the field be lost? All is not lost; the inconquerable will, And study of revenge, immortal hate—" I trailed off, licked my lips with my dry tongue. I'd had a classical humanist as a social worker, and had been infected with a love of books at an early age. The classics had sustained me all through the schoolyard hellhole of Rigger Hall.

I shuddered, remembering that. I didn't like to think about the Hall, where I'd learned reading, writing, and 'rithmatic—and the basics of controlling my powers. Where I'd also learned how little those powers would protect me.

He turned away from the fireplace. *"And courage never to submit or yield,"* he finished. His eyes were like black ice and green flame at the same time, and there was a mark on his forehead that I didn't look at, because I found I had dropped my gaze.

The demon Jaf sank down to one knee, rose again.

"You're late," the Prince of Hell said, mildly.

"I had to paint my nails," my mouth bolted like a runaway horse. "A demon showing up on my doorstep and pointing a gun at me tends to disarrange me."

"He pointed a gun at you?" The Prince made a gesture with one hand. "Please, sit, Miss Valentine. May I call you Dante?"

"It's my name," I responded, uncomfortably. *The Devil knows my name,* I thought, in a kind of delirium. *The Devil knows my name.*

Then I gave myself a sharp mental slap. *Quit it. You need your wits about you, Danny, so just quit it.* "I would be honored," I added. "It's a pleasure to meet Your Lordship. Your Highness. Whatever."

He laughed. The laugh could strip the skin off an elephant in seconds. "I'm referred to as the father of lies, Dante. I'm old enough to know a falsehood when I hear one."

"So am I," I responded. "I suppose you're going to say that you mean me no harm, right?"

He laughed again, throwing his head back. He was too beautiful, the kind of androgynous beauty that holovid models sometimes achieve. If I hadn't known he was male, I might have wondered. The mark on his forehead flashed green. *It's an emerald, like a Necromance,* I thought. *I wonder why?* Necromance emeralds were set in the skin when we finished basic schooling at about eight; I didn't think the Prince of Hell had ever gone to primary school.

I was rapidly getting incoherent. "Excuse me," I said politely enough. "It's getting hard to breathe in here."

"This won't take very long. Bring the lovely Necromance over to a chair, my eldest, she's about to fall down." His voice turned the color of smooth cocoa mixed with honey. My knees turned to water.

Jaf dragged me across the room. I was too relieved to argue. The place looked normal. *Human,* without the weird geometry. *If I ever get back to the real world I'm going to kiss the ground,* I promised myself. *I've read about people going to Hell astrally. Lucky me getting to visit in the flesh.*

He dropped me into a chair—the one on the left—then stepped around to the side, his arms folded, and appeared to turn into a statue.

The Prince regarded me. His eyes were lighter but more weirdly depthless than Jaf's, a sort of radioactive silken glow. Thirty seconds looking into those eyes and I might have agreed to anything just to make it stop.

As it was, I looked down at my knees. "You wanted to see me," I said. "Here I am."

"Indeed." The Prince turned back to the fireplace. "I have a mission for you, Dante. Succeed, and you can count me as a friend all the years of your life, and those years will be long. It is in my power to grant wealth and near-immortality, Dante, and I am disposed to be generous."

"And if I fail?" I couldn't help myself.

"You'll be dead," he said. "Being a Necromance, you're well-prepared for that, aren't you?"

My rings glinted dully in the red light. "I don't want to die," I said finally. "Why me?"

"You have a set of...talents that are uniquely suited to the task," he answered.

"So what is it exactly you want me to *do*?" I asked.

"I want you to kill someone," he said.

CHAPTER 6

Whoa." I looked up at him, forgetting the hypnotic power of those green eyes. "Look, I'm not a contract killer. I'm a Necromance. I bring people *back* to ask questions, and lay them to rest when necessary."

"Fifty years ago, a demon escaped my realm," the Prince said mildly, his voice cutting through my objections. "He is wandering your realm at will, and he is about to break the Egg."

Did he say crack the egg? Is that some kind of demon euphemism? "What egg?" I asked, shifting uncomfortably in the chair. My sword lay across my knees. This felt too real to be a hallucination.

"The Egg is a demon artifact," the Prince said. "Suffice it to say the effects will be very unpleasant if this particular demon breaks the Egg in your world."

My mouth dried. "You mean like end-of-the-world bad?" I asked.

The Prince shrugged. "I wish the Egg found and the thief executed. You are a Necromance, capable of seeing what others do not. Some have called you the greatest death-talker of your generation, which is high praise indeed. You are human, but you may be able to find the Egg and kill the thief. Jaf will accompany you, to keep your skin whole until you accomplish your task." He turned back to the fireplace. "And if you bring the Egg back to me I will reward you with more than a human being could ever dream of."

"I'm not so sure I want your reward," I told him. "Look, I'm just a working girl. I raise the dead for issues of corporate law and to solve probate questions. I don't do lone-gun revenge stuff."

"You've been dabbling in the bounty-hunting field since you left the Academy and with corporate espionage and other illegal fancies—though no assassination, I'll grant you that—for five years to pay off your mortgage and live more comfortably than most of your ilk," he replied. "Don't play with me, Dante. It is exceedingly ill-advised to play with me."

"Likewise," I said. "You've got a fully armed Necromance who knows your Name sitting in your inner sanctum, Your Highness. You must be desperate." My mouth dried to cotton, my hands shook. That was another lie.

Despite being more research-oriented than most of my kind, I didn't know the Devil's Name—nobody did. In any case, he was too powerful to be commanded around like a mere imp. I doubted even knowing Tierce Japhrimel's Name would do more than keep him from outright killing me. Lucifer's Name was a riddle pursued by Magi, who thought that if they learned it they could control the legions of Hell. The Ceremonials said Lucifer's true Name was more like a god's Name—it would express him, but didn't have power *over* him. The exact nature of the relationship between Lucifer and the gods was also hotly debated; since the complete verification of the existence of demons the various churches that had survived the Awakening and the Ceremonials had conducted experiments, largely inconclusive. Belief in the power of the words to banish imps was necessary—but sometimes even that didn't work unless the demon in question was extremely weak. As Gabe's grandmother Adrienne Spocarelli had remarked once in a footnote to her *Gods and Magi*, it was a good thing demons didn't want to rule the earth, since you couldn't even banish one unless it was a bitty one.

"And you must be greedy." His voice hadn't changed at all. "What do you want, Dante Valentine? I can give you the world."

It whispered in my veins, tapped at my skull. *I can give you the world...*

I actually thought about it, but Lucifer couldn't give me anything I wanted. Not without the price being too high. If I was sure of nothing else in this situation, I was sure of *that*. "Get thee behind me," I whispered, finally. "I just want to be left alone. I don't want anything to do with this."

"I can even," he said, "tell you who your parents were."

You son of a bitch. I rocketed to my feet, my sword whipping free. Blue runes twisted inside the steel, but neither demon moved. I backed around the chair, away from Jaf, who still looked like a statue, staring at my sword. Red firelight ran wet over the blade, blue runes twisting in the steel. "You leave my parents out of this," I snapped. "Fine. I'll do your job, *Iblis Lucifer*. If you leave me alone. And I don't want your trained dog-demon over there. Give me what information you've got, and I'll find this Egg for you."

For all I knew my parents had been too poor to raise me; either that or they'd been too strung out on any cocktail of substances. It didn't matter — since my Matheson index was so high and they'd had me in a hospital, they hadn't been able to sell me as an indentured. That was the only gift they'd given me — that, and the genetic accident that made me a Necromance. Both incredible gifts, when you thought about the alternative. It wasn't the first time somebody had twitted me about being an orphan.

Nobody ever did it more than once.

Lucifer shrugged. "You must take Japhrimel. Otherwise, it's suicide."

"And have him double-cross me once we find this Egg? You must not want word to get out that someone took off with it." I shook my head. "No dice. I work alone."

His eyes came up, bored into my skull. "You are under the illusion that you have a choice."

I lifted my sword, a shield against his gaze. Sweat trickled down my back, soaking into my jeans. It was damnably hot — *what else, in Hell? You were expecting a mint julep and a cool breeze?*

I didn't even see Jaf move. In one neat move he had the sword taken away, resheathed, and the gun pressed into my temple. One of his arms was across my throat. My feet kicked fruitlessly at empty air.

"You are intriguing," the Prince of Hell said, stalking across the room. "Most humans would be screaming by now. Or crying. There seems to be a distressing tendency to sob among your kind."

I spat an obscenity that would have made Jado-sensei, with his Asiano sense of decorum, wince. Jaf didn't move. His arm slipped a little, and I fought for breath. He could crush my windpipe like a paper cup. I stopped kicking — it would waste what little oxygen I had left — and *concentrated*, the world narrowing to a single still point.

"Let go of her," the Prince said calmly. "She's building up Power."

Jaf dropped me. I hit the ground and whirled on the balls of my feet, the sword blurring free of the sheath in an arc of silver, singing. *No think,* little nut-brown Jado in his orange robes yelled in my memory. *No think, move! Move!*

I didn't even *see* Jaf move again. He stepped in close, moving faster than a human, of course, twisted my wrist just short of breaking it, and tore the sword from my fingers. I punched him and actually connected, snapping his head back. Then I backed up, shuffling, away from the two demons, my two *main-gauches* whipping out, one reversed along my left forearm, the other held almost horizontally in front of me, ready for anything.

Anything except this.

Jaf dropped my sword. It chimed, smoking, on the floor next to the scabbard. "Blessed steel. She *believes*," he said, glancing at the Prince, who had stopped and was considering me.

Of course I believe, I thought, in a sort of delirium. *I talk to the god of Death on a regular basis. I believe because I must.*

"Do you think you can fight your way free of Hell?" the Prince asked.

"Do you think you could be polite?" I tossed back. " 'Cause I have to say, your treatment of a guest kind of sucks." I gulped down air, a harsh whooping inhalation. It was slow suffocation, breathing in whatever gas these demons used for air.

Lucifer took a single step toward me. "My apologies, Dante. Come, sit down. Japhrimel, give her sword back. We should be polite, shouldn't we, since we are *asking* her for her help."

"What's in the Egg?" I asked, not moving. "Why is it so important?"

Lucifer smiled. That smile made me back up until my shoulders hit a bookcase. "What's in the Egg?" he said. "None of your concern, human."

"Oh, boy." I gulped down air. "This is *so* wrong."

"Help me, Dante, and you will be one of the chosen few to claim my friendship." His voice was soft and persuasive, fingering at my skull, looking for entrance. I bit savagely at the inside of my cheek, the slice of pain clearing my head slightly. "I swear to you on the waters of Lethe, if you retrieve the Egg and kill the thief, I will consider you a friend for eternity."

I tasted blood. "What's the demon's name?" I asked. "The one that stole it."

"His name is Vardimal," Lucifer said. "You know him as Santino."

I considered throwing my left knife. It wouldn't kill him, but the blessed steel might slow him down long enough for me to juke for the door or the window. "Santino?" I whispered. "You slimy son of a—"

"Watch how you speak to the Prince," Jaf interrupted. Lucifer raised one golden hand.

"Let her speak as she wishes, Japhrimel," he said. For the first time, he sounded...what? Actually weary. "Value the human who speaks truth, for they are few and far between."

"You could say the same for demons," I said numbly. "Santino..." It was a longing whisper.

—*blood sliding out between my fingers, a chilling crystal laugh, Doreen's scream, life bubbling out through the gash in her throat, screaming, screaming*—

I resheathed my knives.

Lucifer examined me for a few more moments, then turned and paced back to the fireplace. "I am aware that you have your own score to settle with Vardimal," he continued. "You help me, I help you. You see?"

"Santino was a demon?" I whispered. "How—" I had to clear my throat. "How the *hell* am I supposed to kill him?"

"Japhrimel will help you. He also has a...personal stake in this."

Jaf gingerly picked up my sword, slid it into the sheath. I watched this, sweat trickling down my forehead. A drop fell into my eyes, stinging. I blinked it away. "Why doesn't *he* just kill Santino?" I asked. My voice trembled.

"A very long time ago, during the dawning of the world, I granted this demon a gift in return for a service," Lucifer said. "He asked for an immunity. Neither man nor demon can kill him."

I thought this over. "So you think I can, since I'm neither."

"It is," Lucifer pointed out, "worth a try. Japhrimel will protect you long enough for you to carry out your mission."

Awww, jeez, isn't that sweet of him. I was about to say that, had a rare second thought, and shut my mouth. After a moment I nodded. "Fine." I didn't sound happy. "I'll do it. It's not like I have much of a choice." *And I'll get free from this Jaf guy as soon as I've got the scent. How hard can that be?*

"The rewards will be great," Lucifer reminded me.

"Screw your rewards, I'll be happy just to get out alive," I muttered. *Santino was a demon? No wonder I couldn't find him.* "Can I go back to Earth now? Or is this Vardimal hanging out in the Infernals?" The thought of hunting for a murderous demon through the lands of the not-quite-real-but-real-enough made suicide seem like a pretty good option.

"He is among your kind," Lucifer told me. "Your world is a playground for us, and he plays cruel games."

"Gee, imagine that." I swallowed, a dry dusty click. "A demon who likes hurting people."

"Let me tell you something, Dante Valentine," Lucifer replied, staring into the flames. His back was rigid. "I saw your kind crawling up from mud yesterday, and pitied you. *I* gave you fire. *I* gave you civilization, and technology. *I* gave you the means to build a platform above the mud. *I* gave you the secrets of love. My demons have lived among you for thousands of years, teaching you, molding your nervous systems so you were no longer mere animals. And you spit on me, and call me evil."

My mouth couldn't get any drier. We called them demons, or djinn, or devils, or a hundred other names, every culture had stories about them. Before the Great Awakening they had been *only* stories and nightmares, despite the Magi who had worked for centuries to classify and make regular contact with them. Nobody knew if demons were gods, or subject to gods, or Something Else Entirely.

My vote went for Something Else. But then again, I'd always been the suspicious type. "Lucifer was the very first humanist," I said. "I'm well aware of that, Your Highness."

"Think of that before you open your mouth again," he continued as if I hadn't spoken. "Now get out, and do what you're told. I give you Japhrimel as a familiar, Dante Valentine. Go away."

"My lord—" Jaf began, and I rubbed my sweating hands on my damp jeans. I would need a salt tablet and a few liters of water—the heat was physical, pressing against my skin; sweat drenched my clothes.

"Get *out*," Lucifer said. "Don't make me repeat myself."

I wasn't about to argue. I looked at Jaf.

The demon stared at Lucifer for a moment, his jaw working, green eyes burning.

Green eyes. They both have green eyes. Are they related? Jeez, who knows? I swallowed again. The tension buzzed against the air, rasped against my skin.

Lucifer made an elegant motion with one golden hand. It was a rune, but not one I recognized.

Fire bit into my left shoulder. I screamed, sure that he'd decided to kill me after all, me and my big mouth—but Jaf stalked across the room, holding my scabbarded sword, and grabbed my elbow again. "This way," he said, over my breathless howl—it felt like a branding iron was pressed into my flesh, the *burning*—and he hauled me back toward the door we'd come in through. I struggled—*no not that again it HURTS it HURTS it HURTS*—but when he opened the door and pulled me through there was no hall, just an icy chill and the blessed stink of human air.

CHAPTER 7

M y shoulder ached, a low dull throbbing. It was dark. Rain fell, but I was dry. My clothes were dry, too. I was covered with the smoky fragrance of demon magic.

I blinked.

I was lying on something hard and cold, but something warm was against the side of my face. Someone holding me. Musk and burning cinnamon. The smell drenched me, eased the burning in my shoulder and the pounding of my heart, the heavy smoky pain in my lungs. I felt like I'd been ripped apart and sewn back together the wrong way. "...*hurts*," I gasped, unaware I was talking.

"Breathe," Jaf said. "Just keep breathing. It will pass, I promise."

I groaned. Kept breathing.

Then the retching started. He rolled me onto my side, still holding me up, and I emptied my stomach between muttering obscenities.

The demon actually stroked my hair. If I tried to forget that he had just held a gun to my head, it was actually kind of comforting.

I finished losing everything I'd ever thought of eating. Retched for a little while. Then everything settled down, and I lay on the concrete listening to sirens and hovers passing by while the demon stroked my hair and held me. It took a little while before I felt ready to face the world—even the real human world—again.

I said I'd kiss the ground, I thought. *Not sure I'd want to do that now that it's covered in puke. My puke. Disgusting.*

"I suppose this is pretty disgusting," I finally said, wishing I could rinse my mouth out.

I felt the demon's shrug. "I don't care."

"Of course not." I tasted bile. "It's a *human* thing. You wouldn't care."

"I like humans," he said. "Most demons do. Otherwise we would not have bothered to make you our companions instead of apes." He stroked my hair. A few strands had come loose and stuck to my cheeks and forehead.

"Great. And here I thought we were something like nasty little lapdogs to you guys." I took a deep breath. I felt like I could stand up now. "So I guess I've got my marching orders, huh?"

"I suppose so." He rose slowly to his feet, pulling me with him, and caught me when I overbalanced. He put my sword in my hands, wrapped my fingers around it, then held the scabbard there until I stopped swaying.

It was my turn to shrug. "I should go home and pick up some more stuff if we're going to be chasing a demon down," I told him. "And I need...well."

"Certainly," he said. "It is the Prince's will that I obey."

The way he said it—all in one breath—made it sound like an insult. "I didn't do it," I said. "Don't get mad at me. What did he *do* to me, anyway?"

"When we get to your house, you should look," the demon said, infuriatingly calm. "I hope you realize how lucky you are, Necromance."

"I just survived a trip to Hell," I said. "Believe me, I'm counting my blessings right now. Where are we?"

"Thirty-third and Pole Street," he answered. "An alley."

I looked around. He was right. It was a dingy little alley, sheltered from the rain by an overhang. Three dumpsters crouched at the end, blocking access to the street. Brick walls, a graffiti tag, papers drifting in the uncertain breeze. "Lovely," I said. "You sure have a great flair for picking these places."

"You'd prefer the middle of Main Street?" he asked, his eyes glowing in the darkness. I stepped sideways as soon as my legs seemed willing to carry me. His hands fell back down to his sides. "The Prince..." He trailed off.

"Yeah, he's a real charmer, all right," I said. "What did he *do* to my shoulder? It hurts like a bitch."

"You'll see," was the calm reply. He brushed past me, heading for the mouth of the alley. "Let me move the dumpster, and we'll call a cab."

"Now you'll call a cab, where before you had to drag me through the subway?" I chucked my blade free of its sheath, checked the metal. Still bright. Still sharp.

"It was necessary. Leaving Hell is not the same as entering it, especially for a human. I had to find an entrance you would *survive*, but falling back into mortality is not so hard." He stopped, his back to me. "Not so very hard at all." The light was dim—*I've been in Hell all afternoon*, I thought, and felt an insane giggle bubble up inside me and die away. *Why do I always want to laugh at times like this?* I wondered. All my life, the insane urge to giggle had popped up at the worst times.

"Great," I muttered, shoving the blade back home. "All right, let's go."

He shoved one of the dumpsters aside as easily as I might have moved a footstool. I concentrated on putting one foot in front of the other without keeling over.

Neon ran over the wet street. Thirty-third and Pole was right in the middle of the Tank District. I wondered if it was a demon joke— but then, there was likely to be a lot of sex and psychoactives floating in the air here. It was probably easier to open a door between here and Hell around that kind of energy charge.

We splashed through puddles, the demon occasionally falling back to take my elbow and steer me around a corner. He seemed content to just walk silently, and I hurt too much to engage in small talk. I'd ditch him soon enough.

He hailed a cab at the corner of Thirtieth and Vine, and I fell into the seat gratefully. I gave my address to the driver—a bespectacled, mournful Polish man who hissed a charm against the evil eye when he saw my tattooed cheek. He jangled the antique rosary hanging from his faredeck and addressed all his replies to the demon; he couldn't see that the demon was more of a threat than little old human me.

Story of my life. Guy didn't mind the demon, but would have thrown me out of the cab if he could.

CHAPTER 8

Go ahead and make yourself at home," I said as I locked the door. "There's beer in the fridge. And wine, if you like that. I've got to take a shower."

He nodded. "I should speak of Vardimal," he said. "To familiarize you with—"

"Later," I told him. My shoulder twinged. "Hey."

He turned back to me.

"What did he do to me?" I lifted the sword a little, pointing at my left shoulder with the hilt. "Huh?"

"The Prince of Hell has granted you a familiar, Necromance," Japhrimel said formally, clasping his hands behind his back. He looked a little like a priest in his long black high-collared coat. I wondered where he hid the guns. I'd never heard of a demon with guns before. *I should have studied harder, I suppose. But how the hell was I supposed to know that a demon would show up at my front door? I'm a bloody Necromance, not a Magi!*

"A fam—" My brain started to work again. "Oh, no. I'm not a Magi. I don't want—"

"Too late," he informed me. "Go take your shower, I'll keep watch."

"Keep watch? Nobody knows I'm working for—" I put my back against the door. *How did I get into this?* I wondered—not for the last time, I might add.

"Your entry into Hell may have been remarked," the demon said. "I'll make coffee."

I shook my head and brushed past him, heading for the stairs. "Gods above and below," I muttered, "what did I do to deserve this?"

"You have a reputation for being honorable," the demon supplied helpfully. "And your talents as a Necromance are well-known."

I waved a hand over my shoulder at him. "Fine, fine. Just try not to set anything on fire, okay? Be careful with my house."

"As my Mistress wishes," he said. It would have been hard for him to sound more ironic.

I climbed the stairs, my legs aching. Even my teeth hurt. *An hour into this job and I'm already wishing I was on vacation.* I had to laugh, trailing my fingers along the painted wall. My sword seemed far heavier than it should be. Halfway up the stairs, under the altar niche, was a stash of three water bottles, and I snagged one. I fumbled in my bag for a salt tablet, took it. Dried sweatsalt crackled on my skin. I probably smelled like I'd been stuck in an oven. It was a miracle I hadn't been hit with heatstroke.

I drained the water bottle, dropped my sword on my bed, put my bag inside the bathroom door, and started stripping down. I paused halfway to turn the shower on, and examined my left shoulder in the mirror.

Pressed into the skin was a sigil I'd never seen before, not one of the Nine Canons I knew. I was no demonologist, so I didn't know what it meant, exactly. But when I touched it—the glyph shifting uneasily, ropy scar like a burn twisting under my fingertips—I hissed in a sharp breath, closing my eyes against a wave of heat.

I saw my kitchen as if through a sheet of wavering glass, the familiar objects twisted and shimmering with unearthly light. He was looking at my stove—

I found myself on my knees, gasping. *I've read about this,* I thought, oddly comforted. *I've read about seeing through a familiar's eyes. Breathe, Danny. Breathe. Breathe in, breathe out. Been doing it all your life. Just breathe.* The tiled floor bit into my knees, my forehead rested against the edge of my bathtub. Steam filled the air. *Gods,* I thought. *So that's what they're talking about when they say…oh, man. Heavy shit, dude. Can't take the scene; gotta bail.*

I'd just been given a demon familiar. Magi everywhere would be salivating—it was the high pursuit of every Magi, to achieve a working relationship with one of the denizens of Hell. I'd never done much in that arena—I had more than enough work to keep me busy inside my own specialty. But occult practitioners are a curious bunch—some of us like to fiddle around with everything when time permits. And a lot of the standard Magi training techniques were shared with other occult disciplines—Shamans, Journeymen, Witches, Ceremonials, Skinlin…and Necromances. After all, Magi had been the ones pursuing occult disciplines since before the Awakening and the Para-psychic Act. So I'd been given something most Magi worked for years to achieve—and I didn't want it. It only complicated an already fucked-up situation.

The steam shifted, blowing this way and that. I looked up to see the water running in the shower. I was wasting hot water.

That got me moving. I stripped off the rest of my clothes with trembling fingers and stepped into the shower, loosing my hair with a sigh. I've been dyeing my hair black for years, to fit in with Necro-mance codes, but sometimes I wondered if I should streak it with some purple or something. Or cut the damn mess off. When I was young and in the Hall, every girl's hair was trimmed boy-short except for the sexwitches. I suppose growing it out when I reached the Acad-emy was another way of proving I was no longer required to follow any rules other than the professional ones. Purple streaks would look nice on me.

I'd been mousy blonde at the Hall. Dyeing your hair to fit in with the antiquated dress codes rubbed me the wrong way, but part of being an accredited Necromance was presenting a united front to the world. We were all supposed to look similar, to be instantly recog-nizable, dark-haired and pale with emeralds on our cheeks and accreditation tats if possible, carrying our swords like Shamans car-ried their staves.

Once I retire I'll let it grow out blonde, maybe, I thought, and then the shock of unreality hit me again. I slumped against the tiled wall, my teeth chattering.

I traced a glyph for Strength on the tiles with a trembling finger. It flushed red for a moment—I was dangerously close to shock. And if I went into shock, what would the demon do?

I finished washing up and got out, dried off, and padded into my bedroom, carrying my bag. I was dressed in a few minutes, moving automatically, sticking my feet back into my favorite pair of boots. The mark on my shoulder wasn't hurting now—it just ached a little, a flare of Power staining through my shielding and marking me like a demon to Sight. Black diamond spangles whirled through the trade-mark glitters of a Necromance's aura, and I could see the mark on my shoulder, a spot of pulsing darkness.

Great. This will make work so much easier, I thought, and sighed. I needed food. My stomach was rumbling, probably because I'd puked everything out in a backstreet alley. I yawned, scratched under my wet hair, and scooped up my sword, dumping my salt-crusted clothes in the hamper.

Then I paced over to my file cabinet, passing my hand over the locked drawer. The locks—both electronic and magickal—clicked open, and I dug until I found what I needed. I didn't give myself any time to think about it.

The red file. I held it in a trembling hand for a moment and then slammed the drawer shut. Scooped up my bag from the bed and stood for a moment, my knees shaking slightly, my head down, gasping like a racehorse run too hard.

When I could breathe properly again, I stamped down the stairs, pausing halfway to touch the Anubis statue set in the little shrine tucked in the niche. I'd need to light a candle to him if I survived this.

I found the demon in my kitchen, contemplating my coffeemaker with a look of abstract horror. It was the closest to a human expression he seemed capable of, with his straight saturnine face. "What?" I asked.

"You drink *freeze-dried*?" he asked, as if he just found out I'd been sacrificing babies to Yahweh.

"I'm not exactly rich, Mr. Creepy," I informed him. "Why don't you just materialize some Kona fresh-ground if you're such a snob?"

"Would you like me to, Mistress?" There was the faintest suggestion of a sneer in his voice. He was still wearing the long black coat. I took a closer look at him. Long nose, winged cheekbones, strong chin...he wasn't spectacular like Lucifer, or horrific like the thing in the hall. I shivered reflexively. He looked *normal*, and that was even more terrifying, once you really thought about it.

"Just call me Danny," I mumbled, and stamped over to the freezer, pulling it open. I yanked the canister out. "Here's the *real* coffee. I only get this out for friends, so be grateful."

"You would call me a friend?" He sounded amazed now. It was a lot less like talking to a robot. I was grateful for that.

"Not really," I said. "But I *do* appreciate you holding me up out of my own puke. I understand you're just doing what Lucifer tells you and something tells me you don't like me much, so we'll have to come to some kind of agreement." I tossed the canister at him, and he plucked it out of the air with one swift movement. "You're pretty good," I admitted. "I'd hate to have to spar with you."

He inclined his head slightly, his ink-black hair falling back from his forehead. "My thanks for the compliment. I'll make coffee."

"Good. I'm going to go think about this," I said, turning my back on him. He looked like a piece of baroque furniture in my sleek, high-tech kitchen. I almost wanted to wait to see if he could figure out the coffeemaker, but I wasn't that curious. Besides, demons have been fooling with technology for hundreds of years. They're good at it. Unfortunately for humans, demons don't like *sharing* their technology, which is rumored to be spotless and perfect. It occurred to me now that the demons probably were doing now what the Nichtvren had done before the Parapsychic Act—using proxies to control certain biotech or straight-tech corporations. Cloned blood had been a Nichtvren-funded advance; lots of immortal bloodsuckers had grown very rich by being the stockholders and silent partners in several businesses. I guess when you're faced with eternity, you kind of have to start playing with money to assure yourself a safe nest.

I carried the file into the living room and collapsed on the couch. My entire body shook, waves of tremors from my crown to my soles. I balanced the file on my stomach, flung my arm over my eyes, and breathed out, my lips slackening. Training took over, brainwaves shifting. I dropped quickly into trance, finding the place inside myself that no genemap or scan would ever show, and was gone almost immediately.

CHAPTER 9

*B*lue crystal walls rose up around me. The Hall was immense, stretching up to dark, starry infinity, plunging down below into the abyss. I walked over the bridge, my footfalls resounding against the stone. My feet were bare—I felt grit on the stone surface, the chill of wet rock, the press of my long hair against my neck. Here, I always wore the white robe of the god's chosen, belted with silver, the mark on my cheek burning. The emerald flamed, a cocoon of brightness, kept me from being knocked off the bridge and into endless wells of the dark. The living did not come here—except for those like me.

Necromances.

On the other side of the bridge the dog waited, sleek and black; His high pointed ears focused forward, sitting back on His haunches.

I touched my heart and then my forehead with my right hand, a salute. "Anubis," I said in the not-dream, and my lips shaped the other sound that was the god's personal name, that-which-could-not-be-spoken, resonating through me.

I am the bell, but the god puts His hand upon me and makes me sing.

I breathed out, the warmth of His comfort descending on me. Here in this refuge I was safe even from Lucifer—demons did not tread in Death. At least, I'd never seen one here.

Sometimes, especially after a long stint of working one apparition after another, I wanted to stay. Almost needed to stay. No other Necromance could enter my Hall, even those that could speak to Anubis as their psychopomp. Here I was blessedly alone, except for the dead and the god.

The cipher of the god's presence in the form of a dog pressed closer. I stroked His head. Silently, I felt Him take the crushing weight of the problem and consider it. Blue crystal walls and floors sang a tone that washed through me, pushing away fear and pain as they always did. The souls of the dead rushed past, crystal draperies fluttering and sliding past the edge into the well of souls, impelled down the great expanse of the ballroom of infinity, I curled my fingers in the dog's fur and felt a jolt of warmth slide up my arm.

My left shoulder twinged. The dog looked up, sleek black head inquiring; then nodded, gravely. I found myself laughing. It was all absurd. The demon's mark did not rob me of my ability to walk in Death. I was under the protection of my patron, the Lord of the Dead, what did I have to fear?

Nothing.

I sat straight up, bright metal peeking out between hilt and scabbard. The demon looked down at me, his green eyes subdued now. The file started to slide off my stomach.

I grabbed for the red file, propping the sword to the side, using the floor to brace the end of the scabbard so I could slide the metal back in. It took me a few moments to get situated, but Jaf waited patiently, then handed me a cup of steaming coffee. "Were you dreaming, or Journeying?" he asked.

"Neither." The contact with the psychopomp is private; other Necromances don't talk or write about it easily—and never to strangers or other psis. I would most definitely *not* tell this demon about it. I accepted the coffee cup, sniffed delicately at it. Good and strong.

He'd even added a little bit of creamer, which is how I like my coffee. "Thanks."

He shrugged, folded his hands around the mug he'd chosen. It was the blue one, an interesting choice. Most people chose the white one, a few chose the red geometric TanDurf mug. Only one other person I'd allowed in my house had chosen the blue Baustoh mug.

Maybe the gods were trying to tell me something.

I yawned, scrubbed at my eyes, reached over and hooked up the phone. I'm one of the few people left without a vidshell. I don't want anyone seeing my face unless it's in person. Call me a Ludder, but I distrusted vidshells. And in the privacy of my home, if I wanted to answer the phone naked it was nobody's business but mine.

I keyed in the number. The electronic voice came on, I punched in a few buttons, the program checked my balance and informed me the pizza would be at the door in twenty minutes. I hung up, yawning again. "Pizza's on its way," I said. "You can eat human food, right?"

"I can," he agreed. "You're hungry?"

I nodded, took a sip of coffee. It burned my tongue, I made a face, settled the file in my lap. The tapestry hung on my west wall fluttered uneasily, Horus's eyes shifting back and forth. "I lost lunch *and* breakfast back in that alley, and I need food or I start talking to dead people." I shivered. "*Without* meaning to," I added. "Anyway, I hope you like pepperoni. Make yourself at home while I take a look at this."

He backed away without looking, dropped down in a chair next to a stack of Necromance textbooks holding up a potted euphorbia. Then he just sat, his eyes narrowed, holding the coffee under his nose but not drinking it, watching me.

I opened the file.

Seconds ticked by. I really didn't have the courage to look down yet.

I sipped at my coffee again, slurping, taking in air to cool it. Then I looked down at the file. There was the grainy police laseprint that made my stomach flipflop — Santino getting out of a car, his long icy-pale hair pulled back and exposing his pointed ears, the vertical black teardrops over his eyes holes of darkness. I shut my eyes.

"Get down, Doreen. Get down!"

Crash of thunder. Moving, desperately, scrabbling…fingers scraping against the concrete, rolling to my feet, dodging the whine of bullets and plasbolts. Skidding to a stop just as he rose out of the dark, the razor glinting in one hand, his claws glittering on the other.

"Game over," he giggled, and the awful tearing in my side turned to a burning numbness as he slashed, I threw myself backward, not fast enough, not fast enough—

I shook memory away.

Last seen in Santiago City, Hegemony, it said, and gave a date five years back. *That's the day Doreen died,* I thought, taking another slurp of coffee to cover up my sudden flinch. *He could be anywhere in the world by now.* He had been using the name Modeus Santino, rich and elusive owner of Andro BioMed...we'd thought he was cosmetically modified; the rich got altered to look like whatever they wanted nowadays. After the murder investigation, we found out Andro BioMed was a front for another corporation. But the paper trail stopped cold, since the parent corporation had filed Andro under the Mob corporate laws, effectively rendering itself anonymous.

I hated the Mob like I hated Chill. It wouldn't have hurt any of them to tell us where Santino had gone, it wasn't like we were trying to bring down the Mob as a whole.

We'd squeezed every Mob connection in town and made ourselves a few enemies and finally had to admit defeat. The ancient law of *omerta* still reigned even in this technological age. Santino had vanished.

More pictures.

Pictures of victims.

The first one was the worst because the first one was Doreen lying under the photographer's glare, her legs twisted obscenely aside, her slashed throat an awful gaping smile. Her chest cracked open, her abdominal cavity exposed, her right thigh skinned all the way down to the bone and a chunk of the femur excised by a portable lasecutter. Her eyes were closed, her face peaceful, but it was still...

I looked up at the ceiling. Tears pricked behind my eyes.

Someday someone's going to find out what a soft touch you are, Danny, Reena's voice echoed through years. I hadn't thought of her in a while, no more than I would think of any other deep awful ache. Someone had once accused me of being unfeeling. It wasn't true—I felt it all the way down to the bone. I just didn't see any need to advertise it.

The doorbell rang, chiming through the silent house. I was halfway to my feet before Jaf reached the hallway. I sank back down on the couch, listening. The pizza delivery boy's voice was a piping tenor — *must be the kid with the wheelbike*, I thought. The murmur of the demon's voice replying, and a shocked exclamation from the tenor. *Maybe Jaf tipped him*, I thought, and forced a shaky smile. I already could smell cheese and cooked crust. Yum.

The door closed, and a hot stillness took over the house. The demon was checking my house shields. It was faintly rude — he didn't trust me to have my own house guarded? — but then I set my jaw and turned Doreen's picture over.

Santino hadn't had time to do his usual work-up on Doreen, but there were other pictures, familiar from the case. He had taken different things from each — blood, different organs — but always the femur, or a piece of it. As serial killers went, he was weird only in that he took more numerous trophies than others.

That had been back when the police could afford my services. I still did a turn every now and again, mostly on cases Gabe was working.

I owed Gabe. More important, she was my friend.

He was a demon, I thought. *It all makes sense now. Why didn't he taste like a demon? I wasn't THAT inexperienced . . . and why hasn't Lucifer tracked him down before now?*

I looked up. Jaf stood at the entrance to the living room. My tapestry was shifting madly now, woven strands moving in and out, Horus shimmering, Anubis calm and still, Isis's arms beckoning. "Why hasn't Lucifer tracked him down before now?" I asked. "Fifty years is a long time."

"Not for us," he said. "It might as well have been yesterday."

"Because only *humans* were being carved up." I felt my eyes narrow. "Right?"

He shrugged. The coat moved on him like a second skin. "We don't watch every serial killer and criminal in your world," he said. "We have other ways to spend our time. Our business is with those who want to evolve."

"Get some plates for the pizza, please." I rubbed at my forehead, delicately, with my fingertips. Looked back down at the file.

A teenage girl's eviscerated body peered up at me. Her mouth was open, a rictus of terror. They'd called him the Saint City Slasher in the holovids, lingering over each gory detail, theorizing why he took the femurs, plaguing the cops for information.

I reached for the phone again. Dialed.

It rang seven times, then picked up. "Mrph. Gaar. Huck." Sounded like a monkey with horrible bronchitis.

"Hello, Eddie," I said. "Is Gabe there?"

"Murk. Guff. Ack."

I took that to mean "yes." There was the sound of sliding cloth, then Gabriele's breathless voice. "This had...better be good."

"You got some time tonight for me, Spook?" I asked.

More sliding sounds. A thump. Eddie's cheated growl. "Danny? What's up?"

"I've got a lead," I said. "On the Slasher case."

Silence crackled through the phone line. Then Gabe sighed. "Midnight, my place?" She didn't sound angry. "You know I don't have time for a wild-goose chase, Danny."

"This isn't a wild-goose chase." My jaw ached, I was almost grinding my teeth.

"You have new evidence?" Gabe's voice changed from "friend" to "cop" in under a heartbeat.

"Of a sort," I said. "Nothing that will stand up in court."

"Doesn't follow the rules of paranormal evidence?" She sounded sharp now, sharp and frustrated.

"Come on, Gabe. Don't ride my ass."

The demon paced into the room, carrying the pizza box and two plates. I nodded at him. He stopped dead, watching me.

"Fine." Click of a lighter, long inhale. *She must really be pissed.* "Come over at midnight. You alone?"

"No," I said. I owed her the truth. "I've got company."

"Living, or dead?"

"Neither."

She took this in. "All right, keep your little secret. Jesus. Fine. Come over around midnight, bring your new thing. We'll take a look at it. Now leave me alone."

"See you soon, Spocarelli."

"Fuck you, Dante." Now she was laughing. I heard Eddie growl another question, and the phone slammed back into the cradle.

I hung up and looked across at the tapestry. Horus shifted, Isis's arm raised, palm-out. The great goddess held the ankh to Her chest, protectively. I saw Anubis's head make a swift downward movement.

As if catching prey.

Well, the gods were with me, at least.

"We've got an appointment in two hours with a friend of mine," I told the demon. "Let's go over the file together beforehand, so we're prepared." *Never mind that I'm going to ditch your immortal ass as soon as possible.* I had to fight back the urge to giggle again. "Bring the pizza over, share some space." I patted the couch.

He paused for just the briefest moment before pacing across the room, settling next to me on the couch. I laid the file aside and flipped the pizza box open. Half pepperoni, half vegetarian—I took a slice of either, plopped it on my plate. "Help yourself, Jaf." I prodded him, and he took a single slice of pepperoni. Looked at me. "Haven't you ever had pizza before?"

He shook his head, dark hair sleek and slicked-back. His face was blank, like a robotic mask. A muscle twitched in his smooth cheek. Had I somehow violated some complicated demon etiquette?

I folded the vegetarian slice in half, set the open pizza box on the floor, and took a huge bite. Melted cheese, crust, garlic sauce, and chunks of what used to be vegetable matter. "Mmmh," I said, helpfully. The demon took a bite. He chewed, meditatively, swallowed, then took another bite.

I swallowed, tore into another chunk. Licked my fingers clean. Hot grease and cheese. The food made me a little more solid, gave me some ballast. I had three slices in me before I started to slow down and really taste it. I alternated between chunks of pizza and long gulps of less-scorching coffee. The demon copied me, and between us, we polished off the whole gigantic pizza. He ate three-quarters of it.

"You must have been hungry," I said, finally, licking my fingers clean for the last time. "Damn. That was good."

He shrugged. "Unhealthy," he said, but his green eyes shone. "But yes, very good."

"How long has it been for you?" I asked. "I mean, you don't seem like you get out much, you know."

Another shrug. "Mortal years don't mean that much," he said, effectively stopping the conversation. I squashed a flare of irritation. Served me right, for getting personal with a demon.

"Okay, fine," I said. "How about you tell me why Santino doesn't smell like a demon?"

"He does," Jaf replied. "Just not the kind that's allowed out of Hell. Santino's a scavenger, and a plague, one of the Lower Flight of Hell. But he served the Prince well, and was rewarded for it." Jaf popped the last bit of crust in his mouth, his eyes half-lidding. "That reward allowed him to eventually escape the Prince's strictures and come to this world, with the Egg."

"So what's in the Egg?" *I might as well ask him now,* I thought, *I might not get a chance to later.*

"The Prince told you it's none of your concern," Jaf said, staring blankly at the pizza box. "Is there more?"

"What, three-quarters of a gigantor pie isn't enough for you?" I stared at him. "Why would breaking the Egg be bad?"

"I've rarely had human food," the demon said, and hunched his shoulders, sinking into the couch. "Vardimal must not be allowed to break the Egg. The repercussions would be exceedingly unpleasant."

I blew out a dissatisfied snort. "Like what?" I asked. "Hellfire, brimstone, plagues, what?"

"Perhaps. Or annihilation for your kind," he replied. "We like humans. We want them to live — at least, most of us do. Some of us aren't so sure."

"Great." I toed the empty pizza box. "So what side are you on?"

He shrugged again. "I don't take sides. The Prince points and says that he wants a death, I kill. No philosophy for me."

"So you're on the Prince's side." I wiggled my toes inside my boots, then rocked up to my feet. "You're hungry, huh? That wasn't enough?"

"No." His mouth twisted down on one side.

I scooped up the pizza box and my empty coffee cup. "Okay. Let me see what else I've got. What else do you know about Santino?"

He spread his hands, indicating helplessness. "I can give you his Name, written in our language. Other than that, not much."

"Then what good are you?" Frustration gave my voice an unaccustomed sharp edge. It's usually better to speak softly while a Necromance. Some of us tend to affect a whispery tone after a while. I took a deep breath. "Look, you show up at my door, threaten me, beat up six street punks, drag me through Hell, and finish off the job by eating most of the pizza. The least you can do is give me a little *help* tracking down this demon-who-isn't."

"I can give you his Name, and can track him within a certain distance. Besides, I am to keep you alive," Japhrimel said. "You might find me useful, after all."

"Lucifer said you had a personal stake in this." I balanced the pizza box in one hand. "Well?"

He said nothing. His eyelids dropped a millimeter or so more over burning green eyes. *Lucifer's eyes were lighter*, I thought, and shivered. *Lighter but more awful.*

"You aren't going to tell me anything," I said, finally. "You're just going to try to manipulate me from place to place without telling me anything."

Nothing, again. His face might have been carved out of some golden stone and burnished to a matte perfection. It was like having a statue of a priest sitting on my couch.

That's the last time I try to be nice to a demon, I thought, said it out loud. "That's the last time I try to be nice to a demon." I turned on my heel and stalked away, carrying the empty pizza box. *Fucking demons,* I thought, *rip me away from a nice afternoon spent doing divination and watching the soaps. Now I've got a demon to catch and another goddamn demon sitting on my couch and Doreen . . .*

I folded the pizza box in half, barely noticing. Then I jammed it in the disposer and closed the lid, pressed the black button. "Fucking demons," I muttered. "Push you from square to square, never tell you a goddamn thing. You can take this job and shove it up your infernal—"

Dante. A touch like a breath of cool crystal against my cheek.

I whirled.

The world spun and wavered like a candle flame. I looked down at my hand on the counter, my fingers long and pale, red molecule-drip polish on my nails glimmering under the full-spectrum lights. Necromances can't handle high-end fluorescents on a daily basis.

I could have sworn I heard Doreen's voice, felt her usual touch on my cheek, her fingernails brushing down toward my jaw.

My house is shielded to a fare-thee-well; it would take the psychic equivalent of a thermonuclear explosion to get inside.

A demon could do it, I thought. I blinked.

My sword was in the other room. The living room. I'd left my blade with a demon.

I sprinted down the hall and skidded on the hardwood, turning the sharp corner and bolting into the living room. My sword was where I'd left it, leaning against the couch. The demon sat still with his hands upturned on his knees, his eyes half-closed, a sheet of white paper in one golden hand.

I scooped my sword up and turned on the balls of my feet, metal ringing free from the sheath. Green sparks flashed—my rings were active again, spitting in the charged air. I dropped below conscious thought and *scanned.*

Nothing. Nothing there.

I heard it, I know I heard Doreen's voice. I know I did. I let out a short choppy breath. I'd heard her voice.

My sword rang, very softly, in the silence. The metal was blessed and rune-spelled, I'd spent months pouring Power into it, shaping it into a psychic weapon as much as a physical one, sleeping with it, carrying it everywhere until it was like an extension of my arm. Now it spoke, a chiming song of bloodlust and fear filling the steel, pushing outward in ripples to touch the defenses on my house, making them shiver slightly.

My left shoulder twinged sharply. I glared at the demon, who still hadn't moved.

"Are you expecting a battle?" he asked, finally.

A single drop of sweat rolled down my spine, soaked into the waistband of my jeans. I tried to look everywhere at once.

I heard it. I know I did.

I sheathed my sword, backed up toward my altar, scooped up my bag, and slid it over my head. I needed my knives, would have to go upstairs.

"I'm going upstairs," I told him. "Someone's playing games with me, and I don't like it. I *hate* being played with."

"I am not playing," he told me. He sounded robotic again.

"You wouldn't tell me if you *were,*" I pointed out, and backed out of the room. *Looks like I'll be ditching him right about now,* I thought. *Christ, I'm going to have to leave a demon in my house. This really sucks.*

I made it up the stairs and had my knives on in less than twenty seconds. Then, carrying my sword, I padded to my bedroom window. The chestnut tree that shaded my window had a convenient branch I could drop from.

I had the window open and my foot out when Jaf's hand closed around the back of my neck. "Going somewhere?" he asked in my ear. His fingers were hard, and too hot to be human.

Oh, no, I thought.

CHAPTER 10

I wanted to walk to Gabe's, and the demon had no preference either way. So we walked. The rain had stopped, and the pavement gleamed wet. At least it wasn't darkmoon—that would have been bad all the way around. I get cranky around darkmoon, even with the Espo patch to interrupt my menstrual cycle and keep me from bleeding while I'm on a bounty or just can't be bothered.

I stole glances at the demon as we walked down Trivisidiro Street. Gabe's house was in a bad part of town, but she still had the high stone walls that her great-great-something-or-another had put up. The *real* defenses were Gabe's shields and Eddie's rage. Not even a Chill junkie would intrude on a house held by a Skinlin and a Necromance. Skinlin were mostly concerned with growing things, the modern equivalent of kitchen witches; most of them worked for biotech firms getting plants to give up cures for ever-mutating diseases and splicing together plant DNA with magick or complicated procedures. Skinlin are as rare as *sedayeen* but not as rare as Necromances; most psions are Shamans. Another hot debate between the Ceremonials and Magi and genetic scientists: Why were Necromances and *sedayeen* so rare?

The only real drawback to Skinlin is that they are berserkers in a fight; a dirtwitch in a rage is like a Chillfreak—they don't stop even when wounded. And Eddie was fast and mean even for a dirtwitch.

The demon said nothing, just paced alongside me with even unhurried strides. It was uncomfortably like walking next to a big wild animal.

Not that I'd ever seen a big wild animal, but still.

I lasted until the corner of Trivisidiro and Fifteenth. "Look," I said, "don't hold it against me. You can't blame me for being cautious. You're just here to yank my chain and take this Egg thing back to Lucifer, leaving me in the dust and probably facing down Santino alone to boot. Why shouldn't I be careful?"

He said nothing. Laser-bright eyes glittered under straight eyebrows. His golden cheeks were hairless and perfect—demons didn't need to shave. Or did they? Nobody knew. It wasn't the sort of question you asked them.

"Hello?" I snapped my fingers. "Anyone in there?"

He still said nothing.

I sighed, and looked down at my feet, obediently stepping one after another on the cracked pavement. We had to wait for the light here, Trivisidiro was a major artery for streetside hover and pedicab traffic. "All right," I finally admitted, while we waited for the light. "I'm sorry. There. You happy?"

"You chatter too much," he said.

"Fuck you too," was my graceless and reflexive reply. The light changed, and I didn't look, just stepped off the curb, already planning how to ditch him after Gabe's house.

My left shoulder gave one hot flare of agony. His hand closed around my arm and jerked me back as a warm rush of air blasted up the street. The telltale whine of hovercells crested, and a sleek silver passenger hover jetted past, going well over the speed limit, a sonic wash of antipolice shielding making me cringe.

I should have sensed that, I thought.

I ended up breathless and stunned, staring after the car. Sooner or later a cop cruiser would lock onto it and the driver would end up with a ticket, but right now my skin tingled and roughened with gooseflesh. The demon's fingers unloosed from my arm, one by one.

My breath whooshed out of me. I wasn't focusing on my surroundings. I was too busy grousing to myself over being stuck with a demon. It was unprofessional of me—but more important, it could get me killed. I couldn't afford to lose my focus.

I closed my eyes, promising myself I would *pay attention from now on, okay, Danny? It's no skin off the demon's nose if you fucking well get yourself run over by a frat boy in his daddy's hover.*

I should say thanks, I thought, and then, *If it wasn't for him I wouldn't be standing here, I'd be at home nice and warm and dry. And going on with my life.*

"Thanks," I said finally, opening my eyes and taking a slightly calmer look at the world. "I know you're just doing what you're told...but thanks." *I won't pull a stupid stunt like that again.*

He blinked. That was all the response I got from him.

I checked the street and was about to step out, cautiously, when he caught my arm again.

"Do you hate demons?" he asked, looking out over the empty street. The "don't walk" sign began to flash.

I jerked free of his hand, and he let me. "If what you tell me is true, it was one of yours that killed my best friend," I told him. "She was *sedayeen*. She never hurt anyone in her *life*. But Santino killed her all the same."

He stared across the street as if he found the traffic signals incredibly interesting.

"But no," I continued finally, "I don't hate demons. I just hate being jacked around, that's all. You could have simply asked me nicely instead of sticking a gun in my face, you know."

"I will remember that." Now instead of "robot" he sounded faintly surprised. "Santino killed your friend, then?"

"He didn't just kill her," I snapped. "He terrorized her for months and nearly killed me too."

There was a long silence filled with city sounds—the wail of sirens, distant traffic, the subwhine of urban Power shifting from space to space.

"Then I will make him pay for that," he said. "Come, it's safer now."

I checked again and followed him across the street. When we reached the other side he dropped back to walk beside me, head down, hands behind his back while he paced. My thumb caressed the guard on my sword, wanting to pop the blade free.

If they were right, and I *could* kill Santino, this was the blade that would do it.

Wait until Gabe sees this, I thought, and found myself smiling, a hard delighted smile that would not reach my eyes.

CHAPTER 11

I laid my hand against the gate, let the shields vibrate through me. Gabe's work recognized me, and the gate lock clicked open. I pushed before it could swing closed, slipped through. The demon stepped through almost on my heels, and Gabe's shielding flushed red, swirled uneasily. I bit down on the inside of my cheek and waited.

Gabe's shields settled, turned a deep blue-violet. She'd read what was with me, and wasn't amused.

"Come on," I said, and the demon followed me up the long paved drive. "Keep your mouth shut, okay? This is important."

"As you like," he said. It would be hard for him to sound any more flat or sarcastic.

Just when I was starting to think I might like him, too.

I walked up to the house, my footfalls echoing on pavement. The grounds were ragged, but still evidently a garden. Eddie kept the hedges down and the plots weeded.

I went up the steps to the red-painted door. Gabe's house had layers and layers of shielding—her family had been Necromances and cops for a long time, since before the Parapsychic Act was signed into law, giving psis protected status and also granting citizenship for several other nonhuman races. Gabe's trust fund was humongous and well-managed; she didn't even have to work as a Necromance, let alone as a cop. She had this thing about community service, passed down from her mother's side of the family. I admired that sense of responsibility in her; it made up for her being a rich brat.

I knocked, courteous, feeling a flare of Power right inside the door.

Eddie tore the door open and glowered at me, growling. I smiled, keeping my teeth behind closed lips. The demon, fortunately, said nothing, but a slow tensing of his diamond-flaming aura warned me. The same aura lay over mine, tensing as if to shield me, too.

The shaggy blond Skinlin stood there for a long ten seconds or so, measuring us both. His shoulders hulked, straining at his T-shirt, and the smell of wet earth and tree branches made the air heavy around him. I kept my hands very still. If he jumped for me he wouldn't stop until one or both of us was bleeding.

Gabe resolved out of the shadows, her sword out, soft light sliding on the blade's surface. "You didn't tell me you were bringing a demon," she said, her low soft voice a counterpoint to Eddie's growling.

Gabriele Spocarelli was small and slender, five foot two inches of muscle and grace. Her Necromance tat glittered on her cheek, the emerald spitting and twinkling a greeting that my own cheek burned, answering. She wore a scoop-necked silk sweater and a pair of torn jeans, and looked casually elegant in a way I had always secretly envied. I always wondered what she saw in a dirty misanthropic hedge-wizard, but Eddie seemed to treat her well and was almost fanatically protective of her. Gabe needed it. She got into a lot of trouble for a homicide detective—almost as much trouble as I did.

Almost.

"I'm kind of surprised by that myself," I said. "Truce?" I reached up slowly and pulled cloth away from my shoulder, exposing about half of the red, scarred brand that was the mark of a demon familiar. "I've got a story to tell you, Gabe."

Gabriele considered me for a long moment, her eloquent dark eyes passing over the demon and back to the mark on my shoulder. Then her sword flickered back into its sheath. "Eddie, can you get us some tea?" she asked. "Come in, Danny. You've never pulled a mickey on me before; I suppose you're not pulling one now."

"You can't be serious," Eddie started, his blond eyebrows pulling together. *Why does he never seem to shave?* I thought, letting go of my shirt. I felt better with the mark covered up.

"Oh, come on, Eddie," she said. "Live a little. Tea, please. And you—whoever you are—" Her eyes flicked over Jaf. "If you bring trouble into my house, I'll send you back to Hell posthaste. Got it?"

I saw the demon nod out of the corner of my eye. He said nothing. Good for him.

Inside Gabe's house, the scented dark pulled close. She'd been burning kyphii. I closed my eyes for a moment and filled my lungs. She wasn't the most powerful Necromance around, but she had a quality of precision and serenity most Necromances lacked. Necromances don't often like hanging out with each other. We tend to be a neurotic bunch of prima donnas, in fact. To find someone I actually liked who understood what it was like to see the dead...that was exceptional.

She led us into the kitchen, where Eddie had the kettle on. He had my regular cup out, too, the long sinuous black mug reserved for me. "Tea?" I asked the demon, and he spread his hands, helplessly. "He'll have tea. I've told him not to open his mouth, it'll get us all in trouble."

"Good thinking." Gabe set her sword down on the counter. I prefer a katana-shaped blade, but Gabe went for a two-handed longsword that seemed far too big for her slim hands. And believe me when I say I never want to face her across that edged metal. "So you said, about that case..."

I dug the file out of my bag and handed it to her. "The Prince of Hell wants me to track down this guy. His name's Vardimal—our old buddy Santino."

"The Prince of—" Her eyes stuttered past me, fastened on Jaf.

"Apparently this is the Devil's errand boy," I said, trying to strangle the mad giggle that rose up inside me. It didn't work; I snorted out half a laugh and shivered. "I've had a *really* rough day, Gabe."

She flipped the file open, even though she knew what it contained. Her face turned paper-white.

"Gabriele?" Eddie's voice held only a touch of a growl.

Gabriele fumbled in her pocket, dug out a crumpled pack of Gitanes, and fished one out with trembling fingers. She produced a silver Zijaan and clicked the flame into life. The smell of burning synth hash mixed with the pungent spice of kyphii. "Make some tea, Eddie," she said, and her voice was steady and husky. "Goddamn."

I perched on a stool on the other side of the breakfast counter. "Yeah." My own voice was husky, maybe from the smoke in the air.

Gabe slapped the file closed, not even looking at the demon's addition—the single sheet of paper with silvery lines marking Vardimal-Santino's name in the demon language. "You really think..."

"I do," I answered. "Honestly."

She considered this, took another drag off her smoke. The emerald set in her cheek flashed, popped a spark out into the air; my rings answered with a slow steady swirling. Eddie poured hot water into the cups. I sniffed. Mint tea. "What do you need?" Gabe finally asked.

"I need a paranormal-Hunt waiver on my bounty hunter's license." That was fairly standard and carried no liability for her; all I'd have to do was have her sign off on the paperwork. Now came the big stuff. "I need two H-DOC and omni-license-to-carry, and I need a plug-in for the Net." I licked my dry lips. If I was going to go after a demon, I needed all the policeware I could beg, borrow, or steal. The H-DOC and the plug-in would give me access to Hegemony cop computers and the treaty-access areas of Putchkin cop nets, and the omni license would be nice to have if I needed a plascannon or a few submachine guns to make sure the demon stayed down.

"Christ," Eddie snorted. "And a partridge in a pear tree. Want her fucking left kidney too, Danny?"

I ignored him, but the demon shifted his weight, standing right behind me. My left shoulder throbbed, a persistent fiery ache.

Gabe's dark eyes half-lidded, and she inhaled more smoke. "I can get you the para waiver and one H-DOC and maybe an omni, but a plug-in... I don't know. This doesn't constitute new evidence."

"What if I made a donation?" I asked. My rings spat and crackled. "This is *important*."

"Don't you think I know that?" she snapped. "What the fuck, Danny?"

I accepted my tea from Eddie, who slammed a pink flowered ceramic mug down for the demon. My mouth quirked, turned down at the corners. "I'm sorry," I said. "I just…Doreen, you know."

"I know." Gabe flipped over another page. "I can't get a judge to sign a plug-in for you on the basis of this…but I can ask around and see what the boys can do on the unofficial side. Might even be able to get you some backup. What do you say?"

"I work alone." I jerked my head back at Jaf. "The only reason I let him tag along is because I've been forced into it. You should have seen it, Gabe. It was awful."

She shuddered, a faint line beginning between her perfect charcoal eyebrows. "I have no desire to ever see that, Danny. Graeco Hades is enough for me."

I had never asked who her personal psychopomp was. Now I wondered. It wasn't a polite question—each key to unlock Death's door is different, coded into the deepest levels of breath and blood and consciousness that made up a Necromance. It was like looking in someone's underwear drawer to the *nth* degree.

I blew across the top of my tea to cool it. Gabe flipped grimly through the rest of the file. Her fingers shook a little; she tapped hot ash into a small blue ceramic bowl. Eddie hovered in the kitchen, running his blunt fingers back through his shaggy blond-brown hair, his eyes fixed on Gabriele's drawn-back lips and tense shoulders.

"Gods above and below," she said, finally. "Can that thing actually track Santino?"

I half-turned on the stool. Jaf's eyes met mine. Had he been watching the back of my head? Why?

"Can you track him?" I asked.

He shrugged, spreading his hands again to indicate helplessness. I glared at him. "Ah." He cleared his throat. It was the first almost-human sound I'd heard from him. "Once I am close enough, I can track him. The problem will be finding the part of your world to look in."

"I *need* a plug-in to get information on who's in whatever town I go to," I said softly, swiveling back to look at Gabe. "The nightside will help me trace him, especially if he's up to his old tricks. Dacon can do me up a tracker, but if Santino's a fucking demon and notices me using Magi magick, he might be able to counter." I paused. *"Hard."*

Gabe chewed at her lower lip, considering this. She looked over at Eddie, finally, and the Skinlin stilled. Motionless, barely even breathing, he stood in the middle of the clean blue-tiled kitchen, his blunt fingers hanging loosely at his sides.

She finally looked up at me. "You'll get your plug-in. Give me twenty-four hours."

I nodded, took another sip of my tea. "Good enough. I'm going to visit Dacon and the Spider, and I need to kit myself out. Has Dake moved?"

"You kidding? You know him, can't stand to walk down the street alone. He's still in that hole out on Pole Street," she answered. "You've got to get some sleep, Danny. I know how you are when you hunt."

I shrugged. "I don't think I'll get much sleep for a while. Not until I rip his spleen out — Vardimal, Santino, whoever he is. *Whatever* he is."

"If he was a demon, why didn't we know?" Gabe tapped her short, bitten nails against her swordhilt.

I tipped my head back, indicating Jaf. "*He* says Santino's a scavenger, and they aren't allowed out of Hell. This one escaped with something Lucifer wants back."

"Great." Her mouth turned down briefly. "One thing, Danny. Don't bring that *thing* here ever again."

My rings spat green sparks. It was small consolation that Gabe understood how much more dangerous the demon was than me. I would have thought she'd be a little more understanding, knowing what it was like to be pointed and sneered at on the street.

But then again, a demon *was* something different. "He's not a thing," I remarked acidly, and Japhrimel gave me a sidelong look. "He's a demon. But don't worry, I won't."

CHAPTER 12

I needed to shake out the fidgets and think, and I thought best while moving. I doubted the demon could ride a slicboard, so we walked. The demon trailed me, his boots echoing against pavement. My fingers locked so tightly around my scabbard they ached.

Bits of foil wrappers and discarded paper cups, cigarette butts,

the detritus of city life. I kicked at a Sodaflo can, the aluminum rattling against pavement. Little speckles from quartz in the pavement,
broken glass, a rotting cardboard Cereon box, a pigeon hopping in
the gutter, taking flight with a whir of wings.

Two blocks fell away under my feet. Three.

"That went well," Jaf said finally.

I glanced up at him from my boot toes. "You think so?" I settled
my bag against my hip. "Gabe and I go way back."

"Gabe?" His tone was faintly inquiring. "And you're...Danny.
Dante."

"I had a classical humanist for a social worker." I stroked my
swordhilt. "I tested positive for psionic ability, got tossed into the
Hegemony psi program. I was lucky."

"Lucky?"

"My parents could have sold me as an indentured, probably in a
colony, instead of having me in a hospital and automatically giving
me to the foster program," I said. *Though a colony would have been
preferable to Rigger Hall.* For a moment the memory — locked in the
cage, sharp bites of nothingness and madness against my skin; or the
whip burning as it laid a stroke of fire along my back — rose to choke
me. The Hall had been hell — a true hell, a human hell, without the
excuse of demons to make it terrifying. "Or sold me to a wage-farm,
worked until my brain and Talent gave out. Or sold me as a breeder,
squeezing out one psi-positive baby after another for the colony program. You never know."

"Oh."

I looked up again, caught a flash of his eyes. Had he been looking
at me? His profile was bony, almost ugly, a fall of light from a streetlamp throwing dark shadows under his eyes and cheekbones. His
aura was strangely subdued, the diamond darkness folding around
him.

Like wings.

I was lucky. I didn't know who my parents were, but their last gift
to me had been having me in a hospital and signing the papers to turn
me over to the Hegemony. Even though the Parapsychic Act was law
and psis were technically free citizens, bad things still happened.
Psis were still sold into virtual slavery, especially if their Talent was
weak or their genes recessive. And most especially if they were born
in backroom clinics or in the darkness of redlight districts and
slums.

His black coat made a slight sound as he moved. He had a habit of clasping his hands behind his back while walking, which gave him a slow, measured gait. "So what do you do?" I asked. "In Hell, I mean. What's your job?"

If I thought his profile was ugly before it became stonelike and savage now, his mouth pulling down and his eyes actually turning darker, murderously glittering. My heart jumped into my throat, I tasted copper.

"I am the assassin," he said finally. "I am the Prince's Right Hand."

"You do the Devil's dirty work?"

"Can you find some other title to give him?" he asked. "You are exceedingly rude, even for a human. Demons do not conform to your human idea of evil."

"You're an exceeding asshole, even for a demon," I snapped. "And the human idea of evil is all I've got. So what is such an august personage doing hanging out with me?"

"If I keep you alive long enough to recover the Egg, I will be free," he said through gritted teeth.

"You mean you're not free now?"

"Of course not." He tilted his head up, as if listening. After a few moments, I heard a distant siren. My left shoulder twinged. "Where are we going?"

"I'm going to see Dacon. He's a Magi, he'll just *love* you." My jaw ached and my eyes were hot and grainy. "After that I'm going to get some sleep, then I'll visit the Spider. And by then Gabe should have everything together, and I'll start hunting."

"I suppose you will try to escape me as soon as possible," he said.

"Not tonight," I promised him. "I'm too tired tonight."

"But afterward?" he persisted. "I don't want to lose my chance at freedom for your petty human pride."

"You say 'human' like it's a dirty word." I tucked my free hand in my pocket. My rings were dark now, no longer glittering and sparking. Out here, in the flux and ambient static of city Power, the atmosphere wasn't charged enough to make them react. Instead, they settled into a watchful gleam.

"That's the same way you say 'demon,'" he shot back, immediately. Was he *scowling*? I had never seen a demon scowl, and I stared, fascinated.

I'm not going to win this one, I realized, and dropped my eyes hurriedly back down to the pavement. "You stuck a gun in my face." It was lame even by my standards.

"That's true," he admitted. "I did. I thought you were a door-guard. Who knows what the best Necromance of a generation has guarding the door? I was only told to collect you and keep you alive. Nothing else, not even that you were a woman."

I stopped short on the sidewalk and examined him. He stopped, too, and turned slightly, facing me.

I pulled my free hand from my pocket, stuck it out. "Let's start over," I said. "Hi. I'm Danny Valentine."

He paused for so long that I almost snatched my hand back, but he finally reached out and his fingers closed around mine. "I am Japhrimel," he said gravely.

I shook his hand twice, had to pull a little to take my hand back. "Nice to meet you." I didn't mean it—I would rather have never seen his face—but sometimes the little courtesies helped.

"Likewise," he said. "I am very pleased to meet you, Danny."

Maybe he was lying, too, but I appreciated the effort. "Thanks." I started off again, and he fell into step beside me. "So you're Lucifer's Right Hand, huh?"

He nodded, his profile back to its usual harsh almost-ugly lines. "Since I was hatched."

"Hatch—" Then I figured out I didn't want to know. "Never mind. Don't tell me, I don't want to know."

"You're very wise," he said. "Some humans pester us incessantly."

"I thought you liked that," I said. "Demons, I mean, as a whole."

He shrugged. "Some of us have leave from the Prince to answer the calls of the Magi. I have not had much traffic with humans."

"Neither have I," I told him, and that seemed to finish up conversation for a while. I was glad. I had a whole new set of things to worry about—how Dacon would react, and how the news of me hanging out with one of Hell's citizens would get around town *really* fast, especially if I saw Abra. I couldn't leave the demon behind—he might get into trouble, and besides, I didn't think he'd take to waiting in an alley while I went into Dake's club.

CHAPTER 13

was right. "Absolutely not," he said, his eyes turning almost incandescent.

"Okay, fine, keep your hat on." I looked across the rain-slick street. A few sleek cigar-shaped personal hovers drifted in a parking pattern overhead, and there were several slicboards leaning against the side of the old warehouse, reactive paint glowing on their undersides. I scanned them out of habit and noticed one had a hot magtag; evidently some kid had jacked it. I clucked out through my teeth. Kids stealing slicboards, what next? Then again, since hovers had palmlocks and bodyscans built in standard now, a slic was all a kid could steal.

Pole Street rang with neon and nightlife around us. I shivered, hunching my shoulders, and sighed. "If you want to go in with me, you're going to have to do what I tell you, okay? Let me do the talking and *don't start a fight* unless I start one first. Okay? And try not to kill anyone—just hurt them bad enough to keep them down."

He nodded, his dark hair stuck to his head with dampness. A fine drizzle had started around Trivisidiro and Eighteenth Street, and followed all the way out into the Tank. A block down from us, a group of freelance hookers huddled under an overhang, the neon running wetly off their pleather sheaths and go-go boots. A cop cruiser slid by like a silent shark, bristling with antennas and humming with riot-shields. It drifted to a stop by the hookers, and I wondered if they were scanning for licenses or looking for a little fun.

I licked my dry lips, nervous. "Actually," I said, "can you look scary? It would help."

He bared his teeth, and I had to fight down the urge to step back.

"Okay," I said. "You win. You just look scary and I'll do the talking."

We crossed the street, the demon keeping step slightly behind me, and stepped up on the pavement on the other side. There were two bouncers there—shaved gorillas with black-market augments, three times my size. My fingers itched.

Don't let there be any trouble, I prayed silently.

I came to a stop right in front of the bouncers. The one on the left paled visibly, seeing my tat. The one on my right looked the demon over, his fat cheeks quivering with either terror or silent laughter. I inhaled deeply, tasting night air, hash smoke, and the salt-sweat-sweet smell of Chill. Did Dake know one of his bouncers was on Clormen-13? That shit was nasty, it made addicts psychotic after a while. Taking down a Chillfreak was hard work.

I tilted my head so my tat was visible to both of them. "Dacon Whitaker," I said, pitching my voice loud enough to slice through the pounding bass thudding out the door.

The bouncer on the right nodded. I saw the telltale glint of a comm-link glittering from his right ear, and his throat swelled. He had a subvocal implant, too.

Great. Dake knew I was coming.

"He's indisposed," Shaved Gorilla #1 said. He had muttonchop and some very nice custom-made leather pants straining at his massive legs.

"Either he sees me now, or I tear his club apart and bring the cops down here. He can be charged for interfering with a legitimate hunt." My lips peeled back from my teeth. "I'm doing a bounty, and I'm in a bad mood. It's up to him."

The demon's hot silence swelled behind me. Five seconds. Ten. Fifteen.

"Come on in," the gorilla on the right said. "Go up to the office, the big man says."

I nodded and passed between them, the demon moving close. Together we plunged into a swirling migraine attack of red and orange light, skitters of brightness from the blastball hanging from the ceiling, hash smoke and the reek of alcohol mixing with the smell of sweat and the psychic assault of a warehouse full of people, sunk in the music, most of them dancing. A thin edge of red desperation curled over a smile, a razor-flick against a numb arm.

I was used to the sensory assault, barely paused, my mental shields thickening. There were ghostflits in the corners, riding the air, a few of them silently screaming.

People think that when they die, the Light opens up and takes them. A majority of the time, that's what happens. But sometimes— often enough—the soul is chained here. Sometimes confused, or held by violent death, and sometimes just unable to leave without a loved one, the souls of the dead crowd toward the living any place there's Power enough to feed them and make them more than just a cold sigh against the nape, more than just a memory.

Back before the Parapsychic Act, there was about fifty years of psionics being bought and sold by corporations like chattel — even Necromances. And before that, Necromances were generally locked in asylums or driven to suicide by what we saw — what nobody else could see. Some, like Gabe's ancestors, made it through by keeping mum about their talents, blending in. Others just assumed they were crazy.

I forced my way through the crowd, each person a padded sledge-hammer blow, laid completely open by hash and trance music. I recognized the track — it was RetroPhunk's "Celadon Groove".

If I could stand being around a crowd again, I could dance to this, I thought, and felt a sharp twisting pain. I hadn't danced for three years. Not since Jace.

Don't think about that. My head came up; I scanned the crowd. Like most psis, I disliked crowds, especially riot-crowds or large groups all stoned on hash. Sure, I could jack in and ride the Power created by that much wide-open emotional energy — but I had no need of it. Other psis knew enough to keep their thoughts to themselves, but most normals were sloppy broadcasters, hammering at even the best of shields with the chaotic wash of sense-impressions and thoughts. It was like walking through a field of unmuffled hovers; even if you had earplugs the noise still settled against the pulse and bones, and hurt.

No. Maybe it wasn't the dancing or the crowd that hurt, maybe it was only my heart. I hadn't thought of Jace in at least six months.

Writhing bodies pulsed on the lit-up dance floor. I saw couples twisted around each other, a few shadowed booths in back full of bodies that could have been swooning in love or death. A sharp strain of desperate sex rode the air. My nostrils flared and my rings sparked. I could have jacked into the atmosphere and *used* that Power for a Greater Work, if I'd needed to. I slid between two tarted-up, rail-thin yuppie girls so doped-out on hash it was a wonder they were still vertical; nodded to the bartender.

Behind the bar was a moth-eaten red velvet curtain that the bartender — a skinny nervous man in a red jumpsuit, a cigarette hanging from his lips — pushed aside. A safety door was slightly open, a slice of yellow light leaking out and into the smoky air.

The music shifted. My skin prickled with heat and uneasy energy.

Goddammit, that bastard at the door warned Dake and now he's getting ready. I wanted him off-balance.

I jumped forward, darted through the door, and ran lightly up the stairs. I wasn't in the best shape—my stomach was still bruised and tender from puking and my entire body felt just a fraction of a second too slow—but when I spun into Dake's plasglass-walled office, my sword already drawn, he *did* look surprised. He was up to his pudgy elbows with venomous green snapping Power, and was just turning away from the open iron casket on his desk.

Dacon was a Magi, albeit a weak one. He'd been a few years behind me at Rigger Hall, and I still thought of him as the same pudgy-faced kid with his uniform all sloppy and his mouth loose and wet from too much synth hash. He'd barely managed to produce a low-level imp to qualify for Magi-accreditation, and his tat was a plain round Celtic symbol with no taste. All in all, he wasn't the best for this type of work, but he was the only Magi I could conceivably bully into doing me a tracker for a demon without having to pay an arm and a leg for it.

Even though Dake was a lousy Magi when it came to calling up demons, he was pretty good at the offensive magicks. He couldn't fight much physically, but with enough of a Power charge he was fast and nasty. That, I suspected, was why he rarely if ever left his night-club. I hadn't heard of him being on the street in years. He was as close to a shut-in as it was possible for a psion to get.

And that was also why he was the perfect choice to do a tracker for me. It was a passive offensive piece of magick, which meant it was right up his alley—and he didn't have to leave his nightclub to do it.

"You son of a *bitch*," I said, pleasantly. "You were planning on giving me a little surprise, weren't you, Dacon? Just like the little bitch you are." My blade spat blue-green, light running along its razor edge. The runes I'd spelled into the steel sparked into life, twisting fluidly along the length of the blade. And the demon's aura laid over mine sparked and swirled.

Dacon squeaked, his round pale face suddenly slick with sweat. I felt more than heard the arrival of the demon behind me, and Dacon nearly passed out, swaying, his expensive Drakarmani shirt wet and clinging under his armpits. "You—*you*—" he spluttered, and the green glow arced between his fingers. Sloppy of him.

"Me," I answered. "Of course. Who else would come and talk to you, Dake? Nobody likes you, you have no friends—why are you so fucking surprised?"

Dake's eyes flicked past me. He wore a pair of shiny pleather pants straining to hold his ample legs in. "You have a...that's a...you've got—"

"A demon familiar." My voice was edged with a hard delight that I didn't really feel. "Jealous, Magi? I'll have him talk to you up close, if you like."

The demon moved past me, almost as if reading my mind. The diamond flares of his aura spread, filling the room, closing around the unlucky Magi. I held my sword slanting across my body, the blessed steel a defense from the demon who bore down on Dacon with slow, even steps.

"What the *fuck* you want?" Dake yelled, scrambling back and almost leaping on top of his desk. "*Christ*, Danny, what you *want*? Just tell me!"

The demon paused, again as if reading my mind.

"Information," I said, scanning the room. Something was off here, one instrument was out of tune, screwing up the whole damn band.

My nostrils flared.

Salt-sweat-sweet. The odor of Chill.

I fumbled the paper out of my bag. Silver flashed from my rings. I approached Dake carefully, brushing past the demon, who stood taut and ready. I unfolded the paper, glanced down at the twisted rune that was Vardimal's name. The African masks Dake hung on the walls ran with wet red light through the plasglass windows. People downstairs were dancing, strung out on hash and sex, unaware of the drama going on right overhead.

"I want you to give me a tracker keyed to this name, Dake. And if you're a very good boy, I won't call the Patrols in to get rid of your Chill stash." *You lousy, stupid motherfucker,* I thought. *Chill's going to eat you alive. And how many lives are you going to destroy, dealing here? No wonder one of your bouncers is on that shit. Gods damn you, Dake.*

His round, brown eyes rolled. I held up the paper, ready to jump back if the green glow around his hands struck for me. He stuttered.

"I ain't—I'm not—*Danny*—" A thin thread of spittle traced down his stubbled chin. His mouth worked.

"Don't fucking lie to me!" I snarled, my sword whipping up,

stopping just in time. Razor steel caressed his wet double-chin. "Now, are you going to do me a tracker, Dake, or do I get all catholic and burn this goddamn place down?" *Where did the demon go?* I wondered. *Too much static, where did he go?*

The demon's arm shot past me, fingers sinking into Dake's throat under its slab of fat, pushing my sword aside. I resheathed my blade. "Put. It. Down," the demon said, in a low throbbing impossible-to-ignore voice.

Something metallic clattered on the floor. I didn't glance down. The green glow lining the Magi's hands drained away.

Dake's face crumpled. He began to sob.

Oh, Sekhmet sa'es. *If he starts to cry I'll be here all night calming him down.*

"Let go of him," I snapped. "He won't be good for anything if you make him cry."

The demon made a low, growling sound. "As you like," he finished. Dake whined, gibbering with fear.

I was perilously close to losing my temper. Instead, I curled my fingers into Dake's shoulder as the demon retreated. "Oh, c'mon, Dake, we're just playing around, right? You don't mean to hurt me. You *like* me. You want to be my *friend*, don't you, Dake?" Exactly as I would talk to a four-year-old.

Dake whined and nodded, his lank brown hair flopping forward over his sweaty forehead. Just like school. I'd interfered once when some of the bigger Magi kids had been pushing Dake around, and had to suffer his pathetic attachment for the rest of my career at Rigger Hall. The trouble with Dake was that he had no grit in him; if he hadn't already been broken Mirovitch and Rigger Hall would have wrecked him. For a Magi to lack a magickal Will was bad news; the Power wouldn't obey and his or her spells would go awry. I was of the private opinion that it was a good thing Dake hadn't been able to call up more than an imp inside a chalk circle with a whole collection of more experienced Magi standing guard in case things went wrong; an unwary, cowardly Magi would be easy prey for anything larger than an imp.

And I wondered what would have happened if something like Jaf had shown up in response to Dake's summonings. A Greater Flight demon could kill even from within a chalked circle; that's why they were so hard to call up. Lucky me, getting to hang out with one.

The demon made a low grinding sound, a growl. "Good," I said.

"Good. You'll be my good boy, Dake, and give me a tracker. Then I'll be out of your hair and you can go back to selling Chill and waiting for it to burn out your fucking brain and your Talent as well."

"I'm not *on* Chill," he lied, his eyes shifting back and forth.

I cursed internally. *Does he have enough Talent left to do a decent tracker?* I stepped back, and Dake slid down from the desk, his boots hitting the floor. I half-turned, looked at the demon. Japhrimel's eyes were incandescent green. "Make sure he doesn't move," I said, and didn't wait for the answer.

Below conscious level, the spinning vortex of darkness that was the demon focused on a red-brown pulsing smear. Dake.

My own aura under the demon's shielding held the trademark glitters of a Necromance. I watched those glitters swirl, reacting to the presence of the demon and the nervous spatters of red-brown Dake was giving off. On this level, Dacon Whitaker was visibly in trouble, gaping holes in his aura, Power jittering and trembling out of his control. Dake's Power would escape him, eat him alive as the Chill consumed his nervous system. But not yet—not yet. He had his Power—but not for very much longer.

I snapped back into myself. The demon was absolutely still and silent, his shoulder touching mine, his eyes eating into a trembling Dake.

I held the paper up. "I need a tracker, Dake. Get your kit, and be quick. I've got other shit to do tonight."

When it was finished, the tracker looked like a globe of spun crystal and silver wire, a crystal arrow inside it, pulsing faintly reddish as it spun. "What's the range on this thing?" I asked, almost forgetting that Dake was a Chillfreak now. When he was motivated he did good work, and it was always nice to see another magickal discipline perform.

"Worldwide, baby, it's a Greater Work. Let it settle for about twenty-four hours, then give it the keyword and it'll go live. Use sparingly." Dake coughed into his palm, scuttling back toward his desk. The odor of burning blood in the air had bothered me for the first ten minutes, but my nose was acclimated now.

I've never seen anyone grind up a frog before, I thought, and shivered. I dropped the tracker in a small leather pouch and settled it carefully around my neck. "Okay, Dake. Thanks."

I did not tell him I owed him one.

He blinked at me. "You're not going to kill me?" he whined.

The thudding bass beat of the music downstairs made me nervous. "No," I said. "Of course not, you idiot. Why would I kill you?"

As if he was a goddamn normal instead of a Magi who should know better.

"I know how you feel about Chill," he stuttered, "and if you think I—"

No shit you know how I feel about Chill, everyone knows how I feel about that shit. "I don't *think*, Dake." I turned on my heel and started for the door. "I know. And you'll get yours soon enough. The Chill's going to eat you, Dacon. There's no detox for it. You're a stupid motherfucker."

"It's not my *fault!*" he yelled after me as I swung out the door. "It's *not!*"

"Yeah," I said, and stamped down the stairs into the womblike starred dark of the club below. "Sure it's not, Dacon. Nothing ever is."

Hot salt spilled down my cheeks as I pushed through the crowd of people and finally, blessedly, achieved the coolness of the street outside. One of the bouncers—probably the Chillfreak—sniggered something behind me, and for a single heartbeat I considered turning around and separating him from his liver.

I wrestled the urge down, still striding along the cracked pavement, my shields resounding. I waited until I turned the corner to stop, head down, my ribs heaving. I had jammed my sword into the loop on my belt, not trusting myself with edged metal right now.

"Are you injured?" the demon asked.

I almost flinched. The hard impenetrable darkness of his aura swirled once, counterclockwise, brushed against my aura's sparkling. Checking for damage. I shivered, my shields thickening reflexively, pushing the touch away. It was bad enough to smell like a demon, I didn't want him pawing at me. Even on an energetic level.

"I'm fine," I forced out through a hard lump in my throat. "I just wanted to…I'm fine."

He didn't say anything else. Instead, he only stood there. Another human being might have asked me useless questions, tried to say something comforting. Apparently a demon wouldn't.

I finally wiped my cheeks and scanned the street, deserted except for me and a demon. "Okay," I said. "We've got our tracker. Let's go."

"Is he a friend of yours?" The demon tipped his chin back, indicating the vague direction of the club with one elegant motion. His eyes were darker now, strange runic patterns slipping through the depths of green light.

"Not any more," I said, casting around for a callbox.

There was one down at the end of the street, and I set out for the lighted plasteel box. The demon followed me, moving as silently as a manta ray slipping through dark water.

I passed my hand over the credit square, flushing my palm with Power. The door clicked open, and I stepped into the callbox. It was one of the older ones without a vidshell. *Thank the gods for small favors.* "Hold the door," I said, and the demon put out his golden hand, held the folding door aside.

I picked up the handset and dialed the copshop.

"Vice, Horman speaking," Detective Lew Horman snarled on the other end.

"Horman? It's Danny." My voice sounded normal. A little husky, but normal.

"Aw fer Christ's sake—"

I didn't know he was a Christer. "Don't blaspheme, Detective. Look, I've got a word for you."

"What the fuck now, deadhead? I ain't Homicide!" The high edge of fear colored his voice.

"You know the Chill that's been soaking the South Side? I found out a major distributor."

That got his attention. He literally gasped.

I waited a beat. "Of course, if you're not interested—"

"Goddammit, you deadhead freak. Give it up."

"Dacon Whitaker, out of his club. One of his bouncers is a Chill-freak and so is he now."

"A fuckin magician's a Chillfreak? I thought they didn't—"

"They don't last long, but they're nasty while they do. I'd take some para backup with you. Don't mention my name, okay?"

"Quiet as the grave," Horman snorted.

I let it pass. "You owe me one, Horman," I said, and hung up without waiting to hear his reply.

The demon still said nothing.

I took my hand off the phone and looked out the wavering safety-glass at the dark street, pools of streetlamp glow shivering on wet pavement. "Fuck," I said finally, and clenched my hand. *"Fuck!"*

My fist starred the safety glass in a spreading spiderweb, I pulled back and let another one fly. This punch left a bloody print on the cracked glass.

Then I stopped, gasping for breath, fighting for control. My pulse pounded in my ears.

When I had swallowed the last of my rage, I opened my eyes to find the demon studying me. His eyes were even darker. "What did you do?" he asked, mildly enough.

"I just turned Dake in to the cops," I told him through gritted teeth.

"Why?" It was a passionless inquiry.

"Because he'll kill people with that Chill shit."

"A drug?"

"Yeah, a nasty drug." *A drug that makes mothers abandon their infant babies at the hospital, a drug that eats people whole, a drug that makes punk kids shoot social workers on the street in broad day-light, a drug that swallows whole families and smashes psions. A drug the Hegemony won't get serious about outlawing because the Mob gets too much taxable income off it, a drug the cops can barely stem the tide against because half of them are on the take anyway and the other half are so choked with paperwork they can't stop it.*

Between Chill and the Mob, it was hard to tell which I hated more.

"Why not let those stupid enough to take it, die?"

I considered him, my bleeding hand curled tightly in my unwounded hand. Dake had been at Rigger Hall; I suppose I couldn't blame him for wanting some oblivion. My own nightmares were bad enough; just the thought of that place made my shields quiver.

Valentine, D. Student Valentine is called to the headmaster's office immediately.

And the Headmaster's chilly, precise, dry little voice. *We've got something special for those who break the rules today, Miss Valentine.* The smell of chalk and spoiled magick, the feel of a collar's metal against my naked throat and collarbones...

Thinking about it made the scars on my back ache again, an ache I knew was purely psychic. Three stripes, running down my back; and the other scar, the burn scar, just at the bottom crease of my left buttock. Dake probably had his own scars...but that was no excuse to drown them in Chill. After all, I managed to live without drown-ing mine, didn't I? It was no excuse.

Was it? Or had I just turned him in because I was having a pissy day?

"Because I'm human," I informed him tightly, "and I operate by human rules. Okay?" I wasn't about to tell him about Lewis bleeding to death on the sidewalk, dead by a Chillfreak's hand, his antique watch and Rebotnik sneakers stolen to hawk for more Chill. It was private. And anyway, why did he care why I hated Chill? It was enough that I hated it.

He shrugged. "Your hand."

I stared at him. "What?"

"Give me your hand."

After a moment's consideration, I extended my hand. He folded his fingers over it, still holding the door of the callbox open with his other elbow. My entire hand fit inside his palm, and his fingers were hard and warm.

A spine-tingling rush of Power coated my entire body. His eyes glowed laser-green. The pain crested, drained away.

When he let go of my hand, it was whole and unwounded under a mask of blood. I snatched it back, examined it, and looked up at him.

"I will endeavor to remember human rules," he said.

"You don't have to," I found myself saying. "You're a demon, you're not one of us."

He shrugged. Stood aside so I could exit the callbox.

I let the folding door accordion shut behind me. The light inside the callbox flicked off.

"Okay," I said.

"What next?"

I took a deep breath. Looked at my hand. "Next I go home and try to get some sleep. Tomorrow I'm visiting Abracadabra—a friend. I'll see if she can give me a direction to go in and some contacts. Better not to use the tracker until I'm sure I need it."

"Very well." He still didn't move, just stood there watching me.

A gigantic lethargy descended on me. Why did it all have to be so *hard*? The pressure behind my eyes and throat and nose told me I was a few minutes away from sobbing. I set my jaw and scanned the street again.

Empty. Of course. Just when I needed a cab.

"Okay," I said again. "Come on."

He fell into step behind me, silent as Death Himself.

CHAPTER 14

I lay on my back, holding my sword to my chest, looking up at the dark ceiling. My eyes burned.

I slept with my rings on, and the shifting blue-green glow sliding against the ceiling told me I was agitated.

As if I don't already know, I thought, and my fingers clasped the sword more tightly.

Downstairs the demon sat in front of my fireplace. My shields buzzed and blurred; he was adding his own layers of protection. Even my home wasn't mine anymore. Of course, on the plus side, that meant a better shielding for my house.

If I'd been born a Magi, I would have at least some idea of how to deal with a demon in my house. I probably would have even been excited. Magi worked with circles and trained for years to achieve regular contact with Hell after passing their Academy test and calling up an imp. They paid the rent by working as consultants and doing shielding for corporations, like Shamans. They also ran most of the training colleges and did magickal research. Finicky eyes for detail, most Magi; but when dealing with demons you wanted to be a perfectionist when it came to your circles and protections. The Greater Demons were like *loa*, only more powerful—they didn't exactly have a human idea of morals. And while the *loa* might mislead, it was an axiom of Magi practice that demons outright lied sometimes for the fun of it—again, because their idea of truth wasn't the same as ours.

I sighed, burrowed my back deeper into my bed. I was retreading the same mental ground, going over and over what I knew of demons, hoping I would somehow think of something new that would make me feel better about this.

If I was a Christer, I'd be peeling the paint off the walls screaming, I thought sardonically. Some normals were still Christers, despite the Awakening and the backlash against the Evangelicals of Gilead; the Catholic section, of course, would have tried reading from old books and blessing water to get rid of a demon. Sometimes it might have worked—even normals were capable of belief, though they couldn't use it like a tool as a Shaman or a Necromance could. And the Christers had even believed that demons could get *inside* people, not understanding the mechanics of shielding and psychic space very well.

None of this got me anywhere.

How the hell did this happen? How did I end up working for the fucking Devil?

I didn't have a clue. There had been no warning, from my cards or runes or any other divination. Just a knocking on my door in the middle of a rainy afternoon.

So did they sneak up on me, or are my instincts getting rusty? Or both?

I stared at the greenshift shadows on the ceiling, my mind ticking, sleep a million klicks away.

Breathe, Danny. Start the circle like you were taught. In through the nose, out through the mouth. Breathe deep, deeper, deeper—

The ritual was comforting, born of too many sleepless nights. Outside my window a gray rainwashed dawn was coming up. I yawned, settled myself more comfortably between white sheets.

I wondered if the cops had visited Dake yet. Or if Dake had dumped his stash in panic, guessing I'd turn him in even though we went way back together. Back to the Hall.

Don't think about that.

Mirovitch's papery voice whispering, three lines of fire on my back—the whip, the smell of my own flesh searing—

Do not think about that. I shifted on the bed, the sheet moving, my fingers white-knuckled on the swordhilt. "Don't think about that," I whispered, and closed my eyes. "What you cannot escape, you must fight; what you cannot fight, you must endure. Now think of something useful if you're going to stay awake."

You weren't warned because they haven't been preparing this, the deep voice of my intuition suddenly whispered. *This doesn't have the feel of a well-planned expedition.*

It was a relief to have something else to think about. So even the Devil was scrambling to keep up with current events, so to speak. Maybe he'd gone to use this Egg or look at it, and found out it was gone. Hell was a big place; you couldn't keep track of every artifact and demon.

Which means Santino probably has Lucifer by the balls. And how does this Japhrimel fit in? He's Lucifer's agent. Why wouldn't Lucifer come out on this job himself?

It would do me no good to fret over it. I was well and truly caught.

I closed my grainy, burning eyes, consigning the question to my unconscious mind. With any luck, the bubbling stew of my subconscious would strike me with the answer—right between the eyes— soon enough.

Even Japhrimel has no idea what's going on, I thought. *Even Lucifer. They're playing blind. Which is why they need me.*

They need me. I'm calling the shots here.

The thought was enough to press a smile to my face as I kept breathing, deeper and deeper, waiting for dawn. When I finally fell asleep, the sky was turning gray with morning.

The house was full of the smell of demon, amber musk and burning cinnamon creeping through the air like gas. I came downstairs after a long shower and fresh clothes to find his scent rippling and dyeing the psychic atmosphere with golden darkness.

He handed me a cup of coffee. He looked just the same as he had last night, except a little of the robotic blankness was gone from his face. Now he looked thoughtful, his green eyes a shade darker and not quite meeting mine.

I blew across the steaming mug and yawned, contemplating the kitchen. Late-afternoon sunlight slanted in through the window. The rain must have fled, because golden sunlight edged the wandering Jew hanging over the sink. "Morning," I finally said, slipping past him to stalk to the toaster. "How are you?"

"Well enough," he replied. "Did you sleep well?" He actually sounded interested.

"No. I hardly ever do. Thanks for the coffee." I dropped two slices of wheat bread into the toaster and pressed the button for "just short of charcoal."

"Where is your sword?"

I shrugged. "I don't think I need it in a demon-protected house, do I?" I yawned again. "When we go out to hunt I'll be taking my sword. I won't put it away again until I've brought Santino down. I haven't started yet—this is just saddling my horse." My rings sparked again. This time the shower of sparks was pure gold.

I smell like a demon now, I thought with a sort of grim amusement. *That should make things fun.*

"I see." He still sounded thoughtful. He hadn't moved from the kitchen door.

"Before we go," I continued, "I need you to tell me exactly what having a demon familiar means. I was going to ask Dake, but we didn't have time last night. So I'm forced to ask you."

"I'll do my best not to disappoint you," he said sardonically.

I swung around to look at him, the coffee sloshing in my cup. I fished a butterknife out of the drying rack next to the sink. "You're starting to develop a sense of humor," I said. "Good for you."

"We will get exactly nowhere if we cannot reach an agreement," he pointed out. "I am responsible for your safety, and my physicality is now tied to you by the grace of the Prince. If I allow you to be harmed, it will be most unpleasant for me." His lean saturnine face didn't change, but his voice was colored with a faint sneer.

"Mmh." My toast popped up as I was getting the peanut butter down. "Guess it's bad luck all *over* you, huh?" I set the coffee cup down after a quick, mouth-burning gulp. It was, at least, decent coffee.

"On the contrary," he said. "It is very *good* luck. It appears you need a familiar and I need my freedom. You appear tolerable, at least, despite your foul mouth. And you are occasionally thoughtless, but not stupid."

I looked over my shoulder. He had his hands behind his back again, standing military-straight, his long black coat buttoned up to his chin. "Thanks," I replied, as dryly as I could. "Have you had breakfast?"

He shrugged. "Human food is pleasant, but I don't *need* it."

I was just about to say something snide when the phone rang. I hooked up the kitchen phone and snarled into it. *"What?"*

That was my hello-good-morning voice.

"And a good bloody morning to you too, Danny," Trina chirped. She was the agent for the Parapsych Services Unlimited Message Agency; most psions in Saint City used them. Since I did bounties as well as apparitions, Trina managed my schedule and acted as a buffer between me and the cranks and yahoos who sometimes decided to prank-call psions. I didn't have the time or energy to keep track of when I was supposed to be where, so Trina would coordinate with my datpilot and datband as well as monitor my datband while I was on a bounty. Magick was a full-time job; even Necromances needed secretaries nowadays and it was cheaper to just freelance-contract with an agency. "Quick word?"

"What, another job?" I looked down at my toast, picked up my coffee. "How much?"

"Fifty thousand. Standard."

That would take care of another few mortgage payments. "What kind?" I swirled the coffee in the cup, the steam rising and twisting into angular shapes.

"A probate thing. Shouldn't take more than a coupla hours. Old coot named Douglas Shantern, died and the will's contested. Total estate's fifteen mil, the estate itself is paying your fee."

I yawned. "Okay, I'll take it. Where's the body? How fresh?"

"Lawyer's office on Dantol Street has his cremains. Died two weeks ago."

I made a face. "I hate that."

"I know," Trina replied, sympathetic. "But you're the only one on the continent who can deal with the burned ones, since you're so talented. I'll schedule you for midnight, then?"

"Sounds good. Give me the address?"

She did. I knew the building; it was downtown in the legal-financial district. The holovid image of a Necromance is all graveyards and chanting and blood, but most of our work is done in lawyers' offices and hospital rooms. It's very rare to find a Necromance in a graveyard or cemetery.

We don't like them.

"Okay," I said. "Tell them I'm bringing an assistant."

"I didn't know you had an apprentice." She actually sounded shocked. I have never met Trina face-to-face, but I always imagine her as a stolid, motherly woman who lived on coffee and Danishes.

"I don't," I said. "Thanks, Trina. I'll hear from you again, I'm sure."

"You're welcome," she said, barely missing a beat. "Bye."

"Bye." I hung up. "Well, that's nice. Another little job."

The demon made a restless movement. "Time is of the essence, Necromance."

I waved a hand over my shoulder at him. "I've got bills to pay. Santino won't get anywhere quickly. He escaped fifty years ago; you guys didn't jump right on the bandwagon to bring him down. So why should I? Besides, we're going to visit Abra too, and after I do this job Gabe will have all the things I need and we can start hunting. Unless you're going to pay my power bill this month."

"You are infuriating," he informed me coldly. The smell of demon was beginning to make me dizzy.

"Tone it down a little, Japhrimel." I curled my fingers around the edge of the counter and glared at him, reminding him that I knew his

Name. "I don't have a whole hell of a lot to lose here. You make me angry and you lose your big chance to shine."

He stared at me with bright laser-green eyes. *I think he's angry,* I thought, *his eyes just lit up like a Yulefestival tree. Or is that just me?*

The plate holding my peanut butter toast chattered against the countertop. I held his gaze, wondering if the Power thundering through the air would burn me. My rings popped and snarled, my shields shifting, reacting to the charged air.

He finally glanced down at the floor, effectively breaking the tension. "As you command, Mistress."

I wondered if he could sound any more sarcastic.

I shrugged. "I'm not your mistress, Japhrimel. The sooner I can get rid of you and back to my life, the better. All I want you to do is stay out of my way, you dig? *After* you explain what a demon familiar does."

He nodded, his eyes on the floor. "When would you like your explanation?"

I wiped a sweating hand on my shirt, my combat shields humming as they folded back down. "Let me finish my coffee first."

He nodded, his hair shifting, wet dark spikes. "As you like."

"And pour yourself a cuppa coffee or something," I added, grudgingly. Might as well be polite, even if he wasn't.

CHAPTER 15

Ashton Hutton," the lawyer said, his grip firm and professional. He didn't flinch at the tat on my cheek or at the sight of Japhrimel—of course, lawyers in the age of parapsych don't scare easily. "Nice of you to come out on such short notice, Ms. Valentine."

"Thank you, Mr. Hutton." I smiled back at him. *You fucking shark,* I thought. He was slightly psionic—not enough to qualify for a trade, but enough to give him an edge in the courtroom—and his blond hair was combed back from a wide forehead. Blue eyes sparkled. He had a disarming, expensive grin. The wet ratfur smell of some secret fetish hung on him. I filled my lungs, taking my hand back, smelling something repulsive and dry.

Not my business, I thought, and looked past him into the tasteful meeting room. The windows were dark, but the lights were full-spectrum, and the table was an antique polished mahogany big enough to carve up a whale on.

The family was there: bone-thin, sucked-dry older woman who was probably the wife dressed in a peach linen suit, very tasteful, a single strand of pearls clasped to her dry neck; there were two boys, one of them round and wet-eyed, greasy-haired, no more than thirteen, a ghost of acne clinging to his skin. The other was a college-age kid, his hair cut into the bowl-shape made popular by Jasper Dex in the holovids, leaning back in his chair while he tapped at the table's mirror polish shine with blunt fingertips.

On the other side of the table was a woman—maybe thirty-five, her dark hair in a kind of spray-glued helmet, ruby earrings clipped to her ears. *Mistress,* I thought. Then my eyes flicked past her to the two plainclothes cops, and a whole lot more about this situation started to make sense.

I looked at the lawyer. "What's with the cops?" I asked, the smile dropping from my face like a bad habit.

"We don't know yet," Hutton replied. "Miss Sharpley requested a police presence here, and it was not denied by the terms of the will, so..." He trailed off, spreading his smooth well-buffed hands.

I nodded. In other words, the cops were here because someone was suspected of something, or relations between the wife and mistress were less than cordial. Also none of my business. "Well," I said, and stepped into the room, digging in my bag. "Let's get to work then."

"Who's your associate?" Hutton asked. "I didn't catch his name."

"I didn't throw it," I replied tartly. "I'm here to raise a dead man, not talk about my accessories." I was already wishing I hadn't accepted this job either.

In the center of the table stood the regulation box, heavy and made out of steel, holding the remains of the man I would be bringing back out of death's sleep. I shivered slightly. I hated cremains, worked much better with a body...but you couldn't afford to be picky when you had a mortgage. I wondered why an estate worth fifteen million didn't have an urn for the hubby, and mentally shrugged. Also none of my business. It wasn't my job to get involved, it was my job to raise the dead.

The first time I'd raised an apparition out of ash and bone had been at the Academy; I hadn't been prepared for the silence that fell over the training room when I'd done it. Most Necromances need a whole body, the fresher the better; it was rare to have the kind of talent and Power needed to raise a full apparition out of bits. It meant steady work, since I was the only Necromance around who could do it—but it also meant that I pulled more than my share of very gruesome remains. One of the worst had been the Choyne Towers fiasco, when a Putchkin transport had failed and crashed into the three towers. I'd been busy for days sifting through little bits and raising them for identification, and there were still ten people missing. If I couldn't raise them, they must have been vaporized.

And that was a singularly unpleasant thought. That hadn't made my reputation, though. My reputation as a Necromance had been cemented when I'd almost by accident raised the apparition of Saint Crowley the Magi. It was supposed to be a publicity ploy by the Channel 2004 Holovid team, but I'd actually done it, much to everyone's surprise. Including my own.

But most of what I was stuck with were the gruesome ones, the burned ones, and dead psions. It was Hegemony law that the remains of a dead psi had to be cremated—especially Magi and Ceremonials, because of the risk of Feeders.

I shivered.

I had the candles out and placed on the table when the wife suddenly made a slight choking sound. "Do we have to?" she asked, in a thready, husky voice. "Is this *absolutely* necessary?"

"Chill out, Ma," the college boy snapped. His voice was surprisingly high for such a husky kid. He leaned back in his chair, balancing on two legs. "Smoke and mirrors, that's all, so's they can charge for it, you know."

"Ms. Valentine is a licensed, accredited Necromance," Hutton said thinly, "and the best in the country if not the world, Mrs. Shantern. You *did* ask to have the...questions...resolved."

The stick-woman's mouth compressed itself. On the other side of the table, the mistress's dark eyes rested steadily on the steel box. She was as cool and impenetrable as a locked hard drive, her smoothly planed cheeks coloring slightly as she raised her eyes to mine.

That's one tough cookie, I thought, and looked over at the plainclothes. They didn't look familiar.

I shrugged. Once the candles were secure in their holders I snapped my fingers, my rings sparked, and blue flame sputtered up from the wicks, glowing like gasjets.

I always got a kick out of doing that.

The wife gasped, and the college boy's chair legs thudded down on the expensively carpeted floor.

"If you'd be so kind as to kill the lights, Mr. Hutton," I said, drawing my sword free of its sheath, "we'll have this done in a jiffy."

The lawyer, maybe used to Necromances working in semidark, moved over to the door, brushing nervously past the demon, who stayed close, almost at my shoulder. I hopped up on the table and sat cross-legged, the sword in one hand, and rested my free hand on the steel box. This put my head above everyone's—except the demon and the taller of the plainclothes cops in his rumpled suit. *What are they here for?* I thought, dismissed the question.

"Dante?" the demon asked. It was the first time he had truly used my name.

"It's okay," I said. "Just wait. I'll let you know if I need you."

I am your familiar, the demon had told me, *and I may act to defend you. Any harm that comes to you, I will feel as if committed to my own flesh. I am at your command as long as you bear that mark. If it is possible for me to do, your word will make it so. I am not free to act, as you are.*

I understood a lot more now. No wonder Magi wanted familiars. It was like owning a slave, he had explained, a magickal slave and bodyguard. The trouble was, I didn't want a slave. I wanted to be left alone.

I closed my eyes. Deep circular breaths, my sword balanced across my knees. After the uncertainties of the last few days, it was a relief to have something I *knew* how to do and understood doing. Here, at least, was a problem I could solve. Dropped below conscious thought, the blue glow rising, my hand resting on the steel box.

The words rose from the deepest part of me. *"Agara tetara eidoeae nolos, sempris quieris tekos mael—"*

If you were to write down a Necromance's chant, you'd have a bunch of nonsense syllables with no real Power. Necromance chants aren't part of the Canons or even a magical language—they're just keys, personal keys like the psychopomp each Necromance has. Still, someone always tries to write them down and make them follow grammatical rules. The trouble is, the chants *change* over time.

Blue crystal light rose above me, enfolded me. My rings spat sparks, a shower of them, my left shoulder twinging. Riding the Power, crystal walls singing around me, I reached into the place where the cremains rested, hunting. Small pieces of shattered bone and ash a bitter taste against my tongue.

To taste death, to take death into you... it is a bitter thing, more bitter than any living taste. It burned through me, overlapping the ache in my shoulder from the demon's mark.

I've seen the tapes. While I chant, my head tips back, and the Power swirls counterclockwise, an oval of pale light growing over the body—or whatever is left of the body. My hair streams back, whether caught in a ponytail, braided, or left loose. The emerald on my cheek glitters and pulses, echoing the pulsing of the oval of light hanging in front of me, the rip in the world where I bring the dead through to talk.

My hand fused to the steel box. My other hand clamped around the hilt of my sword. The steel burned fiercely against my knees, runes running like water up the blade. My tattoo would be shifting madly, serpents writhing up the staff of the caduceus, their scales whispering dryly.

Blue crystal light. The god considered me, felt through me for the remains, and the thin thread that I was stretched quivering between the world of the living and the dead. I became the razorblade bridge that a soul is pulled across to answer a question, the bell a god's hand touches to make the sound out of silence...

There was a subliminal *snap* and the wife gasped. "Douglas!" It was a pale, shocked whisper.

I kept my eyes closed. It was *hard,* to keep the apparition together. "Ask...your...questions..." I said, in the tense silence.

The chill began in my fingers and toes. I heard the wife's voice, then the lawyer taking over, rapid questions. Shuffle of paper. The mistress's husky voice. Some kind of yell—the college kid. I waited, holding the Power steady, the chill creeping up my finger, to my wrists. My feet rapidly went numb.

More questions from the lawyer, the ghost answering. Douglas Shantern had a gravelly voice, and he sounded flat, atonal, as the dead always do. There is no nuance in a ghost's voice...only the flat-line of a brain gone into stormdeath, a heart gone into shock.

There was another voice—male, slightly nasal. One of the cops. The numb chill crept up my arms to my elbows. The sword burned, burned against my knees. My left shoulder twisted with fire.

The ghost replied for quite some time, explaining. My eyelids fluttered, the Power drawing up my arms like a cold razor.

There was a scuffle, something moving. The lawyer's voice, raised sharply. I ignored it, keeping the ghost steady.

Then the lawyer, saying my name. "Ms. Valentine. I think we're finished." His voice was heavy, no longer quite as urbane.

I nodded slightly, took a deep breath, and blew out between my teeth, a shrill whistle that ripped through the thrumming Power. The cold retreated.

Blue crystal walls resounding, the god clasping the pale egg-shaped glow that was the soul to His bare naked chest, dog's head quiet and still. White teeth gleaming, eloquent dark eyes...the god regarded me gravely.

Was this the time that He would take me, too? Something in me— maybe my own soul—leapt at the thought. The comfort of those arms, to rest my head on that broad chest, to let go—

"Dante?" A voice of dark caramel. At least he didn't touch me. "Dante?"

My eyes fluttered open. The sword flashed up between me and the pale egg-shaped blur in the air. Steel resounded, chiming, and the light drained back down into the steel box, fluttering briefly against the flat surfaces, limning the sharp corners in a momentary pale glow.

I sagged, bracing my free hand against the polished mahogany of the table, the smell of my own Power sharp and nose-stinging in the air. I could *feel* the demon's alertness.

When I finally looked around the dark room, one of the cops had the younger son—the acne-scarred wet-eyed boy with the greasy hair—in plasteel cuffs. The boy blinked, his fishmouth working. *Goddammit,* I thought sourly, *if I'd known this was a criminal case I'd have charged the estate double. Got to have Trina make a note about this lawyer.*

The wife sat prim and sticklike still, but her eyes were wide and wild with shock, two spots of red high up in her dry cheeks. The mistress sat, imperturbable. The older boy stared at his younger brother as if seeing a snake for the first time.

I managed to slide over to the edge of the table and put my legs down, sheathing my sword. Surprisingly, the demon put his hands up, held my shoulders, and steadied me as I slid down. My fingers were numb. *How long?* I thought, numbly.

"How long?" I asked, forcing my thick tongue to work.

"An hour or so," Jaf replied. "You...Your lips are blue."

I nodded, swayed on my feet. "It'll pass soon, I'll be fine. What *happened*?" I deliberately pitched my voice low, a whisper. Jaf caught the hint, leaned in, his fingers digging into my shoulders.

"The mistress was accused of killing the man," he said softly. "The ghost said it was his son that beat him to death with a piece of iron."

"Ms. Valentine?" the lawyer interrupted, urbanely enough. The cops were dragging the limp kid away. He hung in their hands, staring at me. The shorter cop—curly dark hair, dark eyes, he looked Novo Italiano—forked the sign of the evil eye at me, maybe thinking I couldn't see.

Lethargy washed over me again. I swayed. *An hour? I kept the ghost talking—a full manifestation—for an hour? From a pile of ashes? No wonder I'm tired.* I took deep, circular breaths. The air was so cold from the ghost's appearance my breath hung in a white cloud, and little threads of steam came from Jaf's skin. "I hate the ash ones," I muttered, then faced the bland-faced lawyer. "It just happened to slip your mind that this was a criminal affair?"

"Consider your...ah, fee, tripled." His eyes were wide, his slick blond hair ever-so-slightly disarranged. Maybe I'd scared him.

Good. He'd think twice before trying to cheat a psi out of a decent fee again.

"Thanks," I said, and blinked deliberately.

He was sweating, and his face was pasty white. "I've never—I mean, I hardly—" The lawyer was all but stammering. I sighed. It was a transitory pleasure to scare the shit out of a little scumbag like this.

"I know. I'll be going now. I suppose I can just let myself out?"

"Oh, well—we could—"

"No worries." I was suddenly possessed of the intense urge to get the hell out of this bland, perfect, antique office and away from this stammering frightened man. Maybe he wasn't quite as used to Necromances as he'd thought.

I never thought I would be grateful for a demon. But Japhrimel apparently had grown impatient waiting for me to finish making the lawyer stumble and sputter, because he put his arm around me and pulled me away from the table. I stumbled slightly; the demon's arm was a warm weight.

As soon as he led me past the empty secretary's desk and into the office lobby, I ducked out from under his arm. "Thanks," I said, quietly.

My knees were still a little shaky, but my strength would return quickly. "That was a little draining. I had no idea they wanted a full hour from a bunch of ashes."

"You appear to be most exceptional." Japhrimel's arm fell back to his side. His eyes were half-lidded, glowing so fiercely that the skin around them seemed to take on a greenish cast. Again, there were runic shapes glittering in their infinite depths.

"I don't know," I said. "I'm just a girl looking to pay off her mortgage."

"I am sorry I doubted your ability," he continued, falling in step beside me as I headed for the stairs. The elevator dinged, nearly sending me through my skin; Japhrimel's hand closed around my upper arm. Steel fingers sank into my flesh. "Easy, Dante. There is nobody there."

"Not...the elevator." I forced the words out. If I had to be closed in a small space—

At least he had his own shields, and could keep his thoughts to himself. Raw as I was, if he'd been human I might have torn my arm out of his grasp to escape the onslaught of someone else's emotion. As it was, I let him steer me through the door and into the echoing, gray-painted stairwell. "So you've decided I'm not so bad?" I asked, trying for a light tone. The ghost's voice echoed in my head, just outside my mental range, shivering, a deep husky sound. I would hear him for another few hours, until my psyche recovered from the shock of holding someone else so closely. Training helped lessen the shock, but could not deaden it completely.

"I have decided that you need a familiar," he said flatly. "You seem foolhardy."

"I'm careful," I protested. "I've survived this long."

"It seems like luck instead of care," he remarked. I stumbled, my feet feeling like huge blocks of cold concrete—he steadied me, and we began down the stairs, my footsteps echoing, his silent.

"I don't like you very much."

"I supposed as much."

By the time we reached the bottom floor, my boots were beginning to feel less like concrete and more like they belonged to me. The awful cold retreated slowly, the mark on my left shoulder a steady flame that dispelled the ice. My energy was returning, the Power-well of Saint City flooding me with what I'd expended on the apparition. The ground-floor lobby was plush and quiet, water dripping down a tasteful Marnick wall fountain. I kept my fingers curled around my sword, my bag bumping my hip. As soon as I could walk by myself I shook his arm away. It was a good thing the weakness never lasted long. "Thanks."

"No thanks necessary." He opened the security-lock door, sodium-arc light shining against glass. The parking lot was mostly empty, the pavement drying in large splotches. Night air touched my face, a cool breeze sliding through pulled-loose strands of my hair. I tucked one behind my ear and checked the sky. Clearing up from the usual evening shower. That was good.

"Hey." I stopped, looking up at him. "I need to do something. Okay?"

"Why ask me?" His face was absolutely blank.

"Because you'll have to wait for me," I replied. "Unless you can ride a slicboard."

CHAPTER 16

Hey, deadhead," Konnie said, stripping green-dyed hair back from his narrow pasty face. "Whatchoo want?"

The Heaven's Arms resounded with New Reggae music around me, the sweet smell of synth hash from the back room filtering out between racks of leathers in garish colors, shinguards, elbow pads, helmets. "Hi, Konnie," I said, ducking out of my bag. The demon accepted the strap—I felt a thin thread of unease when I handed my sword over. "I need a board and an hour."

Konnie leaned back, his dead flat eyes regarding me over the counter. "You got credit?"

"Oh, for *fuck's* sake." I sounded disgusted even to myself. "Give me a board, Konnie. The black one."

He shrugged. "Don't suppose you're gonna wear any pads."

"You've got my waiver on file." I ran my fingertip over the dusty counter, tracing a glyph against the glass. Underneath, blown-glass hash pipes glowed. There were even some wood and metal hash pipes, and a collection of incense burners. Graffiti tags tangled over the walls, sk8 signs and gang marks. "Come on, Konnie. I've got a job to do."

"I know." He waved a ringed hand. His nails were painted black and clipped short—he played for a Neoneopunk band, and had to see his hand on the bass strings in pulsing nightclub light. "You got that look again. Who you hunting down this time, baby?"

"*Give* me the goddamn board," I snarled, lips pulling back from my teeth. My emerald sparked, my rings shifting crazily. The demon tensed behind me. "I'll be back in an hour."

Konnie bent briefly, scooped up a slicboard from its spot under the counter. He slid the chamois sheath free, revealing a sleek black Valkyrie. "I just tuned it up. Had a Magi in here not too long ago told me to 'spect a deadhead; I hate that precog shit. You're the only deadhead crazy 'nough to come to the Arms. Why dontcha keep this thing at home?"

I snatched the board. My hands were trembling. The ambient Power of the city helped, soaking into me, replacing what I'd spent in bringing Douglas Shantern back from the dry land of death. But I still wasn't convinced I was still living… "Fine. Thanks."

"Hey, what to do with the stray here?" Konnie called after me as I headed for the front door.

"Try not to piss him off," I tossed over my shoulder, then hit the door. I was running by the time cool night wind touched my hair, my fingers pressing the powercell. I dropped the board just as the cell kicked in, and the sound of a well-tuned slic hummed under my bones.

My boots thudded onto the Valkyrie's topside, the board giving resiliently underneath me. My weight pitched forward, and the board hummed, following the street.

No, I don't want streetside, I thought. *I want to fly. Tonight I need to fly.*

I pitched back, the slic's local antigrav whining. Riding a slicboard is like sliding both feet down a stair rail, weight balanced, knees loose and relaxed, arms spread. It's the closest to flight, to the weightlessness of astral travel plus the gravity of the real world, that a human body can ever attain.

Hovercells thrummed. Up in the traffic lanes, hovers were zipping back and forth. The thing about hover traffic is that it's like old-time surfing waves—catch the right pattern, and you can ride forever, just like jacking into a city's dark twisted soul and pouring Power into a spell.

But if you miscalculate, hesitate, or just get unlucky, you end up splashed all over the pavement. Hovers and freights have AI pilot decks that take care of keeping them from colliding, making driving mostly a question of following the line on your display with the joystick or signing the control over to the pilot deck, but slics are just too small to register. The intricate pattern of mapped-out lanes for hover traffic was updated and broadcast from Central City Hall in realtime to avoid traffic jams, but the slics couldn't tune in to that channel. There wasn't room on a slic for an AI deck, sk8ers and slic couriers disdained them anyway.

I stamped down on my left heel, my weight spinning the slicboard as it rocketed up, and I streaked between two heavy hover transports and into the passenger lane, missing a blue hover by at least half an inch, plenty of room. Adrenaline hammered my bloodstream, pounded in my brain, the Valkyrie screamed as I whipped between hovers, not even thinking, it was pure reaction time, *spin* lean down kick of wind to the throat like fast wine, I dove up out of the passenger traffic pattern and into the freight lanes.

Riding freight is different, the freight hovers are much bigger and their backwash mixes with more hovercells and reactive to make the air go all funny. It requires a whole different set of cold-blooded calculations—freight won't kill you like a passenger foul-up will. Slicboard fatalities in the passenger lanes are called "quiksmaks." Freight fatals are "whoredish." They're tricky, and a mistake might not kill you instantly. It might kill you three feet ahead, or six behind. You never know when a freight's backwash will smack you off your board or tear your slic out from under your feet.

—*watch that big rig there, catch*, fingernails screeching on plasteel, hovercells whining under the load, *board's got a wobble, watch it, lean back stamp down* hard *going up*, ducking under a whipping freight hover, my hair kissing plasteel, rings showering golden sparks, coat flying, weaving in and out of the hovers like a mosquito among albatrosses, *this is what it feels like to be alive, alive, alive...*

Heart pounding, copper laid against my tongue, Valkyrie screaming, lips peeled back from teeth and breath coming in long gasps, legs balancing the slic, the friction of my boot soles the only thing between me and a long fall to the hard pavement below.

I fell in behind a police cruiser that was whipping between freights, going siren-silent. They'd already scanned me—an unhelmeted head on a slic isn't a crime, but they like to know who's riding suicidal— and I played with their backwash, riding the swells of turbulence until they dropped out of the traffic patterns. I rode a little while after that, almost lazily, darting down into traffic and swooping back, tagging hovers.

When I finally dropped back to streetside, hips swaying, body singing, I brought the Valkyrie to a stop right outside the Arms and hopped down. My hair fell in my face, my shoulders were loose and easy for the first time since a booming knock on my door had sounded in the rain.

Japhrimel leaned against the window of the Arms, neon light spilling through the glass and glowing against his wetblack hair. He held my bag and my sword, and his knuckles stood out white against the scabbard.

I tapped the board up, flipping off the powercell, and let out a gusty sigh. "Hey," I said. "Anything cool happen while I was gone?"

He simply stared at me, his jaw set and stone-hard.

I carried the board back inside and gave it to Konnie, used my datband to transfer the rent fee to him, and came out into the night feeling much more like myself, humming an old PhenFighters song. After every Necromance job, I ride a slicboard. I fell into the habit years ago, finding that the adrenaline wash from riding the antigrav worked almost as quickly as sex; the fight-or-flight chemical cascade wiping the cold leaden weight of dead flesh away and bringing me back to full screaming life. Other Necromances used caff patches or Tantra, took a round in a sparring cage, visited a certified House like Polyamour's or any cheap bordello—I rode slics.

Japhrimel handed my bag over, and my sword. His silence was immense, and it wasn't until I looked closer that I noticed a vertical line between his coal-black eyebrows. "What?" I asked him, slightly aggrieved. Rain-washed air blew through the canyon streets, brushing my tangled hair and making his long coat lift a little, brushing his legs.

This is a demon, I thought, *and you're not screaming or running, Danny, you're treating him just like anyone else. Are you insane?*

"I would rather," he said quietly, "not do that again."

"Do *what* again?"

"That was foolish and dangerous, Dante." He wasn't looking at me; he studied the pavement with much apparent interest.

I shrugged. I couldn't explain to a demon that a slicboard was the only way to prove I *was* still alive, after lying cheek-by-jowl with death and tasting bitter ash on my tongue. Neither could I explain to him that it was either the slic or the sparring cage, and I didn't like cages of any kind. Besides, it didn't matter to the demon that I *needed* to prove I was alive after bringing a soul over the bridge and feeling the cold stiffness of rotting death in my own limbs. "Come on. We've got to visit Abra."

"I would like your word that you will not leave me behind again," he said quietly. "If you please, Mistress."

"Don't call me that." I turned away from him, slinging my bag against my hip, and was about to stalk away when he caught my arm.

"Please, Dante. I do not want to lose my only chance at freedom for a human's foolishness. *Please.*"

I was about to tear my arm out of his hand when I realized he was *asking me politely,* and saying please as well. I stared at him, biting my lower lip, thinking this over. A muscle flicked in his smooth golden jaw.

"Okay," I said finally. "You have my word."

He blinked. This was the second time in my life I'd ever seen a demon nonplussed.

We stood like that, the demon holding my arm and staring at my face, for about twenty of the longest seconds of my life so far. Then I moved, tugging my arm away from him, glancing up to check the weather. Still mostly clear, some high scudding clouds and the relentless orange wash of citylight. "We've got to get moving," I said, not unkindly. "Abra gets mean later on in the night."

He nodded. Did I imagine the vertical crease between his eyebrows getting deeper? He looked puzzled.

"What?" I asked.

He said nothing, just shrugged and spread his hands to indicate helplessness. When I set off down the sidewalk he walked beside me, his hands clasped behind his back, his head down, and a look of such profound thoughtfulness on his face I half-expected him to start floating a few feet off the pavement.

"Japhrimel?" I said finally.

"Hm?" He didn't look up, avoiding a broken bottle on the pavement with uncanny grace. I readjusted my bag so the strap didn't cut into my shoulder. I'd left both my sword and my bag with him, and he hadn't tampered with either.

"You're not bad, you know. For a demon. You're not bad at all."

He seemed to smile very faintly at that. And oddly enough, that smile was nice to see.

CHAPTER 17

Abra's shop was out on Klondel Avenue, a really ugly part of town even for the Tank District. *Abracadabra Pawnshop We Make Miracles Happen!* was scratched on the window with faded gilt lettering. An exceptionally observant onlooker would notice that there were no graffiti tags on Abra's storefront, and that the pavement outside her glass door with its iron bars was suspiciously clean.

Inside, the smell of dust and human desperation vied with the spicy smell of beef stew with chili peppers. The indifferent hardwood flooring creaked underfoot, and Abra sat behind the counter in her usual spot, on a three-legged stool. She had long dark curly hair and liquid dark eyes, a nondescript face. She wore a blue and silver caftan and large golden hoops in her ears. I had once asked if she was a gypsy. Abra had laughed, and replied, *Aren't we all?*

I had to give her that one.

Racks of merchandise stood neatly on the wood floor, slicboards and guitars hung up behind the glassed-in counter that sparkled dustily with jewelry. Her stock did seem to rotate fairly frequently, but I'd never seen anyone come into Abra's to buy anything physical.

No, Abra was the Spider, and her web covered the city. What she sold was *information.*

Jace had introduced me to Abra, a long time ago. Since then we'd been friends—of a sort. I did her a good turn or two when I could, she didn't sell too much information about my private life, and we edged along in a sort of mutual détente. I'll also admit that she puzzled me. She was obviously nonhuman, but she wasn't registered with any of the Paranormal voting classes—Nichtvren, Kine, swanhilds, you name it—that had come out when the Parapsychic Act was signed into law, giving them Hegemony citizenship. Then again, I knew a clutch of nonhumans that weren't registered but managed to make their voices heard the old-fashioned way, by bribe or by hook.

The bell over the door jingled as I stepped in, wooden floor creaking. The demon crowded right behind me.

"Hey, Abra," I began, and heard a whining click.

The demon's hand bit my shoulder. A complicated flurry of

motion ended up with me staring at the demon's back as he held two silvery guns on Abra, who pointed a plasrifle at him.

Well, this is exotic, I thought.

"Put the gun down, *s'darok*," the demon rumbled. "Or your webweaving days are over."

"What the *hell* did you bring in here, Danny?" Abra snapped. "Goddamn psychic women and their goddamn pets!"

"Japh—" I stopped myself from saying more of his name. "What are you *doing*?"

"She has a weapon pointed at you, Dante," he said, and the entire shop rattled. "I will burn your nest, *s'darok*. Put the gun down."

"Fuck..." Abra slowly, slowly, laid the plasrifle down and raised her hands. "Psychic women and their goddamn pets. More trouble than anything else in this town—"

"I need information, Abra," I said, pitching my voice low and calm. "Jaf, she's not going to hurt you—"

"Oh, I know that." His voice had dropped to its lowest registers. "It's *you* she'll harm, if she can."

"Isn't that sweet." Abra's face crinkled, her dark eyes lighting with scarlet pinpricks. The shop's glass windows bowed slightly under the pressure of her voice. Dust stirred, settled into complicated angular patterns, stirred again. The warding on Abra's shop was complex and unique; I'd never seen anything like it. "Dante, make him go away or no dice."

"Oh, for the love of—" I was about to lose my temper. "Japhrimel, she's put the gun down. Put yours away."

There was an eye-popping moment of tension that ended with Japhrimel slowly lowering his guns. His hands flicked, and they disappeared. "As you like," he said harshly, the smell of amber musk and burning cinnamon suddenly filling the shop. I had quickly grown used to the way he smelled. "But if she moves to harm you, she'll regret it."

"I *think* I'm capable of having a conversation with Abra that doesn't lead to anyone killing anyone else," I said dryly. "We've been doing it for years now." My skin burned with the tension and Power in the air. The smell of beef and chilis reminded me I hadn't eaten yet.

"Why does she have a gun out, then?" he asked.

"You're not exactly kind and cuddly," I pointed out, digging my heels into the floor as the weight of Power threatened to make me sway. "Everyone just *calm down*, okay? Can we do that?"

"Make him wait outside," Abra suggested helpfully.

"Absolutely *not*—" Japhrimel began.

"Will you *both* stop it?" I hissed. I'd be lucky to get *anything* out of Abra now. "The longer you two do this, the longer we stay here, and the more uncomfortable it'll be for *all* concerned. So *both* of you *just shut up!*"

Silence returned to the shop. The smell of beef stew, desperation, and dust warred with the musky powerful fragrance of demon. Japhrimel's eyes didn't leave Abra's face, but he slowly moved aside so I could see Abra without having to peek around him.

I dug the paper scored with Santino's name out of my bag. "I need information on this demon," I said quietly. "And I need to know about Dacon Whitaker. And I'm sure we'll find other things to talk about."

"What you paying?" Abra asked, her dark eyes losing a little bit of their crimson sparks.

"That's not how things stand right now. You owe me, Abra. And if you satisfy me, I'll owe *you* a favor." She more than owed me—I had brought her choice gossip last year after that Chery Family fiasco. The information of just who was stealing from the Family had been worth a pretty penny, and I was sure she'd sold it to the highest bidder—without, of course, mentioning that I'd been the one to bring her the laseprints. After that, I'd watched the fireworks as the Owens Family lost a good chunk of their holdings from an internal power struggle. It always warmed my heart to do the Mob a bad turn.

Her dark eyes traveled over Japhrimel. "You aren't a Magi, Danny. What are you doing hanging out with Hell's upper crust?"

So she recognizes him as a demon, and what kind of demon, too. That's interesting. "Just call me socially mobile," I said. "Look, *they* came and contacted *me*, not the other way around. I didn't ask for this, but I'm in it up to my eyebrows and sinking fast, and in order to collect on all my balloon payments I need to be breathing, okay? And I need information to keep breathing, Abra." My voice was pitched deliberately low, deliberately soothing. "We've been colleagues for a long time now, and I made you some cash during that Chery Family thing last year, and I'd *really like* to get some usable information. Okay?"

She measured me for a long moment. The demon didn't even twitch, but I felt him tense and ready beside me. My left shoulder was steadily throbbing, the mark pressed into my flesh responding to his attention.

"Okay," she said. "But you'd better not ever bring that *thing* here again."

He's not a thing. I didn't say it, didn't even wonder why I'd thought it. I had all I could handle right in front of me. "If I had a choice, I wouldn't have brought him in the first place," I snapped, my temper wearing thin. "Come *on*, Abra."

She made a quick movement, slipping the plasrifle off the counter. The demon didn't move—but my shoulder gave a livid flare. It had been close. Very close. "Okay," Abra said. "Give me whatever you've got."

I laid the paper down on the counter, face-down. I gave her everything I had—Santino/Vardimal, the Egg, being dragged into Hell, Dacon's addiction to Chill, and the job I'd just been on. That was an extra, for her—she could sell the information that Douglas Shantern had been murdered by his son. I laid the pattern out for her, and Japhrimel drew closer during the recital until his hand was on my shoulder and his long black coat brushed my jeans. Oddly enough, I didn't mind as much as I might have.

Abra took it all in, one dusky finger tapping her thin lips. Then she was silent for a long moment, and put her hand down, fingers stretched, over the paper I'd laid on the counter. "Okay," she said. "So you have a tracker, and Spocarelli'll give you a waiver and a DOC and an omni . . . and you need a direction, and not only that, you need contacts and gossip."

I nodded. "You got it."

"And your tame demon there is supposed to keep you alive until you kill this Santino. Then all bets are off."

Japhrimel tensed again.

"That's my personal estimation of the situation," I said cautiously.

Abra chuffed out a breath between her pearly teeth. It was her version of a sarcastic laugh. "Girl, you are fucked for sure."

"Don't I know it? Give me what you got, Abracadabra, I've got work to do tonight."

She nodded, dark hair sliding forward over her shoulders. The gold hoops in her ears shivered. Then she flipped the paper over, regarded the twisting silvery glyph. "Ah . . ." she breathed, sounding surprised. "This . . . oh, Dante. Oh, no."

The color drained from her dark face. She spread her hand over the paper, not quite touching it, fingers trembling. "South," she said in a queer breathless voice. "South, where it's warm. He's drawn to

where it's warm...hiding. He's hiding...can't tell why. A woman...
no, a girl..."

Japhrimel tensed next to me. I didn't think it was possible for him
to get any tighter strung. He moved a little closer, I could feel the heat
breathing off him, wrapping around me. If he got any closer he would
be molded to my side.

"What about the Egg?" I breathed. Abra's eyes were wide and
white, irises a thin ring around her dilated pupils, splotches of hectic
color high up on her now-pale cheeks.

"Broken...dead...ash, ash on the wind..." Abra's hand jerked,
smacking down on the counter. I jumped, and Japhrimel's fingers bit
my shoulder. She didn't get these flashes often, but when she did,
they were invariably right—though usually not precise enough to be
of any real help.

I had an even more important question. "How do I kill the
sonuvabitch, Abra? How do I kill Santino?"

Her eyelids fluttered. "Not by demon fire...neither man nor
demon can kill him...*water*—" She took in a long gasping breath,
her lips stretched back over strong white teeth. "Waves. Waves on the
shore, ice, I see you, I *see* you, Dante...face-down, floating...you're
floating...floating—"

I leaned over the counter, grabbed Abra's shoulders, and shook
her. When that didn't work, I slapped her—not hard, just hard
enough to shock her. Her eyes flew open, and Japhrimel yanked me
back, hissing something low and sharp in what I guessed was his
own language. Abra coughed, rackingly, grabbing on to the counter
with white-knuckled fingers. She said something quiet and harsh that
I didn't quite catch, then looked me full in the eyes. "This is going to
kill you, Danny," she said, with no trace of her usual bullshit. "Do
you understand me? This is going to *kill* you."

"As long as I take out the fucker that did Doreen I'll be okay," I
grated out. "Information, Abra. Where the fuck is he?"

"Where else?" Abra snapped back, but her chin trembled slightly.
She was paler than I'd ever seen her. "Nuevo Rio di Janeiro, Danny
Valentine. That's where you'll find your prey."

I scooped up the paper and shoved it in my bag. Abra stared at
me, trembling, her teeth sunk into her bottom lip. It was the first time
I'd even seen her even remotely close to scared.

She looked *terrified*.

"What about Dacon and the Chill?" I asked. "How the hell did—"

"Whitaker's hand-in-fist with the Owens Family, has been for years now. He got hooked last year and started skimming from their shipments," she replied shortly, reaching up to touch her cheek where the mark of my hand flushed red. "You *hit* me!"

"You were getting boring," I said before I thought about it. "Contacts in Nuevo Rio?"

"I don't have any," she said. "But as soon as you get there, you might want to look up Jace Monroe. He moved down there a while ago. Doing work for the Corvin Family. He's gone back to the Mob."

I hadn't known that. Then again, I'd never asked Abra about Monroe, even though he'd introduced me to her. I knew he'd been Mob, and suspected he'd gone back to the Mob—but hearing it out loud was something else entirely. I made a face. "I'd rather talk to a spasmoid weasel with a plasrifle," I muttered. "Okay. So what about gossip?"

Abra shrugged. "Word on the street is you're into something big, and there's a warning out there, too. *Don't mess around with Danny Valentine.*"

"I thought that was common knowledge."

"You've got a demon for a lapdog, Danny. Nobody wants that kind of static." She grimaced, rubbing her cheek. "Not even me. Can you go away now?"

I nodded, frustration curdling under my collarbones. "Thanks, Abra. I owe you one."

Her response was a bitter laugh. "You're not going to live long enough for me to collect. Now get the fuck out of my shop, and *don't* bring that thing back here." Her hand twitched toward the plasrifle leaning obediently on her side of the counter. Japhrimel pulled me away, dragging me across the groaning wooden floor, my bootheels scraping. The temperature in the shop had risen at least ten degrees.

He's not a thing, Abra. "I'll leave him at home to crochet next time," my mouth responded smartly with no direction from my brain. "Thanks, Abra."

"If she dies, *s'darok*," Jaf tossed back over his shoulder, "I will come hunting for you."

"Stop it. What's *wrong* with you?" I tried to extract my arm from his hand, with no luck. He didn't let go of me until we were outside the pawnshop and a good half block away. "What the *hell*—"

"She predicted your death, Dante," he said, grudgingly letting me slip my arm away from him. I felt bruises starting where his fingers had been. I dug my heels into the pavement and jerked my arm all the way free of his grasp, irritation rasping sharp under my breastbone.

"What the hell does it matter to *you*?" I snapped. "You're more trouble than you're worth! I could have gotten *twice* the information out of her if you hadn't gone all Chillfreak! You're fucking *useless*!"

A muscle in his cheek twitched. "I certainly hope not," he answered calmly enough. "You walk into a *s'darok*'s den with no protection, you court death with no conception of the consequences, and you blame *me* for your own foolhardiness—"

"I blame *you*? You don't even make any *sense*! If you had just been a little less set on 'psychotic' we could have gotten twice as much information from her! But no, you had to play the demon, you had to act like you know everything! You're so arrogant, you never even—"

"We are *wasting time*," he overrode me. "I will not let you come to harm, Dante, despite all your protests. From this moment forth, I will not *allow* this foolishness."

"*Allow?* What's this 'allow'? What the bloody blue hell is wrong with you?" It wasn't until the streetlamp in front of us popped, its glass bulb shattering and dusting the pavement below with glittering sprinkles, that I realized I was far too upset.

I need to fucking well calm down, I thought. *Too bad it looks like that's not going to happen soon.*

He said nothing in reply, just staring at me with those laser-green eyes, his cheek twitching. The cold wind was beginning to warm up, little crackles of static electricity in the air.

Necromances and Ceremonials both tended to affect a whispery tone after a while. We live by enforcing our Will on the world through words wedded to Power—and a Necromance shouting in anger could cause a great deal of damage. One of the dicta of Magi training ran: *A Magi's word becomes truth.* And for trained Necromances, who walked between this world and the next, discipline was all the more imperative.

I took a deep breath, tasting ozone, my shields flushing dark-blue with irritation, annoyance, and good clean anger. "Okay," I said, struggling for an even tone. "Look, I think we can make some progress, if you just tell me what's wrong with you. Okay? You're making this much harder than it has to be."

His jaw worked silently. *If he keeps that up he might grind his teeth down to nubs,* I thought, and had to bite back a nervous giggle.

I rubbed at my arm. It *hurt*, and so did my left shoulder. The burning, drilling pain reminded me of how quickly my life had grown incredibly fucked-up. Even for me. "I wish I'd never seen you," I said tonelessly. "That *hurt*, you asshole." I was far too angry to care about calling a demon who could eat me for breakfast an asshole.

He reached out for my arm again, and I flinched. His hand stopped in midair, then dropped back to his side. He looked—for the first time—actually chagrined. Or as if he was hovering between chagrin and fury. I'd seen that look before, but only on Jace.

I didn't want to think about Jace.

My hand shook as I massaged my new bruise. "Look," I said finally. "I'm going to call Gabe and set up a meet so we can get our supplies. Then I'm packing for Rio and catching a morning transport out there. I can't be taking time to educate *your* dumb ass on how to catch a gods-be-damned demon in my world. Stop fucking up my hunt, okay?" My emerald spat a single spark out into the night, a brief green flash making his pupils shrink. "I am going to find Santino and kill him. It's *my* revenge. When I tear his spleen out through his nose, you can have your fucking Egg and go back to your fucking Prince and *stay out of my life*. But until then, *quit fucking up my hunt!* You got it?"

He stared at me for another ten seconds, that muscle in his cheek twitching. "As you like," he finally grated out.

"Good," I said. "Now follow me. And keep your goddamn motherfucking mouth shut."

CHAPTER 18

I met Gabe in a noodle shop on Pole Street. I was starving, and managed to get most of a bowl of beef pho into my stomach before Gabe and Eddie drifted in the front door, Eddie silently snarling, Gabe looking cool and impenetrable in a long black police-issue synthwool coat.

Gabe slid into the booth across from me, and Eddie lowered himself down with a single glance at the demon, who sat utterly straight next to me, staring into the distance, a teacup steaming gently in front of him. The tattered red velvet and black-and-white photographs of ancestors and movie stars hung on the walls made the entire place feel warmer than it was, and the sticky plastic of the booths made squealing sounds as they made themselves comfortable.

The waitress brought coffee for Gabe, and Eddie ordered seafood soup. I slurped down another mouthful of noodles. Eddie smelled like dirt and violence, and Gabe had one hell of a black eye. Probably fresh, since she would have used a healcharm on it if she'd had time. I studied her for a long time before letting my eyebrows raise.

"I got called in to do para backup on a Chill raid last night," she said finally, tossing her dark hair back over her shoulder. "Some motherfucking dumbass Magi dealing Chill out of his nightclub. Wouldn't you know."

I nodded. "Sorry about that."

She shrugged. Her sword was propped between her knees, and Eddie was probably carrying some hardware, too. "Not your fault, sweetie. You did the right thing." She slid a bulky package wrapped in brown paper across the table. "An official bounty hunter's license, two H-DOC and omni-license-to-carry, and a plug-in for the Net. A sanctioned plug-in."

My jaw dropped. Japhrimel's lip twitched. He looked down at the table, one gold-skinned finger tracing a single symbol I wasn't able to decipher over and over again on the Formica.

"What the hell?" I asked.

"Someone's put some pressure on the department. Apparently anything you need is okay. You're a real golden girl right about now." Gabe's lips quirked up at the corners. "Knowing the Devil personally has some benefits, I'd guess."

I let out a gusty sigh and slurped some more noodles. "You want to get on my shit list, too?" I asked her. " 'Cause the number of people on that hallowed list is growing rapidly tonight."

"Poor baby," she laughed, while Eddie glared at me. "So where we going? What did Abra say?'

"Abra said Nuevo Rio," I said shortly. "And what's this *we*?"

Japhrimel stared out from the booth, his eyes moving over the entire restaurant in smooth arcs. I got the feeling that even the flies buzzing in loose spirals over the tables and the pattern of grease speckles and neon on the front window were receiving his full attention. Behind us, an old Asian man slurped loudly at his noodles, a curl of cigarette smoke rising slowly into the air. I'd been eating noodles here for six years, and no matter what time of the day or night, the old man was here, and he was always smoking. It was a dependable thing in a very undependable universe.

"Well," Gabe said finally, after studying the demon's impassive face for a few moments, "Doreen was my friend, too, and it was my case. Eddie and I have talked it over, and we're coming with you."

I put my chopsticks down and took a deep breath. "Gabe," I said, as kindly as I could, "I work alone."

She jerked her chin at the demon. "What, he's good enough to come along, but not me?"

"It's not like that," I said. "You know it's not like that." The familiar tension began in my shoulders, drawing tighter and tighter.

"I know you're going to get yourself killed chasing Santino down, and you need backup. Have you read your cards lately?" Her elegant eyebrows raised.

"My last divination session was kind of rudely interrupted," I said dryly.

"Come on, Danny." She batted her long, coal-black eyelashes at me. "I've got some vacation time, and I want to bring this fucker *down*."

"Gabe—"

"She says she's going," Eddie growled. "Means it too. Can't dissuade her."

Since when does Eddie use the word "dissuade"? I thought. *This is lunacy.* "Since when do you use the word 'dissuade,' Eddie? You get yourself a Word-A-Day holovid pro? Come on, Gabe. I don't want to have to watch out for Eddie on a hunt like this—"

"Eddie's got his own hunter's license," she pointed out, "and he's perfectly capable. You're grasping at straws, Danny. We're coming."

I threw up my hands. "Oh, *Sekhmet sa'es*," I snarled. "If you must, I suppose. Gods above and below damn this for a suicidal idea, and Anubis protect us *all*. What did I do to deserve this?"

"You were Doreen's best friend," Gabe reminded me. "You got her out of that—"

I shivered, all levity and irritation disappearing. "Don't," I said tonelessly, looking down at the table. "Don't talk about that. I failed when it mattered, Gabe, that's what I did. So don't go patting me on the back. If I'd been stronger, smarter, or faster, Doreen might still be alive."

Silence descended on the table. Eddie's chopsticks paused in midair, noodles hanging from them. Steam drifted up. The smell of fried food, soy sauce, grease, and dust warred with the smell of demon, making my stomach flip.

The demon looked over at me. He reached out, deliberately, and touched the back of my wrist with two fingers.

Heat slid through my body. The mark on my left shoulder tingled. My other arm, where the bruise was swiftly developing, gave a crunching flare of pain and then eased. He said nothing.

I licked at dry lips and finally jerked my wrist away from him, almost upsetting my almost-empty soup bowl. I caught it, gathered my chopsticks, and dropped them into the plasglass bowl with a clatter.

"I'm catching a transport out in the morning," I said, picking up my bowl.

"We've already got the tickets, for you, too," Gabe replied. "And we're bringing munitions. Being a cop is good for *something*."

"It better be," Eddie muttered darkly, munching on his noodles. I took a long drink of hot beef broth, holding my chopsticks out of the way with my thumb. The demon still watched me.

I ignored him.

When I finished and set my bowl down, Gabe was staring into her coffee cup. "Better go home and get some sleep," she said. "We're scheduled for a 10:00 A.M. jumpoff."

"Charming," I muttered, then poked at the demon's shoulder with the hilt of my sword. "Okay. Come by my house about eight-thirty tomorrow. All right?" I took the bulky package with me, following the demon as he rose gracefully to his feet and moved aside, offering his hand to help me stand. I didn't take it, squirming out of the booth on my own.

"Don't get any ideas about stranding me, kid." Gabe peered around Eddie, who had his face buried in his bowl, supremely unconcerned. "It's hard enough to find a friend nowadays. I don't want you to go all *banzai* on me."

Oddly enough, that made a lump rise in my throat. "You win, Gabe," I said. "You win."

I turned around and headed for the door.

"Nice to be working with you," Eddie burbled through his soup.

We made it out onto the hushed street. The noodle shop's neon-lit windows threw a warm red glow out onto the drying pavement. The demon still said nothing.

My arm didn't hurt anymore.

I could feel the demon's eyes on me. Wouldn't you know, he wasn't bothering looking at where he was going; he was busy looking at me, stepping over a drift of wet newspaper without even looking.

"What?" I finally asked, my eyes on the pavement under my feet. I kicked a Sodaflo can out of the way. "I can feel you wanting to say something, so spit it out."

We walked for maybe half a block until he spoke. "You're distressed," he said quietly. "I hurt your arm. My apologies."

"We could have gotten a lot more out of Abra if you hadn't threatened her," I pointed out.

"I did not want you injured."

"Because it'll foul up your own carefully laid plans," I flared. "Fine."

He was quiet for another half minute, during which we crossed Pole Street. I looked both ways this time. The old feeling of being on a hunt, adrenaline and sour boredom and fierce determination, was beginning to come back.

"You are the most infuriating human I have ever met," he said.

"I thought you didn't often leave Hell." I was so out of sorts that my neck was starting to tingle.

"Why must even an apology be a battle, with you?"

"I thought demons didn't apologize."

"You are testing my patience, Dante."

"Go back to Hell, then."

"If I were human, would you be so cruel to me?"

"If you were human you wouldn't have shown up at my house and dragged me to Hell with a gun pointed at my head and gotten me involved in this mess." I stamped against the pavement, my boots echoing. *Get over it, Danny. You're losing your focus. What is wrong with you?*

Nothing's wrong with me. It wasn't quite true. I thought I had made my peace with Doreen's death, but the ghosts of the past were standing up, shaking out their dusty clothes, and emerging into my life again. I didn't want to face any more memories of pain and terror and death—I had too many already.

And if the memories of Doreen were coming back, why not the other memories I thought I'd locked up and buried for good? *Let's make it a party for Danny Valentine, let's get out all the old terrors and shake her to and fro, how about that?*

"How would you have preferred it, then?" he asked.

"I would have *preferred* to be left alone," I snapped at him. "I thought you were going to apologize."

"I already did. If you weren't so determined to hate me, perhaps you would have noticed."

"You arrogant—" I was again paying no attention to where we were going, so the slight scuffle in the alley made me stop midstride and whirl. Metal sang as my sword cleared the sheath. A good fight was just what the doctor ordered. My lips peeled back from my teeth. *Come on out,* I thought, dropping into guard position, my blade suddenly aflame with blue light. Even the thought of the paperwork it would take to clear up the mess wasn't enough to deter me from stepping forward, unconsciously putting the demon behind me as if to protect him, the blue glow of my sword suddenly reflecting on eyes and teeth and glints of metal.

The demon turned, too, an oddly graceful movement, peering into the alley. He held up a hand, and sudden light scored the darkness, making my eyes water.

Shit, he's destroyed my night vision, dammit—I flicked my sword up into the blind guard, readying myself for a strike. Here on Pole Street, it wasn't likely to be a minigang like on the subway. Here it was likely to be a full-fledged pack of street wolves, and even though I had a sword and a Necromance's tat, it could get really ugly, really quickly.

Then again, ugly was just fine with me. The flood of copper adrenaline was almost as good as riding a slicboard, my breath hissing out through my teeth.

Unfortunately, the demon's little light-ball showed six dark shapes fleeing down the alley, one with a metal glint in his hands. Switchblade or gun, didn't matter. I stood there as the demon calmly flicked his wrist, bringing the white-hot glowing sphere back to rest obediently in his palm. Another flick of his wrist and the light was gone, making me blink my dazzled eyes. Power hummed through the air, the smell of ozone and rain mixing with the sharper smell of garbage, and fear. And over it all, the smoky smell of demon.

"As I said," he said quietly, "you appear to need a caretaker. Were you unaware of being followed? And did you think to protect me?"

His face resolved as my pupils expanded, green eyes glowing and half-lidded, his mouth curled up faintly at the corners. Laughing at the poor stupid human.

"I don't need to be taken care of, especially when it's only a grunge-smelling pack of Pole Street wolves. I need to get this *over* with so I can go back to my life, pay my mortgage, and retire." I resheathed my sword, the blue glow draining from the blade as unspent adrenaline wound my nerves up like a slic set on high. "I'm going home to get some sleep."

He nodded.

I set off down Pole Street, vaguely wishing there *had* been a fight. The demon's disdain was infuriating, even though I shouldn't have cared. It took me about a block to realize I'd been rude. "Hey," I said, looking up at the demon, who paced beside me silent as a shark.

"Yes?" Wary. But he looked puzzled, too, as if I had just done something extraordinary.

"Thanks for the apology," I gave him, grudgingly. "And I tend to take point to protect whoever I'm with. It's not a comment on your ability. I'm sure you're able to take care of yourself."

Did he stumble slightly, or was it just my imagination? He didn't say a word.

CHAPTER 19

*G*et down, Doreen. Get down!"

Crash of thunder. Moving, desperately, scrabbling…fingers scraping against the concrete, rolling to my feet, dodging the whine of bullets. Skidding to a stop just as he rose out of the dark, the little black bag in one hand, his claws glittering on the other.

"Game over," he giggled, and the awful tearing in my side turned to a burning numbness as he slashed. I threw myself backward, not fast enough, not fast enough, blood exploding outward, copper stink.

"Danny!" Doreen's despairing scream.

"Get out!" I screamed, but she was coming back, hands glowing blue-white, still trying to heal.

Trying to reach me, to heal me, the link between us resonating with my pain and her burning hands —

Made it to my feet, screaming at her to get the fuck out, and Santino's claws whooshing again as he tore into me, one claw sticking on

a rib, my sword ringing as I slashed at him, too slow, he was some-
thing inhuman, something inhuman—

"Dante. Wake up." A smooth, dark, old voice. "Wake up."

I sat bolt upright, screaming, my fingers hooked into claws, scrambled back until my shoulders hit the wall, sobbing breaths hitching in through my mouth because my nose was full. My back burned, the three whip scars full of heat, the burn scar on my left ass cheek twinging, and the scars across my belly and up my right side pulsing with awful fiery remembered numb pain.

Japhrimel's hand dropped back down to his side. "You were dreaming." His hair was slightly mussed, as if he'd been sleeping, too. His eyes glowed, casting dim shadows under his nose and cheekbones and lower lip. "I heard you scream..."

My left shoulder ached most of all, a deep desperate pain. I gasped. Blinked at him. The sheet had come free; I clutched it to my chest, trying to control my jagging breath. My rings spat green-gold swirls of light. I rubbed at my left shoulder with a fistful of sheet, my silk nightgown wadded up at my hip. The phantom pain drained away, each wound giving a final vicious sear, promising a return. The whip scars went first, and the clawmarks on my left side lingered until I took another sobbing breath in through my mouth and reminded myself that I was not bleeding.

Not anymore.

I reached for the box of tissues on my nightstand, blew my nose. It was my only admission of the tears, having to wad up the tissue and toss it in the general direction of the bathroom. My heart rate dropped to something like normal, and I found my voice. "You heard me?" I sounded husky, not like my usual self. Frightened.

"Of course I heard you. You bear my mark." He pointed to my left shoulder. He was still wearing that long black coat. *He must not have much of a dry-cleaning bill,* I thought, and a traitorous giggle almost escaped me.

"You're still wearing that coat."

"I usually do. What were you dreaming about?"

"S-s-Santino. When he k-killed D-Doreen..." I rubbed at my shoulder. "Why does it hurt?"

I sounded childlike.

"How did he kill her?" he asked.

I shrugged. "He kills psionics. We thought he was a serial killer, he eviscerates—"

Japhrimel stiffened. "He bleeds psychics? Not just ordinary humans?"

I nodded, pushed strands of my hair back over my shoulders. "He took trophies. Internal organs...he took the femur, or parts of it. It was his trademark...We couldn't figure out what his victims had in common, until I did a reconstruct of a crime scene and we found out all of his victims were psis. Then we went back through...*gods*..." I took a deep breath. "He sent each one flowers. Flowers!"

Japhrimel nodded. His eyes were so bright they cast little green sparkles against his cheekbones. He settled on the edge of my bed. "I see."

"I figured out he was the Saint City Slasher by going through some security tapes on one of the victims' buildings. By that time Gabe was on the case. I think...I think it was my being on the case that made Santino fixate on Doreen. He s-s-sent those f-f-flowers... Gabe agreed with me that Doreen was a target, and we out-thought him...gods, it must have just made him more angry..." I relaxed, muscle by muscle. Took deep breaths. *In through the nose, out through the mouth...*

Moving Doreen from safehouse to safehouse, one step ahead of the killer; living out of our suitcases, me lying awake every night with my hand curled around my swordhilt, listening, my entire world narrowing to keeping Reena alive one more day...

Japhrimel touched my shoulder with two fingers, warmth spreading through my cold bones. Gooseflesh prickled at my skin. "That's a nice trick," I managed around the lump in my throat.

He shrugged. "We are creatures of fire."

The way his eyes were burning, I believed it.

I shut my eyes. That was a mistake, because Santino's face hung in the darkness behind my lids. I stared at the face, the black teardrops over the eyes, the high-pointed ears, long nose, sharp teeth—

I thought he had rich-boy cosmetic augments to make himself look like a Nichtvren, I thought he was psionic and overrode me while I was losing consciousness, even though the cops couldn't find any sign of a memory wipe, I thought he was just a sick twisted human psionic...

"Dante. Come back." His fingers were still on my shoulder, bare skin scorching against mine.

My eyes flew open. He leaned across my tangled bed, his fingers almost melded to my shoulder. My other shoulder—the one that bore his mark—twinged sharply. "Why does it hurt?" I asked, tipping my chin down to point at my shoulder.

He shrugged. "I am your familiar. I suspect it's one of the Prince's jokes."

What the hell is that supposed to mean? "What are you talking about?"

"How much do you know of the bond between Magi and familiar?"

My heart rate calmed down. Sweat dried on my skin. I tasted copper adrenaline and blood—I'd bitten my lip. "I told you, not much. Just that some Magi get familiars, it's the great quest for every Magi...mostly imp-class demons, just little guys. Barely enough to light a candle."

"It's my duty to obey you. It's *your* duty to feed me." He didn't sound like it was any big deal.

"You know where the kitchen is." I took in a deep breath. "Thanks for...for waking me up. I haven't had a bad nightmare like that in... in a couple of years." The lie came out smoothly. The nightmare returned almost every night, punctually, unless I was exhausted. I had plenty of nightmares, from Rigger Hall, from some of the jobs I'd been on, from any number of horrible things I'd witnessed or had done to me. But the replaying of Santino's last assault had top billing for the last few years.

It was my heaviest regret, not being strong enough or fast enough when it counted.

He was quiet, and still. "I don't need *human* food," he said.

I touched my bleeding lip. My sword lay on my other side, safe in its sheath. "So what are you talking about? Power?"

"Blood. Sex. Fire." His fingers fell away from my shoulder. "Imps can feed on alcohol and drug intoxication, but I wouldn't recommend that. You need your wits about you."

"*Anubis et'her ka,*" I breathed. "You're not serious. Why tell me this now?"

"There hasn't been a better time." He settled back, the bed creaking underneath him. "I think you would be most comfortable with blood instead of sex."

"You've got *that* right," I muttered, my head still ringing with the dream. That chilling little giggle, while he took what he wanted, his satisfied wet little sounds while he—

A new and terrible thought occurred to me. We had assumed Santino took trophies. What if he was...*eating* the parts he took? I shivered, opening my eyes as wide as I could.

"How badly did he hurt you?" he asked. "Santino. *Vardimal.*"

I shut my eyes again. "He eviscerated me," I whispered. "If Doreen hadn't...she had her hands on me when he slit her throat. He didn't have enough time to do his entire ritual on her...he just bled her dry and cut out part of her femur...she had her hands on me... she used her last breath to heal me."

"Blood. Why blood? And a human bone..." he asked, very softly, as if to himself.

"You tell me," I said. "What does he need to murder psionics for? Does it have anything to do with the Egg?"

"It is useless to him," Japhrimel said quietly.

"What happens if he breaks it? Apocalypse, right?"

"Of a sort." Japhrimel folded his hands. The mark on my left shoulder gave another deep twinge. "The Egg holds a piece of...of the Prince's power. Decoded on Earth instead of in Hell, it could...upset the order of things. It is a violation of the way things should be."

"Okay." I took a deep breath. This was almost interesting enough to make me forget my heart was still hammering from a nightmare. Was this Egg a Talisman? The way he was talking about it, it seemed likely. "I guess I understand the magickal theory behind that, if it's heavy-duty demon stuff. But what's in it? Why does he want it? If word gets out that it's been stolen, what will—"

Japhrimel's teeth showed in one of those murderous, slow grins he seemed so fond of. "It will mean that the Prince is not strong enough to rule Hell. Demons will test his strength as they have not done for millennia. A Rebellion might succeed...and Vardimal might become the new Prince of Hell."

I chewed on this for a moment. He wasn't precisely answering the question, but his answer opened up so many other questions I decided to let the first one go for now. "So that's why Lucifer can't have anyone know that someone's stolen the Egg," I said. "Funny—I thought you guys were in Hell because you rebelled in the first place."

My attempt at levity failed miserably. He didn't even look like he got the joke. Then again, not many psis studied classical literature and the pre-Awakening Christos Bible Text, which had been discredited and gone out of use in the great backlash against the Evangelicals of Gilead.

"I have heard that story," he answered slowly. His eyelids lowered over his glowing eyes as he glanced down. "Human gods do not trouble us overmuch. It is only that humans were frightened of us, and mistook *us* for gods. There was a rebellion—the Fallen defied Lucifer's will, and died on earth because of the love they bore for the brides... but that is not something we speak of."

I absorbed this. If I was a Magi I'd be peppering him with questions, trying to get him to say more, but I was too tired.

Silence thundered through the dark bedroom. The mark on my shoulder ached, pounding. I was finally beginning to believe that I was awake. The scars went back to sleep until the next nightmare; maybe I could sleep, too. Maybe.

"If he manages to destroy this Egg," I thought out loud, "does that mean you'll be free?"

"Of course not." He dropped his eyes, studied the bed. Little green shadows danced on my blanket, showing me his gaze moving in an aimless pattern from my knee to my hand to the edge of the bed, back to my knee. "Should Vardimal's rebellion fail, I will be left as your familiar, perhaps. Then after your death—which might be swift, since the Prince is not one for slow punishment—I will be punished, for as long as the Prince's reign is secure. If by some stroke of chance Vardimal succeeds, I will be executed—after your death as well. If the Prince wins, I wait another eternity for a chance at my freedom—if another chance is granted me at all."

"You just can't win, can you." I didn't want to sound snide. I swallowed dryly. It seemed like I couldn't win either, since both scenarios involved my sudden demise, too.

"No," he said. "I can't."

"So you really have a lot invested in this."

"It would appear so."

Another long, uncomfortable silence. The world was hushed outside, in the deepest part of night before the flush of false dawn. I didn't feel sleepy, though I knew I should be trying to catch some shut-eye before the morning transport. Once I left the house tomorrow, I'd be on the hunt. I didn't sleep much while hunting.

"You must be pretty hungry," I said finally. "This mark hurts like a bitch."

"My apologies."

It took more courage than I thought I had to extend my hand, flipping my palm up and making a fist. My wrist was exposed, pale in the dimness of my bedroom. The nightlight in the hall shone in through the door, a cool blue glow. "Here," I said. "Blood, right? You need me to cut myself, or..."

He shrugged. "Many thanks for the offer, Dante, but...no."

"You're hungry. I don't want a weak demon. I want a kickass demon who can help me deal with Santino."

"I fight better when I'm a little hungry."

"Fine." I dropped my hand, feeling foolish. "I'm okay now. You can go back downstairs. Get yourself something in the kitchen. If you want."

"As you like." But he didn't move.

"Go ahead," I finally said. "I'm fine. Really. Thank you."

"You will have no trouble sleeping?" he asked, still looking at the bed. The burning intensity in his eyes seemed to have lessened a bit. He ran his hand back absently through his hair—the first sign of nervousness I'd ever noticed in him. Was he nervous? Was it just me, or was he seeming a little more...*human*...with every passing hour?

I managed to dredge up an uneasy laugh. "I always have trouble sleeping. It's not a big deal. Go on and catch some shut-eye yourself. Tomorrow's going to be a busy day."

He unfolded himself from the bed and stood up, hands behind his back. *Why does he stand like that?* I wondered. *And why doesn't he take that coat off?* "Thanks." I scooted back down, pulled the covers up, rested my hand on my sword, still lying faithfully next to me. "For checking on me, I mean."

He nodded, then turned on his heel and stalked for the door. There was a moment of shadow, his bulk filling the doorway, his coat like a shadow of dark wings. I heard his even tread going down the hall, then down the stairs. He went into the living room, and silence pervaded my house again, broken only by the faint hum of traffic and the subliminal song of the fridge downstairs.

I snuggled back into bed and closed my eyes. I expected to be lying awake for a long time, shaking and sweating in the aftermath of the dream, but strangely enough I fell into sleep with no trouble at all.

CHAPTER 20

Eddie dug his fingers into the armrests. He was as pale as I'd ever seen him, his cheeks chalk-white under his blond sideburns.

Gabe, leafing through a magazine, didn't appear to notice, but Japhrimel was studying Eddie intently, his green eyes glittering. The demon lounged in his seat next to me, occasionally shifting his weight when the transport rattled. I tapped my fingers on my sword-hilt and looked out the window. Seeing the earth drift away underneath the hover transport was no comparison to a slicboard, but it was nice to sit and watch city and water drift away, replaced by pleated folds of land, the coastal mountains rising and falling.

"I can't believe I made a ten o'clock transport." I rested my head against the seat-back. Gabe had actually scored first-class tickets. We had a whole compartment to ourselves—Gabe's tattoo and mine took care of that. "I haven't even had coffee yet, goddammit."

"*Someone's* a little cranky." Gabe hooked her leg over her seat-arm and rubbed her ankle against Eddie's knee. "Bitch, bitch, bitch. I had to drag this big shaggy guy out of bed and onto a transport before noon. I should be the one whining."

"You're always trying to one-up me," I mumbled. The demon glanced at me, then leaned forward to look out the window. I caught a wave of his scent and sighed, my eyes half-closing. Once you started to get used to it, being around a demon was kind of absurdly comforting. At least the most dangerous thing in the vicinity was right where I could see it.

"Fucking transports," Eddie said, closing his eyes. "Gabe?"

"I'm here, sweetie." Gabe rubbed her ankle against his knee. "Just keep breathing."

I looked away. So there *was* something Eddie was afraid of.

"What's he doing in Rio?" I asked the air, thinking out loud. "Not a particularly good place to hide..."

"No, not with all the *santeros* down there," Gabe answered dryly, flipping another page. A holster peered out from under her left shoulder, a smooth dark metal butt. *Plasgun,* I thought, and looked over at the demon again. He had disappeared as we navigated the security checkpoints and rejoined us just before boarding, his hands clasped behind his back and his face expressionless. "Hey, you know their Necromances kill chickens to get Power like the vaudun? Then everyone eats the chicken."

I'd studied vaudun at the Academy, so I wasn't entirely unfamiliar with it. "That's weird," I agreed, my eyes snagging on the demon's face. He was looking at me now, studying intently. "What?"

"Why does he reek of fear?" Japhrimel asked, jerking his chin at Eddie.

"He doesn't like high places," Gabe said, "and he doesn't like enclosed spaces. Most Skinlin don't." Her dark eyes came up, moved over the demon from head to foot. "What are you afraid of, demon?"

He shrugged, his coat moving against the seat. "Failure," he said crisply. "Dissolution. Emptiness." His mouth twisted briefly, as if he tasted something bitter.

Silence fell for about thirty seconds before the first in-flight service came along—a blonde stewardess in a tight magenta flightsuit, paper-pale and trembling. Her eyes were the size of old credit discs, and she shook while she poured coffee, probably thinking that we were all going to read her mind and expose her most intimate secrets, or take over her mind and make her do something embarrassing—or that Gabe and I would suddenly start to make ghosts appear to torment her. Instead, I selected a cream-cheese Danish, Gabe got a roast-turkey sandwich, Eddie asked for the chicken soup in its heatseal pack. Oddly enough, Eddie seemed to scare her the most in his camel coat and long shaggy hair, his Skinlin staff braced against Gabe's sword. She looked like she expected him to go berserk at any moment. Japhrimel accepted a cup of coffee from her with a nod, and it was strange to see her give him an almost-relieved smile. Being normal, she couldn't see the dangerous black diamond flaming of his aura.

Sometimes I wished I'd been born that oblivious.

We waited until she was gone. I dumped a packet of creamer into my coffee. "So do you have contacts in Rio, other than a plug-in? Abra couldn't give me any." I settled back, wrinkling my nose at the reheated black brew.

"A few," she said, tearing into her sandwich. "Guess who else is down Rio way? Jace Monroe."

I made a face. "Yeah, Abra told me. Go figure."

"He's good backup."

"Too bad we're not going to use him."

"Aw, come on," Eddie piped up. "You two are so cute together."

I shrugged. "I don't go near the Mob. I thought you knew that."

"He's not Mob no more." Eddie slurped at his steaming soup, wiggling his blond eyebrows at me. He seemed to have forgotten he was on a transport.

"I fell for that line the first time. Once Mob, always Mob." I nibbled at my Danish, finding it bearable. "You remember that when you're dealing with him, Eddie, 'cause I sure as hell won't ever be messing around with him. Once was enough for me."

"I'll bet," Gabe muttered snidely, and I threw her a look that could have cut glass.

My rings swirled with lazy energy. We settled down to a long flight, Gabe flipping through her magazine again while she sipped at her coffee, Eddie finishing his soup in a series of loud smacking slurps, crunching on the crackers. I fished a book out of my bag—a paperback version of the Nine Canons, the glyphs and runes that made up the most reliable branch of magick. You can't ever study too much. I was secondarily talented as a runewitch, and I firmly believed that memorizing the Canons trained the mind and opened up the Power meridians, and why waste power creating a spell when you could use a Canon glyph as a shortcut?

The demon settled himself in his seat, alternating between watching me and studying his cup as if the secrets of the universe were held inside the nasty liquid passing for coffee. At least it was hot, and it had enough caffeine.

It was going to be a long, long flight.

CHAPTER 21

We touched down in Nuevo Rio not a moment too soon. "Eddie, if you don't quit it, I'm going to fucking kill you," I snarled, standing and scooping my sword up.

"You're the one tapping your fingernails all the time," Gabe retorted. "Don't get all up on him."

"Stay out of this, Spocarelli," I warned her.

The demon rose like a dark wave. "Perhaps it's best to have this conversation outside," he said mildly. "You seem tense."

That gave us both something to focus on. "When I want your opinion, I'll ask you for it," I snapped.

"Oh, for the love of Hades, leave the damn demon alone!" Gabe almost yelled. "Off. Get me *off* this damn thing—"

"You're like a pair of spitting cats," Eddie mumbled. "Worse than a motherfucking cockfight."

"Now I know why I don't travel," I muttered, making sure my bag fell right. The airlocks whooshed, and we would have to wait our turn to get out.

Fuck that, I thought, and jammed the door to our compartment open. There are some *good* things about being a Necromance. One is that people get out of your way in a hell of a hurry when you come striding down a transport corridor with a sword in your hand and your emerald spitting sparks. Being accredited meant being able to carry edged metal in transports, and I had never been so glad.

Japhrimel followed me. By the time I stalked through another pair of airlocks and onto the dock, I was beginning to feel a little better. Eddie was next off, with Gabe right behind him, dragging her hand back through her long dark hair. "Fuck," she said, turning to look at the bulk of the transport through the dock windows. Hovercells were switching off, a subliminal hum loosening from my back teeth. "We're in Nuevo Rio. Gods have mercy on us."

"Amen to that," I answered. "Hey, what hotel are we staying at?"

"No hotel," she said, still trying to push her hair back, "I got us one better. We're going to stay with a friend. Cheap, effective, and safe."

"Who?" I was beginning to suspect something wasn't quite right by the way Eddie was grinning, showing all his teeth.

"Who else?" A familiar voice echoed along the dock. People began to pile out of the transport, casting nervous glances at us— two Necromances and a Skinlin, armed to the teeth, and a man in a long black coat. I closed my eyes, searching for control. Found it, and turned on my heel.

Jason Monroe leaned against a support post, his blue eyes glowing under a thatch of wheat-gold hair. He wore black, even in Rio, a pair of jeans and a black T-shirt, a Mob assassin's rig over the T-shirt, two guns, a collection of knives, his sword sheathed at his side. I prefer to carry my blade; he wore his thrust through his belt like an old-time samurai.

He was taller than me, and broad-shouldered, and wore the same kind of boots Gabe and I did. The thorny-twisted tattoo on his cheek marked him as an accredited Shaman just as the leather spirit bag on a thong around his neck marked him as a *vaudun*. Small bones hung from raffia twine clicked together as he moved slightly, twirling his long staff. I caught a glimpse of red in his spiky aura—he must have just offered to his patron *loa*. "Hey, Danny. Give an old boyfriend a kiss?"

CHAPTER 22

I can't *believe* you did this," I hissed at Gabe. She looked supremely unconcerned.

"It's *safe,*" she repeated for the fifth time. "And neither of us has endlessly deep pockets. Who's going to mess with an ex-Mob *vaudun* Shaman in Nuevo Rio? He's established, Danny. He's letting us stay for free and feeding us as well as running interference with the locals. What more do you fucking want?"

"A little warning next time you decide to drop shit like this on me," I said, glancing out the window. Jace had reserved us a cab, said he'd meet us back at his place, and hopped on a Chervoyg slicboard, rocketing away. Leaving us to pile into the cab with our luggage and get dumped at his house like a package delivery.

One thing hadn't changed; the man certainly irritated me as much as he ever had.

Eddie was grinning broadly. "He's still got it for you, you know." He settled back, stretching his legs out, bumping my knee. I kicked him back. For a claustrophobe Skinlin, he seemed extremely comfortable in the close quarters. Maybe it was just big transports he didn't like.

Nuevo Rio sprawled underneath us in a haze of smoke and noise. Here, the Power was more raw, not like Saint City's cold radioactive glow. This was a different pool of energy, and I would have to spend a little time acclimating. As it was, I felt a little green, and when the cab swooped to avoid a flight of freight transports, I grabbed at the nearest steady thing—which just happened to be Japhrimel's shoulder. I dug my fingers in.

He said nothing.

"I don't care *who* he's got *jackshit* for," I snapped. "I told you I never wanted to see him again. And you—*you*—" I was actually spluttering.

Gabe regarded me coolly, her dark eyes level. "What's the big deal, Danny? If you were so truly over him, it wouldn't *be* a big deal, y'diggit?"

"One of these days," I forced out between clenched teeth, "I will make you pay for this."

She shrugged. "Guess we'll be even when all's said and done, won't we?" She looked out the window at the sweltering smoghole that was Rio. "Gods. I hate the heat as much as I hate travel."

I could kill her, I thought. *No jury would ever convict me.* I realized my fingers were still digging into Japhrimel's shoulder and made them unloose with a physical effort. "Sorry," I said, blankly, to the demon.

He shrugged. "He was once a lover?" he asked, politely enough. "He seemed very happy to see you."

"We broke up," I said through gritted teeth. "Long time ago."

"She hasn't dated since," Eddie offered helpfully. "They were a hot team when they did work together—if they could finish a job without ripping each other's clothes off."

I gave him a look that could have drained a hovercell. "*Will* you *quit* it?"

He shrugged, settling back in the seat, bumping my knee again with his long legs. The smell of dirt and growing things filled the car, and the musky perfume of demon that I had only just become accustomed to. "Not my business," he said finally. "Hey, I wonder what time's dinner?"

"Soon," Gabe said. "He told me he'd feed us. Since we're on business."

"What else did you tell him?" I was forced to ask.

"Not much. Said you'd brief him on the hunt. That was his condition, that he get a piece of the—"

"Oh, *Sekhmet sa'es*," I hissed. "You *didn't*."

"What is your motherfucking *problem?*" Gabe snarled.

"Here we go again." Eddie at least pulled his legs up out of the way.

"Strictly speaking," the demon said, "the more cannon fodder, the better your chances, Dante."

I looked at him, my jaw dropping.

Silence crackled in the cab for a good twenty seconds, during which the driver—a bespectacled Hispanic normal with an air-freshener of Nuestra Dama Erzulie de Guadalupe hanging from his farecounter—did his level best to commit suicide by taxi. I stared out the window until my stomach rose in revolt and then shut my eyes, breathing deeply and trying to get a handle on my rage. It would strike at anyone around me if I lost control, my anger taking physical form—and I didn't want that.

Not yet.

"You invite yourself along on my hunt," I said slowly and distinctly, "and you give me trouble about the tech I ask you to supply, and you finish up by inviting *someone else* into my hunt too, someone who may or may not be trustworthy. This is not looking good for future collaborations, Gabe."

"You're the one dragging around a fucking demon," Gabe replied tartly. "And he's right—the more cannon fodder, the better the chances that your sloppy ass will get through this alive. You're losing your touch, Valentine. *Don't* make me come over there and smack some sense into your hard head. Besides," she continued, "sparring with Monroe will take some of your edge off. You haven't had a good sparring partner in years, and you won't eat him alive the way you'd do anyone else. Way I recall it, he always gave you a good run for your money—in and out of the sack. I never saw you so relaxed."

"Do we have to drag my sexual history into this?" I asked. "'Cause if we do, you're going down with me."

Silence. The cab began a wavering descent. My ears popped.

"Do you need combat to ease your nerves?" the demon asked.

I shrugged, keeping my eyes firmly shut as my stomach lurched.

"Hades," Gabe breathed. "Does he live *there*?"

I opened my eyes to look; wished I hadn't.

Jace had either done well for himself or was renting from a Nuevo Rio druglord. The house was large, with an open plaza made of white stone, green garden growing up to the stone walls, a red-tiled roof and the glitter of shielding over it.

The shielding slid briefly through the taxi, flushing slightly as the demon stilled. The mark on my shoulder gave another spiked burst of pain.

"The mark's hurting," I said. The demon's attention fixed on me.

"My apologies."

"What's up?" Gabe asked.

"Don't even talk to me," I said without any real heat. The anger had drained helplessly away. "Not until after dinner, Gabe. *Fuck*."

She shrugged and stared out the window again.

"Thank the gods," Eddie mumbled.

I was just beginning to seriously contemplate drawing a knife when the cab touched down and we scrambled out onto the glittering hard-baked white marble plaza—above the city's smoghole stink, but still blazing under the hammerblow heat of Nuevo Rio.

CHAPTER 23

Jace Monroe hadn't just done well for himself.

He'd gotten absolutely, filthy, marvelously, stinking rich.

I took a long bath in a sumptuous blue-tiled bathroom while the demon laid his own protections in the walls and windows of the suite a hatchet-faced butler had led us to. Gabe and Eddie had their own set of rooms right next door, done in pale yellow instead of blue and cream. I wondered if Jace had picked the furnishings himself or had an assistant do it.

I wondered who he'd bought the house from, and how he'd managed to accumulate enough credit. Mob freelancers usually don't get rich—they usually die young, even the psionics.

I closed my eyes, resting my head against the back of the tub. The water was hot, the soap was sandalwood-scented—I knew that was Jace, he had to remember that I'd always used sandalwood soap—and I felt as safe as it was possible to be, in a Shaman's mansion with a demon carefully laying warding everywhere.

I wondered what Jace would make of Japhrimel. He hadn't seemed to even notice the demon. I wondered what Gabe had told him.

I lifted my toes out of the silky hot water. Examined the blood-red molecule-drip polish on my toenails. The heat was delicious, unstringing muscle aches and soothing frazzled nerves.

Gabe was right, really. This was better than a hotel. And if Jace would feed us, it would mean that we wouldn't have to spend a fortune tracking down Santino. We could spend our credit on *finding* the demon instead of hotels and food...and maybe hiring some merc talent to make things uneasy for him.

Feeding, I thought, and grimaced. *What am I going to do about the demon? Blood, sex, fire. I can't give the last two...and he's refused the first.*

A knock on the bathroom door interrupted me. "Dante, I've finished shielding the room."

"Come on in," I said, sinking down in the milky water. "We've got to have a little talk."

He opened the door. A burst of slightly cooler air made the steam inside the bathroom billow slightly. "Are you certain?"

"For God's sake. I'm sure you've seen a naked woman before. I'm under the water, anyway. Sheesh."

He stepped into the bathroom, his long coat moving slightly. He didn't seem to sweat, even in the fierce Nuevo Rio heat. He examined the mirror over the sink across from the bathtub as if he'd never seen one before, and I thought of asking him to sit down but the only place was the counter next to the sink or the toilet—and the image of a demon sitting on the toilet and looking at my profile was too much. While he studied the mirror I studied his broad back, turned to me and covered with that coat. "You wanted to talk?"

"You need blood," I said, wiggling my toes against the cobalt tiles. My sword leaned against the tub, a comforting dark slenderness. "The mark's hurting me, and I can't do my job with that kind of unnecessary distraction. Okay?"

He nodded, his dark hair beginning to stick to his forehead. He wasn't sweating—the steam in the air was weighing his hair down. "It may be uncomfortable for you."

"Well, you won't take mine, so...Um, how many pints do you need?" *I should have suggested a Nichtvren haunt,* I realized, kicking myself for not thinking of it sooner. Since the advent of cloned blood, Nichtvren social drinking had taken on a whole new context and popularity.

"I can visit a slaughterhouse," he said. "You still have slaughterhouses."

"Oh." I absorbed this. "You don't...oh. Okay." *Silly me. I thought he meant* my *blood.* I slipped my toes back into the water, yawned. Oddly enough, I was tired. "How about tonight? I need to do some recon anyway, get used to the whole place."

He nodded. His eyes were darker, their luminescence veiled. "Very well."

"Is it going to be really messy?" I asked. "We can't afford *him* being warned of our intentions."

"I think it would be best if I went alone, Dante."

I shrugged, water rippling against the side of the tub. "Fine." Another yawn caught me off-guard. "I'm going to finish up in here, and then you can have a turn."

"Not necessary. But thank you." He didn't sound robotic—his tone was merely polite, shaded with some human emotion. Which emotion? I couldn't tell.

I shrugged again. "Okay. Scoot along, then."

He turned to leave, then stopped. "I would not have you see me feed, Dante."

Why should I care? I thought. "Thanks," I said out loud, not knowing what else to say.

He ducked back out the door, steam drifting behind him. *He didn't even sneak a peek,* I thought, and smiled, ducking under the sandalwood-scented water.

When I emerged into the bedroom, wrapped in a towel and carrying my sword, the demon stood by a window looking down into a courtyard full of orange trees. Up here above the main bulk of the city, the smog wasn't so bad, and the heat was bearable due to the high ceilings and chill stone walls. Jace had climate control. But I was going to have to get used to the heat if we were going to be hunting here.

"It's pretty, isn't it?" I said, dropping down on the bed. Water weighed my hair, sandalwood smell drifting around me and warring with the heavy smell of demon. "I wonder how Jace affords this."

"Ask him," the demon replied. "You're tired, Dante. Sleep."

I yawned again. "If I asked him, he'd probably think I was interested."

"Are you?"

"We broke up a long time ago, Japhrimel. Why are you asking?"

"He seems to evoke a response from you." Did he sound uncertain?

"I suppose loathing might be a response," I admitted. "He's infuriating."

"Did you leave him?"

"No," I yawned again, closing my eyes, surprised. I didn't sleep much on hunts. And who would have thought that it could be comforting to have a demon in the same room? "He left me. Three years ago. Came down here, I guess..."

"Foolish of him," Japhrimel said, before I fell asleep.

CHAPTER 24

Gabe settled down cross-legged on the rug across from me. I balanced the tracker in one hand, examining its crystalline glitter. The arrow was spinning lazily, not yet triggered. I wouldn't use it unless I absolutely had to—but it was nice to have. If we didn't find any whisper of the demon here, we could trigger the tracker and see where it led us.

"Where's the demon?" Eddie asked.

"Went out," I replied absently, staring at the tracker. "Needs feeding."

"Hades bless us," Gabe snorted, "Feeding?"

"Well, he said he was going to go to the slaughterhouses. Efficient, right?" I shifted on the green and blue Persian rug, uneasy. "Where's Jace?"

Gabe pulled a black satin card-pouch from the bowels of her blue canvas bag. Her fingers moved with the ease of long practice as she extracted the tarot cards, shuffled them with loud gunning snaps, then turned one over. "He said he'd be back by dark. It's dark, so I suppose either he lied, or—"

"You have no faith in me either," Jace said from the door. He stalked into the room, the bones on his staff clicking together. His hair was damp, sticking to his skull and darker than its usual gold, and his eyes were dark too. *He's upset,* I thought, automatically cataloguing the set of his shoulders, the way his left knee moved a little stiffly, the way his aura shifted through violet and into blue. We'd been lovers once, and it was a mixed relief to find out I could still read him with a glance.

I looked back down at my palm, at the tracker's lazy spinning.

We were downstairs, in a huge high-ceilinged living room holding two long blue velvet couches and a collection of silk and satin floor pillows, ceiling fans turning lazily. The staff of the house were Nuevo Rios, lean brown women in starched uniforms, a black-jacketed butler, none of whom spoke any English.

Gabe glanced up at Jace. "Hey, Monroe. Nice digs." Her tone was neutral, and her expression might have been a warning.

"Anything for the famous Spocarelli. And the pretty Danny Valentine." He paced over to the wet bar holding up one end of the room. "Drinks?"

"Scotch on the rocks for Eddie, vodka Mim for me, and Danny looks like she's in the mood for a brandy," Gabe replied promptly. "What's the word, Shaman?"

He waved his staff briefly, a clicking rattle. "Give me a minute, Gabe. 'Kay?"

I studied the tracker, worrying my lower lip with my teeth. If I could still read Jace...

No. He had never been able to read me.

My left shoulder throbbed. Japhrimel had left as soon as dusk fell. I didn't want to know what he was doing. I kept my fingers away from the mark, not wanting to see through his eyes.

Gabe's eyes rested on me. The clink of glasses, liquid pouring from place to place. "Aren't you going to say anything?" she stage-whispered.

I darted her a murderous glance. She grinned, her emerald twinkling, and a completely uncharacteristic desire to laugh came over me. She was acting just like a high-school girl—or at least, like the high-school girls I'd seen in holovids, blinking innocently and giggling over boys.

I shrugged. I didn't have a reputation for small talk, so I simply concentrated on stuffing the tracker back in its leather bag. *If I have to use this, it had better work,* I thought, *or I'll go back to Saint City and find whatever cell they've stuck Dake in, and I'll make him wish he'd never been born.*

If he hadn't died from Chill withdrawal by the time I got back.

How long would it take to hunt down Santino anyway?

Not long. Not once he finds out I'm looking for him. My skin went cold, my nipples tightening and gooseflesh breaking out over my skin. All at once memory rose, swallowed me, was pushed down.

Jace turned around at the wet bar, and his blue eyes met mine. I hadn't even known I was staring at his back. "I hear you're hunting Santino, Danny," he said quietly. "Is that why you brought a demon into my house?"

I rocked up to my feet, carrying my sword. "Okay," I said quietly. "That's *it*."

Gabe sighed. "I didn't want—"

"Let's get this over with," I snapped, and my thumb caressed the katana's guard. One simple movement would slip it free. "I didn't want to be here in the first place, Monroe. I'd rather live in the filthiest sink of Nuevo Rio than stay in *your* house." I took a deep breath. "And that demon's saved my life more than once since this whole filthy mess started. More than I can say for anyone else here."

Silence. Jace carried two glasses instead of his staff. He walked across the room, handed one glass to Eddie, who was watching me, his hazel eyes narrowed. Gabe turned over another card, accepted the other glass.

I started to feel a little foolish, standing up. Gabe hummed under her breath, a snatch of classical music. *Berlioz,* I placed it, and took a step back, turning on my heel.

"So you're in a bit of a mess," Jace said quietly. "You always did have a talent for getting into trouble."

I rounded on him, my unbraided hair swinging heavily against my back. "It's none of your concern. I wasn't the one that wanted to contact you."

"I know," he answered, straightening a little. His fingers tapped his swordhilt. "Gabe told me as much. I talked her into staying here. It's safer all the way around, especially if you're hunting Santino." His voice dropped. "I heard enough of your nightmares to know that name."

My thumb rested against the guard.

There was a slight sound, and the black-clad hatchet-faced butler bustled in. I took a deep breath, eased my hand away from the guard, clasped the hilt loosely. He directed a stream of liquid Portogueso at Jace, who shrugged and gave a clipped answer. The butler, his dark eyes resting on me for just a moment and skittering away, bowed and scuttled out.

Jace shrugged. "Dinner's in fifteen minutes, sweetheart. I was just curious. He's a tough one, your demon."

I swallowed dryly. My left shoulder gave one last spiked flare of pain; then a wave of warmth slid over my body, my neck easing its aching. "I guess so," I said. "Look, I didn't want this."

He nodded, his eyes holding mine. "I know. It's okay. Come on, let's get something to eat. It's been a long day. I've cleared my calendar for the next month or so, and there's a few contacts we can start on tomorrow—"

"You're inviting yourself in on my hunt, *too*?" My jaw clenched.

Jace's mouth curled up into a half smile. It was his "I-know-best" expression, and the sight of it tightened my hand on the hilt. "Why not? You're a hell of a lot of fun to work with, Danny."

I looked down at Gabe. Her hair fell forward over her face, unsuccessfully hiding her smirk. Eddie still stared at me with narrowed eyes. He was tense, too tense. Eddie expected me to go after Gabe.

That managed to hurt my feelings.

I took another step back, bare feet shushing against the Persian carpet. If I'd been wearing my boots, I might have stalked out of the house. "If everyone's finished having some fun at my expense," I said tightly, "I think I'll excuse myself."

"Dinner," Jace said softly.

"Not hungry," I countered.

"You don't eat, you start seeing ghostflits without wanting to," he reminded me. "Come on, Danny. Don't let that stupid pride ruin a lovely reunion."

I kept my temper with a physical effort of will, my hand clenching on the hilt. Gabe scooted back and made it to her feet, hooking her arm through Eddie's. "Come on, Eddie. Let's let these two have a moment alone." She looked enormously pleased with herself.

"No need," I said. "I'm leaving."

"Don't." Jace said. "Come on, Danny. Bend a little."

I shrugged. "I was never very good at that, was I? That's why you left."

Gabe all but dragged Eddie out of the room, whispering something to him. The shaggy blond Skinlin cast a doubtful look over his shoulder. Gabe kicked the door to the hall closed behind them. And for the first time in three years, I was alone with Jace. His face was interested and open, his eyes now bright blue. His tattoo shifted a little, thorny lines twisting.

"Dante—" he began.

My sword leaped half free of the scabbard, my arm tensing. "Don't."

His own hand drifted down, touched his swordhilt. "That's what you want?"

"I won't hold back," I warned him. "Don't push me, Jace. I'm on a hunt, and Gabe seems determined to bring every halfass mercenary in the world in on it. And I've been dragged through Hell for this, I even have to have a demon tag along with me." I resheathed my blade, then reached up and dragged my shirt down, exposing a slice of the branded mark on my left shoulder.

"Fuck," Jace breathed. "Dante—"

I let go of my shirt. "So don't push me, Jace. Got it?"

The ceiling fans turned lazily, drafts of cooler air sliding across my skin. "I never did," he said. "You were always the one pushing."

"We're old news, Jace. Get over it." I turned away again, but was unable to resist a final parting shot. "At least the goddamn demon can't betray me."

He grabbed my arm, sinking his fingers in hard, his weight perfectly balanced. I recognized the stance—he was ready for me to attack him. I wondered grimly if I should. "I didn't betray you. I would *never* betray you."

I shrugged. My rings crackled in the tension, reacting uneasily with the Power in the air. "Get. Your. Hand. Off. Me."

"No."

"Get your—"

There was no warning. One moment I was yanking my arm away from Jace's grip, screaming, and the next Jace stumbled back, sword ringing free, Japhrimel's right hand up, arm outstretched, the shining gun held level. The demon was between us, his long black coat fuming with Power, the rumbling thunder of his arrival shattering the air inside the room. Jace's defenses resounded, humming into life, crackling with Power, gathering like a cobra gathers itself to strike.

"Stop!" I yelled, and the demon paused, though the gun didn't move.

"Are you injured?" he asked, and his eyes didn't waver from Jace. I thought for one lunatic instant that he was asking *Jace* if he was injured.

"Call him off, Danny," Jace said grimly. He carried a larger sword than mine, a *dotanuki* instead of a *katana*; the steel shimmered under the full-spectrum lights. Second-guard position, balanced and ready, Jace's jaw was set and his eyes burned blue. Burning—but still human.

I curled my left hand around Japhrimel's shoulder. The subliminal hum of that much Power in such a confined space roared through me, heady whine like the kick of a slicboard's speed against my stomach. "It's okay," I said. "Really. Stand down, Jaf, it's all right." It was an effort of will to keep from using more of his name. When had I started to think of him as *human*?

Japhrimel considered Jace for a few moments, then eased the hammer down with his thumb. The gun was bright silver, glittering under the lights. "You're all right?" he asked again.

"I think so," I replied, taking another deep breath. "Where were you?"

"Returning from my feeding," he answered, still not looking at me, his eyes glued to Jace. "I felt your distress."

"I'm not distressed. Just pissed off and tired and hungry and wishing this was all over." I kept my hand on his shoulder. If he dove for Jace, what would I do? Stab him in the back? "Okay? Thanks, Jaf. I mean it. Easy, okay?"

The gun disappeared. Japhrimel half-turned, examined me with one laser-green eye. His mouth turned down at both corners. "You have no further need of me?"

My chest tightened. "Thank you." I meant it. "I'm going to go do some recon."

Japhrimel's shoulders tightened slightly. If I hadn't been staring at his throat, I wouldn't have seen it. *What's with him? He looks ready to explode.* "I will accompany you, then, as is my duty."

I decided it would be wiser not to fight over this one, set my jaw. My head rang with the tension and Power humming in the air. If Jace moved on Japhrimel, or if Japhrimel decided Jace meant to hurt me—

"Danny." Jace's sword slid back into its sheath, whispering. "Get something to eat. And I'll spar with you tomorrow, I'll even let you kick my ass if it'll make you feel better about this."

"Good," I slid my hand down Jaf's arm, found his elbow. "I'll do that. I'll be back in a few hours."

"Hey, demon." Jace's chin tilted up. "Take care of her."

Japhrimel studied him for a bare second, then nodded once, sharply.

I don't need anyone to take care of me, Jace, shut your stupid mouth. I hauled on Japhrimel's elbow. "Shut *up*, Jace. Just shut up. Have a nice fucking dinner and I'll talk to you tomorrow, okay?"

He didn't respond. Japhrimel followed me obediently out into the hall, then pointed to the right. "The front door is that way."

"I need my boots," I said, harshly. My throat hurt, for some reason. As if there was a big spiky lump in it.

"The stairs." Japhrimel pointed, again. I was grateful, even though I had Jace's house mostly figured out. I've deciphered enough city street grids that one overblown Nuevo Rio mansion wasn't a hassle.

I nodded, and we set off. Just to be sure, I kept my hand on his elbow. He didn't object.

CHAPTER 25

Once we alighted from the hovercab Japhrimel had somehow had waiting for me at Jace's front door, I chose a few streets at random. Walked along feeling my shields thicken and thin, taking in the atmosphere. It's a strange process to get accustomed to another city; it takes normal people months. Psionics process a lot faster; it takes up a few days—or if we deliberately sink ourselves into a city's Power-well, a few hours.

We walked, the demon and I, his coat occasionally brushing me. I sweated freely, heat still trapped in the streets, my coat's Kevlar panels heavy against my back. My bag's strap cut into my shoulder. I carried my sword, tapping my fingernails on the hilt.

I might not have held back this time, I thought, as we turned into the redlight district.

Down in the smoking well of Nuevo Rio, I found a *taqueria* and ordered in passable pidgin with a soupçon of pointing. The demon stood uncomfortably close, his heat blurring and mixing in with the heat of the pavement giving back the fierce sun of the day. He said nothing as we stood aside between a bodega and a closed-up cigar shop. Crowds pushed past, Nuevo Rios in bright colors, most of them wearing *grisgris* bags. Vaudun and Santeria had taken over here after the collapse of the Roman Catholic Church in the great Vatican Bank scandal in the dim time between the Parapsychic Act and the Awakening; the revelation that the Church had been funding terrorist groups and the Evangelicals of Gilead had been too much for even the Protestant Christians traditionally opposed to the Catholics. And the Seventy-Day War had put the last nail in the coffin of the tradition of Novo Christos.

Nuevo Rios understood a little more about Power than other urban folk, and would no more go outside without defense from the evil eye or random curse than they would go out without clothing. So Nuevo Rio was heat and the smell of tamales and blood, copper-skinned normals with liquid dark eyes speaking in Portogueso, old crumbling palatial buildings standing cheek-by-jowl with new plasteel skyscrapers, pedicabs and wheelbikes making a crush of traffic on the streets. Sweat, heat, and more heat; I could see why the city seemed to move so damnably fast and slow at the same time. Slow because the heat made everything seem like it took forever to do; fast because the natives seemed unaffected by the thin sheen of sweat on everything.

I bolted the food, hoping I wouldn't get sick. I had the standard doses of tazapram in my bag, but I rarely needed them. Most Necromances had cast-iron guts. You'd think that a bunch of neurotic freaks like us would have delicate stomachs, but I'd never met a queasy Necromance.

When I finished, licking hot sauce from my fingers, the demon glanced down at me. "Did he hurt you?" he asked, incuriously. But his shoulders were tense; I saw it and wondered why. Of course, if anything happened to me Jaf was screwed . . . I wondered if he thought Jace was that dangerous.

I shrugged. "Not really." *Not physically, anyway,* I added, looking away from the demon's green gaze.

He handed me a cold bottle of *limonada* and watched as I opened it with a practiced wrist-flick. We stepped out into the flow of foot traffic, the demon still uncomfortably close, moving with weirdly coordinated grace so he didn't bump or jostle me. "Why was he holding you?" Japhrimel asked in my ear, leaning close so he didn't have to shout.

"I don't have any idea," I said. "I think he's upset at me."

"Do you?" Even though the street was crowded, we were still given a few feet of breathing room. My emerald glowed under the streetlamps, and my rings swirled with color, my shields adjusting to the different brand of Power pulsing out from the people and pavement. "Why did he leave you?"

I shrugged. "I have no idea. I came home from a job and he was gone. I waited for him to come back for a few weeks and . . ." I glanced up as slicboards hummed overhead. The hovertraffic here was chaotic outside of a few aerial lanes, taxis screeching through banzai runs, gangs of slicboarders whooping as they coasted through the smoggy air. "I got over it."

"Indeed." The demon bumped my shoulder slightly. I wished I'd thought to tie my hair back — a stray breeze blew a few strands across my nose. "He seems very attached to you, Dante."

"If he was attached, he wouldn't have left. Don't *you* start in on me, too."

"Understood." He sounded thoughtful. We started to walk, oddly companionable.

I stopped to watch a three-card-monte game, half-smiling when I saw the man's brown hands flick. Streams of liquid Portogueso slid past me. The demon leaned over my shoulder, his different heat closing around me and oddly enough making the sweaty smoggy atmosphere a little easier to handle.

Down the street from the monte, a *babalawao* drew a *vevé* in chalk on the pavement. The crowd drew back to watch, respectful, or hurriedly slipped away, giving her a wide berth. The woman's dusky hair fell forward over her dark shoulders, her wide-cheeked ebony face split with a white smile as she glanced up, feeling the demon's glow and my own Power.

I nodded, the silent salute of one psionic to another. She was too engaged in her own work of contacting her guardian spirit to do much more than give the demon a brief glance — and anyway, Shamans aren't nearly as scared of demons as they should be. To them, the demons are just another class of *loa*. I didn't think so — if demons were just another type of *loa*, Magi techniques for containing a spirit should work for the spirits like Erzulie and Baron Samedi. They don't — only the Shamanic practice of going through an initiation and gaining an affinity for a *loa* of your own does.

I watched the *vevé* take form under her slender fingers, a curl of incense going up. A rum bottle stood to one side, and a wicker basket that probably held a chicken.

"What will she do?" the demon asked, quietly, in my ear.

"She's probably fulfilling a bargain with a *loa*," I replied, tilting my head back and turning so I could whisper to him while still watching the *babalawao*. My knuckles ached, I was gripping my sword so tightly. "Just watch. This should be interesting."

Little prickles of heat ran over my skin. It was uncomfortable, but being this close to a contained burst of Power would help me adjust to the city. I'd studied vaudun, of course, at the Academy. The Magi training techniques borrowed heavily from Shamanism, vaudun, and Santeria in some areas; vaudun and Santeria had been interbreeding ever since before the Parapsychic Act. Eclectic Shamans like Jace picked up a little here, a little there, and usually had two or three *loa* as incidental patrons; this *babalawao* would be sworn to two *loa* at the very most, and would probably intensely dislike being compared to Jace—who was, after all, only a gringo Shaman trained by the Hegemony, not heir to an unbroken succession of masters and acolytes like the *babalawao* would be. Even though the basic techniques were the same, this woman's Power felt different; here in Nuevo Rio she was on her home ground, and her Power was organic instead of alien.

I wish I'd thought to learn Portogueso, I thought, and blinked.

The *vevé* to call the *loa* done, the woman took up the rum bottle, her bracelets and bead necklaces clicking together. She took a mouthful of rum, swirled it, then sprayed it between her lips into the air, the droplets caught hanging, flashing over the *vevé*.

Power spiked, scraping across my shields and skin, prickling in my veins.

A cigar laid across the chalk lines started to fume as the woman flipped open the wicker lid and yanked a chicken from the basket. The bird made a frantic noise before she cut its throat with one practiced move, blood spraying across the *vevé*.

"She'll cook it tonight and eat it for lunch tomorrow, probably," I told him. A swirl of air started, counterclockwise, the chicken's body still scrabbling mindlessly. The blood slowed from a spray to a gush and then to a trickle, and the *babalawao*'s voice rose, keening through a chant very similar to a Necromance's. But this chant would complete the job of making the offering to the *loa*. The rum droplets vanished, eaten up by Power. I felt insubstantial fingers touch my cheek, saw a vague shape out of the corner of my eye—a tall man, with a top hat over his skull-white face, his crotch bulging, capered away through the crowd. A breath of chill touched my sweating back. I didn't mess around with *loa*.

Power tingled over my skin, a wash of fever-heat, the sickening feeling of freefall just under my stomach. The Power-burst would force my own energy channels to change to acclimate to the different brand of Power here if I just gave it enough time. I kept my breathing even. *Just a few minutes*, I told myself. *It'll go away. Just need to relax long enough for it to work, that's all. Stay cool, Danny. Just stay cool.*

It was while I was staring at the *vevé* and waiting for my body to acclimatize to the resident Power, my mind tuned to a blank expectant humming, that the precognition hit.

The demon had my shoulders, drew me back away from the clear space in the pavement, the *babalawao*'s chanting rising against the backdrop of city noise. "Dante?"

My gods, does he sound concerned?

"What's wrong? Dante?"

"Nothing," I heard my voice, dim and dreamy. Precog's not my main Talent; if it was I'd be a Seer. But I had enough of it to be useful sometimes. "Nothing." Darkness folded over me, a quiet restfulness, the sound of wings. The vision trembled just outside my mental grasp. If I simply relaxed and let my minor precognitive talent work, it would come to me, and I would be warned... but of what?

What did I need a warning for? I already knew I was in deep shit.

"Nothing..." I whispered. Hot fingers touched my forehead; my fingers curling around my scabbard, head lolling, I sank into the candleflame of the future, guttering, held in a draft—

"Don't lie to me," he snarled, and I found myself dimly surprised. *Why should he give a shit if I lie to him?* I thought. I snapped back into myself, hot prickles running over my skin, my stomach flipping uneasily, my eyes fluttering. "Dante! *Dante!*"

"I'm fine," I said irritably. "Just give me a minute, okay? Will you?"

"As you like." Heat roiled over my skin. Was it him? A flood of hot, rough Power slid down my spine from the demon's hands. It knocked the premonition—and my hold on relaxation—away like a *jo* staff slamming into my solar plexus. There went any hope of seeing the future.

"—*fuck*—" was all I could say, digging my heels into pavement, curling around the scorching pain in my middle. The Power tipped back and slid into the hungry well of Nuevo Rio. "Gods *damn* it—"

"What's wrong?"

It was too dark. What had—

I opened my eyes slowly. The demon stood, feet planted, green eyes glowing like chips of radioactive gemstone. "I lost it," I said. "A premonition, and I lost it. Ask me before you do that next time, all right?"

The demon shrugged. I looked up. Brick, plasteel, cardboard, and aluminum sheeting, tenements sloped crazily up. Instead of the street, it was an alley. Why wasn't I surprised? Had he dragged me here, thinking I was about to have some sort of fit? "I acted for your safety," he said, quiet but unrepentant. "I feared you were being attacked."

"Who would be stupid enough to attack me with a demon right next to me?" I snapped, and wriggled out of his hands. He let me go, clasping his hands behind his back again, standing straight, his eyelids dropped, hiding his eyes. "Great. A premonition usually means something nasty's on its way, and now I'm not even forewarned. Perfect."

Japhrimel said nothing.

I sighed, filled my lungs with the heavy carbon stink of Nuevo Rio. Curdled smells of garbage and human misery rose around me. My shields were paper-thin, the premonition draining me; I forced myself to breathe through the stink. *"Anubis et'her ka,"* I breathed, shaking my head. "I'd better get back. I think I'm going to crash."

"Very well." Japhrimel took my elbow, guiding me toward the mouth of the alley. "You should take more care with yourself, Dante."

"Nobody ever got rich by being cautious," I muttered. "Besides, what do *you* care? As soon as we find this Egg, you'll be on your way back to Hell, and I'll probably be left to clean up the mess. I'll be lucky to get out of this alive, and you're telling me to be careful." I snorted, concentrating on placing one foot in front of the other.

"I would not leave you without being sure of your safety," he replied, quietly enough. "It would grieve me to learn of your death, human."

"Bully for you," I muttered ungracefully.

"Truly," he persisted. "It would."

"Fuck," I said, the beginnings of a backlash headache starting behind my eyes. "Just get me back to Jace's, okay? My head's starting to hurt."

"Backlash," he said. "Dante, there is something I would—"

If he kept talking I was going to scream. "Just get me back to Jace's, all right?"

His hand tightened on my elbow. I closed my eyes. "Understood."

CHAPTER 26

I stamped into the practice room just as the afternoon heat began to get thick and heavy, black-stacked clouds massing over the city. There would be rain soon, a monsoonlike downpour. Thunder and lightning would accompany the rain, and by the time full dark fell the steaming city might get some relief.

I wasn't wearing my bag or my coat, just jeans and a fresh microfiber shirt, boots and my rings. My hair was wet, braided back tightly, and I'd relacquered my fingernails with the molecule drip that made them tough as claws.

The practice room was a long hall floored with tatami, weapons racked on the wall and three heavy bags ranged in a row near the door. One wall was mirrored, a ballet barre bolted to the mirror (*Now that probably wasn't here before, Jace must have put that in,* I thought snidely) and Eddie faced Jace in the center of the room.

Jace had a *jo* staff, and Eddie had one, too. They both wore black silk *gi* pants, and Eddie wore a white cotton tank top that did nothing to disguise just how hairy he really was. I stopped, leaning against the doorjamb to watch.

Jace, stripped to the waist, held his staff with both hands. Muscle flickered under his skin, the scorpion tattoo on his left shoulderblade moving slightly, his golden hair plastered down with sweat.

Gabe was stretching out, well away from them. She went into a full front split, then leaned forward to touch her forehead to her front knee. *Showoff,* I thought, the ghost of pain behind my eyes reminding me of backlash.

Japhrimel, his arms folded, leaned against the wall on the other side of the heavy bags. The windows were covered with sheer curtains, but the sun pouring in still made it a little too warm. Nobody had flipped on the climate control in here.

I watched as Eddie moved in, Jace parrying strikes, low sounds of effort from both men. I watched the fight, almost feeling the wood balanced in my own hands, jagging in a breath when Eddie smacked upward, meaning to catch Jace in the face. It was a dirty move, but they were both good enough—and with two Necromances standing by, if someone caught a bad strike we were well prepared to handle it.

Japhrimel approached me slowly. "Better?" he asked. Behind him, the sunlight coming through the windows dimmed. The clouds had arrived. That didn't break the heat, though; it just made one more conscious of the awful humidity pressing against skin and breath.

I don't know why heat rose to stain my cheeks. "Yeah," I said, glancing up at his unremarkable, saturnine face. "Thanks."

"I've seen backlash before," he replied quietly. "The best thing for it is Power, and letting the pain pass."

"Thanks," I said again. "It helps, to have someone there during—"

Crack. Eddie's strike wrenched Jace's staff out of his hands. I clicked my tongue. *That's the first time I've seen Jace lose at staves with Eddie.*

Eddie growled. "Quit fuckin' around and give me a fight, hoodoo! Goddammit! You ain't no fuckin good to us distracted!"

"Shut up, dirtwitch." Jace snarled back. "Want to switch to blades?"

"You'll fuckin' kill yourself," Eddie scooped up Jace's staff, tossed it at him. Jace's hand flashed up; he caught the smooth wood, then turned it vertically. "Thanks anyway. Been a while since I saw you make an amateur move like that. Hey, Danny!" He glanced over Jace's shoulder at me. "Come on over here and work his fidgets out, will you? Goddamn boy can't even hold his staff."

I sighed. I had expected this. "Fine," I said, shrugging. "We'd come to this sooner or later." I looked up at the demon's face, quiet and shuttered. "I'm going to spar with Jace. I want you to stay out of it, all right?"

Japhrimel nodded his dark head.

"Cool," Gabe said, bouncing to her feet. "I've missed watching you two fight. Better than a holovid."

I ignored her. *What would piss Jace off most?* I thought, looking up at the demon again. A faint breeze swept through the room, carrying the promise of thunder with it. *Okay.*

I stepped close to the demon, went up on tiptoe, my hand curling around his shoulder, the smell of musk and dark Power enveloping me. "Hey." I pulled on his shoulder and he bent a little, obediently. I kissed his cheek—just a peck, but I heard Jace's indrawn breath and knew I was halfway to winning.

He fought better when he was angry, anyway.

"Thanks." I repeated to Japhrimel, whose eyes had half-closed. He looked surprised. "It helps to have someone there while I'm in pain." My tone was a little more intimate than I'd planned. "I appreciate it."

He nodded once, sharply, and straightened, his gaze flicking away from me. I turned back to the practice room.

Gabe's jaw dropped. She sidled back, almost to the mirrored wall. Eddie followed her, watching Jace, white teeth showing in a wide grin.

Jace walked deliberately over to a rack near the windows and put his staff up, scooped up his scabbarded sword. "I'm game for it, if Danny is," he said quietly, and I had to fight the smile that wanted to pull my lips up. *Careful, Danny. You haven't fought him in a while, ease into this.*

I made it to the center of the room and yawned. I hadn't even stretched out beyond my usual morning routine. Jace carried his sword, approached me cautiously, his booted feet shushing over the tatami. "Hi, sweetheart," he said, his blue eyes locking with mine. It was his usual greeting, usually followed by a kiss. My body remembered the sound of that voice. I let myself smile, then. My rings gave out a low, sustained humming.

"You're in for a treat," Gabe said to the demon. "Jace and Danny are the best in the biz. They used to do naked-blade slicboard duels, back in the day. And—"

"Shh," Eddie said. "I wanta see this."

"Hi, baby," I said quietly, holding my sword, fingers curled loosely around scabbard and hilt. "Missed me?"

"Every damn day." Jace's face was set. His shoulders were loose and easy. *Maybe I didn't piss him off as much as I thought.* "Every single motherfucking day."

"Hmm." I smiled sweetly. "Shouldn't have left."

"Didn't have a choice," he returned.

We circled each other, wary. I shifted my weight forward, playing through the sequence that would end with his head separated from his body. He countered almost immediately, and we went back to circling.

Point for him, he'd made me twitch first.

"Yeah," I said. "You were in such a hurry you didn't even leave a note. Must have been really deep and hot, Jace, for you to just get up and leave." I let my smile broaden. "What was her name?"

"I've been a fucking monk since our last time, sweetheart," he said, the easy smile dropping from his voice.

Second point for me. I'd pushed him too far.

"I hope it's made you a better fighter...than you were as a lover." I tacked that on just to goose him.

"You had no complaints."

"None I told you to your face."

He was smiling again. He moved in, testing, and I countered.

"When are they going to—" Eddie began. I tuned him out.

"Wait." Gabe replied.

I caught a flash of Japhrimel watching, hands behind his back, his eyes almost spitting sparks.

"Try me again, sweetheart," Jace said, his tone low and purring. "I've been dying for it."

"Good for you." I shuffled back, to the side; things were rapidly heating up. "Get used to disappointment."

"You don't want an explanation?"

"Three years too late, Jace. All I want to do now is forget you ever existed." My own voice dropped to a whisper. His eyes narrowed.

"Good luck," he said. "I just bought myself free of the Corvin Family, sweets, and I have some time on my hands. Want to help me fill it?"

"I'd rather turn into a Chillfreak whore." My blade whispered free of the sheath just as his did.

"Now?" Eddie asked.

"Just wait," Gabe whispered back.

"Mmh." Jace said. "You say the sweetest—"

He moved in then, with no warning. Metal clashed and rang. We separated, both of us breathing fast and deep.

"You've gotten quicker," he said.

"And you still talk too goddamn much," I said, wishing I could spit. That would add something to the festivities.

"I should put my tongue to better use," he muttered, and gave me a flash of the famous Monroe grin, the one that had Mob groupies following him around all the time.

"Try it on someone who cares, fucker," I spat at him, and that broke the tension.

We moved in on each other, feet shuffling, sparks spraying from the metal and the Power in the air. He wasn't trying very hard, and I almost got him twice before he realized I was serious and began to scramble. Cut overhand, spin-kick, he tried to lock me into a corps-a-corps where his height and weight could overpower me but that was an old trick, *move move move*, scabbard flying in to jab him in the ribs, it was a cheap shot but every little bit told, I had speed and endurance, he had power and a different type of endurance —

Parry, parry, a short thrust he had to shuffle back to escape, metal sliding, wall coming up fast, was I going to cheat or was I going to —

I cheated.

I popped my left hand forward, the scabbard held horizontal, and a dart of Power flashed from my rings, spattered on his defenses.

We separated, both breathing hard now. It bought me some breathing room.

"Cheater," he said. Sweat rolled down his forehead, his hair truly soaked now. Thunder rumbled outside.

"Anything for you," I answered, showing my teeth. Sweat dripped down the shallow channel of my spine. My ribs flared with deep rasping breaths. "You going to come and get me, baby?"

"You should be so lucky," he said. "We're full-on now, sweetheart? You sure? Last time we did this I spanked your ass."

"I was holding back," I said. "Since you always bitched when you lost."

He grinned. "You sure, Valentine?"

"Come over here and find out, Monroe," I dared him, katana dipping into *guard*. He was coming in low, his shielding swirling with the peculiar spiky turbulence of a Shaman, impossible to predict. I was glowing, glitter spattering through my aura; reacting to his nearness and to my own defenses springing up, locking with his.

We closed in again, and this time he was serious. Metal screamed and Power tore through the air, ozone, smell of musk, the mark on my shoulder suddenly coming alive. Spray of sparks, he was using a pattern I didn't recognize but muscle memory took over again and it was like riding a slicboard, trembling on the outer edge of adrenaline control, fully alive, fully *aware*, kiss of breeze against my sweaty forehead, clap of thunder like angels striking and neither of us flinched, spin, half-falling, *get up get up,* kicked his bad knee, felt the flare of sick pain from his shielding but he was too hyped on adrenaline to slow down, we closed again but I had momentum, *push*, Power crackling, across the room, running, his face inches from mine, eyes locked, my lips peeled back with effort, familiar, every other time we'd fought blurring under my skin, memory and intuition and action —

Glass. Shattering. I drove him through the window, separating from him for long enough to gain footing on the stone walk outside, heavy scent of wet green air rising from the garden on the other side of the strip of stone flags. Boot soles gripping, sliding, cut overhand, he batted it away with more luck than strength. Harsh gasps of air tore at my throat. His shielding flared, trying to throw me off, I reacted without thinking, tearing Power from the air and smashing at him.

Rain spattering against my skin, stinging-hard. Rivulets of water down Jace's face. We were outside now, booted feet crunching in glass, the wild rain pounding on both of us, soaked to the bone and suddenly chill, breath steaming, sparks flying like water as we danced.

Flying. I didn't have to hold back. The rhythm of the fight changed, became insistent, *no think! No think! Move!* Jado-sensei screamed in my memory and I fell, landing on the wet stone scrambling, scrambling, throwing aside one of his strikes, on my feet again, whirling, his scabbard coming in, deflected, I was going to bruise there by tomorrow, didn't care, *alive, alive, see you stay that way, alive, alive—*

Thunder.

He fell, blood striping his face, landing sprawled on the marble. My blade kissed his throat. For a moment I was tempted—*push the blade in, no resistance, you can watch him bleed, watch the soul leave the body, watch the sparks fly, and then—*

"Do you give?" I asked, my voice a harsh croak. My ribs flared.

"Of course," he said, his eyes closed, head tipped back, throat exposed. Steel caressed the vulnerable place where his pulse beat. My hands weren't shaking, but they were close. "Anything you want, Valentine."

"Stay off my case, Monroe." I let the temptation slide away. Not today. I wouldn't kill him today.

Thank the gods, think of the paperwork... I sheathed my blade, suddenly aware that the rain drenched both of us, my shirt stuck to my body, my jeans chafing, boots sloshing in foaming water. I offered him my hand, still tuned to combat, watching his blade just in case.

"Sure." He took my hand; I hauled him up from the stone walk-turned-river. "You still look good when you fight, sweetheart."

I tore my fingers out of his, watched as he sheathed his sword. Both of us were bloody—scraped knuckles, a cut on his scalp, his knee, a shallow slice on my shield arm, my back on fire. "Good match," I said grudgingly. "You've been practicing."

"So have you. That double-eight thing kicked my ass."

"Where'd you learn that little shuffle-trick? That's nice." I pushed a strand of wet hair out of my face—no matter how tightly I braided it, sometimes little bits worked free.

"Around and about. You still do knife-work?" His hair streamed with water, dark and plastered against his forehead.

"When the occasion calls for it." I stepped through the shattered window. "Sorry about that."

"It's okay. It's just a window." I could hear the smile in his voice. "Goddamn, you're good."

"I train with Jado almost every day when I'm not on a job."

"That old dragon? Chango love you, girl, no wonder you're good." He stepped through, shaking the water off his hair and hands, stamping his feet. *That'll foul the mats,* I thought, and wondered if broken glass ground into tatami was a bad idea. *Of course it is. But maybe he can afford it.* "I couldn't even get time with him. Some say he only trains women."

"No, there's men too. But he says women are better. Quicker reaction time. More evil." I found myself smiling. Adrenaline laid its thin copper taste against my palate. Now I wanted a hot bath, and I wanted sex.

Too bad. Nobody here but unavailable men. And I don't want to trust the local escorts.

Jace's hand closed around my wrist. His skin was warm, almost too warm, his shields rubbing against mine. His thumb drifted over my skin, an intimate touch. "Danny."

I tore my hand away again. He tried to keep it. Again. "Danny—" Again.

"No, Jace. Forget it. That's all you're going to get from me."

He shrugged. "It's a shame. I remember how good it used to be after a sparring session." His eyebrow quirked a little. Even with blood running down his face—head wounds are messy—he was still beautiful. I'd always liked blonds. Maybe because I had to dye my hair to fit in with Necromance codes.

"Well, if you hadn't dumped me three years ago you might be a little luckier now," I said, and turned away.

Gabe and Eddie were watching us. Gabe's eyes were round. Eddie's were narrowed, and he looked about ten seconds away from a growl. He had his arm over Gabe's shoulders; she leaned into his body as if she belonged there.

Japhrimel stood bolt-upright, his hands behind him. His eyes were half-lidded and the smell of demon filled the entire practice room, warring with the tide of rain-washed air pouring in through the broken window. His coat smoked and fumed with darkness, a psychic stain spreading out from him.

I don't know if that's really a coat, I thought, and stopped short, staring at him. *What else could it be? Wings? An exoskeleton?*

Jace went utterly still beside me. "Is that it?" he asked. "You're dating a demon?"

"Don't be ridiculous," I snapped, and stalked away from him. "Your dick always gets the better of you, Jace, maybe you should try thinking with your *brain* next time. Thanks for the sparring, I needed it. Next time I'll spar with Japhrimel—he's a real challenge." I was so happy with myself I used more of Jaf's name, and sounded as if I was talking about someone else. The name fit smoothly against my tongue. *Japhrimel.* I wondered what it meant, and if I called him by his full name, what would happen?

"Fucking *hell*—" Jace began, his voice hitting a pitch I recognized.

He'd lost his temper.

"That's enough," Gabe snapped, even though Eddie pulled back on her shoulders. The emerald in her cheek flashed, sending a spear of green light through the heavy air. "Hades, haven't you two finished flirting? Get over it already so we can find the fucking demon and get rid of our Happy Little Pet here!"

"Japhrimel," I said, over the last half of her sentence, "come on. The rest of you, we're going recon in two hours when the rain stops and it gets darker. I'll expect you all to be ready."

"Oh, for fuck's—" Gabe began. Eddie shushed at her.

"Danny?" Jace's voice.

I stopped. Didn't turn around. Japhrimel hovered near my shoulder. I hadn't seen him blink across the intervening space, and that made me vaguely nervous.

"Thanks for the sparring," Jace said. "I love working with you."

"Sorry, Jace," I answered. "It's too late. I work alone."

Then I strode out of the practice room, my anger crackling on the air, hearing Jace's awful silence behind me. I'd won both battles.

Good for me.

CHAPTER 27

Japhrimel didn't say anything until we reached the blue suite. He closed the door behind us, precisely, locking it, the defenses he'd set in the walls humming as soon as I entered the room. "That was not wise," he said quietly. "A jealous man does not work well."

"Jace works better when he's under pressure," I said, unwinding my wet hair from its braid. "And he deserved it." My rings lay dark and silent against my fingers now. I felt better, the headache eased out by pulling on Power from the well of the city now that my body had acclimatized, my back stopping its low-level cramping. I'd stretch out after a hot bath, and be ready for recon.

My hands shook. I'd just faced Jace over a sword again. Three years. Three *years*—and he hadn't even tried to explain yet. Just acted as if—

I took a deep breath. I could feel the weight of Japhrimel's green gaze on my back. Jace didn't matter. I'd said he didn't matter, that I didn't care anymore. I'd sworn many times, out loud and silently, that I was over Jason Monroe. Period. End of story, end of spell, so mote it be, amen, *finis*.

"Nevertheless," Japhrimel persisted. "You should not have used me to prick his jealousy."

I shrugged. "It's his problem. Not mine. My problem is finding Santino and getting that Egg back to Lucifer. Besides, he's only human. It's not like he can hurt you if he decides to do something stupid."

"Perhaps," he replied. "But even demons understand jealousy, Dante."

I started to unbutton my shirt, tossing my sword on the bed. *Safe enough*, I thought. *At least for now.* "Next time I'll spar with you. At least you'll give me a workout."

If my voice had been any more brittle, it would have snapped. If I was over Jace, I was *over* him. Right?

Right?

"You were not sparring with him," the demon pointed out. He leaned on the door, his arms folded on his chest, his eyes half-lidded.

There was a faint red stain on his caramel cheeks. Dear gods, was he blushing? "You were trying to kill him."

"I don't see any other way to play," I tossed over my shoulder as I headed for the bathroom. "I'm going to clean up."

"As you like." He didn't sound too pleased.

I stopped and looked back at him, my shaking fingers pausing on the fourth button. *I didn't do anything wrong,* I repeated to myself. *I simply sparred with Jace and made it clear he doesn't affect me anymore. Now everyone knows what's going on, it's official, it's all aboveboard and time-stamped. I didn't do anything wrong.* "What? Go ahead and say it."

Japhrimel didn't move. He might as well have been a statue, leaning against the door. Warm electric light caressed the planes of his face, sparked in his eyes. The faint reddish stain had drained from his cheeks. "You are . . . trifling with his affections, and using me to do so. The game is exceedingly dangerous."

I examined him. "What are you really trying to tell me, Tierce Japhrimel? That Jace has some sort of feeling for me? Why did he leave, then? Huh? You answer me that."

"If you like, I will find out."

I clutched my shirt together. "I don't want to know. If it was important, he would have sent me a message or something. I'm not interested in his excuses now."

"Then stop needling him. Treat him as an equal."

"Hey, demon, I didn't know if you noticed, but everybody gets the short end of the stick from me."

"Do not use me to make a human jealous, Dante. It is very unwise of you."

"*Sekhmet sa'es,*" I hissed. "I *didn't.* Don't get your girdle in a twist."

"You *did,* Dante. I would advise you not to trifle with him, and not to trifle with me either." He didn't move, but the air swirled uneasily. Thunder boomed outside, muted by the bulk of the house but still enough to raise the hairs on my nape. The demon's stain on my aura moved, drawing closer to my skin, a gentle brush against the edges of my awareness.

"Like *you* care," I said, and turned on my heel, stalking for the bathroom. "Leave it alone, hellspawn. This is a *human* thing."

He said nothing. I stamped into the bathroom and slammed the door, then started peeling off my wet clothes. "Gods *damn* it, " I hissed, yanking my jeans down, kicking them into the corner. *I could really hate them both, couldn't I? I sure could. Especially the gods-be-damned demon. Because?*

I found myself staring in the mirror, wet lank dead-black seaweed hair, indeterminate dark eyes, pale face, dark rings under my eyes, my mouth pulled tight in a bitter grimace, my fingernails *skritch*ing against the counter as my hands tensed. My tattoo shifted uneasily, serpents writhing against winged staff, the emerald turning dark and glittering angrily.

Because he's right. I want Jace to suffer. I want him to lose his temper. I want to win, goddammit. Even if it's a hollow victory. I want him to hurt.

"Fuck," I breathed, looking at my eyes. Dark circles, mouth drawn tight, Power trembling at the outer edge of my control. *Deep breath, Danny. Take a deep breath and get cool with the program, okay? Chill down. Chill down.*

I'm going to die.

"Shut up," I whispered. "If I die, I'm taking Santino with me. I owe Doreen. And I've lived long enough."

It sounded good, but the woman in the mirror didn't believe it. I had a mortgage. I had a life I was just beginning to piece together and go on with. I didn't want to die.

"How much longer would you live anyway going up against Santino, Danny?" I asked myself. "Huh?"

Not very much longer, some deep voice replied. *Just long enough to make him regret it.*

"Good," I said. "So stop fooling around."

I don't want to die.

"I don't have a choice. If the god takes me, He takes me."

I still don't want to die.

"Too bad," I whispered, turning away from the mirror. I couldn't take looking at myself any longer.

CHAPTER 28

El diablo Santino," Jace said, the knife pressed against the thin Hispanic's throat. "Okay?"

Gabe and Eddie had the mouth of the alley and the demon stood behind me. I watched the man's eyes flicker, white rolling around their edges. He was sweating, great drops of water sliding down his face. The reek of fear warred with the smell of demon. The alley was piled with garbage, hot and rank and wet from the afternoon's rain. It was only slightly cooler. My hair, trapped in a braid, was twisted into a knot at my nape. I looked down at my wrist, having just scanned the man in.

The plug-in, clear plasilica smoothed over my datband, lit up with a string of code. "He's got a warrant, Jace," I said quietly. "Do we haul him in?"

The omni and the first H-DOC, slim squares of plasilica with clear Hegemony military-tech flexcircuits, I'd already plastered over my datband. I'd smoothed the second H-DOC over Japhrimel's wrist. We were officially on a hunt now, plugged into the Hegemony police nets and immune to a few laws having to do with general murder and chaos — as long as the murder and chaos served the purpose of bringing our bounty in. The night sky was choked with clouds though the downpour had stopped, and steaming heat closed us in a bubble of damp discomfort. Now I knew what the inside of a rice cooker felt like.

The man babbled in Portogueso, sweating, his eyes rolling. He wore a loose white cotton shirt and frayed khakis, his huaraches digging into the pavement as he tried to back through the rough earth-brick wall behind him. One of his hands hit the dumpster Jace had trapped him beside, and a hollow boom punched the air.

Jace was shaking down his contacts, and none of them looked happy to see him. Considering he was walking around with two Necromances, I didn't blame them. Still, Jace was savage. He was in his element here. The first contact had tried to dive out a fourth-story window onto bare concrete to get away from him.

I was beginning to think that he had a reputation.

Jace said something very low. The man's eyes flicked past his shoulder, fastened on me, and he gibbered something.

Jace went very still. He asked a couple more questions, both answered in a high whine.

Jace laid the knifeblade against the man's cheek. He said something very low and quick, and I caught my name —*Dante Valentino*— and his own name, accented strangely. Then he let the man go, tossed him onto the floor of the alley, the knife disappearing.

As soon as he turned around, his eyes thoughtful, I knew there was trouble. "What was that?" I asked incuriously, looking down at the man moaning on the pavement. He seemed to be in an ecstasy of fear. "And are we hauling him in?"

"No, let him go, he's wetting his pants anyway. Come on, Danny." Jace straightened his shoulders. "We've got to pow-wow."

Gabe and Eddie drifted in from the mouth of the alley. We left Jace's contact scrambling against the cracking pavement and moaning to himself. "Good news," Gabe whispered. "There's a set of heavies coming through the neighborhood, Jace. Not sure if they're looking for you or—"

"They aren't," he said grimly. "Word is the Corvin Family's looking to capture Danny. Alive and unharmed. Someone is putting the squeeze on the Mob down here." Jace's eyes didn't move from mine. He wore dark blue, shirt and jeans, blending into the night. He dropped his hand to his swordhilt, tapped blunt fingers in a pattern I recognized. "Wonder who that could be."

"Santino?" I asked. Why would the Mob get involved, expecially a Mob Family I hadn't ever tangled with? *Then again, the Mob didn't want us to go after Santino last time, because they were in the same corporate bed with him when it came to illegal augments.* The memory made my lip curl. Gods above and below, how I hated the Mob.

Behind me, Jace's contact monkeyed up a splitting, rotten wooden fence and dropped down on the other side.

"Don't think so. I've got enemies too, and you came in on a public transport as Saint City police irregulars. Fun. About as stealthy as a Skinlin berserker." He grinned, lips stretching back from his teeth in a grimace I remembered. Jace was *furious.*

Why? Why would *that* make him furious?

"So what do we do now?" Eddie asked. "They're gettin' kind of close, Monroe."

"Do?" Jace shrugged. "I just told Jose to spread the word that Danny Valentine's under my personal protection. As for those clumsy fuckers moving in, we either run, or we send a message that she ain't going to come cheap. My vote goes for the latter. It will make it easier to get information, scare some people. What do you say?"

Eddie shrugged. "I'm up for a fight."

"Me, too," Gabe chimed in. "Lucky you, Danny, you've got an admirer or two. Or a hundred."

"I can't think of why," I grumbled. "Look at this, I just blew into town and already people want to kill me."

"Not *kill*," Jace corrected. "Capture. Alive and unharmed."

"For how much?" the demon asked suddenly.

"Five million standard credits," Jace replied easily.

Silence. I looked at Gabe. Her jaw dropped. She had her hair in two braids like a demented schoolgirl. One hung forward over her slim shoulder, the other dangled in back. Her emerald glittered in the darkness. Even in a police rig and synthwool coat in the boiling heat, she looked cool, calm, and precise.

Eddie let out a low whistle.

"Take her back to the house," Jace said to the demon. "*Watch* her. Don't even send her to the bathroom alone."

"Now just wait one goddamn second," I objected, relieved that Japhrimel made no move to obey Jace. "This is *my* hunt, I'm not going to be hauled around like a piece of baggage."

"Give us some time to clear the street and do some recon, Danny," Jace said reasonably. But a tic in his cheek was jumping. That meant trouble. *Heavy* trouble. There was something Jace wasn't telling. "It's best. You know it's best."

"This is *my* hunt," I repeated in a fierce whisper. "You are not taking over. Is that clear?"

"This serves no purpose," the demon said. "Dante?"

"Let's go kick some ass," I answered. "Don't fuck with me on my hunt, Jace."

"Danny, you should get under cover until we can sort out who's looking for you." Jace sounded calm and reasonable, but his hand curled around his swordhilt. He was two steps away from rage, and I'd only seen Jason Monroe in a rage twice before.

"I'm not backing down, Jace," I hissed. "Come on."

"Fine," he said. "But after that we're going back and hashing this out."

"Good enough," I gave in. I was hungry anyway, and I wanted a quiet place to think. "Let's go rumble."

"Standard form?" Gabe asked.

"Yeah. Watch out for Danny, everyone, they'll look to net her." Jace didn't look away from me, even when my lip lifted and I snarled openly at him.

"I can take care of myself," I said, thumbing my blade free of the scabbard with a small sound. "Japhrimel, we're going to mix. Kill the opposition, as long as they're not innocent bystanders. Okay?"

"As you like," Japhrimel said quietly. "I will watch over you, Dante. They are coming quickly; we had best go now."

"Oh, *Sekhmet sa'es*," I hissed. "Get moving, standard form. Jace, you take point; Gabe, keep Eddie from going berserk—"

"Danny?" Gabe turned, her right hand sliding below her left armpit. "They're here."

As if to underscore her words, a plasbolt crackled past. I looked up—they'd gotten onto the roofs. *Stupid, sloppy, I'm going to smack Jace hard for this.* "Out!" I yelled, shoving Jace. "Take it streetside! *Go!*"

We ran.

"Twelve of them," Japhrimel said, his voice calm and clearly audible even though the rest of us were pounding down the pavement, Eddie gasping out something that might have been the beginnings of a chant. I snapped out two words of the Fourth Canon, throwing my right hand up. My second ring—amber cabochon—sparked and crackled, and a milky shimmer in the air separated around each of us. Juggling a spell while running was bad enough, but worth the effort because a plasbolt streaked the air and splashed against the shimmershield surrounding Gabe, who let out a short sharp falcon's scream, probably expecting to be flung on the pavement.

My own cry rose with hers, breathless. I pumped Power into the shimmers, drawing from the city's well, grateful I'd already suffered through the migraine of backlash—Eddie and Gabe would be crippled by their limited ability to draw on Nuevo Rio Power unless they had taken the time to acclimatize themselves.

Gabe grabbed half the load on the shimmershields away from me, her mental touch light and deft. "*Do* something!" she screamed, as we plunged into the nighttime crowd. I thought she was screaming at me instead of Japhrimel, so I popped the shields down, freeing them from my conscious control; stopped short (stopping from a full head-on run is a skill, I'll admit I stumbled) and turned, my sword sliding free of the sheath.

"*Danny!*" Jace yelled.

The crowd of Nuevo Rios exploded away from me, making signs against the evil eye. I met the first hired thug with a clash of steel—he didn't have a sword, but he had a machete. I knocked the plasgun out of his hand with a flicker of my scabbard. Metal clashed and rang—he cut overhand, a sloppy move, expecting me to be dumb enough not to expect it—tall, thin Nuevo Rio man in an assassin's rig, black leather straps with various knife sheaths and other things attached. I dispatched him with a short thrust and backed up as they converged on me, six dark-eyed, dark-haired men, one of them a *vaudun*, shaking his staff. The bits of metal and circuit-boards attached to it jingled. Neon ran on the wet street, the sound of sirens and screams of the crowd fading from my consciousness. *Six against one*, I thought, twisting my blade free from the body on the ground. *I'm going to enjoy this. Watch that Shaman, he's the dangerous one.*

I stood my ground, letting them come to me, pavement cracking underneath me, the dark pulsing heartbeat of the city resounding, a tapline open to feed me Power from the city's ambient energy. The shimmershields crackled as more plasbolts raked the ground. The H-DOC on my wrist flashed, reading the layout of the fight, alerted by the spike of plasgun bolts. The cops wouldn't interfere; this was a private hunt.

A dark shape streaked past me, silver gun flashing. Japhrimel met the six with a popping clatter of gunfire. He punched one in the face, sending him flying back. I was left facing the Shaman, who locked shields with me and proceeded to blow a few circuits in my shimmershield with a swift, nasty attack of Power.

He was good. I held my sword level, metal gleaming, rings sparking as I countered, grabbing all available Power in my range, the mark on my shoulder crunching with sudden pain as the demon let out a shattering roar. Jace drove past me, engaging the *vaudun*. *Dammit, Jace, he was MINE!* Jace made a quick motion, and something like a tiger made of solid light and dapples of shadow, Jace's prime fighting construct, tore itself out of the air and descended on the other *vaudun*.

Where are the rest of them? I thought, and heard another one of Gabe's short sharp cries. *Engaged over there*, I thought, turning on my heel, my tapline into the city's dark heart pulsing with Power. I kept the shields steady, juggling them as I bolted back for Gabe and Eddie. Jace could handle himself.

The Skinlin was growling as he fought with another Shaman, this one a wizened old nut-brown man with streaks and dapples of red paint on his face. Gabe, swearing and spitting, her face contorted into a mask of rage, was dueling a tall mercenary—he wasn't a Nuevo Rio, too pale, sandy blond hair, but he wore an assassin's rig and used a short thrusting sword. Plasbolts whined. One splashed against the edge of my torn shimmershield, and the resultant Power-flare nearly knocked me to my knees. I staggered, my forward momentum pushing me, just like riding a slicboard—and I threw myself on the two Nuevo Rios edging for Gabe's back.

One of them clipped me on the shoulder with a thrown knife before I cut him down, pain blooming along my nerves like spiked oil, the other engaged me—he was a huge hulking mass of weight-lifting muscle and black-market augmentations; I smelled salt-sweat-sweet Chill on him before I made my cut and a bright jet of arterial blood splashed out of his neck. He was still trying to come for me when I took off his right hand with the plasgun still clasped in it. I finished by whirling and opening his belly with two cuts, my own battle-yell stinging my throat and dyeing the air red. *Chillfreaks, I hate Chillfreaks. I thought Nuevo Rios were more into hash anyway.*

Then it was over. I stood, panting, watching the blood gurgle, hearing the last choking gasps as the Chillfreak died, his eyes dimming, the spark exiting his chemical-abused body. *"Anubis et'her ka."* I breathed. *That was for Lewis, you sack of Chill shit.* The thought slid across my mind and was gone as soon as it came.

The plasbolts had stopped. Eddie's growling still sounded from behind me, and I heard Gabe taking in harsh tearing gulps of air. Clatter of steel. Running feet. A long, low howl of abused breath, snarling, a flare of familiar Power. Jace.

I stared blankly down at the body in front of me. The street was now deserted, but eyes glittered in the shadows. If we left the bodies, they would be stripped and harvested in minutes.

Chillfreaks, I thought, and shuddered. *I hate the motherfucking Chillfreaks.*

Three things I hated: the Mob, Chillfreaks, Santino. Each one of them had stolen something from me—Santino stole Doreen, the Mob had helped steal Doreen, and Chill and the Mob had stolen Lewis and fucked up too many bounties to count.

Japhrimel's hand closed around my wounded shoulder. I flinched—I hadn't even sensed him behind me. That was starting to weird me out. "You're hurt," he said quietly, and his hand bit down, a hot snarling mass of Power forcing its way into the wound. I gritted my teeth, feeling muscle knit itself together—I'd been so pumped on adrenaline I'd barely noticed the strike. "My apologies."

"Why? You had enough to deal with." I looked down at the body on the pavement. True death had occurred, but the nerves were still glowing with false life—what Necromances called foxfire. The soul was gone. "I hate Chillfreaks," I muttered.

Lewis, his beaky face splashed with blood, leered up in my memory. I'd been collared, on a rare excursion with my social worker, when a Chillfreak had killed him; I'd only been a kid. Unable to protect him—he'd told me to run, and I had. The cops had arrived too late.

Lewis had taught me to read, left me his books and his love of the classics. I had been lucky to have such a gentle social worker, one who was so genuinely interested in me, even if I'd been unable to tell him the truth about Rigger Hall because of the collar. When he died I'd been given a social worker who could have cared less that I was in hell and helpless; she was too busy collecting her checks and getting strung out on synth hash to pay any attention to the kid she was supposed to be looking out for. When Rigger Hall had closed down and the news of what Mirovitch had done to the kids became common knowledge, I never even got an apology from the stupid bitch. After that I refused to see any social workers at all.

I returned to the present with a jolt as Japhrimel sighed.

"I am to protect you," he said, slowly, as if I was a stupid third-grader.

"Up until I face Santino," I told him, "I'm capable of taking care of myself." I looked up.

Eddie held Gabe, kissing her forehead. "You okay?" he said, his blood-dotted face thunderous with worry. She nodded her assent.

I looked hurriedly away. I didn't want to think about why it hurt me to see them together sometimes.

"Danny?" Jace sounded breathless. "*Danny!*"

"I'm fine," I said, my sword whipping through the air, blood splashing from its shimmer. Power smoked along the blade, a habitual cleaning of the bright steel. I slid it back into the sheath. "Dammit, Jace. You took the Shaman. He was mine."

"Sorry," he said, in a tone that suggested he wasn't sorry at all. "Let's move, kids. My instinct tells me that was only the first wave. Leave the bodies for harvest."

"You mind not giving orders on my hunt?" I snapped, and looked up at the demon. His face was set, his eyes sparking with radioactive green. "Thanks, Japhrimel."

He nodded. "Where now?"

"Back to Jace's house. This kind of changes the situation a little."

"They were serious," Gabe said. She'd finally stopped clinching with Eddie. "Five million credits. Holy fuck, Danny, what'd you do?"

"I didn't *do* anything; I've been forced into this," I snapped, and set off down the pavement after scanning the bodies. We should have stopped to search them, but I was too shaken to pause. I wanted a drink. "Come on."

CHAPTER 29

I poured a full glass of brandy, handed it to the demon, and took a long pull off the bottle. It was good stuff, silken-smooth, igniting like a thunderball in my belly.

Jace slugged a hit of vodka. Eddie cursed as Gabe swabbed at his arm with peroxin. I waited a few moments, exhaled, took another pull from the bottle, my other hand white-knuckled on my sword. My bloody sleeve flopped.

"Careful with that, Danny," Jace said. "I need you sober."

"Fuck you," I said. "Why does the Corvin Family want me, Jace? What aren't you telling me?" *You swore you were free and clear of the Mob when you met me, and I believed you. Silly me.*

He shrugged. "Don't worry about the Corvins, sweetheart. I'll take them down if they so much as touch you."

"You still *work* for them, don't you, Jace? That's why you didn't want to talk about it. Once Mob, always Mob. You can't take them down."

Jace's face was bloodless under a mask of sweat, grime, and a spatter of blood high on his left cheek. "I bought myself free of the Corvins, Danny. They don't own me." He took another slug of vodka, smacked the shotglass down on the counter. The sharp sound crackled in tense air.

I took another hit off the bottle, turned to look at the demon. "Jaf?"

He shrugged, too. Goddamn shrugging men.

He's not a man, he's a demon. The thought struck me with almost physical force. I stopped, staring at him. When had I started thinking about him as if he was human? That didn't bode well. I tipped the bottle up to my lips again, but Japhrimel set his untouched glass down on the bar and took the bottle from me, his fingers hot against mine. "No, Dante," he said softly. "Please. I will not allow you to be harmed."

Well, that's comforting, I thought. And oddly enough, it was.

"Okay," I answered, letting go of the bottle. The brandy settled into a warm glow behind my breastbone. "So the Corvins want me alive. What the fuck for? And—" A horrible thought struck me just as I finished turning to face Japhrimel.

He set the bottle down beside his glass, watching my face. "Dante?"

I stood stock-still, frozen, my entire body gone cold. Abra told me Jace is working for the Corvins... *The Corvins want me alive, and they're paying so much... someone else is leaning on them, someone big... Jace and the Corvins. He's one of them. Once Mob, always Mob.*

"Danny?" Gabe must have caught my sudden stillness, because she was staring at me, too, her dark eyes wide. "Danny?"

I swallowed. "I've got to go up to my room," I said, hearing the queer breathlessness in my voice. I sounded like a young girl viciously embarrassed at her first party. "Excuse me."

I was halfway to the door before Japhrimel fell into step beside me. He said nothing.

"Danny, what's wrong?" Gabe called. "*Danny!*"

I found the grand wide staircase and started to climb, the premonition beating under my skin. Premonition—and shock. It couldn't be. It couldn't be.

But he betrayed me once, didn't he? Left without a word—what do you want to bet he was called down here by the Corvins and that's why he left? Abra warned me... she knew. And now he's so willing to help... so very hospitable, stay in my house, it's safer there, he said he bought himself free of the Corvins but I know the Mob, you never get free. Even if he bought something from them, they can squeeze him until he hands over an ex-girlfriend, can't they?

My brain shied away from the cold, logical conclusion. I didn't want to believe it.

The demon stepped behind me, soundless, his musky aura closing me in, a shielding I ignored because I didn't have time or concentration to spare to shake it aside. He only touched me once, a subtle push on my blood-crusted shoulder when I almost got lost in the hallways. When we reached the blue room, I shoved the door open and bolted inside, trembling. Stopped.

The room, instead of blue, was now white. Heavy fragrance drenched the air.

Flowers. White flowers. Lotuses, roses, lilies, scattered over the room as if a snowstorm had dropped its blossoms. Gooseflesh raced up my arm, spilled down my back; my teeth chattered and my nipples drew up hard as pebbles. The flowers lay on every flat surface, even the floor, the smell was stifling, heady, and cloying. They piled on the bed, fluttered near the window, and I could see the bathroom was full of them, too.

Santino had sent blue flowers to Doreen. Great sprays and cascades of flowers in every shade of blue. I still couldn't look at irises or blue roses or cornflowers without shuddering.

"Dante?" Japhrimel definitely sounded alarmed now. He closed the door, then stepped aside, his long coat brushing his legs with a soft sound. "My shields are intact; only the house servants could have—"

"They were probably delivered and brought up by the staff." I sounded like I'd been punched in the stomach. "Look, I need to change. And pack my bag." I flattened my free hand against the door to brace myself. "Can you get me out of here without Jace's shields reacting?"

"Of course," he said, lifting one shoulder and dropping it. *All things should be so easy*, that shrug said. "What is this?" he asked. "Did your former lover perhaps—"

"Santino sent all his victims flowers," I said numbly.

The demon stilled, his eyes turning incandescent.

"He knows," I continued. "He knows I'm here, and looking for him. And I'm a Necromance. He's picked me as his next victim."

"Dante—"

"That means I won't have to worry about finding him," I said. "He'll find me." I laughed, but the sound was gaspy, panicky. The world roared underneath me, spinning carelessly away, almost like a slicboard but my feet slipping, slipping—

"Dante." He had me by the shoulders. "Stop. Breathe. Just breathe." His fingers bit in, and he shook me slightly. My teeth clicked together. I tasted apples, and the sour smell of my own fear.

A whooping breath tore between my lips. My left shoulder gave a livid crunching flare of pain, shocking me back into myself. I found myself shaking, my hands trembling, the demon's chin resting atop my head, his smell enfolding me. His arms closed around me, the feverish heat of Hell flooding my entire body. I was sneakingly grateful for it—I was cold, so cold my jaw clenched, my teeth chattered, and goosebumps rose everywhere. He had my sword—had I dropped it or had he just taken it from my numb fingers? That was three times he'd taken my blade. Was I really getting sloppy? When I was younger, I never would have dropped my blade.

"Breathe," he murmured into my hair. "Simply breathe. I am with you, Dante. Breathe."

I rested my forehead against the oddly soft material of his coat, filled my lungs with the musk smell of demon. Alien. It steadied me. The lunatic urge to sob retreated.

"Calm," the demon said. "Steady, Dante. Breathe."

"I'm okay," I managed. "We have to get out of here."

"Very well." But he didn't move, and neither did I.

"We have to find a place to stay," I said, "and I have to...I have to..."

"Leave it to me," he answered quietly.

"I've got to pack." I sounded steadier now. *"Anubis et'her ka. Se ta'uk'fhet sa te vapu kuraph."* The familiar invocation bolstered me.

He didn't move until I did. I rocked back on my heels and he let me go, his arms sliding free. His face was blank, set, his eyes burning holes. The mark on my shoulder throbbed insistently. He held my sword up, silently, and I took it from his hand. "Thanks." I was shaky, but myself again.

Japhrimel nodded, watching me. I wasn't sure what he was looking for, but he examined my face as if the Nine Canons were written there. Heat, a purely human heat, rose to my cheeks. "It is my honor," he said quietly. "I swear to you on the waters of Lethe, Dante Valentine, I will allow no harm to come to you."

"Santino—" I began.

A swift snarl crossed his face. I flinched.

"We will find a way to kill him, you and I. Pack your bag, Dante. If you are determined to leave this place, let us go quickly." He sounded utterly calm, the kind of calm that could draw a razor through flesh with only a slight smile.

"Sounds like a good idea," I managed. The flowers stirred. More thunder rumbled above the city, and a slight cool breeze stole in through the open window, ruffling petals, swirling the cloying stench of dying blooms against my face. I swayed in place. Japhrimel reached out, his golden fingers resting against my cheek for a moment. The touch made my entire body glow with heat. "Japhrimel—"

"Dante," he replied, his glowing eyes holding mine. "Hurry."

I did.

CHAPTER 30

The bodega was deep in the stinking well of Nuevo Rio, a small storefront marked with the universal symbols of Power: signs from the Nine Canons spray-painted on the front step, a display window showing small mummified crocodiles nestled among *grisgris* bags and bottles of different holy waters, lit novenas crowding on the step, each keyed to a shimmer of Power. The smell of incense from the fuming sticks placed near the door threatened to give me a headache, along with the breathless sense of storm approaching that hung over the city. I adjusted the strap over my shoulder, then rubbed at my dry, aching eyes. Japhrimel leaned on the counter, bargaining with the *babalawao* in fluent Portogueso. The woman had liquid dark eyes and a Shaman's thorn-spiked cruciform tattoo on her cheek; the cross shape and thorns told me she was an Eclectic Shaman—rare here in Rio for a native to be an Eclectic. She eyed me with a great deal of interest, stroking her staff at the same time. The staff thrummed with Power, as did her tiny bodega, and I counted myself lucky that I didn't have to fight her. She was tall, and moved with a quick ferret grace that warned me she was very dangerous indeed.

I was faintly surprised to find Japhrimel knew Portogueso, but I suppose I shouldn't have been. Demons like languages as much as they like technology, and have fiddled with both for a long time.

He finally looked back over his shoulder at me. "Carmen says we're welcome to stay up over the shop," he said. "Come. You need rest."

I shrugged. "How likely is it that we'll be tracked here?"

He showed his teeth. "Not likely at all," he replied, and I didn't press him for details. He probably wouldn't give them anyway. "She is of the Hellesvront—our agents," he continued, immediately proving me wrong.

"You have agents? Hell has human agents?"

"Of course. Human and others."

Then why didn't they track down Santino? I decided not to ask. The bodega felt like Abra's store—dusty, old, the same smell of chilis and beef. Yet the *babalawao* wasn't like Abra—she was powerful, true, but human. Only human. She swept her hair back over her shoulder and regarded me coolly, her eyes moving over my disheveled hair, dusty sweat-stained clothes, and white-knuckled grip on my katana. She asked one question, and Japhrimel shook his head. His inky hair lay still against his skull. He didn't seem to sweat even in this malicious wet heat.

Hell was hotter, anyway.

The woman led us to the back of her store, sweeping aside a curtain woven into bright geometrics that writhed with Power. A narrow staircase threaded up into darkness.

Japhrimel touched the woman's forehead. She nodded, her brown skin moving under his hand, and grinned at me, her teeth flashing sharp and white. *"Gracias, filho,"* he said quietly.

"De nada," she said, and returned to perch on her barstool behind the glassed-in counter. Glass jars of herbs twinkled behind her, and a rack of novena candles threw back the gleam.

I climbed the creaking stairs, the demon's soundless step behind me. We reached a low, indifferently lit hall, and a single door. I opened it, and found myself looking at a small, plain bedroom. An iron mission-style bed with white sheets and a dun comforter, a single chair by the empty fireplace, a full-length mirror next to a flimsy door leading to the Nuevo Rio version of a bathroom. I heaved a sigh. "I like this much better," I said shakily.

"No doubt." Japhrimel crowded past me into the room. It suddenly seemed far too small to contain him. The window looked out onto the street. I shut the door while he made one circuit of the walls, Power blending seamlessly to hide us. I dropped my bag on the bed, wishing I'd had room for more than one change of clothes. *It won't be the first hunt I've finished dirty,* I thought, and flipped open the messenger bag's top flap. I had to dig a bit to retrieve my datpilot. "What's that?"

"I need contacts," I said, waiting while the plug-in and the H-DOC established a linkup with the hand-held device. "Since we can't use Jace's, I'm going to have to look for anyone who has dual warrants in Saint City and in Nuevo Rio. That should give me a place to start. If nobody I know is in town we'll have to buy information, and that could get expensive."

"What information are we pursuing, then?" he asked, finishing his circuit of the room and making a brief gesture in front of the door. The whole building groaned a little, subliminally, and I felt a flutter in my stomach as the Power crested, ebbed. The room was now shielded—and if what I Saw was any indication, also invisible to prying eyes.

I took a deep breath. The medicinal effects of the brandy I'd taken down were beginning to wear off. My knees felt suspiciously weak. "I need to know two things: first of all, if Santino's running the Corvin Family from behind. And second—" I tapped into the datpilot, setting the parameters for the search, "I need to know what Jace has been doing these past three years."

CHAPTER 31

The next day was hot and breathless, thunder rumbling off and on, the light taking on a weird gray-green cast. I spent most of the day trying to sleep, sprawled on the small bed. Japhrimel dragged his chair up to the side of the bed and watched me, his green eyes veiled. I didn't speak much. I slept thinly, tossing and turning, waking with my katana still clenched in my hands and the same muggy heat lying over the city.

And Japhrimel's green eyes resting on me, oddly dark. Glazed.

My mind kept worrying like a dog with a single bone, over and over again.

Jace. The Corvin Family. Jace. Santino.

Jace.

The afternoon was wending toward evening when I finally sat up on the bed, tired of retreading the same mental ground. "Do you think he's betrayed me?" I asked, without even knowing I was going to open my mouth.

"I don't know," the demon answered, after a long, still pause. He rose to his feet like a dark wave. Demon-smell washed over me. He'd kept the window open, but the air was so close and still that the fragrance clung to the room. "You need food."

"I'll be fine. There's hunting to do." I stretched, my back cracking as I arched, then I swung my legs off the bed, came to my feet, and picked up my bag from the floor. A few moments divested it of everything I wouldn't need tonight—I piled extra clothes, the spare plasgun, and some other odds and ends on the bed. Japhrimel watched expressionlessly as I clumped over to the bathroom door, and was still watching when I came out. I buckled on my holster, checked the plasgun, and slid it in. Shrugged into my coat, immediately starting to sweat again. I finally gave my hair a short, vicious combing and braided it back.

"Do you think he's betrayed you?" he finally asked me when I checked the action on my main knives.

"It's looking pretty fucking possible," I said. "If what Abra told me is any indication, he ran with the Corvin Family even before he came to Saint City. You don't ever escape the Mob. And if Santino's running the Corvins from behind, they might be running Jace — or he was using me to pressure them for something. Or maybe just holding me until the Corvins reached a point in negotiations with Santino..." I trailed off. "It's very possible." I slipped my turquoise necklace on over my head, settled the pendant between my breasts. Japhrimel didn't reply. I finally settled my bag strap across my body. "What do you think?" I asked him.

His jaw set. "Do you truly wish to know?"

I nodded. "I do."

He shrugged, clasping his hands behind his back. "My opinion? He wants you far too badly to give you up to this Family," he said. "All the same, it would be foolish to trust him."

"If he wants me so much, why did he leave me?" I flared, then closed my eyes and took a deep breath.

"It seems we must discover this," he answered. "Do you care for him, then?"

"I used to," I said, opening my eyes and looking down at my free hand, clenched in a fist. "I'm not so sure now."

"Then do not decide yet," was his equable reply. But his face was full of something dark. I didn't want to know.

It was my turn to shrug. "You have agents in the city, you said."

He nodded. "They are already searching for information. Quietly, so as not to alert our quarry."

"That's good." My conscience pricked me. But that was ridiculous. He was a *demon.* He wasn't human. He wasn't even close to human. "Hey...you know, I..." Was I blushing? I was. Why?

I don't have time for this.

I approached him cautiously, laid my hand on his shoulder. His smell closed around me, vaguely comforting. "Thank you," I said, tilting my head back to look up into his face. "Really. I really...well, thank you."

One corner of his mouth quirked up slightly. It was by far the most human expression I had ever seen on him. "No thanks necessary," he said quietly. "It is my honor."

"Do you really think I can kill Santino?" I asked.

His face changed. "We have no choice, either way. I will do all I can to protect you, Dante."

"Good enough." I dropped my hand. "Let's go find our first contact."

CHAPTER 32

The police net plug-in gave me a current map of the city and tag-locations of landmarks loaded from my datband to my datpilot; the DOC told me who was in town. It wasn't too hard to find a familiar face. Whatever city Captain Jack was infesting, he always hung out near the prostitutes.

We visited five bordellos before we hit paydirt. I scanned a two-story building and brushed against weak, familiar shielding. After running into Captain Jack on four bounties, one of which had almost cost me my life when he turned traitor and sold me to the criminal I was hunting, I could tell his shielding even through a building reeking of sex and desperation. It was an unpleasant skill. "Come with me," I told the demon, pushing through the crowd. "Look dangerous. Don't kill anyone unless I do, okay?"

"As you like." He shadowed me as I crossed the street. We ended up on the doorstep, two Nuevo Rio prostitutes eyeing us. They made no move to stop me as I strode past them. The heavies guarding the door—two rippling masses of black-market augmentation—examined me, looked at the demon, and stepped back.

It was kind of useful, having Japhrimel around.

Inside, the place was done in threadbare red velvet, waves of perfume and hash smoke, naked women pressed against lace, offering their breasts and other things. One bronzed Nuevo Rio man, reclining on an overdone mahogany and black satin couch with a guitar in his supple hands, plucked out a mellow tune—an accompaniment to the girls' blandishments. Two customers, neither of them Jack, stared at me with wide eyes. Seeing a fully clothed woman carrying a sword in a Nuevo Rio bordello must be a huge shock.

I scanned the room — no, the Captain was up on the second floor. It figured.

The madam came fluttering out in a pink synthsilk robe, a tall and heavily lipsticked woman, her thinning hair padded out with horsehair. She carried about fifty extra pounds, and I felt the skin on my nape prickle. The three whip scars on my back gave one remembrance of a twinge, then subsided as I took a deep breath.

At least being a Necromance had saved me from being a sex worker.

She fired a chattering stream of Portogueso at us, and Japhrimel answered her with a few curt words. She paled, and he held out two folded notes — Nuevo Rio paper. Currency for those without datbands.

She snatched the notes from his hand and leered at me. I turned my cheek so my emerald sparked at her, and she almost fell over backward in her haste to get away. If the Nuevo Rios were easier with Shamans and demons and *loa*, they were even more frightened of Necromances. They had old legends here of the spirits that walked in Death and the humans that could talk to them — while Shamans were mostly acceptable, a Necromance definitely was *not*.

I took the stairs two at a time, following the pattern of instinct, intuition, and Power. A long hall, some open doors with women standing in them, their usual catcalls dying on their lips as I came into sight; other doors were closed, the reek of sex and hash in the air thick enough to cut. I tapped in, shaping the Power deftly, and by the time I smacked the door open and came face-to-face with a half-naked and disgruntled Captain Jack I was all but humming with invisible force. Any more and I'd go nova. It alerted him to my presence, of course, but by then it was too late for him.

"Hesu *Christos* —" he began, and I was on him, driving him to the floor, my sword within easy reach. I had him in an armlock. Japhrimel hushed the naked, screaming girl on the bed by the simple expedient of clapping a hand over her mouth. He dragged her to the door and tossed her out, then tossed a few more Nuevo Rio notes after her. *How much money does he have?* I thought, and leaned into the armlock.

Captain Jack, weedy from hash overuse, his ribs standing out, still possessed a great deal of wiry strength. I was actively sweating by the time he finished cursing and heaving, his sweat-slick skin sliding under my fingers. He'd gotten old. His dreadlocked brown hair was streaked with gray, bits of glittering circuit-wire wrapped around dreads and twisted into runic shapes, dusty from the plank flooring. He called me something filthy. I got my knee in his back and applied a little pressure. He settled down a little.

"What the motherfucking hell do *you* want?" he snarled. The demon, his face expressionless, leaned against the door, his arms folded across his chest.

"What I always want, Jack. To see your sweet face," I leaned over and purred in his ear. "Taking a vacation from Saint City, pirate? I'm on a legitimate hunt and you've got warrants. If you don't want your ass hauled in and cored in a Nuevo Rio prison, you might want to consider being a little more polite."

"Bitch," he hissed. His long thin nose pressed into the dusty planks; spittle formed on his thin lips. He'd pawned his golden earring, I saw it was missing. The tattoos on his shoulderblades—twin dragons, with no significance or Power—writhed on his skin. He was a bottom-feeder, with only enough psi to avoid being taken into wage slavery, not enough to qualify for a trade or even as a breeder. "Whafuck? Don't got nothing on you, I ain't seen you in years—"

"It's not me I'm asking about," I said quietly. "I want to know why Jace Monroe blew into town three years ago. Give, Jack, or I'll break your fucking arm and haul you in, I swear I will."

He believed me. "Christos," he moaned. "All I know's Jace was in the Corvins...bought himself out six months ago, foughta running street war with them. He's...big man now, lots of credit and a mean network. On the way to becoming a Family himself, he's filed...agh, lay *off*—for incorporation."

"*Sekhmet sa'es,*" I breathed. "And? Why did he come here? There must be rumors."

"Corvins made him a deal: Either he come in or they ice some bitch he was seeing. Lay *off*, willya? You're breakin my fuckin arm!"

"I'll break more than that if you keep whining. Who's he working for now?"

"You! Goddammit, woman, he's working for you! That's the word! Let up a little, come on, Valentine, *don't*!"

"Quit your bitching. Who's leaning on the Corvins to put my ass in a blender? Huh? Who?"

"Some big dude!" Jack moaned, his eyes rolling. "Don't know!

Five million credit and a clean slate for bringing you in. Whole city's lookin' for you—"

"That makes you the lucky one, doesn't it." I eased up a little on the pressure. "You must have heard rumors, Jack. Who's pushing the Corvins?"

"Same as always, the big dick Corvin. Jace was their front man in Saint City, man. Goddammit, lay *off*!"

"Jace was their front man three years ago?" That was something I hadn't guessed.

"Hell, he's been working for them his whole life! Ran off about six years ago, worked mercenary, they let him go for a while and then sank their hooks in good when he started seein' some bitch up Saint City way. I ain't been back there for five goddamn years, Valentine, I don't know who he was screwin' up there! Lucas will know, go bother him!"

That was unexpected news. "Lucas Villalobos? He's in town? Where?"

"Man, do I look like a fuckin' vid directory?"

I shoved. He screamed, the sound of a rabbit caught in a trap.

"*Las Vigrasas!* He hangs out at Las Vigrasas on Puertain Viadrid, goddammit, motherfuck—"

I looked up at the demon. He nodded slightly, understanding. It sounded like Jack was telling the truth.

I gained my feet, scooping my sword up; watched Captain Jack struggle up to hands and knees, then haul himself into a sitting position, facing me. "Hesu Christos," he moaned. "Look at this mess. You used to be such a nice girl, Valentine."

"Yeah, I had to grow up. Sucks, doesn't it." My lip curled. "Thanks for your time and trouble, Captain."

"Fuck you," he spat, his watery brown eyes rabbiting over to the demon and halting, wide as credit discs. He crossed himself—forehead, chest, left shoulder, right shoulder—while I watched, fascinated. I'd never seen Captain get religious before. "*Nominae Patri, et Filii, et Spiritu Sancti—*"

Does he think Japhrimel's going to disappear in a puff of brimstone? I thought, feeling a sardonic smile tilt one corner of my mouth. "I never knew you were a Novo Christer, Jack. I thought fucking so many prostitutes would have made you irreligious."

He kept babbling his prayer. I sighed, backed up a few steps, eased for the door. It wasn't wise to turn your back on Captain Jack.

I made it to the door before he broke off long enough to glare at me. "I hate you, Valentine," he hissed. "One of these days—"

Japhrimel tensed. His eyes flared. I reached behind me for the doorknob. "Promises, promises," I said, twisting the knob and opening the door. "If you go running to Monroe, tell him he'd better pray his path doesn't cross mine."

"They'll catch you!" Jack screamed. "The whole city's lookin' for you!"

"Good luck to them," I said, and ducked out of the room. Japhrimel followed me.

"Shall I kill him?" he asked quietly as we made our way down the hall. The entire bordello was silent, waiting. "He threatened you."

"Leave him alone. He hates me for a good reason."

"What would that be?"

"I killed his wife," I said, checking the stairs. Looked safe enough. "Come on. Let's go find Lucas." My jaw set, and fortunately, Japhrimel didn't ask me anything else.

CHAPTER 33

Las Vigrasas was a bar. The street it crouched on lay under a drift of trash, furtive shadows sliding from place to place, danger soaking the air. I shivered, peering at the front of the bar from our safe place across the street. Japhrimel had suggested watching the place for a few minutes, and I'd concurred.

I scanned the place carefully. No real Power here, this was a blindhead bar. It was asking for trouble, walking in there. Some places weren't very hospitable to psis.

A lonely sign with a peeling *L s Vig asa* painted on it swung slightly in the freshening breeze. The air was so muggy, even the breeze didn't help much. Bullet holes and plasgun scorches festooned the buildings.

I took a deep breath. "What do you think?" I asked him.

I can't believe I'm asking a demon his opinion, I thought. *What the hell is wrong with me? Then again, he's my best backup, at least until I find this Egg thingie.*

"I think this is a dangerous place," he said softly. "I would ask you to be careful, but—"

"I'll be careful," I said. "Look, don't hesitate in there. You see someone go for me, take them down."

"Kill them?"

"If necessary." I paused. "I trust your judgment."

His eyes sparked briefly, turning bright laser-green, and then just as swiftly darkened. "You do?"

"I guess so," I answered. "You haven't let me down yet."

He didn't answer, but his eyes held mine for a long moment.

I finally eased out of the shadows and crossed the street, skirting mounds of rubble and trash. I didn't have to look—Japhrimel seemed melded to my shadow. Three steps led up to Las Vigrasas's swinging door; I heard rollicking shouts from behind it, a barrelhouse piano going. I pushed the door open, grimacing inwardly at the feel of greasy wood against my fingers. A roil of smell pushed out— alcohol, vomit, cigarette smoke, the stench of an untended lavatory, unwashed men.

Eau de Nuevo Rio bar, I thought. *I wish Gabe was here.*

That startled me. I wasn't used to hunting with anyone in tow, but it had been nice to have Gabe around. At least she was honest—or I hoped so. Then again, she had suggested staying with Jace, and contacted him.

It truly sucks to doubt your friends when you only have one or two of them, I realized.

I strode into the bar, Japhrimel behind me. Cigarette smoke hazed the air. The dark and sudden quiet that fell over the raucous drunken pit warned me. *Oh, what the hell*, I thought. *In for a penny, in for a motherfucking pound.* My emerald spat, sizzled, a green spark drifting down to the floor.

A long bar crouched on the left side of the room, tables and chairs scattered to my right. I stepped down, my boots making quiet sounds against the wood of the stairs and then a muffled deadened sound as I stepped onto the oiled sawdust.

Dark eyes watched me. Several Nuevo Rios, lean tanned men in clothes very much like mine, plasguns and old-time projectile guns openly displayed. There was a smattering of Anglos—I scanned the bar once, and found a familiar slouched set of shoulders. Lucas stood with his back to the door, leaning against the bar.

I knew better than to think he didn't know who had just come in from the cold.

I made it two steps across the sawdust before the bartender spat something in Portogueso, a long deadly-looking shotgun in his brown hands. He wore a stained apron and a sweat-darkened white shirt, oddly luminescent in the gloom.

Japhrimel said something in reply, and the air temperature dropped by at least ten degrees. Nobody moved, but there was a general sense of men leaning back. I waited, eyeing the bartender, my peripheral vision marking everyone in the room. Lucas wore a Trade Bargains microfiber shirt, like me; run-down jeans and worn engineer boots. But he also wore a bandolier, oiled supple leather against his shirt; his greasy hair lay lank against his shoulders.

The bartender spoke again, but his voice quivered slightly. I watched the shotgun.

Japhrimel said nothing, but the air pressure changed. I felt like a woman holding a plasgun over a barrel of reactive—my pulse ran tight and hot behind my wrists and throat, my nape tingling, my skin bathed with Power.

Five seconds ticked by. Then the bartender dropped his shotgun on the bar. The wood and metal clattered. I tensed, bile whipping my throat. *Do all these places have to smell so bad?* I thought, and then, *If I didn't have Japhrimel with me, someone would have tried to kill me by now.*

It was awful handy, having a demon around.

The bartender raised his hands, backing away from the shotgun. His pupils dilated, the color draining from his face. Pasty and trembling, he slumped against the flyspotted mirror sporting shelves of dusty bottles. Glass chattered.

I pantomimed a yawn, patting my lips with the back of my hand. My rings flashed. I walked across the sawdust, skirting a table where three men had a card game set out. I glanced down at the table—poker. Of course. A pile of metal bits lay in the middle of the table. One of the men caught my eyes and hurriedly looked down at his cards.

I made it to where Lucas leaned against the bar. A glass full of amber liquid sat at his elbow.

"Valentine," he said, not turning around. His voice was a whisper, the same whispered tone Necromances affected after a while. It made me shudder to hear. "Thought you'd come looking for me."

"I hate being predictable," I said carefully. "I want information."

"Of course you do. And I'm the only honest fucker you can find in this town that won't sell you." He shrugged, one shoulder lifting, dipping. "What you paying?"

"What you want?" I kept my katana between us.

"The usual, *chica*. You got it?" His shoulders tensed.

"Of course, Lucas. I wouldn't come here otherwise." *Letting you walk inside my mind isn't a price I want to pay, but I have no choice.*

He turned around then, slowly, and I took a step back. Japhrimel's fingers closed around my shoulders, and I found myself with the demon plastered to my back, my sheathed katana raised to be a bar between me and Lucas Villalobos.

He was five inches taller than me, compact with muscle, his lank hair hanging over a pale, wasted face. His eyes glittered almost-yellow in the uncertain light.

The scar ran down his left cheek, a river of ruined skin. Was that where his tattoo had been burned away? I didn't know, he never told. I gulped. Lucas was a lot older than he looked; something in the hooded twinkle of his eyes and the almost-slack set of his mouth made that age visible. He wouldn't die, though. You could gut him, slit his throat, burn him alive, but he wouldn't die.

Death had turned His face from Lucas Villalobos. Nobody knew why, and it was worth your life to ask.

"You want to know about Jace Monroe," he whispered. His smell, dry as a stasis cabinet, brushed against my nose.

I preferred the stink of the bar. Power pushed at Lucas would simply be shunted aside; he didn't cast spells. No, he merely killed; hired himself out for protection work and assassinations. It was expensive to have the Deathless on your side—but worth it, I'd been told.

I never wanted to find out. Even going to him for information scared me. This was our third time meeting, and I sincerely hoped as I did every time that it was our last.

Nobody else in the bar spoke. Japhrimel was tense behind me, heat blurring through my clothes. The smoky smell of demon began to drown out every other scent in the bar—and for that, I was grateful. My mouth tasted like cotton—and bile.

"Tell me," I said simply.

He shrugged. "Not much to tell. He was born into the Corvins, I think. Far as I know, he's Deke Corvin's youngest son. Word is, he planned his escape for a long time, hoofed out to Saint City, and started doing mercenary work. Then something happened he didn't count on." Lucas shrugged, picked up his glass. Drained it, his Adam's apple working. "Idiot fell in love with a girl. Old man Sargon moved in for the kill, fouled up a job of hers, then let Jace know that if he didn't come back and fly right, he'd take out a contract on the girl. Jace caved, came home like a good little boy." Lucas's yellow eyes mocked me. "Stupid bitch didn't even bother coming out to Nuevo Rio to find out what had happened."

"I'm sure she had her reasons," I said, matching his quiet tone. Our words dropped into the profound silence of the bar like stones into a pond. "Who's running the Corvin Family from behind, Lucas?"

"Nobody I know of," he whispered, setting his empty glass down with finicky precision. "Sargon runs the Corvins, with an iron fist. Jace just bought himself free legally—and extralegally, the streets are still bleeding from his nightside war with the Corvins. He's incorporated under a Mob license of his own. Surprised?"

"Not really," I said. "Once Mob, always Mob. Who's looking for me, Lucas?"

"Whole damn city," Lucas returned. "You're worth hard cash, good credit, and a clean slate to several interested parties. Jace is combing the sinks for you and your pet demon there. Boy's got a real hard-on for you."

"I'm sure it will pass," I said. "Give me something real, Lucas."

"I don't have anything else," he said. "Someone wants you alive and unharmed. Every bounty hunter worth a credit is pouring into the city. You can't hide forever."

"I don't want to hide," I said. "I'm after Santino."

If I'd thought the place was quiet before, it went absolutely still now. Nobody was even breathing once I spoke that name.

Lucas went even paler. "Then you're on the track to suicide," he whispered. "Take my advice, Valentine. Run. Run as fast as you can, for as long as you can. Steal whatever bit of life you can. You're already dead."

"Not yet I'm not," I said. "You can tell whoever you like. I'm gunning for Santino, and I'm going to take him down."

Lucas made an odd wheezing sound. It took me a moment to realize he was laughing. Cold sweat broke out on my back.

Lucas finally wiped tears away from his hooded yellow eyes and regarded me. "You can't kill that fucker, Valentine. Not from what I've heard," he said. "Now get out of here. I don't want you near me."

"What about payment?" My fingers tightened on my katana.

"Don't want it. Get the fuck away from me before I decide to take you in myself."

"Good luck," I said dryly. "I don't want any debt to you, Lucas."

"I'll see you in Hell, Valentine. Get the fuck out of here, now." His eyes slid up, regarded the demon. "Go out and die well."

I didn't wait to be told twice. I backed up, cautiously, Japhrimel moving with me, oddly intimate. Then he slid to the side, and I turned around. He walked behind me as I retraced my steps. I looked back over my shoulder once, when I reached the stairs, and saw Lucas pouring into his glass from a bottle of tequila. He filled it to the brim, then lifted the bottle to his lips and took two long gulps, not stopping for breath. He looked shaken.

Now I had officially seen everything.

CHAPTER 34

The stink of the street outside was almost fresh after the close, reeking air of the bar. I filled my lungs, walking quickly, Japhrimel matching me step for step. He didn't speak, and neither did I. We reached a slightly better-lit part of town. He touched my shoulder and pointed out a small restaurant; I didn't demur.

It was a little hole-in-the-wall cantina, and I ordered two shots of tequila to start off with. The waitress eyed me, nervously touching the *grisgris* bag around her neck. I didn't care anymore. Finally she took Japhrimel's money and hurried off.

I sank back into the cracked red vinyl booth, then leaned forward and rested my forehead on the table, trembling. Thunder muttered in the far distance.

"Dante." His voice was calm. I could feel his eyes on me.

"Give me a minute," I said, my words muffled.

He did.

I took in deep ragged breaths, trying to force my heart to stop pounding. Jace was a Corvin. He'd never told me—and I'd never guessed. Not even when Abra had told me Jace was Mob had I guessed he was a blood Corvin.

The second-to-last job I'd gone on before he left—that had been the Morrix fiasco. I'd barely escaped alive. I'd told Jace about it and he'd been worried, of course—any time your lover gets shot during a routine corporate-espionage, you can legitimately get worried—but he must have had a better poker face than even I'd guessed. He had lied to me about his origins, and I'd swallowed it like the fool I was.

And Lucas turning down payment was unheard-of. Whatever he knew about Santino, he wasn't going to tell—and he considered me already dead.

I was seriously beginning to wonder if he might be right. I was Santino's next victim.

And Jace might be working for the demon who haunted my nightmares.

The waitress brought the tequila. Japhrimel murmured to her, and I heard the rustle of more money exchanging hands. *I wish I'd learned Portogueso,* I thought, and slowly sat up. I took the first shot of tequila and tossed it back, hoping the alcohol would kill any germs on the dirty shotglass. Fire exploded in my stomach and I coughed slightly, my eyes watering.

Japhrimel sat bolt upright on the other side of the booth. I watched the front window of the restaurant for a little while—we'd taken a booth in the back, of course, so I could have my back to the wall. The water from the tequila-burn rolled down my cheeks; I scraped it off with the flat of one hand, keeping my katana under the table.

He examined me closely. I contemplated the second shot of tequila.

Finally, he reached over and took the shot glass in his golden fingers. He lifted it to his lips and poured it down, then blinked.

"That," he pronounced, "is unutterably foul."

I coughed slightly, and giggled. The sound was high-pitched, tired, and more panicked than I liked. "I thought demons liked liquor," I said. The slick plastic tabletop glowed under the high-intensity fluorescents set in the plasteel lamps hanging from chains, made to look like old-fashioned lamps.

"That seems to be something other than liquor," he replied.

I took in a shaky breath. The banter helped. "Do you have any ideas?" I asked him. "Because I've got to tell you, I'm fresh out."

He nodded, the light running over his inky hair and even face.

"There might be something..." He trailed off, closed his eyes briefly. Then he looked at me. "I've ordered food. You must take better care of yourself, Dante."

"Why?" Another jagged laugh escaped me. "I have it on good authority I'm not going to live long enough to have it matter. Everyone keeps telling me I'm going to die." *Including that little voice that happens to be my better sense,* I added silently. I held up a finger. "I'm Santino's next victim." Another finger. "The Corvins want me unharmed, presumably for delivery to an interested party." I held up a third finger. "Jace is a Corvin. A *blood* Corvin. What does this add up to? Me being fucked, that's what it adds up to. Santino's a *demon.* If *you* can't kill him, what chance do I have?"

Japhrimel looked down at the table. He said nothing.

"Lucifer's set me up to die, hasn't he?" I said it quietly. "There's no way I can kill Santino. I'm supposed to distract Santino while you get the Egg. And when I die, it's *too bad, so sad, but she was only a human after all.*" My fingers ached, gripping my katana's sheath. "Tell me if I'm wrong, Tierce Japhrimel."

He placed his hands flat on the table. "You're wrong," he said quietly. "The Prince believes you can kill him. You did survive him once, after all. And now you have me, not a human *sedayeen,* watching over you. I may not be able to kill him myself, but I can help you—and keep you alive and free long enough to kill him. And once we recover the Egg, I will be free." His eyes swung up, found mine. "*Free,* Dante. Do you know what that means? That means I can do as I please, no commands from the Prince, no shackle to my duty. *Free.*"

His eyes blazed, his mouth turning down in a grimace. I watched, fascinated, almost forgetting my sword. It was the most emotion I'd ever seen from him.

I swallowed dryly. I'd never heard of a free demon before. Lucifer must be desperate to drag me out of my house and offer a demon like Japhrimel complete freedom. "What would you do if you were free?"

He closed his mouth, dropped his eyes again. There was a long pause before he shrugged. "I do not know. I have an idea, but...so much may change, between now and then. I have learned not to hope for much, Dante. It has been my only true lesson."

I took this in. I was beginning to feel more like myself now. "All right," I said. "You haven't led me wrong so far. So what's this idea of yours?"

"Eat first," he said. "Then I'll tell you."

I tapped my lacquered nails on the tabletop. "Okay." I checked the front window again, nervous for no discernible reason. "So what did you order?"

"*Arroz con pollo*. I am told it's quite good." He didn't move, hands flat on the tabletop, eyes down, shoulders straight as a ruler. His black coat and inky hair drank in the light, oddly glossy under the fluorescents. "Does it surprise you, that he would not tell you his Flight and clan?"

I shrugged. "I never would have dated him if I'd known," I admitted. "But still."

"Indeed." He waited for a few heartbeats. "He went back to his clan to protect you, it seems."

"He could have told me. Left a note. Something. Look, I don't want to talk about this. Can we pick another subject?"

He nodded, his left hand suddenly moving, tracing a glyph on the tabletop. I watched for a few moments, then looked at his face, studying the arc of his cheekbone, his lashes veiling his eyes, the curve of his lower lip. "I have a thought," he said.

"Lay it on me." I tapped my fingernails on the plastic. My rings were quiescent, dark.

"Sargon Corvin," Japhrimel paused, traced the glyph again. "In the name-language of demons, *sargon* means 'bleeder' or 'despoiler.'" He looked up again. This time his eyes were dark, and I felt my pulse start to hammer again. He looked thoughtful. "So does *Vardimal*."

It was near dawn as we headed back for Carmen's bodega. Japhrimel was right, the world started to look a little less grim once I had some food in me to balance out nerves — and the tequila.

Nuevo Rio was hushed, the night people streaming toward bed and the day people not yet awake. That meant that the crowds had thinned out, and there was less cover for an Anglo Necromance trailed by a demon. I was a little more sanguine now, though. After all, I had a demon on my side.

And I was beginning to think he was trustworthy.

We turned the corner onto a long, empty street with boarded-up windows, Japhrimel pacing next to me, his hands clasped behind his back. I carried my katana a little more easily than I had before, since it didn't seem likely that I'd need it in the next few minutes.

"So what's this grand idea of yours?" I asked, checking the sky.

Pale pearly dawn was beginning to filter through the lowering clouds, and the breathlessness of an approaching storm had intensified, if that were possible. I longed for rain, for lightning, for anything to break this tension. I hate muggy weather.

"You may not like it," he said, his head down and his hands clasped behind his back.

"Does it give me a better chance of killing Santino?" I asked, checking the street again. My nape prickled. Nerves, probably. It had been a hell of a night.

"It does. Yet..." Japhrimel trailed off again. "You do not trust me, Dante."

I shrugged. "I don't trust anyone, not until proven." That sounded rude, and I sighed. "You're okay, you know. But my jury's still out until you tell me this idea."

"Very well," he said. But he didn't explain—instead, he glanced up at the sky too, then down at me.

"I'm waiting," I reminded him.

"I would wish to give you a gift," he said, slowly, as if he was choosing his words carefully. "A piece of my Power. It will make you stronger, faster...less easy to damage."

I thought it over, skirting a puddle of oily liquid. The pavement here was cracked and dangerous, small sinkholes yawning everywhere. My neck prickled again. I was too nervous. Too strung-out. I needed sleep, or a fight...or something else entirely. "What's the catch?" I said finally.

"I am not sure you would wish to be tied to me so closely," he answered. "And the process is...difficult, for humans. Painful."

I absorbed this. "You would...what, make me into a demon?"

"Not a demon. My *hedaira*."

"I've never heard of that."

"It's not spoken of," he said. "It...ah, it requires a...ah, a physical bond..."

Was that *embarrassment* in his voice? Another first, the first time I'd heard a demon groping for words. "You mean like Tantrik; like sex magick?" I ventured, feeling my cheeks heat up. *I'm blushing. Anubis guard me, I'm blushing.*

"Very similar," he agreed, sounding relieved.

"Oh." I mulled this over, stepping over another puddle. Gooseflesh raised on my back, a chill breath on my sweating skin.

Why am I so nervous?

I opened my mouth to say something when Japhrimel froze between one step and the next. I halted, too, closed my eyes, and sent my senses out, winging through the predawn hush.

Nothing. Nothing but the demon next to me, and the persistent static of city Power—

—and a smell like cold midnight and ice.

My entire body went cold, my nipples drawing up hard as pebbles, my breath catching.

"Dante," Japhrimel said quietly. "Run."

"No way," I whispered. "If he's here—"

"Do not be foolish," he whispered fiercely, catching my arm and shoving me. "*Run!*" His hands flickered, came up full of silver guns.

My katana whispered free of its sheath, metal running with blue light and Power, runes twisting along its surface.

And then all hell broke loose.

I'd like to say I was of some use once the fighting broke out, but the only thing I remember was a huge stunning impact throwing me to the ground, my katana still clenched in my hand, and Japhrimel's roar of furious agony. *Plasgun bolt,* I thought, *I didn't expect a plasgun bolt from a demon.* And darkness swallowed me whole.

CHAPTER 35

*C*old.

After the heat of Nuevo Rio, the cold crept into my bones and twisted hard. I moaned, trying to lift my head. My left shoulder burned mercilessly, my right wrist clasped in something hard and chill. Stone under my fingertips.

It took a while before I could open my eyes. When I did, the darkness didn't change. Either I was blind, or locked in a place with no light.

Both were equally possible.

For a few vertiginous minutes after I woke up, I couldn't even remember my own name. Then it all came flooding back.

Plasgun. I'd been hit with a plasgun bolt, set on stun. That explained the temporary blindness—if I was blind—and the way my entire body felt as if it had been ripped apart and put back together wrong. A plasgun charge was the worst thing for psionics; it drained and screwed up Power meridians, as well as giving a hell of a headache.

I moved slightly, and the sound of metal dragging over stone reached my ears.

Chained. I was chained to the stone. A metal cuff clasped my wrist.

I took in a deep ragged breath, moaned again. Yanked on the chain. I was underground, I could tell I was underground, in the dark. My rings scraped stone as I pulled on the chain, metal clanking, another moan echoing against the walls.

Stop it, a cold, calm voice intruded on my panic. *Get hold of yourself. You're not dead yet, so look around. Use that famous wit of yours, Danny, and try to figure out why you haven't been killed yet.*

Santino. He'd been there. Had he snatched me? If so, I *had* to think, I had to.

I shut my eyes again. The squirming worm of panic under my breastbone started to grow. I had to pee, and the darkness was absolute, and the cold leaching into my bones made me shiver, like the cold of bringing a ghost back.

Anubis et'her ka. Se ta'uk'fhet sa te vapu kuraph. Anubis et'her ka. Anubis, Lord of the Dead, Faithful Companion, protect me, for I am Your child. Protect me, Anubis, weigh my heart upon the scales, watch over me, Lord, for I am Your child. Do not let evil distress me, but turn Your fierceness upon my enemies—

Light bloomed, a faint blue glow. I hitched in a shuddering breath. My eyes popped open.

My rings were dead and dark. The glow came from my katana, lying on the other side of the stone cube with my bag and my coat, thrown in a heap. My plasgun was gone; so was the katana's scabbard. *Oh, thank you,* I thought. *Thank you, Lord. Thank you.*

A faint heat bloomed inside my chest. My shoulder ached fiercely, as if a hot poker was being drilled into the flesh. What had happened to Japhrimel?

And why leave me my sword? I was deadly with edged metal.

Then again, Santino had faced me down with a sword before and won; he'd taken the plasgun, which was the only thing faster than a demon. Santino might not fear me even if I had my other weapons.

Let's hope that's his first mistake.

I was trapped in a featureless stone cell with a drain in one corner.

A faint sour smell came up from the drain. I wriggled across the floor, not trusting my legs yet.

The chain fetched me up short. I wriggled around, stretching, but the katana was still a good six inches away and I couldn't twist any other part of my body near enough due to the narrowness of the cell. I finally settled on my stomach, staring at the katana's hilt.

I was drained. I had not even an erg of Power left. Taking a plasgun bolt will do that, scramble and drain your Power meridians. I'd either have to wait for a recharge, or...

I stretched out my left hand. My shoulder burned. The faint blue glow helped immensely, even though I could see no way out of the cube. *Don't worry*, I told myself, *if there's a way in, there's a way out.*

I lay on my back, my left hand out and reaching, stilled myself. *Anubis,* I prayed, *You have shown me Your favor. Give me my weapon, please. Don't let me die chained like an animal. Please, my Lord, help me, for I have served You faithfully—*

I strained, every muscle singing in agony, my heart speeding up, my breathing rising. The blue glow stuttered. I inhaled, waiting for the space inside me where the god lived to open.

—blue crystal pillars, a flash of light, the god's face, turning away from me. My emerald, flashing, a song of creaking agony.

My katana's hilt slammed into my palm. I gasped, shocked heart and lungs struggling to function—the body needed Power to survive; to drain myself so completely was dangerous, my heart and lungs could stop and tip me into Death's embrace.

When I regained consciousness, I had my katana in hand. The Power vibrating in the blade trickled into me. It helped.

In the glow from my blade, I examined the cuff around my wrist. It took a moment to snag the blade on the strap of my bag, and then once I had my bag I dug in to find my lockpicks. They were there—I said a silent prayer of thanksgiving while I worked on the ancient lock. It took a while, and one fit of whispered cursing at my numb fingers, but I finally tickled the lock open.

Wearing my coat helped with the chill. I settled my bag under the coat, against my hip, and held my katana.

There, I thought, *that's definitely better.*

I took a few moments to lean against the wall and breathe. The stone cube was windowless, doorless, with nothing but the drain in one corner. There was no Power in the walls that I could sense, but

when I closed my eyes and felt around me I discovered two things—
that I was still in Nuevo Rio, because the Power here tasted like ashes
and tamales and blood, and that there was a dead spot on one wall,
where the stone didn't resonate like stone should.

First things first. I relieved myself into the drain, wishing I'd
packed some toilet paper in the bag. *Really,* I scolded myself, *you
should have known that you'd end up in a stone dungeon with no
facilities. That's how these things always end up, isn't it? Who kidnapped me? If it's Santino, why am I not dead? And why in the name
of the gods did he leave me my sword?*

Then I zipped myself up and walked over to the dead spot. The
ceiling gave me only about an inch of clearance; if I'd been any taller
I would have had to hunch.

I had enough Power now to reach out and tap into the city's well
again, thankful I'd had a chance to acclimate. Being locked in this
cell with backlash would not have been good.

With the tapline secure and my throbbing headache easing as the
Power soaked back into me, I touched the dead spot on the wall. It
appeared to be stone to my fingers.

I stared at the stone, and my left shoulder gave a crunching flare
of pain. I transferred my katana to my left hand, blade-down so the
glow from the steel would give me light, and reached up with my
right, sliding my hand under my shirt. The ridged loops of scar pulsed
under my fingers. Heat flooded me.

I saw, as if through a sheet of rippling glass, the city underneath
me. Fire bloomed in several different places, and my right hand was
up, clinging to something rough. Rain lashed down, unable to quench
the fires, and there was an incredible noise. Then the world rushed up
to meet me, boots thudding into pavement, and someone's soft throat
gave under my iron fingers.

"If she is harmed," I heard Japhrimel growl, *"I will kill all in my
path, I promise you this."*

I woke up lying curled on the stone floor, my katana's hilt pressed
to my forehead. I would have a nice goose-egg on my temple from
hitting the floor. The tapline resounded as if plucked like a guitar
string. "I gotta stop passing out," I moaned, tasting blood. I'd bitten
the inside of my cheek. "I'll never get out of here."

The tingle of Power told me I'd been down for about half an hour.
That doesn't tell me anything, I thought, *who knows how long I've
really been down here?* Hunger twisted my stomach.

I settled down cross-legged in front of the dead spot, staring at it. The lack of Power here told me *something* was here, and chances were it was an entrance.

I started to breathe, deep circular breaths. Opened the tapline as far as my aching head would allow, soaking up the Power of the city like a sponge. Three-quarters of the influx went into my rings; they started to sparkle against my fingers. The other quarter I used to start fashioning a glyph of the Nine Canons — *Gehraisz,* one of the Greater Glyphs of Opening.

If it didn't blast the door off its fucking hinges, at least it might blow away some of the shell of illusion over the door and give me something to work with. I waited, building the glyph carefully, the faint glow from my katana fading to a dim foxfire glow.

It took a long time for my rings to come back to life, meaning that my Power meridians were settling back into normal. Then all the available Power went into the glyph. It started to pulse, folding up in the air and glowing a fierce silvery-white. Looped and spun, three-dimensional, and I drew it back. Like an arrow, like a cobra coiling itself to strike.

I waited, humming the low note the glyph was keyed to, at the very bottom of my range. I juggled the glyph, forcing an overflow line down into the floor of the cell. If the glyph rebounded or the door was trapped, I didn't want the backlash. Let the stone take it.

There was an endless moment of suspension, everything paused, the world stopped like a holovid still, and then the glyph released, hurling itself toward the dead spot in the wall.

A brilliant flash of light seared my eyes, and my left shoulder sent a bolt of hot pain through me. When I finished shaking my head to clear it, I saw it had worked.

An ironbound door with a handle and a keyhole stood in front of me. I let out a long satisfied breath.

"Okay," I whispered, hauling myself to my feet. My left leg had gone to sleep, and I shifted back and forth, gasping as the pins and needles bit my flesh. "Looks like I'm back in the game."

CHAPTER 36

What felt like an hour but was probably only fifteen minutes later, I pushed the door cautiously open, my katana held ready. Stairs hacked out of stone rose up in front of me, and I sighed. *Of course not. It couldn't be easy, could it?* I climbed cautiously, my shaking legs protesting, my back on fire, my shoulders tense as bridge cables and my glutes singing a song of agony.

I reached the top of 174 stairs and found another door. This one was more resistant to my lockpicking skills, and I was beginning to gasp with panic, imagining being trapped underground, when it finally yielded. It creaked open, slowly, and revealed the very last thing I expected.

A large high-ceilinged room done in white. White marble floor, a large white bed with mosquito netting draped over it, a fireplace made of the same white marble. A white leather chair crouched in front of the empty fireplace, and a white rug lay on the floor at the bed's foot. I had to look twice before I recognized it as a polar bear's pelt. My gorge rose. I pushed it back down.

The tall French doors across the room were open, and the filmy white curtains fluttered on a sultry breeze. I heard the sound of falling rain, smelled oranges.

Out. Get out. Get out of here.

I made it halfway to the windows before he spoke.

"Impressive, Ms. Valentine. Lucifer's faith in you is well-placed, I expected another six hours before you came through that door. I hope your temper has calmed."

His voice was chill, high-pitched, and soaked with murderous Power. And then I smelled it—ice and blood, blind white maggots churning in a corpse, the smell that had soaked my nightmares for five long years.

I turned, my sword held ready. Blue fire ran along the blade, dripped on the floor. Gooseflesh roared over my body.

Get down, Doreen. Get down—

Game over.

He stood by the fireplace, one long hand on the back of the chair, the black teardrops over his eyes swallowing the pale marble light. He wore a white linen suit, cut loose and tropical on his thin demon's frame. His ears poked up through a frayed mat of dark hair, coming to sharp points. My hand shook, but the katana stayed steady. My spare knife slid out from its hidden sheath in my coat, reversed itself along my forearm.

"Santino," I whispered.

"The very same," he answered, bowing slightly. "And you, my beauty, are Danny Valentine. I knew I'd meet *you* again."

"I'm going to kill you," I whispered.

"Certainly you want to," he replied. "But I would like to talk to you first."

That was just strange enough to make me blink. *He's a demon, he's tricky, be careful.*

"Who are you?" I blurted. "Are you Sargon Corvin, or Santino Vardimal?"

He nodded. "Both. And more. Come with me, Dante. Let me show you what Lucifer doesn't want you to see."

"I don't trust you," I snapped. My rings sparked. *Why did he leave my sword and my gear in there with me, if he wanted to kill me?* It didn't make sense.

But I knew how he liked to play with his prey.

"I didn't think you would. However, I have not killed you. If I wanted to, I would have while you lay unconscious in the street and saved myself all this trouble. Surely you can afford to listen before you attempt my murder?" He shrugged, a demon's shrug.

I wish Japhrimel were here, I thought, and hastily shoved the thought away.

"You're being used, human," he said softly. "Come with me. I'll show you."

Without waiting for my answer, he turned his back on me and paced across the room.

Don't follow him, Danny. Take the window, however big the drop is from there you can take it, get out, get out, get AWAY—

I found myself following, advancing, keeping my sword ready. If he tried anything, I'd kill him or die trying. *Why did he leave me my blade?*

The house was massive, mostly floored in white marble, done hacienda style. It would have been beautiful if I hadn't been so terrified. He led me down stairs and through rooms furnished with pieces worth more than I made in a year—apparently Vardimal had done very well for himself.

Just like Jace.

He didn't seem to notice I was following him, but as we walked down a long hall with columns on one side and paintings I didn't look at on the other, he began to talk.

"Lucifer wants me destroyed because I outwitted him. He never could stand that. Yet he is himself the Prince of Lies. He may know that I've managed to do it, I've succeeded where so many others have failed."

"You're not making any sense," I said numbly.

He led me into another hall, this one sloping downward. "You're right. I should tell you from the beginning." A pair of doors in front of him; he twisted the knobs and flung them open. "A long time ago, when Lucifer had finished twisting the genes of humans to fit his plans, the sons of his kingdom looked upon the daughters of Men, and found them fair. They came to earth and lay with them, and in those days giants roamed the earth."

I'd heard this story before. Another hall spun under my feet. *Where are all his guards and everything?* I wondered. *And Lucas told me Jace is a Corvin's youngest son.*

"Are you telling me you've bred with human women?" I said, my boots whispering over the slick marble. I was beginning to feel sick and dizzy from the backlash of Power—and terror. I was following Santino through his own lair. Close enough to kill him. I was close enough to kill the thing that had killed Doreen.

Why hadn't I attacked him?

Something else is going on here, I thought. The premonition buzzed under my skin, the vision Japhrimel had interrupted. Would it have shown me this if he hadn't short-circuited it?

"Of course not. Yet you're far more intelligent than you're given credit for. Human women are some of the most pleasant ways to pass the time. Why do you think Lucifer took an interest in your species? But no, I have not fathered a child. Not in the way you think. "

He turned down another hall, this one lit by high-end fluorescents, most of them turned off so only a faint glow showed me the marble floor and tech-locked doors, each with a handprint lock. "Have you wondered why Lucifer granted me an immunity, Dante? Because I am a scientist first and a demon second. Long ago, I did the grunt work for Lucifer's remodeling of your species. Before demons could *play* with humans, humans had to be...well, helped along a little."

My gorge rose again. He talked about playing with humans as if it were slightly shameful, slightly loathsome, the way a Ludder would talk about going to a sexwitch House. Santino stopped in front of a blank, anonymous door, laid his hand on the printlock. Green light glowed, and the door shushed aside. "Come inside."

I followed him, the chill of climate control closing over my skin. It was a lab—fluorescent light flickered, computer screens glowed, and the temperature was about sixty-five degrees, shocking after the heat outside. Along one wall was something I'd seen before at the Hegemony psi clinics—a DNA map, twisting on a plasma screen, numbers and code running in the lower left corner. One whole wall was taken up with liquid-nitrogen-cooled racks of sample canisters behind glass, each neatly labeled. I had the sick feeling I would recognize the names on some of those labels. Each canister was a life, probably holding an internal organ, or a vial of blood—and a slice of human femur, with its rich big core of marrow. Just the thing for genetic research.

So many, I thought, the racks and rows of canisters gleaming softly under the bright pitiless light. *So many deaths.*

Santino turned to face me again, and I lifted my sword. Blue light ran over the blade. He looked thoughtful, the black teardrops over his eyes holes of darkness. "I'm sterile, Dante," he said. "I couldn't breed with a human woman even if I wanted to. To breed, a demon has to be one of the Greater Flight of Hell—and he must also become one of the Fallen. I can't do that. So I escaped Hell and came here, in search of something very special."

My throat was dry. "You weren't taking trophies," I whispered. "You were taking *samples.*"

He beamed at me, razor teeth gleaming, his high-pointed ears wriggling slightly. "Correct!" he said, like a magisterial professor talking to a gifted but sometimes-terribly-slow student. "Samples. I felt sure that the key to the puzzle lay in psionics. Humanity exhibits some rather bizarre talents as a result of demon tinkering; if I could find a certain strain of genetic code I could reach my objective. I adopted several psionics and sponsored research in the Hegemony, but they move too *damnably* slow, even for humans. I decided to do the work myself, and for that I needed other samples. I was running out of time. I knew that the more time passed, the greater the chance

Lucifer might decide to create another demon, and find the Egg missing." His fingers stroked the glass over the sample canisters, his claws making a slight *skree* against the smooth surface.

"What objective? And what *is* this Egg thing?" *Kill him*, my conscience screamed. *Revenge for Doreen, don't listen to him, KILL him!*

But if I was being used, I wanted to find out *why*. Lucifer had told me none of this. *Japhrimel* had told me none of this. Which brought up the question of what they really wanted—what deeper game was being played here? I'd wondered why they had let him roam around earth for fifty years.

"Come." He led me through the lab, out another tech-locked door, and into a hallway that was more like a colonnade, an enclosed garden lying still and steamy under the Nuevo Rio rain, an assault after the climate control of the lab room. He turned to his left and I followed numbly, the door almost clipping my bootheels.

This garden was lit with a kind of orange glow—the light pollution from the city. He stopped at a techless door, this one white and etched with a strange design of an unearthly bird done in gold leaf. Santino turned to face me, and I shuffled back quickly, raising my blade. He laughed, a high-pitched giggle that echoed my nightmares and made my heart turn to dumb ice in my chest.

"We are an old and tired race, Dante, and our children are few and far between. Almost none are born without Lucifer's intervention, and he is *most* stingy in giving his help. To breed, a demon must go to the Prince as a supplicant." The black teardrops over his eyes somehow managed to convey the impression of a wide smile. "You want to kill me, Dante, because I took those precious human lives. But those lives were taken in service to a greater good—breaking the hold the Prince of Darkness has on your world and mine. I've finally done it, Dante. I've birthed a child that can challenge the Prince himself." He reached behind his back, twisted the doorknob, and backed into the room. "Come and see."

I followed him, cautiously. *Don't trust him, Dante! Kill him now! Kill him or run!*

It was a nursery. Slices of dim light fell through iron bars on the windows. Toys scattered across the hardwood floor, and plush rugs too. I saw a rocking horse, and a set of chairs around a table low enough for a little person. Wooden blocks lay scattered near a fireplace. And on the other side of the room, Santino stalked toward a low queen-sized bedstead wreathed in mosquito netting.

I followed, my boots occasionally kicking a small plush animal. *Dear gods,* I thought, *he has children here? What kind of kids are raised by a demon?*

"Lucifer rules because he is powerful," Santino whispered, his voice buzzing with secrecy. "But not only that—he rules because he is *Androgyne,* almost like a queen bee, capable of reproducing. It took me forty-five human years, but I finally found out how to birth another demon Androgyne. All it takes is the proper genetic material and engineering, Dante." He paused, maybe for effect. "Engineering by the scientist Lucifer used to create humanity in the first place—and material taken from a *sedayeen,* perhaps. A human psionic with the ability to heal, an almost-direct descendant of the *A'nankimel*—the demons that loved human women, and raised families with them eons ago. Until Lucifer, fearing the birth of an Androgyne on earth, destroyed them."

It made a twisted kind of sense. I approached the bed slowly, step by step. Needing to see.

"Demon genes don't lose their potency as human genes do," he whispered. "Witness the growth of human psychic powers, the fantastic blossoming of those powers during the Awakening—"

"Shut up." I sounded choked.

In the bed, under the smooth expensive sheet, was a pale-haired little girl about five years old sleeping the sleep of childhood innocence. Her long hair tangled over the pillow; I heard the faint whistle of her breathing. I tasted salt, and bitter ash. I knew that face—I had seen it before.

She lay on her back, one chubby arm upflung. Her forehead was odd, because there was a mark that glittered softly green on the smooth skin. My cheek started to burn. *An emerald. I wondered why Lucifer had one.* I could tell this emerald wasn't implanted—it was too smoothly and sheerly a part of her skin. Almost like a jeweled growth. It made me deeply, unsteadily sick to think that maybe my own emerald was an echo.

"There are two branches of human psionics that are almost directly descended from the *A'nankimel,* with the necessary recessive genes for my purposes. One branch is the *sedayeen,* who hold the mystery of Life. The other..." He paused again as I stared at the child on the bed.

The child that wore Doreen's young face.

"The other," Santino said, "is the Necromance."

"This is —" My voice was a dry husk. "This is why you —"

"This is why I took samples," he said softly, persuasively. "Who do you think rules both worlds, Dante? Who do you think is the king of all you survey? It's *him*. We are all his slaves. And I have the Egg, and the child that can topple him from his throne."

I swallowed, heard the dry click of my throat. "You killed her for *this*?" I rasped, and my eyes tore away from her sleeping face to Santino's grinning mask.

"Yes," he said. "I made a mistake, though. I shouldn't have killed her. I needed a human incubator, once I harvested the marrow and discovered she had all the requisite characteristics. It took all the cash and illegal gene-splicing that the Corvin Family could supply me with to bring this little one to pass. The human governments are too slow. But I did it. I found the shining path of genes that even Lucifer couldn't find with all his bloody tinkering. Now that I know *how*, I don't have to kill. All I need are female *sedayeen*—and Necromances—of certain Power, to blend with the codex in the Egg. I can make as many Androgynes as I want, capable of reproducing—"

"You killed her for *this*?" My voice rose. The child on the bed didn't stir. I heard her even breathing, slightly whistling through the nose. She slept like a human child, with deep complete trust.

"Think of it, Dante," he said. Softly, persuasively as Lucifer himself. "You can be the mother of a new race that will topple Lucifer from his throne. You'll be the new Madonna. Your every need—"

I backed up, kicking a small stuffed toy. "You killed her for *this*." I could say nothing else.

"What is one small human life compared to freedom, Dante?" He stepped forward. I raised my sword yet again. The blue glow from the blade intensified, and Santino flinched. It was only a small twitch, but I saw it.

A blessed blade will hurt him, at least, I thought. I heard Japhrimel's voice—*she believes.* Of course I believed—I *saw* the gods, I saw the Lord of Death up close. I had no choice but to believe. And that belief itself could be a weapon.

Maybe a blessed blade can even kill him, I thought.

"You didn't just kill Doreen. You slaughtered her while you laughed," I said. "You're no more a scientist than any other lunatic. You're just a different species of psycho, that's all." *There's a window behind me. Oh, gods. Oh dear gods.*

He waved his long elegant fingers, as if I were bothering him with trifles. Just like a fucking demon. "They were the mothers of the future, they died for a *reason*. Don't you understand? *Freedom*, Dante. For demon and human alike. No more Prince of Lies behind the scenes, everyone bowing and scraping to his whim—"

I was about to break for the window when the air pressure changed. Thunder boomed. The mark on my shoulder gave another screaming twinge.

Japhrimel.My heart leapt.

Santino's face twisted into a mask of rage. He lunged for me so quickly I barely saw him move. My sword jerked, blurring down as I threw myself sideways and back, toward the open window. His claws clanged off the blade. There was another shuddering impact, and I heard the unmistakable sound of Japhrimel's roar. The sound tore the air and left it bleeding. Santino snarled, whirling with balletic grace. He bolted for the bed and I scrambled forward, thinking of his claws and the little girl. I was too slow. Shock and the recent loss of Power and the swimming weakness dragged me down.

He scooped up an armful of bedding and the child's slight form, and his clawed hand came up. Metal flashed. The impact caught me high in the chest, the coughing roar of a projectile weapon splitting the air, my boots dragging along the floor in slow motion, my katana clanging on hardwood. I fell, my head cracking against something unforgiving—maybe one of the blocks.

How strange, I thought. *He shot me. Why did he shoot me? You'd think a demon would be more creative.*

I lay there, stunned, for what seemed like a long muffled eternity. Then I tried to roll onto my side. A bubble of something warm burst on my lips. I heard footsteps. Plasbolts. And Japhrimel's scream of agony. Pain bloomed in my chest, a hideous flower.

More footsteps. I tried to roll onto my side again. No dice. Just more pain. Bubbling on my lips—

—blood it's blood I'm dying, I'm dying—

"Oh, my God. Oh, God. He shot her, he *shot* her—" Jace's voice, high and breathless. "Goddammit, *do* something!"

A growled curse in a language I didn't know. But I knew the voice. A gigantic grinding shock against my chest.

"—leave me," Japhrimel snarled. "You will *not* leave me to wander the earth alone—*breathe*, damn you, breathe!"

Another shock, smashing through my bones. My left shoulder, torn from its socket, liquid fire in my veins. I gasped. Darkness tingled on the edges of my vision. I smelled flowers, and blood, and the musky smell of demon, drenching and absolute.

"You will not leave me," Japhrimel said. "You will *not*."

I tried to tell him to chase Santino, to kill him, to save the little girl—but before I could, Death chewed me with diamond teeth and swallowed me just as I hitched in breath to scream.

CHAPTER 37

A voice, reaching into the darkness.

I stood on the bridge, irresolute, my feet bare against cold stone. I felt the familiar chill creeping up my fingers, up my arms.

My emerald flashed as the souls fluttered past me, streaming over the bridge. The cocoon of light holding me safely on the bridge dimmed.

Why was I here? I wasn't pulling a soul back. Was I? I could not remember.

I looked at the other side of the bridge, the other side of the great Hall. The blue crystal walls rang softly, whispering a song I almost understood. I could feel it pressing in upon me, that great comprehension of Death's secret, the mother language from which all Necromance chants derived. The current of souls pushed at me, the emerald's light weakening, my cocoon of safety shrinking.

Yet that voice cajoled, pressed, demanded. I saw the god, His form shimmering between a slender Egyptian dog and some other form, a shape of darkness that seemed to run like ink on wet paper even as I looked at it.

My lips shaped the god's name, but the syllables sounded alien. The crystal walls shuddered, and for a moment I saw stone, a great grim drafty stone hall, with a dour-faced King upon a throne at the far end. The throne was crusted with gems, glittering madly, and at the King's side sat a Queen with a face like springtime. I felt my mouth shaping alien words, desperation beating in my throat. I wanted so badly to understand the secret language, to feel the clasp of the god's arms around me as I laid my head on His chest and let the weight of living slip from me—

BOOM.

The sound startled me. It seemed to take forever for me to turn around. Before I could, the sound came again, as if a gong was being beaten, a brazen sound, pulling me back.

BOOM.

I struggled as if through syrup. I wanted to stay.

I wanted to stay dead.

BOOM.

One of the souls streaming past me halted, held up a pale hand. Formless as all souls were, a crystal drapery of unique energy, still it seemed I knew it, could put a face on it.

BOOM.

"Go back," it said. "Go back."

BOOM.

I opened my mouth to protest. Shimmering, the soul brushed my cheek.

BOOMBOOM.

"Go back," Doreen said. "Save my daughter. Go back."

BOOMBOOM. BOOMBOOM.

Then I understood it was not a gong or a brass bell. It was my heart, and I was called back to the world.

Dizziness. Cold seeping up my arms. Voices.

"Call her back!" Eddie, yelling, the bass in his voice rattling my bones.

My heartbeat thudded in my ears. To be forced back into a body was excruciating, even worse than being shot.

"Dante!" Japhrimel, howling.

"Danny! *Danny!*" Jace screaming at the same time. Cacophony. "Let me *go—*"

Scorching pressed against the side of my face. A hand.

Gabe's chant stopped, the last throbbing syllable shattering inside my head. I gasped a breath like knives. My chest hurt.

A great scalding wave of Power lashed me. I cried out, weakly, convulsing.

"Do not leave me," Japhrimel husked. "Do not leave me, Dante."

"Goddamn you, Eddie," Jace hissed, "let me *go* or I will *kill* you."

Light struck my eyes like a newborn's. I reacted the same way, screaming, raw from the lash of Japhrimel's Power and Gabe's Necromance. Japhrimel closed his arms around me and rested his chin on my head. I gasped, screamed again, muffled against his chest. The scream degenerated into sobbing. I cried because I had been wrong, and because I'd been right. I cried because the comfort of death was denied me. I cried because I had been dragged back into my weary body and shackled again.

And I cried in relief, clinging to Japhrimel the demon. He was solid and warm and *real*, and I did not want to let go.

CHAPTER 38

I was weak but lucid by the time we got back to Jace's mansion.

Eddie covered Jace with a plasgun most of the time. Gabe, paper-pale with exhaustion and bloody all over (most of it was mine), piloted the hover. I didn't ask where it had come from—if it was Jace's, it was all right, if it wasn't, I didn't want to know. All three of them—Gabe, Eddie, Jace—looked as if they had been through the grinder. Eddie's left arm hung limply by his side, Jace's face was covered in blood from a scalp wound and most of his shirt was torn off, stripes criss-crossing his torso. Gabe's clothes were tattered, filthy, smelling of smoke and blood and something suspiciously like offal.

Japhrimel carried me. His face was shuttered, closed, his eyes dark, a smear of my blood on one cheek. Santino had shot me in the chest. Otherwise, his dark coat was pristine. He occasionally stroked my cheek, sometimes glancing at Jace while he did so.

I didn't want to know. I had the uncomfortable feeling I'd find out soon enough.

I was too tired to think. My brain reeled drunkenly from one thought to the next, no logic, nothing but shock.

The city lay under a pall of smoke. It looked as if a full-scale riot had gone down. I saw several craters, but the rain had intensified and was drowning the fires. The aroma of burning filled the air, even inside the hover. When we touched down at Jace's, it was a relief.

Inside, Gabe herded us all into a sitting room done in light blue and cream. Eddie shoved Jace down on a tasteful couch. *I hope he searched this room,* I thought, tiredly, *Jace could have a weapon stashed in here.*

I shivered. It would be a while before I took another Necromance job. If I went back to the borders of the land of Death too soon I would perhaps be unable to come back, training or no training.

"Okay," Gabe said, stalking across the room to a walnut highboy and tossing it open to reveal liquor bottles, "I need a motherfucking drink."

I cleared my throat. "Me, too," I said, the first words out of my mouth since leaving Santino's hideaway. "We need to move quickly," I said, as Japhrimel carried me to the couch facing Jace's. Instead of setting me down, he simply dropped gracefully down himself, still holding me. A little rearranging and I found myself in his lap, cuddled against him like a child.

A child. I shuddered at the thought. But it was comforting, his heat, and the smell of him.

Gabe groaned. "Give me a minute, Danny. I just found out one of my friends is a fucking traitor and yanked you out of Death's arms. At least let me have a bourbon in peace."

I cleared my throat. "Pour me one," I said, husky, my voice almost refusing to obey me. "We've got big-time problems."

"I would never have guessed," Eddie growled. "You get into more fucking trouble, Valentine. That thing nearly burned down the entire goddamn city looking for you."

I barely had the courage to look up at Japhrimel's face. "You did that?" I asked.

He shrugged. "I had to find you," he said, simply.

I let it go. Instead, I started telling my story with the accompaniment of rain smacking the windows. Gabe knew me well enough not to interrupt, and Eddie watched Jace. Halfway through, Gabe handed me a glass of bourbon and settled down stiffly in a chair, her split lip and black eyes combining to turn her thoughtful expression into sadness. I downed the liquor, coughing as it burned the back of my throat, then continuing. By the time I got to the child sleeping in the bedroom, Japhrimel's eyes were incandescent. He had turned slowly to stone underneath me.

When I finished, Gabe drained the rest of her drink. Silence stretched through the room, broken by a low rattle of thunder.

Then she leapt to her feet and hurled her glass across the room, letting out a scream as sharp as a falcon's cry. The shattering glass didn't make me jump, but the scream came close.

She half-whirled, and pinned Jace with an accusing glare. "*Traitor!*" she hissed. "You *knew!*"

"I didn't know a goddamn thing—" he began. Eddie growled.

"Let him talk," I said, quietly, but with a note of finality that cut across the Skinlin's rumbling. "And while he does that, Gabe, can you take a look at Eddie's arm?"

They all stared at me for a moment. Then Gabe moved stiffly to the hedgewitch and touched his shoulder. Some unspoken agreement seemed to pass between them, and Eddie's shoulders sagged just a little. More thunder crawled across the roof of the sky. I was so tired that for once it didn't hurt me to see Gabe press her lips to Eddie's forehead—but I did look away. I looked at Jace, who was paper-pale, the tic of rage flicking in his cheek.

"Talk fast," I told him. "Before I decide it was a bad idea to do that."

"I didn't know a goddamn thing," he said, harshly. Gabe started poking at Eddie's arm, and I felt the vibration of her Power start. She was doing a healing. I shuddered—every time she pulled on Power, it was like another astringent stripe against my abraded psyche. She had pulled me back from Death.

"Why didn't you tell me you were a blood Corvin?" I asked. *Are you part demon, Jace?* The question trembled on my lips. My skin crawled.

"I'm *not*," he said, sagging into the couch back. His hair was matted with blood and water. We were a sorry-looking group—except for Japhrimel, who was untouched except for the swipe of my blood on his cheek. "I was *adopted* by one of the Four Uncles—Sargon Corvin's adopted sons—because of my psi potential. That's what gets you into the Corvins—psi. I hated every goddamn minute of it, Danny. Once Deke Corvin died I made my escape and I ran as far as I could...and then I met you."

"You knew Sargon Corvin, the head of your fucking Mob Family, was Santino?" I asked, very clearly.

"No," he answered. "Gods, no. I swear on my staff, I had no idea. Nobody's seen Sargon for years except the older uncles—they give all the orders, supposedly from him. I thought the great Sargon was a motherfucking myth, Danny. Nobody was allowed into the Inner Complex—where we found you. That's where all the gene research went down, they were heavy into illegal augments and gene splices because it made money—that's what I knew. I didn't know. I thought Sargon was after you for revenge, since my street war with them killed all three of the surviving Uncles. They died hard, too. I've had my hands full while you were up in Saint City moping." He dropped his head back, leaning against the couch, and swallowed, his Adam's apple bobbing. "He would know that the only way to hurt me would be to kill you, Danny. That's why I left you, and why I insisted you stay here during this little hunt of yours."

"Why didn't you tell me you were a Corvin? You should have told me." I tried not to sound hurt and failed miserably. I was just too tired.

He laughed, dropping his chin to look at me. "Everyone knows how you feel about the Mob, baby. I never would have gotten past your front door."

"So you lied to me."

"I love you, Danny," he said, closing his eyes and tipping his head back onto the couch. Dark circles stood out all the way around his eyes. He was unshaven, gaunt. "I didn't have a *choice*. Not if I wanted to stay clean; if I'd told you who I was, you would have ditched me. I wanted to be clean for you. I was *out*, until you went on the Morrix job. They threatened to kill you. The only thing I could do was disappear and hope they would leave *you* alone." He sighed. "Sargon's been too busy to bother with you, I'd guess, while he perfected this fucking process of his and I slipped my chain and started giving him trouble. Until you came back and shoved yourself in his face again. I didn't *know*, Danny. If I had known, I would have killed him myself. Or tried to, at least. Why don't you ask your pet demon what he knows about all this?"

"Watch your mouth, *human*," Japhrimel said quietly, his tone completely cold. "Did the Prince know that Santino has gone so far as to create an Androgyne, he would have brought Hellesvront— Hell-on-Earth—to bear on this Corvin Family, and wiped them from existence. This affects him far more than it affects you."

Jace snorted and opened his mouth. "Shut up," I said. "Just shut up."

Japhrimel lifted his free hand and stroked my hair back from my face. "You should rest, Dante."

"What about the little girl?" I asked, craning my neck to look at his face. "Did you know Santino was trying to breed a new kind of demon?"

"Not a new kind of demon," Japhrimel said. "An extremely rare kind of demon. Lucifer is the Prime, the first Androgyne from whom all demons are descended—the younger Androgynes are either his vassals or his lovers. It is not a thing spoken of to humans."

I let out a long sigh. I was so damnably tired, my eyelids felt like lead. "So you knew. What does it mean, Japhrimel? I'm tired, and I died back there. I'm feeling kind of stupid, spell it out for me."

"The Egg is a sigil of the Prince's reign," Japhrimel said. "It holds the Prince's genetic codex and a portion of his Power—so much Power that he cannot leave Hell without it. Santino can access the genetic codex by virtue of his function as one of Lucifer's genetic scientists, but the Power locked inside the Egg is not his to use. If another Androgyne unlocks the Egg, the balance of power in Hell itself will shift. The Androgyne with the Egg will control Hell—and who will control the Androgyne?"

"Santino," I breathed. I believed it. I didn't need the canisters or the vision of the little girl with Doreen's face to convince me any more than I already was. Demons played with genetics the way they played with technology—some scientists said our own genes were proof of that. It was one of the greatest scientific mysteries, hotly disputed and contested by Magi and geneticists—could demons theoretically interbreed with humans? Only no demon had done so for thousands of years, if they ever had—if you could believe the old stories about demons marrying human women and giants roaming the earth.

I thought of the rows and rows of canisters and shuddered. Santino had figured out how to make another Lucifer, a Lucifer he could use for his own ends? A lovely little malleable, controllable genetic copy of Lucifer—using Doreen's genetic material in the process.

And now he wanted to use mine. Or maybe just my body as an "incubator." *You could be the new Madonna,* his voice whispered in my memory, soft and chillingly inhuman.

I shuddered. I had escaped being assigned as a breeder in Rigger Hall; I didn't want to be turned into one now for a crazed demon. And what about other *sedayeen* or Necromances, possibly kidnapped and forced to incubate more of the filthy little things?

I should have been angry. Japhrimel had omitted to tell me far more than Jace had, but I only felt a weary gratefulness that the demon was here—a gratefulness I didn't want to examine more closely. Silence stretched through the room. Eddie hissed a curse between his teeth, and Gabe murmured an apology, bandaging his arm.

"He's playing for control of Hell itself," the demon said quietly. "And if that happens, he will gain control of your world as well."

"He says it's for freedom," I answered. Exhaustion pulled at my arms and legs, wrapped my brain in cotton wool.

"Freedom for Vardimal, perhaps." Japhrimel shrugged. The movement made my head loll against his shoulder.

I closed my eyes. It was so hard to think with exhaustion weighing me down.

"So what now?" Gabe said.

"Now I get a couple hours of sleep, and I do what I should have done in the first place."

"And what is that?" Japhrimel didn't move, but his arms tightened slightly. If I hadn't been so tired, I might have thought about that.

Sleep was stalking me a little more gently than Death had. It was the expected reaction; most people fell into a deep sleep after being yanked back from death. It was the psyche's method of self-defense, trying to come to terms with brushing the Infinite. "I'm going to get up, and find my sword, and hunt the motherfucker down. Alone."

"Not alone," Gabe said. "We'll tie you up if we have to, Danny. Don't start that again."

I was about to tell her to back the fuck off when I passed out. The last thing I heard was Japhrimel's voice. "If I did not leave her at Death's door, I would not leave her now. I will take her to bed."

CHAPTER 39

I slept for twenty-eight hours.

Plenty of time for Santino to get away.

When I finally surfaced, it was to find myself tucked naked into a large dark-green bed. The climate control was on, so the room was cool, even though fierce early-morning sunlight stabbed through the windows. I blinked at the light, propping myself up on my elbows.

My entire body ached, the reverberation of the plasgun bolt and Power backlash. I'd pushed myself far beyond the limits of pain-free Power use. I would be lucky to escape a migraine in the next twenty-four hours.

My shoulder didn't ache, though. I touched the scarring of Japhrimel's mark and had to steel myself against a wave of painful nausea.

"I'm here," he said, and turned from the window. I hadn't seen him there, maybe dazzled by the sunlight. Maybe he hadn't wanted to be seen. "Rest, Dante."

"I can't rest," I said, tasting morning in my mouth. "Santino—"

"He's being tracked. You will not be helpful if you do not rest." He approached the bed silently, his black coat floating on the sunlight. "Events are moving, Dante. The Prince, now that he knows what Santino was attempting, has placed the full resources of Hellesvront under my control. Every Hell-on-Earth agent is looking for Santino. He will not long escape our attention."

I sat up the rest of the way, gingerly, and rubbed at my eyes. "Unless he goes where there aren't any people," I said. "Human agents aren't any good if he stays out of sight like he's been doing for the past fifty years." And besides, he was *mine*. I'd started this hunt, I was going to finish it.

He shrugged. "Not all the agents are human. Vardimal is a scavenger, despite his contempt for humans. He needs people, hungers for them. Hellesvront will find him."

"What the hell are the demon police getting involved for? They can't *kill* him. I should know, I tried. Where are the others?" I asked, squinting up at him. I wanted to see his face, couldn't.

"The other Necromance and the earth-witch are sleeping. Your former lover is sealed in a spare room, but otherwise unharmed." Japhrimel's tone changed slightly. He sounded... disdainful. His eyes glowed with a light of their own. Backlit by the sun, he looked like a shadow with bright eyes. "I would speak with you of something else, Dante."

"If Vardimal's a scavenger, what does that make you?"

"I am of the Greater Flight, he is of the Lesser. I am not bound by his hungers." Japhrimel shrugged, but the movement wasn't as fluid as it usually was.

"Is that why you're the Devil's assassin?"

He bared his teeth in a facsimile of a pained grin. "I am the Prince's assassin because I am able to kill my brothers and sisters without qualm, Dante. And I am his assassin because he trusts me to do his bidding. I would speak to you of—"

I didn't want to know. "Is it true?" I asked him. "*Sedayeen* and Necromances—is it true?"

He was silent for a long time. Then, "It is true; *sedayeen* and Necromances do carry recessive genes closely related to demons. I would speak to you about—"

Gods. I'm human, I thought. *I'm not a demon. I know I'm human.*
"Later," I said, and slid my feet out of the bed. The blessed warmth of
the covers was matched only by the blessed coolness of the climate
control. "Get the others. We've got work to do."

"You should eat something," he said, stepping back slightly.
Retreating into the sunlight. "Please."

"I'll make you a deal." I gained my feet in a rush, too happy to be
vertical to care if I was naked. Besides, he was a demon, he'd probably seen plenty of naked women before. "You get the others here by
the time I get out of the shower, and I'll eat breakfast while we plan."
I headed for the bathroom, heard his sharp intake of breath.
"What?"

I stopped, looking over my shoulder. My knees were shaky, but I
felt surprisingly good despite having been shot and dragged back
from death.

"Your...scars." Japhrimel's voice was flat again.

"They don't hurt anymore," I lied. "It was a long time ago. Look,
Japh—"

"Who? Who did that to you?" Now there was a tinge of something else in his voice. Was it anger?

It was my turn to shrug. "It was a long time ago, Japhrimel. The...
the person who did that is dead. Get the others. I'll have breakfast
while we plan." I forced myself to take another step toward the bathroom. Another. *That's what you get for walking around naked in
front of a demon,* I thought, and managed to make it to the bathroom,
flicked on the light, and shut the door behind me before I looked
down at the other mass of claw scars on my belly. My ribs stood out,
each one defined, my hipbones sticking out sharply. I'd lost weight.

I blew out a long whistling sigh between my teeth. My legs trembled. I looked up, meeting my own eyes in the mirror. I'd faced Santino again, and survived.

Miracles did happen.

"Maybe this job won't kill me," I whispered, and tore my eyes
away from my gaunt face to go take a shower.

Gabe looked a lot better, especially with her long dark hair clean and
pulled back. Eddie still favored one arm, but Gabe's healing charm
had apparently sped his recovery—as well as hers. Her black eyes
were now a yellow-green raccoon mask, and her split lip looked less
angry.

Jace was unshaven and moving a little stiffly, but his eyes were clear. He lowered himself cautiously into the chair Japhrimel placed for him. Gabe didn't even spare him a look. Eddie, shaggy and direct as ever, stared at him for a full twenty seconds, lip lifting in a silent snarl.

I sat cross-legged on the bed. It felt good to be dressed in clean clothes, and felt even better to be clean myself, my hair damp from the shower and smelling like sandalwood. Japhrimel, expressionless, produced my katana. The sheath was lost, so I balanced naked metal across my knees. "Okay," I said, once we'd all settled in. "Breakfast is due up in a quarter-hour. Japhrimel's checked the staff here and says they're trustworthy. I'm going to start tracking antino as soon as—"

"Wait a minute." Gabe held up her hand. "How in Hades are you going to find him without alerting him? He's got a day's head start, and he's a demon—Magi magick might find him, but if he's on his guard it might just put him in a snit. And we can't afford to have you come down with another case of backlash. There's a limit to the amount of abuse you can take, Danny—*despite* what you seem to think."

I held up my hand. "Gabe," I said with excessive patience, "we may not be able to track *him*, even with Dake's little toy. But he's got the kid. And the kid's at least half Doreen; I shared my mind and my bed with her. I can find the kid, we're bound by Doreen's blood. Where she is, Santino will be."

Gabe shrugged. She glanced at Jace, seemed about to say something, and stopped.

"What about this kid?" Eddie asked suddenly. "What the demons gonna do with her?"

I looked up at Japhrimel, who shrugged. His eyes darkened, more strange runic patterns slipping through their depths—but he looked down at the floor, as if avoiding my gaze. "The Prince will perhaps take her as a lover," he said, "or as a vassal. Androgynes are precious, and she is far too young to challenge his rule."

"Like hell," I said. "I'll take care of the kid. I owe it to Doreen. Lucifer didn't contract me to bring the kid back, he contracted me to kill Santino and return this Egg thing. He doesn't even need to know about the kid. You haven't told him, have you, Japhrimel?"

Please tell me I've guessed right and he hasn't told Lucifer about the kid.

Silence crawled through the room.

"You would ask me to lie to the Prince," Japhrimel said, finally. He stood at the side of the bed, his head down, his eyes hidden, hands clasped behind his back. His coat rustled slightly; I wondered again why he wore it.

"You can't trust a demon, Danny," Jace piped up. I ignored him, watching Japhrimel. His reaction told me he'd kept his mouth shut. If he hadn't told Lucifer about the little girl, he had to have guessed I would ask him not to.

He finally tilted his head back up, his green eyes meeting mine for a long moment. It wasn't hard to hold his gaze anymore. "I have not...told Lucifer of the child, only that Vardimal was attempting to create an Androgyne. I did not think it wise, as Lucifer would perhaps seek a different means of effecting Santino's capture. That would endanger you, Dante." He paused, his eyes holding mine. *Here it comes,* I thought, amazed I'd been able to predict him for once. "However, to *lie* to the Prince after Santino is dead...I will do as you ask," he said, "but in return, I will ask a price."

I shrugged. "I expected as much." My throat went dry. "What price?"

"I will tell you when the time comes," he said. "It is nothing you cannot pay."

"Danny—" Jace sat bolt upright.

"Shut up, Jace," I said, my eyes fixed on the demon. "All right, Japhrimel. It's a deal. Gods grant I don't regret it."

"I would speak with you privately, Mistress," he said, formally, nodding slightly. That managed to hurt my feelings—so we were back to *Mistress,* were we?

You will not leave me to wander the earth alone. Had he really said that, or had it been some kind of near-death hallucination?

I shook the thought away, hair sliding over my shoulders. "Soon enough. Gabe, I need you and Eddie at full strength. Do what you have to do to get there. We're hitting the trail soon as possible. Before twelve hours I need a work-up of every bit of munitions we can beg borrow or steal. *Everything.* Plasguns, assault rifles, projectile guns, explosives, everything. Eddie, I need as many *golem'ai* as you can make before we leave—and firestarters, too. You're the best Skinlin I know, and the mud-things will even the odds for us. Jace—" He flinched as I said his name, his shoulders hunching protectively. "Get yourself up to full strength and outfit us. We need transport, supplies, and passports into Mob Circle."

"Mob Circle?" Eddie actually sputtered. "Are you *crazy*?"

"We can't travel everywhere in the world just on a hunt," I said. "If Santino goes into any Freetowns, Mob Circle passports will give us some kind of protection and a place to sleep. Can you do that, Jace?"

He was paler than I'd ever seen him. "You'd trust me?" he asked, his blue eyes stuttering up to mine then sliding away, as if he couldn't stand to look at my face. "You'd trust me to do that?"

"I'm not going to *forgive* you," I told him. "I'm just going to overlook the fact that you took up a year and a half of my life with a complete lie. You do this for me, and we're even, your debt's paid. After this job, I never want to see your face again. If I see you after this is over, I'll fucking kill you—but if you help me take Santino down, I'll let you go your own way. Alive. All accounts balanced."

"Danny—" he began.

"You lied to me," I hissed. "Every time you touched me, it was a lie. And you didn't come clean when I came here, either—you *kept* lying to me. What, were you thinking I'd never find out?"

"You never would have—" he began.

"Well, we'll never know now, will we? I never had the chance." I shook my head, looking away to where the sheaf of sunlight fell into the green room, pure light glowing on every surface. It was nothing like the clear light of Death, but it was close enough that my heart twisted. The room was beautiful, clean, and made my entire body hurt. I wanted to be home, with Santino dead and the Devil's lies and little games out of my life. "Either you do this for me, or I'll kill you, Jace. It's that simple."

I don't know if it was my level tone or the way my face felt frozen, or maybe it was just the way my fingers touched the katana's hilt, but Jace believed me. He stared at the floor, his jaw working.

"Fine," he finally said. "If that's the way you want it, that's the way we'll play it."

"Good." I looked up at Japhrimel, who was wearing a faintly startled expression. "Japhrimel?"

He shrugged again, one of those faint, evocative movements. Nothing to add or subtract, and he wouldn't talk to me in front of them. Fine.

"Okay," I said. "That about covers it. Let's get moving."

Jace hitched himself up to his feet with a single measuring glance at Eddie. The Skinlin sat absolutely still, his eyes slitted, his hair tangling over his forehead. "I'll start working on passports and supplies," Jace said. "The staff will bring you breakfast, and whatever else you need."

I nodded.

He strode from the room without giving me a second glance.

Gabe whistled, shaking her head. "Are you crazy?" she said. "What if he's still working for Santino?"

"He's not. If he was, we'd all be dead." I sighed.

"You're letting him off easy," Eddie snarled.

I knew it. Ten years ago I might have gone after Jace just on principle. But I was just too tired. And the vision of all those canisters behind that glass shield, Santino's claws skritching against the glass, wouldn't go away. So much death, who was I to add to it? I was a Necromance. It was my job to bring people back. I was so tired of killing.

"Danny?" Eddie snapped his fingers to get my attention. "You're lettin' him off easy. You should fuck him up at the least, break a few bones. He—"

"Relax, Eddie," Gabe broke in, reaching out with her bare toes to rub his knee. "She knows what she's doing. The munitions aren't for a frontal assault on Santino, are they, sweets?"

"Of course not," I said. "They're for erasing whatever's left of the Corvins from the face of the earth. And Jace is going to do it himself. If he fails, we don't get any blowback, because Jace will be dead and his Family just another failed attempt at cutting out turf. If he succeeds, Santino doesn't have a Mob Family to do his dirty work, I'm free of the Corvin Family for good—and Jace will owe me a big-ass favor, since he'll be free too. *Really* free, not just street-war free."

"The *golem'ai* and the firestarters?" Eddie asked, comprehension dawning over his hairy face.

I suppressed a shudder. The *golem'ai*—semisentient mud creatures a Skinlin could create from organic matter and pure magick— made my skin crawl. "Those," I said, "are for Santino."

CHAPTER 40

We had a nice, if hurried, breakfast; the thick Nuevo Rio coffee-with-chicory did a good deal to dispel the cobwebs and ease my pounding head. Japhrimel was oddly silent, watching me eat, occasionally walking to the window and gazing out, his hands clasped behind his back. I didn't want to know. His silence seemed to infect all of us. Maybe there was just nothing left to say. The maids who came to clear away breakfast were both pale, their hands trembling, stealing little glances at me out of the corners of their eyes.

I couldn't even work up enough steam to care. You'd think they'd be used to psions, working for a Shaman.

I finally sent Gabe and Eddie to do their work and yawned, looking down at my katana. Oddly enough, the blade didn't seem to be reacting to Japhrimel's presence — it should have been spitting glowing blue as it had every other time he'd touched it.

Then again, after dealing with Santino and almost dying there was precious little Power left in the steel. I'd have to recharge before I could make my blade burn again. It was a kind of torture — the longer we waited, the more prepared we were to kick Santino's ass, but the more time he had to dig himself into a bolthole it would cost us blood to crack.

The door shut behind Eddie, and Japhrimel turned on his heel, sunlight falling into the bottomless dark of his coat.

"Okay." I slid my feet off the bed and stood up, the katana whirling in an ellipse that ended up with the blade safely tucked behind my arm, the hilt loosely clasped in my hand and pointed downward. "You've been acting weird, even for a demon. What's up?"

He shook his head, light moving over the planes of his face. I took a closer look.

I'd thought he was plain, his face saturnine and almost ugly. I'd never noticed the exact arch of his eyebrows, his thin mouth half-quirked into a smile, or the high impossible arcs of his cheekbones. It was nothing to compare to Lucifer's beauty, of course... but he was actually kind of easy on the eyes. "Spit it out," I persisted. "You said you had something to discuss with me?" My bare feet curled against the hardwood floor, and I shivered. I was so used to the blanket of Nuevo Rio heat by now that the climate control was a little chilly.

Japhrimel took one step toward me. Then another. His eyes burned, seeming to make the sunlight on his face slightly green.

He approached slowly, his hands clasped behind his back, and finally ended up looming over me, less than a foot away. The musk smell of demon drenched me, his aura sliding over mine. I tilted my head back to look up into his face. "Well?"

He shook his head again. Then he unclasped his hands. His left hand came up, cupped my right shoulder, heat scorching through the material of my shirt. His eyes caught mine.

My heart gave a huge thudding leap. "Japhrimel?" I asked.

He slid his left hand down my right arm, and his fingers curled over mine. He took the katana's hilt from my hand, the sword chimed against the floor. I would have lunged for it, but his eyes held mine in a cage of emerald light. "Dante," he answered.

His voice was no longer the robotic, uninflected flatline it had been before. Instead, he sounded…husky, as if he had something caught in his throat. I blinked.

"Are you—" I began to ask him if he was all right, but his eyes flared and the words died in my throat. He didn't sound okay.

Then, the crowning absurdity—he slowly, so slowly, dropped down to his knees, his hand still holding mine. He wrapped his other arm around me and buried his face in my belly.

Nothing in my life had ever prepared me for this.

I stood rigid, uncertain. Then I lifted my free hand, and smoothed the rough inky silk of his hair. "Japhrimel." I said, again. "What—"

"I failed," he said, his breath blurring hot through my shirt to touch my skin. I barely understood him, his voice was so muffled; he pressed against me like a cat or a child. "I *failed* you."

"What are you *talking* about?" My own voice refused to work properly. Instead, I sounded like I had something lodged in my windpipe, strangling my words, making me breathless.

He looked up, his arm still pressing me forward. "I knew you were not dead," he said, his eyes blazing so brightly I almost expected to smell scorching in the air. "For I was not returned to Hell. Yet I did not know what Vardimal would do to you—keep you alive to torture you, or wait until I reached you before he killed you. I *did not know,* Dante. I failed to protect you, and you were taken."

"It's all right," I whispered. "Look, you couldn't know they'd paste me with a plasgun bolt. Even you can't outrun one of those. It's not your fault, Japhrimel."

"I found myself faced with a vision of an existence without you, Dante. It was...unpleasant." His lips peeled back from his teeth in a pained snarl that tried to be a smile.

You will not leave me to wander the earth alone. His voice traced a rough line through my memory.

I smoothed his hair. The inky darkness was silky, slightly coarse, slipping through my fingers. "Hey," I said. "Don't worry about it. It's all right now."

I sounded awkward even to myself. *He's a demon, Danny. What is he doing?*

"You will hate me, Dante. It cannot be avoided."

A jagged laugh snapped out of me. "I don't hate you," I admitted. *Great, Danny. He's too old for you. He's not even human.*

But he came for me, I protested.

Only because he's got a stake in this. He's playing with you, Danny. He's playing. Nobody could ever —

I don't care, I thought. *He doesn't look like he's playing. I don't care.* "But you're a —"

"You must know," he said. "I am no longer demon."

What? I stared at him, my fingers stopping, curling into his hair. "What the *hell* are you talking about?"

"I am no longer demon," he repeated, slowly, looking up at me. He was queerly pale under the even golden tone of his skin. "I am Fallen. I am *A'nankimel*. I have set you as a seal upon my heart; I will not return to Hell." His arm tensed, and so did his fingers holding my right hand.

My mouth went dry. "Um," was my utterly profound response.

He waited, patient and expectant, staring up at my face.

I regained the power of speech in a spluttering rush. "You mean... what do you...I mean, I...um, why do you...ah. *What?*"

"I am yours," he said, slowly, as if spelling it out for an idiot.

"Why?" I could have kicked myself. *How do I get in these situations? I'm chasing one demon and I have another kneeling at my feet and oh my dear gods, what am I going to do?*

"Because you are the only being in eternity who has treated me as an equal," he said, his arm tightening a little more. My knees buckled slightly. "You have *trusted* me; you have even defended me to your precious friends. I have watched you, Dante, in daylight and in shadow, and I have found you fair."

"Um," I said again. "Japhrimel—"

"My price for silence to Lucifer is this: Do not send me from your side," he whispered, still watching my face. "When you have killed Santino, allow me to remain with you."

"Um," My brain seemed to be working through syrup. "Ah, well, you know, I can't have a demon hanging around."

"Why not?" he asked, logically enough. "You court Death, Dante. You have found nothing to live for; you walk alone. I have seen your loneliness, and it gives me pain. Besides, it seems you are foolhardy enough to need me."

It occurred to me that I should protest about this, but it was hard to find an objection in the soup my brain had become. Common sense warned me to be cautious—after all, he was a demon, and demons *lied*. That was the first rule in Magi and Ceremonial training— beings that weren't human had nonhuman ideas about the strict truth of any situation. What was in it for him?

And yet…He had stood behind me when I faced Lucas Villalobos. He'd tried to follow me into Death. And he'd burned down damn near a third of Nuevo Rio looking for me.

But Lucifer has him by the balls, too, I thought.

"What about your freedom?" I finally asked him.

"When we win my freedom, it is mine to do with as I will," he said. "I will stay with you, Dante. As long as you allow it, and per- haps after."

I chewed on my bottom lip, thinking about it. I had no way of knowing if he was telling the truth. "Why now? Why tell me this *now*?"

"I told you there was a way," he said. "I wish to give you a part of my Power, Dante, and I must do it quickly, before I become more *A'nankimel* than I already am. It will bind me to your side and your world will become my domain. There is only a short time for me to bond with you before I fall into darkness and a mortal death." His arm loosened a little, but I couldn't have gotten away if I tried, because he rose to his feet, my right hand still trapped in his left. I had to tip my head back to look at him. My heart pounded and my palms slipped with sweat, and I had the lunatic idea that maybe I would start screaming, once I got my breath back. Something about his eyes was making it difficult to breathe.

"Oh," I said, and wished I hadn't, because he smiled. It was a gentle smile, and my entire body seemed to recognize it.

His free hand came up, cupped the side of my face. "Courage, *hedaira*," he said, softly, his breath touching my cheek. Then he leaned down, and his mouth met mine.

It's said by the Magi that demons invented the arts of love, and I was tempted to believe it. The kiss tore through me, lightning filling my veins, the smell of him invading me, making me drunk. Blood-warm, his darkness folded around me, and I shuddered, my hands coming up and clasping behind his neck. My entire body arched toward his, he tipped me over onto the bed. I didn't care.

He bit his lip, and the smoke and spice of demon blood filled my mouth. I gasped for air, swallowing, choking on the scorching-hot fluid, his Power wrapped around us both. I was too far gone to think, nothing but a welter of sensation, my throat burning, eyes closed, his hands tearing at my clothes, finding bare skin and burning me all the way down to the bone. I cried out twice, shaking and shuddering, wet with sweat, my heart exploding inside my chest. And when he drove his body into mine I nearly lost consciousness, screaming, thrashing away from pleasure so intense it was like the chill-sweet darkness of Death. It was like dying, being held in his arms while the Power tore through me, remade me, and finally drove me down deep into twilight. Again.

CHAPTER 41

The soupy half-conscious daze lasted for a long time. I would surface for long enough to remember where I was—completely naked, in a demon's arms, lying in one of Jace Monroe's beds—and then my mind would shiver back into a kind of halfsleep. My entire body burned, changing. He held me when my bones crackled, shifting into new shapes; things moved under my skin, internal organs changing and moving, my heart pulsing lethargically. He murmured into my hair, his voice taking away the pain and bathing me in narcotic drowsiness.

It ended with a final flush of Power that coated my skin, sealing me away. I came back to myself with a rush.

Japhrimel lay next to me, my hair tangled over his face, my head pillowed on his shoulder. His fingers, no longer scorching-hot but merely warm, trailed up my back and I shuddered. "It's done," he whispered. For the first time, he sounded tired. Exhausted.

"It hurt," I said, childishly. That was the first shock—my voice wasn't my own anymore. Instead, it was deeper, full of a casual power that gave me gooseflesh. Or would have given me gooseflesh, if my skin hadn't been so—

I looked at my hand. Instead of my usual paleness—a Necromance almost never went out in daylight unless forced to it—I found my hand covered with golden, poreless skin. My nails were still crimson and lacquered with molecule drip, I still wore my glittering rings, but that just made my hand look even more graceful and wicked. "Anubis," I breathed. "What did you—"

"I have shared my Power with you," he said. "There was pain, but it's over now. You share a demon's gifts, Dante, though you are not demon yourself. You will never be a demon."

A kind of dark screaming panic welled up from behind my breastbone. But I was too tired—or not precisely tired. I was numb. Too much had happened, one shock after another. I was too emotionally drained to react to anything right now—and that was dangerous. *Numb* meant *not thinking straight*, and thinking straight was the only thing that was going to keep me alive. "You did *what?*"

"You are still everything you were," he pointed out. "Now you are simply more. And Vardimal will not be able to kill you so easily."

"*Sekhmet sa'es*—" I pushed myself up, trying to untangle my body from his. A few moments of confusion ended up with me sitting, the sheet clutched to my chest, staring at him. Bare, hairless, golden chest, his collarbones standing out, and behind him, glaucous darkness lay on the bed. *So that's why he never takes it off,* I thought, and had to put my head down on my knees. *They're wings. Oh, my gods, they are wings*—I hyperventilated for what seemed like ages, Japhrimel's hand on my back, spread against my ribs. The heat from his touch comforted me, kept the gray fuzz of shock from blurring over my vision.

Finally the panic retreated. But it was a long time before I looked up and found that the room was going dark. "How long has it been?" I asked.

"Ten hours or so," he replied. "It takes a short while for the changes to—"

"I wish you hadn't done that," I said. "I wish you'd warned me."

"You would not have allowed it if I had," he pointed out. "And now you are safer, Dante."

"How safe?" I couldn't believe I was having this conversation with a naked demon. Then another more terrible thought struck me. "Am I still a Necromance?"

"Of course," he said. "Or at least, I presume so."

"You *presume* so?" Okay, so maybe I wasn't numb, just stunned. I stared at him, my breath coming fast and short. My heart pounded.

No, not numb. Stunned, and numb, and terrified.

"I presume so," he said. Dark circles ringed his green eyes. "I have never done this before."

"Oh, great," I mumbled, and looked down at the side of the bed. My clothes lay in a shredded heap. "Japhrimel—"

"You could thank me," he said, his eyebrows drawing together. "If you were a Magi—"

"I'm *not* a Magi," I interrupted. "I'm a Necromance. And I'm *human*."

"Not anymore," he said shortly, and levered himself up from the bed. "I told you, I will not allow you to be harmed. I swore on the waters of Lethe."

"Shut *up*." I bolted up from the bed, yanking the sheet with me. It tore right down the middle. I stood there, looking at the long scrap of green cotton clenched in my hand. "Gods," I breathed, and then looked wildly around.

I found myself across the room, with no real idea of how I'd gotten there. As a matter of fact, I collided with the wall, and plaster puffed out in a cloud. *Faster than human*, one part of me thought with chilling calm. *I'm faster than human now. That will come in handy when I go after Santino.*

I untangled myself from the wall, shivering. Stared at my hands. My golden, perfect hands.

"Why?" I whispered. "Gods above, *why*?"

"I swore to protect you," he answered. "And I will not let you leave me behind, Dante. No one, demon or human, has treated me with any kindness—except you. And even your kindness has thorns. Still—"

I clapped my hands over my ears and bolted for the bathroom. Japhrimel watched this, expressionless.

The vision that confronted me in the bathroom mirror made my stomach revolve. *Or do I even have a stomach now?* I thought. I looked...different. My tattoo was still there, quiescent against my cheek, the emerald glittering slightly. But otherwise...my face wasn't my own. Golden skin stretched over a face I didn't recognize— but there were my dark eyes, now liquid and beautiful. I looked like a holovid model, sculpted cheekbones, a sinful mouth, winged eyebrows. I touched my face with one wondering fingertip, saw the beautiful woman in the mirror touch her exquisite cheekbone, trace her pretty lips.

I looked like a demon. There was only a ghost of the person I used to be left in my face. Japhrimel's mark remained on my left shoulder, but it was a decoration instead of a scar, etched into my newly perfect golden skin. And my hair, Japhrimel's inky black—but long, falling over my shoulders in choreographed strands.

My flat stomach, lightly ridged with muscle, showed no more marks from Santino's claws. I twisted around, pulling my hair up, and strained my neck to examine my back in the mirror. No ridged thick whip scars. I couldn't see my ass in the mirror, but I felt along the lower curve of my left buttock and found no scarring there either.

Gone. They were gone. All except Japhrimel's mark on my shoulder. I dropped my hair over my back, shuddering.

The disorientation made me grab at the counter. I tried not to do it too hard, but my nails drove into the tiles. My hair fell over my face, tangling, tempting. I still clutched the piece of green cotton sheet in my other fist.

"Anubis," I breathed out, and closed my eyes, shutting out the vision. I sank down to my knees, sick and shaking, banged my head softly against the cabinet under the countertop. My breath shivered out of me. "*Anubis et'her ka...*" The prayer shivered away from my lips, a more terrible fear rising out of my panic-darkened mind. What if the god no longer answered me? What if the emerald on my face went dark, what if the god no longer accepted my offerings?

I choked on a dark, silty howl that filled my throat. I felt the inked lines of my tattoo shift slightly, and tried to breathe. If I could breathe, if I could just *breathe,* I could find a quiet space inside myself and see if the god allowed me back.

Japhrimel gently freed my fingers from the tile. "Hush," he said, and knelt down. He took me in his arms. "Hush, Dante. Breathe. You must breathe. Shhh, hush, it is not so bad, you *must* breathe." He stroked my hair and kept whispering, soothingly, until my shallow gasps evened out and I could open my eyes. I clung to him, the material of his coat soft against my fingers.

Now that I knew what it was, it made me slightly sick to think about touching it. But he pressed his lips to my forehead, and the warmth of that touch slid through me, exploding like liquor behind my ribs. "You must be careful," he said. "You will damage yourself if you try hard enough. That will be unpleasant for both of us."

"I hate you," I whispered.

"That is only natural," he whispered back. "I am yours now, Dante. I am *A'nankimel*. I have Fallen."

"I hate you," I repeated. "Change me back. I don't want this. Change me *back*."

"I cannot." He stroked my hair. "You have a demon to hunt, Dante."

I couldn't help myself. I started to giggle. Then chuckle, then roar with panicked laughter.

You have a demon to hunt, Dante.

I was still laughing like an idiot when Gabe kicked the door to the bedroom in, Eddie right behind her.

CHAPTER 42

I crouched in the bathroom, a towel haphazardly wrapped around me. My throat burned from laughing until I screamed, and screaming until my voice broke.

Outside, raised voices. Japhrimel had driven them back into the room and stood guard, not allowing any of them to come near the bathroom.

GABE: *I don't care what you think, that's Danny in there. You can't—*

EDDIE: *Used to be Danny. That goddamn thing did something to her!*

GABE: *What the fuck did you do? Answer me, or I'll—*

JAPHRIMEL: *Injuring me, if it is possible at all, will harm her. You don't want that. I can calm her, if you leave. Leave now.*

EDDIE: *Shoot the fucker, Gabe, shoot him!*

JAPHRIMEL: *Shooting me might possibly harm her. And if she is harmed I will kill you both. This was the price I demanded of her, and she has paid. It is a private matter.*

EDDIE: *Shoot the fucker, Gabe! Shoot him!*

GABE: *Shut up* both *of you. Or I'll shoot you both. What the hell happened to Danny? What did you do to her? You'd better start talking.*

Long tense silence. Whine of an active, unholstered plasgun. Then another sound, footsteps. Drawing closer. Feet in boots, a familiar tread.

JAPHRIMEL: *Don't, human. She is dangerous.*

JACE: *Fuck you.*

The door slid open, a slice of light spearing the darkness. I put my head on my knees, curling even more tightly into myself.

He didn't turn the light on. I smelled him, rank with dying cells. *Human,* a smell I had never noticed before. Would I smell it everywhere, this effluvia of decay? How did Japhrimel stand it? How could *I* stand it?

He didn't walk into the bathroom. Instead, he stood in the door for a moment, looking. Then he slowly bent his knees, knelt down, and crawled into the bathroom on all fours.

The darkness wasn't helping. Neither was the electric light that poured through the door. Nothing was helping. Nothing would ever help again.

He stopped just inside the door. I huddled against the antique iron bathtub, making a small breathless mewling sound. The sound wouldn't stop, no matter how hard I drove my sharp new teeth into my perfect new lips. My datband was blinking. It had to be reset — I didn't scan as human now. I scanned like a genesplice, like an aberration... like something *other*. He told me I wasn't a demon, I was *hedaira* — but what the fuck did that *mean*?

Jace eased himself to the side, sitting with his back against the wall. He sat for a few moments, and then, slowly, he reached up into his linen jacket and pulled out — of all things — a pack of cigarettes.

He never used to smoke, I wonder if he got those from Gabe, I thought, and my breath hitched. The small wounded sound I was making quit, too.

"Mind if I smoke?" he said, quietly.

My breath sobbed in.

He lit up. The brief flare of the lighter seared my eyes. I huddled back even further, the soft helpless sound rising to my lips again. But he didn't do anything, just inhaled some synth hash smoke and blew it out. "It's a nasty fucking habit," he said, his tone pitched low and intimate. "But you've always got to have a pack, in case some petty thug you're trying to ease needs one. You know?"

I said nothing. Squeezed my eyes shut. Patterns of Power shifted in the darkness under my eyelids, patterns I had never seen before. Part of a demon's Power. Shaking at the edge of my control, straining to leap free.

He tapped the ash onto the tiled floor next to him. The tiles were dark-green, with lighter green ones scattered every fourth or fifth tile. It was pretty, and kind of soothing.

He took another drag. "I must have seen thousands of these in my time," he said. "Smoked a few, too. Have to take detox every six months, but it's worth it to see someone relax when you offer them a stick. You know they used to call these fags? Used to make them out of tobacco 'stead of synth hash. *Nicotiana.* Eddie still grows some of that shit."

My breathing eased out a little. His tone was so normal, so familiar. I opened my eyes, resting my cheek on my naked knees. Watching him.

He finished the smoke and ground it out on the floor. I heard low shuffling sounds out in the bedroom. Gabe's hiss, the slow static of Japhrimel's attention. Japhrimel was trembling, too, a fine thin tremor racing through his bones. I could feel it in my own body, the demon's need of me.

Like an addiction.

"I remember one time I was talking to this guy," Jace continued, lacing his fingers over his knee and leaning back into the wall, "and I had to find out what he knew. He was uncooperative . . . they'd already put him through the wringer by the time I got there. I took a look at the situation, and settled down in a chair. Then I offered him a cigarette. I had the information in five minutes. Useful things."

More silence. Jace tilted his head against the wall. I caught the gleam of his blue eyes.

"You remember that little slicboard shop we always used to get our boards tuned at? You still ride a Valkyrie?" He waited.

I was surprised to hear my own voice. "After jobs, sometimes."

I sounded flat and bored. My breath hitched; my beautiful new voice was ruined and husky — but still lovely. It still made the broken glass on the floor shiver slightly; I felt Japhrimel listening intently.

"You always loved Valkyries," he said. "I think what you liked best about riding a board was the flying. The adrenaline. Made you feel alive, right?"

A tear trickled down my cheek, touched my knee.

So demon-things can cry, I thought. It was the first sane thought, and I grabbed it like a shipwreck survivor.

"I miss Saint City," he said. "That noodle shop on Pole Street with the fishtank on the far wall. And that hash den we used to drink at — the one with the great music."

My throat was raw. "It closed down," I whispered. "Two hookers ODed in a week. On T-laced Chill."

"Shit," he said easily. "Damn shame. They played RetroPhunk all the time. And Therm Condor."

"Ann Siobhan," I supplied finally, my voice shaking.

"The Drew Street Tech Boys," he said after a considering pause. "Audiovrax."

I seemed to be slogging through mud to think. "Blake's Infernals."

"Krewe's Control and the Hover Squad," he said.

"I hated them," I whispered.

"Did you?" Now he sounded surprised. "You never told me."

"You loved them." My voice caught on a hoarse sob.

"You bought me all eight discs," he said, scratching at his cheek. "Damn."

"I incinerated them," I admitted. "After you left."

"Oh." He paused. "I'm sorry, baby."

It sounded like he meant it.

"Why didn't you tell me?" I whispered, my voice raw.

"I was trying to protect you, Danny. If you'd known, you'd have come riding into Nuevo Rio with your sword out, to 'save' me. That goddamn honor complex of yours would have gotten you killed. Just like you're trying to get yourself killed avenging Doreen."

"I have to," I said. "I *have* to." I choked on the words. Rigger Hall had taught me how to be hard — but to be hard was no use without your honor. Honor was everything. And honor demanded I avenge Doreen, even if it killed me.

Even if it turns me into a genesplice aberration? I wondered, and my breath jagged out, a low moaning sob.

"I know," he answered, softly, intimately. "You can't be anything else, Danny. I always liked that about you. Right out to your fingernails, you just can't be anything other than what you are."

"Look at what he did to me," I whispered.

"So what?" Jace said. "You're still *you*. Still my pretty Danny Valentine. And while you sit in here moaning about it, your prey is either getting away or digging into a hidey-hole." He shrugged, his shirt moving against the tiled wall and making a little whispering sound. "We need you to finish this hunt, Danny. Gabe needs her own revenge on the Saint City Slasher. Eddie needs Gabe happy. I need Sargon Corvin dead so I can start living again and maybe prove to you I ain't so bad. You're letting us down, Danny. Come on."

I shuddered. It should have been a transparent ploy, but it needled me. I *was* letting Gabe down—she'd dropped everything to come with me. And Eddie loved her. It must eat at him to see her unhappy.

A deep racking cough shook me. I wiped at my face with bladed hands—my hands weren't even my own anymore. But they would do what I asked them to do. I finally raised my head to find Jace watching me. He didn't look nervous, but the set of his shoulders told me he was tense.

"I need some clothes," I said huskily.

"You got it," Jace said. "Anything you need, baby."

CHAPTER 43

Gabe examined my face. "Hades," she breathed, then handed me my sword.

I took it, cautiously. But no blue fire bloomed on the blade, and it didn't hurt me.

I glanced at Japhrimel, who stood expressionless by the window. Darkness pressed against the glass, the sound of rain tapering off. I wondered if the city was still burning. "Blessed weapons won't react to you," he said quietly. "Ease your mind, Dante. Your blade is still your own."

I looked at the curved length of steel, closed my eyes, and thought of Santino. Opened my eyes.

Blue ran weakly along the slight curve of the blade. *Anubis,*

I prayed, *I beg of You, answer me.* I let out a shaky breath. Felt my tattoo shift on my cheek, the emerald sparking. Relief burst inside me. It still worked. And if my blade was still blessed, I was still one of the god's own chosen.

"Well," Gabe said. She wore her long black police-issue coat, a plasgun holstered under her left arm. I couldn't see her sword. She put her fists on her hips. "Damn. Better than an augment, I guess."

It was her attempt at humor, and it failed miserably. I was still grateful for it, though. "And so cheap," I said, my own failed attempt at levity.

Silence stretched inside the wrecked bedroom, a thin humming silence. The bed was reduced to matchsticks and springs and strips of material, the chairs splintered. The curtains were torn, and there were a few impact-marks on the walls. I took this all in.

"Sorry about the room, Jace," I finally said, not meeting his eyes. My voice was indeed ruined, husky but still perfect. I sounded like a vidsex queen.

"It's okay." He leaned against the door to the hall. His staff leaned next to him, the bones moving uneasily in the charged air, clacking against each other. "I wanted to redo it anyway."

Eddie, his arms folded, hulked behind Gabe, stealing furtive looks at me and then at Japhrimel, who looked just as he always had—except for the dark rings around his glittering eyes. He looked tired and somehow more human than I'd ever seen him. I felt his unwavering attention, his back to the window but his entire body focused on me.

"Where are we at?" I asked, and didn't dare look Gabe in the eyes. I didn't think I could stand to meet her worried dark gaze.

She cleared her throat. "I've managed to get a nice stockpile of munitions. Eddie can have three *golem'ai* ready for Manifest in two days. And he's put together eighteen firestarters. Forty-eight hours, and we're as ready as we can be." She looked at Jace.

"I've got Mob Circle passports for all of us," he said quietly. "And my second is already handing out the weapons. We've declared war on the Corvins, they just don't know it yet. Funny thing is, there aren't any of the Inner Circle left in the city. They've vanished, probably gone with Sarg—um, Santino. I've given the orders to take out their holdings. As for us, we've got supplies, and world-class transport. I'm ready to go whenever you are."

"You're staying here," I said. "You've got to coordinate—"

"I'm going with you," Jace disagreed mildly. "If you don't like it, tough. I've got my own score to settle with Sargon Corvin. Or whoever the hell he is."

I looked at him, my fingers tightening on the hilt. Gabe stepped back. Eddie slid his arms around her, and they stood, watching me.

A kind of black fury welled up behind my breastbone. I swallowed, looking down at my sword. Blue light glittered along the ringing blade. "Get me a map," I said, finally. "Let's see if I can track Doreen's blood. If I can't, we still have Dake's tracker. We can hope Santino hasn't set up countermeasures."

I felt rather than heard Gabe's sigh of relief. Jace nodded, took his staff, and left the room. Gabe followed, pulling Eddie by the hand. The Skinlin sidled past me. Gabe paused at the door.

"Danny?" she said.

"Hm?" I steeled myself, looking at the glitter of blue fire along the steel. Power. The changes had settled into me, and I felt the same humming force that lay over Japhrimel flooding me. So much Power—I didn't even need the city's well of energy now. My brain shuddered away from the implications. *I could tear this whole damn house apart.*

"You're still my friend," she said, firmly. "No matter what you are, you're still my friend."

Startled, I half-turned to look at the door, but she was gone, dragging Eddie after her.

That left me alone with Japhrimel.

He studied me across the burning air. Finally he moved slightly, clasping his hands behind his back. "I am not sorry," he said.

"Of course not," I said. "You're a demon."

"*A'nankimel.* Not demon. Fallen." His eyes did what his hands didn't, touched my face, roamed over me. "I will not give you up, Dante."

"I don't belong to you," I flared.

"No," he agreed. "You do not."

I swallowed dryly. "Why? Why did you do this?"

"If you were merely human, Vardimal might kill you." Japhrimel cocked his head to the side. "Now you are neither human nor demon. *Neither man nor demon may kill him,* that was the immunity given to him by the Prince in return for his services."

That brought up another question. "What's Lucifer going to think of this?"

For a long moment, Japhrimel examined me. Then one corner of his mouth quirked slightly up. The slight smile made my heart pound. "Ask me if I care."

"Do you care?" My breath caught on the last word.

"No."

Well, that about summed everything up. Except one thing.

I stepped around a pile of splinters that had once been a chair. Approached him cautiously, my boots grinding against the plaster dust and small bits of wreckage on the floor. I held my katana to the side and stopped less than a foot from him, close enough to feel the heat radiating from him. His eyes held mine, but he didn't move.

"Did you mean any of it?" I asked him. "What you said?"

He nodded. "Of course, Dante. Every word."

His eyes glittered feverishly, and a faint, almost-human flush crept up his cheeks.

I believed him. Gods help me, but I believed him.

"You're going to have to tell me what all this means and what exactly I am now," I said finally. "After I kill Santino." *There's a whole lot about my life that I'm going to sort out once that motherfucker's dead.* The thought was welcome—it sounded like me. At least I sounded like myself inside my own head.

"When he is dead, I will explain everything," Japhrimel agreed. "My apologies, Dante. But I am not sorry."

I licked my dry lips. "Neither am I," I said harshly. He deserved the truth. "I...I just...it's a shock, that's all." It took more courage than I thought it would, but I reached up and rested my fingertips on his cheek. "I never thought I'd even *consider* dating a demon." I was still searching for levity and failing miserably.

His shoulders sagged. He closed his eyes, leaning into my touch. We stood there for a few moments before I took my hand away, and his green gaze met mine. His eyes seemed strangely dark now.

"Now come on," I said. "We've got a demon to kill, and the Egg to get back, and Doreen's little girl to save. We'll do some planning."

CHAPTER 44

They ate dinner in the ornate dining room while I examined the map and checked my gear. I'd lost my scabbard, but Jace had an antique katana hanging on his study wall, so I took its scabbard. It was better than nothing.

We weren't anywhere near ready yet, but I felt a whole lot better about the deal.

I settled cross-legged in front of the fireplace, the chill of climate control playing over my face, staring at the map. It unrolled in front of me, Hegemony territories in blue, Freetowns in red, Putchkin in purple, and the wastelands where nobody lived in white. There was precious little white — mostly around the poles and one spot in Hegemony territory, the Vegas Waste where the first and only nuclear bomb of the Seventy Day War had dropped.

Why do all these rooms have fireplaces? I thought. *It's Nuevo Rio, it never gets cold here.*

Gabe and Eddie held a fierce whispered conference, silverware clinking against plates. Jace said nothing, staring at his plate as if it held the secrets of the universe. Japhrimel stood by the French doors leading out into the courtyard-garden, slim and dark and utterly impenetrable.

I held my hand over the map, trying to feel anything. Nothing. Nothing at all.

I sighed. Then I drew one of my main knives out of my coat.

Silence fell.

I set the blade against my hand.

"Dante?" Japhrimel's tone was cool, but the snarl below his voice warned me.

"Calm down," I said. "Easy. Blood's what I'm tracking, let me work."

He said nothing else, but I felt the weight of his eyes on me.

I drew the blade against my palm, willing the blood to come out. The new golden skin was a lot tougher than human skin; I almost had to force my flesh open. A thin line of smoky-black blood welled up.

My breath hissed out between my teeth. The slash began to close almost immediately.

I closed my eyes and my hand, slippery hot blood burning in my palm. Held my hand over the map.

"Doreen," I whispered. *Doreen.*

I had found her while on the Brewster job, the one that had made my reputation as a hunter, not just a Necromance. I'd taken the contract and tracked down Michael Brewster, psychopath and serial killer; brought him back from the Freetowns to the Hegemony justice system, getting shot at, knifed, almost gang-raped by a Circle of Magi, and nearly burned alive in the process. It had been Doreen's distraction at the warehouse that had bought me enough time to escape the Magi and go to ground, and I'd hunted Brewster down with increasing panic after that. The day after he was processed into lockdown, I flew back on the red-eye hover transport and sprung her from that whorehouse in Old Singapore, using most of the bounty credit to pay off her tag fee and threatening the pimp into letting her go.

She'd been in bad shape. I guess that when the rogue Circle couldn't have me, they went for her. One psion almost as good as another, and a *sedayeen* couldn't even fight back like I would have. Might have, if I hadn't been spell-tied and chained.

Who was I kidding? I knew I wouldn't have been able to escape that without her help. Leaving her there was a shoddy fucking way to repay her for that, but I'd had no *choice.*

It had taken a long time for either of us to get any real sleep after I brought her to Saint City — she would scream in the dark for months, nightmares torturing her until I woke her up. My bare skin on hers, her mouth meeting mine, our hair tangled together in the safety of my bed.

You saved my life, she would often say, *I owe you, Danny.*

And I'd always reply, *You saved mine too, Reena.* I wouldn't have survived that job without her. Or the years that followed, while I learned how to work the mercenary field and started tracking down criminals. The house I bought with the bounties became *our* house: she had always wanted a garden and after Rigger Hall I had wanted a space all my own. As a Necromance I needed space and quiet, the house was the only piece of Doreen I had left.

And Doreen had given me the greatest gift of all: she had taught me how to *live* again.

Her pale hair, cut short and sleek; her dark-blue eyes. She'd worked in a Free Clinic in the Tank District and also patched up mercenaries and psis when they played too rough. Quiet and serene, her mouth always tilted into a smile, her eyes always merry. The Saint City psionic population closed around her like a protective wall. Psionic healers—*sedayeen*—were pacifists to a fault, they couldn't stand to hurt anyone. The pain they inflicted would rebound on them. They were helpless. So we all watched out for her—but it had done no good.

The flowers, blue flowers. I knew now that they were Santino's gift to the "mothers of the future," but back then, all I had known was the threat to Doreen's life.

And Gabe had been the only cop who believed me about the danger Doreen was in.

I had moved Doreen from safehouse to safehouse, but the flowers always found her. Gabe and I had taken turns standing guard, frantically trying to dig up the murderer who seemed intent on stalking her. Once we blew his human cover—once we knew it was Modeus Santino we were looking for and his company was seized—he went underground, and we had a week of breathing room before the flowers showed up again and the last desperate endgame started. Always one bare step ahead, moving her around, hiding first in one part of the city, then another—

—and Santino had probably known all the time, I realized. Had probably simply played cat-and-mouse with us, allowing us to spirit her away, drawing out the final coup, finally moving in for the kill—his "samples"—in that warehouse. Gabe had been called away on another case, Eddie had gone for supplies, and it was only me and Doreen, hiding in a shattered hulk of a pre-Hegemony building.

Slippery blood in my palm. I felt the Power take shape.

My cheek ignited, the emerald singing a faint thin crystal note. I *reached* into that place I had not touched since her death, the place inside me where her gentle presence had gone.

—*Slight sound, scraping, a high thin giggle in the dark. Doreen whirled, her pale hair ruffling out. I leapt to my feet, sword ringing free of the sheath, spitting blue fire. I shoved her and she fell, scraping both palms and crying out thinly. Rumbling sound—the freight hovers, rushing past the warehouse; here in the shattered part of town they ran a lot closer to the ground.*

Explosions. No—projectile fire. And the whine of plasbolts. I tracked the sounds—one gunman, firing at us both. No—Doreen was trying to get up, but he was firing at me, he wanted her alive. I pushed her toward the exit.

"Get down, Doreen. Get down!"

Crash of thunder. Moving, desperately, scrabbling...fingers scraping against the concrete, rolling to my feet, dodging the whine of bullets and plasbolts. Skidding to a stop just as he rose out of the dark, the razor and his claws glittering in one hand, his little black bag in the other.

"Game over," he giggled, and the awful tearing in my side turned to a burning numbness as he slashed; I threw myself backward, not fast enough, not fast enough.

"Danny!" Doreen's despairing scream.

"Get out!" I screamed, but she was coming back, hands glowing blue-white, still trying to heal.

Trying to reach me, to heal me, the link between us resonating with my pain and her burning hands—

Made it to my feet, screaming at her to get the fuck out, Santino's claws whooshing again as he tore into me, one claw sticking on a rib, my sword ringing as I slashed at him, too slow, I was too slow.

Falling again. Something rising in me—a cold agonizing chill. Doreen's hands clamped against my arm. Warm exploding wetness. So much blood. So much.

Her Power roared through me, and I felt the spark of life in her dim. She held on, grimly, as Santino made little snuffling, chortling sounds of glee. The whine of a lasecutter as he took part of her femur, the slight pumping sound of the bloodvac. Blood dripped in my eyes, splattered against my cheek. Sirens—Doreen's death would register on her datband, and aid hovers would be dispatched. Too late though. Too late for both of us.

I passed out, hearing the wet smacking sounds as Santino took what he wanted, giggling that high-pitched strange chortle of his. His face burned itself into my memory—black teardrops over the eyes, pointed ears, the sharp ivory fangs. Not human, *I thought,* he can't be human, Doreen, Doreen, get away, run, run—

Her soul, carried like a candle down a long dark hall, guttering. Guttering. Spark shrinking into infinity. I was a Necromance, but I couldn't stop her rushing into Death's arms...

I came back to myself with a jolt. Tears slicked my cheeks. Japhrimel knelt on the other side of the map, his fingers clamped around my wrist. My finger rested on the map, far south of Nuevo Rio, in the middle of a field of white and the paler non-Hegemony blue of ocean.

An island in the middle of a cold sea. Almost in Antarctica. The last place anyone would look for a demon.

"That's where he is," I said, husky, my voice making the map flutter against the floor, held down by my finger. "Right there."

Japhrimel nodded. "Then that is where we will go," he said. "Dante?"

"I'm fine," I said, wiping at my cheeks with my free hand. "Let go."

He did, one finger at a time. I looked over at the table.

Gabe's fork paused in midair. She watched me, her pretty face pale, her emerald flashing as the tat shifted against her cheek. Eddie stood, his chair flat on the floor as if he'd tipped it over. Jace had pushed his plate away and was staring at me, blue eyes wide, fever spots of color high in each pale cheek.

"Finish your dinner," I said. I sounded like Japhrimel, the same flat voice, loaded with a full-scale plasgun charge of Power. "Then get some rest. We've got work to do soon."

CHAPTER 45

The house slept.

Gabe and Eddie were asleep, and Jace had finally stumbled off to bed, rubbing his eyes. They would need their rest.

I didn't want to sleep. Instead, I walked slowly through the empty halls of Jace's mansion, my footsteps echoing. I didn't know where I was headed until the front door loomed up ahead of me, and I put my hand flat against it. The Power contained in Jace's walls resonated, slightly uneasy, and I calmed it as I would a rattling slicboard.

"Where would you go?" Japhrimel asked in my ear, appearing out of the darkness with only a sigh.

I shrugged. "I'm not going anywhere, I just need some air."

"And?" His voice was calm, almost excessively calm.

I didn't answer. Twisted the doorknob, let myself out into the night.

Outside, the plaza in front of Jace's house stretched away,

expanses of white marble. The edges dropped down, sheer rock, until the suburbs of Nuevo Rio splashed against the cliff. He'd chosen this place for security, I guessed, and metaphorical height.

Japhrimel closed the door behind me. I paced out onto the flat white expanse, glancing up at the sky. Clouds scudded in front of a quarter-moon, I had no trouble seeing. Demon sight was far better than human eyes. I could see every tiny crack in the marble, every pebble and dust mote, if I looked for it.

Japhrimel, silent, halted at the bottom of the steps leading to Jace's front door.

"So what am I?" I asked finally. The stink of human Nuevo Rio, the sharp tang of Power, vied with the night wind and the persistent smoky fragrance of demon. "What *exactly* am I?"

"*Hedaira*," he replied, his voice weaving into the night. "I am Fallen, Dante. And I have shared my Power with you."

"That tells me a lot," I said, my hand tightening on my swordhilt.

"Why don't you ask what you truly wish to ask me, Dante?" He still sounded tired. And forlorn.

"Can I kill you?" I asked, in a rush of breath.

"Perhaps."

"What happens to you if Santino kills me?"

"He will not." Stone rang softly underfoot as Japhrimel's voice stroked it. His voice was almost physical now, caressing my skin as nothing else ever had. It reminded me of the barbed-wire pleasure, so intense it was agony, of his body on mine.

I turned back, saw him with his hands clasped behind his back. His eyes gleamed faintly green. The darkness of his winged coat blended with the darkness of night, a blot on the white stone. "That's not an answer, Tierce Japhrimel."

Saying his name made the air shiver between us. He tensed.

My thumb slid over the katana's guard. His dark eyes flicked down, then back up, a glitter showing on their surface from the moon. The pale crescent slid behind clouds again, and he went back to being a shadow. If I concentrated, I could see his face, decipher his expression. "You do not want to question me," he said. "You want to fight."

"It's what I'm good at," I said, wishing he hadn't guessed.

"Why must it always be a contest, with you?" I could see he was smiling, and that managed to infuriate me.

"Why don't you carry a sword?" I avoided the question.

"I have no need of one." He shrugged. "Would you like me to prove it?"

"If you can beat me, Santino will—"

"Santino preys on *humans,*" he said. "He is a scavenger. I was the Prince of Hell's Right Hand, Dante."

"What did you prey on?" I tried to sound rude, only managed to sound breathless.

"Other demons. I have killed more of the Greater Flight of Hell than you can imagine." His lips peeled back from his teeth, one of those murderous slow grins.

I tried to feel afraid. Every other time he'd grinned like that my skin had gone cold with terror. Not now. Now my breath caught, remembering his mouth on mine. Remembering his hands on my naked skin.

I almost drew my katana, five inches or so of bright steel peeking out. No blue glow.

He still smiled, watching me.

"Did you plan this? Or did Lucifer?" I swallowed, wishing for my normal human terror with a vengeance that surprised me. I never thought my own fearlessness would be so scary; I'd lived with comfortable fear for so long.

"Lucifer did not plan this, Dante; he will be exceedingly displeased. No demon *plans* to Fall. To become *A'nankimel* is to give up much of the power and glory of Hell." He shrugged again, his hands still clasped behind his back.

"You can't go back?" I asked. "What about...what about being free?"

He shook his head. "There are other kinds of freedom. My fate is bound to yours, Dante. I am bound to finish the Prince's will in this matter, and then...we shall see, you and I, what compromise we can reach."

I closed my eyes.

You're so sharp and prickly, aren't you? So tough. Someday you're going to find someone you can't bamboozle, Danny, Doreen's voice echoed through my memory. *Someone's going to find out what a soft touch you are, and what are you going to do then?*

I'm not soft, I had replied, and changed the subject. And Doreen had giggled, her fingertips sliding over my hip, a soft forgiving touch.

I'd met Jace at the party we threw to christen the house, and he started coming around after Doreen died, doing repairs, showing up once or twice while I was on a job to watch my back, and going out on a limb for me during the Freemen-Tarks bounty, the one that had given me the worst case of nerves from a bounty ever. I still had nightmares about being trapped in the rain, Tarks beating me with a crowbar until Jace appeared out of nowhere and took him down. Even when Jace had started to actively court me I'd kept him at arm's length. Everything had to be a fight between us, and he seemed to enjoy the battles as much as I did, exchanging sharp word for sharp word, finally a sparring partner I didn't have to hold back and be careful of.

I opened my eyes, looked down at my blade, peeking out between hilt and scabbard. Slid the blade home. It clicked back into the sheath, useless. What was I going to do, try to kill him because he'd made me stronger? If Santino couldn't kill me now, if I was quicker and tougher because of what Japhrimel had done...

I didn't realize I was walking toward him until he moved down off the bottom step, opening his arms, enclosing me in the warmth of a demon's embrace. I sighed, my shoulders dropping, the weight of uncertainty slipping away. In his arms, I could breathe. As if he carried around the only sphere of usable air on the planet.

He kissed my forehead, gently. Fire sparked through my veins, recognizing the touch. "If you wish to fight me, Dante, fight me." His lips moved against my new skin. "If it will ease you, I will play that game. Or we can devise new ones."

I hadn't thought it possible that a demon could seduce me. But seduction was what demons did. Cajoling, enticing, fascinating, tempting—they made it into sport, and had a long time to practice.

He kissed my cheek, the corner of my mouth; I tipped my head back, a small pleading sound escaping me, and his mouth met mine. This kiss wasn't like the first—it was gentler. Softer. A sharp, greedy demon I could fight. Japhrimel, gentle, sharing his mouth with me as if he was human, and mine—I had no defense against that.

Japhrimel led me through Jace's house, his warm fingers in mine. I cried without a sound, tears sliding down my cheeks as he closed the door of yet another bedroom behind us. He wiped away the tears, tenderly, and I forgot to weep as he told me silently everything I had always wanted to hear.

CHAPTER 46

t's a ten-hour hover flight," Jace said. "You said we needed something that could go over water."

I eyed the freight hover, tucking a stray strand of hair behind my ear. It looked like a garbage scow, dirty and blunt-nosed. Her name—*Baby*—was permasprayed on her hull in pink. "Any particular reason why you chose this piece of trash?"

"Watch." Jace lifted his wrist and tapped his datband. He was grinning, an expression he usually reserved for when he'd won a card game.

The hover—almost as big as a freight transport—vanished. My jaw dropped. I saw the marble plaza, the smoke drifting up from Nuevo Rio in the background, hover traffic beginning to slide through the city once more—but no garbage scow.

I lifted my own datband and scanned. Then I dug in my bag and extracted my datpilot, scanned again. I thinned my shields and tried to find any electromagnetic disturbance.

Nothing. If I hadn't watched it vanish, I would never have guessed.

"Gods above and below," I said. "How did you—"

"Hegemony military tech and a little extra," he replied, his golden hair shimmering in the reflected light from the vast marble courtyard. "I've got a great Tech guy, and your demon's been pretty useful. Invisible to radar, deepscan, magscan, and psi. It's faster than it looks, too. And it's combat-equipped, fore-and-aft plascannons—"

"Yeah, but does it have that new-hover smell?" Eddie snorted. He handed me a small plas package full of six gray crystalline nubbins, each as big as my thumb. "Firestarters. Be careful, okay?" But his eyes didn't quite meet mine. I didn't blame him. I had trouble looking in the mirror, and I was living inside this new body.

Gabe shrugged, her coat settling against her shoulders. "I've got the map," she said. "Let's get this show on the road, huh?"

"One second." Jace pressed his datband again, and the hover reappeared. "She only looks ugly, guys. She's got a heart of gold." He produced his chromium hip flask.

An ash-smelling wind touched my hair. Nuevo Rio had stopped
burning, but it would be racked with gunfire again as soon as Jace's
lieutenants moved out into the city. Hours of frantic planning had
narrowed down to this: if his network succeeded, Jace would take
over all the Corvin Family's assets in Nuevo Rio and probably elsewhere in the Hegemony. It was the accepted method for a Family to
start out, in murder and fire after all the legal paperwork of incorporation was done. And we hoped it would distract Santino—he was
arrogant enough to think that if we were attacking the Corvin Family, we weren't going after him, right?

Wrong, I thought.

Jace unscrewed the flask, took a swig. Rolled it around in his
mouth. Tossed it back. "We who are about to die, salute you," he said.
Handed the flask to Gabe, who glanced at me.

"A sort of ritual," I said. "Every time we started a job, we would
take a slug and give a quote. Good luck."

She shrugged, took a hit, and coughed, her cheeks flushing pink.
"Let the gods sort them out," she said, and grimaced. "Hades love
me, that's foul."

Eddie took the flask, took a long swallow. "*Fortis fortunam iuda-
vat,*" he growled. Coughed slightly, blinking watering eyes. "Goddammit, Jace, what *is* that?"

"Jungle juice," Jace replied. He was smiling, and his eyes glittered madly. Fey.

Eddie handed me the flask. If it was a gesture, it was a good one. I
tipped it into my mouth, a long swallow, felt it burn fiercely all the
way down. I coughed, my eyes watering. "*Go tell the Spartans,
passers-by; That here, obedient to their orders, we lie.*" It was just as
awful as every other time I'd tasted it. I gave the flask back to Jace,
who watched me for a moment. Had he been watching the flask meet
my mouth, the way my throat moved as I swallowed? Maybe.

Then he passed it over my shoulder to Japhrimel, who stood dark
and silent as ever. "Take a swig and give a quote," Jace said. "You're
one of us."

I don't know what it cost Jace to say that, but I was grateful. I bit
my lip, sinking my teeth in, but nobody looked at me.

"I suppose he is," Gabe chimed in. "He saved Danny's life."

"And got her involved in this in the first place," Eddie snorted.
She elbowed him, her emerald glittering in the late-morning sunlight. The afternoon storm was just beginning to gather on the hori-

zon, a dark smudge. I could smell approaching rain and nervous peppery adrenaline from them all. Except Japhrimel.

Japhrimel took the flask, lifted it to his mouth. A single swallow. His eyes dimmed slightly. *"A'tai, hetairae A'nankimel'iin. Diriin."* He handed the flask back to Jace. "My thanks."

"Don't mention it." Jace tipped the flask, poured a smoking dollop out onto the marble, and then capped it deftly. "Well, if we're going to make a suicide run, let's get on with it."

"Let's hope it's not suicide," Gabe said dryly. "I've got property taxes. I can't afford to die."

CHAPTER 47

I watched out the window as the dark nighttime ocean slid away underneath us. Japhrimel leaned against the hull on the other side of my window, looking out as well. The hold was fitted with utilitarian seats, the entire back section filled with crated supplies. I hoped we didn't need everything we had brought—we could hunt Santino for months on what we'd packed. If I had to spend months doing this I *would* probably go crazy.

Gabe, strapped into the captain's chair, piloted us with a deft touch. Eddie paced down the length of the hover's interior, silently snarling, whirled on his heel, paced back, stared out the front bubble, then whirled back and repeated the whole process. He was readying the *golem'ai* to be released. They were a Skinlin's worst weapon, the mud-things. I felt a small shiver trace up my spine.

Jace leaned back in his chair, his eyes shut. It was his usual prejob ritual, to sit quiet and still, maybe going over the plan in his head, maybe praying, maybe silently chanting to a *loa*. The thorn-twisted tattoo on his cheek shifted slightly.

And me? I sat and stared at my hands, clasped loosely around my katana's hilt. Golden skin under my rings. Light sparkled under the amber and moonstone and silver and obsidian. They rang and shifted with Power constantly now, demon-fed.

I had far too much now, too much to control. Power jittered in the air around me, working its way into my brain, teasing and tapping and begging to be used. I slid my katana free, just an inch or so, and watched a faint blue glow play over the metal. The song of my rune-spelled blade, familiar, resonated under the whine of hovercells.

I looked up at Japhrimel, who studied the waves, his profile sharp and somehow pure in the blue light. I blinked.

His eyes were no longer bright laser-green. Instead, they were dark, dimming. I gasped, shoved my katana back into its sheath. "Japhrimel?"

He glanced at me, then smiled. It was a shared, private smile that made my breath catch. *I was lying in bed with him this morning,* I thought, and a hot flush slid up my cheeks. "Your eyes," I said, weakly.

Japhrimel shrugged. It was an elegant movement. Would I share his grace? The crackling aura of Power that followed him around? *There are worse things,* I thought, and then flinched. *No. I'm human. Human.*

No, I'm not. I realized for the umpteenth time, my fist clenched on my katana's hilt.

"Dark now," he said. "Probably. I am glad of it."

"Why?"

His smile widened slightly. "It means I am no longer subject to Hell," he said shortly. "Only to you."

"So you're technically free? You could walk away from this?" I persisted.

"Of course not. It simply means that once the Egg is returned to Lucifer, I stay with you."

"I'm not so sure I'm comfortable with that," I answered, and went back to staring out the window. "What is he likely to have on that island, Japhrimel?"

"Several rings of defenses, human guards, other things." Japhrimel still leaned against the hull. "It is impossible to guess. Best just to wait and see."

"Like a standard hit on a military installation," Gabe supplied from the front. "Can't tell until we get there, going to have to just go loose and fast. Not enough time for proper intel."

We'd gone over this before, but the conversation was comforting. Better than the silence, anyway. But something was bothering me, some question I couldn't quite frame.

"Well, if we're invisible, we can recon a little before we send their asses to hell," Eddie growled. Then he glanced at Japhrimel. "No offense."

Japhrimel blinked. "None taken."

I watched the sea heaving below. I'd never liked the sea. Anything that big and unpredictable gave me the willies. Ditto with thunderstorms, some of the Major Works... and demons.

The question clicked into my conscious mind as I sat staring out the window. *Just how exactly did Santino escape Hell?* He was scary, much scarier than any human monster I'd faced. But still... I'd *seen* Hell now, and it didn't seem likely that Santino had possessed the kind of Power necessary to wrench himself out of the Prince's grasp, especially with something so valuable as the Egg. Of course, the Egg wasn't often used... so it was probably guarded.

Guarded by a demon Lucifer thought he could trust.

My eyes traveled up Japhrimel's coat, fastened on his profile. I did *not* want to be thinking this, especially since I'd spent the morning rolling around in bed with him. He hadn't let me down yet; I could ask him the hard questions later.

If there *was* a later.

We had about four hours before we reached the island, and then we had to find whatever installation Santino had there, and then we had to crack it and kill him—and rescue the little girl.

Doreen's daughter. Or Doreen cloned. Lucifer cloned with a bit of Doreen. One-quarter? One-half? How much? Did it matter? Of course not. I owed Doreen. If nothing else, she had given me my body back, made it possible for the terrified girl inside me to finally go to sleep and the adult begin to come out.

Oh, come on, Danny! I thought, lifting my katana, resting my forehead against the sheath. I was glad we were running dark, so I couldn't see my reflection in the windowplas. *What are you going to do with a demon child? Play mommy? Send her off to school and hope she doesn't burn the whole goddamn place down?*

Doesn't matter, I answered. *You can't hand a little kid—Doreen's kid—over to Lucifer. You just can't. What will* he *do to her? You owe Doreen. She saved your life at the expense of her own.*

I sighed. Here I was, sitting in a retrofitted garbage scow, dragging my best friend—and who qualified as my best friend now if Gabe didn't?—and her boyfriend into this. And Jace. And Japhrimel, but *he* could probably take care of himself.

Could he? Why the hell was I worrying about *him*?

I lowered my katana, drummed my fingernails on the hilt. "Japhrimel?"

"Dante."

"Are you...are you vulnerable, now?" I sounded a lot less certain than I wanted to.

"Not to humans," he said, shortly. "To some demons, perhaps. Not many."

"Is Santino one of them?"

He shrugged. "I am not worried about him."

"That's not an answer."

"You have grown more perceptive."

"And you're giving me the run-around. Which means he could hurt you."

"The Power contained in the Egg might conceivably damage me. However, I am not the one he wishes to capture." Japhrimel was a statue of darkness now, only his skin faintly luminescent.

"He *shot* me. I doubt 'capture' is on his laundry list where I'm concerned."

"If he wanted to kill you, he would have eviscerated you, Dante. He could have. Instead, he only shot you, knowing we were close enough that your condition would delay us. He obviously means to recollect you at his leisure. Which means he has a plan."

That didn't help me feel any better. I opened my mouth, but Jace beat me to it. "It doesn't matter," he said. "As soon as my Family moves on the Corvins, all Santino's neat little plans go out the window. He won't have any resources left to fuck around."

"I doubt your move on him is unanticipated," Japhrimel said quietly. The hover rattled. I tensed in my chair, and Eddie growled.

"Still doesn't fucking matter," Eddie growled. "We're taking him down." He swung around to pin us all with a ferocious glare. "I ain't come all this way and been beat up and stuffed in two hovers to let him get off with just a spanking. 'Sides, we got *the* Gabriele Spocarelli. An' Jace Monroe. And Danny Valentine version two, kickass demon Necromance with her own pet demon boy. And you've got Eustace Edward Thorston III, Skinlin sorcerer and pretty pissed-off dirtwitch berserker." He showed his teeth, lips peeling back. "He hurt my Gabby," he continued softly. "And I'm gonna make him *pay*."

I blinked. It was the longest speech I'd ever heard from him.

Gabe didn't twist around in her seat, but I could tell from the set of her shoulders that she was smiling. Japhrimel had turned, and was regarding Eddie with a faintly surprised look. Jace grinned, his eyes closed, his head lolling against his seatback.

I cleared my throat. "Thanks, Eddie. I feel better," I said dryly. And the funny thing was, I did.

CHAPTER 48

"Holy motherfucking shit," Gabe whistled out tunelessly. "Would you look at that."

"What about the radiation scans?" I asked.

"Flatline. They can't see us," Jace said, leaning over Gabe's shoulder, buckling his rig. "Ogoun..." he breathed. "Damn."

"Impressive," Gabe giggled. It was a carefree, girlish sound, but it set my teeth on edge. "Looks like a bad holovid villain's hideaway."

Below us, the icy sea broke foaming against sheer cliffs. The island was a hunk of rock rising from ice-floes, and the castle crouched atop it, spires of stone rearing up from darkness, decked with tiny yellow and blue points of light. It looked like something out of a Gothic fairytale, spire upon spire, screaming gargoyle shapes torn out of the stone.

"Get me a laseprint of that," I said, and Jace's fingers danced over a keyboard. The computers hummed. A laseprinter droned into life. "Are you *sure* we're invisible?"

Eddie tore the paper free. "Looks like antiaircraft batteries here, here, here, and here," he said, smacking the printout down on a small foldout table. "If they knew we were here, they'd blast us out of the sky."

I passed my palm over the smooth paper. We'd done our final equipment checks. All that remained was to actually drop out the side hatch and start causing trouble. "Jace, get me a couple of different views. Gabe, keep us going slow. Magscan shielding is no good unless we drift a bit."

"I know, Mom," Gabe sneered. "Let me fucking drive, okay?"

"They are unaware," Japhrimel said. "Dante, this place is heavily guarded."

"Good," I said. "The more confusion, the better."

Jace laid another two printouts down. "More?" he asked, and my eyes met his. It was a moment of complete accord, the kind we used to have while we were working together.

"Can you penetrate the shielding?" I asked.

"That is no trouble," the demon answered, his eyes never leaving me. "Santino has no demon shielding; if he did, Lucifer could track him. He is naked here, depending on secrecy."

"Good." I spread my hands over the printouts. "Japhrimel, make sure I don't bleed through," I said.

He nodded. "Of course."

I *focused,* looking for the link I'd followed before. It was weak— the child wasn't Doreen, and she wasn't human. But then again, neither was I. Not anymore.

I followed the thread-thin cable stretched tautly over the roiling sea below. Reaching. *Reaching.*

Contact.

—who are you—

The voice was neither male nor female, but it was *familiar,* as familiar to me as my own. A wave of heat sparking up my arms, into my bones, my heart pounding, mouth full of copper.

Disengage, ripping free, link open, too open, salt against raw wound, Doreen, the memory of Doreen tilting her head back, her hands full of blue-white fire, her blood everywhere—

—who are you—

The *contact* stretched. My mental "fingers" froze, unable to let go, as whoever it was—*the kid? But no kid can be this strong—* examined me like a fly caught in a glass.

I stumbled back. Japhrimel caught my shoulders, steadied me, absorbed the backlash of Power. He rested his chin on top of my head. "Dante?"

"Fine." I said. My fingertip glued itself to a space on the printout. *Whatever that is, it's not a kid. It looks like a kid, but it's not a kid. But it's Doreen's, and I promised.* "She's here. We'll hit here hardest and extract her."

"Sounds good," Gabe said. "I'll put ol' Betsy here on autopilot."

I looked up at Eddie. The shaggy blond Skinlin hitched his leather coat higher on his shoulders, then checked his guns for the umpteenth time. "Maybe you should stay here, Gabe," I suggested.

"Fuck that," she returned equably, her fingers tapping an AI pilot deck. Coordinates entered, she slid out of the captain's chair and picked up her rig, buckling herself into it. Projectile guns, plasguns, knives, and triggers for various spells settled into their accustomed places. Even in a rig she looked impossibly elegant. "I'm not about to stay in here while you go have all the fun."

"You can pilot this thing; we need a getaway driver."

"Quit fussing, Mom." Gabe rolled her eyes, shoved a pin through her braided hair. "Why don't *you* stay up here and cover us?"

"That's Jace's job," I returned. Then I looked down at the print-outs. My finger rested over one of the yellow points of light, low down on the south side of the castle, in one of the most difficult-to-access parts. "Japhrimel, can you...umm, fly?"

"I can get you into that window, Dante," he replied. "I can't carry more than one, though."

"Don't worry about us," Gabe piped up. "We brought slicboards."

"I don't suppose I can talk you out of this." I rolled my head back; Japhrimel's lips met my temple. Jace glanced down at the printouts. I tore my finger away from the table with some difficulty, shook my hand out. My heartbeat took on the usual prejob pace—too quick to be resting, too slow to be pounding, adrenaline flooding my bloodstream.

"Wait a minute," Jace said. "I'm not staying here. You need backup."

"I've got Japhrimel," I said, without thinking about it.

There, it was out. Jace's mouth twisted down at the corners. Japhrimel's arms tightened slightly. The mark on my left shoulder flushed with velvet heat.

"We're too small a group to leave someone topside," Eddie said. "We need everyone we've got down there making trouble."

I hunched my shoulders. "You're all fucking crazy." I put my hand out, palm-down, over the table. "All right. We all go in together."

Gabe placed her hand over mine. "All together, and the gods help us."

Eddie covered our hands with his hairy paw. "Fuck 'em all," he growled.

Jace, then. "I won't be left behind," he said. "Not on something like this."

Japhrimel paused, and then slid to the side. He laid his hand over ours. "May your gods and mine protect us," he added judiciously.

"I didn't know demons had gods." Gabe grinned. It was her combat grin, light and fierce.

We broke as if at a prearranged signal, and I looked up at

Japhrimel. "Be careful, okay?" I rubbed my katana's hilt with my thumb.

His face was as grim and murderous as I'd ever seen it. The eerie green glow from the instruments bathed him in a radioactive aura. "Do not worry over me, Dante. I have fought many battles in my time."

I looked down at the printouts, my mouth dry. The place was massive, and I had no clue where Santino would be hiding.

Jace opened the side hatch as the hover drifted. "Datbands?" he yelled over the sudden roar of wind, water, and pressurized airseals. The commlinks in everyone's ears crackled into life. I shook my head—I hated commlinks, but I couldn't spare the concentration keeping a telepathic five-way link open would cost me.

I held mine up, Gabe and Eddie copying me. We were all three keyed into the hover's intranet, which meant we could track each other with our datbands. Gabe extracted a long NeoSho slicboard from a crate in the pile of supplies. I checked my plasgun for the fiftieth time. Eddie took the NeoSho and Jace pulled out his Chervoyg. The hum of powering-up antigrav filled the air.

Gabe grinned. "See ya in the funny papers," she yelled, and ran for the door. Eddie followed, coasting his slicboard out into the jetstream and leaping, the green-yellow glow of Skinlin sorcery limning him. *He's triggered the* golem'ai *to start the distraction,* I thought, and shivered. The mudlike creatures gave me the willies. "Japhrimel," I yelled over the noise, "just cause as much damage as you can once we've grabbed the kid. Level the whole place, if you can."

He nodded curtly, his coat beginning to stream and flap, separating in front. I swallowed hard. Jace dropped out the hatch, two plasguns already in his hands, his sword tucked through his belt. I took a deep breath. "Catch me?" I yelled, and Japhrimel nodded.

I didn't wait for more, simply ran for the hatch and launched myself into the night. Before I could lose my nerve.

CHAPTER 49

We certainly made an entrance.

We were too-small targets for the antiaircraft battery, and by the time I found myself yanked up in Japhrimel's hands, the first *golem'ai* had Manifested. It was seven feet tall, built out of what looked like sentient humanoid mud, with glowing yellow spotlight eyes. It landed on the battlements with a thud, and screams drifted up over the sound of the waves and the punishing icy wind.

Cold. It was brutally cold. The wind sliced through me. Jace bobbed and wove underneath us, skating his slicboard fast through a collage of plasgun bolts—*where are those coming from,* I thought, and tossed a firestarter into the wind. A breath of Power made it arrow off toward the outcropping where human guards crouched, raking us with plasgun fire. The resultant explosion briefly turned the night a lurid orange, and I saw Gabe and Eddie had already reached the south side. Gabe wove among plasbolts with incredible grace, as if she was tagging slow hovers back in Saint City; I heard her voice raised sharply as Japhrimel glided, angling to keep us out of the way of the plasbolt crossfire. One gun emplacement exploded; I caught a whiff of Gabe's Power. She'd used a firestarter.

Picture this, then: the whole battle happening in seconds. Jace's share of the firestarters crackled, he was sowing them in a criss-cross pattern, taking out a whole tower. Stone crumbled, I heard his whoop of bloodthirsty joy. Then he went streaking over the battlements, sword in one hand, plasgun in the other, almost losing his slic as a plascannon bolt clipped the edge of his shielding.

We were on the north side, Japhrimel and I, about to make the sharp banking turn that would bring us back around and drop us into position to run for the spot in the castle where I'd felt Doreen's kid. There was a bank of guns here, too, beginning to move on their gimbals to focus down on the other three. "Drop me!" I yelled, flicking a firestarter, and wonder of wonders, Japhrimel obeyed.

I hit hard, rolling, and he was right behind me. I took the first two almost before I knew what was happening, my body moving with instinctive speed and precision. I leapt, catching the iron bar that the gunner was standing on, found his ankle, and yanked. He tumbled off into the wind, a human cry escaping him, lost in all the ruckus.

"Heavy fire," Eddie gasped.

"I'm on it," I snapped, shimmying up, hearing the clatter of gunfire while Japhrimel dealt with the other human guard. My conscience would prick me later—but they signed up with Santino, they took their chances. I swung the plascannon and yanked back on the triggerbolt, praying—

Prayers answered. The bolts raked the other end of the wall, exploding cannon after cannon and crackling. I scrambled down, whirling as Japhrimel shouted something shapeless I understood anyway, and flicked another firestarter at the cannon as he grabbed me and flung us both out into empty air. "Now, isn't that better?"

Japhrimel coasted around, ducking under a stray bit of debris. "Let's get this over with," he yelled. I glanced down — we were losing altitude fast.

"Direct me, Danny," Gabe's voice crackled over the commlink.

I was happy I could. "Two windows up, straight in front of you, that's where the kid is. Pull up and watch your left, there's a bunch of plasgun coming your way."

"Got it," Eddie snarled, and flame bloomed again. A concussive *boom!* raked the night, stone and glass shattering. I heard thin human cries; another klaxon started to blare. More lights started to blaze in the massive pile of rock. *Holy fuck,* I thought, *we're doing a full-scale frontal assault on a demon's hideaway and getting away with it.*

Then things started to get interesting.

I didn't want to see how Japhrimel was flying — or gliding, actually, since we seemed to be falling pretty rapidly. He aimed for the kid's window and I spent a few moments with my eyes closed, *feeling* for her, letting him take care of it. The flare of her presence was close, so close —

"Dante?" Japhrimel's voice in the commlink.

"We're in," Gabe said. "What the —"

"Danny!" Eddie yelled. *"He's here! He's here!"*

"Burn the entire fucking place down, Japhrimel!" I screamed, and the entire world went soundless white as Japhrimel pulled on all the Power he could reach. A thin white-skinned shape blew out on the backwash of the explosion; my entire body screamed. It might have been Santino, my prey, falling through cold empty air.

If it's him, that won't kill him, I thought. *Not even a drop like that will kill him, he's a demon even if he's a weak one he's too strong, too slow, we're moving too slow* —

Jace nipped neatly inside the hole torn in the south side of the castle. Japhrimel let go of me and I tumbled through empty frozen air, faster-than-human reflexes saving me as I slammed into the stone wall. The *boom!* of another explosion rattled the wall; I jackknifed into the hole, my fingernails plowing stone and cold air plucking at my hair, landed on a wooden floor littered with shards of glass, broken stone, and wooden splinters.

The room was a nursery, again, stone floors holding pastel hangings in a faint attempt to make it less grim. Toys scattered, burning, across the floor. A huge ornate mahogany bedstead crouched in one corner, and I saw a stray gleam of light from the emerald in the child's forehead as it gave one amazing flash of light. My own emerald rang, answering it.

"Oh, no—"

Eddie screamed. The smell—ice and cold blood, maggots and wet rat fur—triggered my gorge. If I'd had anything in my stomach I would have spewed. I didn't know demons *could* throw up. *Santino.* It was his smell, he'd been here, I *knew* he'd been here. So it had been him falling from the room.

Gabe lay, broken and bloody, against the far wall. Of course— she'd been the first in, and Santino had been here, probably expecting us as soon as the commotion started. How badly was she hurt? I didn't have time to think about it; Eddie would take care of her.

Eddie gained his feet, shaking his shaggy head. It looked like he'd fetched up hard against the other side of the steel door to this room; his hair was singed and he was dirty from stone dust. He ran for Gabe. *Don't let her be hurt,* I prayed. *don't let her be hurt—*

Jace grabbed my arm and hauled me up as Japhrimel landed inside the room, coat folding around him as he rolled. He gained his feet and whirled, seeing me, then nodded. He strode toward Gabe and I shook free of Jace, bolting for the bed.

The little girl sat straight up, her dark eyes huge. The only uncertain light came from burning reflected in through the massive hole in the wall, glass from the lamp in the ceiling crunching under my boots. I reached the bed, stared down at the girl.

This is no child, I thought. *What am I doing?*

"Go," Japhrimel said. "Go, take her back to the ship. She'll live."

"He ripped her stomach out!" Eddie screamed, but Japhrimel caught his shoulders, his eyes sparking for a moment with the old green flame.

"I have mended her, she will *live*, dirtwitch. As you value her life, *go!*" Then Japhrimel pushed him away.

"What about Santino?" Jace yelled.

I held out my hands.

The girl looked at me. The cacophony—klaxons screaming, human cries, antiaircraft fire—they were filling the sky with bolts, trying to hit something—faded away.

She has Doreen's eyes, I thought, and the child nodded.

It wasn't just that she was beautiful, because she was. She looked as if Lucifer and Doreen had been melded into one small, perfect entity, the emerald in her forehead singing softly. It wasn't that she put up her hands and smiled at me. It wasn't even that she smelled familiar—some combination of fresh-baked bread and a unique smell that something in my subconscious recognized.

It was the shadow of knowledge in her dark eyes, and the absolute lack of fear. I knew she had somehow been waiting for me. Had somehow *known* I was coming, and accepted it. The knowledge chilled me right down to my new bones.

She's not human, I thought. *What if it's best to leave her with Santino?*

I scooped her up and turned, ran for the others, her hot, chubby arms wrapped around my neck.

Eddie had just finished triggering the third *golem'ai*. Screams. The heavy, ironbound door leading into the rest of the castle resounded with shouts and thuds. They were breaking in. Santino's human army was on its way.

Where did Santino go? How long will it take him to get back up here?

I didn't have time to worry about it.

I shoved the girl into Jace's arms. He took her before he realized what I was doing, and I pushed him out of the hole in the wall, his slicboard whining and taking the kinetic energy I supplied. *Too much Power, sorry about that, Jace*—"Get her to the ship, Jace! *Move!*" Japhrimel hauled Gabe up, Power thundering in the confined space and dyeing the air with diamond-dark, twisting flames. Gabe flopped in his arms, but Japhrimel had said she would live.

Eddie took Gabe's limp weight. Her slicboard lay twisted and useless against the far wall. "He went that way—" Eddie screamed, pointing at the hole in the wall, his face a mask of rage.

I grabbed him by the collar and shook him. "Get Gabe out of here! *Move it!*"

I didn't have to tell him twice. He bolted for the hole in the wall, Gabe in his arms, blood dripping from her long dark braid. *I hope she's still alive, if she dies goddammit Santino I'll kill you twice—*

"Danny, get out of there," Jace yelled, the commlink crackling in my ear. "Hurry up!"

Japhrimel started toward the hole in the wall.

Oh no, I thought. *I am not leaving. I have business to finish here.*

I turned toward the door, my katana sliding free. I dropped the borrowed scabbard, tore the commlink out of my ear, and fitted the plasgun into my left hand. Took a deep breath. Japhrimel twisted away from the hole in the wall, his boots skidding. Had he really thought I would leave without doing what I came to do?

As long as Santino was alive, I would never be able to rest again.

Japhrimel's lips shaped my name as I took in a deep breath, my blade blazing with pitiless blue light that threw sharp reflections through the ruined room. I pointed the plasgun at the door, where a circle of white-hot glow told me they were using lasecutters to break in.

"*Santino!*" I roared with all my newfound Power, and squeezed the plasgun's trigger just as the demon Vardimal broke through the wall behind the bed, mahogany splinters flying like shrapnel, stone turning to dust and icicle shards. The shockwave caught me and threw me against the stone wall, and I almost lost my sword when I hit with a sickening thump that shivered yet more stone from the roof and wall.

Japhrimel let out a sound so huge it was almost soundless and hurled himself at Santino.

Who threw up one clawed hand that held something glittering, made a complicated twisting motion, and tossed the glitter straight at Japhrimel.

The Egg! The thought seemed to move through syrup.

I gained my feet in a shuffle, hearing groans from the ruins of the door. The plasgun bolt had smacked into the cutter's field and caused a chain reaction, plasbolt reacting with the lase energy and freeing a whole hell of a lot of violent energy. It's a basic law of dealing with plasguns: *never shoot at reactive or lase fields.* Nobody caught in *that* would want to fight anymore—not if they were human. If I'd been human the concussion might have killed me.

I launched myself at Santino as the small glittering thing, no bigger than my fist, smacked Japhrimel in the chest—and blew him through the wall and out into the night with a sound that made a gush of blood drip down from my ears and nose. I shook my head, dazed for only a split second. The drilling pain flashed through me and was gone, the warmth of the blood freezing against my skin in milliseconds. My breath puffed out, turned to a tissue-thin cloud of ice crystals, fell straight down.

Japhrimel! I skidded to a stop, facing Santino, whose claws cut the cold air. Our feet crunched in glass and tinkling stone shards as he moved, circling.

He didn't look happy to see me. "*Fool!*" he hissed. "The *fool.*"

My katana circled. The rest of the world faded away. Here he was, right in front of me.

My revenge.

"Santino," I hissed. The entire world seemed to hold its breath, the shape of my vengeance lying under the fabric of reality, rising to meet me. "Or Vardimal. Or whoever the hell you are."

"You can't kill me," he sneered. "Neither man nor demon can kill me. Lucifer assured me of that."

I showed my own teeth, boots shuffling lightly, quickly. "I am going to eat your fucking heart," I informed him. *I'm not a man or a demon, Santino. Your immunity doesn't apply.*

"You could have been a *queen,*" he snarled at me, the black teardrops over his eyes swallowing the light. "You could have helped me kill Lucifer and take the rule of Hell! But no, you stupid, silly *human*—"

"Not human," I said. "Not anymore."

He bared his teeth again. "Who do you think helped me *escape* from Hell?" he screamed, my blade flashing up as we circled. "He's *Lucifer's* assassin! His Right Hand! He's *used* you—"

That answered the question that had been teasing the back of my mind since this whole thing started—of how exactly Santino had escaped Hell. I should have been enraged at Japhrimel for hiding that from me, I should have been wondering what else he'd hidden. What other secrets he might have kept. But with my revenge in front of me and Japhrimel's blood filling my veins, I could have cared less.

"I don't fucking care," I hissed, and my own voice tore more stone from the ceiling and sent it pattering down in a drift of dust. "I've come to kill you, you scavenger son of a bitch, for what you did to Doreen. And every other woman you murdered."

And then there was no more time for talk, because he moved in with that spooky invisible speed of demons.

I parried his claws, my katana ringing and blazing with blue fire. He screamed, a horrible drilling sound of awful agony, the plasgun tore out of my hands but I hooked my fingers and swiped at him, hot black demon blood spraying and freezing in the too-cold air. Something had happened when he'd thrown that thing at Japhrimel. It was too cold even for Antarctica.

He leapt on me, his compact weight knocking me off my feet. We tumbled, and his claws tore at me, a horribly familiar gush of pain. I screamed, forgetting I was no longer human, and did the only thing I could.

I jackknifed my body, using his momentum as well as my own, and flung us both out into the night as I buried my katana in his chest, shoving with every ounce of preternatural strength Japhrimel had given me. The blade rammed through a shell of magick, through muscle and the carbolic acid of demon blood, and the agony of the blade's shattering tore all the way through me.

One of the shards pierced his heart. I flailed at him with my claws, his throat giving in one heated gush that coated my face and hands and instantly froze, almost sealing my nostrils. If I hadn't been screaming, I might have suffocated.

I was still hacking at him with my claws when we hit the water, his slack lifeless body exploding out in noxious burning fragments. The shock of that hit drove all breath and consciousness from me, and I fell unresisting into the embrace of the ocean, waves crackling and freezing closed over my head.

CHAPTER 50

I floated. Face-down.

Stinging. Cold so intense it burned. Lassitude creeping up my arms and legs.

No. A familiar voice. Familiar fingers on my cheek, tipping my head up. *No, don't, Danny. You have to live. You promised.*

I didn't promise! I wailed silently. *Let me go! Let me go, let me die—*

You have work to do. Doreen's voice, gentle, inexorable. *Please, Danny. Please.*

Floated. Sinking. Even a share of a fallen demon's Power couldn't keep me alive for long in this. Something had happened—Santino had done something, that small glittering thing had hit Japhrimel—

Santino. I'd killed him. I'd watched his body dissolve under my fingernails, I'd torn through his throat. He was, indisputably, dead and scattered on the freezing ocean. No little bit of him would be left.

I killed him, I pleaded. *I did it. I got revenge for you. Isn't that enough?*

No, she replied, solemn. *Live, Danny. I want you to live.*

It hurts too much, I keened to her.

Blue crystal glow, the bridge under my feet. For one dizzying moment I was between two worlds — the Hall of Death, its blue directionless light pouring through me, Anubis standing tall and grim on the other side of the bridge; and the real world, where I floated facedown under a sheet of broken ice. For one infinite moment I was locked under the pitiless, infinitely forgiving gaze of the Lord of Death, weighing, evaluating, His black eyes fixed on mine. *It hurts too much,* I told him. *Please don't make me go back.*

He shook His sleek black head, once, twice. I struggled — *no! Let me stay! Let me stay!*

Then He spoke.

The Word boomed through me. It was not His name, or any Word of Power. It wasn't the secret name I held for Him, my key to the door of Death.

No.

It was my name — only more. It was my Word, spoken by the god, the sound that expressed me, the sound that could not be spoken aloud. My soul leapt inside me, responding to His touch. The god took the weight from me, briefly, let me feel the freedom, the incredible *freedom,* rising out of my body, leaving the world behind, the clear blue light becoming golden, the clear rational light of What Comes Next.

Then it dwindled to a single point in the darkness, and I rammed back into my body, fingers clamped in my hair, yanking. I was torn from the water's embrace, glazed with ice, choking, coughing, the landing lights of the garbage scow named *Baby* exploding through the darkness. Jace, his lips blue, tangling the plasnet around us both and we were yanked up together, his arms and legs wrapped around me. We broke through the airseals and into the warm interior of the hover, and the hatch slammed closed as the peculiar weightless pressure of a hover quickly ascending pressed down on me.

I coughed and choked, spluttering.

"*Breathe,* you stubborn little bitch—" Jace shivered and cursed, raging at me. Water washed the decking, rapidly melting ice shrinking under the assault of climate control.

"Is she alive?" Eddie said from the front. After the deafening noise, the quiet of the hover's interior and someone speaking normally was a muffled shock.

"She's alive," Jace said, and flung his arms around me again. Water dripped. My fingers and toes tingled and prickled. "Gods *damn* you, Danny, don't you *ever* do that to me again." He kissed my forehead, examined my fingers and my dark rings, wrapped me in a spaceblanket that started to glow, heat stealing back into me. My teeth chattered. My right hand was twisted into a fist, and I couldn't unloose it.

"G-G-Gabe—"

"She'll live. Your demon friend patched her intestines back together up there in that room, damndest thing I ever saw. She's lost a lot of blood, but she's stable and the medunit's monitoring her." Jace kissed my cheek, pushed sodden strands of dark hair back from my face. "Don't *ever* do that to me again, Danny. I thought he'd killed you."

"The k-k-k-k—" I began.

"The kid's fine. Curled up in a seat with a spaceblanket. She's asleep." Jace coughed. "Look, Danny—"

"Japhrimel?" I whispered.

Jace shook his head. "There was a hover—another hover. It might have scooped him up, I don't know. We looked for him, Danny. We really did. The entire goddamn island's broken down and iced over, I don't think anything survived that. If we hadn't been airborne we'd have been toast. What *happened?*"

"I killed him," I whispered. "I killed Santino. He threw s-s-something at J-J-aph..."

"We couldn't find him," Jace said. "I'm sorry, Danny."

I clapped my fists over my ears, huddled under the spaceblanket, and started to cry. I'd earned it, after all.

CHAPTER 51

Twelve hours later we floated over an oddly quiet Nuevo Rio. Dry and finally warm again, I sat in the seat next to Doreen's daughter (I couldn't think of what else to call her), watching out the window as morning lay over the city. Jace had moved up front next to Eddie, and the comms up there were crackling with messages. Gabe lay across a table, strapped down and deep in a sedative-induced slumber, the medunit purring as it monitored her and dripped synthetic plasma and antibiotics through a hypo into her veins. She'd wake up with a headache and a sore gut and spend a week or so recuperating, but she'd live.

The Corvin Family was gone. Just…gone. They hadn't even put up a real fight. Jace was now the owner of a hell of a lot of Family assets.

When I looked back at Doreen's daughter, I saw she was awake. In the light, her eyes were wide and clear, and dark blue. Like Doreen's.

Exactly like Doreen's.

She watched me gravely, a small child with frighteningly adult eyes, far too much Power and knowledge swimming in their depths. For a few moments, we sat like that, one tired, sobbed-out half-demon Necromance and one small demon Androgyne child.

I can't handle this, I thought. Then, *I have no choice.*

I finally managed to clear my throat. "Hi," I said quietly. "I'm Danny."

She watched me for a few more seconds before she responded. "I know," she said, in a clear light voice. "He told me you would come."

My mouth was dry and smooth as glass. This wasn't normal for a kid.

Like I knew what was normal for a kid. I never spent any time with children if I could help it. "Who told you?" I managed. "Santi— ah, um, your daddy?"

She nodded, her pale hair falling forward over her face. "*He* said he was my daddy," she confided, "but I don't think he was. My real daddy talks to me inside my head at night. He has green eyes and a green stone like me and he told me you would come for me. He said he would send you."

She seemed to expect some sort of reply. It was obvious who her "real daddy" was. Either Lucifer had some way of communicating with her, or she was precognitive, or…My brain stopped sorting through alternatives. It didn't matter. Lucifer already knew about the kid, I'd bet. I'd also bet that Lucifer had known about Santino's "samples." Or if not known, guessed. The Prince of Hell was no fool.

Why then had Japhrimel promised not to tell him?

"I promised your mommy I'd take care of you," I said rustily. *Oh, gods, Danny, you've done it now.*

The little girl nodded solemnly. "You're not like them." She pointed at the front of the hover, where Jace and Eddie conferred in low worried tones. "You're not like my real daddy either."

"I hope not." I shifted uncomfortably in the seat, the spaceblanket crackling as I moved. "What's your name?"

"I'm Eve," she said, matter-of-factly. I flinched. *Of course,* I thought, and watched as her dimples came out. She smiled at me. "Can I have some ice cream?"

"I don't think we have any, kiddo." *Japhrimel had to live on blood, or sex, or fire,* I thought. *What does this girl eat? Oh, you are not ready for this, Danny. Not ready at all.*

The hover circled slightly, and began to drift downward toward Jace's mansion.

"Um, Danny?" Jace called. "You may want to come take a look at this."

I hauled myself up, and the little girl pushed her blanket off and shimmied down from her seat. She held her small perfect hand up. "Can I come, too?" She wore a short white babydoll nightie, and her chubby feet were bare. I fought the urge to pick her up off the hover's cold metal deck.

"Okay," I said, and took her hand. It was warm in mine—a demon's touch.

Like Japhrimel's. Was he dead? Or had Santino's men taken him? What could they do to him? Was he injured?

I made my way up to the front, holding the girl's hand. "What's up?" I peered out the front window.

"Take a look." Jace glanced up at me. "How's the kid doing?"

"She seems okay," I replied.

Below us, the familiar blocky outlines of Jace's mansion grew larger as the hover slowly dropped. On the wide marble expanse of courtyard in front, two sleek limo-hovers crouched, and four police cruisers.

"Fuck me," I breathed, forgetting the child's small hand in mine. "What the hell?"

"I was hoping you could tell me," Jace said. "I'm incorporated and operating under codes, so I'm fairly sure they're not here to roust *me.*"

"Sekhmet sa'es." I was too tired to come up with a good plan. "No chance they're here for you, Eddie."

" 'Course not, unless they'd like to arrest Gabe for fucking almost dying," he said, with no apparent growl in his voice. He must be exhausted. "What do we do, Danny?"

I wish they would stop nominating me as the idea man, I thought. "Nothing else to do," I said. "Drift on down and land, but keep the motor running until we're sure we won't need it. Jace, can I have a commlink?"

"Of course," he said. "What do you want me to do, Danny?"

"Stay here with the kid," I answered, glancing down at Eve. The little girl looked up at me, as if I were the only person in the hover. "If they take me, get the kid somewhere safe and wait for me to show up."

Jace swung out of his chair, not even bothering to argue with me. I felt a weary relief. Was it normal to feel this way? So tired, but unable to sleep.

No sleep. Not until I finished this game. And it *was* a game, I'd been pushed from square to square all along.

I took the child back into the hold and settled her back into the chair, tucking the blanket around her again. When I finished, Jace was standing by a crate of supplies, a strange expression on his face. His hair curled into a halo, drenched in ice water and then dried in climate control. I probably didn't look very good either.

"What?"

"Nothing," he said. "Let me find a commlink."

Eddie piloted the hover down. We landed with a thump. "Sorry," he called back. I slipped the commlink in my ear, settled my wrinkled coat on my shoulders, made sure my knives were easy in their sheaths. My right hand ached deeply, all the way down to the bone. If I were still human, I might be maimed.

I knelt down in front of Eve, who watched me with Doreen's eyes. "I've got to go talk to whoever this is," I told her. "You stay with Jace until I get back, okay?"

She nodded. "It will be all right, Danny. My daddy says so," she said, her clear piping voice oddly adult.

"Great," I answered grimly, and stood up. The ground swayed underfoot, or maybe it was just me. "Jace, I want you to promise. Promise you'll take care of her if I—"

He shrugged. "You know I will, Danny. Go on, get this over with." His blue eyes skittered over to the girl, back up to me.

I nodded, then Eddie popped the side hatch. I hopped down to the marble, almost losing my balance. The heat hammered at me, Nuevo Rio back to its old, bad, sunny self. *I wish I was home,* I thought suddenly, and that surprised me, too. I hadn't felt like Saint City was home for a good two or three years.

One of the limo-hovers opened its side hatch. A set of steps folded down.

I swallowed. I had a fair idea of what could be waiting in there.

I strode across the burning white marble and toward the sleek black hovers, trying to keep my shoulders straight and wishing I wasn't dirty, bloody, air-dried, and so close to crying my throat ached keeping it all in.

CHAPTER 52

The inside of the limo-hover was done in all different shades of red. Crimson, cardinal, burgundy, magenta, carmine, lobster—I blinked, stepping onto plush carpet at the top of the stairs. The air swirled with the smell of *demon,* smoky musk, and I took a deep breath. It was as if I hadn't been breathing until now. Whatever demons used for air, this hover was full of it.

That's why she smells familiar, I realized with no real surprise. *She smells like him. Like Lucifer.*

The Prince of Hell lounged elegantly on a huge circular red-velvet couch, his booted feet crushing the velvet. I gave the surroundings a tired glance—wet bar, tinted windows, doors probably leading to a bathroom and a private bedroom. There was a sunken tub in one corner, bubbling and frothing with a clear viscous fluid that didn't look even remotely like water.

Lucifer's golden hair burned among the redness. He was dressed, of course, all in black silk, loose elegant pants and a long-sleeved, Chinese-collared shirt. The walls were done to look like expensive red damask wallpaper, and heavy velvet drapes muffled every sound.

I swallowed. "The decor sucks," I said, too tired for any bowing and scraping. I cradled my right hand in my left—it was really starting to throb as adrenaline wore off.

"Good afternoon to you, too," Lucifer replied, his voice stroking and tapping at my ears. A thrill like old tired fire ran through me—I was too exhausted to really respond to him. If I'd had any more energy I would have been worried about it. "Have you brought me the Egg?"

"Nope," I said. "But Santino's dead. And you didn't really want me to bring you the Egg anyway, that was Japhrimel's job. Looks like he did it, because you're out of Hell and feeling frisky."

Lucifer held up one elegant golden hand. I could look at his face now, without my eyes blinking and watering. His smell folded over me, teased at my hair, permeated my clothes. My bones rang with his nearness, a vibrating electricity that made me want to go to my knees. I fought the urge.

A fine golden chain wrapped around his beautifully manicured fingers. "The once-demon Japhrimel brought me this," he said, twirling a diamond-glittering oval on the chain. The hum of Power filled the air. I couldn't look directly at the glittering thing, it hurt even my eyes.

My throat was desert-dry. "So that's what that was." Santino had thrown the Egg at Japhrimel, to fend him off.

"Indeed. Vardimal managed to unlock a fraction of the Egg's power and threw it at Tierce Japhrimel. The only thing that could possibly hurt my Eldest—because it is *mine,* and therefore dangerous to my line. Any demon would be grieviously injured by it. Except, of course, myself. I am the Prince." Lucifer sounded amused. He cocked his golden head. "Where is the child, Dante Valentine?"

I shrugged. "That's what you were after all the time, wasn't it? Doreen's kid. The Androgyne. You let Santino alone until he did what you couldn't, and now you have everything."

"The *sedayeen* was never more than a template, Dante. The Egg contains my genetic codex, and pure Power. It is a mark of my reign and a useful tool."

"You knew the whole time. You *knew.* You just couldn't afford to have anyone else know Santino had done what you couldn't, so you had to find a human to do the dirty work. And all that tripe about the Egg being broken—" I shook my head, a lump in my throat. My voice sounded husky and harsh next to his smooth persuasive tones.

"Think if Vardimal *had* managed to raise the child undisturbed, Dante. Imagine him ruling Hell, and our Hellesvront agents on Earth, through that child. That is what 'breaking the Egg' means. Breaking the chain of command, breaking the rule of Iblis Lucifer."

I had one of those sudden flashes of instinct that made my back chill with gooseflesh. *He's not nervous,* I thought, *but he is tense. Where's Japhrimel? What game is he playing now?*

I glanced back toward the side hatch. It had silently closed. I was alone in a hoverlimo with the Devil. And wonder of wonders, it looked for all the world like the Devil was scared of little ol' me. "That hover at Santino's lair—that was you, or your agents. They brought you Japhrimel, and the Egg. And Santino's dead. Case closed, contract terminated, bargain fulfilled." I didn't want to say it, but I had to anyway.

Lucifer tipped his perfect head back, his green eyes crawling over me. "Aren't you going to ask about Japhrimel?"

The thought that had been tormenting me all the way back from the island slammed into the forefront of my mind again. *Who do you think helped me escape from Hell? He's Lucifer's assassin, his Right Hand! You've been used!* "I doubt you'd tell me the truth if I asked," I said. "Why waste my breath?"

"He is *A'nankimel,* Fallen. I can no longer use him, and he has tied himself to you. Besides, I promised him his freedom." Lucifer seemed to sink even further into the cushions. "I never thought to see the day my assassin was brought low by a human woman."

I got the distinct idea that Lucifer was not pleased with this turn of events.

Now we come to it, I thought clinically, wishing I had my sword. "So? He's free. Fine."

Lucifer blinked.

I suppressed a tired urge to giggle.

"Let me be perfectly clear, Dante: you do not want to play with me."

I shrugged. "I'm not playing, Lucifer. I don't care anymore. I just want to go and get some sleep." I spread my hands—my new, golden-skinned hands, sparks from my rings popping in the charged air. It felt like a thunderstorm was gathering.

For all I knew, one was.

He sat up, his boots touching the floor. I tensed. But he only leaned forward, hands on his knees. "Very well then. Here is your choice. Give me the child, and I will give you Japhrimel."

That did it.

I tipped my head back and laughed. It started out as a giggle, blew through a chuckle, and ended up full-fledged howling mirth. I laughed until tears squirted out of my eyes and my stomach hurt. When the laughter finally faded in a series of hitching gasps I wiped my eyes and regarded the Prince of Hell.

"Go fuck yourself," I said pleasantly, "if it will reach. If you think I'm going to hand an innocent kid—*Doreen's* kid—over to you for gods-alone-know-what you want to do to her, you've got another think coming. You made the bargain with Japhrimel that he had his freedom when he finished this job, and he finished it. You can't keep him, you sorry son of a bitch, and I'd like to see you try. He'll eat you for breakfast." I took a deep breath, my rings sparking, Power cloaking me in close swirls. "Let me give you a piece of advice, *Iblis Lucifer*. Don't ever try to double-cross a Necromance. As scary as you are, *Prince*, Death's bigger *and* badder."

I finished my speech with my hands on my hips and my chin held high, my right hand flaring with pain as I balled it into a tight fist. Lucifer didn't move. His eyes glittered, that was all. No wonder he was afraid—if Santino could challenge him with Eve, Lucifer probably thought I could too, if he pissed me off enough.

"How do you think you will feed her, Dante? Or teach her to live in the human world? Hell is separate from earth for a *reason*. You cannot raise an Androgyne." He said it softly, silk brushing my ears, whispering in my veins, tapping behind my heartbeat.

"I promised," I said. "I promised to take care of her. I don't want Hell or any fancy-schmancy deals. You should have told me everything at the beginning, Lucifer. She wasn't part of the deal. Let Japhrimel go."

I waited. The air turned prickling-hot. I didn't move, meeting his eyes, finding out that I only had to be too tired to care before I won a staring match with the Devil.

He finally spoke again. "Japhrimel is no longer a demon," he said quietly. "Any bargain I made with him does not apply. I will keep him in Hell, enchained, tortured for as long as his life lasts. And I will be certain to let him know that you could have saved him from his fate, and did not."

"You really are a piece of work," I said, my left hand creeping toward my knifehilt. Left-handed? I couldn't kill the Devil left-handed. "I am *not* handing a kid over to you, you freak. And if you go ahead and torture Japhrimel—which I don't recommend— you'll just be a fucking grifter. How will that look—the Prince of

Hell has to welsh on a deal? You're already known for being a liar, now you're a cheat, too—"

I didn't even see him move. One moment I was standing there, hands on hips, talking smack to the Prince of Hell. The next instant, he had me by the throat, his grip crushing-strong, holding me against the side of the hover as casually as he might hold a kitten by the scruff. "I am being merciful," he said softly, pleasantly, "because you have been useful. You are under the *illusion*—" His hand tightened, here, and I kicked fruitlessly, "that you have a *choice*. Do not interfere with the child, and I will let you and Japhrimel live out your miserable lives unmolested."

What happened to being my friend? I struggled, black spots dancing over my vision. His fingers were like iron bars even for my newfound demon strength. Something crackled in my throat; he eased up a little. I managed a little bit of air. "Fuck...you..." I croaked, and his eyes blazed. He didn't look so pretty when he was angry.

My left shoulder began to burn. Faintly at first, but steadily. The black spots danced over my vision. I kicked, weakly, once, twice.

"Ah." Staring over my shoulder, out the window, he dropped me like a pile of trash and I coughed, rolling onto my side and rubbing my throat. Blessed air roared into my lungs. It took me two tries to get to my feet. The side hatch of the hoverlimo was open, white sunlight from the Nuevo Rio day pouring up and making a square on the ceiling.

I half-fell out of the hover and down the stairs, sharp edges biting into my hip, smacking my head on one. The skin split and blood dripped down my face. I landed in a heap on hot slick stone and scrabbled to my feet.

The child—Eve—stood by the garbage scow, the fierce sunlight making her hair seem even paler, glittering. Her eyes blazed, incandescent blue.

And Lucifer stood in front of her.

"No—" I choked, scrambling over the marble. "*No!*"

The Prince of Hell knelt slowly, sinking down, a black blot on the carnivorous white of the day. I saw Jace, braced in the side door of the hover, shaking his head as if dazed. Lucifer held up the Egg, and settled the thin gold chain around Eve's neck.

She smiled up at him.

My abused body couldn't go anymore. My feet tangled, and I fell.

Lucifer rose like a dark wave, and the child put her arms around his neck and hugged him, resting her head on his shoulder.

Just like a little girl with her daddy. My gorge rose. But demons weren't human—and human rules didn't apply to them. For all I knew, all of Lucifer's bed-buddies were his children. He was the Androgyne. The first.

Then Lucifer turned on his heel, took three steps, and lifted one golden hand. His hair ran with sunlight, a furnace of gold, glittering unbearably. I heard the whine of hover displacement, didn't care. I saw Iblis Lucifer rip a hole in the fabric of reality and step through as if going from one room to another. Flame licked the corners of the hole he made, and the last thing I saw was Eve smiling over his shoulder, her blue eyes fixed on me, calm and tranquil and utterly inhuman. Power rippled, rent the air, nausea spiking under my breastbone.

Something thudded on the marble. Jace's boots rang—but the thump was from behind me. He reached me, dropping to his knees with a heavy sound, grabbing my shoulders. We watched together as the limo-hovers lifted into the sky, quickly, then dived over the well of Nuevo Rio. The police cruisers made one circuit of the mansion and then slid down into the city, going back to patrol probably.

Game over. Lucifer wins.

Jace cursed, shook me. "Danny! *Danny!*"

"What the *fuck?*" My tongue felt too thick for my mouth.

Jace's arms crushed me. "Fuck, Danny. What happened? The kid heard his voice on the commlink and just walked out; she said her daddy was here to get her."

I groaned. "I hate this line of work," I husked dryly, then looked back over my shoulder, to where the limo-hovers had rested.

Another black blot on the pavement, this one with short ink-black hair.

"They tossed him out," Jace said into my hair. "Danny—"

"Help me up. Help me *up.*"

He dragged me up to my feet, steadying me as I swayed.

"What the *fuck* is going on out there?" Eddie yelled from the hatch.

"Go back," I told Jace. "I'll be fine."

"You're not fine," he shot back at me. "Look at you. Your hand— your *throat*—"

"Go make sure Gabe's okay," I said, and shoved him away. "Go on."

Maybe I shouldn't have done that. He took a step back, his face going cold and hard as the marble under us. I think I watched Jace Monroe age five years in that one moment, his shoulders slumping, his blue eyes gone pale as frost.

"Danny," he said. "You're not seriously..."

The heat poured down on us like oil from Nuevo Rio's blue sky. "Go on, Jace. Go."

I turned away. Limped toward the crumpled dark shape lying against the whiteness. Too still. He was too still.

"Danny," I heard Jace say behind me, shut the sound out. I didn't care.

It took me a long time to limp across the marble. I finally reached him and went down on my knees. He lay twisted against the smooth slick stone, legs shattered, his face unrecognizable. Nothing could possibly be that broken and live.

I flattened my left hand against his shredded chest. His wings lay bent and broken, tattered, draped across him. He had stopped bleeding. Smoke threaded up from his wings, his blood burning, burning.

"No," I whispered. "No."

His eyes were mere slits, glazed over. "Japhrimel?" I whispered. The mark on my shoulder had stopped its flaming pain. Now it was cold, all the way down to my bones. Numb cold, the cold of shock.

No spark of life. I touched his throat, pried up one ruined eyelid and peered at his eye. No pulse. No reaction in the pupil. Just the steady drift of smoke rising from him.

My head dropped. I sighed. The sound seemed to go on forever. My throat pulsed with pain.

I *reached,* with all the Power I had left. I tried to find the spark of life in him. I rested my left palm on his body and closed my eyes, searching, but nothing was there. This was only a shell.

Japhrimel was gone.

Free. He was finally free. Lucifer had killed him—or let him die.

I didn't realize the tears splashing his battered face were mine. I bent over him for a long moment, frantically searching for any sign of life, and then settled back on my heels, cold in the middle of the furnacelike sunshine. The flames began in earnest, eating his demon body, self-combusting with a smell like burning cinnamon.

Then I tipped back my head and howled to the uncaring blue sky.

Epilogue

Gabe was fine. Shaky, battered, weak from blood loss, and possessed of an interesting new set of scars where Santino had ripped her belly open, but fine. She lived, and after a couple of days she called me to say Eddie had stopped rampaging through the mansion threatening to break windows. I stayed in a hotel down in Nuevo Rio, a cockroach-infested place where I had to listen to screaming and the pops of projectile guns outside my window every night. Gabe also told me Jace was going to give them the *Baby,* and they planned to fly the garbage scow back to Saint City. Eddie had wanted a hover anyway.

I said nothing, just listened to her on the phone and then slowly closed the sound of her voice away, setting the receiver down in its cradle. Good for them.

I flew first class in a passenger transport. My right hand was an awkward claw, but I got around with my left just fine. It would take me a long time to bless another sword if my hand ever straightened out.

I carried the urn with me. It was black lacquer, beautiful, and heavy. Pure fine cinnamon-scented ash, scraped together from white marble and carefully placed in the urn's embrace. Every speck of ash I had been able to find had gone into the urn, left by Lucifer as a parting gift maybe. Just to rub everything in.

Jace did not see me off at the dock. I didn't expect him to. I'd left his mansion like a thief in the middle of the night, carrying Japhrimel's ashes with me. Jace hadn't tried to find me or talk to me.

Good.

It was while I was sitting in the hover, resting my head against the side of the seat, that everything became clear. Of course Japhrimel had helped Vardimal escape Hell. It made sense, especially since Lucifer probably *let* him do it, figuring that Vardimal wouldn't find anything of value among humans, even humans carrying the strain of the Fallen—psions. What Lucifer didn't know, and Japhrimel probably didn't know either, was that Vardimal had taken the Egg. And when Lucifer found that out, suddenly Vardimal wasn't so little a threat. If Lucifer hadn't known about the kid then, he'd probably guessed when he found the Egg gone and took notice of the human world again; finding out that Vardimal, true to form, had been taking samples from human psychics and had then disappeared. And at some point, Lucifer had made contact with Eve—way before I did, but probably by following the same link of blood I'd followed. Only his link with the child would be stronger, since it was his genetic material, and I only had the fading echo of my love for Doreen and our shared human link.

And if Lucifer had been unable to leave Hell without the Egg, all of a sudden it became necessary to attack Vardimal from a direction the scavenger demon wouldn't see coming. No demon would think that the Prince would hire a human.

Lucifer had been playing to retain his control of Hell; Eve was another playing piece with potential value as a *created* Androgyne. It would be child's play for Lucifer to reverse-engineer and find Vardimal's "shining path of genes," securing his own grasp on the reproduction of other demons. And it probably piqued the hell out of Lucifer that Vardimal had managed to do something the Prince couldn't.

Vardimal had been playing for control of Hell itself. Japhrimel had been playing for his freedom, and just when it seemed possible that he might live out the game, Lucifer had killed him for letting Vardimal escape—never mind that Lucifer allowed and probably facilitated it.

It was all very logical, once I got a chance to think about it. Simple enough.

Me? Just a human tool. I'd been playing for my life. And here I was alive, and the demon who lied to me was dead. I'd killed Santino at last, but Lucifer had Doreen's kid. If that made us even, it also made me the loser.

Maybe Lucifer hadn't expected Japhrimel to turn me into whatever I was now. And that was a problem—just what the hell was I? Japhrimel had expected to be alive enough to explain it to me when everything was said and done. Maybe he miscalculated just how deeply Lucifer would detest the idea of anyone winning anything from him—even his assassin, whom he'd thrown away anyway.

The transport finally docked, and I waited until everyone else had a chance to get off before I made my way out into the hoverport, breathing in the Saint City stink again, feeling the cold glow of my home's Power rasping against my flesh. It took me bare seconds to adapt, because I wasn't...human.

I caught a cab home, the urn cuddled against my belly, and found myself in my own front yard again, under a blessedly cloudy Saint City sky. A faint light rain was misting down, decking out my garden with small silvery beads of water. I'd need to weed soon, and tear up half the valerian. Dry out the roots to use for sleeping-tea.

If I could ever sleep again, that was.

I unlocked my door and stamped my feet on the mat. My familiar, soothing house folded around me.

I carried the urn into the stale, quiet dimness of my house. The hall had that peculiar odor of a place where nobody has breathed for a while, a house closed up on itself for too long.

Halfway up the stairs, the niche with the little statue of Anubis was just the same as it had always been. Dusty, but just the same. My house was still here, still standing. It was only my life that had been burned to the ground.

I settled the urn between two slim vases of dead flowers—I had forgotten to throw them out before I left—and lit two tall black candles in crystal holders. Then I trudged up the rest of the stairs, one by one. I draped my coat over the banister, unbuttoned my shirt, freed my hair from its filthy braid. Somehow washing off all the crud hadn't seemed worth it.

My personal computer deck stood in the upstairs study, next to the file cabinet where Santino's file had rested. I flicked it on and spent a few moments tapping.

When I finally signed on to my bank statements, I sat and stared at the screen for a long time.

I was no longer Danny Valentine, struggling mercenary and Necromance.

I was rich. Not just rich—*phenomenally* rich. The breath slammed out of me while I sat there, staring at the flickering screen. I would never have to worry about money again—not for a long, long time, anyway.

And just how long would I live, cursing myself, knowing I'd been outplayed by the Devil in a game I hadn't even known I was going to be sucked into? All things being equal, I was lucky to still be breathing.

I looked at the numbers, my pulse beating frail and hard in my throat and wrists. At least Lucifer hadn't welshed on that part of his promise.

I logged out and switched the deck off, then sat looking at my hands in the gathering twilight. The blessed quiet of my house enfolded me.

My hands lay obediently in my lap, golden-skinned and graceful. The right was still twisted into a kind of claw, but if I tried I could move the fingers a little more each day. My wrists were slender marvels of bone architecture. If I scrubbed the dirt off my face I could look in a mirror and see a demon's beauty under a long fall of dark hair, the emerald glowing from my cheek.

Would I still be able to enter Death? I was pretty sure...but I didn't have the stinking courage to find out for sure. Not yet.

Empty. I was an empty doll.

You will not leave me to wander the earth alone. Had he meant it?

Had the only thing Japhrimel not planned for been *me*? Or had I been part of his game?

Somehow, I didn't think I'd been something he'd planned. Call me stupid, but...I didn't think so.

The breath left me in another walloping rush. I blinked. A tear dropped from my eyelid, splashed onto my right hand.

I might have sat there for hours if my front door hadn't resounded with a series of thumps.

My heart leapt into my mouth. I tasted bile.

I made it down the stairs slowly, like an old woman. Twisted the doorknob without bothering to scan the other side of the door. My shields—and Japhrimel's—still remained, humming and perfect over the house. Nothing short of a thermonuclear psychic attack could damage my solitude now.

I didn't want to wonder why Japhrimel's shields were still perfect if he was dead. Maybe demon magick worked differently.

I jerked the door open and found myself confronted with a pair of blue eyes and slicked-down golden hair, dark with the creeping rain. He stood on my doorstep, leaning on his staff, and regarded me.

I said nothing. Silence stretched between us.

Jace shoved past me and into my front hall. I shut the door and turned around. Now he faced me in my house, through the stale dimness.

We stared at each other for a long time.

Finally he licked his lips. "Hate me all you want," he said. "Go ahead. I don't blame you. Yell at me, scream at me, try to kill me, whatever. But I'm not leaving."

I folded my arms. Stared at him.

He stared back at me.

I finally cleared my throat. "I'm not human anymore, Jace," I said. Husky. My voice was ruined from screaming—and from the Devil's hand crushing my larynx. I was lucky he hadn't killed me.

Or had he deliberately left me alive? To wander the earth. Alone.

"I don't care what you are," he said. "I'm not leaving."

"What if I leave?" I asked him. "I could go anywhere in the world."

"For fuck's sake, Danny." He pounded his staff twice on my floor, sharp guncracks of frustration. "Get off it, will you? I'm staying. That's it. Yell at me all you like, I'm not leaving you alone. The demon's dead, you need someone to watch your back."

"I don't love you," I informed him. "I won't ever love you."

"If I cared about *that* I'd still be in Rio with a new Mob Family and a sweet little fat-bottomed *babalawao,*" he shot back. "This is my choice, Danny. Not yours."

I shrugged, and brushed past him. Climbed the stairs, slowly, one at a time.

I hadn't made my bed before I left, so I just dropped myself into the tangle of sheets and covers and closed my eyes. Hot tears slid out from between my eyelids, soaked into the pillow.

I heard his footsteps, measured and slow. He set his staff by the bed, leaning it against the wall the way he used to. Then he lowered himself down next to me, fully clothed.

"I'll sleep on the couch, if you want," he said finally, lying on his back, staring up at the ceiling.

"Do whatever you want," I husked. "I don't care."

"Just for tonight, then." He closed his eyes. "I'll be a gentleman. Buy another bed and clear out that spare bedroom tomorrow..." His voice trailed off.

"I don't care," I repeated. Silence descended on my house again, broken only by the soft sound of rain pattering on my roof. The sharp tearing in my chest eased a little, then a little more. Tears trickled down to my temples, soaked into my hair.

He must have been exhausted, because it took a very little time before his even breathing brushed the air, his face serene with human unconsciousness and age. Sleep, Death's younger sister.

Or oldest child...

I lay next to Jace, stiff as a board, and cried myself into a demon's fitful sleep.

EXIT INTERVIEW
Amadeus Hegemony Academy

Student #: 47138SAZ
Name: Dante Valentine

Interviewer: Mollison Rigby, Guidance Counselor 4A

Good afternoon, Miss Valentine. Congratulations on your achievement.

Thank you.

May I say what a pleasure it's been, having you with us? You're a credit to our Necromance program.

[Silence]

Well, then. *[Nervous laugh]* Let's begin. We've discussed your preference for law enforcement, and you've taken several courses to that effect. Your combat-training scores are very good. I'll ask again, are you planning on entering federal law enforcement, or perhaps a smaller city bureau?

Haven't given it much thought. I suppose I'll see what comes up.

Okay. *[Rustling paper]* You're aware the cost of your Academy schooling is part of a deferred federal Hegemony loan? Have you read the literature pertaining to——

I know what I owe, Rigby. Five hundred thousand standard, give or take a few credits. Interest is at the usual rate. A percentage of any income I receive goes into a fidelity account to be applied against my debt quarterly. I won't be taxed on that income and I'll receive a credit for the interest.

Well, you've done your homework on student loans. I shouldn't be surprised. [*Laughs*] I have to ask, you see. Federal regulations. There's just a few more things, and you'll be free to start living your life as a fully accredited psion. Here. [*Paper rustling*]

What the hell's this?

Since you're past your majority and are accredited, I'm allowed to hand it over. It's the contents of your foster father's savings accounts and the proceeds from the sale of his effects, as detailed in his will, which you'll find a copy of and a full accounting detail for in the red envelope. The blue envelope——

Anubis...I didn't know.

His will was very explicit, providing for his funeral and resting costs as well as ameliorating quite a bit of the expenses incurred as a result of your Academy schooling. It was sealed until you reached your accreditation, you see.

[Indistinct murmur]

What was that?

His books. What happened to his books?

They were auctioned off, for a fair price. He had some fine items.

[*Pause*] *Yes. Yes, he did. Are all of them gone?*

I believe so. [*Pause*] It's quite a sum, and yours to do with as you please. Not every student gets such good news.

[*Sarcastic laugh*] *Thanks. Can I go now?*

Are you all right?

Can I *go* now?

Not just yet. Here's a sealed packet, which is an anonymous survey of the Academy, part of our quality control program. I like to encourage all our students to fill it out thoroughly——we like to know if we're doing a good job.

Better than Rigger Hall.

[*Pause*] Yes, you were there for your primary schooling, weren't you? I hope your time here has been better.

I can't complain. Do we have to do this? You've probably got better things to waste your time on.

It's not a waste, Valentine. In any case, it's routine.

Sure. Fine. Whatever. Can I go now?

I suppose nothing else is of earthshattering importance. Here's the rest of your exit packet. I'm available to help you for the next two years, which is, as I'm sure you know, shown to be a difficult adjustment time in a young psion's——I really don't think you should—— What's in the blue envelope? From Lewis. Do you know?

I don't. You look pale. Are you all——

I'm fine. I have to go now. Thanks, Rigby. See you.

Valentine! [*Sound of door closing*] Dammit. Fucking kids.

Book 2

Dead Man Rising

To L.I.
Peace. The charm's wound up.

Quis fallere possit amantem?
—Virgil

Leaving Hell is not the same as entering it.
—Tierce Japhrimel

Since before the Awakening, the world has been aware of the existence of psionics. And since the Parapsychic Act was signed into Hegemony law, the psionic Talents have been harnessed to provide valuable service to mankind. Who can imagine a world without Skinlin and sedayeen *cooperating to find new cures for every gene-morphing virus, creating new techniques for alteration and augmentation of the human body? Who can imagine a time when the Magi did not probe the laws of magick and alternate realities, or when Ceremonials and Shamans didn't minister to the needs of believers and track criminals, not to mention provide protection for houses and corporations? Who can imagine a world without psions?*

The Necromance's place within this continuum is assured: The Necromance treads in that realm of mystery called Death. At hospital bedsides and in courtrooms, Necromances ease the passing of their fellow humans or provide testimony for the last wishes of the dead. An accredited Necromance's work touches the very mundane world of finance, wills, and bequests at the same time that they peer into the dry land of Death and return with absolute proof *that there is an afterlife. Necromances also work in the Criminal Justice arm of the Hegemony, tracking criminals and murderers. A Necromance requires not only the talent for entering the realm of Death, but also the training and sorcerous Will to come back* out *of Death. This is why accreditation of Necromances is so expensive, and so harrowing for even the Academy-trained psionics whose Talent lies in Necromance.*

On the flap opposite you will see several careers where an accredited Necromance can make a difference…

—Brochure, *What Can Death Do For You?*, printed by the Amadeus Hegemony Academy of Psionic Arts

CHAPTER 1

The cavernous maw of the warehouse was like the throat of some huge beast, and even though it was large and airy claustrophobia still tore at my throat. I swallowed, tasted copper and the wet-ratfur reek of panic. *How do I talk myself into these things? "Come on, do a bounty, it's easy as one-two-three, we've done a hundred of them."* Sure.

Darkness pressed close as the lights flickered. *Damn corporate greed not putting proper lighting in their goddamn warehouses. The least they could have done is had the fluorescents replaced.*

Then again, corporations don't plan for hunters taking down bounties in their warehouses, and my vision was a lot better than it used to be. I eased forward, soft and silent, broken-in boots touching the cracked and uneven floor. My rings glinted, swirling with steady, muted light. The Glockstryke R4 was in my left hand, my crippled right hand curled around to brace the left; it had taken me weeks to shoot left-handed with anything like my former accuracy. And why, you might ask, was I using a projectile gun when I had two perfectly good 40-watt plasguns holstered in my rig?

Because Manuel Bulgarov had taken refuge in a warehouse full of plastic barrels of reactive paint for spreading on the undersides of hovers, that's why.

Reactive paint is mostly nonvolatile — except for when a plas field interacts with it. One plasgun blast and we'd be caught in a reaction fire, and though I was a lot tougher than I used to be I didn't think I could outrun a molecular-bond-weakening burst fueled by hundreds, if not thousands, of gallons of reactive. A burst like that travels at about half the speed of light until it reaches its containment edge.

Even if I could outrun or survive it, Jace certainly couldn't, and he was covering me from the other side of the T-shaped intersection of corridors faced with blue barrel after blue barrel of reactive.

Just like a goddamn bounty to hide in a warehouse full of reactive to make my day.

Jace's fair blond face was marred with blood that almost hid the thorny accreditation tat and the spreading bruise up his left cheek, he was bleeding from his shoulder too. Ending up in a bar brawl that alerted our quarry was *not* the way I'd wanted to do this bounty.

His blue eyes were sharp and steady, but his breathing was a little too fast and I could smell the exhaustion on him. I felt familiar worry rise under my breastbone, shoved it down. My left shoulder prickled with numb chill, a demon's mark gone dead against my flesh, and my breathing came sharp and deep, ribs flaring with each soundless gasp, a few stray strands of hair falling in my face. *Thank the gods I don't sweat much anymore.* I could feel the inked lines of my own accreditation tat twisting and tingling under the skin of my left cheek, the emerald set at the top of the twisted caduceus probably flashing. *Tone it down, don't want to give the bastard a twinkle and let him squeeze off a shot or two.*

Bulgarov didn't have a plasgun—or at least, I was reasonably certain he hadn't had one when he'd gone out the back door of the PleiRound nightclub and onto an airbike with us right behind him, only slightly slowed down by the explosion of the brawl. After all, the PleiRound was a watering hole for illicits, and once we'd moved and shown we were bounty hunters all hell had broken loose. If he'd had a plasgun, he probably wouldn't have bothered to run. No, he would have turned the bar into a firezone.

Probably.

I'd almost had Bulgarov, but he was quick. Too quick to be strictly normal, though he wasn't a psion. I made a mental note to tell my scheduler Trina to tack 15 percent onto the fee, nobody had mentioned the bastard was genespliced and augmented to within an inch of violating the Erdwile-Stokes Act of '28. That would have been nice information to have. Necessary information, even.

My shoulder still hurt from clipping the side of a hover as we chased him through nighttime traffic on Copley Avenue. He'd been keeping low to avoid the patrols, though how you could be inconspicuous with two bounty hunters chasing you on airbikes, I couldn't guess.

It was illegal to flee, especially once a bounty hunter had identified herself as a Hegemony federal officer. But Bulgarov hadn't gotten away with rape, murder, extortion, and trafficking illegal weapons by being a law-abiding jackass who cared about two more counts of felony evading. No, he was an entirely different kind of jackass. And staying low meant a little more time without the Hegemony patrols getting involved in the tangle, which made it him against just two bounty hunters instead of against full-scale containment teams. It was a nice move, and sound logic — if the two bounty hunters weren't an almost-demon and the Shaman who had taught her a good deal about hunting bounties.

My eyes met Jace's again. He nodded curtly, reading my face. Like it or not, I was the one who could take more damage. And I usually took point anyway; years of working bounties alone made it a tough habit to break.

He was still good to work with. It was just like old times. Only everything had changed.

I eased around the corner, hugging the wall. Extended my awareness a little, just a very little, feeling the pulse thunder in my wrists and forehead; the warehouse was magshielded and had a basic corporate security net, but Bulgarov had just walked right in like he owned the place. Not a good sign. He might have bought a short-term quickshield meant to keep him from detection by psions or security nets. Just what I'd expect from the tricky bastard.

Concentrate, Danny. Don't get cocky because he's not a psion. He's dangerous and augmented.

My right hand cramped again, pointlessly; it was getting stronger the more I used it. Three days without sleep, tracking Bulgarov through the worst sinks in North New York Jersey, taxed even my endurance. Jace could fall asleep almost instantly, wedged in a hover or transport seat while I crunched data or piloted. It had been a fast run, no time to catch our breath.

Two other bounty hunters — both normals, but with combat augments — had gone down trying to bring this guy in. The next logical choice had been to bring a psion in, and I was fresh from hunting a Magi gone bad in Freetown Tijuana. From one job to the next, with no time to think, perfect. I didn't *want* to think about anything but getting the next bounty collared.

I would be lying if I said the idea of the two extra murder charges *and* two of felony evading tacked onto Bulgarov's long list of indictments didn't bring a smile to my face. A hard, delighted grin, as a matter of fact, since it meant Bulgarov would face capital punishment instead of just filling a prison cell. I edged forward, reaching the end of the aisle; glanced up. Nothing in the rafters, but it was good to check. This was one tricky sonofabitch. If he'd been a psion it would have made things a little easier, I could have tracked the smears of adrenaline and Power he'd leave on the air when he got tired enough. As it was, the messy sewer-smelling drift of his psychic footprint faded and flared maddeningly. If I dropped below the conscious level of thought and tried to scan him, I'd be vulnerable to a detonation circuit in a quickshield, and it wasn't like this guy *not* to have a det circuit built in if he spent the credit for a shield. I could live without the screaming migraine feedback of cracking a shield meant to keep a normal from a psion's notice, thank you very much.

So it was old-fashioned instinct doing the work on this one. *Is he heading for an exit or sitting tight? My guess is sitting tight in a nice little cubbyhole, waiting for us to come into sight, pretty as you please. Like shooting fish in a barrel.* Sekhmet sa'es, *he better not have a plasgun. He didn't. I'm almost sure he didn't.*

Almost sure wasn't good enough. *Almost sure,* in my experience, is the shortest road to *oh fuck.*

Jace's aura touched mine, the spiked honey-pepper scent of a Shaman rising around me along with the cloying reek of dying human cells. I wished I could turn my nose off or tone it down a little. Smelling everyone's death on them was not a pleasant thing, even if I, of all people, know Death is truly nothing to fear.

Whenever I thought about it, the mark on my shoulder seemed to get a little colder.

Don't fucking think about that, Danny. Nice and cautious, move it along here.

A popping *zwing!* made me duck reflexively, calculating angles even as I berated myself for flinching. *Goddammit, if you heard the shot it didn't get you, move move move! He's blown cover, you know where he is now!* I took off, not bothering to look behind me—Jace's aura was clear, steady, strong. He hadn't been hit.

More popping, clattering sounds. Reactive paint sprayed as I moved, blurringly, much faster than a normal human. My gun holstered itself as I leapt, claws extending sweetly, naturally, my right hand giving a flare of pain I ignored as I dug into the side of a plastic

barrel, hurling myself *up,* get *up,* and from there I leapt, feet smacking the smooth round tops of the barrels. My rings spat golden sparks,
all need for silence gone. The racks holding the barrels swayed
slightly as I landed and pushed off again, little glowing spits and
spats of thick reactive paint spraying behind me as lead chewed the
air. *He's got a fucking semiautomatic assault rifle up there, sounds
like a Transom from the chatter, goddamn cheap Putchkin piece of
shit, if he had a good gun he'd have hit me by now.*

I was almost under the floating panel of a hover platform. Its
underside glowed with reactive paint, and I could see the metal cage
on top where the operator would guide the AI deck through manipu-
lating the dangling tentacles of crabhooks to pick up five racks at a
time and transport them to the staging area. A low, indistinct male
shape crouched on the edge of the platform, orange bursts showing
from the muzzle of the semiautomatic rifle with the distinct Transom
shape. He wasn't aiming at me now, he was aiming *behind* me at
Jace, and this thought spurred me as I gathered myself and leapt, fingers sinking into the edge of the platform's corrugated metal and
arms *straining,* the deadweight of my body becoming momentum as
I pulled myself up as easily as if I were muscling up out of a swimtank.
Almost overbalanced, in fact, still not used to the reflex speed of this
new body, proprioception still a little off, moving through space
faster than I thought I was.

*Don't hit Jace, you motherfucker, or I'm going to have to bring
you in dead and accept half my fee. Don't you dare hit him, you piece
of shit.*

Gun barrel swinging, deadly little whistles as bullets clove the
air. A smashing impact against my belly and another against my rib-
cage; then I was on him, smacking the barrel up. Hot metal sizzled, a
jolt of pain searing up my arm from the contact, then faded as my
body coped with the damage. He was combat-augmented, with reac-
tions quicker than the normal human's, but I'd been genetically
altered by a demon, and no amount of augmentation could match
that.

At least, none that I'd come across yet.

I tore the Transom away and grabbed his wrist in my cramping
right hand, setting my feet and yanking sharply down. An animal
howl and a crunch told me I'd dislocated his shoulder. Fierce enjoyment spilled through me, the emerald on my cheek giving one sharp

flash, the *kia* burst from my lips as I struck, *hard;* ringed fist ramming into the solar plexus, pulling the strike at the last moment so as not to rupture fragile human flesh. My rings turned my fist into a battering ram, psychic and physical power wedded to a strike that could kill as well as daze. The *oof!* sound he made might have been funny if I hadn't felt hot blood dripping down my ribs and the slight twitching as a bullet was expelled from the preternatural flesh of my belly. *Ouch.* It stung, briefly, then smoothed itself out, black blood rising and sealing the seamless golden flesh. Another shirt ruined. I was racking up dead laundry by the ton now.

Of course, I could afford it. I was rich, wasn't I?

Knee coming up, he struggled, but he was off balance and I shifted my weight, hip striking as I came in close, he fell and I was on him; he howled as I yanked both arms behind his back, my fingers sinking into rubbery, augmented muscle fed by kcals of synthprotein shake and testos injections. *Gonna have to pop that shoulder back in so he can't shimmy free of magcuffs. You've got him down, don't get cocky. This is the critical point. Just cuff him, don't get fancy.* He bucked, but I had a knee firmly in his back and my own weight was not inconsiderable, heavy with denser bones and muscle now. The quickshield sparked and struggled, trying to throw me off; it was a sloppy, hastily purchased piece of work—all right for hiding, but no good when you had an angry Necromance on your back. One short sharp Word broke it, my sorcerous Will slicing through the shell of energy—a Magi's work, and a good one, despite being so hurried. I snapped the mental traces aside, taking a good lungful of the scent; maybe we could track down whoever did the quickshield, maybe not. They hadn't done anything illegal in providing the shield; quicks were perfectly legal all the way around. But a Magi this good might have something to say about demons, something I'd want to hear.

"Jace?" I called into the warehouse's gloom. The sharp smell of reactive paint bloomed up, mixing with dust, metal, the smell of human, hot cordite, sweat, and my own spiced fragrance, a light amber musk. Sometimes my own smell acted like a shield against the swirling cloud of human decay all around me, sometimes not; it wasn't the psychic nonphysical smell of a true demon, but the scent of something in-between. "Monroe? How you doing?" *Jace? Answer me, he was aiming at you, answer me!* My voice almost cracked, stroking the air with rough honey. My throat was probably permanently ruined from Lucifer's fingers sinking in and cracking little bits of whatever almost-demons had in their necks. I sounded like a vidsex operator sometimes.

Apparently I could heal from bullets, but demon-induced damage to my throat was another thing entirely.

"You're so much fun to hang out with, Valentine," he called from below. I tried not to feel the hot burst of relief right under my ribs. The bitter taste of another hunt finished exploded in my mouth, my heart thudding back to a slower pace. My left shoulder prickled numbly, as if the fluid mark scored into my skin was working its way deeper. *Don't think about that.* "Got him?"

Of course I've got him, you think I'd be talking if I didn't? "Stuffed and almost cuffed. See if you can find the control panels and bring this sucker to the loading dock, will you?" My lungs returned to their regular even task. My tone resumed its normal, whispering roughness. Most Necromances affect a whisper after a while; when you work with Power wedded to your voice it's best to speak softly. "You okay?"

He gave a short jagged spear of a laugh, he was rubbed just as raw as I was. "Right as rain, baby. Get you in a second."

My right hand clumsily fumbled for the magcuffs. Bulgarov mumbled a curse in some consonant-filled Putchkin dialect. "Shut up, waste." I sank my knee into his heaving back. Short squat man, corded with heavy muscle and dressed in a long-sleeved shirt and jeans under his assassin's rig, a long rat-tail of pale hair sliding out from under the kerchief he'd tied around his head like a kid playing minigang. "Unlucky day for you."

The magcuffs cooperated, and I had to hold him down while I popped his shoulder back into the socket with a meaty sound, eliciting a hoarse male scream. The cuffs creaked but held steady, and just to be sure I dug in my bag and retrieved the magtape, spent a few moments binding the bastard's elbows, knees, and ankles; I gagged him too. I was ready when the hover platform's control board lit up, I kept the man down and watched him cautiously while the platform jolted into life and began to glide on its prearranged path. Bulgarov had escaped last year from a seven-person Hegemony police unit that had him down and cuffed; I didn't want to underestimate him.

Four little girls, six hookers we know he killed for sure, three we're not sure of, and eight men, mostly Chill dealers. I wouldn't have minded the Chill dealers, but the kids... My rings were back to a steady glow: amber, moonstone, obsidian, and bloodstone all swirling with easy Power. I surveyed the mess the bullets had made of the reactive barrels as the hover platform glided over neatly-placed racks and rows. Glowing paint dripped thickly under dim sputtering light from fluorescents turned down for the night pulsing outside in all its shades of darkness. *And he killed them slow. Gods.*

I could understand killing when necessary, the gods know I've done my share. But kids...and defenseless women. Even a *sedayeen* healer experienced with mental illness could do nothing for this man; he was a pure sociopath. No remorse, no hesitation, no conscience at all; he was neither the first nor the last of his kind the world would see. And probably not the last one I'd hunt, either.

The trouble was, I'd had little difficulty tracking him. Thinking like him. *Being* like him, to catch him.

That was starting to worry me.

The hover platform settled with a jolt and Bulgarov thrashed, making a muffled sound behind the gag. It probably wasn't comfortable, lying facedown on a cold metal platform with a stretched-out, busted shoulder and a bruised solar plexus. I might have broken his nose, too, when I had my knee in his back. At least, I hoped I had. My hand tightened on the neck of his jacket as I finished searching him for weapons, finding the trigger to the quickshield—a pretty ceramic medallion with a Seal of Solomon etched into one side—four knives, two projectile guns, and a little 20-watt recharge plasgun fitted into a pocket on the thigh of his jeans.

I turned the plasgun over in my hand. *Gods.* A tremor slid through me, my teeth chattering briefly. *That close to blowing up this whole warehouse, would have taken a good chunk out of the neighborhood here too. You son of a bitch. Thank the gods you didn't use this.*

The assault rifle bothered me, but he could have had it stashed on the airbike. My tat tingled, ink running under my skin, and my left shoulder tingled too. I was used to both sensations by now; did my best to ignore them. I'd smashed my slicboard into the side of a concrete building. If I was still human I'd be dead by now.

Jace met me on the platform. He looked like hell, his clothes torn and his face bloody and bruised. He also looked chalky-pale under his perpetual tan. I'd have to healcharm him, or find a healer to do it.

"You okay?" My throat rasped a little, but my voice still made the air shiver like a cat being stroked.

He nodded, his blue eyes moving over the trussed package on the floor, checking. I reached down, set my feet, and hauled Bulgarov up, nodding toward the pile of weapons. Without the brace of his Shaman's staff, Jace almost-limped on his stiff knee over to the pile, his sword jammed through the belt on his rig. It was a *dotanuki;* heavier than the last sword I'd used. My right hand cramped again, remembering driving the shattering blade through a demon's heart as we both fell through icy air and smashed into the surface of the frozen sea.

Don't think about that. Because thinking about that would only make me think of Japhrimel.

I winced inwardly as I hopped down to the yellow-painted concrete of the loading dock, the shock grating in my knees. I'd gone a whole...what, forty-five minutes without thinking of him? Adrenaline was wonderful, even if I wasn't sure what the demon equivalent to adrenaline was. Now if I could just find another bounty as soon as I dragged this guy in, I'd be all set.

"Chango," Jace breathed. "He had a plasgun."

I could have laughed, didn't. The short man was a heavy limp weight, more awkward than hard to carry; I was a lot stronger than I looked. He'd given up thrashing, his ribs heaved with deep breaths. I caught him straining against the magtape and dumped him on the concrete. Drew one of my main-gauches from its sheath and dropped to my knees, my fingers curling in his greasy hair. This close I could see the blemishes on his skin, blackheads rising to the oily surface. A side-effect of illegal augments, he had a pallid moon-shaped face scarred and pocked by terminal acne. Revulsion touched my stomach. I pushed it down, pulling his head back and craning his neck uncomfortably. It would be easy to give a sudden twist, hear the snap like a dry stick. So easy.

I laid the knifeblade against his throat. "Keep struggling," I whispered in his ear, my voice husky and broken. "I'd love to rid the world of a blight like you. And I'm a deadhead, Bulgarov. I can easily bring you back over the Bridge and kill you twice."

I couldn't, of course. Death didn't work like that; an apparition brought back from the halls of the hereafter couldn't be killed twice, only sent back into Death's embrace. But there was no reason for this bastard to know that. I'd seen the files and the lasephotos. I knew what this bastard had done to the little girls before he killed them.

He went limp for a moment, then struggled frantically against the magtape. I held him down, easy now that he was bound, and used the knife's razor edge to prick at his flesh, right over where the pulse beat. "Come on," I whispered. "Struggle harder, sweetheart. I'd love to do to you what you did to the little blonde girl. Her name was Shelley, did you know that?"

"Danny!" Jace's voice. "Hey, I've keyed in for pickup; we've got a Jersey police transport coming to get us and our little package. Want me to bag the weapons?" Did he sound uneasy? Of course not.

Or did he? I might be a little uneasy if I hung around me. I wasn't hinged too tightly these days. Call it nerves.

"Sure. Make sure that plasgun's sealed." My messenger bag's strap dug against my shoulder as I turned my head, objects inside shifting and clinking a little against my hip. A tendril of dark hair fell in my face, freed of the tight braid I'd put in this morning. Bulgarov had gone limp and still as a fresh corpse underneath me.

I resheathed the knife and let him go, his head thudding none-too-gently against the concrete. My hands were shaking, even my crippled right hand, which rubbed itself against my jeans. I was dirty and tired, no time for a shower while I was tracking this bastard, barely time enough for food to keep Jace going, since my stomach usually closed up tight on a hunt. Jace was looking a little worse for wear, but he insisted on coming along. And I was soft enough to let him — after a bit of bitching, of course.

Anything was better than staying at home, staring at the walls and thinking thoughts I would rather not think. Especially since the only thing I seemed able to do while I was at home was research in Magi shadowjournals and stare at the black urn that held a demon's ashes.

A Fallen demon. Japhrimel.

You will not leave me to wander the earth alone, a soft male voice, flat but still expressively shaded, whispered in my head. I shut my eyes briefly. The mark on my left shoulder — *his* mark, the burning scar Lucifer had pressed into my flesh to make Japhrimel my familiar — hadn't faded with Japh's death, just gone numb as if shot with varocain. Sometimes it was like a mass of burning ice pressed into the skin, pulsing every now and again with a weird necrotic life of its own. I wondered how long it would feel like that, if it would ever fade, and how long it would take for the cold burning numbness to fade.

If it ever did.

Goddammit, Dante, will you quit thinking about that?

Distant sirens began at the edge of my hearing, slicing through the rattling whine of hovertraffic. All this reactive paint, and the bastard had a plasgun all the time. What if he'd decided to take a potshot, take us with him?

Would a reactive fire kill me? I didn't know. I didn't know what I *was* now, other than almost-demon. Part demon. Whatever. I was stuck with the face of a holovid model and a body that sometimes escaped my control and moved far faster than it should, and I was taking down bounties like they were going out of style. Gabe called it "bounty sickness," and I wasn't sure she was far wrong.

I'd be home this week for my usual Thursday rendezvous with Gabe in the back booth they saved for us at Fa Choy's. I'd missed it last week. *That's a good thought,* I told myself grimly as the sirens drew nearer and Jace finished bagging Bulgarov's weapons. *Keep that one.*

But what I thought of, as I watched the shapeless lump of the man magtaped on the floor, was green eyes, turning dark and thoughtful, and a long black coat, golden skin, and a faint, secretive tilt to a thin mouth. Goddammit. I was thinking about a demon again. A *dead* demon, at that.

Does a demon have a soul? The Magi don't know, they only know what demons tell them, and the question's never come up. And what am I? What did he do to me, and why didn't I die when he did?

That was a bad thought. Jace brought the bagged weapons over, his injured knee slowing him a little, and gave me a tight smile. "Fresh as a daisy," he said in his usual careless tone. "I hate that about you."

"Fuck you too." It was postjob banter, meant to ease the nerves and bring us down. It was working.

"Anytime, sweetheart. We've got a few minutes before the transport gets here." His mouth quirked up into a half-smile, and he rolled his shoulders back under the leather straps of his rig. But his eyes slid over the man on the floor, checking the magtape. Professional to the last. A handsome blue-eyed man, spirit bag dangling from a leather thong around his neck marking him as a *vaudun* just as the tat on his cheek marked him as a Shaman. He'd cut his hair like Gypsy Roen's sidekick on the holovids, soft and spiky, a nice cut on him. Especially with his lazy smile and his electric eyes.

Despite myself, I laughed. I tried not to; my ruined voice made it sound like a rough invitation, velvet curled under sweating fists. "You're the soul of chivalry, as always."

"Only for you, baby." The sirens were screamingly close. "Wanna carry him outside?"

"Do I get to drop him headfirst?" I sounded only halfway joking.

So did he. "If you want, sweetheart. Make sure you do it on concrete."

We caught the redeye transport back to Saint City; it deposited us onto the dock amid a stream of normals. I was glad to get off the transport, claustrophobia tends to run in psions. I was also happy to get rid of the whine of hover travel. It settles in the back teeth, hover-whine, and rattles your bones. Normals can't hear it, but they get itchy on long hover flights too. Of course, it could be because all the normals I've seen on transports are a little edgy at being in a compartment with a psion. For some reason they think we want to read their minds or force them to do embarrassing things, though the gods know that the *last* place a psion wants to tread is the messy, open sewer of a normal person's brain. Without the regulation and cleanness imparted by training, minds can get rank and foul very quickly—and they stay that way. I don't know how normals endure it.

I was wearing my last clean shirt, but the fact that my jeans were dotted with black blood that smelled like sweet rotting fruit might have had something to do with the sidelong looks and not-so-subtle avoidance of normals. Or perhaps it was my rings, glowing faintly even in the gray thin morning light, or the rig with the guns and knives, stating clearly that I was combat trained and licensed to carry anything short of an assault rifle on public transport. Or the holovid-star face with velvety golden skin, and dark eyes set above a sinfully sweet mouth; or the way my right hand twisted sometimes into a claw without my realizing it, cramping up as if it was trying to grab a corkscrewed swordhilt. I missed the feel of a hilt and the clean confidence of carrying a katana; knives just aren't the same. But shattering a sword in a demon's heart isn't the best way to keep your swordhand whole. I was lucky; if Japhrimel hadn't changed me into whatever I was now, killing Santino might have killed me instead of just crippling my slowly-healing hand.

Yeah. Lucky, lucky me.

My skin tingled as we stood there, Jace leaning on his staff—

rescued from the hotel room in Jersey—with its raffia twine at the top, small bones clicking and shifting against one another, even though the staff wasn't moving. After a while a Shaman's staff tends to take on a personality of its own, much like any object used to contain Power. There are even stories of Shamans who have passed their staves on to students or children, mostly in the older traditions. Jace was an Eclectic, like most North Merican Shamans; it's hard to work for the Hegemony and only stick with one discipline. Plus, psions tend to be magpies. We pick up a little of this, a little of that, whatever works. The use of magickal and psionic Power is so incredibly personal we'd be fools to do otherwise.

The tingling on my skin was my body adjusting to the flux of Power in the rainy air, the transport well was full so we had docked in an auxiliary outside bay. Rain misted down, a thin barely-autumn drizzle that smelled of hoverwash, the salt from the bay, and the peculiar damp radioactive smell of Saint City.

Home. Funny how the longer I spent chasing down bounties, the more I thought of Saint City as home.

"You coming home?" Jace tapped the butt of his staff against the concrete, but gently. Just a punctuation, not the sharp guncrack of frustration. His wheat-gold hair was beginning to darken and slick itself down with the drizzle; the bruise had faded and I could *see* the faint pulsing of the healcharm I'd laid on him. He'd slept on the transport, I hadn't; but we were both night creatures. Being out in the light of early morning was guaranteed to make both of us cranky. Not to mention he'd need a few hours or so to reaccustom himself to the flux of ambient Power here, we hadn't been gone long enough for his body to set itself to Jersey's Power flux. It was like hoverlag, when the body isn't sure whether it's day or night because of the speed of transport, only harder and if a psion was drained and exhausted enough potentially very painful.

Glancing at the glass doors, I found my voice. Wherever we were going, we could take the lifts down to the street together. If I wanted to. "No, I've got a few things to do."

"I thought so." He nodded sagely, a tall, spare man with a quick famous grin, his assassin's rig easy over his black T-shirt and jeans, the *dotanuki* thrust through his belt and his staff in hand. If it wasn't for the accreditation tat, he might have been a holovid star himself. But there were fine fans at the corners of his eyes that hadn't been there before, and he looked tired, leaning on his staff for support instead of effect. The last ten months hadn't been easy on him. "It's the Anniversary, isn't it."

I didn't think you'd remember, Jace. The last time you saw me do this was years ago. Before Rio. Before you left me. I nodded, biting my lower lip. It was a sign of nervousness I never would have permitted myself, before. "Yeah. I'm glad we're back in town, I...well, missing it would be rough." He nodded. "I'm going to pop in at Cherk's and have a drink before I go home." He tipped me a wink, the patented Jace Monroe grin flashing. That smile used to line up the Mob groupies for him, he never had any trouble with women—as he was so fond of remarking—until he met me. "Maybe I'll get all drunk and you can take advantage of me."

Damn the man, he was making me smile. "In your dreams. Go on home, I'll be along. Don't get too drunk."

" 'Course not." He shrugged and stepped away, heading for the door.

I wanted to go after him, walk down to the street together, but I stood very still and closed my eyes. My right hand lifted, almost of its own accord, and rubbed at the numb spot on my left shoulder. Was it tingling more than it had before?

Stop it, Dante. It was the stern voice of my conscience again. *Japh's gone. Live with it.*

I am, I told that deep voice. *Go away.*

It went, promising to come back later and taunt me. I rubbed my shoulder, scrubbing at it with my knuckles since my fingers were curled under and cramped. At least it didn't hurt anymore. Not there, anyway.

I wondered, not for the last time, why the mark hadn't faded with Japh's death. Of course, Lucifer had first burned it into my skin.

That was an uncomfortable thought, to say the least.

Jace was nowhere in sight when I took the lifts down and emerged blinking again into the gray day. Down on the street the drizzle had turned to puddles vibrating with hoverwash and splashing up whenever an airbike or wheelbike went by, the ground hovertraffic moving a little bit slower than usual. The sidewalks were crowded with people, most of them normals intent on their own business, since the psions would probably be home in bed. It felt good to walk, my hands dangling loose by my sides and my braid bumping my back, my boots light on cracked pavement. Bulgarov had been left in a holding cell

in Jersey lockdown; the fee for the collar plus the extra 15 percent I'd
told Trina to charge was probably safely in Jace's bank account by
now. I didn't need the money, as there was plenty left from Lucifer's
payoff. Even though I had no qualm about using it, I still flinched
internally whenever I looked at my statements or signed on through
my computer deck. Blood money, a payment for the life Lucifer had
manipulated and cajoled me into taking, even though left to myself I
would have killed Santino.

I had *needed* revenge. Lucifer still owed me, both for Doreen's
daughter and for Japhrimel. I didn't have a chance of collecting, but
still. He owed me, and I owed my life to a dead demon.

I winced, pacing through the rainy gray Saint City morning. The
Prince of Hell might still be keeping an eye on me.

I owed him *nothing,* and that was exactly what the Prince of Hell
was going to get from me. End of story.

*Think about something else, Dante. You've got a lot to brood over.
Like Jace.*

Jace had given up his Mob Family for me, just handed it over to
his second-in-command without a word and signed the papers for
cessation-of-ownership. After fighting so hard to get his own Family
he'd turned his back on it and showed up at my door.

*Dante, you are spectacularly good at thinking things you don't
want to.*

It took me an hour to get to the corner of Seventh and Cherry. I
had stopped at a street vendor's for a bouquet of yellow daisies, and I
stood on the south corner under the awning of a grocery store that
had been put in two years ago. The times I'd been here with Lewis,
there had been a used bookstore across the way.

My pulse beat thinly in my temples and throat, as if I was taking
down a bounty again. I clutched the daisies in their plasticine wrap,
their cheerful yellow heads with black centers nodding as I held them
in my trembling right hand. Coming back here every year was a penance, maybe, but who else would remember him? Lewis had no family, substituting the psionic kids he fostered for a real blood link. And
to me, he was the only family I'd known, my caseworker from the
time I was an infant until I was thirteen.

If I was anything to be proud of, it was because Lewis had taught
me how to be.

Memory rose. That's the curse of being a psion, I suppose. The
Magi techniques for training the memory are necessary and ruthless.

A Magi-trained memory can remember every detail of a scene, a magick circle, a canon of runes, a page of text. Necessary when one is performing Greater Works of magick, where everything has to be done right the first time, but merciless when things happen that you want to forget.

The prickling in my shoulder had gone down, thankfully. There wasn't much of a crowd here, most passersby ducked into the small grocery and came out carrying a plasbag full of alcohol bottles or synth-hash cigarettes. I stood just around the corner, tucked out of the way close to the wall, and stilled myself, forcing the memories to come clear and clean.

He'd brought me down to the bookstore, a special treat, and the smooth metal of the collar against my throat was less heavy on that unseasonably sunny autumn day. The crisp cinnamon smell of dried leaves hung in the air and the sky was impossibly deep blue, the type of blue that only comes in autumn. Blue enough to make the eyes ache, blue enough to drown in. Lewis had pushed his spectacles up on his beaky nose, and we walked together. I didn't hold his hand like I did when I was a little girl, having grown self-conscious in the last few years. I had ached to tell him something, anything, about how bad things were at school, but I couldn't find the nerve.

And so we walked, and Lewis drew me out, asking me about the last books I'd read, the copy of Cicero he'd loaned me and the Aurelius he was saving for if I did well on my Theory of Magick final coming up at the end of the term. *And did you enjoy the Ovid?* he asked, almost bouncing with glee inside his red T-shirt and jeans. He didn't dress like a social worker, and that was one more thing to love about him. He had given me my name, my love of books, and my twelve-year-old self had cherished wild fantasies of finding out that Lew really was my father and was just waiting for the right time to tell me.

I enjoyed it, I told him, *but the man was obsessed with women.*

Most men are. Lewis found the oddest things funny, and it was only once I reached adulthood that I understood the jokes. When I was young, of course, I had laughed with him, just happy that he was happy with me, feeling the warm bath of his approval.

I had been about to reply when the man blundered around the corner, jittering and wide-eyed, stinking of Clormen-13. It was a Chill-freak desperate for his next dose, his eyes fastening on the antique chronograph Lewis wore, a glittering thing above his datband and looking pawnable. Confusion and chaos, and a knife. Lewis yelled for me to run, my feet rooted to the ground as the Chillfreak's knife glittered, throwing back a hot dart of sunlight that hurt my eyes. *Run, Danny! Run!*

My eyes were hot and grainy. Drizzle had soaked into my hair and coat. I was standing exactly where I'd stood before I'd obeyed him, turning and running, screaming while the Chillfreak descended on Lewis.

The cops had caught the freak, of course, but the chronograph was gone and the man's brain so eaten by Chill he could barely remember his own name, let alone what he'd done with the piece of antique trash. And Lew, with his books and his love and his gentleness, had left me for Death's dry country, that land where I was still a stranger even if I'd known my way to its borders.

I laid the flowers down on the wet sidewalk, as I did every year, their plaswrap crinkling. The bloodstone ring on my third left finger flashed wetly, a random dart of Power splashing from its opaque surface. "Hey," I whispered. "Hi."

He had a grave marker, of course, out in the endlessly-green fields of Mounthope. But that was too far for a student to ride public transport and get back to the school by curfew, so I ended up coming here, downtown, where he had died almost immediately. If I'd been older, combat-trained and a full Necromance, I could have run off the Chillfreak or mended Lewis's violated body, held him to life, kept him from sliding off the bridge and into the abyss, under the blue glow of Death... *if* I'd been older. If I'd had some presence of mind I could have distracted the Chillfreak, diverted his attention; wearing a collar meant I couldn't have used any psionic ability on him, but there were other ways. Other things I could have done.

Other things I *should* have done.

"I miss you," I whispered. I had only missed two Anniversaries, my first year at the Academy up north and the year Doreen died. Murdered, in fact, by a demon I hadn't known was a demon at the time. "I miss you so much."

Nihil desperandum! he would crow. *Never fear!*

Other kids were raised on fairy tales. Lew raised me on Cicero and Confucius, Milton and Cato, Epictetus and Sophocles, Shakespeare. Dumas. And for special treats, Suetonius, Blake, Gibbon, and Juvenal. *These are the books that have survived,* Lew would remind me, *because they are as close to immortal as you can get. They're good books, Dante, true books, and they'll help you.*

And oh, they had.

I came back to myself with a jolt. Morning hovertraffic whined and buzzed overhead. I heard footsteps, people passing by on Cherry to get to the shops, but nobody going down this side of Seventh because it was apartment buildings, and everyone was gone for the day, or in bed. The daisies, a bright spot of color against cracked hard pavement, glowed under the thickening rain.

"All right," I said softly. "See you next year, I guess."

I turned slowly on my heel. The first steps, as usual, were the hardest, but I didn't look back. I had another appointment today. Jace would beat me home, and he would probably already have a few holovids from the rental shop on Trivisidero. Maybe some old *Father Egyptos,* we both loved that show and could quote damn near every line of dialogue. *What evil creeps in the shadows? Egyptos, the bearer of the Scarab of Light, shall reveal all!*

Uncharacteristically, I was smiling. Again.

CHAPTER 2

Morning had leapt gray into drizzling afternoon when I knocked on the wooden door, the street behind me gathering circles of orange light under each streetlamp. A glowing-red neon sign in the front window—a real antique—buzzed like hovertraffic without the rattling whine, its reflection cast on the bank of yarrow below. I felt wrung-out and a little sore, as usual after a bounty, and the blood on my clothes, with its simmering stink of decaying spicy fruit, didn't help.

The door was painted red, and the shields over this small brick house with its cheerful ragged garden were tight and well-woven. Kalifor poppies vied with mugwort and feverfew, nasturtium and foxglove; there were some late bloomers, but mostly the plants were now merely green or dying back, getting ready for the rainy chill of winter. I smelled the sharpness of rosemary, she must have just harvested her sage too. In summer the garden was a riot of color, the property-line shields smooth and carefully woven, an obvious stronghold. Then again, I'd heard Sierra never left her house. I'd never seen or heard of her around town, and I didn't care either.

No, I came here for a different reason. I blinked against the gray sunlight, wished it was darker. Like most psions, I never feel quite myself during the day; a marker for nocturnalism crops up with amazing regularity in psion gene profiles. When darkness falls is when I feel most alive. At least that hadn't changed, even if everything else about me had.

I was glad I was back in time. I'd missed my appointment last month and been a little out of sorts ever since. I lifted my hand to knock at the door but the house shields had already flushed a warm, welcoming rose color, and the door pulled open. I pushed back a few stray strands of my damp hair and met Sierra Ignatius's eyes.

Her gaze was wide and pale blue, irises fading into the whites, the pupils sometimes flaring randomly. There was an odd film over her eyes; the sign of congenital blindness. Usually blindness is fixed with gene therapy during infancy, but for some reason she hadn't received the therapy then or in later years. Despite that, she moved around her little brick home with an accuracy and assurance some sighted people never achieve. Rumor had it that her parents had been Ludders, but I wasn't curious enough to find out. Her blindness made her, like me, an anomaly; it was probably why I allowed myself to come here.

"Danny!" She sounded calmly delighted, a short thin woman with thistledown hair and a thorn-laden cruciform tat on her left cheek. My cheek burned, my tat shifting. I felt another unwilling smile tug the corners of my mouth up. Sierra looked like a tiny pixie full of mischief, and her aura smelled of roses and wood ash, a clean human smell I somehow didn't mind as much as others. "I wondered if you'd come back. You missed last month."

Behind Sierra, taking her hand off the hilt of her shortsword, was a rangy female Shaman with the kind of tensile grace that shouted combat training and a tat that matched Sierra's. She inclined her chin gracefully, turned on her heel, and stamped away. Kore didn't like me, and the feeling was mutual. We'd tangled over a bounty once, one of her Skinlin friends I'd hauled in for murder and illegal genesplicing. She didn't hold a grudge but she didn't have to like me either, and whenever I showed up for my appointment, Kore took herself upstairs out of the way. I appreciated her restraint.

I would have hated to kill her.

"Sorry I missed last month." I stepped inside, took a deep lungful of kyphii incense and the smell of dried lavender. The air was still and close, and as soon as Sierra closed the outside world out I felt my shoulders relax fractionally. Her front hall was low and dim, candles burning in a niche under a statue of Aesclepius. The walls were wood paneling and the floor mellow hardwood. "I was out on a bounty."

"You've been out on a bounty since I've met you, sweetie. Come on back, the table's set up. What's hurting you today?" She was, as usual, all business, setting off past me with a confident step, faster than I could have gone with my eyes closed. I saw her aura fringing, sending out little fingers of awareness, the perfume of spiced Power trailed behind her, reminding me of Jace. We walked down the hall, through the neat little kitchen with its racks of potted herbs in the window and the suncatcher above lazily hanging on a string. Her counters were clean and the kitchen table clear except for two wine-red placemats and a vase of white lilies that sent a shiver up my spine. There were few flowers I could see anymore without thinking of Santino.

"Hurting me?" As usual, I pretended to give the question my full attention as she led me into the round room at the back of the house, where a fountain of piled black stones dripped. She stepped down onto the plush carpet and moved into the middle of the room where the table sat, draped with fresh white sheets. *Hurting me? Nothing, really. Only my shoulder. My hand. My heart.* "Not much. I feel pretty okay."

"Liar. All right." She smoothed the sheets, a habitual movement. "What do you want me to work on?"

I shrugged, remembered she couldn't see the motion. Slid out of my coat, hung it up on the peg by the door, and undid my rig with the clumsy fingers of my right hand. "My back, whatever else. Like usual. Just work your magic, that's all."

Sierra cocked her pale pixie head, listening as I hung my bag and my rig up. "Cordite," she noted mildly. "And I can smell that sweet stuff. You got clipped?"

I found myself smiling again. I could remember going months without smiling, before Rio. "You're amazing. Yeah, I'm a little dirty. Sorry." I leaned down, working my boots off with my right hand, then padded to the table in my sock feet. "Do you mind?"

If I had still been fully human, I would have had to chemwash to get the blood off. As it was, only my clothes were bloody; my skin had absorbed the thick black ichor. She, like all psions, could see the staining of black-diamond fire in my aura, marking me as something close to demon; she never asked me to chemwash, figuring whatever communicable nasties I had weren't dangerous to her. It was open wounds she had to watch out for, and I didn't have any of those.

Not on the outside, anyway.

"Of course not. Your back, you said. What about that left shoulder of yours?"

I reached up with my right hand, touched my shirt over the mark. "Leave that alone for right now." It was the standard answer, and as usual, she accepted it gracefully.

I stripped down, left my clothes on the straight-backed chair set to the side, and eased myself onto the thigh-high table, squirming onto my belly while Sierra pulled the sheet up over me. I'd told her she didn't have to leave while I disrobed, most psions are pretty comfortable with nakedness. I wasn't precisely uncomfortable, but taking her up on her offer to give me privacy while I undressed seemed weak. I fitted my face into the facecradle, seeing the carpet below me in the flickering wash of candlelight and my braid swinging to the side, and let out an involuntary sigh.

"I live for that sound." She folded the sheet down low on my hips. The bolster went underneath my ankles to take the stress off my lower back, and I sighed again. "Ooh, twice. Must have been a hard month."

"Yeah. Couple of bounties." I closed my eyes as she rubbed her hands together, heating them up, the warm good smell of almond oil blooming. She didn't scent the oil, for which I was grateful.

"Always working." She laid her hands flat on my back, one right between my shoulder blades, the other at the base of my spine. A few moments of pressure, then she rocked me back and forth a little, gauging the way my body mass responded. "Too tense, Danny. When are you going to learn to loosen up?"

"Perfectly flexible," I muttered. "Got to work to pay you, sweets."

It wasn't true, I had enough money now. I had all the money I could ever want. I didn't need the bounty fees. But oh, gods, I *did* need the bounties.

She moved to the head of the table. Then what I'd been waiting for . . . she leaned in and smoothed both her hands down on either side of my spine, digging into my muscles under the tough, perfect golden skin. I let out another sigh. Her hands were cool and forgiving, my skin warmer than hers because of the hiked metabolism. I shivered with delight as she started the usual routine, kneading at me. My right hand relaxed and dangled off the table as I let go, fraction by fraction, Sierra's hands seeking out knots and nodes of tension.

Gabe had bought me my initial consultation with Sierra, and I'd thought it a frivolous gift even after she bullied and dragged me to the red-painted door at the appointed time. The first two-hour massage had ended with me in a languid puddle, more relaxed than I could ever remember. I'd gone home whistling, arrived at my door in the closest thing to a good mood I'd had since before Rio, and promptly burst into tears on my way upstairs. Thank the gods Jace had been out shopping for groceries. I'd locked myself in the bathroom and had a completely uncharacteristic fit of sobbing, then took a long hot shower. As dawn had risen through my bedroom window, I had fallen asleep for the first time in weeks, a thin restless troubled sleep but sleep nonetheless.

That did it, I was hooked. I came back once a month unless I was on a bounty, and each time it was the same: her delicate iron fingers digging into me, smoothing me out. Hers was a touch I didn't have to fend off or worry about what it cost me. I paid her, she touched me, it was that simple. Even and uncomplicated.

Why couldn't everything be like that?

"Are you staying in town long?" Her voice was soft, if I chose not to talk she would be silent.

"A while. Don't know when the next bounty's coming up." I felt the involuntary quiver go through me. She must have, too, because her touch gentled.

"Too much pressure?"

You couldn't hurt me if you tried, Shaman. At least, not without steel or a plasgun and a whole lot of luck. "No. Not too much." *I wish I knew exactly what I was. I wish Japhrimel would have had time to tell me.*

There I was again, thinking about him. I let out a long soft breath, keeping my eyes closed. "Just thinking," I explained, grudgingly.

"About?" Again, the soft tone; if I parried the question she'd let it drop.

About a demon. About a Fallen demon, a dead demon, that I only knew for a short time but I can't stop thinking about. He won't leave me alone. And neither will the only other man I ever loved, the one that betrayed me so honorably. A ghost I can't have and a man I can't touch, and skipping from bounty to bounty isn't helping any. "About the past."

A soft laugh. She kept working at my back, smoothing down the muscles, moving to one side or the other and using her elbow or the flat of her forearm, her entire weight pressing down through tough skin. "Never a comfortable subject."

That's the understatement of the year, sunshine. "No." I shifted in the facecradle a little, the emerald grafted into my cheek digging into my flesh. She moved to my legs, flipping the sheet aside, and I swallowed dryly.

"You have great skin." Tactful of her to change the subject. The spicy smell of kyphii was stronger now, reminding me of Gabe's house. Gabe loved burning that stuff. "Lucky girl."

"Mh." A noncommittal sound in reply. She took the hint and the rest of the massage was spent in blissful silence on her side and increasingly ill-tempered brooding on mine.

It was the bounties that were bothering me, I tried to tell myself. Jace was beginning to look a little ragged. Ten bounties in under six months, none of them cakewalks, and he hadn't uttered a word of protest. Not only that, but he'd insisted on coming along, and I'd caved each time. Allowing it, expecting it, treating him as if it was the old days when he had taught me how to track, how to let my intuition do the work for me, how to find a mark and stick on him, how to scent the prey and become the thing you hunted, how to find clients that would pay for things other than a legitimate tag but short of actual murder.

Admit it, Danny. You don't want to let him out of your sight. You're afraid he'll vanish and never come back, or that you'll come back to an empty house.

It was uncomfortably close to the truth. The fact that Jace never asked about Japhrimel only made it easier to pretend nothing was happening, that we were just living together. Just roommates with a good thing going, a lucrative bounty-hunting partnership and a carefully charted dance where he moved forward and I retreated, but never fast or far enough.

Was he waiting for me to forget Japhrimel?

It was only a few days, Danny. And he was a demon. He lied to you about Doreen's daughter, about Santino, about Lucifer's plans. What is it with the men I fall for and their aversion to truth?

"Time to turn over," Sierra said softly, and I did while she held the

sheet; then she slipped the bolster under my knees and started working on the front of my legs. The sound of water from the fountain in
the corner soothed me, just like the smell of kyphii and Sierra's
strong fingers. She knew just where the aches were. *What I would
have given to know about this when I was human.* But when I was
human I never would have let anyone do this to me, even if I was
paying them and thus absolving myself of obligation.

She even massaged my abdomen but left my shoulder alone, and I
didn't glance down to see the fluid glyph in its pretty scarred lines,
looking more like a decoration than a brand, the mark of a demon. *Is
it his Name?* I wondered, not for the first time. *Or is it "best opened
by this date"? Lucifer put it on me, like Nichtvren mark their thralls.
Maybe it's like a brand.* A swift spill of feeling roiled through my
stomach, revulsion and heat all mixed into one pretty package.
Japhrimel's mouth on mine, his skin against mine, the semaphore of
desire that needed no translation...My rings flashed, went back to
swirling lazily; my aura rang with the twisted black-diamond flames
of demon and the sparkles that meant Necromance. I looked like
nothing else in the landscape of Power now.

The massage ended with Sierra taking my hair out of its braid and
rubbing my scalp. I had never known what kind of tension lurked in
the thin tendons and flat muscles over the cranium. It was unreal. By
far my most favorite moment of the massage was when she undid my
braid; it was like having Doreen play with my hair again.

Doreen. It was turning out to be a day of unpleasant memories all
around. I wished Trina at the agency would call in with the news that
she'd scouted me another bounty. There *had* to be a job out there that
would keep me going so fast I didn't have time to slow down and
brood.

And remember. Memory, rage, guilt. The holy trinity, as far as I
was concerned. Good fuel, channeled into bounties and justice.
Hadn't I ever felt something softer?

Well, we could add shame to the list, couldn't we? My shame, that
I was still grieving for a dead demon I hadn't known more than a few
days, who had augmented me into something even my best friends
had a hard time looking at.

I sighed as Sierra's fingers trailed through my hair, regretfully.
"Better?" she asked.

"Much." I made a mental note to tip her 40 percent this time. I
opened my eyes, my left hand curling as if seeking a slim sheathed

shape. It was a reflex, as if I hadn't just spent almost a year without a sword. My right hand wasn't cramping either. It had straightened out, the fingers relaxed. The mark lay cold and quiescent against the hollow of my shoulder. "Thanks, Sierra."

"No problem. Want some tea, or would you like to let yourself out?"

So tactful. "I'd better let myself out. Thanks."

"You're very welcome, Danny. See you next month." She retreated, trailing the spiky spicy smell of Shaman and the decaying smell of human with her. I took another deep lungful of kyphii and exhaled into the dark air, staring at the white-painted ceiling. The door closed softly behind her, and I rested there against the table for a moment.

See if Trina can find another quick job. Just one more, I told myself. *Then it might be time for a vacation. Close up and magseal the house, go to the islands or something. Start chasing down more Magi shadowjournals and break their codes, see if any of them know what you are. Maybe even see if there's a Magi circle that will apprentice you, even if you are too old. Your initial training's sound, you're not rusty, and who knows how long you'll live now? Demons are virtually immortal unless killed by violence or suicide. Who knows how long I'll be around?*

I hated that thought. It usually waited until the middle of the day while I was trying to sleep, to show up.

All right, Valentine. Get your ass in gear, you need to go home and change. I surged up off the table, taking the sheet with me, was dressed in five minutes and fully-armed in another five. I would let myself out the back door and through the back gate, up to Ninth, cut through the University District to stretch my legs while I did some thinking. I thought best while moving, and that would get me home in time to get some serious trash holovid-viewing in. I tapped my datband, paying Sierra's fee and tacking 40 percent on for a tip; I'd have Trina schedule me another appointment next month.

Outside, the afternoon was wet and fragrant, the smells of Sierra's garden temporarily overwhelming the drowsing stink of Saint City air. I glanced up at the sky, scanned my surroundings out of habit, and felt my shoulders come up under the habitual burden of tension as I stepped back into my life.

CHAPTER 3

Two days later, the buzzing sound jolted me out of an uneasy thready half-trance. Jace muttered something next to me, blowing out between pursed lips. I rolled over, checked the clock, and sighed. The cotton sheets tangled around my legs, I'd been tossing again.

Three PM. Another drunken night of watching old *Indiana Jones, Magi* and *Father Egyptos* holovids shot to hell. There had been a letter in the afternoon mail, an unaddressed vellum envelope with a heavy bloodred wax seal. Even as I picked it up, I'd caught a whiff of heavy, spicy scent. *Demon.* My hands had moved despite myself, trembling, and torn the heavy beautiful envelope open.

Careful scripted calligraphy marched across thick linen paper. *Dante. I would speak to you.* And signed, simply, *L.* As if I wouldn't know who it was from.

The Prince of Hell. Lucifer himself, sending me a little note. I'd tried to tell myself I didn't care, tossed it in the garbage compacter, and matched Jace drink for drink.

Not like it helped. I couldn't even get drunk.

Jace muttered again and turned away, presenting me with his broad, muscled back. The scorpion tattoo on his left shoulder blade shifted uneasily, its black-edged stinger flexing. Thin lines of pale scarring traced across muscle hard as tile, marring skin that had never lost its Nuevo Rio tan. He'd collapsed on my bed for once because the room down the hall was too far away when he was that inebriated. Besides, it was almost soothing to hear him breathing next to me while I lay and tried to sleep, achieving at most a half-trance that tried to rest the mind and left me feeling almost as tired as when I started.

Something's up. Instinct raced along my spine, my rings flashed. A golden spark popped from the amber cabochon on my left middle finger. Of *course* something was up, nobody would call me in the late afternoon unless something was up. And no holomarketer would call a registered psion's number, we tended to be a bad return on that advertising dollar. Even though it was illegal to hex a normal out of spite, some of us had a nasty habit of disregarding possible legal action when it came to bloody holomarketing jackals. It was also expensive for corporations to keep the required coverage that would bring a psion out to remove the hex.

My left shoulder ached, a sudden fresh bite of coldness burning all the way down to the bone. If I touched it, I might almost feel the ropes of scar moving under my fingers. I refrained from touching it, as usual, and shifted position, rolling the shoulder in its socket as I shook the almost-dream away. The phone shrilled again, the most annoying buzz I'd heard in a long time.

I scooped up the receiver, cursing at whoever had thought it was a good idea to plug in a phone up here. It had seemed like a good idea at the time. Which meant I was muttering imprecations at myself. "*Sekhmet sa'es.* What?"

All things considered, it was as polite as I could get. I never use the vid capability on modern phones if I can help it, the thought of someone seeing me inside my own private house without having to get in a goddamn hover and come out just rubbed me the wrong way.

Plus, if I want to answer the phone naked, it's nobody's business but mine.

"Danny." Gabe's voice. Of all the people I could identify with one word, she was at the top of the list. She sounded strained and urgent. "Get your ass up. I need you."

I sat bolt upright, dragging the sheet away from Jace, who made a low, sleepy sound of protest and curled into a tighter ball. "Where?"

Click of a lighter, inhaled breath. She was smoking again. Bad news. "I'm at the station. How soon can you be here?"

I reached over, shook Jace's shoulder. His skin was cool under mine, my lacquered fingernails scraping slightly. He woke up a little more gracefully than I did, sitting up, sheathing the knife he kept under his pillow as soon as he realized I was on the phone instead of under attack. We were both jumpy; going from bounty to bounty will do that to you.

"I'm on my way," I told her. "Hang loose."

She hung up. I dropped the phone back into its cradle and stretched, the ligaments in my right hand cracking as I tried to spread the fingers all the way. I hadn't been dreaming, but it had been the closest I'd gotten to real sleep for a good three weeks, and I didn't like having it interrupted. Bounties weren't good for resting; sleep usually meant your prey was getting away.

Then again, I've always had bad dreams; the only stretch of good sleep I've ever had was when Doreen lived with me. A *sedayeen* could tranquilize even the unruliest Necromance, and that was one more thing I missed about her: the gentleness in the middle of the night when she calmed me down from a nightmare and sent me back into grateful blackness.

I could count the time I'd spent with Japhrimel, but we hadn't done a whole lot of sleeping.

"What's up now?" Jace sounded sleepy, but he slid his legs out of the bed and grabbed his jeans. I was already across the room, pulling a fresh shirt off the hanger with no memory of the intervening space. I'd blinked through the room again, using inhuman speed. *Got to stop doing that.*

Ten months and counting, and I still wasn't used to it. I remembered just how eerily, spookily *quick* Japhrimel could move, and wondered if I looked the same way when my body blinked through space and my mind tried to catch up. *A piece of my power,* he'd said. *To make you stronger, less easy to damage.*

If it wasn't for that gift I might be dead now. Lucky Danny Valentine, tougher than your average psion.

"Gabe. At the station. Wants us there *now*." I didn't need to yawn, but I did take a deep breath, wondering where the weariness came from. If I didn't need to sleep, why should I be tired?

Did part-demons need sleep? None of the Magi shadowjournals or demonology books could tell me, and hunting down bounties was cutting into my research time in a big way. But research just gave me too goddamn much time to fret.

"Fuck." Jace yawned, stretched. He stripped wheat-gold hair back from his face, yanked his shirt down, and shrugged into his assassin's rig. Oiled, supple leather; guns, knives—my own hands moved automatically. My right hand throbbed uneasily until I shook it out, joints cracking and popping. I ducked my head through the strap of my black canvas bag and had to stop, taking another deep breath, settling the strap diagonally across my body.

Maybe it was another bounty. I hoped it was another bounty. A big one, a complex one, one that would keep me occupied with the next thing to be done, and the next, and the next.

It didn't matter. I jerked my coat from its hook, shrugged into it. My two main knives rode in their sheaths; the guns easy and loose in my rig, and my rings popped a few more golden sparks. Familiar excitement mixed with dread deep in my belly, tainted the air I blew out between my teeth.

"Did she say anything else?" Jace rubbed his face, yawning again. His aura rippled, the spiky darkness of a Shaman prickling the air. My own cloak of energy responded, singing an almost-audible answer. "I mean, do I need to bring the rifle?"

"No." I plunged my fingers in my bag and checked for extra ammo clips, the plasgun didn't need them but the projectile weapons did. Sunlight glowed under the edges of my bedroom blinds; I felt logy and slow, as I usually did during the day. "Just your staff. If she needed your rifle she wouldn't have dialed, she'd have shown up personally."

"Good point." How did the man sound so casually amused, especially after drinking three quarters of a bottle of Chivas Red? I could still smell the sourness of his body and Power metabolizing the alcohol, running through the depressant, converting the sugars. "Fuck. I think I'm still drunk, Danny."

"Good." I stuffed another two ammo clips into my bag. It pays to be prepared. "That'll keep you relaxed. Let's go."

CHAPTER 4

Late-afternoon sun made Jace's hair glow like a furnace. I blinked, rubbing at my eyes, and slid out of the cab while Jace finished paying the bespectacled cabby. The man had taken a fifty-credit tip to get us to the Saint City South station in record time. My stomach was still churning. Thank the gods part-demons didn't throw up often.

Or at least, I didn't, and I was the only one I knew of. It made sweeping generalizations a whole lot easier. I've never been a fan of sweeping generalizations, but I'm all in favor of efficiency.

Jace clambered out, stood next to me as the cab lifted off and zipped into the traffic lanes, its underside glowing with hovercells and reactive paint. I took a deep breath of the stink that passed for air in Saint City, full of the effluvia of dying cells, the cloying smell of decay—my nose wanted to wrinkle. I let out a short whistle, my rings swirling with steady light.

"Would you look at that." Jace scratched at his hairline with blunt fingers. He tapped his staff once, sharply, on the sidewalk pavement, making a sound like two antique billiard balls smacking together.

Gabriele Spocarelli was waiting for us. She stood on the steps of the police station, a short woman, slim and graceful as a ballai dancer, her sleek dark hair cut in a short bob that framed her classically pretty face. There was a faint shadow of crow's-feet at the edges of her dark eyes, and her air of serene precision had deepened—if that was possible. A cigarette hung from the corner of her chiseled mouth, unlit.

Yep. She's not happy. If she'd lit the cigarette it would have been different. But unlit cigarette plus strained, tense shoulders and an aura singing with blue-violet under its Necromance sparkles all added up to a very unhappy Gabriele.

Her emerald flashed a greeting. The tattoo on her left cheek shifted slightly, inked lines running on her pale skin. My left cheek burned, the emerald flickering in response, sending an electric zing all the way down to my neckbones. Power shifted, stained the air with electricity.

I approached cautiously, my right hand starting to ache. It was a normal ache, so I ignored it. She watched us both come up the steps, unmoving, her aura flushed a deep purple-red like a bruise.

Nope. Gabe was not amused.

"Well," Jace said from behind me. "Still as pretty as ever, Spooky. How's Eddie?"

"Monroe." She tilted her head slightly, the only mark of respect she'd give him. Neither she nor Eddie had forgiven Jace his treachery, his connection to the demon who had killed Doreen and damn near killed me as well—but they were civil for my sake. I'd only presided over one short, strained meeting six months ago, where we hashed out that nobody was going to kill anyone else and all accounts balanced. Jace hadn't known that the head of the Mob Family he'd run from was Vardimal Santino, and just this once, we agreed, the circumstances were extraordinary enough that Jace could get a pass.

Well, Gabe and I had agreed. Eddie simply glowered and quit threatening to kill him. We were all a lot happier when just Gabe and I met at Fa Choy's once a week.

Gabe's eyes cut away, as if she couldn't bear to look at him anymore. "Sends his greetings. You made good time."

I shrugged. "What good are ill-gotten gains if you can't use 'em?"

The sunlight blurred as my pupils reacted, squeezing down to pin-pricks. That was one thing about having excellent demon vision—bright lights were more painful than ever. "What's up? I assume you didn't call me out here to stand around chatting."

"Fuck you too." She tore the unlit cigarette out of her mouth and tossed it into the trash-laden gutter, maybe for effect, maybe because she was too upset to remember she hadn't lit it. If it was a gesture, it was a grand one; my mouth curled up in an unwonted smile, my cheek burning as the tattoo settled again. "Come on up."

We followed her up the steps and into the police station. Old blue linoleum flecked with little sparkles squeaked underfoot. Fluorescents buzzed—they didn't have the budget for full-spectrum lights in the halls where normals worked, and I shuddered at the thought of working under that soulless light day after day. I followed at Gabe's iron-straight back and felt my hands shake slightly with the urge to touch a knifehilt, caress the smooth butt of a gun. It wasn't like her to be rude. It doubly wasn't like her to call and demand my presence. We met once a week, when I wasn't out chasing bad guys, had dinner, carefully didn't talk about Nuevo Rio or demons. Instead, we traded stories about bounties, bullshitted, and kept a careful distance that was as welcome as it was teeth-grindingly annoying. But I couldn't complain. The distance was there because of me.

Because of what I'd become.

My back prickled slightly, uneasy; fine hairs rising on my nape and the coppery tang of demon adrenaline in my mouth. I could feel it trembling on the edges of my awareness, the scorching smell of fate like the kick of hard liquor against the back of my throat.

Just like a bounty.

Up on the third floor, the Spook Squad hung out. They weren't chained in the basement like in the old days—no, now the parapsychic arm of law enforcement had corner offices, a good budget, and decent equipment at last. Computer decks hummed on desks buried under drifts of paperwork, full-spectrum lamps sat on every desk. I saw a Shaman with a staff made of twisted ironwood prop his boots on his desk, leaning back in his chair, his aura swirling red-orange; three Ceremonials clustered at the watercooler, laughing about something. All three of them wore sidearms—police-issue plasguns—and long black synthwool coats, their accreditation tattoos shifting on their cheeks. The air resonated with Power, my rings sparked again. Heads turned as I followed Gabe.

They weren't stupid and head-dead like normals. Even if they couldn't name what it was, they could see the twisting black-diamond patterns staining my aura like geometric flames.

Part-demon. Unique, even among psions. I could have done without the honor.

We reached Gabe's cubicle, and she dropped into her cushioned ergonomic chair. She pointed at the two folding chairs on the other side of her desk. "Take a load off." Her mouth turned into a hard line. The expression didn't do anything for her pretty face, but it would take a lot more than that to make Gabe look ugly. "You want some coffee?"

I shook my head. My braid tapped against my back. "Jace?"

"Chango, I need a beer." He shook his head, leaning his staff against the cubicle wall. The bones tied to the raffia twine crowning the length of oak clacked uneasily. "But no. What the hell's goin' on, Spooky?"

"I've got a case." Her voice was pitched low and fierce. "I need you, Danny."

Now I wasn't just uneasy. I was heading into full-blown *alarmed*. "What for?" I was curious too. It wasn't like her to pussyfoot.

She pushed the file toward me. There were only one or two clear spots, the rest of the desk taken up with paperwork, a nice custom Pentath computer deck, an inlaid-wood box that probably held a mismatched double set of tarot cards (Gabe was secondarily talented as a tarot witch), an in-box buried under more paper, and two dusty, full bottles of brandy perched precariously near the edge. "Take a look."

I sighed, scooped up the file. "You're a real lady of mystery, aren't you." Flipped it open, the smooth manila giving under my black-painted nails. My back wasn't crawling with gooseflesh — for some reason my new demon body didn't have the reflex — but the sensation of prickling on my skin still remained, a human sensation I would have been glad for if it hadn't been so creepy. To feel goosebumps rising under your skin but unable to press through to the surface is weird, like a phantom limb complete with ghost pain and a reflexive shudder.

They were homicide lasephotos. Of course — Gabe was a Necromance. What else?

The first photo was of a man. Or I assumed it was a man, once I took a closer look at the shape. "Anubis," I breathed, as the shapes snapped into a horrible picture behind my eyes. The worst part wasn't the loops of intestine or the pool of blood. The worst part was one outflung hand, unwounded, the fingers clutching air. The arm was a mess of meat flayed off the glaring-white bone.

Gods above, that's gruesome. "Gods above. When was this?"

"Four months ago. Keep going."

Jace shifted slightly, his chair squeaking. He knew better than to ask. I'd give him the file when I was good and done.

I flipped through a coroner's report, a standard parapsych incident report, the homicide report, neatly laseprinted. No real leads, nothing of much interest except the savagery. Finally, I looked up at Gabe. "Well?"

She pushed another file across her desk. With a sinking heart I handed the first one to Jace and took the second; Gabe's eyes were dead level and gave nothing away. "This one's about eight weeks old."

Jace whistled out through his teeth, a long low note. "Damn." From someone who had seen the type of carnage Jace Monroe had, it was almost a compliment.

I flipped open the second file. "Fuck." My voice held disgust and just a trace of something stronger—maybe fear. Paper stirred uneasily on her desk, stroked into motion by the tension in the air.

This one was even worse, if it were possible. The body lay, exposed and raw, spread-eagled on what appeared to be a cement floor. "Look past the body." Gabe's tone was soft, respectful of the corpse on the two-dimensional glossy paper.

It was hard, but I did. I saw the blurred edges of a chalk diagram, right at the very margin of the photo. I flipped to the next one—the photographer had pulled back, and I could see the chalk lines clearly. It was a double circle, inscribed with fluid spiky runes that twisted from one form to another even as I watched. Even through the lasephoto they seemed to hum with malignant force. They weren't symbols I knew.

That's not from the Nine Canons, I thought, and my skin seemed to roughen with gooseflesh again. I was secondarily talented as a runewitch, and the runes that made up the acceptable and studied branches of rune magick were mostly instantly-recognizable to me. Most psions have a good working knowledge of the Canons, since runes have been used since before the Awakening, when psionic and magickal power began to be a lot more reliable and a lot stronger in certain talented humans. A rune used for so many years, for so many psions, is a good shortcut when you need a quick and dirty spell effect. Not to mention the Major Works of magick that required perfect performance of drawing, defining, naming, and charging runes.

I reached up with my aching right hand and touched my left shoulder, massaging at the constant cold ache of the demon glyph through my shirt. "Looks like Ceremonial work, the double circle and runes." My eyes moved over the picture. A pile of something wrinkled lay off to one side. "Is that what I think . . ." *Don't. Don't tell me it is.*

"The fucker flayed her." Gabe pushed another file at me. My gorge rose, I squeezed it back down. *I don't throw up,* I reminded myself. *I hate throwing up.*

I was grateful that thirty years of that habit was hard to break. I scanned the remainder of the second file and handed it to Jace. Then I took the third one.

"This one was last night," Gabe said tightly. "Brace yourself, Danny."

I opened the file and felt all the blood drain from my face.

Gabe watched me, dry-eyed and fierce. Her tension stirred the dust in her office, made it swirl in graceful patterns in the climate-controlled air. This keyed-up, with the sharp powerful scent of Power on her, she smelled like pepper and musk. It wasn't so bad, not like the usual human stink. I'd toyed with the idea of becoming a Tester to keep my hand in, since I could now smell Power and psionic talent instead of just seeing and feeling it with human senses. That sort of work wouldn't give me an adrenaline jag and keep me from thinking, so the application papers still lay on top of my laseprinter, half-finished.

It can't be. I turned to the coroner's report. There it was in black and white, the name of the victim who had been dismembered in the middle of a circle, bones and gristle and muscle torn into unrecognizable shapes, a murder of exceeding savagery all the more chilling because it was done to a psion like me. However shattered and wrecked the body was, there was just enough of her face for me to recognize.

Christabel Moorcock.

A Necromance.

Like me.

CHAPTER 5

S ekhmet sa'es," I breathed, looking down at the photographs.
"This is…"

"Does it look familiar, Danny? You're way into scholarship these
days, can't drag your nose out of books when you're not out trying to
kill yourself with bounties. Does it look like *anything* you've read
about? Seen before?" Gabe's eyebrows drew together, her mouth
tight. She pulled out another cigarette and tucked it behind her ear,
the slight smell of dry synth hash mixing with the aroma of the cit-
ronel shampoo she used.

I stared at the picture, my eyes heavy and grainy. "No. I've never
seen anything like this. I've been studying demons, old legends, Magi
stuff. When I'm not working bounties." Tore my eyes away from the
pitiless image. "But that's not why you called me down here."

Gabe's voice was heavy. "We've got Christabel down in the
morgue. I need you to bring her out so I can question her."

Jace went completely still beside me. On any other day I might
have found that funny. Or touching.

I swallowed bitterness. Rubbed at my left shoulder as if trying to
scrub the scar away with my shirt. "Gabe…" I sounded like I'd been
punched breathless.

There wasn't much on earth that could hurt me these days, not
since Japh had changed me. Changed, genespliced, molded into
something new — but my heart was still human. It pounded under a
tough, flexible cage of ribs, my pulse thready in my wrists and throat.
Pounding so hard I felt a little faint.

"I know it's hard for you," Gabe continued. "Since…since Rio.
Please, Danny. I can't do it, I've tried, there's just…not enough body.
Or some kind of wall, some barrier. I can't do it. You can. Please."

I stared at the photo. I hadn't gone into Death for ten months.

Not since Nuevo Rio, hunched on a wide, white blazing-stone
plaza running with sunlight, sobbing as I prayed. I remembered cinnamon smoke drifting in the air, as the demon's body in my arms
crumbled bit by bit.

That was a memory I usually kept to torment myself during long, slow daylight while I tried to sleep. I shoved it away, shut my eyes, opened them again. Shapes jumbled in front of me, my vision blurring. My god still accepted my offerings, but I had not gone into His halls.

Sekhmet sa'es, *Danny, call it what it is.* My heart pounded thinly, my eyes unfocused. *You're afraid that if you go into Death, Japhrimel might be waiting for you.*

"Danny?" The concern in Jace's voice was also equally amusing and touching. Did he think I was going to pass out? Start to scream?

Was I? I felt close. Damn close.

I blinked. I was staring at the photo. Gabe was sweating now, tendrils of her sleek dark hair sticking to her forehead. The temperature in the room had gone up at least ten degrees. The climate control would kick on soon and blow frigid air through the vents. Power blurred out from my skin, Power and heat and a smoky fragrance of demon. Tierce Japhrimel had smelled like amber musk and burning cinnamon; I smelled like fresh cinnamon and a lighter musk. *Demon lite, half the Power, all the nasty attitude,* the humorous voice that accompanied bad news rang out inside my head.

I felt my chest constrict as the vision rose in front of me—ash drifting up from white marble, a hot breeze lifting smudges and scatters of it. Ash and the single, restrained curve of a black urn, left as a final cruel joke.

My right hand twisted into a claw.

I owed her too much to easily walk away from. Gabe was old-school. She'd gone with me into hell and nearly been eviscerated on the way. She hadn't ever uttered a word of anger at my rudeness or my distance or about the fact that she'd almost died because of my hellbent need for revenge on Santino. Or about the fact that I held her at arm's length, refusing to talk about Rio or demons or anything else of any real importance that lay in the air between us, charged and ready to leap free.

"I don't know, Gabe." *Why is my voice shaking? My voice never shakes.* "I haven't gone…there…for a while."

And I missed it. I missed communing with my god, feeling ever-so-briefly the weight of living taken from me. I made my offerings and kept my worship, and every once in a while when I meditated the blue light of Death would weave subtle traceries through the darkness behind my eyes, a comfort familiar from my childhood.

But still, if I went into Death, what would I meet on the bridge between this world and the next? Would I see a tall slim man in a long dark coat, his golden hands clasped behind his back as he considered me, his eyes flaring first green, then going dark? Would he tell me he'd been waiting for me?

You will not leave me to wander the earth alone. But he'd left me, burned to death, crumbled in my arms. Seeing him in Death's country would make it final. Too final. Too *unbearably* final.

"You're the best, Danny. You can even hold an apparition out of a box of cremains, you've *always* been the best. *Please.*" Gabe never begged, but her tone was dangerously close. She didn't even shift in her chair, leaning forward, her elbows on her desk. *She's ready for action,* I realized, and wondered just how tense and staring I looked. I was bleeding heat into the air, a demon's trick.

It wasn't just that Gabe was asking me. I closed Christabel's file and met her eyes squarely. At least she didn't flinch. Gabe was perhaps the only person that could look me in the eyes without flinching.

She still saw *me*. For Gabe, I hadn't changed. I was still Danny Valentine, under the carapace of golden skin and demonic beauty. She wasn't afraid of me—treated me no differently than she had ever since we'd become friends. For Gabe, I would always be the same person; the person she had dropped everything, leveraged her personal contacts, and hared off to Rio for. She had never even considered letting me face Santino by myself.

I would go into Death just for that reason alone.

I looked away. "What else is going on, Gabe? Come clean."

"Can't fool you, can I?" She shrugged, reaching again for her crumpled pack of cigarettes. She couldn't smoke in here, but she tapped the pack twice, a habitual gesture both soothing and oddly disturbing. I had never seen her this distracted. "It's not much, Danny. If I had anything more to work with..."

"Give it up." I sounded harsh, my voice throbbing at the lower registers of "human." The brandy bottles chattered against the desktop, my right hand ached. I wished the alcohol would do me some good. If it would have, I would have reached for it.

"Moorcock was found in her apartment. I searched the place, of course, and found exactly nothing. Except this." She held out a folded piece of pale-pink linen paper.

I took it, the black molecule-drip polish on my nails reflecting stripes of fluorescent light. Actually, they looked like nails, but they were claw-tips, just another mark of how far away from human I'd been dragged. My rings shimmered. They were always awake now, not just when the atmosphere was charged—though the air in here was heavy enough with Power and tension to qualify. I was radiating, and so was she. The line of force between us was almost palpable. Jace, of course, lounged like a big blond cat, smelling hungover and human with a soupçon of musk and male thrown in; spiky, spicy Power contained and deadly within a Shaman's thorny aura.

I caught a fleeting impression from the paper—a wash of terror perfumed like cloying lilacs, an impression of a woman. Necromances are an insular community, for all that we're loners and neurotic prima donnas. We *have* to be a community. Even among psions, the juncture of talent and genetics that makes a Necromance is unusual. I had known Christabel peripherally for most of my life.

The paper was torn on one corner. I gingerly opened it, as if it held a snake.

It pays to be careful.

I looked at it. All the breath slammed out of me again. "Fuck," I let out a strangled yelp.

Her handwriting was ragged, as if she'd been in a hell of a hurry. Great looping, spiky letters, done in dragonsblood ink; the pen had dug deep furrows in the paper. Like claw marks.

Black Room, it said. And below, in huge thick capitals, *REMEMBER REMEMBER RIGGER HALL REMEMBER RIGGER HALL REMEMBER REMEMBER—*

There was a long trailing slash at the end of the last letter, daggering downward as if she'd been dragged away while still trying to write.

I gasped for breath. The lunatic mental image of my body flopping on the floor like a landed fish receded; I forced my lungs to work. The world had gone gray and dim, wavering through a sheet of frosted glass. My back hurt, three lines of fire; another throbbing pain right in the crease of my left buttock. *No. No, I don't have those scars anymore. I don't. I DON'T.*

It took me a few moments, but I finally managed to breathe again. I looked up at Gabe, who sat still and solemn behind her desk, her dark eyes full of terrible guilt. "Fuck." This time I sounded more like myself, only savagely tired.

Only like I'd been hit and lost half my air.

Gabe nodded. "I know you went there. Before they had the big court case and the Hegemony closed it down. Moorcock was a few years older than you, she actually testified at the inquiry."

My mouth was dry as desert sand. "I know," I said colorlessly. "*Sekhmet sa'es*, Gabe. This is..."

"Blast from the past?" For once her humor didn't make me feel better.

Nothing would make this feel better.

I realized I was rubbing at my left shoulder with my wounded right hand, fiercely, as if trying to scrub away the persistent ache. I stopped, dropping my hand into my lap as I examined the paper again. There was a tiny ward-glyph at the top of the page, sketched hastily. It held no Power—it hadn't been charged.

Maybe she'd been interrupted by whatever had torn her body apart. Whatever. *Who*ever.

Could a person do this? I'd seen some horrible things done to the human body, but this was...

"When did she write this?" *I actually sound like myself again, maybe because I can't breathe enough to talk. Hallelujah. All I have to do is get the wind knocked out of me, and I'll sound normal. Simple.*

"We can't tell," Gabe said. "We had Handy Mandy try it, but she just passed out. When she came to, she said it was too thick and headed straight for a date with the bottle, hasn't sobered up since. It was on Moorcock's desk in her bedroom; she was in the living room when she was...killed. There was no sign of forced entry—her shields were still in place, fading but still in place, and ripped from the *inside*."

From the inside? "So it was someone she knew?" I wanted to rub at my shoulder again, stopped myself with an effort that made my aching fingers twitch. I smelled something new on the air.

Fear. A sharp, sweaty stink, as if I were tracking a bounty.

Except it was my own.

Gabe's eyes were darker than usual, the line between her eyebrows deepening. "We don't know, Danny."

"What about the other two victims?"

"They're...interesting, too. The first one—Bryce Smith—was registered as normal. Except he lived in a house with some mighty fine shielding, but he had none of those damn chalk marks around his body. And the second, Yasrule—she was one of Polyamour's girls." Gabe's mouth twisted down briefly.

Mine did the same. Polyamour, the transvestite queen of the sex trade in Santiago City. It wasn't her fault, sexwitches were born sexwitches, and the psionic community was too hated as a whole by normals for us to consider shunning our own. Still...I was glad I hadn't been born as one of them.

"A normal, a sexwitch, and a Necromance." I shook my head. A stray strand of silken ink-black hair fell in my face, I pushed it back impatiently. "Gods."

"We can't get anything else from the scenes," Gabe said. "That's when your name came up."

Lovely. The cops call me in when all else fails. Am I supposed to feel honored? The sarcasm didn't help. I swallowed sourness again, looked down at the pale-pink paper. Gabe had made no move to take it back.

REMEMBER RIGGER HALL. The writing glared up at me, accusing. I didn't want to remember that place. I'd done everything I could to forget it, to go on with my life.

I wish I could tell her I'd do this just because she asked me. I tossed the paper back onto her desk, as if it had burned my fingers. I wouldn't have been surprised if it had.

The phone shrilled just as I opened my mouth to tell her I couldn't take the fucking case. I *couldn't*. Nothing could induce me to even *think* about Rigger Hall for longer than absolutely necessary. As a matter of fact, I was eyeing the brandy, wondering how much more than two bottles it would take before the liquor would have some effect. I'd lost interest at about six last time. I suspected I couldn't drink fast enough to cloud my Magi-trained, demon-enhanced memory. Not with my fucking metabolism.

"Spocarelli," she snarled into the receiver. A long pause. "Fuck me...You're sure?" Her eyes drifted up and met mine, and for an instant I saw through her calm.

There were dark circles under her eyes, and her pale skin had a pasty tone she'd never had before. Her collarbones jutted out, and so did the cords in her neck. She was too thin—and there was something torn and frightened in her dark eyes.

Something terrified. And furious. She was a psionic cop, and something had killed two psions on her watch. A normal, maybe one of the Ludders, gone mad and deciding to murder instead of simply protest the existence of psions? But what normal human could do this *and* tear psionic shields from the inside?

Was it a vendetta springing up rank and foul from the deep filth of the place where I'd learned just how powerless a child could be? What revenge would wait this long and be this brutal? A group, working together? Or one person?

"Keep them off as long as you can," she said finally. "I've got Valentine in here right now. We're heading to the morgue." Another long pause. "Okay. See ya."

She dropped the phone back into its cradle with excessive care. "That was the Captain. The holovids have gotten wind of this."

I winced. Then I opened my mouth to say, *No. I can't do it. Find someone else.*

Instead, what came out was, "You weren't at Rigger Hall, Gabe." I knew her career like I knew my own, like I knew John Fairlane's. Necromances were rare among psions, we listened for news about one another. If Christabel Moorcock was dead, there were only three left in the city, two of them in this very office.

Of course Gabe hadn't gone to Rigger Hall, she hadn't been poor or orphaned.

"No." A flush rose to her cheeks. "I went to Stryker. My mom's trust fund, you know. But...Eddie went to Rigger."

Eddie. Her boyfriend. The Skinlin.

He'd gone with us to Nuevo Rio, had almost lost Gabe to my quest for revenge, and been knocked around a good bit himself. And Eddie had been to Rigger—which meant he would have his own nightmares. The net of obligation closed tight around me.

Oh, fuck. "I guess we're going to the morgue."

I was rewarded with a look of relief so profound that I was sure Gabe didn't know how loudly her face was speaking.

Jace made no sound, but he hitched himself up to his feet, scratching at his forehead under a shelf of tawny hair. He stretched slightly, his aura touching mine, thorn-spiked Power offered in case I needed it. I pushed the touch away—but gently. He didn't sway on his feet, but he did scoop his staff up and twirl it, the small bones clicking and clacking together. The familiar sound did nothing to comfort me.

"Hades," Gabe said, "I was afraid you'd—"

"I won't promise anything. It's been a while. I might not be able to do it, might need to practice before I can get back into the swing."

But I felt the tattoo shift on my face, its inked lines running under my skin, and knew I was lying.

CHAPTER 6

The morgue was across the street, in the basement of a county administration building that looked as if it predated the Seventy Days War, graceless crumbling concrete and some oddly-shaped old glass windows instead of plasilica. Fine, thin clouds were beginning to blow in from the bay, and the sunlight had taken on a hazy quality. I could almost taste the barometric pressure dropping. Sudden shifts like that used to give me a headache.

I breathed in the stink of Saint City and once again felt the city press against my shields like a huge animal waiting to be stroked. The security net on the morgue building let us in, the armed guard in the foyer lowering his plascannon. Legal augments rippled and twitched under his black-mirror body armor. He had a chest the size of a small barrel of reactive and a pair of old optical augments set into his cheekbones, mirrored lenses that looked like sunglasses until their polarized magscan capability gave them away. The guard's lip curled behind Gabe's back as he saw us. I toyed with the idea of giving him a grin, decided against it. Gabe wouldn't like it if I got into a scuffle. Not to mention Jace was hungover—why make him fight? Besides, one normal with legal augments wasn't even a challenge, not anymore. Even if I didn't have a sword.

Gabe signed us in at the counter, staffed only by an AI receptionist deck in a gleaming steel humanoid casing. We were given plasilica one-liners to smooth over our datbands, and in we went.

Necromances don't like morgues, but they're bearable. At least inside a morgue there is cold steel and the clinical light of medical science. The aura of dispassionate research helps. Not like graveyards and funeral homes, where grief and confusion and agony and generations of pain dye the air a razor-grieving red. The holovids make it look like Necromances spend all their time illegally digging up bones in graveyards, but truth be told that's the *last* place you'd look for one of us. You'd have a better chance in a hospital or a lawyer's office.

Though hospitals aren't easy either. Any place soaked with pain and suffering isn't easy.

Jace's hand curled around my elbow when we got to the bottom of the staircase, a warm hard human touch. Gabe pushed though the swinging door and we followed her, boots clicking in uneven time over the same blue glittery linoleum as the police station. I didn't shake my arm free of Jace's touch all the way down the hall. The man was stubborn, following me on bounties and picking up after me. I didn't know what debt he thought he was paying.

I didn't even know what debt *I* was paying on now, I had so many due.

I pulled away from his hand as Gabe flashed her badge at the admin-assist behind a sheet of bulletproof. The girl's throat swelled as she nodded, her pink-streaked hair sticking up in the new Gypsy Roen fashion—she had a subvocal implant. Her fingers blurred as she tapped on a datapad. I wondered who she was talking to while she was taking dictation, followed Gabe through the fireproof security door, and swallowed against the sudden chemical stench. *I wish I could figure out how to quit smelling that.*

"Hey, Spooky," a thin geek in a labcoat, carrying a stack of paperwork, called out. "You here for the deadhead?" Then his eyes flicked past her to me, and he stopped cold, unshaven face turning the color of old cottage cheese.

It wasn't as satisfying as it might have been. His stringy hair was cut in the bowl shape Jasper Dex had made popular. It didn't suit him. Neither did the color of his face. His eyes came suspiciously close to bugging out. I wondered why—working in the morgue, he probably saw his fair share of Necromances, between Gabe and John Fairlane.

Then I remembered I was golden-skinned, with a face like a holovid model's and a share of a demon's beauty without the persistent alienness of a demon; my hair was ink-black, longer than it had been and silky, refusing to stay back unless braided tightly, sometimes not even then. I looked like a particularly good gene-splice to most normals, like I'd paid a bundle to look like a holovid wet dream.

The emerald in my cheek would just give normals a reason to fear me; an atavistic fear of psions in general and Necromances in particular. Silly normals sometimes mistake Necromances for Death Himself, loading another layer of fear onto the trepidation they feel about all psions.

If they knew how unconditionally Death loved His children, maybe they would fear Him less. Or more. But psions were feared by normals all over the world, just because we had been born different.

"Yeah, Hoffman, I'm here for the pile of meat that used to be a deadhead." Gabe's voice was a slap bouncing off the hall walls. "This is the big gun. Dante Valentine, meet Nix Hoffman."

"Charmed, I'm sure." The dry tone I used was anything but. My voice echoed, not as hard as Gabe's, but casually powerful; I had to remember to keep toning it down *especially* around normals. The effect my voice had on unsuspecting civilians was thought-provoking, to say the least.

"Likewise," he stammered. "Ah, um, Ms. Valentine—"

"Which bay is the body in, Hoff? Caine's?" Gabe barely even broke stride.

"Yeah, Caine's got it, he's in his office. He was doing toxicology." The young man's eyes flittered over me. I knew what he was seeing— a particularly desirable genespliced woman—and wished I didn't. His pupils swelled. If I flooded the air with my scent I could have him on his knees, begging without knowing why. Yet another side effect of whatever I was now.

Hedaira, a flat ironic voice whispered in the lowest reaches of my mind. I shut that voice away—it hurt too much to hear it. Why was Japhrimel's the voice I used to hurt myself?

"Thanks, jerkwad." Gabe sailed past him, and I did the same, letting out a deep breath between my teeth. I did *not* sneer. It took some effort.

"You've got yourself a reputation," Jace murmured in my ear. I snorted something indelicate. "Oh, come on, Danny. You're too cute. Maybe we should get you one of them Oak Vegas Raidon outfits."

"I can't raise the dead in a black-leather bikini," I muttered back, grateful once again because the damnable urge to smile rose again. Gabe's boots clicked on the linoleum.

"A *studded* black-leather bikini," Jace corrected.

"Pervert." The stench of human cells, dying decaying dead, rose up to choke me.

How did Japhrimel stand it? I wondered, and my left shoulder suddenly *burned* as if something hot was pressed against it, scorching the skin, twisting. I could almost feel the scar writhing on my skin.

I stopped dead. Jace nearly ran into me, stopped just in time, the bones tied to his staff clicking together. His Power stroked me briefly, a pleasant touch that would have unloosed my knees and made my breath catch if I hadn't been struggling to make my lungs work, my skin running prickly with demon Power. "Danny?"

"Nothing." These flashes of heat were getting more and more pronounced lately. I wondered if I was going into demon menopause.

There was another, nastier idea. I wondered if the flashes of heat had anything to do with the Prince of Hell.

What a nightmare-inducing thought. Assuming I could sleep, that is. I put my head down, started forward again, lengthening my stride to catch up with Gabe. "Just a thought."

"What kind of thought?" He sounded only mildly curious, his staff tapping in time with our footsteps.

"The private kind, J-man. Back off."

"Fine." Easy and calm, he let it drop. How he managed to do that I could never guess — it took a lot to ruffle his smooth surface. Maybe it was growing up in a Mob family that did it, made him so hard and blank; impenetrable. Or maybe it was putting up with me. *Why did you hand over your Family, Jace? Just give it up? People have killed to stay in Families, let alone control them. You could have had everything you ever wanted. Why?*

I wished I could find the words to ask him.

Gabe stopped in front of another door. Her bobbed hair swung as she turned her head slightly, a quarter-profile as pure as an ancient marble in a statis-sealed museum case. "Word to the wise. Caine's a Ludder."

I felt my lip curl up. A *genesplice-is-murder, psions-are-aberration, Luddite-Text-thumping fanatic.* They were everywhere these days. "Great. He's going to *love* me."

Gabe opened her mouth to reply, but the frosted-glass window set in the door darkened. The hinges squealed, and I had to kill the sardonic smile that wanted to creep up my face. I had the distinct idea that the hinges were deliberately left dry. *Come into my parlor, said the medical examiner to the hapless police detective.* My right hand tightened, searching for the hilt of a sword. I actually twitched before I remembered I didn't have a katana anymore. My hand ached, one vicious cramp settling into the bones and twisting briefly before letting go. Getting better. It used to ache all the time, now it only ached when I wanted to reach for a hilt and found only empty air.

"Gabriele," the stick-thin elderly man said. His eyes, poached blue eggs over a bloodless mouth and pale powdery cheeks, swam behind thick plasrefractive lenses. His lab coat was pristine, the mag-tag on his pocket read *R. Caine.* He'd chosen a caduceus logo on the tag; it reminded me of my own accreditation tat. A mad giggle rose up inside of me, was suppressed, and died an inglorious death as an almost-burp. "And some company. How charming."

"Afternoon, Dr. Caine." Gabe's voice was flat, monotone. Deliberately noncombative, but slightly disdainful at the same time. "I presume Captain Algernon has spoken with you."

If he could have sneered, he probably would have. Instead, his eyes lingered on me. The pink dome of his scalp under a few thinning gray-white strands of combed-over hair added to the egglike appearance of his head; no cosmetic hair implants for this gentleman. His teeth were still strong and sound, but they were terribly discolored, shocking in this age of molecular dental repair. Like the dry hinges, his teeth were probably deliberate too. "This is most irregular," he sniffed. "What is *that?*"

"Dante Valentine, Dr. Caine. Dr. Caine, Dante Valentine." Gabe moved slightly to one side, still between the doctor and me. I got the impression she was ready to jam her boot in the door if he decided to try to slam it shut.

"Pleased to meet you." I lied with a straight face, for once.

His watery blue eyes narrowed behind the lenses. "What *are* you?"

I set my shoulders. I'd been given the cold shoulder by a lot of normals, he was going to have to work harder than that to irritate me. "The proper term is *hedaira,* Doctor. I'm a genetically altered human." The words stuck in my throat, dry and lumpy. *Wouldn't you love to know, Doctor. I didn't ask for this to be done to me. And I have no idea what* hedaira *even means. The only person who could have told me is ash in a black urn. When I'm not hallucinating his disembodied voice to flog myself with, that is.* "Although I suspect *abomination* is the term you're looking for. Let's get this over with."

"Who did your genesplicing?" He licked his thin, colorless lips. "It looks like an expensive job."

Expensive? I guess you could say so. It cost me my life and someone I loved. I felt it like a sharp pinch on already-bruised flesh. So maybe he *would* manage to annoy me. One point for the Ludder doctor. "That's none of your business. I'm here to view a body in a legitimate murder investigation. Should I come back with a court order?"

My voice made the glass in the door rattle slightly. *I think I'm behaving badly.* A lunatic giggle rose up again inside of me. Why did I always have the urge to laugh at times like this?

Dr. Caine's wiry eyebrows nested in his nonexistent hairline. "Of course not. I know my duty to the police department. *Despite* their habit of sending me cadavers."

"Why, Doctor, I thought it was your job to deal with cadavers." I didn't move, my feet nailed to the floor despite Jace's sudden grip on my elbow. I hated the syrupy sweetness in my voice — it meant that I was about to say something unforgivable. "Perhaps you should retire."

"Not until I'm forced to, young woman. Come inside." He laughed mechanically and didn't look pleased, but ushered us into a small office jammed with a desk, two chairs, two antique and crooked metal file cabinets, piles of papers and files, and a thriving blue-flowered orchid on top of another file cabinet, this one wooden and glowing mellow with polish. That was interesting. Nearly as interesting was the dry-erase board set on the wall across from the second door. Dr. Caine's handwriting was spidery, and it wandered inside the neatly-ruled sections, keeping track of what body was in what bay and what tests needed to be done. At least, that's what I assumed the complicated numbers and letters meant. It looked like a code based on the old Cyrillic alphabet.

"Now I want it to be very *clear,*" he said, once we were all crowded in his office, "this is happening against my will, and under my protest."

"Mine too," I muttered under my breath, taking refuge in snideness. Gabe cast me an imploring glance. I shut up.

The good doctor studied me for a long moment. I noticed he had two lasepens in his breast pocket and a capped scalpel too. "The body is of a Necromance." His lip curled. "Cause of death, as nearly as we can determine, was some type of psionic assault."

That was something new. Dr. Caine noticed my sudden attention. "We can tell because of the MRI and sigwave scans." He directed his words at me. "Bleeding in the cortex in characteristic star-patterns. It seems that, just as manual strangulation leaves petechiae, psionic assault resulting in death leaves these starbursts of blood and scarring in the brain."

Thank you for that incredibly vivid mental image, Doctor. I glanced around his office again. I smelled chemical reek, dying human cells, and pipe tobacco mixed with synth hash. So the good Doc was a smoker. Most medical personnel were. His hands didn't tremble, but they were liver-spotted and thin as spider's legs. I imagined his hands on a lasecutter and had to shudder. *He probably talks to the cadavers. And very patronizingly, too.* I glanced up at the ceiling, where the random holes in the soundbreak tiles almost began to run together and make sense. Dust swirled in the air, forming little geometric shapes as the room heated up with four adult bodies in it— and the extra heat I was putting out. Power trembled at the outer edges of my control, straining to leap free. I invoked spread-thin control, clenching my right fist so hard I felt the claws prick my palm. It felt comfortingly like fingernails digging in as I made a fist.

"What kind of psionic assault?" Gabe asked. "Feeder, Ceremonial, Magi, what?"

"I am unable to determine. I was under the impression that was *your* job." This sneer he directed at me. I ignored it. Instead, I studied the dry-erase board, watching the shape of the letters blur as I unfocused my eyes. With it all hazy, I could almost pretend there was a pattern there too. If I spent a little Power, I could probably decode it, my minor precognitive talent turning a randomness into a glimpse of the future.

I came back to myself with a barely-covered start. Took a deep breath. I couldn't afford to get distracted here. No amount of precog was worth even a momentary lapse in attention.

"What else can you tell me, Doctor?" Gabe was in her element. I almost forgot she was a cop; she looked like a wide-eyed med student. Caine preened under her attention. I overrode the urge to rub at my left shoulder. The mark was burning, a piercing, drilling, fiery pain I only felt rarely over the last year. Was it just because I had allowed myself to think of Japhrimel again? Was thinking of him more frequently now?

As if I ever stopped thinking about him, even while I was being shot at by panicked, psychopathic bounties.

"There is a high likelihood that Miss Moorcock was also sexually assaulted before she was dismembered." Caine's poached eyes glittered. "There was tearing and severe bruising in the vaginal vault. Unfortunately, we were unable to recover any DNA evidence because of contamination by blood and foreign matter in the vagina."

My throat closed again, hot bile rising. *Why do I keep wanting to throw up?* I braced myself. Jace's thumb drifted across my elbow, a soothing touch.

Too bad I wasn't soothed.

Gabe waited.

"There's nothing else," he said finally. I'd have bet my house and the rest of Lucifer's blood money Caine was enjoying this. "We're running toxicology screens and reanalyzing some of the forensic measurements."

"Reanalyzing?" Gabe fractionally raised one eyebrow.

"Either we have made an error, or whatever ripped her into pieces did it simultaneously. Her arms, her legs, her head—all at the same time. As if she was quartered. Are you familiar with quartering, Ms. Valentine?"

His poached-egg eyes rested on me now, his thin mouth curved into the slightest of smiles. I dropped my right hand back down to my side, both my hand and shoulder burning. "I'm somewhat of a student of history, Doctor. I'm familiar with the term."

CHAPTER 7

The tiled vault of the body-bay was chilly. Steam rose off my skin as soon as I stepped through the airseals into climate control. I had to spend a moment's worth of attention readjusting—my internal thermostat was set on "high." I ran very warm these days, not needing a pile of blankets like I used to when I was human. That was one thing Jace had been good for during our affair, even though he ended up kicking off the covers. I supposed it was living in Rio that made him so warm.

Nowadays, if he collapsed on my bed it was because he was drunk, and he slept on top of the covers more often than not, or woke when I poked him in the ribs to haul himself down the hall to his own room.

I scanned the room habitually—nothing but the usual security net and countermeasures; the holovid captures set in strips along the ceiling to get everything in 3-D. Steel lockers took up one side of the room, tools hung neatly, racks of equipment and scanners. My teeth ached until I took a deep breath and made my jaw relax.

The tough blue plasticine bodybag lay on the stainless-steel table. The shape was subtly wrong, of course—there were only parts of Christabel Moorcock left.

I was alone in a morgue with a body. My skin roughened, smoothed out. All of a sudden I was more comfortable than I'd been for almost a year. I knew how to do this. I'd been doing this most of my life.

Then what are you afraid of? a cool, deep voice asked inside my head. I shut that voice back up in its little black box. It hurt too much to hear the shading of male amusement, the flat ironic tone of a demon's voice stroking the most intimate of my thoughts. Why couldn't I just let the sound of his voice go?

What *was* I afraid of? Oh, nothing. Except for maybe finding him waiting for me on the other side of Death's bridge, his hands clasped behind his back and that faint smile on his face. The last time I'd brought a soul out of Death like this, Japhrimel had been with me, watching.

The intercom crackled. "Whenever you're ready, Danny," Gabe said from the observation deck outside. This would be taped, of course, since it would be admitted into evidence as part of the investigation. "Just take it slow."

Take it slow, she says, a nasty mental snigger caroled across my brain. *It's not her ass on the line here.*

It wasn't precisely that I was afraid—after all, I still had my tat and my emerald. My patron god still accepted my offerings. I missed the touch of my god, missed the absolute certainty of the thing I knew I was best at. The contact with a psychopomp is so achingly personal for a Necromance. My god would not deny me.

No, I was only afraid of myself.

I reached up, touched my left shoulder. The mark burned with a fierce, steady ache now. As painful as it was, I welcomed it. It had burned like that when Japhrimel was alive—as if a live brand was resting on my skin. I had never thought nerve-scorching pain could be comforting. The mark would turn ice-cold soon enough as whatever made it heat up faded, and I would be left with the reminder that the demon it named was dead.

Dead, maybe. Forgotten, no. And Lucifer…

I didn't want to think about the Prince of Hell.

I had no sword, but my right-hand knife was good steel, and I held it loosely. Two glassed-in white candles stood on a wheeled cart between me and the body. Cool air touched my forehead, caressed my cheekbones and the shallow V of skin exposed by my shirt. My right hand cramped slightly on the knifehilt, then eased suddenly.

I had to look.

I skirted the cart and approached the table with its plaswrapped burden, the soles of my boots scritching slightly on the easy-to-hose plaslino floor. The silvery drain set below the table gave out a whiff of chlorine and decaying blood.

The intercom crackled again. "Danny?"

You of all people should know that I just can't barge into this headfirst. Though I don't know why, that's my usual style. "Just relax, Gabe. I need to see."

"Danny—"

"I won't touch the body. I'm going to unzip the sheath, that's all. It will make it easier." I heard my own voice, calmer than I really felt; I was a master at sounding like I knew what I was doing.

"For who?" It was a blind attempt at humor, and it failed dreadfully. I glanced up at the observation window, felt my lip curl up slightly. The magshielding in the walls was good, I could only feel them through the window—Gabe a cool purple bath of worry; Jace, spiky, spiced electric honey, every nerve suddenly focused on me; and Caine's dry, smooth, egglike aura, giving nothing away. Blind natural shielding, a disbelief so huge it could protect him from psychic assault. Some normals were like that. They literally wouldn't believe their own eyes when it came to magick.

I wondered what he thought of psions, since he was so disbelieving. Of course, he was a Ludder, he probably thought we should all be put in camps like the Evangelicals of Gilead did during the Seventy Days War. Rounded up, shot, and put in disposal units. Ludders hated genesplicing on principle, but they hated psions with an atavistic revulsion as irrational as it was deep. It didn't matter that we'd been born this way, according to the Ludders we were abominations and all deserved to die.

"Don't ride me, Gabe. It's not recommended." I wasn't amused.

"Then just get this done so you can go home and drink." She wasn't amused either. Guess we were even.

Like drinking will help. I can't even get drunk anymore. My fingers closed around the cold zipper. I drew it down with a long ripping sound.

At least they had put the parts where they were supposed to be.

I wondered what was missing—I hadn't looked at the preliminary report yet. The stink of death belched up, assaulting my sensitive nose.

Sensory acuity was a curse sometimes. No wonder demons carried their personal perfume around like a shield. I wished I could. "Christabel," I said. "*Sekhmet sa'es.*"

The air stirred uneasily. There was no dust here, but I felt the Power in the air—my own—tremble unsteadily, like a smooth pond touched by a hover field. Not rippling but quivering, just about to slide free of control and plunge into chaos.

Well. That's odd.

I backed up. I didn't need to see more than her ruined, rotting face. I retreated to the other side of the room, swallowing hard. A snap of my fingers as I passed the steel cart lit the candles. I used to get such a kick out of doing that.

Back before Japhrimel. "Kill the lights, Gabe."

"All right." A popping sound, and three-quarters of the fluorescents went dim. The ones that remained lit buzzed steadily, maddeningly. It was better lit than the warehouse had been. I briefly wondered where Bulgarov was now, if they'd run him through the courtroom and into a gasbox yet. No, it was too soon. I wouldn't need to testify, I'd only done the collar.

Quit dithering, Danny. The bounty's over. Focus on what's in front of you.

I held the knife up, steel glimmering, a bar between me and whatever happened next. "Here goes nothing," I murmured. "Dante Valentine, accredited Necromance, performing an apparition on the body of Christabel Moorcock, also accredited Necromance." *And I hope like hell she has something to tell us.*

"Got it," Gabe said. "Whenever you're ready."

I sighed. Then I closed my eyes. I had no more time to screw around.

It was easy, too easy. I dropped below conscious thought, into the blue glow of whatever juncture of talent and genetics allowed me to see the dead. I wasn't touching the body—I couldn't stand the thought of resting my hand on that plastic—so I expected there to be a time lag, some difficulty, maybe a barrier between me and the blue crystal walls of Death's antechamber.

I was wrong.

Oh, gods, it feels good. My head tipped back, my loose long hair

streaming on a not-quite-wind. The chant bubbled up from the most
secret part of me, my voice husking on the high accents, Power leaping to fill the words almost before I uttered them. *"Agara tetara
eidoeae nolos, sempris quieris tekos mael—"*

So far so good, I thought hazily, then it swallowed me whole.

Blue crystal light rose above me. My rings spat a shower of sparks,
my left shoulder blurring with pain. Riding the Power, the crystal
walls singing, I reached across space and steel and vibrating air,
hunting. Bits of shattered bone and decaying flesh turned bitter
against my tongue. Christabel's body was no more than an empty
shell, no spark of life still housed in the fragile meat, not even the
foxfire of nerves dying hours or days after the event. The cold, stiffening chill of death walked up my fingers with small prickling feet,
taunting the ends of my toes.

I opened my eyes.

*It was so familiar I could have wept. The chant poured out of me,
sonorous, striking the blue crystal walls stretched up into infinity. I
wore the white robe of the god's chosen, belted with silver that
dripped like chainmail in daggered loops. My bare feet rested on the
bridge over an endless abyss; a silver stream of souls whirling past,
drawn over the bridge by the irresistible law of Death's renewal. I
walked, the emerald on my cheek casting a spectral glow, enfolding
me. The emerald's light was a cocoon, keeping me safely on the
bridge, preventing me from being flung into the well of souls. The
abyss yawned below, the bridge quivering like a plucked harpstring.
I did not have time to see if perhaps a demon's soul waited there for
me. I had been afraid that he would be here in Death's halls, tied to
me. I had been afraid that he would not be here—that mortal death
held no place for a demon's soul.*

*How could my own cowardice have kept me from the thing I loved
most, the only place I felt utterly safe?*

I raised my head slowly. I could not look, did not want to look.

Had to look.

*The god of Death's cipher, His slender dog's head glossy black,
regarded me. The same as He always had, since the first time I had
ventured fully into the blue glow. He sat on the other side of the
bridge, a dog-shape that was only a mask for His true form; the merciful mask that allowed me to come into Death and face the infinite
terror of life's ending. Though I was Necromance, Death's touch
frightened even me; no finite human likes to face the infinite. And yet,*

cheek by jowl with the terror was complete acceptance. Death's touch was cool and forgiving, the laying-down of burdens, the easing of pain, the washing-away of obligation and of memory.

And oh, how I wanted to feel that lightness, even as I struggled against it as all living things struggle, clinging to a life that is familiar even if painful. The agony I knew, not the mystery of what lay beyond the well, the secret Death whispered to every mortal thing sooner or later.

I let out a dry, barking sob in the middle of my chant. Power crested, spilled over me, the god reached through me. The place inside me where He lived bloomed again, a hurtful ecstatic flower, and I became again the bridge a god uses to pull a soul from Death.

Pressure, mounting against throat and eyes and the juncture of my legs, sharp pleasure. My head fell back, and a subliminal *snap!* echoed dryly against tiled walls. The chill numbness rose in my fingers, creeping up my arms. "Ask . . . your . . . questions . . ." I said softly, fierce joy rising and combating the chill. I had done it. I had *done* it once again.

The intercom crackled, Gabe's voice staticky and harsh, and Christabel Moorcock's ghost moaned. There was no modulation to the ghost's voice—of course not, the dead don't speak as we do. There is nothing in an apparition's tone but the flat finality of that most final punctuation to the act of living. The longer a body has been in a grave, the more horribly flat an apparition's voice. People have screamed and fainted when an apparition speaks, and sometimes even other psions blanch. I've seen it happen while watching others of my kind work in training videos.

Nobody likes to hear the dead speak.

What's that? Even in my chanting trance I realized something wasn't right. Christabel's low flat moan scraped across the surface of my words, tautened the Power holding the chant steady, sent a cold fiery finger up my back. It was *wrong.* No apparition should sound so . . . horrified.

This isn't right, I thought, but I held the apparition. Held it to the living, the chill starting in my fingers and toes, the cold marble-block feeling of death.

Gabe asked again, and a feedback squeal ripped against my vulnerable psyche. I screamed, Power tearing through me again, my emerald spitting sparks and my rings crackling, showering golden sparks. Tiles shattered, and glass from a fluorescent tube chimed against the floor. I dug my heels and mental teeth in, the chant spilling and stretching, Power bucking, mental threads tearing with sharp, painful twitches.

REMEMBER! REMEMBER! REMEMBER!

For one vertiginous second I felt the caress of cold, mad fingers against my cheek, a blast of something too inhuman to be called thought, carrying undeniable meaning and repeating the single word over and over again. *REMEMBER! REMEM—*

I tore away. The ghost screamed and my knife flashed up, cold steel between me and the hungry thing lunging at me, feeding from the Power I carried.

"Japhrimel!" I screamed hoarsely. My shoulder gave a crunching flare of pain that ripped through my trance. A gunpowder flash of blue flame belled through the air, and my shoulders hit the wall, cracking more tile. Tile-dust and ceramic shards pattered down as more glass drifted to the floor, ground diamond-fine. Sudden dark plunged through the room—only one flickering, buzzing fluorescent remained lit on the far side of the body-bay.

I slid down the wall, blinking, as Christabel Moorcock's dead body sucked the last traces of her hungry ghost back into Death. I shuddered, my emerald burning on my cheek, and could not stop the dry coughing sobs welling up inside me. Tears slicked my cheeks, hideous relief and fresh grief welling up from a place too deep to name.

Japhrimel was not in Death's halls. Wherever he was now, he was lost to me completely.

CHAPTER 8

Fuck," Gabe said for the twentieth time, rubbing at the back of her neck. "I'm sorry, Danny. Hades, that could have killed you."

I shrugged, using the small plastic stick to stir the coffee-flavored sludge with my left hand. My right lay in my lap, useless and discarded out of habit. The sound of the Spook Squad bustled around us, and I heard a Ceremonial on the other side of the partition dictating into a videorecorder about a suspected-telepath bank robbery. "Don't worry about it, Gabe. I'm a lot tougher than I used to be."

He wasn't there. He's gone. Really gone. I told that voice to go

away. It went without a struggle, but promised to return and taunt me
the next time I tried to sleep.

At least some things in my life were consistent.

"That's apparent." She sighed, looking down at the heaped files
on her desk. One stray dark strand of hair had fallen into her face,
shocking in a woman of Gabe's precision. Her sidearm was briefly
visible as she rubbed at the back of her neck with both hands, massaging away a constant ache. Her eyes were wider than I'd seen them
in a while, but at least she'd lost the cheesy pale color in her cheeks.
"Gods. I'm so sorry, Danny."

"Don't worry," I repeated, suppressing the flare of irritation. *She's
worried about me, she's my friend, she doesn't deserve my bad mood,*
I told myself for the fifth time, leaning back in the chair and shifting
my gaze to the bottle of brandy. Gabe had offered us all a medicinal
swig and I'd taken it, even though it might have been water as far as
my new physiology was concerned. Jace had actually taken three
long drafts before capping the bottle and handing it back to her. "At
least it tells us a few things."

Jace took a long slurp of his coffee, holding the plasticine cup
gingerly. "What does it tell you, Danny?" He sounded only mildly
interested. His face was set and white, blue eyes bloodshot and livid.
The bones on his staff moved uneasily, one clacking against another.
Fever-spots burned high up on each cheek.

I appeared to have frightened them both. I supposed when the
feeling of relief and crazed joy at daring the borders of Death again
wore off, I would be frightened too. But I didn't have the good
sense or manners to be scared right now. I felt oddly as if I'd won a
victory.

There were only a few things that could turn an apparition into a
ravening, hungry, vengeful ghost, most of them having to do with
soul-destroying torture before the act of death. Ritual murders—
what you might call "black magick," Power gained through the
expense of torturing and killing another sentient being—and geno-
cides were high on the list. So was being attacked and contaminated
by a Feeder—a psychic vampire. Among a population where Power
was so common and so frequently used, it stood to reason that some
would develop pathology in their processing of ambient Power and
need to siphon off vitality from those around them, feeding on
magickal or psionic energy in ever-increasing doses, until they got to
the point where they could drain a normal person in seconds and a

psion in minutes, depriving them of the vital energy needed to sustain life. Most Feeders were caught and treated while young, able to live out normal lives as psions with early intervention. When an older psion started to exhibit Feeder pathology, early intervention was key as well.

But Feeders didn't tear their prey apart. At least, not physically.

It looked like a ritual murder to me, but it was too soon to tell. Whatever it was, Christabel Moorcock had suffered something so horrible even her ghost was insane with the echoes of the act.

"Well." I propped my boots up on Gabe's desk, picked a sliver of tile out of my hair, dropped it in her overflowing wastebasket. "It tells us we're dealing with some serious shit. That's nice to know. If we can assume we're dealing with a ritual murder, which would be my first guess, it also tells us that whatever was done to her reverberates after death. So that narrows down the type of magick we're hunting. It tells us that someone is very, very determined; it tells us that a lot of preparation and time went into this. So there are some clues lying around. Nobody can work a magickal operation like that with surgical precision; there's always some sloppy fucking mistake. I learned that doing bounties." I deliberately did not look at Jace, though it was an implicit nod to him. He'd been my teacher, after all; had taught me more about bounties in a year than I could learn on my own in five.

"Great." Gabe rested her elbows on her desk, finally stopping the rubbing at her neck. The white rings around her eyes were starting to go away. I smelled pizza—someone must have decided to grab a quick dinner here. It reminded me I was hungry. As usual. "Caine's having a fucking fit that you destroyed one of his body-bays. The holovids are going to be all over this, Danny. And if word gets out you're working on it, the sharks will go into a frenzy."

"He'll get tax compensation and the Hegemony HHS will step in since his body-bay was destroyed during a routine investigation." My tone sharpened. "And nobody cares what *I* work on."

I was surprised by Jace's snort. He took down half of his scalding coffee in one gulp, reached for the brandy bottle and, apparently changing his mind in midreach, settled back again. The flimsy folding chair squeaked. "Oh, really? You're *the* Danny Valentine, world-class Necromance who retired rich at the top of her game after a hush-hush bounty hunt that nobody can dig up any information on except for the Nuevo Rio Mob War. Of course they're going to eat it up. I'd be surprised if there weren't reporters covering your house already, Danny."

He forgot to mention that I was the Necromance that had raised Saint Crowley the Magi from ashes, as well as worked on the Choyne Towers disaster. And my recent string of bounties had been profiled on a holovid show. Gabe was right, if it surfaced that I was working on the case all hell might very well break loose. Plus, it would be bad for the cops to admit they'd had to bring in a freelancer.

"Fuck." I took a long swallow of the scorching mud that passed for coffee around here. Decided to change the subject. Accentuate the positive, so to speak. "So we've got more information than we had before, and we have a direction."

"What direction?" Gabe asked.

"Rigger Hall." I shivered. "Nightmare Central." *Remember. Remember. Remember.* The memory of the apparition's soulless chant chilled me as much as the thought of Christabel's note. I didn't *want* to remember Rigger Hall. I had done very well for years without remembering. I wanted nothing more than to continue that trend.

Silence crackled between us. The paper on her desk shifted uneasily, stirred by something other than wind.

"What happened there, Danny?" Gabe looked miserable. The chaos of ringing phones and crackle of uneasy Power outside her cubicle underscored her words. The Ceremonial next door swore softly and started over again, I heard the click-whirr of a magnetic tape relay. "The inquiry was sealed, it would take a court order to open it, and that means *more* publicity. I'm supposed to keep this as quiet as possible. Once the press sinks their teeth in, we'll be lucky to avoid a rush of copycats and Ludders attacking psions."

She was right. We would be lucky if nobody found out about it and was tempted to do a little cleansing-by-murder. And the first victim had been a normal. If there was even a *hint* that a murder of a normal had been committed by a psion, people got edgy.

Most psions were well able to defend themselves from random street violence, even the idiots who didn't take combat training. But still, it wore on you after a while, all the sidelong looks and little insults. We were trained in Hegemony schools, tattooed after taking Hegemony accreditation, and policed both internally and externally, but normals still feared us. We were useful to the Hegemony and a backbone source of tax funding as well as invaluable to corporations, but none of that mattered when the normals got into a snit. To them, we were all freaks, and it never did to forget that for very long, if at all.

I said nothing, staring at the brandy bottles and their amber liquid. One bottle was almost empty. Inside it, the liquid trembled, responding to my attention.

Jace hauled himself up to his feet, scooping up his staff. "I'm gonna go check for reporters outside." He was gone before I had time to respond.

I watched him vanish and looked back to find Gabe frowning at me. "What?" I tried not to sound aggrieved, shifted my boots on her desk. My mouth tasted grainy with the glass and porcelain dust from the morgue bay.

"He's upset," she informed me, as if I didn't already know. "What's going on with you two, Danny?"

"Nothing," I mumbled, taking another scalding sip of coffee. "He stays at my house, does bounties with me. He sticks around, but... nothing really, you know. I can't." *I can't touch him. I won't let him touch me.*

Her frown deepened, the crow's-feet at the corners of her eyes deepening as well. "You mean you haven't..." Her slim dark eyebrows rose as she trailed off and examined me as if I'd just announced I wanted a genderchange and augments.

"I don't know what it will do to him." My left shoulder gave one muted throb that sent a not-unwelcome trickle of heat down my spine. *And he's not Japhrimel. Every time he tries to touch me, all I can think about is a fucking demon. Ha, ha. Get it, fucking a demon?* "Can we not talk about my sex life, please?"

"He gave up his Mob Family for you. Just walked away from it. From everything." *And he's human.* She didn't say it, but I heard it clearly nonetheless. Even someone she considered a traitor was better than me mourning a demon, apparently.

"Rigger Hall," I cut across her words. The nearly-empty brandy bottle jittered slightly on the edge of her desk, paper ruffled again. "I don't know a lot, Gabe. But what I *do* know, I'll tell you."

She stared at me for a long fifteen seconds, her dark eyes fathomless, her emerald sizzling with light. Her aura flushed an even deeper red-purple. "Fine. Have it your way, Danny. You always do anyway." She leaned back in her chair, the casters squeaking slightly, and plucked the cigarette from behind her ear. In blatant defiance of the regs, she flicked out her silver Zijaan and inhaled, then sent twin streams of smoke out through her nostrils. A flick of the wrist, and a stasis-charm hummed into life, the smoke freezing into ash and falling on her desk. It was a nice trick.

I swallowed dryly. "Rigger Hall." The words tasted like stale burned chalk. "I was there from…let's see, I was tipped from home foster care to the psi program when I was five. So I would have been there, clipped and collared, for about…eight years before the inquiry." I shuddered. My skin prickled with phantom gooseflesh again.

I looked at my right hand, twisting itself further into a claw. It ached, not as much as it had, but still…My perfect, poreless golden skin was tingling in instinctive reaction, my breath coming short and my pulse beating hot and thready in my throat.

"Hades," Gabe breathed, a lungful of smoke wreathing her face before falling, dead ash, onto the papers drifting her desk. "Eddie does the same thing. What *happened?*"

"The Headmaster was a slimy piece of shit named Mirovitch." My breath came even harsher. My voice was as dry-husky as it had been right after the Prince of Hell had tried to strangle me. "He was part of the Putchkin psi program. Got a diplomatic waiver to come over and reform the Hegemony program with Rigger as an experimental school. What nobody knew was that he was a Feeder, and had been for some time. He was well-camouflaged, and he didn't want to be cured. Instead, he wanted his private playground, and he got it."

"A Feeder?" Gabe shivered. "Gods."

"Yeah. He was slick, and we were just…just kids. It was…" For a moment my voice failed me, sucked back into my throat. I set my coffee cup down on the floor beside my chair, feeling the floor rock slightly underneath me. Or maybe it wasn't the floor—maybe I was shaking. "It was really bad, Gabe. If you stepped out of line—if you were *lucky*—you got put in a Faraday cage in a sensory-dep vault. It was…A couple of the kids committed suicide, and Mirovitch made one of the Necromance apprentices sleep in the room that…He went insane and clawed his own eyes out. They wrote it up as an incorrectly-done training session."

Her eyes were round, disbelieving. "Why didn't anyone—"

"He paid off the Hegemony proctors. Had a profitable little sex-witch stable going on the side, could afford to hand out cash…and other bribes. And if any of the kids really pissed him off, he signed the forms to turn you into a breeder." I shivered again, rubbed at my left shoulder, my eyes blinded with memory.

Gods. If there was any justice in the world, the memories would have faded. They hadn't.

Once, my roommate had tried to tell her social worker what was going on inside Rigger Hall's hallowed walls. She'd paid for it with her life. It was ruled a suicide, of course—but sometimes even a kid has the guts to take her own life rather than be pushed into the breeder program.

Roanna's body hung tangled on the wires, jerking as the electricity zapped her dying nerves, smoke rising from her pale skin, her long beautiful hair burning, stinking. The streak of the soul leaving her body, as if it couldn't wait to be finally free—and the sick-sweet smell of flesh roasted from the inside. The Headmaster's fingers dug into my shoulder and knotted in my hair, squeezing, pulling, as he forced me to watch. I did not struggle; I did not want to look away.

No. This I would remember. And I swore to myself that one day, somehow, I would get my revenge.

The spike of pain from my shoulder brought me back to myself. Phones rang, people spoke in low voices. It was a normal world going on outside the cubicle—or as normal as the parapsych squad of the Saint City police ever got, I supposed. I reached for the brandy bottle, uncapped it, and inhaled the smell since the booze would do me no good. The liquid slopped against the sides of the bottle. I didn't even try to hold my hand steady.

Of course, the kids who went to Rigger didn't have anyone to fight for them. We were the orphans and the poor; most of our parents had given us up to the Hegemony foster program as soon as we tested high enough on the Matheson index. The rich kids and the kids with families went to Stryker, with the middle-class families receiving subsidies to defray the costs of a psion's schooling. And of course, you could run up a hell of a debt after your primary schooling taking accreditation at the Academy up north, but that was different. If you didn't have a family or a trust fund, your primary school was the closest Hegemony boarding school to your place of birth. Period, end of story, full stop.

I took another deep inhale. *I am an adult now. I am all grown up. I can tell this story.* "The story I heard goes like this: Finally some of the students banded together. Mirovitch was eerie, he could always tell who was making trouble . . . But some of them got together and . . .

I heard they cracked the shields and the school security codes, slipped their collars, and caught him in his bedroom fucking a nine-year-old Magi girl. I heard later—now this is *all* rumor, mind you—that one of the Ceremonial students had turned herself into a Feeder and killed him that way, in a predator's duel." My teeth chattered. Chilly sweat seemed to film my entire body, gray mist threatening my vision. The sound of everything outside Gabe's cubicle seemed very far away. *If you go into shock there's nobody to bring you out. You are stronger than this, you are all grown up now. Focus, dammit!*

The chattering shakes receded. "You can't imagine the fear." I stared at the drift of gray ash on her desk. "Or the things that went on. Some of the students stooged for him. Those were the worst. They would avoid punishment by ratting on the others, and they were sometimes worse than *he* was. The beatings...They would turn up the collars and administer plasgun shocks..." I'd had scars, before I'd been turned into a *hedaira*. Three thick welts across my back, and a welted burn scar along the crease of my lower left buttock. No more. I didn't have the scars anymore. I had perfect, scarless golden skin.

Then why are they aching? Three stripes of fire down my back, the red-hot metal pressed against my skin, my own frantic screams, the leather cutting into my wrists, the trickle of blood and semen down my inner thighs...

I am all grown up. I set my jaw, shook the memories away. They didn't want to go, but I was stronger.

For now. When I tried to sleep, we'd see how far I'd gotten.

"Why would Moorcock write that down?" Gabe stubbed the cigarette out in a pocked scar on top of her desk. Her face was caught between disgust and pity for a moment, and I felt the old tired rage rise up in me. If there is anything in the world I hate, it's pity.

"I don't know." I was miserably aware that phantom gooseflesh was trying to rise through my skin. My right hand twisted even tighter, straining against itself, shaped into a knotted claw. Black molecule-drip polish gleamed on my nails. "But I'm going to find out."

"Danny." She pushed herself up to stand behind the desk, her palms braced, bending over slightly to look me in the face. Her sleek dark hair was mussed, and her eyes were dilated, probably catching my own fear. "If I'd known, I wouldn't have asked you. I wouldn't—"

"But you did." I rose, my chair legs thocking solidly into the peeling linoleum floor. "And I owe you. You've done your duty, Gabe. Now it's time for me to do mine."

I didn't think it was possible, but Gabe turned pale. The color spilled out of her cheeks as if tipped from a cup. "It wasn't duty, Danny. You're my friend."

"Likewise." And I meant it. She had her own scars—four of them, on her belly, where Santino's claws had ripped through flesh and inflicted a wound even a Necromance couldn't heal, though we who walked in Death were second only to the *sedayeen* in healing mortal wounds. I was willing to bet Gabe had her own nightmares too, even if she was a very rich woman who played at being a cop. "Why do you think I came down here?"

No, she didn't play. Gabe was good at what she did, working on homicides for the Spook Squad, tickling the dead victims into telling her who killed them. She had a gift. She was the best detective they'd had in a good two decades, ever since her grandmother retired.

"Danny—"

No. Please, gods, no. Don't let her go all soft on me. I can't take that.

"I gotta go." If I stayed here much longer I'd start telling her other things, things she didn't need to know. Things about Rigger Hall, and things about me. "Call me if anything breaks, I'm going to go start looking around. Can you courier copies of the files to my house?"

"You know I can," she said. "Danny, I'm sorry."

Me too, Gabe. Me too. "See you soon, Spooky." I got the hell out of there.

CHAPTER 9

Jace was waiting for me downstairs. "You okay?" he asked, as I pushed open the door to the ancient parking garage. There was an auxiliary exit here to the other side of the block, and holovid reporters wouldn't be able to catch us. There was already a swarm of them drifting across the front steps of the station house. I didn't envy Gabe having to give a press conference, but the holovids probably loved her.

"No," I said shortly.

"Rigger Hall." He scowled, stripping his hair back from his forehead with stiff fingers. "Danny."

"I don't want to talk about it." I glanced around the concrete tomb, police hovercruisers sitting dark and silent on their landing legs. They didn't have the roof space to host all the hovers on the top of the building, and they'd had to widen both the main entrance and the auxiliary, but it was good enough. A lighted booth crouched at the far end, with a whey-faced duty officer sipping coffee and pointedly ignoring us inside.

"I'm sure you don't." He caught my arm. "Danny."

Oh, please, gods, not now. "Don't, Jace. I need to go to Jado's. And I need to drink."

"It won't affect you." Why did he have to state the obvious?

Never mind that he was right—my changed metabolism simply shunted alcohol aside. It had no more effect on me than water. I was still too much of a coward to try some of the more illegal options for disorientation and sweet oblivion.

If this kept up I might get a little braver.

"I can try." My face crumpled, matching his.

"Ogoun," he breathed, and took me in his arms.

I was a little taller than I had been, but still able to rest my head on his shoulder, my face in the hollow between his throat and collarbones. I had to lean carefully—I was much heavier and stronger than I used to be. I always took point on the bounties, always worried about him catching a stray strike or bullet.

All the same, I let him hold me for a little while, listening to the echoing sounds of the garage around us. Sounds overlapped, straining and splashing against concrete, a cruiser hummed in with its cargo of a dusted-down Chillfreak for processing.

I sighed and stepped away from him, scrubbing at my left shoulder. It throbbed persistently and I wondered why. It had been cold before, a spiked mass of ice pressed into my flesh—now it was warm, a live fire twisting against my skin. The flash of heat hadn't gone away like it always did.

Had the Prince of Hell started sending me heat waves?

Perfect. Another thing to worry about.

"Don't ask me about Rigger Hall," I told him. "Okay?"

It wasn't fair. He still looked like hell, the back-to-back bounties were hard on him. Yet he hadn't complained. He'd shown up on my doorstep and stayed with me, watching my back as I flung myself into hunt after hunt, not wanting to think. He'd betrayed me once, certainly, not telling me he was Mob and abandoning me when his family threatened to assassinate me unless he came back and did their dirty work. At the time, I had known only the agony of that betrayal. But since Rio, Jace had always come through in a big way. It wasn't fair to him at all. None of this was fair to him.

True to form, he dropped the subject. "You got it, baby. I've got something better to ask you." He tapped his staff once against the old, dirty concrete, making a crisp sound that sliced through the humming whine of hovercells.

"Shoot." I started off toward the exit, he fell into step beside me, his staff clicking time against the concrete. Bones clattered dryly together; the aura of his Power was sweet and heady. No other Shaman smelled like Jace—a combination of pepper and white wine, overlaid with fiery honey. If it hadn't been a human smell, it would have been very pleasant.

"Did you love him?" To his credit, he didn't sound angry, just curious.

My boots didn't falter, but I felt like I staggered. "What?" *Why the fuck are you asking me this now? Because I yelled his name when that thing came for me?* One of the silent hovers sitting obediently on its landing gear creaked, responding to my uneasiness.

I took a deep breath.

"Did you love him? The demon. Japhrimel." I could almost see Jace's mouth twisting over the name, as if it was something sour.

"Jace." I made the word clipped and harsh. "Quit it."

"I deserve an answer. I've waited long enough." Quiet. Not his usual careless, ironic tone.

"What do you deserve? You lied to me about Santino." *Predictable, Danny. Take the cheap shot. You bitch.*

What else could he say? I wouldn't let him defend himself. "I didn't know."

"You lied to me about the Corvin Family." Another accusation. I couldn't help myself. Why did we have to have this conversation *now,* of all times? Why?

"I didn't have a choice. I did what I did to protect you. They would have killed you then. When you were human."

It was the first time he'd mentioned the painful nonsecret of my changed status. How long had he been thinking it? "As opposed to an abomination? You're turning Ludder now? Going to go march in

front of a hospital with a 'Genesplice Is Murder' sign?" My voice
bounced off the concrete, cold enough to coat my skin with ice. I
could crack the pavement if I wasn't careful. It trembled on the edge
of my control. All this Power, I wondered if Japhrimel had intended
to teach me how to use it, how to keep it from eating me alive.

"You're just what you always were, Danny," he informed me
tightly. "Stubborn and bitchy and rude. And beautiful."

"You forgot abrasive, unbending, and cruel."

"Not to mention overachieving." He sighed. "Fine. You win,
okay? I just want to know, Danny. Haven't I earned it? Did you love
him?"

"Why? What possible *difference* could it make? He's dead and
he's *not coming back,* Jace. Let it go." We started up the ramp leading
to the airseal that closed out dust and trash from the street, keeping
the garage climate-controlled. He matched me step for step, as usual,
his longer legs canceled out by my quicker stride and his stiff knee.

"When you let it go, I might be able to." He snapped off the end of
each word.

"He's dead, Jace. Let it *go.*" I couldn't say it any louder than a
whisper, because my throat closed off as if a large rock had come to
rest there. *Dead, yes. But gone? No. Ask me if he's the reason I can't
touch you. Ask me why I hear his voice in my head all the time. Even
if I've finally found out it's true, demons aren't in Death's country.*

"Fine." His staff pounded the concrete in time to our steps, bones
now clattering with thinly-controlled anger. "What do you need me
to do?"

I swallowed, hearing my throat click in the thick silence. I had
called Japhrimel's name and not his. He had a right to be angry.

"You're in?" I sounded surprised. *You've done your duty, Jace.
Nobody could say you haven't, you've watched my back since Rio.
What the hell does anything else matter?*

"Of course I'm fucking in, Danny. What do you want me to *do?*"
Now he sounded as irritated as he ever had, his words colored lemon
yellow, acrid.

My shoulders suddenly eased a little, dropping down. I shook out
my right hand, hearing the joints pop and snap. I was oddly relieved,
a relief I didn't want to examine the depth of any more closely. "I
need to go see Jado, do some sparring and clear my head out if I'm
starting another hunt." I glanced over at him. His profile was straight

and unforgiving. "Can you get me into the House of Pain? As soon as possible?"

If I didn't know him better, I'd think he went pale when he heard me say that. "Chango love me, girl, you don't ask for anything easy, do you." He actually sounded breathless.

"I don't smell human," I said dryly. "I think they'll let me in. But I need an invite or I won't get anywhere, and you've got the connections to get me one." *Since you were Mob.* I swallowed the words. That was history, wasn't it? *Gods, if I could just let one thing be history, what would I choose?*

He didn't even hesitate. "Fine. I'll get you an invitation. What'll I do while you're talking to the suckheads?"

"You're going to do some research."

CHAPTER 10

Jado lived in the University District, on a quiet tree-lined street that had been eccentric years ago but was now merely deserted. There was little ambient energy in the air here, mostly because of him; his house crouched far back in a landscaped yard. His ancient hot tub stood on the deck on one side, and the meditation garden was pristine. There was even a sand plot, impeccably raked, with a few rough black rocks buried in the smoothness. The aura of peace, of stillness, was palpable.

I rang the bell, then twisted the knob and stepped in. The front hall was bare; no shoes on the cedar rack underneath the coat pegs. I caught no breath of human thought in the place.

Thank the gods.

I worked my boots off, and my socks. I hung up my coat and my black canvas bag; my guns dangling from the rig as I hung that up too. Nobody would dare to touch them here. I didn't even bother with a keepcharm. It would have been an insult to my teacher, implying that I didn't trust the safety of his house.

Barefoot, feeling oddly naked as usual without my weapons, I padded down the high-ceilinged hall and through the doorway into mellow light, and stepped up onto *tatami* mats. Their thick, rough texture prickled luxuriously against my bare soles, and I restrained myself from rubbing my feet just to feel the scratchiness.

Jado sat at the far end on the dais, his robes a blot of orange underneath a scroll with two kanji painted on it. *Ikebana* sat on a low table underneath the scroll; three red flowers on a long slender stem reminding me of the orchids in Caine's office. I suppressed a shiver, bowed properly before I stepped over the border from "space" to "sparring space."

The old man's wizened face split like a withered apple, white teeth flashing. His bald head glistened, charcoal eyes glimmering in the directionless light. His ears came to high points on either side of his head, and his callused hands lay in his lap, in the *mudra* of wholeness.

He looked like a relaxed little gnome, an old man with weird ears, harmless and slow. "Ai, Danyo-*san*. Good thing no students here."

I bowed again. "*Sensei.*"

"So serious! Young one." He shook his head, *tsk*ing slightly. "Well, what is it?"

"I need to think," I said baldly. Not to mention that sparring was the best way to shake off the chill of death. Sparring, slicboarding, sex—anything to flush me with adrenaline and get rid of the bitter taste of death in my mouth, the lingering chill of it in my fingers and toes. "Look, Jado-*sensei,* can we stop the Zenmo crap and get down to business?"

His hand flickered. My right hand moved of its own volition, smacking the dart out of the air. It quivered in a ceiling beam, a wicked steel pinblade and feathered cap. "You are *most* impatient."

I made no reply, watched him. He stood, slowly, pushing himself up from the floor as if his bones ached. My skin chilled instinctively, I dropped into "guard." He clucked at me again. "What would you like? Staff? Sword?"

"I don't have a sword," I reminded him. "Staff or barehand, *sensei.* Either." *Need to move, need to think, and need to ask you a favor.*

"A warrior should have sword, Danyo-san. A sword is warrior's honor."

I was hoping you'd say that. "After the fight, I'll need a sword. Unless you don't think you can take me, old man."

He blinked across the room to the rack of staves, his brown fingers curling around a quarterstaff. My heart settled into its combat rhythm, eyes dilating, every fiber of my skin aware of him. "I begin to think you need lesson for manners," he said gently, avuncular.

He tossed me the staff, and followed a split-second later with a staff in his own slim brown hands. The crack of wood meeting wood echoed through the dojo.

Spin, kick, the end of his staff arcing up toward my face, half-step back, *can't afford to do that with him, he's too fast—*

Wood crackled, he jabbed for my midriff and I swung back, the rhythm of staff striking staff lacking a clear pattern. The end of my staff socked into the floor, and I flung myself forward, body loose and flying, Jado narrowly avoided the strike and folded aside but I was ready, landing and whipping the stave out, deflecting the only strike he could make at that angle. Down into a full split, stave spinning backward—a showy move, but the only one I had. Each moment of a fight narrowed the chain of coincidence and angle, Jado moved in as I bent back. I heard the crackle of my spine as I moved in a way no human being should, front heel smashing into the *tatami* to push me up. My body curved, I landed again and feinted, struck—but his stave was there before me, wood screaming as we smashed at each other.

Propellor-strike, shuffling, my breath coming in high harsh gasps, like flying. Alive. I was alive. The lingering chill of going into Death and bringing Christabel out faded, washed clean by adrenaline, every inch of my body suddenly glowing. *Alive. All grown up and alive.* Another flurry of cracks. We separated, I shuffled to one side, he countered. Then, the first flush of the fight over and neither of us having made a stupid mistake, we settled into feinting; first Jado, then me, him trying to lull me into a pattern, me testing his defenses. I earned a solid crack on the knuckles by being too slow, blurred back, shaking my hand out, staff held in guard. Red-black blood welled up, coated the scrape along my knuckles and vanished, leaving the golden skin perfect.

I still wasn't used to that.

"What is it, Danyo-chan?" he asked, standing apparently easy, holding his staff in one hand. Tilting forward a fraction of an inch, testing; I countered by leaning sideways, my staff lifting slightly, responding.

"Old ghosts, my friend." My breath came harsh, but I wasn't gasping. Not yet. "The goddamn school. Rigger Hall."

I'd never told him about the Hall. I wouldn't have been surprised at anything he'd guessed, though. I'd come to him for training straight from the Academy, having heard he was the best; he had known me longer than just about anyone, except maybe Gabe.

He nodded thoughtfully, almond-shaped eyes glittering and sweat gleaming on his brown forehead. His mouth was a thin lipless snarl, I'd scored a hit or two of my own. It just felt so *good* not to have to hold back; humans were so fucking fragile.

Careful, Danny. You're still human where it counts. I swallowed, eased down a little, watching his chest. Any move would be telegraphed there. We circled; another fast flurry of strikes deflected. Sweat began on my skin, trickled down my back. It felt good.

It felt *clean.*

"And so you bring ghosts to Jado, eh?" He grinned, but the smile didn't reach his eyes. Here on the sparring floor, there was no quarter asked or given.

"At least I can't kill you," I shot back.

"Hm." He shrugged, inscrutable as ever. His robes whispered as bare brown feet moved over the *tatami;* he closed with me in a flurry of strikes. Sweat flew, his and mine. *Move move move!* I heard his voice from other training sessions. *No think, move!*

His staff shattered, my cry rising with it to break in the sunlit air. I held my own staff a quarter-inch from his chest. The echoes of my *kia* bounced off the walls, made the entire building shiver. Dust pattered down from the groaning roof.

"Not bad," Jado said grudgingly. I treasured that faint praise. "Come. I make you tea."

Sweating, my staff still held warily, I nodded. "Have you ever seen anything dismember a Necromance, Jado-*sensei?*"

"Not recently." He brushed his horny hands free of splinters. "Come, tea. We talk."

I racked my staff and followed him into the spotless green and beige kitchen. Early-evening light poured in through the bay window. Jado got down the iron kettle and two bowls, and his pink Hiero Kidai canister that held green tea. I hid a smile. The old dragon was gruff, but he loved little pink things.

Maybe humans are little pink things to him too. I had to swallow bile again. My left shoulder twisted with hot feverish pain.

"So." Jado put the water on to boil while I eased myself onto a wooden stool set on the other side of the counter. "You have been called out of slumber, it seems."

"I wasn't sleeping, I don't sleep," I objected immediately. "I'm just not a social person, that's all. Been running bounties."

He shrugged. He was right, throwing myself into one hunt after another was a way of numbing myself. Trying to exhaust myself so I *could* sleep, staving off the pain with furious activity. It was a time-honored method, one I'd used all my life; but as a coping mechanism I had to admit it was failing miserably.

His robe, rough cotton, caught the sunlight and glowed. I filled my lungs — the lingering smell of human was only a tang over his darker scent of flame and some deep, scaled hole, darkness welling up from the ground, incense burned in a forgotten temple. I didn't know what Jado was, he didn't fit into any category of nonhuman I'd ever read or heard about. But he'd been in Saint City for at least as long as Abra, because I sometimes, rarely, took messages from one to the other; little bits of information. I had never seen Jado leave his home, or Abra leave her shop, and I wondered where they had come from. Maybe one day I'd find out.

It was a relief to smell something inhuman. Something that didn't reek of dying cells, of pain, of eventual abandonment.

Japhrimel's gone, I thought, and the sharp spike of pain that went through me seemed somehow clean as well. "What do you know about Christabel Moorcock? Did you ever train her?"

He shook his head. "She is not of my students." The kettle popped on the stove, heating up. "You wish for a sword, then."

It was my turn to shrug, look down at the counter. I traced a random glyph on the Formica with one black-nailed fingertip. My rings sizzled. The glyph folded out, became something else — the spiked fluid lines of the scar on my shoulder. I traced it twice, looked up to meet his tranquil eyes.

"You have decided to live." Jado leaned on the counter, his own blunt fingertips seemingly arranged for maximum affect. His broad nose widened a little and he seemed to sniff. For a moment, his eyes were black from lid to lid, maybe a trick of shadow as he blinked, his eyes lidding like a lizard's. "Though you still smell of grief, Danyo-*chan*. Much grief."

He's not coming back. Maybe I can grieve instead of trying to avoid it. "I never thought I wouldn't live," I lied. "Look, Jado, it's about Rigger Hall. And I think I need a sword. My hand won't get any stronger if I don't exercise it."

"Christabel." His accent made it *Ku-ris-ta-be-ru*. "She was death-talker. Like you."

With only four of us in the city, it stood to reason he would know. I looked down at my left hand, narrow and golden and graceful. His, brown and square, powerful, tendons standing out under the skin. "I don't think that's what killed her."

A slight nod. "So, you have theory already."

"No. Not even a breath of one. I've got a dead normal, a dead sex-witch, and a dead Necromance who left a little note about Rigger Hall. That's all I've got." *I think it might be ritual murder, but I'm not sure. And until I'm sure, nobody's going to hear a theory from me, dammit.*

"And this means you need sword?" His eyebrow lifted. The kettle chirruped, and he poured the water into the bowls. I watched him whisk the fine green powder into frothy, bitter tea, his fingers moving with the skill of long practice. When my bowl was ready, he offered it with both hands. I took it in both hands, with a slight bow. Black *raku* glaze pebbled under my fingertips. The bowl still remembered the fire that made it strong; I caught the echo of flame even in the tea's strong, clear, tart taste.

We are creatures of fire. Tierce Japhrimel's voice threaded through my memory, slow and silken. I was too busy keeping Jado from bashing me with a staff during sparring, but now the thought of Japh crept back into my head. I had managed a full half-hour, forty-five minutes without pain? Call the holovids, stop the presses, rent a holoboard, it was a banner event.

No. I hadn't stopped thinking of him. I never stopped thinking of him. But he was really, truly, inevitably, finally gone.

"I miss him," I said without meaning to, looking into the teabowl's depths. Now that I knew he wasn't in Death's hall, I could admit it. Maybe. "Isn't that strange."

Jado shrugged, sipping at his own tea. His slanted charcoal eyes half-lidded, and the rumble of our strange paired contentment made the air thick and golden. "You have changed, Danyo-*chan*. I met you, and I saw it, so much anger. Where did anger go?"

I shrugged. "I don't know." *The anger isn't gone, Jado. I'm just better at hiding it.* "I've been doing research on demons. And on

A'nankhimel. Between bounties, that is." My mouth twisted into a bitter smile. I stared into the tea. "He never really told me what he did to me, or the price he paid for it. I still only have a faint idea—it's so hard to separate myth from reality in all the old books, and demons seem to delight in throwing red herrings across the trail." I realized what I was talking about, looked up. Jado examined the window with much apparent fascination.

I sighed. "I used to work so hard at just staying alive, paying off my mortgage, just jumping from one rock to the next. Now I've crossed the river, and you know what? I wish I was back in the middle. At least while I was jumping I didn't have so much goddamn time to brood."

Jado made a soft noise, neither agreeing nor disagreeing, just showing he was listening. Then his dark eyes swung away from the window and came to rest on me. "Perhaps would be best if you did not pursue your past, Danyo-*chan.*"

Remember Rigger Hall. "I'm not pursuing it. It's pursuing *me.* Now I have to find out what Christabel did at Rigger Hall, and what connection the three victims had."

"Why?" He took the change of subject gracefully, of course. If anyone knew me, it was Jado. Even before Rio he had never treated me differently than any of his other students.

How could an old man who wasn't human have made me feel so blessedly, thoroughly, completely human myself? "There's only three Necromances left in the city. Me, Gabe, and John Fairlane. We can't afford to lose any more." Bitter humor traced through my voice, etching acid on a pane of glass.

Jado snorted a laugh as if steam was coming through his nose. "Come, drink your tea. We will find you sword. I think I know which one."

The room at the head of the stairs was just as I remembered. Dying sunlight fell through the unshielded windows, slanting to strike at the polished wooden floor. Dust swirled in sinuous shapes with long frilled wings. The door had been taken off its hinges, a long fall of amber silk taking its place. The silk rippled and sang to itself in the silence.

On the black wooden racks against the wall the swords lay, each humming in its sheath. I glanced down to the space where my sword

had hung; it was empty. There were four empty spaces—four of
Jado's students, out in the world. I wondered if any of the others had
broken their sword in the heart of a demon.

The thought managed to make me feel ashamed. Jado didn't hand
swords out to just anyone, and I'd broken the last one. "*Sensei*," I
whispered, "is it really right?"

He laughed, a papery sound in the bare room. There were two
tatami in the middle of the floor, and he gestured me to one. I folded
myself down as his thick-skinned bare feet scraped against the floor.
An unlit white candle in a plain porcelain holder sat off-center
between the mats. "Ai, even swords come and go. You used Flying
Silk well. But now, something else." He paced in front of the swords,
their wrapped hilts ticking off space behind him. His long orange
robe made a different sound than the silk in the door, I could hear the
rattlewhine of faraway hovertraffic. It was soothing.

I eased down onto my knees on the mat, tucking my feet under
me. It was quiet here; even the dust was serene. My shoulder settled
back into a burning prickle, like a limb slowly waking up. I inhaled,
smelling Jado's fiery smell, and wished, as I often did, that I could
stay with him. It wouldn't work—he was old and liked his space,
and my own neuroses would probably irritate both of us to the point
of murder after a while. But when I stepped over Jado's threshold, I
was no longer a psion feared by normals, or a Necromance crippled
by fear and a clawed hand. I was no longer even a *hedaira,* something
that wasn't even alluded to directly in the old books about demons I'd
managed to dig up. Here, in this house, I was only a student.

And here, I was valued for myself alone. My skill, my bravery,
my honor, my willingness to learn all he could teach me.

"This one." Jado lifted down a longer katana. It was in a
black-lacquered reinforced scabbard, probably made by Jado's own
hands. The wrapping on the hilt was exquisite, and I saw a faint
shimmer in the air surrounding it. I found myself holding my breath.

The first time I had stepped into the dojo after killing Santino my
breath had come short, my heart pounding; my palms had not been
wet but my right hand had twisted into a painful knotted cramp. Jado
had been teaching a group of rich teenagers *t'ai chi* as part of the federal health regimen. I'd waited in the back, respectfully; when class
was finished and the young ones gone, he had stalked across the
tatami and, without a word, took my right hand and examined it,
moving the fingers gently. I let him, even though I couldn't stand to

let anyone else touch me, shying away from even Jace's unconscious skin when he happened to collapse on the couch in an inebriated haze.

Then Jado had grunted. *No sword yet. Staff. Come.* That simply, my nervousness had fallen away like an old coat. An hour later I had dragged myself sweating and shaking to the water fountain after a hard workout; it took a lot more to make me sweat now, but he'd done it. And that, apparently, was that.

No other man could make me feel so much like a child. If Lewis was the father of my childhood, Jado was the father of the adult I had become. I hoped I'd made them proud.

Jado settled down cross-legged across from me. His thumb flicked against the guard, and three inches of steel leapt free. It was beautiful, slightly longer and wider than my other sword. The steel rippled with a light all its own. "Very old. For some reason, Danyo-*chan,* you delight the very old. This—" He slid the blade home with a click, "—is Fudoshin."

The candle between us guttered into life, a puff of smoke rising briefly before the flame steadied. I smiled at the trick, pretending not to notice, my eyes fixed on the sword.

I tilted forward slightly, a bow expressed more with my eyes and upturned hands than anything else, looking up to meet Jado's eyes. "Exquisite."

He nodded slowly, his bald head gleaming with reflected sunlight. The candle's gleam was weak and pallid in the brightness of day. "You delight my heart, Danyo-*chan.* Fudoshin has been with me very long time. He is very old, and very much honor. But I tell you, it is not very good to give this sword."

More time ticked by, the swords singing their long slow song of metal inside their sheaths. Jado breathed, his eyes dark but lit with pinpricks of orange light, his gaze soft as if he was remembering something very long ago.

I always knew Jado wasn't human, but he hadn't truly frightened me until the first time I'd sat across from him in this room. His stillness had been absolute, not the dozing stillness of a human, but a trance so deep it was like alertness. Now I wasn't only human either, and I found myself copying his watchful silence, as if we were two mirrors reflecting each other into eternity.

Finally, Jado drew in a breath, as if wrapping up some long conversation with himself. "Fudo Myoo is the great swordsman. He

breaks the chains of suffering, lives in fiery heart of every swordsman. Fudoshin is dangerous, very powerful sword. He must be
wielded with honor, but more important, with compassion. Compassion is not your strongest virtue, Danyo-chan. This sword loves battle." He looked up at me, his seamed face suddenly seeming old. "So
do you, I think."

I shook my head. A strand of hair fell in my face. "I don't fight
without reason, *sensei*. I never have."

He nodded. "Just so, just so. Still, I give you caution, you are
young. Will ignore me."

"Never, *sensei*." I managed to sound shocked.

That made his face crinkle in a very wide, white-toothed grin. He
offered the sword again, and this time I held my hands out, let him
lay the almost-instantly familiar weight in my slightly cupped palms.
I felt a shock of rightness burn through me, a welcome jolt not from
my shoulder but from the pleasure of holding something so
well-made, something intended for me. "Fudoshin," I whispered.
Then I bowed, very low, over the blade. It seemed right, even though
my braid fell forward over my shoulder and swayed dangerously
close to the candleflame. *"D'mo, sensei."* My accent mangled it, but
his loud laugh rewarded me. I straightened, balancing the sword,
already longing to slide the blade free and see that gleaming blue
shine again. Longing to hear the slight deadly hiss as I freed it from
the sheath, the soft whistling song of a keen blade cleaving the air.

Jado's laugh ended in a small, fiery snort. "Ai, my knees ache.
Ceremony bores me. Come, let me see if you can still perform first
kata."

"It would take more than a few months for me to forget that, *sensei*," I told him. It felt so good to hold a sword again. Complete.
Right.

"It always takes long time, forgetting anything painful." He nodded sagely, and my eyes met his. We both bowed to each other again,
and I surprised myself by laughing when he did.

CHAPTER 11

wasn't paying much attention as I rounded the corner, still loose and easy and smelling of healthy effort. I'd kept my house, and bought the two houses on either side with some of the blood money from the Santino bounty. Knocking the two houses down and building a wall around my place was the best step I ever took for privacy. I'd gotten the idea from Gabe. She inherited her private walls, I had to build my own.

My left shoulder burned with steady hot pain. I wondered if the mark would start to eat at my skin, and the last of my good mood fled.

Lucifer, maybe? What are the chances that he's involved in this mess? But no, there was no smell of demon on Christabel. I'm fairly sure I'd smell that. And this is too much gore for a demon, not even Santino was this messy.

Still, thinking about the Prince of Hell made a slight, rippling chill go up my back. It was fairly obvious he was still keeping an eye on me, for what purpose I didn't like to guess.

Screw Lucifer. He can wait until I've found out who's killing psions.

A click alerted me. I didn't stop, but my shields thinned, and I felt the hungry mood circling my front gate. The defenses on my walls sparked and glittered. The curtain of Power would short out any holovid receiver that got too close.

Oh, damn. Reporters.

They hadn't noticed me yet. The click I'd heard was someone tucked behind a streetlamp, taking stills of my walls. His back was to me, sloping under a tan trench coat, uncoordinated dark hair standing up. Purple dusk was falling, and bright lights began to switch on. He was a normal, and therefore blind to the eddies and swirls I caused in the landscape of Power.

I stood aside in shadow, melding with a neighbor's laurel hedge, and watched them for a few minutes. *Holovids,* I thought, blankly. *What the hell do they want with me? Oh, yeah.* Sekhmet sa'es, *who*

*tipped them off? Less than twenty-four hours on the case and there's
already a leak. Wonderful. Perfect. Great.*

My knuckles whitened against the swordhilt. The sword was a
slightly-heavier katana, a beautiful, curving, deadly blade in its reinforced black-lacquered scabbard, older than the Parapsychic Act. I
had expected it to feel strange to hold a sword again. I'd expected my
right hand to cramp and seize up.

It didn't. In fact, it felt more natural than ever to curl my fingers
around the hilt. Natural, and painless. I could pull the blade free of
the sheath in one motion.

It's not my sword yet. My fingers eased up a little. It would take
time and Power before the blade would respond like my old sword
had, made into a psychic weapon as much as a physical one.

A lance of exquisite pain through my fingers made my hand
spasm around the hilt. I drew in a soft breath, watching the holovid
reporters circle in front of my gate, their klieg lights blaring, trying
to get a good shot of my house. No hovers—they must have gotten
some aerial shots already. *Jace.* Had he managed to slip inside
unseen?

I finally cut through someone's weedy front yard and down the
dirt-packed alley that had marked my neighbor's property line before
I'd bought the place. No reporters back here yet, thank the gods.

My shields quivered, straining. I stopped, staring at my wall; the
layers of energy I'd warded it with were flushing and pulsating a deep
crimson. Demon-laid shields, Necromance shields, layers that Jace
had applied, of spiky Shaman darkness. I calmed the restive energy
with a touch and felt Jace inside, his sudden attention stinging against
my receptive mind.

It was a bit of work to scale the wall; I'd contracted one of the best
construction guys in the city to make it smooth concrete, aesthetic
razor spikes standing up from the top. Demon-quick reflexes saved
me; I hauled myself up and over with little trouble, my boots thudding down in the back garden. Water tinkled from a fountain, the
smell of green growing things closing around me. I inhaled deeply,
the air pressure changing—Jace's silent greeting, one psi to another.

When I slid the back door open, stepping over a pile of flat slate
tiles I planned on turning into divination runeplates, he met me with
a cup of coffee and a grim expression. He hadn't started drinking
yet, but the night was young. I didn't stare at him only by an effort
of will.

"Hey," I managed. "Looks like we've got company."

"Oh, yeah. Fucking vultures." His lip curled. Mob freelancers hate reporters a little more than the rest of us, and Jace was no exception. There's a reason why psis don't work for the holovids.

Well, besides the obvious fact that they would never hire a psionic actor or talking head. It was illegal to discriminate — but the natural antipathy we felt for the way we were shown on the holovids, mixed with the reluctance of the studio heads to put a psion on the air and lose a chunk of Ludder ratings, equaled no psionic actors. Status quo, just like usual.

"Nice sword." That was as close to a comment as Jace would allow himself.

I shrugged. "Thought it was time I started practicing again. How'd you make out?"

A sudden grin lit his face. "Pulled a few old strings, visited a few old friends. Got you the invite, for tonight. You can take a servant with you, it says. Need me?"

I actually considered it for a few moments, then looked at him. There were fine lines at the corners of his eyes, his mouth was pulled into a straight line, and he was bleary-eyed from too much Chivas, too many bounties, and not enough sleep. His clothes were rumpled, and I saw a shadow of stubble along his jaw. It occurred to me that my friends were getting older.

And I looked just the same, when I could bring myself to glance in the mirror. Golden skin and dark eyes, and a demon's beauty. A gift I'd neither wanted nor asked for.

I shook my head. "I need you to research for me, remember?" Even my hair shifted uneasily; the vision of Jace walking into the House of Pain was enough to make me shiver. I wasn't sanguine about going in there myself. Despite the fact that nonhuman paranormals had legal rights and voting blocs, they still didn't like to get too chummy with humans. I didn't blame them. "I need to know a couple of things, and you're just the man to find out."

He folded his arms, his tattoo thorn-twisting on his unshaven cheek. "You are a spectacularly bad liar, once someone knows you," he informed me flatly.

"What?" Now I was feeling defensive, and I hadn't even gotten ten feet inside my own back door yet. The papers lying on the closer end of my kitchen counter stirred uneasily, whispering. I wondered if there was another parchment envelope in today's mail.

Pushed the thought away. *Jace, for the sake of every god that ever was, please don't ask to go to the House of Pain. I worry enough about you on regular bounties.* I closed my lips over the words, swallowed them. That was the surest way to piss him off, implying that he was less than capable.

He planted his booted feet and regarded me with the cocky half-smile meaning he was on the verge of irritation. "I won't break, Danny. I've seen worse than this, and I know how to take care of myself. Quit treating me like I'm second-class, all right?"

"Jace—" This was not the conversation I wanted to have with him right now. *Why does he always pick the worst goddamn time to throw his little hissy fits?*

"Maybe I'm not a demon," he said quietly, "but I used to be good enough for you once. And I've kept up my end of the bounties, haven't I?"

He did not *just say that to me.* My stomach turned into a stone fist, heat rising to my cheeks. The windows bowed slightly, rattling, and I took a deep breath. If I blew my own fucking house down it would be even more fodder for the vultures outside. Instead, I pushed past him, gently enough not to hurt him, only sending him backward a few steps. My teeth buried in my lower lip, I stalked through the kitchen, down the hall, and up the stairs.

Halfway up the stairs, Anubis's statue stood nine inches tall, slim and black, glowing with Power inside the altar-niche. Two unlit black novenas stood on either side; I had scattered rose petals and poured a shallow black bowl of wine for him. The wine's surface trembled as I stopped, looking into the niche.

Set to one side, a black lacquer urn glowed. No dust lay against its slick wet surface. No dust ever touched it, and no whisper of the ashes it held ever reached me. I'd spent hours staring at it, I knew every curve of the smooth surface. I had even once or twice caught myself opening my mouth to say something to the urn. I'd drawn chalk circles and tried solitary Magi conjurings out of shadowjournals; altering the runes and circles, trying to find my key to weaken the fabric of reality and call him to me. I'd tried to use my tarot cards and runes—but the answers I got were always fuzzy, slippery, fading. Nothingness, emptiness, dissolution. My own desperate hope managed to make any information I could get from divination useless.

My shoulder burned. But my right hand, clamped around the swordhilt, did not hurt.

Japhrimel. I didn't say it. My lips shaped the word, that was all.

He isn't there, Danny. Stop torturing yourself.

But had he waited for me there before slipping into the abyss?

Don't think about that, Danny. Sekhmet sa'es, *he's gone. He's not in Death. You've seen he's not there. Stop it.*

I just couldn't help myself.

Who would ask the questions for me if I managed to make an apparition of my dead demon lover appear? Certainly not Jace. It was too much to ask even Gabe for, and she was the only Necromance who might conceivably do such a thing for me.

I heard Jace's short plosive curse downstairs. Was he listening? He could probably tell from any slight sound where I was in the house. That is, if he didn't simply *extend* his senses and See me. He could tell I was in front of the niche. I'd caught him standing here once or twice too, usually after I'd spent my days between bounties in the living room staring at the urn's smooth sides, reluctantly replacing it every time. When I wasn't feverishly researching demons, searching for any clue about the Fallen, that is. I didn't know what Jace would say to Japhrimel's ashes. I didn't even want to guess.

Jace could certainly tell I was standing here.

Well, Anubis is my patron, I thought, my fingers tightening. *I never asked Jace to come here.*

You never sent him away either, the pitiless voice of my conscience replied. Was it me, or did it sound like Japhrimel's? Not the level, robotic voice he'd used when I first met him, no. Instead, it was the deep almost-human voice he'd used to whisper to me while I shuddered, wrapped in barbed-wire pleasure and his arms.

I sighed. The fingers of my left hand hovered centimeters from the urn's surface. What would I feel if I touched it now, my senses raw from pulling Christabel Moorcock's screaming, insane ghost out of Death, my body loose from sparring with Jado and sweating out the chill touch of that dry country where Anubis stood, endlessly waiting for me?

I let out a soft curse of my own and continued up the stairs. It was useless to waste time. I had to get ready. If I was going to the House of Pain, I wanted to be dressed appropriately.

Oh, damn. I'm going to have to take the whip.

CHAPTER 12

Jace stood in the living room, his arms folded, the portable holovid player bathing the room in its spectral pink glow. He hit the mute button as soon as I appeared. I held the cloak over my arm, a long fall of sable velvet; I'd managed a tolerable French twist with my recalcitrant hair. The earrings brushed my cheeks as I tossed my head impatiently, making sure the long, thin stilettos holding the twist steady were not likely to fall out. It would be highly embarrassing to meet the prime paranormal Power in the city and have weapons fall out of my hair.

Jace looked up, his mouth opening as if he would say something. Instead, he stopped, his jaw dropping further open. His pupils dilated, making his eyes seem dark instead of blue.

"What?" I sounded annoyed. "Look, it's the House of Pain. I can't wear jeans and a T-shirt, much as I'd rather."

"You would have before." But his mouth quirked up in a smile. I felt my own mouth curl in response.

"I'd have never gotten an invitation before. They don't *let* humans in, especially not psis. Look, Jace—"

He was suddenly all business. "Research. What d'ya want me to find?" He flicked the holovid off, bent down to touch his staff where it lay against the couch, then straightened, his back to me. "I'll bet you're thinking of some*one* instead of some*thing,* right?"

I hate your habit of anticipating me, Jace. I always have. "I need you to find out everything you can about our normal." I rotated my shoulders back and then forward, making sure the rig sat easy. Before, I'd always carried my sword—*no use having a blade if it's not to hand,* Jado often said, but I'd need my hands for other things tonight. My rig, supple oiled black leather, complemented the black silk of the dress and the sword-hilt poked up over my right shoulder. The back-carry was buckled to my usual rig. Drawing a sword is quicker when the hilt is over one's shoulder instead of at the hip, and it keeps the scabbard from knocking into things too. It was a compromise, like everything else.

Chunky dress-combat boots with silver buckles hid under the

long skirt. I was unwilling to sacrifice any mobility to high heels; I'd already lose out because of the damn dress. The necklace was silver-dipped raccoon *baculum* strung on fine silver chain twined with black velvet ribbon and blood-marked bloodstones, powerful Shaman mojo. Jace had made the necklace for me during our first year together. He had poured his Power into it, using his own blood in the workings over the bloodstones, his skill and his affection for me as well as every defense a Shaman knew how to weave. I had locked it away when he left, unable to burn it as I'd burned everything else that reminded me of him; but now it seemed silly to go into the lion's den without all the protection I could muster. My rings shifted and spat, shimmering in the depths of each stone. "He's our first victim, there has to be a reason it started with him."

"You got it." His eyes dropped below my chin. The dress had a low, square neckline with a laced-up slit going down almost to my bellybutton; my breasts offered like golden fruit thanks to the shape and cut. The slender silver curves of the *baculum* were a contrast against velvety golden skin. The sleeves were long, daggering to points over the backs of my hands. The effect was like Nocturnia on the paranormal-news reports, a sort of elegant old-fashioned campiness. The guns rode low on my hips, the knives hidden in both the dress and the rig, the bullwhip coiled and hanging by my side. I knew I'd be chafing by the end of the night, and probably missing my messenger bag too.

"Did Gabe courier the files?" I tried to sound businesslike. His eyes dropped again, appreciatively, and then he let it go, straightening and scooping up his staff. The bones cracked and rattled—he wasn't quite as calm as he wanted me to think.

For once, I let it go. Dante Valentine, restraining herself. I deserved a medal. Of course, as careful as I was being, he was too. *Give him a gold star. Give him a medal too. Hell, give him a fucking parade.*

I told that snide little voice in my head to shut the fuck up.

He nodded. "Of course. Over there." He tipped his head.

I found them lying atop an untidy stack of ancient leather-bound demonology books. I would have to visit the Library again soon, make an offering in the Temple overhead and go down into the dark vaults full of ancient books. Maybe this time I would find a demonology text that would give me a vital clue about what I was.

I flipped the first file open, took a few pictures; the second and then the third. Christabel's ruined face stared up from glossy lase-print paper, but there was a good shot of the twisted chalk glyphs. I would probably have to visit her apartment too; sooner rather than later to catch whatever traces of scent remained. If nothing broke loose, that was. "I'm going to have to take the hover," I muttered. "Gods."

"Why don't you take a slicboard?" His tone was mischievous.

"In this dress?" I hitched one shoulder up in a shrug.

"Relax, baby. I ordered a hoverlimo." The grin he wore infected my own face, I felt the corners of my eyes crinkle and my lips tilt up. How could he go from irritating me to making me smile? Then again, he liked to think he knew me all the way down to my psychopomp. "No reason not to go in style."

He sounded so easy I could have ignored the spiky, twisting dark-ness of his aura. Jace was furious, his anger kept barely in check. I laid the cloak down, the pictures on top of it, and for the first time crossed the room to stand next to him, silk whispering and rustling against my legs.

His blue eyes dropped. Jace Monroe looked at the floor.

I swallowed dryly, then reached up and laid my fingertips against his cheek. My nails, black and shiny, wet-looking as the lacquer of Japhrimel's urn, scraped slightly. The contact rilled through me. My aura enfolded him, the spice of demon magic swirling around us both.

Why must even an apology be a battle, with you? Japhrimel's voice, again, stroking the deepest recesses of my mind. I had never thought it possible to be haunted by a demon. Of course, if he had truly been haunting me it might have been a relief, at least I wouldn't be torturing myself with his voice. If he was haunting me, at least I would have some *proof* that somewhere, somehow, he still existed.

And was thinking of me.

"Jace?" My voice was husky. He shivered.

Be careful, be very careful; you don't know what it will do to him. The old voice of caution rose. Keeping him at arm's length was an old habit; I still ached to touch him even as the thought made my stomach flutter—with revulsion, or desire, or some combination of the two, in what proportion I wasn't sure.

Oddly enough, I wanted to comfort him. He had suffered my silence and my throwing myself into bounties, playing my backup with consummate skill. He had turned into the honorable man I'd first thought he was.

When had that happened?

"Danny," he whispered back.

"I..." Why did the words *I'm sorry* stick in my throat? "I want to know something."

"Hm." His fingers played with his staff, bones shifting slightly but not clacking against each other. His skin was so fine, so dry... and once I looked closely I could see the beautiful arch of his cheek-bone, the fine fan of his eyelashes tipped with gold. Japhrimel had studied me this intently once, as if I was a glyph he wanted to decode.

Lovely, Danny. You're touching Jace, and all you can think of is a dead demon. "Why did you give up the Family?"

Jace's eyes flew open, dug into mine, oceans of blue. I smelled his Power rising, twining with my own. "I don't need it, Danny," he answered softly. "What good is a whole fucking Family without you?"

If he'd hit me in the solar plexus with a quarterstaff I might have regained my breath more quickly. My skin flushed with heat. "You..." I sounded breathless. My fingers sank into his skin, his desire rose, wrapping around me. The threads of the tapestry hung on my west wall shifted, the sound brushing against sensitive air, and for once I did not look to see what Horus and Isis, in their cloth-bound screen, would tell me.

He tore away from me, his staff smacking once against my floor, and stalked across the room to my fieldstone altar, set against the wall between the living room and the kitchen. He'd set up his own small altar next to it, lit with novenas; set out a half-bottle of rum, a pre-Parapsychic-Act painting of Saint Barbara for his patron Chango, a dish of sticky caramel candy, and a brass bowl of dove's blood from his last devotional sacrifice. The candleflames trembled. "Even the *loa* can't force a woman's heart," he said quietly. "Here's your invitation." A square of thick white expensive paper, produced like a card trick, held up so I could see it over his left shoulder.

"Jace."

"You'd better go." His voice cut across mine. "I hear the Prime doesn't like to be kept waiting, and I had to pay to get this."

"Jace—"

"I'll have any dirt on your normal by tomorrow afternoon. Okay?"

"Jason —"

"Will you just *go,* Danny?"

Irritation rasped under my breastbone. I stalked up to him, snatched the paper out of his hand, and heard the proximity-chime ring. The hoverlimo was here. Jace tapped his datband, keying it in through the house's security net. I pulled the shields apart slightly to let the big metal thing maneuver into my front yard. I took a deep breath, scooped up my cloak and the pictures, and stamped out of the living room.

If I hadn't been part-demon, with all a demon's acuity, I would never have heard his murmur. "I had to give it up, Danny. I *had* to. For you."

Oh, Jace.

I shook my head. He was right, I was going to be late. And in Santiago City, you never wanted to be late while visiting the suckheads.

CHAPTER 13

After the Parapsychic Act, many paranormal species got the vote and a whole new code of laws was drawn up. Advances in medical tech meant cloned blood for the Nichtvren, enzyme treatments to help control werecainism, protection against human hunters for the swanhilds, and a whole system of classification for who and what qualified for citizen's rights. Most of the night world had come out to be registered as voters, some of them reluctantly. The Nichtvren, of course, having shepherded the Act through after decades of political maneuvering and hush money, came out first of all. In more ways than one — Nichtvren Masters were the prime paranormal Powers in any city, keeping the peace and dispensing swift justice to any werecain, kobolding, or any other nonhuman that flew above the radar and made too much trouble. The Nichtvren were courted by both Hegemony and Putchkin, and if you had to deal with the paranormal in any city, a good place to start was with the suckheads. They had their long pretty fingers in every pie.

The House of Pain was an old haunt. Feeding place and social gathering spot at once, it had been a hub of the paranormal and para-psychic community ever since its inception; after the Awakening, it had closed to humans and started catering exclusively to other species. The Nichtvren who ruled it, the prime Power of the city, was rumored to be one mean sonofabitch.

I wouldn't know. Humans, *especially* psions, aren't allowed in Nichtvren haunts unless they're registered as legitimate indentured servants or thralls. I sighed, settling back against the synthleather of the limo's back seat. Several paranormal species didn't precisely like psions, but we were marginally more acceptable than normals. Psions and Magi had been trafficking with paranormals since before the Awakening, trading their own uncertain skills for protection, knowl-edge, and other things.

The population growth of humanity had eaten away at the habitat of almost every paranormal species—and even the Nichtvren had reason to fear mobs of normals with pitchforks, stakes, or guns. To the other species, humans were evil at worst, psions a necessary evil at best. They have long memories, the paranormals, and they remem-ber being squeezed out of their habitats by humanity, or being hunted when they tried to adapt. Silence, blending in, and clannishness had kept them viable as a species; the habits held even though they hadn't had to hide for a long time.

A psion could go her whole life without really interacting with a paranormal, even if she was a Magi or an Animone. The few humans who studied paranormal physiology and culture were given Hege-mony grants and worked in the academic fields, and some anthro-pologists even studied paranormals...but those were few and far between. Despite the stories of psions being taken in by swanhilds or taught by Nichtvren, it just didn't happen that often. Paranormals were more likely to view humans as food—or a disease. Given how we'd treated nonhuman species throughout most of our history, I don't blame them one bit.

The alley off Heller Street was full of milling people, most with press badges. The Nichtvren paparazzi were out big-time; the gothed-out groupies clustered with them, trying to look exceptional and maybe buy a Nichtvren's notice. A faint, listless sprinkle of rain splattered down. Full night had fallen, orange cityglow staining the sky. I saw the thick pulsing of power on the brick wall at the end of the alley, an old neon sign pulsing the word *Pain* in fancy script over the door. A red carpet unrolled from the door down the alley, and red velvet cords on heavy brass stands kept the crowd back. Two hulking shapes I was fairly sure were werecain instead of genespliced bouncers lumped on either side of the door.

"Ma'am?" the driver asked, almost respectfully. His voice crackled over the intercom.

I came back to myself with a completely uncharacteristic sigh. "I'll be out in a few hours. You'll be here?"

"I've been contracted the entire night," the staticky voice said. "Yours until sunup, Miz Valentine. Do you want to get out now?"

Great. I've got a comedian for a driver. I sighed again. "All right. No time like the present."

He hopped out, then the doorhatch clicked and *fwished* aside. The white-jacketed driver offered me his hand, and I took it, careful to place no weight on it as I stepped out of the hoverlimo, my boots grinding slightly on wet pavement. I smelled night and human excitement, and a dash of something dry and powerful over the top—I wished again I could shut down my nose.

Laseflashes popped. They were taking pictures. I blinked, settling the cloak on my shoulders, shaking the folds of material free. The papers, tucked in a pocket I'd thoughtfully sewn into the skirt, rustled slightly. I set my chin, nodded to the driver—a short, pimple-faced young boy squeezed into a white and black uniform with gold braid—and set off down the red carpet. Behind me, the driver's footsteps echoed, then I heard the whine of hovercells as the limo lifted up to float in a slow pattern, joining the other hoverlimos and personal hovers already threading through the parking level above the House of Pain.

"*Hey, Valentine! Valentine!*" Some enterprising soul called my name. I didn't acknowledge it. Soon all of them were yelling, trying to catch my attention. I strode down the carpet, head high, feeling the weight of my hair and the stilettos caught in the twist. *I hate this.*

If Japhrimel had been with me, he would have walked with his head up, his hands clasped behind his back, utterly unmoved by the human hubbub. Jace might have grinned, mugged for the cameras a bit, or caused some mischief. Gabe would have lit a cigarette, and Eddie would have snarled. The thought of Jado or Abracadabra dealing with this was ridiculous enough to be laughable.

But me, I couldn't imitate any of them. I strode toward the lion's den with no time to waste.

The things by the door were indeed werecain, hulking bipeds covered with fur, halfway between human and huntform. I'd taken the required classes in paranormal anatomy at Rigger Hall and beyond, at the Academy, but it was odd to see them up close. In the old days they might have worn clothing or stayed in human form. Now all they wore were ruffs of hair around their genitals. I didn't look.

Instead, I held up the invitation, and dropped the outer edge of my shields. Power blurred, stroking against the building's cold blueblack glow. A radioactive wellspring of Power from Saint City's deep black heart bathed this place. It had been here for centuries, the crackling energy of paranormals gathered in one place seeping into the concrete brick and stone. A heartbeat of music thudded out through the walls.

The werecain said nothing. One of them jerked his chin, motioning me inside. Flashbulbs popped.

I wanted to curl my right hand around my swordhilt. I also wished my left shoulder didn't buzz and burn as if red-hot iron was held just above my skin. Anger curled through my stomach, a welcome thread of familiar heat. I would be damned if I would be treated like a second-class citizen to be hustled into this goddamn place, even if I was human.

I measured both werecain with a slow, steady gaze. *I could take them. I could take them both. I could gut them. I've got a sword again.*

Then I remembered I wasn't just human anymore, but I still didn't back down, holding eye contact and playing the dominance game. It would be a bad start to act weak here at the door.

Finally, one of them gave me a jerky half-bow. "Come on in, lady." His voice, shaped by lips and tongue and teeth no longer human, sounded thick and grumbling. "Welcome to the House of Pain."

I gave them a nod and swept past, my head held high. *Who am I? I would have never done that, before.*

CHAPTER 14

Inside, a migraine-attack of red and blue lights throbbed, and the music was a slow haunting melody over a pounding bass beat. Nothing I recognized. There was a time when I would have known, back when I used to go dancing with Jace, his spiky aura closing me off from the backwash of crowd-feeling. Inside the House, there was no tang of humans or human desperation, no sweet knifeblade of human desire or straining sex in dark corners; there were no ghostflits riding the edges of the crowd's heat. No blur of alcohol, no swirls of synth-hash cigarette smoke either.

Instead, Power rode the air in swirls and eddies, a lazy bath of energy that made me shiver slighly, my lips parting, my entire body stroked and teased in a hundred different ways. If I'd known—

No wonder they don't let humans in here. A psion could get addicted to this, they could have a whole community of Feeders in here. The overcharge of carnivorous Power in here would addict a human psion faster than Chill would hook a junkie, and they would keep coming back for more—or looking for the same charge out on the streets, draining anyone they could to feel the crackling feedback of Power. I was lucky to be safe behind a demon's shielding, closed off from the dozing, razor-toothed buzzing that could swallow me whole. Good thing I'd left Jace at home, too.

The place was warehouse-sized, and full of bright glittering eyes and long hair, beautiful pale faces, and the massive shapes of werecain. I saw a gaggle of swanhilds in one corner, their feathered ruffs standing erect around their heads, and a group of something I recognized as kobolding in another, downing tankards of beer. Each time one of the squat gray-skinned things took down another pitcher, the others would cheer.

Long floating sheets of material hung from the ceiling. I glanced up, wished I hadn't, and glanced back down. *Cages on the ceiling,* I thought incoherently, swallowing. I couldn't afford to gray out from shock now. If Japhrimel had been here—

Stop thinking about that. The image of a lean saturnine face and piercing green eyes rose in front of me, I shoved it down. Set off across the cement floor. A few steps in, slick stone reverberated under my feet. They'd paved the whole place in marble. The sound bounced and echoed. I shook my head slightly, wishing once again I could shut my ears off, or turn the volume dial down just a little.

The area that vibrated most intensely with power was a booth done in red velvet, facing the bar. I skirted the dance floor, trying not to notice the infrequent pattering drops from the cages overhead, or the bright, inhuman eyes peering at me. The Nichtvren didn't act as if they noticed my presence, but I sensed a few of them trailing me. They dressed in silks and velvets, some of them in ultrahip modern pleather and spiked hair, gelglitter sparkling on pale cheeks. One of them, a tall man in bottle-green velvet with fountaining lace at the cuffs, smiled widely at me, showing his fangs. My right hand curled into a fist. I considered stopping, reaching for my sword—but my legs had already carried me toward the booth, as if set on automatic.

This was dangerous. I couldn't afford to lose focus now.

I blinked slowly, the pain in my shoulder spiking, then easing a little. I could tap into the Power here and blow the whole goddamn place down, if I wanted to. Without even the slightest hesitation or hint of backlash. Now was not the time to be glad that Japhrimel had altered me, but...I still felt glad. A little. In a weird, heart-thumping kind of way. Playing with the big boys now, Danny Valentine was in a whole different league.

I stopped in front of the booth. Two men that looked almost human, both with a glaze of Power and the musty, deliciously wicked smell of Nichtvren on them, stood on either side. One of them eyed my swordhilt and opened his mouth to say something. I fixed him with a hot glare.

"Let her in." The voice cut through the pulsing noise. The dance floor seethed behind me, a sharp spiked flare of Power matching a rise in the music's tempo. I hoped my hair wouldn't fall down.

Nikolai, the prime Power of Saint City, leaned back on the red velvet of an antique couch carved to within an inch of its life. An equally antique table rested in front of him, pocked with gaps I recognized as bullet holes. He was tall, broad-shouldered, and dressed in nondescript dark clothing that looked silky. No amount of simplicity could disguise the weltering onslaught of Power he commanded.

I would have been impressed if I hadn't dealt with Power all my life. As it was, I cocked a hip for balance and leverage in case anyone came at me, looked into his cat-sheened dark eyes, and held up the invitation.

He had a shelf of dark hair falling over his eyes, a wide generous mouth, and high sculpted cheekbones. He would have been hand-some without the flat shine of his eyes, like a cat's eyes at night when the light hits them just right, and the utter inhuman stillness he set-tled into. He wore a dark button-down shirt, probably silk, and a pair of loose silken pants, a pair of very good Petrolo boots, and no jewelry.

Beside him, leaning forward with her elbows on her knees, sat a Nichtvren female with a fall of long, curling blonde-streaked hair, her dark-blue eyes liquid and fixed on me. She had no catshine to her eyes, and none of Nikolai's immobility—instead, her fingernails tapped at the air, her lush lips parted slightly, the tips of her fangs showing; she wore a frayed red V-neck sweater and a pair of dark ratty jeans, beaten and scarred combat boots, and a thick silver cuff-bracelet with a tiger's eye the size of a mini credit-disc on her right wrist. She measured me from head to foot, and then smiled, half of her mouth pulling up.

I'm glad someone's having fun. I stepped forward, into the booth through a sticky sheet of Power that snapped shut behind me. Instantly, the noise they called music went down in volume, and I gave an involuntary sigh of relief.

Nikolai said nothing, examining me. It was like being eyed by a wild animal that hadn't quite made up its mind to eat you or simply crush you with a clawed paw.

I nodded at the female, knowing that his Consort was the way into his good graces. Rumor had it she was the only thing in the entire city that Nikolai valued. Rumor *also* had it that he went crazy if he even *thought* someone had messed with her.

Aw, now ain't that sweet. "I'm Danny Valentine, and I'm grateful you agreed to see me, ma'am. Sir."

Anyone who knew me would have expected the words to sound sarcastic. I was faintly surprised they didn't.

Nikolai still didn't move. The Nichtvren female laughed. The deep, husky sound surprised me and made my hackles rise, her eyes flared a dark luminous blue. She was exquisite, and I caught a thread of an odd scent; some type of musk that reminded me of sexwitch over the musty caramelized-dark-chocolate scent of Nichtvren. "Hi," she said. "Sit down. Nik's just in a mood. We have to see a werecain delegation after you, and he finds that unpleasant. Want something to drink?" Her accent was old Merican, the vowels shaped oddly, like they used to be around the time of the Parapsychic Act but before the great linguistic meltdown of the Seventy Days War. So she was old too.

Not nearly as old as him.

I wouldn't trust the liquor in here, lady. I shook my head, let my cloak fall to the floor. It was a good gesture, it showed I had nothing but the ordinary weapons. I settled myself on the couch to their left, easing down gingerly, wishing I could hold my sword across my lap. Steel would be better than empty air between me and these two.

Nikolai finally moved. "What is it you require?" he asked, and the woman's pale expressive hand came down on his knee; the tiger's eye on her bracelet flashed with light. He had been immobile before, now he looked over at her, and a stone would have looked frenetic next to him.

"Be polite, sweetie. She's new at this." The woman rolled her eyes, then rested her elbows on her knees again. "What can we do for you, Miss Valentine?"

Now that was unexpected. I drew the papers out of my pocket, making sure to move very slowly. All the same, Nikolai's eyelids dropped a fraction. A chill, prickling weight of Power covered him.

I don't think I'd ever want to see him pissed off. The thought was there and gone in a flash, I pushed the sudden swell of almost-fear down. I had nothing to worry about, I was here on business, and I wasn't just human.

Am I? What's the protocol for an almost-demon dealing with a Master Nichtvren? This wasn't ever covered at the Academy. Maybe I should write to the Hegemony Educational Board.

I laid the papers on the table, swallowing the choking panicked giggle rising in my chest. "The police have asked me to look into this. Have you ever seen anything like it? I know you'll have access to texts I don't. If you can narrow this down, it would help me immensely."

She scooped the papers up. Nikolai didn't move, but he seemed to give the impression of a twitch. She settled back, moving with pre-ternatural Nichtvren grace, and cuddled into his side.

That managed to make him move. He slid his arm over her shoulders and looked down at the top of her head. My heart slammed into my throat. For some reason, he reminded me of Eddie watching

Gabe, his face softening slightly, his eyes lighting up. It was a startlingly human expression on a being who hadn't been human for a long, long time. No man had ever looked at *me* like that.

Would you have noticed, if they did? the deep voice asked me.

I decided to not even dignify that thought with a response. Sekhmet sa'es, *I'm even ignoring my own bloody self. I'm losing my mind.*

Velvet rustled as I shifted uneasily. I wished I could have worn jeans to this. *At least if I'd worn jeans I could have ridden a slicboard.* I licked dry lips and watched as she scanned the pictures, her mouth tightening.

She shuddered, her blue eyes lighting with a flare of something almost-panicked, gone in an instant.

Nikolai's eyes flicked over me.

"Nik?" She held up the papers. "Take a look at this."

He stirred himself to glance, a faint line grooving between his eyebrows, taking the laseprints from her slim pretty hand.

"It's Ceremonial." She moved slightly, her body shifting closer to his. "But I haven't seen this variation. Have you?"

"It stinks of evil, Selene." His eyes lost their catshine for a moment and turned dark. For a moment, there was a flash of how he might have looked as a human man, and I found myself staring, hoping to catch it again.

"Have you seen it?" she demanded, her hand flashing out to catch the other side of the sheaf of paper. There was a long, breathless pause.

"No, *milyi*." His eyes searched her face, still dark and horribly, awfully human. "I have not seen this exact variation. And yet..." He trailed off, his gaze moving slow and gelid past me and out over the dance floor. *He looks just like a lion looking over a herd of zebras,* I thought. *Or a pimp checking out a flock of unregistered hookers.*

"You're killing me here, Nikolai." She pushed a dark-blonde curl out of her face. Her lips quirked downward before she smiled. Bits of light from the blastball suspended over the dancefloor flicked over the smooth planes of her face. "Can we just once have some information without it being a huge production?"

Hear, hear, I seconded internally. I'd thought it was going to be a relief to be in a place without human stink. Instead, it creeped me out. My hackles rose, almost-goosebumps roughening my skin. They clustered through the whole building, the Nichtvren, alien as demons, even if originally human. The only way to become a Nichtvren is to be infected, bitten and transformed with a blood exchange; it usually takes two or three exchanges for the Turn to happen. Bones change, the jaw becomes distended and cartilaginous, the eyes transform, able to see in complete darkness, and the thirst races through their veins. It's a combination of retroviral infection and some etheric transfer from Master to fledgling that modern science, for all its bio-mechanical wonder, can't replicate. They were different from normal humans and different from me, yet I still felt something odd: a type of kinship.

Most of the Nichtvren here had been Turned into something else, altered away from human and into something different. Something more.

Like me.

I wonder if people feel like this when they look at me. I shifted slightly on the uncomfortably hard couch. Velvet rasped against my skirt. The air inside the sticky shield turned chill, pressing against heart and throat and eye. If I'd still been human, this would have made me draw my sword, a feral, bloodthirsty current swirling through the air. I would have looked for a safe wall to put my back to. It felt like someone was going to get hurt.

"It looks like Feeder glyphs." One of Nikolai's hands crept up, touched her cheek. The gesture was so tender, blood rose hot in my cheeks, I felt like a voyeur. His eyes took back the gold-green sheen of a cat's, flicked between the photos and then her face. "Why have I heard nothing of this?"

I shrugged. "It started with a normal, and then a sexwitch. One of Polyamour's girls. Then it was a Necromance. Christabel Moorcock." I quelled the shiver rising up my spine. "They're Feeder glyphs?" Feeder glyphs were illegal except for research purposes. Twisting the Nine Canons to serve a Feeder was heavy-duty magick, lethal to some, it was hard to protect against spells using runes that could bolster a Feeder's talents.

"They appear to be," Nikolai answered, his eyes still locked on Selene's face. She moved slightly, her mouth softening, and I dropped my gaze to the bullet-scarred table. *You'd think Nichtvren would have proper furniture,* I thought sourly, and inhaled deeply to calm myself. My left shoulder eased slightly, not so much of the crunch-ing, living glare of pain. The music outside melded into RetroPhunk, their *Celadon Groove.* A chill finger traced my spine. The last time

I'd heard this music had been in Dacon Whitaker's old nightclub before I'd turned him in for running Chill. When I'd blown back into town after Rio, I'd found out Dake was dead of Chill detox, eaten alive by the drug. It wasn't a pleasant thought, just like everything else I'd been thinking lately.

Nikolai spoke again, his voice slicing the noise like a silvery scalpel through mauled flesh. "This thing killed a *tantraiiken?*"

I had to think before I remembered that was one of the old—very old—words for a sexwitch. Sexwitches used to be rare, their ability to heal and need to live off the etheric and psychic energy raised by sex combining to make them prized paranormal pets before the Awakening. It also contributed to a lot of them getting killed off young in some very nasty ways before they had Hegemony protection. I nodded, the stilettos a reassuring sharp weight in my hair.

"Then you shall have assistance in hunting down the perpetrator." Nikolai shuffled the papers back together with one brisk movement. "You are welcome here, Miss Valentine. When you have dispatched this criminal, come back. It seems my Selene fancies you."

The female rolled her eyes again, a reassuringly human movement. "That's his way of saying you can step in without an invitation," she translated, plucking the papers from his hand and leaning forward to offer them to me. My fingers were numb. I forced my right hand to close around the laseprints and tuck them back in my pocket.

"Thank you," I managed through my dry lips. "Ma'am."

"It's Selene." Her eyes flicked out over the dance floor. It was a glance very much like his, maybe an unconscious imitation, but it still made my skin crawl. "There's the delegation," she sighed. "I think that's all we can tell you. Nikolai's got this thing about anyone messing with *tantraiiken.*"

I don't know why I asked. "Why?" *Curiosity killed the cat, Danny. Just get out of here. Get out of here now.*

She shrugged. It was a beautiful, loose, fluid movement. "Maybe because I used to be one. Stay and have a drink if you like, the bar's got stuff for just about everyone. Come back sometime."

"I might." I made it to my feet, my shoulder throbbing. "Thank you."

Nikolai lifted his hand. "One moment, demonling."

I froze. *He recognizes me as demon? Of course, he's Nichtvren.*

He can see Power. If he came over the table at me I could carve his heart out, but she was something else. The hard glitter in her dark blue eyes and the nervous way she twitched was almost scarier than his rocklike stillness. And the Power that cloaked them both was impressive, even if it was nothing like a demon's. Then again, nothing in the wide world was like a demon when it came to Power—except for a god.

And I had no desire to meet any god other than my own, thank you very much. I could even go the rest of my life without having to deal with a demon ever again too.

Now if I can just convince the Prince of Hell to forget I exist.

"I have a library." Nikolai's flat cat eyes looked straight through me. The music pounded behind me. I wasn't sanguine about going back out into the sonic assault. Or about having them at my back. Or about staying in this goddamn place any longer than I absolutely had to. I didn't look up at the cages on the ceiling—but the effort cost me dearly. My stomach fluttered uneasily, and I had never in my life wished to vomit more than I did at that moment. "Among my acquisitions are several texts supposedly written by demons. You may find them useful."

Where were you the last year or so when I had time to come and bury my nose in a few books? I nodded. "Thank you." It was all I could say.

I turned on my heel and plunged through the sticky shield, pausing only to scoop up my cloak and swirl it around my shoulders. The music slammed into my whole body like a backdraft from a reactive fire. *Get me the hell out of here. I have got to get out of here; dear gods, get me out of here—*

There was only a millisecond's worth of warning before the lights died. The music failed as well, which was a relief. Instinct sent me into a fighting crouch, and my hand blurred up toward my swordhilt. Sudden dark settled into the walls and floor, I heard whispers and shuffles, the lamplit pricks of Nichtvren eyes firing through the gloom.

I heard something else, too. A low, vicious growling.

My sword whispered free of the sheath. My heart gave one incredible leaping thud, my skin coming alive. I cursed the skirt of the dress even as the demon equivalent of adrenaline flooded my system. Whatever was coming, if anything got near me I was going to kill it.

Oh, yes. This was what I *lived* for.

Screams. Something snarled and soft padded feet slapping the floor.

A thundercrack of Power slammed out from behind me, bearing the unmistakable cold acid tang of Nichtvren. "I am *not* amused," Nikolai said softly, the weight behind each word pummeling the air in concentric rings of razor-edged glass.

That seemed to break the stasis. Chaos screamed into being, snarling and scrabbling boiling through the darkness. Roaring filled the air. I tracked the sound, coming up out of my crouch in a fast, light shuffle, blade whirling, the familiar feeling of racing on the thin edge of adrenaline rising from that old place of instinct and terror. The cloak fell for the second time, it would only tangle me up. My boots squeaked as I half-turned, steel coming up with a faint sound as it clove heavy air.

Tchunk. My blade carved cleanly through whatever it was. I whirled on the balls of my feet, avoiding bloodspray, took the second one with a clash. Low hulking shape, my pupils dilated, demon-eyes taking in every available photon and squeezing the usefulness out of it. There wasn't much light here, even for me.

My left-hand main-gauche, reversed along my forearm to act as a shield, took a hell of a strike. I cried out, more in surprise than pain— the damn thing was *fast*. The emergency lights came up, a wash of crimson stinging my eyes but I was moving on instinct anyway, punching something hairy in the face with my fist braced with the knifehilt then leaping, landing between two hulking shapes. Quick kick behind one's knee, the hairy shape bellowing and folding down; spinning to engage the other. The smell of blood and wet fur exploded out, gaggingly strong, my shoulder burned even more fiercely. Claws raked up my side, and the whole world seemed to go white for a moment, a sheet of fire blinding me. Black, demon blood pattered on the marble, *my* blood, redolent of spice and sweet rotting fruit. *How did I get into this? I'm fighting off a couple of fucking werecain, bad luck I suppose, I was just in the way. Goddammit.*

It hit me like a freight train, fur and stink and claws. I smashed up with my left and again; *too close to engage with the sword, get a little distance, move move move.* I took the easy way out, dropping and rolling to scythe the 'cain's legs out from underneath it. The 'cain spun aside, twisting in midair with unholy fluidity, and the scar on my left shoulder blazed into agonized life. My body gathered itself, new strength suddenly coursing through my veins, and I kicked up with both legs, my back curving as momentum jolted me up off the floor and onto my feet. My right foot lashed out, catching the 'cain I'd just tripped on the nose. A flurry in the corner of my eye was another one bearing down on me. Steel flashed. Fudoshin described a sweet, clean arc, deadly steel singing low, and more blood exploded. The 'cain leaping for me dropped, its intestines slithering wetly out as I landed, spinning to feint with the main-gauche and then *cut;* followed with a one-handed side-downsweep that missed because the 'cain was shuffling back.

It was my turn to attack, my wrist turning so the blade fell into position again, every motion as natural as breathing. I bolted forward, boots shuffling and the battlecry rising in my throat; my *kia* shivered the air as I engaged with the werecain again. Its snarl turned into a falsetto squeal as I rammed the main-gauche home between two ribs, then leaned, sword coming in from the side, because the side-downsweep turned naturally into the rib-splitting cut. The werecain gurgled as Fudoshin bit deep—deep enough, I hoped, to cut the abdominal aorta. I twisted the blade against the suction of preternatural muscle, smelled the stink of a battlefield and of werecain blurring together, and the 'cain in front of me slumped away from my sword. I backed up, blood hissing free of shining blade as I whipped it through the cleaning-stroke; faint blue fire etched itself along the razor edge. The process of making the sword *mine* had begun with the first blood shed together.

I half-spun, ready to take on the next enemy, but as soon as it had begun the fight was over. Dead werecain lay scattered about, the last one flopping until Nikolai casually reached down, Nichtvren claws extended, and tore its throat out.

There were more bodies piled over the red velvet couch he and Selene had just been perched on, and still more bodies further away toward the dance floor. For every one I'd killed, Nikolai had killed three. "Most distressing." His voice throbbed in the lowest register, like a huge pipe organ. It was a voice that could tear through bones and thump against the heart itself, a sound felt more than heard in the crackling silence that followed the death of the music.

"Well," Selene answered, over his shoulder. "You left nothing for me."

"My apologies, *milyi*." He straightened. "Søren will have much to answer for." His eyes came up, dark holes in his face under the shell of crimson lighting. "You fight well, demonling. And you attacked my enemies."

That most emphatically does not *make me your friend,* I thought, clamping my teeth so the words couldn't escape. The *last* thing I needed right now was more trouble. *If I hadn't been in the way they would have ignored me, and I would have been happy to just get the hell out of here.* "Thanks for the compliment," I managed, my jaw set tight as I bent down to wrench my knife free of a werecain's ribs. "Why..." I trailed off, not wanting the explanation anyway.

"The werecain are embroiled in a territorial dispute." He straightened as I did, immaculate. His face was a thoughtful Renascence stone angel's, set in its perfection and unremarkable as a statue compared to the welter of Power surrounding him. Selene stood behind him, dyed and dipped in crimson, her hands on her hips. She didn't look happy. "This is the faction unhappy with the decision I was required to arbitrate. I am sorry for the disturbance. I do not like a guest of mine being forced to fight, it reflects badly on me. Accept my apology."

It's hell being top of the heap, isn't it? The merry, sardonic voice inside my head almost made it out of my mouth. There was a time when I would have let it. "Oh. No worries." Then, "Have a nice night."

"It is extremely unlikely." He half-turned to look over his shoulder at Selene, his gaze falling in one swift sweep down her body, as if checking her for damage. "But you have my thanks, demonling. Good luck."

Great. I couldn't help myself. "I'm beginning to think I'll need it," I said, and got out of there while I still could.

CHAPTER 15

I had the hoverlimo for the rest of the night; there was no reason not to use it. So I gave the driver Christabel Moorcock's address.

I should have started with the puzzling Bryce Smith, or with the sexwitch Yasrule. I should have gone to salvage whatever traces remained, yet I went to Christabel's. I tried to tell myself I was violating procedure because of instinct, and that the other two scenes were too old.

The hoverlimo spiraled down to land on the roof of her brownstone apartment building at the edge of the Tank District. The driver scurried around to open the door before I could reach for the handle; his eyes were wide and dark. The hoverlimo rose afterward to circle in the parking-patterns overhead.

This close to the Tank District, the smell of garbage and synth hash swirled through the air, mixing with sharp spikes of illicit sex from the hookers prowling the strips and the deep wells of the nightclubs, glittering like novas in the psychic ether. Cool wind touched my hair as I stood for a moment on the concrete landing-pad, feeling the atmosphere of the Tank press against me. If Saint City was a cold radioactive animal wanting to be stroked, the Tank was the pulsing heart of that animal, so fiercely cold it burned. The throbbing that forced vital energy through the rest of the city, through the sluggish brain of the financial district and the arteries of the pavement. The Rathole was buried in the depths of the Tank, a deep pit of vital energy whistling a subsonic note at the very bottom of my sensing-range.

My city. It did indeed feel like home.

My datband got me in through the building's public-access net; Christabel's magsealed apartment was on the top floor. Since Gabe had keyed me into the Saint City police net with access to the scenes, the magsealing parted for me.

The air was stale, tinted with the chemical wash of Carbonel, used to get blood out of fibers. The cleaners had come in to get rid of the blood and matter once the forensic techs had gone through the place; I caught a lingering trace of jasmine perfume and the tingle of a powerful awareness. A Reader had been here to capture every aspect of the scene; it had probably been Beulah McKinley. She did good work, and whatever scene she had processed always held a breath of jasmine.

I wondered if she, like Handy Mandy, had caught sight of whatever had driven Christabel's ghost mad.

The front door had been shattered, splinters peppering the wall opposite and the carpeted hall. Christabel's shields were slowly fading, the giant rents torn in them patched with Gabe's trademark deftness. A shuntline hummed into the street outside to carefully and

safely drain away the ambient energy and fold Christabel's shields up
so no trace of murder and agony remained to create psychic sludge
for other inhabitants of this quiet building. The temporary magseal
door shut behind me with a click.

I was inside Christabel Moorcock's house.

The carpet was wine-red. The hall was dark, but I caught geometric patterns painted over the walls; protection charms. I glanced into
the dining room and into a bathroom with an amber-glowing
fleur-de-lis nightlight. In both rooms the painted walls were covered
with an intaglio of protection runes, each knot of safety carefully
daubed. They resonated uneasily, the ones near the door spent and
broken; long waving fronds of Power flowed toward the front door.

Huh. That's odd.

The entry hall, the dining room, and the two bedrooms were carpeted. The bathroom was tiled, the kitchen and the living room in
mellow hardwood. The second bedroom was a meditation room, a
round blue and silver rug in the middle and the ceiling painted with a
wheeling Milky Way.

Quite an artist, Christabel. I did not turn the lights on yet.

I inhaled deeply. I smelled traces of Gabriele's kyphii-tainted
scent, the Reader's jasmine, other faint human scents overlaying a
more complex well. Closing my eyes, I shut away all the more recent
smells, including the sweet, decaying fruit of the blood drying on my
ruined dress.

That left me with a powerful brew of female psion, a healthy
astringent scent. Christabel had smelled like molecular-drip polish
on long nails, slightly-oily hair, and strong, sweet resin incense.
Resin was cheap and high quality, readily available in metaphysical
supply stores, and it brought back a swirl of memories from my
school days.

*So you used schoolgirl incense. A little surprising, but I suppose
it isn't any stranger than Gabe and her kyphii.* The furniture was
overstuffed, no hard edges. Her bookshelves weren't dusty, but there
were no houseplants. No pets either, not even cloned koi.

The altar in her meditation room held a bank of white candles in
varying heights, and a statue of Angerboda Gulveig Teutonica, glittering gold leaf on Her robe worked with flames and the Teutonica
heart symbol. There was another statue set off to one side, a black
dancing Kali of the old school, graphic and bloody.

There was a fresh offering in front of Kali, a shallow dish of something sticky that smelled of wine and faint traces of human blood. Also interesting.

Christabel's bed was neatly made. A copy of Adrienne Spocarelli's *Gods and Magi* stood on the bedstand, a ritual knife laid across its cover. The clothes hamper was full of dirty clothes that smelled of lilac powder. A sleek, gleaming Pentath computer deck stood in the corner at a precise angle to her mauve bed. Her bathrooms were spotless.

To go from this order to the chaos of the living room was a shock. Great gouges had been torn into the wooden flooring, and the waning chalk marks on the hardwood were barely visible under a dark stain no amount of cleaning could scrub away. The couch was destroyed, the table reduced to matchsticks. Little drawstring bags of herbs, protective amulets all, hung from the dark ceiling fixture. Splashes of blood had baked onto the full-spectrum bulbs; I was glad I could see in the dimness. There had been a hell of a fight in here.

I let out a long, slow breath. Both Gabe and a Reader had been here. There was nothing for me to see. Wherever Christabel had allowed herself to truly live, it wasn't here. This place was more like a stage set than anything else.

Paper lay scattered across the gouged floor, the same parchment she had written her last message on. A spilled bottle of dragonsblood ink lay near the entrance to the kitchen. Try as I might, I couldn't find the pen among the drift of chaos.

My own voice startled me. "I'm here." It was a whisper, like a child's in a haunted house. "If you want to talk, Christabel, I'm listening."

Silence gathered in the corners. I felt like a thief, here in the middle of this carefully constructed world. I didn't want to resurrect her mad raving ghost; I wanted some breath of the living Necromance.

None came. Even the flowering stain of thick-smelling violence in the air was smooth and blank, nothing for my intuition to grab onto.

The other scenes won't tell you anything either, the deep voice of certainty suddenly spoke inside my head. I paused, velvet and silk rustling as I turned in a slow circle, my eyes passing over the chiaroscuro of protection runes painted on each wall. *The answer to this puzzle doesn't lie here. You know where it lies.*

I did. The only clue I had likely to unravel this tangled skein was encapsulated in three words scrawled on parchment by a terrified dying Necromance.

Remember Rigger Hall.

"I would much rather not," I muttered, and the air swirled uneasily just like my skirt. I suddenly felt ridiculous, overdressed, and very, very young for the first time in years.

But if remembering the Hall would keep someone else from dying, I would do it. I'd survived that place once. How hard could remembering it be?

The three stripes of phantom fire down my back twinged in answer. So did the vanished scar along the crease of my lower-left buttock. The scar on my shoulder burned, burned.

My hand tightened around Fudoshin's scabbard. I was no longer weak or defenseless.

"All right, Christabel." My voice bounced off the walls. "You're my best clue. For right now, you lead the dance."

I had the not-so-comforting feeling that the air inside her wrecked living room had changed, becoming still and charged with expectation. As if it was... *listening.*

My knuckles were white on the scabbard. My mouth had gone dry, and when I slipped out again through the temporary magseal door I should have felt relieved to leave the scene of the carnage behind.

I wasn't. All I could think of were three little words, chanted over and over again by a shrieking, insane ghost who had once been a woman inhabiting a neat, orderly, soulless little apartment.

Remember. Remember Rigger Hall.

I knew what I had to do next.

CHAPTER 16

The night was getting deep when the hoverlimo dropped me off on the concrete landing-pad in my front yard, and I tipped the driver well. He muttered his thanks and lifted off before I reached my front door. The garden rustled uneasily, dappled with darkness and the orange glow of citylight.

My hands were shaking. Not much, but enough that I could see the fine vibration when I held them out in front of me. Even my right hand, that twisted claw that had so gracefully held a sword and defended me tonight, was shaking, the fingers jittering as if I was typing a Section 713 Bounty Report.

I made it inside, shut the door, and leaned against it, scabbard digging into my back. The dress was stiff and crusty with blood along my left side that I noticed for the first time. *"Anubis et'her ka."* The god's name made the air stir uneasily. "That was unpleasant."

Jace wasn't home. He was probably off digging through public records. Because psions so often worked at night, public buildings rarely closed before two in the morning.

It was a pity. I could have used some easy banter.

I lifted my left hand because my right was shaking too badly, examined the black molecule-drip polish and the graceful wicked arches of my fingers. The fingers flexed, released.

The smell of lilacs still clung to my dress. Lilacs, and terror. The quiet dark inside my house suddenly made the flesh hang traitorously heavy on my bones — slender, arching frames, architecturally different than human bones but not agreeing with demon physiology in any of the books I read. Stuck in between, trapped like a butterfly halfway out of a glass chrysalis and frozen, popped into a kerri jar stasis. I didn't belong here in my old life, had nothing and nowhere to move into despite all my frantic thrashing on bounties. Stopped, frozen between one step and the next like a holovid still.

What butterfly wants to go back into the chrysalis? Or revisit being a caterpillar?

Remember. Remember Rigger Hall.

Bile rose, I forced it down. A rattling tremor slid from my scalp to my booted toes. I could feel it circling, the panic attack deep and needle-toothed, combat and the shock of memory both catching up to me.

Hey, Danny, the lipless mouths of my nightmares said. *Thought you shook us loose, huh? No way. Let's get out the old fears and rattle them around, let's dance in Danny's head and shake her left and right, what do you say?*

"Why am I shaking?" I asked the still darkness of my refuge. Took a deep breath and realized how musty the place smelled. I rarely cleaned anymore, and there was only so much Jace would do. Besides, we were gone all the time, tracking down criminals.

Compassion is not your strong suit. Jado's voice careened inside my skull, echoed, stopped as if dropped down a well.

My left shoulder crunched again. I bent over, retching, my hair coming loose and the stiletto chiming on the hardwood floor. Almost a year of hiding behind the image of a big, tough bounty hunter hadn't changed a goddamn thing.

It never would.

Japhrimel was gone.

The floor grated against my knees and palms, cold and hard. The world went gray. *I'm going into shock. And nothing around to bring me out.* The layers of shielding energy over my home shivered, singing a thin crystalline note of distress, like a thin plasglass curve-edge stroked just right.

"You will not leave me." A voice like old, dark whiskey. Familiar.

My entire body leapt to hear that voice.

I looked up. Saw nothing but my front hall, iron coatrack, the mirror, a slice of warm gold from the kitchen. Jace had left the light on.

"You will *not* leave me to wander the earth alone." The voice slapped at me, yanked me up off the floor, and shoved me back against the door, pressure like a wave-front of Power against my entire body, squeezing around me, forcing away the gray shocky cloudiness.

I'm being smacked around by a ghost. A ripping unsteady laugh tore out of me. I opened my eyes, saw the empty hall again. Fragrant, sweet black blood was hot on my chin—I'd bitten my lip almost clean through. It stung before it healed over, as instantly as any other wound. "Lucky me," I half-sang. "What a lucky girl, lucky girl, I'm a lucky girl, Necromance to the stars."

"Dante." Merely a whisper, but I felt it all the way down to my bones.

"It's not fair. I want you back." Then I clapped my hand over my mouth, and my entire body tensed, listening.

Listening.

A long silence greeted this. I made my hands into fists. Careful. I always had to be so stinking careful. Had to hold back, so as not to damage the less resilient. The *humans.*

A long sigh, and the voice—more familiar to me than my own, by now—brushed my cheek. "*Feed* me…"

I scanned the hall. Empty. The entire house was empty.

No human. No demon. No *nothing.* Nothing in my house but me, dead air, my possessions, and the lingering smell of Jace. Dust, and the smell of stale grief. That was all.

Great. The dead will talk to me, but never the way I want them to. Never the useful way. Oh, no. The dark screaming hilarity in the thought was troubling, but it was like a slap of cold water across the face of a dreaming woman.

I am an adult, I told myself. *I grew up, goddammit. I am all grown up now.*

I peeled myself away from the door, silk rustling around my legs as I strode for the stairs. Halfway up, I stopped so quickly I almost overbalanced and fell on my ass all the way back down.

The niche stood as it always had. No dust on the scorching black urn.

Anubis dipped his slender beautiful head, examining me. The wine was gone.

The god had accepted the offering.

The rose petals were withered too. Dry. Sucked dry.

"This is crazy." My shoulder throbbed. "I've got a killer to hunt down. A killer that uses Feeder glyphs in some kind of elaborate Ceremonial circle. And I can't afford to be haunted by..."

But being haunted by Japhrimel was better than missing him, was better than grieving for him. "Are you talking to me?" The urn's gleaming curves mocked me. "Please tell me you're talking to me."

Of course, no reply. Nothing but the still hot air teasing at my face, the statue of Anubis shifting, as if demanding my attention.

I met the statue's eyes. Was it a hallucination, or did the god appear to be smiling slightly?

"I've missed you." This time, I was talking to the god. My voice sounded thin, breathless. It was true. I'd missed the sense of being always held, protected—the god of Death was the biggest, baddest thing around. Even Nichtvren feared Death.

Even demons did.

I always wondered if that was why I was a Necromance. A helpless, collared girl pushed into the Hegemony psi program because of her Matheson scores, an orphan sent into Rigger Hall like all the rest—and in the Hall, you either found a protector or you didn't last long.

Death was the best protector. At least I didn't have much to fear; when I finally died it would be like going into a lover's embrace.

There were whole months of my schooling when I merely endured through the day, going from one task to the next, one foot in front of the other. I would wait for every visit with Lewis, but I was getting older and couldn't see him as often. I had only the books.

At night, I would read by the light of a filched flashlight under my covers, every book Lewis had left me. When I could read no longer, when I finally closed my eyes, I would slip into the blue-fire trance of Death.

That kept me going. I was special, both because Lewis had given me his books and because Death had chosen me. I withdrew mostly into myself after Roanna's death, learning to live self-contained, a smooth hard shell. But I always had the books and the blue glow, twin lines going down into the heart of me, feeding me strength. Telling me I could endure.

I aced every single Theory of Magick class, every single Modern Classics test. I was academically perfect no matter how bad it got, having absorbed Lewis's love of study.

More importantly, I never doubted that I would survive. Lew had given me a primary gift: a child's knowledge that she is loved completely. And though the punishments were bad, some of the teachers had been dedicated, true masters of their craft. There were good things about the Hall—learning to control my abilities, learning who could be trusted and who couldn't, learning just how strong I really was.

And always, always, there was Death.

I was too young to tread the blue crystal hall or approach the Bridge, but I would feel the god's attention, a warm communion that gave me the strength to become self-reliant instead of withdrawing into catatonia or developing a nervous tic like some of the other kids. Sometimes, even during the worst punishments, I would close my eyes and still see that blue glow, geometric traceries of blue fire and the god's attention, *my* god's attention, and I had made up my mind to be strong.

I had *endured*.

And when Mirovitch was dead, the inquest finished, and the school shut down, I went on through the Academy and my schooling up to my Trial, that harrowing ordeal every Necromance must pass to be accredited, the stripping away of the psyche in an initiation as different as it is terrifying for every individual. You can't handle walking in Death until you've actually died yourself, and what is any initiation but a little death? I'd had an edge over every other initiate: I never doubted I would survive my Trial. And afterward, with a few white hairs I dyed to make them the standard black of a Necromance,

I'd gone on and never looked back. Never stopped in my steady march, moving on.

But all the time, I hadn't had a goddamn idea what I was marching *toward.* I still didn't, but I knew one thing for sure: I didn't want to go *back.*

And yet that was what Christabel was asking me to do.

"Rigger Hall." My eyes locked with the statue's. "I swore I'd never go back."

You must. The eyes were blank and pitiless, but so deep. Death did not play favorites—He loved all equally. *What you cannot escape, you must fight; what you cannot fight, you must endure.* The god's voice—not quite words, just a thread of meaning laid in my receptive mind—made me shudder, my knees bumping the wall. That had been my first lesson when they clipped the collar on me at the Hall. Endurance. The primal lesson, repeated over and over again. Even later, when I seriously doubted I would get out of some new horrible situation alive, a thin thread of me down at the very core of my being had merely replied, *You will.* And that was that.

I've been called suicidal, and crazy, and fey; I've even been called glory-hungry and snobbish. I don't think that's accurate; I simply always knew I would survive, a core of something hard and nasty in me refusing to give in even at the worst of times. Better to face what frightens you than to live cowering in fear; and if Death frightened me I need only go further into the blue glow of His embrace until even fear was lost and the weight lifted from me.

I had nothing to fear. I kept my honor intact. An honorable person was only as good as the promises she kept, the loyalty she showed. My honor was unstained.

A familiar touch against my shields warned me—Jace coming back, probably on a slicboard. He was dropping in fast, probably to avoid being seen or shot by the holovid reporters outside. I felt the security net slide away to let him pass.

I made it almost all the way down the stairs before my legs started to tremble alarmingly. I slid down to sit, my knees giving out so I thumped inelegantly onto the second step. When Jace opened the front door I was perched on the steps, leaning against the wall, my knees drawn up.

He kicked the door closed. "Danny?" His voice, blessedly normal, *sane,* made me shut my eyes again. I rested my chin on my forearms, braced on my knees, the silken cascades of the dress falling to either side. The wall was doing a damn fine job of holding me up.

Three scars, dipping down my back, and the brand laid along the crease below my left buttock. I smelled the sick-sweet odor of burning flesh again, heard whistling soft laughter and my own throaty screams, felt blood and semen trickling down my inner thighs.

And I heard something else: Headmaster Mirovitch's dry, papery voice whispering while the iron met my skin. I forced myself to stare unflinchingly into the memory, the door inside my head a little ajar, showing me what I'd locked away so I could go on living.

"Danny." Jace stood in front of me. "You okay?"

I lifted my head. His hair was messy, windblown, and his blue eyes were humanly kind. I didn't deserve his kindness, and I knew it.

My eyes burned, but my left shoulder had quieted. It took me two tries to reply through a throat gone dry as reactive paint. "No. I'm not. Get the shovels, Jace. We've got some digging to do."

CHAPTER 17

The garage housed garden implements and a sleek black hover, dead and quiescent on its landing gear. This space had been empty before I'd gotten rich. I had always meant to turn it into a meditation room, but I ended up avoiding it and doing my meditating in the living room or bedroom.

I pushed a stack of boxes aside, my hands trembling, and looked up to find Jace watching me, his wind-ruffled hair a shock of gold in the light from the bare full-spectrum bulbs.

"Listen." He pushed his hand back through his windstruck hair. The motion achieved absolutely nothing in terms of straightening it, only made it stick up raffishly. He looked like Gypsy Roen's sidekick Marbery, all angles and cocksure grace under a shock of hair. "Why don't we call this off and get drunk? Tackle this tomorrow night."

"You might be able to get drunk. I can't." I was surprised by how steady my voice was. The smell of the garage, the hover on its leaf-spring legs and cushion of reactive smelling of metal and fustiness, clawed at my throat.

"Well, why don't we just fall into bed and shag until we forget this, huh?" He tried to make it sound like a light, bantering offer. Just like prejob bullshitting to ease the nerves. Unfortunately, his breath caught and ruined the effect.

Oh, Jace. I actually managed a smile, then pushed again. The boxes of files scraped along the floor, cardboard squeaking against smooth concrete. I looked down, saw the wooden door set in the concrete. A round depression in the center of the trapdoor held an iron ring.

"You truly are amazing." Jace propped the two shovels over his shoulder like an ancient gravedigger. "This is right out of a holovid."

Irritation rasped at me, but my retort died on my lips. He was too pale, sweat standing out on his forehead. We were both claustrophobic, and he...what was he feeling? If I touched him I would know. Bare skin on skin, I might have been partly-demon but I was still the woman who had shared her body and psyche with him. Almost a decade ago, but that kind of link didn't fade.

Was that why I couldn't quite let go of him? Or was it because he reminded me of the person I had been before Rio, a feeling I couldn't quite remember for all the sharpness of my Magi-trained memory?

"You don't have to come down." I closed my hand over the metal ring. It was so cold it scorched—or was it that my fingers were demon-hot? Dust stirred in the still-hot air; I was radiating again. *I'll never need climate-control again, maybe I should hire myself out as a portable dryer. Rent your very own psionic heater, reasonable rates, sarcasm included.*

"And let you face this alone?" He shook his head. "No way, sweetheart. In for a penny, in for a pound."

Words rose in my throat. *I'm so sorry. I wish I could be what you needed.*

Instead, I wrenched the trapdoor up.

A musty smell of sterile dirt exhaled from the square darkness. I felt around under the lip of the hole. "Probably not working," I muttered. "That would just cap the whole goddamn day."

My fingers found the switch, pressed it, and a bare bulb clicked into life. I let out a whistling breath through a throat closed to pinhole size.

"How was the suckhead convention?" Jace's tone was light, bored. I glanced up at him, suddenly intensely grateful for his presence. If I owed Gabe and I owed Eddie, what did I owe to Jace?

The answer was the same in each case: too much to easily repay. Debt, obligation, honor; all words for what I would keep paying until I took my last breath, and be damn grateful for the chance.

It was better than being alone, wasn't it?

It sure as hell was. "Interesting. He says he's got some books on demons I'm welcome to come by and peruse." I managed not to choke on my own voice.

"You do have a way of making friends." Hipshot and easy, Jace Monroe examined the trapdoor, the bare bulb's glare showing a drop bar and a square of pale, dusty dirt.

"Must be my charming smile." I leaned forward, catching the drop bar in both hands. The dress slithered as I trusted my weight to the iron, pulling my legs in and dropping them, then slowly lowering myself down. Thank the gods my swordhilt didn't snag. I hung full-length for a moment, then dropped the three inches to the dirt floor. "There was a werecain attack while I was there."

He hadn't mentioned my torn dress or the black demon blood crusted on the side of the bodice. I would never have believed him capable of such restrained tact. If I went upstairs to change out of the dress, I would find some way of putting this off.

"I can't leave you alone for a moment, can I." Jace handed the first shovel down, the second. He took his sword from his belt and handed it to me.

"Guess not. I went by and checked out Christabel's apartment." Bits of garden dirt still clung to the rusting metal of the first shovel. The second shovel was new. Why had I bought it? Was my precognition working overtime again?

Sometimes I hated being gifted with precognition as well as rune-witchery. Being gifted with precognition is like being shoved from square to square on a chessboard, you're never sure if your intuition is working or if you're just getting paranoid. There's precious little difference between the two. Out of all the Talents, precogs — Seers — go insane the most.

"Find out anything interesting?" He leaned over, caught the drop bar, and levered himself down gracefully. His T-shirt came untucked when he curled down and I caught a flash of his tanned belly, muscle moving under skin. His boots ground into the dirt, and he scanned the unfinished space. "Anyone else would have a *ladder,* Danny."

"You think I come down here often enough for that? And yes, I found out something interesting, at least at the suckhead convention. The Prime and his Consort identified the circles as being marked with Feeder glyphs."

I felt cold just mentioning it. Feeders were nothing to mess with. It's every psion's worst nightmare, tangling with a Feeder.

Jace whistled tunelessly, taking both shovels from my unresisting hands, leaving me his sword. I was abruptly warmed by the implied trust. "That's...well." His sandy eyebrows drew together, his lips compressed.

I studied the perfect arc of his cheekbone, the corner of his mouth. He had always been so very attractive; and his air of self-assuredness was compelling too. I wondered if I'd fallen for him because he'd always seemed so damn sure I would, and my own well-camouflaged uncertainty made his confidence even more magnetic. I had always secretly wanted to be as *sure* as he seemed to be, instead of faking it as I usually did. His façade never cracked, his good humor rarely faded. "What did *you* find out?"

A shrug, a brief snort of frustration. "Exactly zip. Our Mr. Smith was registered as normal on his datband. He worked as a jeweler, but his birth certificate's vanished and his utility bills were paid by a trust."

I pushed past him, glad the ceiling wasn't lower. "What kind of trust?" I'd bought this house partly because of the crawl space being basement-sized; Doreen hadn't minded as long as it had a garden. It had been abandoned and rundown, but the foundations were sound; we'd celebrated the final round of remodeling by throwing a huge party for the Saint City parapsych community. I'd met Jace at that party, though I hadn't seen him again until after Doreen's murder.

Thinking of that made me shiver again. I quelled the shudder, rubbing my right hand against my ruined skirt. Dried black blood crusted the velvet, scraped against my black-lacquered nails.

"A blind sealed trust. No way of breaking in. The same trust that covered the names of his clients under corporate confidentiality. A full search of public records turned up a big fat nothing except for the name the guy's slicboard was registered to." Jace sounded disgusted.

I found the corner at the far end of the house, under a closet I never used. I stopped, my heart pounding. The left side of the dress's bodice crackled with dried blood as I took in a deep breath. My heart beat thinly. "A jeweler with a slicboard? What name?"

"Keller. Just the one word. No last name. Bought at a dealership out on Lorraine that's since gone out of business." His aura roiled with spikes—Jace didn't like being down here either. I felt the warmth of his body across the air separating us as I turned back to him. The smell of peppered musk and honey was soothing even if it carried the decaying tang of human.

"The plot thickens." My voice shook. I reached for one of the shovels.

"Goddamn thick enough already." Jace shouldered me aside. "Let me, I've been up to my elbows in paper and public records for hours. I could use a little sweat. Where do I dig?"

I pointed at the corner. "Just start going down."

He gave me an extraordinary blue-eyed glance. In this corner of the basement, the light was dim enough that I couldn't see the fine lines beginning at the corners of his eyes and mouth.

Unless I concentrated.

I chose not to. Instead, I watched him drive the shovel down and start to dig. The concrete foundations were very close here. The earth was dusty and pallid. Having nothing else to do, I lowered myself down and sat on the ground, shifting inside my rig until the sword rode comfortably, balancing his scabbarded blade across my knees.

"Jace?"

"Hm?" He tossed another shovelful of dirt with a clean, economical movement.

"Thank you." The words stuck in my throat. As if I could ever thank him for what he was doing right this second, digging so I didn't have to.

"Anytime, baby." Another shovelful of pale dirt and small stones. "What am I digging for?"

"Metal. I buried it deep. Really, I mean it. Thank you."

"You're going to ruin that dress." His muscles flexed under the black T-shirt.

I swallowed copper fear, wished there was more light. Shadows pressed thickly in the corners. "It's already ruined. And I'm never wearing a dress again. If jeans and a Trade Bargains shirt isn't good enough, people can go fuck themselves."

"I've always liked you in jeans. That cute little ass of yours." He was beginning to get serious about digging, breathing deep and loosening up. Starting to sweat, drenching the air with the smell of a clean human male having a good workout.

I shivered, looking up at the ceiling. "I'm sorry." It came out as easy as an apology ever had. Which meant it tore and clawed its way out of my chest while I watched him excavating something I never wanted to see again.

His even rhythm didn't stop, but his shoulders tensed. "For what, baby?"

"I'm not very nice to you." *That's the understatement of the year, isn't it. I'm a right raving bitch to you. You deserve someone who can at least be affectionate.*

If I was telling the truth to myself, I might as well let him in on it.

He was silent for a full three shovelfuls. The hole was beginning to take shape. Chills crawled over my skin. My jaw clenched tight so my teeth wouldn't chatter. "No. You're not." He tossed another shovelful of dirt, didn't look at me.

"You're better than I deserve."

That made him laugh. Jace Monroe had an easy laugh, sometimes used as a shield, sometimes genuine. This one was genuine. "You worry too much, sweetheart. What am I digging for?"

"Metal."

"What's inside?" He was beginning to get a respectable-sized hole. My teeth chattered, since my jaw had unloosed enough to talk. I hugged myself, cupping my elbows in my palms, squeezing, feeling my fingernails poke at my arms. Wished I could go back up into my house and forget about the trapdoor again—bury the memory deeper than I'd buried the rest of everything that had to do with the Hall.

"Books. Other things." I couldn't even pretend to have a steady voice.

"Great. Other people bury bodies, Dante Valentine buries books." He warmed to the work, I could feel the heat coming from him. Human heat, animal heat. Familiar heat.

Why did I feel so guiltily grateful for that warmth? For his mere breathing presence?

"They're going to be useful, Jace." I dropped my head, staring at his sword in my lap. A *dotanuki* instead of the katana I usually carried; he'd had it since I'd met him. A bigger hilt for his bigger hands, more weight, I'd sparred with him before. I'd beaten him even before Japhrimel made me into what I was now. But Jace was dangerous, tricky; he was the type that would take a cheap shot. I used to think it was dishonorable of him.

Now I wasn't so sure.

I trailed my fingers over the hilt-wrapping, catching flashes of

Jace as he handled the blade. There were memories locked in that steel. I tapped the scabbard, touched the hilt again.

"Danny, baby," Jace said, "you keep stroking him like that you're going to give me a hard-on."

I glanced up. He was watching me, leaning on the shovel. His eyes were dark and hot, I didn't need a dictionary to read the look on his face. Jace Monroe had never made any secret about wanting me, which had made his abandonment of me all those years ago so much more shocking. And then, Rio, and now this penance he was paying by staying with me, watching my back, and forcing me to live.

Of all the things I had to be grateful for, Jace was probably the biggest. Who else would have put up with me?

"Sorry." I laid his sword aside. *That's it exactly, Jace. I don't know what would kill me, but I think losing Japhrimel was damn close to it. Did you think I'd hurt myself? Is that why you came back?*

He gave me a brilliant, unsettled smile. *Well, what do you know. Claustrophobia strikes again.* "It's okay. I kind of like it. What did you find at Christabel's? Anything?"

I snorted and hauled myself to my feet, scooping up the other shovel. "Nothing I didn't already know. Let's get to work." And I walked toward my grave with sweating demon hands and a sour stomach.

"Chango love me, girl." Jace used his forearm to wipe sweat from his face. "You buried this fucker *deep*."

"Only way to stop the dead from rising." I tossed the shovel. It was a passionlessly accurate throw, ending with the shovel neatly stowed up on the surface, out of the way. The second shovel followed, its blade chiming against the first. I laced my fingers. "I'll give you ten up and hand it to you."

The deep gloom of the hole meant I saw the gleam of his teeth and the whites of his eyes as he grinned a little too widely. "Sounds good. I need a shower."

"Me too."

He stepped into my fingers and I lifted him easily enough, careful not to overshoot. He caught the edge and levered himself out.

One good thing about demon strength, I never would have been able to do that before.

Then I lifted my coffin, an old-timey footlocker from before the Seventy Days War. Hefted it with more ease than I'd lifted him.

Something chinked inside, and the sound made a cold shiver trace all the way down my spine. I bit back a moan, it died as a strangled gasp.

Jace dragged it up out of the hole. Then I leapt, catching the lip just like the side of a swimtank, hauling myself up. *"Sekhmet sa'es,"* I hissed between my teeth. "I hate this. I just started this hunt and already I'm six feet deep and sinking fast."

"Keep paddling, baby." Jace yawned. "We gonna fill this in?"

"We'd better." I rubbed at my forehead, feeling gritty grave dirt clinging to my skin. "Let's get it over with so we can wash up."

"We could probably use some dinner too." He stretched, then gamely went for the shovels. I laid my hand on his arm.

He went still, looking down at me.

"You go on up, get washed up. Get something to eat. I'll be up in a few." I don't think either of us believed I was dealing with this well.

"I'll help." He shook his golden head, stubborn, his face streaked with dirt.

"Come on, Jace." I took the path of least resistance. "I'm *hungry.* This way, by the time I get up there I can take a shower and eat something. Okay?"

He examined me for a long moment. " 'Kay," he said finally, just like a pouting little boy.

"Thanks." Impulsive, I went up on tiptoe and kissed his dirty cheek. What else can you do for the man that just dug you up out of your grave?

He scooped up his sword. When he was gone the entire cellar seemed to close around me. The darkness seemed full of exhaled danger, my nape prickling, my breath coming short and harsh.

I picked up the shovel, considered it, set it down. The hole mocked me. The dirty, rusty footlocker mocked me. My sword, riding my back, mocked me.

I lifted my right hand. It was actually doing pretty well, not cramping or seizing up. Maybe holding a sword was all it needed.

Instead of using the shovel, I started pushing at the pile of dirt with my bare hands, like an animal. I pushed and pushed, scooping great armloads of sterile earth, shoving it, kicking it. My lips pulled back from my teeth. The dress's bodice, never meant for this sort of treatment, tore. One of the laces snapped, and it took me a few moments to undo my rig and shuck myself out of the dress. Piling my weapons to one side, I tossed the fall of silk and velvet into the hole and continued to fill it in. My new golden skin didn't bruise, but I felt as if it had, all the way down to my bones. My hands shook again, so badly dirt spilled between them, dry pebbles clinking and grinding together. It wasn't until I stamped the earth down with my booted feet that I realized I was making a low throaty noise of rage. My left shoulder throbbed dully and the vanished scars on my back felt as if they'd broken open, bleeding phantom blood. A collage of scars. An art statement made of suffering.

And I *laughed.*

I had, after all, survived everything I'd buried. I had fought so long and so hard, I had taken bounty after bounty, taken on the Prince of Hell himself. What was down here that I needed to be afraid of?

I collapsed on top of the disturbed mound of lifeless dry dirt, laughing until I choked, my knees grating against small pebbles. My teeth clicked together painfully. I hugged myself, bare breasts pressed together, hunching over until I presented a small target. Naked except for my boots, I hugged myself and shook like a rabbit, tasting shock bitter and flat against my tongue as I screamed with dark hilarity.

After all, it was a child's fears I was feeling. There was no longer any need for me to huddle in the corners sobbing, like I used to.

Rigger Hall. Goddamn.

How old did I have to be before the name itself didn't make me shiver? Who did I have to be grateful for—Doreen, who had taught me how to be vulnerable again? Japhrimel, who had taught me that love was not strictly a human phenomenon? Gabe, whose friendship had never wavered? Or Jace, who was still teaching me about who I could trust?

I was grown-up now. Rigger Hall could no longer hurt me.

Then why was the child inside me still screaming? Hadn't I grown past that, fought past it?

It was a long time before I heard footsteps again, Jace's stiff knee giving his gait a familiar hitch. He didn't say a word, I pushed myself up, and thankfully he didn't try to help me, just waited until I got to my feet and offered me a robe I dragged on with shaking hands as I shuddered with tired laughter. I felt like I'd just run through five sparring matches and fought in all three theaters of the Seventy Days War without a break as well.

He'd scrounged a ladder and pushed me up it, then dragged me upstairs. I wasn't unwilling, I just let him lead me. He didn't bother trying to get me in the shower. He just slid the robe off my shoulders and pushed me into bed, worked my boots off, then shucked his clothes, dropped down and held me.

He was not Japhrimel, but he was warm and he was human. I took what comfort he offered gratefully, his naked skin against mine, while every tear I had swallowed during eight years of Rigger Hall broke out of its black box and leaked out of my eyes, shaking me as if an animal made of grief had me in its teeth yet again.

CHAPTER 18

He slept heavily, lying on his side, his face relaxed without its shield of good humor. Dirt smudged his cheekbones and his forehead. His hair was stiff with dry sweat and dust. Grime worked into the small, thin wrinkles that were beginning to etch his flesh, the lines that would grow deeper soon. He *was* getting older. So was Gabe.

I lay on my side, my leg hitched up over his hip. He was sweating, grime clinging to both of us even though I never seemed to sweat; I traced his cheekbone with a gentle fingertip. Black molecule-drip polish glinted in the dim light from the hall.

The curve of his lower lip unreeled below my touch. His breathing didn't alter. He was out cold, it had been a long day. And whatever else he was, Jace was no longer young.

I pressed his hair back, gently. Traced his eyebrow, drew my finger down his cheek, the rough stubble of his chin made my mouth twitch. He smelled of human, of decaying cells and honeyspiked Power, of grave dirt and sweat.

I can't be what he wants, I reminded myself for the thousandth time. *I don't even know what it is he wants.*

Then again, I'd never bothered to ask him, had I?

I took my hand away and moved, slowly, infinitely slowly, until we were chest to chest, my face inches from him. His breath mingled with mine, a heady brew of demon, Necromance, and Shaman.

My lips touched his, a feathery touch.

He exhaled. I shuddered. It wasn't like Japhrimel. It could never be like that again. My skin crawled, remembering the screaming, intense drowning of being clasped in a demon's arms. The loathing wasn't for the memory—it was as if my body revolted at the thought of another lover. Mutiny in my cells.

I was pretty sure I could push that aside; I didn't need to enjoy sex. I'd had plenty of sex without enjoyment; I could probably even fool Jace into believing I was having a great time. I remembered what it was like with him before: sex between us was another form of sparring. A chess match, a game, each touch a challenge, the prize in the other's final abdication of control.

Sex as war, as a game, hadn't it been that way for him? Another question I had never asked.

Would I forget he wasn't Japhrimel once I reached a certain pitch of excitement? If I let myself go, did what I wanted to do, what would it do to Jace? I remembered the blinding pleasure, heart straining, lungs forgetting their function, ecstasy wrapped in barbed wire and rolled across exquisite nerve endings. A form of Tantra, sex magick, reaching into the deepest level of genes and psyche to remake me.

Remake. In whose image?

I hesitated, my lips touching Jace's. Would it kill him? Remake *him?* I doubted it. I had no illusions about the amount of Power I had—not enough to rival Japhrimel even when he had Fallen. And yet the research I'd managed to do between bounties had made me no wiser about the exact limits of what I was. I probably wouldn't change him into anything, but I didn't *know.* I knew nothing.

I knew nothing, and I couldn't betray Japhrimel. It was an impossible situation. I needed Jace. I wanted to be kind to him, I had a debt to repay to him and one to collect, and yet...

My shields quivered, shuddering restlessly. Someone was coming in on a slicboard, coming in fast, and the quick brush against my shields was familiar, garden dirt and the smell of beer and sweat.

I'd expected him to drop by.

I was up and out of the bed in one motion, grabbing a handful of neatly folded clothes as I ran for the bathroom. It was 3:00 AM, late afternoon for most of us who lived on the night side, and I felt him slide through my shields as I ducked into the shower and twisted the knob all the way over to "cold" as a penance.

It took a little longer than I liked to scrub the grime off, but when I came downstairs, braiding my hair back the way I used to, he hadn't come in past my front hall. I stopped at the end of the hall next to the stairs and took him in.

Eddie slumped against the wall, fingers tapping his staff. There were only three people that could key in through my shields like that: Jace, Gabe, Eddie. Anyone else attempting entry would be denied, whether by the security system or by the cloak of Power over my house, the triple layer of shielding. I realized with an abrupt jolt that I was lucky to have three people I could let into my home with no question. Three... friends, people who went into danger for me when they didn't have to.

The net of obligation and duty might trap me, but it also protected me and kept me from falling into an abyss. Which abyss I couldn't quite say, but I had felt its cold breath enough to suddenly be very grateful for the man sleeping upstairs, the woman who had pulled me into this, and Eddie in my front hall.

Shaggy blond Eddie of the hulking shoulders and long hair, the smell of fresh dirt hanging on him like it did on every Skinlin dirt-witch berserker. He seemed to carry a perpetual cloud of shambling earthsmell with him, his blunt fingers seeming too indelicate for any fine work. For all that, Eddie was the most dangerous dirtwitch I'd ever met in a sparring match.

I guess he had to be, to keep up with Gabe.

He wore a long camel-colored coat and a *Boo Phish Ranx* T-shirt strained on his massive hairy chest. I studied him for a moment. He stared back, meeting my eyes for once. Shifting his weight from foot to foot, tapping his staff with callused fingertips, his aura roiling, he made the house shields quiver and my own defenses go tense and crystalline. "Eddie."

"Danny." He lifted one shoulder, dropped it. "Guess you wanna ask me a few."

I shrugged. "Why, you know something?" He said nothing, and my conscience pinched me hard. "Not if you don't want to talk," I amended. It was the least I could give him; the gods knew *I* didn't want to talk about the Hall. An act of mercy, not requiring of him what I wouldn't want to do myself.

But Eddie wouldn't be here if he didn't have vital information. And if it would stop another death, he would force himself through it.

He was as cottage-cheese pale as I'd ever seen him. "Dunno if it's useful, but you better hear it."

I nodded. "Let me get my sword."

"Time was you would'n answer the door without it."

Time was I wouldn't have let even you or Gabe key in through my shields and use the key to my front door, Eddie m'man. Guess I've grown up. "Someone would have to be pretty fucking stupid to come in here and start trouble. If they could get in at all without my approval."

"So you got another sword?" He lifted one shaggy eyebrow. For him that passed as tact; he must have been taking lessons from Gabe.

"Figured it was time I stopped fucking around."

"Amen to *that*," he sniffed.

Dear old Eddie, always dependable. I was Gabe's friend, therefore I was—no matter how sarcastic he got—worthy. That was the thing about Eddie Thornton, if you were all right in Gabe's book, Eddie would go to the wall for you. There was no deception in him, no subterfuge. Either you were worth his support, or he would cut you loose. He had no middle ground.

Gods above, but that was refreshing.

I took Fudoshin down from the peg where my old sword had hung. My bag was already slung diagonally across my body, I shrugged into my coat. "My slic's outside with Jace's. Let's go."

CHAPTER 19

We went to the old noodle shop on Pole Street. It was absurdly fitting. The place hadn't changed a bit, from the dusty red velour hanging on the walls to the old Asiano man sitting in the back booth slurping his tea and eyeing everyone suspiciously, a curl of synth-hash smoke drifting up from his ashtray. Two bowls of beef pho later, I was beginning to feel a little less raw.

"Okay." I grabbed a hunk of rice noodles with plasilica chopsticks. Eddie sucked at his beer and blinked at me.

The fishtank in the back of the store gurgled softly.

I took the mouthful of noodles, slurped it down. Beef broth splashed. I had to suppress a small sound of delight—eating was the only thing that gave me any pleasure anymore. Thank the gods I had a hiked metabolism, or I'd be as fat as a New Vietkai whore.

Well, I got enjoyment from hunting down bounties too. But it wasn't a clean enjoyment. Each bounty was a brick in the wall between me and the uncomfortable thoughts that rose when I had too much time on my hands.

Eating, however, was all mine. I didn't have to think while I ate.

"You're still a goddam pig." Eddie grimaced.

"Says the man who eats with his fucking fingers?" I fired back. "Spill, Eddie. I left a warm bed for this."

"How warm?" He smirked through blond-brown stubble. "Jace finally tie you up? Or did he put on horns and a pitchfork?"

I laid my chopsticks down. It had taken me a year to learn to eat with my left hand wielding the silverware. Now my right hand felt clumsy, as if all it wanted to do was curl around a swordhilt. "That's *one,* Edward." My tone made my teacup rattle against the table. "Now why don't you quit being an asshole and tell me what you've got?"

"I might know something." He went even paler, if that was possible. Looked down at the table. Gulped at his beer. I suddenly longed to get drunk. This would be so much fucking *easier* with chemical enhancement.

I picked up the thick, white china teacup. Said nothing.

He squeezed his eyes shut. His hand trembled as he set his glass down. "I was there," he mumbled. "Rigger Hall."

I'd known that, of course. He'd been a few classes ahead of me.

Like Christabel.

Great beads of sweat stood out on his forehead. "There was...a secret." His throat worked, his Adam's apple bobbing. "I don't know much, but..."

Rigger Hall was full of secrets, Eddie. I felt the glowing metal pressed against my skin again, heard Mirovitch's papery voice. Cleared my throat, set my teacup down. "Eddie..." My voice was harsh, harsher than it had to be. The glass of beer rang uneasily. *I have got to get some kind of control over myself.* My left shoulder burned dully as if in agreement. *"Anubis et'her ka,* don't do this to yourself."

His eyes flew open. "You don't tell me what I do or don't gotta do," he growled, leaning back. "I can't go home, I can't fuckin sleep, and people are *dying.* I got to get this done."

I shrugged. My heart beat thinly under my ribs, hammering with impatience and adrenaline combined. Picked up my teacup again.

He took another long gulp of beer. "'S a wonder anyone made it out. I wasn't in it, not the Black Room."

I shuddered. His eyes flew open, as wide as I'd ever seen them. "No, not *that* one," he hurriedly amended. "No, that was the name of the Secret. 'Cause they met in that old shed off the lake. You remember?"

I nodded. Christabel's ghostly screaming rang inside my head, I pushed it away. "I remember." Cold sweat lay on my skin. *Black Room, remember Rigger Hall. That's what Christabel meant.*

His eyes were the eyes of a child reliving a nightmare. "You was in the cage?"

He meant the Faraday cage in the sensory deprivation vault under the school. It had been intended to help telepaths who needed a short-term respite from their gifts. Instead, it had been turned into a punishment. Psions—especially strong ones—can only stand a cage for a very short time before their psyches begin to crack under the lack of stimulation. If you weren't a telepath seeking relief, being in a cage was like being trapped in a black void—no light, no sound, and no access to the ambient Power that fed magickal and psychic talent. It is the closest thing to insanity I had ever known, and I still couldn't step into an elevator without shaking and feeling the walls close in. The cage of an elevator or hoverlift was uncomfortably similar to the cage of Mirovitch's Black Room. "Four times," I replied, husky.

"I had two. Two was enough."

"*Never* would have been enough," I forced out past teeth clenched so tightly my jaw hurt. *If it was before Rio, would I shatter my own teeth and swallow them?* The thought of the sensory-deprivation vault and the cage, and the *blackness* rising through me to eat at the very foundations of my mind—"*Sekhmet sa'es,* Eddie..." I swallowed dryly several times, my throat clicking. *Got to get control. Goddammit, Danny, get a hold on yourself!*

"The secret...Christabel was one a 'em. I wasn', but I got friendly wi' one."

I waited. He would come to it in his own time. The least I could do was give him a few minutes to work up to saying whatever he had to say.

"Steve Sebastiano," he said finally. Was he *blushing?*

Now I had officially seen everything.

My jaw dropped. "You got friendly with *Polyamour?*" Polyamour the transvestite, one of the most famous sexwitches in the world? The sexwitch rumored to be so fantastic in bed that Hegemony heads and even some paranormals paid just to call on her socially? Her house took a healthy chunk of cash just to be put on the waiting list. Polyamour, who used to be Steven Sebastiano, a few classes ahead of me and already the source of whispers and rumor at school. I heard she'd been tutored by Persephone Dragonfly down in Norleans at the Great Floating House, and done an internship in Paradisse as part of an exchange program.

And one of her sexwitches had been a victim. The piece fell into place neatly, and I felt the little click of intuition inside my skull.

The first link in the chain, the first arc of the pattern, was always the hardest. It would only get quicker from here.

Thank the gods. I don't think I can stand to look at another dead body.

Eddie shrugged, looking down into his half-empty glass. "We was roommates. Bastian was one of Mirovitch's sexwitch stable. Fucked him up royal."

A sexwitch in Rigger Hall? "Fucked up" would be an understatement. "I'll bet. So what happened?"

Eddie's sleepy hazel eyes were haunted, no longer the eyes of a fully grown man. Instead, they were the deep wells of pain in the face of a terrified child.

I didn't need a mirror to tell me my own eyes were just as dark. Just as wide, and just as deep—and just as agonized.

"Mirovitch," I persisted, my throat dry and tight. "Who did him in?"

The Skinlin shrugged. "I dunno. I just know Bastian was in it with Christabel. They had code words."

"Like what?"

"*Tig vedom deum.*" Eddie took down the rest of his beer in two long drafts. He was sweating. I could smell the fear on him, rank and thick and human. Was it any consolation that my own fear now smelled like light cinnamon and musk?

My left shoulder began to throb again, evenly, almost comfortingly. "Part of the Nine Canons. Second canto, line four." I shifted on the vinyl bench, looking down at the remains of my second bowl of soup. *I've lost my appetite. Go figure.* "For sealing a spirit in its grave."

"And for short-circuiting a Feeder." Eddie's bushy eyebrows drew together. He glared at the table as if it had personally offended him.

"Any truth to the rumor that one of the students was a Feeder?" *And why would that have jackshit to do with these murders? Miro-vitch is dead. The Hall's closed down.*

"I dunno, Danny." He looked miserable. I didn't blame him.

"There's a lot of shit you don't know." Frustration turned my voice sharp and angular. My teacup rattled slightly, I took a deep breath. Power swirled the air in lazy waving tendrils.

If I didn't know better, I'd say it's gotten stronger. I've gotten stronger.

I shoved that thought as far away as it would go. I didn't need another problem.

His eyes flickered up to my face, slid away. He could barely stand to look at my new face, and my heart squeezed inside my chest. "Don't ride my ass, Danny. I've given you all I got. Now go and get this thing done so I can go home and sleep again."

"Why are you afraid? You weren't part of it."

He shrugged. "Don't look like this thing's too fuckin selective, if it'll kill a normal."

Thank you, Eddie. I realized that was precisely what was bothering me. Why would whoever-it-was kill a normal to start off with? Unless it was practice, a dry run—but that didn't seem too likely. Once you've mastered Feeder glyphs and enough power to charge a Ceremonial Magick circle, dry runs lose their usefulness. The higher up you go, the more everything depends on Working perfectly under pressure—getting it right enough to work the first time.

"Unless the normal wasn't so normal." But the coroner's scans would have caught it, if he'd been a psion. I stared at my water glass, my index finger tracing a glyph on the table. A loose, spiked, fluid, twisting glyph in another magickal language.

A glyph scored into my own flesh. If I kept tracing it, fiddling with it, would I eventually get an answer? A whole year of longing hadn't brought me anything but grief.

Quit daydreaming, Danny. "What are you aiming at, Eddie?"

"Seems like someone's cleaning up some loose ends, don't it? I called Bastian. He'll see you soon as you want." Eddie sank down further in his seat, studying me. "You lookin' better, girl."

"Thanks." I don't think my tone could have been any drier or more ironic. "You got me a personal interview with Polyamour? Just how friendly *were* you?"

There it was again, that flush. I never thought I'd live to see Eddie acting like a blushing teener. I'd planned on interviewing Polyamour anyway, but having an introduction would make it much easier.

"Friendly 'nuff." Eddie reached for the second full glass of beer, downed it in one long gulp, his throat working; smacked it back down with a little more force than necessary. He looked at the two empty steins with a mournful expression, his lips pulled down and his sleepy eyes pupil-dilated and dark under his frowsty, bushy blond hair.

"You want another one?" My tone was uncharacteristically gentle.

"No. Danny..." He trailed off, tapped his blunt fingertips on the table.

"What?" I had, for the first time ever since Japhrimel altered me, lost my appetite. I pushed the remains of the second bowl of beef pho away. Took a drink of tea.

"Nothin. Just...be careful."

I let out a short bark of a laugh. "Since when have I ever been careful, Eddie?" *I never would have guessed Eddie knew the most famous transvestite sexwitch in the western half of the Hegemony well enough to get me an immediate interview. Wonders never cease in this wide, wide world.*

"You mighta been once or twice. When you was young." Eddie's lips pulled back in a brave attempt at a smile.

"Maybe. When I was young." I set my teacup down, extended my hand over the table. "Eddie? Thanks. It..." The words failed me. If I still had nightmares about Rigger Hall, he probably did too.

And if my reaction to having the Hall resurrected were enough to make me laugh like a crazed lunatic into the dirt under my own home, what was Eddie going through? Hadn't we suffered enough, both of us?

"Yeah I did." Eddie looked at my hand. His eyes flicked back up to my face; he extended his own hand, touched fingertips with me. His Adam's apple bounced as he swallowed, convulsively. "I got to be able to sleep again, Danny."

It was the first time he had ever voluntarily touched me. We are skittish about being touched, we psions.

My throat was dry.

I swallowed, and I spoke my promise. "I'll catch him, Eddie. Or her. Whoever's doing this. I swear it."

He snatched his fingertips away. "Yeah. You do that. Word of advice? When you do catch 'em, don't bring 'em back alive. Anything to do wit' Rigger Hall is better dead."

You better believe it, Eddie. "Including us?" I sounded wistful, not at all like my usual self.

Eddie moved, sliding his legs out of the booth and standing up. He tapped at his datband, then looked down at me. "Sometimes I think so." His eyes were still haunted wells. "Then I look at Gabe, and I ain't so sure."

I found nothing to say to that. Eddie stumped away toward the door, and I let him go. I touched my own datband, and found out he'd paid for my dinner.

Nice of him. *Oh, Eddie.*

I sighed and took one last mouthful of tea, rolling it around in my mouth to wash away the taste of fear before swallowing. It would take something stronger than tea to get that taste off my tongue, though.

CHAPTER 20

I came in the back way, dropping into my backyard with a whine and a rattle. My board needed servicing. The media vans sat squat and dark at my gate, bristling with fiberoptics and satellite dishes to catch footage if I ever came in through the front door. I toyed with the idea of giving a press conference. It wouldn't help anything, but it would put off what I had to do next.

I let myself in the back door. Jace looked up and yawned, pulling his T-shirt down and buttoning his jeans. His golden hair was mussed, sticking up in all directions, but at least he was clean. "Hey, baby. What did Eddie have to say?"

I shook my head. "Got any coffee? We're going to Polyamour's as soon as possible."

His mouth curled into a grin. "I didn't think you liked bought sex, sweets. And I didn't think a fempersonator was your type."

I made a face at him before I could help myself, sticking my tongue out. He laughed, blue eyes dancing, and I was surprised by the way my heart squeezed down on itself. "Turns out Eddie knows her. They were chums at school. And Poly might know something about this group of students that took Mirovitch down." *I guess that wasn't a rumor after all. I wonder what else wasn't a rumor?*

"Good." He poured me coffee, brought it over. I folded my hands around the cup, grateful for the warmth; both of the cup, and of his concern. "Do you think that's what happened?" Carefully-reined curiosity sparkled behind his eyes.

"It's as good a place as any to start, it's our first break. Eddie's nervous, says if the murderer started with a normal then he obviously isn't too picky about his prey." I stared down into the thick black liquid. I liked Jace's coffee. He was the only one who made it strong enough.

"I know that look." He leaned hipshot against the kitchen counter, cocking his head. Breathless morning darkness pressed against the kitchen window. "What are you thinking, Danny?"

What doesn't bother me about this? It's going too slow. I should have latched onto something before this. "Something about that normal bothers me. Why would he have a sealed trust? Why would he have shields? It doesn't make any *sense*."

He nodded, tapping his fingers against his swordhilt. Took a gulp of his coffee, made a face as if he'd burned himself. "Yeah, it's weird. And who is this Keller?"

I shrugged. "Maybe Polyamour can tell us."

"You want me to go with you?" He didn't sound surprised, but he did arch one eyebrow. He took another long draft from his coffee cup and grimaced. If it didn't hurt going down, it didn't feel like real coffee to him.

"Sure. I hear Poly likes pretty boys." I caught myself smiling, tilting my head slightly to the side and regarding him. "She might tell you more than she tells me."

"You're using me for my looks." He mock-pouted.

"I guess so. Does that bother you?" The smile felt natural, so natural the corners of my eyes crinkled.

"Naw." His grin answered mine, widened. "I kind of like it."

The footlocker lay silently in the middle of the living room, dusty with sterile earth. I took a deep breath, regarding it from the doorway the way a mongoose might stare at a particularly poisonous cobra. Jace, behind me, didn't ask what was in it.

I'd waited for false dawn, pearly gray light beginning to flower through the windows. The upswing of hovertraffic buzzed in the distance; Saint City's heartbeat quickened slightly, shaking off dreaming and getting ready for the day. I still waited, watching the gray metal as if it would sit up and accuse me. Jace was absolutely still at my shoulder, obviously curious, wanting to ask, not daring to.

Why was this so hard? I had grown past Rigger Hall. Hadn't I?

I was beginning to think I wasn't as far past it as I had hoped.

I glanced at the tapestry on the west wall. Isis's arms were crossed protectively, and Horus's ferocious Eye gazed serene and deadly. The gods were not actively involved... but their backs were not turned either. Whatever I did, they would witness.

That's not as comforting as it could be. I finally took a deep breath. Both my fieldstone altar and my main altar were humming with Power, and the house shields were thick and carefully laid. Nothing could harm me here. This was my home, my sanctuary.

Nothing in there can hurt me now. I swallowed dryly, heard my throat click. The locker's closed metal face taunted me. *Yeah. Right.*

My left shoulder burned steadily. It felt as if the ropy scar was pulsing, sliding against itself, straining. I took the first step into the room and approached the footlocker cautiously, placing each footfall carefully, as if I was on unsteady ground.

I sank down beside it on the hardwood floor, my knee on the thick, patterned rug I used for meditation. I had to remind myself to breathe. The padlock—I used a bit of Power, and it clicked open with a sound like a frozen corpse's jaws wrenching open.

My teeth chattered until I clenched them together. *Strong,* I told myself. *I am strong. I survived this.* I laid the padlock aside and opened the top slowly, hearing dirt caught in the unoiled hinges squeal like a scream.

"Valentine, D. Student Valentine is called to the Headmaster's office immediately."

The bright eyes of the kids in my class, all solemn and horrified and squeamishly glad their name hadn't been called. Woodenly reaching my feet, setting my battered Magickal Theory textbook aside; the teacher's—Embrose Roth, a Ceremonial and one of the worse at the Hall—ratty little face gleaming with curiosity, mousy hair pulled up in a tight bun, aura geometric and cold blue. Roth staring at my back as I trudged to the door, her attention like the filthy prick of a rat's claws against my nape.

Squeaking of my shoes against the stairs in the main hall, heading to the Headmaster's office; the collar far too heavy on my neck.

Frantically trying to remember an excuse, any excuse, that would keep me from being beaten or worse.

At Rigger Hall it was likely to be worse.

My fingers trembled, my nails scraping against the metal as I pushed it all the way open.

"Chango, Danny," Jace breathed. "You're pale. You don't have to do this."

Yes, I do. I looked down.

There, laid on top, was the collar, a curve of dark metal.

Waves of shudders rippled down my back. My shoulder burned, a fierce pain I was glad of. It kept me anchored. I'd faced worse than this, hadn't I? I'd killed Santino. I'd faced down the Devil himself.

I didn't have anything to fear from the detritus of my past. I denied the trembling that rose up in me.

"That's a collar." I heard the fear under Jace's heartbeat.

Every psion hates the thought of collars. They're supposed to protect the normals from us, but the deadheads are not the ones who need protection. They are in the majority, no matter how many holovids have psions in their storylines. They make the rules, and those of us with Talent have to dance to their tune. Collars make them feel better, sure.

But there's only so much of being collared a human being can take.

"Shut up, Jace." My voice trembled, but it still sliced the air. The house shields went hard and crystalline, on the verge of locking down as if I was under attack.

I blew out a long breath, tried to make my shoulders a little less tense.

The arc of dull dark metal with circuit etching on one side was dead and quiescent. Without a power-pack and the school security net, it was useless. Still, I handled it as if it was live, flipping out a knife and using the bright blade to lift it, laying it aside. I still remembered the hideous jolts—with a collar live and locked on, a psi couldn't protect herself. It short-circuited most types of Power; the teachers had controls to change the settings in order for the students to practice. The principle behind collars was to keep a psion from harming anyone while she learned to control her gifts.

I suppose it was a good idea—but like all good ideas, someone had found a way to make it go horribly wrong. When a collar was live, a plasgun shock administered from a prod hurt like hell, burning through every nerve, as if you were being electrocuted. It didn't leave much in the way of permanent scarring—not on the outside, anyway.

Underneath was a pad of dirty green cloth, rough synthwool cut from an institutional bedspread in the long, low girl's dormitory. I flipped that aside, keeping one eye nervously on the collar.

My last school uniform. Plaid skirt, the white cotton blouse dingy with age, knee-socks, the heavy shoes I had always hated. The navy synthwool blazer with the crest of Rigger Hall worked in gold thread. I'd put the other five uniforms into an incinerator, but this one was the one I was wearing when the Hegemony had finished the inquiry and pronounced Mirovitch posthumously guilty. After the inquiry, we were free to wear normal clothes, and the Hall was visited by social workers every week. The psis were uncollared for visits with their social workers, and surprise inspections became the rule. The new Headmistress, Stabenow, had supervised the closing of the school after my class graduated. The younger students had scattered to other Hegemony schools, hopefully better-policed.

I lifted each item out reverently and laid it aside, still neatly folded. Jace was completely silent.

Tears welled up. I denied them, pushed them down. Invoked anger instead, a thin unsteady anger that at least did not choke me.

Under the uniform, books. Schoolbooks, mostly, each with their brown-paper cover decorated with glyphs done in pen, numbers, notes. And eleven slender books bound in maroon plasleather, with gold-foil lettering on the side.

Yearbooks.

I lifted them out carefully. Some junk jewelry and a threadbare teddy bear were wedged into the remaining space; the teddy's plastic eyes glinted at me.

Lewis had given me the teddy.

I survived, goddammit. I survived because I was strong enough to put this behind me, strong enough to go into Death itself. Don't start feeling sorry for yourself, Dante Valentine. Pull yourself together and do what has to be done, like you've done all your life. Do this. You will only have to do this once.

I decided I could look at this just once. Just this once. I was strong enough for that. I swallowed bile. My rings sparked and swirled uneasily. The mark on my shoulder crunched with pain. I inhaled, smelling dust and must and old things. Felt the phantom blood drip down my back again.

In the very bottom of the locker was the only thing I've ever stolen without being paid to do so. It was a long flexible whip, real leather, with a small metal fléchette at the tip. It was still crusted with rusting stains.

Bloodstains.

Jace exhaled sharply as I touched the whip with one finger. The shock jolted up my arm—pain, fear, sick excitement. I snatched my hand away.

"Roanna," I whispered. "She was *sedayeen*. She tried to tell her social worker what was happening at the Hall, but the bastard wouldn't believe a kid and had a nice little conference with the Headmaster." My voice was flat, barely stirring the air. "Mirovitch whipped her almost to death and then signed the papers to make her a breeder. She committed suicide—threw herself on the fencing with her collar turned all the way up."

"Danny..." He sounded like he'd been punched.

I ran the back of my hand over my cheek, bared my teeth as if I was facing a fight. I stacked the schoolbooks on top of the whip, pushed the teddy back in his place, then put the uniform and the sheet of green cloth back. I used a knifeblade to lift the collar up, laid it on top. Closed the top, wincing as the hinges squealed, and let out an unsteady barking breath that sounded like a sob. I flipped the padlock up and jammed it closed, the small click sounding very loud in the stillness. I resheathed my knife and slid my hands under the stack of eleven yearbooks. "Clear off the table in the dining room, will you?" I gained my feet and turned around, the negligible weight of the books in my arms seeming much heavier.

Jace's face was set and white, his mouth a thin line. His eyes burned. Fury boiled in the air around him, his aura hardspiked and crystalline. Despite that, his tone was dead-level. Calm. "They did that to you. Didn't they? I always wondered who made you so afraid."

Afraid? That puzzled me. It wasn't in me to be afraid, was it? I was supposed to *fight*. The classics Lewis had poured into me had taught me that much: the only way to kill your fears was to fight them. *Be as frightened as you want,* Lewis's voice whispered in my head. *Then do what you have to do. That's what he's saying here, in this passage.*

"I got whipped once. Put in the cage four times. B-branded. I was lucky it wasn't more." *Lucky nothing happened that broke me. Nothing big. Nothing I couldn't handle, Jace.*

"Lucky." His aura flushed with fury. "Danny—"

"Clear off a space on the table, Jace. The sooner we get this done, the sooner I can bury this again." *And by the grace of Anubis, I can't* wait *to bury this again.*

He stared at me for a few more moments, jaw working, then turned on his bootheel and stalked away soundlessly. I knew that set to his shoulders, the controlled angry grace. Jace was *furious.* I had only seen him in a rage twice, but both times had given me a healthy respect for his anger. I wondered if I was going to see it again, hoped not.

If he went nova I might draw steel on him, and I didn't quite trust myself with edged metal right now.

I carried the books into the dining room. He moved jerkily, clearing a space on the table. Other texts on demonology and basic Magi theory, drifts of paper where I'd made notes, and the talismans Jace had been working on—he stacked them all to the side, and I put the eleven yearbooks down. Blew out a heavy breath.

"Who are we looking for?" He set a four-book set of Tierley's *Democria Demontia* on one of the chairs with excessive delicate care. I picked up a piece of fine parchment, a twisted glyph that was Japhrimel's name branded into my shoulder repeated over and over again in different permutations. I hadn't even realized I was doodling it.

I cleared my throat, suddenly more grateful for his presence than ever. I had to force myself to speak quietly. "Well, after we visit Polyamour we'll have some more names. But I want to find out if Christabel's class had anyone named Keller. Can you get my bag and your datpilot? I want to see if there are any Ceremonials in town."

"Hm. Why Ceremonials? You're thinking they might have a connection to this?"

Ceremonial magicians weren't as rare as Necromances or as common as Shamans. They worked with the Nine Canons and the Seven Seals, charging and containing Power in objects, working with talismans, and providing permanent defenses for corporations, not to mention doing theoretical work and research into magick and the science of Power. Most teachers and trainers were Ceremonial magicians.

But there was a simpler reason why I wanted to find out who was in town. I met his worried blue eyes and gave him a smile that didn't feel natural at all. "I want to find out if any of them have gone Feeder."

Because, out of all psions, it was the Ceremonials—those who dealt with the theory of containing Power—who most often turned Feeder in adulthood. And if we had a Ceremonial on our hands who had gone Feeder and was hunting down former Rigger Hall students, the whole city's collection of psions would have to be alerted.

I would need all the help I could get.

CHAPTER 21

We were into the third book when the phone rang. I stretched and yawned while I padded into the kitchen. Jace tapped another name into his datpilot, glancing up briefly as I passed him. Late-morning light glowed in the windows. I leaned a hip against the counter and picked the phone up. " 'Lo."

A click and a pause, as if the call was on relays. My spine went cold, as if my body recognized the truth before I did.

"Dante Valentine. It is a singular pleasure to speak to you again."

My entire body turned to ice. There was only one being in the entire goddamn world that could strangle me with fear in just two sentences.

The voice was smooth as silk, persuasive, crawling into my head. My phone had no vidshell, for which I was now doubly grateful. If I had to face down the Prince of Hell again, even over a holovid shell, I wasn't sure I would come away from the experience quite sane.

The letter. I'd chucked it into the garbage. I owed him nothing. There was no reason for the Prince of Hell to want to talk to me. I'd done what he wanted, and I'd paid the price. I had screamed as Japhrimel turned to ash in my arms. Wasn't he happy? Wasn't that *enough?*

Why would the Devil call me on the *phone* instead of sending another demon to collect me if he wanted me? He'd done it before, sending Japhrimel and asking me to hunt down Santino, perfectly aware I had my own reasons for wanting that bastard dead.

Anubis protect me. The jolt of fear that smashed through my throat tasted like iron. *What if Lucifer is involved with the murders?*

My entire body went cold. My throat was dry. My hand tightened, digging clawlike fingernails into the countertop. Ceramic screeched under the pressure of my fingers, claws springing free and dimpling the tough tiles. "I can't say the same," I husked, my throat burning with the memory of the Devil's hand crushing my larynx. "What the hell do *you* want? Leave me alone."

"Polite as ever." Lucifer's voice held a weight of amusement I wasn't sure I ever wanted to hear again. "I must speak with your lover, and I am unable to contact him in the usual manner. You will not respond to my missives. Therefore, I am forced to use the human channels of communication."

What the motherfucking hell is he talking about? My lover? Has Lucifer been spying on me? My entire body flushed hot, then cold again; my nipples drawing up, my skin going cold and tight as an icy glove.

"Is this some kind of joke?" I could actually *feel* my temper grow thin and brittle, rage rising to wash away sick, deadening fear. "I don't have time for this, *Lucifer.* You killed Japhrimel, you bastard *demon;* are you calling to remind me? You think I'm going to hand Jace over to you? Get a *life.*" *And he's not my lover either. Though that's none of your goddamn business, is it, you sack of diseased shit.* The cupboards rattled as my voice turned sharp and cool, Power spiking under the harsh, throaty croak.

But the suspicion, once voiced, wouldn't go away. *Oh, my dear sweet fucking gods, is Lucifer involved in this?* My entire body turned to ice. A solid block of ice.

If this was something to do with demons, I was dead in the water. But Christabel's body had held no hint of demon, no scent of spice and dark flame.

There was a pause. "Can it be you have not resurrected him?" The Prince of Hell actually — chalk one up for me — sounded shocked.

I seem to have a habit of nonplussing demons.

My voice was a choked whisper. "Resurrected?" What the hell did *that* mean? Jace wasn't dead. And if I could have resurrected Japhrimel, I would have already done it.

Then I shook myself. Demons lied. The Prince of Hell was no exception. So he'd sent me a little love note, and now he was graduating to obscene phone calls. I had no fucking time for this, not when I was trying to deal with every goddamn ghost from my childhood trying to climb up through the floor and throttle me.

"Go away," I enunciated clearly through the scratching in my throat. "You don't need me, I'm not your errand-girl anymore. Japhrimel is dead, you can't hurt *him* anymore. You're just lucky I don't come after you for kidnapping Eve. Now if you'll *excuse* me, I have real work to do and a killer to catch." I slammed the phone down so hard the tough plasteel base cracked.

I wanted to pick it up again, see if he was still on the line. I wanted to scream, I wanted to dial the operator. *Hello, Vidphone Central? Hook me up to Hell. Tell the Devil he can have me, if he just brings Japhrimel back. Tell him I'll do anything he wants, if I don't have to face this alone.*

Then welcome fury crawled up between the words. *Tell him, while you're at it, that if he's involved with this he'd better say his prayers. Because he's meddled in my life one too many times, and if he's killing Necromances in my city I'm going to see how much demonic flesh my blade can carve. We're even, sure, but I have a score to settle with you, Lucifer Iblis.*

Despite my brave words, I couldn't rescue Doreen's daughter. I stared at the phone, longing to reach through and throttle the Prince of Hell. Why call me now? He'd left me to rot in Rio, stewing in the aftermath of Japhrimel's death and savage guilt that I hadn't been able to save Eve. The fact that Eve was a demon Androgyne—a child I had no hope of raising—didn't salve the ache. Doreen's ghost had asked me to save her, and I'd tried.

Tried and failed. Lucifer had Eve now. That I'd had no hope of fighting the Devil to keep him away from her didn't ease my conscience one iota.

Failed. Just like with Japhrimel, lying dead on the white marble plaza under the hammerblow of Nuevo Rio sun, dead and gone. I kept my hand away from the mark on my shoulder only with a titanic effort of will that left me shaking, sweat for once springing up along my scalp and the curve of my lower back.

I drove my teeth into my lower lip, the sweet jolt of pain shocking me back into some sort of rational frame of mind. Too bad rational never worked where demons were concerned. *Stop it. You don't owe the Devil jackshit, you're free. He can't hurt you now.*

That was a lie. The Devil could hurt me plenty if he bestirred himself to do it.

"Danny?" Jace, from the dining room.

I backed away from the phone, eyeing it as if it would rise up and strike me. Given what I knew of demons, it was a distinct possibility.

"Danny? Who is it?"

I cleared my throat. "Wrong number," I called back, my voice as harsh as if Lucifer had just half-strangled me again. *The same wrong number that sent a letter I never let you see.*

Silence. I glared at the phone, daring it to ring again.

It didn't.

Leave me alone. Leave Jace alone, leave my city alone. You killed Japhrimel and stole Eve, you leave me alone or so help me, I will...

What could I do? A big fat nothing. Fat gooseflesh rose rough on my arms, bumps struggling up under golden skin. I took a deep, racking breath in. I couldn't worry about demons now too. *Let's just hope he was playing with me, what do you say, Danny? Just torturing the human, making sure I still know who's boss. Who's keeping an eye on my life in case he needs a goddamn hand puppet again.*

Finally, my shoulders dropped slightly. Why would Lucifer pick *now* to start playing mind-games on me again? I hadn't done any divination for a week or so, but even when I had, there had been no whisper of demons in my cards.

Then again, last time there hadn't been any warning either. And the letter, with its fat blood-red seal...

Don't think like that, Danny. You're going to get paranoid, and paranoid is exactly what you do not need. Paranoid people don't think clearly.

Despite the fact that paranoid people usually survived better than the foolhardy, I told myself sardonically. Besides, if Lucifer thought he could use me again, he was going to have another think coming. A long, hard think, preferably a painful one.

"Danny, I think I have something," Jace called.

I swallowed, my throat clicking. Turned away.

The phone rang again. Twice. Three times.

No. My hands shook.

"Danny?" Scrape of a chair, Jace was getting to his feet.

I scooped the phone up, pale crimson fury spilling through the trademark sparkles of a Necromance in my aura. "Look, you son of a bitch—" I began, the cupboards chattering open and closed, a mug falling from a rack and hitting the wooden floor with a tinkling crash.

"Danny?" It was Gabe. "What the hell? Are you okay?"

I swallowed. Jace skidded into the room, his guns out. "I'm fine," I said to both of them. My throat was full of scorching sand. "What's up, Spooky?"

"Saddle up, I've got another body." Gabe was trying to sound flip and hard, but her voice shook. I could almost see her pale cheeks, the trembling around her mouth.

"Where?" I shook my head at Jace, whose hands blurred, spinning the guns back into their holsters. He scanned the room, then stared at me, the question evident in his blue eyes.

"Corner of Fourth and Trivisidero, the brick house with the holly hedges." No wonder Gabe sounded uncomfortable—that was precious close to her own home. "Get here quick, we're holding the scene for you."

"I'll be there in ten." I dropped the phone back into its cradle. "Let's go, Jace."

"You might want to take a look at this first. Are you all right?" His eyes dropped from me to the shattered mug on the floor. Shards of ceramic dust—my anger and fear had shattered the mug, ground into it, compounding injury with insult. It was the blue Baustoh mug.

The one Jace liked, the one Japhrimel had chosen for his use the only time he'd drunk coffee in my house.

Anubis et'her ka. I didn't want to think about it.

"What have you got?" I rubbed delicately at my throat with my fingertips, my nails pricking, claws threatening to spring free. My right hand actually *itched* for my swordhilt, and the sensation was so eerie I almost couldn't feel relieved that it wasn't cramping.

"It occurred to me to look at the last yearbook that listed Mirovitch as Headmaster, the year he died. Guess who was on the Student Yearbook Committee?" Jace looked up from the glossy blue shards of ceramic, and the question in his eyes remained unspoken. I was grateful for that, more grateful than I ever thought I would be to him.

"Who?"

"Christabel Moorcock."

CHAPTER 22

I suppose we had to give the reporters something; besides, it was too hard to talk while on slicboards with the wind rattling and howling around us. So we took the hovercar. The flashes from pictures being snapped bathed the underside of the hover. I glanced out the window, my lip curling, glad of the privacy tinting. Jace drove while I looked through the yearbook from my eighth year at school. "Check page fifty-six," he said, and I flipped through the heavy vellum pages. "Now look at Moorcock's picture."

Christabel Moorcock, known as "Skinny." She grinned out of the page of holovid stills, a tenth-year student with long dark hair and wide dark eyes. She was pretty but alarmingly thin; her cheekbones standing out and her heart-shaped face a touch too long. The cupid's-bow of her mouth was plump and perfect, her eyebrows winged out. The picture was a headshot, it showed only the very top edge of her collar.

Below were the usual lists of interests, including Faerie Ceremonial magick—and a small black mark shaped like a spade in a deck of playing cards. I rubbed at it, thinking it an ink blot, but it didn't blur. "The black mark?"

"Now try page fifty-eight. Steven Sebastiano." Jace's fingers danced over the touchpad, and the AI pilot took over inserting us into hovertraffic. I felt the familiar unsettling pull of gravity against my stomach, swallowed hard. *Can it be you have not resurrected him?* Lucifer's soft, beautiful voice teased at my brain.

Resurrect a demon? It's not possible. But then again, I'd been researching only to try and find out how Japhrimel had altered me. I had never thought that...It wasn't possible that I could bring him back, was it?

Was it?

I want him back. That was a child's plaint. I wanted each dead person back. I wanted every person I'd ever loved back.

And I, of all people, should understand the finality of Death.

"Danny?"

I shook myself back into the present, closed the yearbook with a snap, not bothering to check Sebastiano's picture. "You're a sneaky bastard." I tried to sound admiring. "Good work, Jace. I wouldn't have thought of that. Have you looked to see —"

"I haven't made a list yet. But I thought it was worth looking into, seeing as how that's the only link between Christabel and Polyamour I can find in the yearbook."

The year Mirovitch died, Christabel was on the yearbook committee. Why would she leave a mark? If she did leave a mark, that is. It would be stupid. On the other hand, Mirovitch was dead by the time they finalized the yearbook, it came out at the end of the year, after the inquest. It's probably nothing, some primary-school bullshit. Still, it's the only clue we've got. "I wonder who lives on Trivisidero." I looked out the window, seeing the city roll by underneath, its daylight geography gray with concrete and splashes of reactive paint marking hover bounce pads, the towers of high-density apartment buildings scrolling down Lossernach Street. If I focused, I could see the strings of Power underlying every street and building, the green glow of any trees and gardens that managed to survive. And underneath it all lay the pulsing radioactive smolder of the city's heart, seething in a white-cold mass of Power.

"Gabe does." The hover dropped out of the traffic pattern into a lazy spiral.

"Gabe didn't go to Rigger Hall." I reopened the yearbook, scanned the pages, looking for more black marks. "We're going to have to make a list."

"Here we are," he said. "Danny? Who was it on the phone?"

It was the goddamn Devil, Jace. "Nobody," I muttered, my right hand reaching up to massage my burning left shoulder through my shirt. "Gods."

Can it be you have not resurrected him?

"'Kay." We were keyed through the police security net. Jace piloted the hover down to land in the driveway of an immaculate brick house. I remembered the place from walking to Gabe's so many times. The holly bushes outside were green and healthy and the walls behind them covered with the strangely geometric shielding of a Ceremonial. There were other police hovers there, including a squat black coroner's hover.

"Great." I triggered the door lock. "Well, what do you know. Digging that coffin up wasn't useless after all."

I hopped out, the hover's hum diminishing as Jace turned off the drive. The springs groaned a little as the hover settled.

The house was three stories high and immaculate, the gardens largely ornamental. I saw several rosebushes and a monkey puzzle tree. The roof was new, plasilica made to look like slate, gleaming wetly from last night's rain and the afternoon sunlight. There were officers milling all over the front driveway, a wide circular field of crushed white stone. At the top of wide granite steps there was a police guard at the massive wooden front door, two Saint City blues; I saw Gabe's familiar figure come out blinking into the sunlight. She lifted a hand, I saw one of the blues at the door flinch.

My nostrils flared. I smelled fear and blood, and death. And the sharp stink of human vomit.

It must be bad. I stuffed the yearbook in my bag and curled my left hand around my sword, then struck out for the front door, my boots crunching on the rocks. A strand of long black hair fell into my face. I blew it back, irritably. "Yo, Spooky!" I called, as soon as I got to the bottom of the stairs. "I should be home in bed."

"So should I." Her shields flushed purple-red. My own shielding reverberated, answering hers; she stopped and looked down at me as the emerald on her cheek sparked a greeting. "You look different, Danny."

"Must be exhaustion and digging up old bodies." I paced up the stairs, aware that Jace was right behind me. His staff tapped on the granite. My cheek burned, the twisted-caduceus tat shifting its inked lines against my flesh. "What do we have here?"

"Ceremonial." She ushered me past the blues, who both recoiled slightly. I guess my reputation preceded me. It was one time I was glad of it—at least if they were recoiling they weren't staring at me.

The emerald on my cheek burned as I stepped over the threshold, a deep drilling warning. "The shielding's torn." I looked up. "From inside."

Gabe nodded. "Just like the other three. It's Aran Helm."

I remembered him. He'd gone to Rigger Hall too, in my class. He'd been a tall blond babyfaced Ceremonial, with blue eyes and a habit of sucking on his lower lip; I'd had him in a Philosophy of Religion class and a few other electives.

Jace swore. "This is Helm's place?" He smacked the butt end of his staff against the marble flooring, one sharp crack echoing through the foyer. "Gods*dam*mit."

"You know him?" I asked, looking up. Apparently Helm's taste had gone for high ceilings, a coat of antiquated mail on a stand, and a tall grandfather clock that chimed as we walked in. A long, overdone staircase went up to the right. I followed Gabe, my fingers trailing the balustrade. The feel of defenses wedded to every stair crackled against my skin, humming uneasily. I smelled beeswax, and a frowsty scent that told me only one human lived here. Apparently Aran Helm lived alone; in a huge house full of silence and loneliness.

"Ran with him for a while, when I was dating you," Jace replied easily enough. "Worked with him on a couple jobs — did some wetwork together. Never met at his house though. Dodgy."

"Wetwork." *Assassination.* A long time ago I would have been willing to swear there was nothing I didn't know about Jace, but here I was finding out something new. I had balked at doing assassinations, though he'd said it was good money. I hadn't asked what his own jobs entailed; I'd trusted him blindly. "How was he?"

"Good," Jace said. "Cold. Not overly troubled with hesitation." His aura touched mine. I shivered.

Not like me; the only time you mentioned assassination to me I almost bit your head off. How many wetwork jobs did you come home from and climb into bed with me? Did you ever want to tell me, Jace, or did you think I'd never find out? I swallowed the anger. It was ancient history. I didn't have to think about it, did I? Not right now with a killer to catch and the Prince of Hell calling me again.

It was a relief to find something unpleasant I *didn't* have to think about.

"He's up in the bedroom." Gabe's shoulders were tense under her long dark synthwool coat. "It's . . . well, you'll see. Have you got anything so far, Danny? Anything at all?"

It wasn't like her to sound desperate. "I'm going to see Polyamour as soon as possible. It seems Steve Sebastiano was part of the conspiracy that got Mirovitch." I laid it out in a few clipped sentences, including the marks in the yearbook, which were probably nothing but the closest we had to a link. At the top of the stairs Gabe led us down a hall past another two blues standing guard, and I didn't need her to tell me which room Aran was in. The hacked-open door and thick cloying smell of blood spoke for itself. After you've smelled death for a while, the smell of blood stops bothering you much . . . at least, consciously.

The lingering traces of other smells in the air were more interesting. I inhaled deeply — protections, even more protections, laid thick and tight over every inch of wall and floor. A marble bust of Adrien

Ferriman, legislative creator of the Parapsychic Act, stood on a blackstone plinth, his familiar jowled scowl apparently directed down the hall.

Laid over that was the raw, new smell of human from the blues, Gabe, and Jace. I sniffed deeply, closing my eyes. Human blood, human sweat, protection magick, and...

I filled my lungs. *There it is.* I smelled offal, magick, and the reek of aftershave. I filled my lungs, closing everything else out, even the throbbing burn in my shoulder.

I knew that smell. Dust, offal, magick, aftershave, chalk, and leather.

The smell of the Office. The Headmaster's Office.

I shivered, the shudder going from my heels all the way up to the crown of my scalp. Nerve-strings tight and taut, singing their siren song of bloodlust and the path of the hunt laid in front of my feet. But laid over that shudder was fear, nose-stinging and skin-chilling fear. The fear of a child locked in a room without light.

Be careful, Japhrimel's voice whispered at the very back of my brain. *He cannot hurt you now,* hedaira. *You are beyond his reach.* I felt a warm hand touch my face, an intimate trailing down my cheek, pausing at the pulse in my throat, then sliding down to the curve of my breast.

I came back to myself with a jolt. *What the hell? I didn't smell this at Christabel's. That damn lilac perfume of hers, maybe. Or maybe the scent had faded.* "I can smell it."

"Danny?" Gabe paused before the doorway. "You okay?"

No, I wasn't. I was hallucinating my dead demon lover's voice. But it didn't matter. Getting the smell of the quarry is important in any hunt. And if imagining Japhrimel's voice helped me get through this, I was all for it no matter what price I would have to pay afterward, when the hunt was over and I had to face the fact that he was truly gone.

"I'm fine," I rasped. A pattern was starting to appear under the shape of events. "Let's take a look at Mr. Helm." I stepped past Gabe and looked into the room. "He certainly did believe in protection, didn't he?"

"Either that or he was afraid of something," Jace said grimly. "Chango..." It was a long breath of wondering disgust.

I agreed. Past the hacked and battered door was an orgy of blood and bits of what had once been a human body. The chalk marks on the floor were familiar but hurried, scrawled instead of done neatly. The circle was sloppily and hastily finished. Had the killer been interrupted? "Who found the body?" My nose wrinkled. The only thing worse than the effluvia of dying cells around living humans was the stench of rotting ones.

You think that as if you're not human, Danny. I shivered again.

"Housekeeper," Gabe said. "Apparently was paid a good deal to come in and work ten hours a day cleaning this pile. And to keep her mouth shut. The body's a few days old, she wasn't supposed to come into this part of the house very often. Once she found the body, she didn't know whether she should call the police. She brought the question to one of her cousins, who's a low-level retainer for the Owens Family and a stooge for the Saint City PD. He brought it to us. If the shields hadn't already been cracked we would have called you in to crack them."

"Gods." Jace looked definitely green, yet another new and amazing thing. I felt a little green myself. "There's only pieces."

Check that. I wasn't just feeling a *little* green. I felt green as a new crop of chemalgae. Nausea rose, twisted hot under my breastbone. I forced it down. I'd seen a lot of murder and mayhem in my time, but this...the smell of blood wasn't bothering me, but the visuals were beginning to become nightmare-worthy.

I should know, I've had my share of wonderful nightmares.

I looked into the bedroom. This was evidently where Aran Helm truly lived. Scattered papers and dirty clothes strewn about, a huge four-poster bed with wildly mussed covers now spattered with blood and other fluids, and burned-out candles in many holders. Between this and Christabel's careful obsessive order, I wasn't sure which I preferred.

I stepped delicately inside the room, wishing once again that I could shut my nostrils down, and saw something.

A human hand, severed at the wrist, clutching a bit of consecrated chalk.

A few more bits of the pattern fell together. "*Sekhmet sa'es,* Gabe. We've got it all wrong. The marks weren't made by the killer."

"What?" Gabe stopped at the door. "What are you talking about?"

"Look." I pointed at the hand. "The victims made the marks. I need a laseprint of these. If I can figure out what they were trying to defend against—"

"You don't think it's human?" Hope and dawning comprehension lit her face.

"I wouldn't say that," I answered slowly. "I can't tell. But if the marks are *defensive,* I've been going about this all wrong." I whirled. "If Jace gives you a list, can you find out who on the list is still in Saint City? And who's still alive?"

"All things should be so easy." Gabe's eyes lit up. She looked a few years younger. "You're sure, Danny?"

"Not sure." I gave the room one last look. "But it's better than any other theory I had. There's something else, too."

"What?" She almost twitched with impatience, and I suppressed the desire to giggle nervously. Couldn't she *see?* Why did she need me to tell her?

"This door's hacked *in.*" I looked back at them, saw Jace was watching me, his blue eyes bright against the shadow of the hall. A deeper shadow slid over his face, and I would have recoiled if my feet weren't nailed in place. When I looked again, the shadow was gone, and I had to chalk it up to nerves.

I was chalking a lot up to my nerves lately. It was a bad habit to get into.

"What?" Gabe's tone wasn't overly patient. I had drifted into silence, staring at Jace, my forehead furrowed.

I shook myself and met her dark worried eyes. "I don't think the attack started here."

CHAPTER 23

I was right. We found his *sancta* in the basement, a hexagonal stone room with nudiegirl holoposters gummed to the rough walls. A pentacle was etched into the discolored granite floor—Aran had done well for himself, if he could spend time and Power etching stone. I was uncomfortable looking into the room—after all, a Ceremonial's *sancta* is like a Necromance's psychopomp, the deep place they trust to work their greatest magicks. Apparently, Aran Helm had derived a great deal of his power from sex; it didn't look like he had many partners, however. He must have done a lot of Power-raising with his right hand.

A drawer in a low armoire was pulled all the way out, showing shiny sharp implements. Bloodletters and weights. I sucked in a breath, delicately touching the wood of the drawer with a fingertip. The shiver that went through me wasn't entirely unpleasant—blood and sex, and pain. Good fuel for magick.

And very tempting for demons. Even part-demons like me.

Interestingly enough, there was only one door to the *sancta,* and it was hacked open—but from the *inside.* I cast my gaze over the hexagonal room.

Jace leaned in the door. Gabe's voice raised in the corridor beyond, giving orders. Jace's staff glowed golden, a faint light edging it and the bones tied with raffia clicking together. Here in another sorcerer's *sancta,* any Shaman would be uncomfortable. And the lingering trail of terror and bloodlust on the air would only add to that discomfort.

Cigars lay fanned under a twisted statue of The Unspeakable. *So he was a Left-hander,* I thought. That was valuable information—no wonder he'd been in the business of assassination. Left-handers wouldn't sacrifice humans to gain magickal energy, but they *would* sacrifice other things. Dogs, cats...monkeys, sometimes. Insects. There was a whole branch of Left-handers that dealt with the power released by killing snakes as slowly as possible, since snakes were living conduits of magickal energy. Cats were popular too, and goats. About the only animal a Left-hander wouldn't touch was a horse, since plenty of Skinlins worshipped Epona and their goddess took a very dim view of sacrificing equines. Of course, there was the question of what to do with the body afterward. The old joke was that a *vaudun* and a Left-hander would both kill a chicken—but the *vaudun* would eat the chicken afterward.

Most of the time, after a Left-hander was finished, there wasn't much of the sacrifice *left* to eat.

A half-bottle of very good brandy sat on the altar too. His ceremonial sword, its blade twisted into an unrecognizable shape, was a two-handed broadsword, pretty but cheap metal. If he did wetwork it was with knife or projectile gun, not honest steel. Aran Helm had used the human deaths to pay for his house, and animal death to fuel his magick.

I wondered if either had troubled him.

"Here," I murmured. "Here was where it started. How could it come from inside?" I turned to the door. Gabe had already repaired Christabel's shielding by the time I got there, but the bits from the door had all been on the *outside,* in the hall. "Christabel's shields breached from the inside? And the other two, the sexwitch and the normal?"

Jace shrugged. "Moorcock yes, sexwitch yes, normal no. That's what Gabe said. I'll ask again if you want." But he stayed there, looking at me, his eyes oddly shadowed and burning at the same time. "Danny, what are you thinking? You look..."

"I'm not sure yet." *Why are we so sure the normal's part of this? But I am sure, sure as I can be. It started with our mysterious normal and hasn't ended yet. Something I'm missing, something critical. And Christabel, making marks and shouting "Remember."*

I blinked, knelt down. Caught in the pentacle's deep-carved lines was a glimmer of something. My fingertips brushed stone, and I caught a glimpse of a man who had to be Aran—blue-eyed, his greasy blond hair cut in a flattop, stumbling back as Power whipped like a serpent from the statue of The Unspeakable. "Was he a very good sorcerer, this Aran Helm?"

I felt more than saw Jace's shrug. "Good enough. Better as an assassin, I think. Otherwise, how would he pay for this?"

"True." It was a fine silver chain, a necklace. The clasp was broken. Attached to it was a charm the size of my thumb from distal joint to fingertip—a silver spade, like on an antique playing card. "Ace of spades." I held it up delicately between index finger and thumb. "I think you're onto something, Jace. Good work." *Stupid to put a mark in a yearbook, Christabel. Why would you do something like that? It's a pity I can't bring you out of Death and ask you.* Shivers rilled up my spine.

One corner of his mouth lifted into a half-grin. "Good to hear it. Can Gabe's team start up in the bedroom?"

"I think so." I made it to my feet, holding the necklace. "We need to go through this yearbook and make a list."

"You got it."

A new thought struck me as I rose from the floor. I paused, holding up the necklace. "I wonder if Christabel had one of these."

Jace turned and murmured to Gabe. She said something, then looked over his shoulder at me. "Danny?"

"Did Christabel have one of these?" I held the necklace up so she could see it.

"She did. So did the sexwitch. I chalked it up to junk jewelry."

Gabe's tone was uncharacteristically harsh. No cop liked to miss a piece of evidence.

"The normal didn't have one?" I asked, just to make sure.

"Not that I remember. I'll go through the evidence manifest again, if you want."

"Do that." I stared at the nudiegirl posters on the wall. They fluttered as my attention brushed them. Nothing behind any of them. No way into the room but the door, and the door hacked open from *inside*.

I tore the yearbook out of my bag and stalked for the door. "Gabe. Get me the list. *Everyone* in here who has that mark next to their names. I need to know who's still living and where, especially in Saint City. Send it to my datpilot, will you?"

She nodded. "What's up?" At least she knew enough not to bother me with questions that needed long explanations.

"One of Polyamour's girls was the second body," I said, and watched Gabe's eyes light with comprehension. She was looking more relieved by the second. At least we had a connection, however tenuous; a direction to go in was good news to any cop. "I'm going to drop in on Poly *now*. If one of her girls was downed and she has more bits of the puzzle, she's going to be very nervous, very guilty—or the next goddamn victim."

Gabe nodded. "Go. Go on."

I gave her a quick smile and pushed the yearbook into her hands. "I need this back." *So I can bury it again. Maybe deeper this time.*

"Understood. Now go." Her tone wasn't just a *thank you*—it was relief and gratitude all rolled up together and lit with birthday candles.

Jace followed me, his staff tapping on the marble. The spade necklace dangled from my fist, and I stuffed it in a pocket without thinking. My fingers tightened around the katana's scabbard. *I should have gotten a sword long before this so I could have a blade I could depend on.* A chill finger touched my spine. My rings flashed, demon-fed, and the atmosphere of Aran Helm's palatial house shivered. I reached out without thinking, calming the runaway energy like a restive horse. Helm had put so many layers of protection on his home that the air itself would have been dead and stifling if not for the giant rent whoever—or whatever—had torn in the shielding.

From the inside. I wonder if he invited his killer in. Why, if he was so obsessive about protection?

It was a relief to have this puzzle, so I didn't have to think about Lucifer's soft voice burrowing in through the phone line. *I must speak with your lover, and I am unable to contact him in the usual manner.*

I wondered what the "usual manner" was and felt my skin go chill again.

Can it be you have not resurrected him? Taunting, soft, and corrosive.

I decided I didn't fear him as much as I had when I was human—and that was bad. After all, I wasn't a demon, only a *hedaira,* whatever that was. And even if I had been a demon, Lucifer was the Prince of Hell.

So maybe the Prince of Hell was starting a new game. I had to go carefully, or I might be caught like I was last time. Of course, any game the Devil started was rigged from the beginning; but last time I'd had no warning whatsoever. Now at least I *knew* something awful was about to happen.

Cold comfort, if any.

"Danny!" Jace caught my arm. Sunlight fell down on the crushed stone. I'd walked out of the house and toward the garden wall. A few more strands of my hair fell in my face. My boots seemed rooted to the ground now. "Hey. The hover's this way."

I blinked at him. "Jace." I'd been so deep in my thoughts I had literally forgotten about him. The sunlight was kind to him, made his hair catch fire and his eyes glow. Had he followed me through the entire house, trying to get my attention? "I'm sorry. I was thinking."

"It's not like you to wander around deaf to the world." He shook his staff for emphasis, the bones clicking and twirling on their raffia twine. "It's that phone call, isn't it." His voice was flat.

Once before, I'd been so wrapped up in my own thoughts I hadn't been aware of my surroundings. Japhrimel had pulled me out of the way of a speeding streetside hover. I had no demon to watch over me now; I gave myself a severe mental shake, pushing away uncertainty. I'd deal with Lucifer after I dealt with this mess.

After I deal with a crazed killer from Rigger Hall, the Devil might almost be a vacation. Black humor tinted my mental voice, gallows humor. The type of macabre humor every Necromance and cop used to distance him or herself from the horror of what people could do to each other with gun and knife and club.

My fingers tightened on the scabbard. "Are you coming with me to Polyamour's?" I looked up into Jace's face.

He nodded. His jaw set, a muscle in his cheek flicked. "Of course. Do I get to play bad cop?"

You'd be better at that than I would. How many other things did I not know about Jace?

Did it matter?

Not to me, not now. Whatever he hadn't told me could stay in the past. What mattered was that he'd given up Rio for me, moved in with me, and stretched his human body to the limits trying to help me. And gods help me, I could forgive him everything for that.

"We're not going to frighten her," I decided. "Not unless I think she's guilty." I touched his shoulder, my hand closing, my thumb moving gently. It was almost a caress. "Thank you. For... for everything. I mean it."

His face eased slightly, mouth relaxing into a genuine smile. "Hey, no problem, baby. Hanging out with you is better than a holovid game."

An unwilling smile tilted my lips up even as my heart sank. Jace Monroe, the man I'd thought abandoned me years ago, loved me. But I still couldn't stand the thought of anyone but Japhrimel touching me. If Japhrimel could be resurrected... "I'll choose to take that as a compliment. Let's go."

CHAPTER 24

Polyamour's was in the Tank District, on the very northern fringe between the Tank and the financial heart downtown. Of course, she had to be close to her clients; and her clients had to be rich. To afford a liaison with Polyamour, or one of her contracted sexwitches, took a chunk of hard cash or credit that Lucifer himself might have balked at spending. She was evidently expecting us, for the security net acknowledged my hover; Jace spent a few minutes tapping on the deck, and the net's AI linked with ours, brought the hover down in a circling pattern to land with a jolt on the roofpad. It was broad daylight, so the roof lot was empty except for one sleek gleaming hoverlimo.

I spent a few moments studying the roof and the shielding. The place was well-shielded, both magickally and electronically; I wouldn't have wanted to crack it. The roof entrance was a sort of small gazebo seemingly made of stone and strung with glittering plaslights; stairs descended. I exchanged a glance with Jace and shook my right hand out. It threatened to cramp. My shoulder eased a little; maybe the thin shell of calm over my deepening panic was fooling the demon-made mark.

We went down the stairs and finally came to a beautifully carved mahogany door. Venus glowed from one half, her wooden face serene; Persephone with her pomegranate on the other. Others might have mistaken it for art, but any Magi-trained psion would know better. The sexwitch's realm was Eros and Thanatos, the life-urge married to the reality of Death itself, pain turned to pleasure turned to Power; that it was offered for clients dispelled none of the mystery.

Some theorists said sexwitches were the bridge between *sedayeen*—the healers—and Necromances, those who tread in the realm of Death. I didn't believe it.

Still, I couldn't dismiss the power of sex itself. No psion who deals with the deepest urges of the body and psyche can.

Sex was the least of what sexwitches offered. Redemption, delight, the chance to play with the deepest and most forbidden of fetishes and fantasies, companionship, vulnerability—sexwitches offered all the power of the physical body to soothe, all the power of sex to enlighten, to loosen, to liberate. It was heady stuff, and people paid in buckets for it, making sexwitch House taxes a top revenue source for the Hegemony government.

Two full-spectrum lights made to look like gaslamps burned behind the silvery lattices of ornate carriage lamps. I inhaled and smelled kyphii, sex, and synth hash.

"Great," Jace murmured. "The one time I go into Polyamour's and it's during the *day.*"

I laughed. The sound bounced off the creamy marble walls. "I wonder what these stairs are like when it rains."

"Slippery. But think of the possibilities."

"Slipped disk. Cracked skull." I kept the laughter back only by sheer force of will.

He snorted, a short chuckle. "You have no imagination."

"More like too much." The banter to ease our nerves was so familiar I began to relax fractionally. Then the doors gave a theatric creak as they began to open, a slice of glowing almost-candlelight widening.

We waited, my right hand closing around the hilt of my sword. Jace let out a short sound that wasn't quite a whistle and nowhere near a word. When the door was fully open, it revealed a dimly lit hallway hung with red velvet and decorated with tasteful marble statues. And there, standing in the middle of the hall, was the transvestite Polyamour, the most famous sexwitch of our generation.

She was tall, and her face was as beautifully made as any architectural triumph: caramel skin; long, curling black hair; and amazing gray eyes fringed by thick charcoal lashes. She had long aesthetic legs, lightly muscled and revealed by a fluttering pale-pink silk dress. Her feet were bare and surprisingly small, the nails lacquered deep blood-red. One dainty ankle was graced with a thin gold bracelet, and gold hoops hung from her perfect ears. High on her left cheek was the inset ruby, aesthetically placed, which any datscan would reveal as encoded with a powerful protective chip. If a plasgun or projectile discharged anywhere near her or if the ruby were removed, the police would automatically be called. A datscan would also reveal her as a licensed sexwitch, immune to several laws applying to other psionics—and worth ten years in a federal prison if she was assaulted. The Hegemony received far too much in tax profit from sexwitches to look kindly on any harm done to them—not like the fifty years before and after the Parapsychic Act, when sexwitches had all but died out due to the abuse they received from being bought and sold like chattel, worse than any other sort of psion.

Her quick intake of breath showed a pair of shallow high breasts under the silk. I wondered if they were augments, or if she'd taken hormone courses.

Her Power reached out, caressed the edges of both my shields and Jace's. The familiar smell of sexwitch—sex and vulnerability and pure sugary musk heat—rolled out from her in waves.

Anubis, she's powerful.

"Dante Valentine. And Jace Monroe." She tilted her beautiful head slightly, an acknowledgment that sent her perfect ringlets cascading. "I thought you would be along sooner rather than later. The holovids just reported Aran Helm's death." Her voice was caramel with a slight astringency, too deep for a woman's but too light for a man's.

I sniffed. Something smelled odd here: a rank edge of fear under all the perfume.

I saw a glint of silver at her throat.

I dug in my pocket, pulled out the broken necklace. The spade swung at the end of it. *"Tig vedom deum."* My voice stroked the hall, made the velvet hangings flutter. I was forgetting to be careful.

Polyamour actually turned pale and stepped back. She reached up to her sculpted throat and touched her own necklace. If my eyes hadn't been so sharp, I might not have been able to see it in the shifting, dim light. But there it was, a silver spade. I felt a jolt of sick happiness, one more connection sliding into place. I was getting closer. *Are you happy, Christabel? I'm remembering, and I'm dragging other people through remembering it too. Are you fucking happy?*

"You were not a member, but you know." Her voice was less smooth now. Her eyes slid over me again. "I suppose you should come in."

"I suppose we should." I moved down the steps, heard Jace behind me. "The way I see it, either you're part of it or you're a potential victim. If it's the former, I'll get you first. If it's the latter, you could do worse than have my protection."

She laughed, but the sound was unsteady. Polyamour turned on one soft bare foot and started off down the hall. "I was told you were direct. That seems a bit of an understatement."

"One of the victims was a girl of yours." I moved after her, my boots clicking softly. "Why didn't you say anything?"

She cast me one extraordinary dark glance over her shoulder. The sway of her hips under the silk was almost a woman's. I looked back at Jace, who seemed bemused. "You were at the Hall," Polyamour said. "You know the habit of silence can be hard to break. I didn't *know* anything useful about Yasrule's death until Edward brought me the pictures. Then I knew."

"What exactly do you know?" She wasn't moving very quickly. My boots, and Jace's, thudded in the murmuring silence, all sound dulled by the velvet on the walls. The doors closed behind us on whisper-soft hinges.

"Let's have some coffee. We can be civilized, can't we?" She had recovered. Her voice was back to smoothness. But her aura shifted uneasily, and my own Power reached out, caressing her vulnerable edges. Sexwitches were still nicknamed "beggars" in some circles; the natural physiological processing of Power triggered chemical cascades of pleasure in them, endorphins that made them pleading and vulnerable. As a part-demon, I had more Power than most sexwitches ever encountered; if Polyamour wasn't fully-fed she would be distracted, and I would have to be very gentle. If I was careful of my new body's effect on normal humans, I was doubly careful of what I could do to an exquisitely sensitive sexwitch.

Other halls began to open off this one. I caught sight of round couches, spears of daylight picking out details: a large harp, the glowing green leaves of some trailing plant, a sleeping white Persian cat on a round cushion of black velvet. All in all, it seemed pretty tame.

As if reading my mind, Polyamour laughed. It was a practiced sound, with a rill of uneasiness underneath. "These are only the reception rooms. Have you ever been inside a House, Ms. Valentine?"

"Call me Danny," I said automatically. "No. Some bordellos and brothels, but never a House. It's very beautiful."

She accepted the compliment with a queenly nod. "My private quarters are a few floors down. If you don't mind."

"It would be an honor." Something that was bothering me became painfully clear. "Where are your bodyguards? I'd think your intra-House security would be a little tighter."

"What good would bodyguards do if Dante Valentine wants me dead?" Her tone edged on the whimsical. "No. For personal reasons, I'd prefer to keep this meeting private." The end of the hall rose up in front of us and two shielded doors opened, revealing an elevator. I swallowed, my jaw setting, and Jace's hand closed around my elbow. "Besides, I am not without a slight precognitive Talent. It comes in handy."

We stepped into the elevator. Polyamour's aura pressed against mine, the air roiling with Shaman, sexwitch, and almost-demon. The doors closed. There was a time when I would have drawn steel and started struggling to escape such a confined space, but now I set my teeth together and tightened my left hand around the scabbard. My rings popped and sparked. Jace's touch on my elbow loosened for a second, but then he drove his fingernails in savagely.

The bright diamonds of pain were negligible, but they helped.

Polyamour studied my face. In such close quarters, I could see the line of her jaw, too strong for a woman's. There was an old, faint scar running just under her right ear, under the jawbone to the bottom of her chin. Her forehead was a little too broad too. But those eyes more than made up for it. "You're exquisite," she said. "I could get you a ton of work."

I managed a tight smile. Maybe she didn't assume I'd been

genespliced. Then again, she could see the black stain on my aura. *Thanks for the compliment. I don't want to look like this.* "Not many would like to fuck a Necromance." *And I can't touch a man without thinking of a dead demon and how he held me.*

Nothing seemed to throw her. "You'd be surprised." The elevator made a soft sound, and the doors opened. Disregarding safety or politeness, I was the first one out, tearing free of Jace's hand but dimly grateful that he had choked up on my elbow.

This hall was plain, wood-floored, and white-walled. Sunlight poured in from the windows, but gauzy white curtains diluted the force of the light. I blinked, my pupils contracting, and smelled coffee. Polyamour led us through a plain wooden door and into a large comfortable room with a fireplace, a tumbled king-size bed, two blue linen couches, a battered Perasiano rug, and a woman wearing nothing but a collar and long chain standing in the middle of a small kitchenette, pouring coffee from a silver samovar.

"Please, sit." Polyamour strode across the room, silk fluttering, and draped herself across one of the couches. "Diana will bring the coffee."

I lowered myself down gingerly, the sword across my knees. Looked up at Jace, who wore a faint scowl. He stood to the side and folded his arms, *watchdog* written in every line of his body. "I suppose we might start with the obvious," I said. "Someone's killing the members of the Black Room. Why?"

She gave one elegant shrug, the silk whispering as she moved. The naked woman padded over softly, bearing a silver tray. She glanced at Polyamour, who nodded slightly.

"Cream?" the naked woman asked, her breasts moving gently as she knelt to place the tray on a low ebony table. Her pubic fleece was smoky darkness, her hair a long rippling fall of chestnut. She was a sexwitch too, a ruby glittering in her cheek. She seemed utterly unself-conscious of her nudity, almost to the point of parody. Her aura was at a low ember, fully fed, but she still made a subtle, inviting movement as soon as the edge of my aura touched her. "Sugar?"

"Just cream." *If this is a game to see how I react, Poly, you're going to be very disappointed. Even when I was human I didn't go in for this.*

She looked up at Jace, who shook his head.

The naked woman handed me an antique silver cup full of expensively smooth coffee and chicory, cut with heavy cream. She spent a few more moments preparing Polyamour's drink, handed it to her, and sat back on her heels, waiting.

"You may go, Diana. I will be quite all right. Come back in two hours." Poly waved her away.

The woman bowed, her breasts moving, hair falling forward to veil her face momentarily. Then she rose, looped the chain from the leather collar over her arm, and left, closing the door with a quiet click.

Polyamour seemed to shrink slightly at the sound of that click. "I suppose you want to know how they did it."

I took a sip of the coffee. "This is very nice."

She acknowledged the compliment with a small nod.

Let's get down to business. "The more I know, the better prepared I am to stop this thing."

"I'm not sure you *can* stop it." She crossed her legs, demurely, but a faint sheen of sweat showed on her forehead. I wondered if she'd had her chin laser-treated to get rid of stubble, or if hormone treatments had taken care of it. "It's probably Destiny coming home to roost. Do you believe in Fate, Danny Valentine?"

I shrugged. "No more than the next Magi-trained Necromance."

She gave a coughing little laugh. "That's very funny. I was involved in a conspiracy to kill a Hegemony officer. Are you going to arrest me?"

It was my turn to laugh, a laugh that dropped and shattered in pieces on the wooden floor. "Not fucking likely. Any truth to the rumor that someone turned into a Feeder and took him on in a predator's duel?"

"In a way, I suppose." Polyamour shivered.

My nostrils flared. I Saw her fear, rising in trails that rippled and eddied like heat. A sexwitch's fear is perfumed, and smells like something fragrant and wanting, pheromones pressing hard against anyone in the room. Humans and Nichtvren like the smell, psions are particularly sensitive to a sexwitch's pheromones of fear or excitement; werecain and kobolding aren't affected at all.

And me? It was difficult for me not to look at the curve of her throat where the pulse beat. She smelled like food. She also smelled— just a hint—of amber musk and burning cinnamon, a smell that made me think of Japhrimel's body against mine, his spent, shuddering sigh as he buried his face in my throat, the tang of demon blood burning my mouth. *It's not real. It's only chemicals and Power. She's just scared.*

Her long caramel hand came up and touched the spade necklace. She curled her fingers around it, then broke the chain with a flick of Power, held the necklace up. "They made it stop." Her eyes moved with the spade as it dangled back and forth, glittering. "Or Keller did."

I breathed shallowly, trying not to inhale any more of the delicious, electric, mouthwatering scent. "Keller?"

Her mouth quirked slightly. "Our fearless leader. I..." She was trembling. Abruptly, Polyamour swung her legs off the couch, set her coffee down on the tray, and rolled up to her feet. The one quick movement told me she'd had some combat training, and that was very interesting. Sexwitches don't normally go for combat; fear turns into desire for them, crippling their ability to respond. "You know," she said tonelessly. "You *know* how bad it was."

I swallowed. The coffee turned to ash in my mouth, but the taste of it cut through the tantalizing scent. I wondered if that was why she'd offered it. "I was in the cage four times. But I know the sexwitches had it rough."

"Oh, rough." She waved a hand, pacing away from us. I could breathe again, without her pheromones drowning me. "Rough. We were fucked every which way but loose, Valentine. That's not *rough*. The rough part was having that bastard pawing away at your *mind* while he or one of his cronies stuck whatever they wanted in their orifice of choice. If you're a sexwitch, you learn early that your body betrays you—it's your *mind* that has to stay impregnable. Your soul. To have that filthy old maggot fingering inside your head..." Her cascade of dark curls shuddered as she turned her supple back. She was *shaking*.

"*Sekhmet sa'es,*" I whispered. At least the few cubic inches inside my skull had been all mine. No matter how much of a smoking wasteland it became, it was still my wasteland. What was that old fable?

Why do you eat your own heart? Because, O King, it is bitter, and because it is my heart.

Even in the middle of my blackest moments, I'd had my books. The hard kernels of immortal stories, each one a reminder of how deeply Lewis loved me, of how strong I could strive to be. My books and my god, steady sources of strength in the impregnable fortress of my head. I *had* been lucky.

Lucky. I never thought I would think *that*.

Polyamour turned back to us. The beauty of her face had become harder, more brittle; her eyes were dark holes. "I learned early that I wanted to be strong. Or at least have a strong protector. And so, I built this. But would you believe I still have nightmares?"

"I believe it." My eyes flickered over to the mantel. Hung above it was a restrained, priceless Mobian print, the famous black-and-white of the woman's back tattooed with a rising dragon. I would bet it was the original. The subtle shades of gray and stippled black were alive to my demon sight. I could have contemplated it for hours. "I believe it." *I had Anubis, and you had nobody. Should I feel guilty about that? Lucky? Or guilty about feeling lucky?*

"Would you believe I actually felt guilty?" Her throaty, husky voice broke on the last word. The sharp pinch of my own guilt settled in, twisted hard. The scent of her fear still lingered on me, and it took an effort of will to calm my own racing pulse.

If I could, Poly, I'd walk out of here and let you get back to trying to forget all about it. Because as soon as I finish this, I intend to forget every-fucking-thing that has to do with Rigger Hall too. "Poly, I need to know who. I need to know what you did. And why the Feeder glyphs are supposed to protect you against it."

She dropped her head, stood with her carefully ringletted hair around her face. After a moment I realized the sound in the room was her. She was breathing like a horse run too hard, her fear rising in waves like heat from pavement. Her aura swirled in blue and violet, trembling, about to go nova.

I was off the couch before I knew it, leaving my sword behind. I approached her softly, my own aura stretching; my rings swirled steadily. When the gold glow of my aura touched the edges of hers, the result was startling—her light yearned toward me, the classic response of a sexwitch. They need to feed, either on sex or the power sex raised; pure Power always raises a sexual response in them. That is what makes them so vulnerable—their bodies beg for it, slaves to the deepest urges of the body itself. The smell of her fear rose to drench me, but my own demon-scent overlaid it, a fiery, smooth kick like brandy igniting in my stomach.

Gods above, I could get drunk on this.

I'd forgotten how much more I was. How much more Japhrimel had made me. The outer layer of my defenses dropped, and a thin, humming sonic note of Power slid through the air like oil into a glass.

Her head tipped back. Even though she was taller than me I caught her nape and wrist easily, the demon-hard calluses on my golden hands from daily knife-drill rasping on her soft skin. Then my aura closed around her, the full-scale plasgun charge of power sinking into her veins. Her eyelids fluttered shut and she moaned, helpless against the riptide.

Was that what I looked like when Japhrimel changed me? I shook the thought aside. Pleasure scraped against my nerves, sparked through my bones. It *was* just like alcohol, a thorny electric lassitude like the best stage of every drunk I'd ever been on. Yet I was in control, not helpless in its grip. Gently, ever so gently, I stroked down Polyamour's spine with a feather-touch of Power. She moaned again, the silk of her dress whispering as her hips jerked forward. I kept one hand steady on her nape, my skin roughening slightly as the wave of her pleasure wrapped around me. My other hand touched her chin, her skin startlingly soft. My fingernails scraped slightly as I traced the scar on her jaw. This close, I saw that her skin was flawless; her eyelids fluttered again, eyelashes as thick and dark as a young boy's.

I could do anything I wanted to her. The thought shook me. I had *power,* more power than I'd ever had in my life. And Polyamour was helpless, as helpless as we had been under Mirovitch.

Shock jolted me out of the haze of sensation. *No. I'm not like that. I want to help her, dammit. I'm trying to help her.*

I exhaled, disengaging, the flow of Power slowing to a trickle. Waited until she stopped trembling and made sure she had her balance. She leaned toward me. I pressed a kiss onto her cheek, smelling the peculiar musk of sexwitch laid over the smell of human. It was oddly pleasing, but now the edge of fear was gone, and so was the buzzing, blurring pleasure slamming through my nerves. *Do demons feel like that when they scare us?*

Had Japhrimel felt that when he frightened me?

"There," I murmured. "Isn't that better?"

She blinked. Consciousness flooded back into her eyes. She tore away from my hand; I let her go, backed up two steps, and paced back to the couch. Jace stood in the same place, studying the Mobian. He wasn't blushing—but I could smell his arousal. It didn't smell nearly as good as hers. My shoulder wasn't burning—the mark had settled back into a dim glow. I picked up my cooling coffee cup, my hand stopping halfway to my mouth. My head suddenly cleared, swept clean by the jolts of sensation.

Can it be you have not resurrected him?
You will not leave me to wander the earth alone.
Feed me.

Sexwitches needed feeding. *I* needed feeding—but thankfully I could use human food. Japhrimel had needed blood. He had visited a slaughterhouse in Nuevo Rio.

I would not have you see me feed. His voice, old and fiercely dark as whiskey. I stared into the coffee. Polyamour stood with her back to us for a few minutes, taking in deep ragged breaths; but her aura smoothed out. When I could talk around the lump in my throat, I repeated myself. "I need to know who. I need to know what you did. And why the Feeder glyphs are supposed to protect you against it."

She let out a clipped little laugh, then swung around to face us. "I'll tell you what I know. You've paid for it, after all, with that little display."

You enjoyed it. But that was unfair. So had I. "For fuck's sake. You could be next, Sebastiano. Quit fucking around with me and tell me what I need to know or I'll leave you to it and track it down from the other end."

Polyamour held up the spade necklace. It glittered, a venomous dart of light. "I'm dead anyway. We couldn't kill Mirovitch, we were just kids. It was Keller's idea that they...they each take *some*." Her hand jittered. The spade danced, more barbs of light spitting. "I don't know all of it, Valentine. My job was to get them into Mirovitch's private rooms past the security. Keller couldn't take *him* on by himself. And nobody wanted to take *him* on in a Feeder duel. Nobody wanted to become a Feeder, hunted down, despised even after treatment. So Keller came up with the idea. They each take a *part*."

I blinked. *That's part of why the inquiry was sealed.* If word got out that a circle of psions—just kids—had slipped their collars and murdered the Headmaster of a school, especially one as experienced as Mirovitch...

That would be even worse than the public-relations fiasco of a school with a Headmaster gone awry. It was publicly more palatable for the Headmaster to abuse the students. Psions were already hated and feared equally in some places, uneasily accepted at best. The Hegemony needed us, we were protected under the law—but publicity was another thing entirely.

My stomach turned sour. It was the reality of living in the modern world, but it still nauseated me. It was more *acceptable* for him to abuse us than for us to turn on him. Because after all, if psions could kill when they were children, where did that leave the adults? Too dangerous to be left alive, maybe. That was the logical extension to that thought, wasn't it?

Jace shifted slightly. I caught his meaning as if he'd laid it in my brain with a telepath's light open touch.

"Keller?"

"Kellerman." Polyamour sighed.

The name didn't ring a bell. "I must not have met him."

Her voice took on a scraping note of sarcasm, elegantly done of course. "I doubt you'd remember it even if you did. He was eminently forgettable."

"Kellerman?"

Polyamour shivered, her hair trembling — I didn't bother to speak softly, and the entire room reverberated, the tray ringing softly against the creaking table, the walls groaning slightly, the curtains over the windows blown back, throwing gauzy shadows over the walls. I wondered if her body was betraying her, if she was fighting the urge to come back and drop at my feet, fawn on me.

I suppressed a shiver. I thanked my gods I hadn't been born a sex-witch or been sent out as a breeder. Or indentured to a colony. Or any of the thousand other things that *could* have happened.

Still... it would be so easy to scare her a little, just a very little, and feel that delicious drowning feedback again.

"It was a nickname. Kellerman Lourdes. His parents were Novo Christer, died in a colony transport crash." Polyamour let out a low breath. "What else do you want?"

"Why the Feeder glyphs? And who else was in this?" The pattern was rising from the depths of coincidence like a shape breaking up through smooth glassy water, pieces falling into place. But not enough pieces, and not nearly quickly enough.

"Only Keller knew. We'd meet him in that boathouse on the grounds — you remember that shack? Anyway, none of us knew about anything other than the person we recruited — never more than one more — and Keller. He took secrecy very seriously. I was only recruited to get Keller and the others through the security."

"The others?" *You'd think she'd be spilling everything she ever even thought she knew about this Keller and Mirovitch,* I thought sourly. But she was pale and shaking, only the flush of my power keeping her from collapsing. If memory could reopen the scars on my back and almost force me into shock, echo in Eddie's head loud enough to make him shake even after all these years, and push the fabled Polyamour into losing her careful control, then she deserved a few seconds and all the gentleness I could muster.

Especially since I was almost trembling with the urge to do something unforgivable, just so I could have a few moments of oblivion. I had never understood bought sex before, *never*.

Not until now.

"I think Yasrule was one of them. Maybe. I don't *know*." Tears thickened her exquisite voice, welling in her dark, haunted eyes.

"You weren't there? How could you short out the security and—"

"*He* liked orgies." When she mentioned Mirovitch, it was obvious; her voice took on a weight of whispery fear and utter loathing that scraped the air and made it bleed. "So I brought fresh meat, and I brought Keller. I had to get close to *him* and—"

"*Sekhmet sa'es*," I whispered. "Your one recruit and Keller."

She nodded. "Once we were inside, Keller slipped his collar and bought enough time for me to get the security circle down. Then I dragged the meat away—she was a Magi, Dolores Ancien-Ruiz, she didn't know anything. That's why I hate myself. *He* was busy with her while Keller started his...plan...and I worked on the net." Polyamour held up her caramel hand, examining her shaking fingers as if they belonged to someone else. "I do hate myself for that."

I had to know. "Why?"

Her shoulders dropped and she pulled them back taut again. "Dolores committed suicide two years later. She was eleven when she hung herself."

Shit. I would have wanted to question her too. The thought of an eleven-year-old girl hanging herself...I pushed it away.

"I hauled her out of the Headmaster's House. She was screaming. They went past me—they were all wearing sk8 masks, but I thought I recognized Yasrule. And Aran. And Hollin."

"Hollin? Hollin Sukerow?" *Him* I knew, by reputation at least. I glanced up at Jace, who was pale, a sheen of sweat on his forehead. It wasn't a comfortable story. He was vulnerable to Poly's pheromones, too. I wondered what he smelled when she drenched the air with fear.

"The very same." Polyamour's chin lifted, a faint note of challenge. "Are you almost done? I have an appointment I would rather not miss."

As if you have anything more important to do. But it might just have been that she wanted us gone, that she wanted to start forgetting the fear that made her helpless. I made it to my feet, this time scooping up my sword. Paced over to her, avoiding the low table. I don't know what she saw in my face, but she dropped her eyes, her entire body shifting just a few millimeters. It was amazing how she could express complete but grudging submission with such a subtle movement. I wished I had body language that expressive.

Less than a foot from her, I halted. My fingernails scraped her hand as I took the spade necklace from her slackening fingers. This close, with my aura blurring and wrapping around her, she sighed, leaning forward as if she would lay her head on my shoulder.

I stuffed both spade necklaces into my pocket and caught her nape again with my free hand, holding my sword well clear. Polyamour's forehead touched mine. Her skin was fevered, but still not as warm as mine. She exhaled, I smelled human breath, coffee, and sexwitch musk. If I kissed her, she would melt against me, and Jace would be left standing on the couch. It had been a long, long time for me; and she...

But I want to scare her. I don't think I could control myself. The thought frightened me, because it was so goddamn tempting, and would be oh so very easy.

What have I become?

Her aura turned gold as I pushed Power into her, more and more and more until she cried out hoarsely, her body shuddering and hips jerking helplessly forward again. My fingers suddenly turned to iron to brace her. "Full-up," I whispered. "Now for a few nights, you don't have to feed. Take a vacation. And stop beating yourself up over Dolores." My own breath caught as I inhaled, struggling for control. Kept it. *I don't do that. I don't use people like that. I DON'T.*

Oh yeah? For once, the snide voice of my conscience didn't sound like Japhrimel. *What about Jace?*

I drew in a deep ragged breath. "Chances are it wasn't you, Bastian. Lots of kids killed themselves rather than handle the fallout from that place. Who knows what she suffered before she helped bring Mirovitch down?" My voice sank into its lowest registers, a throbbing contralto husk, swirling into her skin as I tied mental strings in a complicated knot, sealing the Power into her. For a few days, Polyamour would be free; she wouldn't have to feed. The power-charge I gave her would last longer if she didn't attempt any spells—and if she was attacked, she now had a full charge to fight with. It was poor payment for what I'd just put her through, but all I could give.

One thing was certain. Our killer wasn't Polyamour. Sexwitches didn't turn Feeder. Their capacity to hold a charge of Power was finite; they couldn't feed from anything other than sex. Not only was our killer not Polyamour, but she wasn't implicated in the mess. She was clean.

She gained her balance, and I let go of her neck. "And the next time you need another few days of rest, Poly, you come see me." I forced myself to step cautiously, then turned on my heel and tilted my head at Jace. "We'll let ourselves out."

Jace turned too, preceded me to the door. His hand touched the knob.

"Valentine!" Polyamour's voice didn't quiver. I halted, not looking back. If I looked back I was going to do something I shouldn't. My left hand almost creaked, I clutched the scabbard so tightly.

"You bitch." Now her voice broke like a teenage boy's. "Thank you."

If you only knew how close I was to scaring you, to using you, you might not thank me. "No problem." I touched Jace's shoulder, he pushed the door open, and led me out into the hall beyond.

"We're going to have to do the elevator again," he said. I let out a sharp breath, closing my eyes. My hand dug into his shoulder. He leaned into it. If it hurt him, he gave no indication. "Don't worry, Danny. I'm with you."

It was more comforting than I expected. "Good." My voice was still low, it made a shiver run through Polyamour's House. *That was close. That was so fucking close. And I invited her to call me again. She needs it, every sexwitch needs it.* Loathing crept up my spine, skin-crawling dislike. *No. I can offer her some help. That's all. Payment for what I almost did to her, for what I was tempted to do. I am not a demon. I'm human. Human.*

But that exquisite sensation, the blessed relief from pain, the *pleasure* of smelling her fear, sweeter than anything I'd tasted since being locked in a demon's arms...

No. *No.* I was human, goddammit. I was going to stay that way, no matter what. Genesplicing didn't make a human less *human,* and neither would this. Only my body had changed. The rest of me remained the same.

Didn't it?

Oh, Anubis, I prayed, *don't let me be wrong on this one.*

"Danny?"

I let out a ragged breath. "Yeah?" *Don't ask me, Jace. Don't ask me if I can give you any more than what you already have from me. The best thing I can do is finish out this case, however it ends up, and try to find some way to set you free to live your own damn life. I can't do this anymore.*

But once again, he surprised me. "Where we going next? Let me guess. To find Hollin Sukerow."

I opened my eyes again. The mark on my left shoulder throbbed against my skin, and I felt hot fingers trail up my back. Dead fingers. *Japhrimel's* fingers. Had my fear smelled like that to him? Had he loved the smell of my terror? Had it strained his control? I wrestled the thought away with an almost-physical effort, forced it down. "You got it. But first we're going to rendezvous with Gabe."

And as soon as I can, I'm going to see if there's a slaughterhouse in Saint City that will do me a blood vat.

It was a good thought, one that made my heart lighten. The one that came after it made my entire chest sink. *But what if I'm wrong and I dump Japhrimel's ashes in a vat of blood and ruin them? Lucifer lies, and the rest is just guesswork. What if he's taunting me?*

If the Devil was taunting me, he was doing a goddamn good job of it. I would have to finish this goddamn hunt and then find every book I could lay my hands on about resurrecting demons. No more bounties.

I'd grieved long enough, goddammit.

CHAPTER 25

The station house was a seethe of activity, and we made it to the Parapsych floor from the underground parking garage without trouble. I guess my hover was known to the cops, because their parking-lot AI deck took care of bringing the hover in. Jace said very little, and his face was thoughtful. I had finally managed to unclench my left hand and convince myself I hadn't just tempted Poly to call me again. I'd only been offering an exchange, fair payment to her for making her remember the Hall.

So what if I felt the lightest touch of sweat prickling along my forehead and under my arms when I thought of her? I didn't sweat easy anymore, it took phenomenal effort that left me numb and hungry to wring water out of my skin. But there it was.

Gabe stalked into her office with a stack of paper to find us waiting for her. Her dark eyes glittered with something close to rage, her sleek hair ruffled. She stopped, seeing us, and tossed the paper on the desk. "Find anything useful?" A slight snarl turned her pretty face feral.

Yeah. I found out that I can get drunk off scaring a sexwitch. How about you, Gabe? "Lots of interesting, and possibly useful." I blinked at her. "What's up, Spooky girl?"

"I made a list of the kids in the yearbook that had that mark. One of 'em I can't find. *All* of the few still living are still in Saint City. The others are dead."

"How many?" Jace leaned against the wall of her cubicle, folding his arms. I tried to tell myself I didn't want to know what *he* smelled in Poly's fear.

Lying to yourself is a bad habit to start when you're a Necromance.

"Nine outside Saint City dead." Gabe's mouth turned down at the corners. "It looks like they scattered to the winds: three of them in Putchkin territory, two in Freetowns, and the rest in Hegemony territory as far away from Saint City as possible."

"Let me guess." I dropped down in a chair and leaned back, closing my eyes. Thank the gods, something else to think about. "The one you can't find is Kellerman Lourdes."

"Sounds like you've had a productive few hours," she said sourly. "Here's the thing: all of the nine are dead. It started in Putchkin territory, then in the Freetowns, then coming closer and closer to the city. Then this last string of killings in the city itself. And nobody's caught on. Guess when the first killing was."

I shrugged, reaching up and rubbing at my temples as if I had a headache. I wondered if part-demons ever got headaches, or if a psychosomatic headache would explain the way my head was pounding. "Tell me." *Not in the mood for guessing games, Gabe. Sorry.*

"Exactly ten years to the day after Mirovitch's death. The victim, Anders Cullam—"

"I remember him." I shivered. "One of Mirovitch's stooges." The phantom scars on my back started to burn, three stripes of fire; the branding along the lower crease of my left buttock gave one flare of pain and then settled down. My left shoulder spread a prickling heat down my chest, velvet fire threading through my veins, soothing me just as I'd just soothed Polyamour.

I was almost happier with a demon mark that was cold and quiescent than one that seemed to have a mind of its own. Especially since I wondered if the mark was reacting to *my* fear. But that was impossible. I was not a sexwitch.

Gabe dropped down into her chair. "He had one of those spade necklaces and a serious case of being ripped limb from limb. The Putchkin police had the case cold-filed after they hit a wall and no other homicides in the city fit the profile. Look, Danny, I don't understand just one thing. The normal, Bryce Smith. How the hell does he fit in?"

It was a small, sour reprieve to have a puzzle to think about. *Neither do I. That's the thing that bothers me the most.* "Don't know yet. Can you pull his records? Everything not covered under the blind trust?"

Gabe shrugged, dug in the pile of paper drifting up on her desk, and retrieved a thick file. "Already did. Let's see. He didn't have one of those spade necklaces either."

"He *was* a jeweler. His slicboard was registered to someone named Keller," Jace piped up. "Guess what Kellerman Lourdes's school nickname was, according to Polyamour."

"No shit?" Gabe shook her head and flipped the file open. "Bryce Smith. Applied for a Putchkin visa as a 'technological advisor,' which would put him in that territory at about the right time...hmm. He took someone else with him, but it doesn't say who. Goddamn diplomatic seals." Her eyes came up to meet mine. "Goddamn, Danny. It's good to have you with me."

That managed to bring a weary smile to my face. I leaned forward to take the file. "I live to serve. You have a list of the ones living in Saint City?"

"I do. Seven of them settled here and are assumed alive—"

"Take Polyamour off the list. And Kellerman Lourdes. That leaves five. Is Hollin Sukerow on the list?"

"Yep. Is Kellerman our suspect, Danny?"

I took a deep breath. My brain clicked over into "work" mode, and it was a relief. "I don't know." *I'm working on blind instinct here, Gabe. You keep expecting a miracle.*

Well, wasn't that what blind instinct was? Wasn't that what *magick* was?

"Why are the people in Saint City still alive?" Gabe's eyebrows drew together.

"Because Rigger Hall is located here. That's where it started—so that's where it will stop." The prickling heat from my left shoulder slid down my back, the phantom scars turning to liquid fire and then subsiding. I blew out through my teeth, a whistling tone that served as punctuation. "All right then. Let's get this hover in the air. What are we going to do?" I was slightly surprised my voice didn't shake. I sounded normal except for the throatiness left over from Lucifer crushing my windpipe. Time hadn't taken the sting from that memory—or from any other, for that matter. A Magi-trained memory is both a blessing and a curse; there were so many things I wished I could forget. The list seemed to be getting longer lately. Much longer.

Do you believe in Fate, Danny Valentine? Polyamour's voice, terrified and low. I hadn't really answered her, because the answer was too...scary.

For a moment I contemplated telling Gabe that some things *should* be left to Fate, that something was being worked out here, some horrible equation being finished. I wondered what she would say if I told her that I was beginning to see the pattern, and that it was a terrible one, complete in its infinite awfulness.

Then I had another thought, rising like bad gas from the darkest vaults of my mind. They—whoever it was in that dark room after Polyamour dragged away a screaming nine-year-old who had probably suffered more than *any* child should have to face—had fed on Mirovitch, torn him into psychic pieces and perhaps physical ones too, since physical dismemberment would definitely help the psychic mutilation. And now, decades later, they hadn't contacted the police when they felt danger closing in. Instead, they had retreated to their sanctums and drawn circles with consecrated chalk. Were they the same circles and glyphs Keller had altered and used to drain the life out of a monster wearing the Headmaster's clothing?

I was suddenly, chillingly sure that something had risen from those circles and torn them to pieces. Had Christabel wondered if this might happen all those years ago and marked those she knew might be in danger? A Necromance knew that the dead stayed dead, but could she have suspected something would rise from an unquiet grave and...

I shook the thought away, my braid bouncing against my back. She hadn't been a full-fledged Necromance at the time. But maybe Christabel had started to wonder about things... And maybe she was like me, with a small precognitive talent that had whispered to her to mark her fellow conspirators, maybe as a *fuck you* to the world that hadn't saved them from Mirovitch, forcing them to do the unthinkable to save themselves.

Remember Rigger Hall. Remember.

My hand dropped to my pocket, feeling the small bumps from the silver necklaces. *Maybe I should just let this take care of itself.*

I couldn't believe I'd just *thought* that. It had to be the fear talking.

I didn't even recognize myself anymore. The old Danny Valentine would never have thought so, would never have entertained the notion that perhaps it was better for *this* circle to be closed. That this murderous cycle might best be left to finish itself out unmolested.

No, the old Danny Valentine would know that whoever had killed Mirovitch was due a debt of gratitude, if nothing else.

The old Danny Valentine wouldn't have wanted to scare a sex-witch just to get a few cheap moments of enjoyment either.

Come on, Danny. Think about it. There is a circle being closed here. You get in front of something with this type of momentum and it could run right over you. And besides, this is not your fight, is it? If it's vengeance, it's a vengeance you have nothing to do with.

It was a dishonorable and uncomfortable thought. A thought not worthy of someone Gabe could count on, a thought unworthy of the woman Jado had given another sword, unworthy of the terrified Necromance Japhrimel had tried his best to protect and the woman Jace was even now protecting as best he could.

But still, the thought persisted. Like the Devil's perfumed, silken voice, crawling in the corners of my mind, searching for entrance.

The Devil's voice — or Mirovitch's.

Besides, I had vengeance of my own to mete out. For Roanna, who had tried so hard to tell her social worker what was happening. And for myself, too. For the child I had been.

Eddie's voice floated through my head. *I can't go home, I can't fuckin sleep, and people are* dying. *I got to get this done.*

I looked up at Gabe's worried face. I had no choice. It had been too late the moment Gabe picked up her phone and dialed my number. *In for a penny, in for a pound.* "Do?" I shrugged. "I'm going to go visit Hollin Sukerow. You try to find out more about this Bryce Smith." *Good luck, if he was a tech advisor you can't break the blind trust; it's standard for Hegemony-Putchkin work trades.*

"Do you think he was Keller?" she asked.

It was an idea. It would have been nice and neat, except for the fact that it made no sense at all. Keller was a psion, or he wouldn't have been at the Hall. "I don't know. We don't even know for sure who Bryce Smith was, only that his body scanned normal and had some genelocking they checked to verify identity. Until we find out more, it'd be useless to assume everything. You know what they say about assumptions."

That earned me a sniggering laugh. She was looking better by the moment. Give Gabe a clear-cut string of probabilities to work, and she was just dandy. Uncertainty and blank dead ends bugged the hell out of her. "All right. You ever thought of working for the cops?"

I rolled my head back, stretching out my neck. "I'm not too good at playing politics and taking orders. I like being a freelancer."

Gabe laughed. It was a low, brittle sound, but better than nothing. "Actually, my ass is gold right now. The Nichtvren are putting pressure on the mayor and City Hall to give me anything I need. Whatever you did when you visited the Prime Power must have impressed him."

"I killed a couple werecain." I rocked up to my feet. *And I'm planning on paying the Prime and his Consort another visit and raiding their library soon.* "I'm going to go visit Sukerow. Can you give me a copy of the list?"

She grinned. "It's already on your datpilot. Hey, Danny?"

I paused, looking up at Jace, who started scraping himself off the wall. There were dark circles under his eyes, and he looked like he needed about twenty-four hours of sleep. I had to remember his limits. "What?"

"Thanks. For talking to Eddie. He came home last night."

I winced inwardly. "No problem, Gabe. After all, you're my friend."

That being said, I paced out of her office, Jace following me. "We heading to Sukerow's?"

I glanced down the hall, unease prickling at my neck. "No. Home. I need to pick some stuff up, and you need some sleep. I'll visit Sukerow, and hook up with you in twelve hours or so. Then we'll—"

"Goddammit, Danny. I can handle it." He sounded irritated. We took the stairs down to the parking level again. Our boots rang on the linoleum steps, the sound bouncing off concrete walls. I was breathing easier now, but the prickling on my nape meant bad trouble coming.

"I know you can handle it, Jace." I wondered if the excessive patience in my tone was going to piss him off even more. It was damn likely. "I just don't want you to if there's no need. In twelve hours or so I'm going to need you big-time."

"Why?" Faint tone of challenge in his voice. I could sense the tension in him as he slammed down the steps behind me, his staff thwocked the wall with a hollow sound. *Dammit, Jace, let up on me, all right? I'm not having a good fucking day here.*

"Because when I finish with Sukerow and the others on the list, I'm going to Rigger Hall. And I'm going to need you there." My voice was at least as brittle as his. *And when this is all over I also have something I need to do, something that doesn't concern you. Something you wouldn't understand. Something that concerns a blood vat and a demon's ashes, and me praying a whole hell of a lot that Lucifer just isn't yanking my chain again. You can't waste your life on someone who can't give you what you need, Jace. As soon as this is all finished, all over, I have to tell you that. Make you understand.*

"At least let me go to Sukerow's with you. My 'pilot says it's right near here."

I stopped on the stairs and looked up at him. He carried his staff, his sword was thrust through a loop in his belt, and he'd been silent about us for far too long. I'd guessed it couldn't last—it had been long enough to strain anyone's patience. Even Jason Monroe's.

He shoved his datpilot back into the inner pocket of his coat, his blue eyes meeting mine. There was a time when I would have sworn that I knew every thought crossing through those blue eyes. He'd come after me, and dealt with me being generally unsociable and rude, never losing his temper, not even pushing me for sex. He had simply been there, a comfort and support.

Why? Especially when the Danny Valentine he knew would never have forgiven him, no matter how much penance he peformed. I was no longer the terrified, swaggering, half-cracked Necromance he'd fallen in love with. I was someone else, and so was he.

Who was he in love with, who I used to be or what I'd become? And who was I trying to protect by keeping him close to me? Jason Monroe, or my own silly self?

The stairwell echoed with silence. I balanced my right hand on the round handrail covered in chipped blue paint; my left hand curled around the sword. It had quickly become natural again to have my left hand taken with the slender weight; I could almost forget everything was so different now. I could almost forget the intervening years; I could almost forget Nuevo Rio, the heat, and the ice of the island we had tracked Santino to.

I could almost forget everything when I looked up at him, the faint fans of lines coming from the corners of his eyes, the way he favored one injured knee, the familiar slope of his broad shoulders, and the way his mouth quirked at one corner even when he was being serious. I had imagined, sometimes, how he would look when he got older, back in the painfully intense days of our first love affair. I'd even toyed with the idea of having a kid with him, once the mortgage was paid off. There was still something about Jace Monroe that made my shoulders relax and my mouth want to curl up in a smile. He could irritate me the way no other human being on earth could—and the memory rose of his hand around my elbow in Polyamour's elevator, his fingernails digging in, silently giving me the pain to anchor myself.

I could almost forget everything except the one thing that stood between us, the shadow-ghost of a tall not-quite-man with his hands clasped behind his back, his long Chinese-collared coat smoking with demon power, green eyes gone dark and watching me. The one thing I could never forget, the one thing Jace would never be able to fight his way through or understand his way around.

Japhrimel. Tierce Japhrimel.

But still, my heart ached for Jace.

He's protecting me the only way he knows how. I eased up another step. My right hand closed around his shoulder, carefully, delicately. "Jace," I said quietly, "if there was anyone in the whole world I would...be with now, it would be you. The only reason I...well, I don't know what it would do to you. The last time I had...sex...with anyone, it was Japhrimel." My voice miraculously didn't break on

Japhrimel's name, for once. I couldn't bring myself to tell Jace that I couldn't give him anything more. It was cowardice, plain and simple; cowardice and need, dressed up as a gentle fiction to spare his feelings. "I'm *different* now. I don't know what it would do to you, and I don't want you... hurt. I don't think you're less capable than you were, Jace. I just don't... I don't feel weariness like I used to. Or pain. I can go for longer without resting. That's all. It's not because I don't trust you."

Who else do I have to trust? You, Gabe, Eddie. More than I've ever had in my whole life. I loved you, Jace; I still do. The very thought was shaded orange with bitterness. Why couldn't he have stayed with me instead of disappearing? Why couldn't he have trusted that I could protect myself instead of thinking he had to return to Rio to "save" me? *Why?*

I would have taken on Santino, taken on Lucifer himself, for Jace; I would have counted it small potatoes. But now, with the shadow of a demon between us, I could not give Jace what he needed. Whether I could resurrect Japhrimel or not, I couldn't be what Jace wanted me to be. Who I used to be. The woman he'd fallen in love with.

Maybe it was time to let him go.

He looked down at me, his blue eyes dark and his mouth a straight line. "I've never seen you the way you were with Polyamour," he managed, finally. "And I... *Chango,* Danny. This is all fucking wrong."

You can say that again. And I wasn't doing Poly any favors, no matter what it looked like to you. "I know." I swallowed dryly. The words I could never say to him, the silences he'd used against me, hung between us; an even bigger wall than the demon who had Fallen and altered me. I settled for giving in. "Fine. Come with me to Suke-row's. But then I want you to get some rest. If I go back into Rigger-fucking-Hall, I need you fresh. Okay?"

He nodded. Some weight he'd been carrying for a long time seemed to slip from his shoulders, and he sighed, pushing his blond hair back with stiff fingers.

It lasted only a moment, the dark caul sliding over his head. I blinked. His face turned into a deathshead, and my entire body chilled, nipples peaking, my breath catching. The stairwell seemed to go dark, the emerald on my cheek spat a single green spark — and the moment passed, my eyes opening, Jace looking just the same. His lips were moving.

"—Sukerow's, I'll catch a few winks. Sounds good."

I stayed where I was, afraid to move, staring up at Jace's face. He looked down at me, his eyes soft, and then lifted his free hand. His knuckles brushed my cheek. "You don't have to explain, Danny. 'Slong as I get to hang around you, I'm a happy man. 'Kay?" There was no hint of sarcasm or of the anger we used against each other. Just simple tenderness, a tone I'd heard Eddie use with Gabe. My heart rose into my throat, lodged there.

The stairwell was empty except for Jace and me. There was no breath of threat or magick other than my own pulsing demon-fed Power and Jace's bright thorny Shaman glow. I swallowed my heart, hearing a dry click from my throat. "Jace, I—"

"We better go get Hollin Sukerow and see what he has to say," he said. "I'll drive."

I nodded, turned on wooden feet, and led Jace down the stairs.

CHAPTER 26

Sukerow's home was a ramshackle brownstone apartment building on Ninth. We clambered out of the hover streetside, then the AI deck took the hover up to hold in a parking-pattern. I slid my sword partly free and checked the blade, good bright steel, then blew out a long breath. Moved my head from side to side, stretching out my neck muscles.

Jace examined me, his fingers tapping his swordhilt. He'd left his staff in the hover, and he touched the butt of a plasgun. "You look like you're expecting a less-than-warm welcome."

No shit. So do you. What else could fucking go wrong today? I winced inwardly. It was tempting Fate to even *think* that too loudly. "I've got a bad feeling about this." I glanced up at the building. "According to my datpilot, he's up on the third…" The sentence trailed off. *Hang on. What the hell's that?*

The third-floor corner apartment had a fine set of shields blending with the physical structure of the building. Sukerow was a Skinlin, and his balcony was green even this late in autumn. He probably rented a plot in a co-op garden, but would grow some of the more common things at home. As I watched, some leaves fluttered on a breeze contrary to the desultory chill wind swirling anonymous trash along the sidewalk. The shields pulsed, a streamer of energy spiraling through them, and I drew my sword, the scabbard reversed along my left forearm to act as a shield. *"Fuck!"* I yelled. "Call Gabe! *Stay here!"* Then I bolted for the building.

I could have leapt for the balcony, but that would mean using an amount of Power that would react with Sukerow's torn shields, which were quivering and sending out staticky bursts of fear. Instead, I ripped the maglocked security door open with a quick snapping jerk, streaked into the lobby, and started pounding up the stairs.

Second floor. The tops of my toes barely touched every fourth step, demon speed making me blur. My sword whirled and tucked up behind my arm, the hilt pointing down in my right hand, vibrating with my uneasiness. I reached the third floor, kicked the fire door open, and dove into the hall.

Sukerow's door, apartment 305, was slightly open. Yellow electric light leaked out around its borders. I rolled up, gaining my feet, and pounded down the hall.

The next few moments take on a hazy shutter-click quality. First click — a short hallway, a spreading sticky stain of Power dyeing the air with leprous blue light. Linoleum square in front of the door, a welcome mat of twisted and knotted raffia and strands of plasilica. Each knot held a protective charm, and I shatter every single one of them, the entire rug bursting into flame.

Click. Down the short hall inside the apartment, my sword up, blue light twisting on the steel. What would have taken me months before Japhrimel altered me — months of pouring Power into the blade, shaping it, sleeping with it, breathing my life into it — is done in a few seconds, sparks popping, the steel made *mine,* answering to *my* will. At the end of the front hall, I see hardwood-looking laminate flooring and the edge of a chalk circle. The leprous blue light grows intense, a small starlike point of brilliance.

I see Hollin Sukerow on his knees in front of a thin, tall shape I had only seen in nightmares for the past two-and-a-half decades. The tall figure stands, elbows akimbo, silhouetted against the light in its hand, something pulled from the yawning mouth of the Skinlin's shattered body.

Click. Blood explodes. Footsteps behind me. Raising my sword, the *kia* sharp and deadly as it had ever been in Jado's dojo, blowing the glass out of the windows and stripping the light away, making it stream in twisted livid flames. My boots skidding on the laminate as I fling my weight back, trying to stop.

Click. Jace hurtles past me, his own battlecry ripping the air with thorns, a Shaman's glow suddenly streaming from him. He moves without thought, heedlessly fast, as if he's trying to protect me, place his body between me and the shadow-thing that curls in on itself like paper in a hot flamedraft. My left hand drops the scabbard, shoots forward to haul Jace back.

Click. The shape spins, the light gives a glaring flash like a holovid reporter's stillcam. The iron smell of blood in the air mixes with a reek of dust, offal, magick, aftershave, chalk, and leather. The scent I know, the scent of my quarry in this hunt.

I hear a high, thin giggle that dries all the saliva in my mouth and makes the scars on my back reopen. They blaze, sharp agony making my back arch as if the lash and fléchette had just split open my skin for the first time. My fingers close on empty air. Jace dives, his *dotanuki* blurring upward to slash through the figure.

Click. A coughing roar. Hollin Sukerow's last despairing, choked scream. More blood explodes. Jace yells hoarsely, his sword ringing in one awful high-pitched cry of tortured and stressed metal. Backlash of Power fills the air, smacking at the walls. My boots grind long scars in the floor as I am flung back, my left elbow crumpling the edge of a wall and denting the steel strut just under the plasticine and Sheetrock.

Click. I see the face—pocked with the scars of teenage acne, dark eyes soulless and mechanical, greasy dark-blond hair and the wink of silver at his throat. A pad of fat under each jawline, the ravages of age clearly visible. He looks oddly familiar, though I don't recognize him.

Click. The leprous blue light gives one last flare. The stick-thin shadow vanishes. Another burst of that fetid stench—the rancidness of the Headmaster's Office—and footsteps run toward the window. A high, piercing giggle drives me to my knees, the gray of shock closing over my vision, the mark on my left shoulder squeezing down and sending red agony through me, shocking my heart back into beating.

I cough. Time snaps and speeds back up. I hear sirens.

It had taken only a few moments, all told. I crawled forward, my sword clattering to the ground, and took Jace in my arms. "—*oh gods*—" My voice sounded small after the thunderclap of demon Power.

Jace's blue eyes were glazed and thoughtful, the thorny Shaman tattoo on his cheek stock-still. His body was light—too light—even in my demon-strong arms. Too light because his throat and belly had been torn open, both in one painless gush.

I reached blindly for Power, my rings sparking, but it was too late. He was already gone. Sometimes not even a Necromance can bring back someone whose internal organs have been yanked out; whose throat has been slashed as well. We are the healers of mortal wounds, we who walk in Death's shadow, but this wound I could not heal.

The bathroom stench of a battlefield rose up around me. Hollin Sukerow's body lay inside a messy, uncompleted chalk circle, the Feeder glyphs wavering and a tide of quick-decaying ectoplasm covering everything in its wet slug-trail gleam, steaming as it rotted away. The glyphs tore and twisted—his hand must have been trembling.

And standing beside him had been a man whose face seemed only slightly familiar. But if I paged through my yearbook, I knew where I would find the younger version of that face.

Right next to Kellerman Lourdes's name.

And I knew what I'd seen, even if my eyes were blurred with tears. I'd seen the stick-thin figure of Headmaster Mirovitch, his hands on his hips, silhouetted against the diseased blue light. I had *smelled* him.

Blood and other fluids bathed my arm. "Jace," I whispered. His head lolled back obscenely far, throat slashed all the way down to the vertebrae; the wet red of muscle sliced too cleanly for a blade. The flesh had parted like water; I saw the purple of the esophagus, a glaring white chip of cervical spine.

His sword, the blade twisted into a cockeyed corkscrew, chimed against the ground as his hand released it. "*Jace*." My tattoo burned as I drew on all the Power available to me. The room shook and groaned. Books fell off shelves, and glass implements broken by my *kia* and the welter of backlashed Power from the Headmaster and Keller shivered into smaller pieces. I poured out every erg of my demon-given strength to do what a Necromance should do—bring a soul *back,* and seamlessly heal a hopelessly shattered body.

The light rose from him. I could still see it, the shining path made by a soul leaving the body, the foxfire of dying nerves giving a last painless flash. The blue crystal hall of Death rose around me, my emerald drenching the hall in swirling green light as I stood on the Bridge over the abyss. *Jason!* I howled his name, the crystal walls humming with the force of my distress, and then the God of Death came.

Anubis stalked to the very edge of the abyss in His full form, the obsidian-black, smoothly muscled skin of His arms and legs gleaming wetly. His ceremonial kilt rang and splashed with light, gold and gems glittering; His collar was broad and set with more jewels. The god's slender dog's head dipped, regarding me with one merciless, pitiless Eye, a black Eye that held a spark of crystalline blue light in its orb. He stood at the end of the Bridge anchored in the hall of Death, the Bridge I had walked so many times to bring a soul back.

His arms crossed, one holding the ceremonial flail, the other holding the crook. His will stopped me on the Bridge, my not-self wearing the white robe of the god's acolytes, my golden feet bare on the stone. Please! *It was an agonized cry, with all the force of my Will behind it—the sorcerous will I had learned to use, used all my life; the will that pushed Power to do my bidding, the will every practitioner had to create and use if he or she expected to cast any spell. My throat swelled with the agony of that cry, a physical ache in a nonphysical space.* Please, no! No! I will give you anything, I will go in his stead, please, my Lord, my god, give him back!

The God of Death looked down on me, His daughter, His faithful servant, and shook His head.

Bare, laid open, I struggled against that kind implacability. I offered it all: my own life, my service, every erg of power and heat and love I possessed. I could never give Jace what he wanted from me, but letting him go down into Death's dry country...No. The stubbornness flared, and for the first time in my memory, my god paused.

One hand extended, one finger, weightless, touched the crown of my head. There was a price for the balancing of Death's scales. Was I prepared to pay? Was that what he was asking me?

Anything, *I whispered.* I will give You anything I have, anything You ask.

And Death paused again. I read the refusal in His ageless, infinite eyes, and struggled uselessly against it. My cheek burned, the emerald flaring with drenching light, driving back the blue flame for one eternal moment. On and on, the strings of my psyche snapping, tearing, rent...

I was shoved back, pushed out of the space between worlds,

rammed choking and sobbing back into my body. I cradled Jace's empty husk to my chest, tilted my head back and screamed again, a sound so massive it was soundless, rising out of me like light from a nuclear fission. I was still screaming when the cops arrived, still screaming when Gabe fought through the press of sound, her nose bleeding from the wall of psychic agony. She fell to her knees, taking me in her arms. Her human warmth folded around me while I sobbed, mercifully robbed for a short while of every shred of demon power. I screamed again and again with only a broken human voice while I clutched the breathing, living body to my chest.

Breathing, yes. Living, yes. But nobody had to tell me that the soul inside was gone. My demon-given Power had mended Jason Monroe's shattered body in a mimicry of a *sedayeen*'s miraculous ability to heal, but he was dead all the same.

CHAPTER 27

I folded my hands carefully around the paper cup while late-afternoon sun slanted over the street. Gabe spoke softly to someone, they were processing the scene. I huddled in the back of an ambulance hover, a brown woolen blanket around my shoulders, my clothing stiff with dried blood and noisome fluids. I shivered, the black liquid masquerading as coffee inside the paper cup slopping against the sides.

It had been the middle of the day, everyone at work, nobody home except Hollin Sukerow. Which was a good thing, my scream and the explosion of loosed Power had taken out a good chunk of the building. Debris littered the street, smoke clearing on the air. It looked as if a wandering shark had just cruised by and taken a big half-circle bite out of the brownstone.

I shut my eyes. Gray shock closed over the darkness behind my eyelids again. Again the spiked warmth from the mark on my shoulder fought it back. Tears leaked hotly between my eyelids, dripping down my cheeks. My tangled hair was full of dust and blood and dirt.

They had taken Jace's body to the hospital. He was breathing, his heart beating, everything apparently fine...except it wasn't. It was an empty shell, an empty house, the soul fled but the housing that contained it intact. All the Power granted me by a demon's touch could not change Death's decree.

My sword, tucked up against my leg, hummed softly. I sat on the cold rubberized floor of the ambulance hover and exhaled softly. The whine of a slicboard rattled over the scene, and I realized my lips were still shaping the prayer to Anubis.

Anubis et'her ka. Se ta'uk'fhet sa te vapu kuraph. Anubis et'her ka. Anubis, Lord of the Dead, Faithful Companion, protect me, for I am Your child. Protect me, Anubis, weigh my heart upon the scales, watch over me, Lord, for I am Your child. Do not let evil distress me, but turn Your fierceness upon my enemies—

I stopped, choked on the rising tears, and forced them back down. Just like a kid, crying because a toy had been taken away, sobbing messily and completely.

No. I was not a child. I would never be a child again.

"Thank the gods you're here," Gabe said.

I opened my eyes to see Eddie heeling his slicboard as the cell powered down, ending with the board neatly racking itself against the step of the ambulance hover. "How is she?" For once, Eddie didn't growl or sneer. Instead, he pushed his shaggy hair back from his face and stole a few worried glances at me in between examining Gabe. He didn't even glance up at the hole in the side of the brownstone.

Gabe shrugged, an eloquent movement. "Danny?"

Both of them approached me, Eddie's rundown boots scraping the wet pavement. His long dirt-colored coat flapped. His aura, smelling of earth and pines, sweat and beer, meshed with Gabe's swirling Necromance sparkles.

I swallowed bile, looked up at their worried faces. Sunlight glittered in my reactive-dry eyes. I blinked.

"I didn't grab him in time. He was moving quicker than I've ever seen him move. He threw himself at Keller and Mirovitch—" I repeated it through the lump in my throat, my voice barely recognizable. Hoarse and wrecked, the voice of a stunned survivor of some natural disaster on the niner holonews. Change the channel, flip the station. Repeat as necessary.

Gabe's hand closed around my right shoulder. She squeezed just a little. "You already gave your statement, Danny. You don't have to."

"I should have caught him." Why did my voice, as hoarse and ruined as it was, sound so young? "I should have caught him." I held up one golden hand. "All the strength Japhrimel gave me, I should have *caught* him." My face crumpled again, soundlessly contorting into a mask. A tragedy mask, the darker half of laughter's coin. The mask I'd seen on so many other faces when a loved one passed on.

Gabe whispered something to Eddie.

"Goddamn." The dark circles under his eyes were almost gone. He looked better. "Look, Danny, I'm gonna take you to our house. We can clean you up, maybe get you something to eat."

"I'll be fine," I said tonelessly, hoarse. "Got work to do. The others on the list—"

"They've been taken to safehouses," Gabe said. "The building security net included stillcams. We've got a few good shots of Lourdes. They're all over the holovids, make the press work for us for once. Someone will call him in, and we'll take him down." Her mouth twisted slightly to one side. "Hard."

It was a promise of revenge, one that should have made me grateful. I felt nothing; the numbness of a razor drawn swiftly through flesh, the breathless moment before the pain starts, before the blood begins to flow.

"Nobody will see him." The ectoplasm had vanished, leaving only a faint shimmer on the bodies; the other victims had been found too late, no trace of ectoplasmic attack remaining. If we'd seen the slimy eggwhite of a *ka* taking shape in the physical world, we would have been more cautious. A *lot* more cautious. "Any more than anyone would see you if you really wanted to stay invisible. And he's...I think...Gabe, he's got Mirovitch...inside him."

"You saw Mirovitch? But I thought you said he..." She looked as confused as I felt.

Focus! The sharp stinging slap of the deep voice of my conscience jerked my head up. I'd been staring at my boots. "Gabe. Look. Poly told me that the kids all took a *piece* of Mirovitch. What if Keller took the last piece? Or somehow...I don't know. The first death was a decade after Mirovitch's...disappearance. Maybe the Headmaster wasn't as dead as everyone thought."

Gabe nodded. Her sleek hair dipped forward over her shoulders. "So he's out for revenge?"

"Revenge, maybe, who knows? But most certainly *collecting.*" I waited until Gabe absorbed this, then tossed the cup of coffee into the street. Steaming liquid spilled out. I watched as the steam twisted into angular shapes, dissipated. "I don't know if safehouses are going to be any good. I don't know how he's tracking them."

"You think Mirovitch is *inside* Lourdes?" Gabe's eyes were wide and dark. It was the stuff of nightmares, a psi carrying something like that around. A mule carrying a Feeder's *ka.*

A Feeder, hungry for Power. And instead of feeding from random victims, or having a mild case of being Feeder, Mirovitch was inside Keller, and taking back whatever the kids took from him years ago. Claiming his own. It made sense. The worst, absolutely *worst* type of Feeder. Hungry, hard to kill, and so very close now to collecting the leftover pieces of itself and becoming a fullblown *ka,* moving from mule to mule and draining each one as it went, turning them into soulless zombies—or worse, into Feeders too. A spreading contagion, replicating itself wherever it could.

"I'm guessing it's a *ka,* Gabe. Nothing else seems to fit." My throat stung, my eyes watering from the sunlight. Yes, only the sunlight. "I have something I have to do." Straining for politeness. It was a long reach.

"Danny. Please. Go with Eddie. Get some food. Get cleaned up and come to the hospital. We'll do this together."

I shook Gabe's hand from my shoulder. She backed up half a step, and I saw the sudden flicker in Eddie's aura. "You don't have to worry," I told them both, still in that little-girl voice I had no idea I still possessed. I heard the hurt clearly in my voice, too worn to camouflage or swallow it for once. "I'm not going to lash out at you. You could have a *little* more faith in me."

"I know you wouldn't," Gabe said. "But you've got that look again, Danny. That scary look that says you're about to go hunting, and gods help anyone in your way."

"That's about right." The ambulance hover rocked a little on its springs as my tone turned chill. Eddie shivered. The wind rose slightly, keening through the broken edges of the brownstone above. "I was too fucking young to kill Mirovitch all those years ago. I should have, I wished I could. I used to dream about it. This time, I'm old enough and armed enough to do it." I looked up at the smoking hole torn in the building. "I need to find out about this Bryce Smith guy—if he was just a cover for Lourdes. What the connection is. We still don't know that."

Gabe nodded. The purposeful milling around the scene continued behind her. Two coroner's hovers lifted off, the whine of hovercells cutting through the sound of the gathered crowd behind the yellow plasilica tape marking off the borders of the investigation. I saw flashes pop, and guessed the holovid reporters were out in force. My eyes followed the hovers as they rose gracefully, then banked and flew away toward the station house and the morgue. Sunlight stung my eyes even more, making hot tears roll down my cheeks. "Hospital." I winced at the childlike breathiness of my voice. "They've taken him to the hospital?"

Gabe nodded. "Yeah. Come with us, Danny."

No. Please, no. "His sword. You don't need that for evidence, do you?"

Eddie made a brief restless movement. I was being rude again.

I was too tired to care. Japhrimel had never told me about the weariness of demons, the weariness of a being that didn't need sleep. A weariness that seemed to sink into every bone, every thought. Or was it a weariness peculiar to *hedaira?* I had nobody I could ask.

I was adrift again, as if I was twelve years old and shipwrecked by the death of the only family I had ever known. Again.

"You know it's yours." Gabe actually looked hurt. "I'm so sorry, Danny. I know you loved him."

My lips puckered as if I tasted something sour. Maybe it was only failure. *I didn't even know that myself, Gabe.* "Thanks." My voice sounded as if it was coming from someone else, someone whose harsh tone was flat and terribly loaded with Power. If the god hadn't temporarily denied me the ability to use the demon Power I'd been granted, I might have leveled the building. Or even more.

Probably more.

Definitely more.

"Don't, Danny." Eddie was uncharacteristically serious, examining me. His shoulders slumped as if under a heavy weight. The wind plucked at his coat, mouthed his untidy hair. "Don't do this to yourself."

Don't do this to myself? Don't DO this to myself? "Who else should I do it to? I'm kind of out of victims, in case you hadn't noticed. Everyone who gives a damn about me dies sooner or later. You should be getting as far away as—"

I didn't realize I was shouting until Gabe clapped her hand over my mouth, stepping close. Her dark eyes—*human* eyes—were bare inches from mine; she was much shorter than me, but I was sitting on the edge of the hover's step, so her nose hovered next to mine, her mouth on the other side of her hand. Her breath brushed my face, and the smell of kyphii and her perfume mixed, driving through my nose. My demon-based scent flared, a wave of musk and spice, and her pupils dilated slightly. That was all.

"Shut the fuck up, Dante," she said softly, conversationally. "We're using your hover. You're coming to my house to get cleaned up, and we're going to the hospital. We'll catch this fucker, and when we do, what we do to him is going to make a werecain kill look sweet and clean. I dragged you into this, and if you want to blame someone, fine, blame me and we'll do some sparring later to hash it out. But for right now, sunshine, you're with us. You got it?"

It was ridiculous. It was ri-*fucking*-diculous. I was part *demon,* stronger and faster than her, with enough power to level a building when a god wasn't stopping me. Hunger began, a faint cramping under my ribs. But hunger wasn't what was making my hands shake so that I had to clasp my sword, *hard,* to keep them still.

I stared into Gabe's eyes, her irises so dark her pupils seemed to blend into them. This close I could see the fine speckles of gold in her irises, and the faint freckles that dusted her perfect patrician nose. Her aura closed around me, the comfort of another Necromance, not seeking to minimize the pain. Her cedary perfume spilled through the shield of demon scent, and I was grateful for it.

Her eyes looked directly into mine.

I have only stared that intensely into one other pair of eyes, and those had been brilliantly green, glowing green. As it was, wordless communication passed through her into me, a zing like an electric current, stinging all the way down to the quick. It was a different kind of communion than the one that passed between me and Anubis, and still different than the alien ecstasy of Japhrimel's hands on me while he stared unblinking through my humanity. No, this was purely female communication, something as deep and bloody as the depths of labor pangs.

And for all I'd never had a child, I still *knew.* Every child knows. Every woman knows, too.

"I'm with you, Danny," she finally whispered. "You owe him being at the hospital. You know what we have to do."

My vision blurred. It wasn't shock, it was hot tears. Gabe's eyes were gentle and utterly pitiless, but still grieving.

I nodded, slowly. Her hand fell away from my mouth, but she didn't look away. She offered me her hand, and I took it gently, my fingers sliding through hers.

Eddie hunched his shoulders. He said nothing as Gabe pulled me to my feet.

Soft beeps and boops from the machines monitoring pulse and respiration filled the air, and a tide of human pain scraped at my skin. Hospitals aren't comfortable for psions. All the advanced technology in the world can't hide the fact that a hospital is where you go when you're sick, and the terminus of getting sick is dying. Even the Necromance, whose entire professional life is bound up with death, doesn't like being reminded that he or she is finite and will one day tread the same path as the clients.

The room was small, but at least it was private. There was even a window, showing the thin sunlight outside and clouds massing in the north. We were up on the third floor, the curtains pulled back, smooth blue plasflooring under our feet...and Jace Monroe's body, lying perfect and breathing like a clockwork toy on the tethered hoverbed with its white sheets and dun blanket. His hair glowed in the pale light; he finally looked relaxed and about ten years younger.

The chair sat stolid and empty on the other side of the bed. Eddie stood at the foot, and I found myself next to Jace's hand, looking down.

Gabe exchanged low fierce whispers with someone at the door. She was a licensed Necromance and the investigating detective, and if she said he was dead her word held in a court of law. With two Necromances in the room and an EEG showing flatline, there wasn't any doubt: Jason Monroe was *dead,* and this was a flagrant use of Hegemony medical facilities for no good reason. Still, Gabe made them go away so we could say goodbye to the soulless body on the bed, probably invoking the second clause of the Amberson Act.

I didn't care. Was past caring. I was scrubbed down and wearing Eddie's shirt and a fresh pair of jeans—not Gabe's, she was too small, and I didn't want to ask why they had a pair of pants in my size at their house. My boots were still wet, but at least they'd been rinsed off. My hair lay wet and tightly braided in a rope against my back that bumped me whenever I shifted my weight.

Gabe closed the door with a firm click. I felt the tingle of Power and glanced over to see her place a lockcharm on the handle. The rune sank in, barring the door with its spiked backward-leaning X; simple and elegant like all of Gabe's magick.

Silence fell. She turned away from the door, her long police-issue synthwool coat moving with her. I hadn't taken my coat off either, and we both were fully armed. Add to that a Necromance's reputation for being a little twitchy, and no wonder the hospital staff was nervous. And if it wasn't that, the sudden appearance of holovid crews outside the hospital would have done it.

Gabe blew out between her teeth, met Eddie's eyes. Communication passed between them, like the look Jace would give me when he wanted to ask if I was all right but didn't quite dare to.

Jace. My throat was dry. "Gabe." The word cracked on the air.

"Take your time," she said.

I closed my eyes, tried not to sway. I needed all my courage for this. All of mine, and more. "You could do it." I whispered, helpless to stop myself. "You could bring him back. He could—"

Eddie made a brief, restless movement. Said nothing. But his aura tightened, the smell of fresh dirt and beer suddenly foaming through the room. He was a dirtwitch berserker, if he got angry enough he was well-nigh unstoppable. There was no reason for him to get angry at me, though.

Not yet.

Gabe sucked in a small breath. "You know I can't." Her voice hitched. "He's gone, Danny. Let him go."

Wonder of wonders, calm precise Gabriele sounded choked. As if something was stuck in her throat. My rings sparked dully. I reached down, saw my own graceful, golden-skinned hand. It hovered above the human hand lying on the fuzzy dun coverlet, callused and scraped from hard combat, white scars from knifework reaching up his wrist. There was a time when I would have known every scar, would have kissed each one. "An apparition." My throat was dry as sand. "Just this once. His body's living, he just needs to come *back*."

"You know it doesn't work like that." Gentle, relentless, but there was a sob behind every word. "We have to let him *go,* Danny. We have to."

I never thought to hear my own voice raggedly pleading at a bedside, though I'd helped many a client over the border and safely into death, making sure their families could hear their last words and say their own final codas. My right hand cramped, but only a little, as I reached up to scrub the tears away from my cheeks. I had promised not to cry, hadn't I?

Anubis et'her ka. Anubis, my Lord, my God, please help me. Please, help me.

Nothing happened. I took in a jagged breath freighted with the smell of human pain and Jace's fading peppery scent. Without his soul in the body, the smell of his Power would leach away, just like the perfectly functioning clockwork of his body would begin to atrophy. He was, for all intents and purposes, gone. Pulling an apparition back from the dry land of Death and trying to force it back into the body wouldn't work. If his soul had stayed, miracles could be worked, but Death had claimed him.

The next prayer that rose was tinted blood-red in its intensity, sweeping over my entire body like a rain of tiny needles, clouding my vision.

Japhrimel. That was all, every scrap of longing poured into one single word. I tipped my head back, jaw working, the murdered animal inside my chest scrambling for escape. The mark on my left shoulder began to tingle, prickle, and finally burn, sinking in through my skin as if the nerves there were slowly waking up after a long cramped sleep. *Please, Japhrimel, if you can hear me, help me out here. Help me.*

Then the shame started as I tipped my head back down. Here I was at Jace's bedside, and I couldn't stop thinking about a dead demon. If Japhrimel could be resurrected, I would have resurrected him by now. I wasn't worth either of them, goddammit.

I snatched my hand back. "I can't." The words tasted like ash in my mouth. I lifted my left hand, weighted with my sword, let it drop heavily back down to my side. "Gabe, I c-can't."

Silence. Was she looking at Eddie? Was he looking back, sharing her pain? Pain shared, pain halved. How many times had I leaned on Jace, letting him take my pain, blind to everything but my own selfishness? And yet he'd given up everything, including his life, thinking he could protect me from still more. I stumbled back a blind two steps, and Eddie's arm closed over my shoulders. I flinched, almost ready to drive an elbow into his ribs and duck away, but control clamped down on combat instinct just in time. The Skinlin's arm tightened, and the heavy edge of his coat brushed mine. He was warm, very warm for a human, and smelled most of all like freshly-turned earth.

He said nothing. It was a new world record, Eddie refraining from a snarky comment for longer than ten seconds. A bloody fucking miracle.

Gabe stepped up to the bedside. She had unsheathed a knife, cold steel. It was, after all, traditional. She didn't glance at me. Instead, her pretty face was set and white as she looked down at Jace's still form, its chest rising and falling with macabre regularity. "Would you like to say anything, Danny?" The familiar question, only I was usually the one that asked it.

"You think he can hear me?" I tried to sound brave. But my voice was too high-pitched and breathy, again lacking the terrible velvet weight of demon's seduction or the ruined hoarseness of Lucifer's final gift to me, when his fingers crackled in my throat.

She smiled, still looking down at his face. He looked peaceful, the lines smoothed away and his hair combed back from his face. As if he was sleeping. "The dead can always hear us, Danny. You know that."

And gods help me, but I did. Only the knowledge held no comfort, even for me. My shoulders hunched. Eddie's arm tightened. I swallowed ash, tasted bitterness. "I'm sor—" Gulped down air, tried again. "I'm sor—" And again, the sounds that were choked halfway. I couldn't say it now, when it mattered most of all.

"Gods," Eddie whispered. "Gabe." He was shaking, a fine tremor that leapt to me as if we were both drunk or sick. I think my knees may have buckled, because I leaned into him.

She understood, and moved forward, one pale narrow hand resting on Jace's forehead, the other holding the knife tucked back against her forearm. Her sleek dark hair gleamed in the light, and the sparkles of her aura began to pulse. "Jason Monroe," she said quietly, her voice carrying ancient authority, "travel well. Be at peace."

Noooooo ... I swallowed the moan, locked my teeth, refused to let it out. Still, a low hurt sound came, whether from me or from Eddie I couldn't tell. Didn't want to know. Gabriele's aura flashed, and for a moment I seemed to see blue flame crawling up her arm. The knife flicked, steel glittering in the weak autumn sunlight, and a sigh echoed through the room. The machines stopped their beeping and booping. Silence rang like a bell through the room, a silence I had heard so many times but never like this, never when I was the one trying to scream and utterly unable to do so.

"And flights of angels sing thee to thy rest," Gabe whispered softly, tenderly. His eyes were closed, but she laid her hand over them anyway, as if closing them. Her aura faded back to its usual sparkles, her shielding humming as it settled into place. Tears glittered on her pale cheeks. The blood had drained from her face, and fresh shame bit me. What had it cost her to do this for me, something I was too weak to do for myself?

Jace. Jason...

I managed to find my balance, slowly. Eddie let me go as soon as I pulled away from him. I took the deepest breath of my life, seemingly endless, my ribs crackling as I inhaled, and inhaled, and inhaled. My aura throbbed.

I stepped up to the side of the bed. Gabe didn't look at me. She studied Jace's sleeping face as if the secrets of the universe were printed there. For all I know, they might have been.

Two fingers, tipped with black molecule-drip polish, I touched the back of his hand. Nothing there, not even the low glow of nerves slowly dying out, what Necromances call foxfire. She had done a good job. Her knife sang as it slid back into its sheath, softly, gently, clicking home.

It was too hard to look up. I stared at his hand. "Thank you." Amazingly, the words didn't stick in my throat. My broken voice sounded like sandpaper honey. The plain beige curtains ruffled uneasily.

Her free hand found my arm and squeezed once, hard. "You're my friend, Danny." She sounded tired. "You understand? There's no debt between friends."

Maybe it's just that the debt gets so high you stop counting it. I freed her fingers from my arm gently, delicately. "Thank you." It sounded more natural now, more like myself. More like Danny Valentine.

Who the hell was she, though? I no longer knew.

"Danny—"

I turned, digging my heel in, my boot scraping on the plasfloor. Then I headed for the door. Two long strides. I heard Eddie move and tensed, but his hand didn't close on me.

The words sent a chill up my spine. "Let her go," he told Gabe. "Gods above and below, just let her *go*."

It was too late. The door was closed. I was already gone.

CHAPTER 28

It was child's play to slip back into my house without the reporters seeing. I came over the wall again, twisting to land lightly on my feet, and brushed my hands off. My lungs burned from running for so long, literally blurring through the streets, moving with a speed close to the eerie darting quickness of a demon. Close, but not close enough.

The god of Death did not bar me from using my strength now.

The sun was sinking, high dark clouds massing in the north. The first of the winter storms, not coming in from over the bay but sliding down the coast. I took a lungful of Saint City air, chill with approaching winter. My garden was ragged, unkempt; I had been too busy running bounties to keep up with the weeding.

I stopped a good twenty paces from my house, eyeing it critically. Bought with Doreen, as an abandoned dump when cheap property was the rule in this neighborhood because of the gang wars and derelicts, paid off completely with blood money, my haven and sanctuary rose above me, glowing with some freak ray of evening light.

I kicked my front door open, the doorframe shattering and spraying little splinters into my front hall. Choked, had to swallow cold iron. Tears, and grief. And something so huge I was afraid it would choke me.

The shields shivered, each layer of energy vibrating. The layers of shielding Jace had applied were fading; it would take a long time for them to fully vanish without his reinforcing. Months, maybe, if I didn't put a shuntline in and take them down myself. But I didn't have that sort of time, did I?

I stalked into the front hall, into my living room.

The candles on Jace's altar were out, the smell of burned wax filling the air. The dove's blood had splashed up out of the brass bowl, the painting of Saint Barbara rent and tattered.

So Jace's *loa* knew. Of course they knew. The spirits always know.

I looked at the tapestry on the west wall. Isis's face was turned away, and Horus's wings rustled uneasily, threads shifting against each other with soft, whispering, grieving sounds.

A cream-colored flash on my fieldstone altar caught my eye. I approached it slowly, each footstep seeming to take an eon, my boots making hard clicking sounds against hardwood and muffled thuds on my meditation-rug.

Propped against the inlaid wooden box holding holostills of Lewis and Doreen, the envelope crouched. Vellum, with its proud screaming seal of red crimson wax, it grinned at me. I resisted the urge to turn in a tight circle—there was nobody in my house. Not now.

The sound surprised me. A low keening hum vibrated in my chest, my back teeth clicking together as my throat swelled with the effort of keeping the scream in.

Lucifer. Dipping his elegant little fingers in my life again. Taunting me. Polluting even my grief. He couldn't stand to leave me alone. Japhrimel was dead, Jace was dead, and the Prince of Hell had just poked me one goddamn time too many.

This has gone too far. This voice was new, a stiletto of steely-cold fury turning in the center of my brain. I stared at the crimson seal, hearing the creaks and flutters of my house as my rage communicated itself through the air, pressing against the walls, touching the tapestries, ruffling the paper. From the kitchen came a dim crash as cupboard doors chattered open and closed, I heard smashing from the dining room and the tinkle of broken glass upstairs. My throat swelled, a stone caught in its center, my eyes hot and staring as I struggled to contain the fury.

There was no containing it. An almost-audible *snap* resonated in the middle of my chest, a locked door shattering open and sterile light flooding out. The circuit of rage snapped closed, and a humming filled my brain.

I. Have. Had. Enough.

The choking wrath eased, turning into sharp clarity. There were things to do. Places to go.

People—and not-people—to *kill.*

I turned on my heel, stalked upstairs. My fingernails had turned to demon claws. I tore the borrowed clothes off as I went, shreds of fabric falling away. I ripped my shirt into pieces, sliced the tough denim of my jeans. I tripped halfway up, my jeans tangling around my ankles. My head hit the balustrade with stunning force, shattering the wood. The sounds that came out of me smashed the plaster from my walls, scorched the paint, made the glass of each picture I'd hung shatter. The noise of plasglass breaking almost managed to cover my wrenching sobs.

I tore the covers from my bed; they still held Jace's scent and mine. I threw them across the room. Then I punched my computer deck. Plasilica broke, my tough golden skin sliced but closing almost immediately, the black blood welling up and sealing away the hurt. Sparks popped, a spray of them from the deck's monitor, little squealing sounds as my rage smashed the circuits.

My demon-callused feet ground in shards of plasglass, since I'd broken the shower door and the mirrors. I got dressed—a microfiber shirt, another pair of jeans, dry socks, my boots were still damp but I pulled them on anyway. I slid the strap of my messenger bag over my head. The necklace I'd worn to the House of Pain went over my head, settled humming against my breastbone.

I dug the two spade necklaces out of my bloody coat. My hair streamed over my shoulders, heavy and soft, the braid had unraveled. The necklaces went into my bag.

Then I strode down the hall to the end. The holostill of Doreen to my right, smiling her gentle smile, fell. The plasglass of the frame shattered in a tinkling burst. I hit the door at the end of the hall open with the flat of my hand; a hollow sound thudding through me.

Jace's room blazed with the last dying rays of sunlight. A golden square from the window lay over his bed with Doreen's blue comforter. I smelled the lingering sweetness of a psion metabolizing alcohol wedded to the smell of human male, and my heart twisted. The lamp by the bed—a Merican Era antique with a base made of amber glass—rattled as I stood in the doorway. I could go no further.

Neatly-made twin bed, plain pine dresser with empty Chivas Red bottles making a collage of mellow glowing plasglass, each tightly capped and with a small lightcharm wedded to each one. At night the bottles would glow softly, each limned in gold or blue; it was a trick most often seen in Academy dorm rooms, where drinking was a hobby raised to an art form. The closet door was half-open, showing neatly hung dark clothes, the long low bench where he made his own bullets and prepared his charms and amulets rested along the wall, organized with amulets in different stages of completion, as well as jars of dried herbs and interesting bits of bone and fur and feather. A threadbare red velvet cushion sat precisely placed in front of the bench. His nightstand held a stack of music discs and a personal player, the headphones stowed out of the way; a short wickedly curved knife; and a Glockstryke R4 projectile gun gleaming mellowly in the thick golden light. No pictures or holostills on the walls. His spare rig hung neatly on a peg near the door, as did his old coat, with its several pockets and leather patches against the tough canvas.

I reached out, gently took the coat down, and shrugged into it, switching my sword from one hand to the other. It still smelled like peppered honey that tingled with the memory of thorn-spiked Shaman's aura.

I filled my lungs with the smell of my Power and Jace's, the mixed scent of a part-demon and a Shaman, the bitter smell of my own failure tainting every mouthful, every inch of oxygen. Then I backed away, closing the door gently, as if someone was sleeping in the room beyond.

It was time to pay my toll to the dead.

I turned, went down the hall and down the stairs, stopping at the niche. The statue of Anubis I wrapped in a square of black silk sitting under it, the resultant bundle went into my bag, with a quiet apology to the god. I picked up the lacquered urn, surprised again by its weight. *Oh, Japhrimel. I'm sorry. Gods forgive me for what I have done. Forgive me for what I am about to do.*

My cheeks were wet again. I sniffed, spat to the side. My rings loosed a shower of golden sparks.

Urn in one hand, my sword in the other, I continued downstairs. I looked into the kitchen, at the dining-room table, where the stack of yearbooks taunted me. I'd forgotten to turn the coffeepot off, and it had no shut-off switch. The smell of cooked coffee made my gorge rise.

What rough beast's hour has come at last? I almost seemed to hear Lewis's voice, from the long-ago dim reaches of my childhood. The poem had always made my hackles rise, it had been my favorite. *And where will it be born, after it slouches through my life?*

I looked at my fieldstone altar; at Jace's altar, my couch, the plants he had watered and nursed between bounties because I'd been too busy running headlong from one thing to the next. I took another deep breath, a thin sound breaking free as I exhaled, catching sight of the vellum envelope and crimson seal.

My bootheels clicked on the floor. I smelled smoke.

I drew my sword.

The blade shone blue, runes twisting on the steel, answering my will as if I'd spent months stroking it and pouring Power into it.

Jace...

His name choked me. I could not say it.

Anubis had denied me entry into Death for the first time. The Lord of Death didn't bargain, and I couldn't have brought Jace back even with a demon's Power—his body had been too wounded, internal organs pulled out and shredded. It had been hopeless even before I'd spent all my strength in a futile rebellion against Death's decree. A *sedayeen* might have been able to do it right after the initial injury, but I was no pacifist healer. Or maybe Jace's soul had been tired of living, finding itself freed of the body for a moment and bolting away from the cruelty of life?

My failures rose to choke me. I hadn't been quick enough as a human to kill Santino, and if Japhrimel hadn't given up a large share of his demon Power for me he might have been too tough for Lucifer to kill so easily. And even with the strength and speed Japhrimel had given me, I had not been able to catch Jace when he rocketed past me to protect me from whatever twisted sorcery had dredged up Mirovitch to torture seemingly everyone who had survived Rigger Hall.

The glyph took shape at the end of my sword, encased in a sphere of lurid crimson. It was *Keihen,* the Torch, one of the Greater Glyphs of Destruction, a little-used part of the Nine Canons.

I don't love you, I had told him after Rio. *I won't ever love you.*

And his answer? *If I cared about* that *I'd still be in Rio with a new Mob Family and a sweet little fat-bottomed* babalawao. *This is my choice, Danny.* And stubbornly, over and over again, he had proved his love for me in a hundred different ignored ways.

I had never even guessed how much he meant to me.

There was only one thing I could give up, one penance I could pay, for the mess I'd made of everything. If Japhrimel could be resurrected, it was probably too late; he had Fallen. Lucifer's word meant nothing; hadn't he always been called the father of lies? If a Fallen demon could be resurrected and Lucifer wanted him, he could have sent another demon to collect me and the urn, or just the urn. I was part-demon, sure, but no match for a real one.

None of it mattered. All that mattered was that I had tortured myself with hope, when I had known all along there *was* no hope. Japhrimel was never coming back, and neither was Jace. If I survived taking down a Feeder's *ka,* I'd live afterward with the knowledge that I had denied myself even the faintest slim chance of resurrecting Japhrimel.

My toll to the dead: my hope. It was the only penance big enough.

I took my time with the glyph, no shuntlines, no avenues for the Power to follow except one simple undeniable course. The crimson globe spat, sizzled, and began to steam. Vapor took angular shapes, tearing at the air. I clamped my teeth in my lower lip, ignoring the pain, and stood in my front hall, Japhrimel's urn tucked under my arm and the house shields quivering uneasily but calming when I stroked them. The glyph twisted inside its red cage, trying to escape. I flicked it off the tip of my sword, in the hall between the stairs and the living room, and held it spinning in the air with will alone, my sword sliding back into its sheath.

I got a good grip on Japhrimel's urn. I had to hold the glyph steady while it strained like a slippery fiery eel. I spat black blood from my cut lip, sank my teeth in again until I worried free a mouthful of acid-tasting demon blood. This I dribbled into my palm and smoothed over Japhrimel's urn, the rising keening of the glyph inside its bubble of crimson light beginning to scorch the ceiling. The heat blew my hair back. The paint blistered on the walls, bubbling, and I smelled more smoke.

I tossed Japhrimel's bloodied urn straight up. My sword rang free of the sheath, a perfect draw, the sound of the cut like worlds colliding. Ash pattered down, the cleanly-broken halves of the urn smacking the floor and shattering, but I was already shuffling back, my sword held away from my body. Running with every ounce of demon speed, I reached the door before the bubble holding the glyph...burst.

There was an immense, silent sound, felt more in the bones than heard. I spun aside at the door and leapt, but a giant warm hand pressed against the back of my body and threw me clear. I landed and rolled, instinct saving me. I came to a halt panting, my head ringing with flame, my bitten lip singing with pain until black blood coated the hurt and sealed it away.

My left shoulder came alive with agony. I screamed, the force of my cry adding to the explosion that shook the ground. Flame bellowed up, and bits of the garden igniting and crumbling to ash. The heat was like a living thing, crawling along my body, only the shield of my Power kept my clothes from smoking and catching fire.

There. Both the men in my life, gone. I had read, long ago, of the

Vikings sending ships out to sea alive with flame, burial barges to go with the dead into the afterlife. Now I sent my house into Death as well as Japhrimel and Jace. If I was lucky, when I died they might be waiting for me.

The only thing left now was anger. Fury. Rage. A crimson wash so huge it shoved all other considerations aside. Easier to fight than to cry. Easier to kill than to admit to the pain.

And oh, anger is sweet. Fury is the best fuel of all. It is so clean, so marvelous, so ruthless. Eye for eye, tooth for tooth, rage against evil is better than sorrow. Sorrow can't balance the scales.

Vengeance could. And she would too, if I had anything to say about it.

I was already on my feet, unsteady, walking away. I made it to my front gate as the layers of shielding on my house imploded, fueling the Power-driven flames. There would be nothing left but ash and a deep crater. My head rang and my shoulder crunched again with pain. I inhaled, staggering.

I had always wondered what the limit of my powers was. The wall was scorching, concrete turning black and brittle on the outside. My garden was swallowed alive with flame, kissed with choking ash. I dimly heard human screams, and wondered if the shockwave would break a few windows. The gate itself was beginning to melt and warp. It almost seared my hand when I touched it, tough painted pla-silica bubbling and smoking.

I opened my front gate, stepped out.

A few enterprising holovid reporters tried to take pictures. I no longer cared. I stalked through them like a well-fed lion through a herd of zebra. Some of them were cowering behind their bristling hovers. Fine hot flakes of ash drifted down. I heard sirens, and thought that the house was past saving. I did feel a moment's pity for my neighbors, but it passed.

It was three blocks before I remembered to sheathe my sword. The mark on my left shoulder settled into a steady burning that was not entirely unpleasant, except for one last flare that stopped me for a full thirty seconds, head down as I breathed heavily, ribs flickering as my lungs heaved. Then I pushed my hair—dry now from the fierce heat, and crowned with tiny flakes of ash—back, and continued on my way. The sun had sunk below the rim of the bay in the west. The column of smoke from my shattered home blazed a lurid orange, underlit by flame.

Night had fallen.

And it was going to be a long one.

CHAPTER 29

Four hours later I stopped in a coffeeshop in midtown, ordered five shots of their best espresso, and stood at a table. My sword tucked into a loop on my belt while I tapped at my datpilot. The shop's holovid feed was on, and I saw without much surprise that my house had made the evening news.

I didn't look after seeing the first few moments of scrambled footage: the column of flame going up an impressive couple of thousand feet, making a mushroom cloud of smoke that led some hysterical people to think that there had been a nuclear attack on Saint City. There had been no hovertraffic overhead, since my house was outside the main lanes, and the force of the explosion had been channeled up instead of outward, so apart from some broken windows and traumatized holovid reporters, there was precious little damage to anything other than my house.

Which was, of course, what I'd wanted. Something I'd done right, for once.

I took down the five shots of espresso at once. The mark on my shoulder had settled back to a satisfied glow, spreading over my body like warm oil. I looked at my datpilot. The information Gabe had sent was interesting, to say the least: a summary of all the bodies so far, dates of death, and thumbnail digitals of the crime scenes. She'd also had an analysis done of the glyphs, and it was this that I studied, going from one to the next while my datpilot glowed. It took a couple of hours of standing there, my eyes glued to the screen, to really get a sense of how the Feeder glyphs altered from the regular Ceremonial alphabet of the Nine Canons, and how twisting each rune in a particular fashion would serve the purpose of strengthening a psychic vampire. My secondary talent as a runewitch helped.

I felt the gnaw of hunger just under my breastbone. For the first time, I had truly extended my powers, and I found I was starving. I ignored it, for now.

My eyes felt dry and grainy. I locked my jaw against the slight moaning sound I wanted to make. *Grieve later,* I told myself. *Work now. Grieve later.*

The door to the coffeehouse opened, and I glanced over. Nothing impressive, just a slicboard kid, his hair done in wild spikes of blue and green, wearing three torn, layered Fizzwhackers T-shirts and loose plasleather shorts with a chain for a belt, along with the newest and most expensive gleaming white Aeroflot sneakers. He looked at me with the supreme unconcern of the very young, and my blood turned to ice when I thought I recognized his face. Then the moment passed. He was too young to have been at Rigger Hall. Far too young, and normal besides. Not a psion.

I noticed for the first time that the shop was very quiet, and glanced up. The three employees were trying not to stare at me, and uneasiness roiled in the air. I set my jaw, put my datpilot away, and left, no doubt to their great relief.

Walking through Saint City at night is always interesting, due to the fact that the city rarely sleeps. In some districts, it never sleeps at all except during daylight. I wandered, head down and hands more often than not clasped around the katana's scabbard. I wasn't quite thinking. It was more like a sort of haze, shot through with different crystal-clear images.

Like the corner of Thirtieth and Pole, a hooker leaning against a streetlamp opening her mouth to proposition me but retreating rapidly as soon as she saw my tat, the call dying on her lips as streetlamp light kissed and slid over her tired human face.

Or a neon-lit alley, where I paid the entrance fee and went into a screaming shuddering nightclub, going to the bar and paying also for a shot of vodka I didn't drink; the atmosphere of synth-hash smoke, sex, and frantic clinging as painful as the loud screeching noise that passed for music. Then, turning away from the bar, wandering aimlessly through the dancers and the occasional ghostflit riding the waves of sound and sensation, and finally going out the front door again onto the black streets.

Or a deserted street, wet because rain had started to fall, patterns of street light swimming against the gleaming concrete. Shapes I almost knew flickered through the gleam of the falling droplets as the storm moved in, washing the air clean.

I penetrated the tangle of alleys in the Bowery, the deepest part of the Tank District. They led to the Rathole, and I spent a little while standing on an abandoned shelf looking down into the huge sinkhole that used to be a transport well, watching the little firefly flickers that were the sk8 tribes getting ready for their nightly cohesion of slicboard deviltry and community-building. Each young slictribe kid down there whirling on a slicboard through the ramps and jumpoffs was a star, reactive paint glittering as they swooped and yelled with joy; I felt the meaning of the patterns of their chaotic dance tremble at the edge of my understanding.

The idea swam just under the surface of my mind. I always thought best while moving, and this aimless back and forth did qualify as moving. I had read once that sharks in the ocean's cold depths couldn't stop swimming or they would drown.

I understood.

Dawn came up in a glow of rose and gold, the storm passing to the south after having dropped its cargo of water. I found myself up on a rooftop in the University District, the spell of night wearing off and the furnace of the sun breaking free of Earth's darkness. I saw dripping trees in Tasmoor Park below me, heard the hovertraffic overhead take on a new urgency to begin the day, felt my dry burning eyes wanting to close.

When the sun had been up for a while, I got up from lying on the wet, cold concrete of the rooftop and climbed down the rusty fire escape to the alley below, and went in search of a callbox. It took some doing—on this edge of the U District the last riots had destroyed a few callboxes, and phone companies were loath to put more in when everyone had datpilots with voice capability—but I finally found one on the fringe of the Tank District on the edge of an abandoned lot. I stepped into the lighted box, my wet clothes sticking to my steaming skin, and dialed a familiar number.

"Spocarelli, Saint City Parapsych." She sounded hassled and tired. Behind her, frantically ringing phones and raised voices, shuffling papers. It sounded busy.

"Gabe." My voice was a husk of its former self. "It's me. Any news?"

One lone second of silence was all I got. Then, "Holy *fuck*," Gabe whisper-screamed into the phone. "Where the *fucking* hell are you, Danny? Eddie and I been looking everywhere for you! What the *fuck* are you doing? We thought Lourdes had taken you out too! What are you *doing?*"

This struck me as an excellent question. What was I doing? "Thinking. Been thinking. Look, the other four on the list—"

"Three," she said grimly. "It was a busy night. He got a Shaman named Alyson Brady last night and killed four cops to do it. It's like he has some sort of link with them, he's hunting them down like a bloodhound. We had all of them in safehouses. Now we're moving them every two hours. The holovids are having a field day. They're calling him the Psychic Ripper. Chief just got finished chewing my ass out over this. I sure hope you have a good fucking idea in that steel box you call a head, I have been worried *sick* about you, goddammit! Why didn't you call me? Goddamn you and your theatrics, Valentine!"

I closed my eyes. Four Spook Squad cops down, and Brady. I'd known Brady, even worked on a mercenary job or two with her. I might have even seen her wearing that spade necklace. We'd never discussed Rigger Hall at all, not even when we were crouched behind a pile of wreckage with three desperate bounties shooting at us, me bleeding from my head and her bleeding just about everywhere else. That had been the Gibrowitz job; the bounties were wanted for the rape and murder of the Hegemony senator's daughter. We'd brought them in a little worse for wear. Brady, in particular, did not like rapists.

The necklaces.

Instinct clicked under my skin. I actually gasped, cutting off Gabe's frustrated swearing.

If I hadn't been so tired, so physically and emotionally exhausted, I might not have seen it. "Gabe." My voice took on a new urgency. "Look. Do they still have the spade necklaces?"

"I don't...I know Brady had one." Gabe's tone sharpened suspiciously. "Danny, what are you thinking?"

"Get those necklaces from them. Do it now. Take 'em to the station, and *don't touch them* if you can help it. Leave them on your desk for me and *clear out.* I think that's how he's tracking them. Get all the necklaces together. I'll be there in an hour to get them. Draw him off."

"Danny, we still don't know what we're dealing with!" The high edge of panic colored her voice. "If it's a *ka*—"

"I think I know what's going on. And he killed Jace because he couldn't kill me, Gabe. I'm the best equipped to track him down, goddammit, if it's a *ka* I'll take my goddamn motherfucking chances." My voice was infused with a certainty I didn't feel. Then something else occurred to me. "Why did you think Lourdes had taken me out?"

"Your *house,* you idiot! Didn't you see the footage?" Phones beeped and buzzed behind her. I heard someone shouting about a Ceremonial trace. More shuffling papers. Click of a lighter and a long inhale—she was smoking again.

I think that is the very first time you have ever called me an idiot, Gabe. "What footage?"

"Hades, Danny. It's been all over the news. Your house was wrecked and they have footage of you wandering off looking like you'd been hit on the head. Worrying the *fuck* out of me, I might add! I thought Lourdes was following you, I thought you might be *dead!*"

A slight, shaky laugh boiled out of me. "I *am* dead, Gabe. I just don't have enough sense to lie down and admit it. Get the necklaces. I'm coming to collect them, and I'll take care of Lourdes or Miro-vitch or both or *whoever* this is. And Gabe, if you've got the neck-laces there in the building and you start to feel hinky, *run.* Don't take him on."

"But—*backup,* Danny! For the love of Hades—"

"No fucking backup." My voice was flat and level. "You saw what he did to Jace, he's already killed enough of your people. I'm part *demon,* Gabe. If anyone can take this on, it's me; if I think I need backup or a goddamn thermonuclear strike I'll call in and *tell* you. Don't you fucking *dare* put anyone in danger by sending them after this guy. He's *mine.*"

"Danny—"

"Your word, Gabe. I want your word."

Long crackling silence. If I had to worry about human psions behind me getting hurt my effectiveness would be halved, and I was, after all, stronger, faster, and able to take more damage. Gabe was in an unenviable position—throw more of her coworkers in the line of fire and hope this man, whoever he was, didn't kill them, or send me and trust me to finish the job. Trust the lying certainty in my voice. There was only one choice she could make. Sacrifice the many, or trust me to handle it.

"Fine. You're on." But Gabe's voice shook. Another inhale, a long exhale of synth-hash smoke I could almost taste over the phone line. "I'm glad you're alive, Danny."

That makes one of us. A choking laugh ripped its way free of my throat. "Thanks, Gabe. Be careful."

"You got it. Don't do anything stupid." She slammed the phone down. I rested my head against the metal and plasilica of the phone booth, laying the receiver back into its cradle. Hunger twisted under my breastbone. A wave of weakness slid over me.

Doreen. Eve. Japhrimel. Jace. The litany kept going under my conscious thought, the sharp spurs of guilt sinking in, poisoning all they touched.

"I need food," I muttered.

...feed me...

Can it be you have not resurrected him?

"Can't now even if I want to, sunshine," I said, with a kind of grim humor. "Look at this. I'm talking to myself in a phone booth. Come on, Danny. It's time to go get some food."

Another thought stopped me. I keyed in another number from my datband's clear plasilica display. It rang four times.

"The House of Love," a male voice purred out of the receiver. "What is your wish?"

"This is Dante Valentine," I said, low and fierce. "I need to speak to Polyamour. Now."

"Well, everyone has to—" The sound clicked off. I heard something, moving material, and then another voice. Female, dark and smooth, and raising the hair on the back of my neck.

"Ms. Valentine. Lady Polyamour thought you'd call. Just a moment."

"Lady" Polyamour? I was too tired to even find that funny.

Another click. No hold-music, just staticky silence. I looked out over the abandoned lot and felt terribly exposed. The skin on my back roughened. The dawning gold of sunrise edged even the weeds in the empty lot with gold, touched the sky with blush. Thin cirrus clouds trailed across the sky—the night's rain was pushing eastward, inland, leaving a fresh-washed pale blue and pink in its wake.

Then another click. "—punishment. I told you to tell me if she called." Polyamour's voice. I smiled slightly, my skin feeling as if it was going to crack. I needed food, lots of it, and soon. "Ms. Valentine. I thought you would call again."

"I hate to be predictable. Look, Poly, I need to know something. The necklaces. The spade necklaces, the reminders. Where did you get those from?"

"Keller got them from a jeweler..." She was silent for a moment, probably trailing the name through memory. It didn't take long—a Magi-trained memory is a well-trained memory. "Smith. Bryce Smith. His uncle."

I let out a long, satisfied breath. The normal living in a house with excellent shields—what else does a psionic kid do for his loving uncle? I'd bet the shields were Keller's work, after the kid left school.

After he'd left school—and before Mirovitch had broken free of whatever deep psychic vault Kellerman Lourdes had locked him in, maybe believing him dead. "That's what I needed, Poly. Thanks. Lock your fucking doors and stay under cover, okay?"

"Thank you for your concern, but I'm quite well-protected. Dante?"

"What?" I leaned my forehead against the metal again. The clear plasilica windows were starting to steam up.

For once, she didn't sound disdainful or controlled. Instead, her voice was tinged with something foreign—respect. And not the fawning respect of a courtesan for her callers—*genuine* respect. "Thank you. You're welcome here anytime you choose to come."

Oh, gods above, don't tempt me. "Thanks." I hung up. *Food. I need food.*

In the Tank District there were eateries that still served real meat instead of protein substitute. I stopped at a taqueria, bought and wolfed two huge steak burritos; then went to the burger stand next door and took down three triple-cheeseburgers in ten minutes. Next was another burger stand and three more cheeseburgers, this time with soy bacon. Then, with the edge of the blowtorch hole in my gut slightly taken off, I walked into a Novo Italiano cafe and ordered spaghetti and garlic bread, with bruschetta to start off with, stuffed mushrooms, and a double order of calamari. I barely even tasted it. I would have ordered more, but they took too long to bring it to the table.

When I finished there, I stopped in a convenience store and bought a twelve-pack of plascanned weightlifter shakes, meant to help those with black-market augments keep their muscle mass. Ten minutes later, in an alley, I dropped the last can and wiped my mouth.

The hunger was only blunted, but I'd told Gabe I'd be at the station in an hour and had only fifteen minutes left. Made it just in time, bolting up the stairs and reaching the third floor, whirling in through the door and finding Gabe's office empty. On her desk were four silver necklaces, their chains tangled together.

The entire third floor was eerily silent and empty. Of course, with a Feeder killing psionics — both cop and civilian — and the suspected trigger to his tracking on Gabe's desk, she would have little need for persuasion to clear the place out. They were probably watching, waiting to come back after I left the building.

I didn't blame them.

I scooped the necklaces up, looking around. Finding a blank piece of paper proved to be a little tricky. In the end I wrote on the backside of a laseprinted burglary report.

The first victim — the normal was Lourdes's uncle. He made the necklaces. I know where Lourdes is. I'm going to make him fucking pay. Do NOT send anyone after me!

I paused, then wrote, *THANK YOU.* Underlined and circled twice. It didn't seem enough, so I laid my hand on the paper and let a tingle of Power down, shaping stray ink into a glyph — *Mainuthsz,* a Greater Glyph of the Canons, shaped like the suggestion of a rider on a horse twisted into an inky line sketch. It meant unconditional love, a partnership — something she and Eddie had, something I had always wanted.

The swift dark stream of guilt roared under the surface of my mind for a few moments before I wrestled it down. I was going to expiate the guilt in the oldest of ways — with blood. But to do that, I needed to think clearly.

Revenge is best served subzero, because revenge is no fucking good if you don't *think clearly.* I was perfectly prepared to die, yes — but I was not prepared to waste myself. Before I was through, Keller or Mirovitch — or both — were going to be sent to Hell, with all the ferocity and cunning I could muster, and all the clinical coldness I was capable of.

I picked up the pen. There was nothing else that could have expressed what I felt for her, or what I had to do. I hesitated, scrawled one more word.

Goodbye.

I ducked out of her office. The place was deserted. I made it down the stairs and out of the station, the spade necklaces dangling in my hand before I remembered what and who I was, and stuffed them in my pocket.

Come and get me now, Mirovitch, I thought, waiting for the lash of pain down my back, waiting for the phantom wounds to reopen.

They didn't. Instead, an ice-cold wall of fury closed around me, impenetrable, shutting me away. My quarry was in front of me, the track clear, my revenge assured. I was going to make him pay, no matter who he was. Lourdes, Mirovitch, the fucking King of the Rats—I was going to kill him.

Now it was personal.

CHAPTER 30

I still needed food. Seven restaurants later, the late-afternoon sun glittered in my eyes as I ended up in a pub in the eastern fringe of Saint City, sandwiched between the city and the lake. I was working my way toward the Bridge going east on instinct, from one meal to the next. The necklaces were a weight in my pocket. I hadn't precisely lied—I didn't know *exactly* where Lourdes was, but I could feel a little tingle in my subconscious. I'd hunted down too many psychopaths and criminals not to know that little tingle. It meant that I was close and on the right track. The bounty hunter in me was satisfied, and that was good enough for now.

I set down the pint of beer, wiping my lips with the back of my hand, and studied the demolished large-size pizza in front of me. I hate the taste of beer, but it provides a lot of carbs in a very short time, and I needed fuel. I felt like a goddamn glutton, but I was *hungry.*

I sighed. From a back booth, my eyes tracked through the dark pub. The holovid feeds were showing an advert for the newest series about a group of Ceremonials in East Los Dangeles-Frisco. *For hating psions so much they certainly love to watch us on the holovids,* I thought, as I always did.

Then the feed switched and it showed my house, the familiar grainy images of the column of flame rising. I watched, my fingernails tapping the table. Gabe had thought Lourdes and Mirovitch had gotten to me in my own house, or trailed me away from the burning wreckage. She must have been worried, worried sick. A better friend than I deserved; Gabe had never let me down.

I watched, my eyes nailed to the display. Inside the column of flame, something twisted.

Something dark and swirling like obsidian smoke.

A vaguely human shape stretched in the middle of the fire, spreading its slender black wings, hands upraised. Then the column of fire was sucked back toward the figure, a shockwave rattling the camera.

I watched, my jaw dropping. *What the fucking hell?*

The flames didn't stop, but they were pulled back in, wreathing around the dark figure, which lifted its head as if searching. Then, maddeningly, the picture stopped, dissolving in a burst of static. My face flashed on the holovid, a thumbnail up to the right of an announcer. I saw with a slight twitch of aggravation that it was my new face. Someone had managed to take a stillcam holo of me. My hair was pulled back, tendrils falling softly and beautifully in my face, so I would bet it was taken at the House of Pain.

The announcer was of the type always chosen for holovids— slightly androgynous, high cheekbones, sculpted mouth. This one had sleek blond hair and a pair of bright green eyes that made my stomach turn over. I paid and got out of there in a hurry, my boots barely touching the stairs that took me streetside. The pub's antique wooden door swung shut behind me.

What was in my house? Was it Lourdes? Had he somehow been there, stalking me while I was blind with grief, and my torching the house had taken him by surprise? My throat went dry, my right hand clenching into a fist.

But I hadn't sensed Mirovitch or Keller. And even crazed with grief I was sure I would have noticed the cloying psychic stench of the Headmaster.

It couldn't be. It *couldn't* be.

Can it be that you have not resurrected him?

"Impossible." My voice startled me. I glanced around, catching a few frightened looks from the normals who were giving me a wide berth. "Im-fucking-possible."

Figment of the imagination. Or, if not... Santino had used the Egg against Japhrimel, and Lucifer had finished the job by beating him to death once he was already wounded. Would fire and Power do what I'd thought blood *might* do, and bring a demon back to life? Rebuild a demon's shattered body from ash? Even a Fallen demon?

Don't get distracted, Danny. Every moment you delay is another moment he has to kill someone else.

But I had the necklaces, didn't I? I was the target now.

I walked down the street, my hands clasped around the scabbard.

My sword hummed inside the sheath, a subliminal song of Power. After a while I noticed that people were spilling out of my way while I walked. When I passed into a belt of residential buildings and the sidewalks were empty under old trees turning red and orange and white for winter, it was a relief. I crunched through wet-smelling fallen leaves and kept moving.

The sun was setting by the time I made it to the Bridge.

With hovertraffic being what it was, the huge Bridge was in a state of disrepair. But slicboarders can't go over water, and foot or wheelbike traffic needed the Bridge. A thriving traffic rumbled over the lake, and there was a rail line to take land supplies that for one reason or another couldn't go by hover transport.

I needed to go east, and I wanted to walk, so it was the Bridge or nothing.

On the west side, the old main roads zigzagged down the hill. I cut through the bands of shrubbery and wished I'd thought to keep my slicboard, or rent one. The edge of the river curled away under the beginning of the Bridge, I smelled cold iron and the dead, chemical-laden water. There were colonies of homeless people living on the banks, renegade psionics, all sorts of human driftwood. It made the Tank District look like a *sedayeen* commune. I kept walking.

The Bridge lay on the surface of the glass-calm lake, an architectural triumph when it was made five hundred years ago, revamped every few decades. The original concrete was crumbling, but haphazard repairs are done every year, and plasilica and new steel had been hammered in a few years ago during a grand reconstruction funded by Hegemony grants and City Hall. Algae drifted thick on the lake, harvested and distilled by the biotechs or anyone with a chem degree and a few thousand credits' worth of equipment. The last wave of additive-laced Clormen-13 had come from here; tainted and cut with some thyoline-based substance to make it more harsh and addictive. Not like Chill needed any help.

I could have been over the Bridge in a short time if I'd gotten a slic or used some of my demon speed, but I shivered, continued walking. The pond that the boathouse on the Hall grounds stood near fed into the river, I was sure of it. Even being this close to water that had touched the grounds of that cursed place was enough to make my blood turn cool and loose in my veins.

The more I thought about it, the more miraculous it was that the

Black Room had managed to meet anywhere on the grounds, especially in the same place more than once, even if Keller only took the members there one at a time. Mirovitch had been uncanny, sniffing out hidden stashes of contraband, seemingly always one step ahead of every upswell of rebellion in the student population, as well as any student conspiracies. No matter where you turned, someone was reporting to the stooges, or being punished, or simply withdrawing into their own little shell, just trying to survive.

What other secrets had Rigger Hall kept?

After an hour's steady walk I reached midspan, pausing to look over the dark algae-choked surface of the lake. I had no warning.

My left shoulder came alive with pain, as if a clawed hand had curled around and dug in. I went to my knees in the middle of the road, steel creaking under me. I found my claw-cramping right hand under my shirt, my fingertips touching the writhing ropes of scar that was Japhrimel's mark. The slight pressure—fingertips against scar—made the world swim as if a pane of wavering glass hung in front of me.

Saint City seen upside down, the lights shimmering on the Trans-Bank Tower, hovertraffic zipping by. Need burning hot in the veins, dropping, wings furled, breaking the fall at the last moment, booted feet slamming into pavement. Following a scent that was not a scent, a sound that was a touch, a fire of need in veins old and strong, drawing . . . eastward.

I came back to myself, ripping my fingers away from the scar. My knees dug into the Bridge, which swayed like a plucked string. I heard yells from both ends, used my scabbarded blade to lever myself up.

Can it be you have not resurrected him?

Lucifer's voice, taunting me. And the dark winged figure in the middle of the flames . . . Fire, enough fire to perhaps feed a demon?

Enough Power to perhaps bring one back, rebuild a demon's body from ash?

Ridiculous. Insane. If Japh—

If *he* had been alive, even just barely clinging to life, I would have known when I clasped his burning body to my chest. I would have known every time I touched the glassy lacquered urn. I would have *known*. I was a Necromance, death was my trade, and I was as exquisitely sensitive to the spark of life and soul as a sexwitch was to Power.

But what about the *soul?* A demon's soul...or a Fallen demon's soul, the soul of an *A'nankhimel*...

I wished again that I'd been able to study more about demons. Or, more precisely, about *A'nankhimel,* Fallen demons, and the *hedaira,* their human brides. But none of the books had anything other than old legends garbled to the point of uselessness. The demons didn't like to talk about the *A'nankhimel,* for whatever reason; and the Magi for all their fooling around with demons, didn't know about anything the demons didn't care to talk about. The Magi's natural jealousy and obfuscation surrounding each practitioner's research and results didn't help. I couldn't even *question* a Magi about demons, they wouldn't talk unless it was to members of their own circle, and even inside circles each Magi had his or her own secrets.

What if I turned back now? I could find out. I could touch my scar and go wherever it led me. I could leave this horrible circle of murder and death and foulness behind and look for my dead demon lover instead of revenging myself and every other soul who had suffered at Rigger Hall. And if my sanity snapped, I could look anywhere in the world for him, anywhere at all. I could spend my life uselessly hunting down something that didn't exist, fooling myself into believing he was still alive, around the next corner, just out of reach.

No. If he had not come back before now, he wasn't going to. All the longing in the world couldn't fool me into knowing otherwise.

I squeezed my eyes shut, hot tears dripping down to the Bridge deck. I was just hallucinating, trying to hoodwink myself. Japhrimel was dead, Jace was dead, and I was hunting a Headmaster who refused to die.

Where did Kellerman Lourdes fit in? Was he carrying Mirovitch like a poisonous seed in his own thoughts? Was he a mule for the Headmaster's twisted psyche and soul, his slime-drenched Feeder *ka?* Or had Mirovitch taken over completely, grown inside Lourdes's body, driven out of his own middle-aged body by the assaults of the other kids?

None of it made much sense. It was ridiculous anyway. I'd shattered his urn to remove the hope of Japhrimel coming back. It was my penance, and by every god that ever was, I was going to pay my penance and have my revenge.

I swayed on the middle of the Bridge. Another thought chilled me—maybe the Power I carried, like a plasgun over a barrel of reactive, was going to eat me up. Maybe the only reason I'd survived so long was because I hadn't used the full extent of my capabilities, wasting myself on grief, bounties, and torturing Jace. Maybe it was rising, and it would burn me to ash—just like Japhrimel.

Just like my house.

I'm going to take him with me. Mirovitch, Keller, whoever he is, I'm taking him with me when I go. If I go.

What if I managed to kill Mirovitch? What then?

I was so tired, weary with a weariness that went all the way down to my bones and even further. I had read about despair of the soul, and never thought it possible until now. Even the part of me that had fought all my life, the stubborn refusal to give in that had colored my entire existence, was dully muted, hanging its head. There comes a time when even simple endurance can't carry you through.

I knew what it would be like, laying my head on Death's black chest, feeling the weight of living rise away from me. The clear light would break out from the horizon of What Comes Next, and I would go gratefully into that foreign land.

But not before Mirovitch. Or Keller. Or whoever the hell he was.

I looked out over the algae-choked, glassy surface of the lake, reflecting the orange glow of the city on every shore. I lifted one foot, uncertain, and then put it back down. Remained standing where I was.

The last few dregs of light squeezed their way out of the sky. Night folded over Saint City and the Bridge—and me—with all the softness of black wings.

I shook my hair back, ash falling free of the black silky strands, and continued on.

CHAPTER 31

Walking up Sommersby Street Hill at night was a strange experience. The last time I'd seen this place had been in broad daylight decades ago, when I'd walked to East Transport Station to board the transport that would take me north to the regional Academy for my specialized Necromance training. While at the Hall I had rarely seen the street at night; students weren't allowed off the school grounds after dark, and I'd never come east of the Bridge in all my after-Academy years of living in Santiago City. I'd been all over the world hunting bounties, but this place so close to home I'd avoided like the plague.

Given my druthers, I would have continued doing so.

Fog was rolling in off the bay and the lake, a thick soupy fog that glowed green near the pavement and orange between the streetlights. With the fog came the smell of the sea—thick brine—and the smell of fire, burned candle wax, and ash. Or maybe the smell of a burned, smashed life was only mine, rising from my clothes.

I paced up Sommersby Hill, my bootheels clicking, and saw with a weary jolt of surprise that the Sommersby Store was still open.

While I was at the Hall, the Store was where all the kids went in our infrequent free time. We bought cheap novels and fashion mags about holovid stars, candy bars to supplement the bland Hall food, and synth-hash cigarettes to be smuggled on campus. The Store used to have a counter that sold tofu dogs and ice cream and other cheap fare, but I saw that part of the building was boarded up now. With Rigger Hall gone, most of the Store's customers would be gone too. It was a miracle that even the main part was still there.

For a few minutes I stood, my hands in the pockets of Jace's coat, the sword thrust through the loop on the belt of my weapons rig. I watched the front of the Store, its red neon blurring on the dirty glass. The newspaper hutch standing to one side of the door was gone, a paler square of the paint of the storefront marking where it had stood; but the slicboard rack was still there. The boarded-up half of the storefront was festooned with graffiti, a broken window on the second story blindly glared at me. I stared at the glass door with its old-fashioned infrared detector, the plasticine sign proclaiming *Shoplifting Will Be Prosecuted* still set above the door's midbar, dingy and curling at its corners.

I finally slid my sword out of the loop on my belt. Holding it in my left hand, I crossed the street.

I'm about to be swallowed by my own past. It wasn't a comfortable feeling. After all, my past had teeth. And what would I become when it finished digesting me?

Will you stop with the disgusting thoughts? Please, Danny. You're even irritating yourself.

The motion detector beeped as I stepped into the warm gloom. It looked dingier and even more rundown, but there was the same ice machine and rack of holovid mags, shelves of crisp packets and junk food in bright wrappers, and a plasilica cabinet holding cheap jack-knives and datband add-ons, gleaming like fool's gold. The floor was still white and black squares of linoleum, dirt and dust drifting in the corners. Memory roiled under my skin. I expected to look down and see my scabbed knees under a plaid skirt, feel the stinging weight of the collar against my vulnerable throat and scratchy wool socks against my calves.

"Help ya?"

The voice was a rude shock. Even more of a shock was the man—fat, almost-bearded, dressed in a stained white T-shirt, oily red suspenders, and a pair of baggy khaki pants. I let out a breath. My left hand, holding the sword, dropped. "Hi." My eyes adapted to the gloom. Red neon cigarette-brand signs buzzed in the windows. *Tamovar. Marlboro X. Gitanes. Copperhead.* "I'm here for a pack of Gitanes. Make that two. And that silver Zijaan, in the case." I picked up a handful of Reese Mars Bars—my favorite during school years. I rarely had any money left over from my state stipend after it was applied to tuition and my uniforms. Even though Rigger Hall was for the orphans and the poor, the kids with families usually had a little more pocket change.

A psion was state property, their upbringing supposed to be overseen by trained professionals, the family just an afterthought—nice if it was there, but not terribly necessary. Had I missed my family? I'd had beaky, spectacled, infinitely gentle Lewis, and my books. The pain of that first loss seemed strangely sweet and clean to me now, compared to the sick, twisting litany of grief and guilt caroling under the rest of my thoughts. I'd had Roanna, my first *sedayeen* friend, the gentle ballast to the harshness of my nature even then. And my connection with my god had sustained me; I had always known, from the moment I read my first book on Egyptianica, that Anubis was my psychopomp. Some Necromances reached their accreditation Trial without knowing what face Death would take, I was lucky.

The library, the hall where we were taught fencing, a few of the teachers that weren't so bad... there had been good things too, at the Hall. Things that had sustained me. I hadn't missed the mother and father who had given me up at birth. I hadn't known enough to miss them, and still didn't.

I shook myself out of memory. Couldn't afford to be distracted now.

What else? I cast around.

There, on the rack, was a holovid mag that showed a picture of Jasper Dex leaning against a brick wall, his bowl-cut hair artistically mussed. It was a retrospective issue; memory rose like a flood again. I pushed nausea and memory down, trying not to gag at the smell of unwashed human male.

Mrs. DelaRocha had been behind the counter in my younger years, balefully eying the collared kids from the Hall, suspiciously peering at you, following you down the two aisles of the store, breathing her halitosis in your face when you asked for cigarettes. I squashed the guilty idea that if I turned around I would see her right behind me, her skirt askew and her cardigan buttoned up wrong, lipstick staining her yellowed teeth, her hook nose lifting proudly between her faded watery hazel eyes.

I laid the candy and the magazine down on the counter. He looked at me curiously, but got the cigarettes and the lighter for me. "The Zijaan's full-up. You want lighter fluid?"

"No. Thank you." I paid with crumpled New Credit notes instead of my datband, because that's what I would have done as a kid. He pushed everything back over the counter at me, glowering as he counted out my change—three single credits, everything in the store was priced in whole numbers and the Hegemony never indulged in the antique custom of sales tax like some of the Freetowns did. They had other ways of getting your credits.

The candy and the magazine went into my battered messenger bag. My emerald glittered, a sharp green spark crackling in the dimness. The man jumped nervously. The sight of all that blubber quivering made a completely reprehensible desire to giggle rise in my throat. It was suppressed and died away with no trouble at all. His T-shirt was filthy and barely covered his hairy chest; stub-ends of cigars lay in a plastic ashtray shaped like a nude woman with her legs spread. No doubt a commemorative item, the ashtray was half-pushed behind a stand-up holoshell calender.

Today is (blank spot). The last two digits of the year blinked— *75*. I shivered. The calendar was a good twelve years slow.

The extra pack of Gitanes went into my pocket. I opened the first pack, took my change, and stalked out of the store, ignoring his sarcastic "Havva good evenin'."

It's extremely unlikely I'll have anything of the sort. I stepped out into the fog-laden street. My hands shook only slightly as I clicked the Zijaan with my free right hand and lit the first Gitane. The smell of synth hash rose up, nearly choked me. I blinked. My eyes watered. I walked across the street again, head down, dawdling like I used to do on the afternoons when we were free to leave school grounds. Then I glanced back at the Sommersby Store.

A chill ruffled my spine.

It was dark and boarded-up, no neon in the windows. Abandoned like all the rest. No sign of lights, of neon, or of the fat hairy storeowner.

CHAPTER 32

My mouth went dry, and the gray of shock fuzzed around the corners of my peripheral vision. I forced it away, bent over, my right hand twisting into a claw once again. The red eye of the cigarette taunted me. I inhaled smoothly, down into the pit of my belly as I'd been taught.

"Holy shit. I just bought Gitanes from a ghost." My voice sounded high and childish even to myself. Did this mean that the gods were with me? Or was I hallucinating again? Both were equally likely.

I re-crossed the street. If anyone was watching, they would probably think I was a lunatic. I poked at the boards over the shattered glass door I'd just walked through whole, went on tiptoes to peer inside the cave of the store. A heady brew of wet decay and other garbage-laced smells poured out; my demon-sharp eyes caught sight of a magazine rack upended, a few holomags scattered, drifts of trash on the floor. The plasticine counter was shattered too, and I saw a scraped-clean circle off to one side and a blackened scorch mark on the floor. Probably a fire some transient had made inside the abandoned building.

I dropped the smoking cigarette, then opened up my bag. The magazine was gone, and the candy, but one pack of cigarettes was there. I fished the other pack out of my pocket and stared at them, turning the unopened one over to read its warning label; there was a sweepstakes to win a free hover blazoned on the back.

I crumpled both packs in my fist, feeling the sticks break inside, and dropped them heedlessly. Then I drew the silver Zijaan from my pocket.

The breath left me in another gasping rush. The lighter was battered and scratched with hard use, and etched into one flat side was a
cursive *C* wreathed with another cursive *M*.

I blinked. Flipped the lighter open, spun the wheel with a click,
and orange flame blossomed. I snapped it shut. I ran my fingers over
the carved letters.

For once in my life, I was completely at a loss. I looked up at the
boarded-up storefront again, smelled decay and that strange, indecipherable scent.

CM? Christabel Moorcock?

"Christabel?" I said, tentatively, my voice echoing against the
soggy shredded interior of the abandoned store.

No answer. Except the memory of the scraping awful scream—
remember, remember. The lilac smell of terror clinging to pale-pink
paper as Christabel wrote her last message. The memory of her bed,
neatly made; her bookshelves religiously dusted, her kitchen and
bathroom spotless...Everything in its place.

In all my years of dealing with Power and the strange logic of
magick, I had never come across anything even remotely like this. I
held up the lighter. Swallowed dryly.

Then I slipped the lighter in the breast pocket of Jace's coat.
*There's a circle being closed here. Just like a Greater Work of
magick.*

It was vaguely comforting. It meant some other agency might be
working with me to bring Mirovitch and Keller down. Maybe
Christabel was helping out another Necromance. Who knew?

Or perhaps it meant I was to be offered as a sacrifice. That was a
little less comforting. I blew out a long breath between my teeth, a
tuneless whistle that fell flat on the foggy air. I backed away from the
store, finally hopping down from the sidewalk and into the street. I
decided to go up the Hill and—

"Valentine! Hey, Valentine!" A girl's voice, light and young, and
the patter of quick, light, running feet on concrete. My ears tracked
it, the footsteps sounded as if someone was running up right behind
me. My neck prickled.

I gasped, whirling, my hair fanning out. Sommersby Street
yawned, the abandoned buildings and boarded-up houses mocking
me. The concrete pavement was cracked and pitted here, and no hovertraffic lit the sky. Without the Hall, this district had probably gone
into slow decline.

A perfect place to hide.

My own voice caught me by surprise. "Christabel?" *Okay, that's it. I have had enough of this. Everyone out of the swimtank. No more voices, no more illusions, no more delaying.* I straightened, my jaw set, my right hand cramped around the hilt of my sword. When I could walk without staggering, I continued up the middle of the street in defiance of any streetside hovertraffic, my bootheels clicking on the pavement. Winter had come early here up on the Hill, and frost rimed the darker places where the sun didn't reach during the day. Under trees and in shadowy corners, winter was creeping in without the benefit of the rest of autumn.

I continued up Sommersby and turned right onto Harlow. At the end of Harlow the gates rose up, wrought-iron with plasilica panels, an *R* done in gothic script on one half, an *H* on the other. On the top of the gates, dagger-shaped finials lengthened up like claws.

I stopped in the shelter of a doorway, looking at the gates. *Be careful, Danny,* Jace's voice brushed my cheek. *It only looks quiet. Don't trust nothin' in there.*

"You don't need to tell me that," I muttered.

The first illegal job I'd gone on had been as a result of Jace's tutelage, a few months into our relationship during a dry period. I'd complained that I didn't have enough to make my mortgage even with the apparitions and bounties I worked on, and he'd looked at me, his head propped on the headboard of my bed, and said, *How would you like to make some* real *money, baby?*

I'd done bounties and I'd tracked down stolen objects, but I'd never done corporate espionage or thieving before. I'd never even thought of doing mercenary work, but the money was good and Jace and I were a fantastic team. At the time I hadn't wondered at it, but no doubt Jace's Mob Family connections had come in handy. Under his tutelage, I'd become so much better at tracking bounties it wasn't funny, spending just half the time it normally took to bring them in.

The memory was strangely fuzzy, even the sharp sword of pain at the thought of Jace was oddly muted. I stared at the gate I'd seen for years in my nightmares, and my hand tightened on the scabbard once more. My heart thundered in my chest.

"Okay, Christabel," I murmured. "You're still leading the dance. Let's go."

CHAPTER 33

wondered why the geography of a place I'd tried so hard to forget
was burned so deeply into me that I had no trouble calling up a
mental map of the entire complex. Behind the gate, the driveway
would curve up the gentle hill, the pond to the right, the shack of the
boathouse just visible on the other side. The main house, with class-
rooms, the cafeteria, and the gymnasium, would rear up in front of
the driveway. An ancillary road would curve off to the left, leading
to the four Halls, each one shock-shielded and stocked with supplies
for practicing the standard Magi disciplines, intranet security and an
automatic fail-safe on each one.

Behind the main building were the dormitories, two for girls, one
for boys (since the X chromosome carries Talent far more often than
the Y) and the fencing salle/dojo, the swimtank building, and, in the
very back, the Headmaster's House. Further up the hill and also to
the left was the Morrow building, containing the Library, more class-
rooms, and a fully stocked alchemical lab, as well as hothouses for
the Skinlin trainees closed around a courtyard that held a co-op garden for the Skinlins and hedgewitches.

The only thing missing was the stink of childrens' fear—and, of
course, the tang of Power as well as the glimmer of a security net:
deepscan, magscan, and a full battery of defensive measures. Not to
mention the chain-link fence, six foot tall and topped with razor wire
Mirovitch had erected inside the older, more aesthetically pleasing
brick wall.

Who did that to you, Danny? Jace's voice, harsh with anger, during one of our old fights. *Who made you think you were worthless?
Tell me who. Goddammit, who did that to you?* And he'd turned in a
tight half-circle, jerking away from me as if the offender might be
hiding in the living room.

"Jace," I whispered to the empty, foggy street. "I don't want to go
in there again."

Whether I was caught in some magick of Fate or just too stubbornly, exhaustedly determined for my own good, I was called upon
to finish it. And who, after all, was left to finish it if I couldn't?

My right hand throbbed and ached. I dropped it, touched the pocket holding the spade necklaces. If I was right—and I goddamn well hoped I was—Keller would be tracking me now. I would draw him like a lodestone draws iron filings, like a broken-down hover in the Tank District draws techstrippers. Like a fight in Rio draws the organ harvesters.

Thinking of this, I reached down into my pocket and drew out four necklaces, leaving one behind. I cupped them in my palm, examining them closely. There was no thread of Power I could detect. But of course, if it was only a passive charm keyed to Keller I might not be able to see it at all, even with a demon's acuity. When it came to tracking spells, passive usually meant *weak,* but it also usually meant *invisible.*

I closed my right hand into a fist, the sharp pricks of the spade charms digging into my skin. The trickle of Power slid down my wrist like a razor, heat welling up under my skin. It pooled in my palm, melting, swirling, straining to escape.

I stared at my hand, the trickle of superheated Power making my fingernails glow.

Memory rose.

Crack. *The worst thing about the whip is not the first strike, laid hot against the back. For the first few microseconds it is almost painless—but then the red-hot fléchette, fueled with Power, scorch-splits open every nerve, and the entire body becomes the back. Not just the back, but the entire* world *becomes the lash of agony. The scream rises up out of the deepest layers of the body, impossible to deny. No matter how much the will nerves itself not to scream, the body betrays begging, pleading, breaking.*

I opened my fist.

Valentine, D. Student Valentine is called to the Headmaster's Office immediately.

The fléchette gleamed in my hand, long and thin and razor-sharp. Made of Power and the metal in the necklaces, it rang softly as I touched it with a forefinger. I blew a low tuneless whistle between my teeth and looked up toward the gate.

It was open slightly, fog wreathing through the bars. *Come into my parlor, said the undead Headmaster to the wary ex-pupil.* The lunatic singsong sounded a little bit more like me. I grabbed at the thought, sucked in another breath, and dug in my messenger bag. I had no sheath that would fit the fléchette, so I wrapped a supple piece of plasilica around it and stuck it in my pocket with the last spade necklace.

I don't think I'm going in through the front door. I melted out of the shadow of the doorway to vanish into the fog.

CHAPTER 34

It was still there, the old drainage tunnel. Trash drifted in the bottom of the round concrete cave, looking a lot smaller now that I was at least a foot taller. Several years of fallen leaves were turning into sludge at the bottom. I examined it carefully, reaching out to touch the concrete. Here, where the drainage ditch went through a hummock under the fence, someone had once cut through the iron grating covering the school side. Generations of students had carefully covered the hole with rotting wooden scraps from the woodshop, enough to let the water drain and cover the fact that the metal grille was broken. Since the hole went underground, it didn't register on the shields, psychic or electronic—or if it ever had, it had been forgotten. As far as anyone knew, this was one secret the students had successfully kept. Sneaking out to roam the streets at night was a Rigger Hall tradition, indulged in even in the darkest days of Mirovitch's reign. We were, after all, only kids. There was nowhere else to go, not as a collared psion. We were Hegemony property.

After hearing about the Black Room, I wondered if other secrets were kept. I would have thought it was impossible to keep anything from Mirovitch or his stooges. Now, with an adult's sense of circumstance and complexity, I found myself thinking a little more charitably about the stooges and rats. They had just been terrified kids, like me.

But I'd never broken. I hadn't broken even when he'd forced me to watch Roanna die—and now I wondered if he had known she would slip through his old, hard fingers and fling herself at the fence after we had refused to betray each other.

I had never broken, not even afterward when Mirovitch dragged me back into his office to punish me, demanding to know just what my *sedayeen* roommate had told her social worker—and if she had told anyone else. I knew now that he had been almost frantic at the thought of losing his personal playground, not to mention the punishment that would have been meted out to him; swift execution, most likely in a gasbox. After that, he'd had it in for me. My defiance outraged him, but I was still only one small girl in a large school. I frequently managed to stay beneath his notice.

I ducked into the end of the tunnel, my boots slipping in the scudge. Water sloshed. The air was absolutely still, and the fog made it eerily quiet. Complete blackness made the tunnel into an abyss, despite my demon sight. There were no streetlights on either side of the concrete pipe, and the thick fog cut visibility even for my eyes.

I lifted my sword, thumbed it free. The slight click of the katana easing loose of the scabbard was loud in the cottony silence. Three inches of steel slid free, and a faint blue glow flowed along the metal.

I saw the tunnel, still sloping slightly upward, a knee-high spill of water and leaf sludge coating its bottom. Permaspray graffiti tangled along the walls, some of it even glowing with Schorn's algae when the light from my blade touched it. The concrete was crumbling, but still sound. I couldn't see anything blocking it, and the water was still coming, so I bent down to step cautiously into the opening.

Halfway through, I paused and lifted my blade, looking at the left-hand wall. My boots sloshed; I moved very carefully, peering through the dark.

There it was. In black permaspray, the crudely-done drawing of a slender Egyptian dog with long ears, reclining; a copy of an ancient statue. I remembered biting my lip as I marked the wall, the sharp chemical reek of permaspray, and the satisfaction I'd felt when it was done. It was the mark of my personal war with the school, my badge of honor for not breaking. I smiled, holding my sword up a little higher, shaking my hair back. In the dim light, shadows shifting and crowding, it seemed the dog's head dipped once, nodding at me. I set my jaw and nodded back, then carefully stepped away.

The tunnel was shorter than I remembered. At the end, I pushed aside a sheet of rotted plaswood, setting foot for the first time in decades inside the walls of Rigger Hall again. I took a cautious sniff, smelled only leaf mold, grass, and salty fog. Strained my ears, but heard only the thick silence of a cloud-wrapped night. I held the cloak of my Power close but sensed no shields on the walls; when they closed the school, a team of Hegemony psions had come out and dismantled the defenses, earthing the power. And there were no electronic countermeasures. If Keller was here, he was counting on invisibility to keep him safe.

The familiar loose tension invaded my body, my heartbeat speeding up. *I chased down a demon even the Prince of Hell couldn't catch. I survived two run-ins with the Devil. I'm the best Necromance in Saint City. I'm listed as one of the top-ten deadliest bounty hunters in the Hegemony.*

That thought caused a sniggering little laugh to jerk its way out of me. One of the biggest hunts of my life, and I wasn't going to make a red credit off of it.

That was a very adult thought, and I was glad. I still had to check to make sure I wasn't wearing the plaid skirt, and every time the denim of my jeans touched my knees I had to suppress a guilty start.

The grass was no longer manicured but knee-high, weeds lying thick and rank and edged by frost in the deeper shadows. I saw the familiar bulk of the dormitories' roofs over the hill, decided to go uphill and angle toward the Headmaster's House. I could cut around the back of the dojo and avoid any possible patrolling teacher or stooge.

As if there was anyone here.

For all I knew, nobody *was* here…but just because I felt like I should sneak around to avoid Mirovitch's hounds didn't mean it was a *bad* idea to exercise a little caution.

I'm being eaten alive by my own childhood. Gods above. Why me? The answer came in a flash. Why not? Who, after all, was better equipped than me?

I reached the top of the hill and hunched down instinctively, the edges of my shields roughening. *Dust, offal, magick, aftershave, chalk, and leather.* I retreated, almost as if scalded, gasping and dropping flat as the wall of magick passed overhead. He was scanning the grounds.

Well, now I know he's here. I tried to remember if I had any consecrated chalk in my bag. Then it occurred to me that I was doing exactly what a scared teenager would do—hiding, and waiting for Lourdes to find and trap me like a rabbit.

Which brought up another glaring hole in my plan. I didn't even have one. I was operating on a sort of half-ass instinct I hadn't used since I was twelve. A miserable instinct that was just what any stupid kid would use. The fact that it was impossible to plan for something like this didn't exonerate me from feeling a little dumb.

Time to start thinking, Danny! A whisper that sounded like Jace's in my ear, hot breath touching my cheek, warm fingers on my nape. It felt so bloody *real* I gasped, throwing myself down and rolling, instinctively throwing up a flare of Power that stained the hillside crimson for a moment.

Well, I just blew any chance I had of secrecy. I made it to my feet and bolted away at a different angle. This would take me directly to the Headmaster's House, keeping me below the sight line of the hill.

I heard boots crunching on gravel, which told me two things: that he was on the other side of the hill and behind me, and also that he had been at the front gate or in the dormitories.

For a moment, I considered veering up and engaging him head-on; but I was already running soundless as an owl. I heard the footsteps on gravel slow and strained my ears, suddenly and, for once, blessing my demon-acute senses.

A short yell of pain and the sound of something falling, hitting the ground hard. Then a mad gravel-crunching scramble, and footsteps on grass. I didn't stop, came around the side of the hill's breast, and found myself faced with the track leading up to the Headmaster's House.

Polyamour came this way, with a nine-year-old girl and Keller. Bringing them to Mirovitch. My gorge rose. The track was paved, and I ran over it using all the speed and silence my new body could give me.

I had just come over the slight rise, leaping over a pothole, when I heard a hissing crackle. I threw myself aside and the bolt flung past me, crackling and spitting as it went, and buried itself in the Headmaster's House.

The prim, two-story neo-Victorian was clearly abandoned, plaswood over the windows. Uncertain foggy light showed great cracks in the peeling paint—the same kind of leprous blue light I'd seen in Sukerow's apartment. Only this time, the blue light spread, crackling and hissing. I wondered for a split second if the unhealthy looking glow would give me a radiation burn. It certainly *looked* like the diseased glow of a coremelt.

The explosion was deafening. I ended up lying in the long grass on the side of the road, the shockwave smashing me down, a warm trickle of blood coming from my nose.

"Plenty more where that came from," I heard from my right, down the hill in the bushes. The bolt had streaked past me from my right, which meant that he'd been scrambling behind me.

The fléchette, he's probably tracking the fléchette.

And the last necklace that I had in my pocket.

"Who are you?" The wheezing, slightly asthmatic voice came again. Chills worked up my spine, spilled down my arms. It sounded odd, strangely distorted, as if passed through a synthfilter—but I *knew* that voice. My entire body went cold and strained against shock at the sound, my fingers digging into the earth, the smell of crushed wet grass and damp earth rising around me and warring with the heady, spicy fragrance of demon.

The Headmaster's House was burning merrily, orange flames instead of blue now, casting a livid light up into the fog. I had only a few seconds before he crested the rise and saw me.

Then I heard a horrible, chilling scream. *"No! NO! Stop it! STOP IT!"* This voice was different, a baritone, with the unmistakable tang of Skinlin. I only heard one set of footsteps—but then I heard a thrashing, like a fight.

"Whoever you are, *run*! Run for your life!"

I intended to run, but not for my life.

I intended to run for *his*.

"—*down*," Mirovitch hissed. "And *stay* down. In your place, boy."

I didn't stick around to hear more. I ran.

CHAPTER 35

I suppose the last place either Mirovitch or Keller would have expected me to go was the cafeteria. There was a wall of boarded-up windows on one side, two lone leftover tables stacked against the wall, and insulation hung from the ceiling in long swathes. It was tactically exposed, and I'd had to break open a door to get in here— and if the sound of screeching metal and my own jagged breathing didn't bring Mirovitch, what I was going to do next would.

I was only a few steps in before my foot came down on something

soft. My sword whipped out, and I found myself looking at an innoc-
uous sleeping bag, lying tangled on the floor. The smell of canned
beef soup hung in the air, and I smelled candle wax as well. Candle
wax and unwashed human—and the cold, fetid reek of Mirovitch,
dust and magick and feces and chalk and aftershave.

I'd found a lair. The trouble was, I wasn't sure of *what.*

I dug in my bag with one trembling hand. My sword glowed blue.
My frantic fingers couldn't find any chalk, though I knew I had some.
I could almost feel time winding down, the clocksprings of whatever
was going to happen ticking away, closer and closer, rising through
the water to sink its teeth into my thrashing legs.

I pulled my hand out of my bag and took a deep breath flavored
with human and not-so-human scents, my own smoky demon smell
suddenly strong as a shield in my nostrils. Reached into my pocket,
fingers closing around the fléchette in its plasilica sheath.

The touch of cold metal shocked me back into some kind of sense.
I crouched down on the floor in the middle of the caf, a swordsman's
crouch, my blade held out to one side, the fléchette in my left hand.
What do I need chalk for? I'm part demon.

The circle swirled in the air, dust scorching as the fire in me rose,
whipcracking in small, controlled bursts, a tattoo of Power burning
into the concrete under the linoleum. It took bare seconds. By the
time it was done, I had a tolerable approximation of a double circle
scored around me with red-glowing Power—and between the two
circles, the subtly altered shapes of the Feeder glyphs Kellerman
Lourdes had created writhed. Every candle Lourdes had placed in
here burst into flame, suddenly alive with fire, their glow warm and
welcoming. The fléchette began to hum, metal glowing, heating up
in my hand. My pocket, the one holding the leftover spade necklace,
began to smoke. I didn't have a hand left to fish it out, so I just
crouched, on guard.

One of the plaswood windows blew in. Then another. Another.
Splinters skidded across the floor.

Silence descended. Here was where it would end.

Do you believe in Fate, Danny Valentine?

I gulped down air, the three phantom scars on my back alive. The
vanished brand along my lower-left buttock began to ache, dully at
first, and then with increasing pain. A curl of smoke drifted up from
my pocket. I waited.

The door I'd wrenched open creaked as it was pulled wide, then ripped off its hinges. And into the cafeteria shambled Kellerman Lourdes.

Now that I saw him up close, I vaguely remembered him as a tall, gawky, acne-pocked Skinlin, always on the periphery of whatever activity was being conducted. His career at Rigger had been singularly free of rumors and whispers. It was as if nobody noticed him at all. The invisible man.

Part of the puzzle became clear as I studied him. He stepped into the caf and watched me, dead dark eyes sparking with blue pinpricks, his thick wattled cheeks quivering ever so slightly.

"You were a Feeder already." Breathless, I sounded like I was fourteen again.

And scared.

That was why he'd been invisible; and that was why he could get close to Mirovitch that fateful night with Polyamour and Dolores. He'd had a Feeder's camouflage; it was no use being a psychic vampire if you shouted it to the heavens. No, they were all-but-invisible, especially to children, which was what made them so bloody dangerous. In a normal Hegemony psi school he would have been tested, treated, and more than likely saved, free to live out a normal life as a psion. But in Mirovitch's kingdom he was left untreated... and so he used that camouflage to kill Mirovitch with the others, probably taking Mirovitch's death into his own psyche and sealing his own fate as a Feeder—or even worse, a Feeder's mule. A physical body for the *ka* of the dead Headmaster to ride.

He stared at me fixedly, his face slack and wooden. Then something swirled in the bottom of his eyes, crawled for the surface, and tried to speak. "You're... not... one. Of. Them." He cocked his head to the side, his throat swelling as he wrestled for control of his own voice. "Get. Get out. Out of here. I can't... hold..."

"He's riding you," I realized out loud. "You're a Feeder's mule. But you kept him down for ten years." I felt a thin burst of satisfaction at having guessed right, along with a flare of guilt for how stupid I'd been. It was all plain as day now.

"I *can't*—" Kellerman Lourdes gasped, spittle flying from his lips. He twisted, hunching down, some terrible battle being waged for control of his body. "I *can't stop him* now. You... run..."

Then his head jerked forward, like a snake's quick whipping strike. The fléchette in my left hand abruptly cooled, the cold stinging my fingers far more than heat would have. I held on, grimly. Waiting.

Then blue light bloomed from the circle of glyphs I'd scratched into the floor. The necklace, still in my pocket, fell as I shifted. It had burned a hole straight through the Kevlar-reinforced canvas of Jace's coat. It fell, the chain writhing like a live thing, and hit the floor with an oddly musical tinkle.

The circle cracked. Blue light flared like a thunderclap, and I saw Kellerman Lourdes's entire body jerk as ectoplasm streamed from mouth and nose and eyes and ears, a coughing mass of it. I dove back as Mirovitch's *ka* streaked for me, its inhuman hands turned into venom-dipped claws. Only this was not Mirovitch, the stoop-shouldered tweedy Feeder Headmaster who liked to prey on children.

This was the *ka,* grown monstrous and foul, Mirovitch seen through the eyes of a child, with claws and fangs and the leprous blue-burning eyes of a closet-hiding goblin.

I screamed, scrambling back, forgetting I was holding a sword. The backlash of the circle's cracking and breaking from inside poured up my spine and jerked a coughing yell from my throat as the Headmaster descended on me, his claws raking my belly, one catching in my ribs. A hot gush of demon blood boiled out, I convulsed, and Mirovitch dove for my open mouth, gagging reeking ectoplasm forcing down my throat.

CHAPTER 36

Gagging. Retching. Agony, as the claws tore in through my skin and organs, viscera spilling in a hot stream, my eyes bugging out as everything behind them *pushed* like depressurization.

"Student Valentine is called to the Headmaster's Office immediately."

Walking, every step a dread drumbeat, up the wooden stairs. Mirovitch's smile as his dry papery hand landed on my shoulder. We've got something special for those who break the rules today, Miss Valentine. *Meeting Roanna's eyes, feeling the sick thump of knowledge behind my breastbone. She'd told her social worker, and Mirovitch had found out.*

Jerking, crackling, her body on the fence, Mirovitch's fingers sinking into my arm as he dragged me back into Hell...and the brand, glowing red hot. Leather against my wrists as I screamed until my voice broke, after he was finished with me and the red-hot iron burned my skin as his semen trickled down my thighs; the chair's hard slat in my midriff, unable to breathe, the sound of his papery laughter filling the universe as that last shameful memory crashed out from behind the locked door—the door I'd closed and locked when I left Rigger Hall, the door that had *to close so I could go on living. Surviving.*

Fingers. In my head. Scraping, tearing, ripping. *Burning.*

No wonder Christabel couldn't be brought back—

The alien thing in my mind recoiled. That thought wasn't part of the feedback loop that would keep me helpless while it destroyed me. I grabbed onto it with the last shipwrecked vestige of my strength, sank my mental teeth into its hide, and began to *fight.*

Polyamour, tilting her head so slightly. "You learn early that your body betrays you—it's your mind that has to stay impregnable. Your soul. To have that filthy old maggot fingering inside your head..."

It howled with rage, this thing bent on rape and destruction, and tore into me all the more savagely, battering down even more mental doors, tearing great gaping holes in my psyche.

And I fought back.

Two dark eyes, the last flaring of emerald light in them. Green eyes in a saturnine face, the demon's mouth warm as he mouthed my neck, my shudder against him, spent, his murmur in my ear.

Memory, twisting and whirling, Putchkin Roulette with the inside of my head, the *burning* as he forced his way in, battering down doors, bursting locks, trying to find...what?

"Even the loa can't force a woman's heart..." If I hadn't been part-demon, I would never have heard his murmur. *"I had to give it up, Danny. I* had *to. For you."*

It screamed, recoiling from that memory too. Of course, the memory of Jace was underlaid with a clean pure well of emotion, shame and love and guilt twisted together but still mine, still a source of strength, inimical to the unholy thing. I had weapons, if I could just reach them, find them, *use* them. Good things, anything.

Smoke belched up, the unholy sick blue light forcing its way into me, lesions cracking on my skin, demon blood boiling, trying to heal me.

A convulsive effort. I was winning, if I could only remember.

Remember, Christabel keened. *Remember everything.*

Remember Jace's face, sleeping and peaceful in the bed you shared with him so long ago. Remember Doreen's soft touch, the light in her eyes. Remember Lewis's hand in yours, so strong, so sure. Remember the books he gave you, each one telling you that you were precious because he trusted you. Remember Japhrimel's last sigh as he sank down on your body. Remember reading under the covers with your heart in your mouth and your breath stale in your throat. Remember Gabe, doing for you what you could not do for yourself. Remember Eddie, holding your shoulders, remember Japhrimel throwing himself between you and Santino, determined to protect you. Remember, Dante.

Remember everything.

My fingers tightened on the fléchette. I gagged. Black spots over my vision. Passing out. Oxygen...even a demon needed some kind of air. And then what he did to my mind would be done to my body.

—fucker flayed her alive—

Christabel's raw scream, the shattering of tiles as she lunged for me. No wonder—even Death might not take this agony from me.

But I would win. As long as I could *remember.*

Remember, Dante. Remember everything.

I flung the fléchette as I fell backward, the thing that was Mirovitch forcing its way into my mouth and nose, ramming its way into my mind. I struggled, the memories fading as I tried desperately to keep them, to keep them and to stand, to *endure.*

The splinter of metal and Power pierced the wall of blue glow, shone like a shard of ice, and glowed as it bulleted in a perfect arc—

—and buried itself in Kellerman Lourdes' neck. *Kill the mule and the Feeder should die, please, Anubis, please...*

It was the only way I knew of to kill a *ka.* I would win, if I could just hold on.

If I could just remember what mattered.

Falling, then. Falling, falling, *fell,* concrete smacking my head and back, its claws twisting in my belly but I could not scream, it was in my throat, pushed past my gag reflex, forcing its way in, my nose burning and stretching, it was tearing at my jeans with one probing finger of ectoplasm, *it'll get in any way it can,* convulsing, darkness not just spots but a glaucous sheet closing over my vision.

Remember, Dante. Remember. Christabel's voice, not insane with an apparition's flat terrible finality, but as if she stood next to me, a skinny girl with bruised knees and folded arms, terrible knowledge in her childlike dark eyes. *Remember. Remember.*

I could remember nothing but one last despairing cry. The name that beat behind my heart, inside my head, the prayer I had left when all else failed.

Japhri—

My left shoulder suddenly crunched with an agony even greater, as if my left arm was being torn out of its socket one hard millimeter at a time. I managed a strangled noise past the suffocating thing stuffing itself down my throat, black demon blood pattering on concrete, and then the world exploded.

Fire. Red fire.

I heard a sound like thunder smashing the jars of the universe, every star exploding and raining fiery destruction, the grinding of an earthquake and the crackle of ice calving on every mountainside at once. Then blessed cold air seared my throat.

Searing. It hurt almost as much as what Mirovitch had done, my body blindly scrabbling for survival, every demon-tainted, demon-strong cell fighting to *live.* The wet tearing sound as my battered viscera spilled back into my stomach cavity, bones crackling as the scream bubbled past ectoplasm in my throat, a burst of Power forcing its way along my skin.

Something had happened.

Remember, Dante. Remember. Christabel's voice, grown huge, a bell filling the world, as she stared at me with her dark eyes. *Remember. Remember.*

I rolled weakly onto my side, coughing, choking the smell of dust, chalk, and aftershave out of my mouth, blowing out through my nose, slick egg-white gobbets of ectoplasm streaming away and rotting in seconds. I retched again, but didn't throw up.

—do part-demons throw up? The thought made me laugh. I giggled, a high, thin sound of insanity, and made it to hands and knees. My belly ran with fire, tender tissues stretched and straining. Grabbed for my swordhilt. Found it, my right hand curling around wrapped metal slick with noisome fluids, Power jolting up my arm with a force that made me cry out weakly. Then I collapsed again, my sword solid in my cramping right hand, my shattered shields trying to close over me, Power bleeding out into the night air. Another convulsion, my

forehead smacking concrete, a grinding pain flared in my middle as my abused insides rebelled again.

"Dante." The voice was soft and full of fire, smooth like old brandy going down to ignite in the belly. "What have you done?"

I screamed again, weakly, scrabbling against the floor. Yet another convulsion racked me. I vomited a long jet of shuddering, writhing ectoplasm tinged with black, smoking demon's blood and immediately felt much better — only three-quarters dead and burning instead of all the way dead and insane to boot.

Warm fingers closed over the back of my neck, under my tangled hair. "Be still." And then an amazing bolt of Power lanced through me. My shields mended in one explosive flare, but the ragged bleeding wounds in my mind still smoked raw and deep.

On my side. Arms around me, the stroking of a warm hand on the side of my face. "Truly you are foolhardy, *hedaira*," he said softly. "I suppose you have your reasons. Be still, now."

But I struggled up, my body obeying me now, the tearing pain inside my chest now soothed. The whistling empty hole in my chest left by his absence, the hole I had stopped noticing, was gone. My left shoulder didn't hurt. Instead, the mark sent waves of hot, soft Power down my body, each a little warmer and deeper than the last. "No," I whispered, my voice a pained croak. Then I coughed and spat another amazing gob of ectoplasm to the side. It hit the floor with a dull *splat,* and my stomach turned violently again. "No. You *burned.*"

I raised my head.

His dark eyes met mine, just the same. A lean, saturnine face, his cheekbones balanced, his mouth a straight unforgiving line. The demon Tierce Japhrimel touched my cheek, his knuckles brushing my skin. The contact sent a shudder through me, my body recognizing him before the rest of me could dare to. "You burned," I managed, before another fit of retching and gagging shook me. "You burned — you were *ash* —"

"While you live, I live." The corners of his mouth turned down, an expressive movement that managed to give the impression of a grim smile. "I suppose nobody told you."

I shook my head weakly. His smell — the scent of a demon, cinnamon incense, amber musk — wrapped around me, filled my lungs. I felt like I could breathe again, without every breath being tainted by the stench of dying cells. The smell of him seemed to coat my abused insides with peace, and flow down into the middle of my body to spread through my veins. "I tried," I whispered. "Books—Magi." I filled my lungs again. While I could, before what was undoubtedly a hallucination vanished. Gasped again, a great rasping breath blessedly free of the stink of dying human cells.

Human. *Human* cells. The thought of humans reminded me of where I was.

I tried to scramble to my feet but he caught me, his strength embarrassingly more than mine, especially at the moment. "Be still. There is no danger."

"But...the...*Mirovitch*—"

"Is that his name?" Japhrimel moved aside slightly.

Spread-eagled on the floor, coated with ectoplasm, was Kellerman Lourdes. He looked dazed, his eyes rolled back into his head, his body limp. I could see one leg was twisted the wrong way, it looked like a fracture of the lower femur. I flinched. The pool of goo coating him pulsed, and as I looked Kellerman opened his mouth to scream. The cracked bone started to mend itself, creaking and snapping.

Christabel's voice still echoed in my head like a gong, like the circuit of Fate completing itself.

Remember, Dante. Remember for us.

My stomach rose in revolt again, was ordered back down, and subsided. Japhrimel's hands were at my shoulders. "Dante? I suppose you would not care to explain." He sounded mild, but the fractional lift of one eyebrow told me he was very close to violence.

My eyes drank him in. If he was a hallucination, I wanted to store every detail. But there was no *time*—Lourdes gurgled, a sound of choked agony.

"Up. Help me up."

My hallucination of my dead demon lover stared at me, his dark eyes thoughtful. Once they had been a brilliant piercing green, like Lucifer's eyes. But when he had made me into whatever I was now, his eyes had gone dark. Without the incandescent light behind them, they looked like ageless human eyes, infinite in their depth and as familiar to me as my own. Hot tears rose, I pushed them down.

Lourdes curled into a fetal position, some inhuman effort pushing him over, up on his hands and knees. Then he collapsed, broken as a rag doll, his half-mended leg twisted impossibly to one side. He rasped out something indecipherable. The blue glow pulsed. Lourdes screamed with a human voice, the end of the scream trailing off into a writhing gurgle.

"Explain *later*," I said, every word an effort. "Help me up *now*."

As usual, Japhrimel wasted little time with human questions. Instead, he hauled me up effortlessly. The long, high-collared black coat he wore was the same, wings masquerading as clothing, but instead of black jeans he wore a very dark blue denim and worker's boots, new and unscarred. It was the same, yet different.

Flakes of the ectoplasm drifted to the floor, cracking and crackling on my skin and clothes. "You found me." The words broke on a sob. I had thought I'd destroyed any chance of his resurrection. That was my penance. What was I going to do now?

"Of course. You bear my mark. Did you think me dead, Dante?"

Yeah, for almost a year you looked pretty damn dead, you looked like a pile of fucking ash and Lucifer kept sending me letters. "You're going to have to explain this," I muttered, as if I believed he was real. He moved gracefully aside, I started limping toward Kellerman. My right leg dragged a little, not quite obeying me. I was in a sorry state. Hallucination-Japhrimel stayed on my left side, out of the way of my swordhand, his hand weightless on my shoulder, those soft intense waves of Power pulsing down my body. Repairing. Mending.

I wondered if Power alone could heal my mind.

I didn't allow myself to look up at Japhrimel. If I looked, would I find out he wasn't there, and this just another hallucination, my starved brain dreaming in color and holo before dying? Even demons needed air, I wondered if a strangled and mindraped almost-demon would have a deathdream.

Was I still alive? Or were starbursts of blood rising to the surface of my brain, so that when they autopsied me Caine would say, *A classic example of psychic assault resulting in death* in his dry disdainful voice?

Caine would probably enjoy cutting me open.

I looked down at Kellerman Lourdes. He convulsed again, his leg straightening, the bone sounding as if it was shattering to tie itself back together. My right hand twitched, bringing the tip of my sword up. Blue light ran down the blade, a healthier shade of blue than Mirovitch's diseased glow.

His eyes rolled back down, and it was Lourdes, craning his head up and to the side, looking at me with human eyes. He stared up at me. His lips tried to shape the word, *who?*

Oh, gods. "Danny Valentine," I husked. "Couple years behind you, Keller. We never talked."

Comprehension lit his eyes. He dropped his head. "Pl-please," he rasped. "Before *he* comes back..."

"You're a Feeder, and a mule," I said. "There's no cure. Not at this stage."

Weariness settled over his face. Weariness, and a bravery that hurt me a little to see. "Do...it. Are...any...left?"

"Polyamour—*Bastian.* And three more." I lifted my sword a little, paused. "One question. *Why?*"

I had to know.

"Revenge..." His eyes fluttered again. "I...Took *him.* The others...couldn't. I took...the last...piece. Should have...killed myself. Couldn't..."

Of course not. By the time Keller knew what he carried, knew that Mirovitch wasn't dead, the *ka* would have had its hooks in deep. Keller could not destroy himself once the *ka* reawakened.

I thought of Gabe at Jace's bedside, doing what I could not. One act of bitter mercy for me, one for Keller. Even, each side of the scale balancing. I swallowed, tasted bile. Filled my lungs. The smell of rotting ectoplasm, dying human cells, and the Headmaster's cloying reek warred with the smoky fragrance of demon. Japhrimel's aura, twisting diamond flames, covered mine, the mark at my shoulder spreading and staining through my battered shielding, melding together the rips and holes. When it finished, I would have a demon's shielding again.

Christabel's voice faded. *Remember,* she whispered. *Remember everything.*

Was she real, or a memory? Was she here, invisible to me? And if she was, who else was with her? Every child damaged by Rigger Hall, or just one?

Just me?

My sword swung up, both hands locked around the hilt. I braced myself, my right leg threatening to buckle. "It's over," I whispered. "Be at peace, Kellerman Lourdes."

How many times at hospital beds had I said those same words, now bitter in my mouth, tainted with death? Necromances were brought to the side of the dying, to offer comfort and ease the transition. And not so incidentally, to make sure the deceased didn't come back.

He must be wielded with honor, but more important, with compassion. Compassion is not your strongest virtue, Danyo-chan. Jado's voice whispered, memory bleeding through the present like sluggish water through a filth-choked ditch.

Compassion? For Lourdes or for me, or for both of us? Or for every damaged soul shattered by Rigger Hall?

For all of them, then. For Roanna, for Aran Helm, for Dolores. For Christabel, who had left me the clue for whatever reason, whether adolescent hubris or nascent precognition. Whether she was haunting me or whether some other intelligence had her voice and was spurring me to finish this didn't matter. It was the mercy that mattered. Mercy for all the survivors, for Eddie and Polyamour.

For all of them, and for me.

And for him most of all, the invisible kid who had thrown himself in harm's way to save us all just as Jace had thrown himself forward to save me. All accounts balanced, except for the low sound of a swordblade as it clove the air and closed the circle.

Lourdes closed his eyes. But then they popped open, the cold blue glow filling them; Mirovitch looking out through Keller's eyes.

Compassion is not your strongest virtue, Danyo-chan.

Yes, it is, I told myself. *Gods grant I don't forget it. For all of them. For all the children.* I swung my sword down. It was a clean cut, with all my force behind it, gauged with perfect accuracy. My *kia* rose, short and sharp as a falcon's cry or the deathscream of an alley cat. Blood fountained up; arterial spray. Japhrimel pulled me back as the high-tension jet bloomed from Lourdes' neck. The sword shrieked, sparking, an intense blue-white streak of living metal. Blood flew free of steel, the blade clean and shining, muscle memory carrying it back into the sheath with a click, all in one move.

A shattering psychic wail rose as Mirovitch scrabbled blindly for life, the *ka* frantically seeking something, anything to latch onto, to replicate itself, ectoplasm bubbling and burning. I sagged against Japhrimel's shoulder. He again didn't ask any useless questions, just stood watchful as the pressure behind the bloodspray lessened. The tide of blood mixed with the ectoplasm, and I smelled the reek of released bowels.

"Japhrimel." My voice caught. "Burn him. Please. Every bit."

I didn't have to ask twice. The Fallen demon raised his golden hand, and fire leapt to obey him. It dug into the concrete, red liquid demon flame, drops of blood spat and sizzled. A breath of sick-sweet smell like roasted pork filled the air. Shadows writhed and jabbed against the cafeteria's dark walls. Heat boiled up, making the linoleum char and the paint on the ceiling bubble and blister.

Finally, the flame died down. I turned my face into Japhrimel's shoulder. "You're going to disappear," I said into his coat, not even caring that I knew what it was made of. "Just stay for a moment, just please just for a minute, a second—"

"Dante." His fingers came up, tangled in my already-tangled hair. "I heard you calling me. I tried to answer."

"Just for a few seconds." I buried my face in his coat, his other arm closed around me. I inhaled the smell of cinnamon, of amber musk, the deadly smoky nonphysical fragrance of demons. Filled my lungs with the breath of life. "Before I have to burn this whole fucking place down."

"Be still," he answered. "I am here, I have never left your side. I told you, you will not leave me to wander the earth alone."

I closed my eyes. The strength spilled out of my legs. Mirovitch was dead, Kellerman Lourdes was dead.

Jace was dead. The circle, closed.

My knees buckled. Japhrimel caught me, murmured into my hair. I started to cry. The sobs shook me as if a vicious animal had me in its teeth. There, with the bloody smoke filling the cafeteria, the scorched ash that had once been Kellerman Lourdes stirred only by a faint breeze passing through the shattered plaswood-covered windows. I did not stop crying until, exhausted, I passed into a kind of gray deathly haze broken only by the slight murmurs of Japhrimel's voice as he carried me away from that place of death—and the sound of rushing flame as he did what I asked and leveled the whole nightmare of Rigger Hall to the ground.

CHAPTER 37

Sunlight spilled through the station house windows, but in Gabe's cubicle the glow of a full-spectrum bulb painted the air. Paper stirred on her desk, and the two empty brandy bottles were in the wastebasket with a drift of frozen gray cigarette smoke turned to ash.

"You caused a helluva lot of damage," Gabe said, her arms folded. "You *razed* Rigger Hall, there isn't a stick left. We didn't even get to recover a body. We only have your word—"

"Have there been any more murders?" I asked. "No? Good."

She sighed. "I believe you, Danny. I just…goddammit. Did you know? Did you know it was a Feeder's *ka* for sure?"

I shrugged, looking down at her desk. What could I tell her? The circle had been mine to close. Had I been the only one strong enough to close it, or had I just been picked by blind chance?

Did it matter? It was over. It was *done.* I no longer heard Christabel's whispering in my head. Wherever she was, I hoped she was resting more comfortably.

Phones rang in the background, I heard someone's raised voice—the punchline of a joke. Guffaws greeted the attempt. My nose filled with the scent of humans, and my own fragrance rose to battle the stench.

I knew enough to do that, now.

"I'm sorry, Gabe. He was…it was…" My sword, lying scabbarded across my knees, rang softly. I pushed a strand of inky hair back, tucked it behind my ear. "Anyone else would have been a liability instead of a help, you know that. He would have killed a hell of a lot of cops if you'd gone in to take him down." Amazingly, my voice didn't crack. I swallowed. "Keller must have been an incipient, natural Feeder. Taking from Mirovitch triggered that propensity, but the *ka* was dormant and he might have thought he was safe. He held out for ten years, thinking Mirovitch was dead, getting as far away from Saint City and Rigger Hall as he could. His uncle even went to work in the Putchkin under diplomatic contract—I'd guess to get Keller away." *Leaving no trail for us, because all diplomatic-visa workers have their personal information under blind trusts.*

"And then, Mirovitch finally breaks free." Gabe shuddered. "Hades."

I nodded. "The necklaces were an etheric link: nice, passive, and undetectable. Mirovitch would drive his mule right up to their doors. He didn't have to crack their shielding—that was done from inside, by the necklaces themselves. Fed by the very glyphs Keller had taught them. They thought they were protecting themselves from Mirovitch's echo—but that very defense killed them." *And Mirovitch pawed through their minds to get the pieces of himself they'd torn away. No wonder none of the victims were able to talk—that kind of psychic rape right before death echoes for a long time.*

That was what had saved me, the fact that there was no piece of Mirovitch inside my head for him to retrieve, my refusal to give in. The simple act of remembering.

That, and Japhrimel.

I shivered, thinking again of the clawed maggot fingers blindly squirming inside my head. My skin went cold, and the mark on my shoulder pulsed once, flushing me with heat. I straightened in the chair again, looking down at the lacquered scabbard. My reflection, ghostly and distorted, stared back at me with wide dark eyes.

"Why kill the uncle, then?" Gabe shifted her weight, leaning back slightly and regarding me. I looked up and saw without any real surprise the touch of gray at her left temple. It was only a few strands, and she had a lot of fight left in her.

I shrugged. "Here in Saint City, the uncle was a liability. If anyone started tracing former Rigger students, the uncle probably knew enough for an investigator to get the picture with the right questions. Either that or the uncle found out. We'll never know. That's why the shields on Smith's house were intact—Keller didn't need to rip them to get out."

And without Christabel's clue, I might not have caught on so quickly. Had she been looking over my shoulder? I didn't care to guess. That was one mystery I was happy to consign to the gray land of *just-don't-think-about.*

Silence stretched between us, a taut humming full of other questions. Other things neither of us could ever say. She didn't ask where I'd vanished to for three days after Rigger Hall was leveled, didn't ask where I had washed up, and especially didn't ask me if I was okay. Instead, she kept her distance, a brittle fragile professionalism presented to me during the two hours of my taped statement and this less-formal wrap-up. Case closed. Crime solved.

Game over.

"Danny." Gabe leaned her hip on her desk, regarding me with her pretty, serene eyes. "You're...different. I...Look, I know what Jace meant to you. If you want to talk, if you need anything—"

I nodded. "I'll call," I promised.

I saw the crows'-feet at the corners of her eyes, the fine lines beginning to take over her face. Gabe was getting too old for the Saint City Parapsych crap. She was a cop right down to her bones;

she'd take it all the way up to retirement and probably do security work afterward—but she was tired. Too tired, even though she had her own deep share of stubbornness.

And me? I wouldn't age. I would look just the same. And when Gabe died, who would I have left that remembered?

When she no longer remembered *me,* would I be dead too?

"Gabe?" I made it to my feet in one movement, caught myself. My right leg was still a little unsteady, despite my body's fantastic ability to heal. I struggled to find the words I wanted, failed, tried again. "Look, I just . . . be careful, all right? Take care of yourself."

"You sound like you're going to your own execution instead of on vacation." She laughed, her shoulders had relaxed. She was possibly looking at a promotion from this case. The most tangible benefit she'd received was a gold medallion and a silver credit disc. The credit disc would get her into Nikolai's office building downtown if she ever needed help. The gold medallion was an award for "superlative police work." Add to that a fat raise she didn't need and the goodwill of the Prime Power of Saint City, and she was as well-off as I could possibly hope for. I could rest for a little while, knowing she was safe.

I had one last question. "How's Eddie?"

She shrugged. "Okay. Dealing with it, I guess."

I nodded. That was good news. "Tell him . . . Tell him I killed Mirovitch myself. He isn't coming back." My stomach fluttered briefly, the papery whisper of Mirovitch's voice echoing in the darker corners of my mind. "Tell him Dante gives her word Mirovitch is *dead.*"

It was her turn to nod, thoughtfully, the emerald on her cheek flashing. "Danny." Her voice was soft, as if she'd forgotten we were standing in her office. "Look, I . . . I'm really sorry. If you . . . I mean, you—"

I felt my face tighten. I stepped forward, balanced on both feet, and put my sword down deliberately on the chair I'd just vacated. Then I spread my arms. She stared at me for a second, jaw dropping, and then moved haltingly forward, flinging her arms around me. She was so short her chin rested against the top slope of one of my breasts, but I hugged her anyway, carefully. She squeezed me with all her wiry strength, earning a slight huff of breath out of my lungs for her efforts. "You're my friend, Gabe," I whispered, my ruined voice creaking and breaking. "*Mainuthsz.*"

"*Mainuthsz,*" she echoed. Then she sniffed, as if her nose was full. "You'd better believe it. Go on, go on your vacation. And if you need me, call me."

"Likewise. Give Eddie my best." We untangled ourselves. I scooped up my sword. Turned away. Took four steps.

Taking the fifth step, out of her cubicle, was the hardest thing I'd done so far.

I did it, and was just about to turn the corner when she called out. "Danny? One last question."

I looked back over my shoulder, brushing my hair back with my left hand, the sword's scabbard bumping my cheek, my emerald spitting a single spark.

Gabe leaned against her desk again, her arms folded. Tears glimmered on her cheeks, her eyes were red and overflowing. She looked wavery through the welling water in my own eyes. "Why did you burn your house, Dante?"

What could I tell her? In the end, I settled for a simple answer.

"That was a toll. A toll paid to the dead." I felt the smile tilt the corners of my mouth up even as a tear slid down, touching my emerald and rolling across my Necromance tat. "Gods grant they stay there. Goodbye, Gabriele. May Hades watch over you."

Outside, the sky was cloudy, night falling early as it always does in winter. There were no holovid reporters — they were busy covering a scandal (having to do with a judicial candidate, three hookers, two million credits, and a plasgun) in the North District. I was now, to my profound and everlasting relief, yesterday's news and probably already forgotten by a great many people.

A gleaming black hoverlimo broke free of its holding pattern overhead and drifted down, landing with a sigh of leafsprings, the side hatch opening. I barely waited for it to open all the way before I climbed up, ducking through the airseals into climate control and filling my lungs.

Inside, everything was crystal and pale pleather, gleaming softly. Fitted into a rack on the wall was a twisted, scarred *dotanuki*, its blackened blade still seeming to vibrate with the last strike made against an enemy it had no hope of defeating. If Japhrimel had been there, Mirovitch couldn't have attacked me — and Jace would probably still be alive.

The sharp pinch of guilt under my breastbone retreated. I would pay my penance in my own way, in my own time. For right now, I couldn't stand to think about it.

I made a slight sound, wiping my cheek with the back of my right hand.

Japhrimel sat tensely on one side. I made my way over to him as the hatch closed. The whine of hovercells crested, rattling my teeth as it always did, and my stomach flipped as the hover ascended smoothly.

I dropped down onto the pleather seat next to him, letting out a sigh that seemed to crack my ribs.

"You are done?" He sounded as flat and ironic as he had when I'd met him; he stared straight ahead, giving me his profile. It had taken some doing to convince him to stay out of sight in the hover while I finished the hunt I'd started. He had remarked dryly and fiercely that after coming back to physical life, tracking me through Saint City, and finding me trying to fight off Mirovitch, he now knew what fear was, having never felt it in all the long time of his life as a demon.

The admission, pulled out of him as if by force, had broken me into a sobbing heap. And he had agreed to let me finish up with Gabe alone.

"That was the last bit of business," I said. "The case is closed. Gabe can go on now. And nobody needs to know about you. It would just raise more questions."

"Hm." He opened his arm as I slid next to him. I settled against his side, letting out another deep sigh as his familiar heat and aura closed over me. I laid my head on his shoulder and was rewarded with the pressure of his cheek against the top of my head, a subtle caress. "And you?"

I shut my eyes. It seemed they were leaking again. I had thought I was done with crying. "I thought you were dead," I said for the hundredth time. "I keep thinking you'll vanish, and I'll wake up."

"I told you, while you live, I live." He sounded calmer now, the tension leaving him. He settled back into the seat, and I leaned into him, grateful. "I would not abandon you, Dante."

"So if I'd dumped the . . . the *remains* into a vat of blood, would it have . . . brought you back?" A flare of embarrassment stained my cheeks with heat. It had been hard to leave him in the hover while I went into the police station; I still wasn't sure he was real. The throbbing of his mark on my shoulder, sending waves of heat through me, had remained a steady reassurance. But I wanted to hear him tell me again, I wanted him to keep talking, and above all else I wanted to feel his arm around me and feel the proof and comfort of his skin on mine.

He repeated his answer for me, again. "Most likely. The first... resurrection... is always the hardest."

"The fire, and the shields on my house collapsing—"

"I am here, am I not?" Now he sounded amused. He stroked my cheek, and my breath caught. It was almost enough to drown out the persistent scratching sound of Mirovitch's last scream. "It was not so long a time, Dante. Not for us."

"Long enough," I muttered, my heart twisting again. "And if I'd known—if someone would have *told* me—Jace would still be alive."

"You said yourself the god denied you entrance into death. Perhaps it was his time." Japhrimel now sounded thoughtful. His coat shifted slightly as he moved against the seat. The driver made one low swooping turn over the city, banking to head southeast. The setting sun glittered on the water, rippling on the bay's surface, the shadows of transport hovers like the shapes of great fish drifting against the ground. I sat up to look out the window past his profile, studying the familiar geography of Saint City falling away under the hover while he studied my right hand loosely clasped in his left, lying in his lap. "I am sorry. I should have sought to tell you more."

"There wasn't time while we were hunting Santino. It doesn't matter." It did matter, but who was I to tell him that? If he wasn't going to make a fuss over me leaving him for dead in a burning house, I wasn't going to blame him for not having a chance to tell me more about what I was. Even enough for me, for once. More than I deserved. "Where are we going?" And the more important question, "Are you... are you angry with me?"

Anubis help me, I still sounded like a kid. Could he forgive me for using Jace to remind myself of what I used to be? Could he forgive me for loving a human, even if it was no match for whatever it was I felt for him?

A demon.

My demon. One of the many. Only this one, I hoped, wouldn't hurt me.

He stirred slightly, freeing his left hand to gently cup my chin, forcing my eyes to meet his. A spark of green flared to life in his dark eyes, like a flash at the bottom of a deep, old well. "You are asking if I am jealous. I recall a certain swordfight not too long ago, and the outcome—and my warning you not to use me to make the Shaman jealous."

I was glad part-demons didn't blush. At least, I hoped I didn't. My cheeks were on fire. The green spark vanished, leaving his eyes dark and thoughtful as they had been since his resurrection; his skin on mine made pleasant shivers rill down my spine. Seeing him brought home how little I knew about him—and how little I knew about what he'd made me into.

A *hedaira*.

Whatever that was. Maybe now I could learn what it meant.

His thumb stroked my cheek. My eyes half-closed. When he spoke next, it was very softly, his voice an almost-physical caress against my whole body. My flesh tightened like a harpstring. I swallowed hard against the wave of liquid heat. "How can I possibly be jealous when I know you spent your time grieving for me, Dante?"

That reminded me of something else. "Lucifer," I reminded him. "He said he'd been trying to contact you. That was the first clue I had that..."

Japhrimel shrugged. "What do you owe him?" He leaned closer, a fraction of an inch at a time. My heart sped up, anticipation beating just under my skin with my pulse.

I swallowed dryly. My eyes were dry and grainy, and bright diamond needles of pain sometimes rippled through my head. I couldn't think of Jace without my chest hurting and my eyes filling—couldn't think of Rigger Hall without shuddering, my hands shaking like windblown leaves. It would take time for the effects of Mirovitch's mental assault to fade, time for my almost-demon body to heal. It would be quick, Japhrimel told me—but his idea of quick wasn't exactly mine. Yet.

And being near him would speed the healing even more. But the grief and the guilt, would those go away? Did I want them to, would I still be *human* if I no longer felt that pain?

"Dante?" Japhrimel asked.

"Last time I checked, I was even with the Devil. He got the Egg back." My breath hitched in, almost a silent gasp. *Though he's been sending me letters. If he sends another one, Japhrimel, will you throw it away? Or will you open it? And if he knows you're alive, what will the letter say?*

I couldn't bring myself to worry about it.

"Then let him wait," Japhrimel said, and his mouth touched mine. I didn't ask him again where we were going.

It didn't matter.

THE NINE CANONS: AN INTRODUCTION

Lecture at the Stryker Lee Hegemony School of Psionic Arts

Are we all present, then? Or at least physically here? (*Faint laughter.*) Very well. Let's start immediately, shall we?

Writing is an old art, one of the oldest abstract arts known to man. We presently believe the Sumerians to be the first to practice it, but given the perishable nature of much written work we may have overlooked other civilizations entirely—including the theory that somehow demons learned writing first and taught it to humans. (*More faint laughter.*) I see the Magi students are not chortling. Good.

The cuneiform of the Sumerians represents for us a critical development in human understanding: the need to convey reality with symbols.

Ever since its inception, writing has been regarded as an art that smacks of the magickal. For example, a large part of Egyptianica sorcery was focused on writing. The *Book of the Dead* (here I refer to both the Egyptianica and Tibetan manuscripts of the same name) qualifies as an act of religion, which in several important aspects is indistinguishable from an act of sorcery, not the least in which it presumes that the written or spoken word—human language itself—can alter the behavior of an immutable law (namely, death), and another state of being, the afterlife. We are all familiar with the concept of Logos here, the magical act of naming to enforce one's will on the world? Good.

It is *critical* to understand one simple thing about the Canons.

This is a magickal law you have had drilled into you ad nauseum, and I will repeat it again.

There is no such thing as an empty word. Write that down, underline it, brand it into your memory. The psionic arts are tightly regulated and accredited practitioners are held to a high standard because of this simple fact. Word wedded to will—intent, that is—produces change in reality, which is the heart of even simple sorcery. Words are an extension of action; an action wedded to intent is sympathetic magick, the First Great Branch of sorcery. The Second Branch, encompassed by but distinct from the First, is runewitchery and other magickal writing. The propagandists of the twentieth century fumbled with this law, and their shortcomings as well as triumphs will be studied later this semester.

Let us take a short look at the Canon itself before we dive into theory, shall we?

The Nine Canons we have now had their nucleus in *one* Canon, from a manuscript dating to just prior the Seventy Days War. As you will no doubt recall, just prior to the War, the Awakening was beginning, and a renascence of occult knowledge as well as workable techniques for controlling Power were flourishing, both in the subversive stratum of noncitizenry in the Republic of Gilead as well as in what we now refer to as the Putchkin Alliance. This particular Canon, today known as the Jessenblack Runes and the first half-canto of the Nine, was codified by a nameless person in Stambul. It was first distributed among the ceremonial magicians in that city as a set of broadsheets, stapled together and extremely perishable. The great revolution in the Jessenblack Runes was their accessibility—they are never more than two syllables, and were distilled from several different occult traditions. They are more properly glyphs than runes—Question? No? Very well.

We know very little about who discovered the actual technique for distilling a rune, but history has provided us with some interesting candidates, any one of whom would be an excellent subject choice for your term paper, by the way. Let us explode one myth right now: Saint Crowley the Magi had nothing to do with the Jessenblacks, though his strain of magickal theory certainly fed the spirit of experimentation that bore such fruit during the Awakening itself.

The easiest and best theory is that the Jessenblacks were simply in the right place at the right time. Due to the explosion of psionic ability during the Awakening, any set of runes would have done just as well. However, the Jessenblacks were easy, they were simple, and they worked nine times out of ten—which is far more than many other pre-Awakening occult practitioners could say.

The rest of the Canons were added in dribs and drabs over the next century of magickal experimentation, leaving us with the Nine we know today, which encompass by themselves an entire branch of magick. Not only that, but the fact that the Nine have been used by so many psions for so long has given them a quantum increase in the amount of untapped Power each rune possesses.

This is of course a simplification. The Canons are not powerful in and of themselves. Like any symbol, they are fueled by human intent. Think of it this way, especially those of you talented as runewitches: The Nine Canons are a set of doors. It remains up to you to expend the effort of opening the door. Once opened, the door will stay open as long as you hold it, and the combined weight of expectation—of Power—built up over successive uses of the rune is there to be tapped.

Now, can anyone tell me what holds the door open? Yes, Miss Valdez? (*Indistinct murmur.*) Very good!

Your sorcerous Will holds the door open, which is why practice is so important to runewitchery. This is a feedback cycle. Your Will is strengthened and trained by attention and practice, allowing you to hold the door open and incidentally adding the weight of your expectation to the symbol countless other psions have used. This is the reason the Canons are required study for every psion, not just runewitches or Ceremonials.

Now, if you will open your books to page eleven, we will begin the first Canto...

(*Fadeout.*)

NEITHER FRIEND NOR FOE

Term Paper: Magi Studies 403

East Merican Hegemony Academy of Psionic Arts

Dacon Whitaker

The current strain of Magi thought has undergone a complete reverse in past years. This paper examines the attitudes most current among active Magi practitioners and touches on how this change came about.

The pre-Awakening view of demons was hazy in the extreme, tainted by the Religions of Submission. Of all spiritual practices, only Vaudun and Santeriana came close to a workable theory of interaction with noncorporeal or sometimes-noncorporeal beings. This had begun to change by the end of the twenty-first century, when a vibrant counterculture existed, most notably of those study-ing Saint Crowley's work. However, the Republic of Gilead inter-rupted most serious experimentation in this area, and the confusion of the Seventy Days War, as well as the social and economic disloca-tion caused by the Awakening, further interfered.

Between the Awakening and the advent of Adrienne Spocarelli's work, demons were defined as primarily noncorporeal as well as eth-ically unsound and morally capricious—in essence, trickster demi-gods, against whom humans are essentially powerless and can only beg for favors from. Magi theory at that time held that whatever place demons existed in prior to and after their visits to our physical plane was an environment unsuitable to flesh-and-blood beings. This attitude was widespread even though Broward, in his classic study, points out that demons do indeed seem to breathe and bleed (witness the woodcuts of the Sterne collection and the holostill captures of the Manque Incident.) Broward's observations were treated with the assumption that when demons enter our physical plane, they take on a physical body and so, can be hurt. (Adrienne Spocarelli, in her famous essay *What's Flesh Got To Do With It?*, remarked wryly that a thermonuclear strike might even work to kill a demon—with a whole lot of luck.)

It was Spocarelli's work with a reliable method of calling and constraining imps that finally answered the question. Spocarelli claims to have been able to induce an imp to write in Merican on the hardwood floor of her study inside a circle; the imp's claws would scratch out a word or two in response to her carefully-phrased questions. The complete transcript sounds like a conversation between a lawyer and a mischievous five-year-old, but several important points can be deduced.

First of all, whatever place demons come from, they *are* physical there as well as here. Much ink and breath has been wasted on trying to determine actually *where* they come from, whether different plane, dimension, planet, or simply state of being; Spocarelli's greatest revolution was declaring that she didn't care where they came from, she simply wanted to find out how they affected *our* home plane and planet—and why they seem so damn interested in it. As physical beings, they only seem to violate natural laws; in reality, they may well be made of a stuff that conforms to different laws only because of its basic alienness but conforms to laws all the same. In other words, just because hover technology superseded petrolo does not mean that either violated natural law. And just because demons supersede humans in magickal technology does not mean that humans or demons violate natural laws.

Spocarelli's other great revolution is so simplistic as to seem obvious and is predicated on the first. While other practitioners looked upon demonic lying with several layers of shock and disapproving prudery, she pointed out that demonic *culture* may be so different from ours as to make their "lying" simply a different set of social interaction rules. If they are physical sentient beings, they have a culture; if they have a culture, they may even have prohibitions against whatever they define as "lying." All verbal brinksmanship on both sides aside, Spocarelli declared that she wanted to discover how and why demons are seemingly addicted to interaction with humanity, and that it might be worthwhile to apply anthropological and archeological tools as well as magickal theory to our interactions with demonkind.

The effect of this simple suggestion cannot be overestimated. At one stroke, Spocarelli disposed of any lingering superstitious worship of demons, reducing them to the level of beings that could be studied with scientific techniques; she also made it possible, though reactionaries loudly trumpet against her, to put the Magi in a position of power instead of supplication when it came to these beings.

The next thing that can be deduced from Spocarelli's transcript of the imp's replies is this: demons are as fascinated by humans as we are by them.

Spocarelli, while often scoffing at the notion of demonic involvement in human evolution, nevertheless does not completely rule it out. Again, she is utilitarian: whatever involvement demons might have had in shaping human genetic code is irrelevant at this juncture. What matters is that they are now seemingly enthralled by and disdainful of humanity at the same time, much as Nichtvren are. But while Nichtvren have the advantage of once being human, demons do not. Why, then, are they so fascinated?

Even pre-Awakening sources (Caplan, Perezreverte, Saint Crowley, Saint Goethe, and the anonymous author of the Illuminatis Papers, to name a very few) agree that demons are possessive and controlling in the extreme. A human who catches a demon's attention does not easily escape meddling. Even Spocarelli herself seems to have had some murky trouble with a particular demon, though reports of this are sketchy at best and mixed up with legends about other members of her famous family.

Perezreverte, in his classic *Nine Gates*, postulates that demons are hungry for human adulation, that it feeds them in some way. This is sound magickal theory and a good working hypothesis, even if demons presumably had other means of gaining Power before the advent of humanity. Perezreverte also seems to think demons are lonely, sometimes bored with their own kind, and turn to humanity for momentary diversion. He seems to give some credence to the ancient tales of fleshwives, though any mention of *that* myth tends to drive Magi to fits of frustration. Dealing with demons is hard enough without pulling in outright fabrication to muddy the issue.

This leaves us with something important to remember: We simply do not know what demonic motivation is yet. They are jealous and possessive when they deign to take notice of humanity, and the Circles working with Lesser Flight demons often note how one or more Magi within the circle will be singled out for positive or negative attention, often with almost-disastrous results on the Circle's cohesive magickal Will necessary to keep a demon under control (if such a thing can ever be said to be done.)

The logical extension to these new strains of thought is a deeper examination of reported instances of demon behavior, especially when the demon attaches himself to a particular human, whether as familiar or nemesis. Many Magi circles are reporting positive signs in dealing with imps and certain Lower Flight demons with anthropological cultural-sensitivity guidelines establishing their behavior. The amount of information available about demon anatomy and hierarchy has quintupled since Adrienne Spocarelli's time, and instances of severe harassment seem to be on the decline. However, this may not prove anything, as Circles are not likely to report ignominious failures, and actively demon-harassed Magi rarely live long enough to report their experience.

To sum up, having accumulated enough data since the Awakening, the Magi community was simply ripe for someone to put into words a few laws about dealing with demons in a way free of pre-Awakening superstition. Genius often consists of simply seeing what was there before, something Spocarelli seems to have excelled at. On the other hand, her utilitarianism has earned her severe criticism, mostly from hard-core academes who consider her as throwing the baby out with the bathwater and not practicing proper caution. On the other hand, Spocarelli survived far past the median age for actively demon-consorting, solitary Magi. She must have been doing something right.

We do not yet know why demons are so fascinated with humanity, or whether they are at heart friendly or inimical to human interest. The gamut of opinion runs from the ever-cautious old-fashioned Magi who think extreme caution must be taken to defend the greater mass of humanity from demonkind to those who insist that it is humanity's prerogative to bargain with demonkind for superior magickal training and technology, to the benefit of both sides.

Whether friend or foe, demonic intervention in human affairs does not seem likely to cease. And that is the strongest reason for the Magi to continue research, to find out exactly what they want from us.

Note: The electronic notation on this document reads: "B-. Wonderful paper, Mr. Whitaker. Who wrote it for you?"

Book 3

The Devil's Right Hand

For Kazuo, my best friend

Non satis est ullo, tempore longus amor.
— Propertius

Warlord: You are looking at a man who can run you
    through with this sword without batting an eye.
Monk: You are looking at a man who can be run
    through with that sword without batting an eye.
—old Korean folk tale

The last of the theories is the most intriguing: what if the Awakening itself was prompted by a collective evolution of the human race? Psionic talent before the Awakening was notoriously unreliable. The Parapsychic Act, by codifying and making it possible to train psionic ability, cannot alone account for the flowering of Talent and magickal ability just prior to its signing into law—no matter how loudly apologists for Adrien Ferrimen cry.

A corollary to the theory of collective evolution is the persistent notion that another intelligence was responsible. The old saw about demonic meddling with the human genetic code has surfaced in this debate so many times as to be a cliché. But as any Magi will tell you, demonkind's fascination with humans cannot be explained unless they somehow had a hand in our evolution, as they themselves claim.

For if there is one law in dealing with demons, it is their possessive nature. A demon will destroy a beloved object rather than allow its escape; in this they are like humanity. A second law is just as important in dealing with demons: as with loa *or* etrigandi, *their idea of truth is not at all the human legal definition. A demon's idea of a truth might be whatever serves the purpose of a moment or achieves a particular end. This leads to the popular joke that lawyers make good Magi, which this author can believe.*

In fact, one might say that in jealousy and falsity either we learned from demonkind, or they caught these tendencies like a sickness from us—and the latter option is not at all likely, given how much older a race they are....

—from *Theory And Demonology: A Magi Primer*
Adrienne Spocarelli

CHAPTER 1

I t's for you," Japhrimel said diffidently, his eyes flaring with green fire in angular runic patterns for just a moment before returning to almost-human darkness.

I blinked, taking the package. It was heavy, wrapped in blue satin, with a wide white silk ribbon tied in a bow. I pushed the large leatherbound book away and rubbed at the back of my neck under the heavy fall of my hair. Long hours of reading and codebreaking made my vision blur, the white marble behind him turning into a hazy streak. For just a moment, his face looked strange.

Then I recognized him again and inhaled, taking in his familiar smell of cinnamon and amber musk. The mark on my shoulder burned at his nearness, a familiar sweet pain making my breath catch. The room was dark except for the circle of light from the antique brass lamp with its green plasilica shade. *"Another* present?" My voice scraped through my dry throat, still damaged; I didn't have to worry about its soft huskiness, alone with him. The tattoo on my cheek twisted, and my emerald spat a single spark to greet him.

"Indeed." Japhrimel touched my cheek with two fingertips, sending liquid fire down my back in a slow, even cascade. His long dark high-collared coat moved slightly as he straightened, his fingers leaving my cheek reluctantly. "For the most beautiful Necromance in the world."

That made me laugh. *Flattery will get you everywhere, won't it.* "I think Gabe's prettier, but you're entitled to your opinion." I stretched, rolling my head back on my neck, working out the stiffness. "What's this?" It was about the size of my arm from wrist to elbow, and heavy as metal, or stone.

Japhrimel smiled, his mouth tilting up and softening, his eyes dark with an almost-human expression. It looked good on him—he was usually so fiercely grim. The expression was tender, and as usual, it made my entire body uncomfortably warm. I looked down at the package, touched the ribbon.

The last present had been a copy of Perezreverte's *Ninth Portal of Hell* in superb condition, its leather binding perfect as if it had just been printed in old Venizia over a thousand years ago—or been sitting in a stasis cabinet since then. The house was a present too, a glowing white marble villa set in the Toscano countryside. I'd mentioned being tired of traveling, so he presented me with a key to the front door one night over dinner.

My library breathed around me, deep in shadow, none of the other lamps turned on. I heard, now that I wasn't sunk in study, the shuffle of human feet in the corridors—servants cleaning and cooking, the security net over the house humming, everything as it should be.

Why was I so uneasy? If I didn't know better, I'd say the nervousness was a warning. A premonition, my small precognitive gift working overtime.

Gods, I hope not. I've had all the fun I can stand in one lifetime.

I rubbed at my eyes again and pulled at the ribbon, silk cool and slick against my fingers. Another yawn caught at my mouth—I'd been at codebreaking for a full three days and would need to crash soon. "You don't have to keep giving me—oh, *gods* above."

Satin folded away, revealing a statue made of perfect glassy obsidian, a lion-headed woman on a throne. The sun-disk over her head was of pure soft hammered gold, glowing in the dim light. I let out a breath of wonder. "Oh, Japhrimel. Where did you…"

He folded himself down into the chair opposite mine. Soft light from the full-spectrum lamp slid shadows over his saturnine face, made the green flashing through his eyes whirl like sparks above a bonfire. His eyes often held a green sparkle or two while he watched me. "Do you like it, Dante?" The usual question, as if he doubted I would.

I picked her up, felt the thrumming in the glassy stone. It was, like all his gifts, perfect. The funny melting sensation behind my ribs was familiar by now, but nothing could take away its strangeness. "She's beautiful."

"I have heard you call upon Sekhmet." He stretched out his long legs just like a human male. His eyes turned dark again, touching me, sliding against my skin like a caress. "Do you like it?"

"Of course I like her, you idiot." I traced her smooth shoulder with a fingertip, my long black-lacquered fingernail scraping slightly. "She's *gorgeous.*" My eyes found his and the mark on my shoulder pulsed, sending warmth down my skin, soaking through my bones, a touch no less intimate for being nonphysical. "What's wrong?"

His smile faded slightly. "Why do you ask?"

I shrugged. A thin thread of guilt touched me. He was so gentle, he didn't deserve my neurotic inability to trust anything simple. "A holdover from human relationships, probably. Usually when a guy gives a lot of presents he's hiding something." *And every couple of days it's something new. Books, the antiques, the weapons I barely know how to use—I'm beginning to feel spoiled. Or kept. Danny Valentine, Necromance and kept woman. Sounds like a holovid.*

"Ah." The smile returned, relieved. "Only a human suspicion, then."

I grimaced, sticking my tongue out. The face made him laugh.

"Oh, quit it." I was hard-pressed not to chuckle, myself.

"It pleases me to please you. It is also time for dinner." He tilted his head, still wearing the faint shadow of a smile. "Emilio has outdone himself to tempt you away from your dusty papers."

I grimaced again, setting the statue on the desk and stretching, joints popping. "I'll get fat." *This code seems a little easier than the last one. Probably a Ronson cipher with a shifting alphanumeric base. I hope this journal has more about demon physiology—I can always use that. The one treatise on wings was invaluable.*

I had never before known what a tremendous show of vulnerability it was for a Greater Flight demon to close the protective shell of his wings around another being.

"You think so?" His smile widened again. "That would indeed be a feat. Come with me, I need your company."

It abruptly warmed me that he would admit to liking my company, let alone *needing* it. "Great. You know, I've gotten really fond of this research stuff. I never had time for it before." *I was too busy paying off my mortgage. Not to mention chasing down bounties as fast as I could to keep from thinking.* I stretched again, made it into a movement that brought me to my feet. I scooped the statue up, wrapping it back in the blue satin, and offered him my hand. "I suppose you're going to try to talk me into dressing for dinner again."

"I so rarely see you in a dress, *hedaira*. The black velvet is particularly fine." His fingers closed over mine as he rose, putting no weight on my hand. He stepped closer to me and slid his hand up my arm, my shirtsleeve giving under the pressure. I wore a silk T-shirt and a pair of jeans, bare feet. No rig, no weapons but my sword leaning against the desk, its Power contained. It rarely left the sheath anymore, except during sparring sessions.

I still kept my hand in, unwilling to let my combat reflexes go rusty. I probably shouldn't have worried—demon muscle and bone would still keep me quicker and tougher than any human. But I've spent my life fighting, and that isn't something you just lay aside no matter *how* safe you feel.

The idea that he was right next to me and my sword was just out of arm's reach didn't make me feel unsteady or panicked like it used to.

Go figure, the one person on earth I trust while I'm unarmed, and it's him. I leaned into Japh, my head on his shoulder. Tension slid through him, something I hadn't felt since our first days of traveling away from Saint City. The only thing that would soothe him was my nearness, I'd learned it was better to just stay still once in a while and let him touch me, it made things easier for both of us. I was getting used to the curious feeling of being practically unarmed around a demon.

A Fallen demon. *A'nankhimel,* a word I still had no hope of deciphering.

"You're talking about the black velvet sheath? Half my chest hangs out in that thing." My tone was light, bantering, but I let him hold me.

Bit by bit, his tautness lessened, drained away. "Such a fine chest it is, too. The very first thing I noticed." His tone was, as usual, flat and ironic, shaded with the faintest amusement.

"Liar." *The first thing you noticed was my annoying human habit of asking questions and being rude.* I rubbed my cheek against his shoulder to calm him. It had taken a long time for me not to care what his long black coat was made of. I was getting better at all of this.

"Hm." He stroked my hair, his fingers slipping through the long ink-black strands. I often had wistful thoughts of a shorter cut, but when he played with it I always ended up putting off the inevitable trim. At least I no longer had to dye it, it was black all the way through naturally now. Silken black.

The same as his. Just as my skin was only a few shades paler than his, or my pheromonal cloak of demon scent was lighter but still essentially the same.

"Japhrimel?" The huskiness that never left my voice made the air stir uneasily. My throat didn't hurt anymore, but something in my voice was broken all the same by the Prince of Hell's iron fingers.

"What, my curious?"

"What's wrong?" I slid my free arm around him and squeezed slightly, so he'd know I was serious. "You're...." *You're in that mood again, Japh. The one where you seem to be listening to something I can't hear, watching for something I can't see, and set on a lasetrigger that makes me a little nervous. Even though you haven't hurt me, you're so fucking careful sometimes I wish you'd forget yourself and bruise me like you once did.*

"What could be wrong with you in my arms, *hedaira*?" He kissed my cheek, a soft lingering touch. "Come. Dinner. Then, if you like, I will tell you a story."

"What kind of story?" *Trying to distract me like a kid at bedtime. I'll let you.*

It didn't often show, how old he was; I suspected he deliberately refrained from reminding me. Perfect tact, something I'd never known a demon could exercise. They're curiously legalistic, even if their idea of objective truth often doesn't match a human's. Another pretty question none of the books could answer. How close *is* legalism to tact?

He made a graceful movement that somehow ended up with him handing me my sword and turned into a kiss — a chaste kiss on my forehead, for once. "Any kind of story you like. All you must do is decide."

Emilio had indeed outdone himself. Bruschetta, calamari, soft garlic bread and fresh mozzarella, lemon pasta primavera, a lovely slate-soft Franje Riesjicard, crème brulee. Fresh strawberries, braised asparagus. Olives, which I didn't like but Emilio loved so much he couldn't imagine anyone hating. We were, after all, in Toscano. What was a meal without olives?

The olive trees on the tawny hills were probably older than the Hegemony. I'd spent many a late afternoon poring over a solitary Magi's shadowjournal written in code, Japhrimel stretched out by my side in the dappled shade of a gnarled tree with leathery green-yellow leaves, heat simmering up from the terraced hills. He basked like a cat as the sky turned into indigo velvet studded with dry stars. Then we would walk home along dusty roads, more often than not with his arm over my shoulders and the books swinging back and forth in an old-fashioned leather strap buckled tight. A schoolgirl and a demon.

I had basic Magi training, every psion did. Since the Magi had been dealing with power and psychic phenomena since before the Awakening they were the ones who had the methods, so the collection of early training techniques was the same for a Magi as a Necromance, or a Shaman or Skinlin or any other psion you would care to name. But actual Magi nowadays were given in-depth magickal training for weakening the walls between worlds and trafficking with Hell. It was the kind of study that took decades to accumulate and get everything right—which was why most Magi hired out as corporate security or took other jobs in the meantime. Japhrimel didn't stop me from buying old shadowjournals at auction or from slightly-less-than-legal brokers, but he wouldn't speak about what being Fallen meant. Not only that, he wouldn't help me decode the shadowjournals either...and good luck apprenticing myself to a Magi circle, if any would take me while Japh was hanging around. They would be far more interested in him than in me, even if I could convince one to take on a psion far too old for the regular apprenticeship.

Dinner took a long time in the high, wide-open dining room, with its dark wooden table—big enough for sixteen—draped in crisp white linen. I was happy to savor the food, and Japhrimel amused himself by folding some of my notes—brought to the table in defiance of manners—into origami animals. I always seemed to lose some when he did that, but it was worth it to see him present them almost shyly after his golden fingers flicked with a delicacy I wouldn't have thought him capable of.

Emilio, a thick, round Novo Taliano with a moustache to be proud of, waltzed in carrying a plate with what looked like...it couldn't be.

"*Bella!*" His deep voice bounced off warm white stone walls. A crimson tapestry from the antique shop in Arrieto fluttered against the wall, brushed by soft warmth through the long open windows, my sword leaned against my chair, ringing softly to itself. "Behold!"

"Oh, no." I tried to sound pleased instead of horrified-and-pleased-plus-guilty. "Emilio, you didn't."

"Blame me." Japhrimel's lips curved into another rare smile. "I suggested it."

"You suggested Chocolate Murder?" I was hard put not to laugh. "Japhrimel, you don't even *eat* it."

"But you love it." Japhrimel leaned back in his chair, the origami hippopotamus squatting on his palm. "The last time you tasted chocolate—"

Heat flooded my cheeks, and I was glad I didn't blush often. "Let's not talk about that." I eyed the porcelain plate as Emilio slid it in front of me. A moist, heavenly chocolate brownie, gooey and perfect, studded with almonds—*real* almonds grown on trees, not synthprotein fooled into thinking it was almonds. Nothing but the best for a Fallen and his *hedaira*.

The thought made me sober, looking down at the still-hot brownie mounded with whipped cream and chocolate shavings, cherries soaked in brandy scattered in a flawless arc along one side of the plate. I could smell the still-baking sugars, could almost taste their delicate balance of caramelization. "Oh," I sighed. "This is *fantastic*, Emilio. Whatever he's paying you, it isn't enough."

He waved his round arms, his fingers thick and soft, not callused like mine. Our cook didn't take combat training, nobody wanted to kill a rotund Taliano food artist who wore stained white aprons and spoke with his plump hands swaying like slicboard wash. For all that, he was very easy with me—one of the few normals who didn't seem to fear my tat. "*Ch'cosa, s'gnora*, I don't cook for him. I cook for you. Take one bite. Just one."

"I'm almost afraid to, it's so beautiful." I picked up the fork, delicately, and glanced at Japhrimel, who looked amused. The hippo had vanished from his palm. Emilio waited, all but quivering with impatience. "I can't do it. You have to."

Emilio looked as horrified as if I'd suggested he cut up his own mother and chew on her, his mustache quivering. I offered him the fork.

"Please, Emilio. I really can't." I blinked, trying not to look like I was batting my eyelashes. "You made this, it's beautiful, you deserve to break it."

He shook his head solemnly. "No, no. Wrong." He waved a blunt finger at me. "You don't like the Chocolate Murder?" His voice was laced with mock hurt—he was *so* good at laying on the guilt. His accent mangled the Merican; I still hadn't learned Taliano.

I laughed, but an uneasy frisson went up my spine. I glanced at Japhrimel, who now studied me intently.

His eyes were almost human, dark and liquid in the light from the crystal chandelier hanging overhead. "Thank you, Emilio. She loves it, but she simply can't trust a gift. It's in her nature to be suspicious."

I let my lip curl. Even a demon had a better time of dealing with normals than I did. "I never said that." To prove it, I broke through the pristine whiteness of the whipped cream, took a scoop of brownie, and carried the resultant hoverload of sinful k-cals to my mouth.

Bittersweet darkness exploded, melting against my tongue. I had to suppress a low sound of pleased wonder. No matter how many times Emilio made this, I was still surprised by how bloody *good* it was. It's supposed to be a cliché, women and chocolate, but damn if it didn't have a large helping of truth. Nothing else seems to satisfy.

"*Sekhmet sa'es.*" I opened my eyes to find both Japhrimel and Emilio staring at me as if I'd just grown an extra head. "That's *so* good. What?"

"Thank you, Emilio." Japhrimel nodded, and Emilio, satisfied, bounced away out of the dining room. My eyes strayed to my pile of notes. Japhrimel's fingers rustled among them. "I shall make you a crane. A thousand of those are said to buy a space in heaven."

That managed to spark my interest. "Really? Which heaven?" Warm wind blew in from the Toscano hills, making the house creak and settle around itself. The shielding—careful layers of energy applied by both demon and Necromance—reverberated, sinking into the walls as Japhrimel calmed the layers with a mental touch. The sense of him listening to something I couldn't hear returned, and I watched his face. "Elysium? Nirvana?"

"No. Perhaps I am wrong, and it only buys good fortune." His mouth turned down at the corners. "Is it good?"

"Have some." I balanced a smudge of brownie and whipped cream on my fork, managed to scoop up a brandied cherry as well. "Here."

He actually leaned forward, I fed him a single spoonful of Chocolate Murder. I don't know what Emilio called the dessert, but I'd called it *murder by chocolate* and Japhrimel found it amusing enough the name had stuck.

He closed his eyes, savoring the taste. I examined his face. Even while he concentrated on the dessert, his fingers still moved, folding the paper into a crane with high-arched wings. "That's very pretty." I took the fork back. "I had no idea you were so talented."

"Hm." His eyes flashed green for just a moment, a struggle of color losing itself in a swell of darkness. "Inspiration, *hedaira.*"

"Yeah." I took another bite, the siren song of chocolate ringing through my mouth. "The man's a genius," I said when I could talk again. "Give him a raise." *Since we don't seem to be hurting for cash. I'd ask you where it comes from, but demons and money go together. Besides, you'd just change the subject, wouldn't you. As usual.*

"For you, anything." But he looked grave. The crane was gone. "Days of poring over Magi scribbles seem to have taxed you."

"If you'd just tell me, it would be a lot easier." I took another bite, adding a brandied cherry to the mix. He was right, it was heaven. Took a sip of wine, sourness cutting like a perfect *iaido* strike through the depth of chocolate. "What does *hedaira* mean, anyway?" *Just one little clue, Japh. Just one.*

Demons wouldn't talk about *A'nankhimel*, I guessed it was an insult to imply they could Fall. Asking a demon about the Fallen was like asking a Ludder about genesplices: the whole subject was so touchy with them that precious few demons — if any — were capable of discussing it rationally. Japhrimel was highly reticent about it even with me, and I was the reason he was where he was.

I wondered if I should feel guilty about that, tried not to ask him. Couldn't help myself. It was like picking at a scab. He never stopped me from researching, but he wouldn't provide anything more than tantalizing hints. If it was a game, the point of it was lost on me.

"*Hedaira* means you, Dante. Have I told you the story of Saint Anthony?" One coal-black eyebrow lifted fractionally, the mark on my shoulder compressing with heat as he looked at me. "Or would you prefer the tale of Leonidas and Thermopylae?"

I stared at the remains of the brownie. It would be a shame to waste it, though my stomach felt full and happy. I was pleasantly tired, too, after three days of slogging through code. *Why won't he answer me? It's not like I'm asking something huge.*

It was always the same. I had a real live former demon living with me, and I couldn't get him to answer a single damn question.

I used to be so good at finding things out. I scooped a brandied cherry onto the fork, chewed it thoughtfully while I watched him. He was busy looking through my notes. As if they could tell him anything he didn't already know.

The paper rustled, a thin, familiar sound. "Shall I make a giraffe for you?"

"They're extinct." I laid my fork down. "You can tell me the one about Saint Anthony again, Japhrimel. But not now." Silence fell between us, the wind from the hillside soughing in through the windows. "Why won't you tell me what I am?"

"I know what you are. Isn't that enough?" He ruffled through my notes again. "I think you're making progress."

You know, if I didn't like you so much, we'd have a serious problem with your sense of humor. "Progress toward what?" Silence greeted the question. "Japhrimel?"

"Yes, my curious?" He folded another small sheet of paper, over and over again, the spidery ink scratches of my notes dappling the paper. The mark on my shoulder throbbed, calling out to him. I was tired, my eyes strained and my neck aching.

"Maybe I should go back to Saint City. The Nichtvren Prime there has some demonology books, he and his Consort invited me to stop by anytime." I watched his face, relieved when it didn't change. He seemed to be concentrating completely on folding the paper again and again. "It'd be nice to see Gabe again. I haven't called her in a month or so." *And I think I might be able to go back to Saint City without shaking and wanting to throw up. Maybe. Possibly.*

With a lot *of luck.*

"If you like." Still absorbed in his task. It was uncharacteristic of him to concentrate so deeply on something so small while I spoke to him. That look of listening was back on his face, like an unwelcome visitor.

Night breathed into the room through flung-open windows. Uneasiness prickled up my back. "If something was wrong, you'd tell me, wouldn't you?" *I sound like an idiot girl on a holovid. I'm an accredited Necromance and a bounty hunter, if something's wrong I should know, not him.*

"I would tell you what you needed to know." He rose like a dark wave, his coat moving silently. Green flashed through his eyes. "Do you not trust me?"

That's not it at all. After all, who had rescued me from Mirovitch's deadly *ka* in the ruined cafeteria of Rigger Hall? Who had I left Saint City with, who had I spent every waking moment with since then? "I trust you," I admitted, softly enough my voice didn't break. "It's just frustrating, not knowing."

"Give me time." His voice stroked the stone walls, made the shielding reverberate. He touched my shoulder as he passed, pacing weightlessly across the room to stare out the window. His long dark coat melded with night outside. I caught a flash of white—did he still have the animal he'd made out of my notepaper? "It is no little thing, to Fall. Demons do not like to speak of it."

That did it. Guilt rose under my ribs, choked me. He had Fallen, though I had no idea what that meant beyond a few hints gathered from old, old books. He'd shared his power with me, a mere human. Never mind that I was more than human now, never mind that I still *felt* human every place it counted. "Fine." I pushed my plate away, gathered up my notes. "I'm tired. I'm going to bed."

He turned from the window, his hands clasped behind his back. "Very well." Not a word of argument. "Leave the plates."

I stacked them in a neat pile nonetheless. It doesn't pay to be sloppy, even when you have household help. I've washed my own dishes all my adult life, it feels wrong to leave them to someone else. When I spoke, it was to the ruins of the brownie. "If there's something you're not telling me, I'll find out sooner or later."

"All things in their proper time." Damn him, he sounded amused again.

Dante, you're an idiot. "I hate clichés." I brushed my notes into a scarred leather folio and crossed the room, carrying my sword, to stand beside him as he looked out onto the darkness of the hills under a night as rich as blue wine. The smell of demon—amber musk, burning cinnamon—rose to cloak us both, the deeper tang of sun-drenched hills exhaling after nightfall making a heady brew. "I'm sorry, Japh. I'm an idiot." Easier than an apology had ever been, for me. Which meant that it only hurt like a knife to the chest, but didn't claw its way free.

"No matter. I am a fool, as any Fallen is for a *hedaira*'s comfort." He forgave me, as usual, and touched my shoulder. "You mentioned being tired. Come to bed."

Well, that's another sliver of information. For a hedaira*'s comfort.* "Give me back my notes, and I will." I sounded like a kid throwing a tantrum for an ice-cream cone. Then again, he was much older than me. How old was he, anyway? Older than the hills?

Lucifer's eldest child, Fallen and tied to me. *As any Fallen is for a* hedaira*'s comfort.*

Did that mean there was something so terrible he was actually doing me a favor by not telling me?

He made a single brief movement, and an origami unicorn bloomed in his palm. I took it delicately, my fingertips brushing his skin. "Where did you learn to make these?"

"That is a long story, my curious. If you like, I will tell it to you."
He didn't smile, but his shoulders relaxed and his mouth evened out,
no longer a grim thin line. The listening look was gone, again.

For once, I opted to take the tactful way out. "Sounds good. You
can tell me while I brush my hair."

He nodded. The warm breeze stirred his hair, a little longer over
his forehead since I'd met him. "Heaven indeed. Lead the way."

*Now what the hell does he mean by that? He knows this house better
than I do, and I'm the one always following him around like a puppy.*
"You know, you get weirder all the time, and that's saying something.
Come on." I reached down, took his hand. His fingers curled through
mine, squeezed tight enough to break human bones. I returned the pressure, wondering a little bit. It wasn't like him to forget I was more fragile; he was usually the very first to remind me. "Hey. You all right?"

He nodded. *"A'tai, hetairae A'nankimel'iin. Diriin."* His mouth
turned down again as if tasting something bitter, his fingers easing a
little.

"You're going to have to tell me what that means someday." I
yawned, suddenly exhausted. Three days locked in a library. Scholarship was heavier than bounty hunting.

"Someday. Only give me time." He led me from the dining room,
my hand caught in his, and I didn't protest. I left the folio behind on
the table. Nobody would mess with it here.

"I'm *giving* you time. Plenty of it, too." Behind us, the sun-flavored
night crept in through the windows. What else could I do? I trusted
him, and all he asked for was something I had plenty of nowadays.
So I followed him through our quiet house, and ended up letting him
brush my hair after all. Once again, he'd distracted me from asking
what I was—but he'd also promised to tell me eventually, and that
was enough.

CHAPTER 2

I woke from a trance deeper than sleep, a dreamless well of darkness.
I had been unable to sleep for almost a year while Japhrimel was
dormant; it seemed now I was making up for it by needing a long,
deathlike slumber every few days. He told me it was normal for a

hedaira to need that rest, during which the human mind gained the relief it needed from the overload of demon Power and sensation. I'd done some damage by pushing myself so hard. Now, each time Japhrimel soothed me into blackness I felt relieved. Every time I woke, disoriented, with no idea of how much time had passed, he was there waiting for me.

Except this time.

I blinked, clutching the sheet to my chest. Moonlight fell through the open floor-length windows, silvering the smooth marble; long blue velvet drapes moved slightly on a warm night wind. Here in Toscano the houses were huge villas for the Hegemony rich. This one was set into a hillside looking over a valley where humans had farmed olives and wheat for thousands of years and now let the olive trees grow as decorations. My hair lay against my back, brushing the mattress, silk slid cool and restful against my skin.

I was alone.

I reached out, not quite believing it, and touched the sheet. Japhrimel's pillow held a dent, and the smell of us both hung in the room, his deeper musk and my lighter scent combining. My cheek burned as my emerald glowed, and I saw the altar I had made out of an antique oak armoire lined with blue light. I turned my head slightly, and the spectral dart of light from my emerald made shadows cavort on the wall.

I slid out of bed naked, my fingers closing around the hilt of my sword. The blade sang as I pulled it from the lacquered sheath, a low, sibilant sound of oiled metal against cushioned and reinforced wood. More blue light spilled on the air, runes from the Nine Canons—the sorcerous alphabet that made up its own branch of magick—sliding through the metal's glowing heart. Jado had named the blade *Fudoshin*, and I rarely drew it.

I had nothing left to fight.

It had been a long time since my god spoke to me. I approached the altar cautiously, sinking down to one knee when I reached the invisible demarcation between real and sacred space, rising and stepping into the blue glow. My hair moved, blown on an invisible breeze as blue light slid down my body like Japhrimel's touch.

Where is he? Does he leave while I sleep? He's always here when I wake up. I discarded the thought. If my patron psychopomp wanted me, I was safe enough, and it didn't matter yet where Japh was. I had never seen him sleep—but I didn't care. This was private, anyway.

I stood in front of the altar, my sword tucking itself back behind my arm, the hilt pointing down and clasped loosely in my hand. The metal's thrumming against my arm intensified as the katana's tip poked up past my shoulder. My cheek burned, the emerald sizzling, the inked lines of my tattoo shifting madly under the skin.

The new statue of Sekhmet glowed, set to one side of my patron Anubis — all I had left of the altar I'd set up in my old house in Saint City. Anubis, dark against the blue light, nodded slightly. The bowl set before him as an offering was empty, the wine I'd poured into it gone. I reached up, touched my cheek with my fingertips, felt my skin fever-hot, hotter than even a demon's blood.

Then the blue light took me. I did not quite fall, but I went to my knees before the gods, and felt my body slide away.

Into the blue crystal hall of Death came a new thing.

I stood upon the bridge, an oval cocoon of light from my emerald anchoring my feet to the stone. I wore the white robe of the god's chosen, belted with supple silver like scales. My new sword, glittering with fiery white light as if it too lived, was clasped in my hand for the very first time.

I had not ventured into this place since Jason Monroe's death.

The fluttering crystal draperies of souls drew very close around me. I was used to it — I was, after all, a Necromance — but the one soul I sought I did not see. No unique pattern that I would recognize, no crystallized streak of psychic and etheric energy holding the invisible imprint of shaggy wheat-gold hair and blue eyes.

I looked to find him, and I was grateful he was not there. If he was not there I would not have to face him.

Instead, my eyes were drawn irresistibly to the other side of the bridge, where Death stood, His slim dog's head dipping slightly, a nod to me.

Behind my god stood a shadowy figure, flames crackling around the shape of a woman, Her lion's head surrounded by twisting orange. A rush of flame and rise of smoke dazzled me for a moment, I lifted my sword blindly, a defense against a Power that could burn me down to bone.

Coolness rolled along my skin, dispelling the heat. The blade glowed fierce white instead of the blue I was used to. Steel shivered as Power stroked its edge and the mark on my shoulder flared with a deep bone-crunching pain I had not felt in years, sending a stain of twisting-diamond demon fire along the cocoon protecting me. Even here in Death I was marked by Japhrimel's attention, though my god didn't care.

Anubis knew I was His. Even a demon could not change that. I am Necromance. I belong to Death first, and to my own life second.

The god spoke, the not-sound like a bell brushing around me. Yet I am the bell, the god puts His hand on me and makes me sing.

Anubis bent, His black infinity-starred eyes fixed on me. He spoke again. This time the sound was like worlds colliding, blowing my hair back, the edges of my emerald's glow shivering so for a moment I felt the awful pull of the abyss beneath me. My fingers loosened on the hilt, then clutched, the sword socking back into my grip.

—a task is set for you, my child—

Comprehension bloomed through me. The god had called; I was asked to do something. This was warning and question both, a choice lay before me. Would I do as He asked, when the time arrived?

Why did He ask? I was His. For the god that had held me, protected me, comforted me all my life, it was unnecessary to ask. All You must do is tell me Your will, I whispered soundlessly.

The god nodded again, His arms crossed. He did not have the ceremonial flail and hook, nor did He wear the form of a slim black dog as He usually did. Instead, His hand lifted, palm-out, and I felt a terrible wind whistle as my skin chilled and my ears popped.

Then She behind him spoke, rushing flame like a river, the dance of unmaking the world taking another stamping step. I fell backward, my knuckles white on the sword's hilt, a long slow descent into nothingness, waiting for the stone to hit my back or the abyss to take me, the words printed inside my head, not really words but layers of meaning, each burning deeper than the last, a whisper of a geas laid on me. A binding I could and would forget until the time was right.

CHAPTER 3

I surfaced, lying on my side against chill, slick marble. Warm sunlight striped my cheek. I'd been out a long time.

Hot iron bands clamped around my shoulders, lifted me. "Dante." Japhrimel's voice, ragged and rough as it had only been once or twice before. "Are you hurt? *Dante?*"

I made a shapeless sound, limp in his hands. My head lolled. Power flooded me, roaring through my veins like wine, flushing my fingers with heat and chasing away the awful, sluggish cold. I cried out, my hand coming up reflexively. Steel fell chiming as Japhrimel twisted my wrist. He was so much stronger than me, I could feel the gentleness in his fingers as well. So restrained, careful not to hurt me. "Easy, *hedaira*. I am with you."

"They called to me." My teeth began to chatter. The chill of Death had worked its way up past my elbows, past my knees, turning flesh into insensate marble. How long had I been away, on the bridge between here and the well of souls? "Japhrimel?" My voice cracked, a child's whisper instead of a woman's.

"Who did this?" He pulled me into his arms, heat closing around me, his bare chest against mine. My back was brushed with softness— he had opened his wings and pulled me in. I shivered, my teeth chattering, more Power burned down my spine from his touch, warmth pulsing out from the mark on my shoulder. "What were you doing?" He didn't shout—it was merely a murmur—but the furniture in the room groaned slightly as his voice stroked the air. It didn't sound like my voice, the tone of throaty invitation. No, Japhrimel's voice loaded itself with razorblades, the cold numbness of a sharp cut on deadened skin.

"The g-g-gods c-c-called—" My teeth eased their chattering. He was warm, scorching, and he was *here*. "Down for a long time. Gods. Where were *you?*"

He surged to his feet, carrying me. I felt the harsh material of his jeans against my hip, heard the clicking of bootheels as he carried me to the bed and sank down, cradling me. My sword rang softly, lying on the floor.

Japhrimel held me curled against him like a child, warmth soaking into my skin. "What were you thinking? What did you do?"

It had been a long time since I'd felt the cold of Death creeping up fingers and toes, sinking into my bones. "You were gone." I couldn't keep the petulant tone out of my voice, like a spoiled child with a hoarse, grown-up voice. "Where were you?"

"You're cold." He sounded thoughtful, rubbing his chin against my temple, golden skin sliding against mine, a hot trickle of delight spilling up my back. "It seems I cannot leave for even a moment without you doing yourself some mischief. Stay still."

But I was struggling free of him. "You left me. Where were you? What did you do? *Where were you?*"

"Stay *still*." He grabbed my wrist, but I twisted and he let me go, my skin sliding free of steel-strong fingers. I arched away, but he had my other wrist locked, an instinctive movement. It didn't hurt me— he avoided pressing on a nerve point or locking the rest of my arm, but it effectively halted me, making me gasp. "Just for a moment, be still. I will explain."

"I don't want *explanation*," I lied, and pushed at him with my free hand. "Let *go*."

"Not until you hear me. I did not want to leave you, but a summons from Hell is not ignored. I could not put it off any longer."

My heart thudded up under my collarbone, and I tasted copper. "What are you *talking* about? Let go!"

"If you do not listen I will make you listen. We have no time for games, *hedaira*, though I would gladly play any game you could devise. But *the Prince has called*."

The words didn't mean anything for the first few seconds, like all truly terrible news. Most of the fight went out of me. I slumped, and Japhrimel's arm tightened. He released the wristlock and I shook my hand out, my head coming to rest on his shoulder. He pulled me closer, his wings brushing softly against my shoulder and calf. It was incredibly intimate. I knew enough, now, to know that a winged demon—those of the Greater Flight that had wings, at least—did not suffer those wings to be touched, or open them for anything other than flight or mating.

Lucky me. Lucky, lucky me. Dear gods, did he just say what I think he said?

"Do you hear me?" he whispered into my hair. "The Prince has called, *hedaira*."

I have been unable to contact him in the usual manner. Lucifer's voice purred through my head. That had been during the hunt for Kellerman Lourdes and Mirovitch, the Prince of Hell sticking his elegant nose into my life again. In the mad scramble of events afterwards, I'd forgotten all about it. Psychic rape and the death of one of your closest friends can do that to you.

Japhrimel was telling me that life was about to get very interesting again. I raised my head, hair falling in my eyes, and looked at him.

His mouth was a tight line, shadows of strain around his dark
eyes, a terrible sheen of something that could be sadness laid over the
human depths I thought I knew.

My hands shook. It had taken a long time for me to stop seeing
Mirovitch's jowly face printed against the inside of my eyelids, a long
time before the aftermath of facing down my childhood demons of
Rigger Hall faded to a nightmare echo.

It still wasn't finished. My entire body chilled, remembering the
ka's ectoplasm shoving its way down my throat and up my nose, in
my ears, trying to shred through the material of my jeans while Mirovitch's spectral fingers squirmed like maggots inside my brain, rap-
ing my memories. The only thing that saved me was my stubborn
refusal to give in, my determination to strike back and end the terror
for everyone else.

That, and the Fallen demon who held me, who had stopped the *ka*
from killing me. Who had searched until he found me, and burned
my childhood nightmares to the ground simply because I *asked*.

I looked at Japhrimel. The morning sunlight didn't reach the bed,
but reflected golden light was kind to his high balanced cheekbones
and thin mouth. A terrible, paranoid thought surfaced, and I opened
my big mouth. "You're leaving me?" I whispered. "I . . . I thought—"

His eyes sparked green. "You know I would not leave you."

It was too late. I'd already said it, already *thought* it. "If the Prince
of Hell told you to, you might," I shot back, struggling free of his
arms, my feet smacking the floor. He let me go. I scooped up the
fallen scabbard and made it to my sword, steel innocent and shining
in the rectangle of sunlight from the window. Scooped up my blade
and slid it home, seating it with a click. "What is it this time? He
wants you back, you just go running like a good little demon, is that
it? What does he *want?*"

My shoulder flared, a tugging against the mark branded into my
flesh. I ignored it.

"You misunderstand, my curious." Japhrimel's voice was terribly,
ironically flat. "The one the Prince seeks audience with is *you.*"

CHAPTER 4

I turned so quickly my hair fanned out in a loose arc. Sunlight warmed my hip and knee, pouring in through the window. Japhrimel had stood up, and his long dark Chinese-collared coat was back, wings folded tightly as if armoring himself.

As if he was the one who needed the armor.

He watched me, his hands clasped behind his back again. "It seems that once again I am to ask you to face the Prince, Dante. There is...terrible news."

I swallowed dryly. "Terrible? When you say that, I suppose it means something different than when I say it." Then the absurdity hit me—I was standing here naked, my entire body gone cold and tense with foreboding, talking to a demon. How did I get myself into these things? "Am I allowed to get dressed, or does Lucifer want to see me in the buff?"

"If you wish to present yourself as a slave, I can hardly stop you." The edge to his voice glittered and smoked like carbolic tossed across antigrav. "Try to rein your tongue for once. If I have meant anything to you, you must *listen* to me."

Slaves are naked in Hell? Yet another demon custom I don't know about. The mad urge to giggle rose up inside of me and died away again. My jaw set itself like plasteel. "You have no idea what you mean to me," I informed him, just as flatly as he'd ever spoken to me.

"And vice versa. You are a selfish child sometimes. It could even be your particular brand of charm."

I lifted the sword slightly. "Do you want a sparring match, or do you want to explain to me why you left me while I was unconscious? And defenseless, I might add?"

"I cannot imagine you defenseless." Japhrimel stepped forward once. Twice. He approached me slowly, as if I might bolt at any moment. I stood trembling at the edge of the sunlight and let him come near, my hand with the sword dropping. "I gave up my place in the Greater Flight of Hell for you. I am of the Fallen, and I have chosen to bind my fate to yours. Remember that."

The mark on my shoulder sent a burning tingle all through me. His hand brushed my elbow, slid up my arm to polish the bare skin of my shoulder, then slid under my hair, curling around my nape. He didn't have to pull me forward, I leaned into him like a plant leans toward a window. "I have fended off the polite requests Lucifer has sent for your presence, and I have parried his less-than-polite requests. He has stopped asking and started summoning, *hedaira*, and he is an enemy we cannot afford to make. Not if we expect to keep living, and I find I have grown fond of life with you. Even this pale world has its beauty when seen through your eyes." He dropped his face, spoke the last sentence into my hair. He inhaled, a slight shudder passing through him. My sword dropped the rest of the way, my arm hanging slack, the scabbard resting in my hand. "At the very least, I ask you to come and listen. Will you?"

The lump in my throat made it difficult to talk. "Fine," I rasped. "But don't expect me to be happy about it. I hate him, I *hate* him, he killed you and I hate him."

The tension running through him drained away. "He did not kill me. I am here."

I couldn't argue with that, so I let him pull me back to the bed and run his fingers through my hair. I let him kiss my shoulder, my cheek, and finally my mouth. I sighed as he folded me in his arms and spoke to me the way I understood best—the language of the body, an instinctive semaphore used to tell me once again that he was real. His mouth against mine, his body against mine, and the rough hungry fire of my own desire swallowing me whole—but tears slid down my cheeks as I gave myself up to him.

I should have known things wouldn't stay perfect forever.

CHAPTER 5

It took a long time for my heartbeat to return to normal. I lay in his arms, my eyes closed, feeling the weight of his body against mine. The Magi say that demons invented the arts of love, and after years of living with Japhrimel I didn't just believe it—I *knew* it, all the way through my veins.

It was too bad he couldn't have been human in the first place. Would I have loved him so much if he was?

I propped myself up on my elbow, my hair sliding over my shoulder as he threaded his fingers through and pushed it back, tucking it behind my ear. The silky strands clung to his fingers, unwilling to let go. "All right," I said, my legs tangled with his. "Time for you to come clean. What's going on?"

He shrugged, his touch trailing down my arm and skipping to touch my ribs. As usual, slow fire followed, unstringing my nerves, soothing me. His eyes, half-closed, still held sparks of green circling in their depths. "You have been buried in your books, my curious. While you have done so, there has been unsettling news. The air is full of... disturbance. For Lucifer to request a *hedaira*'s presence is a thing unprecedented in the history of Hell. The Three Flights—Greater, Lesser, and Low—now know of Vardimal's rebellion. A demon escaped Hell and lived among humans for fifty mortal years, and even created an Androgyne. Now they think it is possible to leave Hell unremarked—and they think perhaps Lucifer is weakening, or his grip on Hell is slipping. Mutters of discontent rise everywhere. The fact that Lucifer lost his assassin to a human woman does not help."

"I'm missing the part where that's my problem," I muttered.

He brushed my cheek with his knuckles, a gentle, careful movement. "If Lucifer loses control of Hell, do you think demons will cavil at settling old scores with me? We have notoriously long memories." A swift snarl crossed his face. A long time ago, it would have frightened me. "Not to mention that it is the Prince's will that keeps demon-kind from meddling further with your world. *That* is something you should be devoutly grateful for." His pause sent a chill down my back. "Our kind play cruel games."

That makes sense. Too much sense to be comforting. I sighed and sank down into the pillow, untangling my legs from his and turning on my back. The rectangle of mellow sunlight moving across the room reminded me I should be in the library. I could only acquire shadowjournals from the estates of solitary Magi, since circles burned shadowjournals when a member passed, or kept them in heavily guarded libraries that were destroyed if the circle died out.

Each solitary Magi had a different code, and each text required months of patient work to break that code and strip-mine whatever information the Magi let slip about demons, hoping for a word about the Fallen. It was slow, frustrating, difficult going, and now I might never finish.

Japhrimel's hand slid down to spread against my belly. It reminded me of claws digging into my guts, the sick leprous light of Mirovitch's *ka* burning the air, my own helpless screams. My skin had healed without a scar. I had no scars left except the fluid twisted glyph on my shoulder, the mark of my bond with him. "So what does Lucifer want with me? I'm no use to him."

"My guesses are unpleasant, and it is better not to guess where the Prince is concerned." Old bitterness shaded his voice. He didn't like to talk about his life as Lucifer's Right Hand; I might have understood more if he'd told me even a little about it.

"So when you told me nothing was wrong, you were lying? Like when you didn't tell me you helped Santino escape from Hell?" I closed my eyes, staring into the mothering dark behind my eyelids. Japhrimel's aura swirled, black diamond flames sliding through the trademark sparkles of a Necromance, showing I was linked to him. *Dante, for the sake of every god that ever was, don't do this.*

"I did so under the Prince's direction." Was it me, or did his voice sound even more bitter? "I had no *choice*. Not until I Fell, and you freed me by completing your bargain with him."

I blew out another long, frustrated breath. "So he wants to see me. Posthaste."

"We have until nightfall. Then I will take you to the meeting place. I was told we will meet a guide there who will take us to a door into Hell. Once we pass into Hell, you will be required to do the speaking for us."

Another arcane custom? "I am *not* ready for this." A new thought struck me. "Lucifer wants a bargain?"

I could feel his eyes moving over me, the weight of his gaze like amber silk and honey against my skin. "I would assume so."

Does this mean I have a chance of.... "Then I can bargain for Eve?"

Japhrimel froze, his hand tensing. He made a slight sound, like a bitter snort of laughter. After a long pause, his fingers gentled against my abdomen. "It would be most unwise, Dante. *Most* unwise."

"He *took* her. She was Doreen's. He had no *right*." *Plus he almost strangled me, and he killed you. The Devil owes me, and if he needs something from me I'm going to make him pay with interest.* It was hollow bravado at best. I had no illusion of being able to win in any game involving the Devil. Humans just don't win when they tangle with him.

But I had Japh on my side, didn't I? That had to be worth something.

"How would you have raised her, Dante? You do not even truly understand a demon, let alone an Androgyne. He took her for a reason." His tone was soft, reasonable, and did not mollify me in the least.

I don't care why he took her. "He nearly strangled me in the process, Japhrimel. Or did you forget?" *If I don't understand demons, whose fault is that? You won't tell me anything!*

"You survived, did you not? For him, that passes as a light warning. Must I beg you to be cautious?" His hand tensed again, his thumb moving slightly, a light caress.

"I'm *plenty* cautious. Especially where demons are concerned. Last time I didn't come off too badly, did I?"

"I was pleasantly surprised." Levity, his own particular brand of dry humor. We both knew how close it had been.

I sighed, opened my eyes, saw the blue velvet canopy flutter. How many times had I awakened to this bed? How many times had Japhrimel soothed me out of a nightmare, stroked my back and shoulders until I could stop trembling? How many times had I sobbed out the names of my failures and listened to his calm voice making everything better?

If Japh needed me to, I'd take on the Prince of Hell and more. What else *could* I do? "All right. If you want me to, I'll meet the Devil again."

I hadn't realized how tense he was until he relaxed, the silent crackling static of his attention swirling out of the air. I took a deep breath of the scent we made together — amber musk, burning cinnamon, something spicy and overwhelming to a human but the equivalent of a shield for a demon; a defense against the mortal world and its pervading odor of dying. It was also the equivalent of an air bubble, climate control and some indefinable gas making breathing easier. I used to think the smell of a demon wasn't physical. Now that I was part-demon it was all *too* physical.

"I will protect you, Dante." His tone was low, a promise. "Never doubt that."

Silence rose between us. Before, quiet had been something shared. Now it was dangerous.

"What aren't you telling me?" I swallowed the next question: *Do you mean it when you say you're staying with me?*

I wouldn't have been surprised if he'd heard it anyway. I did some quick mental calculations. It had to be months that we'd lived here, quite how many I didn't know. Time got away from me nowadays, especially when I was in the library.

However long it had been, I hadn't doubted a single word that crossed his lips until now. "And how long has Lucifer been asking for me?" I added.

"Since I was resurrected, my curious. We have had more time than I ever thought possible. You needed it." He stroked the curve of my hip, rounder now since I'd put on a little weight. Not much, but a little.

"You *lied* to me." Flatly. I shouldn't have been so upset. Even as I said it, I knew I shouldn't have.

You forgave Jace, didn't you? He lied to you about Santino too. My conscience, of course, piped up loud and clear. But Jace had stayed with me, putting up with my grief and my inability to stop moving, pushing his aging human body to its limits to keep up with me on bounties, watching my back. I *had* forgiven him. He'd earned it. Danny Valentine, the woman who swore that even one lie was a treasonous offense, had forgiven Jace everything, even if I couldn't be what he wanted or needed.

But Japhrimel...was different. The thought of Jace lying to me had filled me with untinctured rage and contempt at the time; the thought of Japhrimel hiding something from me, no matter the reason...hurt. As if my heart had been replaced with a live coremelt. Tears rose behind my eyes, I pushed them down. Blinked furiously. *Why does it hurt like this? What's wrong with me?*

He sighed, tracing the arch of my rib without tickling. I almost wished he would tickle me—that would end up in a wrestling match, and *that* would mean I wouldn't have to think for a while. "What would you have done, had you known? You were a shadow. Whatever ghost I rescued you from crippled you. I feared you might die of despair, and if you locked yourself in the library at least you were not grieving." His fingers were so gentle, he stroked my skin delicately, soothing. I had never been touched so carefully by a human lover; even Doreen's comfort had lacked the deep softness of Japhrimel's. Who would have thought a *demon* could be so gentle? "To know that Lucifer was asking for you was a burden you were not ready for."

It wasn't so much the chain of his logic as the infuriating tone of reasonableness and *I-know-best* he used that made me spitting mad. The fresh anger and irritation was like a tonic against the clawed pain in my chest, fear sparking fury as a defense.

All in all, I was taking the news rather well.

"I'll decide what I'm ready for," I snapped, rolling up and pushing his hand away. "You should have told me." I gained my feet, scooping up my sword, and strode for the bathroom. If I was going to meet the Prince of Hell again, there were things I had to do first.

The mark on my shoulder warmed, a prickling of heat.

"What of *your* secrets?" His voice rose from the tangled bed behind me, a silky challenge. "What of the dead you bear such guilt for? You grieved for me while living with your human paramour, and I have never asked you to explain *that*."

I actually stumbled. I hadn't believed he would throw Jace at me, especially since it was salted with the pinch of truth. I took in a deep breath, my head down, tendrils of my hair slipping like living things over my shoulders. Then I lifted my head, regaining my balance. "At least Jace didn't lie to me," I flung back over my shoulder, and slammed into the bathroom before he could reply.

It wasn't quite true. Jace never told me he was Mob, and part of the Corvin Family to boot. But I'd flung it at Japhrimel. Now who was the liar?

CHAPTER 6

If I was going to visit the Devil, I wanted to be fully armed. So I opened up the huge dresser in the corner of the bedroom. Japhrimel was nowhere to be seen. I knelt on naked knees, my hair drying in a thick braided rope against my back. Pulled out the lowest drawer and saw with faint surprise everything was still there.

Well, why wouldn't it be there? You put it there. You're being ridiculous, Danny. Get moving.

Trade Bargains microfiber shirt, sheds dirt easily and doesn't smell no matter how long you wear it, thanks to antibacterium impregnation. Butter-soft, broken-in jeans, cut to go over boots and treated to be water and stain resistant, patches tailored in to accommodate holsters and with the crotch inset so side-kicks are possible. The old explorer's coat, too big for me because it was Jace's—supple tough Kevlar panels inset in canvas, one pocket scorched where a silver spade necklace had turned red-hot and burned its way free. The rig, still oiled and spelled, not cracking like regular leather. Knives, main-gauches and stilettos, and the two projectile guns, cartridges neatly stacked off to the side. And in its deep velvet case, the necklace Jace had given me in the first days of our affair. I'd worn it all through the last job—tracking down Kellerman Lourdes. Even after I'd finished, that job had almost killed me

I could admit as much now, if only to myself.

The necklace was beautiful. Silver-dipped raccoon baculums on a fine silver chain twined with black velvet ribbons and blood-marked bloodstones as well as every defense a Shaman knew how to weave, all twisted together in a fluid piece of art. He hadn't given any other woman something like this—at least, not that I knew of. He had spent months making it, a powerful mark of his affection for me.

If I went into Death again, if I used the necklace he'd worked so hard on or the sword twisted with his death to call his apparition up, what would he have to say to me?

Maybe something like "I loved you, Danny, and I was human. Why couldn't you love me?" Maybe something like that. Or maybe "Why did you let me die?" Or "What took you so long to come find me?"

Any or all of those questions were equally likely, and equally viciously hurtful. Which one would I pick to answer, if I could?

"I'm not brave enough to find out," I whispered, and picked up the necklace with delicate fingers. I fastened it, and spent a moment arranging it so the baculums hung down, each a curve of silver against my golden skin, knobbed ends pointing out. "Or am I?"

I felt as if a shell had been ripped away, as if my skin was hitting the air for the first time. I'd spent so long living on the edge of a sword, taking one bounty after another, jobs other Necromances wouldn't touch, honing myself into a weapon to still the voices whispering in my head. *Not good enough, not strong enough, not brave enough, not tough enough.* Now, instead of feeling properly terrified, I felt a type of giddy glee. Soon I'd be facing down some new kind of danger, feeling as if my heart was going to explode from adrenaline. I had said that all I wanted was a quiet life, to be left alone.

I'd actually believed it when I'd said it, too.

Under the necklace were my rings, chiming as they tangled together. I lifted them one by one—amber rectangle, amber cabochon. Moonstone. Plain silver band. Bloodstone oval, obsidian oval. Suni-figured thumb ring on my left hand. They began to glow, sullenly at first, then brighter as my Power stroked at them. I sighed, feeling the defenses and spells caught in each stone rise to the surface, tremble, and settle back into humming readiness.

I dressed quickly, my fingers flying as they hadn't for a long while. Buttoning up my shirt, my jeans, finding a pair of microfiber socks. My boots were a little cracked, but everything still fit. Living soft hadn't made me fat yet, though I'd lost the look of being starved. A demon metabolism, every girl's best friend.

I picked up the rig with trembling hands. Shrugged myself into it, buckled it down. Tested the action of the knives. They were still sharp. The plasgun went into its holster under my left arm. The projectile guns rode easy in their holsters. I slid clips in them both, chambered a round in each, and found the little clicks comforting to hear.

The only thing left was my tattered canvas messenger bag—the bag that had gone into Hell with me, back to the nightmare of my childhood with me, the bag I'd carried on every job since Doreen had bought it and sewn in the extra pockets and loops of elastic to hold everything down.

I scooped up the bag and the six extra clips, paced over to the bed, and dumped everything out. Scraps of paper, containers—blessed water, salt, cornmeal mix, my lockpick set, extra handkerchiefs and ammo clips and my athame, still glimmering with Power inside its plain black leather sheath. The chunk of consecrated chalk—my fingers trembled, touching its dry surface. I'd been searching for it desperately in the abandoned cafeteria of Rigger Hall with Lourdes chasing me, carrying the poisonous remnant of Mirovitch inside his brain like a cancerous flower. A silver Zijaan lighter with a cursive-script *CM* etched into it. A battered paperback copy of the Nine Canons—the runes that Magi and other psions and sorcerers had been using since before the Great Awakening—that I'd had since the Academy. My tarot cards in a hank of blue silk. Rough bits of quartz crystal, a few more bloodstones, some chunks of amber. More odds and ends.

My hands knew what to do. I laid Jace's coat down, my fingers moving, checking, stowing everything in its proper place. I picked up the bag, gave it an experimental shake, and let it settle. I ducked through the strap and settled the bag on my hip, under the holster carrying my right-hand gun. I rolled my shoulders back as everything settled in, then shrugged into Jace's coat. Picked up my katana.

"Ready for anything," I muttered.

The house was oddly quiet. I listened and heard nothing, not even servants moving. I realized how used to the sound of human hearts beating I'd become. The maids didn't talk to me—I didn't speak Taliano, and they didn't speak much Merican, so I let Japhrimel translate and was grateful none of them looked askance or forked the sign of the Evil Eye at me. None of them set foot in the library unless it was to dust while I was sleeping or to leave a box of new books inside the door. Only Emilio seemed completely unafraid, both of me and of the demon who shared my bed.

I stood for a few moments, the room resounding with small sounds as my attention swept in a slow circuit, brushing the curtains of the bed, sliding along the walls, caressing the framed Berscardi print above the low table where Japhrimel kept a single lily in a fluted black glass vase. The lily was gone, the vase dry and empty. The curtains fluttered. I sighed.

I turned on my heel, my boots clicking, and strode out of the bedroom, down the hall. The doors rose up on either side of me, never-used bedrooms, a small meditation room, a sparring room with a long wooden floor and shafts of light coming in every window.

The sparring room almost quivered with the echoes of sessions between Japh and me, combat as intimate as sex, his greater strength and speed giving me the ability to push myself harder, faster—I didn't have to worry about hurting him, didn't have to hold back. The only times I'd ever fought as hard were in Jado's *dojo,* training to take on the world.

I found the door I wanted unlocked, hit it with the flats of both hands. It swung inward silently, banging against the wall. Dust flew. This wasn't a place anyone entered often.

The room was long, a wooden floor glowing with layers of varnish. At the far end, barred by two shafts of sunlight, stood a high antique ebony table, and on this table lay a scarred and corkscrew-twisted *dotanuki*, its hilt-wrappings scorched.

Jace's sword. Still reverberating with the final agonized throes of his death.

A blot of darkness hunched on the floor in front of the table.

Japhrimel, on one knee, his back turned to me, his coat lying wetly against the floor behind him.

Of all the things I expected, that was probably the last.

He didn't move. I strode up the center of the room and came to a halt right behind him, my boots sliding on the floor. I dug my heels in—going too fast. It seemed I would never learn how to slow this body down. My rings spat, swirling with color, each stone glittering.

I waited. Japhrimel's head was down, inky hair falling forward to hide his face. His back was utterly straight. He didn't speak. Sunlight fell like honey, but the sun was sinking down in the sky. We were going to go find this door into Hell soon.

I finally settled for stepping close and laying my hand on his shoulder. He flinched.

Tierce Japhrimel, Lucifer's assassin and oldest child, *flinched* when I touched him.

I didn't choke with surprise, but it was damn close. "Japhri—"

"I have been here, asking the ghost of a human man for forgiveness." His voice slashed through mine. "And wondering why he has more of your heart than I do."

It was the closest thing to jealousy I'd ever heard from him. I closed my mouth with a snap, found my voice. "He never did," I finally said. "That was the problem."

Japhrimel laughed. The sound was so bitter it dyed the air blue. "Are you so cruel to those you love?"

"It's a human habit." The lump in my throat threatened to strangle me. "I'm sorry."

Even now, saying *I'm sorry* didn't come easily. It tore its way out of my chest with razor glass studded along every edge.

Japhrimel rose to his feet. I still couldn't see his face. "An apology without a battle. Perhaps there is hope."

I knew he was using that black humor again, like a blade laid along the forearm to ward off a strike. It still hurt. "If I'm so bloody bad why don't you go back to Hell?" *Great, Danny. Lovely. You're really on edge, aren't you? This is really adult. No wonder he treats you like a little kid.*

"I would not go back, even if Hell would have me. I seem to prefer your malice." He turned on his heel, away from me, the hem of his coat brushing my knee. "I will wait for you."

My voice had turned ragged, but even that couldn't stop the dripping sweetness along its edges. "Don't run away from me, dammit."

He paused. Stood with his back to me still, his shoulders iron-hard. "Running away is your trick."

You little snot of a demon, why do you have to make this so fucking hard? "You're an arrogant son of a bitch," I informed him. The air turned hot and tight, the twisted corkscrewed sword lying on the table ringing softly, its song of shock and death cycling up a notch. Catching the fever in the air, maybe. We were both throwing off enough heat and Power to make the entire room resound like an echo chamber.

"I am what you make of me, *hedaira*. I will wait for you outside the door." He strode away, every footfall a clicking crisp sound. Anger like smoke fumed up from his footprints. His coat flapped as if a wind was mouthing it.

"Japhrimel. Japh, wait."

He didn't pause.

"Don't do this. I'm sorry. *Please*." My voice cracked, as if Lucifer had just finished strangling me again.

Two more steps. He stopped, just inside the door. His back was straight, rigid with something I didn't care to name.

I folded my arms defensively, the slim length of my sword in my right hand, a bar of darkness. "I'm *frightened,* Japh. All right? I woke up, you weren't here, and you drop this on me. I'm fucking terrified. Cut me a little slack here, and I'll try to stop being such a bitch. Okay?" *I can't believe it, I just admitted being scared to a demon. Miracles do happen.*

I thought he'd continue out the door, but he didn't. His shoulders relaxed slightly, the hurtful static in the air easing. It took the space of five breaths before he turned back to me. I saw the tide of green drifting through his eyes, sparks above a bonfire. His mouth had softened. We looked at each other, my Fallen and I. I tried to pretend I wasn't hugging myself for comfort.

"There is no need for fear," he said finally, quietly.

Yeah, sure. We're about to go meet the Devil, for the third time in my life. I could have done without ever meeting him at all. He's probably got something special planned for us, and the Devil's idea of a little surprise is not my idea of a good time. "You've got to be joking." I sounded like I'd lost all my air. The mark on my shoulder turned to velvet, warm oil sliding along my skin from his attention. "It's the *Devil.*" *I don't think he's likely to be in a good mood, either.*

He came back to me, each footfall eerily silent. Stopped an arm's-length away, looking down to meet my eyes, his hands clasped behind his back. "He is the Prince of Hell," he corrected, pedantically. "I will let no harm come to you. Only trust me, and all will be well."

I've trusted you for a long time now. "Is there anything else you haven't told me?" I searched his face, the memorized lines and curves. He had his own harsh beauty, like a balanced throwing-knife or the curve of a katana, something functional and deadly instead of merely aesthetic. Funny, but when I was human I had thought him almost ugly at first, certainly not *beautiful* by any stretch of the imagination. The longer I knew him, the better he looked.

He shrugged. Gods, how I hate demons shrugging at me. "If I told you what I guess, or what I anticipate, it would frighten you needlessly. Until I am certain, I do not wish to cloud the issue with suppositions. Best just to go, and to trust in your Fallen. Have I not earned as much?"

Goddamn it, I hated having to admit he was right. Even *I* knew that anticipating something from the Prince of Hell was likely to end in a nasty surprise. Japh had never let me down. "I do." My voice dropped, the soft ruined tone of honey gone granular soothing the last remains of tension away. "Of course I trust you. Don't you know that?"

I thought he'd be happy about it. Instead, his face turned still and solemn as we looked at each other, the mark on my shoulder pulsing and sending a flood of heat down my skin. "Cut it out." I could hardly get enough air in to protest. It was as intimate as his fingers in my hair, as intimate as his mouth against my pulse. "Let's just get this over with."

A single sharp nod, and Japhrimel offered me his hand. I let him take my right hand, my sword hand; it made me nervous as hell to know that he could very easily keep me from drawing just by tightening his fingers a little.

I don't want to do this. I don't. Japhrimel led me out of the room, and the doors closed behind us, silent on their maghinges. *But if I have to face down Lucifer, at least I've got Japh with me.*

It wasn't as comforting as I'd thought it would be, since Lucifer had killed him once before. Dead, or driven him into dormancy — gods, I didn't want to try to figure out the difference again. Even with Japh on my side, seeing the Prince of Hell was likely to be hideously unpleasant.

Still, I'd do it. What you can't run away from, you have to face.

Living with the ghosts inside my head had taught me that much, at least.

I just hoped facing this would leave me alive.

CHAPTER 7

The town of Arrieto has dozed in the middle of wheat fields and olives for centuries, drowsing in southern sun. We caught a transport in the town square, a piazza still picturesquely cobbled with worn-down stones. Here in a historical preserve of the Hegemony, there was no urban sprawl and no great flights of hover formations — but every sunbaked house had a bristling fiberoptic array and invisible security nets humming. Slicboards were racked outside cafes, and a Necromance was still local news.

By the time we lifted off, me in the window seat and Japhrimel in the aisle, I had already had enough of stares and whispers hidden behind hands. I've walked the streets of Saint City, one of the biggest metropolises in the world, and had my armor hold up. But this little town's obvious fear got to me. Normals always think psions want to read their deep dark secrets, or use mental pressure to force them to do something embarrassing. Not one normal seems to understand that to a psion, touching a normal's mind is like taking a bath in a festering sewer. Messy thoughts, messy emotions, messy fantasies all stirred together, randomly emitting and decaying; a normal mind was the *last* place a psion wanted to find herself in. The psions that *did* take advantage of normals very quickly found themselves subject to bounty hunters and dragged in to answer felony charges.

I should know. I've dragged more than a few in.

Still, all the holovids are full of evil psions and occasional psion antiheros, taking down the bad guys while crippled by their own talents. The fact that psions don't work in the holovid biz only makes it worse.

None of the normals could tell what Japhrimel was, but I had a tat on my cheek, the emerald flashing, and my sword. Only an accredited psion can carry edged metal in transports and guns on city streets. Only an accredited psion or the police, that is. So I stuck out, and Japhrimel blended in.

Sort of. It's kind of hard to hide a tall, golden-skinned demon in a long black Chinese-collared coat. To normals he probably looked like he'd only been genetically augmented, which was a little odd but not way out of the gravball court. A genescan would show him as a different species but no weirder than a werecain or kobolding. No, it would take a psion to see the twisting black-diamond flames of his aura. They would know what he was. But there were no other psions on the transport.

I leaned my head back against the seat. The flight was quiet, only ten people—we had plenty of empty seats around us in every direction. Nobody would want to crowd me; Necromances have a reputation for being a little twitchy. "So we're going to get a guide, and go through a door," I said.

"Yes."

I wanted this all *very* clear. "You'll negotiate our passage, but you're not going to talk—once we pass *through* the door."

"No." Japhrimel's eyes were closed. He leaned back into the seat, his mouth a straight line, his hands cupped and upturned in his lap.

"Because that would look as if I was weak."

"Yes."

"If you don't speak and you stay behind me while we're in Hell, you're just a bodyguard—and not responsible for anything impolite I do." *Which is bound to be something, since I have the worst manners in the world. Don't think I'm going to make a special effort for Lucifer either.*

"Yes."

"Don't touch anything, don't take anything from the Prince, and especially don't eat or drink." I looked out the window. The whine of hover transport settled against my bones. I hated it, my back teeth grinding together before I could make my jaw unloose. "And you don't know what he wants me for. Won't even venture a guess."

"I have my guesses. None of which are pleasant."

I couldn't help myself. "Care to clue me in?"

That earned me a quirk of a smile. "If we go to meet death, I would prefer it to be a surprise for you. I do not want you dreading it and becoming distracted."

I couldn't tell if he was joking, for once. His sense of humor was a little strange, when it wasn't mordant black wit or irony it was a particular brand of macabre I was beginning to recognize as purely demon. "Oh, how comforting." I tapped the sword's hilt with my fingernails. I'd been painting them with black molecule-drip polish for so long the polish was starting to maintain itself on my nails. I knew how to make my fingers into claws now, I was stronger and faster than any mortal.

Fat lot of good it would do me against Lucifer. Every culture has its stories about nonhuman beings—beings whose beauty didn't conceal their essential difference, beings who didn't necessarily believe in the human idea of truth. The fact that we can separate them into *loa, etrigandi,* demons, or what-have-you doesn't make them any less dangerous.

The Old Christers had called Lucifer the Father of Lies. I was beginning to think they'd had the right idea, even if their conception of gods was so narrow as to be laughable in this day and age.

"Japhrimel?"

He moved slightly, restlessly. "What is it, my curious one?"

"If I died, what would happen to you?"

One eye opened a fraction of an inch, glanced at me. "There is little cause to worry, *hedaira.* Even Fallen I am still the one who was Lucifer's assassin, and that is your safety. There are not many demons who would challenge me, weakened as I am."

I shouldn't have felt guilty. I hadn't *asked* him to Fall. If he'd told me what he'd intended to do I would have done everything possible to dissuade him, including drawing my sword or lighting out to track Santino on my own. I hadn't had the faintest *clue* of what he'd intended when he'd changed me.

Still... I did feel guilty. Right up under my breastbone and slightly to the left, the place where my heart still kept steady time. "I'm sorry. That you're... weakened."

I watched, fascinated, as his right hand curled into a fist. My own right hand had been spoiled and knotted for a good year or so after I'd killed Santino. I'd been unable to draw another sword until Gabe called me in to work on the Lourdes murders.

That thought sent another hot prickle of guilt up my spine. She'd sent some news clips about the murders and some other messages through my datpilot, and I called her as frequently as I could stand to. The conversations were usually short. *Hi, how are you. Not bad, Eddie's good? Oh you're busy? Sorry about that. Okay, well, catch you later.*

Ghosts of the words we could never say to each other crowded the phone line, robbing us both of breath. She tried to apologize for bringing me in on the Lourdes case, I didn't let her. Each time she started, I would tell her not to.

I would try to thank her for performing a Necromance's duty at Jace's bedside. She would tell me not to. Everything that lay between us stopped the words in both our throats.

Why was it so damn hard to talk to the one person I could have said anything to?

I wished now that I'd spent more time on the phone with her. I would have given a lot to call her, maybe even use my datpilot's fiendishly expensive voice capability. But she didn't even know Japhrimel was alive. I had, for the first time, lied to her when I'd left Saint City. Even if only by omission, it was still a lie told to the one person on earth I should never have misled. Gabe had gone through hell for me.

You can't do anything about it now, Dante. Focus on the task at hand.

I raised my left hand, threaded my fingers through Japhrimel's. It took some doing—he didn't fight me, but his fist was clenched. I finally pried it open, and the touch of his skin on mine rewarded me. "Talk to me," I said, so softly only a demon's sensitive ears could have heard.

He let out a quiet breath. His anger could blow the transport to pieces, but no whisper of it escaped. Except for the mark on my shoulder, burning as it twisted its way more deeply into my skin.

"You are cruel and gentle, in the manner of your kind," he said finally. "You have never treated me as anything less—or *more*—than human. As one of your own."

I thought about that for a moment. I had fallen into the habit of treating him just like another human early on in the hunt for Santino and never quite grown out of it. Was that what he was talking about? "It wouldn't be fair otherwise."

"Fair?" His hand relaxed slightly. His eyes were closed, but I would have bet hard credit and the emerald in my cheek that he knew the location of every person on the transport and had them evaluated down to the last millimeter. "Life is not fair, Dante. Even demons know this."

"It should be," I muttered, looking at my swordhilt.

"I dislike the pain you inflict on yourself." He stroked my wrist with his thumb, an intimate touch making me catch my breath. "We will arrive exactly nowhere if we do not reach an agreement."

Memory rose around me. He'd said the same thing in my kitchen, all those years ago, during the first stages of the hunt for Santino. One terrified Necromance bent on revenge and a demon without the sense to keep from falling in love with her, and the Devil pulling all the strings behind the scenes.

"An agreement? How about *I* try to be a big girl and keep my mouth shut, and *you* try not to keep things from me from now on?" *I'm pretty sure I can keep my half of that bargain if you can manage to keep yours. What do you say, Japhrimel?*

His thumb stroked the underside of my wrist again. My breath hitched. "There." He sounded less tense and more like the Japhrimel I knew. "That is the Dante I know."

I could have laughed at the parallel thoughts. Instead, I studied my swordhilt. Jado-*sensei* was an old crafty dragon, and I wondered if he'd given me a blade that could cut the Devil himself. Yet another thing I missed—Jado's nut-brown wrinkled face framed by long pointed ears. Maybe I *did* want to go back to Saint City.

The thought made my heart pound. I took a deep breath. "Japhrimel?"

A slight, subtle shift, he leaned toward me in his seat. "What?"

"Don't hide things from me. Even if you think it'll scare me."

"You're persistent."

It was like one of our sparring sessions. During the first few I'd held back, afraid of hurting him because he so rarely used a weapon. It was only after the third time he took my blade away from me without even seeming to try that I started to get angry—and I hadn't held back since. The same sense—of slashing at an opponent who simply melted away from my strikes then blurred in to take my weapon away—was there in our conversation.

"Don't change the subject." I kept my temper by a thin margin. "Please."

"Even if it is for your own good, *hedaira*?"

I scowled at my sword. *Even then, Japh. I'd rather be scared than have you hide something from me.* "Who are you to decide that?"

"Your *A'nankhimel*, Dante. The one who Fell through love of you."

"I didn't ask you to." *I didn't make you Fall. I just treated you like a person. Was that so wrong?*

He moved again, still leaning toward me. "And yet, it happened.

Enough. I will tell you truth, but I will not bother you with trifles or distract you unnecessarily."

It was no use. He wasn't going to budge. *It's going to be goddamn hard to get through this if you don't tell me little things like "Oh, Dante, the Devil keeps calling and wants to talk to you." That kind of sounds like need-to-know information to me, Japhrimel.* I bit the inside of my cheek to keep the words from spilling out. I was already in a hell of a bad mood.

Not the best way to meet the Devil at all.

CHAPTER 8

Venizia lay atop its lagoon, shimmering gilt and pearl. Once, long ago, the city had been at the mercy of a rising sea. Climate control, antigrav, and reactive had changed all that. Now the entire city was mythically beautiful, its buildings arching over canals gleaming crimson as the sun died its daily, fiery, bloody death.

After the failure of the celebrated Gibraltar Locks Project, the Hegemony had funded a massive retrofit to keep Venizia afloat. Everyone was mildly surprised when the Locks architect (an Academy Magi dropout-turned-engineer named Todao Shikai) was assigned to the task, and slightly more surprised when he actually pulled it off. He collapsed and died of a massive cerebral hemorrhage six months after the retrofit was finished. Rumor was he had called up a particular imp after the Locks project failed and bargained away his life for a career success. I'd always discounted the old story — but I was on my way to my second official meeting with the Prince of Hell.

Meeting the Devil does tend to change the way one looks at gruesome old legends — the more gruesome, the more thought-provoking.

The transport floated down, hovercells whining as it held steady above the water for a few moments before gliding onto the dock and landing with barely a thump. Whoever the pilot was, he or she was highly capable. AI decks can't land without jolting everyone aboard; it takes a human touch.

I sat looking out the window, as everyone coughed and shuffled off the transport. Japhrimel, his fingers warm against mine, said nothing. There was a time when I would have fought tooth and nail to get *out* of the damned transport as quickly as possible, but for now I was content to let everyone else go their merry way first. Well, maybe not *content*. Maybe I just didn't want to get out of the hover.

"We must go, Dante," Japhrimel said quietly. His thumb touched the underside of my wrist again, the heat flushing through me and washing away sharp cold fear. The man was dangerous to my pulse. "I would ask you something."

"Hold that thought." I blew out between my teeth and stood up. He moved too, without relinquishing my hand. We went down the central aisle, my bag bumping against my hip. He had to bend slightly, a little too tall for a human transport. His coat rustled, sounding like soft cloth-leather; he must have been agitated for all his face was calm and his aura perfectly controlled.

We stepped off onto the dock washed with sunset light. I glanced into the sky, looked across the dock to where water glittered and foamed under the antigrav. Shikai had done a good job — the retrofit was seamless; Venizia was now truly a floating city. Unfortunately, that much antigrav meant that the whole city whined with a sound inaudible to most normals. Most psions can't stand the sound of hovers for long, it settles in the back teeth and rattles the bones. I sighed. My shields swirled, taking in the quality of the Power here — people and stone and reactive, a taste like sour oily water on the back of the throat, overlaid with coffee fumes and synth-hash smoke. What would have taken me hours before I met Japhrimel — acclimatizing to a new city's Power well — was done in seconds, my almost-demon metabolism shifting through the necessary adjustments. "I bet there aren't a lot of psis here," I muttered, then looked up at him. "What is it you're going to ask me?"

Japhrimel finished scanning the dock, his eyes glittering and that look on him again — the look of listening to something I couldn't hear. His jaw was set, golden skin drawn tight over his bones. I wondered what it felt like to him, to be going back into Hell. Then again, he'd gone last night, right?

I wondered what it was like, seeing what he'd given up for me. Hell was no place to party if you were a human — but he wasn't, and it was his home. Was he homesick?

Then he looked down, and that rare smile lit his face. I couldn't help myself — I caught my breath, smelling pollution-dyed water and sunwarmed stone, and a thread of synth-hash smoke. The pilot and copilot of the transport had just come out of their cockpit access hatch, the gold braid on their uniforms twinkling. The pilot had a synth-hash cigarette dangling from her lip.

"I ask you again to trust me, Dante. No matter what befalls us. And I ask you not to doubt me."

"I'm here, aren't I?" I hunched my shoulders, a faint breeze off the Mediterane touching my braided hair. As usual, a lone strand had come free and fell in my face. It seemed the longer my hair got, the more of an independent consciousness it possessed.

"You are." The smile faded from his face. "*A'tai, hetairae A'nankimel'iin. Diriin.*" It might have been a prayer, the way he said it, but it wasn't a prayer I knew. He had only taught me a little of the language demons used among themselves, saying it wasn't fit for my tongue, and anyway we had time.

Now I wished we had more time.

"What does that mean?" I searched his face as the sun finished its slow slippage under the horizon. I took a deep breath—the wind off the sea was warm, but with a promise of later chill. Lights flickered in the city atop the lagoon. The antigrav made the ground feel as if it was thrumming underfoot, like the deck of an old ship or a balky slicboard.

"Promise me. Say you will not doubt me, no matter what happens."

"It would be a lot easier if you would tell me exactly what's going on," I said irritably. "Are we going to get this over with or not?"

"Promise me." He wasn't going to budge. Stubborn demon, stubborn human woman—only I wasn't fully human anymore.

I set my jaw and glared at him. "I promise." *After all, who do I have left, Japhrimel? Tell me that. You and Gabe, and Eddie by extension. That's all.*

I'm damn near rich, having even that much.

"Say you will not doubt me, no matter what."

And he called *me* persistent. "I promise I'll trust you and I won't doubt you," I chanted as if I was back in primary school. "No matter what. Now can we get this *over* with?"

"I will never understand your tendency to hurry." But his face had eased. Now he looked thoughtful and almost relaxed. It was only a millimeter's worth of difference or so in the lines around his mouth but it shouted at me. At least I knew him well enough for that.

If I have to do this, I want to get it over with. Then you and I are going to have a little chat about our relationship. It's high time we got a few things straight. My heart leapt into my throat, I lifted my sword slightly. "I'm armed and ready to face the Devil, Japhrimel. Let's go."

I wish I could say I saw more of Venizia. The city is a treasure trove of pre-Hegemony art and artifacts; its architecture alone is worth a lifetime's careful study. As it was, I looked down at my feet, barely marking the turns we made and fixing them into a mental map, letting Japhrimel navigate me over bridges and through darkening streets not big enough for even single-passenger hovers. The people here used narrow high-prowed transports on the canals—some of them open-air transports, which gave me a shudder—and slicboards to get around. The fourth time I got tagged by the wash from a slic-board's localized antigrav I made up my mind to draw my sword the next time one came near me.

I almost did it too, but Japhrimel closed his fingers around my right wrist, a bracelet as gentle as it was inexorable. "You *are* out of sorts," he murmured, making me laugh. The sound sliced through the street, rattled away against the hoverwhine pressing against my back teeth.

"I'm going to smashtip the next kid who buzzes me right into the canal," I said through gritted teeth.

"No need. We're here." He halted in front of a soaring pile of stone, I tilted my head back—and back, and back.

The cathedral rose in spires toward the sky just beginning to take on the look of a city at night, reactive and electrical light and freeplas all conspiring to wash the vault of heaven with orange. I saw a round window, real glass repaired with bits of plasglass, in the shape of a rose that would glow red inside when the sun hit it. "The entrance to Hell is in a temple?"

"No." He shook his head, his eyes flaring with runic patterns of emerald green for a moment. "This is simply where I was told to meet our guide. Though most temples are very good places to find a door into Hell." He led me up the steps, and I ran the fingers of my right hand over the waist-high iron railing. The hand that had killed Santino—it had twisted into a claw after I had driven the shards of my other sword into the scavenger demon's black heart.

I touched my swordhilt, lifting the slim scabbarded blade in my left hand.

Did Jado give me a blade that can kill the Devil?

I hadn't thought to ask him at the time, too busy thinking about Rigger Hall and too sick with mourning Japhrimel. Besides, how could I have known the Prince of Hell would start messing with my life again? I thought he'd had enough of me the first time around. I had certainly emphatically had enough of *him.*

I looked at Japhrimel's back as he paused at the double doors, one golden hand lifting to touch them. I'd thought him dead once.

Dead and gone. Grieving for him had almost killed me. So he'd said nothing about Lucifer asking for me, trying to protect me. He was right, if I'd had to deal with Lucifer *and* the echoes of Mirovitch's papery voice rustling in my head, I might have gone gratefully, howlingly insane.

No extenuating circumstances, my conscience barked. *What happened to the old Danny Valentine, the one nobody would dare lie to?*

I did something I'd never done before—tried to shut that voice up. It didn't go gracefully.

"Japhrimel."

He turned his head slightly, keeping both me and the door in his peripheral vision.

"I never would, you know. Doubt you." *I've violated one of my biggest rules for you.* I couldn't bring myself to say the rest of it, and hoped he understood.

His lips thinned, but the mark on my shoulder was suddenly alive with velvet flame, caressing all the way down my body. I took a deep breath, bracing myself.

He pushed the door open, glanced inside, and his shoulders went rigid for half a breath. Then he turned back to give me one eloquent, heart-freezing look, warning me something was wrong, and stepped inside. He paused just inside the door, his attention moving in a slow arc over the church's interior. I waited.

He finally moved forward. A heavy fragrance boiled out of the opened door, and my heart rose to lodge in my throat again like a lump of freeplas. Smoky musk, fresh-baked bread, the indefinable smell of *demon.*

Not just any demon, either. I knew that smell. Had hoped to never, *ever* smell it again.

I stepped into the church, Power brushing along my skin, teasing, caressing. My mouth had gone dry. My heart fell down from my throat into my stomach, somersaulted, then started to pound in my chest, my wrists, my neck. I even felt my pulse in my ankles, my heart worked so hard.

Well, would you look at that. The doors slid along the floor behind me, closing of their own will—or *his*. Ranks of pews marched all the way down the cathedral's interior, but on the altar was a massive Hegemony sunwheel; other gods had their own niches in the halls going to either side. Candles flickered in the dimness, I smelled the faint tang of kyphii. My nose filled with the heatless scent of generations of worship, guilt, and fear, and the later tangs of Power: Shamans and Necromances and *sedayeen* and Ceremonials coming to make offerings, dyeing the air with energy all mixed together to make a heady charged atmosphere.

Most old temples and later cathedrals were built on nodes, junctures of ley lines. During the Merican Era churches had stopped being built on nodes and started to spring up like mushrooms. After the Vatican Bank scandal and in the beginning of the Awakening, the old churches started turning back into temples; the process only accelerated after the Seventy Days War and the fall of the Evangelicals of Gilead. The Parapsychic Act and the codifying of psionic abilities meant that only temples and cathedrals on nodes survived, others were inelegantly torn down to make way for urban renewal.

This place had been reverberating with Power and worship for a very long time. And there at the altar rail was a tall, black-clad figure with a shock of golden hair glowing with its own flaming light. A figure slim and beautiful even from the back, and obviously not human.

We hadn't needed a guide into Hell after all, despite all Japh's careful preparations.

Anubis et'her ka. My throat closed. For one frantic moment I wanted to scramble back for the doors, wrench them open and *run*, anywhere was fine as long as I could get *away*; the feel of Lucifer's steely fingers sinking into my throat rose like an old enemy, taunting me. This was the last chance I had to bolt. I almost made it, too, my body straining against horrified inertia.

Japhrimel half-turned, caught my arm, pulled me forward. He ended up walking just behind me and to my left, to protect both my blind side and my back. The mark on my shoulder flared with heat again. I choked back what I wanted to say and instead moved up the central aisle, each booted footfall echoing along stone and harsh wooden edges. Just like doing a slicboard run through Suicide Alley in North New York Jersey; the only thing you can do is hold your breath and go full throttle—and hope it doesn't hurt too bad on the way through.

I stopped at the front pew. Lucifer stood at the rail, his golden hands loose at his sides. My heart thudded.

I thought we were going into Hell to meet him. The frantic idea that I might almost have preferred the trip into Hell just so I could have a few more moments before I had to face down the Devil made a gasping, breathy laugh rise up in my throat. I killed it, set my jaw so tightly I could feel my teeth squealing together. A worm of suspicion bloomed; I didn't want to think that my gentle Fallen, the lover who had nursed me through the double blow of Mirovitch's psychic rape and Jace's death with more patience than anyone had ever shown me, could still be on the Devil's side.

It's not possible, Danny. It's just fear talking. Just stupid, silly fear.

I said nothing. Japhrimel went still as a stone behind me, radiating a fierce hurtful awareness. I had rarely felt this kind of pressure and tension from him. It was the same feeling—him listening to a sound I could not hear, seeing something I could not see—only magnified to the *n*th degree.

Finally—probably after he thought I'd stewed enough—Lucifer turned slowly, as if he had all the time in the world.

He probably did.

He was too beautiful, the kind of androgynous beauty holovid models sometimes have. If I hadn't known he was male, I might have wondered. The mark on his forehead flashed green, an emerald like a Necromance's only obviously not implanted, the skin smoothly turning into a gem. Lucifer's radioactive, silken green eyes met mine, and if I hadn't had practice at meeting Japhrimel's green gaze—and later, his dark eyes so much older than a human's—I might have let out a gasp.

Instead, I stared at the emerald. He might think I was looking him in the eye if I focused on the gem. The emerald grafted in my own cheek burned. I tried to remind myself it wasn't like his; my emerald was a mark of my bond with my personal psychopomp, the god whose protection I carried, the mark of a Necromance.

It didn't work. I still felt nauseated.

Silence stretched between us, humming. Japhrimel was tight as a coiled spring next to me, and I felt a little worm of traitorous relief inside my chest. As long as he was on my side, I might conceivably get out of this alive.

Still, I wished I could talk to him. I wished I could turn and look at him. My curse—I was so fucking *needy*. I wanted constant reassurance. My big flaw when it came to relationships—questioning the loyalty of anyone crazy enough to date me. After all, I was damaged goods. Had *always* been damaged goods.

You're being ridiculous, Danny. Keep your wits about you. This is Lucifer you're dealing with. You show any weakness, and he'll eat you alive.

I concentrated on staying quiet.

Lucifer said nothing. *I'll be damned if I give the Devil the first word.* I tightened my left hand around the reinforced scabbard.

Power blurred, singing in the air, a physical weight against heart and throat and eye. The demon part of me wanted to drop to my knees; the human part of me screamed silently, resisting with every single fiber of stubbornness I could manage to dredge up from my stubborn, painful life.

I suppose I should have been grateful I'd had practice in enduring the unendurable.

It was close. *Very* close. I had no time to worry how Japhrimel was staying upright, I was too busy keeping my own knees locked, mentally digging my teeth in, *resisting*. My rings spat golden sparks, defiant.

Finally, the Prince of Hell spoke.

"First point to you, Dante Valentine." The voice of the Devil, stroking, easing along every exposed inch of skin, a flame so cold it burned. "I have left Hell, I have come alone, and now you force me to greet you. You must be certain of yourself."

Irritation rasped under my breastbone, lifesaving irritation. It broke the spell of his eyes and bolstered my knees. "Goddammit," I rasped, my voice as hoarse as if he'd just tried to strangle me again. "I don't play your little games. I didn't even know you wanted me until today." I met his eyes, then, something inside my chest cracking as their deep glow burned against my face. "Just get to the point, *Prince*. Use small words, and can the goddamn sarcasm. What do you *want*?"

Lucifer regarded me for a hair-raising moment, during which I had time to curse my big fat mouth.

Then he tipped his head back and laughed, a sound of genuine goodwill raising my hackles. My right hand closed around my sword-hilt, Japhrimel's hand came down on mine, jamming the sword back into the sheath, stinging me. His hand vanished as Lucifer looked back down, and all of a sudden I was glad, deeply glad, that I hadn't drawn steel. The thought of trying to cut him, this being so much older and more powerful than anything short of a god . . . no. *No.*

"I think I have missed your unique charm, Dante." He sounded almost as if he meant it. "I want your service, Necromance, and I am prepared to pay any price necessary."

Go fuck yourself. I don't work for the Devil. I learned my lesson last time. My mouth was dry as a barrel of reactive. "What do you want me to do?"

"You are most honored among humans, Necromance," Lucifer said slowly, his mouth stretching in a shark's grin. "I need another Right Hand."

CHAPTER 9

I blinked. I couldn't help myself—I glanced down at the end of his right arm and counted his fingers. Five. Just like a human. Or four fingers and one thumb if you wanted to get really technical.

"You seem to still have yours," I cracked, and the smile fell from Lucifer's face so fast I was surprised it didn't shatter on the stone floor. The cathedral rang with soft sound—whispers, mutters, laughter. Nasty laughter, the type of laughter you hear in nightmares.

"Do *not* taunt me, Valentine." The emerald in his forehead sparkled, a gleam that reminded me of Japhrimel's eyes back when I had first met him. The meaning caught up with me—Japhrimel had been Lucifer's Right Hand. His eldest son, trusted lieutenant—and assassin.

Right Hand? What the hell? I can't live in Hell. A fine edge of panic began curling up behind my thoughts.

Then someone laughed.

I almost didn't recognize Japhrimel's voice. It boomed and caromed through the entire cathedral. Dust pattered down from the roof, I heard stone groaning. One of the pews rocked back slightly, wood squealing under the lash of sound. The mark on my shoulder blazed with fierce hurtful pleasure, as if his hand was digging into my flesh, keeping me still as his voice tore the air.

I froze, keeping Lucifer in my sights. The Devil looked past me to his former assassin, and the snarl that crossed his features was enough to almost send me to my knees. "You find this funny, *A'nankhimel?*" His voice scraped through the air, cutting across Japhrimel's laughter.

I found my own voice again. "Leave him alone," I snapped. "You're bargaining with me."

He could turn on a red credit's thin edge. The snarl was gone, his eyes so bright they all but cast shadows on the floor. "So we're bargaining now?" His sculpted lips curled up in a half-smile. He was so goddamn beautiful it hurt to look at him, actually *hurt* the eyes, like looking into a coremelt, stinging and blinking against the glow humans were never meant to see.

I tore my eyes away from him. Looked over at Japhrimel, who had stopped laughing. Funny, but he didn't look amused. Instead, his eyebrows were drawn together, examining Lucifer as if a new kind of bug had scuttled out from underneath something and Japh wanted to give it his entire attention.

Then Japhrimel's eyes slowly, so slowly, flowed over to meet mine. The mark on my shoulder eased, sending a wave of heat down my body.

Relief and fresh faith burst inside my chest. Japh was with me. What could Lucifer do, with his assassin on my side?

Oh, be careful, Danny. He could still do plenty. You know he can.

Japhrimel's gaze held mine.

I quirked my eyebrows slightly, a silent question.

He gave an evocative shrug, little more than a fraction of a millimeter's lifting of one shoulder. He couldn't tell me or he didn't care, either way. Then he tipped his head back slightly, raising his chin. *I am with you, Dante.* His mental tone was gentle, laid in my brain like one of my own thoughts.

Had he always been able to do that? Given the depth of the bond between us, it wasn't unlikely. The mark on my shoulder pulsed insistently, a taut line stretched between us. At the moment, it was a good thing, a way to confer with him without Lucifer hearing.

Or at least, I hoped Lucifer couldn't hear him.

I swallowed and looked back at Lucifer, who watched this exchange with a great deal of interest.

"What do you need an assassin for, Prince?" My tone came out flat, not as powerful as his or Japhrimel's, but still something to reckon with. The Hegemony sun-disk ran with a sudden random reflection of light.

He doesn't own me. Anubis owns me; the Devil can't do anything but kill me. The thought wasn't as comforting as it could have been. Death never is, even if you're a Necromance.

"Four demons have escaped Hell. The others I can deal with, but these are of the Greater Flight, and I wish their capture or execution to be both swift and...public. It will go a long way toward easing the...unrest...in my domain. Who better to hunt my subjects than my former Right Hand and the woman who killed Vardimal and returned my daughter to me?"

That did it. My temper snapped. For him to claim my murdered lover's daughter, to act like he hadn't half-strangled me and left me to deal with the fallout after playing his little game and getting control of the Egg and Hell back in one neat stroke—fury smashed through the fear, a familiar anger at injustice, held back and choked for most of my life.

"*Your* daughter?" My voice rose, the sun-disk rocking back on its stand, squealing. "*Your daughter?*"

"Mine," Lucifer replied silkily. "The human matrix means nothing, Dante. Only the Androgyne matters."

She isn't yours. She's Doreen's, and you stole her. "You arrogant son of a bitch," I snarled. "No way. Go fuck yourself, Lucifer, if it will reach." I spun on my heel, static gathering on the air, and would have stalked away with my back exposed if Japhrimel had not caught my arm.

He said something to Lucifer in their demon tongue, sliding consonants and harsh, hurtful vowels. I stared up at Japhrimel's face, his hand burning on my arm—he didn't squeeze, but his grasp was firm enough that I knew he meant business. He wouldn't have broken my arm, but he would have kept me there, and an undignified struggle in front of the Devil wasn't something I wanted.

What the hell was he saying? I didn't even know what *hedaira* meant. All I knew of demon language was Japhrimel's name and the hissing sibilance of their word for *no*. And, oddly enough, the word for *sunlight*.

Lucifer made a reply. Not even his golden voice could make that language sound good.

Japhrimel asked something else, the intonation clearly a question.

Lucifer's reply was brief and pointed enough that I looked from Japhrimel back to him, craning my neck.

This went on for a few minutes, question and reply; the horrible sound of that tongue crawling along my skin with prickling venomous feet. Finally, Japhrimel said something quietly, and the Prince of Hell's lip curled. He nodded, once, curtly. His eyes were bright and avid, resting on me. I felt the weight of that gaze like a load of coldly poisonous sedation, flooding my veins and making me shiver.

Japhrimel looked down at me, his eyes flaring green again for a moment. "Very well," he said quietly. "A moment to speak to my *hedaira*, Prince."

"Granted." Lucifer eyed both of us, then turned away to look back up at the sun-disk. He wore a very slight, very *nasty* smile that dried up all the spit in my mouth.

Japhrimel dragged me down the aisle a few steps, his coat separating in front, then spread his wings slightly and drew me in. He rested his chin atop my head. *Dante.* It was a calm, quiet sound in the very middle of my head, a thread of meaning. *We have no choice.*

Bullshit. We had a choice. There was always a choice. I closed my eyes, rested my forehead against his bare chest. Fine tremors walloped through me, each successive wave beating at the cocoon of Power Japhrimel held me in. My sword hilt dug into my ribs, I held the blade with creaking knuckles.

Japh's voice continued, inexorable. *Either we bargain with the Prince, or we make an enemy of him as well as of the demons that have escaped his control. At least if we bargain with him we have a chance of continuing our life together.*

I didn't want to "bargain." I wanted Lucifer to leave us alone. I got the distinct impression that if I made *any* bargain with the Prince of Hell, I'd come off as badly as I had last time — crippled, barely alive, and possibly with another long, despairing time of trying to resurrect Japhrimel on my hands. Or the whole thing could end up with *both* of us dead, and no way was I in the market for that.

Then let me negotiate. I have, after all, bargained before.

I swallowed, let out a soft breath against his skin. Felt his sudden attention as his arms tightened, pressing me against his body. His fingers traced up my back through my clothes, a wave of familiar fire curling through me. He was taller, his shoulders broad, and with his wings around me I was completely enclosed. The small shudder of response—the proof that I affected him—comforted me much more than it probably should have.

"Fine," I whispered. "You go ahead, then." We weren't in Hell, the rule about him not talking probably didn't apply. Besides, he was more likely to come out ahead when it came to fencing verbally with the Devil.

He nodded, his chin moving against my hair. "Courage, *hedaira*," he said very softly, mouthing the words. I shivered.

I have plenty of courage. I just don't have any assurance Lucifer isn't going to turn on us both.

Japhrimel led me back to the altar rail and waited until Lucifer faced us, green eyes sliding over us both. I saw a flash of something odd on the head demon's face, just a flicker, his eyes darkening and his mouth turning down.

What the hell was that? Did Lucifer actually look guilty? Or envious?

Actually, I was betting on *enraged*. Or *murderous*.

Danny, your imagination just works too well.

"Five years of service," Japhrimel said. "The full control of Hellesvront. Your word on your Name that you will protect Dante with every means at your disposal, forever."

The Devil's eyes closed slowly, opened again. Some essential tension leaked out of the air. Now it was a bargaining game, cat and mouse, bartering for my life. Well, last time I hadn't been able to bargain; it had been pretty goddamn simple. *Do what I tell you, or be killed.* This was a step up.

Not really.

Lucifer countered. "Twenty years, with a meeting to discuss renewal. Full control of Hellesvront, and my friendship to Dante Valentine as long as her life lasts."

"Seven years, full control, and swearing on your Name to protect her until eternity ends, Prince. *That* is nonnegotiable."

"What else?" The Devil didn't look amused now. As a matter of fact, he looked sour. It didn't mar his beauty, but it fascinated me.

Japhrimel paused for only a moment. He said something in their language again, something very slow and distinct.

What the hell? I looked up at Japhrimel, then over at the Devil. *What the hell is he doing?*

Lucifer's eyes glowed. I set my jaw, trying not to feel as if I was burrowing into Japhrimel's side. *Anubis, et'her ka,* I prayed. *Lord of Death, watch over me.*

"You *dare*?" Lucifer snarled, his face suffusing with rage. If I could have made any sound at all I might have whimpered. I'd never seen the Devil truly angry before—and I didn't want to. "*Abomination.*"

Japhrimel shrugged. "I learned too well from you. You should not have offered me freedom, Prince—even if you never intended to ful-fill that offer."

Oh, Anubis, don't piss him off. I don't want to see the Devil in a really bad mood. Japhrimel's arm was tight and reassuring over my shoulder. He'd been the Devil's assassin. If Lucifer lost his temper would Japh be able to get me out of here alive? I certainly hoped so. The entire temple vibrated with Lucifer's anger, stone groaning and air swirling, freighted with a soundless fiery static. One of the pews cracked down the middle, the sound loud as a gunshot. I didn't jump—but it was close.

Damn close.

"I would not have, if your service had not been exceptional." Lucifer bit off the edges of the words. Then he darted a look at me, and I would have sworn his green eyes lit up with *glee*. The Power cloaking him swirled once, spread out to haze through the cathedral. "Well, Dante. What do you think of your Fallen now?"

I waited for Japhrimel to warn me not to reply, but he did nothing, standing curiously still. I cleared my throat. "I trust him a *hell* of a lot more than I trust *you*." That, at least, was unequivocally true.

That made the Devil's eyes light up. Was he actually looking mis-chievous? Wonders never ceased.

Then again, the Devil in a mood to play with his prey was not something I ever wanted to see, either. I was suddenly fiercely glad I wasn't completely physically human anymore, for the very first time. A human would never have been able to stand the welter of razor-toothed Power in the air or the way Lucifer's eyes suddenly drifted down to touch my throat. My heart gave an unsteady leap.

"Well-matched, the pair of you. Very well, Tierce Japhrimel. Seven years, full control, and my protection sworn on my own inef-fable Name for the miserable Necromance, for eternity. I accept your other terms." His voice was brittle as glass. "Is there aught else?"

I could have left it there. I *should* have, Japhrimel's arm tightened around me. But I couldn't help myself. "Eve," I said.

Lucifer's entire body tensed. "Be very careful," he warned me, in a chill, beautiful, hurtful voice. "You do not know what you say."

I cleared my throat. If the Devil truly needed me, I had a way to erase at least one name from my long list of failures. "Freedom for Doreen's daughter, Lucifer. That's *my* condition, on top of Japhrimel's." My lips skinned back from my teeth. There comes a point past which terror gives you a crazy type of courage; maybe I'd reached it.

His eyes blazed. He took a single step forward, the shadows in the cathedral suddenly pulling close, red eyes glowing in the dimness, the susurrus of flame or wings beating in the vaulted space.

I didn't see Japhrimel move, but he was suddenly a little in front of me, his shoulder pushing me aside and back. That put him mostly between me and the Devil, and my heart thumped sickly against my ribs at the thought of him facing down Lucifer. "Enough, Prince." His voice cut through the thunderstorm of Power. "Have we reached agreement?"

"Seven years. Full control. Protection for *her*. And you, Japhrimel, restored to your place of pride in the Greater Flight. I agree."

My heart slammed into my throat. I couldn't help myself. I looked up at Japhrimel, who was utterly still, pale under his golden skin. *What the fuck?* The full meaning of the words slammed home.

"Done." Japhrimel's jaw tightened after the word. His eyes flared, angular green runic shapes sliding through the darkness.

"Done," Lucifer repeated. His eyes turned to me.

Oh, gods. Gods, no. He's going back to Hell, I thought numbly. *What did he just do? But Eve—*

"I am waiting for your agreement, Necromance." Lucifer's voice turned silky. "I counsel you to take this bargain; it is the best you will receive from me."

"Done," I said, tonelessly, shocked. I had no choice—Japhrimel had already agreed, and if I pushed it, he might not be able to keep Lucifer from ripping me a new spleen or two.

Trust me, Dante. Do not doubt me.

The first rule of dealing with nonhumans: their idea of *truth* isn't the same as ours. Maybe Japh had grown tired of hanging out with a damaged human, maybe I'd pushed him too hard. He'd maneuvered me into agreeing, played me neatly as a synthesizer. Eve's freedom wasn't a part of the bargain.

It hit me again, like a thunder-roll after lightning. Japhrimel was going home to Hell for a while, and I was sold to the Devil for seven years.

Great.

Lucifer's elegant lip lifted in a sneer. "Send her away, Tierce Japhrimel. I will wait."

I didn't struggle, but Japhrimel had to drag me away, my boots scraping the floor. The last I saw of Lucifer, he had turned back to the altar, his golden hand resting on the rail again. His black-clad back rippled, as if some force streamed away from him. "Fools," he hissed, and I wondered if he meant humans in general, or demons, or just me.

CHAPTER 10

Japhrimel closed the cathedral door behind us, hauling me into the smoky dark of a Venizia night as if I weighed nothing. The whine of hovercells settled against my bones again, not only because of the city but because a sleek black hoverlimo was now waiting, a plasteel stepladder flowing down from the side entrance to touch the cathedral's steps.

Oh, look. Mad glee bubbled hot and acid in my throat. *The boys send Dante home in style. Pack the human off until we need to use her again.*

"Go home," Japhrimel said. "Wait for me."

"Wait for what? You're coming back?" I asked numbly. Or maybe I just thought it, a roaring filled my head. My bag bumped my hip, and I was glad I'd suited up. If I'd had to deal with this without my weapons I would have started to scream. "Wait a second— Japhrimel—" My fingers tightened around the sword. If I drew it now, what would he do? What could *I* do?

"There is no time for explanations, Dante. Do as I say."

"You asked to go back to Hell? Is that what happened? Are you coming back?" This time I was sure I'd spoken, but I didn't recognize the small, wounded voice as mine.

He made a short sound of annoyance and dragged me down the steps. Something hard and clawed rose in my throat, I closed my teeth against it. Denied it.

I'm not *going to cry. It doesn't hurt. I am not going to cry. It doesn't hurt.*

Number one rule for anyone who practices magick, *don't ever lie to yourself*. I knew, with miserable clarity, that I was breaking that rule. "You *bastard*. Are you going back to Hell? For how long? What's going on? At least say it out loud if you're not coming back, at least *tell* me, the least you could do is *tell* me—" Instead of sounding angry, I only sounded tired. Curious numbness spread through my chest. Numbness like metal must feel when a blowtorch kisses it.

Japhrimel stopped. He caught my shoulders, and before I could back up he pressed a hard, closed kiss on my mouth. I would have struggled, would have tried to break free, but his hands were like steel claws.

"*Listen* to me." His voice held none of the plasgun-charge of Power he'd used inside. Instead, he sounded carefully restrained, almost human. His eyes were full of green sparks, dancing in their depths like fireflies. "I will come for you. I will *always* come for you. Wait for me at home, do *not* open the door to anyone. I will be with you soon. Now *go*."

What could I say to that? I simply stared at him, my fingers nerveless-tight around my sword.

He shoved me up the steps and into the hover. "Go, and wait for me," he repeated, then leapt back down from the steps. I collapsed on the pleather seat, all the strength running out of my legs. The door closed, I heard the whine-rattle of the hovercells beginning to take on flight frequency.

What just happened in there? If he goes back to Hell and leaves me alone, how long will I last against four Greater Flight demons? What did he really ask Lucifer for? I thought he couldn't go back! The thought rose like bad gas in a reactive-painted shaft. I let out a choked sound that rattled the glasses in the rack over the wet bar.

The driver didn't speak. I wondered for a lunatic moment if it was one of Hell's human agents or just autopilot.

He's going back to Hell. For how long? When will he come back? Soon, he said. What's a demon's idea of soon?

Abandoned. Again. All my life I've been left behind—by parents, lovers, friends. I'd thought this time was different. Would I *ever* learn?

I scooted over as the hover rose, pressed my forehead to the window. I had one glimpse of Japhrimel, his face upturned like a golden dish, standing on the cathedral steps and watching as the hover rose into the night sky. His black coat fell down, melded with the shadow lying over the steps, then he was gone.

Vanished. Back into the cathedral.

Back to Lucifer.

Back to Hell.

I collapsed back against the seat. The trembling got worse, running through my bones like hoverwhine.

"Gods," I breathed, and closed my eyes.

It wasn't numbness burning cold inside my chest.

It was a pain so immense I immediately drove my fingernails of my left hand into my palm, squeezing my hand with every erg of demon-given strength. My rings popped and snapped, a shower of golden sparks filling the air. Panic. I was panicking. *Stop it. Ride the pain, Dante; come back, get a grip on yourself. Get a goddamn grip. You're alive. You're still alive.*

For how long? The smell of my own black blood rose to assault my nose. I opened my eyes, lifted my blood-slick hand, dragged it back over my hair to wipe it clean. The nasty ragged half-moon marks from my claws sealed themselves away, closed seamlessly.

The hover banked, turning to go over land. So I wasn't going to be dumped in the sea.

Good to know.

As soon as I realized the thin keening sound was coming from me, I swallowed it. The hole in my chest got bigger. The mark on my shoulder flared with heat, one last caress burning all the way down my body. I'd lived without Japh for a little under a year last time, when he was ash in a black lacquer urn, waiting for me to figure out how to resurrect him. I *never* wanted to do that again. It hurt too goddamn much.

I moved again on the seat, and paper rustled.

What the hell?

I looked down. There was a brown-paper package on the seat I was sure hadn't been there before.

"Well," I said out loud. "That was interesting." My voice broke.

I will always come for you. Don't open the door.

"Gods." Seven years, was that what I'd agreed to? Seven years of working for the Devil. Not just a hunt like last time. Lucifer was probably sitting in Hell right now laughing his immortal ass off. Seven years of working for the Devil, and if Japhrimel went back to being in Hell where did that leave me? Was I going to turn back into a human, without him around? Would I like it? I hoped the process wasn't too painful.

Goddammit, Dante, wake up. You saw the Devil again and lived through it. You should throw a party. A big one. With lots of booze. Fireworks. And a goddamn military marching band.

Only who would show up? Who would even care?

I reached down with shaking fingers and touched the package. It was tied with twine, wrapped in brown paper, bigger than my clenched fist. I picked it up as if dreaming.

The twine and paper fell away.

It was a wristcuff made out of oddly heavy silver metal. Etched into its surface was a complicated pattern that reminded me of a Shaman's accreditation tattoo, thorns and flowing lines twisting through each other. The inside was smooth and blank except for two daggered marks that looked like fangs. It had the slightly alien geometry of something demon-made.

Great. A party favor? An afterthought? What was this?

I touched the cuff with one finger, feeling smooth silver. I traced one etched line.

Oh, what the hell. Nothing can get any worse. I winced at the thought—thinking that was the surest way for some new and interesting twist of awfulness to show up. Any Magi-trained psion knows better than to tempt Fate, even if only inside one's own head.

I picked it up, slid it around my left wrist, twisting so the open part of the cuff lay upward, the flat demon-carved surface along the underside of my arm. It settled against my skin as if it belonged there, a little higher than my datband. It looked barbaric—I've never been one for jewelry, despite my rings. I like all my accessories to have lethal capability.

He knew I wanted Eve free. He knew it. Why did he back away from pressing for Eve? What did he really say to Lucifer? Why did he ask to go back to Hell? Does that mean he's tired of me? He said he would come back. Even told me to lock the doors at home.

Home. Like it's home without him.

Had he wanted to be free of me? Had all the presents just been a way to tell me so?

Sekhmet sa'es. I was even disgusting myself. If he wanted to break up with me, there were better ways of doing it. He'd given me presents because he wanted to. *You know him, Danny. He'll come back.*

But what then? I hadn't the faintest.

"Gods," I whispered. "Anubis. *Anubis et'her ka. Se ta'uk' fhet sa te vapu kuraph.*" The prayer rose out of me with the ease of long repetition. *Anubis et'her ka. Anubis, Lord of the Dead, Faithful Companion, protect me, for I am Your child. Protect me, Anubis, weigh my heart upon the scale; watch over me, Lord, for I am Your child. Do not let evil distress me, but turn Your fierceness upon my enemies. Cover me with Your gaze, let Your hand be upon me, now and all the days of my life, until You take me into Your embrace.*

I crumpled the paper in my fist and tossed it across the hover, a passionlessly accurate throw. Sparks popped from my rings again.

Japhrimel gone back into Hell, to return as gods-only-knew-what, gods-only-knew-when. And me, sent home to wait for further orders, and working for the Devil again.

To hell with tempting Fate. "It can't get any worse," I said out loud, and curled up, bracing my heels against the edge of the soft cushioned seat. My bag shifted and clinked against my side. I wrapped my arms around my legs, buried my face in my knees, and struggled to stop hyperventilating.

It took a while.

CHAPTER 11

The house was still, dark, and silent. The hoverlimo let me off on the landing pad; clearly it was on autopilot. As soon as I jumped down from the side hatch, my boots thudding on concrete treated to look like flat white marble, the whine of hovercells crested and the sleek black gleaming vehicle rose, circled the house once, and drifted away very slowly, far more slowly than it had carried me home.

I stood, and shut my eyes. A Toscano summer night folded around me, warm and soft, the kind of night I could spend in the library, my eyes glued to the page. Or a night I could spend curled against Japhrimel's side in the comfort of our bed, listening to his quiet voice as he told me stories of demons and history, sometimes true, sometimes only rumors. My own voice would answer his, a lighter counterpoint, and sometimes a soft laugh would break the silence.

No more. Lucifer had stopped all that.

I set my shoulders, walked down the steps between the masses of fragrant rosemary growing on either side. The flagstone path to the front door was there, dark and inviting. *Stay inside, don't answer the door, wait for me.* But for how long?

I was grateful none of the servants were there, especially Emilio. Japhrimel must have quietly and efficiently taken care of sending them away, maybe guessing he wouldn't be back tonight.

Did he want to go home? What the hell does Lucifer need me *for, if Japh's going back to Hell?* I shook the thought away, it was useless. What the Devil wanted, the Devil got, and he wanted both of us for some reason.

I pushed open the front door. The security net recognized my datband and genescan; the shields—Japhrimel's careful demon-laid work and my own trademark Necromance shields, layers of energy rippling over the place we called home—parted to let me through.

The mark on my shoulder was quiescent, not throbbing in time to Japh's heartbeat or burning with his attention to me. I did not reach up to touch it. If he was in Hell, I didn't want to see through his eyes. I just hoped the awful empty feeling in my chest would go away sometime soon.

I made my way through silent halls and death-quiet rooms, my bootheels clicking against marble or sinking into rugs. I tried not to look at any room Japhrimel might have walked through. *Gods, Danny, can't you just calm down? Just wait for him. He'll be back. You know he will.*

Most of me knew he would. A small, critical, half-buried part of me still wasn't so sure. The part of me that trusted no one, believed no one; the hard, cold streak of stubborn doubt I hated myself for. I was always waiting for someone to hurt me, maybe because most of the people I'd loved or trusted—or who had power over me, especially when I was a child—had either died or misused my trust. Betrayed me. Hurt me.

Abandoned me.

I finally reached the double doors. Pushed them open, gently. They whispered across the floor.

The long room, dappled with low light, looked just the same. I paced down the middle of the floor, put my palms together, and bowed slightly to Jace's sword. *Why the hell am I in here? What am I doing?*

The sword rang softly, a slow low song of distress from the death of its owner still reverberating in the steel. I wondered sometimes if the shards of my old katana, rusting in frigid ocean depths with rotting bits of Santino, sang with the same aching agony. Only I hadn't died, just been crippled—and lost Japhrimel as well as my own humanity.

I reached up with my free hand, touching the slim, hard shapes of silver-dipped raccoon baculum. The protections wedded to the necklace hummed and shifted, a gentle touch closing around me. Between the necklace, the cuff, and my rings, I was beginning to feel quite the fashion holoplate.

I have been here, asking the ghost of a human man for forgiveness. And wondering why he has more of your heart than I do.

Did he really think that? Had he really thought I was that petty or disloyal? I *had* loved Jace. Loved him and been unable to touch him, unable to return his own affection for me. He had been one of the last links to the person I was before Rio, before I'd ended up half-demon and tied to Lucifer's assassin.

I'd loved him. But I *needed* Japhrimel, the way I'd never needed Jace.

"I'm doing okay with this," I said out loud to the dim dappled half-light and the twisted, blackened sword's moan of agony. My voice startled me, I almost jumped. My heart settled into a fast high pounding. *Japhrimel. Japh. Where are you now, what are you doing? How long am I going to wait here?*

"As long as it takes." My voice startled me again. I shook my head, the thick braided rope of my hair bumping against my back. My fingers gentled on the scabbard, losing a bit of white-knuckled panic. I took a deep breath, turned on my heel, and stopped dead.

A shadow melded with the gloom at the other end of the room. My heart hammered, leaping wildly. I tasted copper.

Blue eyes glittered. A shock of golden hair—gone. The dust in the air swirled, coalesced into a thorn-twisted Shaman tattoo before a stray breath of air smashed through the delicate pattern. I knew that tat as well as I knew my own, as well as I knew Gabe's.

"Gods," I whispered. A breath of warm night wind blew through the room.

Stop it. You're imagining things. You're in shock. You've just had a nasty experience and you're wishing someone, anyone was here. Quit imagining. That's deadly, for a Necromance to start hallucinating.

But the air was full of the scent of tamales, and blood—and the smell of midnight ice and wet ratfur.

Chills rilled up my spine. My right hand blurred to my swordhilt, and I drew the blade free in one fluid motion. Blue fire began to flow along the metal's edge, dappling the floor with reflections as the sword slanted slightly up in first guard, the position so habitual and natural I barely realized I'd drawn steel.

The smell of tamales and blood and Power was Nuevo Rio, Jace's hometown. But the other smell gagged me, made my hackles rise and a thin gleam of light jet from the emerald set in my cheek. The tattoo shifted under my skin, my cheek burning. My rings boiled with sparks for a moment, gold spangles drifting down to touch the floor and wink out.

Ice and wet ratfur was the scent of a demon I'd indisputably killed, with a huge helping of luck and a lot of berserker rage. I'd torn through his throat, plunged the shards of my blade through his heart, and shredded what muck remained of him into the ocean, that great cleanser. Japhrimel had assured me Vardimal was completely dead.

Of all the times to be haunted by a dead demon, it just has to happen when Japh's not here to help.

Rage rose up inside me, a red sheet of fury crackling along my skin, popping sparks off the edge of my blade. I lifted the scabbard in my left hand, held along my forearm with about three inches protruding from my fist for striking at an enemy's vulnerable point. I lowered myself slightly, almost crouching, my back to the wall behind the ebony table. I slid along the wall, backed into the corner, and waited.

The most nerve-racking part of any attack is the waiting—for both attacker and defender. Once Jado and I had held our positions across the tatami mats of his sparring room for a good half an hour, neither of us moving except to blink. I am never the most patient of fighters, preferring to attack and turn the enemy's incipent force back on itself—but that didn't mean I *had* to attack.

Quite frankly, right now I didn't feel in my best fighting shape. I felt like my heart had been ripped out and stabbed—my eyes blurring with tears and my chest aching with swallowed sobs. I *missed* him, a horrible sinking feeling of missing him boiling up inside my chest.

I heard the whine of hovercells too. Was someone coming to visit me?

Take a number, I'm busy with another enemy. Japh told me to stay inside, am I going to have to fight a guerilla action inside my own house?

Cold fury dilated inside me, blue light sliding over the walls, lighting the long room clearly. I inhaled again, filled my lungs. The smell had disappeared—both the smell of Nuevo Rio and the smell of Santino/Vardimal.

It isn't Santino. I killed Santino. It's something like Santino maybe, or something playing a trick on me.

The outer edges of my shielding thinned. Nothing could get in here, could it? Not through Japhrimel's shields. Not through mine. Right?

Japh told you to come here. He insisted on it. He wouldn't have done that unless it was safe. Right?

Of all the times to have a thought like that, now was the worst.

Settle down, Danny, a soft male voice I never thought I'd hear again said inside my head. *Don't second-guess yourself. You smelled it, and your body knows what's up. Just stay put a minute, just wait.*

It was good advice, even if it came from a dead man. Fine time to think of Jace Monroe now, wasn't it?

I waited, my heartbeats thudding off time. Premonition itched under my skin. I wasn't at all sure the house was a safe place to be right now. After all, *someone* had to know we were living here. Being where your enemy expects you is not good tactics.

Why would he tell me to wait here, then? He was very clear about it.

I saw it as the whine of hovercells returned more loudly; a shadow flitting along the window—*outside*. Too quick to track even for my demon-acute eyes, but I was already moving, even as the shields shivered under an assault that threatened to throw me to my knees with the backlash. I let out a short cry, pumping available Power from the reserves below the house and a generous portion of demon Power into a flare that knocked whatever-it-was off. Had to be physical, no magickal assault would feel quite so thumpingly real.

Japhrimel had told me to stay inside, but if someone crashed a hover into the house I didn't want to stick around to see it.

No route like the short route. I gathered myself and leapt. The crash and tinkle of breaking plasglass filled the air, I landed cat-silent, cat-quick, and streaked along the wall of the house, making for the corner. It was a relief to have something to fight at last.

I rounded the corner and saw it, a low black vaguely humanoid shape moving with blurring speed. I let out a short, sharp curse just as it twisted away from the wall of the house, which was resonating like a struck bell, stone singing with the stress of the Power wedded to it *stretching*. Another magickal attack, and I'd gotten out of the house just in time. The shields sang a low feedback squeal I didn't like at all, the night suddenly alive with half-heard chittering and shrieking. I heard a terrible glassy growl float from the front of the house just as the shields shuddered from that direction, taking another massive impact and going hard and crystalline, locking down.

The thing I was chasing bolted across the field on the west side of the house. I jabbed my left hand forward as I ran, making a complicated nonphysical gesture. The bloodstone ring on my left third finger shot a single bolt of thin red light. I'd sunk four or five trackers into this ring, little runespells meant to latch onto a bounty, an unshakeable magickal bloodhound. I was secondarily talented as a runewitch, able to use the runes of the Nine Canons with more accuracy and ease than most; I could make my own trackers rather than buying them from a Shaman or a Skinlin dirtwitch.

I gathered myself and hurtled forward, following the thin smear of red light, using every iota of demon speed. Heard the whining sound as the tracker slammed home. Then, something *shifted*.

POW!

There was a massive sound like every bell in the world struck at once. I dropped to my knees, all speed gone. Reflex took over, earthed the Power, red crackling along my skin in rippled lines. The Power meridians along my skin burned, subsided as I shook my head, my hair slipping forward over my shoulders. My braid had come loose. I sat there on my knees, blinking, my sword gone dark since I no longer needed it.

The thing, whatever it was, had done something...strange. Just popped out of existence and thrown the tracker back at me.

Nothing human could do that. The trackers were meant to hang on to even a combat-trained human psion. I should have been able to follow that thing to the ends of the earth.

We're not dealing with earthly things here, Danny. Get with the program, will you?

I levered myself to my feet, reflexively. If I'd still been human, the backlash would have knocked me out, possibly even burned me physically along my Power meridians. As it was, I shook the stunning sound out of my head, gained my feet, and took a deep breath, my almost-demon body taking a split second to deal with the burning from the snapped tracker. I cocked my head. "What the bloody blue *fuck*?" I barely even realized I was whispering aloud.

The whine of hovercells crested with an abused squeal of antigrav, and a massive shattering sound slammed into me. I was tied to the shields on the house, so I felt a sharp pain, like a tooth yanked from its socket, as the layers of energy, both mine and Japhrimel's, imploded. It would take unimaginable force to break those shields, even with both Japhrimel and me away. Only one thing could supply that kind of force.

Well, two, actually. A god, which was unlikely—gods just don't attack people like that. They have other ways to make their displeasure known.

Or a demon. If presented with a choice like that I wouldn't even lay odds on it; there wasn't any point.

This just keeps getting better.

I sheathed my sword again, and turned to look back at the house just as fire lanced the sky.

For the second time in as many minutes, my legs spilled out from under me. A white-hot column of flame boiled up from the house.

Holy shit. I laid on my side as the shockwave rolled over me. *That's reactive and plas!* Blood slid from my nose in a painless gush, my body trying to cope with this new demand. I waited for the aftershock, half my face tingling where it was exposed to the scorching air. The smell of cooking grass simmered in my nose, I felt another wave of fruitless rage rise up.

Jace's sword. My altar. My books. Goddammit. Heat boiled over me, then aid hovers began to wail in the distance.

My brain started to work again.

Someone had just seriously tried to kill me.

Lucifer, or one of the demons he said he wanted me to hunt? Which would mean they already know the Devil's hired me—which means I'm not going to survive for long without Japhrimel around.

Four of the Greater Flight of Hell, and I'm Lucifer's new little errand girl. All on my own, without Japhrimel. Who told me to stay in the fucking house and get killed. Goddammit. I spared myself one grim smile and shook my head, rolling onto my stomach and bringing myself up to hands and knees, my sheathed sword braced against the earth in my left hand.

I made it to my feet in two tries. There's a limit to what even my body can handle. If Japhrimel's return to Hell and reclaiming his place as a demon undid my change and made me human again, I was looking at a very short, exceedingly uncomfortable lifespan.

The mark on my left shoulder tingled faintly. I closed my eyes against a wave of dizziness. Then I patted myself down.

Bag, knives, gun, plasgun, sword. Everything there. Including all my fingers. Hallelujah.

I looked at the inferno my home had become, suddenly glad none of the servants had been there. The stone itself was warping and twisting, the structure of the marble weakened by the interaction of reactive and plas fields, the very molecular bonds broken down. This was why you never discharge a plasgun near reactive, why shooting a plasgun at a hover isn't used even as an assassination technique. The interaction of reactive paint and a plasfield creates a chain reaction that propagates at roughly half the speed of light, burning and warping molecular bonds, leaving giant scars on the earth unless contained and decontaminated. Even after that, the effects linger in living things, trees grow brittle and other plants wither and die. It's a hugely messy way to kill someone, but pretty effective if you don't care about being fined for contamination and ecological irresponsibility.

And if you were pretty sure *you* could outrun the shockwave.

"Anubis," I breathed. My statue of the god, the obsidian statue of Sekhmet Japhrimel had given me, Jace's sword—probably gone. Had the vision of a dead Shaman been a warning, one my god knew I would heed? "Thank you, Lord Death," I whispered. "For saving my life."

The first of the aid hovers from Arrieto crested the rise, lights flashing. I looked around for cover. They would dump plurifreeze on the flames to keep them from spreading and damp the reaction field, then stamp out any grass fires. I didn't think any of the attackers would stick around after this, they would think they'd trapped me when the house shields went into lockdown. Gods alone knew what had been loosed inside the house when the shields broke, the reaction fire consuming all evidence and mopping me up if I'd survived.

Wait in the house, don't answer the door. As advice goes, Japh, that was terrible.

I faded into a small stand of olive trees, leaning against one, my hand resting on warm bark. There would be a scar on this hillside until the plant life recovered from stresses in cellular structure caused by the reaction and the heat. More glowing aid hovers crested the hill, some of them already beginning to release a fine silvery mist of plurifreeze. Decontamination from a reaction fire this big would take a while, two days at least. The books Japh had bought me were gone, and gods alone knew if anything else might survive. It wasn't likely.

I blew out through my teeth, my free hand coming up to touch the necklace. If his sword was destroyed, this was all that was left of Jace except his ashes, kept safely in Gabe Spocarelli's family mausoleum as a favor to me.

Anger rose in me, sharp and hot. Useless fury that I had to turn into cold clarity if I expected to get out of this mess alive.

I didn't even know who was trying to kill me yet. The list of suspects was getting longer by the hour.

Stay in the house. Lock the doors.

Yeah. Right.

I sighed, gauged the distance between me and the aid hovers, and disappeared into the night.

CHAPTER 12

The first train I could catch from the station rocketed across the landscape on its cushion of antigrav, part of a rail network so old the banks on either side of the tracks have risen to overshadow the sleek trains in some places. That bounced the antigrav back at itself and made everything feel queer and light, but it was a quick way for me to get out of Toscano and to a major Hegemony city—in this case, the great hub of Franjlyon. Once in a big city, I was confident I could hide—but out in the Historical Preserve I stood out like a black-market augment at a Ludder convention.

In Franjlyon I could catch transport for anywhere and start plugging into the bounty-hunter network. If I could find a few Magi, I might have a fighting chance of staying alive for a little while; I also had a fighting chance of staying out of sight for a few days. If I could find a Magi—circle or solitary—I could persuade to part with a few trade secrets, my chances would get even better. Screw decoding old shadowjournals. I wanted to find out what I was and if I would turn back into a human once Japh was a full demon instead of *A'nankhimel.*

I was getting to the point of not being too choosy about how I extracted that information, either.

I settled myself deeper into my seat, wishing I could find a way to make the carriage a little darker. I wasn't exactly inconspicuous, with the tat on my cheek, the emerald glittering there too, my sword and guns, and the flawless lovely architecture of my face. I had grown a little more used to seeing a holovid model's face in the mirror, but it was still a horrendous jolt if I wasn't ready for it. Lots of normals did double- and triple-takes, as if I was a holovid star gone slumming. Or as if I was a psion. Ha ha.

It wasn't so much the overlay of demon beauty that bothered me. It was that every time I caught sight of my face in the mirror, I had a weird double image — my old human face, tired and familiar but *changed*, turned into loveliness even I had trouble looking at. I hated even catching glimpses of myself in windows, like I was doing now.

I focused out the window, seeing nothing but strips of orandflu lighting and the meaningless smear that was the ghost of my face. Orange stripes blurred together, telling me the hovertrain was gliding along with no trouble at all in the reactive-greased furrow we still called "tracks" even though no train had run on tracks since about twenty years after the discovery of reactive and antigrav.

That's great, Danny. Think about historical trivia instead of how you're going to stay alive past tomorrow. If demons are looking for you, the world gets really small really quick, and I'm not exactly inconspicuous. I even smell *like a demon — good luck hiding.*

Nobody else was in the compartment. I'd been alone since I boarded the train. Not many tourists took the red-eye from Turin Station to Franjlyon.

My eyes dropped to the silver cuff on my left wrist. It sank into my skin, and the gap between the curved ends seemed smaller. I couldn't believe I'd fit even my wrist through there. When I'd been human my wrists had been big, corded with muscle from years of daily sword drill. Now they were thinner, looking frail even though they held a great deal of strength in their flawlessly powerful demon bones and claw structure.

The cuff felt good, though my left hand was frozen around my scabbard. I reached over with my right hand, touched the fluid etched lines. It was beautiful. Japhrimel had never given me an ugly present. Was it from him, or was it something I shouldn't have picked up? One of Lucifer's little jokes?

I wondered if it was a tracking device. But it felt so impossibly right, snugged against my wrist as if made for me. I couldn't quite bring myself to take it off, despite the uneasy idea that perhaps the bracelet was *growing* closed around my wrist.

I looked out the window again. Rested my head against the back of the seat. The black demon blood I'd wiped in my hair smelled like perfumed fruit, absorbing back into black silky strands.

The trouble with traveling like this was that I had too much time to brood.

I sat there mulling over the situation and not coming up with anything fresh for a good two hours. The train bulleted through a mountain tunnel, the peculiar directionless sense of being underground raising my hackles. I needed a quiet stationary room and some time to myself—and some food. I was beginning to feel a little strange, lightheaded, as if I was going into shock. The world was going gray, color leaching out of the orange strips outside the window, the blue pleather seat across from me losing its shine, a sort of fuzz creeping over my vision.

I closed my eyes but that made it worse.

The train rocketed out from under the mountain, and the mark on my shoulder began to tingle.

There was no sound but the whining lull of the train and a faraway murmur of other minds, *human* minds full of the random stink of normal human psyches. I reached up with my right hand, touched the mark through my shirt, rubbed at it. If I touched it with my bare fingers I would see out Japhrimel's eyes. It was very, very tempting— though if I looked out his eyes and into Hell, would I come away from the experience quite sane?

The thought that the scar might burn off my skin if he became a demon again was unpleasant, to say the least. I racked my brain for demon sigils and magickal theory but couldn't come up with anything that applied even vaguely. I didn't have a clue what would happen, and that was uncomfortable. To say the least.

I blindly trusted him the same way I'd blindly trusted Jace. But Jace had been human...and Jace had ended up giving up his life for me. Japhrimel had given up his power as a demon, shackling himself to me, and there was a time when I could have sworn he didn't care.

Maybe going back into Hell without me last night had made him care again. The more I thought about it, the more I wondered.

How quaint. I'm pretty much a dismal failure at relationships with two species now.

No. He'd said he would come back. He had promised. I was just going to have to wait and see.

Wonderful. My favorite kind of magickal riddle: one where you just sit and wait for the unpleasantness to begin.

I wasn't an idiot. I knew I had trust issues. Plenty of bounty hunters do. You don't go into bounty hunting without being a little paranoid, and if you survive you get even more paranoid. My parents had left me before I was ten days old, my social worker had left me for Death's country, my friends—when I made them at all—either betrayed me or died as well. Except for Gabe.

Always excepting Gabe.

And let's not even talk about my lovers. I'm overreacting. Who wouldn't overreact, when Lucifer starts playing with them? Japhrimel will come back, Dante. He promised.

Still, I wondered. I *doubted.*

I rubbed at my shoulder through my shirt, rubbed it and rubbed it. The buzzing, prickling tingle in the mark intensified.

Then it gave one incredible, crunching flare of pain that ate right through the gray blanket of shock. I sat bolt upright, four inches of steel leaping free of the sheath, disappearing as I shoved the sword back home. There was no enemy to kill here—just one flare after another of deep grinding pain in my shoulder.

What if the mark vanishes? What will I do then? I tried to focus on my breathing, deep and serene.

The trouble was, I felt less than serene. My entire body ached for Japhrimel. I knew I wouldn't be able to sleep; in fact, I'd probably go insane from lack of rest. I'd survived almost a year without him before, but the bond between us was too established by now. My research, fragmented as it was, told me one thing for sure, *I* certainly couldn't break it.

But with a demon's power, *he* might be able to.

Will you stop it, Dante? He'll come back for you. It's just when *we have to worry about.*

The pain in my shoulder eased little by little. I tucked my chin, reached up, and pulled my shirt away from my chest. Ropy lines of scarring twisted in the golden-skinned hollow of my shoulder, looking decorative rather than scarlike. They also flushed a deep, angry red.

An amazing, searing bolt of Power hit the mark, spreading down my skin like oil. My hips jerked forward as my head snapped aside and I gasped, suddenly glad there was nobody in the compartment with me. The hovertrain rocked slightly on its cushion, I gulped down stale recycled air, panting. It felt like I'd just slammed a hypo of caffeine-laden aphrodisiac, pleasure spilling and swirling through my veins, tautening my body like a harpstring.

The cuff on my wrist reacted, etched lines suddenly swirling with green light. I tipped my left hand over and stared at the design, fascinated, as the lines moved on the metal, shaping themselves into patterns I could almost recognize. They looked like demon glyphs, mutating and twisting, as beautiful as they were alien—and as beautiful as their language was hurtful.

What's it doing? I probed at it delicately with my nonphysical senses, felt nothing. Was it just a decoration, a pretty but useless thing? If it kept glowing I was going to have problems—it would be hard to hide.

I tipped into a half-trance, looking at the colored lines sway and slide over the metal's surface, still probing at it. For all magickal intents and purposes, it was invisible. That in itself was strange, as most things have a psychic "echo" of one kind or another.

The Power continued pulsing down my skin, each successive wave deeper and warmer. It was nice, I supposed—but *why*? Was Japhrimel reaching for his mark on my skin, trying to locate me? Did that mean he was out of Hell and feeling frisky?

I will always come for you.

Was he looking for me? I hoped like hell he was. But staying one step ahead of demon assassins might also make it hard for him to find me.

This drowsy, dreamy thought occurred to me as I stared at the cuff's little lightshow. I blinked.

When I looked again, the lines were frozen into a single symbol.

Hegethusz, one of the Nine Canons. Shaped like a backward-leaning angular H with a slash through it, a simple stark rune of a simple stark nature.

The Rune of Danger.

There was only one door. I rocked up to my feet, reached it in two steps and slid it aside, pressing the lock-lever. Any transport employee would have the keycode for the outside lock, so it would be easy to pick out of an unprotected brain. Just one more reason why people feared psions. If you didn't mind getting a wash of uncoordinated jumbled filth with any usable information, a psion could probably do all the things normals were so afraid of. The thought of the effort it would take to clean out my mind after pickpocketing something from a normal's head made my skin crawl.

The corridor between the windows on the other side of the train and the blank plasteel walls broken by doors into individual compartments was barely wide enough for an anorexic techna-groupie to get through. I turned my back to the windows—I was fairly sure any incoming fire wouldn't be coming from there, we were going too fast—and stuffed my sword in the loop on my rig. The corridor was too narrow for swordplay, and if I had to do knifework I didn't want to do it here.

So it was guns. I slid the two projectile guns out of their holsters. A plasbolt might interact with any reactive paint on the outside of the hovertrain, and I had no desire to see another reaction fire up close. I was glad the train was all but empty. Collateral damage was *not* something I wanted happening if I could help it. Silly of me to worry—demons were sneaky, powerful, and not overly concerned with loss of human life. I was already playing under a handicap and worrying about casualties would make it worse.

I edged down the train toward the back, one gun on either side, my arms stretched out. If any normals came out I was going to look silly—and if anything else showed up I would shoot it. *Please don't let anyone out. Let them all stay in their compartments. If I have to shoot please don't let me hit anyone innocent, Anubis witness my plea, please don't let me hit anyone.*

The mark on my shoulder pulsed again, another soft wave of Power sliding down my skin, burrowing in toward my bones. Why? What was happening?

I couldn't afford to holster a gun and reach up to touch the mark. If he could track me through the scar, could another demon do so too? I shone through the ambient landscape of Power like a demon myself, but without the heavy-duty shielding Japhrimel carried. Stuck between two worlds, too strong for human psions and too weak to combat demons, I was just powerful enough to be visible and not powerful enough to protect myself if a serious demon came gunning for me. And this was the second attack in twelve hours.

I was really racking up the score in this gravball game.

My feet shuffling soundlessly, I covered both ends of the train, looking back and forth, wishing I had eyestalks like the Chery Family bodyguards were all augmented with. It would have been good to be able to see both ways at once.

I felt it, then. A quick fluttering brush against my shields, retreating almost as soon as it occurred. Training took over, clamped down on my hindbrain as adrenaline flooded my system. Too much adrenal juice and I'd be a jittery mess. Other trained mental reflexes locked down the direction, complex metaphysical calculations and intuition all slicing in an arc that pinpointed the location.

That smell again—ice-cold moonlight, wet ratfur—assaulted my nostrils. The thing that had thrown my tracker and disappeared or something that smelled like it—was now on the train. Probably just appearing out of thin air, the way demons had a nasty habit of doing that according to the demonology texts. Especially the Lesser and Low Flights. The Greater Flight liked more dramatic entrances.

At least some of my grueling, piecemeal demonology research was now useful. I knew that some demons could send the Lesser or Low Flight of Hell to do their bidding in the human world. If the demon had enough Power...or if the demon was given permission by Lucifer.

Lucifer's permission was invoked before every conjuration a Magi solitary or circle attempted to bring a demon through, and I got the idea from Japhrimel that there was a bureaucracy in place to handle the requests. Since Magi were traditionally so jealous of the methods they found to weaken the walls between the world and Hell to get their messages through, it sometimes it took years for the proper method to be found to reach a demon one could control or make a familiar. No Magi ever attempted to contact more than the very lowest echelons of the Lesser Flight. If a Greater Flight demon showed up in a Magi's conjuring circle, the practitioner was either especially lucky or incredibly painfully doomed.

Most likely the latter.

Demons weren't under that type of restriction. It was thought fairly easy for a Greater Flight demon to bring a Lesser Flight demon through, and even easier for them to bring one of the Low Flight.

Which all added up to bad news for Danny Valentine.

I turned my back to the rear of the hovertrain. Backed up one slow step at a time, the guns held steady, pointed down the front of the corridor, Power beginning to glow in my hands. The bullets alone might not do much against whatever this thing was, but hot lead wedded to fiery Power made a lethal combination for most things. It wasn't as elegant as blessed steel, and it was so messy and draining not many psions could do it—but I was no longer human, for however much longer I wore Japhrimel's mark. As long as I had the capability, I might as well use it.

I had almost reached the end of the train when it came for me.

Hovertrains are long flexible snakes, each plasteel carriage connected to the next by plasreactive cloth. This means that pleats of the material separate the compartments, rattling and flexing as the hovertrain twists, bounces, and curves its way through a shallow, reactive-laden groove that provides the necessary relief from friction and gravity. This *also* meant I was staring down a long corridor lit only with orandflu light and fluorescent tubes in thickly grilled floor divots, watching the tunnel stretch and twist like the digestive tract of some huge creature, when a small, pulsing movement alerted me.

It melted out of the shadows, crawling forward on hands and feet—and when I say *hands and feet,* I mean that its palms rested flat against the floor, fingers spread, claws extended. Its feet were flat on the floor too, which made its femurs rotate oddly in their sockets. Human ballai dancers would have sold their souls to have that kind of turnout.

It was vaguely human-shaped, white-skinned like the underbelly of a blind fish, with black diamond teardrops painted over its eyes making them into oubliettes. Its ears came up to high sharp points on either side of its oily bald head, and my skin went cold.

The face was different, thank the gods. It wasn't Santino's face.

This was a ruined chubby dollface twisted up like a demented child's, with soft cheeks and pudgy lips. It wore the remains of a red robe, tied at the waist with a bit of what looked like hemp cord; but the robe was kilted up by its posture and I saw its genitals flapping loose.

Well, now we know where the expression "three-balled imp" comes from. The lunatic desire to laugh rose inside my chest as it always did. Why did I *always* feel the urge to laugh at times like this?

If I hadn't been studying what I could of Magi-coded demonology all these years, the resemblance to Santino might have made me start to scream. Instead, I held my ground, pointing the guns at it, thanking the gods again that the compartments around me were empty. I didn't want anyone caught in this crossfire.

It was a demon, a scavenger. One of the Low Flight, I was betting, since it looked like something I could possibly kill if I had a lot of luck. It stood to reason that if some of the larger demons had escaped, one or more of them might have brought a few friends.

No other demon was on the train, though. I would have bet my life on it—I was *going* to bet my life on it.

It was a demon, and I was only a *hedaira*—but I was *hedaira* to the Devil's assassin himself, at least until the mark faded—*if* it faded. I hoped that was enough to buy me my miserable life. I maybe overmatched the imp in Power, but it might have more speed—especially since it was born in a demon's body, and I still didn't have complete control over my inhuman-fast reflexes. The close quarters favored it, it was smaller. I would have preferred edged metal when dealing with this thing, but beggars can't be choosers.

All this flitted through my mind in less time than it takes an unregistered hooker to vanish from a Patrol. Then it coiled on itself, its terrible child's face twisting and slavering, and threw itself down the hall at me.

I squeezed both triggers, the recoil jolting all the way up to my shoulders; Power tore out from me too, matching the physical velocity of the bullets. I had no time to care about stray fire catching anyone else now that the fun had started. Again, again, again, tracking the thing, it was unholy quick, throwing myself backward, *got to get enough speed got to get enough speed*—

The *kia* burst from me as my back hit the rear of the hovertrain. Metal squealed. Physics, insulted, took her due revenge, and I tumbled out of the speeding hovertrain with the imp's left-hand claws sinking into my chest.

CHAPTER 13

Falling. Fire in my chest. Right-hand gun slammed back in holster, hand blurring.

I meant to reach for my sword, demon-quick reflexes just might save me yet—but the thing snarled and twisted on itself, bleeding momentum, and we crashed into the side of the hovertrain trough, all the breath driven out of my lungs. The tall banks on either side of the train-trough were hard clay dirt instead of stone, thank the gods, I coughed up blood as I slid downward. Cool night air touched my face, steam rising from my skin. I spat, clearing my throat, reflex forcing me clumsily up to my feet, almost overbalancing, hilt of my sword socking into my palm, blade singing free of the sheath as the imp snarled and chattered.

I almost understood the words.

It was definitely one of the Low Flight, incapable of anything other than demon speech. If it was trapped inside a Magi's conjuring circle I might have been able to force it to my will, but it was loose in the world, obviously told to come and make life difficult for me. Had I been a Magi I probably would have known something to do to trap it so I could question it, but I was a Necromance. Demons weren't my trade, for all that I'd been screwing one for a long time now and trying to decode documents about others.

It smacked down inside the hover trough and howled, leaping up as if stung. Blood trickled down my chest, hot and black and thick, too much blood. Why wasn't it healing the wounds?

The imp clung to the clay wall and yowled at me again, a sound like rusty nails driven through screeching nerves. I held my sword in second guard, scabbard reversed in my left hand—had I holstered my left-hand gun? I must have. Either that or dropped it, didn't matter. *I'm standing in a hovertrain trough with an imp yowling at me*, I thought, not without a certain macabre humor. *My life certainly gets interesting sometimes.*

I took a deep breath flavored with night air and the dry chemical reek of reactive, pain flaring through me as the thing's clawswipes burned deeper, whittling like hot blades. *Did it have poisoned claws? That would just cap the whole goddamn night, wouldn't it.* "Come on," I whispered, my sword dipping slightly as it shifted position. Here on open ground with my sword, I felt a little more sanguine. A little? No, a lot. There's just something about a bright length of steel that makes a girl feel capable of kicking ass. "Come get me, if you want me."

It howled at me, its baby's face distorted and reddened. But it didn't leap.

Great, I can stay here until another hovertrain comes along and pastes me, or I can try to climb up a fifteen-foot clay wall while trying to fend off this thing. What a marvelous choice.

Well, no time like the present. "*Come on!*" I screamed, stamping my foot. "*Come and get me!*"

It leapt, a marvel of uncoordinated fluidity, and muscle memory took over. I heard Jado's voice, as I often did in a fight—*Move! No think, move!*

The sword, given to me by my *sensei* to replace the blade I'd killed a demon with, carved the thing's head from its shoulders. Half-turn, the hilt of the blade floating up to protect me, the tip whipping faster than the eye could follow, a solid arc twisting like a Möbius strip. The imp's stomach cavity opened, noisome fluid gushing out. Another strike, lightning-quick as the last, and the thing's right arm fell too.

Panting. A few passes of true combat take more energy than any amount of sparring. I shuffled, ready to strike again if the shattered, sliced body should twitch. My feet slipped in the thick bouncy greasiness of reactive paint, a layer of rubbery stuff at least six inches deep giving resiliently under me.

The thing collapsed, twitching. Smoke rose up from its corpse. I watched as its skin and tissues interacted with the reactive, not looking away. Partly because if I looked away, I wasn't sure I would see it if it twitched again—and partly because of Jado. *Watch the death of your enemy if you can, for you have caused it. When you have killed, watch the consequences of your actions.*

It was a good thing I'd killed it, too. I didn't think I could take another pass or two of combat. I was savagely tired, the mark on my shoulder pulsing, another soft, warm wave of Power sliding down from it. That was beginning to get downright distracting. Was he looking for me?

I will always come for you.

How long did it take to turn an *A'nankhimel* back into a demon, back in Hell? What would happen to me if he found me, assuming he was even back in my world again? Could the genetic reshaping he'd done to me be undone? Last time it had taken a mixture of genetic shaping and tantric magick, a remaking from the center of my bones outward. I still wasn't sure of the extent of what it had done to my psyche, but as long as I was still a Necromance it didn't matter.

Maybe. But still, I wondered just how human I was anymore.

I waited until the imp was just a bubbling streak on the reactive before the point of my sword dropped slightly. I hadn't known reactive would do that. I wondered what it would do for other demons. It was cheap and easy to obtain, and maybe I could think of something to do with it that would make my life easier.

Like maybe plasgunning Hell? The thought made me chuckle grimly, pain from the clawmarks in my chest suddenly slamming back into my awareness as the one-pointed concentration of combat eased. The laugh turned into a half-gasp. I sheathed my sword, blew out a long, soft breath between my teeth. Hopefully the hovertrain would make it to the next stop; hopefully nobody would do anything stupid like fall out the hole in the back; hopefully nobody would even notice a huge gaping hole in the back of the train.

Yeah, right. And Ludders will suddenly start riding slicboards.

The sides of the trough began to vibrate, another train was on the way. I took a few running steps and leapt, my claws digging into clay. My chest tore open, I screamed, bit back the scream halfway. Forced myself up the bank, boots scrabbling, claws frantically grabbing at the hard-packed material. Something else ripped free in my chest and I whimpered. Why weren't the wounds healing?

Another hot flush of Power from the mark on my shoulder gave me strength to haul myself up over the edge of the wall. I collapsed and lay panting along the top, closing my eyes and blessing the gods. "Thank you," I whispered. "Thank you. Thank you."

The rumbling whistle of a hovertrain—antigrav and screaming air pushed too fast—began to mount. Another train coming; would it have another imp on it? I rolled away from the hovertrain track and half-fell down a gently sloping embankment, landing with a splash in something cold and wet.

Oh, great. I lay and listened to the rumblewhine.

My arms and legs were weighted with lead. The mark pulsed again, this time all the way down my left arm and out my fingertips. I coughed, turned my head to the side, and vomited an incredible mass of ice-hot writhing poison; it jetted out of my nose and mouth and I almost choked on a lunatic giggle thinking that it might blow out my ears too. It seemed to take forever, but when it was done, I immediately felt much better. Scrabbled myself over onto my other side, hooked my claws in the solidity under the wet slimy stuff I'd landed in—*please don't let it be slag*, I prayed—and began to struggle away from whatever I'd thrown up. My chest no longer burned.

I reached the top of another shallow slope and the scent of pines closed around me. I rolled, and ended up against something soft— tree branches drooping down to the ground.

They made a lovely little tent. I wriggled my way underneath, getting a confused impression of mountains and trees. It was as far away from the track and possibly being seen as I could get. I wanted to hide further away, but I couldn't manage the energy to move. I curled up into a ball and fell into a deathly doze.

CHAPTER 14

Four days later I made it into Freetown New Prague.

I wouldn't have chosen a Freetown. I was a Hegemony citizen, and even the Putchkin Alliance was safer than a Freetown. I would have been able to plug into the bounty net in a Putchkin or Hegemony town. In a Freetown, I'd have to depend on luck and wits, both severely strained by recent events. I'd come a lot further on the hovertrain than I'd thought, and striking out across open country seemed more dangerous than just following the hovertrain trough and finding a station where I could get a transport or buy a slicboard. I'd found a station all right. The only trouble was, I'd somehow gotten on a nonstop train that ended up in New Prague.

I came into the city tired and grainy-eyed, the mark pulsing softly on my shoulder, and found a room in the red-light district. I don't speak Czechi, but Merican is the trade-lingua in most Freetowns, so after a bit of pidgin-laced negotiation and the exchange of a handful of New Credit notes I found myself in possession of a few square feet among the bordellos and hash dens for a few days.

Strictly speaking, the bordellos and hash dens were my type of places; I've hunted many a bounty down in whorehouses and bars. More importantly, the psychic turmoil of sex, synth hash, and—since it was a Freetown—real hash, Clormen-13 and other drugs, desperation, and violence would keep some of what I was hidden. Not for long—I'd have to live with being hunted for a while—but the longer I could stay alive, the more I could find out about the demons Lucifer wanted tracked down. Since I had nothing left to do and was already being attacked, hunting down four demons was where I was going to start. Better to face death on my feet doing what I could, I couldn't assume Japh would find me in time.

I warded the room well and dropped down on the narrow bed, sinking into another type of deathly doze, sleeping just deeply

enough to let the mind rest a little; not the deep velvet unconsciousness Japhrimel could lull me into.

Stop thinking about him. He'll find me. He said he would.

*Yeah, but when? And what else might he have said to Lucifer
when he was sure you couldn't understand? Answer me that.* I tossed
and turned, fretfully.

Stop it. This doesn't do you any good. Rest.

I lay and tossed, tried not to think about it, failed miserably. The
room was small—a pink-flowered rug on the floor, a retrofitted
plas-powered radiator giving out heat I didn't need, a bed, a dresser I
didn't need either, and a bathroom. It was a far cry from a villa in the
Toscano hills.

I didn't need to use the toilet, but I did fill the bathtub and scrub
the dirt off my skin. Then I soaked in the warm water, and then spent
some Power on cleaning off my clothes. I *had* landed in slag after
killing the imp, and if I was still human my skin might be burning
with slagfever by now as my body struggled to cope with the aftermath of a cocktail of chemical sludge. It took a long time to get my
clothes free of the stink.

Finally, clean enough to pass for human, I scanned the wards
again. Nobody had noticed me, but I was still cautious. I didn't catch
a whisper of anyone even *looking* at the thin, subtle glow of warding
meant to keep away notice and guard my door.

I had one other thing to do. The only thing I had was a knife, and
it took a long time of hacking at my hair before I managed to get most
of it off. The resultant shaggy mass around my face was short enough
that I wouldn't lose out on visibility, and nobody should recognize
me right away unless they knew my tat. Only other psions were likely
to be capable of distinguishing the fine differences between one
psion's accreditation tat and the next, so it would make me a little less
likely to be caught.

Or so I hoped. Then again, I looked like a holovid model and
spread out through the psychic ether with the unmistakable flame of
demon. But the people who knew my face might just know my *human*
face, and a demon would probably simply be able to smell me. In any
case, I'd have to risk it; it was the best I could do. I toyed with the
idea of trying a glamour to change my appearance, or even buying
some skinspray to alter my complexion; but a glamour would just
attract the notice of more psions and demons. Besides, I didn't know

how my dermis would react to skinspray. The last thing I needed was to break out in hives.

Though that might have been a good disguise strategy, too.

I slipped out through the third-story window and down the rickety iron fire escape, leaving the door locked — I had another day paid for — and I didn't leave anything behind.

The alley below was filthy, but I was relatively comfortable in my own bubble of demon scent. I found a mound of garbage and threw down the heavy mass of curling black hair, then used a very small bit of Power to spark the strands. They smoked and smelled awful, but they burned. I finally stamped the fire out and kicked garbage over it to hide the stench and the crisped ash. I tried not to feel victorious, but I didn't try very hard. I'd survived for five days — not bad when you're matched against demons.

I stepped out into the wilds of Freetown New Prague on a chilly afternoon just as the sky was beginning to cloud over. I decided to look around the bars a bit and see if I could get lucky. After all, everyone went to the bars to hook up, and I might be able to find a mercenary or bounty hunter I knew, either personally or by reputation. It was more than likely that someone I had met once or twice would be hanging around — New Prague was that kind of town. Once I found someone I knew, things would get a whole lot easier. I could hire someone to help me hide, or maybe find a Magi I could "persuade" to give me a crash course in what to do when demons were looking to kill you.

Six bars and one short, vicious fight in an alley later, I stepped into a dingy *pivnice,* a watering hole tucked under a bridge. I brushed at my sleeve — one of the group of normals who'd thought I'd be easy prey had bled on me. I hadn't killed any of them, but I'd been tempted. Human flotsam tends to collect in Freetowns. Sometimes their greed overpowers their good sense and they decide to find out if a psion carrying steel is combat-trained.

I can never understand why any accredited psion — someone legally allowed to carry anything short of an assault rifle on the streets — would *not* undergo combat training and stay in shape. Even non-accredited psions are allowed to carry steel and one projectile weapon, though non-accrediteds usually didn't go in for bounty hunting or anything else that would make a weapon necessary. Still… it doesn't make sense to me *not* to both carry steel *and* know how to use it. Life is just too dangerous, especially for a psion. Normals hate and fear us enough that the less law-abiding are often tempted to think of us as targets.

The silence that fell in the *pivnice* when I entered was enough to make me think I'd done the wrong thing. It was a low, smoky room, three steps down from the sidewalk outside, a first floor that might have been at street level a hundred years ago but was now halfway to being a basement.

I scanned the place once. Normals, no shielding on the walls, and an atmosphere suddenly charged with fear and loathing. A deadhead bar. I would have backed out, but a familiar pair of almost-yellow eyes met mine.

Well, isn't this par for the course. Shock and unfamiliar fear slammed into my stomach. A queasy sense of unease boiled under my breastbone. Of all the people I expected to see here, *he* was the last.

But I'd been looking for someone I knew, and this was better than I'd hoped for. *If* I could convince him not to try to kill me.

I paced away from the door, through the haze of synth-hash smoke and the effluvia of unwashed human. This was a rough place — for once I didn't look out of the ordinary with my weapons. Freetowns don't have the type of legislation covering who could carry what the Hegemony or Putchkin have; it's largely up to the ruling cartel of each town to make the rules and enforce them. So I saw projectile guns and shortswords, a few machetes, assorted other odds and ends. No plasguns.

That was a mark in my favor. I had a bounty hunter's license, and here in the Freetown I could carry whatever I wanted if I kept my nose clean and didn't interfere with Mob Family wars or cartel turf disputes.

Lucas Villalobos sat in a heavily shadowed back booth, a bottle on the table in front of him. I picked my way between tables, giving the bartender in his stained apron one glance when he opened his mouth. My tat shifted on my cheek, burning, my emerald spat a single green spark. I saw a few normals around me flinch.

Don't say anything. I really don't want to kill anyone today.

The bartender, a stolid heavy Freetowner with a long, drooping black moustache, closed his mouth and wiped his hands on his apron. I felt no gratitude or relief.

Lucas had his back to the wall. There was nothing I could do — I slid into the other side of the booth, my back prickling at the thought of the door behind me. It was an implicit gesture of trust. Lucas wouldn't get many clients if he let them get shot in the bars he frequented. He was known for taking difficult, complex jobs most generally involving assassination; if you had enough cash to hire him, he would kill whoever you asked. He only had one rule—*no kids.* He wouldn't kill anyone under eighteen.

At least, not unless they got in the way during a job. I'd heard unavoidable casualties didn't bother him too much.

His eyes met mine. A river of scarring ran down the left side of his narrow face. I shivered. Word was—now, this is only pure rumor, I don't know for sure—that he'd once been a Necromance, and committed some act so awful Death had denied him.

I couldn't imagine. To be a Necromance, to be protected by Death, and to have that protection snatched away; to be able to see other psions but unable to touch, unable to perform in that space where a Necromance is most fiercely alive...that would be torture. I could have pitied him, if he wasn't so dangerous.

He examined me, blinking slowly like a lizard. His almost-yellow eyes brightened a little, and his lipless mouth curled up slightly. "Well," he said, lifting one finger and tapping his ruined cheek. "You come up in the world, *chica.*" He used the same whispery tone most professional Necromances adopt after a while. Or maybe it could have just been something wrong with his throat. Sometimes a whisper's more effective than a shout for scaring the blue lights out of people.

I felt a prickle between my shoulderblades. Did *not* look back over my shoulder, did not dare even shift my weight. "I wasn't sure you'd recognize me."

"I'd know that tat anywhere. You still move the same, too." His hair lay lank against his skull. He smelled, as usual, of a dry stasis-cabinet, and I realized it wasn't a *human* smell. Whatever he'd once been, he wasn't strictly human now. "You owe me."

I'd bargained with him in Nuevo Rio, while hunting Santino. "You turned down payment that time," I reminded him. Shivered at the thought of paying him what he usually asked of a psion. There was a reason most of his clients were corporations and Mob Families. I heard he even did secret work for the Hegemony sometimes. "You thought I was dead."

His face didn't alter in the least, his expression was blank uninterested boredom. "Ain't you? I don't see much of what you once was in your face, Valentine."

A hot plasburst of relief exploded in my stomach. So he *did* know who I was, he wasn't just bluffing. Or if he was bluffing, he'd bluffed right. "Every day is a death," I quoted, tapped my fingers on the table. "I've got a question and an offer for you, Lucas."

He looked at me for a long time. There was a time when I would have raised my sword between me and his gaze, a time when the demon Japhrimel had been melded to my shadow while I faced down Lucas and I'd been damn glad of the backup. Now I held his eyes, hoping he wouldn't see how desperate I was. I kept my thumb on my katana's guard and my right hand near the hilt, just in case. I might be almost-demon, but Lucas was truly dangerous. They don't call him the Deathless for nothing.

He finally scooped up the bottle, lifted it to his lips, took a swig. Set it down with a precise little click. "What you want, *chica*?"

Relief, sharp and acrid. I didn't let it show. He wasn't averse to bargaining, or being hired. Maybe I could pull this off. "Are you afraid of demons?"

That won a small whistling wheeze from him, Villalobos's version of a laugh. I watched his face crinkle, scarred flesh pleating. "They die just like everythin' else," he finally whispered.

I'm not even going to ask you how you know that. "All right. How would you like to work for the Devil, Lucas Villalobos? The Prince of Hell?"

He measured me for a long moment. "You're fucking serious?"

I held his eyes for longer than I would have thought possible. "I'm fucking serious. Pay's negotiable; the boss is a bitch, but you get to kill things the like of which you've never seen before." *At least I hope you've never seen them before. Or maybe I hope you have, and you know what to do to keep me alive.*

He thought about it. I hoped he was tempted, too.

Dante Valentine, alive despite demons for maybe a little while longer, tempting a man who couldn't die. I thought temptation was a demon trick.

Maybe I'd learned it from the best.

"Pay's negotiable?"

I set my jaw, stared into his eyes, and nodded. "Negotiable, Lucas. What do you want?"

The faint twitch at the corner of his eye warned me. I slapped his hand aside, locking his wrist, the knife buried itself into the table. I found myself sitting across from him, my slim golden fingers locked in a vise around his hand on the knife.

Lucas Villalobos smiled, the river of scarring down one side of his face wrinkling. He hadn't meant to attack me, just see if I was on my toes. His other hand was loosely clasped around the bottle.

I've never seen anyone human move that fast. If I squeezed, I could probably break a bone or two in his hand, and my fingers would sink into plasteel if I extended my claws.

His pupils dilated, turning his almost-yellow eyes a darker shade. "What's the job?" he whispered. His skin was dry and surprisingly fine, but I could feel the tense humming strength in his arm. No, he wasn't human anymore.

If he ever was. It's only rumor when it comes to him, Danny. Be careful.

I took a deep breath. "Keep me alive long enough to kill four Greater Flight demons, and be my eyes and ears." I quelled the urge to look behind me. The mark on my shoulder was soft heat now, wrapping around me, each pulse of Power sliding through my veins and bones. Distracting—but I could use the Power. Was Japhrimel tracking me even now?

Oh, gods, I hope so.

Lucas made that whistling, wheezing sound again, as if he was being slowly strangled. "You're never boring," he said in a low, choked voice. "Let's go out the back door."

Relief made me feel a little weak, but I didn't look away. "What do you want in return, Lucas?"

"The usual." His mouth twitched. "Or I'll think of somethin' else."

Oh, gods. Gods above. My skin seemed to chill. But here was an opportunity, and he was *definitely* the lesser of two evils. I was slightly nauseated at the thought of what I was about to agree to.

Slightly? *More* than slightly. But when it comes to a choice between nausea and dying in some hideous way, I'll take a little bit of indigestion.

"Done." My voice husked through the word, like sodden silk dipped in honey. "One thing." I paused, my hand still clasped around his. The knife creaked in the tabletop, a muttering tide of whispers rising through the *pivnice*. The town would soon be buzzing with the news that Villalobos had found a new client. "What are you doing in New Prague?"

He rasped out a laugh. I wasn't sure I liked being the butt of Lucas Villalobos's humor. "Abracadabra." He pulled a wad of rumpled New Credits from his pocket and tossed a few on the table. "I was in Saint City way; she told me to go to New Prague and you'd find me. Bad news always turns up. I owed her a favor."

The Spider of Saint City wasn't quite a friend, but she wasn't an enemy either. We'd done each other some good turns in the past—and she had warned me about Santino and given me the direction to track him. So she'd used a favor to send Lucas to me, which meant I owed her now.

Oddly enough, I found myself not minding. And unsurprised that Abra knew I'd turn up in New Prague. I wasn't quite sure what she was, but she wasn't human either, and she always seemed to know far more than she should even with her thriving trade in information.

But there might be more to this. "What were you doing visiting Abra?" I loosened my fingers, and he worked the knife free of the tabletop and made it vanish back into his clothing. I watched, but he didn't so much as twitch toward another weapon.

"I drop in every twenty years or so. Nice to have a client that doesn't age." He stood up, and I slid out of the booth as well. Now I could see he was only about three inches taller than me (instead of the five-inch edge he used to have), and bandoliers still crisscrossed his narrow chest. He wore a blousy cotton shirt, yellow with age, and old broken-in jeans. The heels of his boots were worn down. "Let's go, Valentine. From now until the fourth demon's dead, I'm your new best friend."

I let out a sound that wasn't quite a sigh. Lucas was a viper, deadly and unpredictable—but if he said he was my man, it was a bargain. Villalobos didn't back down from his word. He still scared the hell out of me, but if you're facing down a clutch of demons you could do worse than have the Deathless on your side.

CHAPTER 15

When you spend decades doing assassinations, it pays to have a bolthole in a major city or two. I was just glad Villalobos had one here.

I followed his shuffling feet and slumped shoulders through twisting narrow streets in the Old Town, marking each turn in a Magi-trained memory that has seen many cities; it's amazing how much they start to look alike after a while.

We ducked down an alley and into the sewers through the basement of a crumbling building that now housed a colony of slicboard couriers, Neoneopunk music pounding through the air and the sharp smell of Czechi cooking filling my nose, sparking hunger. I already had a good basic grasp of the shadow side of the city after my six-bar odyssey. Now Lucas took me underneath.

Here under the Stare Mesto, water dripped in chilly rivulets down stone, twisting its dark way from the rounded ceilings of the old sewers. Lucas pressed the scanlock on the round door, after making sure we weren't followed by doubling back a few times.

Claustrophobia filled my throat with acid and made my heart pound. I didn't say a word. The door creaked open. I lose a lot of my sense of direction underground, but I was fairly sure I could make it to the surface and give anyone chasing me a good run. *If* I didn't expire of hyperventilation when the walls started to close in on me. I do *not* do well with closed spaces; most psions don't. I have memories that don't help either, memories of the Faraday cage in the sensory-deprivation vault under Rigger Hall, where the darkness was like worms eating the foundations of my mind and the air itself turned to solid glass, choking and slick.

Better claustrophobic than dead. I can live with an awful lot when demons are trying to kill me.

Beyond the door, mellow full-spectrum light played over wood and tile. I stepped through the round hole and let out a soft breath of wonder.

Lucas's lair in New Prague was in a long, vaulted chamber, well insulated from psychic or physical attack. If I knew Lucas, there would be a few little surprises hidden in the room, as well as quick ways to get out that didn't involve the front door. But for a moment, I simply stopped to admire as he closed the door behind us.

I saw two beautifully restrained maplewood tables with the distinctive den Jonten curve to their legs. A restrained red Old Perasiano rug, a Silbery lamp. A near-priceless Mobian print—a naked man sitting on a wooden table, his legs pulled up and head resting on his knees, a tattoo of a scorpion on his bicep straining against the skin— hung on the wall over two low, graceful Havarack chairs.

I remembered a different Mobian print, the one hanging in Polyamour's house in Saint City. A sudden, intense longing to see the noodle shop on Pole Street, or Gabe's house on Trivisidiro, or even Abra's pawnshop, stole the breath from my lungs. I'd lived in Saint City nearly all my life.

My *human* life, that was. Now that I had no chance of getting there, I found myself longing to go back.

Lucas paused behind me.

"It's beautiful," I said. "I like Mobian."

"Valuable," he returned dismissively. "Sit down. You hungry?"

I was *starving*. I was lucky to be able to fuel myself with human food instead of sex or blood, but I hadn't had the chance to eat as much as I'd've liked. "Yeah." *I don't think I've ever seen you eat, Lucas.*

"There's a kitchen through there. Help yourself. I'm going to go bounce through town and see if anyone's looking for you, pick up a few things." I heard him moving behind me, my back prickled. *Lucas Villalobos is behind me. I can't see what he's doing.*

I nodded, turning slowly to face him, telling the ridiculous jolt of panic to go away. He wasn't going to stab me in the back, or at least, I didn't *think* he would. Instead, he was planning on doing what I would have done if our situations were reversed, checking to see if there was any static on the new client. "Is there another exit?" I asked. "In case the front door's compromised?"

He studied me for a long few moments, his almost-yellow eyes empty of all expression. I suppressed a shiver. I was crazy, contracting Lucas to help me; still, a man who couldn't be killed was far from the worst ally when it came to dealing with demons. I had no *choice*.

Dammit, Dante, quit being such a whiner. Until Japh finds you, you're on your own.

He nodded. "Come over here."

Behind a painted Cho-nyo screen he showed me a small depression in the tiles, just big enough for a hand. It triggered a slice of the wall to swing inward, and if you were quick, you could drop down into another tunnel that would take you to the surface. Push the door closed from the other side, and nobody would be the wiser. "But be careful, it's slippery." It hurt to hear him talk. He sounded like he had a lung infection, wheezing out the words.

"Good enough. Thank you, Lucas."

He gave another whistling, snorting laugh. "Don't thank me, Valentine. I'm only taking this because I'm fuckin' curious."

"About what?" I followed him out from behind the screen and almost to the door. Our footsteps echoed, and I was suddenly cold, thinking of when he shut that door and I was alone. Underground. In a windowless room. *Oh, gods.*

"Maybe the Devil can kill me," Lucas Villalobos said, triggering the scanlock on the door. "The gods know I've waited long enough."

CHAPTER 16

The kitchen was where he said it was, and down a short hall was a bathroom and — oh, Anubis — a tiny womblike bedroom. I looked longingly at the plain missionary-style bed, exhaustion weighing me down. It was the first time in my life I'd faced Lucas Villalobos without feeling almost too terrified to talk.

I suppose that possibly losing your ex-demon-soon-to-be-real-demon-again boyfriend and fighting off a three-balled imp behind a hovertrain — not to mention getting your house shattered and blown up — would make anyone a little too worn out to feel the proper fear when facing the man Death had denied. Besides, I was different now. Tougher than a human, capable of taking more damage.

For how much longer, though? If Japhrimel was a citizen of Hell again, was I going back to being a human? I wouldn't have thought a genetic remodel like mine could be undone, but demons have been tinkering with genetics for so long I wouldn't put much past them. Some people even say demons might have been responsible for humanity's evolution, but nobody likes to think about that particular theory. It leaves a bad taste in the mouth.

Japh had changed me in the first place, after all. Reversing the change might not be so big a deal to him. It might even happen just-because.

I sighed, rubbing at my temple with my right hand. This was getting ridiculous.

Ridiculous or not, you need to rest so you can think. So just settle down, sunshine. Relax. Wait for Lucas to come back.

My hunger was sharp, but Lucas's taste ran to heatsealed meals. They taste like cardboard and sit in the stomach like bowling balls, not providing enough in the way of nutrition—especially for my metabolism. So I did the next best thing, dragged two blankets from the bed behind the Cho-nyo screen and propped myself up against the wall, my right hand loose around my swordhilt. I closed my eyes, listening to the quiet. I rarely if ever heard complete silence, being a child of the urban age. Being underground meant the psychic noise of so many people was shut out. The only thing left was Power itself, filtering in through the ground like water, and the peculiar directionless static that meant "you're underground."

Maybe I'll have to go to ground like an animal for the next seven years. The prospect was alternately comforting and horrifying, depending on whether my eyes were open or closed.

I dozed in Lucas Villalobos's lair, feeling a little safer now. Time slid away as I tipped my head against the wall, the back of my neck curiously naked. I hadn't had my hair this short since Rigger Hall. I shivered, thinking of that place again. Afterward, in the Academy, I'd started growing my hair out almost immediately. It was messy to dye to fit in with Necromance professional codes—codes dating back to the Parapsychic Act, to present a united front to the world and make us instantly recognizable—but when Japhrimel had changed me, my hair had turned the same inky black as his.

I was back to Japhrimel again.

Stay inside. Don't open the door. Do not doubt me, no matter what.

I'd walked into that church and faced Lucifer with him. My mind kept pawing lightly at the memory—the speaking in their demonic language, the maneuvering me into the position of having to agree... and here I was, almost everything I owned in the world gone in a reaction fire and demons chasing me down. I was damn lucky that I'd only tangled with one imp so far—an imp Japhrimel hadn't attacked and exhausted first, like he'd done with Santino. I was *damn* lucky to be alive on both counts.

Some demon somewhere knew what Lucifer had bargained me into doing and was looking to get the first shot in. It was predictable—after all, I was the weakest link in the chain leading to the Devil, especially if Japh was a full-fledged demon again. If they killed me messily enough, like a Mob turf hit, it might be a statement to other demons looking to rebel. If Lucifer couldn't even keep one lousy human alive, his reputation would take a hit, and Hell might get even harder to control.

I felt cold at the thought of demons slipping out of Hell and causing havoc in my world. Like it or not, Lucifer was relatively well-disposed toward humanity, and I suspected it might be hard to contact demons mostly because he wanted it that way. The thought of a change in that status quo was enough to give anyone nightmares.

I thought of the temple and Lucifer's eyes on me, his mischievous expression and the cold razor-mouthed beauty of his voice sending another shiver up my spine. I felt goosebumps trying to break through my sleek golden skin but not succeeding, a sensation like a phantom limb's pain. He had neatly outmaneuvered me, as a matter of fact. I hadn't even managed to stick up for Eve's freedom.

Eve. A little girl, her pale hair a shining sleek cap, her indigo eyes too wide and too calm with awful, chilling maturity. Doreen's daughter, birthed from Lucifer's genetic material and the marrow and blood Santino had murdered Doreen for. One of my biggest failures, one of a long string.

Why do I keep going from one subject I don't like to another? I shifted uncomfortably, rubbed my head against the chill tile wall. Since I was so much warmer than human now, it was nice to feel the coolness seeping into my skin.

Sometimes.

Of course Japhrimel will turn you back into a human, a little voice of self-loathing spoke up inside my head. I shifted restlessly again, tried to shut it up. *You're too cold, too hard, too damaged. You've locked yourself up with your books—he's said so himself—and you used Jace to taunt him, didn't you? No wonder he went back to Hell, it was probably more fucking fun than hanging around with* you.

The thought that perhaps Lucifer could be behind the blowing-up of my house or the imp attack wasn't comfortable either. But Japhrimel had made such a big deal of asking for my protection, and he'd told me not to doubt him. No matter what.

Stop it, Danny. Stop it. If you can't trust Japhrimel you're dead in the water. Don't start doubting him now. He's never let you down before; he'll come through. Whatever happens, he'll do all he can to help you.

After a few hours of fruitless brooding, I opened my eyes and sighed again. I was just about to shift so I could lie down on the floor when my demon-sharp ears heard the sound of stealthy movement out in the tunnel leading to Lucas's door. I hadn't even realized I was listening so intently, straining my ears for any whisper of motion.

I froze, my left hand palm-up, clasping my sword. My eyes dropped to the almost-forgotten wristcuff. Its etched lines were moving again, and even under the full-spectrum lights they glinted eerie bright green.

I didn't need a demon-language dictionary to know that meant nothing good for me.

I let out a long soft breath through my open mouth, pushed up to my feet, and started hunting on the wall for the small depression.

CHAPTER 17

Night had fallen when I reached the end of the long slick tunnel, the wristcuff held up to provide me with a little light. Demon-acute sight is a blessing in the dark, but even demon eyes need a few photons to work with; they're not like Nichtvren with their uncanny ability to see in absolute blackness. It was a long, slippery, stumbling walk. Even my preternaturally quick reflexes and sense of balance had difficulty. Imagining Lucas struggling up for the surface through this dark, slimy, slanting passage wasn't comfortable either. I heard squeaks, and once or twice saw beady little animal eyes.

I suppose it was silly to be worried about rats—or any other urban critter—when I was possibly being chased by homicidal demons, but I was getting sillier by the moment.

The wristcuff's glow was steady and green. I was beginning to wonder about this bracelet. Twice now it had warned me of danger. The shifting green lines came together, flowing like water over the smooth surface. I still couldn't feel anything when I probed it for magick; it was oddly invisible.

Was it a gift from Japhrimel? I'd assumed so. He'd told me to accept nothing from Lucifer, especially not food or drink but most importantly, to accept *nothing* from the Devil. Had I done something stupid by putting it on? But it had *warned* me. A backhanded gift from the Devil wouldn't stir itself to keep me alive, would it?

The thought that if I was hit it would mean trouble for Lucifer's prestige was comforting. Unless, of course, Hell wouldn't care about a human Necromance.

Then why would they look to kill me?

I wasn't *all* human either, was I? Not anymore. *Hedaira.* For how much longer?

Dammit, Danny, will you quit it? You're even starting to annoy yourself.

I found myself coming out under another heavily patched concrete and plasteel bridge, with a thin trickle of water sliding from the bottom of the pipe I had been bent almost double traversing. The pipe mouth widened until I could almost stand upright. I heard thunder rumble far away over New Prague, smelled incipient rain heavy and wet and chemical-laden against my palate. A staircase led up to the street, and I picked my way up the crumbling narrow stone steps cautiously, scanning the street above. It was deserted.

This part of New Prague looked bombed-out and deserted, but several ruined buildings had thin columns of cooking smoke rising into the night air. I scanned in a circle with eyes and other senses, my attention moving over the buildings. Nothing dangerous, no shimmer of bloodthirsty intent.

Now that I was aboveground I started to feel a little vulnerable. Who could find Lucas's lair? He was a professional, he wouldn't have led anybody back down to me. Would he? Certainly not willingly, unless he was a double agent. But that seemed paranoid. Maybe a demon could follow Lucas without his knowing?

Either way, the bracelet had warned me of the imp on the hovertrain, I wasn't foolish enough to disregard it now.

What if Lucas was really working for someone who wanted me dead?

Dammit, if that was it he would have leapt on me when my back was turned. I'm starting to get paranoid. Starting? No, I'm a full-blown flower of paranoia. A fucking garden full.

I heard the tooth-grating whine of hovercells, and my nape tingled.

Instinct took over. I ducked back down the stairs, my body moving with preternatural speed, and slid under the cover of the bridge just as a sleek black hover swept into sight from around the shattered hulk of what looked like an apartment building. Light stabbed down from its underside. I caught the bristle of relays on the bottom, like spines on a poisonous fish.

A search hover? I bit my lip as I watched, drawing back in the shadows and hoping they didn't have infrared. I'd show up like a Putchkin Yule Tree with my demon's metabolism radiating heat against the cool night air.

The hover swept the area again in a standard quartering pattern. I was tempted to scan it—but if I tried that, any psion aboard would feel my attention and tell I was close. Despite the interference from the deep well of New Prague's ambient Power and the fact that I was pressing myself into stone and willing it to hide me, they still might be able to tell my general location. It was good to have a share of a demon's Power—but it was not the most circumspect way to get around.

And let's face it, Dante, who knows how long it will last?

I told that voice to shut up and leave me alone. When the hover drifted out of sight I waited, then went slowly up the stairs again, and looked around. Underground. I had to either find a way to get underground again or find a way to contact Lucas.

What the hell am I thinking? I've got a big target painted on my back. If I stay alive long enough, Lucas will find me. Gods know there's only a limited number of places I can hide.

I closed my eyes for a moment, willing myself to *think*, and opened them to find another faint green glow coming from the wristcuff.

What's the one thing they would never expect? Just like that, the answer came.

You must decide to fight or flee, Jado's voice whispered in my head. When attacked, sometimes your enemy's force could be turned back upon itself, and I was rapidly running out of options. I needed to know exactly how the battlefield was arranged against me.

I planted my feet, my left hand curled around the scabbard, and centered myself. I inhaled, smooth and deep—and threw up a very huge, very *loud* burst of Power.

I didn't expect it to flame into the visible spectrum. It did, a sparkling crackling bolt of blue-green lanced up from my outflung right hand and arrowed for the clouds above. It would disperse over the city, but not before it was remarked. If Lucas was near, he'd come find out what the fuss was.

With that done, I ran for the abandoned apartment building. No smoke drifted from its broken windows, and it stood in the middle of a tumbled wilderness of concrete blocks next to an impressive crater hosting a few twisted scrub trees that had managed to grow amid the wreck.

In other words, a good defensible position. If I had to retreat from it, I'd have plenty of cover. Of course, anyone sneaking up on the building would have plenty of cover, too, but life couldn't be perfect.

I'd settle for just living through the night, really.

I heard the whine of antigrav before long, and the sleek black hover came back just as I shinnied through a space between two boards nailed to the broken windows. The hem of Jace's coat tore a little on ancient broken glass, real silica glass instead of plasglass, and I managed to bolt toward the side of the building that would give me a view of the hover.

Trash littered the bottom floor of the building, and a gigantic hole had been blasted through several floors. I could glimpse the sky as I gathered myself to *leap*, claws sinking solidly into crumbling concrete, every nerve alive, *twist* and throw the body upward again, landing cat-soft in my boots. Then I ducked and ran, blurring through the debris littering the third floor. I finally reached the side where I could see the hover and peered out through a broken window, sheltering myself behind a crumbling wall.

The hover yawed, strings tangling down from its underbelly. Had people bailed out on jumpcords? I'd missed something. The sleek black shape slid to the side as if something was terribly wrong, but there was no hint of *what.* It was oddly, eerily silent except for the whine of its hovercells and the stabilizers giving out a ratcheting overloaded squeal.

I looked below and saw dark humanoid shapes flitting through the broken cover. Some moved like humans.

Others did not.

They had to have been in the neighborhood, or came down the jumpcords from that hover. Did they see me coming in here? I thought this over, biting at my lower lip. The hover heeled alarmingly again, and a puff of bright green light showed from inside its tinted windows; quickly seen and just as quickly snuffed.

What the hell is going on here?

I decided a bit more altitude would be a good thing and retreated to the hole blown in the building, trying not to feel like I'd trapped myself. At least now I *knew* they were after me, and I was fairly sure I could fight my way out if I had enough cover to hide behind while I got close enough to conduct a little guerilla action. A few more leaps and I was on the sixth floor, levering myself in and rolling away just as I heard a shuddering boom.

I made it to the window just in time to see the hover grounding itself, throwing up chunks of dirt and stone, its plasteel sides ripped open as it smashed into the bridge I'd hidden under. The ground shook, the building swaying under my feet. I wished for a slicboard— I could get out of here fast with one. Instead, I skirted the gaping hole on owl-soft feet, fleeing for the more broken-down area of the building. It was dangerous since I was denser and heavier than a human, but I could also handle a higher fall.

So a hover had been downed, but not with a plasbolt. A reaction fire would bring this whole damn building down and burn a scar into the city to boot. It had been downed quietly, all things considered, which probably meant some kind of EMP pulse, probably fairly unremarked since we were out of the main hover lanes. That meant, possibly, two groups of enemies tangling with each other.

Good for me.

Fight or flee? I heard Jado's voice yet again, calm and considering.

I found a blind corner and waited. I'd be able to see anything that moved on my floor, I'd be able to shoot anything that came up through the hole. It looked as if this place had been bombed, maybe even in the aftermath of the Seventy Days War or a local brushfire action. If I had to, I could drop out of the building and tear my way through a search ring or two, make enough time to lose myself in New Prague. I'd have the benefit of knowing who was after me and what resources they could scramble on short notice.

The air pressure changed, heaviness sliding against my skin. The cuff tightened, squeezing. I bit back a gasp and folded up inside myself, trying to stay as small and still as possible. The air turned hard and hot, and my throat stopped as I held my breath, unconsciously.

Below, I felt the arrival of something with an aura full of twisting diamond flame. The smell of heavy oranges and bloody musk filled the air.

Another demon. I trembled like a rabbit.

I hadn't felt this since the first time Japhrimel showed up at my door. The black, twisting diamond flames of demon Power warped through the building's physical space. I gauged the distance between me and the window.

Fight, or flee? There was no way I could take on a demon. But if it managed to trap me, I would have to see what I could come up with.

The soft, chilling voice echoed up from below. "Right Hand," it said in Merican, the words making the building quiver like a plucked string. "Kinslayer. I wish to speak to you. Come and face me."

What the hell? That answered a question—he wasn't babbling in Czechi, whoever he was. Speaking Merican meant he was probably after me.

The answer to a question like that is almost worse than having to ask that question in the first place. I had to swallow a wild braying laugh. Why did I always feel the urge to *laugh* at times like this? I had to breathe; took in a shallow, soft sip of air. Smelled the oranges and musk again, a heady scent.

I stayed where I was, waiting.

"I know you are here," the voice continued. Too deep to be female, full of an awful welter of bone-chilling, nerve-twisting Power. Japhrimel's voice had *never* been this uncomfortable. He had occasionally sounded furiously cold or threatening but never so... inhuman. "I can *smell* you."

Good for you. I'd give you a prize but I don't think you'd like it.

My right hand tensed around my swordhilt. *If a demon comes for me, I want it to be on my terms.* I was pretty sanguine about my chances against humans or even werecain, but I didn't know enough about this terrain to be comfortable facing something bigger. Now I knew there was at least one demon in New Prague, and that he was most likely looking for me.

And that he could smell me, mistaking me for Japh.

My mouth gaped, my breathing soundless. I gathered myself, centimeter by centimeter. Like a coiled spring. Japhrimel had taught me how to do it, conserve my body's need for motion, then explode into demon-swift action.

Don't think about him—think about getting out of here. Quickly. Now that you know what you're facing, get the fuck out of here.

Movement below. If it was easy for me to haul my carcass up here, it would be even easier for a demon. Especially one of the Greater . Flight.

Stillness, a killing silence like radiation-burn. *Demon down there, and what else? What else is waiting to make my life miserable?*

The cuff tightened on my wrist again. Its glow had dampened, as if it didn't want to give away my location. I went so still I could imagine my molecules slowing down their frenetic dance. I could imagine the flashes between my nerves slowing down too. I could imagine too goddamn much, as a matter of fact.

"Show yourself." The voice mouthed along the dark well of the hole slicing through the building. "I come to speak of—"

The unthinkable happened.

Pressure crackled in the air. Another arrival. Just like a damn transport dock. *Gods above, this just keeps getting better.*

Chaos exploded underneath me. The noise was so instant and so huge I tore my sword out of its sheath, blue flame exploding along the blade.

I heard a howling snarl, then another chilling scream cut the air. This one froze all the blood in my veins and rather rapidly altered the entire situation. One demon who didn't know where I was I could handle. Two demons in a melee I could most definitely *not* handle, but it would give me enough cover to get the fuck out of here.

I barely thought, all the compressed energy in my body tearing loose at once. I bolted for the window and hit it with Power and flesh both. Wood exploded out, the momentum carrying me far, I braced for impact, tumbling through the air.

Plasgun fire streaked past, and the coughing roars of projectile weapons. I slammed down, my boots cracking concrete, the shock jolting all the way up to the crown of my head, and took the first two opponents with a clash. All things considered it was actually a comfort to have a clear-cut problem in front of me.

Mercenaries, human, each with guns and blades. It barely slowed me down, I didn't even kill the second one, just knocked him aside and streaked over smoking rubble, bowling over another two mercenaries. Plasgun bolts crisscrossed my path, I heard a rising scream I didn't recognize, a sound of lung-tearing female effort. Something brushed my cheek like a whip, a line of fire against my face. The screaming sound was mine, a howl pushed past all endurance and smashing aside crackling yellow plasbolts. They were firing at me because I was moving too fast to engage now.

I burst out into a street, deserted but lit with streetlights, flashes of buildings as I ran using demon speed, hearing the footsteps behind me, pounding. They sounded even swifter than mine—I had to do something quick, gaining on me, gaining on me.

Time to think of something else, Danny.

There comes a point past which running is useless. I saw an intersection ahead of me and could have jagged to try to throw off pursuit, but my body decided otherwise, streaking instead for the shelter of an alley. I burst into noisome darkness, no Power left to make a shield to ward off the smells of human death and decay. Iron burned against my palm as I leapt over a dumpster, shoving it back in the same motion. The end of the alley was what I'd hoped for, a blank brick wall, and I twisted in midair, boots thudding against it, and completed the motion by leaping lightly down facing back the way I'd come, ready now, my sword singing as it clove the air. My lips peeled back from my teeth. If I was going to die, I was going to die in combat, face-on, with my back to the wall.

My ribs flared with deep panting breaths. Adrenaline soared and sang through me, pushing me past rational thought and into the tearing-claw frenzy of an animal brought to bay and prepared to go down fighting.

He stood less than ten feet away, the darkness burning around him with a sound like voices whispering, chattering, sneering. My heart slammed into my throat, I dropped into guard, my blade suddenly glowing with harsh, hurtful blue light. The mark flared against my shoulder, soft velvet heat scoring into my nervous system.

His eyes. Anubis et'her ka, his eyes.

His eyes were like Lucifer's, piercing intense green. And his aura, the diamond-twisting black flames of a demon; he was the same as he had been the very first time I'd ever seen him on my front step.

Tierce Japhrimel was a demon again, and the look on his face froze my blood. My heart smashed against my ribs, my sword blazed blue-white, every nerve in my body sang with the furious urge to kill.

I dug my heels into the concrete and prepared to sell myself dear if he came for me.

CHAPTER 18

Japhrimel cocked his head, watching me. His face was shuttered, blank, only the terrible burning fire of his eyes to show he was something more than a statue. I swallowed copper. I knew how eerily fast he could move. My heart threw itself against my ribs as if it intended to explode and save everyone involved the trouble of killing me.

We stood like that, Fallen-no-more and *hedaira*, for about thirty of the longest seconds of my life. My blade, the weapon of a Necromance, spat blue flame, my head was full of the rushing noise of combat. I was set on lasetrigger, dialed up to ten, and just aching, *aching* to fight.

My patience broke. "If you're going to do it," I rasped, "*do* it, don't make me wait for it!"

A fleeting shadow crossed his face. He looked puzzled.

"What nonsense are you speaking now?"

I was relieved. He didn't sound like the soft evil voice that had crawled up from the bottom floor of the ruined apartment building. I was so relieved that he sounded like he always had—flat and ironic—that I actually let out a sharp breath, my swordblade dipping slightly. More thunder walked through the sky, the smell of rain turning thick and cloying. Whatever weather was crossing the city, it was very near.

Relief turned to whipsawing fear and irritation, riding just under my skin. I hadn't eaten, and I'd expended a *hell* of a lot of Power. My shields trembled once, snapped back into place. The mark on my shoulder pulsed, another hot wave of Power soaking into the mass of exposed nerves I was fast becoming. *Get it while you can,* I thought in a lunatic singsong. *Get it while it's good.*

"Dante?" He didn't move. His eyes flicked down my body, took in my feet in ready stance, the blue-glowing blade, came back up to my face.

"What happens now?" My breath jagged in my throat. My swordblade dipped even further, blue flame glowing, my rings flaring with golden sparks. "What *now*, Tierce Japhrimel?"

Comprehension lit his face. In that one moment he looked completely human despite the lasers of his eyes. My chest gave a horrible
squeeze. His eyebrows drew together again, and I braced myself for
it. *This is going to hurt. This is going to hurt worse than Jace, worse
than Doreen, worse than anything. Oh gods, I've been wrong, he is
planning on making me human again, he's going to tell me...how is
he going to tell me? Japhrimel, please—*

"If you think I am about to fight you, Dante, you are exceedingly
stupid." Now his voice held a faint note of disdain, or was it anger?
Irritation?

I wished I could tell.

My throat closed. "Oh." I braced myself. "Are you sure?"

He made a curious little grimace, sighed. Clasped his hands
behind his back, his inky hair falling over his forehead, longer than it
had been the first time I saw him. His shoulders relaxed infinitesi-
mally. "Someday, Dante, I will discover how your mind works. When
I do I will be able to live content, having solved one of the great mysteries of Creation."

What? "What?" I blinked. My shoulders relaxed. It was going to
be all right. He was here.

But the red bath of instinct under my skin wasn't so sure. The
animal in me wanted to *fight*, wanted hot blood and a deathscream,
and I was so twitched-out on adrenaline and fear I wasn't sure I could
stop myself.

"Have you lost your senses?" Definite anger, reined in, controlled,
and burning out through his eyes. When had he learned to wear such
a human face, the expressions flitting over his expressive mouth plain
as day to me? "I *told* you I would come for you."

"There's a lot that expression can mean." My stupid mouth bolted
like a runaway horse. "You told me to stay inside the house. They
cracked the shields, if I hadn't gotten out of there the reaction fire...
and the imp, there was an imp, and back there—"

"Ah." He nodded thoughtfully. "I see."

Silence again, crackling against the alley. My breathing began to
smooth out. Slowly, so slowly, the tension and bloodlust faded, my
pulse slowing down, and he made no move. I was still on the fine
edge, pushed almost past rationality by the crazed burst of relief and
fresh fear, I had just *escaped a demon* and now here was another one
in front of me, and even though I knew him, I still felt pretty *damn*
nervous. Each moment he just *stood* there scraped my nerves raw.

My nerves were jagged enough. I hitched in a breath. "Don't just *stand* there!" I shouted at him, twitching as if I meant to attack, sword dipping slightly.

He didn't even move. Just examined me, his hands behind his back and his shoulders straight.

"God*damm*it—"

"Hush." He shook his hair back, a quick flick of motion. "You must come with me, now. It isn't safe here for you."

"You're telling me." The sky lit overhead with a few thrown bolts of light. More thunder, seeming to send hot prickles through my aching, strained body. "I thought...I thought you would..." I couldn't bring myself to say it. My heartbeat slowed, but each pounding beat felt thick and heavy.

"Whatever you thought, I am here now. I am losing patience, Dante. Come."

My sword dipped the rest of the way. The blue fire along its edges spattered briefly, went out. The sudden darkness stung my eyes. Even the wristcuff had gone dark, and that was some comfort. It had been warning me of other danger, not of Japhrimel. I took a deep, lung-searing breath. My hands shook.

"You promised not to doubt me." Silken, the reminder. "There would be unpleasant consequences to breaking a promise to me."

What the bloody fucking hell are you talking about? I have just had one fuck of a bad week, and I'm a little twitchy, so just give me a minute. I am so fucking frightened right now I don't care who comes for me, I'll kill them. Kill. I bit the words back. Settled for a choked, "Why didn't you tell me you were going to do that? Huh? Why didn't you *tell* me?"

"There are more pleasant ways to pass our time than this." He took a single step forward, the Power cloaking him pressing against me. "I returned as quickly as I could. You bear my mark, I am still yours."

My brain struggled with this, chewed it, and spat it back out. "You're a *demon* again. What happens *now*? What are you going to do to me?" I sounded scared to death, and not exactly in my right mind.

Amazing. For once I sounded exactly how I *felt*. I was too fucking panicked to be very coherent.

He took another step. "I am *A'nankhimel*, but given back my Power as a demon. I believe the term the Prince used is *abomination*." His eyes glowed. "And if you do not come with me now I will force you, and that will be unpleasant for both of us."

I dug my heels in against the compulsion in his voice, the pressure to do as he said; it was harder to resist than Lucifer's chill weight of command. Was it because Japh had so much more Power now, or because his mark was burned into my skin? "Don't. Just give me a minute, okay, and tell me *why*. That's all I'm asking. That's reasonable, Japhrimel. It really is. Just fucking tell me. I *need* to know." My voice broke, spiraling up into a jagged half-gasp, and wind brushed through the alley, bricks groaning uneasily behind me as Power jittered at the edge of my control.

He studied me for a moment. My sword hung to one side, loosely, and I was sure he could see me shaking like a Chillfreak. With each breath I dragged in I calmed down a little more, but not nearly fast enough.

All things considered, I am handling this very *well.*

"I took a risk, my curious. I thought it likely Lucifer needed us far more badly than he would admit. I could not warn you; he is far better at reading you than you may comprehend. Your reaction convinced him he could drive a wedge between us, cause trouble. Perhaps he was right." He paused. "I am sorry."

I measured his face, he let me. The mark still burned against my shoulder, waves of Power teasing at my skin. Sinking in, caressing, cajoling.

"You promised to trust me, and not to doubt me." His tone was kind, very soft, and familiar.

I didn't need the reminder. I set my back teeth, then slowly, slowly, sheathed my sword; heard the click as the blade slid home. Thunder rumbled in the distance. The storm was closing in. "I know." My voice was harsh, clipped. "You have exactly ten seconds to explain what the *fucking* hell just happened. Slowly. In great detail."

"It will take slightly longer." No hint of irony in his voice, just simple quiet reasonableness.

"I've got time," I shot back, and slid the sword all the way home with a click. "Lead on, lord demon."

Was it my imagination, or did he flinch? He stepped forward, deliberately, and approached me, each footfall silent but distinct. I didn't move, just shut my eyes. My lungs burned, I kept breathing. When his hands met my shoulders I sagged, and he pulled me forward, into the shelter of his body. "Do not, *hedaira*." His breath was hot in the tangled, chopped mess of my hair. "What I have done, I have done to protect you. Have faith in me. Just a very little, that is all I ask."

"I do," I whispered against his coat. "I knew you'd come."

His arms tightened, briefly. He kissed the top of my head, and some of the skittering panic rabbiting under my heartbeat eased. Just a little. "We must go. It is not safe for you here."

Funny, this seems like the safest place in the world to be. But I said nothing, just set my jaw and stepped away when he reluctantly let go of me.

CHAPTER 19

We walked together under the rumbling sky, Japhrimel with his hands behind his back and a familiar thoughtful expression on his face. I kept my hand on my swordhilt and tried to look everywhere at once, the sour taste of fear in my mouth and all my nerve endings scrubbed raw and bleeding. Japhrimel didn't look at me, but he seemed intensely aware of our surroundings. Rain pressed low in the clouds, restless spatters touching the pavement and steaming away from the diamond glow of his aura. He was bleeding heat into the air, which made me think that maybe he wasn't as calm as he wanted me to think.

Of course, being a demon and having the resources of Hellesvront—the deep, wide net of agents and financial assets Lucifer had created on earth—Japhrimel had a suite in a high-rise hotel in the Novo Meste. True to form, he simply ignored the fawning of the hotel employees when he appeared with one tired and battered Necromance in tow.

The hotel was a pile of glittering plasteel and plasglass, soaring above the Rijna na Prikope. Here in the Novo Meste, hoverlimos drifted under steely orange clouds and the buildings were clean and high, like the financial district of Saint City. It was in the Staro Meste that the trash piled up and the bordellos rollicked all night; that would have been the part of town I was more comfortable in. This just felt too exposed.

Of course, my nerves were so jagged I would have felt naked anywhere.

I had to swallow harshly when Japhrimel stopped in the lobby, half-turning to consider me with those new, awful glowing-green chips of eyes. "Are you able to take the elevator?"

I nodded slightly, my chin dipping. "Fine." My voice was a battered husk, still velvety with a demon's seduction. "You still haven't explained a damn thing." *That's okay, I'm not in a mood to listen. I need to fight someone, anyone, but if I start now I'll go crazy and I won't stop until someone's dead. Or sex. That would be good too. Come on, sunshine. Take a deep breath. Calm the fuck down.*

It was impossible. I wasn't going to be calm anytime soon.

"Patience, my curious one." He made a slight movement, as if reaching for me. His hand fell back to his side when I shied away, my bootheel scraping the immaculate floor. It wasn't him I flinched from. It was that the elevators were very close and he obviously expected me to get into one, my hands threatened to start shaking again at the thought. My breath came hard, harsh, my ribs flickering. "Soon enough."

The normals in hotel uniforms drew back as he stalked through the lobby. I suppose a wild-haired, wide-eyed Necromance with a white-knuckle grip on her sword and the static of bloodlust and rage following her like a cloud wasn't exactly their usual clientele. The lobby was nice, I supposed—red velvet couches in baroque style, synthstone glowing white, a statue of a woman in a traditional Czechi costume with water pouring from her bucket into a rippling pool below. I tried to ignore the sudden swirling of fear and worry in the normals, followed Japhrimel's back. The tattoo on my cheek shifted.

One of the elevators opened as we approached. It was empty. It stayed open, and Japhrimel stepped inside.

No. Please, no.

I couldn't back down. I *had* promised, I'd said it was fine. Backing down now would be weak.

So I stepped into the elevator and fought down the hot sourness that rose in my throat as the doors slid closed. All the air seemed to vanish. I couldn't close my eyes to shut out the terrible feeling, so I stared at Japhrimel's feet, pressure building behind my eyes. The push of antigrav helped by pulleys made the bottom of my stomach drop out.

"Japh?" I sounded about a half-step away from panicking, my voice breathless and cracked.

A long pause. "Yes."

"Could you . . . is it possible for you to turn me back into a human?" *I have to know. I won't get any peace until I know. It's just one of those questions I have to ask. Just . . . I have to know.*

His boot-toes didn't shift. "Would you want to?" Was that *hurt* in his voice? Wonders never ceased.

"Will you just tell me? I need to know." *Had* to know. *Sekhmet sa'es,* he was a demon again, with all a demon's Power.

Did he still want me?

It's not that he's back to his old self. I stared at his boot-toes. *It's that I have no control. He could make me do whatever he wants. He could do anything he liked to me, and I wouldn't be able to stop him. That scares the hell out of me. How am I supposed to deal with that?*

"Even if I wanted to, I could not grant you mere humanity again." His tone was so chill the air cooled a perceptible five degrees. "The changes have settled in, and you would not survive such a thing. You will not escape me that easily."

You know, I would have settled for a simple yes or no, Japh. I sighed, my shoulders hunching with tension. The air inside the elevator was beginning to run out, precious little oxygen left. I needed to breathe. I *had* to breathe. My throat began to close, my hand cramped on my swordhilt. *Anubis et'her ka. Se ta'uk' fhet sa te vapu kuraph.* The prayer rose, and a blue glow rose with it inside my mind. I could have cried with the relief. My god had never denied me comfort, even before I'd passed through my Trial to become an accredited Necromance.

That, of course, reminded me of my altar and the shape of fire behind Anubis as he laid the geas upon me. I had studied geas in Theory of Spirituality classes, the gods asking of a specific service; they were rare even among Necromances. Gods, demons—*everyone* was messing with my life now. I tried to remember what the gods had asked of me. Couldn't.

I just had to wait. But the thought of *that* waiting didn't fill me with terror. I didn't think my god would ask me for anything I couldn't do.

The door opened and I bolted from the close confines, searching for a wall to put my back to. Japhrimel stepped out, soundlessly, and waited. He knew better than to touch me, but his aura did what he refrained from, wrapping around mine in an almost physical caress.

When I looked up and nodded, taking in harsh gulps of blessed air, he led me down a quiet, red-carpeted hall and opened a pair of double doors. Once I followed him through, they sighed closed behind me on maghinges.

The suite was done in gold and cream, and a large mirror hung over the nivron fireplace, which was cold and empty except for a fire screen decorated with peacocks. And I wasn't alone in the room with Japhrimel. I caught a confused sense of movement and threw myself away, my back meeting the wall with a thump between a bathroom door and a tasteful, restrained end table made of spun plasglass.

Lucas Villalobos looked over from where he leaned against the mantel, his lank hair lying slick against his forehead. "Relax, *chica*," he said in his softest voice, but he was grinning like a maniac. Thunder rang under his words, the expensive plasglass windows shivering in their seatings. I could feel the building sway underfoot. "You're among friends."

"Friends?" My own voice cracked. My nerves were too jangled for me to be polite to anyone right about now. I was slowly, slowly coming back from the edge. "If these are *friends*, I'll take my enemies."

I didn't mean it. My mouth just bolted like a runaway hover.

Villalobos laughed, the crackling wheeze I was beginning to be uncomfortably familiar with. I had no idea when he started to find me so fucking funny.

Four other men and a woman watched me. A Shaman, a Magi, a Nichtvren—and two men without the glow of psions, but who weren't normals either. They weren't werecain, or kobold, or swanhild, or Nichtvren. I took this in as Japhrimel held perfectly still, his glowing eyes on me.

"Introductions." Lucas sounded maniacally calm. "Danny Valentine, meet everyone. Everyone, Danny Valentine."

Thanks, Lucas. That really helps.

The Nichtvren rose, a tall male with a shock of dirty-blond hair and the face of a holovid angel, his eyes curiously flat with the cat-sheen of his nighthunting species. Below the shine, they were a pale blue. He wore dusty black, a V-neck sweater and loose workman's pants, his feet closed in scarred and cracked boots. I had only seen this kind of Power once before in a Nichtvren, a heavy blurring onslaught of a creature built to be both a psychic and physical predator. He felt like Nikolai, the Prime of Saint City. "Tiens," he said.

I blinked.

Prickles of almost-gooseflesh touched my back. Nichtvren don't make me as nervous as demons do—but anything that fast, that tough, and with that much Power made me nervous enough. "What?" I managed, blankly.

"I am Tiens." He smiled broadly, showing white teeth; fangs retracted to look like ordinary canines. No wonder he'd been Turned— Nichtvren were suckers for physical beauty. I guess immortality was easier when you could collect pretty toys. The rolling song of a different dialect tinted his voice, it sounded faintly like Franje or Taliano. "At your service, *belle morte.*"

"Nice to meet you," I lied. "Look, I don't mean to—"

"I'm Bella Thornton. I worked for Trinity Corp." The female was a Shaman, her tat a curved symmetrical thorn-laden cruciform. It shifted, stabbing her cheek. "Seem to remember you cracked us once." She had wide dark eyes and a triangular Neoneopunk haircut, her bangs falling in her face. Her rig was light—only carrying four knives and a scimitar. The sword lay across her lap, in a beautifully made leather scabbard, not reinforced by the look of it. I would have bet hard credit the steel inside was only decorative.

"Might have been me." It *had* been me, if she was talking about the corporate espionage I used to do with Jace. I'd done Trinity a few times. "I hear Trinity had the best shields in the biz while you were there." It was a lie—I'd been before her time, and I knew it. She couldn't be more than twenty, so unless she was working as an intern there I wouldn't have cracked her shields.

She preened a little under the compliment and jerked her chin toward the Magi, a thin, intense-looking young Asiano man whose muddy hazel eyes sharpened as he took me in. "Ogami, my partner. He doesn't talk much." The Magi's tattoo was a Krupsev, bearing the trademark swirls; he carried a longsword that reminded me of Gabe, and from the way his hand rested on the plain functional hilt I thought maybe he knew how to use it.

This is absurd. I shot a glance at Japhrimel. He watched me, the green light from his eyes casting shadows further down on his golden cheeks.

"Pleasure," I rasped. Rain began to smack the window in earnest, driven by a restless wind. A harsh spear of lightning flashed in the distance.

The other two, both spare, rangy men, watched me. Japhrimel finally stirred as the sound of thunder reached us again, a low grinding counterpoint to the tension in the air. "Hellesvront agents." His voice stroked the air with Power. "Vann, and McKinley."

Vann was brown, from his chestnut hair to his rich warm eyes and tanned skin. He even wore brown—a fringed leather jacket and tough construction-worker's pants, a pair of supple, soft moccasins. *That* was a surprise; most people I met in my line of work wore boots, especially if they were, like him, armed to the teeth. Knives, guns, plasguns, spinclaws... even the butt of a plasrifle stood up over his right shoulder. I was surprised he didn't jingle when he shifted his weight, his eyes meeting mine and flicking away.

"Hey," Vann said.

"Hey." I sounded choked even to myself. *I've had a hell of a night, two demons and a goddamn elevator. Now I'm supposed to be polite?*

McKinley, on the other hand, was dark. Glossy crow's-wing hair, dark eloquent eyes, pale skin, and unrelieved plain-black clothing. Only two knives I could see. The only color on him was the sparkle of a strange kind of metallic coating on his left hand. He stared at me for a few moments, then lifted himself from the couch.

He moved like oil. I set my back against the wall and returned his stare, the back of my neck prickling.

He approached me, slowly, one step at a time. When he was almost past Japhrimel my sword leapt up from the scabbard. Four inches of bright steel peeked out. I swallowed. I didn't know who the hell he was, and the way he moved made me uneasy. "Don't come any closer." *If you come near me, I'm not going to be able to stop myself. I am not safe right now, kiddo. Not safe at all.*

McKinley studied me for a long moment. His eyes flicked down to my left wrist. He glanced at Japhrimel, whose eyes had never left my face. When Japhrimel didn't move, the pale man nodded. "Impressive." His voice was almost like a Necromance's, low—but not whispering. Just quiet, as if he never had to raise it to get something done.

"Glad you approve." Lucas heaved himself up from beside the fireplace. "I'm going to bed. G'night, kids."

"Lucas—" For a moment, I actually considered appealing to him for help. Then I regained my senses. "What the *hell* is going *on*?"

"Isn't it obvious?" Villalobos didn't even look back as he paced from the room. "Your green-eyed boyfriend made good on your promises. Consider me paid and on the job. 'Night."

"Tomorrow," Japhrimel said, and they took it like a prearranged signal. They filed past me to the elevator, while Lucas slid into another room, shutting the door and immediately almost vanishing even to my senses. McKinley edged past me, gave me a long look before stepping through the maghinged doors, and I shuddered at the thought of being in an elevator, unable to fight, unable to breathe.

Japhrimel stayed where he was. Watched me. The elevator door slid closed, the maghinged doors closed too, and I let out a mostly unconscious sound of relief. I was beginning to feel a little silly pressed against the wall. Rain-heavy wind moaned against the windows. "I'm still waiting for that explanation," I informed him. My hands were still trembling, just a little. *What did you pay Lucas? How did you find him?*

"And yet, here you are." His eyes traveled down me once, the mark on my shoulder responding with a flare of heated Power, staining through my shielding. My entire body ached with unspent tension under that caress. Lightning flashed outside the window, the sharp jab of electricity echoing in my shielding.

Sparks popped from my rings. His eyes sharpened, and he looked straight through me. "I came out of Hell to find our home burning and my *hedaira* vanished. The smell of a scavenger overlaid your trail, and when I tried to locate you, I felt resistance. I thought you taken or tortured, or too weak to respond."

What happened next surprised me. He actually snarled, a swift brutal expression crossing his face. "Do you know what it is *like* to search for you, thinking you taken or worse?"

I jammed my sword back home in the sheath. "Were you hoping another demon would find me before you did?"

I have never had his gift for dry irony, it surprised me to hear something so horrible come out of my own mouth. It had sounded funny inside my head, but not so funny now hanging in the air between us.

Japhrimel took a single step toward me, his eyes burning. The air turned hot and tense, the plasglass table next to me beginning to sing softly, one trembling crystal note stroking the air. I considered slipping my sword free again. The storm outside settled into its predetermined course.

"Go ahead," he said softly. "Draw. If it will please you."

"I don't draw without reason." *So help me, I am so close to the edge now. Don't push me.* "Just fucking give me a few minutes, Japh."

"You're angry." He didn't even have the grace to sound ashamed.

"Of *course* I'm fucking angry!" Why did I sound like a hurt child? My voice hadn't broken like this since my first social worker had died, knifed by a Chillfreak for an antique watch and a pair of sneakers. "You pulled one *hell* of a bait-and-switch on me, and I just got chased and—"

"I did what was necessary. You may keep your precious scruples, because I did so." Dismissive. His eyes half-lidded, the green glow intensifying—as if that were possible.

I couldn't believe this. I was so happy to see him, and yet I was shaking with the urge to punch him. As if it would have mattered; I didn't think I could have hit him anyway, he was too fast. I searched vainly for a way to hold onto my temper. "My 'precious scruples' worked for you once," I said tautly. "I finished dealing with Lucifer. And if I hadn't burned my house down, you'd still be a pile of ash. Right?"

He shrugged. "I would have come back to you, one way or another. You know this."

Why were my eyes watering? He *had* come back, he had searched Saint City to find me and helped me destroy Mirovitch's leprous blue *ka*; he had spent so much patient time nursing me through the effects of the psychic rape Mirovitch had inflicted on me.

The anger went out of me. I could almost feel it go with a helpless snap. There are some things even I can't fight, and I was being ridiculous. No sleep, no food, and being chased by demons was not guaranteed to leave me in a good mood, but he didn't deserve the sharp edge of my temper. My muscles began to ache, a sure sign I was coming down from the raw edge of homicidal fury. "I'm just...gods. I could have done without this, you know. I *really* could have done without this. That's all. Can you just...I don't know, give me a little credit for *not* being mad at you but at the goddamn motherfucking situation Lucifer's trapped me in?"

"Dante." He took another step, approaching me cautiously. I glanced past him, toward the window running with rainwater, showing the sky jabbed with spears of light whose holoflashes showed the bridges over the Vltava. Reinforced plasglass. I would be able to leap, but I didn't know what *this* fall would do to me. The thought flashed through my head and was gone in less than a second. "I am sorry." More thunder underlaid his words. The magscan shieldings on hovers glowed with coruscating whirls as the craft disregarded the storm, whipping between high buildings.

I let out a long breath. "Me too." I didn't mean it to sound so sharp.

He repeated himself patiently, as if I was being an idiot. "I am sorry if you ever thought I could abandon you. Do you think I am *human*? Do you think I would throw away Hell for you, then tire of your company?"

For the sake of every god that ever was, I'm trying to be conciliatory here, for once in my goddamn life. Will you just quit it? "Well, you got Hell back, didn't you?" I responded ungracefully.

Japhrimel tipped his head back, closing his eyes. It took a few moments before I realized his jaw was working as his fury circled the room like a shark, looking for an outlet. It took about thirty seconds for his hold on his temper to come back. I stared, fascinated. It was like watching a reaction fire trying to contain itself. I had never seen this level of frustration in him.

"Were I to go back to Hell," he informed me, his tone dead level, "I would be shunned. I am abomination, an *A'nankhimel* who has bargained with Lucifer for a demon's Power. Every moment I spent there would punish me even more thoroughly. I have removed myself irrevocably from Hell, and I have done it for an ungrateful, spiteful child."

I'm trying *to be* nice *to you!* Guilt twisted my heart as if a hand had reached into my chest and squeezed. *Why won't you* tell *me these things?* "Good for you." My hands were back to shaking. "Do you want a cookie or a pat on your widdle demon head?"

He shook his head, as if beyond words. I recognized the gesture — Jace used to make one like it when he'd reached the point of speechless rage during an argument with me. Then he took a deep breath, the crackle of Power dyeing the air around him with black flame.

"Punish me with sharp words if you like." He opened his eyes and regarded me. "Your time would be better spent laying plans. There is a demon to this city, one who thinks it would be tactically sound to kill Lucifer's new Right Hand before she can capture him."

"Great. Another thing that's my fault." *Come on. Lose your temper, Japh. I know you want to.* I could hardly breathe, both from the weight of Power in the air and my own self-loathing. Why did I have to taunt him?

Well, at least I know I have an effect on him. The thought made me wince. I did feel strangely satisfied, as if by pushing him into losing his temper I could regain a little control over the situation. Gods above, I needed a little control.

"Not your fault. Mine. I was frantic, and too conspicuous in my search for you."

The admission took any remaining anger and drowned it. I slumped against the wall, my hand dropping away from my sword-hilt. The wristcuff on my left arm warmed abruptly. "Lovely. More people who want to kill me." *I'm sorry, Japh. I know I'm not a nice person.*

"Is it any consolation that they are not 'people'?" Familiar dry irony. I sagged against the wall, my legs refusing to quite hold me up. I knew that tone in his voice, knew it all the way through my veins. It was the voice he used while we lay tangled against each other, his skin against mine, the most human of his voices. The most gentle.

"Why were you so frantic?" I tried not to sound as if it mattered. Tried not to sound like I wanted, *needed* to hear him admit to it.

He shook his head. Rain murmured and hissed behind him, I saw more jolts of lightning stabbing between heaven and earth. "You are not stupid, Dante. Why do you ask?"

Didn't he *know*? It took courage I didn't think I had to tell him why. "Because I need to hear you say it."

Long pause, moments ticked off in silence. The window was starting to look pretty good, rain or no rain. If I did decide to throw myself through it — just hypothetically, of course — how would I break the glass? And the fall, would it kill me? Could I lay the odds on that? I'd give myself three-to-one chances; I was pretty tough these days. I'd fought off an imp, hadn't I?

One lousy little Low Flight imp.

"I was afraid for you." Japhrimel turned on his heel. Stalked away from me, toward the wall of plasglass, trailing a streak of bright crimson across the air. He stopped, staring down at the lights of New Prague's Novo Meste underfoot, at the clouds crackling with storm-light. "You will not leave me to wander the earth alone, my curious little Necromance. I thought that was clear enough even for your stubborn head."

Oh, gods. He'd said that before, after Santino had shot me and Gabe dragged me back from Death. "You were afraid?"

"Yes." Just the one simple affirmation, no embroidery.

"*Sekhmet sa'es,*" I hissed, and watched his shoulders tighten. "I can't believe I...Japhrimel? Look, I'm sorry. I'm just...this just...."

He shook his head. "Not necessary, *hedaira.*"

"It is. I'm sorry. Okay? I'm sorry. I didn't know what to do, and

I'm *scared*. You should have told me something! You should
have —"

"Stop." He rounded on me, his fists clenched. Against the backdrop of the sky's theatrics, his eyes blazed and his black coat rustled.
"Do you seek to drive me into a rage? You are safe, you are whole;
well and good. You are angry that I used the Prince to gain a measure
of safety for you, you are angry at me because I Fell, you hate me
more than you can admit because I cannot be human, well and good.
But *do not taunt me.*"

*He thinks I hate him? How could he think I hate him? Where the
hell did* that *come from?* "I don't hate you. That's been the motherfucking problem ever since I *met* you, hasn't it? I *can't* hate you. I
keep treating you like you're human."

As usual when an uncomfortable truth is spoken, it hung reverberating in the air, unwilling to die. I looked down at my boot-toes,
grimy from slogging through New Prague; the stains on my
jeans from the puddle of slag I'd landed in after fighting off the imp.
"I shouldn't have said that," I finished lamely, my left hand loosening
so the scabbard slid through, lowering the sword. I wasn't going to
use it.

Not on him.

"I should not have said that either," he said, from very close. His
breath brushed my cheek. The velvet wash of his aura slid down
mine, enfolded me. Then, slowly, he reached up, his fingers wrapping around mine where they rested against the swordhilt.

I didn't look up. I closed my eyes, the last few ounces of resistance leaving me. The touch of his skin on mine sent heat down my
spine, wrapped me in comfort. I was acutely aware I hadn't really
slept, that my body trembled on the edge of deep shock.

Please, Japhrimel. Help me. I can't do this on my own.

I let out a long trembling breath, the shaking in my bones intensifying until the scabbard of my sword tapped the wall behind me, a
tiny embarrassing sound. No control left.

"You will do yourself damage if you do not cease your struggling." His breath ruffled my hair. "That will be uncomfortable for
both of us."

*How much more do you want from me? Why don't you under-
stand?* "Japh?" I leaned into him, and his free hand slid up my right
arm and around my shoulders. I rested my forehead on his chest, the
terrible aching under my ribs easing. The shakes came in waves,

passing through me and draining away as my nervous system struggled to deal with ramping up to such a high pitch and having nowhere
to spend the energy.

"What, my curious?" Was that relief that made him shake, or was
I shaking so hard I was jostling him?

Did I care?

"What demon was it? Back there? Which one?" My voice cracked
again, husky with invitation. I couldn't help myself, I always sounded
like a seduction, like rough honey and damp skin. Why couldn't I
sound cold and ruthless, like a demon?

He shook his head, a movement I could feel even through my
trembling. "Later." He kissed my cheek, then my mouth; I melted
into him. Relief cascaded through me. He would make it *stop*—the
jittering in my hands, the helpless rabbit-pounding of my heart, the
sour taste of terror.

When he led me into the bedroom, I didn't even protest.

CHAPTER 20

I wish I could say I made him work for it, but I was too relieved. He
took his time with me, as usual; sex was the only language we truly
shared despite all our time together. Even when he was talking Merican we had precious little common vocabulary. I can't ever remember being frustrated to the point of tears by my inability to *explain,*
before he came along.

I had a sneaking suspicion he felt the same way.

He didn't let me tell him what had happened until we lay tangled
against each other in a hotel bed, my leg over his hip, his fingers in
my hair, his mouth against my forehead. I told him the entire story,
pausing occasionally while he lifted sweat-damp strands of my hair
and combed them with his fingers, his shoulder tensing under my
cheek as I yawned. Softness draped against my hip, my back, his
wing closed protectively over me.

I finally felt as if I'd survived.

Japhrimel turned slowly to stone as I explained about the reaction
fire and the cracking of the house shields, and I could feel a fine humming tension in him when I told him about the hovertrain. He lis-

tened thoughtfully to the story about the reactive and the imp. His wing tightened, lying along my skin like a sheath around a knife.

He in turn told me of descending into Hell and of Lucifer's granting of his request only in the briefest of terms. He had come back to collect me and explain, found the house burning and the hoverlimo that had carried me part of the wreckage, an imp's trail mixed with mine. He had traced me to the hovertrain, taken one himself, lost my trail and caught it again, and arrived in New Prague shortly after the other hovertrain—the one with the huge hole torn in its back—had been remarked but before I rode into town. Hellesvront had been alerted, the two agents sent and set to finding a Magi worth the trouble of recruiting. Japhrimel started combing the city for me—and when Lucas Villalobos had started making inquiries, Japhrimel had gone to meet him personally, heard of the bargain I'd made, and had come to bring me in.

They found the door to Lucas's sanctum hacked open but no sign of a demon; the hidden escape-hatch hadn't been found. It looked like an imp just came in, found I wasn't there, and left to go topside to track me. From there it was a race to get to the end of the tunnel I'd slipped and slithered through. Then my flare of Power had brought all sorts of fun to the table.

"Do you know who it was?" I asked. "Which demon, I mean? Either of them?"

He shrugged. The movement tightened his wing against me. "I am not sure; he fled as soon as I arrived. I was too busy weeding through the human shields to find you."

"Human shields?"

"And a few imps. They may have been mercenaries to buy him time to escape—or to overwhelm a tired *hedaira*. I do not know, I left none alive." Japhrimel's voice chilled. "Enough of that. We have other matters to attend to."

"Why not let Lucifer drown in his own stew? I know, I know. We've made a bargain." I yawned again, rubbed my cheek against his shoulder. My body sparked pleasantly, languidly, comfort wrapped around me.

"Sleep, my curious." His voice was soft, he pressed a soft kiss onto my forehead. "You attract far too much trouble for my comfort."

"Hm. Would have been more trouble if not for the bracelet." It felt good to be still, to not lay there cataloguing every sound and feeling my skin twitch with alertness.

"The bracelet." He didn't sound particularly happy about that, I wondered if I'd violated another arcane demonic protocol.

I forced one eye open to see him examining my face, his eyes two chips of light in the darkness of the hotel room. It didn't smell like home; but Japhrimel's scent and mine dyed the air, a soft psychic static. "It was in the hover. I thought it was from you." I wriggled a little to free my left arm from under me, bent my elbow, and lifted the wristcuff to his examination.

Japhrimel touched it with one golden finger, his eyes luminous in the dimness. "Ah," he said. "I see.... So."

"So what?" I yawned again. He touched my left hand, curled his fingers around it, lifted it to his mouth. Pressed his lips against my fingers, one at a time, each touch a star in the darkness. Thunder shook the sky, but it was warm and quiet under his wing.

"Tomorrow is soon enough to begin. Sleep."

"But what is this thing, if you didn't give it to me?" The darkness was closing in, I was about to fall. He was the only truly safe haven I had ever known.

"I suspect it is Lucifer's comment on you, Dante. Sleep."

I slept.

CHAPTER 21

When I woke, the bed was empty. Weak rainy sunlight fell in through the windows, outlining Japhrimel as he stood, hands clasped behind his back, looking out onto the Freetown. The light ran over his long black coat and the darkness of his hair—slightly longer now, falling softly over onto his forehead instead of a flat military cut. I liked his hair longer, it made him look a little less severe.

I pushed myself up on my elbows, the back of my neck naked without the heavy weight of long hair. I gathered the sheet, held it to my chest. Saw the glitter of the wristcuff, my rings sparking as another rushing wave of Power slid over me. It was nice, I decided. Maybe a side effect of him being...whatever he was, now.

Demon. Again. But still Japhrimel.

Still my Fallen.

I scrubbed at my face, my rings scraping. Ran my fingers back through my hair, wincing a little as chopped strands rasped against my skin. It was so silky the tangles would come out fairly easily, but so thick that combing promised to be a frustrating process. I looked at Japhrimel's back, and the rest of the night crashed back onto me.

As if he felt my gaze, he turned away from the window. I felt the humming in the walls — he'd shielded this room so well it was almost invisible. His eyes scorched green in the gray light, his face was just the same otherwise. Except for the faint line between his charcoal eyebrows, the way one corner of his mouth pulled down slightly, and the odd shadow over his cheeks.

" 'Morning," I yawned.

He nodded. "More like afternoon. How do you feel?"

I took stock. Hungry, still a little shaky from the adrenaline surge of last night, and still not sanguine about getting through Lucifer's newest game in one piece. "Not too bad," I lied. "You?"

He shrugged, an evocative movement.

We both studied each other. Finally, I patted the bed next to me. "Come on, sit down."

He approached the bed soundlessly, dropped down. I touched his shoulder through the coat, rubbed my palm over the velvet-over-iron, trailed my fingers up the back of his neck, slid them through his hair. Touched his face — he closed his eyes, leaned into my fingers with a silent sigh. I brushed his shadowed cheek, smoothing away the wetness.

I hadn't known demons could produce tears.

I touched his cheekbone, the wonderful winged arch, teased at his lips with a fingertip until the bitter little grimace went away. Then I traced the line between his eyebrows until it eased out. Brushed my thumb over his eyebrow. His eyes half-closed, burning against their lids.

"What does that feel like, to you?" I whispered, my heart in my throat.

There it was, that slight tender half-smile he used just for me. "It's quite pleasant."

"How pleasant?" I found myself smiling back.

"Pleasant enough, *hedaira*." He submitted to my touch, his face easing. His aura enfolded mine, stroked up my back as I soothed him.

"Japhrimel."

"Dante." His mouth shaped my name, softly. He leaned slightly into my fingers, a small movement that managed to make my heart, trapped in my throat, leap.

"Why did you ask Lucifer to give you back a demon's Power?"

His expression didn't alter. "It was too good an opportunity to miss. Why did you cut your hair?"

"Camouflage. I don't think I could use skinspray, and if I used a glamour psions would get curious." I paused, acknowledging his wry expression. He appeared to find that extremely amusing. "I'm sorry. I was on a hair-trigger last night." I offered it in the spirit of conciliation. I had to admit, a full-fledged demon on my side dramatically improved my chances of getting through this.

"I am not some faithless human, Dante. I *fell;* I am Fallen, and my fate is bound to yours. It disturbs me, that you forget it." His eyes were still closed. He tipped his chin up, exposing his throat, I ran my finger down the vulnerable curve under his chin and he shuddered.

Oddly enough, it was that little shudder of reaction that convinced me. Did I need convincing when I'd slept next to him again? Shared my body with him again? "If you'd just talk to me about this, I wouldn't get so tangled up. Is that so much to ask?" *I think it's reasonable, Japh. Far more reasonable than anyone who ever knew me might think I was capable of being. I'm not known for forgiving people.*

"You promised not to doubt me." His voice was low, rough honey.

That's beside the goddamn point. It's because I trust you that I'm asking you this. "If you'd *tell* me what's happening when people are trying to kill me, I'd have an easier time," I repeated, but without my usual fire. "You just spun a complete one-eighty on me in front of Lucifer—how was I supposed to feel?"

"You had to appear shocked. It was necessary." He said it so kindly, so reasonably, that I felt like an idiot for still pressing the point. His eyes glowed green, a shade that reminded me of Lucifer's eyes even though they lacked the inherent awfulness of the Devil's gaze. I couldn't say exactly *how* it was different, but he looked more...human. Even with the glowing force of his eyes and the strangeness of his face, harshly balanced between severity and beauty, he still looked more human than he ever had.

"Necessary." I didn't like the way my hand shook. "Gods, Japhrimel. Don't ever do that to me again."

"Can you not simply trust in me?"

I never thought I would live to hear a demon plead. A new experience to add to all the other new experiences. They were coming thick and fast these days. The oldest curse in the book: *may you live in interesting times.*

"Listen." I tried another tack. "You've got all this power, you can make me do whatever you want. Can you understand that I might feel a little uneasy? I don't like being jerked around. Being *forced.* You know that, it's been there since the beginning. You know everything about me, but you won't tell me a single thing about what you've made me, or about this whole goddamn situation. I do trust you, I trust you more than I've trusted anyone else in my whole *life*, but you've got to help me out here."

His mouth turned down at the corners, almost bitterly. If I had to guess at the expression on his face, I would have called it frustration. Why couldn't he understand something so eminently reasonable?

"Let's bargain," I said finally, when I could talk around the lump of ice in my throat. "I'll do whatever you think's best if you promise to *talk* to me. Don't spring things like that on me. Deal?"

"I cannot, Dante." He sounded sad, now. Another first. His mouth actually *trembled* instead of being pulled into its habitual grim line. "There are things you must let me do. One of them is act for your safety."

"How is asking Lucifer to turn you into a demon again safe for me? How is any of this *safe* for me?" I kept a firm hold on my rising irritation. The ice slid down my throat and into my chest, like the creeping numb chill of Death.

"I am not demon, Dante. I am *A'nankhimel*, a Fallen with a demon's Power. There is a *difference.*"

If you would just bloody well talk to me, I would know there was a difference. I thought this over, playing with the rough silk of his hair. "Gods." My breath hissed out. "I'm warning you, Tierce Japhrimel. You pull another one of those and I'll...." I wasn't used to speech-lessness. What *could* I do to him?

Another tremor slid through him, shocking in someone so con-trolled. "Fearing for your life is punishment enough, *hedaira.*"

I decided to let it rest and touched his collarbone through the coat, he shivered again. "I suppose you hired all those people?"

"Hellesvront. If we are hunting demons, if makes sense to use the resources available. There will be more if we need them." He looked like he wanted to say more, his eyes opening wider and a short breath inhaled. I waited, but nothing came out.

I ruffled his hair affectionately, he smiled again. An unwilling smile touched my own mouth. *I'd do anything you wanted if you just explained it to me, Japh. It's not that hard.* "I don't work well in groups, Japhrimel."

"Neither do I, my sweetness. Neither do I."

I let it go then. He had never called me that before.

CHAPTER 22

You're kidding." I braced myself on my hands as I leaned over the table. "This is *all*?"

"All we really need." Vann leaned back in his chair. "Just the nameglyphs for three of them."

"Oh, *Sekhmet sa'es*," I hissed. "What good is that?" How were we supposed to track down demons with only three runes? Not even their complete names, just the demon version of nicknames, short-hand. Demons kept their truenames a closely guarded secret, which is the reason for all those stories of a quick-thinking Magi solitary using a name to stop a demon.

I've always suspected those stories aren't anywhere close to the truth. I have difficulty believing a simple word will stop a demon, and I'm a Magi-trained psion. I work my magick by enforcing my Will on the world through words and will, so I of *all* people have a healthy respect for the magic of names. But still...*demons*. If you can't kill it with cold steel, hot lead, or a plasgun, I have a little diffi-culty believing a simple name spoken by anyone will stop it.

I never wanted to put it to the test, either. It was one of those ques-tions I could go my whole life without answering definitively. Funny how the older I got, the more of those I had.

"We know how to deal with demons, ma'am. We have a Magi," Bella pointed out. "Give Ogami the glyphs, let him work."

I threw up my hands. "Great. Just great. Have I mentioned yet how *useless* this is?"

"Many times," Lucas wheezed, looking over some magscans of New Prague. There were a couple of places with enough interference to hide a demon, mostly in the Stare Mesto. "Pointlessly. At great length. Shut up."

I subsided. He was probably the only person on earth other than Gabe who could have gotten away with that, if only because I had a healthy respect for him. I might not fear him as much as I had when I was human—but a man who couldn't die was a bad enemy to make. Lucas had a reputation for professionalism. If he told me to shut up, it was because I was being ridiculous.

Vann handed the file folders over to the Asiano, who gave me a long dubious look and retreated to a chair next to the fireplace. Japhrimel stood where he had for the last hour, in front of the rain-spotted window, his hands clasped behind his back. He seemed to be ignoring the rest of us, uninterested in events.

The storm had blown itself out, and the rain was dying in fitful gasps. I poured myself another cup of coffee. The Nichtvren had gone to ground and wouldn't be up until nightfall. Hell, *I* didn't even want to be up until nightfall. Thirty-five years of being a night-walking Necromance was a hard habit to break even after years as a *hedaira* and only needing sleep every third day or so. My body-clock was all shot to hell, and I was suddenly conscious of time passing in a way I hadn't been since the hunt for Kellerman Lourdes. I'd grown used to days that ran endlessly into each other, spent with Japhrimel's steady attention and my books. Now, suddenly, I was in a hurry again.

I didn't like it.

The other nonhuman agent—McKinley—was gone on some errand for Japhrimel. The two of them freaked me out—not human, but no other species of paranormal I'd ever seen before either. They didn't even *smell* human, which irritated me on a very basic level. They smelled like burning cinnamon and a faint tang of demon. And McKinley was seriously creepy; he just rubbed me the wrong way.

The rest of them were getting on my nerves too. I was still scrubbed too raw, all hyped up on adrenaline with nowhere to go. Sex had taken the edge off, true...but I was still twitchy.

As soon as I realized it, I tapped on my swordhilt, my claw-tip nails making a clicking sound. "Is there a sparring room in this pile?"

Silence met my words. Japhrimel turned away from the window. "You need combat?" It was a shock to see his eyes glowing green again. I'd grown so used to a human darkness in them.

An A'nankhimel with a demon's Power. All the Magi shadowjournals and demonology texts I'd read had never spoken of such a thing. If I *was* Magi, I'd have a better chance of knowing or guessing. I couldn't even do what a Magi might and call up another imp to answer my questions. I never wanted to see another damn imp ever again.

"I think I'd best get out of the way." I left my coffee cup on the table as I straightened. *A waste of good java, I'm too keyed up to even enjoy it.* "The only demon I hunted down was Santino, and I already had his trail from Abra. Until we get a direction to go in, I'm just going to fret and pull my hair out. Besides, I think better when I'm moving. Sparring qualifies as moving."

Bella glanced at me, her eyes widening. Then she cast a look at Vann, who shook his head slightly. As if cautioning her to keep her mouth shut. That irritated me far more than it should.

I'm tight-strung enough to hurt someone accidentally. That bothered me. If I hurt someone, I want it to be meant.

"There's a sparhall near here," Lucas said over his shoulder. "You could find something there. Lot of bounty action, psions. Rent's reasonable, ten New Creds an hour."

Relief smashed into my breastbone. A sparhall full of psions—I could rent a cage or a circle and get some action or just work through a few katas. "Thank the gods. Which way?"

"Due west, gray building on the Prikope. Can't miss it, got a cage hanging from the side." Lucas appeared to forget all about me, studying a map of New Prague. He was absorbing this with an incredible amount of equanimity. Then again, he hadn't batted an eye the time he'd seen Japhrimel with me in Rio. I wondered just what Lucas knew about demons, and how soon I could get him alone to pick his brains.

Vann's sad brown eyes flicked from me to Japhrimel and back again, for all the world as if asking for direction. Japhrimel's face didn't change.

"I will accompany you," Japhrimel said. "It is not perhaps quite safe for you to go alone."

As if I was stupid enough to want to wander around alone with demons out looking to kill me. "Sounds good. Let me get my bag."

Japhrimel nodded. I headed for the room I'd slept in last night.

"My lord?" I heard Vann say quietly. "Does she intend to continue—"

Japhrimel said nothing. I ducked inside the room, grabbed my bag and Jace's coat, and made it out just in time to see Japhrimel shake his head.

"No," he said. I got the feeling I'd missed something. "I will not."

"But—" Vann flinched as Japhrimel's eyes rested on him. "Forgive me, my lord."

Japhrimel nodded. "Be at peace, Vann. There is nothing to fear."

Ogami, his eyes wide, stared from his chair. I caught him examining me as if I was a new and interesting type of bug.

"What's up?" I asked. Lucas was apparently absorbed in the maps, as if he wasn't listening. I didn't believe it for a moment. *I think you and I are going to have a little chat, Villalobos.*

"Nothing," Japhrimel's eyes met mine. "Vann thinks I am too forgiving of your disobedience."

I looked at the brown man. I could almost feel one of my eyebrows quirk. Time to get everyone on the same page about Danny Valentine. "Really? Let me clear everything up right now, then. I don't *obey*. I haven't since primary school." For a moment, my skin roughened, remembering Rigger Hall. The phantom scars across my back didn't burn, and I was grateful for that. Maybe I was starting to heal.

Maybe. "I'm generally reasonable when I'm *asked* instead of *told* what to do. But let's just get this straight: I don't take orders well. You got a problem with that?"

Vann's brown eyes widened as if I'd called his mother something unspeakable. "No ma'am," he said hurriedly, his gaze flickering over to Japhrimel, who merely looked bored and ever so slightly amused, just the smallest fraction of a smile tilting a corner of his lips up. "Not at all."

"Good. I'm going to go and get my head cleared out. When I come back, we'll try this again."

Outside the room, I stalked for the elevator. I had the odd feeling someone wasn't telling me something, but I chalked it up to being tense and decided to revisit the whole chain of thought once I was cleared out from some hard sparring. I *was* getting paranoid.

Then again, paranoid would help keep me one step ahead of the game, wouldn't it? *Paranoid* meant *careful*, and careful was good. I jabbed at the button for the elevator.

Japhrimel moved closer. I sensed crackling static in the air as his aura covered mine again briefly, a caress. The mark on my shoulder burned, a soft velvet flame. The elevator dinged and opened. I stepped in, familiar nausea and breathlessness rising. Japhrimel followed me, waiting until the doors closed to curl his hand around my shoulder. "Easy, Dante. There is enough air."

Says you. I couldn't spare the breath to say it aloud. There was *never* enough air in small spaces. It was like some sort of thermodynamic law. Small space plus no windows equals no goddamn *air*, equals me gasping in panic. What a blow to my tough-girl image.

His hand slid up and around, warm fingers touching my nape. It helped, but not nearly enough. "I am with you."

I swallowed, closing my eyes. "Yeah. For how long?" My voice sounded gasping, panicky. *I didn't mean to say that, I didn't. Oh, gods.*

"As long as you allow it. And perhaps after."

I can't imagine that. I leaned against his fingers. "I wish I could go slicboarding," I muttered. That would work all my fidgets out.

"Do you truly wish that?" A curious, husky tone; my stomach flipped as the antigrav floated us down. He leaned closer, his solidity comforting.

I shrugged. "It's okay. I know you don't like that. I was just talking." *Just shooting my mouth off to keep from screaming, that's all.*

"If it would please you, I would learn to live with it."

I opened my eyes, saw him leaning close and examining my face, his fingers hard and warm against the back of my neck. His eyes glittered green, casting shadows under his cheekbones and drowning me in emerald light. I had always tried to avoid looking him in the eye before, when he'd been demon instead of Fallen. "Too dangerous," I said finally, as the elevator fell to a stop. The chime rang, couth and discreet, and I bolted out of the cage and away from his eyes.

Why am I so scared? It's only Japhrimel.

That was like saying it was only a hungry tiger. Living with him had only brought home how much more than human he was, and now that he had a demon's Power back he was something else again. I had been pretending that he was only a man. Bad idea when it came to *anything* nonhuman. But still, I couldn't think of him as anything *other* than human. I couldn't stand to think of living in a world without his quiet, dry humor and steady hands. Go figure—the one guy I had a bad case for, and it was a demon who had already proved he wouldn't necessarily tell me things I *really* needed to know. Here I was, still hanging out with him. How was that for crazy?

I wasn't thinking clearly. I couldn't throttle back the irritation I felt, steady low-burning irritation that was buried rage trying to work itself free. When you live your life on the edge of adrenaline and steel, you can get really jittery. It's best to clean it all out with exercise, cleanse the toxins from the body and clear the mind.

I stalked through the hotel lobby, ignoring the normals—guests and employees—scattering out of my path. Japhrimel fell into step behind me, close as my shadow. Just as he had since he'd met me. "You're running away," he said in my ear as I gave the door a push and stepped out, blinking, into the pale watery sunlight.

I didn't dignify the obvious with a response.

Cracked pavement and a crowd of normals greeted me. I glanced up to get my bearings and turned to my left, heading generally westward and lengthening my stride.

New Prague is old, having been settled well before the Merican Era. The buildings are an odd mix of new plasteel and old concrete, as well as some biscuit-colored stone. The shape of the buildings is different from Saint City's, echoing a time before hovers and plasteel, a time before accredited psions, even though Prague had been a town known for its Magi and Judic Qabalisticon scholars.

It is also a town full of history. Here was where Kochba bar Gilead's last Judic followers had been killed by laserifle fire in the overture to the Seventy Days War, and where Skinlin had first learned the process of creating *golem'ai*, the semisentient mud-things that were a dirtwitch's worst weapon. This town was *old*, and I wondered if Japhrimel had ever been here before on Lucifer's business.

I wished I could find a way to ask.

One of the *good* things about being a Necromance is that even in a Freetown people get out of your way in a hell of a hurry when you come striding down a sidewalk with your sword in your hand and your emerald flashing. Many Necromances only use their blades ceremonially—there's nothing like good edged steel to deal with a hungry ghost or to break the spell of going into Death. The ones who, like me, deal with bounties or law enforcement are combat-trained. There's also a subculture of Mob and freelance psions who are generally very tough customers. Most normals are more frightened of a psion reading their mind than they are of the weaponry we carry, something I've never understood.

Jace had been Mob freelance. He'd been very good, but I'd had to hold back sometimes while sparring with him.

Thinking of Jace, as usual, made a lump of frustrated grief and fury rise to my throat. I slowed down a little, Japhrimel's soundless step reverberating behind me. He was demon, and all but shouted it

now that I was *hedaira* and peculiarly sensitive to him I could feel
the harpstrings of Power under the physical world thrumming in
response to his very presence. Part of it was sharing a bed with him,
my body recognized him.

But that wasn't it, was it? I frowned, trying to figure out why it
felt so different. Was it just because he was a full demon again? I
stalked along the sidewalk, one little corner of my mind focused on
tagging the people around me, cataloguing their various levels of
dangerousness. There weren't a lot of psions out on the streets—of
course, it was during the day. Hard to find a psion in the morning,
unless you spot one heading home to bed.

I still hadn't figured it out by the time we reached the sparhall, a
large gray building due west of the hotel with the universal signs of
violence-in-training—magscan and deep combat shielding, a twisted
sparring cage dangling from a hook bolted into the side of the building high enough that slicboarders could tag it and make it rock,
slicboards racked along the front of the building, and the blue psychic
haze of adrenaline and controlled bloodlust waving like anemones in
the air.

Oh, yes. This was what I wanted—effort, maybe enough to
sweat, a few blessed seconds where I wouldn't have to *think*, only
move. No memory of the past, no thought for the future, only the
endless *now*.

Japhrimel said nothing as I stepped inside, but his golden hand
came over my shoulder and held the door open for me. I tapped my
swordhilt with my fingernails and met the wide blue eyes of a Ceremonial behind the front desk.

Her tat curved back on itself, she wore a rig with more knives
than I'd ever seen before. Propped next to her against the desk was a
machete with a plain, functional leather-wrapped hilt. I measured
her, she measured me, and her hand leapt for her blade.

"Whoa!" I lifted my hands. "I'm here to hire, not to drag anyone
in." I didn't blame her one bit, I was popping with almost visible
twitchy lasetrigger anger, and I looked like a demon to otherSight.
Not to mention the fact that I was being followed by a very tall
definitely-demon.

Her hand paused. I felt Japhrimel's attention behind me, drew
myself up and leaned back into him. He was wound just tight enough
to go for her if she twitched. I didn't like to consider how I knew *or*
my instinctive response both to soothe him and to keep him away

from her. I wasn't sure I could stop him if he started, but keeping myself in between them seemed like a *really* good idea. I'd never seen him in this mood before, not even during the hunt for Santino.

I heard the faint sounds of a sparhall behind soundmuffling — little sounds of effort, the clang of metal, the clicking of staves.

The Ceremonial eyed me, said something in Czechi.

Oh, damn. She doesn't speak Merican?

Japhrimel replied over my shoulder in the same language. *I am really going to have to learn a few new languages,* I thought as I caught a flicker of motion.

The roll of New Credit notes landed on her desk as Japhrimel said something else, short and harsh. I felt the air pressure change, and knew without looking back that he now wore a small chilling little smile.

I'd seen that smile before, and I hoped my reaction was less visible than hers. She paled, the inked lines of her tattoo suddenly glaring on her cheek. Her aura flared with fear, the air full of the rough chemical tang of it. The smell was pleasant, not drunkening like a sexwitch's fear but still enough to make my breath catch.

She reached slowly for a communit on the desk, spoke into it. I heard the ghostly tones float through the rest of the building as she made an announcement in Czechi.

The sounds of metal clashing and heated exclamations trailed off. I restrained the urge to look back at Japhrimel, instead watched the Ceremonial's right hand as it hovered near the hilt of her machete.

She relaxed a bit, scooping up the roll of notes and riffling through them. She glanced up at Japhrimel, jerked her chin up fractionally at me, and rose. She picked up her machete, carefully keeping her fingers away from the hilt. She said something that sounded vaguely conciliatory, then backed away to put her shoulders against the wall.

I didn't blame her one bit. I'd had that reaction before too.

"We may go in," he said behind me.

"Great. You're making friends all over, aren't you."

"It must be my personality," he replied, deadpan. I actually laughed, surprising myself.

I went past the desk to a pair of heavy airseal doors, pushed at them. They opened easily, the whoosh of airseals and the chill of a sparring room's climate control washed over my skin, roughening the smooth gold. *Hedaira* don't often get goosebumps — but I felt awful close for a moment.

The air swirled uneasily. If there was a place to find psions during the day, this was it.

Several Shamans, each of them holding a staff and eyeing the door uneasily. Three more Ceremonials, males each with edged steel, gathered around a watercooler, sweat gleaming on tats and wide shoulders. A few Skinlin and one Magi were scattered around. At the far end of the room a heavy bag shuddered as a double oddity — a male Necromance, with the trademark spatters of glitter in his aura — worked it low and dirty, throwing an occasional elbow, paying no attention to anything else. I took all this in with a glance.

The building was an old warehouse, the floor fitted with shockgel and full-spectrum lights boiling down from the ceiling. Shafts of sunlight lanced down from windows overhead, and weapons were racked in stasis cabinets along two walls. Dueling-circles were painted into the shockgel flooring, I finished my inspection by testing the magscan and combat shielding. Nice and deep, laid with skill and reinforced punctually.

Lucas was right. This was a good place.

"How long do we have?" I slipped my bag over my head and hung it on a peg near the door next to several similar bags, all glowing to Sight with different defensive charms. I shrugged out of my coat, unbuckling my rig at the same time and hanging both up over my bag. Flicked my fingers, my obsidian ring sparking slightly. A keepcharm blurred in the air, settling over my bag and coat to keep them safe from prying fingers. Not that I worried much — the very last place you'll usually find a pickpocket is in a sparhall. Few thieves are *that* suicidal.

"As long as you need." Japhrimel's eyes finished their own circuit of the room. The thuds from the Necromance working the heavy bag didn't diminish. "It seems we will have an audience."

So *he* was going to spar with me. I thought I'd have to find a psion partner and hold back. "Fine by me." I was hard-pressed to keep my tone businesslike, my pulse rose in my throat to choke me. I stepped out onto the shockgel, my right hand curling around the hilt. "You going to use a blade?"

"Not unless it becomes necessary." Was it just me, or did he sound amused? "I think I am equipped to handle one angry *hedaira*."

It was the first time he'd ever goosed me before a sparring match. It worked.

I turned on my heel, my eyes coming up and meeting his. We stood like that, demon and *hedaira*, his eyes burning green, a spatter of golden sparks popping from my rings. "I think I'm angry enough to give you a little trouble." My voice was so harsh it sounded as if Lucifer had tried to strangle me again, and I was grateful I didn't sound like a vidsex queen right now. "I'm wound a bit tight."

Just a little tight. Just like Lucifer's a little scary.

He shrugged, spreading his hands. "I expected no less."

"Are you sure you want to do this?" It was my last-ditch effort to give him a graceful way to back out. I needed to work off my adrenaline, true—but I could spar with someone else, couldn't I?

Couldn't I?

No, I realized, as the Power began to shift between us, straining. We were heading for something, some shape of an event already lying under the surface of the world. There was a collective in-breath from the assembled psions. The steady thudding of the Necromance's fists against the punching bag paused. A few more good solid hits, then the sound stopped altogether.

Japhrimel nodded. Never one to use words when a single gesture would do.

I half-turned, walking sideways, keeping Japhrimel in my peripheral vision as I headed for the center of the warehouse.

I don't just want to spar to work my nerves off. I want to make him pay for making me afraid. Gods, I'm not a very nice person. I want to fight him, I have to fight him, to prove I'm not afraid.

The realization shook me. I looked down at my hand wrapped around the swordhilt.

"Dante," Japhrimel said softly, "you cannot hurt me."

That did it. *We'll just see about that.* I drew the blade free, the slight ringing sound of steel slicing thick air. Heat bled away from my skin, the demon-fed heat of a *hedaira,* it would make the climate control start to strain after a while.

I saluted him with the shining length of steel. Blue fire began twisting in the metal depths, runic patterns slipping like raindrops down a window, sparkling. I must really be upset for my sword to be reacting this way, usually blessed steel didn't react to his presence. It hadn't since he'd Fallen.

But he's demon again, isn't he? And so much more powerful than I could ever be. My rings crackled. I shook my head a little, forgetting my hair was a chopped-short mess.

"All right," I breathed. "If we're going to do this, let's do it. Come and get me."

CHAPTER 23

He paused for just the briefest moment before moving in, deceptively slow, his feet soundless against shockgel. My sword flicked, he slapped it aside. I used the momentum, whirling, shuffling back as he moved in; I darted forward and almost caught him. He actually had to take two steps back, bending slightly to the side to escape the whistling arc of my blade.

I blew out through my teeth. Held the scabbard in my left hand, resting it along my forearm to act as a shield. The sword kept moving, painting the air with blue flame. I learned long ago not to keep the blade still when sparring with him, he could take it away easier if I did.

We circled, Japhrimel's boots soundless, mine shushing, his hands actually, maddeningly, clasped behind his back again. His eyes burned green. His face wasn't set or angry. The only expression I could decipher was indifference with the faintest trace of amusement, his combat mask. Anger rose, tightly reined in and stuffed to the back of my mind. If I got angry this would be over far too soon.

I didn't want that. I *needed* to work this off, get the poison of adrenaline out of my system so I could think again.

I moved in on him, slashing and feinting, he melted away from each strike with impossible grace. His hand blurred, his claws nearly tearing the sword from my grip. A loud clang shot through the air, sparks spraying from my rings as our shields locked together, a psychic engagement as well as a physical one.

He'd never done that before either.

My throat went dry. "You're serious, aren't you."

"You're holding back," he said quietly. "Come at me, Dante. You feel I betrayed you in some fashion. Make me pay for it."

It didn't sting that he was right about my holding back—but it *did* sting that he guessed I wanted him to pay.

I should have come alone and contracted a cage. Or taken a slicboard. Goddammit.

I used to love slicboarding, especially after a Necromance job. But Japhrimel didn't like it when I was on a board; it would be too easy to tip me off and since I had the mark, he said, it would be uncomfortable for him if I died or was injured.

I wondered just *how* uncomfortable.

I showed my teeth, a feral smile. "I just want to spar, Japhrimel." It wasn't precisely a lie—I had thought that was all I wanted until I got here and realized just how furious I still was.

"Then spar. You are wasting time."

"Oh, do I *bore* you?" My voice rose, took on an edge as he batted the sword away again. It doubled back on itself, hilt floating up, I cut overhand and struck with the scabbard in my left hand at the same time. He slid away from both strikes and we went back to circling, my breath beginning to come deep and fast. "I *bore* you. Maybe you want something more *interesting*—a nice little Androgyne copy of Lucifer to keep you warm instead?"

Even I couldn't believe I'd said that.

The only warning I got was Japhrimel's eyes narrowing before he blurred toward me, and I saw the bright lengths of knives reversed along both forearms. He'd gone to blades without warning me.

Another first. Well, wasn't this a day for surprises.

Knife-work is close and dirty, and his speed and strength gave him an edge. But my katana kept him just out of reach, scabbard flickering in to dart at eyes or to smack at his wrist; wall coming up fast and I was losing ground, giving way under the slashes. Parried a strike, metal ringing, hurt like hell and would have broken a human's arm, my sword followed the path laid out in front of it, blurred up in a solid arc and we separated, Power crackling as he pushed at me and I shunted the energy aside.

A thin line of black blood kissed his cheek before it sank in, sealing away the wound, golden skin closing over itself. Perfect. Flawless.

I had rarely been able to touch him, before. Was anger giving me speed to match his? If so, it wouldn't last.

I backed up at an angle to give myself more room. My sword-tip moved in precise little circles.

"You see?" Japhrimel said, both knives laid along his forearms, left arm in guard position, right hand held oddly, low and to the side. "I even let you wound me." His voice stroked along the edge of my defenses, a physical weight. I was overmatched and I knew it. He had too *much* damn speed. I was harder to kill now that I was *hedaira*—but I was no match for a Greater Flight demon.

Not even one that was being kind about it.

Fuck that. I licked my dry lips. *I killed Santino.*

But Santino had only been a Lesser Flight demon, brought to bay by Japhrimel. Killing him had almost crippled me.

Almost killed me.

"Don't do me any favors," I spat, and moved in on him.

Speed. Pure speed. Sword flashing, clanging off knifeblades, heard Jado's voice yet again. *No think! Move!* Scabbard ripped out of my hand, my wrist momentarily numb, sword whistling as I slashed in return and caught air, ducking under his arm and striking in, forcing him *back.*

My left hand closed around my katana's hilt under my right, my ribs flaring with deep breaths. We circled again. I don't usually fight with two hands on my sword — being smaller than most mercenaries meant I was at a distinct weight disadvantage while I was fully human. So I trained to use every ounce of speed I could get as well as the defensive measure of my scabbard.

But since I'd lost the scabbard and gained some demon strength I might as well make every stroke count.

He darted in, I took the only move I had at that point, leaping back like a cat avoiding a snake's lunge, sword streaking blue fire, chiming against a knifeblade, whipping down with all my weight and speed behind it in a solid silver arc. He faded away from under the strike then came back, slashing for me, my boots landed on the shockgel. Parried one strike, coiled myself, and *leapt.*

Tumbling, boots thocking down again, whirling to ward off another strike, now I had the entire length of the warehouse to retreat before I had to think of something good.

Breath coming tearing-hard, body alive and crackling, smashing aside a stroke of Power along the front of my shields. Adrenaline singing, clatter of metal against metal, his eyes narrowed and glowing behind the silver gleams of knifeblades streaking the air. One slash after another, each one just barely batted aside, giving ground but making him work for it, every single inch he gained paid for with effort. His shields locked with mine, shoving, an engagement no less psychic than physical. The entire Freetown could have gone up in reaction fire and I wouldn't have noticed, my entire world narrowing to the man in front of me with his knives and his habit of fading away under my strikes.

The idea came, laid inside my brain like a gift. I didn't hesitate.

Breathing harsh, feet stamping the shockgel, I blurred forward. The *kia* rose from the very depths of me, a scream of rage and despair lifting from a smoking destroyed part of me, metal clashing and shivering and I slashed, he ducked—

—and my blade tore through the air as my foot stamped down again, following unerringly the path of his retreat, and kissed his throat.

Just as his knifeblade blurred in and touched my own pulse beating high and wild and frantic in my neck.

I stared at him, his eyes glowing green. A single trickle of black blood eased down from the corner of his mouth. He'd bitten his bottom lip, sharp teeth sinking in. Oddly enough, that made me feel like I'd won.

His aura wrapped around mine, enclosing me. The mark on my shoulder flared to life, burning through layers of shielding, my body tensing.

Ready to push the blade home.

The bright length of my katana rose over his shoulder, the razor edge about five inches from the hilt against his tough golden skin. I could fall backward away from his knife and slash, twisting my wrist through the suction of muscle.

I *could*.

"Give?" I asked, without any hope that he would.

"Of course," he answered without hesitation, his eyes locked with mine. "Anything you want, *hedaira*."

I felt a second prickle. His right-hand knife, against my floating rib. He could open my belly with a flick of his wrist.

He'd won.

Then why had he conceded?

The knives vanished. He clasped his hands behind his back and looked down at me, my blade still tucked under his chin. My hand shook slightly. I could push the steel in, step forward and twist, all momentum boiling down to one simple, undeniable movement.

I was no longer bloodthirsty enough to do it.

I took a step back. Coughed rackingly. My throat was dry. I could feel the back of my neck crawling. "Why do you make this so hard?"

"I will do what I must to protect you," he answered, inflexibly.

"Even if it means losing me?" Like there was any way in hell I was going to walk away from him. I was in too deep, and I knew it.

He smiled, the amused tender expression that made my breath catch. "We have nothing but time, my curious one."

It didn't satisfy me. My sword lowered, rose into second guard. I examined him. He tilted his chin up slightly, a subtle movement. Offering his throat.

The air was hot and still. I barely noticed the other psions against the walls, shields gone crystalline, the perfume of human awe and fear staining the air. Even other psions were afraid of me. Or afraid of Japhrimel first, and me only by association.

The blade blurred as I reversed the katana, dropping the tip and ending the movement with the blade tucked behind my arm, blunt edge against my shirt and the hilt clasped in my hand. I wasn't sweating—demons don't sweat and neither do *hedaira* without a *lot* of effort—but my ribs flickered with deep heaving breaths and my entire body hummed like a reactive mill. But I felt oddly cleansed. I'd got what I wanted, after all.

"We have demons to hunt." Now his voice was back to flat, with a tinge of... what? Gentleness? Pity?

No, not pity. Didn't he know how I *hated* pity? I would call it gentleness, from him.

I swallowed dryly. "Four demons. Then what?"

"Then we see what pleasures the world holds for us. Seven years is not so long."

Not for you, maybe. "Is there anything else you want to tell me?" I wasn't holding out any particular hope.

He shrugged, a fluid movement. I *hate* demons' shrugging. His coat ruffled a little, his wings settling completely.

I shook myself, like an animal shedding water. Blew my hair out of my eyes. "We'd better get back."

He nodded. I cast a glance around the sparhall.

The light had changed slightly. I met the human eyes locked on us. Bright eyes, accreditation tats shifting on human cheeks of every shade. Then I saw the other Necromance.

He leaned against the wall, his dark hair slicked back with sweat, unshaven cheeks hollow. Dark eyes over high balanced cheekbones. His tat was circular, thorns twisting in a yin-yang symbol; his emerald sparked a greeting and my cheek burned, answering it.

He nodded, lifted his left hand. He carried a katana too. He wore a Trade Bargains shirt over the tank top he'd been working the heavy bag in, and his boots were scarred from long use. He looked faintly familiar, but I'd never worked with him. I couldn't quite place the face, which was a first for my Magi-trained memory. Everything about him shouted "bounty hunter."

The nod was an invitation to spar.

I felt my eyebrows rise. Looked at Japhrimel, who had gone utterly still. "I think someone else wants a match with me."

"Be careful." His eyelids dropped fractionally. Did he look angry? Why?

The mark on my shoulder flared suddenly, heat rising to my cheeks. "I think I'm done." I lifted my sword and my right fist, bowed correctly to the Necromance, honoring him and respectfully refusing his offer. "We've got work to do, anyway."

Then I turned on my heel and stalked away from all of them. Sparring was supposed to make me feel better—and I did. Clearer, cleaner, with the fidgets worked out. But most of what I felt was something hot and deep and squirming behind my breastbone.

It was shame. For a moment I'd thought of hurting him, and he'd offered his throat to the blade. Made himself vulnerable to me.

How could I have doubted him?

CHAPTER 24

Japhrimel said nothing as we hit the street outside. Rainy sunlight still fell down, but darker clouds were rolling and massing; I smelled wet heaviness riding the air. That was worth a nose-wrinkle, and I wondered if another storm was moving in. I walked with my head down and my left hand holding my sword, my eyes fixed on the pavement and only occasionally lifting to check the crowd and the sky above.

Urban dwellers learn quickly to be peripherally aware of hover and slic traffic. Practically all Freetowns have realtime AI traffic controllers just like Hegemony and Putchkin cities. Freetown New Prague was no exception. The distinct swirls of hover traffic with slicboards buzzing in between were almost complex enough to use for divination.

The thought of hovertraffic divination made me smile. I glanced up again, my eyes tracking the patterns, my nape tingling.

Why was I so uneasy?

This is too easy. If there's a demon in New Prague who knows I'm here, why hasn't he thrown everything but the kitchen sink at me? Just a lone imp and one attack in a ruined building doesn't qualify as a real battle. Either he's more frightened of me than is possible . . . or he's laying plans.

Another, more interesting thought occurred to me. Why would Lucifer bargain to have me as his official Right Hand and not Japhrimel? What purpose did that serve?

Maybe the sparring *was* what I needed to shake my thoughts loose. I cast around for a likely place and saw a noodle shop, its door half-open.

Lunch and some heavy thinking. I ducked out into the street, dodging a swarm of pedicabs. There was some streetside hover traffic too, but the hovers were in a crush of pedicabs and people and had to move at a creep, anti-grav rattling and whining, buffeting people out of the way.

Making it across the street in one piece, I slid into the noodle shop. The smell of cooking meat and hot broth rose around me; I had made it almost to the counter when Japhrimel's hand closed around my upper arm.

"This is unwise," he said. I hadn't quite forgotten he was with me, but I was so deep in thought I hadn't even spoken to him. Taking it for granted he would follow me, understanding my need for serious contemplation of this problem.

I set my jaw. "I'm hungry, and I need to think." My tone was sharp enough to cut glass. "Something about this smells."

Amazingly, he smiled. "Now this is revealed to you?"

I swear, he could sound caustic as carbolic when he wanted to. I scanned the interior of the noodle shop—plascovered booths, the counter with three Asiano normals behind it, two staring at me and another one chopping little bits of something that smelled like imitation crabmeat. Holostills of Asiano holovid stars hung on the walls. The ubiquitous altar to ancestors sat near the front door with a small plashing antigrav fountain floating above it, coins shimmering underwater in its plasilica bulb just like miniature cloned koi.

"You're getting testy." I tried not to smile. The jitter of adrenaline bloodlust was gone, I felt like a new woman.

He gave a liquid shrug. I hate a demon's shrug; it usually means he won't answer your questions anyway. "I will not deny a certain frustration."

You're not the only one. I indicated a booth with a flick of my swordhilt. "Fine. Sit, eat, talk, relax. Just like old times, right?"

He shrugged. *Again.* "We should go back to the hotel."

"Not only do I hate the goddamn elevator, but all someone has to do is drive a hover through the windows and there goes our entire team," I said acidly. "We should go to ground. Somewhere safer, and somewhere without a goddamn elevator."

At least he didn't immediately disagree. A curious expression crossed his face, half thoughtful, half admiring. "Where?"

I slid into the booth. "The red-light district. Enough static and interference to hide most of our team—except for you and me. And that's where a demon's going to do his recruiting if he's fresh out of Hell and needs human hands. Ergo, it's where we're going to hear the most whispers and gossip."

Japhrimel slid into the seat across from me. His back was to the door, mine to the back of the restaurant—as usual. We had fallen into that habit during the hunt for Santino, him courteously allowing me to put my back to the wall. My eyes flicked over his shoulder and checked the front window. People passing by, the soft roar of a crowd of normals, the staticky heartbeat of the city. New Prague smelled like pedicab sweat and paprikash, a spicy unique smell tainted with stone and the effluvia of centuries of human living. With a dash of burning cinnamon over the top of it.

The smell of burning cinnamon was demon. Two demons and a *hedaira* in a city, and the whole place started to smell. Something about that bothered me, but I couldn't quite wrap my mental lips around *what*.

It'll probably come back to bite me in the ass pretty soon. I should have told Lucifer to go fuck himself again. Should have told him that and taken my chances the first time.

It was empty bravado. I'd needed revenge on Santino, I couldn't have walked away from the deal even if I could by some miracle have fought off Japhrimel, Lucifer, and the rest of Hell *and* made my way back to my own world.

"Anyway," I continued, "Lucas is one of our biggest assets, and he's best on the shadow side—has a lot of connections. I've also got a nasty thought, Japh. Why isn't this demon throwing everything but the kitchen sink at me? And why did Lucifer ask for *me* to be his Right Hand instead of you? You're the one he can count on here."

One of the Asianos came to the table. She bobbed her dark head, smiling at Japhrimel and casting a little sidelong glance at me.

He ordered in a clicking tongue that sounded like Old Manchu. I frowned at the shiny plasilica tabletop, tapping my right-hand fingernails with little insectile ticking sounds. The problem boiled and bubbled away under the conscious surface of my mind, sooner or later I'd hit the answer. Half of any problem, especially for a psion, is simply trusting intuition to do its work.

Of course, sometimes intuition only kicks in too goddamn late and you figure everything out as you're neck-deep in quicksand. I winced inwardly at the thought.

The Asiano bowed slightly and hurried away, her slippers hushing over the slick linoleum. Japhrimel's glowing eyes met mine. "The Prince can trust you, Dante. You are honorable. I, however, have bargained with him in the past. I am known to be somewhat...unruly."

Lucifer can trust me? I thought my eyebrows couldn't get any higher. "You? Unruly?"

"I won my freedom, did I not? And I am Fallen. That means I am dangerous."

"Why? What's the big deal? You won't tell me anything about the Fallen, and you complain when I try to research it on my own. Why are you suddenly so dangerous to Lucifer?" *Just one little shred of information, Japh. It won't kill you.*

"Why do you think he destroyed the original Fallen? They were a direct threat to his supremacy on earth. It was only a matter of time before a Fallen and his *hedaira* conceived an Androgyne. Then... who knows?"

Oh. I swallowed dryly. Lucifer controlled reproduction in Hell, and the Androgynes were the only demons capable of reproducing. Santino's creation of Eve had been a blow to Lucifer's power, one he couldn't cover up or simply ignore. Hence Lucifer's throwing me into the snakepit the first time.

The waitress came back with heavy real-china teacups, poured us both fragrant jasmine tea with shaking hands. She set the pot down and retreated in a hurry, her bowl-cut black hair shining under the fluorescent lights.

"Why didn't Lucifer kill us both when you...Fell?" I didn't expect him to answer.

He surprised me once again. "I suspect he thought he might have further use for us. In any case, I know better than to try to breed." Japhrimel's eyes dropped to the tabletop.

The steam rising from my teacup took on angular, twisting shapes. I cleared my throat. There had only been one time in my life that I'd even *contemplated* having children, and that time was long past. Still.... "What if *I* wanted to breed?"

I felt his eyes on me, but I looked at my teacup. Silence stretched between us.

"Never mind," I said hurriedly. "Look, let's just focus on one problem at a time. We should get everyone out of that damn hotel and into a safer place. Then we can start figuring out which demon's here in New Prague and what he's likely to be planning."

"Do you want children, Dante?"

He could turn on a red credit's thin edge. No more sarcasm. Instead, his tone was quiet and level. Of all the varied shades of his voice, I liked this one best. I stared at my teacup, willing the lump in my throat to go away.

"No," I said finally. "I have enough trouble trying to deal with *you*."

That made him laugh, a sound that chattered the teacups against the table. I stole a quick glance at him; looked back down at the table. I knew every line and curve of his face, almost every inch of his skin. It wasn't enough — I wanted to know what was going on behind those glowing green eyes, under that perfect poreless golden skin, behind that face that wasn't as gorgeous as Lucifer's but somehow enough for me, beautiful the way a katana's deadly curve was beautiful.

I wanted *inside*. I wanted to crawl inside his head and know for sure that he wouldn't abandon me.

"Japhrimel." My voice cut through his laughter. "What gave you the brilliant idea to bargain for a demon's Power again?"

He sighed, shaking his head. His hair was almost longer than mine now, falling over his eyes in a soft shelf. "I wanted it for one simple reason. To protect you, Dante. A *hedaira* is only as safe as her *A'nankhimel* can make her." It had the quality of a proverb, recited more than once.

Way to seize the moment, Japh. "I thought you said there weren't many demons who could threaten you, even Fallen."

"After we are done killing for the Prince, he may find us expendable." Japhrimel's tone had turned chill. "If that happens, I want every iota of Power I can possibly gather. I will not give you up. Not to Lucifer, not to your own folly—and not to your precious Death either. Therefore, I saw a chance and took it. It was not premeditated."

I stole another glance at his face. He looked over my shoulder, his eyes moving in a smooth arc. His right hand, resting on the table, had curled into a fist.

"Oh." I certainly couldn't argue with my own continued survival. "Well. That was a good idea, then, I guess."

He said nothing, but his eyes met mine. It was just a flash, but I could have sworn he looked *grateful*.

The woman arrived with the food—beef and noodles for me, a plate of something that looked like egg rolls for Japhrimel, who thanked her courteously. I scooped up a pair of plasilica chopsticks and set to with a will.

He didn't touch his food.

I looked over his shoulder, through the windows at the street. Marked traffic. Uneasiness returned like a precognition, swirling around me. I finished a mouthful of noodles, took a sip of tea. "So what do you think is going on? You have any ideas about these demons? Anything that might be useful?"

He moved finally, spreading his hands against the tabletop. "Enough to begin hunting, and enough to understand there is another game being played here."

I caught a bit of beef with my chopsticks. It was a relief to be able to eat with my right hand again. And it was nice to be in a Freetown, where you could be reasonably sure the meat wasn't protein substitute. Substitute is a good thing, but it leaves me still hungry, as if I haven't eaten real food. "What kind of game? Lucifer seemed to blame me for not knowing he was asking for me, too. What was that all about?"

"You were vulnerable. He could have broken you, Dante." Japhrimel paused. "He still might."

It was time for a subject change; not only was he *not* answering the question I asked, but he was telling me something I already knew. I lifted up my left hand, the wristcuff glittering in a stray reflection of light from the street outside as I took another slurping mouthful of noodles. "Mind telling me what this is?"

He shrugged, his eyes dropping back down to his plate. I didn't think he was going to eat any of the eggrolls—after all, he didn't need human food—but I was wrong. He picked one up, bit into it. "A demon artifact," he said after he finished chewing. If I hadn't thought him incapable of nervousness, I would have thought he was actually stalling.

I waited, but that seemed all he would say. "Meaning what? What does it do?"

His tone was quiet. "I don't know what it will do for you."

Or to you. The unspoken codicil hung in the air.

I looked down at my soup. It was the damnedest thing. I'd have sworn I was hungry. Ravenous. But all of a sudden I'd lost my appetite. A chill prickled down my back. "Do you have a datpilot code for any of the others?" My eyes flicked over the front window, tracking a stray dart of light; it was a reflection off an airbike's polished surface. I looked back at Japhrimel, uneasiness turning my stomach over.

He didn't look surprised. "You wish to contact them?"

"I want to tell them to get out of there now. I don't like this. My neck's prickling."

Japhrimel reached under the table, for all the world as if digging in a pocket. If I didn't know what his coat was made of, I would have believed the pretense. He extracted a sleek black datphone from under the table, pressed a button, and lifted it to his ear.

I looked back over his shoulder. The unease crystallized as I heard him murmur in what sounded like Franje. A true linguistic wonder, my Fallen.

I slid out of the booth, gaining my feet in one smooth movement. My thumb clicked the sword free of the sheath's embrace. I heard a gasp from a normal behind the counter, ignored it.

Japhrimel looked up, his hair falling over his eyes. "Dante?"

"Are they getting out?"

"Of course. I respect your instincts. I suppose this means we won't finish lunch?" Damn him, he was back to sounding amused.

"I'll pay." I meant it, too; but he rose from the booth like a dark wave, tossing a few New Credit notes down. Of course, money means less than nothing to a demon, he never seemed to need it but it appeared whenever there was any question.

"My pleasure. What do you sense?"

"I'm not sure. Not yet." *But I will be soon.* The precognition rose through dark water, aiming for me...and passed by, circling. If I could just relax, the vision would come to me. Precog isn't my strongest talent; it's only spotty at best. But when it comes it's something to be reckoned with, for all that it usually comes too late.

The first dark, rain-heavy clouds slid over the sun. Shadow crawled over the street, hoverwhine rising and settling in my back teeth, the vision of something about to happen jittering under my skin. I didn't need to look down at the wristcuff to know it was glowing green. Me and the fashionable accessories. My skin crawled at the thought that Lucifer had given this to me and I had blindly put it on.

I met Japhrimel's eyes for a long moment. It was a relief that I still could, despite their radioactive green. "Out on the street, Japh. Move low and silent." I thought about it for a second. "And kill anyone who moves on us," I added judiciously.

"Of course." He sounded calm enough, but the mark on my shoulder flared again, velvet smoothing down my skin as another wave of demon-fed Power pulsed through the air between us.

I really wish I could decide if I like that.

A few desultory spatters of rain pawed at the crowd as we made our way slowly down the sidewalk, heading on a winding course back to the hotel through the Stare Mesto's narrow, ancient streets. I wanted to give the others plenty of time to get the hell out of there, I didn't want any of them catching blowback from a strike aimed at me.

That was mostly why I work alone. I don't want anyone else paying for my fuckups. Hell, *I* don't even want to pay for my fuckups.

Too bad that's part of living.

I would have liked a long, leisurely brooding lunch over some beef soup, but that wasn't meant to be. We were halfway back to the hotel when I stopped in the middle of the sidewalk, the hair raising on the back of my naked neck, something wrong I couldn't quite figure out until I glanced up instinctively, checking the hovertraffic.

And the big, oddly silent silver hover bearing down on us.

Well, isn't that creative. Smash us with a hover.

Then I thought of something else—the imp, screaming as it turned into a bubbling streak on the greasy slide of reactive paint. What would the thick glowing layer of reactive on the bottom of a hover do to Japh?

My heart thudded into my throat, lodged there. I glanced back at Japhrimel, who was looking up with an amused expression on his face, opening his mouth to speak just as I gathered myself and leapt, my boots connecting solidly to kick him back, sending him flying as a plascannon bolt smashed into the hover and the soundless white flare of reaction fire exploded against my eyelids.

The burning tore through my entire body. I hoped I'd thrown Japhrimel clear enough that the reactive wouldn't affect him.

CHAPTER 25

Gray. Everything gray. Shot through with veins of white flame. The burning. Everywhere, burning. Creeping fire. Every inch of skin, inside my eyelids, the sensitive canals of my ears burning, burning, my mouth burning. Teeth turned to molten chips. *Burning.*

Screaming. A raw agonized voice I barely recognized, breaking on a high note of suffering.

My own.

Cheek on fire. *Emerald. My emerald.* But no blue fire, no hovering of Death.

Wasn't I dead? At last?

"Hold that." Quiet, a male voice I didn't recognize, breaking through my agonized cry. "Goddammit, *hold* it, she's not dead. Don't know where she is, but she isn't dead yet."

Power, flaring out of my control. Sound of smashing plasglass. No blue glow. Only a ragged chant, nailing me in my body, a voice I didn't recognize.

Funny, every other time I'd been this hurt I'd gone into Death and begged the god to take me.

How hurt was I?

It hurt. It *hurt.* It tore along every nerve, worked inward, creeping up my arms and legs like the slow icy crawl of Death. But something fought it — my left arm, braceleted and shoulder-torn in agony, sending out waves of fiery cold, fighting with the other pain for control of me. Back and forth, tearing at me until I screamed, thrashing.

Caught. Held, my arms and legs stretched as I convulsed again.

"Stop." Japhrimel's voice was ragged. "Give me another unit."

A splash against my skin. A collective gasp. "More. As your gods love you, if you do not wish my wrath, *more.*"

Chanting, a Necromance's chant; I didn't recognize the voice behind it. But I wasn't dead. No blue fire, no god of Death. Nothing but the ragged breathless male voice chanting, and the agony, tearing at my skin, working inward, collecting in every joint and rending tender tissues. Motion, spiked air dragging against my nerves, I was being taken somewhere. Or was the world just spinning away underneath me?

Flesh moving on my bones, literally crawling. Crawling as the chant melded with Power to knit together shattered and burned skin and muscle. Warmth, then, forced down my throat. Someone massaging my neck. Making me swallow. It burned all the way down, fire exploding out from the inside now as well as burrowing into my skin from the outside.

"More," Japhrimel said again. His tone had smoothed out. He no longer sounded ready to kill. That was good, I felt queerly unable to move, couldn't talk to calm him down.

Rich wet scent of rain. Was I outside? No, the air was too still. Another storm approaching?

There always is. A deep voice worked its way up through my racked brain. The voice of my instincts, quiet and sure.

"She'll live." The colorless voice that had been chanting, slow and slurred now. Tired, with a weariness that drew down to the bone.

"Help him, Tiens. McKinley?" Japhrimel's voice, chill and hurtful, impossible to disobey. He'd never spoken like that to me, and I was grateful.

"Here." McKinley's voice, soft and respectful.

"Question the humans. Get even the smallest piece of information. Do not fail me."

"Of course not." McKinley's low voice. I struggled, thrashing weakly, a hand closed around my wrist. Sharp inhale.

My body convulsed, a small weak sound torn from my lips.

"The Magi. What does he have?"

"He says it's close. That's all." Bella's voice, quivering. *She sounds so young. Did I ever sound that young? What is she doing involved with this?*

"Not enough. Go back to work."

"He needs sleep, he's exhausted. The countermeasures are—"

"Take what you need, but beware. Time is of the essence. Go." Dismissive. Again, a tone he'd never used on me.

Footsteps retreating. "Gods." I heard my voice crack, hoarse and shattered. It sounded like it belonged to someone else. "Gods. What *happened*?"

"First time I've ever seen a woman take on a hover," Lucas said, his voice wheezing and terrible with amusement. "It was *loaded* with reactive. Lovely. We're going to have the Freetowners crawling up our ass."

"The damage was contained," Japhrimel snarled. "What more do they want?"

Lucas was silent. Probably wise of him.

"More blood," Japhrimel said, his voice stony. Light pierced my eyes. It hurt.

I whimpered.

"Easy, *hedaira*." Something stroking my burning forehead. Ice-cold fingers, painful but also strangely comforting. Thank the gods, his voice was softer now, no trace of that chill hurtfulness. He sounded like himself again. "Let me work. You will not be scarred."

"The hover—reactive—*Japhrimel*—"

"Just because it affects an imp does not mean it will affect *me*. Now lie still."

"Japh—" I struggled with my unwieldy body. The reactive—the vision of the imp bubbling and screaming into a grease stain on the reactive rose again. "*Japhrimel*—"

"I am well enough. Ease yourself."

Relief. I collapsed, hearing a slight whistling sound as I let my breath out. "I'm not hurt," I managed, despite the awful burning sensation. It was no longer blind white agony, only a hard, sharp weight against my nerves. Like the touch of sun on already-burned skin. Or the awful creeping rash of slagfever. "The others?"

"Safe. They left the hotel in time. I must admit your instincts are finer than mine." A warm wave of Power, something else splashing against my skin and sinking in. Something gelid and spicy like demon blood. "You *are* hurt, Dante, but not badly. Lie still."

Another voice. Tiens. Was it night now, the Nichtvren up and about? "The human's locked in a room."

"Feed him, keep him close. He is not a prisoner." Japhrimel sounded chilly again, used to command. Why had I never heard this tone from him before? "Tell him he has my thanks."

"Is she—"

"She will live, Tiens. Do as I say." Thin razor-edge under the command. Japh might be calmer but he was still on a lasetrigger.

Tiens apparently didn't consider it a big deal. "Of course, *m'sieu*. More blood?"

"No. I have enough. Get out."

Blood? That means Japhrimel's feeding. He never wanted to feed on blood in front of me, he preferred to visit slaughterhouses or feed on sex. I didn't think I'd be up for any bedgames for a little while. "Japhrimel?" I sounded delirious, wondered why. *Is he all right? The reactive...he sounds all right. I hope he's okay.*

"Be still, now. Let me work." Power, pulsing along my abused nerves. Coating them with honey. A crackling sound, then a chill as something peeled away from my flesh. Air hitting damp skin, cold and full of knives but still somehow better than the burning.

Peeling away. Fingers in my hair, stroking gently, spinning out the silky strands. A low humming sound of Power sinking into my skin, swirling and dyeing the air green; diamond-black flames twisted over me, working down toward my bones. Shadows began to form, coalescing against the bright white light. "Am I blind?"

"No. Let me work."

Now that the furious pain was gone I could *think* again. "My emerald—"

"Still there. Still alive with your god's presence. Be quiet now."

The strength ran out of my arms and legs. I felt something hard under me, Japhrimel's arms around me. A tickling touch over my face, down my throat, over my breasts, flowering down my body. A different type of tension stirred in me, my hips jerked forward. I heard a low moan—my own.

What, I'm a sexwitch now? The thought was panicked and dark, laden with uncomfortable hysteria—not at all like my usual self. Power had *never* evoked a sexual response in me.

Never.

It ran out my toes, a crackling tide of burning leaving me molten and shaken. I blinked several times, something fine and dusty falling from my eyelashes. Closed my eyes, still blind. Let my head tip back like a heavy fruit on my limp stem of a neck.

I still had eyelashes? Had someone said a hover laden with reactive? I'd been too busy trying to get Japhrimel out of the way to think about anything else.

Reaction fire. What was it with these people chasing me and the reaction fire?

Is it any consolation that they are not "people"? Japhrimel's voice, deep and amused, sounded in my memory.

Had a demon tried to smash me with a hover? It didn't seem like them, I somehow got the sense that demons liked to do their work a little more up-close. When you've got eternity to play in, bloodsport needs to be personal; anything else is just too boring. Or so I think, having studied what I can of demons.

Something else is going on here. Lucifer winds me up and sets me in motion—but he also takes the chance and makes sure I'm separated from Japhrimel. Someone sends an imp after me—but any Greater Flight demon would guess I would be almost capable of taking care of an imp. It was just to keep me running. And a hoverload of reactive—if it won't kill Japhrimel, it might not kill me, but it will slow us both down. So someone needs time to do something.

But demons had all the time in the world. Lucifer only contracted me for seven years. The *smart* thing to do was lie low and wait until I was no longer the Right Hand. Seven years was an eyeblink for a demon.

Someone was trying to throw me off the track. Someone wanted me to chase my own tail.

Or someone was using me for another purpose, bait or distraction.

Lucifer? An escaped demon? *Who?*

All of the above?

I opened my eyes. Saw darkness. Blinked, saw glowing green eyes. A familiar face.

"Japhrimel," I breathed. My body felt made out of lead, my mouth strangely numb.

His fingertips stroked my forehead. "Dante," he breathed back. "Did you think to protect me?"

"As a matter…of fact, I did." I blinked again. "Someone's trying…to delay…us. Or…use…."

"Now this is revealed unto you?" He stroked my forehead again, bent to press a kiss onto my cheek. "Think no more on it. Sleep, and heal."

I fell into darkness, still trying to think through the soup my brain had become.

CHAPTER 26

The next time I woke, it was to find myself in a small, cheap room in Freetown New Prague. Thick curtains were pulled tightly over blind windows. Day or night? I didn't know.

I rolled up, pushing aside the softness of Japhrimel's wing. Examined my hands. Thin tendrils of hair fell forward, brushed my cheeks. It was too long, past my shoulders, as if I'd chopped it months instead of a few days ago. Hair? I'd been in the middle of a reaction fire, I shouldn't have any hair left.

I shouldn't have any *skin* left. Not to mention bones, muscles, or blood.

My hands looked like mine. My shoulder looked like mine, with the scarring decoration of Japhrimel's mark. Even my legs were familiar, down to the velvet hollows behind my knees. Even my feet were mine.

I made it up to stand, unsteady. Japhrimel lay on his back, motionless, one arm flung over his eyes, his wings a soft darkness, one draping off the bed, the other curled close to his side where I had pushed it. The blankets were pushed down to his hips—he didn't like anything covering his wings when he lay next to me. He was warm enough I didn't mind.

A slice of light showed from a white-tiled bathroom. I bolted for it and scrambled inside, blinking against the sudden assault of light. Found the mirror, stood trembling in front of it, my fingers curling around the lip of the porcelain sink.

The same face, a ghost of my human looks bleeding through the lovely golden features. My mouth pulled down at the corners as I examined myself, dark eyes moving over now-familiar arches and curves. For the first time, I felt relieved to see the marks of what Japhrimel had made me in the mirror.

My accreditation tat showed sharp and strong against the golden skin of my left cheek. The emerald glittered, spitting a dart of light. My hair wasn't as long as it had been—but it wasn't a chopped-short mess either. It brushed my shoulders in silky disarray.

And so much simpler than going to a salon, the voice of merry unreason caroled inside my head.

I closed my eyes, my fingernails driving against the porcelain with a small screeching sound. Tried to concentrate.

It didn't work, so I dropped down on my knees. Rested my forehead against the porcelain.

It took a few breaths, but it finally came. My jagged gasping smoothed out, I drew in a few more deep circular breaths and dropped below conscious thought, into the space where a pulse other than my heart thrummed.

Blue crystal walls rose up around me. The Hall was immense, stretching up to dark starry infinity, plunging down below into the abyss. I walked over the bridge, my footfalls resounding against the stone. My feet were bare—I felt grit on the stone surface, the chill of wet rock. The emerald flamed, feeding a bright cocoon, kept me from being knocked off the bridge and into the well of souls. The living did not come here—except for those like me.

Necromance.

On the other side of the bridge the sleek black dog sat back on his haunches, waiting, his high pointed ears focused forward. I touched my heart and my forehead with my right hand, a salute I would give to no other god, demon, or human. Only Death ruled me. Anubis. My lips shaped the other sound that was the god's personal name; That Which Cannot Be Spoken resonating through me.

What would you have of me, my Lord? A thread of meaning slid through my words, laid in the receptive air of the hall like a glittering silver strand. I am Your child.

He cocked His slim head, warmth flowing through the not-air. A thin vibrating elastic stretched between us, my emerald sparking as my rings did, a shower of sparks. Each spark a jewel, each jewel a tear on the cheek of infinity.

The god spoke again.

The meanings of His word burned through me, each stripping away a layer. So many layers, so many different things to fight through, each opening like a flower to the god.

The geas burned at me, the fire of His touch and some other fire that moved through him combining. I had something to do—something the god would not show me yet.

Would I do what the god asked? When the time came, would I submit to His will and do what He asked of me?

I bowed, my palms together; a deep obeisance reaching into the very heart of me. My long stubborn life unreeled under His touch. How could I resist Him?

I am Your child, *I whispered.*

The god's approval was like sunshine on my back. Then He spoke again, the Word that expressed me in all its complexity, and I had to go back. I was not even allowed fully over the bridge, to touch the god and feel the weight of living taken from me for one glorious moment. Instead, the god closed me away from Death gently, allowing me to see the well of souls, the bridge, the blue crystal walls—and the shape of Death shifting like ink on wet paper as He raised one slim paw—a hand, laden with dark jewels. No, it was a woman's hand, with a wristlet of bright metal that ran with green fire.

Wait. The god of Death had never changed for me; a psychopomp was coded into the deepest levels of a Necromance and didn't change. Ever. No Necromance's psychopomp had ever changed. At a Necromance's Trial, she suffers the initiation of the mystery of Death and the psychopomp appears. Unlike other disciplines, Necromances have to be accredited, have to pass a Trial and face the ultimate abandonment of control in the face of that most final of mysteries, the passage into the clear rational light of What Comes Next.

I could not even ask a question. My god's voice rang in the blue crystal hall as He spoke one more word, this one sadder than the last, so sad I found myself fleeing the terrible burning sorrow, blindly lunging back toward my body and the familiar pain of living.

I surfaced, my forehead against chill, slick porcelain. Japhrimel's hands circled my wrists, he pulled me into the shelter of his arms. I collapsed against him, gratefully. He pressed a kiss onto my forehead. Said nothing.

The shudders eased. Warmth rushed back into my fingers and toes. "Something's wrong," I said into his shoulder. "None of this makes any sense."

"It rarely does in the beginning stages. This game is deeper than I thought."

"Great," I managed. "Why don't I find that at *all* comforting?"

A low laugh. He kissed my forehead again. "Am I forgiven yet?"

I shrugged, feeling the slippery weight of hair against my shoul-

ders again. Tipped my head back so I could see his expression.
"We've got to work on our communication."

"Is that a yes, or a no?" How could a voice so flat sound so
amused? He watched my face as if the Nine Canons were written
there, his eyes bright and depthless with their demon glow.

Why does he even ask me that? I'm still here, aren't I? "Forgiven for
what? Yes, sure. Now can I get dressed, or did my clothes burn off me?"
I tried not to notice the way my heart leapt as his wrist brushed my skin,
as he watched me with the intensity he seemed to have only for me.

A faint smile touched his lips, and I swallowed dryly. I knew that
look. "Your clothes are beyond repair, but I managed to save your
sword. And your bag."

I eased away from him. He stroked my shoulders, let me go.
"Guns?" *I need firepower, the more the better. No time for games,
Japh. Though I have to admit it's tempting.*

"Of course." He nodded. Thin tall demon, green eyes glowing in
the face I knew. I reached up, traced his cheekbone with one fingertip, my black-lacquered nail brushing his skin. Winged eyebrows, a
straight mouth, his jaw set but not clenched. "You do not have to protect me," he murmured finally.

I tried to stop myself, but I sighed anyway, rolling my eyes. My
hair slid against my shoulders, a caress as gentle as his hands. "It
wasn't exactly like I was thinking, Japhrimel. I saw what the reactive
paint did to that imp. If anything happened to you I'd . . . ."

"You would what?" If I thought his look was searching before, it
was scorching now. I half expected his eyes to turn into industrial
lasers.

He had been ash, after Rio. Cinnamon-smelling ash in a funeral
urn, left either as a cruel joke or a hint by Lucifer. I had thought him
dead, destroyed his urn as a penance; I had faced the idea of a world
without him. The empty yawning abyss of that world wasn't anything I even wanted to even *think* about ever again. "I thought you
were dead once. Once was enough. Now can I get dressed? We've got
a demon to hunt, and I think I'm beginning to have an idea."

"May all the hosts of Hell protect me from your ideas, *hedaira*."
But he smiled. Not the smile of invitation, but the warm smile I liked
almost as much, wry amusement and irony combining.

I levered myself to my feet, glanced down as he rose, his boots
scraping against the small white pebbly tiles. "Clothes, Japhrimel.
And get the others together."

"What if I like you better unclothed?" A slight quirk of his eyebrow. I folded my arms over my breasts, hoping I wasn't blushing.

An uncomfortable heat rose in my cheeks. "You can give me my sword, too."

He laughed, dropping his chin in a nod that managed to convey the impression of a respectful bow. I was actually a little disappointed when he took me at my word and went to find me some clothes.

CHAPTER 27

He not only brought me clothes — a new Trade Bargains microfiber shirt and jeans, socks, underwear, and my sword — he also had a new rig for me, supple oiled leather that might have been custom-made. New projectile guns (9 mm; anything less is useless when you're facing a determined foe) and a new plasgun, a reliable SW Remington in the 40-watt range. Some bounty hunters use 60-watt, but the chance of blowing up your own hand if a core overheats is exponentially higher with a 60. Give me a good 40 any day — what you lose in power you more than make up for in reliability.

Along with the guns were a new set of knives, even a thin fine polyphase-aluminaceramic stiletto to slip into my boot. The main-gauches were beautiful blue steel, sharpened to a razor edge and with a strange dappling in the metal. I tested the action of each knife and was impressed despite myself. It was nice that Japhrimel understood good gear. Of course, one couldn't expect any less from the Devil's assassin. The curtains rustled slightly, I glanced nervously at them and shrugged myself into the rig. I wanted to find something to tie my hair back, too.

As soon as I suited up and had a look at my slightly-charred but still-whole messenger bag I started to feel much better. Then Japhrimel flicked his wrist, and Jace's necklace dangled from his hand. "This I saved also. I have repaired some small damage to it, but it seems largely unharmed. It is . . . fine work, really."

I dropped down on the bed, all the strength running out of my legs. "Oh." My voice was a wounded little whisper. I looked up at him. "Japhrimel—"

He carefully bent over, his fingers gentle and delicate, slid his hands under my hair to fix the clasp and settle the necklace in its familiar arc below my collarbones. He even frowned slightly while he did so, a look of utter concentration that sent an oblique pang through me. His hair fell in his eyes, and his expression reminded me of a boy at his first Academy dance, pinning a corsage on his date. "I do not think," he said, his fingers lingering on my cheek, "that I understand you well enough. My apologies."

My heart hurt. It was an actual, physical, piercing pain. "Japh... it's okay. Really, it is. I...thank you." *Thank you. That's the best I can come up with, two silly stupid little words. Goddammit, Danny, why can't you ever say what you mean?* I caught his hands, held on as he looked down at me. "I'm sorry I can't be...nicer." *Nicer? I'm sorry I seem to be utterly incapable of anything but raving bitchiness. You're better than I deserve. I love you.*

"You are exactly as you should be, *hedaira*. I would not change you." He squeezed my hands, gently, and let go, pacing across the room and picking up a familiar slender shape.

"I wouldn't change you either." The words burst out of me, and the moment of silent communication as his eyes met mine was worth anything I owned.

He presented me with my sword as properly as Jado might have, the hilt toward my hand and a slight respectful bow tilting him toward me. I accepted the slender weight and immediately felt like myself again. "It is the strangest thing, but your sword seemed unaffected by the fire."

"Jado gave it to me." *Did he give me a blade that can kill a demon? I certainly hope so, I might need one soon.* "Japh, the reaction fire. How did you—"

"My kind are creatures of fire," he reminded me. "No flame can hurt me, even a flame humans unlock from atoms. Steel, wood, lead, fire—none of these things will harm me in the slightest." He clasped his hands behind his back.

I wish I'd known. "Fine time to tell me." A sharp guilt I hadn't even been aware of eased. I finally felt like we understood each other. I didn't like fighting him, I wasn't any good at it.

"I have told you I will not bother you with trifles; I considered that a trifle." He paused, thoughtfully. "I thought it would alarm you to speak of it. If it will ease your mind to know such a thing, I will tell you."

If he had jumped up on the dresser and announced his intention to

become a half-credit unregistered sexwitch trolling the sinks of Old
Delhi, I would have been a little less surprised. "Good enough." I
popped my sword free, looked at four inches of bright metal. Japhrimel
was right—the sword was unaffected. I could see no weakening in its
blue glow, no unsteadiness that would warn me the steel had become
reaction-brittle. I probed delicately at it with a finger of Power, encountered exactly the right amount of resistance.

"I wonder who you really are," I said, not knowing if I was talking to my sword, my Fallen lover, or the demon we were chasing.

Or to myself.

The old Dante would have fought to escape from Japhrimel,
would have tried over and over to push him away, would never have
forgiven him one omission, one misleading statement. Would never
have listened to his explanation, never mind that it was a good one.
Dante Valentine, the best friend in the world—as long as you don't
betray her. I had cut people completely out of my life for less.

Then again, I had forgiven Jace. Any lie he told me, every omission
he made, had eventually not mattered when weighed against his determination to protect me. Or against the debt I owed him for his quiet,
stubborn, careful love of a grief-crazed part-demon Necromance—
and his love for the damaged, brittle woman I'd been. I had forgiven
him, even though I'd sworn I never would.

Was I getting soft? Or just growing up?

And the strangest thing of all: if it hadn't been for Japhrimel, I
wouldn't have learned to forgive anyone, least of all myself. A demon,
teaching me about forgiveness. How was that for bizarre?

Japhrimel's soft voice interrupted that chain of thought. "I am
your Fallen. That is all you need remember. Are you ready?"

"To try and figure out who's been trying to hit me with a hover?
More than ready." At least I *sounded* like myself again, there was no
betraying tremble in my voice. All in all, I was dealing with this
really well.

Wasn't I?

"Dante ...." He let my name hang in the air as if he wanted to say
more. I waited, but nothing came. Instead, he stood with his hands
clasped behind his back, his eyes glowing and his hair softly mussed.
His coat moved slightly, settling around him, and I saw his face
change. Just a little.

"What?" I bounced up off the bed and jammed my sword home.
"I'm ready."

He shook his head, then turned to lead me from the room. "Hey," I said. "Thank you. Really. For saving the necklace. And my sword." *But most particularly, for saving me.*

Did his shoulders stiffen as if I'd hit him? He nodded, his hair moving ink-black above the darkness of his coat, and continued out of the room.

I didn't have time to wonder about that, just followed him.

CHAPTER 28

The suite was on the third floor of a cheap hotel in the middle of the worst sink in New Prague, and that was saying something.

This section of New Prague's Stare Mesto had been the Judic Quarter, back in the mists of pre-Merican history. During the Awakening it was here that the first Skinlin had been trained by Zoharic and Qabalisticon scholars in their words of Power and the secret of making *golem'ai*. After the Seventy Days War and the absolute genealogical proof of the extinction of the line of David, the backlash of disbelief had risen against the Judics; their prewar alliance with the Evangelicals of Gilead had only sealed their fate. There were plenty of genetic Judics all over the world, but the culture they had kept alive so successfully foundered under the double shock of the miscarrying of their prophecies and their alliance with the Evangelicals— and, oddly enough, with the Catholica Church. War makes strange bedfellows, but even the most incisive of scholars could not explain why the Judics had allied with both factions of their old enemies. The Gilead records might have offered a clue, but they'd been destroyed in the War. The only theory was that Kochba bar Gilead had been persuasive, and quite a few—psions and humans alike—had believed him to be a messiah, if not *the* Messiah.

Curiously enough, most Judic psions turned out to be Ceremonials, gifted with using their voices to sing the Nine Canons and alter reality. The only remnant of Judic culture left was the Skinlin's pidgin mishmash of their language used to sonically alter plant DNA with Power wedded to voice. That, and the *golem'ai*.

If I'd been a little less worried about a demon trying to kill me, I might have gone looking for some historical sites of interest, especially the corner of Hradcany Square where the last of the Judic followers of Gilead — the stubborn band that had shown its hand too soon against Merican StratComm's final wrenching of political power away from Kochba's old guard — had been mown down by laserifle fire. As it was, scholarship would have to take a back seat to figuring out who the hell was trying to kill me now. On the bright side, I could always come back.

If I survived.

It was obviously night, since the Nichtvren leaned against the wall by the door, his arms folded. He wore the same dusty black sweater and workman's pants, but a new, shiny pair of boots. "There she is." He sounded lazily amused, the catshine of a night-hunting predator folding over his eyes. "You look better now, *belle morte.*"

I heard rain pattering on the sides of the building, stroking the windows behind his words. No thunder, though. The storm had passed.

"I should." I stripped my hair away from my face. I *really* had to find something to tie it back. "Last time you saw me, I'd just been hit by a hover. Where's Lucas?" I wanted a little tête-à-tête with him, to touch gravbase and also — more importantly — to ask him what they talked about when I wasn't in the room.

"Gathering information." The Nichtvren inclined his head, his gaze flowing slow and gelid over my body. "I would have loved to Turn you, *cherie.*"

That was a high compliment from a Nichtvren, but I never want to hear a bloodsucking Master contemplate any of *my* vital fluids.

"Thanks for the compliment." I settled for a shrug worthy of Japhrimel. My eyes flicked over the room, full of heavy pseudo-antique furniture. Drapes pulled tight over the windows, a nivron fire in a grate. The room was done in red and brown, a graceless slashed painting of a bowl of fruit hung over the fire. Two tables, a collection of heavy chairs. Bella crouched by the fire, her eyes closed. The Asiano Magi hunched over a table spread with papers, his sword close at hand. Today he wore a Chinese-collared shirt and a long brown coat, as if he was cold. He also looked extremely nervous. He was pale under the rich color of his skin, and his hair was sticking up like a crow's nest.

Vann peered out the window, tweezing the ancient curtain aside. He held a very respectable Glockstryke laserifle, with an ease that told me he knew how to use it. "McKinley should be back by now," he said darkly.

I looked past him—a fire escape going down to a dark alley. A good escape route, or a good way for an enemy to sneak up on us. I shook my head, backing away from the window. My hair fell in my face again, I pushed it back.

"He can look after himself," Japhrimel replied. "Do not worry on his account."

The Necromance I'd seen in the sparhall tipped me a lazy salute from a chair set in a dark corner, his long legs outstretched. His emerald spat a single spark, my cheek burned again in answer, the inked lines of my tat running under my skin.

Gods above. "What the hell are you doing here?"

"Nice way to thank a man who saved your life," he answered in a low, clear voice. "I was following you; saw you get hit with that hover. Your... ah, demon there, he shunted the reaction fire straight up and repaired the damage. Damnedest thing I ever saw." He rose easily; he was tall when he wasn't hunching. Dark eyes, dark hair, unshaven cheeks blurring his tat a little. Nice mouth. Lines around the eyes— he wasn't young. "I'm Leander Beaudry."

My jaw didn't quite drop, but it was close. "*The* Leander? The Mayan reconstructionist?" *I knew he looked familiar. What's he doing here, and why isn't he laser-shaved according to the Codes?* It was time to measure him out.

He grinned, the corners of his eyes crinkling. I'd seen that smile on holovids, no wonder he looked familiar. He'd made his professional name sorting out the skeletal remains of ancient Centro and Sudro Merican sacrificial victims, in some cases raising their apparitions so linguists and anthropologists could question them; then he'd moved to Egypt and worked on the tombs there. I hadn't heard any gossip about him for a while. "And you're Danny Valentine. I'm honored. I'm working Freetowns." He indicated his fuzzy cheek.

Ah. No Necromance codes out here. He was trained Hegemony, but he works bounties. Probably not very good at following orders, been doing freelance for a while. Nice to know. "I read about Egypt. Raising Ramses for the Hegemony Historicals. Nice work—I saw the holovid." *You kept his apparition up for a good forty-five minutes, very nice work indeed. I heard you're pretty good with an edged weapon, you brought in Alexei Hollandveiss alive and trussed up like a Putchkin Yule turkey. That's right, you specialize in cold-case bounties.*

He completed the psionic equivalent of dogs sniffing each other's rumps by meeting my eyes. "Well, mummies are easier than cremains.

You're the one who raised Saint Crowley the Magi. And the Choyne Towers."

That managed to make me shudder. It was one of the jobs that had made my reputation as the best Necromance in the world, one capable of raising apparitions from bits of bodies instead of the whole corpses, the fresher the better, that other Necromances needed. A Putchkin transport had failed and crashed into the three Choyne Towers, and I'd worked for weeks raising and identifying the dead— all but the last ten, who must have been vaporized. *Thanks for reminding me.* I looked down at his hands, scarred and bruised from swordfighting and working the heavy bag. "Why were you following me?" A faint tone of challenge.

"Not every day I see a tat I recognize on the face of a holovid angel. Was curious. Did a few stunts with Jace Monroe in Nuevo Rio before he went solo. He always talked about you."

"Did he." I looked away first, down at the floor. My chest tightened. He'd talked about me? What had he said? "Well, you've fallen into bad company."

"Looks like you've got a hunt going. I want in."

Everything I'd ever heard said he was direct. "Ask Japhrimel." I tipped my head back. Japh had gone still and silent behind me, the mark on my left shoulder turned molten-hot. I paced over to the table the Magi was hunched over and pulled out a chair, dropping down and presenting the Necromance with my profile. "I normally don't work in groups, but it seems I'm overruled." I looked down at the papers, started shuffling through them. Maps of New Prague, magscans, sheets covered with cramped, crabbed Magi codewriting. I glanced at the Asiano, who said nothing. His eyes glittered at me, and I saw how tight his hand was on his swordhilt.

He's afraid of me. Why? My left hand tightened on my scabbard as I stared back at him. The room had gone hot and tense. "What do we have?"

The Asiano shifted in his seat, said nothing.

I heard Leander move, leather boots creaking. "If you're hunting demons, you'll need every hand you can get. I'm trustworthy, I've got a reputation to protect just like you do."

The Asiano handed me a blue file folder. The mark on my shoulder crunched with heat, another flush of Power tingling along my skin. "Fine." I glanced up at Leander, flipped the file open. "I told you to ask Japh. I'm not the one in charge here."

"Could have fooled me," Leander muttered. He turned on his heel, facing Japh. "What do you say, then? I've done bounties in every Freetown on earth, and I'm bored. A demon should be a nice change."

"If you like." Japhrimel sounded chill and precise. Why? It wasn't like him to care about something like this. "You are here on Dante's sufferance, then, Necromance. Since you rendered her aid."

Amaric Velokel, I read. Then a twisted, fluid glyph—the demon's name in their harsh unlovely language. The glyph had lines scratched out and redrawn, obviously the Magi was working on figuring out if there was more to it. A combination of divination and codebreaking, feeling around for a demon's Name, sidestepping countermeasures and protections that the demon would use to keep its identity a secret.

I felt the familiar thrill go through me, shortening my breath and prickling at my skin. A new hunt.

All the shutting myself up in a library hadn't managed to change the way I felt about bounties. Sure, they paid well—most of the time. But the real reason I took them was for the hunt. The feeling of pitting myself against an enemy both strong and fierce; just like a sparring match and a battlechess game all rolled into one. The year that Japhrimel spent dormant I had flung myself into bounties, working one after another after another, always feeling nervous and edgy if I didn't have a hunt started or under way. Gabe called it "bounty sickness."

I hated the danger of bounties—they had almost killed me more than once—but I'd grown to need it. Almost addicted. Hate and love, love and hate, and need.

I had said all I wanted was a quiet life. Had I been lying? Or was it just that I was angry now, being jerked around by demons once more?

I turned the page over. More conversation in the room, but I closed it away. I turned over the next sheet too and looked down at a drawing, finely shaded in charcoal. A face—round and heavy, square teeth that still looked sharp, cat-slit eyes that seemed light-colored. The face wasn't human, for all that a human hand had drawn it. The eyes were too big, the teeth too square, and the expression was... inhuman.

This was the first demon, then. Was it the one hiding out in New Prague?

I spread my left hand over the picture, looking down at the wrist-cuff. Heard a slight sighing sound. Glanced up.

Ogami stared at the wristcuff, before his dark eyes flicked up to my face. He was pale under the even caramel of his skin, his thin mouth drawn tight in a grimace.

Bingo. We've hit a Magi that recognizes something about this. Maybe I can get him alone and ask a few questions.

I looked back down at the wristcuff. It flared with green light, the lines twisting back on themselves. Was this thing like a Magi tracker? It seemed to react to demons. Was that why Lucifer had given it to me? Why didn't it glow when Japhrimel was around?

Well, no time like the present to ask. "Does this cuff work like a tracker? Is this the demon in New Prague? 'Cause it seems like this thing lights up whenever a demon's prowling around looking to kill me."

Long pause. I looked up. Vann's eyes were fixed on me, his mouth slightly open. Ogami stared too. Bella, crouched by the fire, had craned to look back over her shoulder. Her hair was mussed, and the triangular haircut didn't suit her. Her chin was too sharp.

The Nichtvren leaned back against the wall, his eyes half-closed and his fangs dimpling his lower lip. I hoped he'd visited a haunt and was well-fed. A chill traced up my spine—I had never really dealt with Nichtvren in my human life. They didn't like Necromances much. I suppose bloodsuckers who prize their near-immortality—and all of them do—might not look too kindly on Death's children.

Japhrimel approached me soundlessly. Leander dropped back down into his chair, his katana placed at a precise angle across his knees. He was staring at me like I had grown another head. Why? I hadn't *done* anything.

"It is certainly possible." Japhrimel's hand curled around my shoulder. "Given the reaction of the Gauntlet, it's likely he's close."

Okay, finally. A usable piece of information. "So who is this guy? And what's the Gauntlet?"

"Velokel is of the Greater Flight." His hand tightened on my shoulder. "In an earlier age he was called the Hunter. He hunted the Fallen and their brides, and killed many."

A lump rose in my throat. "Great." I looked down at the wristcuff. "So what is the Gauntlet?"

"The Gauntlet is what you're wearing," Vann said quietly. "It's a mark given by the Prince. It means you're his champion, and any demon who doesn't bow to his authority is your enemy."

Oh, yeah. This just keeps getting better and better. I twisted in the chair to look up at Japhrimel. "When were you going to tell me about this?" *Why does everyone else seem to know more than I do? You'd think they'd be falling all over themselves to tell me everything they possibly could.*

He shrugged, his coat rustling. "It provides you with some protection."

The fact the Lucifer had given me the bracelet made my bones feel cold and loose inside my skin, but I had other fish to heatseal at the moment. "He hunted *hedaira*? This Velokel guy?"

"He did. Nor was he the only demon who did so." Japhrimel's hand slid up my shoulder, curved around, and rested intimately against my nape. Heat rose up my neck, and I hoped I wasn't blushing. "But the *A'nankhimel* were only Fallen, no more." He paused. "They did not have the luxury of bargaining to regain their place, as I have."

"Great." *I can't tell whether to feel comforted or doomed.* "So what can you tell me about this guy, Japhrimel?"

"Intelligent. Resourceful. A good foe." Japhrimel paused. "He hates Fallen almost as much as he hates Lucifer, but I would have thought him too wise to leave Hell."

I looked down at the drawing, then met Ogami's eyes. "You drew this?"

The Asiano nodded. His eyes were so eloquent it was hard to believe he didn't once open his mouth.

"Good." I said. "Give me a full-body one. And write down in Merican what *you* know about this guy."

CHAPTER 29

I pored over the magscans again as Ogami drew. Tiens stirred against the wall. I had almost forgotten he was there—he was that still and quiet. "The Deathless approaches." He moved gracefully aside from the door. "Rather quickly, too."

I heard the footsteps, light and shushing. Lucas's distinctive almost-shuffling gait—when he wasn't as silent as a knife to the kidneys, that is.

"Get all this together," I said, my neck prickling. Bella began shuffling the papers together. "Hurry. If Lucas is running, it's bad news. You." I pointed at Vann. "Watch the alley. *Anything* out of the ordinary, yell. Nichtvren, slip down to the foyer, take a look. Make sure Lucas isn't being followed. Get those papers together *now*."

Thankfully, none of them glanced at Japhrimel to make sure they were supposed to do what I said. I gained my feet with a single lunge, the chair scraping back. "Leander, I want you to hang out with Bella and Ogami. You're protection detail for our Magi."

"Gotcha." He levered himself up out of his chair, the trademark glitters swirling in his aura. If this Velokel was half as canny as Japhrimel said, he wouldn't think twice about taking out the Magi. And there would go my best link to him.

How well could a demon hide, though? They were huge magickal smears on the landscape of Power. Shouldn't Japh be able to track him better than a human Magi?

My eyes snagged on the magscans again. Intuition clicked into place as the answer I'd been searching for burst out like colors under full-spectrum lighting, shapes falling and locking together to create a picture. *Oh, crap. Right in front of me.*

Lucas opened the door and half-fell inside. Tiens had vanished, a slight shimmer leaching out of the air. The chill returned, touching my back—he must be old, and obviously a Master. A Nichtvren performing that trick in front of humans was something I'd never seen before, though I'd read accounts of it and taken the standard Paranormal Behavior classes at the Academy.

I wondered just how trustworthy a Nichtvren working for the Devil's agency on earth would be.

Lucas's hair was wildly disarranged. A splash of blood painted one yellow-pale cheek. His left hand was buried in his stomach—or what remained of his stomach, it was a mess. My entire body went cold. "I got hit, there's a net out there," he rasped, then glanced over at Leander and grimaced. "What the hell is he still doing here?"

"What do you have, Lucas?" I wanted his eyes on me, started forward. He needed a healcharm, something to stop the bleeding, and I wanted to take a look at the wound. "You look like shit."

He flung out his free hand, fingers splayed, and I stopped dead.

"Keep the fuck away from me, girl. I got gutshot. It'll mend. Got a name around the sinks—Kel. The Hunter. He's lookin' for you just as actively as you're lookin' for him."

I opened my mouth, but Tiens blurred into being right inside the door. "Time to leave this charming place, *n'estce pas?*"

"I threw the pursuit, but the net was already here." Lucas doubled over, shoving his hand even further inside the ragged mass of his belly. My gorge rose, and I started forward again. I wasn't a *sedayeen*, but Necromances were the next best thing when it came to healing a serious combat wound.

A net? Thinking to sneak up on us, and Lucas comes back just in time. I sent up a silent prayer of thanks, my mind starting to click through alternatives, my pulse spiking. I tasted metal against my palate, the nervous excitement of a fight approaching.

"*Stay the fuck away!*" Lucas's voice scraped awfully as he backed up two shambling steps, his hand still outstretched to stop me. "I ain't fuckin' safe right now, bitch! Stay off and get the rest of these fuckin' nacks outta here!" He doubled over again, going ashen, and my heart trip-hammered in my chest.

"Out the window," I snapped over my shoulder. "Tiens, Japh, you first, clear the alley for the rest of us."

"You should go with Vann," Japhrimel said, as if I hadn't spoken.

I half-turned, grabbed his shoulders, and shoved him toward the window. He moved, shaking my hands away. "I'm safer up here until you clear that goddamn alley. I'll be right behind you—just *go!*"

Japhrimel made a slight movement, tipping his head, Tiens nodded. For all the world as if I hadn't just told them what to do.

Goddammit, if there's one thing I hate, it's being ignored in a situation like this. Why even have me along if he's not going to listen to what I say? That was an interesting thought, but one I had no time for.

Vann pulled the window up, helped the limping, bleeding Lucas out. Villalobos was moving much faster than I'd expect a gutshot man to move, and I filed this away for further thought. He said he wasn't safe, but Vann—

Think about it later, Dante. Cover their retreat now. You'll have plenty of time to ask questions later. I whirled back toward the door, shoving my sword into the loop on my belt. My hands curled around the projectile guns. "Tiens, how many?"

"Four that I saw, *belle morte*," he said over his shoulder, ducking out the window. Bella followed, and Ogami.

Leander actually blew me a kiss before he ducked out, a knife glittering along his left forearm. His sword was thrust through his belt, and he looked fey. I promptly shoved Lucas and the Magi out of my thoughts—if they couldn't make it through with that kind of protection there was nothing I could do now. My job was to stop whoever came through the door and give them time to get to cover.

Japhrimel's eyes met mine, glowing green and suddenly much more frightening. "This is dangerous," he said softly. "Stay with me."

"Why aren't you listening to me? I told you to clear the alley." I ghosted across the room and put my back to the wall on the other side of the door, right where Tiens had been leaning. The hammers of the projectile guns clicked easily as I pulled them back, I settled against the wall and made it a point to breathe deeply, calmly. My heart pounded. A net, Lucas said, an encirclement. Expensive, and meant for capture or elimination, most likely the latter. And they'd managed to hurt the Deathless.

Lovely.

"Vann and Tiens are more than capable of protecting the humans." He went utterly still, his eyes flaring.

I shrugged. Listened.

Demon-acute senses are useful most of the time. Since Japhrimel had finally taught me how to control them, they had become even more so. I heard slight shuffling sounds—human feet. Two sets of soft padding footsteps that weren't quite human; the back of my neck wasn't just prickling now. It was flat-out *crawling*.

What the hell is that? I looked at Japhrimel, my eyebrows raising.

He clasped his hands behind his back, watching the door. I almost pitied the sad sonsabitches coming through, human or not.

Wood snapped, groaning, and something slammed into the wall at my back.

Of course. Imps don't need to use doors, Danny. I flung myself away from the wall.

Japhrimel made a short sharp sound of annoyance and moved forward as I rolled. I ended up on my side, hitting the table with a sickening *crack*. Another impact shattered the wall, splinters flying, dust smashing out. I squeezed the triggers, tracking two shapes that skittered away from the coughing roar of the guns. I clipped one human done up in assault gear—nightvision goggles, Kevlar, edged metal and an assault rifle. No plasgun I could see.

Two humans—no, three. Four. And two imps.

Why didn't I hear the other humans? Why didn't Tiens tell me there were imps? Goddammit. Made it to my feet, wood cracking again as I leapt up, boots slamming down hard on the groaning floor. Right hand moving, holstering gun and closing around swordhilt. Japhrimel moved, blurring between me and the two imps. They looked just like the other ones—babyfaces, sharp snarling teeth, black teardrops over their glittering eyes. I promptly forgot about them—Japh could take care of it.

I had other problems. The humans were just *crawling* with illegal augments, twitched out on neurospeeders and muscle spanners to make them quicker and deadlier than human even as it shortened their lives. Even a psion would have a hard time four-on-one with these guys; not only were they augmented, their gear was also top-of-the-line. Whoever sent them was making money no object.

Great. Time to dance.

My sword left the sheath with a long sliding metallic sound. Half-step forward, blade moving in a complicated whirling pattern; one man went to one knee by the door, raising his assault rifle. My left hand came up, gun roaring; he dropped. Smell of cordite, of blood, the man I'd clipped leapt for me, rifle reversed to use as a battering weapon. *Fast for a human, goddamn neurospeeders.* I ducked, my blade whooshing down in a half-circle. *Where's the other one, don't see him, where is he?* Sword flickering, slicing through Kevlar as my *kia* split the air, intestines falling in a shimmering wet slither, a human sound of pain. More movement boiling into the room, slippery padding demon movement; I ignored it. I had *enough* to deal with.

Whirling, feet slipping in bloody mess. Two other men, both moving in, one lifting the rifle to his shoulder. Shot him, recoil jolting up my left arm; moved forward so quickly I collided with the last one as I ran him through, twisting the katana to break the suction of muscle against metal, tearing it free from between his ribs as the smell of death assaulted me. Blood exploded as I jammed the gun under his chin for good measure, saw blond stubble on his cheeks, smelled human sweat and effort.

Anubis, receive them kindly. I squeezed the trigger.

Blood steamed in the air. I turned in a tight half-circle, sword whirling up as something streaked for me—clashing as an imp's claws rang off the blade, an impact jolting all the way up my arm. *Holy fuck! Where's Japh?*

No time. Backing up along the wall, sword a streak of blue flame as the imp lunged for me again, soft cheeks smeared with gleaming saliva as it champed and foamed, its claws clanging off the sword with a grating shock, its breath hot against my cheek as it drove forward. I smashed my back foot down and *lunged,* shoving it back from the corps-a-corps. That gained me a few moments and freed my sword. I gulped down air, almost backed into the corner next to the fireplace. If it came for me again what was I going to—

The imp chittered at me—and squealed, black blood exploding as Japhrimel's claws tore through its belly from the back, twisting up through its chest. He carved through demon flesh as if it was water, finishing with a single swipe that opened the thing's throat. Its squeal died on a burbling rush of black blood. Japhrimel flicked his fingers and the imp turned into ash, white flame flickering through it in a strange veined pattern before it exploded in a cloud of grit. "Dante?"

He sounded furiously, coldly calm. I'd never seen such a casual use of Power from him before. The grit sifted to the floor in with a soft pattering sound.

"I'm good." My breath came harsh and tearing in my throat. The humans had been tricked out for serious night work—the nightvision goggles alone were worth a fortune. Not to mention the augments. "Any more?"

"Downstairs." He straightened, impeccable, hands clasped behind his back again. His eyes glowed, not an inky hair out of place. I swallowed. I could never be prepared for how spookily *fast* he moved; my own speed was scary enough, but his was flat-out terrifying.

I was suddenly, appallingly, completely glad he was on my side.

"There's one wounded." I pointed out into the hall. My breath came fast but even, and I holstered my left-hand gun. Slid my sword back into its sheath. There was a *lot* of that fine, sparkling ash on the floor, swirling through the air. Just how many imps had come? None were left. "I just shot him once. Question him?"

"No need, the imps told me everything I need to know. Quickly. Out."

I didn't stop to argue. Ran for the window, wrenched it open—

—and ducked back as bullets chewed at the wooden frame, splintering the glass. Cursed savagely, Japhrimel's hand closing around my arm.

"This way."

Now this is more like it. I can see a demon doing this—but smash-

ing me with a hover? No. "What did the imps tell you?" Dappled green light flared from my wristcuff, I held it up as Japhrimel pulled me out the shattered door, turning right, stepping over the moaning, bleeding man I'd shot. Japh didn't quite drag me down the hall, but I had a hard time keeping up with him. His hand had turned to iron on my arm; he didn't hurt me but I couldn't have broken free if I'd tried.

"Enough that I see the wisdom of leaving this place *now*," Japhrimel said. "Later, Dante. For right now, let us go."

He didn't have to tell me again.

Up the stairs. I heard something—thundering footsteps. Claws *skritching* against wood, a chilling glassy squeal. It didn't sound human, whatever it was. Memory replayed itself, matched the sound— I'd heard it in the abandoned building, only that time it had been a sort of snarl. What was chasing us? More imps? But they didn't sound scratchy, they sounded soft, padding, and almost wet, like strangling fingers in the dark.

One flight. Two. Three. It was getting closer, smashing against walls. It sounded *big,* and I smelled heat. Tang of smoke against my nostrils. The wristcuff squeezed my left arm, a terrible wrenching pain that made me gasp; the mark on my left shoulder flared in response. Japhrimel's face was set, his eyes glowing so fiercely they cast shadows under his cheekbones, spots of green light flickering as he checked each hall.

Sixth floor. No more stairs, he whirled and headed down the hall, his boots soundless against threadbare carpet. I was too busy trying to keep up to ask him what the hell he was doing. I certainly hoped he had an idea, at least, because I was fresh out. He kicked another door open, my nose filling with the smell of dust and human desperation. I caught a quick flash of a room—done in green instead of red, a cheap table and four chairs, the remains of takeout cartons scattered on said table—before he pivoted and aimed for the window. "Brace yourself."

I grabbed his shoulder, his other arm circled around me. *What do you mean, brace myself?*

He launched us both out the window, plasglass shattering and bullets screaming past. Fire dug into my right shoulder, and Japhrimel twisted, Power burning incandescent in the darkness. Clattering gunfire, a yell from high up on my left, the sound of a falling body. Whoever the sniper had been he was now dead—Japhrimel had shot him.

Anubis, this is going to hurt.

Impact. Too soon, I wasn't ready, the breath driven out of my lungs in a long howling gasp. Japhrimel hauled me up, his fingers slipping in black blood dripping down my right shoulder. Orange city-light glinted off the gun in his hand. My breath plumed in the chilly air. Desultory rain steamed as it met Japhrimel's aura. He literally *burned* with a mantle of Power so intense it was like looking into a furnace of black diamond flames. I had to blink fiercely to screen out my otherSight and see the real world.

It wasn't the street below, but another rooftop. He finished pulling me to my feet as easily as I might have picked up a piece of paper. *Well, that was wonderful; can't wait to do that again; gods, what* was *that thing?*

I gasped again, this time dragging a breath in as the hurt in my shoulder sealed itself away. Fine drizzling mist kissed my cheeks. "*Sekhmet sa'es,*" I hissed. "Warn me next time, will—"

He pushed me behind him so hard I skidded across concrete roof-top, my back slamming into a climate-control unit. I found myself squeezed between him and the unit's plasteel side. He went suddenly motionless, both arms up, two shiny silver guns in his hands. His aura spread over me, hazing and sinking in through my skin. I blinked furiously, trying to *see*, relieved when otherSight retreated. He was damn near blinding me with that trick.

I swallowed. He so rarely used a weapon it was almost shocking. If he had both guns out like this instead of one, it was *bad.*

"Dante," he said quietly, "if I tell you to, *run* down the fire escape on the other side of the roof. Do you understand?"

"What is it?" I whispered. "It didn't sound like an imp."

"It is not an imp." His voice was so chill and sharp I could feel cold air touch my cheek. "As you love life, *hedaira*, do as I tell you this once. Will you?"

I gulped down another breath, lungs burning. My pulse pounded in my throat. "What is it?" *It doesn't hurt to ask, does it?*

"Hellhound." Steam rose, twisted into angular shapes. "Be still, now."

Hellhound? That doesn't sound good. That doesn't sound good at all. I froze, barely even breathing. Watched the gaping hole in the building we'd just burst out from. The moisture wasn't even enough to qualify as rain, more like a heavy mist, tapering off. It steamed away from Japhrimel's aura, and I wondered why I felt so cold. "They're going to try to flank us," I whispered. "Japhrimel—"

It bulleted out from the hole in the side of the hotel, a low, stream-lined lethal shape. I forgot about being quiet and screamed, the mark on my shoulder squeezing, my bloodslick right hand closing around my swordhilt. Japhrimel moved forward, the guns speaking in his hands, fire puffed out in small bursts from the side of the building as he tracked it. It moved with the same eerie speed he did, its eyes glowing unholy crimson. My sword sang free of its sheath. Blue fire crested, spilled free of the blade, the steel's heart flamed white.

It was shaped like a leaner version of a werecain, low and four-legged with hulking shoulders and long claws that snick-snacked as it landed on the rooftop and snarled. It was made of *blackness,* a dark so deep and fiery it burned. A vapor trail followed, its heat scorching the water in the air.

So this was a hellhound. None of the Magi texts had ever mentioned anything *close* to it.

I'm going to have to tell the Magi a thing or two. Just as soon as I get out of this alive.

Teeth made of obsidian snapped, Japhrimel faded aside; he shot it twice. Watching him fight was always strange, he moved with such speed and precision it was impossible not to be impressed. He kicked the hellhound, a sound like a watermelon dropped on a scorching-hot sidewalk. It howled, a long screeching sound, and its eyes swept across the roof, locking on me.

My sword flamed blue-white, etching shadows on the roof. My rings sparked, a cascade of gold; the emerald on my cheek burned.

The hellhound let out an amazing screeching yowl. Its claws scrabbled.

Japhrimel hit it from the side again, his booted feet connecting solidly. It rolled, twisted on itself, and streaked for me.

"Dante! Go!" Japhrimel bolted after it.

I set my feet in the concrete, my sword dipping, sudden knowledge flaring under my skin. I would *not* run, I would *not* let him face this thing on his own, no matter how good or inhumanly hard to kill he was. *"Anubis!"* I screamed, my cheek suddenly flaming with pain as the emerald answered, I leapt forward—

—and was knocked aside by a solid weight slamming into me, rolling in a tumbling mess of arms and legs, me trying to keep my sword from splitting my own flesh. I hurled a curse at whoever had hit me, got an accidental elbow in the face—a brief, amazing starry jolt of pain.

The hellhound streaked through where I had been standing, crashing into the casing. Sparks flew, hissing steam as the climate control circuits blew. Blue-white sparks fountained up. I cried out, throwing up a hand to shield my eyes, the light searing through dark-adapted pupils. Heard more snarls, more claws, and a curse in the spiky hurtful language of demons that made my blood run cold.

McKinley rolled free, gaining his feet in one fluid movement, I spat blood. Shook the dazing impact out of my head. There was a massive crunching sound, another scrabble of claws. *Sekhmet sa'es, it sounds like more than one of them, oh please, Japh, don't get hurt, I'm on my way—*

McKinley, dark eyes blazing, held up his left hand. The oddly metallic coating on it sparkled like quicksilver. "Come on," he said, low and taut. "Come *on!*"

Who the hell is he talking to, me or the hellhound?

The hellhound snarled—and Japhrimel, his coat flaring behind him, shot it twice in the head. Japh descended on the thing. I levered myself painfully up, watching as he moved gracefully, avoiding the thing's dying clawswipe as he tore the life out of it. Then he gained his feet, black blood smoking from his hands, and spat a single word I covered my ears against, the hilt of my sword digging into my temple. There was another low slumped shape—a second hellhound, lying twisted and broken on the rooftop. *Where the hell did that one come from? Anubis et'her ka,* two *of those things?*

The bodies twitched, convulsed, and began to rot right in front of me. Noisome fluid gushed out of slack-jawed mouths, streaming between the sharp glassy teeth. The smell smacked into me, I took two steps back, cement gritty under my boots. They were literally melting in front of my eyes.

I swiped at my face with my free hand. Blood from my nose crackled as I scrubbed it away, resheathed my sword. Japhrimel looked at me.

"Are you hurt?" His voice was so cold I half expected the foggy air to freeze between us despite the steam wreathing him, twisting into angular shapes like spiked demon runes. I gasped, unable to catch my breath, looking down at myself. I didn't *think* I was hurt.

"N-no." I glanced at McKinley, who had a gun out and trained on the closest body as it rotted. His black eyes blazed, and the metallic coating on his hand shifted a little, settling back into his skin. *Where the hell did he come from?* "Where did you come fr—"

"Time to go," McKinley said. "Transport's waiting. There are more on the way."

"Human, or otherwise?" Japhrimel's eyes swept the roof. Where had the second hellhound come from? They were so goddamn *fast*.

"Yes." McKinley's dark eyes flicked over me once. He went back to watching the hellhound's bubbling body. "My lord?"

"Come." Japhrimel arrived at my side, grabbed my arm, and gave me a once-over, nodded briefly to himself. "Leave it, McKinley. It's dead."

The Hellesvront agent holstered his gun. "Fire escape." He pointed.

"I told you to run." Japhrimel's voice was the color of steel. His eyes were furious, and his mouth a thin line. The mark on my shoulder turned hot, melting into my skin.

"I couldn't leave you to face that thing alone." I yanked my arm free of his hold. He let me, his fingers opening as if I'd struck him. "Let's go."

CHAPTER 30

I closed my eyes, leaning against Japhrimel's side. Subway lights flickered as the hovertrain tore down reactive-greased tracks. McKinley watched the interior of the car from where he slumped in a seat, scowling. His crow-black hair was wildly mussed. We were alone on a New Prague subway train, fluorescent light buzzing overhead.

Japhrimel pressed his lips to my temple. He hadn't spoken, guiding us down through subway tunnels and finally onto this train. McKinley said nothing, too. I shuddered again, Japh's arm tightened around me, another wash of Power burning through my nerves as my eyes flew open. It was pleasant, and it kept me out of shock—but I was beginning to wonder if Japhrimel even realized he was flooding me with Power. It was an uncomfortable thought.

"That's not something I ever want to do again," I whispered finally. *Where did the second one come from? I didn't even see it. Gods.*

He kissed my temple again. "I told you to go. McKinley was

waiting to cover your retreat while I dealt with the hellhounds," he murmured.

Goddammit. Just like a demon. "That was awful." I contented myself with a noncommittal reply for maybe the first time in my life.

"I prize you, my curious. I would not lose you." He spoke this into my hair, his breath scorching-hot.

"You won't." I tightened my right arm around him, my left hand aching as it squeezed the scabbard. "You killed it. Both of them."

"Hellhounds for a *hedaira*. They could have killed you." He sounded like he was just realizing it. I leaned into him a little more, suddenly very, very glad he'd found me. I had been extremely lucky not to run across any of those things on my lonesome.

"You were there. So everything's okay." *I sound like a drippy heroine on a holovid. But it's true.*

He wasn't mollified. "If we face another, you *must* do as I say. Do you understand me?"

The train rocked, bulleting through the underground tunnels. McKinley closed his eyes. He didn't look sleepy. Maybe he was giving us some privacy. Polite of him. I still had no idea what the hell he was, or how he had appeared out of nowhere and knocked me down—or why, when I looked at him, I felt the rasp of irritation and distaste rise under my breastbone. I just instinctively didn't like him.

"Dante? If we face another hellhound, you must do as I tell you." Japh repeated it slowly, as if I was an idiot.

I suppressed another flare of irritation with a healthy dose of fear. The thought of Japhrimel taking on those things alone chilled me. Even though I knew he was capable and was glad he was there... still. "I'm not going to abandon you," I said finally. "Don't ask me to do that."

"You *must* live, Dante. While you live, I live." He stopped abruptly, as if he'd intended to say more and changed his mind.

"If I run, another one of those things might be lying in wait. We've got a better chance if we stick together." I didn't think he'd go for it, but he sighed, his face still in my hair. It was comforting, I decided, my body beginning to finally believe I was still alive. My shoulders went loose, thankfully. I blew out a long breath, leaning into the comfort of Japhrimel's warmth. I was alive, we were relatively safe, it was time to ask a few questions. "You said the imps told you something. What?"

"The hellhound might be Velokel's trick. He is the Hunter, and rode with hounds when your kind was not even a dream in the Prince's agile brain." Japh paused as the train bulleted around a bend. I felt his attention flare, scanning our surroundings. Finally, satisfied, he continued. "We may not be the only hunters the Prince has contracted. This was...not unexpected, but something I thought unlikely."

I absorbed this, worked it around inside my head, and tested it against the flash of insight I'd had while studying the magscan maps. It was worth saying out loud, at least. "The Hunter, right? He might be looking to take me out first, and you think Lucifer may have sent someone else too." I worried gently at my lower lip with my teeth. "All right. I've got an idea."

"Save me from your ideas, my curious. What is it?"

I wanted to look up at his face, but his arm was like a steel bar. The tension thrumming through him warned me; I didn't struggle. Instead, I rubbed my cheek against his shoulder. *Calm down, Japh. You scare me when you're like this.* "Try this hover for float, Japh. Lucifer wants these demons dead — but he doesn't trust either of us, especially after you pull your stunt. So what does he do? He smacks me with a few hovers and an imp, making as much noise as possible to distract and draw out whatever demon is around; then he sends another group of hunters in to do the real dirty work. Only this Velokel is a few steps ahead of Lucifer, shows up in New Prague just after me — because I've made a hell of a lot of racket with the imp on the hovertrain — and he takes to the underground, because the earth will hide him better than the red-light district. Lucas had his hidey-hole underground, there's a *reason.* Lucifer never said anything about us being the *only* ones after these demons, and he may have even wanted to clean us up as loose ends." *Though that wouldn't explain why he gave you back a demon's Power. Unless that doesn't matter to him, unless he can easily take it away or kill you anyway.*

My imagination just worked too goddamn well when it came to the possible perfidy of the Prince of Hell. Japhrimel was silent. His thumb stroked my arm.

"Well?" I persisted, as an automated voice speaking Czechi blared from the loudspeaker grilles. We were coming up to a stop. "What do you think?"

"It explains much of the chain of events. And yet...."

Right. And yet. I'm missing some crucial piece, a piece you probably have. Help me out here, okay? "It makes sense to paint a big target on my back and send me out. The demon in that building called me *Right Hand*. Even if he mistook me for you because we smell alike, how could he know you were working for Lucifer again so soon? Unless Lucifer made a *point* of leaking the information. If I was him, looking to get rid of me in the most efficient way possible and still use me for maximum benefit, that's what *I'd* do." *But I'm not Lucifer. I wouldn't ever do this to someone, use them in a trap to catch a bigger predator.*

"Indeed." He sounded grudgingly admiring. The train began to slow, resistance clamping down. I leaned into him. He kissed my temple again. "I would not want to be your enemy, *hedaira*."

"Huh." I manfully restrained from pointing out that he'd probably thought of all this before me. "Good. I'd hate to have to hunt you down."

McKinley swung up to his feet. Japhrimel's arm loosened on me. I breathed in deeply, shaking my hair back. I was almost beginning to feel like I'd survived again.

"There will never be a need." Japhrimel managed to sound, of all things, amused. He braced me as the train slid to a stop. McKinley swung out the door as soon as it opened, scanning the station.

Fluorescent light ran wetly over pre-Hegemony yellow tile, and a framed picture of a jowly, scowling man with a thick black moustache was set behind plasglass. Some kind of muckey-muck who had negotiated the Freetown's charter, probably. Permaspray graffiti tangled over tiles that hadn't been sonicwashed on the last maintenance run-through. The station was deserted; I had little idea of where I was, since this was underground. "Where are we?"

"The outskirt, near Ruzyne Transport," McKinley said, blinking his black eyes once. "I don't think we were followed."

I rolled my shoulders back, checking my rig. It was good gear, and had just come through its first engagement with flying colors. "I don't think so either. Where do we meet the others?"

Japhrimel shrugged. I looked up at his face, noted that he had a vertical line between his dark winged eyebrows. When he did that, pulling the corners of his mouth down, he looked even more grim and saturnine. He didn't immediately answer me.

Finally, he sighed. "Vann will take the others from the city. From here, the hunt is mine."

I felt my own eyebrows rising. "Um, hello?" I snapped my fingers in front of his face. McKinley frankly stared, his jaw dropping; it was the first sign of surprise I'd ever seen from him. "Excuse me, but I believe *I* was contracted for this hunt, Japh." A new thought struck me, one so terrible I almost choked.

My heart began to pound as I stared up at him, my hand frozen in midair. "They were simply bait, you wanted the Magi to draw out the demon so you could see it." I couldn't believe I had been so blind. "You're not surprised by any of this. You wanted me to go with the others so they could drag me clear of the blast zone, and you wanted me to run to McKinley so he could.... You arrogant *bastard*." My stomach flipped over. No wonder Bella had looked so frightened, she'd figured out she and her partner were bait and my assumption that they were hunters instead of support staff must have scared her silly.

"I am concerned more with your safety than your wounded pride." He caught my hand in his, pushed it down to my side. "It makes no difference. I prefer you where I can see the mischief you intend, anyway. I expected you would not accede."

"I have *so* many problems with this," I muttered. *Would it kill you to share a little information with me? And I will not be a party to using other people as a lure, Japhrimel. I won't do it.*

"I counsel you to caution." His eyes blazed. "I am no longer your familiar, I am your Fallen—not bound to obey, only to protect. You would do well to be silent, my temper wears thin."

I closed my eyes and tipped my head back, feeling my jaw work as I struggled to bite back the words rising toward the surface. When I was fairly sure I had my *own* temper under control I gave him a level glare, bringing my chin back down and half-lidding my eyes. "I *suggest* you go a little easier on the autocracy, Japhrimel. I don't like being ordered around and kept in the dark. What do you think I am, some kind of idiot you can just—"

I barely even saw him move. The next thing I knew, I was pinned against the tiled wall, his fingers twisted in my rig and my feet a good half-meter in the air. He held me up by the leather straps one-handed, as negligently as a mama cat might dangle a kitten, his arm fully extended, his lips pulled back from his teeth and his eyes green infernos. I kicked, struggling, my fingers sinking into his hand; he simply shook me, my head bouncing. He gauged it carefully—my skull didn't hit the tile.

Then he sighed, fluorescent light running through the inky darkness of his hair. I couldn't even grab for my swordhilt, I was too busy sinking my right-hand fingers into his hand, trying fruitlessly to get him to let *go.*

"I have been endlessly patient with you," he said softly, each word crisp and distinct, "but we cannot have any more of this. If you will not do as I ask without question, I will shackle you, give you to McKinley, and continue alone." He didn't even shift his weight as I kicked again, somehow he avoided the strike without moving, his eyes never leaving mine. "There is something in this game I do not understand, and until I understand fully I will not allow further disobedience. The Prince means to kill you with this errand despite his oath, and someone has almost succeeded in his desires twice already. I am *through* with playing. Do as I ask, and you can force a penance from me later at your leisure. But for the next seven years, *hedaira,* you are under my guard. Make it easier for both of us, and simply *obey.*"

"*Stop it!*" My voice bounced off the tiles, smashed and echoed, the straps of my rig dug into my flesh. "Goddammit, Japhrimel, *stop it you're scaring me!*"

He shook me once more, maybe just to drive home how he could keep me if he wanted to, and dropped me. I landed hard, the shock jolting from my heels all the way up to my neck. I rubbed at my sternum where his knuckles had pressed, rubbed it and rubbed it. Had I been human, I'd have been bruised. *This puts a whole different complexion on things.* My eyes instinctively flicked toward the stairs leading to the surface. If I—

He caught my chin, cupping delicately, his fingers gentle but iron-hard. I caught a flash of McKinley standing with his arms folded, a study in disinterest though his eyes had a gleam I didn't like. "Don't even think of it." Japhrimel's tone was oddly tender. "It is for your own good, my curious. You *will* do as I say."

I jerked my chin free of his hand. "You didn't have to do that." My pulse beat high and frantic in my throat, and I sounded breathless even to myself. I pushed myself back, the tiled wall meeting me with a thump. He stayed where he was. The snarl on his face was gone as if it had never existed. My head was full of rushing noise; the mark on my shoulder flared with heat sinking all the way down through my chest, spilling through my bones.

He was still for a long moment, his face expressionless. He moved as if he would touch me, but I flinched back from him, the tip of my scabbard striking the tiled wall, scratching along like a blunt claw.

My right hand closed around the hilt, and I stared at him as if he was a stranger, my mouth suddenly dry and the noise inside my head much worse.

Japhrimel stopped. His eyes dropped, taking in my stance and my white-knuckled hand on the hilt. "I am careful with you," he said, softly, still in that oddly intimate tone, the one that made him sound more horribly human. "I am so very careful. Can you imagine what would happen, were you caught by a demon who did not care for you?"

I swallowed dryly. It was one thing to be afraid he would use his strength and speed to force me into whatever he wanted. It was a completely different thing to have him actually *do* it. My chest ached. My cheek stung as the emerald spat a single glowing spark; my rings spiked and swirled with Power. "You shouldn't have done that," I told him, numbly.

"I will do what is necessary to protect you. Have I not proved it?"

"You shouldn't have done that." I could think of nothing else. Tears rose behind my eyes, a hot blurring weight of water. I swallowed them, set my jaw.

He sighed, shaking his head, the fluorescent light running wetly over his hair and the long fluid severe lines of his coat. His aura closed around me, a touch I tried to push away, couldn't. "This serves no purpose."

"How could you?" I whispered, rubbing at my sternum again. He hadn't hurt me, not physically, not yet. But I still rubbed at the spot where his knuckles had pressed. "How could you do this to me?"

"I do what I must." He grabbed my arm and dragged me away from the wall. "Come. We have a transport to catch."

Oh, gods. Anubis, help me. "Where are we going?" I could barely force the words out through numb, shocked lips. I didn't precisely fight him, but I did resist just enough to make him work for it. He cast me one extraordinarily green glance, but it was McKinley who answered.

"Another Freetown," he said, grinning. I didn't like that grin — it was too wide, too white, and too satisfied with current events. McKinley looked very happy to see me put in my place. "The Sarajevo DMZ."

Sarajevo? But why? They don't allow humans in there.

I could have dug my heels in and made him carry me, but the thought made me feel sick. I felt nothing more, except maybe a disbelief so huge it swallowed me whole, a disbelief only broken by a single phrase caroling through my head. *How could you, Japhrimel? How could you?* And under that, an even simpler phrase, repeating over and over again.

I trusted you.

CHAPTER 31

New Prague had a transport dock—Ruzyne—on the outskirts. Japhrimel simply walked through security. McKinley and I did the same, and I found myself ushered aboard a sleek gleaming-black hover. My skin roughened—I hadn't had much luck with hovers lately. I couldn't even bolt for freedom on the dock—McKinley led us, and Japhrimel followed me, one hand on my shoulder. Exquisitely gentle, his thumb occasionally stroking my nape, but I'd just gotten an object lesson in how fast he was when he wasn't playing nice. It would be ridiculous to try to escape him.

Besides, if there were more hellhounds out there, I didn't stand much of a chance anyway.

I dropped into low black pleather seat, laid my katana across my knees, and proceeded to stare out the window at the lights of New Prague. No wonder Bella and Ogami had been frightened. No wonder Japhrimel hadn't seemed worried with the group's progress— he'd just been waiting for the enemy to show himself. Just playing patty-cake with me in the meanwhile, callously using the humans as bait. The fact that he'd sent them out with Vann and Tiens didn't excuse the pitilessness of the action. No harm done, but still.

I'd been a *part* of it. He'd made me a part of it. If it had gone bad, I would have been partly responsible.

Now I also knew why he'd been so damn close-mouthed about the Fallen. If I'd had any intimation that he was no longer bound by the rules of a demon familiar, I might have dug my heels in a little more and *demanded* he tell me everything. If I'd had any *warning*.

I hadn't had any warning. I hadn't even known the Devil was asking for me, hadn't even had a clue. Japhrimel hadn't acted guilty, or as if he was hiding *anything*, he had spent every waking moment with me. That led me to an uncomfortable wondering about just how often I'd been left alone while I slept, lulled into defenseless uncon-sciousness and abandoned while Japhrimel met with Lucifer. It could have happened easily. I'd *trusted* him.

He'd changed plans midstroke, bargained with Lucifer for a demon's Power, and dumped me in the hover to be flown home just like a kid. *Never mind about Dante, she's so easily led. So easily manipulated. Only a human, after all.*

I closed my eyes, searching for calm and an idea. Neither came.

McKinley took the hover's controls while he held a murmured conference with Japhrimel. I shut my eyes, opened them again, star-ing at the lights. Floating streams of hovertraffic threaded between the glowing cubes of high-rises.

The nagging sense of something wrong had gone away. Some-thing hadn't jelled, hadn't seemed right—and this was why. Japh had never had any intention of letting me do what Lucifer's Right Hand was supposed to do.

The thought that I wouldn't have minded playing second fiddle on a hunt like this if he'd just *explained* to me what was going on wasn't very comforting either. Demons were nasty, tricky, and mostly too strong and fast for even a *hedaira*. Never mind that I'd killed an imp. If it hadn't been for the reactive paint things might have been very different indeed. And the hellhounds...my skin chilled, roughened into actual goosebumps. I most definitely wouldn't mind backup when facing *them*.

Most chilling of all was the logical extension to my line of thought—Lucifer had been angling to snare Japhrimel, use me for bait or distraction, and possibly kill Japh all along. If by some mira-cle we succeeded, we would still have to deal with the machinations of the Prince of Hell. Chances were if this plan failed, there would be another one. And possibly another after that.

I didn't think the Devil believed in giving up easily.

Japhrimel lowered himself into the seat opposite me. I stared out the window, my fingernails tapping at the hilt. He'd been holding back while sparring with me the whole time. The *whole time*. He'd even let me cut him once or twice.

Just to make me feel better?

Silence. Hoverwhine settled into my back teeth. A lump rose in my throat, I pushed it down. My sternum hurt, but that was because I kept rubbing it, reflexively, unconsciously.

He stirred, went still, and moved slightly again.

As if expecting me to say something.

I held my tongue. I was tempted to scream. Should have screamed. Should have busted out the hover windows and thrown myself down. Gone limp. Nonviolent resistance. *Something.*

Anything instead of just sitting there.

What you cannot escape, you must fight; what you cannot fight, you must endure. An old lesson, my first true life lesson—but I wasn't enduring. I was simply unable to *do* anything. I was in a glass ball of calm, a type of shock insulating me from the world. He had used his strength on me, something I'd thought he'd never do. He was going to force me to do what he wanted. I was trapped, by the very last person I'd expected to trap me.

"I do not require you to forgive me, or to understand," he said finally. "I demand only your cooperation, which I will get by any means necessary."

"You should have told me." Point for him, he'd made me talk. I didn't recognize my own voice—none of my usual half-whispering. I said it as if I was a normal discussing dinner plans, the velvet weight of demon beauty in my voice taunting me. "I asked you. You should have *told* me all of this."

"You would not have agreed to any of it." Quiet, silken. "Especially my request for you to retreat while I deal with things beyond your strength."

Gods damn you. You might be right. "We'll never know now, will we."

"Perhaps not." A small tender smile. I could barely stand to see that expression on his face, his eyes softening and his mouth curving. Didn't he understand what he'd just *done* to me?

I couldn't help myself. "I could really hate you for this." *You asked me to trust you, I did, and this is what I get? You hurt me, hold me up against a w-wall*—I could still feel the casual strength in his hand as he held me helpless, my legs dangling, his knuckles digging into my chest.

"You will outgrow that." He still smiled, damn him.

I don't think I will. I shut my eyes again, closing him out. The hover banked, my stomach flipped. "You shouldn't have done it. You shouldn't have done that to me." *I sound like a broken holodisc player. Come on, Dante. Snap out of it.*

"I will do what I must. I am your Fallen." He didn't sound contrite in the least.

That would mean something to me if you hadn't just held me up against the wall and admitted lying to me. "I only have your word for that." It wasn't true—I had Lucifer's word as well as my own experience. But if I couldn't hurt him with steel, all I had left were words. The darkness behind my eyelids was not comforting, I could still see him, the black diamond flames that meant *demon*.

Was it just me, or did he seem to pause uncertainly? "I only wish to keep you safe. You are fragile, Dante, for all that I have given you a share of my strength."

I'm strong enough for some things, Japh. Go away. "Leave me alone."

"I will not." Flat, utter negation. I had rarely heard him sound less ironic and more serious.

"I mean it, Tierce Japhrimel. Leave me alone. Go finish your goddamn hunt and play patty-cake with Lucifer." I wanted to pull my knees up, curl into a ball, and wait for the tearing pain under my breastbone to go away. I didn't think it would go soon, but I needed to find a nice dark quiet place to hide in for a little while. "I want to go home."

Wherever that is. The whine of hover transport settled in my back teeth. My stomach roiled. I hadn't felt this unsteady, this *defenseless,* since...since when?

Since I'd been about twelve, that's when. My twelfth year, when the man who had raised me since infancy had been knifed by a Chill junkie. Losing Lewis had left me adrift in a world too big for me, and I felt the same way now, my breath choked and my fingers and toes cold as if I'd just gone treading into the hall of Death, my skin far too sensitive for the brutality of the world.

I felt very, very small.

Of course, he knew the thing to say that would hurt me the most. "Do you have a home, Dante?"

I hunched my shoulders. *Saint City's close enough. That's where I lived most of my life before you showed up to ruin it. Ruin everything. Dragged me into Hell, turned me into an almost-demon, died and left me alone, come back and finished off by ... by ...* I couldn't finish the thought. Still felt the tile, cold and hard against my back, and his fingers gone hard instead of caressing. *I thought you were my home, Japh.*

My skin crawled. I'd shared my body with him, let him into private corners of myself I had let no other lover access. Even Doreen, who had taught me to have a fierce pride in my body and its needs again, her gentleness opening up whole new worlds to me.

Even Jace.

The thought of Jace made the glass ball of calm numbness closed around me crack a little. I set my jaw, determined not to break.

I will not break. My teeth ground together, my hands tightened on my sword, my emerald spat a single defiant spark.

He sighed again. "Our legends warn of the price of becoming *A'nankhimel.* I cannot be human, Dante, not even for you. Can you not understand?"

What was it in his voice that hurt so badly? Pleading. He was definitely pleading.

Fury rose inside me, my right hand curling around my swordhilt. My eyes flew open. He'd just held me up against the wall of a New Prague subway station, and he wanted me to *understand*? "Understand you? I thought I did! I thought I—I thought *you*—" I seemed to lose all capability of speech, though I didn't splutter. It was close, though.

He nodded, leaning forward, elbows braced on his knees, fingers steepled together. "Rage at me, Dante. Be angry. Extract your vengeance later; I will allow it. As long as you will have me and after, I am yours. There is no escaping it, not now."

I shook my head, as if shaking away water. "I would have done anything you asked if you were just *honest* with me," I said miserably, tears welling up. I hated myself for crying. I hadn't cried through the hell of Rigger Hall, I had rarely cried afterward. It was the tone he used, I think, the gentle tone my body responded to. More than the softness in his voice was the betrayal. It was the betrayal that hurt the most.

Or was it the softness? I couldn't tell. I found myself rubbing at my sternum again, my knuckles scraping against my shirt under the diagonal leather strap of my rig. *I thought I knew you.* The lump in my throat swelled bigger each passing second, as if I was trapped in a windowless room.

"You are still in the habit of being human, Dante. It will take time." He didn't even sound sorry. At least when a *human* guy beat his girlfriend up, he makes a show of being contrite afterwards.

A hot tear rolled down my cheek. I couldn't even *fight* him, he was too strong. "I could hate you," I whispered.

"I warned you that you would. But you will outgrow that too."

I glared at him. *Jackshit I'm going to outgrow hating you. How could you, Japhrimel?* My eyes narrowed slightly, I dropped my right hand with an effort, tapped my swordhilt. Said nothing.

"You are contracted for seven years to the Prince. I will make sure you survive them. If I must chain you to my side I will." His jaw set and his eyes glowed. I believed him.

Oh, I'll survive all right. I'm good at surviving. And if I die I have nothing to fear, my god will take me. Maybe you won't follow me there.

I closed my eyes again. Leaned my head against the back of the seat. It was actually very comfortable. Nothing but the best for the Devil's henchmen.

"You do not have to forgive me," he repeated. "But I *will* have your cooperation."

"You know," I said, keeping my voice level, "you could really teach the Devil a thing or two." The blackness behind my eyelids was tempting. Unfortunately, I could still see him, the tightly controlled black-diamond flames of his aura, still reaching out to enfold me, the mark on my shoulder burning softly, Power spreading down my skin like warm oil. Soothing, like fingers stroking my skin, working out the knots in my muscles, easing away tension.

There was a faint rustle as if he'd moved, his coat shifting with him. "I am the lesser evil, *hedaira*. Remember that."

There was nothing I could say. If it was either the Devil or Japhrimel, where did that leave me?

Screwed, that's where. Painted into a corner by a demon.

Again.

CHAPTER 32

Demilitarized Sarajevo is still almost-contested territory. It took two Nichtvren warlords and a whole cadre—seven Packs—of werecain to restore order after the nightmare of genocide following the Seventy Days War. Nowadays, it's the kind of place where even psion bounty hunters don't go—because human bounties don't either.

The northern half of the city is the Demilitarized Zone itself, where most nonhuman species have their enclaves; the southern half is patrolled by werecain whose only boss is the Master of the territory, a Nichtvren named Leonidas who was the final winner of the scramble for power. It's one of the four nonhuman Freetown territories in the world, a zone from the Adriatic to the forward border of Putchkin Austrio-Hungaro, bordered on the south by Hegemony Graecia. The last humans fled after the final Serbian uprising was put down by Leonidas and a werecain alpha named Masud about a century after the War, and the Hegemony and Putchkin negotiated absorbing the ethnic minorities and resettling them in the cultural areas that most closely resembled their former home. Linguists and culture-historians were busy for years sorting the tangles out.

Leonidas, probably understanding that even a Nichtvren can't argue with joint Hegemony-Putchkin thermonuclear attack, made sure most of the surviving humans were released unscathed.

A few humans tried to go back, but nobody ever heard from them again. For a while there was a movement to reclaim the territory, especially the psychic whirlpool of the Blackbird Fields, but in the end the Nichtvren paid off whoever they had to and the whole issue became a moot point. Any human dumb enough to go into DMZ Sarajevo was either dead or Turned within twenty-four hours—and that went for psions too. Even accredited psions with combat training and bounties under their belt don't go there.

There are rumors, of course, of people desperate enough to go into Sarajevo and bargain to be Turned. There are also rumors of indentured servants and slave trading—but those are only whispered in dark corners. The Hegemony and Putchkin largely paid very little attention as long as Leonidas kept order and nothing thermonuclear was smuggled out of the territory.

I'm actually in Sarajevo, I thought with dazed wonder, looking out the hover window.

"We've got clearance." McKinley looked back over his shoulder. "They'll meet us at the dock."

Japhrimel merely nodded. He had sat there the entire flight, watching me. After a while I had dropped all pretense of sleeping and instead had studied the darkness outside slowly falling under the hover. A faint grayness had begun in the east, the herald of dawn. I saw fewer lights than most cities, slices of complete darkness in certain districts north of the river, lots of neon as we banked over the DMZ, McKinley piloting the hover with a sure, deft touch.

"My lord?" McKinley asked.

Japhrimel finally stirred, swinging the seat to look toward the front of the hover. "Yes?"

"Is she...." It sounded like he couldn't find a polite way to phrase it. What was he asking? If I'd been taught my place yet? If I was all right? If I was still alive? Why the fuck should he care?

"That is not your concern." Nothing shaded Japhrimel's voice except perhaps a faint weariness.

"Yessir." McKinley turned back to the front. After a few moments, I saw the console begin to flash as a hoverdock AI took over. McKinley eased himself out of the seat and stretched, joints popping. The metallic coating on his left hand shone dully with reflected light.

He didn't look at me. I was happy about that.

Japhrimel turned back to me. "Your cooperation, Dante. I want your word on it."

That managed to wring a laugh out of me, a jagged sound that made the air shiver. "You sure you want to trust my word, demon?"

"You will give me little else." The mark burned on my shoulder, velvet flame coating my nerves. The sensation had once been pleasant. Comforting.

Now I hated it. The feeling of my skin crawling with loathing under the Power was new, interesting, and awful. It was the way I imagined an indentured servant would feel, helpless impotent loathing and rage. My sternum still throbbed with raw pain, maybe because I'd kept rubbing it, scrubbing it with my knuckles, trying to scour away the helpless feeling of being trapped and betrayed at once.

"I will make you pay for this," I whispered. My throat was full, my eyes hot and grainy. *You shouldn't have done that, Japhrimel.*

"No doubt. Your cooperation, Dante. Full and *complete* cooperation. Your word on it."

"Or what, you'll kill me?" I tried to make it sound like a challenge. "Hold me up against a wall again? Maybe you'll beat me up a little. Slap me around. Teach me my place."

A muscle in his sleek golden cheek twitched, but his voice was still soft and even. "I can think of more pleasant things to do with you, my curious. Your word."

I glared out the window, faintly surprised when the plasilica didn't crack. *You're going to regret this, you bastard.* "Fine. You have my word. I'll cooperate." *Cooperate with what and who, though? That's the question.*

He studied me. I let him have my profile, kept my gaze out the window. "You will cooperate with me for as long with our bargain with the Prince lasts."

"You get seven years from the day I negotiated with Lucifer," I returned tautly. *The first chance I have I'm ditching you, I can "cooperate" from anywhere in the world.*

The bravado was pure reflex, and I knew it. If I left him, how long would I last on my own?

"I have your word?" Damn him, he was pushing me. I could tell from the faint shadow of carefulness in his tone that he had probably gauged just how *far* he could push me without me snapping and trying to run him through.

If I did leap at him now, what would he do? Take my sword away? Cuff me with plasteel cuffs or the shackle of a demon's magick? *I am no longer your familiar; I am your Fallen. I am not bound to obey, only to protect.*

To a demon, "protection" might not mean what it meant to me. He was being careful, but he could force me to do just about anything. I had the same chance of escaping him as a stuffed and cuffed bounty has of escaping a good hunter.

In other words, no fucking chance at all unless I got a little creative and *very* lucky. But even if I managed to pull anything, what then? "I already said so." I bit off the end of the sentence. "Don't fucking push me."

McKinley didn't look at me, but he flinched. That was interesting. I had the not-so-comforting idea that the agent thought Japhrimel was still playing nice with me. Or that I was recklessly suicidal. Welcome irritation began to flow back into me like a tonic, giving me the strength to take a deep breath and measure Japhrimel with open eyes and defiantly lifted chin. *Even if you can force me to do anything you want, I'm still going to fight. I can make this difficult for you.*

Maybe he'd get tired of it after a while. I hoped so.

The hover descended. My ears used to pop every time a transport sank. Now I just felt a funny sinking sensation in my stomach. *Hedaira* don't usually throw up unless poisoned—I knew that much—but I was feeling pretty sick. It was anybody's guess whether that was from the hover or from recent events.

Japhrimel still wasn't done. "Be careful what you make of me."

As if I was somehow responsible for him treating me like this. As if it was *my* fault. Just because he was stronger than me didn't give him the right to do that to me, did it? I set my jaw, looked down at my sword. The thought — *did Jado give me a blade that could kill the Devil?* — circled through my brain.

Then, like a gift, an idea began to form.

Are you crazy? my practical, survival-oriented half screeched. *It doesn't matter if he's a goddamn demon, he's still your best chance of staying alive! What happens if you run across another hellhound?*

A deeper voice full of stubborn determination took shape in the middle of my chest, right under the scraped and throbbing spot between my breasts. *It doesn't matter. 'Tis better to die on your feet than live on your knees, Danny. Rigger Hall taught you that. Santino taught you that. Every goddamn thing in your life that tried to break you taught you that. If you don't fight this, you're going to lose all the goddamn self-respect you've ever earned.*

I looked up at Japhrimel. "You have no right to treat me like an indentured servant," I said softly, shaking my head. A tendril of ink-black hair fell in my face, I blew it away with a short sharp whistling breath. "Just because I'm human doesn't give you the right to manipulate me or scare me into doing what you want."

I rocked up to my feet and stalked toward the front of the hover, looking down at the control deck. It would have been satisfying to smash it — but instead, I simply stood there with my head down, looking out the window and scanning the dock we were headed for. Japhrimel said nothing. It was gratifying to get the last word, for once.

Nichtvren, clustered at one end. A couple of werecain hulking behind them. I marked one Master, a large geometrical stain of Power; several Acolytes with their own shields depending on the Master's like satellites, and a few human thralls. I suppose the thralls didn't quite qualify as human, but still... it gave me a pause to see them there.

McKinley glanced at me, his back set against the partition between the cockpit and the rest of the hover. I was close enough to slip a knife into him.

The temptation was almost overwhelming.

I said nothing while the hover docked, the AI landing us with a slight thump. I closed my eyes briefly, reaching out —

— and retreating back behind my own demon-strong shields. The air outside was alive with creeping Power, like the House of Pain back in Saint City. No wonder they didn't let humans in; this many paranormal species in a city that had been soaked with pain and suffering made for a charged psychic atmosphere.

Charged like a reaction fire. I winced, wishing I could stop thinking about reactive.

Okay, Dante. Imagine you're held by enemies and in DMZ Sarajevo. Keep on your toes, stay loose, and look out for opportunity. He can't pay attention to you every single moment of the goddamn day.

At least, I hoped he couldn't. All it would take was a momentary lapse of attention and I'd have a chance to at least make Japh work for it, if not escape outright.

The good news was, if I could by some miracle get away from Japhrimel, I might be able to find someplace to hide and try to come up with a half-assed plan that would leave me alive.

The bad news was, if I ran across another demon, or even another hellhound, I might end up dead anyway.

It was looking more and more likely all the time.

CHAPTER 33

The Nichtvren Master was none other than Leonidas himself, a spare, slim, blandly beautiful man only a little taller than me, with oily black hair elegantly corkscrewed and hanging down his back. He is the only person I've ever seen wear a microfiber toga with a broad purple stripe and sandals strapped to bare caramel-colored feet. One of his Acolytes held a parasol overhead. I was too busy checking out the lay of the land, so to speak, and so I missed most of the elegant bow he swept to Japhrimel.

His greeting, however, smacked me into full attention.

"Well. If it is not the Eldest Son and his beloved. Welcome to my humble city." He spoke, of all things, passable Merican—probably more because it was the language of trade than in deference to my limited linguistic capabilities. His voice was soft, smoothly accented, and carried enough Power to set off a plasgun charge. He wasn't as eerily, creepily Powerful as Nikolai, the Prime of Saint City.

But he was close.

Very close. Which was surprising, since by my guess, Leonidas was the older Nichtvren. Age usually, but not always, means power among them.

If I'd still been completely human, I would have been frantically searching for a wall to put my back to. As it was, I didn't reach for my swordhilt only because Japhrimel's left hand circled my right wrist, a casual movement as effective as a spun-steel manacle. My rings rang with light, though they didn't spark. I kept myself as tightly reined as a collared telepath, almost shaking with the urge to draw my sword.

Japhrimel nodded. The Nichtvren's Power was a candle flame next to the reactive glow of his, but I still felt more uneasy about the bloodsucker than I did about the demon.

Go figure. Though Japh was rapidly catching up, wasn't he? The raw spot on my chest twinged, the pain fading. I wanted to rub at it again, quelled the urge.

"My thanks for your kind welcome. I am here to hunt, young one, and I am not in a mood for trifles." Japhrimel sounded bored, but McKinley grinned on my other side, a twitchy dangerous grin. I was the shortest person on the dock. One of the Acolytes, a massive blond man, showed his fangs when he caught me looking at him. Blue lines swirled over his face, tattoos from before he was Changed. Nichtvren skin doesn't scar.

At least, I don't think it does, not from what I could remember in my Paranormal Anatomy courses at the Academy. The blond wore what looked like moth-eaten wolf skins slung together in a kind of tunic. His eyes were dead pools, tarns that could suck a whole struggling human in to drown in their depths. The Power here smelled deliciously, mustily wicked, of Nichtvren with a sharp, nose-cleaning tang of werecain that faded in and out — reflecting the peculiar qualities of 'cain pheromones in most species' nasal receptors. Over that was the flat copper scent of blood dried in fur, an alien smell that made every human instinct in me scream like an unregistered hooker caught holding out on her pimp. This was Power that could eat a psion alive.

But I was no longer fully human, and instead of eating me, the Power-well tickled deeper recesses in my psyche, bathed me in a chill bloody weight of seductive whispering. *Get a hold on yourself, Danny.* I gave myself a sharp mental slap, scanned the dock again. I couldn't afford to sink into the atmosphere. The channels responsible for circulating Power through my body tingled, fluxing; it took me a little longer to adapt to the sheer amount of energy in the air. I shivered, and Japhrimel's thumb caressed the underside of my wrist again. It was probably meant to be comforting.

Watch. Wait. Sooner or later, Japh or McKinley would slip or be distracted. I'd given my word, true—but I'd given it under duress, I hadn't promised to stay nailed to Japhrimel, and after what he'd done I was sure it didn't count anyway.

Are you really sure? Unease rippled up my back. *It's your word, Danny. Your Word. Anyone who uses magick can't afford to break their word. Your magickal will depends on your word being truth.*

But I only promised to cooperate. I didn't promise to stay with him. I can cooperate from a distance just fine.

I suppose dealing with demons rubs off on you after a while. I would never have dreamed of wriggling out of my word before.

It was also stupid. How long would I last on my own?

"Very well. But I have a message to give you, Eldest." Leonidas's heavy-lidded eyes closed like a lizard's, opened again. "There is one who wishes audience with your pretty companion. A demon with a green gem to match hers."

That could only mean one thing. *Lucifer wants to see me? Again?* The pit of my stomach was suddenly full of cold metal snakes, my heart thudding dimly in my chest.

Japhrimel was utterly still for a full five seconds, enough time for me to nervously check the entire dock again. I was fairly sure I could take the Nichtvren and I'd killed werecain before, but McKinley was a question mark. I didn't even know *what* he was. He wasn't demon, but he wasn't human either.

And Japhrimel? I had no chance. So I had to find something to distract him, to throw him off-balance. But what if—

What-ifs won't keep you alive, woman. Focus! It was a familiar male voice, laden with impatience, Jace's tone when he felt I wasn't paying proper attention during a sparring match. I was getting used to hearing Jace's voice in my head telling me to stay cool. Or maybe I was just talking to myself and using his voice. It's an occupational hazard for psions, the voices in our heads sometimes change into the people that matter most to us—or frighten us.

"When and where?" Japhrimel finally asked.

"The Haunt *Tais-toi*. Neutral ground. Tomorrow night, midnight. Alone." Leonidas grinned, exposing his fangs, Japhrimel's fingers didn't tense on my wrist but the mark on my shoulder went live again, a honeyed string of heat pressed into my flesh. "I will vouch for her safety, Eldest. There have been assurances given."

"By whom?"

That made the Nichtvren shake his blond head, clucking his tongue. "Now, can I tell you? I suspect your business lies with another demon, though."

"Perhaps. I am here on another errand. I wish to speak to the Anhelikos." Concrete groaned slightly, taking the weight of Japhrimel's voice. Most of the Acolytes stepped back, and the Master paled under the even caramel of his skin.

Anhelikos? What the hell is that?

Leonidas spread his expressive, slender hands. I wasn't fooled. Nichtvren have amazing strength, the older ones can shatter concrete with a negligent blow from a frail-looking hand. No wonder they're pretty much the top of the heap when it comes to paranormals. "I am neutral." But there was a definite glint in his black eyes. "Try not to destroy too much of my city, eh? I have been a good friend to you."

"Of course you have." Japhrimel nodded. "Very well. My thanks, Leonidas."

The Nichtvren seemed to find that funny. "He thanks me! Very generous. Well, dawn is coming. You will excuse us, I hope?"

I searched for something to say, found exactly nothing. Japhrimel stood still and silent as the Nichtvren faded into the darkness; the werecain loped away and vanished down a concourse that probably led to a hovertrain system to take visitors into the city. I glanced back over my shoulder — yes, dawn. A little more pronounced than before, a definite graying in the east.

We were soon alone on the hoverdock, cold air soughing gently through the cavernous half-shell structure.

"Well," Japhrimel said. "What do you make of that?"

"Don't send her alone," McKinley replied immediately, as if he'd been dying to say it. "It's a trap."

"What *kind* of trap? That is the question." Another shade of grim amusement to Japh's tone. He'd never spoken to *me* like that.

I was beginning to get that there was a history between these two — and another history between Japh and Leonidas. Curiosity pricked me, but I bit the inside of my cheek and studied the dock one more time, what I could see of the concourse and the half-shell roof supported with huge plasteel struts.

McKinley was no longer grinning. "A green-gemmed demon.

Either the Prince or an Androgyne, which is the same thing. Here in the same city as the Anhelikos Kos Rafelos. I don't like it."

The whoosis whatsis? I wondered pointlessly if the Hellesvront agent knew anything about *hedaira*, and how I could trick him into telling me if Japhrimel left us alone. Unfortunately, if Japh left me alone with him I might be tied up or worse, unable to make an escape attempt.

"It is not technically a summons." Japhrimel looked down at me. "What do you think, Dante?"

I swallowed bitterness, hearing him say my name so calmly. *What the hell is an Anhelikos? Do I want to know?* "I'm not here to think," I said flatly. "Only to *cooperate.*"

McKinley stared at me, his dark eyes wide. "My lord—"

"Quiet." Japhrimel's voice made the entire dock groan softly. I set my jaw and stared at my boot-toes. "We shall seek the Anhelikos, then shelter."

McKinley nodded. He shut up too, which was a pity. I would have liked to hear what he had to say about me.

Just wait, Danny girl, Jace's voice murmured inside my head. I moved forward obediently enough when Japhrimel did, mulling over this new turn of events. So Lucifer wanted to see me again. I was getting mighty popular with the denizens of Hell nowadays.

And what was the Anhelikos? Looked like I was about to find out.

I put my head down so that my hair fell forward, hiding my face. My lips moved silently, shaping a prayer to Anubis. It was habit, when I found myself in a hopeless situation, to pray. Even a combat-trained part-demon Necromance is human enough for *that.*

Sarajevo is dark, its cracked streets faced with old sloping, crumbling buildings that look deserted except for the curious lack of broken windows and graffiti. The wind is drenched with the stinging, fading-and-returning reek of werecain, as well as the dry feathery smell of swanhild and the musty delicious perfume of Nichtvren, dyeing the air in ripples. The darkness itself seems alive.

Not to mention hungry.

McKinley followed as Japh made turns seemingly at random, my footsteps echoing in the eerie silence between a demon and a Hellesvront agent. I walked, my right wrist still caught in Japhrimel's gentle but inexorable grasp, stealing little glances now and again to fix the city in my Magi-trained memory. The darkness here was deeper than in human cities, where orange light from hoverwash and freeplas reaches up into the sky; the streetlamps here were mostly dark though not broken. It looked like paranormals don't go in for breaking plasglass the way humans do.

The Power in the air stroked my shields, teased at me even through the heavy weight of Japhrimel's aura over mine. It was the end of that long dark time of early morning that is late afternoon for psions, when the normals have gone to bed and the streets unroll like ribbons alive with secrets, the time when old people in hospitals die smoothly and silently. Here in Sarajevo the air moved soundlessly, crackling with force and full of the peculiar music of a thriving city, strangely hushed but still audible. I heard a few hovers, faraway sirens, and the indefinable sound of conscious beings moving around. The faint grayness of dawn was growing stronger, but sunrise was still a way off.

Japhrimel finally stopped on a corner, looking down one more featureless Sarajevo street. I could smell the river when the explosive furry reek of werecain vanished from my overloaded nasal receptors. I could also smell a faint, delicious smell I had to think about before I could identify — bread baking, with a drier tang. Like feathers.

"We are visiting a...being." Japhrimel's voice took me by surprise. His fingers were gentle around my wrist, but I didn't bother to try to pull free. "McKinley will wait outside for us. You will not be in any danger."

Well, isn't that comforting. I stared at the pavement, letting the spiderweb cracks blur as my eyes unfocused. *Would you tell me if I was?*

That was unfair, but I wasn't feeling too fucking charitable right at the moment. I settled for holding my tongue, taking refuge in childish silence. I wondered who or *what* he was visiting. It could be anything from a *gaki* to a kobolding, I'd already seen werecain and Nichtvren. I wondered where a demon would go for information, and what Japhrimel was likely to be asking, and who he was likely to be asking it *of.*

Wild werecain wouldn't have dragged the questions out of me.

He didn't add anything to that, just led me across the street. My bootheels clicked against the pavement, I could hear McKinley now, soft footsteps echoing mine eerily. I got the idea he was doing it deliberately, whether as a comment or a joke I didn't want to guess.

I looked up when Japhrimel paused. There was a high wall, older stones set in smooth concrete and humming with Power. The smell of werecain returned, stinging my nose. The shielding over the wall was something I'd never seen before, a violet haze that looked strangely diaphanous but still sparked and hummed as Japh drew near. There was a small, narrow wooden gate vibrating slightly, moving back and forth like the oscillation of a heartbeat. I couldn't see what was behind the gate, and the hazy shielding was enough to make me hinky. I had never seen this type of defense before. *Unknown* was synonymous with *possibly dangerous* when it came to magick, especially shielding. I stiffened, and Japh actually stopped.

"There is no danger," he said, as if I was a primary-school kid scared of the dark. I didn't bother replying, just took a step forward, tugging against his hand.

Now I had to act like I wasn't frightened.

McKinley stepped to the side, leaned against the wall, and folded his arms. The metallic glow over his left hand sparked with a flush of pale purple light that deepened to an indigo glow as he seemed to sink into the smooth surface, his eyes turning even darker. My jaw threatened to drop as he almost vanished, not only to my physical but also to my psychic senses. Japhrimel set off again, I stared at where McKinley had literally blended with the wall. *How did he do that? What the hell* is *he?*

Japh tented his fingers against the gate and pushed it open. I hung back as far as I could, then passed through the hazy shield. It slid over the edge of Japhrimel's aura, sparkling gold as it interacted with the scorching mark of a demon in the landscape of Power. My rings swirled uneasily, my sword rattling inside its sheath. I inhaled, found myself still alive and under the cloak of Japh's aura. Cautiously decided maybe I was all right.

Inside the wall was a garden. The persistent smell of werecain and Nichtvren died, replaced by the scent of damp earth, rosemary, and lilies. The pungent breath of sage touched my face; the breeze inside the walls was warm and full of the smell of spicy, lush growth.

The walk underfoot turned to flagstones. I saw an oak tree in full leaf, its trunk as big around as an illegally augmented Family bodyguard, and nasturtiums with leaves the size of small pizzas trailed over a stone bench. Night-blooming jasmine scented the air, and I smelled honeysuckle and the sharp tang of rue. A persistent breath of dry, oily feathers drifted by, making the garden even sweeter. It didn't smell like the very beginning of winter, nor was it as chilly as it had been outside the wall. It felt like summer, a perfect summer night in a flawless garden.

It reminded me of Eddie's garden in Saint City, of sitting on the lawn chairs and smelling the *kyphii* Gabe liked to burn, drinking old wine or Crostine rum-and-synth lychee while Eddie fussed over the antique synthcoal barbecue and Gabe's soft laughter drifted over the immaculate beds. I'd taken both Doreen and Jace over to Gabe's at different times, so I could remember Doreen sending little flickers of Power dancing through the fireflies, making them chase each other in complex runic patterns. I could also remember Jace searing steaks or reclining on the lawn, shaping the smoke from Gabe's synth-hash cigarettes into marble-sized globes drifting through the yard, Gabe lazily flicking her fingers in stasis-charms and freezing them into ash. They were good memories, and I found myself wearing a completely unfamiliar smile.

Rising above the garden was a temple, high and narrow with a Novo Christer symbol—an uneven *tau* cross—worked into the pre-Merican Era stained glass over the front door. I shivered, thinking of the Religions of Submission and their war on psions. Stone steps eased up from the flagstone walk, and I was almost up the steps before I realized I was still grinning foggily.

Wait a second. I'm smiling. Why am I smiling?

The air was soft as silk, laden with good memories, Gabe and I weeding a plot of feverfew together on a mellow spring evening, Eddie and I practicing with staves, Doreen in a wide straw hat turning earth in the garden she'd planted, Jace with a bandanna tied around his golden head and muscle moving under his skin as he helped me lay shingles on the roof....

"What the hell is this?" I whispered as Japhrimel set his foot on the first step.

"Anhelikos." He glanced down at me, his mouth turning down at the corners. "Is it pleasant? The beginning stages usually are."

That doesn't sound good. I struggled to think clearly. "What is it?" *What have you dragged me into this time?* But looking up at him sent another cascade of memories through me—offering him my wrist after he'd soothed me out of a nightmare during the hunt for Santino, his gentle refusal. His voice as we lay in bed, my cheek against his shoulder, his patient work repairing the gaping holes in my psyche after Mirovitch's *ka* had almost killed me, Japhrimel stroking my back as I dialed Gabe's number, our linked hands swinging between us as we walked down a dusty Toscano road.

He stopped, his fingers gentle on my wrist. "Only a side effect, part of its lure. It will fade."

"Would it kill you to tell me what's going on?" I couldn't muster any anger, though I knew I *should* have been angry. It was odd to *expect* to feel it, but to be so curiously removed from any anger, as if a reflex circuit had been disabled. The breeze caressed my hair, touched my jeans, seemed to swirl around me.

"Watch, and wait." But he let go of my wrist, sliding his fingers down to lace through mine. "Come."

CHAPTER 34

Inside, mellow candlelight played over the soaring interior. All unnecessary interior walls had been taken out. The choirloft was an empty space, and the belltower had no steps anymore. The floor was stone, polished to a low shine by centuries of foot traffic. The path up the middle toward where the altar would have been was still visible, and the pattern of darker stone where pews would have marched in ordered rows. Up on the dais, thick white pillar candles crouched on holders of every shape, their drenching, flickering glow burnishing every surface with mellow gold. I heard a soft, deep whirring, and it landed softly on the floor.

I say *it*, because it was strangely sexless. Lucifer had his own brand of pure androgynous beauty that was nevertheless tinted with absolute masculinity. This being lacked the hurtful razor edge of the Devil's golden immaculateness. Pale skin feathering into platinum hair, winged colorless eyebrows, slim bare shoulders and a long white silken vest; it wore loose fluttering trousers and had shapely bare white feet. Its eyes were bleached but glowing, a blue that reminded me of the winter sky in certain parts of Putchkin Russe on sunny days when the wind comes knife-edge over the permafrost and slices straight through the best and warmest synthfur. That blue is as intense and fathomless as it is cold, a faded color that nevertheless looks infinite and manages to drench everything underneath it with eerie, depthless light. The eyes were set in a face that could have shamed every genespliced holovid star by comparison, a marvel of delicately flawless architecture.

Japhrimel stopped. I wanted to look around, take in the territory just in case, but the creature looked at me and its wings ruffled.

Did I mention the wings? Much taller than the creature, who towered a head and a half above Japhrimel; the wings were soft white and feathered, wide and broad like a vulture's. It actually mantled as it landed, bare feet soundless on stone floor. The smell of feathers mixed with a deeper, sweeter fragrance I couldn't place, a warm breeze redolent of baking bread and that sweet smell kissing my face. I stared, I'll admit it. I gawked like a primary schooler arriving at Academy for the first time.

It examined us both. Its mouth moved, and a low sweet sound filled the air. The voice sounded like bells stroked gently, a melody against my ears that eased aches I hadn't even known I was carrying. The meaning arrived complete in my head without passing through my ears, as if the speaker was a class 5 telepath.

My greetings to you, Avarik A'nankhimel. And to your bride.

"Greetings, Anhelikos Kos Rafelos." Japhrimel spoke in Merican, maybe for my benefit. The winged being's eyes didn't leave my face, I noticed a slender hilt at its side, attached to a long slim sword-shape. Who would want to fight this creature? It was tall but thin, and looked fragile. "I trust your wings have not faltered."

Not yet. Nor your own, Kinslayer. You are not the first of your kind to come to me lately. The bell-like tone drifted through my head, leaving a sense of lassitude in its wake.

"Ah." Japhrimel tilted his head to the side. I tore my eyes away from the Anhelikos, looked at him. The candlelight touched his face, slid over it kindly, and I was surprised by a jolt of starry pain lancing through my chest. It didn't matter, nothing mattered but his fingers in mine, warm and solid. I began to feel distinctly woozy. "I wondered if that might not be the case. Has the treasure left your keeping, then?"

The wings mantled again. Soft white feathers scattered, the redolent breeze ruffling my shirt and fingering my hair. *It has left my keeping, but not in the way you imply. It has gone on its ancient route to the Roof of the World, as was agreed between your Prince and our kind. How did you come to regain your pride after Falling? You do not seem weakened.*

Japhrimel didn't dignify the last question with a reply. "Who else came, Rafelos?" His voice was harsh and clipped compared to the music of the Anhelikos. Harsh, but somehow cleaner. I frowned, trying to figure out just what I was feeling. Relaxed, very relaxed...but also unsettled. Deeply disturbed. Like a fly struggling in a narcotic web, tiring itself as it thrashes.

I pushed the mental image away with an exhausting effort.

I can so rarely tell you apart, Kinslayer. But this one hunted the A'nankhimel and their brides. I recognize him from the fall of the White-Walled City and the Scattering of the Fallen. The creature's eyes met mine again. Wooziness spilled through me, ignited inside my head as if I was human again and drunk. The only other time I'd felt this inebriated was when I'd questioned a terrified sexwitch during the hunt for Kellerman Lourdes. Did this creature also flood the air with pheromones so strong they could turn me inside-out? How could I fight *that*?

The creature's slim fingers tapped at the bone swordhilt at his side. Hanging a sword off the belt is not generally recommended, it's best to have the blade to hand if you think you might need it. Barring that, the best place to have a sword is strapped to your back, easier to draw and less likely to bang on things when you turn around. But having wings probably made things a little different. I swayed, Japhrimel's fingers tightening in mine.

The swirling disorientation poured through me. *Why does it feel so weird? Then again, weird is my life now. Why can't I be a normal psion?*

Has your Prince lifted his ban, then? The creature's hand caressed the swordhilt; I finally figured out what the look on its beautiful, feral face was.

It looked suspiciously like *hunger*.

My lips parted. "Japhrimel—" It was a whisper, I was barely aware of saying the word and wished I hadn't, because the thing's attention centered on me. *This scares me. Oh, gods, this scares me more than you do. Why did Lucifer pick me to inflict this on? I could have lived my entire life without getting this close to a demon or this...whatever it is. My entire, entire life.*

"Of course not." There was an edge to Japhrimel's voice, grim satisfaction and sudden comprehension. Not to mention terrible anger. The kind of anger that could tear stone apart with a word. "*A'nankhimel* are under the sentence of death, wherever the Prince finds them. And if one cannot kill a Fallen, their brides are ever so fragile."

Ah, yes. So vulnerable. So trusting. The creature blinked, first one eye, then the other.

The mark on my shoulder crunched down on itself, a jolt of pain spearing through the languor wrapped around me. I found myself leaning against Japhrimel, our hands clasped between us, the butt of a projectile gun caught between my hip and forearm. The harder I fought, the more limp and relaxed my body became. I tried to stand up, lean away from Japh, *anything*. The strength spilled out of my legs, if I hadn't been propped against him I might have gone down in a heap.

The creature stared at me. A pale tongue flicked out, passed over its colorless lips. The blue eyes were hooded now.

"My thanks for your aid, Kos Rafelos." Japhrimel nodded briefly. "We will trouble you no more."

Oh, please. Just one little taste. They are so sweet, after all. Its mouth stretched into a lipless smile, showing a bloodless tongue and suddenly sharp teeth.

Japhrimel laughed. The sound sliced through the languid air, I gained my feet with a massive effort, bracing myself with his fingers laced through mine. Stiffened my knees, fighting, *fighting* to stay upright. "Not today, Kos Rafelos. This little one is not to your taste; she has a sharp spine. Good night, Anhelikos."

The creature's hand clasped around the hilt. I saw the muscles in its thin, wiry arm tense, flickering under smooth pale skin.

My left hand jumped of its own volition, scabbard blurring, wrist flicked back, hand palm-upwards; fingers closed around the hilt of the sword and the hand snapping down, blade singing free as the inertia of the scabbard slid it from the sheath. Strength returned, flooding me like freeplas fumes, igniting in my head as I jerked against Japhrimel's hand. He didn't let go as I stepped forward, my knees unsteady, reflex brought the sword up and over in my left hand, held steady and slanting, a bar between the creature's pale gaze and my own level glare. The scabbard flew in a perfect arc behind us, striking the wooden door with a thin snapping sound. *Hope I didn't break it*, I thought, instinct pushing me away from Japhrimel, giving me enough room to fight without getting tangled in him.

"Draw that blade," I said, my voice slurring a little but still steady, "and you'll have more goddamn trouble than you can handle, wingboy."

The voice of self-preservation made its appearance, as usual, a good two seconds too late. *Danny, what are you doing? This thing is goddamn fucking dangerous and you're as drugged as a New Vietkai whore! Let Japh take care of this goddamn thing if it draws down on you!*

Japhrimel's hand was suddenly not clasped in mine, it was closed around my right shoulder. "Easy, *hedaira*." Did he sound, of all things, amused? Damn him. "There is no danger."

The creature's face *shifted*, from one moment to the next. Instead of sexless, transparent beauty, the jaw jutted forward and the nose turned to slits, the pale incandescent eyes bulging. It was only a flicker, there and gone so quickly I gasped, stumbling backward. Japhrimel dug his fingers in, holding me up.

The entire interior of the church rattled with a slow even hiss, the creature's supple body melting bonelessly into a serpent's fluid curve before it snapped back into a recognizably humanoid form. The wings ruffled, more white feathers boiling free, the smell of baking bread and sweet perfume turned cloying-thick.

A hedaira *seeking to protect the Kinslayer.* The thing's voice burrowed into my head, the bell-like tone suddenly gone brittle. *Surely the time of reckoning is upon us now.*

I wasn't trying to protect him. I was going to kill you if you drew, goddammit. I couldn't make my mouth shape the words.

"It makes no difference." As Japhrimel drew me back, I didn't look away from the creature. Its hand dropped from the swordhilt, wings smoothing as we retreated, step by careful step. The mark on my shoulder pulsed with soft, oiled Power. "If others of my kind come, you may tell them what you like. Only be sure to add this: as long as the Prince endures, my *hedaira* enjoys his protection. That means I am disposed to consider his...*requests*...most kindly."

My knees almost gave out on me again as I realized what I'd just done. The candle flames hissed. Japh dragged me out the door, the night air sparkling clean after the cloying interior of the temple. He somehow bent to retrieve the scabbard on the way out, too, though his hand never left my shoulder. He handed it to me as we stood on the top of the steps, the wooden door closing behind us. I heard another hissing, chuckling sound from inside as a wave of thick sweet clotted perfume belched out through the rapidly narrowing crack between the door and the jamb.

The Prince will not allow a hedaira *to live, Kinslayer. Especially* not your *hedaira*. You would do well to remember the White-Walled City and the screams of the Fallen—

The door clicked shut. The garden rustled, leaves rubbing against each other with the sibilant sound of feathers rasping. I coughed, the smell of dry feathers and bread coating the back of my throat. My eyes watered, but I could still resheathe my blade; the action was habitual enough not to need sight.

Japhrimel pushed me down the steps. I stumbled and he held me up. His arm came over my shoulders, but I didn't care. I simply wanted to get *out* of this place as soon as possible. My boots echoed on the flagstone path, Japh's were silent.

What was the White-Walled City? The roof of the world? This thing was holding a stash of something and now it's gone. What's Japh looking for? Goddammit. Frustration rose, fighting with the way my arms and legs tingled numbly, clumsy. "Gods." I coughed again, wanted to spit to clear my throat, didn't. "What the..." I couldn't get enough breath to finish the sentence. Little bits of plant life touched me—leaves, branches; they all felt like tiny grasping fingers.

"Anhelikos." Japhrimel's tone was even and thoughtful. "They feed on anger. And hatred. You are perhaps the first human to have seen one in almost five hundred years." He pushed open the narrow wooden gate, the heat of him cleaner than the thick clotted scent left behind us. I shivered galvanically as we passed through the diaphanous shielding laid over the high wall. His arm tightened, drawing me into his side, and my sword bumped my leg as it dangled in my nerveless left hand. "You are perhaps the only living creature to survive drawing steel inside one's nest. That was ill-advised."

"Sorry." I didn't sound sorry, wanted to shake his arm away, couldn't. My legs felt like I'd just run a thousand-mile marathon, and my head throbbed unevenly. "I feel sick."

"It is a thing inimical to you. The feeling will pass." He glanced at the wall, where McKinley suddenly reappeared.

"Any news?" The Hellesvront agent's black eyes flicked over me, I hoped I wasn't shaking visibly.

It feeds on anger, that's why I felt so drained. Gods. What is that thing? I don't care, I never want to see it again. Gods above.

"Some," Japh replied. "It has been moved, I expected as much. Someone came to fetch it, failed, and triggered the game." He stopped, glanced back over his shoulder at the high, smooth concrete wall. Then he looked down at me. "Did you think to protect me, Dante?"

No. I wanted to kill it before it drew. "It was about to draw, Japh."

"Unlikely." He paused. "I told you there was no danger."

I don't care what you fucking told me. "I wasn't exactly thinking clearly." *I don't even know why I did that. I hate you. I can't hate you. I wish I'd never met you.*

No, I don't. Gods. I was too confused and shaken to think straight. Stepping in front of him had just *happened.* I'd tried to protect Doreen, I'd tried like hell to protect Jace — but they'd been human. Like me.

Japhrimel probably didn't need me at all.

That thought hurt more than anything else.

"So it seems." He studied me for a few moments.

Sekhmet sa'es. I gave up. Leaned into his side, blinking as I stared at the pavement at my feet. My boot-toes seemed strangely far away. "Fine." My quads and hamstrings were starting to tremble, something I hadn't felt since before Rio. I felt about three seconds away from collapsing. "Whatever. Can I sit down somewhere?"

The silence stretched on for a good thirty seconds. I couldn't tell if they were looking at me or each other, didn't care. Finally, Japhrimel spoke. "The weakness will pass. Come."

He set off down the cracked and uneven pavement, I concentrated on putting one foot in front of the other.

Once again, I don't see how things could get any worse. I winced as I thought it. You'd think I would have learned by now not to say that, even to myself.

This being a nonhuman Freetown, the hotel was run by swanhild.

Swanhild, with their ruffs of white feathers and delicate long-fingered hands, are weak when compared to Nichtvren or werecain or even kobolding. But their flesh is extremely poisonous to most carnivorous paranormal species, and a variant of touch-telepathy means that a 'cain or a Nichtvren that kills a swanhild suffers a kind of psychic death in return. It's unpleasant to say the least, and as a result the 'hilds are the paranormal equivalent of Free Territorie Suisse. They function as message carriers and bankers, as well as several other kinds of service providers, for paranormal communities.

Swanhild don't like humans. Something about a pre-Merican Era prince who had trapped one, tried to marry her, and ended up killing

her and committing suicide, I think. There used to be a very old ballai about it, but the swanhild campaigned so effectively it's hard to
even get bootleg holos of old performances. Modern ballai companies
won't perform it for audiences, either.

The hotel was a kobolding-restored building, with the characteristic fluid stone decorations carved into its facade. Inside, the lighting was dim, the windows UV-screened, and a collage of paranormals
hung out in the hotel bar while McKinley checked us in. I saw — for
the first time outside a textbook — a batlike Fumadrin, its snout buried in a bowl of what looked like whiskey but was probably paint
thinner. I saw a red *gaki* with a long black drooping mustache talking
to a blond man in a long black coat with a sword strapped to his back.
The man looked human enough, but he had a crimson-black stain of
an aura, which told me he was probably a host for something. A gaggle of swanhild gathered at one end of the bar, clicking and chirping
back and forth; a single Nichtvren yawned as she paid her tab with a
fistful of New Credit notes, wiping a red stain away from her exquisite lips. Two kobolding slumped in a corner, their table almost
groaning under the weight of empty beer tankards; the bartender was
a husky golden werecain whose yellow eyes flicked over the hotel
lobby every now and again.

Japhrimel kept his arm over my shoulders, his thumb stroking my
upper arm every so often. I kept looking down at the floor, though I
was feeling a lot better. The languid, drained feeling had faded within
a couple blocks of the Anhelikos's temple. I wasn't feeling a hundred
watts, but I was all right. Except for the way my chest hurt, especially
the rubbed-raw little spot under the diagonal leather strap of my rig.

Thankfully, we didn't have to use an elevator to get to the third
floor. McKinley led us up a long, sweeping red-carpeted flight of
stairs lifting from the marble-floored lobby. A sharp right-hand turn
past a glowering werecain guard, and I was ushered into a room that
was dim and soft and luxurious, with antique blue velvet chairs and a
silky cream-colored carpet I immediately wanted to foul in some
way. A wet bar gleamed. There was even a canister of cloned blood
in a stasis cabinet under the shelves of liquor. A plasma holovid player
perched on a wide cherrywood dresser, and the beds were huge and
looked soft enough to sink into.

There were, unfortunately, no windows. The walls were smooth
and blank. A Nichtvren room, safe from daylight. Airless.

As soon as I realized this I looked up at Japhrimel, already feeling the air grow thick. "No. Please, no." My voice cracked, my throat closing with claustrophobic weight. If McKinley hadn't been right behind us I would have tried to backpedal. As it was, I tried fruitlessly to tear myself out from under Japh's arm, failed. "You don't have to do this. I'll be a good little prisoner and stay."

He shrugged, his fingers gentling but still iron-hard. I couldn't break his grip. "I am sorry."

"There's no goddamn windows. You know how I feel about—" I was about to start hyperventilating, I could *feel* it.

"This is *necessary*, Dante." His arm loosened, but I could feel his readiness. Even if I could bowl over McKinley, Japh would catch me before I got to the hallway. The fight went out of me. I could feel it leave, like a splinter drawn out of torn flesh.

"Fine." My voice cracked, making a picture-frame rattle against the wall. "Whatever." I tore away from him, stalked past the beds into the furthest corner of the room, and pushed the chair occupying it away. I put my back to the corner and slid down until I sat on the floor, my knees up, my katana across my lap, right hand clamped over the hilt, left around the scabbard. I leaned my head into the corner, closed my eyes, and struggled to breathe.

Japhrimel murmured to McKinley, I heard the room door open and close again. Peeked out from under my lashes to see Japhrimel walking softly around the end of a bed, approaching me. The familiar breathless feeling of demon magick rose as he warded the walls, demon defenses springing into being under the humming of the hotel's security net and magickal shielding. Cracking a kobold-constructed building run by swanhilds was a tall order indeed. We were probably safe, even if my heart hammered and my throat felt savagely constricted.

I took the only refuge I had left, shutting my eyes and breathing, reaching into the still quiet part of myself that had never failed me. *"Anubis et'her ka,"* I whispered. *"Se ta'uk'fhet sa te vapu kuraph."* My mouth was dry, the whisper was cracked and imperfect. "Anubis, Lord of the Dead, Faithful Companion, protect me, for I am Your child. Protect me, Anubis; weigh my heart upon the scale; watch over me, Lord, for I am Your child. Do not let evil distress me, but turn Your fierceness upon my enemies. Cover me with Your gaze, let Your hand be upon me, now and all the days of my life, until You take me into Your embrace." I breathed in again, tried it again. *"Anubis et'her ka. Se ta'uk'fhet sa te vapu kuraph.* Anubis, Lord of the Dead..."

The blue flame rose up before my inner eyes. I didn't see the hall of infinity, or the bridge, or the well of souls—but the blue light closed around me, and that was good enough. With a grateful sobbing breath, I gave myself up to the comfort of my god.

CHAPTER 35

The room was twenty-four steps long from the blank wallpapered wall to the door that led into a short entry hall, with a huge bathroom off to one side. I know because I counted the steps as McKinley paced it over and over again. Japhrimel was silent, folded down cross-legged on the carpeting a few feet away from me, his eyes closed. Waiting. His coat spread behind him on the floor, a deep, lacquered darkness.

Hours ticked away. I had plenty of time to think through that long weary day, slipping in and out of a hazy blue-flamed trance as I sought the comfort of my god over and over again. My chest hurt. I could barely breathe, and I was hungry, but I shook my head when McKinley asked me if I wanted breakfast. Shook it again when he asked about lunch. A third time when he asked about dinner.

Japhrimel sat, his spine straight, his face closed like the room itself. Tears rose in my throat, pricked at my eyes, I denied them. I would have liked to take a hot shower and cry, but I was damned if I'd give them the satisfaction. Instead, I studied Japhrimel's face, my fingers aching around my swordhilt. I looked at the wallpaper, patterned with gold fleur-de-lis. I examined the edge of the blue velvet bedspread. I looked at the nap of the carpet, found myself looking back at Japhrimel's face. How many times had I run my fingertips over his cheekbones, let him kiss my fingers, lain beside him and told him things I'd never told another living person?

What kind of inhuman patience had it taken to live with me for so long, keeping the fact of the Devil's asking for me to himself? All the presents, the sparring matches, his fingers gentle against my ribs, his mouth against my neck as he shuddered in my arms.

It couldn't all have been a game to him. It *couldn't* have.

I *knew* the Devil meant me no good. I knew other demons would want to kill me because of Lucifer's meddling in my life. But I'd never questioned Japh since his resurrection. After all, he'd Fallen, hadn't he?

Hadn't he? Even Lucifer had said so. But neither the Devil nor Japh had told me very much about what *Fallen* really meant.

I didn't like the way my thoughts were tending. What did Fallen really mean? What had Japhrimel wanted to collect from the Anhelikos? Who was trying to kill me now, and why, and what was Lucifer's endgame in all this? I knew better than to think it was what he had originally presented to me—a straight, simple hunting-down of four demons, badda-bing, time served, Danny Valentine free of demonic manipulation.

Another thought rose, even worse than the first.

Let's just suppose Japhrimel has been ducking out to talk to the Devil while I sleep. Just for the sake of argument, let's say. What do they have planned? Was it all an act?

But Japhrimel had protected me, hadn't he? Tracked me down, found me, asked me to trust him, rescued me from the hellhounds.

That only means Lucifer has some use for you. Ten to one says you're bait too, Danny. It was a puzzle. I'd hunted down Santino for Lucifer, could that have made me an enemy or two? Santino had bred an Androgyne—the type of demon Lucifer was, the most rare and precious because Androgynes could breed. Santino—or Vardimal, as Japh called him—had thought he could create a puppet Androgyne to replace Lucifer on the throne of Hell, effectively crowning Santino as king too, if the Androgyne was malleable enough.

Maybe there were other demons who'd wanted a crack at Santino's patented process of creating an Androgyne, the shining path of genes even Lucifer with all his tinkering couldn't find. So, conceivably, they could want a little revenge for my interference, no matter that I'd been given no choice in the matter. So far this theory was holding up uncomfortably well.

If this was the truth, I was bait for any demons involved with Santino's rebellion. Lucifer had let Santino free to see what he could do, confident in his ability to recapture the Lesser Flight demon anytime he wanted to. Only Santino hadn't played along, had disappeared— and the Devil had started to scramble.

Which led me to another logical extension, chilling in its exactitude.

Try this on for size, Danny. Lucifer leaves Japh's ashes with me, thinking he can pick him up like a dropped toy whenever he wants to—whenever the demons allied to Santino show themselves. When they do, he calls me and plants the idea of resurrecting Japh in my head. I don't listen, because I'm in the middle of hunting down Lourdes. Japh wakes up and starts looking for me—and Lucifer meets him, tells him to keep me alive and take care of me, because I'm bait. Japhrimel does, I fall in with the plan, and when the time is right and I'm ready for my part, I'm called onstage. Only Japh slips in a mickey at the last moment. After all, you can't trust a demon, and he's got Lucifer by the short hairs. Which leaves me with one question.

How far does Japhrimel's protection extend? How expendable am I?

That was a distinctly uncomfortable thought. If Lucifer gave the word, would Japh cut me loose? After all, he had a demon's Power now. Maybe I couldn't be changed back into a human, but maybe Japh could get his freedom and his place in Hell back by bounty hunting these other four demons and finishing it up by tying off the last loose end.

Me.

That's ridiculous, Dante. He's your Fallen. He's kept you alive this far.

Was that just because Lucifer had further plans for me? I *knew* Lucifer was my enemy, was fairly sure any other demon I'd come across at this point was an enemy. Could my Fallen become an enemy too? Especially since he wouldn't tell me what *Fallen* meant? He'd held back during sparring, had kept things hidden from me—had he also only *pretended* some kind of emotional link to me? Or had he been amusing himself, as demons were wont to do in stories?

Do not doubt me, no matter what. I was busy doubting with all my little heart, now.

I considered him, sitting there with his eyes closed. My hand tightened on the swordhilt. I could draw and strike in a little under a second and a half while I was human; I was faster now. I wasn't fast enough to hit him. But what would he do? What could I get away with doing as long as I still had value as bait?

He could tie me up and leave me with McKinley. I shuddered at the thought. *He might, too, if I make any trouble.* I was fairly sure I could break my way out of pretty much any human bonds, given enough time and concentration. But a demon probably knew how to tie a *hedaira* up so she didn't escape. It was probably one of the things they learned in demon nursery school.

The thought of being tied up and having something like the hell-hound attack was chilling, to say the least. McKinley's footsteps continued their even tread. My rings crackled uneasily, golden sparks pulsing in the air above them and winking out.

There was another problem, too. A green-gemmed demon wanting to see me at the Haunt *Tais-toi*, which from the name was probably a Nichtvren haunt. I'd been inside one—the House of Pain in Saint City—and I never wanted to see another.

So Lucifer wanted to see me again. What the *hell* for? To finish me off, now that I'd served my purpose?

Had I served my purpose?

The sense of some missing puzzle piece returned. Gods above, how I hate that missing-piece feeling. It always means I'm about to get deeper into trouble than even I can handle.

Between one moment and the next, Japhrimel's eyes flicked open. He studied me for a long moment, then stretched, the movement turning into a graceful rising to his feet. He offered me his hand. "Dinner first," he said. "An audience has been requested with you, *hedaira*."

How did he sound so bloody *calm*? Was Lucifer planning to kill me or subject me to some incredible new form of torture? Fury rose in me again, was throttled. I wanted to sound at least as calm as he did. McKinley halted. It was a good thing—the pacing was really starting to irritate me.

I made it to my feet on my own, bracing my left hand with my sword against the floor and levering myself up, my legs tingling briefly from forced immobility. I still felt a little shaky, but overall I seemed to have bounced back from the awful draining sensation. "I'm not hungry. I'll go to this meeting, though." My voice shook perceptibly. *Congratulations, Dante. You sound about as calm as a Necromance before her Trial.*

"It could be a trap." Japh's eyebrows drew together.

It's almost certainly a trap. But for who? "I doubt Lucifer wants to kill me. We haven't caught even one of the four demons he wants dragged in yet." *At least, not that I can tell. Though if he has other hunters out there, that might be inaccurate.* I took a deep breath, carried the thought to its logical extension. I was beginning to wish my brain and my imagination didn't work so blasted well. "If he does want me dead, he'll get me one way or another."

A swift snarl crossed Japhrimel's face, green eyes laser-burning. "He will not."

I shrugged. *Not until he's done playing with me and I've outlived my usefulness. If I'm bait, I don't have long to live.* "I'm a Necromance, demon. I'm not going to live forever." I brushed past him, intending to stalk for the bathroom. If I was going to meet the Devil again, I wanted to at least wash my face.

He caught my arm, his fingers gentle but inexorable. Was his hand shaking? Impossible. "Do not say such things to me, *hedaira*."

"Don't call me that." I tugged my arm away from him. He didn't let me go, I set my heels and pulled, not caring if it hurt. "It's *Valentine* to you, demon. Let go of me. I've got a meeting with the Devil to get ready for."

Japhrimel shook me, gently, as if to bring home just how much stronger he was. How much *more*, even though he'd changed me. I tried to yank away from him again, almost feeling tiled wall against my back. Hearing a sudden roaring in my ears, the devouring feeling of helplessness as he held me still.

His voice turned cold. "Why must everything be a battle, with you?"

"Stop it." My breath caught in my throat. "*Stop* it. Let *go*."

He did, and I stumbled, righted myself. My rings swirled steadily. I stalked away from him, past McKinley, who was staring at me again. I was getting tired of being stared at. All my adult life as an accredited Necromance I've been stared at. Too much of anything gets old.

I locked myself into the bathroom, twisted on the cold-water tap. There was a glassed-in shower floored with granite, the entire bathroom was done in kobolding-worked stone except for the deep bathtub and the porcelain stand-alone sink. No toilet—a Nichtvren room wouldn't need one, and I didn't either. That had been one of the harder things to get used to about no longer being strictly human—a female bounty hunter was *always* looking for a decent lavatory. You learned to take bathroom breaks when you could.

The mirrors reflected back a rumpled and tired *hedaira* whose black hair fell messily over her face in seemingly-choreographed strands.

I didn't feel a shock of nausea on seeing my own face, which must have meant I was finally getting used to it. I looked at myself critically, evaluating.

My own dark eyes, liquid and beautiful. Sculpted cheekbones, a sinful mouth now drawn down at one corner as I frowned, winged dark eyebrows. I touched my cheek, and saw the beautiful woman in the mirror brush her exquisite cheekbone, trace her pretty lips with a black molecule-drip polished nail. Japhrimel had made me demon-beautiful, but without the air of *alienness* demons exuded.

If I looked hard enough, I could still see traces of who I'd been in my face — my eyes were still mostly my own, and when I relaxed my mouth still quirked up habitually on one side as if I didn't quite believe what I was seeing. The little half-smile had always seemed welded onto my face before, a professional defense. If I was smiling, it couldn't hurt that bad, could it?

I brushed my hair back with wet fingers, washed my face. Scrubbed my skin dry with a towel. Shrugged inside my rig a little, tested the action of each knife. Checked my bag, scorched and battered but still mine. Extra ammo. I still had my plasgun, too.

I looked at myself in the mirror, the water still running into the bowl of the sink. I wiped the half-smile off my face, watched as the lovely woman facing me grew solemn, the tattoo on her cheek shifting slightly. The twisted caduceus ran its sharp ink lines lovingly over her skin. The emerald set high on her flawless left cheekbone flashed.

There was another green flash, and my eyes dropped. I lifted my left wrist, the breath slamming out of me.

The wristcuff ran with green light, fluid lines scrabbling with humming urgency. A warning.

I drew my plasgun. Left the water running. Edged for the bathroom door. Stopped, and looked at the shower. My eyes snagged on the bathtub, too. A low stone-tiled wall between the bathtub and the shower, only about three feet high. Probably for the plumbing. The bathtub was set in the floor, but behind it was the wall the room shared with the outside hallway.

I bet that wall isn't stone all the way through. It likely wasn't kobolding-made, which meant it wasn't as tough as the exterior wall.

The wristcuff squeezed, a bolt of pain firing its way up my arm. My breath stopped in my throat. Demons. Whether from Lucifer or escaped from Hell, they certainly didn't mean me any good.

You've got to make up your mind, Danny. Let Japhrimel push you around or strike out on your own. Even if you won't last long without him, at least you won't have someone owning you. Forcing you. Lying to you.

Clear coldness settled over me. In the end, everything boiled down to one thing—what I *had* to do. Even if I loved Japh, I couldn't be a slave.

I heard McKinley's voice, low and urgent. Then, a soft light rap on the hotel room's door. Demons, here and knocking at the door.

A static-laden silence smashed through the room. Then a crunching, smashing impact; the bathroom door rattled against its hinges. A low, coughing snarl—a hellhound.

Just before all hell broke loose, I took a deep breath, stepped back, and pointed my plasgun at the wall. Power spiked under my skin, and I squeezed the trigger.

CHAPTER 36

N ight lay thick and heavy over Demilitarized Sarajevo. It felt strange to be in a city of paranormals, but the static in the air was enough to hide even me for once. I crouched in the lee of a dark alley, listening to the snarling as two werecain engaged in a deep philosophical discussion about something out on the pavement across the cobbled square, right in front of the Haunt *Tais-toi* nightclub.

Nightclub is too kind a word. It was a Nichtvren haunt, communal feeding ground, and social gathering spot rolled into one. Instead of thick shielding to keep the hungry Power contained, this had only token barriers—after all, who would be stupid enough to attack a haunt in Sarajevo? And besides, there were no normals or psions around to keep away from the well of carnivorous Power because of the risk of Feeders.

This particular haunt had been a temple once, a twin-towered cathedral in the café section of Sarajevo, facing out onto a wide square now eddying with every conceivable shape and size of paranormal. Species I'd only read about in school lived here in their own enclaves, and night was the time they came out to play.

My shields shivered, demon-strong and flexible. I blinked a few times, feeling a purely human reaction uncomfortably like what any prey would feel in the presence of predators. Maybe I wasn't fully human anymore—but I'd been born one, and something blind and old inside me recognized that to these creatures, the Danny Valentine before Japh's alterations would be walking meat in Sarajevo.

My head still felt tender from the plasgun-plus-Power burst. True
to my guess, the wall hadn't been pure stone, just plasteel struts and
sheetrock with thin marble tiles. It had blown out nicely. I, on the
other hand, had slid into the glassed-in shower. The single low stone
wall between the shower and the bathtub provided perfect cover as I
buttoned myself as tightly down as I could. My feet had crunched on
broken glass from the shower door. The mark on my shoulder bit
down with sudden pain as the demon attackers, followed by McKinley and Japhrimel, streaked out into the hotel. I heard a werecain's
howl — the guard at the top of the stairs. Everyone thought I'd busted
out and was running away — or was being *dragged*.

Jeez, not too bright, I'd thought, my breath still choked in my
throat. Then I'd scrambled out through the hole in the wall, Power
bleeding into the air from where my strike had smashed through
Japhrimel's demon-laid wards. Any other demon's shielding, I probably wouldn't have been able to do so — but I wore Japh's mark, and
his wards weren't meant to strike against or harm me.

Or so I'd hoped, and turned out to be right. Besides, the smashing
against the front door meant the shields were automatically concentrating to throw back the force of that attack and were thus more vulnerable here.

Low and silent, I turned to the left and was around the corner in
another hall before I heard the crashing chaos of a hell of a fight
behind me. I didn't wait around. Instead, I kicked in a door, and —
thank Anubis — found a room with actual windows. A swanhild
room, actually, with a large round nestingbed full of feathery stuff. I
didn't stop to apologize to the screaming swanhild trio that greeted
me, feathers swirling around their shocked faces and narrow naked
torsos. I simply dove out the plasglass window and was gone before
the attacking demons had realized I'd outsmarted them. The drop
hadn't been pleasant, but it hadn't hurt me much.

Finding the Haunt *Tais-toi* had been as easy as getting to a busy
street and politely asking a passing swanhild, then following her
careful directions.

The psychic interference was so intense I couldn't scan the place.
Nichtvren poured in, and I spotted a whole pack of werecain — from
an alpha in a long leather coat all the way down to a few teenage
pups. A few swanhild decked out in silver chains, miniskirts, and not
a lot else waltzed in the front door.

There wasn't a lot of hover traffic. I guess the paranormals around here didn't use them—who needed a hover when you could use the Nichtvren shimmer-trick, or when a werecain could cover ten blocks of city street in seconds? Swanhild were territorial and rarely traveled despite their messaging system, and kobolding hated to leave wherever they'd been hatched.

At least if there aren't a lot of hovers, I might not get hit with one.

I checked the street again. Too many shadows. Any one of them could hold a demon, and the interference was intense enough I wouldn't know it in time.

I was pretty sure I'd shaken all pursuit, and the interference that would hide them would hide me a lot better, since I wasn't as big a disturbance in the Power flow.

Danny, what are you doing? You should be running as far away from here as you can, going as deep into cover as you can.

I couldn't run forever. If Lucifer wanted to kill me, he was welcome to try. I'd die fighting. Besides, why bother to schedule a meeting with me and send assassins for me? Far easier and more satisfying to do it himself.

Besides, this was the one thing Japhrimel couldn't *force* me to do. He was stronger than me, faster than me, more powerful than me. This was my chance to do something by myself.

I finally melted out of the shadows and walked across the street. My bootheels snapped against concrete and patches of cobbles. It was odd to be in a city where the sky wasn't dyed orange with reflected light; it was even more odd when I walked right up to the door of the Haunt *Tais-toi* and plunged into the red-neon thumping bass cave that was the second Nichtvren haunt I'd ever walked into in my life.

The music folded around me, I winced as reflex compensated for the demonic acuity of my ears. *One thing I can thank Japh for, he taught me how to turn the volume down.*

I'd spent so long with him in the forefront of every thought, even while he'd been dormant and I'd struggled unsuccessfully to go on with my life. I suspected I'd miss him for the rest of my life.

The rest of my life might be a very short time, I thought grimly, glancing around the haunt. The dance floor was crammed, prickles of Power racing over my skin from the throng. A bar ran down one whole side of the building, a low stage held four werecain and a Nichtvren. Two 'cain had guitars, one had a bass, another one fingered a Taziba keyboard; the stick-thin, red-haired Nichtvren sang in some language I didn't recognize. He wore leather pants and had his eyes closed, crooning, his voice cutting through the din with little effort, helped along by Power.

The music helped with the interference. I shouldered my way through a gaggle of swanhild and headed for the bar. I was early, according to the timefunction on my datband.

I hoped the Devil was early too. The sooner I could get this over with, the better.

Before, I'd just had to get too tired to care before I could face down the Devil. Now I was tired, hungry, missing Japhrimel, running *away* from Japhrimel, scared out of my mind, and heartbroken.

I was hoping it was enough. It might almost be a relief to have everything over with.

I got to the bar. The bartender was a rarity, a four-armed kobolding. Swanhild and kobolding like to drink, and Nichtvren occasionally take an alcohol chaser with their blood — it doesn't affect them but they like acidic tastes. I hear the stomach cramps are a bitch, though. There were various other stimulants and depressants for other paranormals, and the smell of synth-hash smoke wreathed around me. The thunderous fading-returning odor of werecain, the dry feathery sweetness of swanhild, the deliciously wicked smell of Nichtvren, smoke and stone for the kobolding, other assorted odors.

I let my eyes travel over the place as the Nichtvren's voice hit a new pitch that made my shields shiver. A thread of wonder ran through me. I wouldn't have been able to experience this if I was still human.

There were some things to be grateful for in this new body, however short a time I had left to enjoy it.

Danny, your imagination just works too goddamn well.

I ordered a double shot of Crostine rum and handed the 'tender a fifty New Credit note. My roll was getting pretty thin, I'd have to score some more cash soon. If I used my datband to draw on my accounts, I could be traced. I would have to find a bank and carefully plan a run. Get in, get cash from my accounts, get out and vanish.

Always assuming you live past tonight, sunshine. "Danny Valentine," I said to the bartender. "I've got a meeting."

The 'cain palmed the note and nodded over my shoulder. I whirled, my hand going to my swordhilt.

My heart leapt to my throat. Yellow eyes blazed in a scar-ruined face; Lucas Villalobos grabbed my arm, stopping only to gulp down the double shot and nod to the bartender. "You get into *more* trouble," he wheezed in my ear, his breath laden with rum and the dry scent of a stasis cabinet. He smacked the shotglass down on the bar. "This way."

"What the *hell* are you doing here?" I considered drawing my sword, discarded the notion. I was too glad to see him.

"I don't like losing track of my clients. Puts me in a bad mood." Lucas scanned the building, his oddly flat aura moving like a revolving door. No wonder he was able to get into DMZ Sarajevo, he didn't look human at all on an energetic level. "There's someone you should talk to."

My heart plummeted, then leapt to pound in my throat. *Lucas? Working for Lucifer? No. Let's hope not.* "Great. Is he here?"

"Not *he*," Lucas said in my ear. He'd found a new dark-gray shirt but still wore the same bandoliers I'd always seen him in, his boots were the same rundown pair he'd always had. I wondered how often he got them resoled. "She. And you'd better hurry."

Lucas led me through the dance floor, press of immortal Nichtvren flesh on every side, a knot of werecain twisting in the corner, sweet synth-hash smoke wreathing in billows as a mated pair twined around each other, damn near copulating. I'd always liked dancing, shaking every thought out of my body. I hadn't gone in years.

Not since Jace.

I remembered Jace's hands on my waist, sweat dripping down my neck and spine, a short silken skirt swinging against my thighs as I raised my arms, the music slamming through my bones as I lost myself in one of the oldest communal ecstasies known to humanity.

I shook the memory away. I'd never asked Japhrimel if he liked to dance. Probably not—but he was so graceful. It would have been nice to dance with him.

Will you just quit thinking about him? You'll need all your wits for whatever's going to happen in the next ten minutes.

We reached a dark corner, and Lucas tilted his head at the hulking orange-eyed werecain on its hindlegs in full huntform, a fringe of hair around its genitals. It didn't move as we went past. Lucas's pale hand spread against a door. It opened, disclosing a set of stairs. The reek of werecain faded as the receptors in my nose shut down. He pushed me in, and I went gratefully. The door swung closed behind us, shutting out the wall of music.

I sighed. "How'd you find me?"

"I squeezed the agent—Vann—until he gave up that McKinley had sent a communiqué, said he was headed to Sarajevo. Then I called in a favor and caught a smuggler transport out here. Listen, Valentine, your demon had orders in place that you were supposed to be kept out of the action once we ID'd the first demon. Leander's spittin' mad. He's recruiting in Cairo Giza. We're gonna catch a transport out of here in three hours, but you better hear this first."

"Hear *what* first?"

"I said Abra put me on your trail." He pushed me, the stairs were rickety and groaning under the bassbeat. "I lied. She only told me when to be in New Prague to find you. I was contracted to look after you *before* you showed up in that bar."

What? I pushed the door at the top of the stairs open and stepped into a dimly lit room with a blue Old Perasiano rug, a nivron fireplace full of crackling flame, two heavy mahogany chairs set across from each other—and a dozing hellhound lying against the wall under a small window half-hid behind a blue velvet drape.

My heart slammed into my mouth. Next to the hellhound, his shoulders broad and his catslit eyes glittering icy gray, the demon Velokel stood. His face was round and heavy, square teeth that still looked sharp, and those eyes glowing blue around the vertical slits deep and dark enough to swallow the scream struggling up through my throat. The cuff was quiescent on my left wrist, no dappled green light flaring.

A slim female shape standing by the fireplace half-turned. A flash of dark-blue eyes under a sleek cap of pale blond hair, and a glimmering emerald ringing a soft greeting from her forehead. Power blazed through her; the power of an Androgyne. She smelled like fresh bread, like spiced Power and musk, like . . . .

Like Lucifer.

Anubis, my Lord, my god, watch over me. The prayer rose unbidden, and the thought after that was almost as intense in its supplication.

Japhrimel.

Why was I thinking of *him*? Couldn't I stop thinking of him?

Might as well ask yourself to stop breathing, Danny.

"Don't be afraid, Dante," she said softly. "I won't hurt you, and neither will the hound. Come in, sit down."

CHAPTER 37

I swallowed bile as I eyed the hellhound. And the motionless Velokel, who all but thrummed with lethal power. I found myself absurdly comforted by a single thought, an instinctive weighing of every erg of Power this being possessed. *He isn't as strong as Japhrimel.* The comfort was short-lived. *He can still kill me. He can still easily kill me.*

"Relax, Valentine," Lucas said from behind me, pushing me none too gently. "I was contracted to keep your skin whole."

She wore a loose blue cable-knit turtleneck, khakis with a sharp crease, and a pair of expensive black Verano heels. Her breasts moved slightly underneath the sweater. Velokel didn't move. If he wanted to kill me, he'd had more than enough time. He'd had more than enough time as soon as I opened the door.

My hand dropped away from the swordhilt. Lucas closed the door behind us, leaned against it with his head cocked. "You're too old," I whispered. I sounded choked. My cheek burned, my emerald answering the green gem that flashed on her forehead. "Too *old.*" She should still be a child.

She looked just like Doreen. Just like my *sedayeen* lover, dead on the floor of a warehouse while Santino giggled and snuffled happily to himself, collecting his "samples." My beautiful, gentle, wonderful Doreen, the lover who had given me my soul back. Who had given me *myself* back.

Eve smiled, one corner of her mouth quirking up. It was a familiar smile, but I couldn't quite place it. Doreen hadn't ever smiled like that. "A year in Hell isn't the same as a year on earth. Far from. Please, come in, sit down. It's good to see you."

I eased across the room, staring at her. Velokel might as well have been a statue. My skin crawled. "You...I...*you*—"

"I hired Lucas to find you as soon as I left Hell. It was difficult, but I wanted you to have the benefit of some protection. Someone you could trust. It took him a while to find you; the Eldest had you hidden well." She paused. "We could not locate you for a long time, and when we did, we could not approach. He was too...watchful."

Japhrimel, listening to a sound I couldn't hear. Taut and ready, perhaps sensing someone looking for me. Aware that I was in danger, knowing Lucifer was calling for me. That look on his face, that sense of him listening, hadn't been because he was dissatisfied with me. It had been vigilance, the type of protective attention I'd sometimes practiced while doing bodyguard duty but had never, *ever* thought I would be the subject of. So living in Toscano had been to hide me.

To keep me safe.

"You're in a dangerous game, Dante." She moved slowly, like oil, over to the chair that stood with its back to the hellhound. She sank down gracefully, crossed her legs. "Lucifer has contracted you to kill four demons."

I found myself lowering into the other chair, the katana across my knees. My heart beat thinly in my wrists, my ankles, my throat. In my temples. I swallowed, hearing my throat click. "Yes," I said cautiously. *One of them's standing right over there, pretending to be a block of marble.* I cast a quick nervous glance at him, wished I hadn't. His eyes were fixed on her, he hadn't shifted or moved a muscle but his entire being seemed to yearn toward her. *I can bet you're one of them too. No wonder Lucifer…gods. Oh, gods. Did Japhrimel know? Did he?*

She smiled again, that same half-quirk of her lips that seemed so familiar. "I suppose I'm one of them too, then. The Twins, Kel, and I have all escaped Hell." She leaned back into the chair, looked away from me. Doreen's eyes in her face, staring into the fire. "The fault is mine. I am…unique, it seems."

Then her eyes returned to me. Her gaze was so like Doreen's I was having trouble breathing. The demon and the hellhound were utterly still, Lucas just as still. As if the only two people in the room were Eve and me.

I was almost beginning to believe she was sitting in front of me. "Dante," she said, "listen very carefully. I am about to tell you something nobody else knows. Varkolak Vardimal created me from two genetic samples: one taken from the Egg, Lucifer's genetic material. The other sample was a *sedayeen*—your friend and lover. What Vardimal may not have known, and what the Prince of Hell certainly doesn't know, was that the second sample was contaminated with someone else's material." She paused, maybe for effect. "Yours. You are my other mother, Dante. When Vardimal bled the *sedayeen*, he somehow got your blood in the mix."

Memory slammed into me, swallowed me whole.

"Game over," he giggled, and the awful tearing in my side turned to a burning numbness as he slashed, I threw myself backward, not fast enough, not fast enough.

"Danny!" Doreen's despairing cry.

"Get out!" I screamed, but she was coming back, hands glowing blue-white, still trying to heal.

Trying to reach me, to heal me, the link between us resonating with my pain and her burning hands—

Made it to my feet, screaming at her to get the fuck out, Santino's claws whooshing again as he tore into me, one claw sticking on a rib, my sword ringing as I slashed at him, too slow. I was too slow.

Falling again. Something rising in me, a cold agonizing chill. Doreen's hands clamped against my arm. Warm exploding wetness. So much blood. So much.

Her Power roared through me, and I felt the spark of life in her dim. She held on, grimly, as Santino made little snuffling, chortling sounds of glee. The whine of a lasecutter as he took part of her femur, the slight pumping sound of the bloodvac. Blood dripped in my eyes, splattered against my cheek. Sirens howling in the distance— Doreen's death would register on her datband, and aid hovers would be dispatched. Too late, though. Too late for both of us.

I passed out, hearing the wet smacking sounds as Santino took what he wanted, giggling that high-pitched strange chortle of his. His face burned itself into my memory—black teardrops painted over the eyes, pointed ears, the sharp ivory fangs. Not human, *I thought,* he can't be human, Doreen, Doreen, get away, run, run—

Her soul, carried like a candle down a long dark hall, guttering. Guttering. Spark shrinking into infinity. I am a Necromance, but I couldn't stop her rushing into Death's arms....

I stared at her, my nape prickling and my mouth full of copper. It *could* be true. We'd certainly both bled enough when he killed her. But wouldn't Santino have known? A demon geneticist was perfectly capable of telling a contaminated sample from a pure one. There was no reason for him to even *keep* a contaminated sample.

Unless he'd guessed he might find a use for it.

She looked back at me. Her mouth curled up in that little half-smile again. "Vardimal may or may not have known. In any case, it was immaterial once he realized the value of what he had—a viable sample. A viable *fetus*." Now her mouth pulled down into a soft grimace, Doreen's little moue of distaste. It was damn hard to think with the smell of her filling the air. I shivered galvanically on the hard seat, my eyes flicking past her to the dozing hellhound and returning, compelled, to meet hers.

Doreen's eyes. My dead lover's eyes.

In someone else's face—a face that held an echo of Lucifer. I was responding to her, unfamiliar desire rising to swamp me. A thin trickle of heat purred through my belly. *Doreen. Oh, gods, Doreen.*

My heart slammed against my ribs. The mark on my shoulder was alive with heat, burrowing into my skin. "Why are you telling me this?" I still sounded choked. *I'm in a room with two demons, a hellhound, and Lucas Villalobos. Anubis protect me.*

"I'm explaining." Her voice was soft, soothing. "Vardimal failed to keep me away from *him*. The call the Prince is capable of exerting on an Androgyne is...immense. We are of his kind and he is the oldest, the Prime. I had very little chance of denying him access to my mind when I was a child. However...the Prince, whenever he creates an Androgyne, also implants several commands before the Androgyne is hatched. One of them is obedience. I wasn't implanted until I was five human years old. The implant held until very recently." The half-smile was back. I realized with a deep chill that I recognized it because I'd seen it in the mirror. It was my own expression. "It seems I have inherited your stubbornness, Dante. That is the only explanation I can arrive at for why the Prince has been unsuccessful in his attempt to break me."

"Break you?" My voice seemed to come from very far away. My hands felt weak and unsteady, as if they were shaking. *What would Japhrimel think of this? Does he know? Did he?*

If Japhrimel had known, and hadn't told me...there was nothing, *nothing* that could make that omission less than a complete and utter betrayal.

Had he thought I wouldn't find out? Of course not. He was certain he was stronger than me, able to force me to do whatever he wanted.

Had he known? Would I ever get to ask him, and could I trust his answer if I did?

My chest split, cracking. *Now I know I have a heart,* I thought inconsequentially. *It's breaking.*

The thought managed to shock me back into rationality. Eve. Here. In the world, free. Maybe not for very much longer, since Lucifer had contracted not only me and Japhrimel but possibly more hunters to track her down. No wonder I'd felt like bait. I *was* bait, a lure to draw her out. To betray her without even knowing it.

"I am the only Androgyne to leave Hell for many mortal years, other than the Prince." She blinked her dark blue eyes at me. Her face was clear, unlined, but mature. She looked like a woman on the cusp of twenty-five, except for the shadow of demon knowledge in her gaze.

She couldn't be more than seven or eight *human* years old. How long had she been out of Hell, if Lucifer had been asking for me all this time?

A year in Hell is not the same as a year on earth. How old was she in Hell years? Were they like dog years? How many to a human year, how old was she, how *long* had she been there, suffering under the Prince of Hell?

Bile rose in my throat, and rage under my ribs. Cold, vicious rage, of a type I'd never felt before in all my long and angry life.

This rage was different. It was pure unalloyed hatred.

My eyes flickered back to Velokel. Returned to Eve.

She continued, apparently thinking I was too stunned to respond. She was right. "I am in rebellion against the Prince. I am Androgyne, and I am determined to stay alive and free." She took a deep breath. "I want your help, Dante. I'm not bargaining, I'm only asking. You're capable of feigning to hunt me and mine, I'm asking you not to try too hard. Distract your *A'nankhimel*. Seven years from now your bargain with the Prince will be done, and I promise you all the protection and aid I can offer." She leaned forward, her eyes sparkling. "*Freedom*, Dante. I want mine, you want yours — together we can provide an alternative to the Prince and his stranglehold on both earth and Hell."

That was uncomfortably similar to Santino's cant about freeing everyone from Lucifer. But Santino had wanted to implant me with other Androgyne fetuses. He had thought he could rule Eve, and through her, Hell. I looked over her shoulder at the dozing hellhound, steam rising gently from its pelt. Velokel still stared at Eve, an expression on his round face I had no trouble deciphering. It was equal parts fierce concentration and protective tenderness, he didn't bother to disguise it. It would have been a human expression except for the blazing intensity in his catslit eyes. He looked obsessed with her. Velokel, apparently, was in love.

If demons could love. I'd seen that look before on another demon's face.

"Gods above," I rasped. "Are you *serious*?"

"I swear on the waters of Lethe, this is the truth. I ask you only for time. I won't twist your arm and try to force you like *he* would." It was obvious who "he" was, every time she mentioned Lucifer her pretty face twisted.

You know, I understand. What would it be like to live in Hell, to live with that goddamn viper that calls itself Lucifer? She's half human. Half Doreen. What part of her is mine? I took a deep, endless breath. *Let's get this straight.* "You want me to break my bargain with Lucifer. Set myself up against the Devil."

She nodded. "I do."

I blew out through my teeth. *Well, nice to know we understand each other.* "That's one tall order, sunshine."

Velokel stirred. Eve lifted her expressive golden hand, and he stopped, subsiding against the wall. The hellhound didn't move. I snapped a glance at Lucas, who looked supremely unconcerned, leaning against the door. His bandoliers creaked as he shifted his weight, a small sound.

Eve lowered her hand. "Think on it, Dante. *He* fears you. You took the Right Hand and stood a very real chance of denying *him* access to me. Had you not returned to Nuevo Rio, *he* would have been forced to treat with you as a suppliant. Not so long ago, *he* tried to bargain with your Fallen to kill you. Theoretically, in return the Eldest would be restored to Hell. Such a thing is impossible, and well Lucifer knew it. Still, your Fallen refused, I heard it myself. The Prince was desperate to regain his Right Hand. His hold on Hell has been slipping for quite some time."

Wait a second. Back up. When did this happen? Maybe during the time Lucifer was asking to see me and Japhrimel was refusing? My heart leapt inside my ribs. Japhrimel had refused to kill me in order to go back to Hell. Never mind that it was "impossible."

How twisted was it, that I grabbed at that to feel better? But I had another question. "What about the demon who wanted to kill me in New Prague? The hellhound?"

"Kel wished to meet the Eldest and treat with him, but retreated when he realized the Kinslayer had misunderstood his attempt. The hellhounds in New Prague were not part of Kel's pack. Another demon might have rebelled and sought to strike before the Kinslayer could find him—after all, the Eldest is the demon most feared among those who would rebel against the Prince. There are other trackers and hunters after me as well, Dante. The world is full of peril." She tipped her elegant head. Power stroked along my skin, as warm as Japhrimel's nonphysical caress. I was hard put to swallow a slight, betraying sound as my body flushed with heat. "Tell your Fallen this is Kel's pledge—he will not hunt you unless you threaten us."

Velokel seemed almost to leap without moving, his attention suddenly refocused on her. Eve's eyes dropped slightly, and a faint flush rose to her cheeks. Very interesting. I had the idea that this Kel was a little more intimately involved with Eve than he should be.

Good to know.

"Kel." My eyes met his for a long moment. The mark on my shoulder began to pulse, quietly. "The Hunter. The one who hunted *hedaira*?"

Eve tilted her head, her pale hair moving soft and silky. "He did so at the Prince's orders. Were you told who hunted the ones Kel could not?"

No, nobody told me about that. I met her eyes. "Let me guess. The Right Hand."

She nodded. "The Prince's Eldest killed more *A'nankhimel* and *hedaira* than Kel could hope to. He is not called *Kinslayer* for nothing."

My skin chilled. No wonder Japhrimel didn't talk about the Fallen, if he'd killed so many of them. He must have never expected to end up as one of them.

Oh, gods. Japhrimel. Did you know about this? About her?

I licked my numb lips. "I can't say for sure. But if it's possible, if can do it, I'll help you." Then I spoke the words. "I promise."

If she did manage to break Lucifer's hold on Hell, what would happen? Would there be uncontrolled demons roaming the earth? I was no Magi, but I knew enough about Hell's citizens that the prospect filled me with an uncomfortable feeling very close to terror.

But what else could I do? What the *hell* else could I do?

Eve opened her mouth to reply, but a thin growl rose through the air. I looked past her shoulder. The hellhound's head was up, its teeth bared. It didn't look at me, it looked at the door.

Velokel spoke, a single word, sharp and weighted with the

consonants of the demons' strange, unlovely language. He was suddenly tense, his broad shoulders corded with muscle. He reminded me of a bull, powerful and slow, but I was willing to bet he had the same spooky, blurring speed as other demons.

"Time to go," Lucas said. "Come on, *chica*."

I made it to my feet like an old woman. One shock after another, I was starting to feel like a punch-drunk cagefighter. My hand fastened on my swordhilt as I stared at the hound. Oddly enough, I was more scared of the hellhound than of Velokel.

Eve stepped close to me. Her smell, the smell of an Androgyne, a scent that threatened to unloose my knees and spill me to the floor, caressed me. My head filled with heat, my lips parted. I'd never responded like this to Lucifer—I'd been too terrified to feel anything close to desire for him, even though he was beautiful and lethal. I had *never* had a sexual response to pure Power before, but she was heir to all Lucifer's crackling force and she wore Doreen's face like a sexwitch wears submission, like a perfume. The face of my *sedayeen* lover, the person who had taught me the prison of my body could be a source of joy as well as pain.

You feel everything, don't you? Doreen had asked me once. *But you don't like to show it. You keep that mask of a face up, and people think you don't care. But you do, Danny. You care.*

She had been the only person, *ever*, who understood that about me. She had been the only lover who hadn't asked more of me than I could give.

I had given her all I had.

What wouldn't I do, if only for Doreen's memory, if only to expunge the guilt of my failure to protect her?

"Don't decide yet. I'll contact you when I can." Eve's breath touched my cheek, warm and forgiving.

I nodded, beyond words. Was it true?

Did my blood mix with Doreen's? Was my genetic material part of Eve's?

Was she my child as well? My daughter, the only daughter I would ever have. I couldn't see myself breeding with Japhrimel. *Sekhmet sa'es*, no. Not now. Maybe not ever.

He refused to kill me. He turned Lucifer down. Gods. I stood frozen as she stepped away, beckoning to the hellhound. It got up, shook itself, and paced after her as she walked to the nivron fireplace. Then, wonder of wonders, she stepped *into* the fire, flame lifting to caress her body like a lover, and promptly vanished. A high squealing note of Power split the air, my rings spat and the wristcuff rang with green light. Velokel gave me one narrow-eyed, lip-curling look and followed. The hellhound looped on itself and leapt through the fire after them. Vanished.

What the hell, were we supposed to hunt her when she can walk through fucking walls? Why didn't Lucifer mention that?

Of course he hadn't told me. I would never have agreed to hunt Eve, no matter what he threatened me with.

Japhrimel. Had he known?

He refused to kill me to go back home to Hell, and he'll at least keep me alive. I'm feeling pretty fucking charitable toward him right now. Except for the little matter of him possibly keeping this to himself.

Lucas was at my shoulder. "Don't stand around, Valentine. Somethin' tells me we better get out of here. We got a transport to catch."

"Gods," I said. "*Gods.* Did you believe a word of that?"

"Analyze later," he said, just as the mood of the building underneath — sex and feeding and music blurring together — tipped strangely. A single thrill of fear slid up my spine. "Move *now*." He flung the door open and began down the stairs.

"We're not going out the window?"

"Nope," Lucas flung over his shoulder. "Sheer brick wall straight down to a blind alley, we'll be trapped like rats. Come on, *chica*. I'm s'posed to keep you alive."

CHAPTER 38

We jolted down the stairs and burst out into the music. The werecain guard at the door was gone. I checked my datband, lifting my left hand, weighted with my sword.

Quarter to midnight. I was beginning to think I might still be alive and not dead of shock. Power spiking in the air cleared my head, and I noticed the crotch of my panties was uncomfortably damp. I had *never* responded like that before. Never.

She was Doreen's child, and maybe mine. That I reacted to her was a shameful secret, nothing more. She did, after all, wear my dead lover's face. I wasn't attracted to her, I told myself. No, I was simply determined to keep Doreen's daughter from being dragged back into Hell or killed to salve Lucifer's fucking pride.

I've had just about enough of the Devil. My eyes found the wrist-cuff snugged above my datband.

The cuff ran with fluid lines of green fire, settling into a frozen, scratched rune, a backwards-leaning spiked H.

Danger.

Yeah, like I don't already know that. I was beginning to feel like myself again. If Japhrimel had known it was Eve instead of Lucifer here...had he guessed? Why had he thought Lucifer wanted a little chat with me again? Leonidas hadn't named the demon wanting to see me, and I wondered about that too.

Forget it, Dante. Now it's time to move.

The dance floor still pulsed with writhing bodies. My awareness swept through the interior, and found the swanhild gone. That was interesting. Something feral stalked closer, if I could feel it the 'hilds certainly could, with their exquisite sensitivity to predators.

I took a deep breath tainted with synth-hash and followed Lucas's rigid, bandolier-crossed back through the press of Nichtvren flesh, was jostled by a werecain who snarled at me. The mark on my shoulder heated up again, a live brand pressed into my flesh. It hurt, scorching through the layers of gray numbness threatening me.

I almost welcomed the pain. I wished Japhrimel was behind me. Sure, he was a lying bastard—but right now I was feeling very much like I might not get out of this tangled web without him.

I can't believe I just thought that. He refused to kill me to go back to Hell. He gave up his home for me.

Yeah, and he just "forgot" to mention Eve was out of Hell and giving the Devil a run for his money. Sure he did.

We were halfway across the dance floor when Lucas veered, taking a course that would bring us out near the stage and a glowing green sign in Cyrillic that probably said *exit*. I kept my sword in both hands, left on the scabbard, right on the hilt. The back of my neck prickled, running chills sliding down the shallow channel of my spine. I felt cold even in the middle of the heat and flux of Power, desire draining away and leaving me aching, unsatisfied. A roar went up from the bar—some kobolding playing a drinking game. The kobolding bartender, however, had his back to the mirrored wall holding glass shelves of bottles and stasis cabinets for cloned blood and other things. His yellow eyes glittered as he sniffed. He scanned the place suspiciously, lifting his gray lumpen head.

The shadows thickened near the bar, and I caught sight of a familiar shape. Broad shoulders under a black T-shirt, a black leather Mob assassin's rig, a shock of wheat-gold hair. Recognition slammed through me, and instant denial.

It couldn't be.

I stopped dead on the dance floor, buffeted by moving Nichtvren on all sides. I stared, going up on my toes to get a clearer view.

The man—was it a man? Not in DMZ Sarajevo. But he reached out with one hand and touched a staff leaning against the bar. The staff stood taller then his head, and small bones tied to it with raffia twine clacked as his fingers touched it. That small sound cut through the music and welter of Power, spilling prickles through my veins. My nipples tightened, I gasped.

He swung around. Blue eyes flashed.

Jace Monroe regarded me across a throng of thrashing Nichtvren. He lifted his sword, and I realized I could see *through* him, as if he was made of colored smoke.

I am a Necromance, death is my trade. But I had *never* seen anything like this. Most ghostflits are pale gray smoke, not colorfully lifelike. And this was not where he had died. This was not where his ashes were, the cremains a Necromance could use to bring his apparition through to ask questions—if she was powerful enough. This was not a place Jace had haunted in life.

He should not be haunting it now.

The ghost grinned at me, raising his sheathed *dotanuki,* the same blade that had hung above the altar in the Toscano villa, bent and corkscrewed with the agony of his last strike and death still ringing in the metal. Only his ghost held the sword as it had been, unbent, true and familiar.

My right hand crept up to touch the shape of the necklace under my shirt.

He *winked* at me. Then his face grew grave, and his lips shaped three words.

Run, Danny. Run.

The strength spilled out of my legs. I would have fallen except for the press of Nichtvren flesh around me. The ghost of my dead lover shook his head, the same way he used to when I was too slow during a sparring session.

Go. I heard the word clearly, laid in the shell of my ear, Jace's breath on my nape. My entire body tightened, heat spilling into my lower belly again, my panties soaked as if I'd been necking like a heated Academy teenager. What the *hell* was wrong with me?

I. Am. Not. A. Sexwitch.

Lucas's hand closed around my upper arm again. He made a spitting sound and hauled on me, and I went willingly. We forced our way through the crush of the dance floor, Lucas shouldering aside a pair of Nichtvren Acolytes poured into matching red pleather outfits. We freed ourselves from the press just as the entire building shivered.

Lucas swore. He let go of me—I was thankfully able to walk on my own now. His hands came up with a 60-watt plasgun in each. I jammed my sword into the loop on my belt, keeping my right hand on the hilt. I drew steel, and my newly freed left hand closed around my own plasgun just as all hell broke loose. Again.

CHAPTER 39

I had a few seconds to decide what to do as the second hellhound crashed through the wall, bricks flying. The first hound was busy with four werecain who had unluckily been in its way, and the howling spitting mess crashed into the bar. Plasglass tinkled. Lucas grabbed my shoulder and hauled me back as the second hellhound bulleted forward.

These two were different from the others. Their eyes were green, a fierce glowing green instead of crimson. Heat shimmered and warped away from them all the way across the dance floor.

Lust vanished. Survival took its place, chill fury rising under my skin. The cuff on my wrist made a thin humming sound, like crystal stroked just right.

My sword finished ringing free of the sheath as the second hellhound snarled, a low, vicious sound tearing at the air. The music had halted, but a rising crescendo of screams took its place. Three Nichtvren burned like fatty candles, screeching as the hellhound brushed past them, hair and preternatural skin igniting. Paranormal creatures scrambled for the door, the crowd acting very human for all its Power and inherent danger.

Lucas fired at the hellhound streaking for me. A crimson streak of plasbolt clove the air, smashing into the beast, which snarled and shook its head, crashing to the floor. It literally shook the building. Dust pattered down, I heard the singing whimper of plasteel support struts flexing.

Sekhmet sa'es. It must be dense to rock the building like that. The dragging feeling of being trapped in a nightmare, arms and legs weighted down with sleep while a beast lunges for you, paralyzed me.

"*Go!*" Lucas screamed in his high whistling voice. Paralysis broke.

I backed up, unwilling to turn away from the things. A shattering squealing roar rose from the battle near the bar. Bottles exploded, glass and plasglass flying through the air with little deadly sounds. Alcohol and other fluids ignited, bursts of blue and red flame. Stasis cabinets shattered, and the stink of frying Nichtvren and frying blood filled the air. A line of fire swiped across my forehead, flying plasglass shards, black blood dripped into my eyes. The slice sealed itself before I could even flinch.

The mark on my left shoulder gave one livid burst of pain that almost drove me to my knees. The air was hot and still, popping sounds beginning as the wooden bar caught fire.

Lucas backed up. "I ain't gonna tell you again, Valen—" he began.

Then he was flung back as the second hellhound reached its feet and launched itself at him. It moved so quickly it seemed to simply flash through the intervening space.

"*Lucas!*" I screamed, and flung myself after it. My sword blazed blue-white, a rising song of bloodlust caroling out from the steel. My feet ground in broken glass, shattered brick, and other debris.

Then things began to get *really goddamn interesting.*

I reached the hellhound just as fresh screams started from the door and the air pressure changed. A wave of sickening Power roiled through the air as I chopped down, my *kia* taking on sharp physical weight.

The hellhound's head jerked up and it screamed as my blade, livid with Power, carved deeply into its back. Black blood boiled up, steaming as the glow of my blade made the acid drops sizzle and spatter like hot oil. *Oh, my gods, I actually cut it!*

It turned back on itself with a crackle of flexible bones, and I dropped flat as it flew over me, its momentum making it overshoot. It landed amid a pile of Nichtvren, who tangled and screamed as flame burst through them. Coiled itself, claws raking flesh and flooring both, and I found myself on my feet, the sword slicing down and around as I made sure I had free play in my right hand. It was a swordsman's move, easy and habitual, and the entire world narrowed as the hellhound snarled and launched itself at me again.

It didn't reach me.

A wall of huge Power crashed into my side and I flew sideways, my fingers torn from the hilt. *Wha*—

The hellhound squealed, a sound of glassy frustrated rage. I hit the wall, stone and brick shattering with an almost musical crash. Before I hit the floor he was on me, elegant golden fingers sinking into my throat and the entire world thrumming with the fury of the Prince of Hell.

"*Where is she?*" Lucifer demanded, his eyes glowing so brightly they cast shadows under his flawless cheekbones. His hair glowed too, a furnace of gold like the sun's own flame.

I couldn't have answered even if I wanted to. His fingers tightened, curling almost all the way around my neck. I heard something crackle in my throat—it sounded like a small bone—and did the only thing I could. I kicked, hard, and smashed at him with all the Power I could reach.

His head snapped aside, a thin line of black blood tracing up his beautiful cheek. The emerald set in his forehead spat one single, terrible spark of green so dark it was bloody.

The air chilled as I struggled. His fingers didn't give. Steam drifted up from his skin and mine in thin twisted coils. His hand was so tight I couldn't even tuck my chin to look down at him, instead I saw a rapidly darkening slice of the shattered burning bar opposite. The four-armed kobolding lay twisted and broken like a rag doll in the debris, its body smoking.

"You have meddled for the last time, Necromance," he spat, and I could feel it gathering, breathless electricity. Pain rolled down my skin, vicious little teeth nipping at me, darkness clouding the edges of my vision, struggling to *breathe*.

Oh, gods. I'm dead, I'm dead. I struggled even harder, achieved exactly nothing, darkness closing over my vision, no blue flame though. Lungs burning, burning, heart pounding, my eyes bulging, as if I was in a depressurized cabin and thrashing, struggling, *dying* to breathe.

Had Death forsaken me too?

No. My god would never forsake me.

Crimson light splashed against him, and he dropped me. I collapsed, too weak even to cough, my lungs burning. Whooped in a long gasping breath full of smoke and an awful crisped stench. Paranormal flesh burning: Nichtvren, kobolding, werecain. Ugh.

"You must be the Devil," Lucas wheezed. "Pleasetameetcha. Can you guess m'name?"

I coughed again, hacked, made a low, wounded noise. Frantically scrabbled in the wreckage and dust. *My sword, where's my sword, gods above and below give me my sword, I* need *my sword*—

"Deathless." Lucifer's golden voice stroked the word. I heard a hellhound snarl. A massive impact against my belly—Lucifer had kicked me, an afterthought. I was flung back, hit the wall, a short gasping sound jerked out of me. More plaster and stone shattered, dust poofing out. "You may leave. I have no quarrel with you."

I never thought I'd feel grateful to hear Lucas's grating laugh. There was a gritting sound—he had stepped forward, kicking something out of the way. "She's my client, *El Diablo.* Can't let you kill 'er."

The air chilled even more. Lucifer's attention shifted like a shark swimming through cold water. Brick and plasteel groaned, plaster dust filled the air.

The Devil spoke again. His voice tore the air, left it bleeding, and *hurt* me. "Leave now, or die."

Lucas seemed to find this incredibly funny. At least, he laughed— and fired at the Devil again. The world turned red and I heard the whine of a plasbolt; Lucifer's feet made a light sound as if stroking the surface of a drum.

I moaned. Made it up to hands and knees, coughing. My belly ran with razor fire. The sound of the rest of the world came back in a high towering wave, smashed into my sensitive ears. Crashing. Screaming, deep groaning coughs of werecain in distress. High chilling crystal screams from Nichtvren bleeding or burning.

I scrabbled away from the wall, coughing at plaster dust stuck in my nose. Had to hunch, it felt like Lucifer's kick had ruptured something and my belly ran with lava. *My sword, my sword*—My entire world narrowed to finding my sword. I was in shock, the world graying out, my left arm singing with agony and my throat burning.

More crashes, unearthly screams, and Lucas's laugh again. He was giving the Devil a run for his money, it seemed.

I don't care who hired him. My sword. I need my sword, if Lucifer's going to kill me, I want to die with my sword.

Then, like a gift, I spotted a black-wrapped hilt. My fingers closed on it just as Lucifer's hand sank into my hair and he pulled my head up. I managed to get my feet underneath me, but my spine curved as he yanked my head back, exposing my throat as my knees folded. I crouched, dangling from his hand. My choked cry slammed shut midway, a spear of pain rammed through my stomach.

"I will tear the secret of your talent for inspiring such loyalty from your screaming ghost," he said meditatively in my ear, broken plasglass and plaster grinding as he shifted his weight. Was the Devil crouching over me? "I will only ask once more, *human whore*. Where is she?"

I won't tell you. I will never tell you. Do your goddamn worst, you sonovabitch. I coughed as if choking. I probably was. I couldn't seem to get enough air in.

"*Where is she?*" He shook me.

I took a harsh tortured sip of air. Struggled to *speak*, to say what I had to.

I managed it. Two little words. "Fuck...you."

He made a sound like the earth itself ripping in half. The sword thrummed in my grasp. Hair tore out of my scalp as he hauled on me again, this time hissing in his demonic language. I'd driven the Devil to a sputtering fit of rage.

Huzzah. Lucky, talented me.

I had only one clear, crystalline thought. *Now or never.*

I stamped my feet under me, dug in, and pushed with all the strength in my legs, his hand pulling terribly one last time at my hair. Power sparked, flooded up my left arm, my sword burning white as I twisted, the sharp edge of the katana facing out and the blunt edge along my forearm. As I turned I flexed my wrist, dragging my sword's edge across the Devil's belly.

I felt the blade Fudoshin bite deep.

A tremendous sound, like every key on an ancient pipe organ hit at once and fed through feedback-laced speakers, slammed over the abused air. I fell over backward, my head hitting a pile of bricks and plaster with stunning force. Pain tore through me, something ripping loose inside my abused belly. But I kept my sword, heard metal chime against debris. My fingers were locked around the hilt.

Then I heard something I never thought I'd be so happy to hear again.

"Touch her again, *Prince,*" Japhrimel said coldly, a pall of freezing closing over the demolished interior, "and it will be your last act on Earth."

Silence like a nuclear winter. Ticking of time and plaster dust both falling through empty space. Lucifer spoke again, his voice killing-cold as a nuclear winter. "Did you just threaten me, Fallen?"

"No," Japhrimel said quietly. "I simply inform you of a consequence. It is not fit to treat your Right Hand so."

I dragged in a deep heaving breath, flinched as my gut clenched and broke open with hideous pain. I wanted to close my eyes and curl into a ball, let the world go on without me. So tired, so very tired. Exhaustion dragging down every nerve.

I braced my left hand against the floor. Pushed myself up. It took two tries before I could get to my knees, my left arm braced across my abused stomach. My sword dragged against metal and bricks, too heavy to lift. I coughed, rackingly. Spat black blood. My throat burned as if another reactive fire had been set off inside it to match the one in my middle, below my ribs.

"She was *here,*" Lucifer snarled. He sounded almost speechless with rage, and for once his voice wasn't beautiful. "She—"

"She is your servant, wearing your trinket, and has already suffered violence because of it. Including attack from the other hunters you have sent." Japhrimel's tone was eminently reasonable, and colder than anything earthly. "Are you relieving us of the burden of your service, Prince? I can think of no other reason for such treachery."

Oh, gods above, Japhrimel, what are you saying? I raised my head, muscles in my neck shrieking. It seemed to take forever.

Japhrimel stood in the middle of the wrack and ruin of the Haunt *Tais-toi,* his long wet-dark coat lying on his shoulders like night itself. Lucifer faced him, the Prince of Hell's lovely face twisted with fury, suffused with a darkness more than physical. Japhrimel's hand closed around Lucifer's right wrist, muscle standing out under Lucifer's shirt and Japhrimel's coat as the Devil surged forward—and Japhrimel pushed him *back.*

If I hadn't seen it, I would never have believed it possible. But Japh's entire body tensed, and he forced Lucifer back on his heels.

The Devil stepped mincingly away, twisting his wrist free of Japhrimel's hand. Retreated, only two steps. But it was enough.

Lucifer's aura flamed with blackness, a warping in the fabric of the world. They looked at each other, twin green gazes locked as if the words they exchanged were only window-dressing for the real combat, fought by the glowing spears of their eyes. The two hellhounds wove around them, low fluid shapes. Lucifer's indigo silk shirt was torn, gaping, across his midriff, showing a slice of golden skin—and as I watched, a single drop of black blood dripped from one torn edge. More spots of dark blood smoked on the silken pants he wore.

I'd cut the Devil.

One dazed thought sparked inside my aching head. *Jado must've given me a hell of a good blade.*

Then another thought, ridiculous in its intensity. *Here. Japh's here. Everything will be all right now.*

Childish faith, maybe, but I'd take it. If it was a choice between my Fallen and getting killed right this moment, I'd settle for Japhrimel, no matter how much of a bastard he'd been recently. Funny how almost getting killed radically changed my notions of just how much I could forgive.

Japhrimel's eyes didn't flick over to check me, but the mark on my shoulder came to agonized life again, Power flooding me, exploding in my belly. White-hot pokers jerked in my viscera. My scalp twinged, I tasted blood and burning. My sword rang softly, the core of the blade burning white, blue runic patterns slipping through keen edge and painting the air. I managed to lift it, the blade a bar between me and the Devil facing his eldest son.

The red lights were still flickering, sweeping over the entire building in their complicated patterns, eerie because there were no dancers. "You would have me believe—" Lucifer started. Stone and plaster shattered at the sound of his voice, dust pattering to the wracked floor.

Japhrimel interrupted him again. I felt only a weary wonder that he was still standing there, apparently untouched, his long black coat moving gently on the hot fire-breeze. "We were told by the Master of this city—*your* ally and Hellesvront agent—that you wished to meet Dante here alone. Did you lure your Right Hand here to kill her, Prince? Breaking your word, given on your ineffable Name? Such would conclude our alliance in a most *unsatisfactory* fashion."

I could swear that Lucifer's face went through surprise, disgust, and finally settled on wariness. He studied Japhrimel for a long, tense thirty seconds, during which my throat burned and tickled but I didn't dare to cough.

Japh clasped his hands behind his back. He looked relaxed, almost bored. Except for the burning murderous light of his eyes, matching Lucifer's shade for shade.

I stayed very still, my left arm cramping as my belly ran with pain and my right trembling as I held my sword. A small part of me wondered where Lucas was. The rest of me stared at Japhrimel with open wonderment.

If I survive this, I'm going to kiss him. Right after I punch the shit out of him for lying to me. If he lets me. The nastiness of the thought made me suddenly, deeply ashamed of myself. He was here, and he was facing Lucifer. For me.

He had given up Hell. He had also taken me to Toscano and let me heal from the psychic rape of Mirovitch's *ka,* protecting me from dangers I hadn't had the faintest idea existed. He was loyal to me after all.

In his own fashion.

Lucifer finally seemed to decide. The flames among the shattered wreckage twisted into angular shapes as some essential tension leached out of him. "I rue the day I set you to watch over her, Eldest." The darkness in his face didn't fade, however—it intensified, a psychic miasma.

The tickling in my throat reached a feverish pitch. I *had* to cough, shoved the urge down, prayed for strength. *Anubis, please don't let me attract their attention. Both of them look too dangerous right now.*

Japhrimel shrugged. "What is done, is *done.*" His voice pitched a little higher, as if he imitated Lucifer. Or was quoting him.

The Prince of Hell set his jaw. One elegant hand curled into a fist, and perhaps the other one was a fist too, but I couldn't see it. I think it was the first time I saw the Devil speechless, and my jaw would have dropped if I hadn't clenched it, trying not to cough. I took a fresh grip on my belly, trying not to hunch over. I wanted to see, *needed* to see. My sword held steady even though my hand was shaking, the blade singing a thin comforting song as its heart glowed white.

He finally seemed to regain himself. "You deserve each other," he hissed. "May you have joy of it. Bring me back my possession and eliminate those who would keep it from me, Tierce Japhrimel, or I will kill both of you. I swear it."

Japhrimel's eyes flared. "That was not our bargain, my lord."

Lucifer twitched. Japhrimel didn't move, but the mark twisted white-hot fire into my shoulder, a final burst of Power. The urge to cough mercifully retreated a little. I blinked drying demon blood out of my eyes. I wanted to look for Lucas.

I couldn't look away from my Fallen. He stood tense and ready, in front of the Devil.

"I am the Prince of Hell," Lucifer said coldly.

"And I was your Eldest." Japhrimel held Lucifer's eyes as the air itself cried out, a long gasping howl of a breeze coming from them, blowing my hair back. I felt the stiffness—blood and dust matted in my hair. I was filthy, and I ached. I stayed where I was. "I was the Kinslayer. Thus you made me, and you cast me away. I am yours no longer."

"*I* made you." The air itself screamed as the Prince of Hell's voice tore at it. "Your allegiance is *mine*."

"My allegiance," Japhrimel returned, inexorably quiet, "is my own. I Fell. I am Fallen. I am not your son."

One last burst of soft killing silence. I struggled to stay still.

Lucifer turned on his heel. The world snapped back into normalcy. He strode for the gaping hole torn in the front of the nightclub. Red neon reflected wetly off the street outside. A flick of his golden fingers, and the hellhounds loped gracefully after him, one stopping to snarl back over its shoulder at me.

Well, now I can guess who sent the hellhounds. Probably Lucifer himself, to make sure I fulfilled my intended role as bait. You bastard. You filthy bastard. I sagged. My sword dipped, and the urge to cough rose again. It felt like a plasgun core had been dropped into my gut.

The Prince stopped, turned his head so I could see his profile. "Japhrimel." His voice was back to silk and honey, terrible in its beauty. "I give you a promise, my Eldest. One day, I will kill her."

Lucifer disappeared. Vanished. The air tried to heal itself, closing over the space where he had been, and failed. He left a scorch on the very fabric of existence.

Japhrimel was silent for a moment, his eyes fixed forward. He didn't look at me. I was glad, because his face was full of something terrible, irrevocable, and devouring.

"Not while I watch over her," he said softly.

CHAPTER 40

I finally coughed, a racking fit that ended with me spitting more black blood. It felt like I'd been torn in half. My legs were made of insensate clay. I doubted I'd be able to stand.

Japhrimel knelt beside me, caught my right wrist and pushed my sword away with simple pressure. He said nothing, but immediately slid his other hand under my left arm, pressed flat against my shirt. His fingers burned.

A jolt of Power seared through me. I cried out, hunching over, and retched; a deep, amazing hacking sound. He swore, passionlessly, and I tipped into his arms as the awful tearing agony went away. *All right. Everything's going to be all right. He's here.* The ludicrous, childlike certainty welled up, I choked back tears.

Right then I didn't care what he'd done to me before. I was just damn glad he'd shown up in time.

He kissed my forehead, my cheek, hugged me. Spoke into my hair. *"A'tai, hetairae A'nankimel'iin. Diriin."* His voice was ragged now. "Why, Dante? *Why?"*

What are you asking me for? I'm just trying to stay alive. I hitched in a breath. Another. It rasped terribly against my abused throat. What was it with demons and crushing my trachea? "Lucas," I rasped. "Took on Lucifer...is he—"

"Check for the Deathless," Japhrimel said over his shoulder. "Hurry."

Who else is here? The thought was very far away. Shaking. Shivers roaring through me. Why? I wasn't cold. "J-j-j-japh—"

"Be silent. You're hurt, and you need rest." His tone was clipped now. "Do not fight me, now."

"Japhrimel—" I tried to tell him. "I...I saw...*before—"*

He didn't listen. "No more of this."

I tipped into blackness, but not before I heard Lucas's wheezing voice.

"Goddammit, that *hurt.* Get your ass moving, we have a transport to catch."

*   *   *

Long hazy time of darkness. When I woke, slowly, I found myself on my side. Warmth closed over me, and softness. Power pulsed down my skin, sank in, ran along my bones. I heard Japhrimel's voice, quiet, saying something in his native tongue. Something stroked my forehead, a touch that sent a sweet gentle fire through my entire body. He traced my hairline, touched my cheek, ran his knuckle over my lips.

Hoverwhine. I felt the peculiar humming sensation of antigrav transport. Was I on a hover?

I don't think I like hovers anymore.

I opened my eyes. Dim light greeted me. I felt my swordhilt, both hands locked around it. The sword lay with me, its subliminal hum of Power good and right against my palms.

Japhrimel moved as soon as I looked up at him, straightening and stepping back. I was on a medunit table bolted to a wall behind a partition, and the curve of the plasteel walls told me it was a fairly good-sized hover. The table was hard, but I wasn't being strangled and I didn't feel ripped in half. I was still breathing, and I had all my original appendages.

It felt *great.* I closed my eyes, opened them again, and he was still there.

"Gods," I rasped. "I'm glad to see you."

He managed to look surprised and gratified at once, his saturnine face easing. "Then I am happy. You are well and whole, your friend Lucas has mended, and McKinley and Vann are no worse for wear. Tiens will meet us in Giza. The humans have gone back to their lives, except for your Necromance." His mouth turned down slightly at the mention of Leander.

I nodded. It was getting hazardous to hang around me, and humans were fragile.

I felt only a twinge of guilt for thinking that. After all, I'd been wholly human once, hadn't I?

Was Japhrimel right? Was it no more than a habit? I didn't want to think so. I was human *inside,* where it counted.

He leaned forward, his eyes still bright and green. I examined his face as he examined mine, something new in the silence between us.

He broke it first, for once. "He could have killed you."

I nodded, my hair sliding along a crisp cotton pillowcase. Where had the pillow come from? "He certainly wanted to." The question spilled out of me. "Did you hunt the Fallen, Japhrimel?"

He froze. I would never get used to his particular quality of stillness, as if his very molecules had slowed their frenetic dance. Then his face darkened. It was all the answer I needed.

"Why won't you talk to me?" It came out plaintive instead of angry. I was too emotionally exhausted to be angry. "If you would just *talk* to me—"

"I see no reason to tell you of every assassination I committed at the behest of the Prince." There was no mercy in his tone; it scorched with bitterness not directed at me. "Why will you not *trust* me? Is it so hard to do as I ask?"

You could make me do whatever you wanted; you could force me. You probably will. And I'll fight however I can, no matter how much I love you. You can't control me. "I *want* to trust you," I whispered. "You make it hard." I had one last question. "Did Lucifer offer you your place in Hell back if you got rid of me?"

He stared at me for an endless moment. Then comprehension lit his face, comprehension and savage anger. "Vardimal's Androgyne."

"She wanted to meet me." I opened my mouth to tell him the other half of it—that she'd said she was my daughter too—and shut my lips.

He didn't need to know that. That was private. That was human, between Doreen and me. It was *mine.*

"Ah. *Now* it makes sense." Japhrimel straightened, and turned away from me. His shoulders shook, stiffly. He tipped his head back, his inky hair falling away from his forehead, and I felt the slight tremor that raced through the hover.

"Japhrimel?" I didn't expect him to listen, but he did. "Please, don't."

His reaction told me everything I needed to know. He hadn't kept the knowledge of Eve's escape from me, he hadn't even known. I was willing to believe it.

Are you believing it just because you want to, or because it makes sense?

I didn't care.

The earthquake of his fury eased. I could barely tell anyone else was on the hover, it was so silent.

When he turned back to me, I almost flinched. His upper lip drew back, exposing his teeth; his eyes were incandescent. He looked far more lethal than Velokel the Bull. "An Androgyne out of Hell," he said tightly. "Of course. Of *course.* I suppose the Hunter and the Twins are in league with her?"

"I think so." I freed my right hand from my swordhilt, started to push myself up on my elbow. The softness—it was one of the new microfiber spaceblankets, warm and soft at the same time—crinkled as it folded down. He was immediately there, helping me; I felt clean, my clothes were soft as if freshly laundered. Probably cleaned off with Power; he knew how I hated to be dirty. I was vaguely surprised to find my sword had a new reinforced sheath, deep indigo lacquer. "Japhrimel, she asked me to distract you. To just wait out the next seven years and pretend we can't find her. She wants to—"

"She is in rebellion against the Prince." He stroked my hair back from my face with his free hand as he steadied me. "She cannot *possibly* win. She is young, untutored, without any support."

"She can win if you help her. You're..." I couldn't believe I'd said it, and apparently neither could he, because he set his jaw and looked away, a muscle flicking in his golden cheek.

"No." Just the one word, forced out through his lips.

"Japhrimel—" *Please,* I was going to say. I was going to plead, to beg if that was what it came to. Stopped myself just in time. Begging was weakness.

But she was part Doreen's, and part mine. It was worth any weakness if I could make him understand, if I could convince him to *help* me.

He spoke before I could muster the words. "You are asking me to endanger your life by throwing our lot in with a rebellion that cannot possibly succeed. No, Dante. I will not risk you."

"Lucifer wants to kill me anyway." It came out flat and hopeless. What chance did I have if the Devil wanted me dead?

"I can keep him from you." His hand bit into my shoulder. "Have I not kept him from you so far?"

Oh, Japh. Please. Help me out here. "She only asked, Japh. She didn't demand, she didn't manipulate, she didn't force me. She just *asked.*"

That seemed to make him even angrier. "She's demon. We *lie,* my curious one, in case you have not noticed."

Oh, I've noticed. Believe me, I've learned to count on it. "What about you?"

He leaned in close, his nose an inch from mine, his eyes filling mine with green light just like the wristcuff's warnings. "Judge me by what I *do.* Have I not *always* kept faith with you?"

I opened my mouth to retort, but he had a point. All I had to do was breathe to understand the answer to that particular question. "The Master Nichtvren didn't say it was Lucifer, he just said it was a demon with a green gem. You *did* lie."

No response. My heart pounded. *You gave up Hell for me, and you just lied to the Prince of Hell for me.* "You lied to protect me from the Devil. And you pushed him back. You *stopped* him."

He shrugged, his coat moving with a whispering sound. Said nothing.

I reached up with my right hand, touched his face. He sighed, closing his eyes. Leaned into my fingers.

If he hadn't been so close, I might have missed the single tear that slipped out beneath his eyelashes and tracked down his cheek in the semi-darkness.

Oh, Japhrimel. My heart broke. I could actually feel it cracking apart inside my chest.

"What am I going to do with you?" I managed around the lump in my throat. "You tried to force me to do what you wanted. You *hurt* me."

His face contorted, I smoothed his mouth down with my fingers. "I am sorry," he breathed. He leaned into me, his lips brushing my skin so that he kissed my hand with each word. "I should not have, I *know* I should not have. I was afraid. Afraid of harm coming to you."

Oh, gods. I traced the arch of his cheekbone, the shape of his bottom lip. Felt the tension go out of him as I leaned forward, pressed my lips to his smooth golden cheek. "You idiot," I whispered, my lips moving against his skin. "I love you. Do you have any idea how much I love you?"

He flinched as if I'd hit him. "I am sorry," he whispered. "Do not doubt me."

He'd actually apologized. Miracles were coming thick and fast now.

I couldn't say anything through the lump of stone in my throat, but I nodded. I swallowed a few times.

When his eyes opened again, I almost gasped, their green was so intense. He studied me up-close, then pressed a gentle kiss onto my cheek. He made sure I was steady, sitting up, then straightened, backed up two steps and clasped his hands behind his back. "You're hungry. We land in half an hour."

Understanding flashed between us. His eyes said, *Forgive me. Teach me how to do this. You are the only one who can.*

My heart leapt. *Just trust me, and don't doubt me either. That's all I need from you.*

There was more, but I couldn't have put it into words. The softening in his mouth told me he understood. For that one split second, at least, we were in total accord. My heart twisted inside my chest and my cheeks flamed with heat. Whatever *Fallen* meant, Japhrimel loved me. Hadn't he proved it enough?

The rest could wait.

I nodded. Held up my sword. "Thank you. For the scabbard." My voice was back to rough honey, granular gold. Soothing.

That wasn't all I was thanking him for, and he knew it.

His slight smile rewarded me. Then he reached up, opening a small metal stasis cabinet. He lifted down something small but apparently heavy and took a single step forward, handing it to me. I had to lay my sword down to accept it. "A small gift, for my beloved."

He vanished through the opening in the partition as I brought my hands down and found them full of a familiar weight. The statue was obsidian, glowing mellowly through a scrim of heat-scarring from the fire that had destroyed our house. The woman sat, calmly, Her lion's head set firmly atop Her body, the sun-disc of hammered gold still shining. I could see traceries of Power, careful repair work, where Japhrimel had spent his demon-given Power to repair the weakening of molecular bonds the reaction fire had caused. It would have taken unimaginable Power and precision to repair the glassy obsidian, phenomenal strength and inhuman concentration.

All for me. A gift, the only gift he knew how to give. His strength.

Tears spilled hot down my cheeks.

I'd misjudged him, after all. Just as badly as he'd misjudged me.

CHAPTER 41

Lucas slumped in a chair, blood stiffening on his torn shirt. Sunlight poured in the hover windows, I pushed my hair back behind my ear and examined him.

He looked like hell, gaunt and sticky with dry blood everywhere except for a swipe on his cheek where he'd probably rubbed the dirt-dusted gummy crust off. He still held one 60-watt plasgun, tilted up with the smooth black plasteel barrel resting against his cheek. His legs stretched out, clad in shredded jeans. At least his boots had survived. His yellow eyes, half-lidded, were distant and full of some emotion I didn't want to examine too closely.

Something like banked rage, and satisfaction.

I lowered myself down in the chair opposite him. This hover was good-sized but narrow, with round porthole windows like a military transport. I didn't know where Lucas had gotten it, but it was taking us away from DMZ Sarajevo, and that was all I cared about.

McKinley and Japhrimel held a low conference up front in the pilot booth—this hover was old enough to have an actual booth instead of a cockpit—and Vann leaned against the booth's entrance, his arms folded. He scowled at Lucas. There were horrible livid bruises on his brown face, and one eye was bandaged.

I didn't want to know.

There was no smell of human in the hover. The agents smelled like dried cinnamon, with the faintest tang of demon, Lucas smelled like a stasis cabinet and blood dried to flakes, and Japhrimel and I... well, we smelled like demon. Of course.

I leaned back in the chair, my katana across my knees.

I have a blade that bit the Devil. Gods grant me strength enough to use it next time. I'm sure there's going to be a next time.

"Who are you really working for, Lucas?" My voice was quiet, stroking the air, calming.

He shrugged, his eyelids dropping another millimeter. "You," he said, in his painful whisper. "Since New Prague. I was contracted by Ol' Blue Eyes to meet you, look after you. Figured the two jobs tallied."

I nodded, my head moving against the chair's headrest. Thought about it. Decided. It was only fair, after all.

"If you want to go on your way, I won't blame you. You stood up to the Devil for me." *Gave him a bit of trouble, too. We might almost have had a chance.*

Not really. Not without Japhrimel.

He gave another one of those terrible, dry, husking laughs. He certainly seemed to find me amusing nowadays.

"Shitfire," he finally wheezed. "This's the most interesting thing I seen in years. Ain't gonna stop now. Four demons, eyes an' ears. Until the fourth demon's dead, *chica*, I'm your man."

I nodded. Braced myself. It was always best to pay debts before the interest mounted, and I owed him. If not for him, Lucifer would have killed me before Japhrimel could reach me. "I told you the pay's negotiable. What do you want?"

"Your demon boyfriend paid me, Valentine. Consider yourself lucky."

Well, it was certainly a day for surprises. I shifted uneasily in the seat, then rested my head against the seat's high back.

"Do you think she was telling the truth?" I meant Eve. He'd been in the room, after all.

"Don't know. I ain't no Magi." He shifted a little in the chair, as if he hurt. "Explains a helluva lot."

"Are you all right?" It was a stupid question. We'd both gotten off lightly, for tangling with Lucifer.

"Devil damn near pulled my spleen out through my nose. It hurt." Lucas sighed. He sounded disappointed. "Guess even he can't kill me."

"Give him time." I didn't mean for it to sound flippant. Then I leaned forward, running my hand back through my hair. "Lucas, do you have any friends? I mean, real friends?"

An evocative shrug. His yellow eyes fastened on me.

"If you had a friend," I persisted, "and he lied to you but it was for a good reason, what would you do?"

Silence. Lucas studied me.

The hover began a stomach-jolting descent then rose again, probably to avoid a traffic stream. I folded my left arm across my belly; it wasn't tender, but I was still cautious.

Finally, Lucas hauled himself upright, leaned forward. Rested his elbows on his knees. "You askin' me for advice, *chica*. Dangerous." He rasped in a breath. "I seen a lot of shit on the face of the earth. Most of it pointless. The only thing I can tell you is—take what you can get."

I weighed the statement, wondering if it was any good. *Take what you can get.* Was that even honorable? "So you don't have any friends?"

He shrugged again.

I closed my eyes, leaning back into the chair's embrace. "You do now, Lucas." I paused, let the fact sink in. "You do now."

After all, he'd shot the Devil. For me. Who cared if it was just a job to him?

Take what you can get.

Eve wanted her freedom. Lucifer wanted her dead or captured—most likely captured, since he had used me as bait to draw her out. Lucifer also wanted me kept so busy with "hunting" down his escaped children that I didn't have time to find out it was Eve he was really after. Japhrimel probably wanted to keep us both alive long enough to figure out which was the winning side, and I didn't blame him. Lucas was curious, and he might have thought Lucifer could finally kill him.

Take what you can get.

What did I want out of this? I didn't even know yet.

We were going to land in Giza, meet Leander, and figure out what course to follow next. I had to decide if I was going to hunt down Doreen's daughter for Lucifer, or if I was going to risk my life—and Japhrimel's too—taking on the Prince of Hell.

Who was I fooling? I already knew what I was going to do.

The trouble would be talking both myself and Japhrimel into it.

Excerpt from *"A Face for Death"*

Hegemony Psionic Academy Textbook,
Specialized Studies

By Fallon Hoffman

Sirius Publishing, Paradisse

In classical antiquity, the psychopomp was merely any god relating to death or the dead. The term narrowed with the advent of the Awakening and narrowed even further after the Parapsychic Act was signed into law. The psychopomp—defined as the god or being a Necromance sees during the resurrection phase of the accreditation Trial—is thus an ancient concept.

Necromances are unique among psions because of the Trial. Borrowed from shamanic techniques born in the mists of pre-Awakening history, the Trial is nothing more than a specific initiation, a guided death and rebirth for which every Necromance is carefully prepared through over a decade and a half of schooling and practice in other magickal and psionic techniques.

There is no such thing as a non-practicing or non-accredited Necromance. The nature of a Necromance's peculiar talent demands training, lest Death swallow the unpracticed whole. In pre-Awakening times, those gifted with this most unreliable talent usually ended up in mental hospitals or prisons, screaming of things no normal could see.

During the Awakening, it became much more dangerous and common to slip over the border into what any EKG will label the "blue mesh," that particular pattern of brainwaves produced when a Necromance triggers the talent and creates a doorway through which a spirit can be pulled to answer questions. Many nascent Necromances were lost to the pull and chill of Death, their hearts stopping from sheer shock. Unprepared by any schooling, meditation training, or Magi recall techniques, the Necromance faced death defenseless as a normal human—or even more so.

The solution—a psychological mechanism of putting a face on Death—was stumbled upon in the very early days of the Awakening. Unfortunately, we have no record of the brave soul who first made the connection between the psychopomp and a managed trip into Death, instead of the less-reliable techniques such as soul-stripping or the charge-and-release method. Whoever she is (for Necromances, like *sedayeen,* are overwhelmingly female), she deserves canonization on par with Adrien Ferrimen.

The reason the psychopomp is so necessary is deceptively simple. Death is the oldest, largest human fear. To create a screen of rationality between the limited human mind and the cosmic law of ending, the defense mechanism of a face and personality makes the inhuman bearable and even human itself. A psychopomp is no more than a graceful fiction that allows a human mind to grasp the Unending. It is the simplest and most basic form of godmaking, hardwired into the human neural net. It is much easier to believe in a god's intercession than in a random mix of genetics and talent allowing what our culture still sadly views as a violation of the natural order—bringing the dead back, however briefly.

A psychopomp is unutterably personal, coded into the deepest levels of the Necromance's psyche. Gods are mostly elective nowadays, except for those rare occasions when they choose to meddle in human affairs. But to plumb the depths of mankind's oldest fear and greatest mystery, a human mind needs a key to unlock those depths and a shield to use against them. That key needs to be strong enough, and rooted deep enough in the mind, to stand repeated use.

The psychopomp serves both functions, key and shield. First, it gives the psyche a much-needed handle on the concept of Death. Intellectually, the human mind knows death is inevitable, that it visits every single one of us. Convincing the rest of the human animal, not to mention the animal brain, is impossible. Death is disproved by every breath the living creature takes, by every beat of a living heart. The psychopomp allows empirical evidence of the living body and of the non-space of Death to coexist by providing a framework, however fragile, to fix both concepts in.

Psychopomps also function as a defense against the concept of death itself. Necromances, when interviewed, speak of "Death's love"—not the worship of Thanatos but an affirmation of Death as part of a cosmic order and the Necromance as a necessary part of that order, helping to keep the scales balanced. The idea of balance is intrinsically linked to any god dealing with Death, proof again of the psyche's grasping for reason in the face of the eternal.

Necromances speak, often at great length, about the emotional connection to their psychopomp. This is necessary, otherwise the fear reflex might crush even the most finely honed sorcerous Will. Indeed, the outpouring of emotion lavished on death-gods by Necromances is only matched by the propitiatory offerings made in temples by normals in hopes of Death passing them by. The idea that Death can be reasoned or bargained with haunts humanity with hope.

The psychological cost of trips to the other side of Death's doorway shows itself in several ways, from the Necromance's common need for adrenaline boosts to the compensatory neuroses detailed in Chapter 12. Were it not for the useful concept of a god as guardian, gatekeeper, eternal Other, and protector, Necromances might still be going mad at puberty, which is when the talent commonly manifests itself...

FILE HFS-IW-104496B
INTERNAL

Classification Level 4

Hegemony Federal Service File
Internal Watch
104496B
CLASSIFIED
EYES ONLY

Subject: Dante Valentine (birth name: ******* *** ********) HD# ***-**-**** **

    Last Known Location: Santiago City, North Merica, Hegemony

Detail: Subject is thirty-two years old, brown and brown, height 1.64 meters, slim build, weight variable. Subject is accredited Necromance (Amadeus Academy graduate #47138SAZ) and bounty hunter. Some illegal activity suspected, mostly in industrial espionage/ illicit bounties. Psych profile normal despite childhood trauma (see HFS-IW-*******) and high probability of deconstruction under severe stress. (See HFS-IW/P-*******) Compensatory reflexes within normal range, with significant exceptions as detailed in psych profile.

Incident Date/Time/Duration: **/*/**** / Beginning approximately 1300 / 10 days (tentative)

Incident Prime Location: Nuevo Rio, Sudro Merica, Hegemony
Secondary Location(s): Inapplicable / Classified

Incident: Class 5 interaction with dimensional rift. Class 3 and suspected Class 5 interaction with nonhuman (sp: demonic) forces.

Abstract: Several sources claim subject has been 'transformed' by Class 5 nonhuman being (demon, level 1). Possible interference with sealed Hegemony Directive 2048-E (Project Eden) due to prior contact with FS source Prometheus (HSF-IW-002399Z) in the course of source's collection of viable samples for Project Eden. Project Eden met, of course, with a premature end after initial success. Two sources (codename: Vickers and Preacher) link subject to failure of Project Eden. However, neither source is considered reliable.

Detail: Subject exhibits radically altered genetic profile and has received large sums of hard credit from unidentifiable source. Sources claim a level 1 demon (codename: Starstrike) carried out genetic reshaping on subject in return for unspecified services relating to the interruption of Project Eden. However, the prime mover of Project Eden (codename: Veritas) has insisted subject be kept only under light surveillance. Given the training and background of subject, analysis agrees. Chance of unacceptable information dispersal if surveillance moves above 'light' is calculated at an unacceptable 80% (+/− 2).

The incident in question centers around destruction caused to roughly 40 percent of Nuevo Rio's buildings, presumably by Starstrike in reprisal for an unidentified interaction between Prometheus and subject. The incident definition has expanded to include the destruction of Project Eden's laboratory and refuge (cross-ref, HFS-IW-*******) and the services of Veritas in tying off Project Eden.

Casualties in Nuevo Rio were kept to a minimum (critical loss estimated at less than 4 percent). Incident was declared a federal disaster zone, sealed and repaired within 83.6 hours, emergency funding dispersed under sealed Hegemony Directive 0003-A.
    Damage done to diplomatic relations with Veritas has been contained. Information dispersal to subject (classified as slight) is considered acceptable, in light of overriding factors such as Starstrike's

suspected interference and Veritas's claim of ownership of subject (pursuant to sealed Hegemony Directive 2048-F, ownership of human genetic material transformed by Class 5 nonhuman interference). Subject has been confirmed unsuitable for advancement of Project Eden.

Suggested Action: Continued light surveillance of subject. Consideration of recruitment of subject for high-level wetworking has been advanced several times, despite analysis of subject's psych profile providing high chance of deconstruction and high unsuitability for impersonal motivations for such activity.

Notes: Project Eden may be considered a limited success. Necessity of keeping diplomatic relations open with Veritas dictated a less-than-satisfactory endgame in relation to ownership of Project Eden's greatest success (codename: Omega). Monitoring of Omega is almost impossible due to dimensional interference. Reclaiming Omega is of prime importance to the FS despite low chance of success.

Claims of Starstrike's demise are being investigated by Internal Watch, Division 5. (See HFS-IW-*******) Various methods have brought no conclusive proof. Chance of survival is calculated at 53 percent (+/– 40).

Book 4

Saint City Sinners

For Maddalena Marie.
Never forget who loves you, baby.

A woman always has her revenge ready.
—Molière

In revenge and in love woman is more barbarous than man.
—Nietzsche

The rate of success for female bounty hunters, once one takes into account the statistical weighting of the X chromosome carrying psionic markers more often than the Y, is still two and a half times that of their male compatriots. More male psions go into bounty hunting, but female psions are better at it, bringing in their bounties quicker and with less destruction of lives and property.

This is balanced by the fact that male psions are embarrassingly better than their female counterparts at assassination. There are very few female psions operating in the assassination trade. Morley's quip that perhaps they are better at keeping their identities from authorities need not be mentioned more than once.

However, when comparing female assassins to male, one fact stands out with crystal clarity: the psionic females who do deal in assassination are by far the most thorough, tending to engage far less in messy "personal" kills (Datridenton, On Criminal Justice, *pp. 1184–1206) in favor of getting the job done efficiently with whatever tool is best. This very thoroughness necessarily means they are higher-priced and far less likely to be indicted.*

What conclusion can we draw from this? Morley, tongue-in-cheek as usual, concludes, "It may be well for men, especially men married to psions, to speak softly to their wives and girlfriends." This researcher would submit differently: that we are indeed lucky, given how good psionic women tend to be at coldly planned bloodshed, that most appear uninterested in it....

—from *Ethics and Gender Differences in the Psionic World,* by Caitlin Sommers, Amadeus Hegemony Academy of Psionic Arts

Overture

*J*aphrimel stood in the middle of the wrack and ruin of the Haunt Tais-toi, *his long wet-dark coat lying on his shoulders like night itself. Lucifer faced him, the Prince of Hell's lovely face twisted with fury, suffused with a darkness more than physical. Japhrimel's hand closed around Lucifer's right wrist, muscle standing out under Luci-fer's shirt and Japhrimel's coat as the Devil surged forward—and Japhrimel pushed him* back.

If I hadn't seen it, I would never have believed it possible. But Japh's entire body tensed, and he forced Lucifer back on his heels.

The Devil stepped mincingly away, twisting his wrist free. Retreated, only two steps. But it was enough.

Lucifer's aura flamed with blackness, a warping in the fabric of the world. They looked at each other, twin green gazes locked as if the words they exchanged were only window dressing for the real combat, fought by the glowing spears of their eyes. The two hell-hounds wove around them, low fluid shapes. Lucifer's indigo silk shirt was torn, gaping, across his midriff, showing a slice of golden skin—and as I watched, a single drop of black blood dripped from one torn edge. More spots of dark blood smoked on the silken pants he wore.

I'd cut the Devil.

One dazed thought sparked inside my aching head. Jado must've given me a hell of a good blade.

Then another thought, ridiculous in its intensity. Here. He's here. Everything will be all right now.

Childish faith, maybe, but I'd take it. If it was a choice between my Fallen and getting killed right this moment, I'd settle for Japh, no matter how much of a bastard he'd been recently. Funny how almost getting killed radically changed my notions of just how much I could forgive.

Japhrimel's eyes didn't flick over to check me, but the mark on my shoulder came to agonized life again, Power flooding me, exploding in my belly. White-hot pokers jerked in my viscera. My scalp twinged, I tasted blood and burning. My sword rang softly, the core of the blade burning white, blue runic patterns slipping through its keen edge and painting the air. I managed to lift it, the blade a bar between me and the Devil facing his eldest son.

The red lights were still flickering, sweeping over the entire building in their complicated patterns, eerie because there were no dancers. "You would have me believe—" Lucifer started. Stone and plaster shattered at the sound of his voice, dust pattering to the wracked floor.

Japhrimel interrupted him again. I felt only a weary wonder that he was still standing there, apparently untouched, his long black coat moving gently on the hot fire-breeze. "We were told by the Master of this city—your ally and Hellesvront agent—that you wished to meet Dante here alone. Did you lure your Right Hand here to kill her, Prince? Breaking your word, given on your ineffable Name? Such would conclude our alliance in a most ... unsatisfactory fashion."

I could swear Lucifer's face went through surprise, disgust, and finally settled on wariness. He studied Japhrimel for a long, tense thirty seconds, during which my throat burned and tickled but I didn't dare to cough.

Japh clasped his hands behind his back. He looked relaxed, almost bored. Except for the burning murderous light of his eyes, matching Lucifer's shade for shade.

I stayed very still, my left arm cramping as my belly ran with pain and my right trembling as I held my sword. A small part of me won-dered where Lucas was. The rest of me stared at Japhrimel with open wonderment.

If I survive this, I'm going to kiss him. Right after I punch the shit out of him for lying to me. If he lets me. *The nastiness of the thought made me suddenly, deeply ashamed of myself. He was here, and he was facing Lucifer. For me.*

He had given up Hell. He had also taken me to Toscano and let me heal from the psychic rape of Mirovitch's ka, protecting me from dangers I hadn't had the faintest idea existed. He was loyal to me after all.

In his own fashion.

Lucifer finally seemed to decide. The flames among the shattered wreckage twisted into angular shapes as some essential tension leached out of him. "I rue the day I set you to watch over her, Eldest." The darkness in his face didn't fade, however—it intensified, a psychic miasma.

The tickling in my throat reached a feverish pitch. I had to cough, shoved the urge down, prayed for strength. Anubis, please don't let me attract their attention. Both of them look too dangerous right now.

Japhrimel shrugged. "What is done, is done." His voice pitched a little higher, as if he imitated Lucifer. Or was quoting him.

The Prince of Hell set his jaw. I saw one elegant hand curl into a fist, and perhaps the other one was a fist too, but I couldn't see it. I think it was the first time I saw the Devil speechless, and my jaw would have dropped if I hadn't clenched it, trying not to cough. I took a fresh grip on my belly, trying not to hunch over. I wanted to see, needed to see. My sword held steady even though my hand was shaking, the blade singing a thin comforting song as its heart glowed white.

He finally seemed to regain himself. "You deserve each other," he hissed. "May you have joy of it. Bring me back my possession and eliminate those who would keep it from me, Tierce Japhrimel, or I will kill you both. I swear it."

Japhrimel's eyes flared. "That was not our bargain, my lord."

Lucifer twitched. Japhrimel didn't move, but the mark twisted white-hot fire into my shoulder, a final burst of Power. The urge to cough mercifully retreated a little. I blinked drying demon blood out of my eyes. I wanted to look for Lucas.

I couldn't look away from my Fallen. He stood tense and ready, in front of the Devil.

"I am the Prince *of* Hell," *Lucifer said coldly.*

"And I was your Eldest." Japhrimel held Lucifer's eyes as the air itself cried out, a long gasping howl of a breeze coming from them, blowing my hair back. I felt the stiffness—blood and dust matted in my hair. I was filthy, and I ached. I stayed where I was. "I was the Kinslayer. Thus you made me, and you cast me away. I am yours no longer."

"I made you." The air itself screamed as the Prince of Hell's voice tore at it. "Your allegiance is mine."

"My allegiance," Japhrimel returned, inexorably quiet, "is my own. I Fell, I am Fallen. I am not your son."

One last burst of soft killing silence. I struggled to stay still.

Lucifer turned on his heel. The world snapped back into normalcy. He strode for the gaping hole torn in the front of the nightclub. Red neon reflected wetly off the street outside. A flick of his golden fingers, and the hellhounds loped gracefully after him, one stopping to snarl back over its shoulder at me.

Well, now I can guess who sent the hellhounds. You bastard. You filthy bastard. I sagged. My sword dipped, and the urge to cough rose again. It felt like a plasgun core had been dropped into my gut.

The Prince stopped, turned his head so I could see his profile. "Japhrimel." His voice was back to silk and honey, terrible in its beauty. "I give you a promise, my Eldest. One day, I will kill her."

Lucifer vanished. The air tried to heal itself, closing over the space where he had been, and failed. He left a scorch on the very fabric of existence.

Japhrimel was silent for a moment, his eyes fixed forward. He didn't look at me. I was glad, because his face was full of something terrible, irrevocable, and devouring.

"Not while I watch over her," he said softly.

CHAPTER 1

Cairo Giza has endured almost forever, but it was only after the Awakening that the pyramids began to acquire distinctive etheric smears again. Colored balls of light bob and weave around them even during daytime, playing with streams of hover traffic that carefully don't pass over the pyramids themselves, like a river separating around islands. Hover circuitry is buffered like every critical component nowadays, but enough Power can blow anything electric just like a focused EMP pulse. There's a college of Ceremonials responsible for using and draining the pyramids' charge, responsible also for the Temple built equidistant from the stone triangles and the Sphinx, whose ruined face still gazes from her recumbent body with more long-forgotten wisdom than the human race could ever lay claim to accumulating.

Power hummed in the air as I stepped from glaring desert sun into the shadowed gloom of the Temple's portico. Static crackled, sand falling out of my clothes whisked away by the containment field. I grimaced. We'd been on the ground less than half an hour and already I was tired of the dust.

One worn-out, busted-down part-demon Necromance, sore from Lucifer's last kick even though Japhrimel had repaired the damage and flushed me with enough Power to make my skin tingle. And one Fallen given back the power of a demon pacing behind me, his step oddly silent on the stone floor. The mark on my left shoulder—*his* mark—pulsed again, a warm velvet flush coating my body. My rings swirled with steady light.

My bag bumped against my hip and my bootheels clicked on stone, echoing in the vast shadowed chamber. The great inner doors

rose up before us, massive slabs of granite lasecarved with hiero-
glyph pictures of a way of life vanished thousands of years ago. I
inhaled the deep familiar spice of *kyphii* deeply as my nape prickled.
My sword, thrust through a loop in my weapons rig, thrummed
slightly in its indigo-lacquered scabbard.

A blade that can bite the Devil. A cool finger of dread traced up
my spine.

I stopped, half-turning on my heel to look up at Japhrimel. He
paused, his hands clasped behind his back as usual, regarding me
with bright green-glowing eyes. His ink-dark hair lay against his
forehead in a soft wave, melding with the Temple's dusky quiet;
Japhrimel's lean golden saturnine face was closed and distant. He
had been very quiet for the last hour.

I didn't blame him. We had precious little to say now. In any case,
I didn't want to break the fragile truce between us.

One dark eyebrow quirked slightly, a question I found I could
read. It was a relief to see something about him I still understood.

Had he changed, or had I?

"Will you wait for me here?" My voice bounced back from stone,
husky and half-ruined, still freighted with the promise of demon
seduction. The hoarseness didn't help, turning my tone to granular
honey. "Please?"

His expression changed from distance to wariness. The corner of
his mouth lifted slightly. "Of course. It would be a pleasure."

The words ran along stone, mouthing the air softly.

I bit my lower lip. The idea that I'd misjudged him was uncomfortable, to say the least. "Japhrimel?"

His eyes rested on my face. All attention, focused on me. He
didn't touch me, but he might as well have, his aura closing around
mine, black-diamond flames proclaiming him as *demon* to anyone with
otherSight. It was a caress no less intimate for being nonphysical—
something he was doing more and more lately. I wondered if it was
because he wanted to keep track of me, or because he wanted to
touch me.

I shook my head, deciding the question was useless. He probably
wouldn't tell me, anyway.

Was it wrong, not to hold it against him?

I heard Lucas Villalobos's voice again. *Take what you can get.*
Good advice? Honorable? Or just practical?

Tiens, the Nichtvren who was yet another Hellesvront agent,

would meet us after dark. Lucas was with Vann and McKinley; Leander had rented space in a boarding house and was waiting for us. The Necromance bounty hunter seemed very easy with the idea of two nonhuman Hellesvront agents, but I'd caught him going pale whenever Lucas got too close.

It was a relief to see he had some sense.

Then again, even I was frightened of Lucas, never mind that I was his client and he'd taken on Lucifer and two hellhounds for me. The man Death had turned his back on was a professional, and a good asset... but still. He was unpredictable, impossible to kill, magick just seemed to shunt itself away from him—and there were stories of just what he'd done to psions who played rough with him, or hired him and tried to welsh. It doesn't take long to figure out so many stories must have a grain of truth.

"Yes?" Japhrimel prompted me. I looked up from the stone floor with a start. I'd been wandering.

I never used to do that.

"Nothing." I turned away, my boots making precise little sounds against the floor as I headed for the doors. "I'll be out in a little while."

"Take your time." He stood straight and tall, his hands clasped behind his back, his eyes burning green holes in smoky cool darkness. I felt the weight of his gaze on my back. "I'll wait."

I shook my head, reached up to touch the doors. The mark on my shoulder flared again, heat sliding down my skin like warm oil.

He was Fallen-no-more. I would have wondered what that made me now, but he hadn't even told me what I was in the first place. *Hedaira,* a human woman given a share of a demon's strength. Japhrimel just kept saying I would find out in time.

With Eve to save and Lucifer looking to kill me, I just might die before I found out. Wouldn't that be a bitch and a half.

I spread my hands—narrow, golden, the black molecule-drip polish slightly chipped on my left fingernails—against rough granite, pushed. The doors, balanced on oiled mag-hinges, whooshed open easily. More *kyphii* smoke billowed out, fighting briefly with the burning-cinnamon musk of demon cloaking me.

The hall was large, all architectural space focused on throned Horus at the end, Isis's tall form behind him, Her hand lifted in blessing over Her son. The doors slid to a stop. I bowed, my right hand touching heart and forehead in the classic salute.

I paced forward into the house of the gods. The doors slid together behind me, closing Japhrimel out. Here was perhaps the only place I could truly be alone, the only place he would not intrude.

Unfortunately, leaving him outside meant leaving my protection too. I didn't think any demon would try to attack me inside a temple, but I was just nervous enough to take a deep breath and welcome the next flush of Power spreading from the scar.

Another deep breath. Panic beat under my breastbone. I told myself it was silly. Japh was right outside the door, and my god had always answered me before.

Still, ever since the night Anubis had called me out of slumber and laid on me a geas I couldn't remember, He had been silent. Losing that compass left me adrift in a way I'd never been before. If I'd ever needed direction and comfort, it was now.

Cairo Giza had been Islum territory in the Merican era, but Islum had choked on its own blood during the Seventy Days War, along with the Protestor Christers and the Judics, not to mention the Evangelicals of Gilead. In a world controlled by the Hegemony and Putchkin Alliance, with psions in every corner, the conditions that gave rise to the Religions of Submission have fallen away. After a brief re-flowering of fundamentalist Islum during the collapse of petroleo use, it became just another small sect — like the Novo Christers — and the old gods and state religions had risen again.

The single biggest blow to the Religions of Submission had been the Awakening and the rise of the science of Power. When anyone can contract a Shaman or Ceremonial to talk to the god of their choice, and spiritual experiences becoming commonplace — not to mention Necromances proving an afterlife exists and Magi definitively proving the existence of demons — most organized religions had died a quick hard death, replaced by personal worship of patron gods and spirits. It was, in all reality, the only logical response on humanity's part.

Here in Egypt those old gods have returned with a vengeance, and the pyramid Ceremonials are slowly taking on the tenor of a priesthood. Most psions are religious only to the extent that the science of belief makes Power behave itself. Necromances are generally more dedicated than most; after all, our psychopomps take the faces of ancient gods and act a little differently from the average man's deities.

Part of that probably has to do with the Trial every accredited

Necromance has to face. It's hard not to feel a little bit attached to a god who resurrects you from the psychic death of initiation and stays with you afterward, receiving you into Death's arms when it is finally time to go into What Comes Next.

The debate remains—could a Ceremonial be a priest or priestess, and what exactly did the gods *want* anyway? Only nowadays, people aren't likely to murder each other over the questions. Not often, anyway. There's a running feud between the priestesses of Aslan and the Hegemony Albion Literary College, who say the Prophet Lewis was a Novo Christer, but only ink is spilled in that battle, not blood.

I turned to my right. Sekhmet sat on Her throne, lion-headed and strangely serene, heat blurring up from the eternal fire in a black bowl on Her altar. The heady smell of wine rose; someone had been making offerings. Past Her, there was Set, His jackal-head painted the deep red of dried blood. The powers of destruction, given their place at the left hand of creation. Necessary, and worshipped—but not safe.

Not at all safe.

Japhrimel's last gift before breaking the news that Lucifer had summoned me again had been a glossy obsidian statue of the Fierce One. That same statue, repaired and burnished to a fine gloss, was set by the side of the bed in the boarding house even now. *Please tell me She isn't about to start messing around with me. I have all the trouble I can handle right now.*

I shivered, turned to the left. There, behind Thoth's beaky head, was the slim black dog's face of my own god, in his own important niche.

I drew *kyphii* deep into my lungs. A last respectful bow to Isis and Her son, and I moved to the left.

Thoth's statue seemed to make a quick movement as I passed. I stopped, made my obeisance. Glanced up the ceiling, lasepainted with Nuit's starry naked form.

Plenty of psions worship the Hellene gods. There are colleges of Asatru and Teutonica as well as the Faery tradition in Hegemony Europa. The Shamans have their *loa,* and there are some who follow the path of the Left Hand and worship the Unspeakable. The Tantrics have their *devas* and the Hindu their huge intricate assemblages, Native Mericans and Islanders their own branches of magick and Shamanic training passed down through blood and ritual; the Buddhists and Zenmos their own not-quite-religious traditions. *There are as many religions as there are people on the earth*, the Magi say. Even the demons were worshipped one long-ago time, mistaken for gods.

For me, there had never really been any choice. I'd dreamed of a dog-headed man all through my childhood, and had taken the requisite Religious Studies classes at Rigger Hall. One of the first religions studied was Egyptianica, since it was such a popular sect—and I'd felt at home from the very beginning. Everything about the gods of the Nile was not so much learned for me as deeply *remembered,* as if I'd always known but just needed the reminding.

The first time I'd gone into Death, Anubis had been there; He had never left me since. Where else would I turn for solace, but to Him?

I reached His niche. Tears welled up, my throat full of something hard and hot. I sank down to one knee, rose. Stepped forward. Approached His statue, the altar before it lit by novenas and crowded with offerings. Food, drink, scattered New Credit notes, sticks of fuming incense. Even the normals propitiated Him, hoping for some false mercy when their time came, hoping to live past whatever appointed date and hour Death chose.

My rings sparked, golden points of light popping in the dark. From the obsidian ring on my right third finger to the amber on my right and left middle, the moonstone on my left index, the bloodstone on my left third; the Suni-figured thumbring sparked too, reacting with the charge of Power in the air. The Power I carried, tied to a demon and no longer strictly human myself, quivered uneasily.

My Lord, my god, please hear me. I need You.

I sank down to my knees, my katana blurring out of its sheath. Laid the bright steel length on the stone floor in front of me, rested my hands on my thighs. Closed my eyes and prayed.

Please. I am weary, and I hunger for Your touch, my Lord. Speak to me. You have comforted me, but I want to hear You.

My breathing deepened. The blue glow began, rising at the very corners of my mental sight. I began the prayer I'd learned long ago, studying from Novo Egyptos books in the Library at Rigger Hall. *"Anubis et'her ka,"* I whispered. *"Se ta'uk'fhet sa te vapu kuraph. Anubis et'her ka.* Anubis, Lord of the Dead, Faithful Companion, protect me, for I am Your child. Protect me, Anubis, weigh my heart upon the scale; watch over me, Lord, for I am Your child. Do not let evil distress me, but turn Your fierceness upon my enemies. Cover me with Your gaze, let Your hand be upon me, now and all the days of my life, until You take me into Your embrace."

Another deep breath, my pulse slowing, the silent place in me where the god lived opening like a flower. *"Anubis et'her ka,"* I repeated, as blue light rose in one sharp flare. The god of Death took me, swallowed me whole—and I was simply, utterly glad.

The blue crystal walls of Death rose up, but I was not on the bridge over the well of souls. Instead, the crystal shaped itself into a Temple, a psychic echo of the place my body knelt in. Before me the god appeared in the cipher of a slim black dog, sitting back on His haunches and regarding me with His infinitely-starred black eyes.

I had not come here of my own accord since Jace's death.

I had wept. I had raged against Him, set my will against His, blamed Him, sobbed in Japhrimel's arms about the utter unfairness of it. Yet I know Death does not play favorites. He loves all equally, and when it is time, not all the grief of the living will dissuade His purpose.

This, then, my agony—how do I love my god and still rage against His will? How do I grieve and yet love Him?

Here I wore the white robe of the god's chosen, belted with silver dripping like fishscales. My knees pressed chill against blue crystal floor, the emerald burning against my cheek like a live brand. It was His mark, set in my skin by humans but still with His will, the gem that marked me as Death's chosen. I blessed whatever accident of genetics gifted me with the Power to walk in His realm and feel His touch.

I met His eyes. I was not bringing a soul back from Death, so I did not need the protection of cold steel—but my hand ached to close reflexively around a swordhilt. His gaze was blackness from lid to lid, starred with cold blue jewels of constellations none of the living would ever see and glazed with blue sheen. Galaxies died in Death's eyes as the god's attention rested on me, a huge burden for such a small being—though I was infinite enough in my own right, being His child. That in itself was a mystery, how I could contain the infinity of the god, and how He could contain my own endless soul.

He took the weight from me, certainty replacing the burden. I was His, I had always been His. From before my birth the god had set His hand upon me. He could no more abandon me than I could abandon Him. Though I had set my will against His, even cursed Him in the pain of my grief—and still, sometimes, did—He did not mind. He was my god, and would not desert me.

But there was Lucas, wasn't there? The man Death had turned His back on.

Thought became action instantly in this space; my question leapt, a thread of meaning laid in the receptive space between us, a cord stretched taut. The sound brushed through me, an immense church-bell gong of the god's laughter. The Deathless's path was not mine, Anubis reminded me. My path was my own, and my covenant with Death was always unbroken, no matter if I cursed him in my human grief.

I am clay—and if the clay cuts the hand of the potter who created it, who is to blame?

He spoke.

The meanings of His word burned through me, each stripping away a layer. So many layers, so many different things to fight through; each opening like a flower to the god. There was no other being, human, god, or demon, that I would bow my head in submission to. And so, my promise to Him. I accepted.

The geas burned at me, the fire of His touch and some other fire that moved through him combining. I had something to do—something the god would not show me yet.

Would I do what the god asked? When the time came, would I submit to His will and do what He asked of me?

Bitterness rose inside me. Death does not bargain, does not play favorites, and had already taken people I loved.

Doreen, Jace, Lewis, Roanna . . . each name was a star in the constellations filling His eyes. I could have raged against Him, but what would be the point? His promise to me was utter certainty. The people I loved went into Death and He held them; when my own time came I would see them again. No matter what else What Comes Next contained, I could be certain it held the souls of those who mattered to me in life, whose love and duty still lay upon me, a welcome weight of obligation.

That weight was the measure of my honor. What is honor without promises kept?

As for myself, going into Death's embrace would be like welcoming a lover, a celebration I feared even as I ached for it. Every living creature fears the unknown. To have even a small measure of certainty in the midst of that fear is a treasure. Unlike the poor blind souls who have to take my word for it, I know *who will clasp my hand when I die and help me through the door into What Comes Next. Knowing helps the fear, even if it does not lessen it.*

I bowed, my palms together; a deep obeisance reaching into my very heart. My long stubborn life unreeled under His touch.

I am Your child, *I whispered.* Tell me what I must do.

The slim black dog regarded me with awful, infinitely merciful eyes. Shook His head, gravely. Even the geas was only to tell me what choice was required when the time approached. I was free. He only asked, and in the asking, did not promise to love me less if I denied Him.

Such perfect love is not for humans.

There was no other answer I could give, for all the freedom He granted me.

I would not deny Him, it would be denying myself. His approval warmed me, all the way down to my bones. How could I have doubted Him?

There was one more question I had, and meaning stretched between us again, a cord strained to its limits.

I could not help myself. I lifted my head, and I spoke his name to the god. Japhrimel.

The emerald on my cheek flared, sparks cascading down. The god's face changed, a canine smile. His eyes flashed green for the barest moment.

My god released me, unanswered—and yet, with a curious sense of having been told what was important, holding the knowledge for one glorious heart-stopping moment before the shock of slamming—

—back into my body drove the understanding away. I gasped, bent double, my cold, numb hand curling reflexively around my swordhilt. I leapt to my feet, my boots slamming against stone floor. My heart pounded inside its flexible cage of ribs. I swallowed several times, blinked.

The entire Temple was full of shadows, soft nasty laughter chittering against its high roof. Demon-acute sight pierced the gloom, showed me every corner and crack, down to the flow and flux of Power wedded to the walls. There were no other worshippers, and that was strange, wasn't it? It wasn't like a temple—especially this one—to be empty, especially in the middle of the day.

Copper-tasting demon adrenaline jolted me. The chill of Death flushed itself out of fingers and toes. Other Necromances use sex or sparring to shake the cold of Death and flush the bitter taste of it away. I used to go slicboarding, using speed and antigrav danger to bring myself back to the land of the breathing. This time, I was brought back by the sense of being *watched*.

No. The *knowledge* I was being watched.

But I saw nobody. My heartbeat finally returned to something like normal, and I let out a soft sigh. I was in a temple, under the gaze of my god and with Japhrimel right outside the door. What could harm me here?

My sword sang, sliding back into the sheath. *Fudoshin,* Jado had named it, and it had served me well. Very well, considering it had bit the Devil's flesh without shattering. There was some Power locked in the steel's heart my *sensei* hadn't told me about.

You're not thinking what I think you're thinking, are you Danny? You can't kill the Devil. It can't be done. That's why he's the Prince of Hell, he's the oldest of demons, the one they're all descended from. It's impossible.

I couldn't. But maybe Japhrimel could—he had, after all, pushed Lucifer *back.* Away from me.

Or, if Japh couldn't *kill* him, he might at least *persuade* the Devil to leave Eve alone. It was the least I could do for Doreen's daughter.

My daughter, too. If she could be believed.

I looked up again, at the god of Death's face. He deserved an offering, though I had precious little to give Him right at the moment. Everything I owned had gone up in flames, one way or another.

Including my relationship with Japhrimel. I love him, but how am I going to convince him to leave Eve alone? And how the hell am I going to get him to stop simply using his strength to force me to do anything he wants me to? He's apologized, but the precedent's been set.

I slid one of my main knives free, steel glittering in the light from the forest of novenas. Set the blade against my palm, worked it back and forth to penetrate tough golden skin. This earned me a handful of black demon blood I tipped carefully into a shallow bone dish full of strong red wine, someone else's offering. I used the knife to saw off a handful of my hair—longer now, since Japhrimel had brought me back after the hover incident. Shoulder-length instead of hacked around my ears—but it was still odd to walk around without a braid bumping my back whenever I turned my head.

I bowed again, the cut on my palm closing, black blood sealing away the hurt. "I wish I had more for You," I said quietly to the statue, knowing He would hear and understand. "My thanks, my Lord."

Did the shadows move to cloak Him? I blinked, the sense of being watched strong and inarguable. It wasn't like my sight to be clouded—I'd had excellent vision even before being gifted with demon-acute senses. I stared up at the dog's head above the narrow black chest, the crook and flail held in his long black hands, the kilt of gems running with reflected candlelight. *Strong One,* we who followed Anubis called him; *Protector.* And also, the most loving name—*the Gentle One.* The one who eased all hurts, the god who never left us, even at life's end.

"Anubis et'her ka," I repeated. "Thank you."

As I paced away, the statues didn't move. I wondered if I should offer to Sekhmet, discarded the notion. It was dangerous to attract Her attention—I had all the destruction I could handle in my life right now. I bowed one last time to Isis and Horus, made my way to the granite doors. They opened inward for me, Power sparking and spiraling through their cores, and when I stepped out into the entry hall Japhrimel still stood in the same spot, his hands clasped behind his back, examining the walls.

The doors swung closed behind me. Finally, his eyes returned to mine. "Did you find what you needed?"

The air between us was brittle and clear as thin crystal. He was trying so hard to be careful with me.

I'm trying too, Japhrimel. I love you, and I'm trying. I shrugged. "Gods." I gave him a smile that tried to be natural. "I'm hungry. Did you mention food?"

CHAPTER 2

The boarding house was a large sloping mudbrick building, stasis and containment fields glimmering over every window and door. The heat was almost as tremendous as the blowing sand. I spent a few moments on the sidewalk outside the building, basking in sunlight. Japhrimel, a blot on the tawny day with his long black coat, waited silently.

There were spots of green, of course. Water pumped up from the brown ribbon of the Nile and local areas of climate control made for gardens, plenty of date palms, an oasis tucked in every courtyard. The technology of watermakers was in its infancy, but here it was being used to its fullest extent—which wasn't very far, but it was nice. There would at least be enough water to bathe with, a far cry from the recent thirty-year drought that had gripped the entire northern half of Hegemony Afrike. They were still hashing out the environmental consequences of the technology, but life was beginning to spread away from the river and into the desert. There was even talk of making the desert green again, but the environmental scientists were up in arms about *that*.

I'd run a few bounties down in Hegemony Afrike. There was the Magi-gone-bad I'd tracked through the back alleys of Novo Carthago and the Shaman I'd caught in Tanzania—thank the gods for antivenom and tazapram, that's the only time I've ever been poisoned so bad I thought I'd die. I had almost gone into Death's arms after being bitten six times by a collection of boomslangs the Shaman had tickled into regarding me as an enemy. I hadn't known he was secondarily talented as an Animone.

Then there was the gang of four normals, combat-augmented and hyped on thyoline-laced Clormen-13, who'd thought the Serengeti Historical Preserve would hide them. I'd had to dock my fee 50 percent for bringing in two of them dead and the other two in critical condition, but they shouldn't have shot me and beat me up. And they additionally shouldn't have left me tied up and gone to slam hypos of Chill cocktail.

They should have killed me when they had the chance.

My memories of Hegemony Afrike are all of heat, dust, danger, and heart-thumping adrenaline. Not to mention pain. If I got in a transport when we were finished here without getting into a fight, it would be the first damn time I ever lifted off from Hegemony Afrike soil without bleeding.

Well, a girl could hope, couldn't she?

One thing I'll say for being almost-demon, I don't mind hot weather the way I used to. I used to hate sweating, but nowadays I like heat—the more the better, like a cat in a square of sun.

When I followed Japhrimel in through the containment field, shuddering as it tickled and nipped at my skin, we found square brown Vann waiting for us in the cool, shaded lobby. The Hellesvront agent's face looked better; he was healing much faster than a human but not as quickly as with a healcharm. The bruises Lucas had given him were going down and the bandage had come off his right eye, revealing a wicked slash down his forehead through his eyebrow. He was lucky he hadn't lost that eye, and I felt a little guilty. After all, I'd hired Lucas—but he'd been squeezing Vann for information on my whereabouts so he could show up just in time to save my life.

I was fairly sure Lucifer would have killed me if he could. Just one more time I'd tangled with the Prince of Hell and come away with my miserable life. I was beginning to feel lucky.

Not really.

Vann nodded at me, his brown eyes turning dark. I nodded back cautiously. The desk in the lobby was deserted, a holovid player glowing pink in the office behind it. I caught the sound of a human heartbeat, a cough, shuffling feet. The floor here was an intricate mosaic pattern in tiles of blue and yellow; a dracaena grew in a brass pot near the door, next to a rack of newspapers and cheap holomags.

"News." Vann's tone held uneasy respect, as if I was a poisonous animal he wanted to avoid offending. I looked longingly at the little café tucked into the boarding house's first floor. I was *hungry.*

"Go find a table, Dante," Japhrimel said quietly. "I will join you in a moment."

I weighed hanging around to hear what Vann would say, and decided I probably didn't want to know. I'd find out eventually, and if there was something Japhrimel didn't want me to be told Vann wouldn't say it anyway. I might as well get something to eat for my trouble. "Fine." I couldn't resist a bad-tempered little goose. "I suppose if there was something you didn't want me to know he would wait to mention it to you later anyway, right?"

With that, I turned on my heel and would have stalked away, but Japh caught my arm. I knew better than to struggle—he was far stronger than me. It would do no good.

"Stay, then. Hear everything." His eyebrows drew together as he examined Vann. "Well?"

"It left Sarajevo, we don't know where for. McKinley says there's something going on in Kalif that sounds suspicious, but I don't think anyone would be stupid enough to look *there.* We're collating the reports right now. I'd bet it's following the route with no problems." His tone, as usual when he spoke to Japh, was utterly respectful and curiously unafraid.

Japhrimel nodded thoughtfully. His thumb moved on my arm, a gentle absent caress, and I cast back through memory to piece this together.

Something had been in DMZ Sarajevo, something Japhrimel had wanted to collect. The Anhelikos—a feathered thing living in an old abandoned temple—had told him it had been taken to the Roof of the World, whatever that was.

Thinking about Sarajevo made a shiver go through me, suddenly cold in the climate-controlled interior. A town full of paranormals and Lucifer's fingers closing around my windpipe—my belly was still a little tender from the Devil's last kick. A parting gift.

Japh's thumb moved again, soothing. "The treasure is moving," he said meditatively. "Such a thing has not happened for millennia."

"Millennia?" Vann didn't sound surprised. He scratched at his bruised face with blunt fingertips, grimacing slightly. "You're sure about the route?" It was rhetorical instead of doubting.

Japh shrugged, a fluid lovely movement. "I was the one to leave it with Kos Rafelos, and it had just left his care when I arrived. The game has begun. Now it is the Key they will seek."

Key? What key? And who's they? I didn't say it out loud, but Japhrimel glanced at me, as if gauging how much he should say. I swallowed sudden impatience. He'd earned a little bit of slack, though I still wasn't happy about being shaken like a naughty puppy and held up against the wall in a Sarajevo subway station. The thought of him using his superior strength to force me to do something still filled me with a combination of unsteady rage and sick anticipation, as if bracing myself for a gutshot.

But he had kept Lucifer away long enough to give me a chance to heal my shattered psyche. He had hidden me so well other rebellious demons couldn't find me and even lied to the Prince of Hell to protect me.

Not only that, but he'd given up all chance of returning to his home. For me.

He had, indeed, earned a little slack.

I bit back impatience and simply listened, my eyes moving over the graceful curve of balustrade going upstairs. *Go figure. Danny Valentine, holding her tongue for once. Let's mark it on the calendar and call the holovid reporters; it's a frocking miracle.*

Vann made a sudden movement, as if he couldn't contain himself. The leather fringe on his jacket swayed, whispering. "You're just going to let her walk around? You know what they're after. If they take her, it could mean the end of everything."

That brought my eyes around in a hurry, but he stared at Japhrimel, whose gaze had gone distant, focused on the far wall of the foyer, an intricately-carved screen showing the fresh green coolness of the garden beyond. His thumb moved again, caressing my upper arm.

"My lord." Vann gave me a nervous glance, forged ahead. "It might be better to act first and apologize later. This is dangerous. *Truly* dangerous."

"Act first, apologize later." Japh sounded thoughtful. "What do you think of that, Dante?"

He's actually asking what I think? Another banner occasion. Call the holovid reporters again. "Sounds risky," I answered, carefully. "If *who* takes her? And what's the Key?" *And what the bloody blue fuck are we talking about here? Me?*

Vann's cheeks actually flushed. "My lord." He was beginning to sound desperate. Was he sweating? "I've served you for years and never questioned your orders or methods. But this is *dangerous*. If *he* finds out, *he'll* kill her, and possibly the rest of your vassals too."

Japhrimel shrugged. "At present I am too valuable for him to risk anything of the sort."

"Vassals?" My voice cut across his. "He who? Lucifer? Kill me? He's already tried. If he finds out *what?*" *Served Japhrimel for years? That's news, too.*

Vann winced when I spoke the Devil's name. I didn't blame him, but I was too busy staring up at Japh's profile to worry about his tender feelings. "Japhrimel?" I heard the quiet, deadly tone in my voice. "Care to shed some light on this? I'm a little lost."

I thought he wouldn't answer, but he blinked, as if returning from a long and unpleasant chain of thought. "This is not the place for such a discussion," he said, finally, slowly. Choosing his words with great care, a tone I'd rarely heard from him before. "I would prefer to see to your comfort first, and explain privately. For now, will it satisfy you if I say you have suddenly become far more important to the Prince than even *he* realizes, and Vann is worried because your life is so very precious?" His eyes flashed green as he turned his head slightly, looking down at me with a very faint, iron-clad smile touching his lips. "If you are taken or killed, I will be unable to protect those whose allegiance lies with me, and they may find it... worrisome."

I don't think I've ever been struck so speechless, and that's saying something. I am normally not the type of girl to be at a loss for words. I turned this around in my head once or twice, the mark on my shoulder pulsing softly again with velvet heat. Then I realized he hadn't answered either of my questions.

Still, that's more than he's given me since this whole mess began. I suppose it's a step up. I thought it over, and Vann visibly braced himself.

What does he think I'm going to do? "Okay." I nodded, sharply, once. My hair fell over my shoulders, tumbled in my face. "I'm going to go get something to eat. Come along when you're finished, and you can explain to me over breakfast."

Japhrimel shook his head. "I would prefer to explain in private, Dante." He paused. "If it would please you to accede."

Well, I can't very well argue with that, can I? We were being so very careful with each other, I might have burst out laughing if it hadn't been so deadly serious. "Sure. After breakfast, then. We'll head up to our room and you can explain everything."

Vann was crimson under his bruises. He also looked shocked. I got the idea he wasn't used to hearing Japhrimel express a preference instead of just telling someone what to do. I was pretty surprised myself. And pleased. He was trying, at least.

Japh nodded. "As you like." He let go of me slowly, reluctantly, and I found myself smiling as I backed up two steps, then turned and headed for the small café, an unaccustomed light feeling under my breastbone.

To my surprise, Lucas Villalobos sat at one of the tables, his almost-yellow eyes wide open as he looked over a menu. He'd cleaned up, gotten out of his blood-stiff rags and into a fresh microfiber shirt and jeans, bandoliers crossing his narrow chest and his lank hair lying clean and damp against his shoulders. He had his two 60-watt plasguns, and the river of scarring down the left side of his face looked pink and rough-scrubbed.

He looked none the worse for wear despite being almost eviscerated by the Prince of Hell.

Just how fast did the Deathless heal, anyway?

I scuffed the floor deliberately as I threaded between tables and finally dropped into the chair opposite him, my sword resting in its scabbard across my lap. He was working for me, but still…he was

Lucas. It doesn't pay to be lazy even around people you employ. "Hey." *Gods, I'm grinning like an idiot. Japhrimel asked me, he asked me, he's treating me like an equal. Thank the gods.*

Lucas's eyes flicked over me once, descended back to the menu. "Valentine." His whispering, ruined voice almost hurt my own throat. "Where's your pet demon?"

I suppose for him that passed as a polite greeting. "Getting news from one of his stooges." *Proving he's one of the good guys, as far as I'm concerned.*

The café was windowless, but one whole pillared wall of graceful arched doorways gave out onto the courtyard garden, where green flowered lush under a shimmer of climate control. Linen napkins, heavy silverware, the glasses real silica instead of plasglass, a tiled floor and smooth adobe walls—if the outside of this place looked shabby, the inside at least was very nice. There was a breath of warm breeze from the garden, heavily spiced with jasmine that would fairly drench the place once night fell. "So what's good here?"

"Don't know. The Necromance recommended *huevos Benedictos*." Wonder of wonders, Lucas shuddered. "No matter how old I get, I ain't gonna eat that shit."

I was startled into a laugh. If I'd still been human I would have been too terrified to enjoy any of his jokes. "I don't blame you. How are you feeling?"

It was a stupid question, and his yellowing eyes simply came up and dropped back down to the menu. He didn't respond, and my good mood soured only a little. Lucas wasn't a small-talk type of guy.

The waitress came, a sloe-eyed Egyptiano in jeans and a blousy cassock of a shirt, traditional lasetattoos on her dark hands. The shirt, fine cotton, was embroidered with red around the cuffs and collar; her hair, long and black, pulled back in a simple ponytail. She still looked exotic, helped along by the gold nose-ring and the thin gold rings on each finger as well as the slim chiming bangles on her slender wrists, startling against dusky skin. "Would you like today sirs?" she chirped in passable Merican, taking no notice of my tat or Lucas's scarred face—or the fact that both of us were armed.

Most normals blanch or flinch on seeing my cheek. They think psions have nothing better to do than rummage through their messy, stinking minds. It never occurs to them that going through a normal's psyche is like wading neck-deep in festering shit. Even corporate and legal telepaths don't like dealing with normals and always use a filter between their own sensitive, well-ordered minds and the untrained sludge in most people's heads.

Besides, I was a Necromance, not a Reader or a legal telepath. The emerald on my cheek shouted what I was; there was no reason for normals to be afraid of me unless they were running from the law or attacked me first. I've been feared by normals most of my life, but it never gets any easier. Not even when you're part-demon.

I picked up a flat plascoated menu. One side was in Erabic, the other in Merican and Franje. I scanned the offerings while Lucas ordered curry, a small mountain of rice, and coffee.

She looked at me, smiling. Her teeth were very white. I asked for the same thing — Lucas probably knew what he was about, despite his show of ignorance. I did ask for a synthprotein shake too, but just because I felt peckish.

She accepted the menus with a smile. It was comforting to sit in a café as if I was on vacation — even though Lucas had his back to the safe spot and I had to put mine to the archway leading from the lobby. That made me nervous.

Then again, he'd taken on the Devil for me. Like Japhrimel.

Besides, Lucas's reputation would suffer if one of his clients got hashed at the breakfast table with him. I was pretty sure he cared about his reputation, if nothing else. There was a story that he'd once taken on a whole corporation's security division when a stray shot had accidentally killed his target before he could get to it.

The rumor further was, he'd won — *after* being knifed, shot, blown up, knifed again, shot five more times, and blown up the last time with a full half-ounce of C19. No, you didn't mess with Lucas Villalobos *or* his reputation.

I watched the waitress sway away. There was only one other occupied table — a normal male in a hoverpilot's uniform buried in a huge broadsheet newspaper covered with squiggles of Erabic. It looked a little like Magi code and I narrowed my eyes, staring intently at the inked lines. My left hand was solid around my katana's sheath.

I finally felt as if I'd survived Sarajevo. *And* my last meeting with the Prince of Hell. Getting kicked around and half-strangled by the Devil was getting to be almost routine, by now.

Not really. That sort of thing *never* gets routine.

I let out a long breath, my shoulders dropping. It was going to be a long time before I could smell baking bread again without being reminded of the Anhelikos in the empty temple, its wings mantling and cloying perfume brushing through my hair as my legs turned to butter.

It was going to be a long time before I could begin to forget Lucifer's hand circling my neck, little things creaking and crackling in my throat. My husky broken voice bore no relation to what it had been while human. What was it with demons and strangling me?

"What you gonna do?" Lucas asked finally.

I found him studying me, his dark eyebrows drawn together and his thin mouth twisted down at one corner. "About what?" *Dammit, I never used to wander off in the middle of conversations. Got to keep focused.*

He gave me a look that could have cut plasteel. "The Devil. And Ol' Blue Eyes."

Eve. Lucifer had contracted me to kill or capture four demons, without mentioning Doreen's genetically-altered daughter was the fourth. The more I thought about it, the more it seemed like he'd been using me to draw Eve out.

But if he wanted her dead or captured, the other hunters he'd sent after her — and her cohorts — would be more than enough, wouldn't they? To christen me his new Right Hand, wind me up, and send me after her fellow rebels while simultaneously throwing noisy obstacles in my way and showing up to capture or kill her himself . . . what game was that part of? It wasn't like the Devil to crawl out of his hole personally before everything was all neatly wrapped up.

Bait. And some other game is being played here. Lucky me.

Japhrimel had to know I wouldn't agree to take Eve down or return her to Lucifer. And last but *definitely* not least, what the hell did it have to do with this treasure, the Key, and me?

"I don't know," I lied. "I can't hunt down Doreen's daughter, Lucas. Santino killed Doreen, and I killed Santino." *Boy, is that ever an understatement.* For a moment my right hand cramped, but I spread my fingers under the table and it passed. My good mood was fading even more. "Lucifer took Eve. She . . . ."

She said I was her mother too, that the sample Vardimal took from Doreen was contaminated with my genetic material. I hadn't told Japhrimel, it was too private. Too *personal.* It was different from the omissions he'd made to me, I told myself.

Wasn't it?

"You contracted me for four demons," Lucas reminded me.

And she's one of them. The remainder of the funny, light feeling under my breastbone disappeared, returning me to sour anticipation and a faint headache. I looked away from the table, out toward the garden, steaming sweet green under the glaring hammerblow of desert sun. "I know."

Maybe I would have said more, but the datband flashed on my left wrist. I looked down, my eyes snagging on the silvery wristcuff above my dat, carved with its fluid lines. The Gauntlet, Lucifer's little calling-card, marking me as his extra-special deputy. My skin crawled at the thought of wearing it, but there hadn't been a chance to take it off. Getting chased around by hellhounds and half-strangled by demons will cut into any girl's accessorizing schedule.

My datband flashed again. I had a message. I dug in my bag for my datpilot, wrinkling my nose a little. The heavy black canvas bag had gone through hell with me—literally. Both to the home of demons when Japhrimel had been sent to fetch me the first time and the other hell of my return to Rigger Hall.

My skin prickled with phantom gooseflesh. I took a deep breath, dispelling the feeling. The bag was singed and smelled of hard use and gun oil, its strap frayed but still tough. I fished my 'pilot out, flipped it open, and tapped at the screen while it genescanned me and decided I was, after all, Dante Valentine.

I was glad the electronics recognized me. Some days I didn't even recognize myself anymore. Ever since that rainy Monday when my front door resounded with shattering knocks, my life had taken a definite turn into "gigantic mess."

The screen flashed, cleared. Then the message came up, priority-marked urgent, I knew who it was from. There was only one person it could be from, only one person whose messages would go straight to my datband.

Gabe. Gabriele Spocarelli.

I blew out between my teeth. The icon flashed, waiting for me to tap it to bring the message up. The waitress came with thick aromatic coffee you can get in Hegemony Afrike or Putchkin Near Asiano, syrupy-sweet and fragrant. She also set down my synthprotein shake and gave me a bright smile, her dark eyes passing over my tat with nary a hitch. I looked up at Lucas, who studied his shotglass with apparent interest before lifting it slowly to his mouth with the air of a man embarking on a sensual experience.

I tapped the icon. I'd spoken to Gabe a couple months ago, one of our semi-regular calls. Like most psions, I wasn't good with a regular schedule unless I had a datpilot and a messenger service to keep my life straight; I would sometimes think only a few days had gone by before my 'pilot would beep and tell me it had been a month or three and Gabe was due for another call. Time had taken on a funny elasticity, maybe because I was hanging out with a creature older than even *I* had any idea of.

Usually I dialed, she picked up, and we both did our best to sound like the things we couldn't say to each other weren't crowding the telephone line like apparitions pulled from fresh bodies, shimmering and seeming-solid. We talked about old cases and bounties, told a few jokes, and generally said nothing of any real importance whatsoever.

She didn't mention Jace Monroe. I didn't mention Japhrimel, who observed a strict silence during the phone calls when he didn't withdraw to another room, granting me privacy. Nor did Gabe and I engage in anything even remotely resembling real conversation. Still, I called regularly, and each time I called she picked up. It was good enough for me.

Better than I deserved.

The screen flashed, and a chill touched my nape. The message was simple. Too simple.

> *Danny,*
> *Mainuthsz.*
> *I need you. Now.*
> *Gabe.*

"Who is it?" Lucas's eyes flicked over my shoulder. I looked, seeing Japhrimel. He skirted the tables, obviously intending to join us. My heart began to pound, and if I hadn't been so hungry I might have bolted from the table. Not to avoid him, but because the need to *move* suddenly all but throttled me.

I sat very still, searching for control. It came slowly, tied to the deep breathing I began. All the way down into the belly, blow the breath out softly through the lips. *Anubis grant me strength. All right, Gabe. I'm on my way.* "A friend." I flipped my datpilot shut with a practiced flip of my wrist. "Let's have breakfast. Then I've got a transport to catch."

CHAPTER 3

I waited until after breakfast—the curry was fantastic, searing hot over fluffy rice, washed down with more of the fragrant coffee and plenty of ice water. The shake also took the edge of hunger away, leaving me feeling a bit more solid. I had the standard doses of tazapram in my bag, but my stomach had seemed to get even stronger as a *hedaira*. If it was edible, it mostly looked good to me; I wondered if there was anything I *couldn't* eat. Most Necromances had cast-iron guts anyway, funny for a bunch of twitchy, neurotic prima donnas.

Oddly enough, it reminded me of Emilio, the round Novo Taliano cook at our house in Toscano. He used to beg me to eat, considering it an insult if I didn't consume as many k-cals as he deemed appropriate on a daily basis. When I thought of our house, I thought of Emilio, his pudgy hands waving; he was one of the few normals who didn't seem to fear me at all. He seemed to view me as a pretty and pampered but not-too-bright daughter of a rich family, who had to be bullied and petted into eating properly. It should have irritated me, but *damn* the man could cook.

The meal was quiet. Japhrimel drank a glass of silty red wine, probably more out of politeness than anything else. Lucas didn't ask any more questions about my little message, and I spent the time thinking of how to break the news to Japhrimel.

I didn't think he'd take it calmly. Besides, there were a couple of things we still had to sort out. Like what the hell the Key was, and what the bloody blue hell was going on *now*.

After breakfast—which Japhrimel paid for, as usual—Lucas excused himself to go upstairs and catch some sleep. And probably to give me a chance to talk to Japh, since I'd been monosyllabic all through the meal. I stared at my coffee glass and tried to think of the right words.

Japhrimel waited, his eyes scorching green. Normals didn't seem to notice he wasn't human. Other psions could see the black-diamond flames twisting through his aura, and could call him what he was. Demon.

Only not quite demon. *A'nankhimel,* Fallen.

His fingers played with the wineglass, the long dark Chinese-collared coat as wetly black as the lacquer urn I'd once kept his ashes in. I drew in a deep breath, gathered my courage, and opened my mouth.

"Japh, I have to go to Saint City. I just got a message from Gabe. She needs me."

Japhrimel absorbed this, staring into his wineglass. Said nothing.

I took another gulp of coffee. I really wasn't doing service to it, swilling it like cheap freeze-dried. But I was nervous. "Japhrimel?"

"The Necromance." Faintly dismissive, as if reminding himself. "With the dirtwitch mate."

I swallowed roughly. "She's my friend. And she says she needs me, it's an emergency. Everything else is going to have to wait." *Including Lucifer. Especially Lucifer.*

His eyes half-lidded. The look was deceptively languid, but the mark on my shoulder turned hot and aching under his attention. His hair fell over his forehead, softly, my fingers itched to brush the inky strands. Trace down his cheek like I'd done before, maybe run my fingertip across the border of his lips while he submitted to my touch, his eyes darkening for just a moment.

Stop it. You've still got a few questions to answer, Japh. Like what the hell's going on. Explanations, remember?

But still... *One day,* Lucifer had said as I crouched, my throat on fire and my belly running with pain, *I will kill her.*

Not while I watch over her, Japhrimel had replied.

The more I thought about it, the more it seemed like a declaration of war. I wasn't sure how I felt about that, except gratefulness that I was still alive.

"I'm catching the first transport I can," I told him. "I'm going back to Saint City. You can come with me if you want, but not before you explain everything to me. In detail. Leaving nothing out. Clear?"

He took another sip of wine. His eyes burned. A soft weight of Power folded around me, eased against my skin as if he had wrapped me in Putchkin synthfur. "You swore allegiance to the Prince as his Right Hand. You have four demons to hunt, *hedaira.*"

I winced. *Well, it's now or never, I suppose.* "I won't hunt Eve, Japhrimel."

A single shrug. I was beginning to hate the way demons shrug all the goddamn time. I suppose most of what humans do deserves no more than a shrug—but still.

I struggled with a sharp bite of irritation, took another swallow of coffee. "I mean it. I promised Doreen I'd *save* Eve; I won't hunt her. And I was bamboozled into this Right Hand thing, fine—but my promise to Doreen predates my promise to Lucifer. He can...." *He can go to hell,* I meant to say, realized how absurd it was and swallowed the rest of the sentence. "It's not like it matters," I continued, bitterly, forgetting to pitch my voice low and soft. The cups rattled on the table. "He's sent others to hunt her down. I'm just another game piece."

Not to mention the fact that Eve asked me not to look too hard for her. Simply asked. No manipulation, no lying, no trying to twist me into a game I'm bound to lose. I had to admit she was the demon I was most likely to feel good about helping.

He set his wineglass down and laid his hand over my left wrist. Incredibly gentle, his warm skin against mine; he could have crushed the small bones if he'd wanted to. Instead, his thumb stroked the soft underside of my wrist. Fire spilled up my arm, through my shoulder, made the mark burn again. I had to catch my breath, biting the inside of my cheek savagely. The pain reminded me again I was a Necromance, that I didn't respond sexually to Power.

Though I'd responded to Eve, hadn't I? And Japhrimel knew me, we'd shared a bed for a long time. It's hard to fight someone who knows your body that intimately.

"You are not simply a game piece, Dante. You are my *hedaira,* and you must trust me to do what you cannot."

What the hell does that mean? "What does that mean?" I cast a quick glance around—the garden was empty, the waitress leaning in an arched doorway and exchanging soft laughter with an invisible someone I guessed was the cook. The pilot folded his newspaper, tucked it under his arm, and tapped at his datband to pay his bill.

Japhrimel smiled. It was a sad smile, his eyes flaring with laser-green intensity; another human expression. There was a time I would have been glad to see any feeling on his face, especially his rare smiles. But this expression made cold prickles ripple down my back. I don't get goosebumps, but it felt awfully close. The breeze from the garden filled my nose with green sweetness, overlaid with demon musk. "What you cannot do, I will. Don't trouble yourself. It is, after all, what I am meant for."

After facing down the Devil, I never thought I'd be frightened of anything else again. I was wrong. I stared at him, my pulse beating thinly in my throat. When I could speak, it was no more than a strangled whisper. "You leave her alone. I swear, Japhrimel, if you—"

"Do not." His voice cut through mine, he shook his head. "You know better than to swear such an oath. You must live to your word, Necromance."

I tore my wrist out from under his hand. He let me. I rocketed to my feet, the chair scraping along tiled floor, my sword in my left hand. My fingers tightened on the scabbard. Our waitress stiffened, looking back over her shoulder, the dark sheaf of her ponytail contrasting with the cotton of her shirt.

I leaned forward, my hair falling over my shoulders, ink-black as his. "Don't push me on this, Japh. That's Doreen's daughter." My tone, flat and cold, rattled the entire table. It might be an empty threat—he was, after all, so much stronger and faster than me, and had proved it too many times.

But by my god and my sword, I didn't care. She was Doreen's daughter, most of all. But maybe she was mine too. If she was, it was my job to protect her. My *duty* to protect her.

He had nothing to say to that. I straightened. My bag lay heavy against my hip, I still had my guns and my knives. And my sword, the blade that bit the Devil.

I wasn't able to hurt Japhrimel, not in a fair fight—but if he killed Doreen's daughter or tried to return her to the Prince of Hell we were going to see just how sneaky and inventive I could get when facing down a demon.

A Fallen demon. A man I happened to love, even if he wasn't strictly a man. Wasn't it less than an hour ago I'd promised myself I would give him the benefit of the doubt?

"I swear it, Japh." My right hand closed around my sword hilt. He was too damnably quick—I knew from sparring with him. Even though he sat at the table, looking down at his wineglass, I still felt the nervous urge to back up, get some distance in case he decided to move on me. "By all I hold holy, I *will*."

A fluid shrug. He rose slowly to his feet, his chair scraping more quietly than mine had. "What is it you want me to say?"

I don't know. "I'm going. With or without you, I'm *going*." *Goddammit, Danny, he dangled you up against a wall once before. You keep pushing him, he's going to do it again. Or worse.*

"You will not leave my side until this matter is finished. I thought I explained as much in words even you could understand." How could he sound so calm? As if it didn't matter what I said or did, he had spoken and that was that. A breeze drifted through the garden outside, filled the café suddenly with the scent of growing things and the cinnamon-musk of demons; it was the psychic equivalent of static, dyeing the air around us both. I was radiating again. If I wasn't careful I would start affecting the sloe-eyed waitress and any other human in the place, flooding them with pheromones I couldn't fully control.

I tensed, my left thumb ready to click the blade free of the scabbard. Eyed Japhrimel. *Don't push me. We were just doing so well; don't push me on this.*

His gaze moved over me, from the top of my tangled black hair down to my scuffed boots, the loose easy stance I dropped into, though I didn't draw just yet. "Ever a battle, *hedaira,*" he said quietly. "I will go with you, to see what has befallen your fellow Necromance."

Thank you, gods. Thank you. My breath came harsh and hot. I stared at him. "You mean it?"

Did I imagine the shadow of pain that slid over his face? Probably. "I prefer you where I may see the mischief you intend. I see no reason why we may not stop in Santiago City."

I couldn't help myself. "Really?"

He moved, a single step. Another. Closer, but he didn't look at me. Instead, he looked over my shoulder. His fingers closed around my right hand, the sword kept home in the sheath. "Save your blade for your enemies, *hedaira.*"

I do. Oh, I do. Closed my lips over the words. "Japhrimel?"

"What?" He still looked over my shoulder, a muscle flicked in his golden cheek. As if he expected me to yell at him, maybe. His fingers slid up my arm, cupped my shoulder, tightened but didn't hurt me. I swallowed dryly. He was so close the heat of him blurred through my clothes, less intense than the sun outside but scorching nonetheless.

"Explanations. Remember?" *This is going too well. We're going to hit a hitch soon.*

He still didn't look at me. "When we are finished with your business in Santiago City, I will give you all the explanations you are ready to hear."

Goddammit, Japh. I knew you were being too reasonable. "You promised." I heard the hurt in my voice, couldn't help myself.

"You accepted a bargain with the Prince. That is a promise too."

"It's not the same thing." *It's not. Goddammit, you know it's not.*

He switched tactics. "What did the Androgyne tell you, Dante? She is *in rebellion,* she has no hope of winning. I will not allow you to be dragged down with her." He waited for me to speak. When I didn't, he tried again. "What did she say to make you so stubborn?"

I set my jaw. *I knew you'd ask sooner or later.* Said nothing.

His fingers tensed, hard iron against my skin. "Dante? Tell me what she said to you."

Silly me. I should have known. "Does it fucking matter? You aren't going to explain anything to me. *You* make promises you never intend to keep." The words were flat, final, and terribly sad. *Am I really standing here in the middle of a Cairo Giza café, trying to persuade a demon to explain something to me? How do I get myself into these things?*

"Tell me what the created Androgyne said to you, Dante." Did he sound *pleading?* It couldn't be. Japhrimel had never begged *me* for anything. "What did she tell you? What did you *believe* of what she told you?"

I believed enough. My arm ached, his fingers tense and hard, digging into my flesh. I looked down, the tiles on the floor melting together as my eyes unfocused. It was an old trick, learned back in primary school—if I unfocused my eyes and let the roaring fill my ears, whatever happened to the rest of me wouldn't matter. It didn't work if the physical pain reached a certain level, but short of that....

Japhrimel's fingers loosened. I still felt his hand—if I was still human I might have been bruised. It was so unlike him. He was normally so exquisitely careful not to hurt me. *What does it matter what she told me, Japh?*

"Dante." His tone was quiet, dark with something too angry to be hurt. "You *will* speak of it, sooner or later. You cannot hide from me."

I took a sharp shuddering breath. The café was utterly still. I wondered if the waitress was staring at us or if she had decided to retreat to the kitchen. "I need a transport out of here as soon as possible." It took work to keep my voice level, not weak but quiet. *I'm not backing down on this one, Japh. Do your worst.*

"As you like." He stepped away, dismissing me. "Leave it to me. I suggest you rest."

The scar in the hollow of my left shoulder throbbed. *I don't care. He can do whatever he likes, what happened between me and Eve is private. It's none of his business.*

What I did next surprised me. I caught his arm, the sleeve of his long dark coat—I knew what it was made of, and it hadn't bothered me for a long time. I tensed my fingers, clawtips sliding free to prick the lacquered material. I squeezed as hard as I could, in turn. It probably didn't matter, I wasn't able to hurt *him*. "You hurt me. Again." *Gods, I sound like a whining little girl. But it's true.* "You promised you wouldn't."

I was looking at his boots, so I missed whatever expression that produced.

"Do you truly think I would harm you?" He tore his arm out of my fingers, the material of his coat slick against my fingers. It was wings masquerading as clothing; he was literally of the Greater Flight of demons. He could have killed me without even trying.

How do we define "harm," Japhrimel? I'm not bleeding or dead, so I'm fine? Is that it? "Fine." I turned on my heel, headed for the stairs up to the rooms Leander had rented.

I barely saw the stairs through the welling water in my eyes. But I blinked it away. Crying wouldn't do any good.

CHAPTER 4

Y ou're what?" The emerald on Leander Beaudry's cheek sparked, the thorny yin-yang accreditation tat on his left cheek twisting under the skin. My own cheek burned, my gem answering his in greeting.

"I've got some business in Saint City." I dropped down in a lyre-backed, overstuffed maroon chair and stared at the room. Japhrimel was downstairs with Vann, making arrangements for us to blow this town. "Getting on the next transport. I'm putting the hunt on hold for a while." *For as long as I possibly can. Thank you, Gabe.*

Lying cheek-by-jowl with the throbbing ache in my scarred shoulder was a new, unsteady panic. Gabe wouldn't call me like this unless it was dire. She wouldn't have sent that particular message unless it was a personal matter instead of another job for the Saint City PD. *That* added up to only a few possible scenarios: revenge, a bloody personal bounty, or *bad* trouble.

Add yet another layer of welling mistrust about Japhrimel's

motives, and I was bound to be a nervous wreck before long. He'd given in too easily. *Far* too easily. I'd expected a full-out fight instead of just an aching shoulder and verbal fencing over whether or not I was "hurt."

"What's the business in Saint City?" Leander pushed his hand back through his dark hair.

I squashed a flare of irritation. It wasn't an unreasonable question—after all, he'd signed on to the hunt after spending a lot of Power after that hover incident in Freetown New Prague. Then he'd come to Giza and started making arrangements for further hunting. He was a good Necromance if what I'd read about him was true, and he seemed honorable. Plus he was a bounty hunter, which meant he could probably handle himself in any normal situation.

Too bad nothing about this was normal.

And he's human. I squashed that thought too, sent it packing.

It refused to go quietly.

I sank into the chair. Gravity suddenly weighed down every inch of my skin. "A debt to an old friend. She's called for my help."

He studied me for a few moments, leaning back in his chair with his long legs stretched out, his katana laid across his lap. For a moment he reminded me of someone, though I couldn't think of quite who.

The room was large and airy, containment fields humming over tall windows. Red tile decorated the plaster walls, heavy low furniture sat obediently in prearranged places; through a half-open door I saw the edge of a bed swathed in mosquito netting. Another bedroom door was closed—Lucas, getting some shut-eye. McKinley was nowhere in sight, and I was grateful for that. The black-clad Hellesvront agent with his oddly metallic left hand made me uneasy.

"And?" Leander's eyebrows raised.

I've got to go. Not only that, but I've got to figure out a way to keep Japhrimel occupied so Eve can... what? What is she doing? I hope she has some kind of plan. "I don't know the specifics." I strangled another hot welling of irritation. "She's called, she'll tell me what she needs when I get there. It's that simple."

He absorbed this. "Your friends are lucky. Not many people would fly halfway around the world just on the strength of a phone call."

"It was a datpilot message." I leaned my head back into the chair's embrace, closing my eyes. "I made a promise. That's a magickal law, isn't it? *Thy word is thy bond.*"

I could tell by his faint exhaled laugh he recognized the quotation — attributed to Saint Crowley the Magi, no less, though it didn't sound much like the treatises I'd read. I wish someone would tell my bounties that." The wryness of the comment matched the dry humor in his tone. "Well, it's Saint City then. All right."

And that, apparently, was that. I let one eye drift open just a crack. "You're not required to come along."

He shrugged. A human shrug — it didn't irritate me the way it did when Japhrimel gave one of his evocative noncommittal movements. "Call it my curiosity. I've got some time."

"Might not be too healthy to hang around. People have a distressing habit of dying around me." *You're human. Fragile. Or at least, more fragile than I am, and I'm not doing too well when it comes to facing down demons and the like. When did my life get so freaking dangerous?*

I'd never considered forgoing combat training and hunting bounties. Freelance law enforcement had always seemed the only possible route for me; Jace had taught me about mercenary work and corporate espionage when I'd been desperate for cash after my Academy training and a few years in the field. It had only been a small step — I was, after all, familiar with the idea of fighting.

What you cannot escape, you must fight; what you cannot fight, you must endure. Life was dangerous in and of itself, I was privileged to know the fact from a young age.

It meant I wasn't as nastily surprised as I got older.

"I'm a Necromance." His tone managed to convey disdain and excessive neutrality in one pretty package. In other words, *Death's my trade too, kid.*

Yeah, but I'm tougher than you and I'm having trouble keeping myself together here. Do I really want to be looking out for you? "Me too." An unfamiliar smile spread over my face. It's rare to find a Necromance I enjoy talking to; we're such a bunch of neurotics. Using Power and psionic talent means most of us have distinctly odd personalities as well as a fair helping of *Schadenfreude,* and dealing with Death like we're trained to will make even the most courageous human paranoid on one hand and adrenaline-addicted on the other.

Case in point? John Fairlane, the other Necromance left in Saint City besides Gabe. I couldn't stand Fairlane; his white linen suits and pretentious lisp drove me up the wall. The feeling was most emphatically mutual. Two Necromances in the same room usually ended up with either a catfight or a pissing match. "You know what? You're all right."

"Thanks. That means something, coming from you." Dry, ironic, and amused. He had a nice voice.

That won a tired giggle from me. His own laugh was warm caramel, the air suddenly relaxing between us. On the ebb of that laughter, Japhrimel entered the room and I heard the door close softly. The silent static of anger—*his* anger—touched me, made the mark on my shoulder turn hot and soft.

I wasn't ready for that. I'd expect the mark to hurt when he was mad at me. It had certainly hurt plenty before, usually when I was already in dire trouble and sinking fast.

My eyes flew open. I turned my head to see him standing by the door, his hands clasped behind his back as usual. "The next transport for a hub leaves past midnight," he said. "We can be in Paradisse by late morning, North New York by the following nightfall, and Santiago City by the next afternoon. Slow, but more efficient than layovers."

Too slow, Gabe needs me now. "What about the hover Lucas had? That would be faster."

He shrugged. The crackle of anger around him hadn't abated. What did *he* have to be upset about? "Vann has already taken it."

The faint, precious good humor I'd been feeling drained away. "Why?"

"To convince the Prince we are hunting in good faith instead of following your whim." His voice was a little harsher than its usual even irony. "I suggest you rest, Dante. We will not leave until tonight."

I would have liked to settle down in a bed and do some heavy brooding, but being ordered to do it took all the fun away. Instead, my eyes swung over to Leander, whose hand was just a little too tight on his katana. He was muscle-ropy and probably deadly with his blade, but I wasn't quite human anymore. My strength and speed were closer to a demon's—though not close enough.

Not *nearly* close enough for what I had to do.

"Well, I'm here in Cairo Giza and there's a couple hours to kill before we can catch transport. It'd be a shame to miss the Great Souk. I can probably even pick up a little something for Gabe." I stretched, yawned, and made it to my feet. "Hey, boy, this is your town. You want to show me around?"

"Happy to." Leander turned his own leaning-forward into a

graceful movement bringing him up to his feet. "You've never seen the Souk? You're in for a treat."

"Good. Guess the day's not going to be a total loss, then." Was it just me or did my cheerfulness sound forced?

Then again, *cheerful* didn't seem to be on the menu lately. Here I was about to go running back to Saint City, to a disaster in progress. Lucifer would be breathing down my neck soon. I was under contract to the Devil himself to hunt the escaped demons down, which meant I had to think of some way to keep Japhrimel away from Eve for the length of that contract—a cool seven years of fun and games.

And Japhrimel was hiding some new nasty surprise from me, not to mention making it eloquently clear I was by far the weaker half of our partnership. There was a time I'd thought I'd learned to know him, when I'd thought nothing could break the bond between us— but all that crashed down when Lucifer started poking his nose in my life again.

I glanced down at the metal cuff on my left wrist. The space for my arm to slip free *had* narrowed, or maybe my wrist had gotten bigger. The Gauntlet's fluidly-etched lines weren't glowing green, but the feel of the warm metal against my skin suddenly turned my stomach. The feeling of being watched returned, my nape prickling.

You don't survive as a bounty hunter by ignoring that feeling.

Well, we can start fixing what's wrong right here. I shoved my sword into the handy loop on my rig and dug my fingers in, curling them around the metal, twisting. It didn't want to let go of my skin but I pried it loose, finding that I *could* just squeeze my wrist through the slim opening.

I stuffed the heavy barbaric silver in my bag, and looked up to find a demon and a Necromance both staring at me.

"Let's go." I almost hoped Japhrimel would stay behind, the faint line between his eyebrows and slight downward tilt to the corners of his mouth told me he wasn't pleased at all. My pulse pounded thinly in my throat, fear and sharp defiance mixing.

You can't control me, Japh. I love you, and you're stronger than me—but I won't let you win.

When I followed Leander out the door, Japh was right behind me, the weight of his disapproval a stone in my throat.

The Great Souk of Cairo Giza seethes under fierce sun, dust and sand drifting on a vast rectangular stone plaza glowered over by plasteel-reinforced mudbrick buildings. Climate control and the floating shadows of hovers in parking patterns overhead provide some relief from the heat, but not much. Plenty of the Souk hasn't changed in hundreds of years. Vast baskets of dates, figs, and other delicacies; whole hanging sides of slaughtered animals—I shuddered to see those, but even in Saint City they still have fresh meat— with stasis fields humming to keep the flies away, children laughing and playing among the shifting crowds, professional pickpockets and thieves scamming through the tide of humanity, every conceivable merchandise on display.

You can get just about anything in the Souk, from vat-grown diamonds to legitimate indentured servants to not-so-legitimate slaves—though that trade is relegated to back alleys and in perennial danger of Hegemony police coming through and cleaning them out. You can buy drugs, augments, or enzyme treatments; the *sedayeen* communes have open-air clinics and biolabs, and Skinlin sell herbal remedies. A Ceremonial or Magi can do a quickshield or tell a fortune. There are even paranormals who have their own booths—swanhilds run messages, werecain sell bright woven rugs or rent out as protection duty. And plenty more.

There's an advantage to being sandwiched between a demon and a Necromance in a crowd, you do get a certain amount of space. The Egyptianos seemed less likely than other normals to look askance at my tat and Leander's; they didn't seem to have much of the fear of psions I'd seen in other parts of the world. Japhrimel looked normal, but the breath of *alienness* he carried seemed to communicate itself to them more readily and he was given more strange looks than either of us psions. Maybe it was the long black Chinese-collared coat in the heat, or his straight face, or maybe it was the way he loomed behind me.

I won't admit to uncritical delight, but I will admit to feeling a lot better than I had in a long time. Haggling was the rule here. It took only a few times of watching Leander artfully bargain in pidgin Merican before I got an idea of the going prices, and soon I was munching on the dates he'd bought while fiercely arguing down the price of a pair of beautiful Erabic daggers. They were the finest in the stall, perfectly balanced for throwing—and metal that doesn't need to be filed down for throwing is a rarity indeed. Their hilts were dark wood, plain and serviceable, but the shape of the blades and their balance made them works of art.

We finished bargaining, I paid the man with New Credit notes and stuffed my thinning bankroll back into my bag. The keepcharm on my bag bristled — not many quick fingers would try a Necromance's bag, but you never know. I accepted the knives from the hawk-faced stall proprietor, who bowed, touching his forehead with his right hand and crying out his praise. I must have been smiling, because Leander gave me a curious look. "You do that like you've lived here for years." He handed me another date.

If you only knew how much time I've spent haggling around the world. "I'm a quick study. Is there statuary here?"

"Down on the west side; take us a while to get there." We pushed back out into the milling mass of people come to buy or sell. An ice-seller's traditional plaintive cry split through the noise, a bright thread drawn through the dark surfroar. "Want to go through Jeweler's Alley, and then the rugs?" Leander shouted over the crowd noise, dark eyes dancing. I wrapped the two sheathed knives together and put them in my bag as well.

"Lead the way!" I shouted back. I normally don't like crowds — the messy overspill of emotion from each normal presses against a psion's shields, takes energy to push away. But I was enjoying this. For the first time since hearing that Lucifer wanted to see me again, I was almost content.

Except for the nagging worry about what trouble Gabe had landed in. And the nervous sense of being watched, of disaster hanging just around the corner.

Japhrimel followed as we made our way through the dappled shadows of hovertraffic. I checked the sky more than usual — getting hit with a few hovers will make a girl nervous — and took in the kaleidoscope of sound, color, and throbbing Power that was the Souk.

If I'd still been human I would have been acclimatizing to the different flow of organic energy here. But being almost-demon meant my body had taken to this new sea of Power within seconds. Here in Cairo Giza the pyramids were sonorous bass notes at the very edge of psychic "hearing," throbbing against bones and viscera like a subsonic beat. The well of Power tasted like sand and spice with the faint heavy odor of animals from the pens on the outskirts, goats and camels mostly. Add the heavy spiced langorousness from the coffee, and it was a heady brew indeed.

Maybe that was why I let Leander buy the bag of candied almonds.

We shared them out under the overhang of a rugseller's tent, and even Japhrimel took a handful when I pressed them on him, his skin warm and dry and his face still and set.

A thin trickle of sweat kissed Leander's pale temple, and I sipped from one of the bottles of *limonada* I'd bought while Leander cracked his open with a practiced twist. The jewelryseller's alley glittered under the sun, gold and silver and gems, both vat-grown and natural, flashed.

I was suddenly fiercely glad I was a Necromance. Most normals never get the chance to see more than a little slice of the world; I'd been all over and was even now standing in the Great Souk, something I'd seen in holovids and mags but never thought I'd get around to experiencing for myself. It must have shown in my face.

Must have? Well, I was grinning like a fool. Any minute all hell might break loose, between Lucifer, Japhrimel, and whatever was going down in Saint City; but for right now I was actually—was I happy?

I guess so. Gabe must be right about credit therapy. "Shopping is the perfect antidote, Danny. Just remember that."

Thinking of Gabe, I sobered. But I still felt my cheeks swell with the smile.

"Like it?" Leander asked.

"It's something." Was I being idiotic? The mark on my left shoulder burned, sending waves of Power through me like heatshimmer above pavement. I tried not to feel it, tried to forget the way my shoulder still twinged every now and again with Japhrimel's attention. "It's really something."

"Nothing like it on earth," was his easy reply.

"Ever been to Moscow?" I tried again to banish the smile from my face, failed.

"Yep. Did some work there for the Putchkin Politburov, and some less-legal stuff for the Tzarchov Family. You been to Freetown Emsterdamme?" He swiped at his forehead with the *limonada* bottle, condensation gleaming on his skin.

"Took down a bounty there once. Great light, they still have the tulip fields instead of clonetanks. What about Free Territorie Suisse?"

"Oh, yeah. On vacation though, no work. The Islands?"

"Which ones?" A cool breeze brushed my naked wrist without the weight of the bracelet, I wondered why I felt so vulnerable without it.

The sense of being watched had faded, but still prickled at the corners of my awareness.

"Let's say Freetown Domenihaiti. I spent a year at the Shaman college out there, they've got this amazing vaudun festival."

"Been there. What about the Great Wall? I had a bounty run all that way." The memory didn't hurt that much now, oddly enough. That job had almost killed me.

"You hunted down Siddie Gregors out that way. Even the steppe couldn't hide that motherfucker." He sounded complacent and awed at once.

I laughed. So he knew about the Gregors bounty. "I used to have a scar." I lifted up my left wrist. "From here—" Touched my inner elbow. "To here." Indicated my wrist. "A plasilica knife. Had to get patched up by an Asiano Yangtze doctor. Foulest-smelling herb paste I ever had smeared on me, but it healed up like a dream and even the scar went away after a couple of years. Gregors was a real bastard, I didn't sleep the whole time I was bringing her in."

"I did this bounty in Shanghai once—"

The conversation went on like this for a while, swapping stories as we moved down Jeweler's Alley. We stopped for quite some time at a booth with rings, I looked over their glitter spread over scruffy black velvet. I'd bought my rings one at a time from ethnic shops in Saint City's Tank District, but I'd dearly love to have a memento of this. Something for Gabe would be nice too.

I took my time, sipping at *limonada* and exchanging yet more stories with Leander. Finally, I selected a dainty cascading silver fire-opal bracelet for Gabe, but didn't see anything for myself. I paid for the bracelet with no haggling—it was a gift—and spotted something else.

I hadn't seen it before, which was odd in and of itself. The piece was even odder, a short delicate spun-platinum chain holding a star sapphire the size of my thumb from distal joint to tip, glittering mellowly in the afternoon light. It was plain, restrained, and cried out to me with its own tongueless voice.

I pointed. "There. That one."

Again, I paid without haggling, explaining to the woman running the stall that it was a gift and I couldn't bargain for gifts. She dropped the price by twenty credits when I told her that, and I paid with my datband—she had an old-fashioned creditswipe. The necklace and bracelet went carefully wrapped into my bag as well, and I looked up to find Leander examining me again. "I'm done," I said. "Thanks."

"It's a pleasure," he replied, and we plunged into the crowd again. I had almost forgotten Japhrimel, he was so silent behind me. I looked over my shoulder a few times to find him thoughtfully looking at something else each time. Was he bored as well as angry? What the hell did *he* have to be angry about? I was the one he manhandled.

I wondered if he was enjoying himself. It didn't seem likely.

That's a real shame, I thought, but then Leander started telling me about the Souk's history, and I listened, fascinated, as we drifted with the crowd until dusk started to paint the sky.

CHAPTER 5

I dropped down to sit on the bed, laying my sword aside and wriggling my toes with relief. It was nice to be out of my boots; I wasn't footsore from wandering through the stone-floored bazaar, but it was close. Japhrimel closed the door, his golden hand spread against it for a moment and his head bowed.

"Japh?" I dug in my bag. "Hey."

He didn't move. Stood with his head down, his eyes closed, leaning his entire weight against his hand on the door. His shoulders slumped, as if he was tired.

"Japhrimel?" I saw no complex twisting of Power that would tell me he was performing a work of magick. Saw nothing but the same black-diamond glitter of his aura, hard and impenetrable, shouting his essential difference. He was demon, he wasn't human.

I'd almost forgotten that, before. *Never again,* I promised myself. Still... I couldn't help trying to get through to him. I was an idiot.

For him, I seemed to be nothing but.

He looked back over his shoulder, his face arranged in its usual ironic mask and his shoulders coming back up to their accustomed straight line. "You should rest, Dante."

"Come on over." I patted the bed next to me. Plasilica whispered as I lowered the bag with my most important purchase in it to the floor. I'd bought another small statue of Anubis to replace the one I'd lost, this one easily able to fit in my palm and carved out of a single chunk of black marble veined with gold. The other thing that mattered—the statue of Sekhmet, repaired with infinite care—sat on the bedstand, glassy obsidian glowing mellow. "Please?"

He crossed the room slowly, lowered himself down. The bed creaked. I finished digging in my messenger bag, easing the strap over my head and settling the bag itself on my other side with a sigh. Carrying the damn thing never got any easier.

"Close your eyes." The remains of my good mood and the excitement of the Souk made me smile. *I'll just try this one more time.*

He studied my face for a long few moments before complying.

I undid the clasp and leaned close, my bag clinking as it slid against the bed. Then I settled the sapphire against his coat and fiddled with the clasp, my fingers suddenly clumsy. It took a little while, and when I retreated I found he'd opened his eyes. He looked at me like I'd just done something extraordinary.

"There." I felt very pleased with myself. "I think it suits you."

He said nothing.

A little bit of the good mood slipped away. Then a little more. He examined my face, his eyes moving from my forehead to my mouth to my cheeks to my chin to my eyes and then repeating the process again.

Great. He doesn't like it. He probably doesn't like me very much either right now. If he'd just listen *to me.*

Shame rose inside me. Rebuffed by a demon, a new low even in my dating life. "If you don't like it, I—"

"No." He set his jaw. "It's beautiful, Dante. Thank you."

He didn't sound thankful. He sounded flat, and a little amused, and terribly furious. I wondered if he was going to hurt me again, and kept his hands in view. He could move with eerie blurring demon speed, but I might still have a little warning if he decided to get nasty with me again.

It didn't take much sometimes to tell what he was feeling—you only had to look closely enough to see the tiny changes, a millimeter's quirk to the eyebrow, a fractional lift of a corner of his mouth, a slight flaring of one elegant nostril. The ever-so-tiny lift of one shoulder. I used to think he wasn't as beautiful as Lucifer, used to think he just looked blandly normal.

Well, Dante, you were wrong on that one.

My chest was on fire, a pain that wasn't from any physical wound lying against my heart. *Why does this hurt so much?* "You don't sound happy." I was too tired to keep the hurt out of my voice. "Did I just violate some arcane demon protocol by giving you a present?"

He shook his head. I waited, got nothing else.

"Fine." I turned away, grabbed my bag's strap and my sword, and slid off the bed. Padded around to the other side, then dropped down and stretched out, wiggling my bare toes and almost groaning as comfort closed around me. My bag settled against my stomach, I clasped my sword in my hands. "Take it off and burn it if you don't like it. I don't care." *After all, you held me up against a wall and lied to me. You're a bastard.*

Why can't I hate you?

Long pause. Silence ticked through the room, only slightly marred by hovertraffic and desert wind outside, the call of a candyseller on the corner, the humming of the containment field over the window. Mosquito netting on the bed, pulled aside, swayed on the breeze. I saw a corner of a chair and a slice of plaster wall before tears blurred my vision and I closed my eyes.

"What would you have me do?" Japhrimel's voice, surprisingly, was raw and hoarse. Probably with fury.

It took a few swallows before I could reply through the stone in my throat. "Give a little," I managed. "Tell me what's going on. Don't lie to me. Quit manhandling me when I don't do what you want. And for the sake of every god that ever was, quit being so . . . so —"

"Inhuman? Is that the word?" Terrible sadness weighted his tone. "How many times must I tell you that I will act to protect you; I will not bother you with trifles? You need only obey my requests, Dante, and this will be easier."

Obey? Are you going to start beating me like a pimp beats his favorite hooker? "Don't hunt Eve." My voice was muffled, I pressed my left hand against my mouth. "Please. If you ever cared about me at all, *don't* do it." *I'll do anything you want, Japh, just leave Doreen's little girl alone. Hurt me if you have to, but leave her alone.*

"I will not risk you in a rebellion doomed to failure. The Androgyne is young, untested. She *cannot win,* Dante. I will not lose you to her foolishness. Why will you not understand?"

The injustice rose to choke me. I swallowed it, tried again. "You don't have to declare yourself on her side. We can look anywhere in the world for her, Japh. We just don't look too *hard*. In seven years the contract's over, we're free, and you—"

His voice drained all the warmth from the room, made the air stir uneasily. "How *free* do you think the Prince will leave us if these four are not caught and brought to his justice? It is a choice between them and us. They will die, or we will. And if *she* has clouded your head with some appeal or treachery, it becomes my task to save you from yourself."

Silence. Soughing of the wind as it rose at dusk, the sun sinking below the arc of the horizon and night reaching up to fold ageless desert and ancient city in its embrace.

"You want to save me from myself, and you'll hurt me if I don't do what you want. Is that it?" I swallowed dryly. Tensed myself, waited for him to explode.

"I am sorry. I am a fool." Well, chalk it up to a miracle, he *sounded* sorry for once. "I do not mean to hurt you. You do not understand, and it frustrates me past all reason when you will not listen—will not *see*. When the escaped are brought to Lucifer's justice, you may extract whatever penance you desire from me. Until then, we are at *war*. It is *us* or it is *them,* and I will not have it be us."

"It's not a choice between them and us, Tierce Japhrimel." It was my turn to sound sad. "It's your choice between me and Lucifer." A bitter laugh rose up in me, was savagely repressed, escaped anyway. "Guess I know where your real loyalty lies."

"If it pleases you, continue to think so." He rose, the bed creaking slightly as his weight moved. "When this is finished, I will ask an apology for that accusation."

You might get one, if we can hash this out between now and then. If we have time, between whatever's going down with Gabe and whatever Lucifer's cooking up next. I would have cursed, but he closed the door to the bedroom before I could. I clamped my left hand around my katana's scabbard, the right around the hilt, and settled down to brood before we had to catch the transport. The tears dried up, leaving my eyes dry and hot, scoured by a whole desert's worth of sand.

CHAPTER 6

hate traveling transport, and my recent experiences with hovers falling on me hadn't cured me of it. It was with profound relief that I stepped onto the concrete dock under a familiar plasilica dome and filled my lungs with soupy chemical-laden tang, the familiar cold radioactive glow of Saint City's power well rising to greet me.

Goddamn, it's good to be home. The thought surprised me; I'd never considered the place *home* before. Never thought about what *home* would feel like.

Lucas jostled me from behind, Leander sighing as he worked the kinks out of his neck. "Damn transports," the Necromance said, and I felt sneakingly glad my own claustrophobia was shared by at least one member of our little troupe.

I looked over my shoulder. To the side, Japhrimel murmured to McKinley, who had showed up on the transport dock at midnight in Cairo, along with Tiens. The Nichtvren left to help Vann with whatever errand Japhrimel had sent him on, and the black-clad Hellesvront agent had boarded the transport with us. I didn't like that. The man—if you could call either Vann or McKinley a "man"—made me nervous. The oddly silver metallic coating on his left hand puzzled me too. I still didn't have the faintest idea what the Hellesvront agents were, precisely, but they were part of the net of financial and other assets the demons had in place on earth. Vann had said something about "vassals." Maybe they were organized into a feudal system, like some federated Freetowns.

Which meant that Vann and McKinley were loyal to Japhrimel — if they weren't exclusively loyal to Lucifer. Either way, neither of them was likely to be any help to me, or to give me any information. The Nichtvren didn't seem very likely to help me either.

Which left me with Lucas, Leander, and my own wits. Put that way, I seemed damn near rich. The Deathless and another Necromance were far from the worst backup I could have.

Don't say that, Danny. You're dealing with demons. All the backup in the world might not be enough.

As I watched, McKinley nodded and set off for the other end of the dock, apparently given his marching orders. Japhrimel watched him for a moment, but the mark on my shoulder was alive with heat. No matter that he was looking the other way, Japh's attention was all on me.

I wasn't quite sure how I felt about that. "Lucas?"

"Huh?" His whispering, painful voice barely reached through the sound of people disembarking. The North New York–Saint City transport run was a full one since both cities were hubs. That hadn't stopped us from having a whole first-class compartment to ourselves all the way from Cairo. Maybe Japhrimel had arranged for that, I didn't know.

Didn't care, either.

"Two things," I said out of the corner of my mouth. "Find out what Japhrimel's business in Saint City is, and tell Abra I'll be coming by to see her. Good?"

"You got it." He detached himself from us and melted into the crowd. It was a relief to have a professional in my corner. Whatever Japh was up to, Lucas was my best bet of finding out sooner rather than later.

Leander raised an eyebrow as Japhrimel approached us, threading through a string of disembarking normals who didn't even look at him twice but cut a wide swath around the human Necromance and me.

I thought I'd grown past being hurt by that sort of thing. My mouth tipped up into the same faint half-smile I'd worn as a shield through so many bounties and apparitions as a Necromance. My cheek burned, the tat shifting under golden flesh, I wondered suddenly why my tat hadn't vanished like my other scars when I'd become *hedaira*. "I'll have a job for you too," I told Leander. "Just wait."

"Take your time." Amused and confident, his smile widened.

I grimaced, good-naturedly. He sounded like Jace.

The thought of Jace pinched hard deep in my chest, in a place I'd thought was numb.

Guess it isn't so numb, after all. If I took a slicboard and rose up into the traffic patterns, I would eventually see the huge soaring plasteel-and-stone pile that was St. Ignatius Hospital, where Gabriele had done what I could not and freed the empty clockwork mechanism of Jace's body from the illusion of life.

Leander's low laugh combined with the surfroar of crowd noise —

different from the Souk's genial roar and tainted with fatigue from the long transport haul. I'd slept between Paradisse and North New York, my head propped on Japhrimel's shoulder; the black dreamless nothingness I needed every two or three days. How odd was it that I could only sleep when he lulled me into it, when he was close?

I brought myself back into the present with a jolt. *Stop wandering, Danny. Why are you getting so distracted? It's not like you.* "First things first, though. Can you get us a cab?"

"All things should be so easy."

"You are truly a master," I called after him as he loped away to find and reserve us a hovercab in the queue that would be waiting outside along Beaumartin Street.

It was regular bounty-hunter banter meant to ease our nerves. When Japhrimel reached me, his fingers braceleted my left wrist. I controlled the nervous twitch — that was the hand holding my katana, as usual.

Did he think I was going to run now? Especially when he knew I would only go to Gabe's, a place he'd been before? "McKinley will search for information and find us accommodation." His voice cut through the crowd noise like a golden knife. "I thought that would please you."

There was no sign of the necklace I'd given him, and I had too much pride to ask what he'd done with it. Instead, I tried to pull my wrist out of his hand and got exactly nowhere, though his fingers were gentle. "There's no need for this. We should get going."

"I feel a need." His thumb stroked once across the underside of my wrist. Fire spilled up my arm again, I tugged harder. Achieved nothing. He might not be hurting me, but he wanted me to stay put. "This is unwise, Dante. I am not to be trifled with at this moment."

What the hell? Sekhmet sa'es, *what the fuck are you talking about?* "I'm not the one who's *trifling,*" I hissed back. "You're the one who won't tell me a damn—"

"I will tell you something now," he said in my ear as if we weren't surrounded by a crowd of normals who shuffled toward a transport or away from one. Above us rose the vast dome of the transport well and the different levels of huge hovers docking like blunt whales at each level, the spine of the AI's relays bristling around each floor, fail-safes and double-synaptics glowing and humming with electrical force and reactive-painted buffers.

I went still, closed my eyes. My shields shivered. "Fine." *I would never have thought a demon could throw a tantrum.* My rings popped, sparking, I wondered what the normals around us made of this. His aura covered mine, pulled close and comforting, but I felt the echo of his attention. He was doing it again, listening to a sound I couldn't hear, set at a harsh watchful awareness I couldn't imagine anyone keeping up for very long.

Why? I'm only here for Gabe, but Japh seems to think I'm in danger. Of course I'm in bloody danger, there are demons after me. Still—

"I never knew dissatisfaction before I met you, *hedaira.* The only time I feel any peace is when you are safe and I am near you. Be careful who you spend your smiles on, and be careful of what you make of me." Japhrimel paused. "I am seeking to be gentle, but frustration may make me savage."

In all the time I'd known him, he had never said anything even remotely like this. My throat went dry, my heart banging at my ribs and in my neck, the darkness behind my eyelids suddenly blood-warm. "You mean more savage than you already are?" I pulled against his hand again. I might as well have been chained to the dock.

"You have no idea of the depth of my possible savagery." It wasn't so much the content of his words as the way they were delivered, with a chill even tone I could have thought was indifference except for the well of sharp rage behind it. Japhrimel for the first time in my memory was *furious,* holding himself to control with an effort of will. "I tell you again, be careful. And again, I do not expect your forgiveness or understanding. I require only your cooperation, which I will get by any means I deem necessary. We are here to see what is so urgent with your Necromance friend, well and good. But do not taunt me."

Taunt you? "Taunt *you?* I'm not the one who keeps playing manipulative little games here, Japh. It's you and Lucifer who have the corner on that one. Let go of me."

Much to my surprise, he did. I almost stumbled, the release of tension against my arm was so quick. I opened my eyes, the world rushing back in to meet me, and lifted my left hand slightly. The katana's weight was reassuring. "We've got a cab to catch," I said over my shoulder. "Unless you're going somewhere else."

He didn't dignify that with a reply. It was probably just as well.

Gabe's house crouched on Trivisidiro Street, behind high walls her great-great something-or-other had built. Her family had been cops and Necromances for a long time, passing along Talent and training in a haphazard way before the Awakening and the Parapsychic Act. They had survived because they were rich, and because they did everything possible to blend in before the Act made it possible for psions to come out of the shadows.

I deliberately did not look when we passed over the block that held a huge pile of stone with high holly hedges and walls. Aran Helm's house, where I'd begun to figure out just what nightmare had risen from the depths of Rigger Hall.

I didn't want to see if Helm's house still stood.

The first shock was that the neighborhood had changed. The winds of urban renewal had swept through what had once been a bad part of town, I saw several little boutiques and chic eateries as well as other restored homes.

The second shock, when we got out of the hovercab and Japhrimel paid the driver, was that the shields over Gabe's walls had changed. The hovercab lifted away with a whine, and my skin chilled again. I was really getting to hate hovers.

I caught Japhrimel's arm. He stilled, looking down at me. Leander stood on the corner, his eyes moving over the street and probably marking it in his memory; it was the same thing I did in an unfamiliar city. "Her shields are different," I said quietly, knowing I had Japh's full attention. "Look, can you and Leander wait for me?" He moved slightly, and I interrupted him before he began. "I give my word I won't go anywhere but into Gabe's house, I promise I'll come back out to you. I *swear*. But please, Japhrimel, this is private."

"You continually try to push the limits of—" he began and I squeezed his arm, sinking my fingers in. I couldn't hurt him, but just this once, I *wanted* to. I wished I could. My claws slid free, pricking into his coatsleeve, my entire hand cramping with the effort to stop them.

"*Please,* Japh." My voice gentled, it took an effort that would have made me sweat in my human days. Something suspiciously like tears pressed against the inside of my throat, so it came out muffled and choked instead of only soft. "Don't make me beg you over something like this." *I can't stand begging you over something so simple. I can't stand begging you at all.*

"You do not have to." He nodded, once, sharply. "An hour. No more. Or I will come in for you, Dante, and I will demolish her precious shields. If I even *think* you may be in danger—or seeking to escape me—I will do the same. Is that clear?"

"Crystal." I let go of his arm, finger by finger. *When did you get so arrogant? You were so gentle in Toscano, Japh.* Drew in a sharp deep breath flavored with the smell of dusk in Santiago City—the taint of chemicals, damp, and mold rising from the ground, the tang of the sea and the further iron-rich smell of the lake to the east, the throbbing whine of hover traffic. "Thank you." I didn't sound grateful, but I suppose I might have been.

"There is no need to thank me, either. Go." A muscle flicked in his golden cheek again.

I moved away, across the sidewalk, and stepped up to Gabe's gate. Brushed against her shields, a familiar touch, and realized what was wrong. The shields Eddie had put up, the spiky earth-flavored magick of a Skinlin, were fading rapidly, as if they'd been mostly dismantled and left to shred away from the other defenses.

A curious flutter began under my pulse. Eddie and Gabe had been together so long they seemed eternal.

She was home, and awake. One of the things about visiting psions, when we have a minor in precog we're usually home when you need us. Her shields flushed red as I laid my hand against the gate; the lock clicked open as Gabe's work recognized me. I pushed at the gate before it could close again and stepped through.

The gardens were another shock, full of weeds. Eddie had always kept them pristine—of course, a dirtwitch's trade is in his garden. Skinlin are mostly concerned with growing things, like hedge-witches, but hedgewitches are more interested in using plant material to accessorize spellwork. Skinlin are the modern equivalent of kitchen witches; most of them work for biotech firms, getting plants to give up cures for mutating diseases and splicing together plant DNA with sonic magick or complicated procedures. Their only real drawback is that they're berserkers in a fight. A Skinlin in a rage is like a Chillfreak—they don't stop even when wounded. Eddie was fast, mean, and good; I never wanted to fight him.

I trudged up to the front door as night began to breathe in the garden, more disturbed than I could have ever admitted. The mark on my shoulder pulsed steadily like a heartbeat. Japhrimel, keeping contact with me the only way he could.

Is it the only way he can? I've heard his voice inside my head before, been able to call him without words. The thought froze me on the step, my hand raised to knock on Gabe's red-painted door. The house simmered above me, three stories of brownstone with even more shielding wedded to its physical structure. Would I know it if Japhrimel was inside my mind right now, a thin shadow under my thoughts?

The idea called up a nervous flare of something close to panicked loathing. Communication was one thing, but thinking the cubic centimeters inside my skull might not be wholly my own was...

You learn early that your body betrays you—it's your mind *that has to stay impregnable.* Polyamour's voice echoed in my memory, husky and beautiful. I shivered, pushed the thought away.

The door opened. Gabe regarded me with her dark eyes. The final shock was the worst one, I think, the one that made the world go gray and the mark on my shoulder smash with pain that shocked me, brought me up and made me gasp. My emerald burned on my cheek, answering hers.

Gabriele Spocarelli, Necromance and my friend, had aged.

CHAPTER 7

Gabe made tea, moving around her kitchen; the house smelled of dust and I saw... well, there were toys scattered through the hall, toddler's toys, blocks and small hovercars made of primary-colored nontoxic plasilica. Other things. A small shoe in one corner of the kitchen, the heavy spice of *kyphii* in the air mixed with other smells no longer familiar.

She hadn't said anything about a kid during the phone calls. Not a single word. Not even a hint.

Gabe's long dark hair was threaded with gray since she'd stopped dyeing it, and the wrinkles fanning from the corners of her eyes spoke of frequent smiling. She was still slim and strong, shorter than me and with an air of serenity and precision I had envied so many times. I wondered if she still carried her longsword, a piece of sharp metal far too big for her. When I'd been human, I often thought I never wanted to face her for real over that steel—she was capable of cool clinical viciousness not many other fighters possessed. She'd been a cop all her life, going from the Academy into the Saint City PD, fighting the good fight.

She wasn't *old,* not by any stretch—but being a cop had marked her, turned her hair prematurely gray. That gray alone told me volumes. For Gabe to go against Codes and not dye her hair black was either exceeding vanity or a sign she wasn't working professionally anymore. She still moved with the ease of combat practice and flexibility; she hadn't gotten sloppy like some old bounty hunters or cops do. But there was a slight stiffness, a shadow of slowness, that hadn't been there before. She had graduated from the Academy a full five years ahead of me; one of the few psions to have taken a break between primary training at Stryker and entering for her accreditation. She'd spent those years in Paradisse becoming a cosmopolitan, then come dutifully home and done what her family had always done—gone through advanced schooling, taken her Trial, and settled into being a cop.

We'd been friends a long, long time.

I sat at the old breakfast bar, looking at the fall of fading sunlight through the kitchen window, and felt the full consciousness of time settle in on me.

She had aged, and I hadn't. I still looked the same as I had when I opened my eyes in a Nuevo Rio mansion to find a demon had Fallen and shared his power with me. My hair was shorter, true; but otherwise I was the same. On the outside.

They were only tiny changes, the lines on her face and the threads of gray in her hair. If I'd stayed in Saint City I probably wouldn't have even noticed.

"How long has it been?" *I should know. I should know how long it's been.*

She cast me a shuttered, dark look. "You've lost track? Of course, you disappeared. And time's not your strong suit."

I opened my mouth to defend myself, shut it. I *had* disappeared. With Japhrimel, and she didn't know. We'd settled in Toscano, and I'd buried myself in decoding Magi shadowjournals, searching for the clues that would tell me what I was because he would not. I thought it was a matter of embarrassment—most demons are very touchy about the whole subject of the Fallen, and I thought perhaps Japh didn't want to speak of something painful and degrading.

Now I wondered.

Her bitter laugh brought me back to the present. "Only a couple years. Don't worry, Danny. I understand, as much as I can. I saw you after the Lourdes case, remember? You were dead on your feet, sunshine. I'm just glad to see you now."

"You called." I couldn't produce more than a croak. "*Mainuthsz.* Of course I came."

Her back stiffened as she faced the kettle on the stove. "I wasn't sure you would."

"You know me better than that." *Or at least you should.* Was I hurt?

"You and your damn sense of honor." She cleared her throat. "There's two things I want from you, Valentine. I'll make you tea and we'll talk."

I nodded, though she was facing the other way. Her aura, bright with the trademark sparkles of a Necromance, swirled steadily. Where was Eddie? I couldn't imagine him leaving her.

Memory swallowed me again.

"I'll catch him, Eddie. Or her. Whoever's doing this."

He snatched his fingertips away, his dark eyes scarred holes above hollow unshaven cheeks. "Yeah. You do that. Word of advice? When you do catch 'em, don't bring 'em back alive. Anything to do wit' Rigger Hall is better off dead."

"Including us?"

Eddie moved, sliding his legs out of the booth and standing up. He tapped at his datband and looked down at me, his shaggy blond hair tangling in his eyes. "Sometimes I think so," he said, quietly, and his eyes were haunted wells. "Then I look at Gabe, and I ain't so sure."

I found nothing to say to that. Eddie stumped away toward the door, and I let him go.

No, I could not imagine Eddie leaving her.

I surfaced. This was proving to be harder than I'd thought, past swallowing present as it so often did these days. Was it because I was older too inside this slim golden body? I had been no spring chicken when Japh changed me. Most bounty-hunting psions have a short shelf life, despite genesplicing repair bodies under constant hard use.

Gabe poured the tea. I stayed silent. She'd tell me what she wanted, she would either solve the mystery or not. If not, it would be obvious she didn't want to talk about it, and the least I owed Gabe was a measure of tact. If anything happened to her, the last person who remembered my human self—*truly* remembered my human self—would be gone.

How would I go on then? Getting more and more distracted,

shackled to Japhrimel, maybe forced into ever more complex games with Lucifer when he had some further use for me, trying to preserve some shred of my humanity...

Stop it, Danny. You'll go nuts if you keep thinking like that. Just stop it.

Chamomile tea for me, in a long black sinuous mug familiar enough to make a funny melting sensation begin under my breast-bone. Chai for her, in a new mug—a sunshine-yellow one. That was a change. She usually wasn't a sunshiny-yellow type of person.

I wonder if it's having a kid that does it. Where is the little person who plays with the toys, Gabe, and why didn't you tell me? That qualifies as major life news. I would have liked to have been here for that.

She hadn't told me, hadn't even hinted. Why? Of course, I hadn't ever hinted I was living with a demon who had resurrected himself from ash, either. One secret balancing out the other?

She leaned against the breakfast bar, her fingers clasped around the tea mug. I saw the beginnings of a papery dryness on the fragile skin on the back of her hands, and felt that melting sensation again. Swallowed hard against it.

"No questions?" Gabe smiled. "No, you wouldn't ask me a damn thing, would you. You'd wait for me to tell you, or never mention it if I didn't. Hades, I forgot what it's like to talk to you." She turned away, stalked across the kitchen, and scooped something up from the cluttered counter. The clutter was something new too, her house had always been neat before. Dishes were stacked in the sink, a few holomags scattered across the far end of the breakfast bar, and dust lay on the counter next to me.

"I hope it's pleasant." It was just the thing Japhrimel might have said.

"Sometimes." She tossed it on the counter in front of me. It was a file folder. "I want you to help me kill whoever did this," she said tonelessly, and I realized she was holding onto her serenity by the thinnest of threads.

"Okay," I said promptly, opening the folder. *Consider 'em dead, Gabe.*

I would have agreed to it because I trusted her. I *also* would have agreed to it because looking at the first sheet in the folder—a nice glossy laseprint—showed a body lying on a white floor, a wrack and ruin of shattered glass winking up and dusting the blood that had dried sticky, spreading out in an impossibly large stain. But what drove the breath from my lungs was the face at the top of the ruined mass of flesh.

The mark on my shoulder crunched again, dragging me out of shock. I swallowed something that tasted like human bile. "Eddie," I whispered.

It was his body, indisputably dead. The experience of many other murder scenes rose under my skin, I noted the bullet holes clinically. Projectile weapons, a good way to take out a raging Skinlin. His shaggy head, the arc of his cheekbone as his chin was tipped back, the dark-blond whiskers telling me he hadn't shaved for a day or so before his death. Mercifully, if age had ravaged him, it wasn't visible in the picture.

"When?" The sinuous black mug chattered against the counter-top, I reined myself in with an effort.

"Ten days ago." Her hands tightened again around her mug. I could almost taste the gunpowder anger roiling off her, used like a shield against the shock of loss.

I knew that territory. I'd seen it as a Necromance in the families of the departed, and been through it myself when Doreen, and later Jace, died. Two events, seeming as if they happened to different people, completely different Danny Valentines. Then there was the terrible almost-year I'd spent mourning Japhrimel as he lay dormant, ash in an urn. I remembered the abyss of loneliness and black despair, the mind bumping against the single word *gone* because the word *dead* was too final, no matter that Death was my trade.

We all think we're immortal, even Necromances. Necromances, really, should know better. And yet we never do.

"There's one more thing," Gabe said. "Before you agree."

"Too late. I've already agreed." My throat was dry and raw as a scraped-clean coremelt. *"Mainuthsz."*

She made a low hurt sound, but when I looked up her eyes were dry. She reached down under the counter, as if she was digging in her pocket, and brought out another small piece of paper. I took it, and found myself looking down at a laseprint of a beautiful little toddler with Gabe's dark eyes and Eddie's wild blond hair, wearing a pair of denim overalls and grinning up without a care in the world. Behind her, the green of a laurel hedge writhed.

So this was who had been using the toys. The world had indeed changed while I'd been in Toscano, burying myself in books. Had

she been pregnant during the hunt for Kellerman Lourdes? Either
then or right after, it was a distinct possibility.

Why didn't you tell me, Gabe?

"My daughter," Gabe said tonelessly. "When I die, Danny, I want
you to look after her. Swear to me you'll protect her, and if I . . . I want
you to raise her."

I choked. *What the hell? I can't—a kid? But—* My fingers tightened, almost crumpling the laseprint, she tore it out of my hand.
"Gabe?"

"Swear it, Dante. *Swear.*" Her lips peeled back from her teeth, her
face dead-pale and her eyes flashing with something I'd never seen in
her before.

I had to tell her. "Japhrimel's alive, Gabe."

She froze. Her pupils dilated. The perfume of fear and rage poured
out from her in waves, a coppery chemical smell. "I know," she said,
and my heart almost exploded inside my chest. "The fire at your
house. The shadow inside. With wings."

I nodded. Black guilt rose, choked me, I pushed it fiercely away. I
couldn't afford to stop now.

"I lied. I'm sorry. I *couldn't* tell you, Gabe." *I was . . . I was afraid
of what you'd think of me. I'm afraid of what you think of me now.*

"You stupid bitch." Cold as the creeping chill of Death. "Of course
I knew. It doesn't matter. *I* need you now." Tears stood out in her eyes.
One fattened, slid down her cheek, leaving a shiny trail behind.

If she'd slapped me, I would have been less surprised. I would
have deserved it.

"I'm here." I held her eyes across the air suddenly gone hot and
straining between us. My rings crackled, spat, her emerald shifted
with light. "As Anubis is my witness, Gabriele, I'll do it. I'll do anything you ask." My voice made a few holomags flutter off the end of
the counter, their soft smacks hitting the hardwood floor.

She gazed into my eyes for a good thirty seconds, neither of us
blinking. Then she held up the laseprint. "Swear," she said, and I saw
the hardness in her. Gabe would not stop until Eddie's killers were
dead. "Swear to me. On your name and the name of your god."

I didn't hesitate. "I swear to you, Gabriele Spocarelli, on my name
and on the name of my god Anubis lord of Death, I will help you hunt
Eddie's killers. I will kill them myself if you're unable to. And for the
rest of my life I will look after your child and her children." *Since I
don't know how long I'll be around.* "I give my word."

The world rocked slightly underfoot. There. It was done.

I owed her this much, and so much more. She'd been my friend, my only friend, since the Academy. She had tried to help me protect Doreen. She had gone into the icy hell of Santino's lair with me to hunt down Doreen's killer, and nearly died herself. It never occurred to her to bow out of that hunt, any more than it occurred to me I might bow out of this one.

Not only that, but she had done what I couldn't, and let Jason Monroe go. Performed the duty of a Necromance at his bedside, for me. It had been an act of mercy, one I didn't deserve and would never be able to repay.

Japhrimel's not going to be happy with this.

On the heels of that thought came a second, colder and harder. *I don't fucking care. Let him try to stop me. This is more important than the fucking Devil.*

Gabe slapped the laseprint down. "Good fucking deal." Tears trickled down her cheeks. "Now go away. Take the file with you. Come back tomorrow, ready."

You better believe it. "Where's your daughter?"

"In a safe place." Gabe's fingers curled around the counter, blood-less white with clenching rage. Her aura trembled. She was very close to losing control. Going nova, her aura exploding with pain, loss, fury, abandonment. If that happened, she'd come at me, and while I was fairly sure I could fend her off without hurting her I wasn't at *all* sure how Japhrimel would react if even a breath of what was happening got out to him. "Now get *out.* I'm not safe right now, Danny."

I know. Hadn't I once burned my house to the ground after I'd lost someone?

Someone once tried to tell me grief is passive. Whoever says that doesn't know women, and doesn't know Necromances either.

I left my mug there, but I took the file. I backed away from the counter. My left hand clenched around my sword's scabbard, her anger echoing in my own shields. The air spat, sparks showering from my rings. When I backed down the hall, out of sight of the kitchen, I turned around and left her house, walking as quickly as I could with eyes blinded by tears.

I owed her that, too.

I didn't want to think about the hot salt spilling down my own cheeks and dropping onto my shirt. I especially didn't want to think about the low hoarse sobbing sound I made as I flung myself out of her gates and straight into Japhrimel's arms.

CHAPTER 8

L eander didn't ask any questions. I chalked it up to tact and was grateful, at least.

The "accommodations" were the Brewster Hotel on Ninth Street, cozy, expensive, and vulnerable enough to attack that I should have protested. I, however, did nothing of the sort. I merely banged through the hall and into the room Japhrimel indicated, dropped my bag containing its horrid new cargo, and fell onto the bed with my sword clutched in my hands, staring at the awful pale blue wallpaper with its tasteful pattern worked in gold spongy paint. Night had fallen over Saint City, a night I would have felt comfortable in years ago.

Now the night here had knives, all of them pointed at me.

Japhrimel exchanged some words with a mystified Leander; I heard McKinley, too. "I'll get him settled," the agent said, and the door to the suite closed softly.

Japhrimel's soundless step reverberated as the humming intensity of demon magick rose around the walls of the room, wards and layers of shielding that would make this space psychically almost-invisible.

He stood for a little while in the doorway. Then he paced quietly over the plush carpet and the bed sighed as he lowered himself down on the side my back was presented to.

Don't touch me. Don't fucking touch me, and for the sake of every god that ever was, if you try to manipulate or hurt me now I swear I will try to kill you, I don't care what it takes. Please, Anubis, don't let him push me now.

Another long pause. He moved, stretching out and lying down. Power smoothed down my body, a soft velvet caress.

His fingers touched my hair, stroking evenly. Soothing. He found a knot in the silky strands, worked patiently at it until it was gone, untangled with infinite care. He continued, pulling his fingers expertly through, massaging my scalp. Little rills of pleasure slid down my spine, fighting with the trembling that had me locked in its teeth.

Tears leaked out between my squeezed-shut eyelids. Just when I thought he was going to act like a bastard, he turned around and did something like this. I needed his quiet, even touch; I *needed* the feel of his fingers in my hair, of his arms around me. For just one god-damn minute I wanted to let down my defenses and let go of some of the awful, crushing, terrible burden of being myself.

But that would leave me vulnerable, wouldn't it.

Gods, please. Please. I know how to suffer through a beating, but I can't take this. Don't let him be gentle. Please.

The mark on my shoulder went hot, sustained heat like a candle-flame held close to the skin. Power poured into me, stroking along my flesh, sparkling like impulses between the gaps of dendrites and axons, an electricity that would have been painful and prickling if not for the fact that my body cried out for it. Craved it.

My fingers, tipped with chipped black molecule-drip polish, shook. The sword, inside its indigo lacquer sheath, hummed.

Bit by bit, Japhrimel slid one arm under me. His other hand worked down to my neck, slid over my shoulder, skimmed down my tense, shaking arm. His fingers, blunter than mine but with unerring delicacy, slid between mine, loosened the grip on my sword. After a short struggle, he pushed the blade over the side of the bed and I made a small moaning sound like a rabbit in a trap.

I *needed* my sword. It was the only thing that made me feel safe.

His arms tensed, drew me back into him. Still he said nothing, his breath warm against my hair, his arms closed around me like chains. Like a support.

He simply held me.

The sobs came. Not slow ceaseless trickling from my eyes, not the smothered sounds I'd tried to keep to myself all the way to the hotel while Japhrimel's silence grew more and more obdurate and Leander's puzzlement and curiosity more obvious and restrained. No, there was no secrecy left in these. They tore out of me in deep hurtful gasps, each one worse than the one before. Shaking all the way up from the deepest blackest pit inside me, I convulsed with agonized guilt and grief.

It took a long time for the sobs to judder into little hitching broken gasps, my eyes streaming and my nose full, the mark on my shoulder hot through the ice creeping up my veins from my fingertips and toes. The heat fought for me, pushed back the ice of numbness, Japhrimel's arms tightening until I could barely breathe. It made lit-tle difference — I could not breathe through the gasps anyway.

He murmured something I didn't catch. Probably in his damnable demon language, the one he wouldn't teach me because he said it wasn't fit for my mouth.

The one he'd used to bargain with Lucifer, without my understanding, getting me involved in this whole damn clusterfuck in the first place.

His left hand, fingers threaded through mine of both hands, squeezed. Reassuring, not hurtful.

I don't know how long it took. Finally, I lay hot-eyed and limp in his arms, staring at the wallpaper and the edge of a chunky antique table that held plasticine-wrapped information sheets about how to call for room service and what to do in case of a fire or general catastrophe.

I wished one of them had a guide to deal with being a part-demon whose loved ones were going to die; or maybe a few words about how to live with the utter shame of knowing you'd failed your few friends when they needed you most. I wished one of the plasticine sheets could have told me what to do about the sudden feeling of empty loneliness, so intense my entire body felt like a stranger's.

And why not? It wasn't *my* body; it was the body Japhrimel had given me, altered, made into a *hedaira*'s. He wouldn't even tell me what that was. He was hiding things from me even now. I was a fool if I thought otherwise.

Japhrimel pressed his lips against my hair. Said something else, too low for even my demon-acute senses to hear. The drilling heat from his mark on my shoulder finally flushed the last of the ice out of my fingers and toes. I closed my eyes, squeezing out hot tears. Opened them again. His arm curled under me, wrapped around me, his flattened hand pressing into my belly.

"I'm all right," I whispered finally, raw and uncertain.

Did I feel his mouth move with a smile? "I do not think so, beloved." Soft, the tone he used in the dead regions of night or the laziness of a hot Toscano afternoon.

It made me giggle, a forlorn broken sound. "You never used to call me that." I heard the note of tired hurt in my voice, wished I hadn't said it. Exhaustion pulled at my arms and legs, as if I was human again.

I wish I was. Oh, gods, how I wish I was human again.

"What do you think *hedaira* means?" He hugged me again, the soft pulsing of the mark on my left shoulder turning into a golden spike for a moment.

"You won't teach me anything." My eyes drifted closed. The weariness swamped me, made my arms and legs turn to lead.

"Have you ever considered that perhaps I cherish you as you are?" He sighed, a very human sound. "Were I to teach you too quickly, my curious one, you might well decide to fear me unreasonably. I prefer your anger. You will learn soon enough, in your own time. And I will wait, as long as I must, and with more patience than I have shown so far." Another kiss, pressed onto the top of my head. "What does your friend want of you?"

I swallowed several times, dryly, and told him. The darkness behind my eyelids was comforting again. I couldn't fight him when he was like this. Gods, all he had to do was be *gentle* with me, and I wouldn't be able to stop him from doing anything he wanted. I would even *help* him.

If he was gentle. If he could just remember to tell me the truth.

For a long few moments he was silent. Could I feel the thoughts moving through his alien brain? He'd been alive far longer than me, far longer than *anyone,* even Lucas or the Nichtvren I infrequently met. How could I possibly deal with something that old, that essentially different?

Never mind that I had thought it possible, never mind that I'd trusted him with my life, slept with him, told him things I'd never told anyone else. I'd treated him as if he was human, and he'd responded by becoming *A'nankhimel.* Fallen.

Whatever that was. I doubted I knew even a quarter of it. If I ever thought I did, in the future, all I would have to do is touch my shoulder, feeling the scar twist on the surface of my skin. Or remember being held up against the tiled wall of a New Prague subway stop, shaken like a disobedient puppy while his knuckles dug into the thin skin over my breastbone.

"She's my friend," I went on, barely pausing to take a breath. "Fuck Lucifer, I owe Gabe, I owe her *everything.* I don't care what you think, I'm—"

"Your debts are mine," he interrupted. "Rest, Dante. Shock is still a danger for you."

"You'll help me?" I sounded amazed even to myself. *Ask him about the treasure, Danny. He seems to be in a talkative mood, ask him what the Key is and why all of a sudden everything's so different. Use this.*

Another hot helping of shame boiled up under my breastbone.

Even in the middle of a crisis I was still trying to figure out how to manipulate him back, trying to play his game.

He made a small sound, as if annoyed. "The sooner this is over, the sooner I may return to the task of seeing you alive through the demands the Prince has placed on us. I worry it may be too much of a task even for my skill." There was a curious inflection to the words, as if he had chosen them with finicky care. I was too tired to think about it, too warm, and too grateful for him.

Even if he was a lying demon. "I can't imagine a job *that* big." I yawned and settled further into his warmth.

"Hm." His arms tightened, just a little. "Besides, you obey your honor, Dante. I can do no less. I am your Fallen."

My sudden question surprised me as much as it might have surprised him. "What does *A'nankhimel* mean, Japhrimel?" My voice was slurred, heavy, the sound of a woman in a nightmare that didn't stop when she opened her eyes.

He kissed the top of my head again. "It means *shield*. It also means *chained*. Go to sleep, my curious. You are safe."

I shouldn't have rested. But I was still tired, aching from Lucifer's last kick, and craving grateful oblivion. There wasn't enough sleep in the world to make me feel better.

But I'd take what I could. Just for that moment, there in Japh's arms.

CHAPTER 9

Despite waking up warm under the covers—with Japhrimel sitting across from me in a chair situated so the thin rainy light of a Saint City afternoon fell over him, turning him into an icon of dark coat and golden skin with jeweled eyes—the day started out unsatisfactorily. For one thing, it was still strange to be up during daylight hours. I've been a night creature all my human life—most psions are, something about our metabolisms and a gene marker for nocturnalism. During the day I felt sluggish, not slow enough to handicap me in a fight but as if a veil of misty fatigue was drawn over the world. It was when night fell that I truly felt alive.

I finished tugging my boots on and pushed my damp hair back.

One thing I haven't grown out of is my love of hot water; even though I rarely sweat I like to have a daily shower. I've gone without on too many bounties not to appreciate being clean.

The other unsatisfactory thing? Leander was gone.

"What do you mean, *gone?*" I fixed McKinley with a steely glare the Hellesvront agent bore all too easily. He glanced at Japhrimel, who said nothing.

Apparently deciding that meant I could know, the agent went on. He still wore unrelieved black to match his hair and eyes, and only two knives. McKinley didn't appear to need much in the way of weapons. I'd seen him with a gun once, on a rooftop in New Prague, never again. "Not in his room this morning. No luggage, not that he had much to begin with. I can comb the city...." He didn't sound too concerned, I realized.

"Not necessary." Japhrimel stood slim and dark, his hands clasped behind his back. "Perhaps he had an attack of good sense."

There it was again, that faint note of disdain. Why didn't Japhrimel like him? *"Anubis et'her ka.* So what if he's human? I am too, remember?" *Still human where it counts, Japh.* I rose to my feet, stamped to settle my boots, and slid the strap of my bag over my head, settling its weight properly against my hip. Rotated my shoulders to make sure my rig was all right. Closed my left hand over my sword. "I swear, you're as bad as a normal. Always thinking that a human can't be good enough for anything, just like normals think all psis are mind-stealers." I stalked between them, toward the door of the suite, wishing the room wasn't done in pale blue with old Merican Era fustibudgets for decoration. Even in Sarajevo the rooms had been better decorated.

Japhrimel fell into step behind me, McKinley said nothing. He was going to stay behind, thank the gods.

I made it out the door and down the hall, pushing the door to the stairwell open. I would be damned if I'd take an elevator. My nerves were raw enough.

My footsteps echoed on the stairs; his were soundless. I could have moved quietly, but what good would it have done me? Besides, I was in a mood.

I felt Japhrimel's eyes on me as I stalked through the lobby and out through the climate control, into the familiar cold chembath of a rainy Saint City early afternoon.

Immediately, habitually, I checked hovertraffic and reached out

with all my senses to take in the mood of the city. The flux and glow
of Power here was so familiar another lump rose in my throat.

*Stop it. You've barely ever cried before in your life; stop being an
idiot and use those brains you're so famous for.*

The feeling—which I had to examine thoroughly before admitting it was relief and a sense of being home again—filled my entire
body with an odd combination of lightness and a completely uncharacteristic desire to weep-angst like a holovid soap star. I swallowed
the blockage in my throat, glancing down Ninth to see the familiar
bulk of the skyline lifting its scallops and needles around the bay. I
wanted to get to Gabe's quickly, of course; but still I walked.
Japhrimel, saying nothing, walked behind me.

Three steps behind and to my left, soundless as Death Himself,
his presence felt like sunshine on my back. His mark on my shoulder
was warm, comforting. The streets were familiar, resounding under
my boots. One moment I wanted to dance with crazy joy.

The next I felt the weight of my bag, with the folder inside it. Then
my eye would fall across a slight change—a new building, an old
building remodeled, something *different*—and the change would hit
me hard in the solar plexus.

It was small consolation that with a war shaping up between Lucifer and Eve, and something else in the offing Japh couldn't be prodded
to tell me about, I might not live long enough to see other changes.

I finally hailed a hovercab at the corner of Fifteenth and Pole,
right at the edge of the Tank District. The driver—an Asiano man—
didn't look happy to find out his fare was a psion, but he'd descended
and flipped the meter before seeing my tat. Japhrimel gave the driver
Gabe's address in flawless unaccented Merican. His control of the
language—indeed, of most languages—was phenomenal.

Then again, demons like languages just as they like technology,
or genetics, or meddling with humans.

Meddling with humans—but not feeling any affection for them.
Or Falling, for them.

The unsteady flutter of my stomach as the hovercab rose into the
sky intensified as I studied Japhrimel's profile. He stared straight
ahead, laser-green eyes burning intently as if they intended to slice
through the plasilica barrier between us and the driver, out through
the front bubble, and cut the sky with a sword of light. "Japh?"

"Hm?" As if startled out of his own uncomfortable thoughts. His
eyes turned to me, and I found it slightly easier to meet them.

"Can I ask you something?" My left hand eased on my katana, I even drummed my fingers a little bit against the scabbard.

"Gods protect me from your questions, my curious. Ask." Did he smile? If he did it was a fleeting expression, moving over his face so quickly even my demon-sharp eyes barely caught it.

No time like the present. Since you won't explain anything else, I might as well ask for the moon. I plunged ahead. "Why did you Fall?"

I expected him to turn the question aside, refuse to answer it. He would always make some ironic reply before, or simply, gently, refuse to tell me anything of *A'nankhimel.* Would tell me myths about demons, old stories, tales to make me laugh or listen wide-eyed with a sweet sharp nostalgic terror like a child's—but never anything I could use to find out what I was, what the limits of my new body were. Nothing about himself, or what his life had been like. He would only talk about things that had happened since I'd met him, and even some of those he wouldn't speak about.

As if he'd been born the day he showed up at my door.

I never knew dissatisfaction before I met you, hedaira.

Today, he cocked his head. Considered the question. I felt his awareness again, closing around me. His aura stretched to cover mine, the mark on my shoulder staining through the trademark sparkles of a Necromance's energetic field with black diamond flames.

When he spoke, it was soft, reflective. "I lived for countless ages as the Prince's Right Hand and felt no guilt or shame at what I did. I still do not."

No philosophy for me, he'd said, during the hunt for Santino. *I don't take sides. The Prince points and says that he wants a death, I kill.*

He was silent for so long, his eyes burning green against mine, that I finally found my lungs starving for breath and remembered to inhale. He'd refused to kill me to gain back his place in Hell. I had it on good authority; better authority than if he'd tried to tell me himself. So what did that *mean?*

"Then, the Prince set me to fetch a human woman and use her in a game that would end with the created Androgyne under his hand. I found myself in the presence of a creature I could not predict, for the first time in my life." He shrugged, a simple evocative movement. "I did not understand her—but knew her in a way that seemed deeper than even my kinship with my own kind. And thus, my dissatisfaction."

"Dissatisfaction?" I sounded breathless. What a surprise—I *was* breathless. Damn hard to breathe when he was staring into my eyes like this.

"I Fell through love of you, *hedaira*. It's simple enough, even with your gift for complicating matters. I don't want your fear of me; I have never wanted you to fear me." He looked as if he would say more, but ended up shutting his mouth and shaking his head slightly, as if mocking himself for what he couldn't say.

I don't want to fear you either. "I don't want to be afraid of you. But you make it so goddamn hard, Japh. All you have to do is *talk* to me."

"I can think of nothing else I would rather do." He even looked like he meant it, his eyebrows drawn together as he studied me, his eyes holding mine in a cage of emerald light. "I cherish my time with you."

That made my heart flip and start to pound like a gymnasa doing a floor routine. *All right, Japh. One more try. One more chance.* "What aren't you telling me?" My fingers tightened on the scabbard.

A long pause. The hovercab began to descend, the driver humming a tune I didn't recognize. There was a time in Saint City when I would have known all the songs.

"Like calls to like," he repeated, softly. "I am a killer, Dante. It is what I *am*."

So, by extension, that's what I am. That wasn't what I meant, I wanted you to talk to me about Eve. I thought about this, turned it over inside my head. "I don't kill without cause." My eyes dropped away from his, to the slender shape of the katana. *Fudoshin.* A blade hungry for battle, Jado had said.

Jado lived in Saint City. I wanted to ask him about this sword. *Yeah, sure. Like I have so much free time.*

"Anyway," I continued, "a killer's not *all* you are. If it was I'd be dead too, right?" *You've never let me down when it counted, Japh. You even stood up to Lucifer—and pushed him* back. *You made the Prince of Hell back off. He's scared of you.*

He had no pat reply for that. The hovercab landed with a sigh of leaf springs. He paid the cabdriver. I wondered—not for the first time—where all the money came from.

Then again, Lucifer had paid me too. Cash was no problem to demons. Some Magi even said they'd invented the stuff. It certainly made sense, given money's seductive nature and the chaos it could create.

I decided to push a little more, since he was so willing to talk. "So what's this Key, and what's going on that's changed everything?"

He didn't reply for a few moments, watching the cab lift off and dart back into the stream of hover traffic. "Later, my curious. When we are finished with your Necromance friend."

Disappointment bit sharp under my breastbone. I folded my arms, my sword a heavy weight in my left hand. "Japh?"

"Hm?" His eyes returned to me. "More questions?"

If I didn't know better, I'd think he was baiting me. "Just a request. Quit being a bully. Stop keeping me in the dark."

His mouth pulled down at both corners. But I'd already turned on my heel and dropped my arms, heading down Trivisidiro just like I always used to do, the click of my bootheels marking off each step. *How about that? I think I finally got the last word in.*

I didn't feel happy. What I felt was uneasy, and growing uneasier by the moment.

I blinked at Trivisidiro Street and cast around, vaguely troubled. If I hadn't been so bloody distracted, I would have noticed it right away. As it was, it took me a few seconds before I realized why I was disoriented.

Gabe's front gate was slightly open. Not only that, but the shields on her property line were torn, bleeding trickles of energy into the early afternoon.

CHAPTER 10

I would have gone first, being accustomed to taking point on any job; it was a habit thirty-odd years in the making and difficult to shake. Japhrimel, however, grabbed my arm in an iron grip that stopped just short of pain and gave me to understand with a single vehement emerald look that *he* was going first, and if I didn't want an argument I would be well advised to just let him.

I was so badly shaken I did. I followed him, my thumb pressing against the katana's guard, right hand clamped around the hilt. I suppose I should have drawn a plasgun, but I was operating on instinct. A blade is the weapon I find most comforting. Give me a sword and some open ground, a clear enemy in front of me, and I know what to do.

It's just everything else in my life that confuses me now. The thought was full of bleak humor. Gallows humor, meant to take the edge off my nervousness but failing miserably.

My mind turned curiously blank as I followed Japhrimel's black coat and inky head. As he stepped through Gabe's gate, soundless, the static of his attention stretching to take in the smallest of details, the bleeding shields on her property line flushed red and began to fizz.

I calmed the restive layers of energy with a mental touch, deftly binding together holes ripped in the shielding. It was strange, but there was no sense of *personality* behind the rips and holes.

If another psion had cracked the shields, there would be a distinct stamp, a flavor to the rents. Something I could track, no matter how good the other psion was. That was part of the trouble with the use of Power, it was so unutterably *personal.* A bounty hunter, like me, developed a set of psychic muscles and sensitivities perfectly suited to tracking. We had to; it was how we did our jobs. I still thought like a bounty hunter, never sitting with my back to a door if I could help it and seeing the world as a tangle of connections, some chance some not, that if pursued systematically with a healthy dose of instinct would lead me to the person or piece of information I wanted. Nobody—especially anybody who has done something to make someone like me hunt them—manages to get through life without randomly bumping into something or spilling some energy into the ether. Everybody fucks up, sooner or later—and fuckups are mostly what a bounty hunter snags on.

But there was no flavor to the rips and tears in Gabe's exquisitely careful, beautiful shielding.

Japhrimel ghosted over the gravel walkways of the garden. The house shields were still intact, vibrating with distress of a peculiarly remote kind. I would have thinned my shields to try and reach for Gabe—after all, we shared magick and deeper bonds—but the mark on my shoulder clamped down with fearful pressure and I realized Japhrimel's aura had hardened into a demon-tough shield around me, on top of my regular shielding.

That was something I hadn't expected he could do, and I looked around the weedy garden with my heart in my mouth. Tension brushed my skin with thousands of delicately-scraping pins, and copper filled my mouth.

I felt alive.

We found her around the back of the house, in the garden near the back wall Eddie had used for his more useful but less happy plants — aconite, horehound, belladonna, poison sumac (for repellant spells and treating slagfever), fireweed 12, wormwood, castor, meadow saffron, foxglove, hellebore, you name it. All the datura had been grubbed up, leaving a rain-softened hole in the dirt, and that was puzzling. If Eddie had died ten days ago, why was his garden weedy? And where had the datura gone?

Then Japhrimel turned to me. "Go to the front of the house," he said, but I pushed past him. He caught my left arm, gently. "Dante. You do not wish to see this. *Please*."

I looked, and I saw. It was no use, all the good-intentioned wanting to protect me in the world couldn't have stopped me from looking.

Gabe lay tangled in a young hemlock. She bent back as if doing an enthusiastic full-wheel pose for a gymnasia illustration, except for the bloody holes in her dark shirt and jeans. *Dead for at least six hours if not more,* the Necromance in me thought, tasting the fading tang of what we call foxfire — the false glow of nerves slowly dying. The ground around her was chewed with bullets, white underbark and broken green things glaring through the rainy day. Mist had collected on her face, the angle of her jaw upflung, her hair a hanging skein of gray and black silk.

Her feet were bare and very white.

Her sword, blackened and twisted with her death, spilled out of her right hand. Her eyes were closed, and except for the bloody hole in her left cheek where a bullet had ripped through the flesh and shattered teeth she looked peaceful.

My pulse beat a padded drum in my ears.

The *click* sounded in my brain. I looked at her feet, down at the gravel path. Glanced back toward the house. She had to have come over the lawn, barefoot and in a hell of a hurry. Why?

The part of me that had seen so many murder scenes jolted into operation, like an old-fashioned gearwheel. It slid into place evenly, and I thought quite clearly, *I'm going to feel this soon. Before I do, I need to think. Think, Danny. Think.*

I examined the angle of the bullets, where they had torn through plants and dug furrows in the wet earth. The smell of death rose with the perfume of fresh green garden, newly-churned dirt. The computer deck inside my head took over, calculated angles and wounds, came up with an answer. I looked over my right shoulder, up over the wall at a point some twenty feet above. There was a rooftop there, just right for a projectile assault rifle.

Why was she still lying here? That much hot lead whizzing through the air—someone should have called the cops. Heard something. *Done* something, especially in this neighborhood.

Why had Gabe come out here? Her property-line shields were torn and her house shields vibrating, probably with the psychic shock of her death. I was a Necromance, here with a fresh body—but if I went into Death now, I might not come out. I was too tired, too distracted, and too goddamn upset. To top it all off, Japhrimel would have to question Gabe; he might not know the right questions to ask to elicit the underlying logic of what had happened. There were *rules* to questioning the dead, rules he might not know any more than I knew the arcane rules of demon etiquette.

More than that, something deep and colored a smoking red in me rose in revolt at the thought of using Gabe's body as a focus. She had gone into Death, into the halls she'd walked so often before, and into the clear rational light of What Comes Next. If there was any justice in the world, she was with Eddie now. I wouldn't pull her away from that.

Admit it, Danny. You're afraid of facing her after you've failed her again.

A litany of my life's failures rose before me, all the dead I'd loved. *Roanna. Lewis. Doreen. Jace. Eddie.* And now a new name to add to that long string. *Gabe.*

A long, despairing scream rose inside my chest, was locked away by an iron hand descending on my heart and *squeezing,* its bony fingers sinking into warm flesh and spreading the cold of stone. Cold. Like the gray fuzzy chill of shock, only deeper. This was a killing cold, ice to be polished, sharp as my katana and deadly as the demon standing beside me.

Gabriele. The final echo of the promise I'd made her yesterday sounded a brass gong inside my head.

Whoever did this I won't just kill. I'm going to erase them. I swear to every god that ever was, I am going to make them pay.

"Dante." Japhrimel's voice, quiet. "I am sorry."

My mouth worked silently for a moment. I considered screaming. Then my jaw shut with a click of teeth snapping together. Harsh dragged-in breath tore at my throat with the smell of fresh dirt. My right hand cramped once, viciously, around the hilt of my katana. Released. I shoved the sword into the loop on my rig. Looked at the statue of Gabe's body.

Gone. The word echoed in my head. *Gone.*

Failed again.

The knife whispered out of its sheath. Japhrimel cast me a measuring look, as if weighing whether I would use it on him. I set it against the flesh of my palm and ripped down in one unsteady movement, dropping the blade now smoking with black demon blood.

I lifted my hand, made a fist. Black blood dripped between my fingers, squeezed so hard I heard my own bones creak. My throat locked around a black well of screaming.

This I swear on my blood. I will find who is responsible for this, Gabe. And I won't just kill them. I will make them pay.

"Dante!" Japhrimel grabbed my hand, a hot pulse of Power sealing the wound even more quickly than welling black demon blood.

I blinked at him. *Gods, does he sound frightened? Never heard that before.* I finally found my voice. "Don't worry," I rasped. "That was just a promise." *Am I in shock? I don't feel like it. I feel like I'm thinking clearly for the first fucking time in a long time.*

He studied me. "I am sorry." His eyes measured me. As if he wanted to express more than sorrow, as if there was something else he wanted to say.

I doubted there was anything in all the languages he knew that would suffice.

I pulled my hand away from his. Bent to scoop up my knife, approached her body. The air steamed around me, heat bleeding out from a demon metabolism struggling to cope with the killing cold creeping into my chest.

He said nothing, but the shield of Power around me moved uneasily.

I bent carefully, dug in her right-hand jeans pocket. Almost choked as I leaned over a pool of her blood, diluted by the fine misting rain. Her datband was blinking. Why hadn't aid hovers been dispatched from the central AI well as soon as her datband's pulse monitor figured out her heart wasn't working? A *sedayeen* with an aid unit might have been able to help her.

No, with that much lead in her—especially in her chest—she'd probably bled out in seconds.

Still, why wasn't there a cadre of cops here with a Reader, examining the scene?

A rectangle of laseprint paper crinkled under my fingers as I drew it out. Gabe's daughter grinned up at me, the edges of the glossy paper wrinkled with blood. I tucked the picture securely in my bag, reached up to push a strand of wet heavy hair out of her face. My fingertip slid over her emerald, dead and lifeless now; the tat that would never shift to answer mine again. My cheek burned, though her emerald was dark.

A slight crackling buzz sparked between the gem and my fingertip. *An EMP. Of course. They trigger an electromagnetic pulse, and everyone's so busy trying to get their holovids reprogrammed they don't notice a Necromance's murder. But what about the AI well? Her pulse monitor would have sent distress signals every half-second! Unless...unless it was a focused EMP pulse, that would reset the hardcode.*

I touched the datband with one finger. It flushed red. Hardcode wiped. It was about as useless as plain plasilica now. A focused EMP pulse, cop or Hegemony hardware.

Which meant I was dealing with someone very serious about killing her for some reason. Someone who had the funding and hardware to get away with triggering an EMP pulse within the borders of the city's hoverzones.

"I have to go inside." I straightened, my fingers leaving Gabe's cold motionless wrist reluctantly.

"We must be quick." Japhrimel cocked his head. "I hear sirens."

In a city this size, of course you hear sirens. It was useless, he had some way of knowing the cops were finally coming. Hours too late.

Why? Why were they coming *now*?

I took one last long, lingering look at Gabe's body. Fixed every line, every curve, every drop of blood in my Magi-trained memory.

Roanna. Lewis. Doreen. Jace. Eddie. And now, Gabe. My throat swelled again, I swallowed the scream. Some of those deaths I had avenged, never enough to assuage the deep sleeping sense of guilt; there is only so much satisfaction to be had from spilling blood for vengeance.

But I owe it to her. To both of them, to Eddie and Gabe.

I turned on my heel and stalked away. Japhrimel fell into step behind me, silent again. The pressure of his attention wrapping around me helped to keep the scream inside—I couldn't let it out while the velvet fingers of his aura stroked my skin, the mark on my left shoulder burning deeper and deeper into my flesh.

Gabe's house shields quivered. They would eventually lose Power and become no more than shadows, holding the psychic impressions of her family, generation upon generation of Necromances and cops. But since her family had been shielding this house for a very long time, it might well take hundreds of years for the Power to fade.

The back door was unlocked and open, and I peered in. Let out a sharp breath. This door gave into the kitchen, and I could see smashed plates and appliances. Someone had tossed the hell out of Gabe's beautiful, expensive, comfortable kitchen.

My boots ground on broken ceramic and plasglass as I picked my way inside. Japhrimel laid a hand on my shoulder. "I do not like this," he said quietly.

I inhaled. Sage, and salt. Someone had been cleaning up in here, erasing psychic traces. "Her shields aren't torn here. Someone she knew, then. Someone who didn't have to break in."

Which pretty much ruled out demon involvement. I was fairly sure this had nothing to do with Lucifer, which was a huge bloody relief. Finally, something the Prince of Hell *didn't* control.

The thought of Lucifer turned my stomach over hard, splashing its contents against the sides of my ribs.

I slid through the hall—even the pictures had been torn down, some yanked out of their frames. The first-floor living room, where Gabe and Eddie had done their meditating and had their altars, was a shambles. Gabe's exquisitely painted ceramic statue of Graeca Persephonia lay smashed on the floor, Persephonia's sad flat eyes gazing up thoughtfully at the ceiling. The tang of sage was very thick here, nose-stinging, overpowering Gabe's *kyphii*.

I made my way to the stairs, counted up to the seventh one, and knelt below it. My fingers ran along the bottom of the wooden lip of the seventh step.

"Dante? They are drawing closer. Do you wish to be seen here?"

I ignored him. My fingers found the slight groove, pressed with a small tingle of Power along my nails, and the nonmagickal lock yielded. The top of the step came away in my hands. I let out a low sigh.

There, in the hidey-hole, were four sheets of heavy-duty paper with Skinlin notations—snatches of musical notes, ancient Judic symbols, and complicated chemistry equations. There were also four vials of a white, grainy substance. Otherwise, the hole was empty and suspiciously clean. Gabe must have hoped I'd find this—or hoped nobody *else* would.

Her house exhaled around me, shaking free of sage-reek, the frowsty smell of old construction and uneven, sloping, renovated floors mixing with the heady spice of *kyphii* and the comfortable soft scent of a well-lived-in home. Faint tang of synth-hash smoke—she'd been smoking, probably not around the kid.

Where exactly was Gabe's daughter? Had she been kidnapped? *In a safe place,* Gabe had said. I wondered where, and hoped the place was safe enough.

What the hell is going on?

I scooped everything up. Paper crackled in my hands. "Let's go."

CHAPTER 11

Leander still wasn't back at the hotel, and Lucas was nowhere in sight. I stalked past McKinley without a glance, into the suite I'd slept in. Dropped down on the bed, laid my sword down carefully, and dug in my bag, retrieving Eddie's murder file. Pearly sunlight fell through the window, making a thin square on the blue carpet. I swallowed a scorching curse, my rings sizzling and sparking. Tasted bile.

Japhrimel closed the bedroom door and leaned back against it, his arms folded and his eyes alight. I looked at the file, set it aside with the sheets of paper covered in Skinlin scribbles, and held up one of the vials.

The grainy substance inside glowed faintly in rainy afternoon light. Silence stretched inside the room. The curtains fluttered uneasily, once, and were still. Between Japh's taut alertness and my own furious, tightly-controlled pain, the walls groaned a little and subsided.

My chest ached. My eyes burned, dry and determined to stay that way. Nevertheless, my hand shook a little, making the fine grains inside the glass vial tremble and spill from one side to the other.

The mark on my shoulder lay quiescent against my skin now, no longer burning or spurring me away from shock. But the deep prickling sense of Japhrimel's attention remained, sliding around me the way a cat might, rubbing its head against its owner. Offering comfort, maybe.

Was it so bad of me to want to accept it? Things were as hopeless as ever between us.

I looked over at the door. His eyes were half-lidded, the green glow muted; perhaps for my sake. Still, they were the most vivid thing in the room, so bright they cast shadows under his high cheekbones.

We paused like that for twenty long seconds, each ticked off with a single deadly squeeze of my heart. My traitorous pulse still beat, reminding me I was alive.

"She's dead," I said finally, dully. *Who is that, using my voice? She sounds defeated. Hopeless.*

"I am sorry." It was the first time I heard his voice shake with sadness, ever so slightly. "If I could make it otherwise for you, I would."

I almost believed him. No, that's a lie. I *did* believe him. How was that for ironic? If he could have torn Death away and brought her back, he would have. Simply another present for his *hedaira,* a token of his strength given because he did not know what else to give me. How else to make me *happy.*

It was a shame he couldn't do it. I would have begged him for it, if he could have.

But Death will not be denied. I knew that, even as something old and screaming inside me rose up in rebellion that was quelled by what had to be done now.

I held up the vial again, shook it gently. The grains inside rattled softly, mocking me. "What do you suppose is in this?" The words hitched, caught. I closed my eyes, dropping my hand. It was getting harder to breathe. The air had turned to clear mud.

I heard him cross the room, his booted feet making noise for my benefit. He stopped by the bed, and his fingers slid through my hair again. The touch was gentle and intimate, a gesture he habitually performed in Toscano to request my attention away from my feverish research. He trailed his fingertips down my temple, over my cheek, infinitely gentle.

"I would almost prefer your weeping." His voice stroked the air, turning it to golden velvet. Soothing, a tone so far divorced from his usual flat dry irony he hardly sounded like the same person. "What would you have of me? Tell me what to do, Dante."

My bag clinked as it shifted against my hip. "How savage can you be?" The words turned to ash in my throat. "Because when I find whoever did this, I want them to *suffer.*"

Another long pause as he stroked my cheek again, his sensitive fingertips skimming my skin, sending comforting tingles and ripples of fire down my back. My breath caught, the spiked mass of pain inside my chest turning over.

"Demons understand vengeance." He touched my upper lip, tracing the curves.

Gods. "What *don't* demons understand?"

"Humans." He said it so promptly and ironically I laughed, a forlorn little chuckle that didn't sound like me at all. I scooped up three of the four vials and handed them to him.

"Keep these. They're safer with you." *If I can trust you to give them back, that is. But this is nothing you'd be interested in, I'm betting.*

His fingers flicked, and the small plasglass containers disappeared just like the tiny origami animals he'd made out of my notes. He said nothing else, simply stood and watched me, waiting.

Thinking of how fast his hands were made me wonder where all the little folded-paper animals had ended up. Now that I thought about it, I really couldn't remember seeing creases in any of my notes; I couldn't remember seeing any piece of paper he'd selected to fold and amuse me with ever again.

Dammit, Danny, don't lose your focus. Your problem isn't Japhrimel. Not right now, anyway.

You know, if it wasn't so grim, that'd be a relief. Guilt scored me even as the black humor of the thought helped.

I let out a long shuddering sigh. Held up the small vial again, shook it. I opened the file, scooting back and pulling my legs up onto the bed, retreating from him. "Come take a look at this, if you want. It's Eddie's homicide file." *Hooray for me. I sound almost normal, except for the way my voice cracks.* I sounded like a vidsex operator, my ruined throat giving each word a rough husky pleasantness. Except for the unsteady fury smoking under the soft surface.

"The dirtwitch." Japhrimel settled on the bed next to me. Did he sound uncertain? "He was...he was a good man."

What, for a human? But that was unfair. Japh was trying to be kind. I swallowed around the hard lump in my throat, tasting bile. "He was." I steeled myself. Looked down to find the laseprint of

Eddie's mangled body glaring accusingly up at me. "Gods above." A shocked whisper, as if I'd been punched.

"Perhaps you should be still for a moment." Japhrimel leaned back until he half-reclined on the bed, propped on his elbows. It was a curious pose for someone so controlled, especially with his hair slightly ruffled. A vulnerable stance, exposing his stomach.

Are you crazy? I just got up late and found my best friend—my only friend—dead. I'm not resting. Not for a long, long time. I shook my head. "No." The lamp rattled on the bedside table, pushed by the plascharge of Power in my voice. My rings sparked again, golden crackles in the charged, swirling air.

The temptation to draw my sword and start hacking at the grace-less, ugly furniture was overwhelming.

I looked back down at the file. Hot bile whipped the back of my mouth, and my blade rang softly inside its sheath.

Japhrimel reached over, his golden fingers closing on the file. He pulled it away from my unresisting hands. I heard the rattling whine of a hover outside the hotel's windows, human footsteps in the hall. I heard the walls groaning their long slow songs of stress and wind-shift, heard the faint sound my hair made as it slid against my shoulders.

He closed the file, set it aside. Then, deliberately, he lay back on the bed, his fingers laced behind his dark head. I felt the weight of his eyes on my back, looked down at my hands.

Chipped black molecule-drip polish on my nails, the graceful architecture of demon bones, the fragility of my wrists. "I should look at it. I have to start . . . finding out what I can. I *have* to."

"I know," was the quiet answer. "But not yet, Dante. Not just yet."

"Why not?" *Goddamn you, why not?*

"There is nothing you can do at just this moment. Be still. A hunter does not rush blindly after prey." A thread of gold in the room, his voice brushed the paint, ruffled my hair, touched my cheek. The soundless static of his attention filled empty space; I wouldn't have been surprised to find he was aware of every dust mote, every fiber of the carpet, every stitch in the curtains. Japhrimel was tense, edgy.

Ready for anything.

It didn't help that he was right. I was so keyed-up I would maybe miss something important—or crucial—by forcing myself to look through the file now. I had to think clearly. I had to be cold, chill, logical; I *had* to be.

So what could I do?

Think about it. Just sit still. Study.

But sitting still only made me more aware of the weight behind my eyes, the clawing in my chest. Wine-red, wine-dark, sharp as my sword and chill as the ocean I'd been dumped into after I'd killed Santino —

I shuddered. *Don't, Danny. Don't think about that.*

I jerked, moving as if to lever myself off the bed, but Japhrimel caught my wrist and pulled, catching me by surprise. My balance tipped, I landed hard enough to drive a small sound out between my teeth, ending up trapped in his arms with my sword between us, my rig creaking, the holster of a plasgun digging into my hip and a pro-jectile gun higher up, shoved painfully against a floating rib. Knife-hilts dug against my ribs and pressed into my back.

"Be *still,*" Japhrimel hissed in my ear, his breath touching my skin and sending a hot spill of sensation through my flesh. "Please, Dante."

I kicked him, twisting to get free, the plasgun digging even deeper into my hip. "Let me *go!*"

"No."

I wriggled, tried to knee him, but his arms turned to iron bands. It was a novel kind of sparring match. He was demon; I was only a lousy human infected with demonic Power. No contest. I started to struggle in earnest, earning myself a starry jolt of pain when I cracked my head against his shoulder and finally collapsed, breath-ing heavily, his leg over both of mine, his arms almost crushing me.

"Let go," I said into the hollow between his throat and shoulder. I contemplated biting him. "What are you fucking *doing?* Let *go* of me!"

"You are in a mood to harm yourself." His breath was warm in my hair. "When you are calm I will let you go, not before."

Goddamn him, he's right. I was in a fey space between agony and revenge, I could easily see flinging myself out the window, running, smashing my fist through the wall just to break something, hurt something, *kill* something. "I am not going to harm *myself,*" I whis-pered. "I'm going to kill whoever did this to her."

"Very well. This is only a hunt like any other. You are starting ill and will finish badly if you do not calm yourself." He was breathless too; the spice and musk smell of demon drenched the bed, filled my nose, coated the back of my throat.

Damn demon pheromones. He smells safe, dammit. Oh, gods. Gods help me. I choked back a panicked giggle. After a long pause, he rested his chin atop my head. I shut my eyes tightly, willing the stone egg inside my chest to stay hard and smooth. Impenetrable.

It didn't help that I could see the cool logic of what he was saying. If I started out half-cocked and crazy, I'd get nowhere—and Gabe might be unavenged.

Like Doreen had been unavenged for so long.

If I'd been smarter or faster—or a Magi—I might have recognized Santino for what he was, and Doreen might still be alive. If I'd been stronger and not half-crippled from killing Santino, I could have kept my promise and saved Eve. If I'd been faster, able to use all the preternatural speed Japh had given me, Jace might still be alive. If I'd been home instead of hiding out with a demon in Toscano, Eddie and Gabe might still be alive.

If, if, if. I *hated* that dried-up, prissy, disapproving little word.

I'd even blamed myself for Japhrimel's first death, though he had indisputably come back. Had it been death at all, or a kind of sleep? The word he used—*dormancy*—conveyed only a type of rest. A sleep of a body ground to cinnamon-smelling ash, with only a will to survive left in its crystalline matrices, calling out to me.

Japhrimel drew in a long, soft breath. "Calm," he whispered into my hair. "Calm, my curious one." He said more, but I didn't listen. It wasn't the words, it was the rumble in his chest telling me I was safe, that he was with me, that I had to calm down.

A small *click* echoed inside my head, the same sound a work of magick makes sliding whole and complete into place. It was the sound of a hunt starting, of the right moment to begin. I inhaled deeply, drawing musk-spice smell all the way down to the bottom of my lungs. Here was a demon who had lied to me, misled me, hurt me, dragged me into working for the Prince of Hell again—but he still comforted me. He'd *protected* me when it mattered most. He had even matched his strength against Lucifer's and come away the winner.

I was still soothed, listening to the strong slow beat of his pulse echoing mine.

How was that for crazy?

"I'm all right," I managed. "Really."

"I doubt it." He kissed my hair, a slight intimate movement. I was glad I don't blush easy. "If you continue in this manner, you may well drive me mad."

Drive you mad? What the hell does that mean? When he didn't continue, I wriggled impatiently and he eased up a little. His arms were still tense; if I tried to escape he'd just clamp down again. "What?"

"I do not like to see you in such pain. What will you do first?"

I contemplated the question, trying to find a comfortable way to lie with my rig on. It didn't happen. I took in another deep breath of his smell, male and spice and demon musk, felt my heartbeat slow just a little. "Japh, let me up. I've got a plasgun trying to burrow into my hip and a projectile gun looking for my spleen the hard way. Okay?"

"Perhaps I like holding you. We have had little closeness, of late."

We may not have a whole lot in the foreseeable future, either. "If you'd quit hiding things from me and pushing me around, maybe we'd have more." I didn't have time to get into a spat with him. I really didn't.

"I am not your enemy." He stroked my hair, his fingers slipping between the silky strands.

My reply startled me. "Oh, yeah? Prove it." Then I felt like an idiot; I sounded like a spoiled brat.

"If you like." He laughed, as if genuinely amused. That only irritated me more. The fresh frustration was tonic, pushing aside the numb blackness of shock and grieving horror.

I bit his shoulder, sinking my teeth in, and he sucked in a breath. But his arms didn't loosen, and his body tensed in a way I was all too familiar with.

Well, now. Don't I feel silly. The taste of musk and night and demon filled my mouth, as intimate as a kiss, the material of his coat slick and pulsing with Power against my lips. It reminded me of just how long it had been since I'd had him, felt the blessed relief of not having to think, trusting him with my body. I tried to pull away from him again, achieved nothing.

Dammit, quit treating me like a kid! "Japhrimel—"

His voice cut across mine, soft and inflexible. "Not just yet, Dante. I am not yet convinced you are quite in control of your temper."

It was too much. One thing after another, from Sarajevo to Saint City, so much death and destruction piled on top of an already-strained mind. How much more could I stand without breaking?

I'll show you temper, you supercilious son of a bitch. I pulled back, inhaled, and held my breath, my eyes squeezed shut. Fifteen seconds. Thirty.

The blackness behind my eyelids exploded with pinwheels and bursts of color, far more vivid than real life. The blue glow of Death rose too, the place inside me where the god lived opening like a flower. For the first time, I didn't want to escape into that glow, kept myself away by a sheer effort of will, lungs crying out, pulse throbbing in my ears and throat and the rising tide of desire along my skin swamped by the sudden urgent need for oxygen.

Even demons need to breathe, don't they? A second thought, *I'm acting like a kid. Well, he treats me like one, I might as well. I've reverted to a spoiled three-year-old.*

The fact that I understood I was acting like an idiot couldn't stop me, for once.

Japhrimel's arms loosened. He shook me, hard but just short of hurting, my hair rasping against the pillow. Pent-up air rushed out, I breathed again. Opened my eyes to find him watching me.

The arc of his cheekbone took me by surprise, as it always did. The sculpture of his lips, now pulled tight and thin into a straight line, his eyebrows drawn together, a faint line between them. His eyes were incandescent, silken green. For a moment, he looked like Lucifer. The resemblance was so sudden and striking my heart slammed into my throat and demon adrenaline jolted my entire body, leaving me gratefully alive and thinking clearly for the first time since passing through Gabe's front gate that day.

"Do not," he said quietly, in a voice like the Prince of Hell's, "*ever* do that again."

Bingo, Danny. We've found something that works to irritate him. I felt equally childish and vindicated, as if I'd suddenly gained some kind of control over the situation. "Or what?" I finally worked my way free of his arm. If my voice hadn't been shaking so badly, I might have almost sounded tough.

"Or I will *teach* you not to do so." The bed creaked as he flowed away and to his feet, without a single hitch in the movement. "Think what you like of me. I begin to believe you will anyway."

Gods above and below, does he actually sound hurt? I could barely believe my ears. He stalked away, and I was too badly shaken to say a word. Lucifer called Japhrimel his Eldest, and I wondered how on earth I could live with a being that old, that powerful — and that *alien*. He wasn't human, for all he'd successfully mimicked it for me.

Not human. *Inhuman.*

But then I was no longer fully human either, was I? Maybe only human inside my head. Or my aching, pounding heart.

Wherever I'm still human, it will have to be enough.

The bedroom door closed behind him. I hunched on the edge of the bed, buried my face in my hands, and shoved down the tears. After a long, shaking moment or two, I sighed and dropped my fists into my lap. Looked over at the file, lying innocent against the now-rumpled bedspread. Japhrimel was right, I hadn't been thinking straight. Even if he'd irritated me past human endurance, he had still helped me clear my head.

First thing I've got to do is wait for nightfall. It was a relief to have a single, clear, definable thing to do in the complex mess my life had become.

Then I've got to go see Abracadabra.

CHAPTER 12

I lay curled on my side, my sword clasped in my hands, my rig at the end of the bed near my booted feet. I puzzled over the idea of the Key and the Roof of the World, I thought of what I would do when I saw Abra, and I thought of what I would do to whoever had hurt Gabe.

I brooded most on that, and on how I would find Gabe's daughter. I chewed over the problem in my head, not coming up with anything new.

I tried not to think about acting like a spoiled little brat. I was beginning to deconstruct under the stress. I needed a good clean-out meditation session to keep my head straight. The faster and harder I ran, the more I'd need a clear head and a sure hold on my temper.

First, though, I had to rest.

A twilight doze fell over me near dinnertime, just as I heard Japh and McKinley speaking in the other room. It was hard to ignore, my hearing was so acute, and I strained for the sound of Japhrimel's voice despite myself.

"Tiens is right. You should—" McKinley, getting braver by the moment.

"I did not ask for your opinion on this matter, McKinley." Japhrimel didn't let him finish the sentence, which was irritating in the extreme. "I asked for your loyalty as my vassal. There is a difference."

A long pause. "I've served you faithfully. I'd be remiss in my duty if I didn't warn you it is *dangerous* to allow her to treat you like this."

"What do you suggest? I should chain her in a sanctum like a Nichtvren's plaything? Or that I should allow her to commit a foolhardy suicide and fall with her into darkness?" Each word was underlit with savage anger. I snuggled deeper into the softness of the bed, drowsily glad Japh never spoke to *me* like that. And fuzzily alarmed at what I was hearing.

Foolhardy suicide? Just what does he think I'm going to do? Of course, he can't have too high an opinion of my maturity right now. I actually winced at the thought.

It was time to get a few things straight with him. I lay utterly still, pieces of both puzzles revolving inside my head. Waiting for dark, when I could uncoil like a snake under a rock. And begin hunting.

"You put it that way, it gets a lot clearer." McKinley sounded like he was smiling, for once.

I was tired. My eyes were heavy, and the mark pulsed and rang with soft Power, sliding down my skin, easing me into relaxing. I couldn't cry anymore, could barely dredge up the energy to keep listening.

I listened anyway.

"It is no small choice." Japhrimel sounded heavy, and sadder than I'd ever heard him. "Her hatred or her pain, I do not know which is harder to bear."

If you'd just talk to me, Japh. Precognition tingled along my skin, prickling with tiny diamond feet. It isn't my strongest talent, not by a long shot, but sometimes when the quicksand is getting deeper and deeper I can get a flash of something useful.

Sometimes. But not when my heart was aching this badly. Not when I all but vibrated with the blood-deep hunger for *revenge*. I wanted to start killing, and I wasn't too choosy about who I started with.

Anyone would be fine. And that alarmed me a little.

The precog refused to come. Just the sense of danger, and a creeping sensation against the flesh of my wrist, above my datband. I'd taken the Gauntlet off, but my skin still tingled with the feel of it. Loathing touched the back of my throat, I forced it away.

Relax, Dante. Nothing you can do right now. Just breathe, and wait. Hold yourself still. Don't even think. Just breathe.

I did.

I tipped over the edge into gray nothingness. It wasn't the dead unconsciousness Japhrimel could lull me into, the sleep that was a restorative for my human mind. No, this sleep was more like the restless tossing I'd had all my mortal life, my conscious mind paralyzed by too much stress and sliding out of commission like a disengaged gear, spinning fruitlessly while the deeper parts of me worked, intuition and insight grinding finer and finer until they would present me with the wrench jamming the works.

Inducing a precognitive vision is hard goddamn work, and I failed miserably. But something else happened, something I hadn't done since I'd been human.

I *dreamed.*

This was not the hall of Death.

I gathered up my skirts as I negotiated a wide, sweeping staircase; the vast parquet floor of the ballroom below shimmered mellow under many layers of wax and care.

I recognized this place.

It was the Hotel Arméniere in Old Kebec. I'd stayed here once on a bounty hunt ending with a clean collar in the teeming sink of the Core in Manhattan. The Arméniere was expensive, but a Hegemony per diem had covered it and right after Doreen's death I hadn't cared if it was pricey; it was magshielded, had a sparring hall, and the staff were mostly psi-friendly. That was worth a little credit. Besides, I'd just been knifed, shot at, and hit on the left arm with a ringbar while engaging in a slicboard duel with the bounty I was tracking. I figured I deserved a little relaxation while I waited for him to screw up and give me something to work with to bring him down.

The ballroom had been one of my favorite places, mostly deserted during the day; quiet and full of space where I could run through katas without being gawked at or challenged to a sparring match I wasn't in the mood for. Long narrow windows looked out on a night pulsing with neon and citylife, I heard distant traffic and the thump of a nightclub on the other side of the wall by the stairs. That told me it was a dream — the Arméniere was on a busy street, but the walls

*were thick and you would no more hear a nightclub than you would
hear the staff whistling the Putchkin anthem.*

*The other clue that I was in a dream was the fantastic pre-
Merican-era illustration of a dress. Red silk, long whispering skirt, a
bodice just short of indecent, and long sleeves that belled over my
hands.*

My human *hands, not gold-skinned demon hands. I saw the
well-healed scar on my right thumb, the different texture of pale
human skin, the crimson molecule-drip polish I used to use. A fading
bruise was turning yellow on the back of my right hand.*

*With the fuzzy logic of dreams, it all made perfect sense. Even the
dream-copy of the necklace Jace made for me, silver-dipped raccoon
bacula and blood-charged bloodstones, was there. The real necklace
was on my sleeping self, but this copy hummed with Power, throbbing against my collarbones.*

*I reached the bottom of the stairs, my pulse pounding like the
thump of bass coming through the wall. I felt naked—I had no sword,
none of the familiar weight of a rig against my shoulders. Crimson
silk mouthed the floor as I moved, cold waxed wood and the grit of
dust against my bare tender human feet.*

You look beautiful.

The necklace's throb settled into a sustained heat. I whirled.

*He leaned against the wall between two windows, his face in
shadow except for the bright points of light in his blue eyes. A stray
breeze touched a sheaf of wheat-gold hair, and my mouth turned dry
and slick as desert glass.*

*Jace Monroe hooked his thumbs in his belt. He wasn't armed
either.* Hey, Danny. Spare a kiss for an old boyfriend?

I'm dreaming, I thought. Dreaming. Have to be.

Of course you're not dreaming. *His lips shaped the words, but the
air didn't move. Instead, the meaning resounded inside my head. Like
the tone of psychic music that was a god's communication, fraught
with layers on layers of complexity. A wash of amusement, bitter
spice of regret, a thin thread of desire blooming through and sparkling like an iron wire to hold it all together. Under it, the smell of
peppered honey that was Jace's magick, the smell of a Shaman, the
smell I'd missed without knowing.*

He moved forward into the dim light. Don't think much of the
choice of venues, sunshine. Never did have you pegged as a romantic.

Another shock. He was the young Jace of the days of our first affair, moving smoothly and without the telltale hitch from his injured knee, his face smoother without age and the bitterness that had crept up and glazed over him like varnish. Even his haircut shouted it— shaggy, but obviously expensively trimmed. I'd forgotten that about him, forgotten the antique Bolgari chronograph he used to wear glittering over his datband. Forgotten the lopsided, charming smile he used to use on me, the one I'd fallen for.

He folded his arms. This has got to be the first time I've ever seen you speechless. Don't talk too soon, I'm enjoying it.

You're dead. *My lips shaped the whisper. The pulse in my temples and throat was made of glass.* Mirovitch killed you. Gabe set you free in the hospital. You're dead.

Of course I'm dead. *He shrugged.* But am I gone? Not on your life, Danny girl. I don't have much time right now, you're heading into dangerous waters. I'll help all I can.

A shuddering impact hit next door, the wall behind the stairs creaking. Dust pattered down from the ceiling. I flinched, my right hand searching for a weapon that wasn't there. I didn't just feel naked without my sword. I felt lost, and panicked, and uncomfortably like I was having a nightmare.

Jace's hand closed around my wrist. I damn near levitated— anyone getting that close without my knowledge spooks me. Listen to me, *he said, his skin warm and dry and blessedly human against mine.* You have to wake up now, Danny. No time for fun and games. Wake up and get moving. You got a lot of trouble on your tail.

I opened my mouth to say something, anything, but he shook his head again. I drank in his face, the angle of his jaw, each small detail lovingly polished. It was lifelike, incredibly vivid, right down to the individual grains of grit under my bare feet. Jace's fingers burned, clamping down hard on my left wrist, clasping like chill heavy metal quickly warming to my skin.

Wake up, Danny. Wake up.

I don't want to! *I wailed. My hair slid forward—my old human dyed-black, dead dark lifeless hair. I never thought I'd be so glad to see split ends again.* I don't want to wake—

Another shuddering boom. A visegrip clamped around my right shoulder and ripped my body free of its moorings. I felt the snap as whatever space holding me was torn away and I fell, arching my back, screaming and—

—landing on the floor beside the bed, an undignified squeak cut

short as my teeth clicked together *hard*. I blinked up, a pair of familiar yellow eyes meeting mine; the tip of my blade caressed Lucas
Villalobos's throat. Blue flame ran through my sword, its heart showing a thin thread of white fire; I had also lifted my left arm instinctively into a guard position when I'd landed on my ass. My eyes
snagged on my raised wrist—clasped against my golden skin, the
cuff of silvery demon-wrought metal glowed.

I didn't put that back on. I choked. I wasn't sure what surprised
me more—a human dream, or finding out I was still *hedaira*. The
thin hitching sound of a sob rose in my throat; I denied it.

"Time to go," Lucas wheezed. Darkness broken only by the glow
of a small nightlight fastened into a wall plug filled the room like
deep water, shadows lying over the top of unfamiliar furniture. "Get
up, Valentine."

My sword whispered back into its sheath. It was small consolation
that I'd been ready to kill him, he could have slid a knife between my
ribs while I was lost in whatever trance had taken me. My eyes were
grainy, and my entire body felt torpid, like I'd been shaken out of a dead
sleep in the middle of the afternoon. It was a very human feeling.

It was also profoundly unsettling. *Where's Japhrimel? What's
going on?*

Of all the things I could have said, I settled for the most predictable. "What the *hell?*"

"Had to wait until your boyfriend left, *chica*. Come on." Lucas's
sleeve was torn and floppy, soaked with blood. His yellow eyes were
dead and dark, his lank hair fell in his face, and he wore the widest,
most feral smile I had ever seen on him; either post-coital or post-
combat, it was wholly scary. His teeth gleamed white in the dim bedroom. "Abra wants to see you tomorrow. I found out some o' what the
demon's up to."

"Great." I ducked into my rig. *Where's Japhrimel? I thought he
wasn't going to let me out of his sight.* I didn't smell him, and the
mark on my shoulder pulsed softly, absently, coating my skin with
now-familiar Power. A few seconds worth of buckling had all my
weapons riding in their accustomed places, I passed the strap of my
bag over my head, shrugged into my coat, and was ready to go.
My katana weighted my left hand as I followed Lucas out into the
rest of the suite.

Which was, to put it kindly, a shambles. The furniture was
destroyed, chairs and tables smashed, the holovid player shattered,

and a large imprint rammed into the wall between the suite and the bedroom. Japhrimel was still nowhere in evidence; I wondered where he'd gone. *"Sekhmet sa'es,* I slept through *this?"*

"You been sleepin' a lot, *chica.* Even on your feet. It ain't like you." Lucas jerked his chin at a shape lying on the floor by the nivron fireplace. It was McKinley, bleeding from the nose and ears and gagged with an anonymous bit of cloth held down with magtape, trussed with a thin golden chain that shivered and smoked in the light from the upended lamp. The carpeted floor groaned under him as he caught sight of me and started to struggle.

Leander, now shaven-cheeked, his accreditation tat twisting under his skin, nodded from the windowsill. He stood with one hip hitched up against the sill, his sword shoved into his belt and a plas-gun in his right hand, peering down into the street below. His dark hair was wildly mussed. "Hi, Danny." His tone was excessively even. "Sorry I had to bail, I thought it best I didn't stick around after the demon warned me off." His emerald sparked, and one corner of his mouth pulled down.

Warned you off? What the hell? I contented myself with a non-committal noise. "Mh. What the hell's that?" I pointed at McKinley, whose black eyes narrowed. He was either furious or terrified, I couldn't tell. A whiff of burning cinnamon and dry naptha scented the air, as if his glands had opened to pour out chemical reek.

"The demon left him here, probably to watch out for Sleeping Beauty." Leander sighed, shrugging, but his dark eyes flicked nervously over the room as if expecting company any moment. "Let's go, the back of my neck's itching."

So was mine. *Left him here? What the hell?* It wasn't like Japhrimel to leave me alone. Where the hell was he?

The last time Japh had left while I was unconscious, it was to go into Hell and start the process of dragging me back into a huge mess full of demons. One happy little home in the Toscano hills burned to smoking rubble in a reaction fire and my life crashing down around my ears again.

What was he doing *now?*

"What's Japh been doing, Lucas?" My hand dropped to a knife-hilt as I contemplated McKinley, who went absolutely still. He was bruised all over his face and I was sure one shoulder was dislocated by the way it rotated too far back. This was twice Lucas had faced down a Hellesvront agent and come away the winner.

I am so glad I hired him. Well, technically, Eve started out hiring him, but I'm glad he's working for me. With a clear-cut emergency in front of me, I felt better than I had since I'd received Gabe's message.

Gabe.

I pushed away the thought of her broken body, the emerald dark and lifeless in her pale cheek. *Focus, Danny. Goddammit, focus!* Broken plasilica ground into the carpet under my boots. The dangling almost-chandelier light fixture had been yanked out of the ceiling. The wet bar was a chaos of broken glass and the simmering stink of alcohol, reminding me of DMZ Sarajevo. A shiver bolted up my spine, was ruthlessly quelled.

"There's another demon in town, and word is your green-eyed boy is tracking it down, as well as some other interestin' shit. I got you an interview with a Magi who might know what the fuck's goin' on." Lucas shrugged. "Let's get the hell out of here. The whole fuckin' city's seething. Something about a dead Necromance and your name tangled up together. I can't leave you alone for a fuckin' minute, can I?"

Gabe. So someone knows. Chill fury boiled up behind my breastbone again, was suppressed. "Guess not." I drew a knife with my right hand. McKinley's black eyes met mine, and he strained against the gag, making a low muffled anonymous noise.

One problem at a time. Japhrimel was hunting Eve's rebellion here in Santiago City. Why hadn't he *told* me?

You must trust me to do what you cannot, then. Japhrimel's voice, even and chill. He rarely said *anything* he didn't mean.

And here I thought he came along because I needed him. Silly me. Yellow bitterness coated the back of my throat. *Stupid and blind, Danny. He's doing the same thing he did before, going behind my back.*

Of course. Why expect him not to? It was what he *did*. Too bad I was only finding out now.

The knife flicked from my right hand, burying itself in the carpeted floor with a *chuk,* less than an inch from McKinley's nose. He flinched, barely but perceptibly, and I tried not to feel the hot, nasty wave of satisfaction curling through me. *You told Japh it was better to tie me up and do whatever he wanted, didn't you? And he left you here alone with me. You son of a bitch. No wonder you work for demons.*

"Tell Japhrimel," I said quietly. "Tell him *exactly* what I am about to say, McKinley. If he comes after Eve, he's going to have to get through me first."

That spurred the agent to frantic motion, twisting like a landed fish inside the thin golden chain. I didn't even *want* to know what it was made of. Another desperate smothered noise pressed against the gag as his eyes rolled.

My thumb caressed the katana's guard as I stared down at him. The blade thrummed, hungry inside its sheath.

Lucas pushed me. "That won't hold him forever. Come on."

You're right. I don't have time for this, I have other hovers to fly. There was a time when the thought of Lucas Villalobos touching me would have made my skin crawl with frantic loathing and send me scrabbling for a weapon to protect myself. He was *dangerous,* as dangerous as a big venomous snake or a Mob Family Head. Just because he hadn't bitten me yet didn't mean he wasn't going to.

But along with being dangerous, Lucas was professional. He was indisputably working for me—and in any case I was no longer human. I was fairly sure I could outrun him. Besides, he'd taken on the Devil for me. Something like that will make a girl feel mighty charitable even when it comes to Villalobos.

Leander ducked out the window onto the fire escape, I did too. At least the window wasn't shattered. Someone was going to owe the hotel a bundle for that room—the noise had probably already been remarked.

Outside, the night was cool and cloudy, orange glowing on the clouds and hovers moving in silent formation overhead. The cuff was heavy on my left wrist above my datband; I wondered if Japhrimel had put it on me before he'd left. While I'd been dead to the world, unconscious or tranced into a high-alpha state.

Dreaming of Jace. Or not-dreaming.

The Gauntlet shimmered, my skin crawling underneath it. It bothered me more than I wanted to admit. I wanted to stop and peel the damn thing off again, but we had precious little time and I didn't want to have my hands full of jewelry if the other shoe dropped.

"So where are we going?" I asked Lucas, who had taken a position just behind my left shoulder, watching my back and scanning the street in front of us at the same time. "Where's this Magi?"

"In the Tank District," Lucas said easily. "Just follow Leander, *chica.* We'll get you there."

CHAPTER 13

Anwen Carlyle lived in a rickety, filthy apartment building in the Tank District; and not a nice part of the Tank either. This close to the Bowery, the worst festering sore in the middle of the Tank, the air was full of pain. Bloodlust, desperation, Chillfreaks, pimps, hookers, Mob runners, and other human flotsam congregated there. The Tank is where you go if you're a rich technoyuppie slumming, or a bounty hunter looking to connect with the shadow side. It's also where you *don't* go if you want to get through the evening without a fight. It isn't as bad as the Core in Manhattan or the Darkside in Paradisse, but it's bad enough. The urban renewal that had gone through Trivisidiro hadn't visited this part of the Tank, it was likely none ever would. This close to the Rathole where the sk8 tribes congregated, renewal wasn't a priority. Survival was.

The smell inside the sloping tenement was incredible: dirty diapers, piss, desperation, food cooked on little personal plasfires. "What the hell's a Magi doing here?" I asked, quietly enough, as I followed Lucas up the stairs. There was an elevator, but it didn't work. I didn't mind, even through the titanic stink of human despair and dying cells. I'd rather smell stink than be caught in an elevator, unable to breathe as claustrophobe terror crawls down my throat. "She can't make rent?"

Leander, behind me, made a low snickering sound. "Taken in by appearances?" His tone was light, a welcome distraction from the close dank quarters that almost triggered latent claustrophobia. My sword was heavy in my hand, and the cuff was chill against my skin.

I ignored the itching, nagging desire to take the thing *off* again. "Lucas?"

His bloody sleeve flopped as he climbed the stairs with shambling grace. "Anwen don't like company, *chica*. But she owes me."

I shivered at the thought of what a Magi might owe Lucas. I wondered if he liked to keep a few debts in reserve, for just such an emergency. My skin chilled at the thought of the price he usually demanded from a psion, anyone with Talent would have to be *really* desperate to hire him.

Japhrimel had paid him. What would a demon pay the Deathless?

I decided I could live without knowing. "Great. So she owes you." I looked at the intaglio of graffiti rioting over the walls in permaspray. Most of the lights were broken or burned out. The ones that remained gave enough of a glow I could see every crack and splinter, every patched and unpatched hole in the wall, every small bit of trash and scuttling cockroach. Demon eyes need a few photons to work with, not like Nichtvren and their uncanny ability to see in total dark.

The thought of Nichtvren sent another shiver up my back. For some reason they scare me more than demons. It's an atavistic fear; a human fear of something higher up the food chain. It's also completely unrealistic, a demon will kill you quicker. But I was more scared of suckheads. Go figure.

Let's just get this over with so I can go talk to Abra and start untangling this mess. Impatience rose; I pushed it down. I didn't want to be here in the Tank, I wanted to be somewhere else, anywhere else, tracking down a killer.

Gabe's killer, Eddie's killer. I had revenge to get started with. But if I could also find out exactly what Japh was up to, I had to at least *try.*

What wasn't he telling me, and where the hell *was* he? I didn't like my protection—the only protection I was certain of—vanishing while the inside of my head turned into a bad holovid show. I was sinking fast, as usual, without any clue what the hell was going on now.

Well, we're here to figure some of it out, aren't we? A Magi who owes Lucas. Let's hope she has something useful to tell me.

We reached the sixth floor, Lucas and Leander both breathing a little more raggedly than usual. My own breath came deep and slow, the mark on my shoulder pulsing softly with Power, I wasn't winded in the least.

"One thing," Lucas wheezed. He smelled like copper, dried blood, and the dry throat-stinging tang of a stasis cabinet, under a screen of male effort and stale sweat. "Try not to scare her, Valentine."

"I'll do my best." My left hand tightened on my sword. "Why anyone's scared of me when *you're* around . . ." *Good gods above, I'm actually bantering with Lucas Villalobos. Christer Hell must be frozen over by now.*

Amazingly, he gave a whistling, wheezing laugh as he pushed the heavy fire door open. I saw a glimmer down at the end of the hall—

shields, powerful subtle shields. "I'm a reasonable man, Valentine. You ain't."

Not reasonable, or not a man? I feel pretty damn reasonable, considering my best friend was just murdered and the man I love won't give me a straight answer when it comes to the Prince of Hell and why I'm suddenly such a high-priced chip in this goddamn game. "I'm reasonable," I muttered darkly. "Considering everything that's going on, I'm pretty *damn* reasonable." My throat was dry, my voice soft and seductive in the dark despite or maybe because of my damaged trachea.

"Hear, hear." Leander bumped into me, maybe his human eyes couldn't pierce the dark like mine could. He still smelled like sand and the thick langorously-spiced coffee of Cairo Giza under the cloak of dying cells that meant *human.*

I wondered why the smell sent such a frisson of distaste up my back. I liked him, didn't I? And Lucas's dry stasis-cabinet scent was no better.

"Shut up, deadhead," Lucas snarled. He seemed to have no trouble navigating over the debris in the hall—soymalt bottles, empty takeout cartons, rancid clothing, other shapeless bits of stuff. "I do the talkin' here."

"Leave him alone." My own tone was flat and bored. "He knows enough to keep his mouth shut when dealing with an edgy Magi." *Although how dangerous a Magi who chooses to live in a dump like this is, I won't venture to guess.*

Villalobos didn't dignify that with an answer. We reached the end of the hall, apartment 6A; he knocked once, twisted the knob, and pushed the door wide.

Well, that's interesting. I watched the shimmering layers of Power shunt aside from his aura, magickal energy refusing to touch him. It was something I'd noticed about Lucas, he didn't use Power himself, but it couldn't be used against him either. An impasse, and food for thought...if I could figure out what to think about it.

A breath of *kyphii*-scented air puffed out, caressed the hall. I followed Lucas, stepping nervously through a cascading sheet of energy that parted to let me through before flushing a deep beautiful rose-spangled gold as whoever inhabited this place felt the Power flux change around me. *Female. Magi. Not too young, but not old.* I took a deep breath, all the way down to the bottom of my lungs, tasting the air as if I was on a bounty. Leander followed, sweeping the door shut behind him, and we found ourselves in a hardwood-floored entryway, smelling mellowly of beeswax, *kyphii,* and Power.

Anubis et'her ka, she's powerful, whoever she is. The shields were carefully done, a subtle taint of demon spice threading through them telling me she was an active, demon-dealing Magi.

Like "Shaman", "Magi" is a catch-all term for a wide range of variously-talented psions. A Magi might or might not know what to do with a demon when it pops up, depending on their study—and depending on the demon. Magi have been trafficking with Hell since before the Awakening, but before that great collective human leap forward in psionic and magickal Power, their methods had been spotty and uneven at best. Still, when the Awakening happened, the Magi were the only ones who had an idea of how to train psionic talent, or a framework for making Power behave. Nowadays all psions are Magi-trained in memory, Power-handling, and theory of magick, but that doesn't make us all Magi.

I knew how to call up an imp and constrain it in a circle now; I knew how to consecrate tools to be used in closing an etheric portal into Hell and send a Low Flight demon *back,* I even knew a few more things about demon anatomy than I had before. But demon-dealing Magi are secretive in the extreme, committing information about their successful experiments in breaking the walls between our world and Hell to only one apprentice at a time and writing their shadowjournals—the equivalent of a Skinlin's mastersheets or a Ceremonial's grimoire—in codes that could take months to break. Even if they work with circles, they don't share many of their private secrets, and I couldn't lay my hands on the great books of magick the accepted circles had access to. Another impasse, this one frustrating in the extreme because I *needed* to know more about what I was.

What Japhrimel had made me.

The inside of the apartment was a surprise. It held no trace of clutter or poverty; the floor was polished hardwood and the walls painted varying shades of rose, pale pink, and white. Lucas led us into a living room decorated with an altar draped in silver cloth and sporting a three-foot-tall statue of Ganej the Magnificent, the elephant god. There was a restrained fainting-couch done in rose velvet and a Vircelia print on the wall, an original if my eyes didn't fool me, and the windows were cloaked with heavy silken drapes.

Ganej. The Remover of Obstacles. Odd, but an effective choice now that I think about it. What better way to break the barriers between here and Hell than with the help of a god who surmounts barricades? The statue was an antique, creamy marble veined with gold, and thrumming with Power. So this Magi took her god seriously, as seriously as I took mine.

I cautiously decided to reserve judgment.

There was a click from the doorway opposite the one we'd come in through, and my sword left the sheath in a singing blur as I stepped instinctively in front of Leander.

After all, I knew I could take more damage.

The Magi, a slim caramel-skinned woman with long dark-brown hair and a pair of wide gray eyes, stared at us. She held a very nice 9 mm Glockstryke projectile gun in her right hand, her stance braced and professional. She was pretty in an unremarkable way that wasn't helped along by the design of her tat, which wasn't flowing or graceful; she'd chosen an angular Varjas design, like a Ceremonial. It didn't do a thing for her face, being too thick-lined and sharp. But her aura flamed with Power; she was strong for a human.

Gods, did I just think that? I'm human too. I am. "Drop the gun, girl. Or I'll make you eat it." My voice stroked the drapes, made the walls groan.

"Fuck me with a hover," she breathed, her gray eyes flicking from Lucas to me, settling on me, and widening. The gun dipped slightly, ended up pointing at the floor. She wore jeans and a pretty blue wide-sleeved, square-necked shirt embroidered with Canon runes around the collar and cuffs. "*This* is your client, Villalobos?" The high edge of fear colored her voice, and a rill of excitement slid down my back. Her aura jittered slightly, her dread coloring the air like wine.

It wasn't quite as drunkening as Polyamour the sexwitch's fear, but it was still pleasant. Because Carlyle's terror was tinted with the edge of attraction, a promise that filled the air like the smell of anything fragrant and good, and comprehension flowered in those wide-spaced, rainy-gray eyes.

She knew something. A Magi that knew something, and owed Lucas a favor.

My sword slid back into the sheath, clicked home. "That's right." My pulse pounded in my throat. "I'm his latest employer. And I think we have some things to talk about, Magi."

She didn't offer us anything to drink. Instead, she pointed us toward a pile of cushions on one side of the living room, then stood with her back to her altar and her gun trained on Lucas. I didn't blame her, if I'd been human it's what I would have done.

Her eyes kept flickering over to me, no matter how steady the gun was. "So it's true," she said finally, her voice low and pleasant and reeking of terror. Her tat shifted and strained uneasily under the skin of her left cheek.

"What's true?" I didn't sit on a cushion but I did try to keep my aura close and contained, not wanting to scare her more than was absolutely necessary. After all, she'd just let a part-demon, a Necromance, and Lucas in her front door. The Necromance she was probably sure she could handle—Leander was human, just like her. But still.

Lucas gave me a slanting yellow-eyed look, pushing his lank hair back from his forehead. His breathing had evened out, and he was back to looking like every psion's worst nightmare. "Just tell her what you told me, Carlyle."

She licked her lips, examined me. The gun shook just a little, her sleeve trembled, and her aura shivered right on the edge of going hard and crystalline, locking down. Her pulse throbbed under the damp mortal skin of her throat. *Was that what I looked like when I met Lucas in Rio? Was that what I looked like to Japhrimel? So fragile, and so scared?*

And the even more uncomfortable thought, *Do I still look that way to him? Does he smell my fear, and does it taunt him like hers taunts me?*

"This cancels the debt?" Her voice shook. There wasn't a psion in the building, but the psychically-dense atmosphere kept her shields from being seen. She was almost perfectly hidden, like a scorpion under a rock. Not many people would brave both the Tank and the filth of the building outside to intrude on her privacy. Even if she did have to live with the psychic noise and stench of so many angry scrabbling people, it was a fair trade-off.

I wondered what type of work she did, and I also wondered how she'd managed to turn this apartment into such a clean, luxurious nest. She was combat-trained, the way she held the gun—the way she *moved*—told me as much. It struck me that I was looking at someone very much like the person I had been.

Before Rio. Before Japhrimel.

"Mostly," Lucas rasped. "I did you a *big* favor, Carlyle."

That made her aura turn sharp and pale. "I paid you," she insisted. "I may not be able to kill you, but I can hurt you plenty."

Irritation and impatience rose under my skin, spiked and deadly. *Will you two just get on with it so I can do what I have to do?* I took a deep, sharp breath, kept a firm hold on my temper. The vision of Gabe's body retreated just a little.

Just a very little. I wasn't going to be able to see Abra before the next sunset, so I might as well spend my time getting some information on demons and *A'nankhimel*.

I was hoping like hell she knew something about *hedaira* too. It would be a regular Putchkin Yule down here in the Bowery if she did.

I was suddenly aware of three pairs of eyes on me. Gray Magi eyes, Lucas's almost-yellow, and Leander's dark worried gaze a weight I could feel even though he was behind me. I must have been radiating, despite trying to keep my aura close and contained. "I don't have time for petty bargaining," I finally said, softly. "So if you two could finish up sometime this week I'd appreciate it. I've got a lot of business to handle."

Lucas raised an eyebrow. "Tell her what you told me, Carlyle. I promise I won't make any sudden moves. Unless you get jumpy again." His smile, stretched over his pallid thin face, was enough to send a faint shiver down even *my* back.

She cleared her throat. The perfume of her fear made the mark on my shoulder throb, pleasantly. Was it because she was a Magi? I'd damn near drowned in Polyamour's pheromones before; this was a sharper feeling, like synth-hash spiked with thyoline.

A stimulant, like Chill.

She cleared her throat. "There's talk going around. There are demons boiling through the Veil to our world. Imps have been sighted in ever-growing numbers, and there've been some...disturbing signs, at the collegia meetings." Her eyes flicked over me again. "Gods. It's true," she whispered. "It has to be. You're...you were *chosen*."

My eyebrows threatened to nest in my hairline. *Imps coming through, and she's mentioned collegia. I thought they were a myth, secret societies of Magi getting together to work collective magicks across Circle affiliations. Wow.* My pulse abruptly slowed to its usual regularity. *At last we're getting somewhere.* "Chosen for what?" I kept my tone absolutely dead level, reined in. Controlled. Still, the husky honey of my voice turned the air dark. Not like it needed any help—the only light was from the novenas ranked under Ganej, his eyes twinkling merrily in the flickering gloom.

"To be a…human bride. A fleshwife." Her pupils dilated, and the salt tang of her fear filled my mouth.

Goddammit, none of the bounties I hunted made me feel like this, psion or normal. What's wrong with me?

"I believe the proper term is *hedaira*," I corrected, dryly, as if I knew what the hell I was talking about. My emerald spat a single green spark, and she flinched. "Why don't you tell me everything you know about it, and everything you know about what's going on with the imps and these 'disturbing signs'? I'm sure Lucas will be very satisfied with that."

She eyed Lucas, eyed me, her cheeks were cheesy-pale under the even caramel. Then, far braver than I would have been in her shoes, she eased the hammer of the gun back down with a small click. "I don't know much. But what I do, I'll tell you. And this cancels the debt, Villalobos." Her sharp chin lifted defiantly. "If anyone, Magi or demon, knew I was talking to you like this, my life wouldn't be worth a bag of Tank trash."

"You got it," Lucas rasped. "I'll even let you talk to her alone." His grin was wide and chilling in its good-natured satisfaction. "Your kitchen still in the same place?"

Her hands were shaking, but she glared at him. I was beginning to like her. "Don't drink all the wine, you greedy bastard. Go. And don't touch anything else. You, too, Necromance." Her lip didn't curl when she said it, but she still sounded disdainful. I wondered why, it wasn't like a psion to be so dismissive of another.

Then again, precious little about this woman was normal even for a Magi.

Lucas shuffled out of the room, deliberately noisy with his worn-down bootheels. Leander touched my shoulder before he left, an awkward gesture that oddly enough didn't irritate me.

Immediately, Carlyle became a lot calmer. She holstered the gun at her hip and took a few steps away from the altar. "When did it happen? The change. You're not Magi, how did you convince the demon to do that? Which demon was it? Can you call him anytime you want, or—"

What the hell? "I came here for answers, not to be interrogated," I said frostily. The smell of *kyphii* made me think of Gabe, and the sharp well of pain behind my breastbone made water start in my eyes. "Keep it up, and you'll owe Lucas more."

She actually flinched, again. Her hair fell down over her forehead in a soft wave. Then she collected herself. "May I see it?"

See what? "See what?"

Was she blushing? She appeared to be *blushing.* "The...ah, the mark. If it's not in a sensitive...place."

Huh? I reached up with my right hand, pulled the neckline of my shirt out of alignment, popping a button so she could see a slice of the twisting fluid scars that made Japhrimel's mark in the hollow of my left shoulder. "It hurts sometimes." I let go of my shirt. *So having the mark is something that's supposed to happen. But I got it from Lucifer when he made Japh my familiar. On the other hand, it's the only scar that stayed after Japh changed me. And it seems to be a link between us. I wonder, does the link go both ways? He said he could use it to track me, to find me, and I can see through his eyes if I touch it. That qualifies as both ways.* "What can you tell me about *hedaira?* And *A'nankhimel?*"

Another flinch, as if I'd pinched her. "I only have one book that mentions this," she said. "I got it out when Villalobos asked me. Shaunley's *Habits of the Circles of Hell,* Morrigwen's translation. The relevant passages are on pages 156–160." She sounded like she was reciting for an Academy thesis defense, her gray eyes suddenly soft and inward-looking. A Magi-trained memory is a well-trained memory; she could probably see the page in front of her right now. "I remember it because it's so utterly unlike anything else I've ever read."

I nodded and folded my arms, the sword in my left hand bumping against my ribs. *Any time now, lady. I don't have all fucking night.*

But if I hurried her along, I might miss a critical piece of information. I couldn't see Abra until tomorrow now, so I supposed I *did* have all fucking night. Impatience rose hot as bile in my throat, I swallowed it. My hair brushed my shoulders, I could almost feel the tangles breeding. Since the hover incident I hadn't bothered fastening it back.

"Shaunley says he came across old texts that assert the relationship between demons and human women goes back to pre-Sumerian days, back in the times when demons were seriously worshipped as gods. Of course, they were worshipped as late as the Age of Enlightenment, off and on, but that's neither here nor there. The point is, priestesses in the temples—and other women—were sometimes *chosen.* The term Shaunley used is *fleshwife,* but he also used a very old Graeco term for *courtesan;* it's close to a word that means more like *companion* or *beloved* in the demon tongue. Apparently there were quite a few of the Greater Flight who bound themselves to mortal women, granting a piece of their power and receiving something in return—nobody knows quite what." She leaned back against her altar, probably taking solace in the nearness of her god. Her hand rested on the butt of the 9 mm, the cuff of her sleeve falling gracefully down; I wondered where her other weapons were. She wasn't carrying steel.

I made a restless movement, stilled myself. *What did Japh get from this? He said my world is his in exchange for Hell, but...* I waited. This was confirming several guesses I'd made, but I needed more.

"They were wiped out in a catastrophe that took plenty of humans with them," she finished heavily. "There haven't been any more."

Except me. Wonderful. I took a firm hold my temper. The silk drapes fluttered as Power pulsed out from the mark again. "So the *hedaira* is what, half-demon? A quarter?" *Give me something I don't know, anything, come on!*

"It's not that simple." She inhaled. "As close as I can figure, the demon and the fleshwife are literally *one* being. Whenever they're written about, it's in the singular, as if each pair is one person. The demon survives in our physical world through the fleshwife."

While you live, I live. Japh's voice echoed in the bottom of my head, smooth and fiery like old dark whiskey. "So what happens if the fleshwife dies?" It was the one question I never expected to be able to answer.

Carlyle brightened. She was into the explanation now, like a yuppie bursting to tell someone about a new techtoy. Her eyes actually sparkled. "If the fleshwife dies, the Fallen demon is sentenced to a slow fall into a mortal death, since she's his link to *our* world. That's straight from an inscription, Shaunley actually made a rubbing of the original. The demon seems to be a lot harder to kill, you hear of them almost dying and they're fine again on the next page."

Comprehension swirled through me. I knew I could resurrect Japh, I'd done it once before, hadn't I?

What if he couldn't resurrect *me?* It had never occurred to me to put things in that light. Even a Necromance doesn't like to contemplate her own messy, imminent demise, especially when trying to stay one hop ahead of the Devil. I'd never thought of what might happen to Japh without me.

It certainly put a different complexion on things. "Oh, boy." My mouth went dry and I dropped my arms to my sides. The candleflames flickered, drenching Ganej's supple curves in light. "Whoa."

She shrugged. "That's all I know. I'm sorry."

It confirmed a few pleasant and unpleasant guesses, and with my grounding in magickal theory I could make a few more assumptions. Good enough, and not a bad bargain for her or for me. "What about these disturbing rumors? And the imps?" I braced myself for the worst.

She didn't disappoint me. "There's a war going on in Hell, Necromance. Someone's rebelled against the hierarchy of demons, and there's chaos. Four Magi in the last two weeks—dead when they summoned an imp and got *something else* entirely. There are things riding the air, and demonic activity we haven't seen on earth since the Awakening. They're looking for something, I don't know what."

Chills crawled up my spine. I stared at her, hoping I didn't look like an idiot, my mouth gaped open like a fish's.

Looking for a treasure and a Key. Japh took me to visit the Anhelikos, who had the treasure, but who had sent it, probably along a prearranged route. So there's something demonic bouncing around in the world, and a key to it, and all Hell will probably break loose when someone gets their hands on it. Lucifer? Or the rebellion?

The logical extension to that line of thinking unreeled inside my skull. *Or me?*

A thin finger of ice traced up my spine, remembering the Anhelikos and its wide white wings, the smell of clotted sweetness and feathers, and a predatory face once its beautiful mask slipped. If Japhrimel hadn't been there... but he had, and he'd treated the thing like it was no big deal.

Quit it. Be logical, Danny. Eve is the rebellion, isn't she? But maybe she's not all *the rebellion. They're testing Lucifer because Santino got away, and nobody knows Japhrimel was acting under orders and setting Santino free.*

My head began to hurt with complex plot and counterplot. No wonder Japhrimel hadn't told me any of this. I'd visited the Anhelikos with him and seen Eve afterward; if Japh thought Eve was after this treasure he probably wasn't sure what I'd told her—or what I was *likely* to tell her.

I had to admit, if she'd caused a war in Hell and was making this amount of trouble for Lucifer, I was feeling more fucking charitable toward her all the time.

I didn't give a good goddamn about most of it. The only thing I was worried about right now was getting to Abra's and starting to track down Gabe's killer. "Okay. Anything else you can tell me before I get Lucas out of your hair?"

Carlyle sagged against the altar. "You mean it?" Her dark eyes were wide and haunted. "This cancels my debt?"

I don't know what he did for you, sunshine, but if I was you I'd be happy to still be alive. I forced myself to shrug, my rig creaking slightly as good supple leather sometimes did. "That's between you and Lucas. He's reasonable."

"Far more reasonable than the alternative." She tipped her head back. The perfume of her fear was stronger, taunting me, she was giving out pheromones like a sexwitch. "You...are you staying in Saint City?"

I nodded. "I have some business to sort out." *Someone to kill. And Gabe's daughter to find, wherever she is.* "In a safe place." *I wonder.* "Why?"

"If you want to come back." She swallowed, and I wasn't sure I liked the gleam in her rainy eyes. "I'll trade, for information. About demons."

I had a sudden, nasty mental image of bringing Japhrimel here, quickly shoved it away. "I don't think you'd like that," I hedged. "They're worse than Lucas, Carlyle. Much worse." *You should know that.* A chill, unhappy thought surfaced. *What if she smells like that because she's a demon-dealing Magi? Polyamour smelled good because she's a sexwitch, what if this Magi smells good because she's been dealing with demons and I'm somehow picking up on it?*

"I've called imps." Her eyes were definitely bright and moist. Her mouth pulled down in a grimace, the smell of *kyphii* tanged with the deeper brunette scent of adrenaline-laced fear. "Properly constrained in a circle, they—"

Sekhmet sa'es, *you have no goddamn idea, woman.* "No." My right hand curled around my swordhilt. I'd taken on an imp once and gotten poisoned claws through my chest; the only reason I was still alive was because, of all things, reactive paint had turned the Low Flight demon into a bubbling greasy streak. The memory of a soft maggot-white babyface snarling as the imp came for me in the rocketing flexible tube of a hovertrain made the sensation of gooseflesh rise under my golden skin, hot and prickling. "Forget it, Magi. Just forget it."

Curtains moved slightly at the closed window, and I stilled, glancing at them. I hadn't done that. The Gauntlet turned cold on my wrist, a tugging sliding against the surface of my skin.

What the hell? What was the damn demon-thing doing now? It had warned me of attacks before, but it had never done *this.*

I shook the sensation away and eyed the Magi, whose cheeks had gone back to that alarming pale shade. Her hands shook. *Wait a second.*

"Lucas!" My tone was sharp, and my hand curled around my swordhilt. Three inches of steel leaped free, and I had to clamp down on my control not to draw the rest of the way.

"You bellowed?" he said from the door, and the look he gave the trembling Magi could only be described as *predatory.*

I squeezed down the temptation to voice my sudden certainty that Carlyle might be having other visitors soon, visitors who would be very interested in us. It was a faint mercy, at best.

But no matter what side of the demon's field she was playing, she was scared to death of Villalobos, and I remembered that feeling so well I had no desire to put her through any more of it. I wondered bleakly if she was a Hellesvront agent, or if Japhrimel was looking for me and it was just easier to find me when I hung around a demon-dealing Magi.

The Gauntlet chilled again, a hard frost clamped to my wrist. The feeling was like icy water closing over my head. I surfaced, blinking, and the premonition passed me by again.

Dammit. I hate it when a precog just won't land.

The other possibility, of course, was that it was another demon looking for me, or this Magi was working for someone other than Japhrimel. Since Japh was off doing gods-only-knew-what.

Still, when she looked at Lucas I was reminded of being human, of feeling that gutclenching fear I couldn't even admit to myself now.

Be human, Danny. Prove you're still capable of it.

"Time to go," I said shortly. "Her debt's canceled. Come on."

CHAPTER 14

I spent the daylight hours pacing the inside of a cheap Cherry Street hotel room, wishing I could get *out* and do something productive, shoving away the mental image of Gabe's body, the bite of frustration sharp and smelling of gun oil as I ground my teeth. Leander slept, Lucas settled in a chair by the window and contented himself with oiling and cleaning his projectile guns before falling into a healthy doze. Night was the time to go see Abra; she didn't truly open up until dusk. Darkness would also give us some cover.

There was another component to my unease: we were near the same patch of sidewalk where the man who had raised me since infancy, had been knifed dead by a Chill-freak because his old chronograph looked pawnable. I used to visit the site every year, hadn't since the hunt for Mirovitch. I wondered about going back, maybe buying some flowers. Wondered if I would be alive for the anniversary of his death, wondered if I could make up for the recent time spent with Japhrimel, when I hadn't brought myself to the site because of distance or just plain cowardice.

Time had become fluid while I lived with Japh. I wasn't even sure what month it was. Only that the trees had lost their leaves but the streets weren't cold enough for dead winter yet.

Finally, after dark, Leander led us up Ninth Street and cut over on Downs, probably meaning to work down on Fiske to Klondel. I could have told him to take Avery instead—after all, Fiske would take us right through a really ugly part of the Tank District—but I was too occupied taking note of all the other changes that had happened to my city.

I kicked at a Plasmalt Forty bottle; it clanked against the sidewalk. Downs was deserted this time of night, since all the reputable frowning businesses patronized by normals closed about seven. At Fiske and Twentieth we would start to see some nightlife, it was the edge of the hooker-patrolled part of the District. Even though Downs was deserted I could see changes—graffiti scrawled in permaspray, magbars on some windows—that warned of the Tank spreading this way. Trivisidiro was getting better; Downs was getting worse.

Lucas and I also had other things to talk about. "A dead Necromance and my name. Lovely." Someone had linked Gabe and me. It wasn't surprising, given how often we'd worked together.

"Yeah, you managed to stay incognito a whole twelve hours. Now everyone knows you're back, and plenty know you look like a serious genetic remodel. Abra's is getting hot, what with people coming and asking about you." Lucas scanned the rooftops, blinked like a lizard, and massaged his left shoulder. It bothered me to see his clothes stiff with dried blood, though I couldn't have said why.

"Who's asking about me?" *When did I get so fucking popular? And do any of these people want to know about me so they could figure out if Gabe had time to talk?* It felt good to consign all my problems with demons to the back of my brain. Even if the image of Gabe flung over the hemlock wouldn't go away, making a strange choking sensation rise in my throat. I pushed it down.

"Courier messages from the Tanner Family, four or five bounty hunters. A werecain—some shaggy bastard with striped fur. A Nichtvren girl; she left you an envelope. Couple slic couriers, a Shaman who works on a clinic out on Fortieth—"

"*Sekhmet sa'es,*" I breathed. "Fuck."

He gave a small, whistling laugh. *There he goes again, finding me funny. When did I become so amusing?*

"That's not all. A corpclone from Pico-PhizePharm, too. *Everyone's* lookin' for you; lucky me findin' you first." Lucas's steps matched mine on the sidewalk. Ahead of us, Leander turned on Fiske Avenue. His shoulders were level under his rig. He hadn't flinched once. The streetlamps painted his hair with soft darkness, and he moved with the caution all bounty hunters acquired after a few successful but hard-fought collars.

I like him, I decided. *I'm glad he didn't skip out on me.*

Lucas's eyes followed mine. "Good kid," he said grudgingly. "Came and found me at Abra's. Told me the demon was slipping out while you were asleep."

I don't know what's he's doing or where he's gone. Par for the course, just when I could have used him. "Well." My fingers ached around the katana's scabbard.

Trust me, Japhrimel kept telling me. *Do not doubt me.* He'd faced down Lucifer to protect me, and now he was gone hunting Eve and leaving me behind like a piece of luggage. Just when I thought I had Japh pegged as a good guy or a bad guy, he did something to confuse me all over again.

"Beaudry also told me Boy Black warned him to stay away from you. Seems your demon's jealous." Lucas sounded far too interested and amused for my comfort.

I shivered. Did Japhrimel think I belonged to him? Demons were possessive, everyone knew that. *Way* possessive. Had I put Leander in danger just by smiling at him? Enjoying his company?

Well, let's be honest here, Danny. You like the man; he's a bounty hunter, and he's human. Human, something Japh isn't. You like hanging around him, and Japhrimel reacted the way any jealous lover would.

I decided a subject change would be a fantastic idea. "How are we going to get in Abra's front door without anyone noticing? If so many people are looking for me, at least one of them will figure out just to stay near Abra's until I show up." It was a dumbass question, and the sidelong look Lucas gave me showed he didn't think much of it.

"Abra's spread a quiet rumor that there's bad blood; you gypped her on the payment on that hush-hush Rio bounty. Said she's going to take it out of your hide if you come near. Figured that was enough to keep most of 'em away. I'm gonna take you in the back door, Leander will waltz in the front and see if we have any eyes." Lucas coughed, spat to one side. He sounded horrible, like a man dying of slaglung.

"Good." *I didn't even know Abra had a back door.* "So any more word on the demon Japh's after? Other than your Magi's, I mean." *Eve. Is she here? If she is, where is she hiding? Why would she come here?*

Why would so many people—and other species—be looking for me? And bounty hunters too. Goddammit, Gabe, what's going on?

Gabe couldn't answer, but it felt good to think of her as if she was still alive.

I swallowed the lump in my throat, felt the rage rise again. Corralled it, again, with an almost-physical effort that made my rings ring with light.

I couldn't *afford* to get too angry, too soon. The trouble was, my control was wearing thin. The Gauntlet was so cold against my wrist, the metal heavy and dissatisfied. I shivered again, the feeling of a precog rising, pressing maddeningly out of reach.

"Hope you got something worthwhile out of that bitch, that was an expensive favor I did her. All I've heard is there's a demon in town and it's dug in deep, gonna take a lot to blow its bolthole. But if anyone can, it's your sweetheart." Lucas let out another wheeze of amusement. I wondered why he always sounded so choked.

"Don't call him that." I scanned the street again, the back of my neck prickling. "Lucas, we're being watched." Or had the sensation of being examined just stayed with me all the way from Cairo Giza?

"Probably. You gonna give the demon a niner, Valentine? Or maybe send him a datflash breakup?"

Maybe he thought he was being funny, but irritation rasped against my skin, along with the maddening feeling of something I'd forgotten to think about. "I'll deal with Japhrimel."

He had the great tact not to laugh. *A bloody great success you've been at that so far, Danny.* My bootheels clocked against the pavement. The sense of being watched faded a little. Maybe my nerves were just raw...but just to be sure, my rings swirled and sparked again, anger turned to good use, bled off so I could think clearly. Saint City was big enough that the flux of Power would confuse my trail, but a half-decent Magi might be able to find me. After all, I was linked to a demon. "Lucas, do you know any other Magi that could be induced to talk?"

"Depends on what you want to talk about." He looked around again, a quick reptilian movement that made his lank hair swing. "Thought you said her debt was canceled."

"She gave me enough, Lucas. I just want to find out more. Another Magi might have a piece of the puzzle, might be able to tell me more about what I...am." *And tell me more about this little rebellion in Hell. I've thought all along that there were more players in this game than just Lucifer and Eve; it doesn't make sense otherwise.*

"You don't *know?*"

Imagine that. Lucas the Deathless, sounding shocked. "I don't know *all* of it. I've got some good guesses, I'm figuring everything out." I checked the hovertraffic again, rolled my shoulders back under the rig. Why was I so uneasy? It felt familiar, a half-remembered sensation of my skin crawling with little prickling teeth.

It's not a premonition. Then what is it?

"You're an idiot." Lucas wheezed out another laugh. His lank hair ruffled with the night breeze, and I was struck by the fact that the unscarred side of his face was actually not bad-looking. I'd been too terrified to see it before, but he was almost handsome in a pale, yellow, wolfish sort of way.

Well, except for the scars. And the slightly reptilian cast to his eyes. And his thin colorless lips.

If you only knew how much of an idiot I really am, Lucas. I kicked another Plasmalt Forty bottle. Someone had a taste for something a little more expensive than soymalt. It *must* be bad around here, for the streetdrones not to come through and collect the bottles. Paper trash rustled wetly in the uneasy wind. The graceful arcs of plasteel streetlamps cast sickly orange circles on the street. No streetside hover- traffic, and the sudden sense of a storm approaching. "*You* try shacking up with a demon and killing Santino. Then try hunting down a rabid Feeder and having your brains turned into a barrel of reactive mush. I'm *figuring it out,* Lucas. Don't fucking ride me, I'm not in the mood."

"What's got you in a twist, *chica?*" True to form; my snarl didn't even make a dent.

Leander's footsteps slowed. We caught up to him, but before Lucas could open his mouth I dropped my news. I had to tell him sooner or later.

"Gabe Spocarelli's dead. So's Eddie—Eddie Thornton. Something got them both hit—but before she was hit, Gabe got my promise to hunt down Eddie's killers. It's personal." *You may decide it has nothing to do with you, Lucas. If you do, we're going to part ways.*

I got a full five seconds of deathly silence before Lucas sighed. "Don't suppose it would have anything to do with the bounty hunters or the Mob, would it?"

"Or the Nichtvren or the werecain? Could be Lucifer playing with the mix again." For a moment chills danced along my skin, the Gauntlet heavy on my left wrist. I wondered if somewhere in Hell, the Devil heard me when I spoke his name.

The anger simmering in my belly rose to a fresh pitch. I should have never answered my door that rainy Monday morning. I should have never followed Japhrimel out of my house and into the subway.

You must trust me to do what you cannot, then. The thought of Japh somewhere out in my city, hunting Doreen's daughter despite anything he felt for me, made me glance over my shoulder and check the street. The whine of hover antigrav overhead made me want to look up. The silent street itself made me itch to get under cover. *I told him not to hunt Eve. I told him I couldn't let him hurt her. I warned him.*

"I hate to interrupt," Leander said quietly, "but I think we're being followed."

My thumb caressed the katana's guard. "This is personal, and it looks *big.* It's not what you two contracted for. You can take a vacation until I finish looking into—"

I didn't even get a chance to finish the sentence before a low sleek shape melded out of an alley on the west side of Fiske and loped down the street toward us. Lucas cursed, stepping away from me, a 60-watt plasgun appearing in his hand. Leander's jaw dropped, and my sword clicked free of the sheath, my right hand closing on the hilt as the shape shook itself. A pleased little squeal sliced the bleeding air, ending with a rib-shaking growl as the hellhound hunched its massive corded shoulders and looked straight at me.

Its eyes were glowing red coins. Heat smoked off its lithe, lethal body of living obsidian. It raised its head, sniffing like a dog scenting fresh meat. The cuff of metal on my left wrist suddenly ran with cold fire, blazing with lines and whorls of green flame over its smooth silver surface. And to top off the fun and games, Japhrimel's mark on my left shoulder crunched into painful life as I tasted copper.

"Leander," I said quietly, "get behind me. And for the sake of every god that ever was, when I tell you to, *run.*"

Lucas faded left, moving out into the street in a gentle arc to put himself between me and the thing. My right arm tensed, three inches of burning-blue steel leaping free of the scabbard. *Gonna have to drop the scabbard and go for a plasgun, Lucas shot the other hellhounds, and it stunned them.*

The thing seemed indisposed to attack, just crouched there watching us. Watching *me.* I finished drawing my sword, and the steel's heart turned white again, flaring with sharp pavement-drenching light. Runes of blue fire curled along the edges of the blade—a blessed weapon, but one that had its own strange ideas.

Yet another thing to add to my rapidly growing to-do list: go visit Jado and ask him about this sword.

Right after I visited Abra and started unraveling whatever had happened to Gabe. And hopefully before Japhrimel got back to find his agent tied up and me gone. I was getting very good at running away from him.

He was getting very good at finding me. Now *there* was an uncomfortable thought. Of course he was good at finding me; I carried his mark and was referred to in the singular.

Maybe he wouldn't find me too quickly this time, though. After all, I was on home ground. Even a few years away shouldn't have changed the boltholes and fluxpoints of the city *too* much. If there was one place on earth I felt capable of hiding in, it was Santiago City.

Hiding sounds like a good idea. Just as soon as we figure out what to do about this thing.

The hellhound paced forward a step. Two. Its eyes were still fixed on me, crimson coins in the shifting seaweed shadows. It hugged the opposite side of the street, and I began to feel a little...well, nervous. *Fine time to wish Japh was here, at least now I'm absolutely sure he has a vested interest in keeping me alive, not just something as fragile as caring about me. Always assuming, of course, that Shaunley's right and a Fallen demon suffers a mortal death if his* hedaira's *killed.*

The hellhound's slow, gelid growl rattled the air. Cool wind kissed my face, rich with the promise of rain.

Okay, I was a *lot* nervous. My sword dipped, instinctively taking the guard against attacks from below. What was the thing *doing?* A hellhound had never hesitated before. No, they'd just come straight for me.

A very nasty assumption began to surface under my conscious mind. I stepped forward, my sword ringing softly. Leander had turned to a stone, his aura flushed deep purple-red like a bruise. "Kel?" I whispered. "Velokel?"

The hellhound growled again, and launched itself at me.

Lucas shot four times, streaks of red plasbolt sheeting the air. I held my ground, dropping my scabbard and clasping the hilt in both hands, an instinctive decision that might cost me my life. But Lucas already had a plasgun, and he'd missed.

Four times.

"Run!" I barked, not looking to see if Leander did because the thing—dense heavy hot demon animal—crashed into me. It was appallingly quick, blurring with spooky demon speed, my sword chimed off claws as I spun aside, the mark on my shoulder lighting up with a fierce spike of pain. The cuff blazed green, a thin crackling whip of fire snaking out to lick at the hellhound, which let out a basso yowl of rage.

What the hell was that?

The swordhilt floated up, blade blurring, I made a low sound of effort as shining metal streaked down, sinking into the hellhound's haunch with a deadly low whistle. It coiled on itself, I gave ground, shuffling back. My entire world narrowed to the threat in front of me; streaks of blue fire painted the air as my sword wove a complicated pattern.

I had the oddest sensation—as if a rope attached to the cuff on my left wrist was jerking my arm around, quicker than I was meant to move. Didn't matter—I set my teeth as the hellhound came for me again, another pass that drove me back. It was trying to pin me against the buildings on either side of the street, a death sentence. I remembered how eerily fast the hellhounds were in Freetown New Prague and was vaguely surprised to still be alive. The world narrowed to one thing—the hellhound, its scraping scrabbling nails on pavement and my own harsh breathing, its low plasglass-rattling growl and my boots stamping as I smashed down with my blade and leapt like a cat, narrowly missing getting three glassy obsidian claws as long as my hand slicing into my midriff. I'd been eviscerated twice, had no desire to ever go there again.

It was too quick. I could barely hurl aside its claws and had to fade to the side as it looped impossibly, turning with a much smaller radius than something so big should be able to. Its spine crackled as it jerked fluidly, turning. Black smoking blood striped the beast, and it favored its left forepaw as it hunched and snarled at me, apparently chiding me for my lack of ability to die respectfully when it attacked me.

I snarled back, lips peeling from my teeth. Frustrated fury rose under my breastbone. I was happy to have the outlet—too happy, adrenaline overtaking good sense. I'd make a mistake, this thing was too quick for me to have a chance of winning the fight. Heart pounding, sweat sliding down my back and soaking into the waistband of my jeans—it took a lot of effort to make me sweat, nowadays.

It backed up, one slow fluid uncoordinated step at a time, growling all the while. I considered advancing, my ribs flaring with deep harsh breaths. My left leg burned, high on the thigh—had it gotten me? I honestly couldn't remember.

Darkness breathed between streetlights. Fiske Avenue was utterly still. My aura pulled close, demon shields pulsing, my rings spitting golden sparks. The mark on my shoulder had settled into a slow steady burn, as if flesh had been partly torn away but not yet started to bleed. The wristcuff squeezed mercilessly, I almost heard small bones in my wrist splintering. A ragged *huff* of breath left my lungs; I tried frantically to think of something *else* to do. Throwing a rune-spell or two at it, or a tracker, would probably not work—I'd tried a tracker on an imp once, and gotten a head-ringing case of backlash for my trouble. Japhrimel had made the other hellhound rot with a word in the demon language, but he had also refused to teach me any of his native tongue.

A plasbolt raked in from the side, splashing on the creature's hide. It shook its head, stunned, and I threw myself back as Leander and Lucas, both firing, yelled something shapeless.

The hellhound thudded to the ground, its hide smoking.

I looked up. Leander was white-faced, staring at me like I'd grown a new set of kobolding arms. Lucas's upper lip curled. He looked grimly pleased, yellow eyes blazing.

I tried not to gasp, failed miserably. My heart raced, thudding as if it intended to fling itself out through my ribs and dance a few night-club kicks on the pavement of Fiske Avenue. Sweat dripped, sting-ing, in my eyes. "We'd better...get out...of here."

"You think it's dead?" Lucas kept his gun trained on the loose lump of hide and shadow. I saw no flicker of movement, was unconvinced.

"No. Probably just stunned. Come *on,* let's *go!*" I regained my breath with an effort, Lucas tossed me my scabbard. My hand flashed, caught it, the cuff was back to dull silver on my wrist. I flipped my hand palm-up, palm-down; there was no space in the Gauntlet any-more. *Dammit, how did that happen?* It was a solid band of metal welded to my wrist above my datband, and its sudden chill was enough to cause a swift flash of pain through my temples. *Not going to think about that right now. It just helped save my life, good enough, let's go! "Anubis et'her ka,* let's not stand around!"

We left the stunned hellhound lying slumped in the middle of the street, and I had the uncharacteristic urge to glance over my shoulder all the way to Abra's. I even *did* glance back once or twice, unsure of what I expected to see—another low fluid hellhound shape, or a pair of green eyes and a long black coat.

It's anyone's guess which would have scared me more.

CHAPTER 15

This part of the Tank District had grown even more forlorn. Half the streetlamps on Klondel were dead and dark, either broken or fallen out of service. From the rooftop of the row of buildings Abra's pawnshop was in, the darkened streetlights looked like spaces left by broken teeth. A flock of unregistered hookers milled in dark doorways, and hovers with privacytint and magcoding crawled streetside, cruising the strip. I smelled sour human sweat, decay, synth-hash and the salt-sweet odor of Clormen-13.

Chill.

Chill always raises my hackles. Chillfreaks in Saint City seem to smell worse than anywhere in the world. Maybe it's the radioactive cold of the city's Power well. Maybe it's just the rain giving everything a musty smell. I hate Chill anyway; the drug is instantly addictive and a blight upon the urban landscape. I've lost good friends to Chill and Chill junkies, starting with my foster-father Lewis and continuing down the years in successive waves. Each time a new flood of Chill hits the street someone—or several someones—dies.

Leander came through the shadows, flitting down the street as if trying to stay unremarked. He did a good job, showing just enough of a flicker of movement to make an onlooker believe he wanted to stay unseen.

"Let's go in," Lucas wheeze-whispered in my ear. He stood by the hatch, I melted away from the low wall sheltering Abra's roof. "After you, *chica*."

I jammed my sword into the loop on my belt and dropped into the dark hole, negotiating the slick iron ladder with little trouble. It took my weight easily, something I was glad of. Denser muscle and bone gave me more strength, but also made me a little too heavy to trust sometimes-rickety human construction. My left leg throbbed, my jeans flopping loosely. Black demon blood had coated the slice from the hellhound's claws and healed it, but I still moved gingerly.

Lucas followed. I heard the whine of an unholstered plasrifle as my feet touched dusty wood floor.

"Dammit, woman," Lucas rasped. "Put that thing away!"

"Sorry." Abra didn't sound sorry at all. She rarely did.

I turned slowly, keeping my hands away from weapons. The attic was low and dusty, the roofhatch sealed and magshielded now, and I felt the crackle of magickal shields springing back into place. Abra had been expecting us.

My nostrils flared, demon-acute eyes piercing the dimness with little trouble.

She looked just the same.

Abracadabra had long, dark, curly hair and liquid dark eyes, a nondescript triangular face with a pointed chin. A blue and silver caftan fell to her slim ankles, sandaled brown feet met the floor but rested only lightly. Large golden hoops dangled in her ears, peeking out from under her hair.

The shop's smell—beef stew with chilies, dust, human pain— was the same. But Abra, of course, didn't smell human. She smelled like sticky dry silk and short bristly hairs, a smell that rubbed me the wrong way. Japhrimel hadn't liked her, and if his instinctive response was anything like mine I could see why. But I'd never had any trouble dealing with her while I was human. Even afterward, running infrequent messages between her and Jado, I never had cause to complain. She was always the same, mind-numbingly cautious and looking to drive a hard bargain. She never left her pawnshop, and I had amused myself several times by trying to deduce exactly which paranormal species she was.

The Spider of Saint City blinked her long lashes at me. "Valentine. Might have known. You're trouble all over."

Oh, if you only knew. "It's not my fault I'm a popular girl, Abra. How are you?"

Her lip curled. "Be a lot better if Nichtvren and 'cain weren't showing up at my door. Where's the demon?"

So she knew Japhrimel was in town, and connected to me. Sometimes I wondered how much she knew that she didn't tell. "I left him at home tatting lace. And you *like* being in the thick of things; you get all your information that way."

Abra tilted her head. "The Necromance is here. Your idea?"

"Lucas's." I moved aside as Lucas leapt down, landing cat-silent. "Are you sure you trust him unattended?"

"What, like he'll steal from me?" A mirthless little-girl giggle, she made a complicated parade-drill movement, ending up with the plasrifle slung over her shoulder like an old-time bandido. "Come on down, I'll make tea. This is a *complex* situation."

"You better believe it. Abra, Gabe Spocarelli's dead. So's Eddie Thornton. And I'm hunting their killers." Dust stirred in the air.

Silence. Finally, Abra sighed. "Come on down." Was it my imagination, or did she sound weary? "You're not going to like this."

Abracadabra Pawnshop We Make Miracles Happen was stenciled on the front window with tired gold paint, and the windows were dark with privacy-tint. That was a new trick, Abra had never been the tinted type before. Racks of merchandise stood neatly on the wood floor, slicboards and guitars hung up behind the glassed-in counter that sparkled dustily with jewelry. Her stock did seem to rotate fairly frequently, but I'd never seen anyone come into Abra's to buy anything physical.

No, we come to the Spider of Saint City for *information.*

There was a rack of the new, hot Amberjion pleather jackets, with shoulderpads up to the ear; a display of antique chronographs stood in a plasilica cube on one counter. Otherwise, it looked just the same as it always had.

Nice to have a friend that doesn't age.

Leander leaned hipshot against the counter, studying a display of necklaces. His eyes flicked every so often to the door, and his hand rested on his swordhilt. "Any eyes?" I asked.

"Two. A 'cain two alleys up, and someone right across the street." He shrugged. "I made sure both of them saw me." His dark eyes were alive; he was enjoying himself.

Not too much, I hope. I sighed, rubbing at my eyes with one shaking hand. I'd just fought off a hellhound.

A *hellhound.* Japhrimel had told me to run if I ever saw one; they had been used to hunt *hedaira* in the time of the first *A'nankhimel,* the Fallen Lucifer had destroyed because one of them might possibly breed and spawn an Androgyne, a demon capable of reproducing.

Like Lucifer himself. Like Eve.

Now I had more of the story verified. Temples and priestesses, and the demons who traded a piece of their power and got something in return.

Japh bargained to get a demon's Power back—he's different now. And so am I, if I share some measure of that Power.

I shivered, and Abra handed me a screaming-orange pottery mug. She looked a lot more comfortable perched behind the counter in her habitual space. "Here. Tea." By far the most civil she'd ever been. "You and Spocarelli were tight, weren't you." It wasn't a question.

Lucas took up a position on the far side of the room, settling between a rack of slicboards and a wooden box holding different-sized pairs of combat boots. His yellow eyes slitted but I wasn't fooled, he didn't look tired at all. Despite the floppy blood-crusty rip in his shirt, he looked very alert indeed. We matched, both of us bloody and air-dried.

I was beginning to believe I was still alive. The mark on my shoulder remained curiously numb. Was Japhrimel tracking me?

I hope so. This is getting ridiculous. I nodded, blew across the top of the mug to cool the liquid. "Way tight. Someone pumped Eddie full of enough projectile lead to trade him in at the metalyard, they did the same to Gabe in her own backyard." I didn't mention Gabe's daughter. One thing at a time. My tone was flat, terribly ironic through the lump in my throat. "I promised Gabe I'd take out Eddie's killers. He was working on something, I guess."

"I know. I got a visit from a Shaman—Annette Cameron. Works at that clinic on Fortieth, a *sedayeen* commune attached to a Chill rehab." Abra's lip curled.

"There's no rehab for Clorman-13," I muttered habitually. "Okay."

Abra didn't respond. Everyone knows how I feel about Chill. "Seems Eddie was working with the *sedayeen* out there. You might want to try it. Anyway, Annette was anxious to find you."

"Just like everyone else." *I'm just the most popular girl around nowadays. Even demons want a piece of me.*

"Yeah." Abra reached slowly beneath the counter and drew out a white envelope with a heavy, old-fashioned blob of wax sealing it. "And a Nichtvren came, with this. Said to give it to you."

I broke the seal without looking and tore out a piece of heavy hand-made linen paper that felt rich and perfumed against my fingertips. The dusty, deliciously wicked smell of Nichtvren clung to the paper.

It was a very brief note.

Miss Valentine, I have information for you. Come to the nest at your convenience; I'm not hard to find.

It was signed **Selene**. The consort of the Nichtvren Master of Saint City, the prime paranormal Power. Nikolai.

One scary son of a bitch.

"Wonderful," I muttered. "The suckheads love me."

"If they love you, the 'cain must hate you. There's a contract going around, two hundred thou for your delivery, alive even if messed up, to a buyer on the East Side. Bounty hunters, werecain, and mercs are all jumping at the bait." Abra's jaw set, her caramel skin tight over her bones. "I don't have to tell you what it's costing me to keep quiet."

I tucked the note in a pocket, picked up my mug, and took a cautious sip. Vanilla-spiked tea, very sweet, oddly calming. "And here I thought we were friends." *Bounty hunters?* "If bounty hunters are after me, there must be a claim registered with the Hegemony 'net."

Abra shrugged. "Not necessarily, if they want to keep it quiet.

There was also some spliced son of a bitch from Pico-PhizePharm, name of Massadie." Her gold earrings quivered as she shook her head. "Threw money at me and acted like he was going to pay me more if I dug up anything on you. Stupid. But what you should be worried about is the Mob. They've got some serious hard-on for you. If I didn't have such a good working relationship with the Tanner Family they might have tried to torch my shop."

Tanner Family? They must be new. "What about the Chery Family?" There was no love lost between me and the Mob, but if I could play one Family off against another I might be able to continue on my way unmolested.

Abra made a short snorting noise of disapproval. "Chery's been eradicated, along with every other major player. Tanner's the only game in town."

When did that happen? Gods, I'm out of touch. "Great."

"For their profit margins, yeah. Not so good for the rest of us."

I nodded. "Thank you, Abra. Now give me the real dirt."

The ensuing silence was so long I set the mug down and let my eyes meet hers. Her long dusky finger lay alongside her long, slim nose. Her hair was glossy and her cheeks slightly pink. Abra looked plump, well-fed. Business must have been good lately.

"I hate to say it, Danny, but what are you going to pay me?" Her eyes were dark and velvety, fixed on mine, and I saw a sparkle deep inside them. The sparkle off bloody bits of metal as a survivor picked through the battlefield, dispatching the wounded and picking pockets.

Picking pockets? Like Gabe's pockets, soaked with blood and holding a holostill of a toddler with merry eyes?

I don't even remember moving. The next thing I knew, I had Abra against the wall behind her counter, my left hand around her throat and her feet dangling as she tore at my fingers with her slim brown hands. She gagged, my aura turned hard and hot, and I heard Leander swear. Lucas blurted something shapeless that ended with, *"— get it, she's fuckin' crazy, back off!"*

I *squeezed.* Abra's dark eyes bugged, she made a thick strangled noise. The cuff on my left wrist rang softly, and so did my sword.

I was past caring.

"You listen to me," I said, very softly. *I sound like Japhrimel.* A horrible nasty laugh rose inside of me, was squashed, and died away. "I like you, Abra. Any other hunt I'd pay you anything your little heart desired. But not now." My tone didn't reach above an even whisper, a Necromance's usual voice. The wall shivered behind her, plasglass display cases and windows creaking and groaning as the mark on my shoulder lit with a fierce, pleasant pain. I felt as if I stood in the center of a humming vortex of magick, as if a Major Work had been triggered and was gathering itself to leap through time and space to work my Will, undeniable and absolute. "I don't care who's after me. I don't care who would pay you how much for jackshit. *This is personal.* Whoever killed Gabe and Eddie is going *down.* You get in my way and I will go right *over* you. Clear?"

I eased up a little, and she hissed, her eyes lighting with inhuman fire.

"Clear?" I didn't shake her, but it was close. So close. I trembled with the urge, fire spilling through me from the mark on my shoulder. I'd actually *drawn on it,* pulled magickal force from the scar.

How the hell—I didn't know I could do that! But it made sense. I was Japhrimel's link to the human world, and the scar was the link between us. There was Power there for the taking—and I wasn't as wary as I should be about using it.

Any tool to get the job done, Danny.

"Clear," she rasped. Her eyelids flickered, and she'd gone chalky under her dusky skin. I dropped her. I'd never been behind the counter before, and was vaguely surprised to see that the floor here was just like the rest of the store—mellow dusty hardwood. Nothing special except a few weapons and shelves of paper-wrapped oddments waiting for different people. It was a little disappointing.

Abra rubbed her throat and darted me a venomous glance. "That wasn't necessary," she rasped.

I felt suddenly sick under the bald edge of rage. I'd been held against a wall and throttled, I knew what it felt like. Why had I done it to Abra, of all people?

The vision of Gabe, lying broken and dead, rose in front of me again. *That's why. Because you were too late to save her, you slept in. Maybe because of Japhrimel, maybe not. It doesn't matter. Now the only thing left is revenge.*

If I was going to go for revenge, I might as well go all the way. Which brought up an interesting question: would I be able to stop when I killed whoever had slaughtered Eddie and Gabe? I might as well declare open war on Japhrimel for going after Eve—and pursue revenge on Lucifer himself for the mess he'd made of my life.

I realized with a kind of horror that I had no real problem with that. It was only a question of *how.* Access to whatever Power I could draw through the scar was in the asset column, but my own chill rational consideration of ways and means frightened me. *When did I get so cold? Something's very wrong with me.*

"Let's take it from the top." My voice sounded just the same— flat, whispering, and sharp as a razor drawn over numb skin. The Gauntlet chilled, sending a wave of cold up my arm, pushed back by the heat of the scar. "In great detail, Abra."

Oh, gods above. I don't sound like Japhrimel.

I sound like Lucas.

CHAPTER 16

The tea had turned to cold swill, but I finished it anyway and dropped the last of my bankroll on Abra's counter. She could tell me precious little—just that a biotech company was somehow tied up in Eddie's work, perhaps bankrolling it; someone wanted me dead; the Mob wanted me brought in; the Nichtvren wanted to see me, and the werecain—who knew what they wanted? Revenge, maybe, I'd killed a couple 'cain awhile ago during the hunt for Miro-vitch. They have long memories.

Or maybe it was something else.

In any case, I owed her, both for the information and for losing my temper.

She looked at me, rubbing her throat. "Put that away." She was still hoarse. "I don't work for you, Danny."

"I know you don't." The apology stuck in my throat. *I'm sorry, Abra. I shouldn't have done that.* I didn't touch the money, just left it there. Backed up two steps, my eyes not leaving hers.

She shrugged, the thin gold hoops shivering against her cheeks. "What are you going to do?"

I never thought I'd live to see Abracadabra ask me that with her eyes wide like a frightened child's. I looked away, toward the privacy-tinted windows. Out there in the streets were Mob freelanc-ers and assassins, corpclones and bounty hunters—not to mention werecain and Nichtvren—all waiting for a piece of me. Lucky me, dropping into the middle of a turf war and not even realizing it.

"First I'm going to go out your back door," I said tonelessly. "Then I'm going to start digging. I want you to put the word out, Abra. Tell everyone who comes to you that whoever hit Gabe and Eddie should put their estate in order. 'Cause when I get finished with them, even another Necromance isn't going to be able to bring them back." I paused. It wasn't for effect, but Abra's eyes widened.

"Danny...be careful." She folded her arms. "Although you're never careful, that's how you ended up smelling like a demon."

That reminded me. "You know of any Magi willing to let go of trade secrets for a price, Abra?"

"No." The gold hoops shivered as she shook her dark head, looking puzzled. "Closemouth bastards. Why?"

The mark on my left shoulder pulsed slightly, responding to the thought of Japhrimel. The almost-constant pulses of Power had settled into a rhythm, one I welcomed despite the way they made my skin crawl. *I drew on this mark, I could do it again. Will that tell Japhrimel where I am?* "I need to get some more answers about demons. And Fallen. And *hedaira.*"

Her jaw dropped. "You mean you—"

If one more person said *You mean you don't know?* I was going to scream. I knew enough, I just had to figure out how to make it work for me.

I headed for the stairs behind the *Employees Only* door. "I'm going out the back. Spread the word, Abra. Whoever hit Gabe and Eddie is dead, they just don't know it yet."

Lucas fell into step behind me.

"Valentine?" Leander sounded uncertain.

He's human, and he could have died back there facing down a hellhound. I'm too dangerous to hang out with, even for combat-trained psions. This is going to get real interesting really quickly. "Go home, Leander. Forget all about this." I ducked through the door, my boots moving soundlessly. "We're even."

"Valentine — *Valentine!* Dante!"

But I shut the door and threw the deadbolt, sure Abra would have a key and just as sure she wouldn't give it to him right away. She was never one to *give* anything, and Leander couldn't effectively threaten her. If he decided to go out the front door she'd delay him for a few minutes, long enough for Lucas and me to vanish.

Lucas matched me step for step. We made it up the stairs, he pushed in front of me and led me up the ladder to the attic in the top hall; we pulled it up after ourselves, hinges squeaking. "Which one we gonna do first?" he finally asked as I fitted the attic hatch back into its seating. He fiddled with the trapdoor leading to the roof.

"The werecain. He's the bigger mystery. We'll get him roped up and then you can chat with our other set of eyes. Meet me tomorrow at the corner of Trivisidiro and Fourth, at dusk. Have I thanked you lately, Lucas?"

"No need, your boyfriend fuckin' paid me." *Now* he sounded irritated. I shrugged, though he probably couldn't see it in the darkness of Abra's stuffy, dusty attic. Her house shields vibrated uneasily, then pulled back a little so we could slip out the back door. I wondered again just what she was, and felt shame rise behind my breastbone. Had I really half-strangled her against the wall?

Just like Lucifer. Just like a demon.

The thought spilled cold down my back. When you hunt monsters, you have to be a monster—but not too much of one.

Bounty hunting taught me as much.

How close to the edge of monster was I? "What did Japhrimel pay you, Lucas?"

"Enough that I'm going to see this through." Cold air sparkled through the trapdoor as he eased it open. "You comin', Valentine?"

I shoved my sword into the loop on my rig. "You better believe it."

We dropped on the werecain two alleys away. Literally dropped, I went over the edge of the roof soundlessly and landed cat-light, my main knives reversed along my forearms. Lucas actually landed *on* the 'cain, destroying the advantage of surprise, but the eight-foot-tall bundle of muscle and fur was so busy with him it gave me time to streak up through piles of stinking human refuse.

I willed myself to ignore the thunderous odor as I slashed at the 'cain's hamstrings. The alley was too narrow for swordwork and I didn't want to make the noise of plas or projectile guns. Flesh gave like water under my blade and my rings ran with golden sparks. The 'cain would have howled, but I leapt and dragged it back, my slim arm over its throat, strangling its protest. Hot copper stink of blood, the blade of my left-hand knife singing against my forearm, my right-hand blade pricking just under the 'cain's floating ribs on the left. I could work the knife in here and go for a kidney, if my knowledge of werecain anatomy was sound. It was in full huntform, and not *that* different from a human if you knew where to jab.

The amber rectangle on my right-hand second-finger ring sparked as I yanked on Power, deftly snapping invisible weights tight around the werecain's wrists and ankles. It would cost me — but better to be safe than sorry where an eight-foot bundle of lethal muscle and claw is concerned.

Besides, all the Power I would ever need sang through the demon mark on my shoulder. I didn't precisely *want* to use it — gods alone knew what the price would be — but if it came down to it, any tool at hand was all right by me. I'd deal with consequences later.

If there was a later.

In short order, Lucas had the 'cain trussed-up with a length of discarded plasilica fiberoptic grubbed up from the floor of the trash-strewn alley. *I'd almost suspect you've done this before, Lucas,* the lunatic voice of hilarity in the middle of an impossible situation caroled through my brain.

The Deathless vanished into the shadows at the alley's entrance, going to take care of the other pair of eyes. I promptly put both problems out of my mind.

I kept my arm across the cain's throat as it pitched and struggled, trying to throw me off. The advantage of almost-demon strength was a thin one — I was breathing hard by the time I got him wrestled to the ground, my knees braced against cold wet concrete that smelled like...well, garbage.

Mercifully, my nose shut off. Something about 'cain scent, it overloads nasal receptors in everyone other than swanhild and other werecain after a while.

Given how most of them reek, it's a goddamn blessing.

"Cooperate with me," I snarled in his ear, "or I'll use psi on you. I *mean* it."

The eight-foot hulk writhed one last time under me and went still. Harsh breathing echoed in my ears, I heard a low growl and choked up on its throat again.

Werecain don't like psions. As a species, they're generally vulnerable to psychic attack. Nichtvren and pre-Paranormal-Species-Act Magi used that vulnerability against them too many times. The big advantage werecain had was their longer lifespan — when human psions get old and weak 'cain can struggle free of psychic enslavement and make life difficult. They are also — mostly — pack animals. A pack of werecain can even take on solitary Master Nichtvren and give them a hard time. Enough 'cain in a pack spells bad luck even for a preternaturally powerful suckhead.

"Your choice." Fur rasped against my shirt and my chin. "Either you play nice or I'll clean the inside of your head out like a transport toilet flush. Just try me."

The 'cain snarled, struggled . . . and subsided.

I eased up a little on its throat. "Who you looking for, huh? Who you waiting for out here?"

"Necromance," he growled. Definitely male. I could have told by the genital ruff, but the light wasn't good enough to be staring at a werecain's crotch. Never mind that I could use demon sight, right now I was too busy making sure Wolf Boy didn't heave me off and snap his bonds, or shift shape and slither free. They tend to be pretty big as humans, six-four to six-eight; shifting to a smaller human form would let him get his hands out of the bonds. I was only an inch or so taller than I had been while human, topping out at five-six, I needed leverage to deal with him no matter which form he was in. A 'cain in human form can still shift a hand into claws and strike before you realize what's up. "Long dark hair, pretty tan. Smell like a goddamn bakery in heat. You."

"How sweet." My heart began to thud. I did probably smell like a bakery, thanks to the cinnamon sweetness of almost-demon. With the musk underneath it, it was probably extremely distinctive to a 'cain's sensitive nose. "Who were you going to deliver me to, furboy? Huh?"

"Agh—" He gurgled, I eased up a little. "You know I can't." His voice was choked not only by my arm across his trachea but also by a mouth not truly shaped for human speech. Too many sharp teeth and a wrong-sized tongue.

"Give it up, or I'll brainwipe you." To give the threat a little more credence, I extended the borders of my awareness and *pressed*, very gently, on the edges of his mind. Curiously unprotected, the cranial fire of his consciousness shivered under my touch like a dog begging to be stroked. It would be so *easy*, so very easy—and he was para-normal; his mind wasn't the open sewer of a normal human's.

I caught a breath of something—more musk, the smell of oranges, and heart-pumping fear. *Demon.*

This sparked a few more moments of furious struggling, ending up with me yanking back and choking until he went limp. Then I eased a little. *Wait a second, how did a demon get mixed up in this? Or is it just that anyone following my trail is going to come across demon stink?* "Names, furboy. I want *names*."

"Mob!" he half-barked. "I think he's Mob, he *acts* like Mob, corner of Fifth and Chesko, East Side. Paying two hundred thou for you. Fifty thou for information; where you are, who you visiting."

"A bargain, all things considered."

The werecain didn't see the humor in it. I suddenly longed for Japhrimel. He'd get the joke, it was just the kind of thing *he* might have said. Another few seconds of furious struggle, and the 'cain began to whine a little, far back in his throat. The sharp stink flooded my nostrils again, my nasal receptors suddenly waking up. Garbage, wet fur, werecain—what a combo.

"Relax. I'm not going to brainwipe you, you've been a good boy. Spread the word: Dante Valentine's back in town, and she's on the warpath. Whoever knocked off Gabe Spocarelli is already dead. Got it?"

A growl was the only answer I received. I could have pistol-whipped him a few times to give myself enough room to get away, but that would have been too much. My arm loosened a little, he drew in a whooping breath, his flexible strong ribs heaving under me.

I was at the mouth of the alley before I realized it, my body moving too fast for me again. I still wasn't used to how damnably *quick* my demon reflexes were.

It was a good thing too, I heard scrabbling and a snarling roar behind me. *Time to move, time to move*—I almost wasted precious moments worrying about Lucas while I blurred through patches of streetlight shine, the wind making a soft sweet sound in my ears, combing my hair back. I was fairly sure I was fast enough to outrun a werecain—but it wasn't just the running I was worried about, it was breaking my trail. Werecain are *extremely* good trackers, and the only thing keeping them from putting psion bounty hunters out of business is the fact that criminal psions are generally unwilling to be brought in without exploiting a 'cain's psychic vulnerability. And normal criminals aren't averse to hiring out a little work from a psion to keep 'cain away. Not to mention the fact that the Hegemony only licenses 'cain to hunt down criminals among the other paranormal species.

Running. *He's not still behind me, he can't be, got to be sure....* Breathing coming hard and harsh, muscles burning. Burst out into the confusion of Klondel and Thirty-Eighth, streaking through the crowd and probably bowling over a few of them; I went for the darkest alley I could find and crouched in the garbage, shuddering and hyperventilating, the mark on my shoulder numb as if I'd been shot up with varocain. As I crouched there, my back against the damp brick wall of the alley, I silently berated myself.

He's not following you, a 'cain knows better than to follow a wary combat-trained psion. He's going to head straight to the East Side to sell his information, and this possibly-Mob connection is either going to pull up the stakes and vanish in a hell of a hurry or hire a hell of a lot of security posthaste. Probably the latter if he has to stay put to receive information and possibly your own sweet self trussed up like a Putchkin Yule turkey. You can't fight off every mercenary and paranormal in the city, Dante. You just can't.

Besides, what was the breath of demon I'd caught in the 'cain's memory? What if the people watching Abra's shop weren't there because of my search for Gabe's killer? Or what if only some of them were, and the rest were the hunters looking for Eve, or looking to snatch me because I was suddenly so goddamn important?

More important to the Prince of Hell than even he realized, Japhrimel had said.

Great. I have such a choice of enemies it's not even funny. I leaned my head back against the weeping brick. The smell of a demon rose around me, a cinnamon-laden filter to keep out the reek of human filth.

"I've got to steal a slicboard," I whispered.

CHAPTER 17

I massaged my numb shoulder while melding into the shadow of a large holly hedge, watching the intersection of Fifth and Chesko on the East Side of Saint City. My skin prickled with harsh hurtful awareness and my heart pounded a little too rapidly. The icy cuff of metal on my left wrist didn't help, taunting me with its dull dead surface.

This made only the second time I'd been on the east side of the river since boarding the transport to take me to the Academy. I suppressed a guilty start every time I realized where I was — and found, without any real surprise, that my hands were shaking a little. So I braced them with my sword in its scabbard, and settled down to watch. The slicboard I'd stolen—a nice sleek Chervoyg deck—leaned against the hedge next to me, hot-taped and magwired. I'd lifted it from a rack outside a yuppie club in the Tank District. More than likely some rich kid gone slumming would have to take a hover-cab home, I wouldn't have stolen a slic courier's deck.

I waited, my knuckles almost white as I clutched the scabbarded blade. I hoped I wasn't too late.

I couldn't even enjoy the fact that I'd ridden a slicboard again. It used to be after every Necromance job I'd take a slic up into the hoverlanes until the adrenaline hammered my heart and brain into believing I was *alive*. Now the rushing speed and sense of being balanced on a stair-rail, sliding down with knees loose and arms a little spread, was oddly diluted.

Maybe because I was on the East Side again. On the same side as Rigger Hall.

I looked back over my shoulder again, checking the empty street under its drench of streetlamp light. At any moment I might hear a soft sliding footstep, or catch a whiff of chalk, offal, and aftershave.

Stop it. Mirovitch is dead. You killed him. You scattered his ka and Japhrimel cremated Lourdes. He burned Rigger Hall to the ground, wiped that cursed place off the map. Just stop it. Stop.

A different set of memories rose. Japh touching my back gently, his fingers digging into cable-strung muscles as I sobbed and shook with the aftermath of Mirovitch's psychic rape tearing through my vulnerable head. My own hands clenched in fists, my wild thrashing when the flashbacks returned, Japhrimel catching my wrists in a gentle but inexorable grip, stopping me from beating my head against the wall or flinging myself into damage. The pulse beating in his throat as we lay in the darkness, his voice a thread of gold holding me to sanity.

I let out a soft breath. *I wish he was here.* It was a traitorous thought—would I be in this position if he hadn't maneuvered me from square to square in Lucifer's game? He'd been sneaking out while I was asleep, maybe hunting Eve, and keeping important information from me.

What choice did he have, Danny? Lucifer trapped him, just like he trapped you. Japh's doing what he has to do. You can't argue with his methods if they're keeping you alive. And who was it that just held

Abra up against the wall and scared the hell out of her? You're losing your moral high ground here.

I could have done with a little backup at the moment. Where *was* he?

A flicker of movement caught my eye. There, a quick feral flash, leaping over the fence of the mansion on the northwest side of the intersection.

Well, what do you know. Idiocy strikes again.

I eased myself out of the shadows—or I would have, if the air pressure hadn't changed and a faint shimmer coated the air beside me. I pressed back into the spiny greenness of the hedge, my right hand closing around my swordhilt—and the figure of a tall, slim, dirty-blond and blue-eyed holovid angel appeared, resolving out of bare air. One moment gone, the next *here,* Tiens closed his hand over mine, jamming the sword back into its scabbard. "*Tranquille, belle morte,*" he whispered, stretching his lips and showing his fangs. "Do not go in there. It is," and here he sniffed disdainfully, "a trap."

Nichtvren generally only Turn humans if they are either exceptionally pretty or exceptionally ruthless; I've never seen an ugly Nichtvren. Truth be told, I've barely seen *any* Nichtvren despite the mandatory Paranormal Anatomy and Interspecies Communication classes I'd taken. In the relatively short time I'd been an almost-demon, I'd met more Nichtvren than in my previous thirty-odd years combined.

Then again, Nichtvren don't like Necromances. What species that prizes immortality would like Death's children?

Tiens was a tall male with a shock of dirty-blond hair and a beautifully expressive masculine face, his eyes curiously flat with the cat-sheen of his nighthunting species. Below the shine, they were a pale blue. He had a slight flush along his cheekbones—he'd fed somewhere. He wore dusty black, a V-neck sweater and loose workman's pants, his feet closed in scarred and cracked boots; he looked just the same as he had in Freetown New Prague.

Though I'd begun to feel a little easier around Lucas, I was still *very* wary of a suckhead Hellesvront agent. Suckheads scare me more than demons, and a suckhead working for demons is enough to make my hand itch for my swordhilt.

He was right, the house at Fifth and Chesko was a trap. It didn't take much more than a few moments for the werecain to come back out. When he did he circled the block and plunged back over the wall again. If I'd just arrived—or been chasing him all along—I might have been fooled. Maybe my own blind panic had actually served me.

Tiens's warm fingers eased off my hand as he looked back over his shoulder, noting the werecain's re-disappearance with a slight smile as if at the antics of a not-too-bright child. *"Cretin."* The word was softened by an accent as ancient as South Merican. "Come. Here is not the place for you, *belle morte.*"

"I'm not going anywhere with you," I told him quietly, and he cocked his head, smiling. For some reason that smile chilled me more than a snarl would have—especially since his fangs were slightly extended, dimpling his exquisite lower lip just a little. His eyes lit up with cheerful good humor, as if it was a foregone conclusion that I *would,* indeed, go with him, once he found the proper way to explain to me I had no choice.

"An old friend wishes a word with you." His eyes passed down my body and back up again. His smile widened a trifle, appreciative; I shuddered. *Appreciation* is not what I want to see on the face of any Nichtvren. "Selene, the Prime's Consort."

"Where's Japhrimel?" *And just what "errand" did he send you on, suckhead? A Nichtvren working for demons, there's no reason for me to trust you any farther than I can throw you.*

"*M'sieu* should be with you." Tiens shrugged. "Since he is not, I will remain. We shall go swiftly. You are expected, *le chien* there was obviously meant to lure you. There are soldiers hidden behind the walls, with tranquilizer guns."

I examined him in the difficult light, demon eyes piercing shadows to show me his faint, charming smile. His eyes all but sparkled. Nichtvren eyes, capable of seeing in total blackness. He was at the top of the night-hunting food chain. While I was fairly sure I could handle individual werecain, Nichtvren—especially Masters—were something else entirely. The few suckheads I'd met since I'd become almost-demon were scary if only for the amount of Power they carried.

Let's face it, they were also old enough to make me feel like an idiot child. Too old to be strictly human anymore. If I survived, how long would it be before I was like them?

That was the scariest thing of all.

"You go in front of me." I shoved my sword in the loop on my rig and bent to pick up the slicboard. "Where I can see you." A few quick flicks of my fingers stripped the magwiring off, a press against the controlpad activated the home-return function. Then I dropped it. It would be picked up by the next maintenance bot and returned to its owner, a little worse for wear, maybe. I wasn't strictly a thief.

Not of something so paltry as a slicboard, anyway. The next thing I would steal would be a life.

My left arm felt cold and clumsy. The scar throbbed, holding back the chill from the Gauntlet. I wished I had time to figure out how to take the damn thing *off.*

He made a slight, pretty moue with his sculpted mouth. "You do not trust me?"

"I'm getting to the point where I don't trust *myself.* If you really don't know where Japhrimel is—"

"He should have been with you, *belle morte,* guarding his prize. If he has left your side, it is something *extraordinaire.*" Tiens took one graceful backward step, making a fluid gesture with his hands, expressing surprise and resignation all at once. The flat sheen of an alleycat's eyes at night closed over his blue eyes as he contemplated me, folding his arms. "I think we shall go slowly, for your sake."

I took a deep breath, struggling with irritation and the fresh urge to draw my sword. "Just tell me where the Nest is, and I'll go. You can do what you like."

"If I am to do as I please I shall accompany you, pretty one. A pleasant job in a world full of unpleasantness, *non?*"

And while you're keeping an eye on me you'll be hoping for Japh to show up. I gave up, and followed him. It wasn't worth a fight. Besides, I wanted to see Selene and Nikolai anyway.

CHAPTER 18

The Nest was downtown on Ninth, in a building that looked like a renovated block of apartments. It was incongruous in the middle of a parklike lawn, prime downtown realty treated like a suburban estate by a Nichtvren. Then again, Nikolai was the Prime of the City; he could afford it. For him to have a grandiose lair was expected.

Inside, the halls were dim and restful. I smelled lemon oil, beeswax, polish, and the delicious wicked perfume of Nichtvren. They smell so distinctly sweet, maybe it's the decaying blood. But there's also a hint of sinful dark chocolate, wine, and secret sex to them. My Paranormal Anatomy professor at the Academy had called them "the pimps of the night world" once, right before he was fired. I guess Doctor Tarridge had a bone to pick with Nichtvren.

Lots of people do.

The cloak of Power laid over the Nest was cold and prickling, full of defenses and the weight of a Master's will. My own shielding drew close, my numb shoulder prickling a warning.

I saw nobody but was sure we were watched. When Tiens swept open a pair of double mahogany doors and led me into a firelit hall floored in parquet worthy of the Renascence, I had to suppress the urge to applaud sardonically. My eyes were hot and grainy, my shoulders tight, and I was *hungry*. I hadn't noticed it before, but when the adrenaline faded I was reminded I hadn't eaten for a while. I needed the physical fuel—not like Japhrimel.

Will you stop thinking about him? He's fine, he can take care of himself. Besides, he left you with McKinley. He can't have been too worried about your well-being.

A tall broad-shouldered shape stood in front of the fire, his hands hanging loose and graceful at his sides. Selene, the Consort, was thrown down in a huge red-velvet wingback chair, one leg hooked over the arm, her head resting against the high back. She tensed and flowed to her feet as we approached, pulling down the hem of her black sweater with one graceful yank. "Valentine." She managed to sound happy and disapproving at once. "Thank you, Tiens."

He swept a courteous bow. All he needed was a feathered hat, like in the old Dumas holovids starring Bel Percy. "For you, *demoiselle,* anything."

Nikolai stirred. He was a tallish Nichtvren male, dark eyes under a soft shelf of dark hair and a face an Old Master might have painted—wide, generous mouth now compressed into a thin line, sculpted cheekbones, winged dark eyebrows. An angel's face, carved in old Renascence stone. Not as sexless or alien as a demon's face could be. "I suppose I have you to thank for this chaos, demonling." Catshine folded over his dark eyes.

One trashed hotel room qualifies as chaos? Does he know about Gabe? "Two of my friends have been murdered and there's a price on my head that shouldn't be there," I replied shortly. "If there's chaos it's not my fault. You promised to look after Gabe."

It hadn't quite been a promise, but he'd sent a credit disc she could use to get into his office building downtown if she was in trouble. And I'd been secure in the knowledge that Nikolai and Selene were looking after Gabe, after the whole Mirovitch thing. Nikolai didn't take it kindly when sexwitches were attacked; Selene had been one before she'd Turned. Whatever story was behind that, I didn't want to know. I only wanted to know why the Nichtvren hadn't stepped in to protect Gabe.

Nikolai inclined his head, and the air went cold and still. Selene moved forward between us.

"Let's not start like this. I asked Tiens to look for her." Her dark-blue eyes were eloquently wide, and far more human than his. "Hello, Dante. I'm sorry for your loss. We *were* watching over Gabriele Spocarelli. Whoever killed her and her husband—"

I almost choked. "Husband?" *Gabe married him? Wow. She didn't invite me to the wedding* or *tell me about her kid. Gods. What, did she think I'd refuse to come?* "Oh." I shook my head. "Go on. I'm sorry."

"We have troubles of our own." Nikolai's voice was clawed silk. "A *sedayeen* clinic under our protection has been firebombed. And there are demons in my city, causing damage and killing Magi. What do you know of *that,* demonling?"

Tiens whistled, a long low sound that sliced the tension in the air. The fire popped and crackled. *What are Nichtvren doing around open flame? I've seen them burn.* I discarded the question, shivering at the memory. My right hand itched for my sword.

Tiens said something low and fast, in Old Franje. Nikolai blinked, his attention shifting from me to the other Nichtvren. He replied in the same language, and Selene shook her head slightly at me, as if I was supposed to listen.

I should have learned a couple of languages instead of slogging through Magi shadowjournals.

I'd been studying shadowjournals and breaking code for years now. All useless, because I knew next to nothing about the Fallen. Nothing about *hedaira* except for what I'd figured out on my own— and what Anwen Carlyle had just told me. I'd have been better off spending my time studying Old Franje and Czechi. Or trying to figure out the language of demons.

The conversation lasted just over eight minutes, but when it was done Nikolai's eyes returned to me. "Well. It appears you are an innocent. I never thought to say that of a demon."

"I'm not demon," I said. "I'm *hedaira*." *But I barely even know what that means. I only know enough to get myself in trouble.*

Selene folded her arms. Every time she spoke or moved Nikolai paid attention to nothing else, the rumor was she was the only thing in the city he cared about. The way he looked at her, I could believe it. "Why don't you come with me, Dante? I have a few things to tell you."

"Selene." Nikolai's voice was soft, warning.

She shook her dark-blonde hair back, the gold threaded through her mane reflecting the ruddy firelight. If Tiens was pretty and Nikolai severely angelic, she was exquisite, every line expressly designed for maximum beauty. She looked almost unreal, especially since she had lost a little of the nervous energy I'd seen in her last time. Besides, she was fragrant even for a Nichtvren—a smell that reminded me of sexwitch musk. If she'd once *been* a sexwitch, that would explain it. "Loosen up, Nikolai."

"Remember our bargain."

I shivered. I'd heard that kind of thing before, and could only guess what sort of agreement could be reached between two Nichtvren. Especially a Prime and his Consort.

"I thought we'd gone beyond bargains." Her attention fixed on a point above my right shoulder, her back presented to him as her shoulders stiffened.

"You make it necessary, *milaya*. Not me." From where I was standing, I saw his face change, softening. He seemed to have forgotten Tiens and me, his eyes focused on Selene's back.

It felt vaguely voyeuristic, to watch his face as he looked at her, his mouth softening and his eyes speaking in a language I didn't need to be Nichtvren to understand. Whatever else happened between the Prime and Selene, he was in it hoverwash-deep over her. It was a very human look, and it made a lump rise in my throat.

She managed to sound disdainful and amused at once. "I don't force you into bargains, Nik. You're the one always trying to *bargain*. You'd think after a few hundred years you would learn it doesn't work."

He shrugged, a fluid inhuman movement she probably felt, even if she couldn't see it. "You are still here, are you not? I keep my promises."

"Good." She moved forward, turning on her heel when she reached me and threading her arm through mine. I twitched—it was my right arm, and if I needed to draw I'd have to shake her off. "And I keep mine. I'm going to help her. You can just sit and rot if you want."

"Selene—"

"No, Nik." Her jaw set.

"Selene—" Was that *pleading* in his voice? It was a unique experience, to hear a Nichtvren Master pleading.

Selene was having none of it. *"No."* Her voice made the pictures rattle on the wall, furniture groaning just a little under the weight of her Power.

"Lena." His voice turned soft, private. I wanted to look down at the floor to give them some privacy, couldn't move.

She tensed. "You don't *own* me, Nikolai. I stay because I *want* to. Do we need to have this discussion again?"

His shoulders slumped, he ran one stiff-fingered hand back through his dark hair. I think it was the only time I ever saw a Nichtvren look defeated. Tiens studied his boot toes, not-paying-attention *very* loudly for such a silent pose.

"Do not leave the nest, *milaya*. Not without me. Please."

So he thought she was going to come out to play with me? Was that it? *Thanks but no thanks.* It was ridiculous of me to be more frightened of suckheads than demons, but there it was.

"I'll think about it." She tugged on my arm. I had no choice but to follow. "Have fun, boys."

Nikolai's eyes rested on me for a long moment. I wasn't sure if he was going to blame me for whatever lovers' spat was happening between him and his Consort. I didn't care—all I wanted to do was pump her for information about Gabe and the *sedayeen* clinic. Eddie was hanging out with *sedayeen* right before he died; and a Shaman from that same clinic had come to Abra's trying to find me. And now the place had been bombed? Was it the same clinic? How many *sedayeen* clinics were at risk of being bombed in Saint City? It was vanishingly unlikely that it wasn't connected.

Well, great. At least I know where I'm going next.

Not to mention the deaths of a string of Magi and demons causing havoc. Nikolai assumed it had something to do with me, and I wasn't sure he was far wrong, no matter *what* Tiens had told him or how little I knew about it.

Selene all but dragged me out of the room and shut the door behind us, then let out a gusty sigh. "Come with me." She let go of my arm, indicating the hall with one graceful movement. "You don't know Franje."

I headed the way she pointed, she fell into step beside me. Our boots clicked against the flooring. "No."

"Tiens told Nik that the green-eyed Eldest is hunting a stray demon in this city, and you were being kept out of the fray for your own good. Nik asked if the Eldest was calling in the favor, and Teins replied there was no favor to be called in, but that the Eldest would be extremely displeased if you were not given some shelter, at least." She sounded grimly pleased with herself. "I don't think Nikolai realizes I've been using hypnotapes to teach myself languages. I *hate* it when he tries to talk to people around me."

I was surprised into a short bitter laugh. "You and me both. What demon is Japh hunting here?"

Her shrug was a marvel of fluidity. "I'm no Magi. Someone demon management wants captured alive, I'm told. That's all."

There was only one demon fitting that bill. Japhrimel *was* hunting Eve, here in Saint City.

And he expected to hide it from me. Even Tiens and Nikolai knew more about what was going on with the demons than I did. I was fairly sure the "green-eyed Eldest" didn't mean Lucifer. Anyway, Lucifer wouldn't want me sheltered. He would want me *dead;* especially if he figured out I'd met with Eve and was determined to help her.

I was beginning to wonder if he would get his wish—and beginning to wonder if there was anyplace on earth where someone didn't owe a demon a favor. "Which clinic?" I asked. Fortieth was a big street.

"Fortieth and Napier. Edge of the Tank District. I remember when that was empty lots, before the first transport well was excavated."

"How long have you been with Nikolai?" It was a rude question, but I was honestly curious—both about that and about why she seemed to have taken such a shine to me.

"Long enough to know he'll come looking for me soon to make sure I'm not doing anything 'rash.' I swear, he gets more paranoid every decade, it's a wonder he isn't suspicious of *breathing.*" She led me through dim, quiet halls, I saw a bust of a Roma emperor and a couple of other priceless artifacts. I was willing to bet she'd done the decorating, it didn't look overblown enough to be a really old Nichtvren nest. A couple of holovid-still mags were exclusively dedicated to paranormal homes; I'd glanced through one or two and come away with the idea that the older Nichtvren got, the more cluttered and tasteless their interiors became, crammed with valuables.

Selene paused in front of a double door made of oak and barred with iron. The shields on the room behind it were tough and spiky, no type of magick I'd ever seen before.

The mercenary in me was appalled—a totally new type of shielding? Gods, I was slipping. The trained Power-worker in me was fascinated. "Who did those?"

"Nikolai. And he hired a couple of Magi to do a few more layers. But don't worry, you're with me." She walked right up to the doors, the layers of energy shimmering and pulsing—then softening as they touched her. It was oddly intimate, even the Prime's defenses recognized her.

It reminded me of Japhrimel's aura closing around mine, and I swallowed as heat rose to my cheeks. The mark on my shoulder was *still* numb, my left arm cold. Not the cold prickling numbness of Japhrimel gone dormant—I remembered that feeling. This was something new. Was he closing me out? Maybe. I'd seen through his eyes before, when I touched the ropy scars with bare fingertips; was he doing something he didn't want me to see?

Or was the mark fading? No, the flushing pulses of Power still coiled along my skin at even intervals, and I'd drawn on the mark, pulling magickal energy through it. I'd given up wondering if flooding me with Power was something Japh was doing consciously. Maybe it was just the overspill from his renewed status as a full demon.

Fallen, with a demon's power. I shivered and followed Selene. "No offense, but why are you being so helpful?" The doors swung open. They looked heavy, even for her slim Nichtvren strength.

"Not many people visit Nikolai armed to the teeth. I was interested. You've got quite a reputation, you know." Her hair swung as she closed the doors behind us. "Then the Eldest visited us. Nice-looking man."

My jaw threatened to drop. "Japhrimel came here?"

"A few nights ago. He and Nikolai were talking in Putchkin Russe, very old Russe. I *still* can't get the hang of that language, but at least it's better than Politzhain. Politzhain is like talking through razor blades. Anyway, Nik was very quiet for a long time after the Eldest left. Still won't say a word about it. But I've still got the books, so...."

So Japh had come here our first night in town. Right after I'd visited Gabe, he'd left me with McKinley, and I'd been dead asleep. *Goddammit, Japh. How could you?*

I found myself in a long, high-ceilinged room full of dimness and a crawling breathless sense of evil. My right hand closed around my swordhilt; Selene held up both white hands, her sweater sleeves falling back and exposing delicate wrists, both scarred with old, white ridged tissue. *Nichtvren don't usually scar. Where are those from?* "Easy there, Valentine. It's just the items." She pitched the words deliberately low, deliberately soothing. She did have a beautiful voice, beautiful as the rest of her.

"Items?" There were glass display cases, some of them holding full bookshelves. A cold exhaled breath of something cruelly evil behind all that glass touched my skin, and I felt it struggle to open one yellow eye before retreating, watching balefully.

"Nikolai collects cursed objects. Says it's better for them to be out of the way." She dropped her hands. "There's something here you should have."

"You're going to give me a cursed object?" I made my hand unclench from the swordhilt. My fingers almost creaked. The Gauntlet's weight grew colder, a shiver jolting up my arm and stopping at the scar in the hollow of my shoulder. The sense of being watched lessened, but still was enough to keep me on edge.

"No. This is where he keeps the demonology books too. I've been studying since we last met. Besides, this is the one place his thralls don't come. We won't be overheard." She glanced over my shoulder at the door. "This way."

I followed her. There, on a high shelf, a spider-shaped idol made of obsidian shifted restlessly as I glanced at it. A venomously glowing yellow orb pulsed on a shelf underneath it. Off to my left, a vaguely hover-shaped thing sat draped in a dustcloth. A rusted bucket perched in a glass case, exhaling desperate sadness.

"*Sekhmet sa'es,*" I breathed. "He collects these? Doesn't he care about the curses?"

"He says he's cursed enough, what does one more matter? Regrettable pessimist, that man. I keep trying to get him to loosen up and have a little fun. Here we are." She stopped, brushed a tendril of dark-blonde hair out of her face. "Dante, there's something else Tiens said, right before I sent him out to find you."

We faced a cube of glass. Inside sat a three-foot-high shelf of leatherbound books. I looked for a hinge or a door, any way into the glass. "What? How are you going to—"

Her slender fist struck with enviable grace. I wouldn't have been surprised to hear a *kia*. Instead, she brushed the glass—*real* glass, not plasglass—from her hand. The entire case crumpled, shivering with a lovely tinkling sound.

"Tiens said the Eldest prizes your happiness and wants you kept unharmed. That's a big thing when it comes to demons."

Prizes my happiness? He's certainly not making me happy with this run-off-and-leave-me-alone business. But my heart gave a funny, melting little skip. "Oh, wow." I couldn't dredge up anything spectacular to say.

She knelt, her knees crunching on glass. Ran her finger along the bottom edge of books. "I was curious after our last meeting. Did some quiet asking around. You wouldn't believe what I paid for this, Esmerelda drives a hard bargain.... Here it is." A slim volume almost fell into her hands. "*Hedaraie Occasus Demonae.* The only copy in the world. It's rumored to be written by one of the last of the Fallen demons, back before they all died in some catastrophe or another. I can't translate it, but maybe you can."

She reached her feet in one smooth movement. My shields thickened reflexively against the danger in the air. Some of the things in here probably weren't asleep.

Some of the curses in here probably never slept.

"Do you know anything else?" My heart beat thinly in my throat. *I don't like the picture I'm beginning to get.*

"Just that it's hard to get anyone to talk about the Fallen. Demons don't like to, the Magi can't force them into talking, and Magi won't let a Nichtvren in on their secrets. And *nobody* knows what's going on with Magi dying and imps running around causing damage. Nikolai's fit to be tied." Her dark-blue eyes were amused. "I do know a few things, though. You're stronger than human, faster than human, and capable of using your Fallen's Power. You're his link to this world, if something happens to you...." She shook her head, the weight of her gold-streaked hair swinging.

"So I'm basically a hostage if any other demon gets hold of me." *And here I was thinking everyone was in love with my sweet disposition and charming smile.* "Great."

"I suppose so." Her eyes were shadowed, now. "I was a hostage once, Dante. It's not comfortable. If I could give you one piece of advice?"

Oh, go ahead. I can't stop you. "What?" I tried to sound gracious.

"Don't be too hard on your Fallen. He's . . . well, he was very worried about your safety, from what I heard before he and Nik switched to Russian." She held the book, swinging it gently, the edge of its cover bumping her hip. "Be kind to the Eldest. Do you know why demons Fall?"

If he was so damn worried, why did he leave me alone with McKinley? Be kind to him? *He lies to me, manipulates me—and you're saying to be kind?* "They don't talk about it." *He says it's love. If this is love, I'll take a sparring session.*

Her smile was wonderful, just a curve of her beautiful lips, her eyes turning inward. "They give up Hell for the love of a mortal. It makes them helpless, and if there's one thing a demon hates, it's helplessness."

"How did you—" *How long did it take you to find that out? Not as long as me, I'd bet. And demons aren't the only ones who hate being helpless.*

"I've twisted a few arms." Selene pressed the book into my hands. "Be careful with this. Now listen, you'd better get out of here. Go to the clinic on Fortieth and Napier. Ask for Mercy or Annette—they were working with your friend's husband. And for God's sake be careful, there's a price on your head. Nikolai and I will do all we can to keep the werecain and other paranormals off your back, but it's tricky. There's a lot of mercenaries in town, and we can't interfere too directly in a human affair *or* in anything involving demons. So don't trust *anyone.* If you need a safe place to sleep, go to the House of Love on—"

"Polyamour's?" I tried to keep the disbelief out of my voice. "She's mixed up in this?"

"No, she's not. Which is why she's safe. She also has something for you—but *after* you take care of your business." She paused. "I wish I could go with you. It's been ages since anything really exciting happened."

"Yeah, well." *I've been abandoned by my demon lover, hit with hovers and reaction fire, and strangled by the Devil—again. Not to mention chased by hellhounds and nearly duped by a dumbass were-*

cain. You can have the excitement, I'll take being bored. "It's not all it's cracked up to be."

Her elegant nose wrinkled. "I remember enough excitement to value boredom too. It's just wishful—" Selene cocked her head. "Oh, *lovely.* Here comes Nikolai. Hurry. Up the stairs there, go through the third door on the left. It's only a two-story drop, and that window has a malfunctioning security latch. I was saving it for the next time I go out dancing. One last thing, Dante: don't trust *anyone.* Including me. Demons are in town, and nobody's safe when they get involved."

Don't I know it. "Thank you," I managed. "You're honorable." *Polyamour has something for me? Of course.* Comprehension bloomed under my skin. I'd been stupid; not guessing it. *One less thing to worry about.*

She waved it away. "Go. I'll delay Nik and Tiens."

CHAPTER 19

The night was old and turning gray by the time I got to Fortieth and Napier. The streets were curiously hushed, even the Tank District; thin predawn drizzle dewed my hair with heaviness and made me acutely conscious of heat from my metabolism sending up tracers of steam from my skin.

My left shoulder was heavy and numb, my entire left arm cold. I almost slid my hand under my shirt to touch Japhrimel's mark. That fleeting contact would be enough for him to possibly track me, and I...missed him.

If there's one thing a demon hates, it's helplessness. Well, that made us about even, I hate being helpless too. But it was a huge stretch to think of Japhrimel at anyone's mercy, including mine. After all, he had no compunction about using superior strength to force me into being a good little obedient *hedaira.* Helpless? *Him?* Not bloody likely.

But still.

The only time I feel any peace is when you are safe, and I am near you.

Maybe the helplessness wasn't a physical thing.

He had actually grabbed Lucifer's hand and pushed the Devil *back*.

The Gauntlet rang softly, like a block of ice touched by a sonic cutter. I didn't want to think too much about that. It made my hands want to shake and my knees go a little softer than usual. Lucifer had intended to kill me, quite probably painfully. I was still looking at a very short lifespan without Japhrimel around to keep my skin whole, even with a demon artifact clapped on my wrist.

I took advantage of the shadows across the street from the Danae Clinic. Their windows were boarded up, a smell of scorched plasteel and plurifreeze drifting across the street. I inhaled deeply, my nose sorting out the different tangs, and extended a tendril of *awareness* toward the clinic.

I retreated as soon as my receptive consciousness touched the shields. Careful, heavy *sedayeen* and Shaman-laid shields, layers of energy pulsing and spiking. They had probably deflected most of the explosion, I caught no flavor of Power in the lingering echoes of the bomb. Just explosives, probably C19 or vaston. Which meant Mob work, most likely.

The tang of *sedayeen*—violets and white mallow—slid a galvanic thrill through my bones. I hadn't sought the company of a healer since Doreen's murder.

That thought made me shiver again, hearing my own harsh breath and feeling the claws tear through my human flesh again. Memory rose, swallowed me whole.

"Get down, Doreen! Get down!"

Crash of thunder. Moving, desperately, scrabbling…fingers scraping against the concrete, rolling to my feet, dodging the whine of bullets and plasbolts. Skidding to a stop just as he rose out of the dark, the razor glinting in one hand, his claws glittering on the other.

"Game over," he giggled, and the awful tearing in my side turned to a burning numbness as he slashed, I threw myself backward, not fast enough, not fast enough—

I exhaled. My fingers were under the collar of my shirt, but instead of the mark they were playing with Jace's necklace. It thrummed reassuringly under my touch, throbbing like a bad tooth implant.

I rubbed the knobbed end of a baculum as I watched the clinic. Small movements in the shadows warned me I wasn't the only one watching the place. I settled against the brick wall, feeling the bite of hunger under my ribs. The temptation to dig in my bag and fish out the book was almost overwhelming, but strictly controlled. I had no time for research now, I was on a hunt that would only get faster.

They're not going to open for a while. Go get some breakfast, Dante.

Not while there was someone else watching. Whoever-it-was was well hidden, blending into the landscape. The brick was rough and cold against my hair as I leaned even deeper into the wall, buttoned down tightly, almost invisible.

Selene was right. There were demons in Saint City, and things were getting unpredictable. The familiar mood of the cold pulsing heart of the city's Power well had changed a bit, spiced and spiked with the musksmell of demons. I've noticed it before—when a demon or two moves in, the whole city starts to smell.

Demons are, after all, credited with teaching humanity how to build cities. Yet another thing we can thank them for.

Go over it again, Dante.

Eddie had been working on something, and a biotech company was involved. He was murdered—and Gabe either wouldn't quit digging or knew something dangerous about what he was working on. So she was executed. The little bottles of granular stuff and the papers with Skinlin notations were either a decoy—or they were what he'd been killed for. And someone who had no trouble getting inside her shields had been willing to spend the time and effort to tear apart Gabe's house and go to the trouble of cleaning up psychic traces.

That made whatever I was carrying a hot property. Not to mention the file—had Gabe lifted it from the Saint City PD before it could be copied? Or were there more copies in a police station somewhere?

I had a few contacts on the police force from the days when I would take a turn doing apparitions to assist homicide investigations. Digging in the police department seemed the next logical choice after I found out whatever was at this clinic.

A quiet place to go through Eddie's file and the book Selene had given me would help. Two mysteries: what had killed my last two friends, and where the hell was Japhrimel? He'd seemed pretty insistent on not letting me out of his sight, and if I could be used to force him into joining Eve's rebellion—and now that Lucifer had made it clear I was living on borrowed time—it made no sense for him to leave me alone with McKinley.

Not to mention the added mystery of this treasure and the Key, whatever they were.

Footsteps. Someone approaching.

I faded even deeper into shadow. Listened, taking deep smooth breaths. Smelled a pleasant mix — the violets and white mallow of a *sedayeen* and the spiced honey of a Shaman.

My right hand closed around my swordhilt. I tensed.

They came into view, two women, neither carrying edged metal. Which usually means *helpless*. It always irks me to see a Shaman or Necromance without combat training — what good is being legally allowed and encouraged to carry weapons if you don't take advantage of it?

The irritation quickly turned to full-flowered anger as I noticed the skittering in the shadows of the alleys opposite me. I caught a glint of metal and heard the soft, definite snick of a projectile assault rifle's safety being eased off.

I was already moving.

Reverse grip on swordhilt, tear the blade up, wet gray stink of intestines slithering loose. I kicked the fifth one, a snapping side kick that smashed his ribs on one side and sent him hurtling back. The momentum of the kick brought me around in a neat half-turn, sword singing up and making a chiming noise as I blocked the downsweep of the mercenary with the machete.

They had good, corporate-laid shields. Some Magi had been paid to lay a concealment on them so their blaring normal minds wouldn't broadcast their presence to psionic victims. That alone told me they were up to no good — if they'd just been surveillance teams, they wouldn't have had both concealments *and* enough projectile-weaponry to start a new riot in the Tank District.

The fight was short, sharp, and vicious, ending with me flicking smoking human blood off my sword, Power flaring to clean the steel before it flickered back into its sheath. I grabbed the last one left alive — the merc whose ribs I'd shattered — and hauled him up, bone grinding in the mess of his chest.

He was maybe thirty, sweating under his streaky gray camopaint, in standard merc assassin gear — a rig like mine, black microfiber jumpsuit, various clinking weaponry. His body shuddered, eyes glazing, my rings popped a shower of golden sparks as I shook him.

"Don't you dare die on me," I snarled. "*Who sent you?* Give me a name and I'll ease your passing."

I heard a low choked sound from the mouth of the alley—the *sedayeen.*

I ignored it, shook the man again as he mumbled. "So help me Anubis, if you don't tell me now I'll rip the knowledge out of your soul once you've passed the Bridge."

I couldn't, of course—I could only have someone question him as I held an apparition, as long as that person was trained in the protocol of questioning the dead. You can get misleading answers if you don't phrase the questions right.

Just like with demons.

I couldn't rip the knowledge free of his soul—but he was normal. He probably didn't know that. I felt less guilty than I should have for even threatening it.

"P-P-Po—" The man choked on blood as he tried to scream. I shook him again, his six-foot frame like a doll's in my slim golden hands. My fingers tensed, driving my claws into his shoulders.

A hand closed over my shoulder, and I almost slashed before I realized it was the *sedayeen.* A familiar deep smooth sense of restful Power slid down my skin, clearing my head and washing away some of the cold fury.

"Let him go." A clear, soft, sweet, *young* voice. "I can tell you who sent them. They're Tanner Family goons."

Blood bubbled on the man's lips. His eyes widened frantically. I saw gold-touched stubble on his cheeks, a crooked front tooth, the fine fan of his eyebrows. He'd just taken a job, after all. He was just a mercenary.

What am I doing?

I let out a short guttural sound and freed my right hand, hooking my fingers; my claws extended as I made a quick sharp almost-backhand movement. Blood gushed free, but I'd already pushed him away. The arterial spray missed me, and in any case, he was bleeding so badly internally it wasn't like he had much blood pressure left.

I tore away from under the *sedayeen's* touch. Had I not noticed her approach or had she slipped under my magscan because she was a healer, and harmless? *Sedayeen* are incapable of harming anyone without horrific feedback, they are the swanhilds of the psionic world, helpless pacifists without the natural advantage of poisonous flesh 'hilds have. *Sedayeen* survived by attaching themselves to the more powerful in the paranormal or psionic world, and they were valuable enough to their protectors to avoid the near-extinction sex-witches had suffered in the chaos just after the Awakening.

She was dressed in a faded *PhenFighters* T-shirt and a pair of jeans, Silmari sandals on her small feet. Short spiked brown hair stood up from her well-modeled head, and a wide pair of muddy brown eyes met mine. She had a triangular face like most healers, a sharp chin and a cupid's-bow of a mouth. Her accreditation tat was the characteristic ankh of the *sedayeen,* this one with an additional short bar through the vertical line and a small pair of wings. She wore a hemp choker with turquoise beads, and looked only about sixteen or so. But then, *sedayeen* age well. It probably meant she was around thirty.

The Shaman, a taller woman with her blonde hair braided back in rows, stood at the mouth of the alley with her oak staff raised. Yellow ribbons knotted around the top of the staff fluttered as a slight morning breeze played with them. Her eyes were a fantastic shade of amber, probably genespliced. Her tat shifted uneasily on her left cheek, the spurred and clawed triquetra of a Billebonge-trained Shaman. She stood a little too tensely to be completely untrained for combat, her hand on the staff was steady and placed just so. I wondered why she had no sword. Shamans with combat training usually like steel.

Tanner Family. Why would the Mob want to kill a healer and a Shaman now? After filling a Skinlin and a Necromance with holes. Is it a Mob war on psions? I shook my right hand out, my claws retracting slowly. My breath came in harsh gasps, not because of effort.

I was gasping because I didn't want to stop. I wanted to *kill.* The seduction of bloodlust whispered under conscious thought, tempting me. It would be so *easy.*

They were, after all, only human.

Stop it, Danny. You're human too. You're too close to the edge. This is too personal, and you're going over the line. Calm down. The cold on my left arm retreated before the heat of bloodlust as I struggled to control myself.

"Annette Cameron," I husked. "I'm looking for Annette Cameron." *Please, Anubis. Give me a little help here. I don't think I'm quite safe right now.* Rage receded slowly, leaving behind a slow smoky feeling of strain.

I'm deconstructing. This is bad. Too much stress and too little rest, my psyche was beginning to fray at the edges.

The worst thing was, I wasn't sure I cared.

The *sedayeen* nodded. Her eyes were a little wide, I think I was too much for even a *sedayeen*'s calm at the moment. "That's Cam." She pointed at the Shaman. "I'm Mercy. Come inside."

"Do you know who I am?" I managed around the lump in my throat. My shoulder was still numb, but underneath the numbness a deep broad pain began to surface.

"You're Dante Valentine." The yellow-haired Shaman's hands shook only slightly, the ribbons atop her staff fluttering. "Eddie described you. He said that if anything ever happened to him, you were someone we could trust."

I'd forgotten what it was like to be around *sedayeen*. Inside the clinic—dark because the windows were boarded up and Mercy didn't turn the lights on—the sense of peace was palpable, stroking and calming even the most jagged of auras. The smell of violets wafted through the air; one of the peculiarities of psion noses is that violet scent doesn't shut off in our nasal receptors like in everyone else's. We're maybe the only humans who can smell violets for a long time.

Call us lucky.

The waiting room had chairs and a children's corner. The sight of brightly-colored plasticine made my heart leap into my throat. I tasted bile and looked away, shoving my sword into the loop on my rig. I didn't trust myself with edged metal right now. The reception desk didn't have an AI deck, I would bet they had a psion there to get an initial read on the patients during open hours. A good idea when dealing with Chillfreaks and human refuse in a free clinic.

A maintenance 'bot retreated as we came in, its red LED blinking. The air was dyed blue with calm, freighted with the smell of flowers and mallow. Mercy led me back through a pair of swinging doors and into a maze of examining rooms, offices, and private labs.

The Shaman—Cameron—kept giving me nervous little sidelong glances. I didn't blame her. I knew what my aura looked like—the trademark glitterlamp sparkles of a Necromance threaded with black diamond demon flames, the mark on my shoulder pulsing and staining through my shifting defenses and cloaks of energy. I tore through the psychic ether like the sound of a slicboard through a Ludder convention, not as loud as Japhrimel but unable to hide with little effort like some other psions could. I looked, in short, like trouble.

It was truth in advertising. I *felt* like trouble now.

"What was Eddie working on?" I asked, as Mercy touched a scanlock to the right of a smooth plasteel door. She actually flinched. *Great, I even scare* sedayeen. "Gabe didn't tell me."

"It's not what he was working on," the healer replied. "It's what he found, what he finished." The door *fwoosh*ed aside, white full-spectrum bulbs popping into life. The light speared my eyes before they adjusted, I found myself looking into a stripped-down, empty lab. "This is where he was working."

This isn't where he died. The lab he was in had different tiles on the floor.

Then I saw the counter under growlights. Blooming under the hot radiance of the lamps, their roots safe in hydropon bubbles, were Eddie's datura plants, blossoming and healthy. Each one of them had frilly double-trumpet flowers, purple and white. Datura, used for binding spells and painblockers, if I remembered right it used to be called crazyweed or jimsweed. Poisonous, and illegal for anyone but a registered Skinlin or *sedayeen* to propagate.

"Datura," I whispered. "What the hell did Eddie find?"

The door whooshed closed behind us, and I turned to face the Shaman and the *sedayeen*. The mark on my shoulder sent a tingle down my arm, a welcome relief from numb coldness. I restrained the urge to reach under my shirt and rub the ropes of scarring that made Japhrimel's name branded into my skin.

"Cam? You want to tell her?"

The Shaman shook her head, but she answered. She stank of a raw edge of fear under her spiked scent of magick, something I understood. I'd be afraid too if I was her. "I was working with Eddie. So was Mercy. We were looking for an alkaloid-based painblocker for Pico-PhizePharm." She took a deep breath, then met my gaze squarely. She had deep dark circles under her amber eyes. "What we found was a goddamn fail-safe cure for Chill."

CHAPTER 20

My jaw didn't drop, but it was close. "There *is* no cure for Chill." I sounded like the air had been punched out of me, again. I was getting to sound like that a lot lately.

Clormen-13 was instantly addictive, it was the nastiest drug on the market. The Hegemony police were constantly fighting a losing war, not only against Chill but against the violence that flowed in its wake. Chillfreaks will do literally *anything* for another hit, and the way the drug lowers inhibitions and stirs psychoses is bad news. Chillfreaks are like dusters; they don't feel pain or exhaustion. All they feel in the last stages of Chill addiction is the *need*.

Unlike hash, Chill is addictive for psions; it supposedly gives a high greater than jacking in and riding a Greater Work of magick. The only problem is, it eats away at a psion's shields and control of Power, consuming from the inside. A psion gone Chillfreak is lethal if you aren't careful, not only for the absolute lack of any inhibition but also because they can explode on a psionic level, the magickal equivalent of walking thermonuclear bombs.

The large broad leaves of the plants stirred innocently. They looked healthy for having been dug up recently. Eddie was—*had been*—one hell of a Skinlin. "No cure," I repeated slowly. "That's why it's so profit—oh. *Oh.*"

That's why it was so fucking *profitable,* once you got someone hooked you could take them for everything they had and all they could steal. There was no cure for Chill, the detox process killed almost as surely as addiction did. A cure for Chill would be worth a lot of money—and would cut into the Mob's profit margin worldwide.

My heart gave a gigantic slamming leap. "Who knew? *Who?*" My voice stirred the plant leaves, rattled the beakers and equipment, made the tiles groan sharply.

"Nobody from Pico-Phize knew yet. Or at least, we didn't think they did. Massadie—our contact—might have stolen a sample. Eddie had five." Mercy crossed her arms over her shallow breasts. Now that we were under full-spectrum lights, I saw the shadows of sleeplessness teasing under her eyes and at the corners of her mouth. I didn't blame her a bit. *Sedayeen* aren't frightened of much—they have a sort of genetic disposition to an almost-maniacal calm, bolstered by their training. But even a healer would lose a little sleep over this kind of thing.

And let's not forget she was faced with a patently murderous part-demon. It was probably a wonder she wasn't running screaming in the street.

"He left four at the house," I said numbly. *Sekhmet sa'es. Holy fuck. A cure for fucking Chill.* Mercy made a restless movement—maybe my voice disturbed her. I licked my dry lips. "*Sekhmet sa'es,* do you have any idea...a cure. A cure for *Chill.*"

"Eddie found out that when he treated the datura alkaloids with a new technique, he got something that looked a little bit like Chill. So he ran some tests, refined it; couldn't believe what he had and brought it to me. We...there was no shortage of volunteers. We chose three. They walked out of here free of addiction. We subjected them to every marker and psiwave test. They were *clean.*" Mercy took a deep breath. "Eddie...he did what he had to do. He moved out of his house and into a shitty apartment on Fiske. He came in and mainlined a packet of Clormen-13. Then we locked him in an observation room until he started to suffer withdrawal. We gave him a hypo of the datura cure."

"You did *what?*" Plasglass beakers rang softly as the words hit a shrill high. I didn't sound very much like a whispering Necromance. The daturas rustled.

"He wouldn't let us say it was a cure until he'd done it himself and knew for sure. He took a hypo of the datura solution. Sixteen hours later, he was clean. All bloodlevels normal, no aura damage—*clean.*"

"No aura damage?" The thought of a cure for Chill made me feel distinctly woozy. *I've faced down Lucifer himself, why do my knees feel weak?*

Gods above, this...it could topple the Mob, it could clear the streets and free millions of addicts, stop 70 percent of inner-city crime.... *Gods. Gods above and below, Eddie, you came up with a cure for Chill? You beautiful, dirty, shaggy bastard. Gods above and below have mercy on you, Eddie. You deserve a frocking state-sponsored sainthood and federal buildings named after you.*

"None." Mercy said it slowly, and very distinctly. She had started to look a little more relaxed. "It's a cure, Valentine. A cure that works on psions and normals, a fail-safe cure for Chill. Eddie didn't want to tell anyone yet, but I'm almost positive Massadie found out."

No wonder the Mob was out for blood. A fail-safe detox for Chill would cut their profits by half if not more, Pico-Phize would be able to get Hegemony *and* Putchkin contracts galore as well as corner the market on other alkaloid painkillers, and other pharm companies would line up espionage agents around the block to get a sneaking peek at the technique. But if Massadie had stolen a sample, why would he be looking for me?

My brain began to work again. There was a certain ironic delight in carrying around a vial of one of the most valuable substances on earth at this point.

Then I remembered I'd given Japhrimel the other three.

Well, there was no safer place around for them. And that *still* left one vial unaccounted-for. Not to mention Gabe and Eddie's kid, in a safe place—for now.

I hoped like hell the hole Gabe had found was deep enough to hide her daughter. *One problem at a time, Danny. One goddamn problem at a time.* "Massadie. He's been leaving messages for me. Any idea why?"

The healer shrugged. "He's probably a little upset. His most profitable researcher's dead and it's appropriations time. We found a few alkaloids, but without our Skinlin and his notations it's hopeless. We'll lose funding and Jovan Massadie will slip another few steps down on the corporate ladder, losing the discovery that can pay for his retirement." Mercy's eyes lit with sudden hope. "Gabe said she was going to call you. Is she okay? And little Liana?"

Notations. The paper's notations, maybe a formula. I looked at the daturas, glowing with health. "Gabe's dead," I said harshly. "I don't know where the kid is, Gabe told me she was in a safe place. Right now I'm just concerned with icing the motherfuckers that did her parents." *Not to mention keeping the Devil off my ass and eluding my Fallen.* It was partly a lie, I did know where Gabe's daughter was, but until this was over nobody would hear it from me. *Liana. So that's her name.*

"Gabriele's *dead?*" The Shaman exchanged a long meaningful look with Mercy and made a sharp, controlled movement. It looked like pure frustration. Or was she reaching for a blade she wasn't carrying? "Son of a *bitch.*"

It jarred me then, a warning note. I stared at the healer, but she dropped her eyes. There was something going on here, something else.

Then again, I was probably only getting paranoid. This was a *sedayeen* and a fellow Shaman, Eddie's coworkers—and in just as much danger as Gabe had been.

"Do you two have anywhere you can go, get undercover?" I flipped the flap of my bag open, dug around inside. Metal clinked. I felt the hard leather edge of the book Selene had given me, the stiff but wilting paper of the murder file. I needed a quiet place to sit and do some reading. "And do you have a commnet for other Chill clinics?"

"Why?" The Shaman twirled her staff, ribbons floating on the air. Her aura, a spiked peppery glow, pulsed uneasily. Her eyebrows drew together, and she cast a meaningful look at Mercy's bowed head, as if warning me to be gentle for the healer's sake.

Irritation made my cheeks hot, made my right hand clench into a fist inside my bag. I met her amber eyes squarely. *Why? Because I fucking well said so, Shaman. If you'd taken the time to sweat a little more in combat practice, you might have been able to look after yourself and that healer. You might have even been able to give Eddie a little protection.* I swallowed, hard, burying the words. "Because I have something I want to spread around the clinic network, Shaman. Are you going to argue with me?"

The *sedayeen* stepped forward, partly to deflect me. "Let's just calm down." She spread her hands. "We can broadcast to the entire West Coast network from here, and they can send it worldwide. Is there something you want to send out?"

"You better believe it. Do you have someplace safe to go?" *Please don't tell me I'm going to have to find a safe place to stash them. I can't afford to be weighed down by a fucking healer and a Shaman too lazy to keep up on combat practice.*

The Shaman laughed. It was a bitter bark, her amber eyes hard and cool. "This *was* our safe place. What the hell *are* you?"

I'm hedaira. *That won't mean jackshit to you, though. I doubt I know half of what it means. Where are you, Japh? Hunting Eve?* My fingers drifted across the leatherbound edge again. It felt too fine-grained to be leather, really, but it didn't feel like plasilica or pleather either. *Maybe this will help—if I can translate it. Wonder what language it's in. Quit it, Danny. You have other chips to fry.* "For

right now, girls, I'm your guardian angel. I'm going to keep you alive."
I paused. "And out of the Tanner Family's greasy little hands."

"Why?" Cam's fingers flicked on her staff, her aura pulsing. If
she was combat-trained, why didn't she have sharp steel? And why
in the name of Anubis was she moving so carefully as if trying to
hide it? I felt the nagging sense of some loose end, some instrument
out of tune that was screwing up the whole holorchestra. Shook the
feeling away.

Because you're bloody well helpless and in over your heads,
that's why. I yanked the two sheets of paper with Eddie's careful
handwriting out of my bag. "Because it's the honorable thing to do.
Where's your commnet?"

"In the office. Cam, please, relax. Eddie said we could trust her."
The *sedayeen* sounded just like Doreen used to when she thought I
was being unreasonable — quiet, soothing, her tone suddenly as soft
as a pampered cat's fur. But her voice shook, and fear tinted the edges
of her shielding.

Gods, what a vote of nonconfidence.

Her soothing voice didn't soothe *me.* I wanted to hear someone
else, a dry ironic male tone just slightly inclined toward sarcasm. It
shook me to realize that the only person I felt like talking to right
now was Japhrimel. I wanted to hear what he'd have to say about
Eddie's jacking himself on Chill to test this cure. I wanted to lean my
head on his shoulder and feel his aura wrapping around mine, that
damnable sense of safety. I wanted the look that sometimes passed
between us, his eyes meeting mine and the feeling of being understood, of silent agreement.

Most of all I wanted him to calm me down, because I wasn't sure
I could do it myself. I was walking around with a skin full of rage
and vengeance, getting twitchy and deconstructing under the
pressure.

Anubis, please, help me. Stay my hand, give me strength. It wasn't
my usual prayer, but it was all I could come up with.

I held up the papers. "Can you tell me if this is a complete
formula?"

Cam stared. Her eyes finally widened, and she looked far more
relieved.

Mercy actually choked. "Where did you — that's Eddie's master-
sheet! A Skinlin would be able to decode and —"

"Great. Communit, girls. Let's go."

*   *   *

I didn't look while Mercy sent out the datafax to all the clinics, being busy peering out the window and scanning the street below. I *did* take the mastersheets back over her protests.

The office was cluttered with paper but otherwise neat, with the powerful smell of *sedayeen* filling the air. I was getting very tired of the smell of violets—I kept expecting to turn around and see Doreen, her eyebrows lifted just slightly and her hands clasped in front of her.

Besides, I was nervous. I felt like I was missing something crucial. The feeling irritated me—was it nerves, the result of being under stress for too long? Or was it my small precognitive talent, warning me of muddy water and danger?

The cold numbness spreading up my arm from the Gauntlet didn't help.

My bankroll was gone, and I had nobody handy to spring for a hotel room. Between them, Cam and Mercy had two hundred New Credits; it would be just barely enough. The mark on my shoulder prickled, the sensation growing to an intensity just short of pain and fading in steady waves. Was Japhrimel looking for me?

I hoped he was. He was my best bet for survival, and things were getting a little too deep for my taste.

Great, Danny. Go crying back to Japhrimel, you spineless wonder. You've got work to do and you're on your own. Even if Japh could help you, he probably wouldn't. He has his own problems, one of which you've got to make a whole lot worse for him if you can.

I hate it when that deep sarcastic voice shows up inside my head. It's usually right. Some new faction of demons was in the mix, and this treasure—and the Key. If Japhrimel couldn't be sure what I'd told Eve, no wonder he wasn't willing to give me more information. I was, at this point, a distinct liability to him, between being hostage material and a possible information-leak. He couldn't trust me not to go running off to Eve as soon as I could.

He's convinced Eve is going to lose, and he wants to be on the winning side. I had to shake my head, my hair tangling forward over my shoulders. *Stop looking at things from his side, dammit! You're furious with him, remember?*

True. But I wanted to see him just the same. Things were getting ridiculous. And even if he did manhandle me a bit, he'd certainly kept me alive in the face of distinct opposition from the Devil. That sort of thing will make a girl feel charitable, even toward a lying, manhandling demon.

I got us to the Vaccavine Hotel on the edge of the Tank District, sending the *sedayeen* in to buy the room and prodding the Shaman up the fire escape to meet her on the third floor. Once I got them both settled, I warded the walls—ignoring the Shaman's gasp and Mercy's open, wondering fear. I'd gotten so used to having access to almost-demon Power, it was a sobering experience to see even other psions acting like wide-eyed normals.

I was fairly sure we weren't followed, but I settled myself in the window with my sword across my knees anyway. Mercy took the bed and was blissfully asleep in moments, a skill I envied. She didn't seem old enough to have an accreditation tat, and I wondered about the relationship between the two women. They seemed very easy with each other.

That made me remember Doreen, and my heart twisted inside my chest.

The Shaman paced. From one end of the room to the other, she wore a line in the cheap red carpet. The ribbons on her staff made soft sweet sounds as she frowned at the floor. She didn't quite dare to scowl at me, but I got the feeling it was a close call.

I pulled Eddie's file out of my bag. It was beginning to look distinctly battered, the tough manila paper crinkling at the corners. "All right, Eustace Edward," I whispered. "Let's see what you have to tell me."

Seeing the first laseprint again was the same shock. Shattered glass and sticky-dry blood, Eddie's head smashed back too far for his neck to support. His hair was full of blood, and broken plasglass winked on his cheek. He didn't have his coat on. Jeans and the remains of a *RetroPhunk 4EVAH!* T-shirt. A winking gold chain around his neck that would probably dangle a marriage chip.

I turned the laseprint over, sourness filling my mouth. Glanced at the infosheet below, a standard Saint City copshop document. Name of victim, age, cause of death, scene specifics—

I read the address twice, then again. *What the hell?*

Eddie had been killed in a Pico-Phize lab downtown. And according to the file, the number-one suspect was one J. T. Massadie.

No way, Danny, I heard a familiar voice whisper in my right ear. It sounded a lot like Eddie's usual laconic growl. *If Gabe woulda had a clear lead to this guy she woulda given you his name.*

Lovely. I was dreaming about one dead man and hearing another while awake. Along with dating a demon, my life was getting too interesting even for *me,* and that was saying something. I wished I had time for some meditation, to clear out and organize my head.

I shifted on my chair, my sword singing softly inside its sheath. Massadie looked to benefit from the cure if Eddie could produce it. His position in the corporate ladder as well as his retirement account would be secure.

There's no way Massadie would have sanctioned this. Greed's a better proof of his innocence than a rock-solid alibi would be.

The investigating officer's name was Gilbert Pontside. And he was a normal. *That* was wrong—the murder of a psion was the jurisdiction of the Saint City Spook Squad. A Necromance or Shaman should have been assigned to the case, it was standard procedure. A Magi or Ceremonial might have taken the case if they had a Necromance partner.

The rules were clear. The murder of a psion had to be investigated by psions, not only because of the dangerousness of hunting psions or a normal dangerous enough to kill one, but because of the risk of Feeders—psychic vampires. Sometimes a dead psion's body, if left uncremated, could give rise to a Feeder's *ka.*

I knew enough about Feeders to shiver.

I wondered if Pontside was Gabe's friend. I wondered if he was on the Tanner Family make. And I most *especially* wondered if she'd opened her door to Pontside, or if her shields knew him and didn't react when he came to toss her house over.

It was a workable hypothesis. No wonder Massadie was trying to track me down. Was he on the Tanner Family payroll too, or just afraid for his own miserable life?

I was thinking this over when the hair on my nape stood straight up. My left shoulder prickled urgently, I glanced at my left wrist. The cuff was quiescent, no green light.

But it was so cold, its surface dead and dark. I wished I had the time and the means to cut the damn thing off my wrist.

I jammed the folder back into my bag and made it to my feet. "Get on the bed," I told the Shaman, my right hand curling around my swordhilt. My brain began to tick over likely avenues of attack, fire angles, and what I was going to do if it came down to defending them both.

"Were we followed?" Her throat moved as she swallowed audibly, her fantastic eyes widening. I would have bet she was closer to forty than anything else, but she looked as young as Mercy at that moment. My sword whispered free, the metal ringing softly as faint blue flame slid along the keen curved edge.

"Get on the fucking *bed!*" *Goddamn civilians.* My heart began to pound. How was I going to protect two helpless humans, take down a Mob family, and keep my head down with demons in town looking to take me hostage?

I didn't get another argument from her, because three light taps resounded on the flimsy door. I ghosted toward the door and to the side, behind the wall the room shared with a small bathroom. My sword lifted just as the shields and wards I'd laid on the room turned purple.

The deadbolt and maglock both clicked open, the hinges made a rough sound, and the edge of the door rasped along the cheap carpet. I glanced back—Cam stood next to the bed, her shoulders stiff. The edges of her oak staff glowed red with a Shaman's defensive spells, and her stance was the basic stave-against-unknown-threat.

So maybe she wasn't completely helpless. Was the soft act just another defense?

"Valentine," I heard a familiar voice from the door. "Stand down. It's a friend."

My heart thudded in my throat. *I don't think you're my friend, mister.*

Footsteps, deliberately loud. The door closed behind him. He halted in the hall. "Relax, milady. You need my help. I've got some really bad news."

I stepped out, the sword held slanting up, and faced McKinley.

He looked like hell, but he'd found a new set of black clothes and his shoulder appeared to be back in its socket. He slid a familiar-looking knife—mine, was that how he'd tracked me?—into a plasticine sheath and made it disappear. His face was bruised and swollen, his nose crooked, and his right hand looked like ground beef. But his black eyes traveled down and back up again, taking in the sword and my stance. He looked almost impressed despite himself.

His left hand, with its silvery metallic coating, raised a little. "Easy there, Valentine. You don't have time to kill me."

Says who? I'm a busy girl but I could probably fit you in.

And oh how satisfying it would be to take some of my rage out on him. Dangling from his silver-coated fingers was a silver chain. Swinging on the chain was a star sapphire that cried out to me in its own tongueless voice.

I'm getting pretty used to the sensation of being hit in the gut, I thought dimly. My left shoulder woke in one vivid flare of pain that threatened to drive me to my knees. I dug in, stayed upright. I was also getting very used to the sensation of my left shoulder being run through a meat grinder. At least that drove the numbness away, down my left arm.

Gee, Dante. It's sucking to be you lately.

"The Eldest has been taken," he said. "By the Twins."

"What are you talking about?" My voice cracked uselessly. "Taken? *Japhrimel?*"

"There were too many of them, and they ran him to ground while he was out drawing them off and away from you. Their next move is going to be to try to acquire you, and they're not the only ones." He offered the necklace. The sapphire swung gently, a spark of blue light caught in its depths. "There are other demons in town, at cross-purposes to both the Prince and the rebellion. It's crawling out there, I've got to get you out. We can catch a transport—"

"I'm not going anywhere," I said flatly. "I have business here. Who's got Japh?"

He swung the sapphire again. My eyes tracked it helplessly. "You don't get it," he said quietly. "He's the Eldest, they can't hold him for long. But if anyone gets their hands on you he's *helpless.* He has to do what they want. If *any* demon takes you we're all doomed."

Helpless. Selene used that word too. "Great speech." My sword didn't dip, blueflame runes twisting and coursing along the sharp edge. The steel's heart flamed white, responding to my sudden pounding heartbeat. "Too bad I'm not convinced."

My left hand dropped the scabbard and blurred toward a projectile gun. I eased the hammer back and leveled it at him. "I'll take all the cash you have, McKinley. You're probably carrying a fair bit. Cam, wake the healer up. Get her up *now.*"

"You're an idiot." McKinley's eyes were deadly glittering black, sharp pieces of jet. "I'm on your side. We have to get you to a transport, get you to a safe place. If another faction catches you and threatens to harm you, he *has* to do as they say. With all the demons in the city, you're going to be tagged sooner rather than later." He didn't smell like fear anymore; he smelled faintly like demon and even

more faintly like dust. Dry and inhuman. His shoulders hunched, he
didn't shift his weight but I knew he was ready to move.

I wondered just what exactly the Hellesvront agents were—not
for the last time, I might add. I wondered if I was quick enough to
take him.

Let's find out, Danny. "You don't listen very well, do you. I have
business to finish, and I'm not going anywh—" My shoulder
crunched with pain again, the world went gray, and things got confused for a second as I crouched instinctively, my swordhilt jabbing
forward as he came for me. A bullet whined and pinged before burying itself in the wall.

If he hadn't leapt at me I might have negotiated with him. As it
was, I was sick and fucking tired of being manhandled. The difference between Japh and McKinley was that the agent, while inhumanly fast, was just a shade slower than me; he couldn't easily
overmatch me the way Japh could. It was a major tactical error on the
agent's part to jump me. I happened to believe him about the danger I
was in, but I was fed up to the back teeth with demon-smelling men
pushing me around.

I came back to myself on top of a struggling McKinley, who was
in an armlock facedown on the floor. The cuff rang with fluid green
light, squeezing until I thought I heard bones grinding again. Strength
poured hot up my arm from the blazing metal, the cuff that had
locked itself around my wrist no longer cold. Would I have to cut my
hand off to get rid of it?

Well, ain't that handy. Get it, Danny? Handy?

I leaned down, my hair brushing his cheek. "Don't fuck with me
right now, sunshine. I'm a woman on the edge." I barely recognized
my own voice. My sword lay on the carpet, but I had the gun pressed
to his temple. He surged, struggling, I pushed every erg of demon
strength I possessed *down.* The floor groaned under cheap harsh red
carpet. "I *mean* it, you demonlicking sonofabitch. *Settle down!*"

*Or I swear, by everything I hold holy, I will not be responsible for
what happens.*

He finally quit thrashing. I was sweating, prickles of moisture
under my arms and at the small of my back. He was a handful,
and if the wristcuff hadn't squeezed again I would have lost him.
"Cam?"

"Here." She sounded grim but not panicked. *Thank the gods for
small favors.*

"Is Mercy up?" My voice made the holovid's base chatter on the clunky half-dresser.

"I'm awake. What's going on?" The *sedayeen,* unfortunately, sounded a little less than calm. Her voice shook, and the fear mixing with the smell of violets taunted my fraying control. What was it with psions smelling of fear that pushed me over the edge so badly?

Anubis, help me. Stay my hand, keep me calm.

"Cam, get all the fiberoptic cord you can from the holovid. Slice down the goddamn curtain-strings too. Mercy, get my sword back into the sheath and come over here. I need you to pick his pocket."

This was apparently open for discussion even though she'd awakened to find me holding down a strange man in our hotel room. "You're robbing him? Who is he?"

I glanced up, my fingers digging into his flesh. "He's bad news, baby. Just trust me and do what I fucking *tell* you."

Every item of furniture in the room that wasn't bolted down rattled. *Gods help me, I sound like Japhrimel.* I took a deep breath. *Trust me, do as I say, I know best.*

Except that I *did.* These two had no idea what was going on, and the fact that I hardly knew more didn't erase the primary fact that I was in charge, goddammit. I was their best bet of getting out of this mess alive, and in order to get them out I needed them to do what I told them.

Looks different from this side of the fence, doesn't it, Danny?

I told that voice to shut up and go away again.

"You're not listening." McKinley's voice was muffled, because I had his face smashed into the carpet. "If they catch you, Japhrimel will have to do anything they demand. He can't risk any harm to you. He *won't* risk any harm to you, he—"

I felt as if a great weight had fallen away from my shoulders. Life was about to get very fucking simple. "You tell Japhrimel this. I'm through being jerked around. This little holovid script won't work. I have had enough of manipulation, enough of games, and enough of demons. Consider this a datflash breakup."

He spluttered, but Cam knelt down cautiously and gagged him with a pillowcase, tying it behind his head. His eyes rolled up and he struggled, but between my strength and the Shaman's nimble fingers we soon had him trussed nice and tight.

Poor guy, he keeps getting tied up. I didn't really feel any sympathy at all, but the merry voice of unreason just kept going inside my head.

The healer handed me my sword. "You're really going to rob him?" She sounded faintly disapproving. I guess when you didn't hunt down bounties and have demons messing with your life you could be awful moral.

What are you doing, Danny?

It was a stupid question. I knew what I was doing—the only thing I *could* do, now. I was taking off my protective gear and slicboarding through Suicide Alley.

In other words, I had officially just gone over the edge.

"I can't access any funds without getting a whole lot of heat on my tail," I said shortly. *Since I don't think any bounty hunter after me will be stupid enough not to put a tag on my datband accessing any credits.* I scooped the sapphire from McKinley's rigid fingers, found a thick roll of cash in his back pocket. Stuffed both in my bag. "And I don't have time to plan how to get in and out of a bank without being caught. We can't hide or hunt for long without money, and I've got both of you to shelter too. Come on, that's not going to hold him for more than a few minutes." *If that. It's a pity, if I could trust him not to drag me off on a hover I could definitely use him as backup. I can't wait to hook back up with Lucas.*

His eyes rolled back in his head, showing the whites, and a low steamy hissing slid out from behind the gag. I felt a trickle of cold Power along my skin, like an ice-cube trailed in a lover's hand against fevered flesh. My rings roiled and spat in the charged air. "Time to go."

Mercifully, they didn't argue after that. I had the Shaman bring up the rear, and led them out of the room. Rage boiled just under my ribs. Japhrimel hadn't wanted the necklace in the first place, he'd given it to McKinley, of all people.

Of all the things that hurt, that was the one that seemed the sharpest pain. Maybe it was only because I was numb, confused, hungry, and hurt all at once.

How many demons were looking for me? What would they do if they found me? It sounded like I wasn't just leverage to be used against Japhrimel, there was something going on with this treasure and the Key....

Don't think about that. Focus on what you've got in front of you, Danny. Where can you hide these guys?

CHAPTER 21

Jado lived on a quiet tree-lined street in the University District, in an ancient house with an equally ancient retrofitted hot tub on the newly renovated deck. His garden was still immaculate, but the sand-raking around the rough black rocks in his meditation garden was newly redone. It was early in the day, and he had a class in session. I could tell by the *thwock* of stave against stave and his voice, cutting through the sharp noise with a general's battlefield authority.

"No think!" I heard him yell. "No think! *Move!* One, two, *kia!*"

A ragged chorus of *kia* filled the air. *Beginners,* I thought, working my boots off. The *sedayeen* leaned against the Shaman, obviously drained and exhausted, her cheeks reactive-pale and her eyes glittering.

The sharp bite of hunger under my ribs reminded me I had to get some rest and food soon myself. "This is a safe place. You should be okay here for a couple days. By then, this will probably be over one way or another. Wait here for a couple minutes." A pause, and I heard another solid barrage of wood meeting wood. It reminded me of a Nuevo Rio sparring-room, Eddie and Jace at staves while sunlight fell through windows onto *tatami* mats and Gabe stretched out, sweat gleaming on her pale skin.

Back when I'd been human. In my mind's eye I saw Japhrimel leaning against the wall, his hair ink-black, his coat swallowing the light.

And his eyes glowing green under straight eyebrows.

So he'd been trapped, and even McKinley admitted they couldn't hold him for very long. Talking about trapping Japhrimel was like talking about beating Vinnie Evarion at cards on the old *Vinnie, Video Sharp* holovid. It just didn't happen. He was just too old and smart. So he'd decided to go off on a solo expedition and leave me sleeping with McKinley, obviously expecting to be back before I woke up. And then what?

When we have finished with your Necromance friend, I will tell you everything you are ready to hear.

Maybe about the treasure, or would he tell me how helpless a demon felt after he Fell? That would have been nice, a little admission of need from him. A little human emotion.

For crying out loud, Dante, keep your mind on business. Japh's not your problem right now. If you don't keep moving, you'll drown. Barefoot but still wearing my coat, rig, and bag, I padded into the main space. There was a narrow strip of wood flooring before the mats started, I carefully arranged myself at the edge between "space" and "sparring space." Bowed respectfully, my sheathed sword lifted in my left hand, my right hand a fist.

Silence fell. Fifteen wide-eyed students in white *gi* and one nut-brown, leathery old man in orange robes looked up. The *ikebana* at the far end of the room under the *kanji-painted* scroll was a different red orchid. In any case, the rest of the room looked blissfully the same.

Helps to have a friend that doesn't age, doesn't it, Danny? This time it was Lucas Villalobos's whisper, painful in my ear. I was talking to myself in some awful strange voices lately. Occupational hazard of being a psion—sometimes the voices in your head are the people who matter most to you.

Or who scare you most.

Jado barked a command and his students went back to whacking at each other with more enthusiasm than skill. All normals, all probably rich kids. The fees their parents paid made it possible for Jado to combat-train psions with potential to become canny, deadly fighters almost for free. The last time I'd been here, there had been four empty spaces in the sword-racked room above, four of Jado's true students out in the world. There might have been more, he trained a lot of psions. But the four missing swords always made me feel good in a niggling sort of way.

Four swords gone. Five, now. But still four students. I wondered who the others were. Jado had refused payment after the first few classes; the normals he taught had subsidized me. For him, that was the equivalent of adopting me. He had some funny ideas about the student-teacher relationship.

So did I, as a matter of fact. If my social worker Lewis was the father of my childhood, Jado was the father of my adulthood, the only male I always felt like trusting. I could never have said that to him, of course...but it was still there, unspoken between us. He was my last resort—but also my best resort.

"Danyo-chan." He stood at the edge of the *tatami*. "It must be serious, *neh?*"

I didn't have time for politeness. All the same, I bowed correctly. "You're looking well, Jado-*sensei*."

"How can you tell?" But the corners of his eyes crinkled. His ears came up to sharp points above the dome of his skull. He smelled of a dry, deep, crumbling, scaled hole; a hot exhalation of cinders and meat charred so thoroughly it smelled like woodsmoke. It was, thankfully, not a *human* smell. "Is good to see you, my student."

"And you, *sensei*." I didn't have words to express how good it felt to see him. Jado didn't play games, he simply *taught,* directly and with the smack of a fist or the deadly whistle of a swordblade. Of all the men I knew, human or not, only Jado might have truly understood me. "I have two little things I need kept safe for me. And I want to ask you something."

His nostrils flared as he sniffed. "A healer and a *kami*-talker." His tone was reflective, easy. Behind him, staves whirled; students darted curious glances at me. "There have been inquiries made of you."

"I'm sorry." I didn't want to bring trouble to his door—but my list of living friends was getting really short. I needed his help.

He waved that away, tucked his hands in his robe. "Take them into kitchen and serve them tea, student. I will make certain you are undisturbed. My house is yours." A slight bow, only the briefest suggestion of a bending in his torso.

I echoed it, my left shoulder throbbing as I moved. I realized the right leg of my jeans was still crusted and flopping from my encounter with the hellhound. I was hardly inconspicuous. "Jado-*sensei?*" There would never be a better time to ask.

"Hai?" He still looked amused, his dark eyes lingering on my face. His bare feet were horny and callused, and barely seemed to move when he walked.

I lifted the sword a little, watched his eyes come to rest on it. He looked pleased, and my heart swelled with probably-inappropriate pride. It *mattered,* that Jado was pleased with me. "Did you give me a blade that can kill the Devil?"

"The sword kills nothing, Danyo-chan. It is *will,* kills your enemy." He made a small clucking sound, shaking his gleaming brown head. "Young, too young. Older, you would not ask silly question." He bowed again, waited for my answering bow, then whirled and bellowed at his class. *"No!* Thousand curses on your eyes, *no!* Fight! No curiosity, fight!"

I took two careful steps back, bowed to the sparring space, and exited into the hall. The Shaman and the healer looked at me strangely, and I found I was grinning like a holovid comic.

All things considered it was the best I could do. It was already afternoon, and I had a date with Lucas at dusk. I left Cam and Mercy with Jado, and had the relieved sensation that I could just forget about them for a while. If they weren't safe there, nowhere in Saint City would shelter them. And now that the Chill cure was circulating among the West Coast clinics, the Mob interest in killing a simple Shaman and *sedayeen* would hopefully lose some plascharge.

But not the business between me and the Tanner Family. That was just starting.

I plunged back into the dense urban wilderness of the city, just one face among many. It says something for city life nowadays that even a part-demon Necromance with a holovid face can pass unremarked on the streets.

I bought two six-packs of synthprotein shakes meant to keep heavily augmented bouncers up to weight and drank them all while I sat on a park bench in the lower city. The park had a nice view of the bay, a hard glitter under the afternoon sun breaking through gray clouds. Each empty can I chucked into a nearby botbin, hearing the whoosh of the crumpler as it swallowed.

When I was finished, I shook myself, got to my feet, and headed for the streets again.

Saint City pulsed under my feet, ringing with every step. I had about four hours to twilight, so I moved a little faster than a human would, slipping between normals. I passed a Shaman at the corner of Marx and Ninth, a thin blonde woman with sodaflo can-tabs tied to her staff. They tinkled and chittered as I passed, but she merely set her back against a wall and regarded the street, wide-eyed, her feet in a stance I recognized. Another combat-trained Shaman with no sword. Who knew there were so many of them around? Her eyes, dark as her hair was golden, narrowed as she watched me go by. Maybe she would recognize me from the hunt for Lourdes, when my face had been plastered all over the holovids.

Maybe not. That had been a long time ago, and my hair was down, tangling over my eyes.

That made me think of Cam, who was a puzzle. I was almost sure I'd caught her reaching for a hilt. But why would she leave any weapon at home while she was squiring a *sedayeen* around?

I made it to the Saint City South precinct house in half an hour. There I had my first stroke of luck in a long time. The man I wanted stood in the usual smoking-alcove near a botbin, curls of synth-hash smoke rising thinly around his gleaming bald head. He hunched his turtle shoulders and shook his head, his hands shaking a little. I judged it about half-past a desperately needed drink. His knee-length tan synthwool coat flapped desultorily in the faint breeze; the clouds scudded in earnest over the sun.

Thank you, Anubis, I prayed silently. *Thank you. I'm about due for something good.*

Detective Lew Horman worked Vice. He and I went way back. I'd done Necromance work off and on for the Saint City police, he'd been my liaison to the normal cops more than once. I'd also dropped several useful pieces of information about Chill dealers to him in the past. Whenever I'd come across any distributors in my journeys through the shadow world of the quasi-legal, I'd turned them over to Horman. Sometimes he couldn't do a damn thing, being hamstrung by procedure, but more often than not he acted on my tips. We'd had a grudging almost-partnership for a long time, despite his disdain for psions and his general slobbishness.

He was also one of the few cops Gabe had ever paid the high compliment of calling "incorruptible."

I started casting around for an inconspicuous way to approach him — hugging the shadows on the opposite side of the street and crossing in a blind spot, scanning the roofs and alleys. No nosy little eyes that I could see. Nothing out of the ordinary. The hair rose on the back of my neck.

You're getting paranoid, Danny. You need a safe place to rest for a few hours. Even if your body's demonic, your mind is still human and you're blurring with fatigue. This one thing, then hole up and rest so you're fresh for tonight. You've got a couple visits to make, and a few hours of rest will help you go over the file again. You can also take a look at the book Selene gave you.

I melted around the corner and found myself face-to-face with my last best chance.

"Hullo, Horman," I said pleasantly. My emerald sparked, sizzling to match my rings. "I need to talk to you."

CHAPTER 22

"What the *hell?*" My voice hit a pitch just under *squeak.*

Horman flinched. He pushed me back into the alcove, stood with his three-quarters profile presented to me, watching the empty street. He smelled of synth-hash, half-metabolized Chivas Red, and the decaying of human cells. Mixed with the chemical wash of Saint City hover traffic and biolab exhalation, it was a heady brew. My own smell rose like a shield, I didn't allow my nose to wrinkle. The heaviness of incipient rain blurred on the freshening wind. I smelled electricity, suspected a storm. "But I *just* got into town!"

His hands shook, a smudge of ash drifting down from his cigarette. "You the suspect now. Half the cops in Saint City are looking to bring you in full of projectile lead as a copkiller, deadhead. The other half won't interfere 'cause they know they'll get their own asses singed with hoverwash."

Suspecting me of killing Gabe. Why? Trying to hang it on me instead of Massadie? "Where does that leave you, Horman?"

Sweat gleamed on his bald pate. "Gabe came to me few days ago. Said she had a line on somethin' big. I told her not to get involved, told her she was retired and should stay that way. She told me you'd show up if anything happened to her. I been spending hours out here waitin' for you." Horman shivered, popping up the collar of his coat with his free hand. He flicked ash out onto the pavement.

Oh, Gabe. Looking out for me again. I swallowed, heard the dry click of my throat. "Listen, what do you know about a guy named Gilbert Pontside?"

"Homicide, Old Division. Hates psis." Horman shrugged. He was swallowing rapidly, sweating Chivas. He knew how dangerous it was to be out on the street, but nobody thought I'd be stupid or suicidal enough to try the cops. That was valuable information right there.

You hate psions too, Horman. "So why is he responsible for investigating Eddie Thornton's murder?" I dug in my bag, but he shook his head.

"If you got the original file, don't let me see it. Lots of people been looking for that, it ain't worth my career to have a peek." He hunched his shoulders even further. "I figgered Gabe lifted the original, tricky bitch." He paused. "Pontside. Investigating a dirtwitch murder? A dirtwitch married to a Spook Squadder? I din't hear that, they got a lid clapped tight on this one."

"Suspicious, isn't it?" I took a deep breath. It was time for me to go on faith. "Eddie was killed because he came up with this." I held up the vial, rescued from the depths of my bag. "It's a cure for Chill. I don't know who killed him yet, but it's beginning to look like the biotech company he was working for and the Tanner Family have something to do with this pile of crap. I'm told a bounty is out on me. Is it official?"

" 'Course it ain't. Official means visible, and someone wants this kept quiet." His eyebrows drew together. "There *ain't* no cure for Chill," Horman mumbled. He shot me a quick dark glance, his forehead wrinkling even further. But there was a ratty little gleam in his eyes I'd seen before. Horman had just made a connection.

A good connection, please. Please, Anubis. "I've got a Shaman and a *sedayeen* who worked over on Fortieth who say different; their clinic was bombed and a bunch of goons tried to off them this morning. Plus, why would a Spook Squadder and a Skinlin be killed like they were, and have it kept this quiet, unless they had something huge, huge as a fucking Chill cure?" I took a deep breath, dangerously close to pleading. "You *know* me, Lew. I'm a psion and a bounty hunter. I paid my mortgage with a little bit of illegal action like everyone else. But I don't go around killing my friends. I never went in for assassination. *Ever.*"

Gabe was about the only friend I had left. Why would I kill her? The thought that I could even be *accused* of killing her made me sick to my stomach.

And feeling just a little explosive.

He shivered. "What you want me to do, deadhead? Gabe trusted you, they say you killed her."

Score one for me. If he believed I killed Gabe, he wouldn't be out here waiting for me. He especially wouldn't ask me what I wanted him to do. *Looks like my luck's beginning to change a bit. About damn time too.*

My fingers were deft and quick. I shoved the vial of Chill cure in his coat pocket, tugging sharply on the material so he could tell what I was doing. "Figure out what this is, see if I'm telling the truth. Visit a couple of your Vice stooges and put the word out that I'm going to erase whoever killed Gabe. Also check the West Coast Chill clinic datanet. They should have the formula for the cure flashed worldwide by now."

"A cure's gonna put me out of a job." He didn't sound upset at this eventuality. As much as I'd lost to the ravening monster that was Chill, he'd lost more. I'd attended the funeral of his teenage son years ago, the kid had gotten hooked on Chill and died on a bad batch of contaminated drugs. He hadn't been the only casualty—the distributor cutting Clormen-13 with bad thyoline had soaked most of the city with it—but it had been the one thing that solidified Horman's innate cynicism.

And his hatred of Chill.

I made a short snorting sound. "You're a Hegemony officer, you'll get a pension. Besides, you can always chase unregistered hookers. That's a lot more fun. Or XTSee brokers, vox sniffers, bitfoxes, permaspray junkies.... Or corporate harassment cases." I didn't have to work to sound amused, the maniacal urge to giggle was rising again. My left shoulder throbbed with pain.

"You bitch." Horman's aura flushed brittle red with fear. His cigarette had burned down to the filter, he pitched it into the botbin with a convulsive jerk. Didn't look at me. "What you doing this to me for, Valentine? I never did nothing to you."

"And you were out here waiting. Call it a favor to Gabe. Consider me just the hand of Vengeance coming home to roost." I slid past him, out of the alcove, as light rain spattered on the sidewalk. Glanced up to check hovertraffic, the streams of cigar-shaped personal hovers and the larger whaleshapes of transports moving in their aerial ballai. "If you can, let some cops know I *didn't* kill Gabe. Let them know Pontside is the officer on record in the original file investigating Eddie's murder. But for Sekhmet's sake don't get yourself in trouble." I paused, my tone turning soft and reflective. "I'd hate to have to avenge your death too."

"Goddammit—" Horman began, but I was already gone. I knew what I needed to know.

Half the cops on the Saint City force might well think I'd killed Gabe. But the other half didn't think so, and Horman had been allowed to stand quietly out in his smoking alcove, taking nips off the bottle of Chivas brought to him by his partner. Someone else knew that a normal was the officer on record for a psion's murder, maybe someone had even figured out from the scene of Gabe's homicide that everything wasn't quite kosher. Despite Horman's shambling exterior, he was well-respected among Saint City cops — one of the good old boys. If he dropped a quiet word, it would get around.

I had just bought myself some breathing room. Or more precisely, Gabe had bought it for me, by telling a fat foulmouth cop who reeked of soy whiskey in no uncertain terms that I was to be trusted no matter what the brass said.

Still looking out for me, Gabriele. Mighty nice of you. Even my mental voice caught on a choking sob.

My chest hurt. My eyes were full of unshed tears, the pavement blurring in front of me.

I needed a place to go to ground. I didn't have one. My shoulder twinged sharply, the pain slicing through my misery. *Pay attention, Dante. Wake up. Just a little longer, then you can rest.*

Four blocks away from the precinct house, instinct poked me hard between the ribs. I stepped aside into an alley. Managed to get all the way to the dead end, brick walls rising up in three directions. I turned around, leaning my back against the blind corner; even if anyone started shooting from the roof I was sure I could make it up the handy fire-escape and away. I braced my legs as the freezing rain started in earnest, tapping the roofs, mouthing the pavement. The peculiar whine of streetside hover traffic during rainfall bounced through the alley and rattled my teeth.

I squeezed the scabbard in my left hand, checked the cuff. No green light, it was back to dead-cold and dull against my golden skin. There was no way to get it off, I couldn't even get a fingernail under its curve. It had welded itself to my skin.

Lovely.

I slid my right hand under my shirt, touched the knobs of the *baculum;* slid my fingertips up my collarbone. Took a deep, slamming breath. The decision was instant, I'd just reached the end of my tether.

I don't care what else is going on, Japhrimel. I need you. You lying bastard of a demon, I need to see where you are and if you can help me.

I touched the ropes of scarring, my fingertips delicate as if I caressed his naked shoulder. Or his cheek. Heat jolted up my arm, smashed through my shoulder.

I saw —

—darkness. The single point of light was a candle, its blood-red flame in a curious stasis. Arms stretched overhead, head hanging, hair curtaining face. The chalked lines of the diagram writhed, fluid with demon Power, Magi script altered subtly to make it more effective. Urgency growing in the bones, spreading outward. The bracelet of cold metal around his wrists softened under the lash of his attention.

Circle holding square holding pentacle, the diagram spun lazily against a smooth glassine floor. A hellhound paced at its periphery, red eyes glowing and massive shoulders writhing under its obsidian pelt. A laugh sharp as a razor cut the air, shivered as the candleflame bent in a nonphysical direction and returned to its stasis, standing straight up. The candle itself was a thick parchment-colored pillar set in a barbarously clawed iron stand.

Head, lifting. Eyes beginning to burn as they wrenched away from the flame.

"I will give you one chance," he said, in a chill hurtful voice.

"At last. She's calling," another replied, high and awful as tinkling bells made of frozen blood. "And he's compelled to answer."

"It was only a matter of time. I wonder who caught her, perhaps Arkhamiel?" Wait. Was this voice like the first? Identical. But the shading was a touch deeper, a slightly more masculine tone. *" 'Twas a fool's move to let us take you, Elder Brother. We will soon have the* lai'arak *and your compliance anyway."*

"I have warned you," he said quietly. The chill had not left the words, a sharp jagged blade drawn over numb flesh. *"Your time is almost done."*

I tore my fingers away. Bent over, shook my head, hair swinging as I tried to clear away the sudden disorientation of seeing through his eyes as if through a sheet of wavering glass, each object freighted with different light and perspective. I choked, my stomach revolving. Black demon blood dripped from my nose and mouth, I'd driven my teeth almost clean through my lower lip.

I slid down to my knees. It was not the best place to have a nervous breakdown, in an alley less than four blocks from the South precinct house, exposed to the stinging pellets of frozen rain and drifted with garbage. I hunched over, hugging myself, my weapons digging into various places, and started to shake.

Someone had Japhrimel in a demon-inscribed circle, with a hellhound pacing its borders. The other voices were demons—nothing human could sound that tinkling and cold. Two voices, sounding almost identical. The Twins. Eve's allies.

That answered two questions. Eve's allies had Japhrimel, and some other faction not loyal to Lucifer was in town too. That meant two groups of demons that had a vested interest in either keeping me alive or simply catching me to make Japh behave. Add that to whoever else Lucifer had sent to catch Eve if she came out of hiding, and there were at least three groups of demons double-dealing and jostling each other in Saint City. And here I was, caught in the middle. It would be a miracle if I could solve the mystery of Gabe's death without getting interrupted by whatever trouble was boiling out of Hell *now.*

I wiped tears away with the blade-edge of one hand, but more came, welling out my burning eyes and slicking my cheeks. *Japhrimel.*

Why did he have to go and get himself in trouble just as I had a Mob Family to take down? It was bad fucking timing in the worst way.

What would they do to him? If he could be caught, even if he would eventually escape—which everyone seemed to take for granted—they might be able to hurt him before he did. I didn't think Eve would hurt him willingly, but he might leave her with no choice if he tried to break free and drag her back to Hell. After all, there was Velokel, her lover, who had hunted Fallen and *hedaira* before. Even if Japh had a demon's Power he was still...vulnerable.

That thought sent wriggling cold panic all the way through me.

Goddammit, Danny! The voice was familiar, raising the hairs on the back of my neck. *You're goin' into shock. Get your ass movin'. Find somewhere to sit down and breathe. And for God's sake stop cryin'.*

It was Eddie's *sotto voce* growl, the one he used for sarcasm. Why was I hearing dead men? Didn't I have enough trouble? Maybe it was my subconscious interfering, dangerous for a Magi-trained psion. My control of Power depended on my having a clean psychic house, so to speak; you can't corral and contain magickal force with a scattered mind. Broken concentration sucks away the sorcerous Will.

I scrubbed at the mark on my shoulder through my shirt. *Stop it. Stop right this second. No crying, no* weakness *allowed!*

Bit by bit, the unsteady trembling feeling went away. I sniffed and smelled rain, garbage, and demon musk. I'd flooded the alley with my scent, glands working overtime. Had to rein it in. Would another demon be able to track me? My rings swirled with uneasy light, my shields trembling on the edge of crystallizing.

Japhrimel was taken, I was on my own. Things did not look good.

That was how they found me, crouched in the alley and sobbing. But my hand was still closed around the hilt of my sword, and I felt them coming bare seconds before they arrived—enough time for me to make it halfway up the fire escape. Plasbolts raked past me, splashing against standard-magshielded walls, plasglass shattered.

Even the toughest bounty hunter around will run when faced with four police cruisers and a cadre of what appears to be augmented Mob shocktroops. And all for one tired almost-demon.

CHAPTER 23

I finally lost the last of the police cruisers by plunging into the old Bowery section of the Tank District. It's possible to find almost anything in the Tank, though not as much as you can find in the Great Souk or the Freetowns. The Tank population doesn't take kindly to police. It's a good place to hide, as both Abracadabra and Anwen Carlyle knew.

The Bowery is the very worst part, the cancerous heart of Chill-fed urban blight, and when I was human I hadn't braved it very often. The Tank, yes. The Bowery, no. Not unless I was desperate.

Two of the cruisers had tangled together as they pursued me through the labyrinth of what used to be the National District. I had another piece of good luck when the third misjudged a lane of slicboard traffic and a slic courier shot in front of the bristling cruiser. The cruiser's AI yanked it into a barrel roll to avoid the collision— Hegemony cop cars are all fitted with that sort of control to make high-speed chases less dangerous for civvies. The courier would get dinged with a ticket, but she was still on her board instead of spread over the pavement. And I was long gone.

The last cruiser lost me in the Hole.

Back when I'd been human, I'd had my board tuned by Konnie Bazileus at the Heaven's Arms. Occasionally I'd gone into the Hole, honing my skill on a board against the sk8s, couriers, skaheads, and flicsurfers. Jace and I had even done naked-blade slicboard duels, back in the first violent flush of our affair.

Even Hegemony federal marshals don't go into the Hole often. It isn't worth it.

The Hole itself is underground; it used to be a transport well until the last really huge earthquake. The quake ripped apart the central well and opened up a sinkhole underneath, so the walls were a collage of relays, eighty-five-year-old fiberoptic spikes and reactive strips, debris from the buildings overhead crumbling into the sinkhole. The slictribe had moved in and made it even more challenging, building ramps and jumpoffs, spikes protruding from the walls, deadzones and hoverpatches that made the air move in unsteady swirls just aching to rip a sk8 off a board.

The tangled alleys leading up to the Hole are narrow and sloping, most of them covered by cobbled-together roofs of flimsy plaswood, plasticine, and other scavenged materials. Every once in a while a few teams of Hegemony federal marshals will sweep through the Hole to pick up "criminals," but they never net much. Around the slictribes, if you don't adhere to strict codes you're out. It's all too easy to flip someone off a board and let them fall into the dark well of the Hole. The worst that comes out of here is gang warfare and XTSee for vance parties, and the authorities are more than willing to let that pass as long as the slictribes only kill each other.

I passed like a ghost through the old way into the Hole, my shoulder burning as the last bullet hole closed. The last clutch of Mob troops had actually forced me to stand and fight, peppered with projectile fire. If I'd still been human, I might be dead.

I still wasn't sure I was alive. My clothes were torn and wet with blood, my stomach burned with fierce hunger, and I still felt the last man's neck crack in my hands like plasilica sticks. Only human.

They hadn't sent any psions after me. Only normals. Fragile, vulnerable humans, no matter if they were legally augmented with neurospeeders and muscle spanners.

Dusk was falling. I was going to miss my date with Lucas. Then again, all he would have to do is follow the sirens and listen to whatever lie the holovids were telling, and he'd know I'd had some trouble.

By the time I reached the Hole itself, I had to stop and lean against a sagging plywood shelter that smelled like humans living with chemshowers instead of regular bathrooms. A fair number of skas lived in shacks around the Hole itself, eking out a living on their parents' credit lines while dealing XTSee and bitfox on the side, tuning boards and generally living as they always have.

That was where I saw the first sign of life. A sk8 who couldn't have been more than ten coasted up on a humming, nicely-tuned Chervoyg almost as long as he was. He brought the board to a stop and hopped onto solid ground, racking the board neatly with a kick as the powercell died down. His hair stood up in gelled acid-green spikes, and his face was streaked with blue camopaint. He glanced around, not seeing me, and pulled a pack of smokes out of his breast pocket. He wore a fluttering flannel shirt and a loose pair of black pleather shorts covered in rippling silver magtape.

This was evidently a little-used part of the Hole, because he proceeded to sit down right at the edge and smoke, looking up as the cloak of night fell across the faraway roof and tiny hole that was the main entrance to the subterranean world. Little drops of light that were antigrav and powercells began to flock through, weaving in complicated patterns.

I made a low noise, scraping against the plaswood shelter. Then I coughed, letting him know I was there.

He made no move. I stepped out cautiously.

He took one incurious glance over his shoulder, his fingers caressing his board's powercell. I stopped, the sweet scent of synth-hash filling my nostrils. He was normal, wouldn't be able to see the disturbance I created in the landscape of Power. But I still probably looked like I'd been run through a few hoverwashes.

Gabe used to smoke. Panic rose under my breastbone. I swallowed, my sword shoved into the loop on my belt. My hands were loose and raised. "Hi. I'm Dante Valentine."

He let out a chuff of smoke and a choking sound. "Fuck. Wonton w'hini."

"I know how to ride a board." I kept a firm hold on my temper. "I just don't have one right now. You can help me with that."

He had wide blue eyes, clashing with his acid-green hair. "Landerfuck," he sniffed with magnificent disdain. "Niners outa clap w'hinioo."

"Innocent until proven otherwise." I gave him a lopsided smile. Some people try to mimic slictribe lingo, I don't. It's enough that I can guess at 80 percent of what they mean. Even Konnie had been hard to understand at times.

It was a long shot, but I decided to go for it. "Konnie Bazileus. Heaven's Arms. He still around?"

I thought his eyes couldn't get any rounder. "Bazzmouth on'yo tribe?"

"I'm not tribe," I said. "I'm lander, remember?"

He shrugged. "Bingya Bazzmouth."

"Thanks." I folded myself down onto the gritty filthy floor of the ledge jutting out into the side of the hole, blood crackling as it dried on my clothes. "Bum a smoke?"

After that it was nothing but waiting. Those of the slictribe don't function in the same timezone as the rest of us; the less charitable say it's because of all the hash and XTSee. He smoked his way through two more cigarettes, generously sharing with me, then stood slowly, brushed his pleather shorts off, and pressed the powercell. He tossed the board and flung himself after it, his new BooPhooze sneakers thudding on the deck's surface. It used to be Rebotniks or Aeroflot were the popular brand, but no longer.

I was getting old. I even *felt* old. Creaky, my bones dry. The synth-hash didn't soothe me as much as I wished it would. As soon as he was gone I stubbed the last one out in the filthy greasy crud masquerading as dirt down here.

I put my head down on my knees and tried to breathe. The blue glow of my god's attention was comforting, hovering at the edges of my mental awareness. I'd just outrun four cruisers and what looked like Mob troops. That wasn't a new trick, cops and Mob working together; sometimes the cops needed a little help from the extralegal side. Of course, the Mob troops had only been legally-augmented, but if they were working for the cops I didn't blame them. Still, it bothered me. I assumed they were Mob, because they hadn't *behaved* like cops, cops would have shouted at me to drop my weapons.

If they weren't from the Tanner Family's war with me, maybe they were from Lucifer pulling strings behind the scenes again, using me to trap Eve. Hellesvront had all kinds of agents on earth, it stood to reason the cops might be part of that network.

What a joy. I've got so many enemies, even I can't decide between them.

The rattling whines of slicboards began to build as the Hole woke up. Sk8s and other slictribers, like psions, generally come out and play at night.

I tilted my head up, watching the aerial ballai. It's impossible to look totally graceful while riding a board—you're always on the edge of spilling—but confidence imparts its own kind of grace. I watched the little darts of antigrav light, spinning in the figure-eight pattern slic riders use for high-traffic zones, others dipping down and peeling away to take runs around the edges. Whoops and high joyous cries echoed through the cavern. The pounding of a vance party in another part of the Hole started to throb like a heartbeat, music meant to shake dancers into a trance and keep them there for hours.

I'd thought before of using the patterns of hover traffic for divination. Now I watched the spots of firefly light that were the slicboarders, and I felt premonition flutter under my skin. Deep, unsteady panic welled up from the pit of my belly.

"Gabe," I whispered, and watched the lights tremble as my eyes filled with tears. I blinked them away.

Konnie still rode a board. And he, of all people, reminded me of just how much we'd all aged while I was letting time pass me by in Toscano. His fingernails were still clipped brutally short and painted with black molecule-drip; he probably still played in a Neoneopunk band.

Kids like Konnie rarely ever grow up. He was still riding, still part of a tribe. That meant he was still fast and mean.

He was still lean, and rode with hipshot ease. Still wearing flat golden plasmetal rings on his right hand; still the same dead flat dark eyes. His hair was different now, dyed magenta and long-braided, studded with ivory beads. He wore—since he was no longer a young punk fashion plate but an aging one—a black V-neck linen shirt, skintight purple viscose-velvet breeches, and supple black fake-shark boots. Fans of wrinkles spread at the corners of his eyes, and his mouth was bracketed with two curving lines. He still rode a Valkyrie—slictribers are nothing if not loyal to their decks.

Konnie had known my old face. My human face. I'd been taking my slicboards to him for servicing since I'd left the Academy, and we'd evolved a useful acquaintanceship over the years—an acquaintanceship I was about to use for all it was worth.

I presented my left cheek subtly as he stood with his back to the ledge, studying me. With luck he'd recognize my tat. The kid with the green hair settled down cross-legged and lit another cigarette. The sweet smoky smell of synth-hash rose and twirled around the other odors of the Hole. I was glad I'd learned to tune down some of the demon acuity in my nose.

Konnie grinned, showing strong white teeth. It was a vidflash expression, there one moment, gone the next. "Deadhead. You get augments?"

"Kind of. Against my will." I lifted a shoulder, dropped it. Blood crackled on my clothes, almost dry now and powerfully fragrant of spice and rotting fruit. Tucked under Konnie's arm was a long slim shape in a chamois sheath. "Nice to see you too, Konnie."

"Been a long wave." He studied me carefully, scrupulously speaking my language instead of slic lingo. "You bringin' trouble. Niners all *over* all the entrances. Been a few scuffs."

"I'm sorry." My eyes burned, and my lungs. The vast dim cavern beat with the pulse of slicboard travel and more vance parties starting, the walls really beginning to bounce. Stray tufts of breeze made the beads in his hair clack together, touched my cheek and ruffled my clothes. "I'm on the warpath, Konnie. I don't want to hurt any slictribers, but my temper's real short. I want a board, and I need to get out of here unseen and send a couple messages. I can pay."

He shrugged, his lip curling. "Pay."

Oh, Sekhmet sa'es. "New Credits, you ass. Not datband dangle. You think I was born yesterday?"

His eyes were troubled as he studied me. "You look awful young."

You have no fucking idea how old I feel. "Not my fault. I lost a game with the Devil, Konnie." *There is no lie like telling the truth, is there?*

Is there, Japhrimel?

Trust me, Japhrimel's ghost replied. *Say you will not doubt me.*

I wish he hadn't left me with McKinley, I wish I'd known not to get angry at him. Maybe I could have convinced him to help Eve, maybe not. I should have tried.

"Devil?" He blew out, a long low whistle between his strong white teeth. Business at the Arms must be good. He wore a datband plugin that registered him as constantly monitored by a security company, which meant he probably had his fingers in a few extralegal pies.

"Don't ask. Look, Kon, are you gonna help or am I going to have to figure something else out? I'm kind of in a hurry." I risked a little rudeness.

He clicked his tongue against the roof of his mouth. "Holy shit." For a moment he sounded much younger, and his dead dark eyes flared to life. The Hole pounded, confused air swirling and buffeting,

making the riding even more challenging. I heard a chorus of yells —
a duel, maybe. "It *is* you. Valentine."

"Don't worry," I told him. "Nobody else would recognize me
either."

"Shit they won't." He weighed the chamois-sheathed package in
both hands, his rings winking in the uncertain light. My own rings
swirled with Power, his were merely human.

Completely human.

"You still got that look," he said finally. "We all know it, that hungry Valentine look. Who you hunting this time, baby?"

"Whoever runs the Tanner Family and killed my best friend."
And anyone else who gets in my way. "Name a price, Konnie. If I
don't have it I'll get it in an hour."

He tossed me the package. I flashed to my feet and caught it, moving too quickly to be human. He didn't flinch, I have to give him
credit. But he made that little clicking sound again, tongue popping.
"You always paid before. Spect you earned a little cred." He jerked
his head back. "C'mon, ride wit' me. Then we figure out how get you
outa here."

I need more, Konnie. "And a couple slic couriers? There's no danger in it, not for them."

"Shit," Konnie said, "this ain't nothin'. You shoulda seen the fight
we had last year between the Pacers and the TankLickers. Anything
a Lander comes up with we can handle."

My heart squeezed down on itself. These were no more than children, even if they were sk8 and slic couriers. *I bloody well hope
you're right, Konnie. I really do.*

CHAPTER 24

The package in chamois was a Valkyrie, sleek and black and beautiful, freshly-tuned and magclean. Good old Konnie. I wondered
how much of my reputation still survived down here in the Hole.

I sent four messages by slic courier, three on paper and one
on air.

The air-message was for Abracadabra, telling her I was still alive
and still going after Gabe's killers. She'd make sure the information

got around and caused maximum confusion. It also had a chance of reaching Lucas, who would be able to pick up my trail in the Hole if he was lucky. I'd feel a lot better about this once he managed to catch up with me.

The first paper message was to Selene. *Tell Tiens Japh's been taken and needs help.* That would also let the Hellesvront agents know I believed them without committing me to letting them "protect" me. Maybe, just maybe, they would concentrate on getting Japh out of hock or sowing some confusion to keep my trail clear of demons. I didn't hope for much — after all, they were probably more interested in finding me and spiriting me away from Saint City before another group of demons got their hands on me. Still, I could hope.

Next message, to the Tanner Family's corporate front downtown. A courier with long orange dreadlocks and the androgynous holovid figure in style now knew where it was and took a short note for me.

Hand over Spocarelli and Thornton's killers or I'll send you to Hell. Nice, sharp, direct, though I intended to pay them a visit soon after they received it. I signed it with a flourish and a certain feeling of grim enjoyment. The orange-haired courier also knew where the Tanner Family mansion was, their nerve center. It was by far the most productive half-hour I'd spent in a while, talking to her.

The very last message was to Jado. To this courier, a short, stocky mean-looking kid with a fuzz of dead black hair and a pierced lip, I gave Eddie's mastersheets, sealed in a magpouch with the homicide file and a note asking him to hide it and apologizing for the inconvenience. This about wiped out my stolen bankroll, between pressing cash on Konnie and paying the couriers hazard fees. I was a hot commodity now; it would have been cheap not to pay them for potentially running across someone who would give them plasflak intended for me.

I finally stood at the edge of another ledge, down in the well of the Hole, far enough down that I felt the dread touch of claustrophobia. This would probably be a very good place to hide if I wasn't so damn nervous in close, dark spaces. The central cavern was huge, of course, but still it was underground, and it was dark, and I could feel the pressure of the dirt overhead and to the sides bearing down on me. Konnie stood next to me, humming an old RetroPhunk groove.

A shiver touched my back. I needed food, I needed rest.

Too bad, sunshine.

A clear piercing whistle floated through the pulsing. Konnie finally tapped at his board, leaning against his leg. "Tribe's movin' to clear out an exit. Think y'can keep up?"

I shrugged. I had demon reflexes and had put in a fair amount of time on slicboards, but he was tribe. He lived on his board when he wasn't running his shop. I knew better than to show any false bravado here, especially as he was doing me a favor. "Just go slow and try not to tip me."

He sniggered. Japhrimel would have caught the sarcasm in my tone, but Konnie didn't. He simply smacked the powercell, tossed the board, and performed the same trick as the other kids, leaping out into space and letting his feet thud on the deck's surface, the antigrav giving resiliently under him. The kick of the kinetic energy meeting frictionless antigrav made the deck bounce violently, but he controlled it and whooshed away as I pressed the powercell on my own board and dropped it on the ledge, jumping and landing hard, stamping my front foot down to propel the board out over the Hole.

Space slid away under me, the board bounced, and I caught my slic legs quickly and dove after Konnie, who circled in a lazy spiral and finally nipped neatly into an archway on the west side. I followed into the choking darkness, hoping he wouldn't lead me astray.

It was a shock to go aboveground. Especially on a slicboard, bulleting past neon and keeping to streetside because the hoverlanes would bring me to the attention of the cops sooner. I hoped nobody had figured out I'd been talking to Horman — and I hoped he hadn't alerted his superiors to my presence. I was depending on him to come through for me.

I went a short way into the Tank and found a nice dark Taliano restaurant that wouldn't cavil at my appearance, got a booth, and started eating. Garlic bread first, and a bottle of chianti; calamari and bruschetta, two orders of spaghetti, and the biggest steak they had. Then another bottle of chianti — the carbs in it would help keep me fueled — and another order of spaghetti, an order of fettuccini alfredo with chicken and broccoli. Finally, comfortably full, I ordered three beers and downed them all one after another. I don't like beer, but it's a cheap source of carbs.

If I hadn't been so hungry I would have read the book Selene gave me while I ate instead of stuffing everything down as fast as I could. Long ago I stopped feeling good about the sheer amount of food I needed. I felt like a glutton, especially when I'd expended a lot of physical power. If Japhrimel had been around it would have been better, I didn't need to eat quite so much when I hung around him.

There I went thinking about Japhrimel again.

I had to pay with my datband, but that didn't matter. I didn't intend to stay in the Tank for long, and by the time any bounty hunters or police reached the restaurant, I would be long gone.

Outside it was raining again, pellets of slushy ice. Wet neon slicked the streets, painted the hovers with splashes and traceries of light. The streets hummed uncomfortably, the well of Power pulsing a little differently. I noticed less psions than usual out in the rain-washed night.

I didn't blame them. Saint City felt carnivorous tonight.

So did I.

I zipped through the streets with wet wind mouthing my hair, splashes and kisses of cold against my skin. My clothes were definitely the worse for wear, full of dried blood and artistically torn, unmarked golden skin showing through the rips and bullet holes. I had a full load of ammunition, thanks to Konnie, plus my plasguns and my sword as well as my knives.

It wasn't enough for a full-scale assault on a Mob Family.

The Tanner Family nerve center was in a rich part of town, an arc of prime bayfront property housing blueblood mansions. This wasn't the corporate front, the legal face of the Mob business. This was their home, where they would entertain and hold their most important meetings. A lone psion would be recklessly stupid to attack a nerve center.

I might be stupid, but I'm fast, I'm mean, I have a sword that can cut the Devil and the will to use it. Whoever's there will just have to die, that's all. After they answer my questions.

All my questions.

I had to approach from uphill, swinging out in a wide arc and staying below the hoverlanes likely to hold police traffic. Slicboards can't go over water, and if I'd had a hover... well, a hover wouldn't have changed anything. Across the water, the lights of downtown glittered like a necklace, the orange glow of antigrav and streetlights staining the rainy sky. My city throbbed and pulsed like a heart, its chambers thudding with Power—a pulse echoed by the Gauntlet, clasped to my left wrist.

There are demons in the city tonight. Something's happened. Has Japh broken free? I don't think so, I'd probably feel it through the mark. But something's shifted.

Let's hope that's good for Eve.

The mansion was low and beautiful, a song of blue Graeco-Revival architecture, with outbuildings just as graceful and flawless. The Family had done well for itself. Good shielding wedded to the walls and property line, the kind of shielding laid for corporate clients. There would be regular security too, magscan and deepscan shields, a whole battery of defenses as well as guards roaming the grounds.

In other words, a great opportunity for me to let loose a little aggression.

I hid the slicboard under a juniper hedge, laying a small keep-charm over it. Then, my jeans and shirt flapping and crusted from my healed wounds, I walked up the broad, well-maintained sidewalk as if I belonged in the neighborhood.

The front gates were iron, stylized teeth writhing decoratively along the top curve. They reminded me of another set of gates on the East Side, gates with a gothic *R H* worked into their metal, standing slightly ajar and beckoning like every trap.

I set my shoulders, gritted my teeth.

The defenses started to quiver as soon as I got within half a block. I tasted the pulsing of the energies used to build them, could *See* the layers of Power thickening, hardening at my approach. By the time I stood in front of the gates the defenses trembled on the edge of locking down.

My sword was in my left hand, sheathed and ready. I would need it soon.

In the old days, I would have found a way to subvert the defenses, broken in quietly and pursued what I wanted. Now I had a share of a demon's Power and no need or desire to act like this was corporate espionage. Besides, I wasn't here to steal. I was here for something else entirely.

The house at the end of its black-paved drive was lit up like a Putchkin Yuletree. I looked at it shimmering on its gentle hill and the rage rose up inside me. Whoever was in that house knew something about Gabe's murder, if they hadn't committed it. Either way, they were going to tell me what they knew. All of it. Quickly.

This time I didn't push the red, screaming fury down. I took a deep breath and jabbed my right hand forward, pushing through the layers of defenses on the property line. They went crystal, locking down—but I was already in, the stiletto of my Will driven like a physical knife between ribs.

My right-hand rings, amber and obsidian, sparked as I pumped Power into them, the mark on my shoulder blazing with soft spurred heat. I *drew* on it, drew on the brand that was Japhrimel's name, past caring that it was a demon's name I was relying on. If he had broken free and showed up here it was all to the good; if other demons came along... well, that was a risk I was going to have to take.

I found myself not minding as much as I should have.

The wristcuff tightened, grinding the bones underneath again too, and sent another ice-burn of welcome strength jolting through my shoulder, into my chest.

I set my feet and *pushed,* a low sound of effort jetting between my teeth. Felt a yielding like fat-rich flesh under a sharp thin blade.

I struck. A short, sharp *kia,* my eyes suddenly hot and blazing as if lasers were popping out of them. Deadly force coiling, smashing loose, I wrenched the tough fabric of the defenses apart as casually as Japhrimel might tear apart an origami animal—a crane, perhaps—in his golden fingers.

Dead silence except for my own harsh breathing. Where were the alarms, the guards? Or was this the wrong house? The orange-haired courier had said this was the place, described it to me, and a few moments at a public infoshell had confirmed that the property was legally owned by one Asa Tanner, head of the corporate identity comprising the legal front of the Tanner Family.

I stepped through the rent in the shielding, now bleeding Power into the rainy air, and pushed the gates. Metal squealed as they swung wide on well-oiled hinges. My boots crunched on the raked immaculate gravel. I drew my sword, shoving the scabbard back in its loop on my belt and taking out a plasgun.

"Hi honey," I called, my voice flashing through the rain, breaking the drops into smaller steaming tracers of mist, spraying out in concentric rings. "I'm *hooo-ome!*"

Gravel crunched like small bones underfoot. I couldn't *feel* them, the guards, hanging back out of sight. But I could imagine them just fine. *Trap.* It was a trap.

So what? Close the trap, and see what happens when Danny Valentine gets really pissed.

I walked through the rain, hair plastered against skull and nape, dripping onto my ruined clothes. Steam curled up from my skin, ice melting before it could hit me. The sword sang in my hand, white flame twisting in its heart, blue runes spilling through the edges of the metal. My shields flared into the visible range, traceries of glittering light shimmering in a perfect globe around me, and Japhrimel's aura of black diamond flames had closed over mine again. As if he was behind me, walking with his soundless step, his hands clasped behind his back and his eyes burning no less than mine.

I felt other minds here, and tasted the acrid tang of fear. There was too much magshielding for it to be a plain civilian's house. I was in the right place, I *knew* I was.

So why weren't they attacking?

I got maybe halfway to the house before thunder rumbled low and ominous in the sky and the hair stood up on the back of my neck.

I swung around, sword lifting, the cuff suddenly flaming the green of Japhrimel's eyes. *"Sekhmet sa'es—"* I hissed, ready to face the trap—but what I saw froze the curse on my lips and made my heart pound thinly in my temples, throat, and wrists.

A low sinuous shadow stalked through the rip I'd made in the defenses. A flash of crimson eyes, a glossy obsidian pelt, an ungainly graceful shamble of a walk.

I dropped the plasgun and closed both hands instinctively around my katana's hilt, screaming my defiance as the hellhound—was it the same one?—finished shouldering through the rent in the Tanner house's shields and bulleted toward me.

I had time to admire each finicky-precise footfall, its head bobbing back and forth; paradoxically, I had no time at all. Gathered myself, compressing demon muscle and bone, then *threw* my body to the side, both hands on the hilt and blade blurring down as a white-fire scythe, the *kia* sharp and deadly. More steam drifted up from the hellhound's body. It turned on itself as I landed, too quick it was too quick it was *too quick,* my feet barely touched down and I flung myself in the opposite direction, gravel sprayed as it skidded and roar-hissed its frustration. Gravel also smashed up, exploding away from the sound, my cry taking on physical weight.

Black blood whipped from my blade as I shuffled back, bringing the shining length up between us. Took the high-guard, right hand over left holding the hilt almost at my right shoulder, instinct screaming under my skin.

The hellhound shook itself, snarling. I snarled back, lips skinned away from my teeth and fury scorching the inside of my throat. Then I did another thing I shouldn't have—I leapt for it, on the attack, driven past rage to fey courage. My shoulder smashed and rang, torn apart with pain as my right side tore too, the cuff singing a thin high smoking tone of cold Power. Blood burst and sprayed as thunder toppled the sky overhead and I fell, seeking vainly to get up *get up,* gravel crunching into my hair and mouth and eyes as I rammed against the hilt of my blade, driving it through smoking demon flesh.

We fell together, the hellhound and I, the bright length of my sword buried in its chest, its claws flexing and tangling with my ribs. I heard faint and faraway yells as the rain spattered on both me and the hellhound and the sky lit up with white-hot whips of lightning.

CHAPTER 25

I sank on my back into a carpet of grass, blinking up at the endless blue depths of the sky. Sunlight touched my bare wrist with warm gold, I pushed myself up on my elbows, blinking. Each blade of grass was detailed, glowing juicy green. The field rolled, bounded only by a broken stone wall, with the purple shadows of mountains in the distance. An oak tree lifted proudly in full summer leaf. At any moment I expected to see a troop of old Christer Amish in their wide-brimmed hats on their way to one of their meetings. Or a coven of witches, carrying their baskets of food for the feast after the magick was done... or a group of Evangelicals of Gilead, the women veiled and the men in suits and bowties, hair parted in the center and held down with pomade under small circular embroidered skullcaps.

I like this better, he said beside me, braced on his elbows and so close I could smell him again, spiced Shaman, pepper and honey. And the clean healthy smell of male, a smell with no taint or tang of demon.

Jace lounged next to me in jeans and a white cotton button-down shirt. The sun made his hair a furnace of gold, lit his eyes with incandescence. Same expensive haircut, same Bolgari glittering on his wrist. Grass pricked at my hands as I sat up and looked down at myself—black T-shirt, jeans. Bare feet, my toes human-pale and painted wicked crimson with molecule-drip polish.

You again. *My lips shaped the dim whisper.* Jason.

One elegant golden eyebrow arched. He had a long blade of grass in his mouth, lazy, like a cigarette. I could see the smattering of freckles across his nose, ones that never showed unless he was in full sun. Even the golden tint to his shaved cheeks was there.

And oh, my heart hurt to see him in such detail.

Muscle moved under his shirt as he sat up straight, crossing his legs tailor-fashion. His knee bumped me. The strand of grass dropped from his lip, vanished into the thick mat of greenery. Absolutely, baby. Miss me?

What are you doing here? *I could do no more than whisper, the breath stolen from me by sunlight, the brush of breeze against my skin, the prickle of sweat under my arms and at the small of my back. I smelled grass, and the richness of air with no hoverwash or biolab exhalation, no sour fullness of human decay. I even smelled the faint woodsy odor of the oak tree and the rich loam of drifted leaves scattered around it.*

He shrugged. Other people get *loa.* You get me.

But you're dead! *My eyes prickled with tears. Was I having my deathdream at last? Where was the blue light and my god? Where was the hall of eternity and the well of souls?* Am I dead? *I tried not to sound pathetically hopeful, failed miserably.*

Jace's face fell slightly, turned solemn. I heard a hawk cry far away, saw the thin white traceries of cirrus clouds and the haze of distance over the faraway mountains.

Love's eternal, Danny. You mean you been dealing with Death all this time and you don't know that? *His mouth curled up in a half-smile, a tender expression. A butterfly meandered past, its wings a blue reflecting the sky's wheeling vault.* You always were stubborn.

He leaned over, reaching out and bridging the gap between us. He stroked my cheek, his callused fingertips gentle. Neither of us carried a weapon here, but his hands were still rough with practice. Then he pushed a strand of my hair back, delicately, and I found myself leaning forward.

Our mouths met. Kissing him had always been like a battle before, greedy and deliciously heated, a combustion. But here it was gentle, his mouth on mine like velvet, his hands cupping my face delicately. His thumb feathered over my cheekbone and he made the low humming sound he always used to after sex. My heart sped up, thundering in my ears.

He kissed the corner of my mouth, kissed my temple, closed me in his arms. You're hurt, *he said into my hair.* But you'll be all right.

I buried my face in the juncture between his neck and shoulder, smelled the human cleanness of him. Gabe, *I said.* Eddie.

He stroked my back, kissed my hair. It felt so real. So real. Eternal, Danny. Remember? That means forever. *His arms tightened.* You have to go back now. It's time.

I don't want to. Please. I don't want to. Let me die, let me stay here.

I felt him shake his head, as the sunlight beat down on us in waves. The hot simmering of a summer day, a cauldron of a field under the bright vault of heaven, all of it—I wanted to stay. I didn't care where this was.

That's not the way it works, baby. Go on now. Be good. I'm watching out for you.

A shadow drifted over the sun, and just like that I—

—snapped into full wakefulness, my hand blurring out and sinking into vulnerable human flesh. I choked out an obscenity I'd learned hunting down a bounty in Putchkin territory, it died halfway and I made my fingers unloose. Leander stumbled back, his dark eyes wide, the emerald in his cheek flashing. My left cheek burned, I felt my tat shifting as his did, inked lines running under the skin. My emerald spat a single, glowing-green spark.

Now I knew who he reminded me of. The knowledge hit me so hard I lost my breath, gasping and scrambling back, casting around for my swordhilt.

He held his hands up. He had a fading bruise on his cheekbone, and moved a little stiffly. "Calm down. Calm *down,* Danny, goddammit!"

I gulped down air. Looked at the room. No window, one door, a bed with a purple cotton comforter and rumpled pale-pink sheets; a stripped-pine nightstand with a pitcher of water. Leander was unarmed—but he held my sword. Gingerly, as if he was afraid it might bite him. He offered it to me as I crouched on the bed, my ribs flaring with every heaving breath.

"What the hell are you doing here?" I rasped.

He shrugged, offered me my sword. "You're safe. I hooked back up with Lucas. There's some news you should hear."

"Where am I?" My throat was on fire, sore and scraped raw. The full-spectrum lights beat down, showed me my own hands reaching for my sword, slim and golden and beautifully graceful.

"In a safe place. Listen, Danny, I want your word. All right? I want you to listen to what we have to say. On your honor." His wide dark eyes met mine, I caught a faint green spark far back in his pupils. It vanished. Had I really seen it?

Honor? Do I have any honor left? "The hellhound," I croaked. "Did it—"

"You killed it. I repaired the shielding. Thought we were going to lose you, but you pulled through." He was chalky-pale under his dark hair, and his hands trembled just a little. He was afraid of me. That managed to smash the last vestiges of resemblance—Jace had never been afraid of me. Enraged at my stubbornness, driven to frustrated fury by my constant poking and prodding, gentle during my moments of weakness, and coldly lethal when we were under fire; but Jace had *never* been afraid of me.

I remembered Rio, when he had crawled into the shattered bathroom where I'd taken refuge, lit a cigarette, and simply talked to me after Japhrimel's change had worked its way through my body. It had never mattered to Jace what body I wore; he loved *me,* but by then it had been too late.

I belonged to Japhrimel. No amount of trying to regain my lost humanity would overcome that one simple fact. No matter how angry or hurt he made me, Japh was the only person who truly knew me—even if he didn't know very much about handling me. Even fighting him, being angry at him, struggling against him was better than relaxing with someone else. After all, who else did I reach for when I finally felt out of my depth, even though he'd held me up against a subway wall and bruised my arm, my heart? I hadn't thought of calling anyone else.

The demon and the fleshwife are literally one being. Whenever they're written about, it's in the singular, as if each pair is one person.

A scream rose up in me, died at the back of my throat, cascaded back down into an endless black hole of bitterness that beat like my pulse inside my chest. My left shoulder felt heavy and full, the wrist-cuff was dry and powdery-pale as it rested against my arm, its cold numbness temporarily gone. I still wore the blood-drenched rags of my clothes; they crackled as I moved on the bed. The spacefoam mattress whooshed a little as I eased myself down from crouching on the bed and stood, swaying and finally making my knees lock. I snatched my sword from Leander and looked him in the eye.

Nothing. Nothing but a great yawning distance between me and this human Necromance I liked. Whose company had made me feel a little better. But that was all.

"I killed it." I should have felt happy. I'd killed something even Japhrimel and McKinley had treated cautiously. My ribs ached on the right, twinging as I moved, the flesh tender as it had been after Lucifer's parting kick.

I felt like shit.

I clicked the blade free of the scabbard, examined it. Blue runes ran wetly in the steel, blazing out as soon as it left the darkness of confinement.

Still blessed. Still mine.

The sword kills nothing, Danyo-chan. It is will, *kills your enemy.*

I'd killed a fucking hellhound. Gods above and below, I had *killed a hellhound.* "All right." I must have sounded a little more together, because Leander's shoulders eased and his hands dropped back to his sides. What sort of courage did it cost him to stand there unarmed and look at me while I had a weapon in my hands? "What is it you have to tell me?"

"Come with me," he answered. "I'll take you to Lucas."

Down a short hall with a framed Berscardi print on one side and a priceless fluid lasecarved-marble statue tucked in a niche, Leander stepped into a circular room holding two leather couches and a fireplace roaring with a real fire, the tang of woodsmoke and a low thunderous reek filling the air. My nostrils widened as soon as we reached the hall, smelling a stasis cabinet and dried blood. When we reached the room Lucas was there, dropped down on one of the couches with his arm flung over his eyes. For once he didn't look the worse for wear—I probably looked bad enough for both of us.

Standing at the only other entrance to the room was a slim tall man with a thatch of chestnut hair and bright blue eyes, his feral clean-shaven face set in an ironclad smile. He wore a shirt that looked like fur until I looked closer and realized it was *pelt;* he wore only a pair of jeans tucked into very good boots, Taliano and handmade by the look of them. The glossy, hairy shirt was flagrant advertising of his status as a werecain. And a dominant one too, he had less of the unprotected shiver around his mental walls than a more submissive 'cain's.

My right hand closed around my swordhilt. I'd already almost been trapped once by a werecain. Had Lucas and Leander betrayed me?

"Put that goddamn thing down," Lucas said, his arm unreeling away from his eyes. He glared at me, haggard and bloodshot. He looked wearier than Death after the Seventy Days War. The flat yellow color of his eyes was accentuated by red rims. He calculated everything about me in one piercing look, and the river of scarring down the left side of his face twitched.

I dropped my right hand to my side. Tilted my head slightly, acutely aware of Leander behind me. Human, werecain, and whatever Lucas was. Add to that the decaying-fruit and spice smell of demon blood drenching my clothes and my own fragrance over the layer of woodsmoke, and it was a heady brew. "What the *mother*fucking *god*damn *shit*sucking *hell* is going *on?*" My voice stroked the bare painted walls, and the werecain made a short sharp movement. A muscle twitched in my right forearm.

"You been played like a fuckin' holoboard." Lucas didn't sugarcoat the pill. "What would you say if'n I told you we had Massadie in the next room?"

I swallowed. My voice was as raspy as his now—I was sounding less and less human all the time, even to myself. "I'd say I'd love to talk to him. Who the hell's the furboy? I haven't had a good time with 'cain lately."

"You've been hanging out with the wrong type," the 'cain said pleasantly, with only the tinge of a growl beneath his words. His fur shirt rippled, and the classic lines of his face changed, becoming more austere. His chin jutted a little further now too, and his teeth shone white and sharp. "You're Danny Valentine. I'm Asa Tanner, Head of the Tanner Family. Nice to meet you."

My sword leapt partially free of the sheath. Lucas was suddenly next to me, grabbing my hand, his breath hot and sour on my cheek. "Fuckdammittall, *listen!*" he snarled in my ear.

"I'm listening," I said calmly enough, ignoring the way my knuckles stood out white against the hilt and my entire body tensed against Lucas's hold. He was *strong,* in a wiry way, I didn't precisely strain against him but both of us were breathing hard by the time he felt safe enough to relax a little. This was the closest I'd ever been to him, his hip pressed against mine and his foot between mine, his hand locking my sword arm down and away.

I was surprised by a flare of relief. It was *Lucas,* dammit, and I was scared of him—wasn't I?

He used to scare me more than anything. Now, the strength in his skinny hands and his body pressed against mine was pleasant. Here was someone I wouldn't have to hold back with, wouldn't have to be so goddamn *careful* not to hurt.

It's Lucas, goddammit! Stop it! He scares you! You're human!

But I wasn't, was I. Not completely.

Not anymore.

Asa Tanner made a low coughing sound. It was suspiciously close to amusement. "I didn't kill Thornton or Spocarelli."

"*Liar.*" I strained forward, Lucas pressed against me as if we were lovers, twisting my right wrist until it felt almost bruised. I finally subsided, pushing away the flush rising to my cheeks. Hedaira *don't blush,* I thought. Then, *It's Lucas, Anubis et'her ka, it's* Lucas, *I don't have to hold back.*

But I did. It cost me, but I *did.*

Asa Tanner shrugged, a marvel of coordinated fluidity. Forget my sudden acceptance of Lucas, I had a better question.

What is a werecain doing as head of a Mob Family? "What's a 'cain doing as head of a Family?"

"You think humans are the only ones who should make a little profit?" His laugh resembled a pained bark. His eyes glowed, not like a Nichtvren's but with an animal heat, like old-fashioned gas flame. "Just like a skin. You're all the same."

"You didn't show up," Lucas hissed in my ear, his dry stasis-cabinet breath brushing my cheek and sending a shiver down my spine. "Sloppy, Valentine."

"I was chased by four fucking police cruisers and..." I trailed off, staring at Tanner. *Hold on. Hold everything.* "So what percentage of your Family is human, furboy?"

His upper lip lifted in a snarl. "Only about thirty. Those that can keep up. We're a mongrel bunch."

But they were all human. The shock troops I'd thought were Mob were *all* human, every stinking one, and carrying very expensive gear as well as being legally augmented. I'd assumed the Tanner Family, as the dominant cartel around here, could afford that type of gear; but it hadn't made sense for them to be only *legally* augmented, especially when they were chasing a half-demon. They should have been spliced and loaded to within an inch of their motherfucking lives.

It also made no sense for a Mob Family with a 'cain at its head to be cooperating with the police for *anything*. As dim a view as most psions take of the cops, a werecain's view is even dimmer. Back before the Parapsychic Act, some police forces had special, secret cadres to hunt 'cain. That's why werecain only work as freelancers when it comes to paranormal-species bounties; they don't cooperate with Hegemony police like kobolding or dracolt do.

It's whispered that some police stations still have hunting cadres, secret fraternities fighting a war against the furred and fanged of the Hegemony citizenry. Not to mention the feathered, winged, and clawed. I didn't know if it was true... but the rumor was enough.

So the shock troops weren't Tanner Family goons. But they hadn't been police troops either, had they? No badges, no insignia.

And there had been no psions among them, if they'd been Saint City PD or Hegemony marshals they'd have had psionic support teams.

Gods above, Danny, you nearly killed the wrong people. I shoved that thought down. I would examine it properly later. Later, later, later. There was a lot I was going to figure out later. If I made it to a later.

But for right now... maybe, just maybe, the Tanner Family wasn't the enemy.

"Fuck me." I was too tired, too hungry, and too goddamn confused. My left arm hurt, from the mark on my shoulder all the way down to the fingertips. "Okay. Let go of me, Lucas." I shook him off. "I'm halfway convinced." To prove it, I sheathed my sword.

Silence rattled through the room. The fire popped.

"You run Chill," I said finally, staring at Asa Tanner. My tone wasn't conciliatory at all, but at least I didn't want to kill him.

Yet.

Another elegant shrug, his furry shirt rippling. He could shift in less than a second and launch himself at me. I was faintly surprised I wasn't more frightened.

Danny, you're not thinking straight. You've got to get some rest, you're going to have a psych meltdown soon if you don't give yourself some slack.

But Asa Tanner was speaking. "It's going to soak the streets anyway. I make sure the distributors don't cut it with anything." He said it like it mattered if the poison was uncut when it hit the streets.

"How very *generous* of you." Contempt edged my tone.

His chin lifted half a millimeter, defiant. He was tense, his weight balanced between both feet; if he came for me I wondered if I could take him.

A shudder worked its way through me. I'd faced down a hellhound.

Again.

And lived, again.

I almost killed the wrong people. "There was a werecain. Said he was working for the Mob...." I wet my lips nervously. His eyes settled on my mouth, and his smile broadened. It was a show of dominance, I realized, exposing his teeth. He was one angry werecain. The reek of 'cain vanished as my nasal receptors shut down—a stunning relief.

"I wouldn't have sent a single 'cain to eye you, Valentine. I'd've sent a full pack with a Moontalker to bring you in." He folded his arms across his broad, hair-covered chest. "Not every fucking 'cain in the city answers to me. Though they should."

Oh, I'll bet you've tried. "Okay." I tore my eyes away from him, looked at Lucas. A fine thin sheen of sweat made his pale forehead glisten, strands of his lank hair sticking to pasty skin. "What the *fuck* is going on?"

"Question Massadie," Lucas answered grimly. He looked relieved, and for a moment I wondered about that. Lucas Villalobos wasn't scared of *me,* was he? "Then you can tell me what *you* think."

Jovan Tadeo Massadie sat in the room's single chair, staring out the window at the ripples of water on the bay. Rain lashed against the wall and the bulletproof plasglass. He was pale, and genespliced to within an inch of his life. No normal human could look that exquisitely buffed, every surface almost poreless, his face remodeled not along the lines of holovid beauty but with a strong-jawed aquiline perfection seen only in classical marbles. He wore a rumpled gray linen suit, and his pale hair was sleek and shining, a little long for a corporate clone. Almond-shaped hazel eyes completed the picture, cat's eyes in a statue's face. The eyes were an artist's choice, maybe.

He didn't glance at the door as I stepped into the room. Instead, he sat, for all the world as if he was meditating. Faroff thunder muttered over the city.

Silence crackled. This room was painted white too. I got the feeling this mansion was more of a stage set than a Family nerve center.

Asa Tanner looked like he'd be more at home in a Tank bordello; I wondered where he *really* slept. Probably in a heap of other furry dozing beasts, 'cain are pack animals.

I wondered what it was like to have a pack, to be sure of absolute loyalty from those who shared your blood and fur. Every single person whose loyalty I never doubted was dead: Lewis, Doreen, Gabe, Eddie. Jace I'd mistrusted, but he'd proved to be just as loyal as Gabe in his own way.

Japhrimel? Loyal to me in his own way, too. And not dead yet. But still.

I folded my arms, my clothing shifting and rustling. I was just glad it covered the decency bits—if this kept up I would soon be dressed in nothing but bloody rags like a zombi in the old *Father Egyptos* holovid.

Massadie still said nothing. He probably wanted me to sweat a little—pure corpclone strategy.

He was practicing hard-line corp psych crap on the wrong person.

My thumb caressed the katana's guard. I'd let out a little of the fury boiling under my breastbone, but there was plenty more. I could easily—oh, so easily—slip the blade free of the sheath. Press it against his throat, watch a bright line of blood well against pale human skin, hear a corporate monster begging for his life.

It would feel good to kill him. It would be wonderful to smell his fear, even if he's only human.

I realized I was smiling. The smile cracked on my face, made a thin rill of fiery Power scream through the air, touching each wall and tearing along every surface. My thumb pressed against the guard.

Such a small movement would click it free.

Massadie bolted to his feet, his almond-shaped eyes wide as he scrambled, overturning the chair. He stared at me, blinking furiously, and I now saw he had been crying. Tear-tracks glittered on his planed cheeks, his mouth trembled but firmed as he faced me, drawing up his shoulders as if preparing for a fight.

The fury leaked away. Mostly. It settled back into a granite egg of coldness in my chest. I shoved my sword into the loop on my belt, shook my hands out, and looked at him.

"You're *her*." His voice was a pleasant baritone, now a little squeaky with fear. "Valentine."

I nodded. Found I was capable of speaking. "That's what they call me." It was a flip answer, but better than what I *wanted* to say. "You have—" I checked my datband, a little bit of theater to drive the point home. "Exactly two standard minutes to convince me not to kill you. Start talking."

"Eddie's dead. I suspect his wife's dead too, or you wouldn't be here." His throat worked as he swallowed dryly. "I know who killed him, and I can guess who killed her."

I folded my arms, sank my fingernails with their chipped black polish into my arms. Japhrimel's mark was warm, pulsing Power down my skin. What if he'd escaped, if he was tracking me? What if he came into the room and found me facing down this human? What would he do?

What would *I* do? "I'm waiting," I reminded him, my voice full of sharp edges. I saw him wince and took another look at him.

Anubis et'her ka. He's a psion.

Not enough for schooling or accreditation, but he had a little shine to his aura, and the clear edges of his personal Power field told me he meditated regularly. Whatever small psionic potential he had, he took good care of it. "That's why Eddie would work with you," I realized out loud. "You're a psion."

"A little bit. Four point three on the Revised Matheson, not even worth teaching."

I nodded. He'd just missed being taken into the Hegemony schools for training; a five on the scale gets you into the program. It wasn't quite legal to think maybe he'd been lucky. "Must be a real asset when dealing with us freakheads." My tone was still sharp and cool. I didn't sound human at all.

His cheeks flushed, a faint blush high on the arc of the bones just like a girl. "Not really."

I guess not. Normals might not trust you if they knew, and we don't trust you either since you're not trained. You're not in either world, are you?

The chilling thought that I wasn't in either world too—not a demon, not truly human, in-between, stuck—made the last few flickering vestiges of killing rage die back. They went hard, tearing at my throat and eyes, but finally left only a black aching hole in my chest. I leaned against the door and met his eyes, the tattoo on my cheek burning.

"Dante Valentine." He lingered over my last name. "Named for a saint whose day became a celebration of fertility and romantic love. Born in a Hegemony hospital, father unknown, mother's name erased under the Falrile Privacy Act. Rated thirty-eight on the Revised Matheson scale, attended primary schooling at Rigger Hall. Attended the Amadeus Academy, graduated with honors and went straight into apparitions. Made your reputation while still in school by raising Saint Crowley the Magi from dust. Also made another type of reputation when you entered the mercenary field under the direction of a Mob Shaman turned freelancer—"

"Stop it." If he said Jace's name I was going to draw my sword. Not because I was angry, but because I didn't think I could stand to hear this polished little god of a man use his mouth on Jason Monroe's name. *"Stop."*

He stared at me. We were even, I suppose. Maybe he wanted to kill me too, his almond-shaped eyes narrowing and burning with something too complex to be hatred and too frightened to be loathing.

"I've done my research," he said. "Eddie mentioned your name when things started to get too deep. Then I found myself with a mystery in front of me, a dead fucking Skinlin, and my name on a hit list."

I folded my arms again, dug my fingernails in. "Eddie found a cure for Chill. And the shock troops chasing me with the cops were corporate crack-squadders." I drew in a slow, soft breath, my hands squeezing. Warm blood trickled down my arms, dropped off my elbows, and plinked on the floor. "Pico-Phize troops."

"No." He shook his head. His eyes locked with mine, maybe pleading with me to believe him. "Probably Herborne Corp. They work with alkaloids, they're one of our biggest competitors in the painblocker field. We were infiltrated. I believe it was routine corporate espionage, but one of the agents happened to...find out. But there's something else. The Pico lab security was taken out by a focused EMP pulse—"

"So was Gabe," I said, but he overrode me, shouting because my voice had risen too. The room groaned under the rough lash of Power in my tone, but his next words cut through mine.

"It was *Saint City Police Department tech!*" he yelled, and I slumped back against the door. I don't think I've ever been reduced to speechlessness from rage so quickly before.

Say what? I replayed mental footage, decided that he *had* said what I thought I'd heard. *Saint City Police Department tech. What the fucking hell?*

Massadie knew he had my attention now. "There is a fuck of a lot of Chill money that goes to the cops, Miss Valentine." His tone was soft, reasonable, and utterly truthful. "Not just from routine payoffs but in other ways. Herborne found out what we had and leveraged every contact it had inside the police force, I'd guess. They're scrambling to keep this quiet. You're creating a lot of trouble for them, and they need to shut you *up* just like they needed to shut Eddie's wife up. She made it goddamn hard for them, yapping at the heels of the IA division about where the Skinlin was getting all the trouble from. It wasn't the first time they tried to kill him."

Not the first time? Oh, Gabe. Eddie. Gods forgive me. "How many?" I whispered. "How many times?"

"Six or seven." He shrugged. "He said it was no big deal. Then I came home to find my house tossed—"

"All fun and games until you get your own fucking hands dirty, right?" The contempt in my tone could have drawn blood. The picture-window shivered, and thunder tore the clouds overhead like wet paper. *Six or seven times and Gabe didn't call me?* The knowledge hit home. She hadn't thought I would show up. She'd known Japhrimel was alive, had she thought I wasn't interested in my *human* friends anymore?

What had I done? I would have dropped everything and come running for her marriage, for the birth of their daughter, for the first attempt on Eddie's life. Hadn't she *known* that?

Had she? Or had she not been sure I would show up, even when she sent me the datpilot message? Had she held off contacting me because she wasn't sure? How could she have *doubted* me? Was I her last hope, because she wasn't sure I'd respond?

How could she have doubted even for a *moment?*

I lied to her about Japhrimel. She probably felt betrayed. Guilt crawled into my stomach. I tasted bile.

"That same night, Eddie's wife was attacked. She had the kid with her. It was them getting attacked that did it, Valentine. Eddie told me they were safe, but..."

"Did Eddie tell you where?" Tension spilled down my back, brought me back to myself. "Where he'd put the kid?"

"He said you'd know. She's safe." He blinked at me. "You mean you—"

You mean you didn't know? If there was one phrase I was beginning to hate, that was it. This time, however, I just wanted to be sure this greasy genespliced son of a bitch didn't know where Gabe's daughter was. "Who?" I interrupted. "Who is it?"

Who betrayed them?

He folded his arms in a copy of my pose. He was sweating, his crumpled suit beginning to wilt. "Are you going to kill me, Valentine? Where's the cure?"

"In a safe place." *Three vials held by a demon in hock and the recipe and the murder file with Jado.* A very nasty thought hit me after I finished the sentence—I'd given one vial to Horman.

I'd been so sure he could be trusted. But right after that four police cruisers had descended on me. And one vial was gone—maybe stolen by whoever Gabe had trusted, whoever had gone in her house and searched it as she lay bleeding and dying in her own backyard, stunned with a focused EMP pulse maybe triggered by a member of her own police force.

Sekhmet sa'es, I'm even suspecting Horman. He wouldn't be mixed up in this; he doesn't play like that. But the suspicion had taken root, and bloomed in my chest with a feeling uncomfortably close to panic.

I was well on my way to being paranoid. Rain slapped the window with rattling spatters of ice. Blood dripped off my elbows, I felt the blades of my claws slide out of my flesh. My eyes dropped to Massadie's chest. "Who?" My voice had dropped a whole octave, it worked its way free of my throat and I tasted the copper fruit-spice of demon blood. *I am not in the mood to fuck around. Don't push me. For the love of every god there ever was, don't push me, you fucking little pile of corporate shit.*

He gasped in a short choppy breath. I twitched, and he yelled the name as he went backward, his shoulders pressed against bare white-painted wall as I found myself halfway across the room, my boots suddenly skidding on the plush blue carpet and my right hand raised, claws springing free. My hand no longer resembled anything human, graceful and golden-skinned, the black-tipped claws glassy and glinting dully as they extended. Black-tipped because I painted the ends just like they were fingernails—or I had, before. The molecule-drip polish was chipped and cracked now.

I stopped. We stared at each other. I blinked. "But...." I trailed off.

"It's true," he squealed, his face no longer the polished perfection of a statue but distorted into a tragedy-mask of fear. "I swear it, I *swear on my mother's grave it's true!*"

I believed him. As fantastic as it was, I *believed* him. It made sense now. Everything about the puzzle clicked into place— everything except who in the Saint City PD had murdered Gabe.

I'd find that out soon enough, though. I was sure of that.

My hair fell in my eyes, but if I moved to swipe it back I wasn't sure I could stop myself from drawing my sword. I swallowed, heard the click in my dry throat. The pattern completed itself, everything in its proper place. "You're a loose end too. So you came running to find me."

"I knew Asa. His...he...Pico, we sell Chill through him." Massadie shook like a junkie in withdrawal. The rich gassy scent of his fear filled the room, went to my head like wine. In that single moment I understood far more about demons than I ever wanted to. It would be so fucking *easy* to kill him, and nobody would blame me. The fear was good. It was *power,* it was warm and heady and I could have gorged myself on it.

The cuff chilled against my wrist. Numbness spread up my left arm, but the heat pulsing from Japhrimel's mark drove it back.

You and your damn sense of honor, Gabe's voice echoed. Had she been surprised that I still kept some shards and slices of that honor? Would she be proud of how I was refraining from killing this polished genespliced leech?

Of course the pharm companies sold Chill. It was high-profit, easy for a fully equipped lab to make, and they could test other acid-based addictives and narcotics with it. So the pharm companies were in bed with the Mob, and the cops were in bed with the pharm companies, everyone got along well and made a tidy bundle. Until, of course, a Skinlin doing routine research came up with a cure and everyone started scrambling to own it and shut him up, not necessarily in that order.

"Sekhmet sa'es." Japhrimel's mark grew steadily warmer, a lasecutter-spot of heat against my skin. I caught a glimmer of green, the cuff reacting. Why? I didn't care just at the moment; I *needed* whatever this corpclone could tell me. "Who's her contact on the police force, Massadie? You give me that and you can walk away, I won't kill you."

"M-my career's r-r-ruined anyway," he stammered, sweat rolling off his perfect skin. How much genesplicing had Pico paid for, to make sure it had a beautiful face to present to the world? A pretty face on top and a mountain of bodies of dead Chill junkies on the bottom—and all the other victims too. Like Lewis, the closest thing to a father I'd had, choking on his own blood because a junkie needed a fix.

"Isn't that a fucking shame." I was having trouble caring. "Who?"

His voice broke. "Some fucker named Pontside. Her stepbrother."

I nodded. Everything came together in a tidy little package. *Her.* The traitor.

I turned on my heel and stalked for the door. The aroma of fear and shed demon blood turned the air velvet-soft, a red-painted scent like the inside of a sexwitch House.

The thought hit me with almost physical force, I almost staggered with a sudden panicked burst of fear. But nobody knew where Gabe's daughter was, nobody but me and maybe the Prime's Consort.

If anything happens to that kid not even a Nichtvren will be able to stop me from killing everyone who might have had a hand in this. Not even Japhrimel.

And that was why, even though I loved him, I could not let him hurt Eve. The fierce feeling under my breastbone was instinctive. Even though I'd never even contemplated having children I still would not let either Doreen's daughter or Gabe's be harmed if I could stop it.

Mine. Both of them are mine now.

I halted near the door, my hand on the knob. "If I see you again, I'll kill you." I didn't bother looking back. *He should be glad he's still alive,* I thought coldly. If he'd been less frightened of being found out as a psion, maybe Eddie would still be alive. Or if he'd just been a little more decent as a human being, he might have warned Eddie they'd been infiltrated instead of just trying to save his own miserable skin.

Why hadn't Gabe called me when the trouble started? I twisted the knob and stepped out into the hall.

I knew why. She probably felt guilty, since she'd asked me to take the Lourdes case and I'd ended up mind-raped and unable to think about the Hall without shuddering like a Chill junkie. Jace had died; how my own grief must have tortured her. She'd probably felt accountable since she'd called me in. When I disappeared without saying anything about Japhrimel she probably thought I couldn't stand to see her again; all the things we couldn't say to each other on the phone convincing her that somehow she was culpable. That she was to be blamed, or that I blamed her in some way for the whole rotten, ugly fiasco. As honorable as I tried to be, Gabe was intrinsically. How it must have hurt her to think she'd been responsible for my pain.

Oh, Gabe. Gabriele. I should have told you. I should have known.

I'd have taken the Lourdes case anyway. Some circles had to be closed; some debts had to be paid, willing or not. I had been chosen to close the murderous circle of Rigger Hall, whether by the gods or the ghosts of murdered and mind-battered children or by Fate itself. It had been my duty.

More than that, though, I would have done it because she'd needed me; she was my friend. My family. My *kin,* though we shared no blood. It had never occurred to me before that she could blame herself. That there was *anything* to blame her for.

Oh, Gabriele. I'm so sorry.

I paced down the hall and stopped, my nostrils flaring. Spice and heat filled my nose. The cuff squeezed, running with cold green light. I felt the bones in my wrist grind together.

Not another hellhound, please. Please, Anubis, not another hellhound.

Something didn't smell right. There was no sound other than the soft slap of rain and the rolling iron balls of thunder. I took the last step, around the bend in the hallway, and saw the room was empty. No Lucas, no Leander, and no Asa Tanner. The drapes moved near the window, wet wind pouring in through the broken window. I hadn't heard the glass shattering. My nostrils flared. The reek of demon was thick and overwhelming.

I heard faint sounds, as if there was a fight outside. Clashing steel, and the roar of a werecain in a rage, and Lucas rasping a crescendo of obscenities.

What the hell—My hand closed around the swordhilt, too late.

The skinny, red-skinned demon slapped my blade aside and backhanded me, the force of the blow like worlds colliding. His eyes glowed yellow, cat-slit, and he exhaled foulness in my face as darker lines of red like tribal tattoos writhed over his skin. The thin, high, chilling giggle raised the hairs on my nape. It was oddly familiar, had I heard that voice before?

Then he was on me, knee in my back, and something that *burned* clapped around my wrists. A noxious cloth pressed against my face, a whispered word in my ear, and darkness took me struggling down into a whirlpool. The last thing I saw was the edge of the drapes, slapping wetly at the wall below the window, and the green glow painting the walls as the wristcuff flared with icy vicious light before guttering out.

CHAPTER 26

I remember only flashes. A face over mine, a face I'd seen in DMZ Sarajevo while a nightclub full of Nichtvren and other paranormals danced to the throbbing beat below and a hellhound dozed at his side. Round and heavy, square teeth that still looked sharp, cat-slit glowing eyes. The face wasn't human, for all that a human Magi's hand had once drawn it in a charcoal sketch. The eyes were too big, the teeth too square, and the expression was...inhuman.

Velokel? The Hunter. Allied to Eve. Anubis, help me.

"She was *not* to be harmed." A harsh unlovely voice, but with its own compelling undertone. A voice that demanded obedience, burrowed along the nerve endings and *hurt* as it yanked at my bones, ran hot lead into my marrow. I moaned softly, half-swallowed the sound. I could barely even *think,* the disorientation was so intense.

"She'll live." Someone else, clear and chill as a bell. I recognized it, didn't I? I'd heard it taunting Japhrimel, when my fingers were glued to the ropy scar of his name against my shoulder.

"Here is your payment." Clink of something light and metallic, a short chuffing inhale of breath. "Consider our alliance renewed."

Darkness took me again as I strained to open my eyes, to see, to *fight.*

The next flash—a candleflame. Red flame, crimson as blood. Standing up straight, then wavering in a nonphysical direction, not guttering but seeming to shudder anyway. I struck out with fists and feet, dimly aware I was in danger. I heard shouts, and someone caught my wrist, a touch that sent fire through me and made my left shoulder crunch with vivid pain.

"Be still," he said, the voice that demanded I *obey.* I struggled against it, against him, felt the python squeeze of another mind close around mine, Power crushing down until my strangled scream choked the air. He *squeezed,* almost as I would with a werecain, but harder, determined—this was no warning, this was a prelude to brutal mental rape.

No. The core of stubbornness in me rose, something hard and ugly as biting on magtape. It was the strengthless endurance that had kept me alive and conscious during some of the worst parts of my life.

What you cannot escape you must fight. What you cannot fight, you must endure.

Scars in the fabric of my mind tore open, bled afresh. Tearing, ripping, my defenses resisted, denying him entrance to my mind, to the innermost core of me. For a dizzying eternity I was back in the shattered cafeteria in Rigger Hall, choking on ectoplasm as a Feeder ripped and stabbed through my psyche—

—shoving against the back of my throat, against my nose and eyes and ears, fingering at the zipper of my jeans, another tide of slime as Mirovitch's ka *tried to force its way in—*

A breathless scream spiraled up out of me. *No.* I would fight, I would *die* before enduring another vicious mental assault. I could not be violated that way again and remain sane.

"Stop." Female, young, and edged with steel, a smell like baking bread and heavy musk, a smell I recognized. The smell of Androgyne.

Eve, Doreen's daughter. Lucifer's child. And maybe mine too.

"*Stop* it. Didn't I tell you not to hurt her?" The sharp guncrack of a slap, and I fell into darkness again, the mental pressure falling away and my slight helpless moaning spiraling into silence.

Next came the gutwrench of hover transport, my stomach turning over in purely psychosomatic reaction to the rattling hum of antigrav. My cheek against freezing-cold metal, the Gauntlet on my left wrist propping my head up. I moaned, soundlessly, my mouth hung slack. Something was very wrong. I felt too weak, too fevered. What was happening to me?

Burning fingers stroked my forehead. "Hush," Eve said, gently. "It's all right, Dante. I'm here now."

I don't want you, I thought hazily. *I want Japhrimel. It should be him saying those words to me. Where is he? Japh?*

Power jolted down my spine, spread through nerve channels still screaming-raw with pain, detonated agony in my belly and my side, as if all the old wounds, from Lucifer's kick to the hellhound tearing into me, were slashing back open. I screamed, more and more Power forced into me, with no regard for pain or humanity.

"There," she whispered, stroking my forehead again. "Better?"

It *wasn't* better. Japhrimel wouldn't have hurt me like that, he had *never* hurt me like that. Childish faith rose up in me, I was too exhausted to fight it. Darkness, since I couldn't open my eyes, the crackling breathlessness of a small space full of demons, a heavy spice in the air that closed around me and soothed even as my nervous system jolted with more electric pain, raw acid tracing through my bones.

"Japhrimel," I heard myself whisper, cracked lips shaping the word.

"Soon enough," she said, and I heard cloth moving. She walked away, but the aura of her scent lingered, sinking into my head, confusing me until I passed out again.

When I woke next, my fingers slid against my breastbone. I lay on my back, on something soft. I felt the arc of my collarbone, the calluses on my fingertips scraping as I reached instinctively for my left shoulder. Then, *contact,* Japhrimel's mark writhing and hot, bumps and ropes of scarring moving under my skin like the inked lines of my tat.

I don't care, I thought hazily. *I need you. Please.*

The vision swallowed me whole, I sank into seeing out through his eyes as if I had never stopped. Had I always resisted before?

—spine straight, sitting in the middle of the circle holding square holding pentacle, the diagram spinning lazily against the glassy floor. Wrists braceleted with ignored agony, shoulders afire, staring straight ahead with dry burning eyes. The candleflame was low and guttering, now and then stretching. A few more hours, and he would be free.

The door opened, slowly, and she had come. As he had suspected, she could not ignore the chance to taunt him. Tall demon, the mark of the Androgyne on her forehead, a sleek cap of pale hair and a half-smile that tore at him, reminding. She was not the woman he wanted to see.

She wore simple blue, the marriage-color, a sweater and loose breeches hiding none of her slender grace. The aura of an Androgyne—spice, the potent smell of possible breeding, the attraction of fertility—teased at him.

It was not the scent he wanted.

"A spider emerges." Forcing the words out between his teeth, no politeness, no petty games of silence. "The trap was baited well."

She shrugged, pushing her sweater-sleeves up. "Sometimes the clumsiest tools are the most effective. You could be free in a single moment, Eldest. All that is necessary is to say the word." Her voice stroked the air, the weapon of an Androgyne, meant to seduce, cajole, entice.

His right hand became a fist, and the flexing of muscle pushed at his wrist, a red tide of pain sweeping up his arm.

She laughed, a low sarcastic bark of merriment. Perhaps he truly did amuse her. "Then I will be forced to treat with your companion, Fallen. She, at least, will listen to reason."

Both wrists burned now as his fists knotted. The candle guttered, recovered itself slowly. "If she is harmed—"

"Why would I harm her? She is so amenable, so willing to please."

It was his turn to laugh, sweeping his eyes across the room at the windows. No sunlight. Another day gone while he worried at the walls of his prison, tearing apart the demonic magick that held him bit by bit, thread by thread. Inhuman patience, a single-pointed will, spurred by the need burning in his veins. Need, like addiction. He wanted to see her again, he needed *to see her again, to reassure himself she was alive, unharmed.*

He needed to touch her.

"You have not found her so?" Eve continued, patent surprise in her tone. "But of course not. And now all her frustrated passion for you will fall upon me. I am, at least, willing to simply ask *her. She does not trust you."*

"She will know better in time." The words scraped his throat raw, he forced down rage. It would blind him, and he needed clear vision now.

"She escaped and killed a hellhound, Eldest. Even now she cries out your name as she lies wounded—no, not by my hand, I assure you. Such a thing has never been seen before, a Fallen's concubine overmatching a Hound."

He shrugged, the movement spilling pain into his shoulders. The heavy liquid of his armored wings slid against his skin. "You do not deceive me."

It was not an answer.

Her tone was gentle. Of course, she did not need to shout. "You are

Fallen, yet with a demon's Power. She is hedaira, *bound to you and sharing in your newfound status. Such a pair could help me topple him, Eldest. Such a pair could name their price for support or service."*

He closed his eyes. "You bore me."

"What side will you choose if she ties herself to me? Answer me that, Deathbringer. Should I add any of your other titles, Right Hand? Kinslayer?"

He said nothing.

"She had this," the Androgyne continued, and he opened his eyes again. Saw, with no real surprise, the book. How had she found it? How had she had time to find it? Or was it another lie? "I think perhaps I should read it to her, I may even teach her the language it is written in. It will make a wonderful bedtime story."

His legs twitched, ready to bring him to his feet. But it was still not yet time. He closed his eyes again, did his best to close his ears.

The silvery laugh taunted him. "Pleasant thoughts, Eldest." The door scraped along the floor as she closed it, and the sound-not-sound of another hellhound appearing, its padded obsidian feet striking against the floor like fingers caressing a drumhead, scored his ears. His—

—fingertips fell away from the mark, and I blinked up at a ceiling made of blue. Deep dark blue velvet hung in waves, stitched with tiny little things that glittered in the low clear light pouring in through a gray, rain-speckled window.

The bed was fit for a princess, four-postered and choked in dark blue silk and velvet. I pushed myself up on my elbows, flinched as my tender head reminded me someone had been messing with my psychic shields. Silk sheets slid cold against my naked skin. There was a nivron fireplace spitting blue flame, and the decor ran to heavy faux-Renascence. A slice of white tiled bathroom gleamed through an open door. Two chairs, both of blue watered silk, and something incongruous—a steam-driven radiator, painted white, set under the window.

I thought there weren't any of those left. If I hadn't been so research-oriented, I might not have recognized it. As it was, I'd swallowed history books whole all my life. A printed page was a psion's best friend—books didn't point, or mock, or beat, or manipulate. They simply told the story.

My eyes closed, slowly, as if my eyelids were falling curtains.

The moments seen through Japhrimel's eyes had taken on the quality of a dream, fuzzy and fading. I sighed.

What dream is this, before my eyes? I heard Lewis's voice, even and deep. *Dreams, the children of an idle brain...I dreamed a dream, and lo my dream was taken from me....*

My head echoed with jabs of pain, poking into my temples. My mental shields had held up, demon-strong—but old scars had ripped apart again, as if my psyche was part of my flesh and torn open. A nervous trembling like voltage through a faulty AI relay quaked up from my bones. I shivered, cold and feverish at the same time.

After life's fitful fever he sleeps well, Lewis's ghost whispered. I could almost smell the coffee he used to drink, thick espresso cut with cream. Could feel my child-self's cheek resting on my small hand as I listened to his flexible voice slide through the ancient words, strangely accented. *Lord, what fools these mortals be. Night and day the gates of dark Death stand open....*

Another voice cut across the recitation. *I will always come for you.*

Japhrimel. My eyes flew open. My sword lay sheathed next to me. My right hand curled loose around the hilt. My bag, a dimple of darkness, lay against the bottom of the bed. I heard stealthy creaks, little tiny sounds, telling me others moved in this place. But the sounds were...different. Too light and quick, or too groaningly heavy. They were not the human sounds of an inhabited house. The air was thick and heavy with crackling Power, the walls vibrating with demon shielding. I recognized it as the type of shields Japhrimel had laid in every room we'd shared. Shielding to keep a room invisible, to keep everything inside safe.

My bedroom in Toscano had been blue, too. But the light in that bedroom had been warm, southern sun flooding every surface. This light was cold, gray, and wet. Saint City light.

I reached for my bag, making a small noise as my abdomen protested. The sight of the Gauntlet, no longer dull silver but turned dark as if corroded, barely stopped me. I couldn't tell if the cold clasping my flesh was from the cuff or not.

I didn't care, either.

I dragged my bag across velvet, flipped it open, and found it unransacked. Even Selene's book was still there. It was small, the size of a holovid still romance, and in the light I saw the cover, too fine-grained to be leather.

Had I really seen the book in Eve's hands, through Japhrimel's eyes? Had Eve slipped it back into my bag? Or was Japhrimel even able to lie to me while I looked through his eyes, since he was no longer a familiar but Fallen?

I wouldn't put it past him. But there would be no way for him to know when I was going to touch the mark. Eve wants my help, she wants his help too; If she can't have both of us she'll take me. I don't blame her at all. I didn't even mind her telling him about my "frustrated passion" for him.

Hey, you can't argue with the truth.

My fingers trembled, the chipped black polish on my nails glowing mellow. My cuff ran and rang with green light, the fluid lines carved in it twisting and straining. Sheets and blankets pooled in my lap, my golden skin unmarked but feeling stretched-thin, too strained.

Hedaraie Occasus Demonae, stamped into the cover with gilt. It looked old, and the faint spice of demons clung to every closely-written page. It was written in a spidery alien hand, the ink deep maroon on vellum pages. It was in a language I had no hope of reading, vaguely Erabic but with plenty of spiked diacritical marks I couldn't decipher. Useless unless I did some more research, found someone who knew what language it was and had time to teach me or translate it. I glanced at a few pages without truly seeing them, examined the binding, and dropped it in my bag as if it had burned me.

It was skin, but not animal skin. Bile whipped the back of my throat. I yanked my bag closed and tightened my grip on my sword.

I sensed her before the door opened, the black diamond fire of a demon's aura. When the door opened—I heard no click of a lock—and Eve stepped in, I sucked in my breath and pulled the sheet up with my right hand, covering my chest and wadding the silk against the mark on my shoulder. My left hand closed around my sword so tightly the knuckles turned white.

She was slim, with sleek pale hair and flashing dark-blue eyes. Today she wore white, a pristine crisp button-down shirt with the tapered sleeves that were fashionable now, a pair of bleached jeans, good boots. Doreen had always worn sandals.

Doreen. The cuff squeezed my wrist again, so hard the bones creaked.

She *looked* like Doreen, the same triangular face and wide eyes, the same way of tilting her head. She folded her arms, a fall of material caught in them, and I breathed in the smell of Androgyne, the Power flooding from her sparking along my nerve endings.

"Dante," she said quietly. "I've brought you clothes. And explanations."

"The h-hellhounds." I sounded like a little girl. The wristcuff above my datband glowed green. "Velokel?"

"Only one was ours, and only supposed to *find* you so I could speak with you. The other, I do not know. Kel would not harm you, Dante. He knows how much you mean to me."

Is that why he tried to tear my head open like a sodaflo can? My throat was dry. "You have Japh."

She nodded. "It was a stroke of luck, capturing instead of killing him." Her pale hair didn't ruffle, it was as sleek as a silken cap. Her skin glowed, burnished gold. "I'd hoped you would be able to distract him."

Me too. "He's persistent." The thin trickle of heat in my belly made my stomach turn. *I am not a sexwitch. I do not respond this way to Power.*

But I did, didn't I? After all, I was staring at her, at the shape of her lips, filling my lungs with the scent of her. Fresh bread, musk, and demon, a smell that whipsawed me between terror and desire, a smell that made it difficult to think straight. Pheromones like a sex-witch, drenching the air. She smelled like Lucifer, but she didn't scare me the way he did.

She sighed. "We've had a difficult time evading the Eldest."

"You and me both. He kept putting me to sleep without my real-izing it. I asked him not to hunt you, Eve. I *begged* him not to hunt you, and not to lie to me." *I sound like a whiny three-year-old.* But it was suddenly very important for Doreen's daughter to understand I'd tried my best to keep him away from her.

She made an expressive gesture with one hand, brushing away the need to explain. "Demons lie, Dante. It's in the nature of the thing." Her lips quirked up into a half-smile, my own expression, familiar. Was it true? Was she also my daughter, the sample Santino took from Doreen contaminated with my blood as well?

Doreen's daughter, Gabe's daughter. Both mothers dead and depending on me.

How am I going to pull this one off? My mouth was dry, my lips cracked. "You too?"

"Maybe. I suppose you'll have to figure out if you can trust me.

There are no guarantees." She held up the handful of material, jeans and something else. "I brought you fresh clothes. Then I'll take you to see the Eldest."

My throat closed up. *He's here. In the same building, maybe? The mark was numb, maybe because whatever they have him trapped in cuts him off from me?* "What if I don't want to see him?" It was a rusty croak. The light caressed her face, ran its fingers over her hair, touched the arc of her golden neck where the pulse beat.

She shrugged. "How else are you going to know if I'm lying?"

I tore my eyes away from her face, away from the slope of her breasts under the crisp white cotton. My eyes fell on my sword's curved length, resting against the velvet in the glowing indigo sheath Japhrimel had given me. "I have a revenge to do." I still sounded like a little girl; high and squeaky, and breathless.

"I won't force you, Dante. I'll ask for your support, but I won't force you." She approached quietly, cloth whispering as she laid the clothes on the end of the bed. "Your weapons are there, on the floor. Whenever you're ready, you may go on your way or see the Eldest, as you wish. If you decide to . . . to throw your lot in with us, we'll welcome you. You killed a hellhound; there's not many that could have done so."

It almost killed me too, it was trying to take my heart out through my ribs the hard way. "The h-hellhound was t-trying t-t-to—"

"The one we sent was supposed to find you and bring you to us, not harm you. I'm sorry, Dante. Events have become . . . complex."

Complex. I was getting to hate that word. When someone said *it's getting complex,* the translation usually was *Danny Valentine's about to get screwed.*

My head hurt. I had revenge to accomplish and Gabe's daughter to collect; I didn't have time for demon games.

My heart thudded behind my breastbone. "Leander. And Lucas. The demon—"

"The demon who brought you to us was uninterested in the others, Dante. Or so he told us. I believe he was led to you in a manner I would not quite agree with." I felt more than heard her back away, toward the door. "Kel mistreated you, and for that I am sorry. I will punish him, if you like."

Oh, gods. I shook my head, speechless. *Leave me the hell out of this. I don't need another demon mad at me.*

"If you like," she repeated, patiently.

"No," I whispered. *Where did they go? Did they sense the demon coming? Gods grant they got out of there in time.* I shuddered again, ice water creeping through my veins. I wasn't thinking straight. "No," I repeated, louder.

The gods knew I didn't want to make another demon enemy. *Just add it to my laundry list,* the merry voice of unreason chirped brightly inside my skull. I choked down a maniacal giggle.

"As you like." She paused. "If you change your mind, all you have to do is tell me."

I shook my head again, and she retreated.

When she closed the door with a quiet click, I scrambled up out of the bed to get dressed. My legs were a little shaky but still solid, and once I had clothes on I felt a lot better. If I kept moving, the vision of Eddie's shattered body—and the vision of Gabe's broken, battered, bloody one—wouldn't torture me so much. If I could just keep *moving* I might be able to get through this.

The clothes were...well, they were almost certainly Eve's. The sweater was too big for me, as was the silk T-shirt. But they were clean, and the jeans fit, and the boots were my size even if they were too new. They would need hard use before they were good.

My head gave an amazing flare of pain, so did my left shoulder. I crouched at the foot of the bed for a little while with my sword in my hands and my forehead pressed into the velvet of the coverlet. The shivers and hyperventilating finally stilled. Even my god was silent. There was no blue glow, no comforting sense of being held in Death's hands. There was only the breathless sense of waiting. For what?

True to Eve's word, my weapons rig was tangled on the floor by the bed. Everything was undisturbed, I buckled myself in and wished for a microfiber shirt and a coat. Jace's necklace still rested against my throat, pulsing reassuringly as my fingers touched the knobs of the baculum. The mark on my shoulder had turned warm but quiescent, feeling like normal skin for the first time since it had been pressed into my flesh.

The cold retreated bit by bit, and the sense of being watched returned, but oddly distant. As if something was trying to see me, through layers of interference. Something deadly and inimical.

The Gauntlet was still dead-dark against golden skin, its surface swallowing instead of reflecting light.

I don't think I'm thinking clearly.

My right hand shook when I held it out in front of me. I tried to stop it, but the harder I tried the harder it vibrated. My fingers jittered like a slicboard needing tuning.

That reminded me of the Valkyrie, under a hedge in the rich bay-front part of town. I wanted the slicboard. It was a ridiculous thing to focus on, but it seemed the only thing that mattered was the sleek black deck, gleaming as I pressed its powercell and flung myself into open air, going fast enough to outrun...what?

First things first, Dante. Get this the fuck over with so you can kill the fucking traitors. Then you can go on living. Everything else— demons, Hell, Lucifer, even Eve—can wait.

I stopped the trembling in my hands by simply clamping them around the sword's slenderness. Once I got right down to it, the world was really simple. All I had to do was just cut out the bullshit and decide who to kill first.

I found Eve waiting for me in the hall, leaning against the wall and looking out a long window while gray light washed her face. She had tucked her pale hair behind her ears and stood slumped, as if tired. But she turned to me with a smile, as Doreen always had, and my heart thudded in my throat. "It's so nice to see the sun," she said, a little wistfully. Her smell mixed with mine, a fleshy ripe combination of musk and cinnamon, demon and female. "I missed that, in Hell."

A year in Hell is not the same as a year here, they all told me. I hoped I'd never find out. I glanced out the window, saw a slice of green and a high concrete wall. The hall was long, with high narrow windows. Blank doors stood at even intervals.

"You weren't ever allowed to come out?" Miraculously, my voice didn't shake. I clenched the sword in my hands, the hilt bobbing a little as my arms jerked.

She shook her head slightly, her eyes dropping. "Coming to your world, is a privilege for us. One earned only by obedience." Eve peeled herself away from the wall, pushing her sweater-sleeves up. "I have not been obedient in the slightest."

The hall was painted white too, with a hardwood floor. It looked like an institutional hall, and the skin on my back roughened to phantom gooseflesh at the thought that it might be a school. Or any old abandoned government building, maybe. Who knew? About all I could tell was that I was still in Saint City.

My arms jerked again.

Eve's fingers closed around mine. She was too close; I flinched.

Demons had a spooky habit of getting too damn close to me; maybe they liked to move in on humans and see them flinch.

Only I wasn't quite human, was I?

The Androgyne's hand was warm, her skin impossibly soft. "*Avayin, hedaira,*" she murmured. "Peace, Dante. Breathe."

I did. It was what Japhrimel always told me—*Breathe, Dante. Simply breathe.* It was enough like him that I felt my shoulders unloose, I closed my eyes. The iron bands squeezed around my lungs loosened a little, I dragged air down into the very bottom of my belly, and blessedly saw the blue glow of Death rise behind my eyelids. It wasn't much—just subtle traceries of blue fire—but it made the shakes settle down.

My god, at least, had never betrayed me.

When I opened my eyes, I found Eve's face inches from my own, her nose almost touching mine. Her eyes were like Doreen's, dark blue, and except for the gold of her skin and the green gem glittering above and between her eyes, it was like looking at Doreen again. The crucial millimeters of difference weren't so visible close up, the overlay of demon that made her so exotic. Was there a similarity to my own face lurking in her bones?

My daughter. All I had left of my *sedayeen* lover.

"Better?" she asked again.

I nodded, just a slight dip of my chin. "I've got to go," I managed through the lump in my throat. "I've got a revenge to finish before I'm free to handle the rest of this." Now my knees were shaking for a different reason. She was so close I drowned in her smell, fire rising through my bones and blood and flesh, a heat I recognized pounding in my wrists and throat—and low in my belly.

I stepped back, breaking her hold on my hands. She let me go. There was a faint smile playing on her lips—an expression that was neither Doreen's nor mine, or even her own.

It reminded me of Lucifer. A slight, cruel lift of the corners of the lips, the eyes lit from within, the entire shape of the face changing from sweet or tired to predatory.

Desire turned to ice, crackling through me. Gray light bleached her platinum hair even further, made her eyes lighter than their usual dark blue. With the emerald glowing in her forehead, her eyes took on a slightly green cast.

Gods—My heart hammered. "Eve?" The word shattered on my lips, fell to the floor.

She shook her hair back and was again familiar. Or if not familiar, then at least more like what I thought I recognized.

Demons lie, Dante. Demons lie.

But Eve hadn't done anything to make me distrust her. As a matter of fact, she was the only demon I seemed able to believe at this point.

"See him," she said. "Please. If you would, Dante."

Weariness swept over me, sucked at my legs. What did it matter? I knew what I needed to know, knew where my revenge lay. Five minutes facing down Japhrimel wouldn't matter one way or another. Would it? "Can he get out?"

Her shrug was a marvel of even fluidity. "He's the Eldest. Even an Androgyne can't hold him for long, even in a circle made harder to break by the use of his *hedaira*'s name. No one except the Prince could hold him, and perhaps not even that." She studied me for a moment, her hands dropping graceful and loose to her sides. "Of course, if you broke even a single line of the circles around him… that would set him completely free. I only ask for a little warning, enough to get my people out of here. We fear him."

The set level look in her blue eyes convinced me. *You used my name in a circle to trap him? No wonder he's pissed.* I swallowed, tasted copper. "There's a bunch of demons running around loose. What's going on?"

Her eyebrows lifted slightly. "My rebellion, it seems, has spread. I suspect that isn't what worries *him* the most, though." As usual, when she mentioned Lucifer her lip curled and her expressive eyes filled with disdain and loathing, not to mention a healthy dose of fear.

I stared at her face. "The treasure." A thin croak, the words turned to dust. "The Key."

"So he's told you?" She looked puzzled.

I shook my head. I felt gawky next to her sleek beauty. She was so comfortable inside her golden skin, and I felt like an imposter every time I saw my face in the mirror. "He wouldn't tell me. We saw the Anhelikos in Sarajevo, though. I didn't have time to tell you."

Eve nodded. "We're searching for something, Dante. A weapon that can change our fortunes and turn our rebellion into a successful coup. It will take time to track it down, but there have been *most* encouraging signs." Her mouth tilted up in a smile, so much like Doreen's gentle, forgiving expression I almost choked. "And once we have that weapon, *he* is welcome to find us."

A weapon. So the treasure is a weapon. "What's the Key?" I asked, my heart sinking.

"Not what, Dante. *Who.* We don't know who the Key is yet, but I have a good idea. I think I'm the only one who does." She was looking brighter and happier all the time. "When the time comes, the Key will be revealed. I think that's what the Eldest is afraid of. If he finds the weapon first, he will be in a position to dictate to the Prince. If I find it . . . he may find himself on the losing side. If that happens, you may well be the only person who can save him. He's too dangerous to be allowed to live."

She sounded as calm as if she was discussing dinner plans. "You mean you'd . . . ."

"For your sake, I want to give him every chance. You are, after all, the only mother I have left." Now her eyes were large and dark. The rainy sunlight fell over the curves and planes of her face, so like Doreen's. "Will you help me, Dante?"

Gods above and below, you don't even have to ask. I'm already in up to my neck because I'm helping you, I might as well drown.

"Okay." My throat was dry, my heart pounding in my wrists and temples. I could even feel the pulsing of my femoral arteries, my heart thundered so hard. "Fine. Lead the way, let's get this over with."

CHAPTER 27

I was right, this had been a school. I knew because they had him in the gymnasia, a huge wood-floored expanse pierced with shafts of cool light from the high-up windows. Bleachers had been pulled away from the walls and taken out so nothing remained but bare stained expanses of painted wall and gravball hoops bolted to either end of the long room. He was in the south end.

It was just as I'd seen it, and I had to shake away the persistent doubled feeling of living out a premonition. Eve had paused near the door and asked if I wanted to be alone, I shook my head and motioned her inside. She closed the door with a precise little click—the maghinge had been taken off—and leaned against it, waiting. Her eyes were dark again, blue and lit from below like a swimtank with cloned koi flicking through its depths.

I squared my shoulders and walked across the wooden floor, the heels of my new boots tapping on the wood. Halfway there, the mellow shine turned to glass underfoot. Seamlessly, a glossy black obsidian sheet rose up and supplanted the flooring.

Demons are such snazzy interior decorators. I grabbed at the darkly humorous thought as if it was floating debris and I was drowning. If I was still cracking jokes, I was okay. Maybe. Kind of.

Not really.

The Key isn't a what, it's a who. And if I can't convince Japh to back off...a weapon that could kill the Devil. My fingers tightened on the hilt, the Gauntlet's heavy cold weight a reminder of the promise I'd made—the one I was about to break. *It could just as easily kill Japh. Then I'd have to resurrect him. I never want to do that again, I don't even know for sure what will bring him back, other than fire. Lots of fire. And maybe blood. He says enough blood would do the trick, but how do I know for sure?*

The air in here was thick and still, curdled with magick. It raised the fine hairs on my nape, coated the back of my throat, almost made my eyes water.

He sat cross-legged in the middle of the circles, his back straight and his long black coat lying wetly against the floor behind him. In front of him, the candle with the blood-red flame now flickered and guttered, the streak of red light a good four inches high. There was about three inches left of wax for it to burn through.

When the candle was snuffed, what would happen? But he'd probably be loose by then.

I could See the layers of magick, woven too tightly and skillfully to be human, glowing with the icy tang of demon Power. I could also See his careful patient unraveling, working at the threads that held the borders of the circles—my eye traveled over them, marking each symbol in a Magi-trained memory. This was demon magick, a kind Japhrimel would never share with me. If it could trap him here like a silkworm in a kerri jar, I could almost understand why.

And if Eve had used my name in the binding, and it held him here this long...I didn't want to think about that. I didn't want to think about how furious he was going to be once I finished what I was about to say.

My hands were shaking again. I clasped them around the sword. Then I remembered something.

I freed my right hand for long enough to dig in my bag, eyeing him nervously the whole time. Japhrimel said nothing, merely sat, his head dropped. Ink-black hair fell down, hiding his eyes. His shoulders were military-straight under the liquid blackness of his coat. His golden hands lay loosely in his lap, I could see no mark on his wrists. His sleeves covered them.

The chain twisted, dangling the sapphire from my fingers. I held it out, swallowed harshly, then forced my shaking hand open and let it drop.

It hit the glassy floor with a tinkling sound, four feet from the border of the outside circle, the one holding the pentacle that nested the square and inmost circle in its heart. I could see the shimmering brittle veils of energy, focused and curved so any direct attack from Japhrimel's side would shunt the force directly back at him. Eve wasn't lying—all I had to do was *touch,* and the outer layers of the magick would crack and fall away. You could not make a shield like this impervious on both sides, even with all a demon's Power.

At the small chiming of the necklace meeting the floor, he slowly raised his head and looked at me, his eyes halting for just the barest moment at my left wrist and the dead black weight of the Gauntlet.

I would have backed up, lifted the sword between me and his laser-green gaze again, but the granite egg inside my chest cracked. Rage boiled up, hot and satisfying, I returned to myself with an incendiary jolt. It felt good to let the anger out, as if a valve had been opened, some of the awful pressure bleeding away.

I narrowed my eyes and stared back, hoping it was just as uncomfortable for him. It wasn't bloody likely, but a girl could hope, couldn't she?

His lips moved. "Dante," he said, quietly. Evenly. With no particular weight of emotion.

Hey, sunshine. Glad to see me? I clamped down on the shudders jolting through me. "Japhrimel."

His eyes bored into mine. The command was immediate, peremptory. "Release me."

Not even a "Hi, how are you?" The fury mounted another pitch. Giving me orders, again. Well, now that he couldn't manipulate me and lull me to sleep while he ran around doing gods-knew-what, I suppose it was about all he had left. It shouldn't have made me angry—but it did.

"What the hell *for?*" I shook my head, my hair brushing my shoulders and spilling into my face. I needed to find something to tie it back with. "I told you, I warned you. I *begged* you not to hunt her, didn't I? I begged you not to lie to me, not to keep things from me. But I suppose that's all a human's good for. *Begging.*"

He shrugged. He *shrugged* at me.

It was a good thing my hands were shaking so badly, I decided. Otherwise I might have done something completely idiotic, like draw my sword and charge through the circles. As it was, I stared at him, my eyes moving over the face I'd thought was familiar. Why was I always so surprised to find him so attractive? His nose was a little too long, his lips too thin, the planes of his cheeks too harsh, his eyebrows too straight. But I liked it better than Lucifer's golden beauty or Massadie's genespliced perfection.

Japh was beautiful like a blade was beautiful, anything well-oiled and deadly dedicated to a single purpose.

Hate surged inside me, all the more intense for the spoiled affection and broken trust underneath it. It wasn't fair to blame him for everything, but it was so easy. So convenient. He was here, and so was my daughter, and I might be the only thing standing between them.

I would have to be enough.

"You *bastard,*" I whispered. "You motherfucking *demon.*"

"I am," he returned calmly, "what you make of me." His right hand curled into a fist. His eyes flicked away to the red candleflame, which began to smoke and splutter. "I warned you not to make me savage, Dante."

My voice hit a pitch just under "shriek." "Me? This is *my* fault? You're the one who deceives, and manipulates, and—"

The candleflame guttered under the weight of his gaze, recovered with a sound like air sliding past a hover's hull. "You are the Prince's Right Hand, and you are implicitly aiding his enemies. Against your own *A'nankhimel,* I might add, the demon who Fell through love of you. Where is your precious honor in *that?*"

I don't think either of us believed he'd said that. The glassy floor creaked and shifted as the circles fought to contain him—and won, but just barely. They were right, he was going to get out soon.

And all the gods help us when he did.

"So it's war," I said. "Me and Eve on one side, you and the Devil on the other."

"Do not be so sure." But his tone was now colored faintly with sarcasm. "I will have your compliance, Dante, one way or another.

Free me now, and I can promise I will deal gently with the Androg-yne and her rebellion. I can perhaps even save some of them."

Well, at least he's being honest about not being on my side, for once. A jittering, thready laugh burst out of me. The gravball hoop nearest us shivered, the bolts holding it to the wall squeaking a thin song of agonized metal. The air sparked and danced like carbolic tossed across reactive paint, glittering and smoking.

"There's not a single thing you could swear on now that I would believe, Eldest." I backed up one step, two, unwilling to turn my back on him. My traitorous eyes still drank in his face. I wished he would look at me, buried the wish as soon as it appeared.

"I could swear on my *hedaira*." He even managed to say it with a straight face.

"Save it for someone who gives a fuck." Each word was bitterness itself, almost bitter as the taste of Death in my mouth as I brought a soul back. "We're *over*, Japhrimel. It's war."

His eyes left the candleflame, traveled slow and scorching across the floor. Met my boots, slid gelid and heavy up my legs, caressed my torso, and finally found my face. The mark on my shoulder crunched with fresh sensation, steel fire braiding into my skin and turning to velvet, driving a fresh wave of numbness back down my arm and almost to the cuff.

I ignored it. I was getting very good at ignoring that feeling. Just like I was getting very good at jamming down the squealing wall of rage. What would happen when I couldn't push it away anymore?

He drew in a sharp breath, two spots of color flaming high on his cheekbones. His eyes were incandescent, and he had never looked so much like Lucifer. "There is *nothing,* on this earth or in Hell, that will keep me from you. *I am your Fallen.*"

I lifted the sword slightly, the hilt mercifully deflecting his eyes from mine. "Whatever weapon Eve's looking for, I hope she finds it. The next time I see you, I'm going to fight you with everything I have." My throat closed on the words, bit each off sharply. Made them a husky promise. Here among demons, I didn't have to worry about the invitation in my voice, the Power that coated my words, my own unwanted ability to seduce. "I *trusted* you, Japhrimel. You betrayed me first."

He said nothing. There didn't seem to be much else to say.

I turned my back on him. I walked away, each footstep echoing. His eyes were on me the whole time, a weight against my shoulders.

It took an eternity to reach the door. Eve slid her arm over my shoulders, and I was glad because I didn't think I could stay upright much longer. She glanced back over her shoulder at Japhrimel and ushered me out into the hall. When the door closed with a quiet click I felt something inside my chest snap like a bone breaking.

I ducked away from under her arm as soon as I could stand. "I need a slicboard and I need to get going. I've got business to finish."

She nodded, sleek hair swinging. "Whatever it is, be quick about it. That won't hold him for long." She looked like she wanted to say something else — maybe something ridiculously human like *are you okay?*

But I knew the answer to that. I was *not* okay.

I was not ever going to be anything close to "okay" ever again. I'd just thrown down the gauntlet, ha ha, and when he got out of there he was going to come looking for me. It was all out in the open now — his lies, and my refusal to live up to my end of the bargain we'd made with Lucifer.

Now it was war. I didn't think he'd fight fair.

I didn't think *I* would fight fair either. Not with Eve depending on me. I squared my shoulders, willed my legs to stop trembling. "I've got some business to finish. Where are we going to hook up?"

She nodded slightly. It was an implicit agreement. I was breaking my word to Lucifer, I had betrayed Japhrimel. It was all over but the screaming, as they used to say.

Now I just need to get this wristcuff off, and we'll be ready to tango.

Her dark-blue eyes held mine, a velvet cage. "If you can, meet me in Paradisse. If not, I'll find you."

Paradisse, in Hegemony Franje, the glittering suspended city of a thousand lights and the Darkside underneath. A great place to hide, especially for a demon. I nodded. My eyes were suspiciously full and hot.

Eve leaned forward. Her breath brushed my cheek, and then her cool scented mouth met my skin.

It was a gentle chaste kiss on my cheek, and very short, but it scorched all the way through me. When she backed away, I found I could stand up straight. I could even unlock my hands from my sword and push back a few strands of my rebellious hair. The hallway quivered, the dust in the air holding its breath.

Does that mean the bargain's struck? Sealed with a kiss. The kiss

*of betrayal. I can't win against Japhrimel, but I can't betray Eve
either. I'm fucking doomed.*

"Thank you," she said gravely. "I won't forget this."

*I have a sneaking suspicion I won't either. I just did the one thing
a Necromance should never do—I've broken my word.* "I know," I
whispered. "Do me a favor and get out of here fast. He's closer to
breaking out than you think."

I called Jado from a public callbox in the University District, leaning
against the side of the booth and watching the crowd of late-afternoon
shoppers contending with the steady persistent drizzle. Another
storm was moving in, I could tell from the way the rain smelled and
the air was full of uneasy crackles. Whether that storm was weather
or trouble, I couldn't tell. I suspected it was both.

Jado could tell me nothing except that Cam and Mercy were gone.
Not particularly surprising; I'd expected it. He still had the sealed
pouch with the mastersheets and file—it would take more than either
of them had to steal from *him.*

He asked if I had found what I was looking for.

"After a fashion, *sensei.*" I hardly trembled at all, though I did
sound husky and ruined. For once, I felt just as tired as I sounded.
"Thank you. I'll keep in touch."

That done, I hailed a hovercab at the corner of University and
Thirteenth. The driver, a fat pasty normal in a blue felt hat, for once
didn't mutter or turn pale when he saw my tat. He seemed blissfully
unaware that I was a psion.

Well, little miracles do happen.

"Trivisidiro, North End. Get me there fifteen minutes ago."

I only hoped I wasn't too late.

CHAPTER 28

Jace taught me more about bounty hunting in a single year than all the
law-enforcement supplements at the Academy had in five. The first
rule, he always said, was to *understand* your prey. When you comprehend the nature of what you hunt, you understand what it is capable
of—and can anticipate its next move.

I watched as dusk fell over Trivisidiro, chill purple shadows gathering in rain-drenched corners. The high walls of Gabe's property line stood mute under a lash of rainy just-above-freezing wind; the shields were still viable, the work I'd done binding them together holding steady. I leaned against the wall of my hiding spot, tucked between another house's high walls and a dripping holly hedge prickling against my hand and shoulder and hip, poking through wet fabric. My skin steamed where the rain hit it, but the steam shredded before it could rise above the hedge and give away my position. I waited still and quiet, counting on the instability of the storm and the flux of Power to keep me hidden—since I was having a hard time keeping myself buttoned down anymore. I needed rest, I needed food, I needed sleep.

I wasn't going to get any of what I needed. Best just to deal with it.

There's a mind-numbing brand of circular mental motion that takes place while you're on stakeout. I thought about Japhrimel, would remind myself not to think about him and wrench my mind into remembering Gabe, lying tangled in a young hemlock. I would think of Gabe's daughter and a holostill smile. Would she have the dimple in her left cheek, like Gabe? Would she have a hoarse little braying laugh like Eddie? Would I be able to protect her while I was running from both Japhrimel and Lucifer, trying to keep Eve alive long enough to make a difference?

Though Eve didn't seem to be doing too badly. What the hell did she need *me* for? What was it with demons being so interested in me?

Which would lead me right back to thinking about Japhrimel. I'd begged him not to hunt her. Yet he'd refused to tell me what was going on, left me with McKinley while he went out looking for her. If he *had* managed to catch her and return her to Lucifer, what would have happened? Would he even have told me?

I shouldn't have been, but I was still surprised. Wearily, heart-wrenchingly surprised, each time I thought of it. He was a demon. His idea of truth wasn't necessarily mine. To him, I might be no more than a valued possession; a pet, even. You love your cat or your cloned koi, but you don't treat it like a human. No, you pet it, feed it, take it to the Animone for its shots and checkups. You don't treat it like a partner, or an equal.

Even if it's referred to in the singular, with you.

Had he thought that it would push me back on Lucifer's side if he appeared to be in danger? Or had he miscalculated, not thinking Eve was strong or smart enough to catch him *or* hold him this long?

Why? If I could have asked him anything, that little word would be it. It would cover so much, if I could trust his answer.

But he had held me while I cried, hadn't he? And no matter what kind of trouble I was in, I usually could count on him to bail me out. That was worth something, wasn't it?

I cherish my time with you. His voice, smoky-dark and smooth.

I tore my thoughts away from him again with an almost-physical effort, wondering about Lucas and Leander. Where were they? Were they even now frantically looking for me? Or had they been killed?

There was no more time for thinking. My prey came down the sidewalk in the early-morning dark, walking arm-in-arm as if they hadn't a care in the world. They might even have believed themselves safe.

After all, what did a *sedayeen* and a Saint City cop have to fear?

Only me, I thought, silent and deadly in the shadow of a holly hedge.

Only me.

I let them get through the shields. The layers of energy flushed a deep blue-green, settled as the healer stroked them. Bile rose in my throat. Gabe would not have denied a *sedayeen* entrance into her house, especially one working with Eddie. So she would have been already *inside* when something alerted Gabe to a possible attack on her property and the defenseless healer inside. Gabe, sword in hand, went out alone to defend her home and got shot. Then it was child's play for the healer to "clean" the psychic traces inside Gabe's house after she and the normals she'd let in through Gabe's shields searched for the vials.

Just like now it was child's play for the healer to slip in through the defenses with her normal in tow.

I let them get inside the dark, silent house, then drifted across the street and touched the shields. Softly, a kitten's brush of a touch, warning them not to react to me. Gabe's work recognized me — how could it not?

Oh, Gabriele. I failed you. I should have stayed. Even though it was hard, I should have stayed. Why didn't you tell me you were getting married, you had a kid, you were afraid for your life? Why? Didn't you trust me to come if you needed me?

No, she hadn't, because I'd lied to her about Japhrimel. With the best of intentions, because it would only raise more questions, because I couldn't stand to admit to her that I loved a demon and I was no longer fully human. Each phone call, with its long silences and the things neither of us could say, was another failure on my part. I should have told her.

It was my fault. I hadn't been here to protect her.

I slid through the layers of energy slowly, so slowly. Gabe's front gate squeaked as I pushed through it, but they wouldn't hear. Even if there had been Saint City PD magshielding or a lock on the place as the site of a homicide, a cop would have no trouble getting clearance, especially a normal homicide deet flush with dirty Chill money.

Everything so neatly arranged. Everything so perfectly planned. Down to the fact that I'd bet hard credit the cop had the missing fifth vial to sell to the highest bidder—the sample the healer had probably talked Gabe into producing after Eddie's death. I didn't know for sure, but that *felt* right.

The front door was open, the shields on the house quivering with the presence of intruders, even acceptable ones. The windows, blank empty darkened eyes, watched as I approached carefully, cautiously, and closed my right hand around my swordhilt. Up the stairs to the massive double door, not the side door that any friend of Gabe and Eddie's knew to go to. I slid through the front door, my new boots soft and soundless.

Just like a thief.

I found the trigger by the front door, my fingers sliding over the base of a bronze statue. The statue was Eros in Psyche's embrace, his wings pulled close around the half-nude female. Eddie had called it Classic Porn, sniggering every time he passed it. Gabe would icily remind him that it was an *antique,* and that it had been in her family for *generations,* and that the artist had been a *close family friend.* I could just see her immaculate eyebrow lifting as she repeated this patiently, as if Eddie was a primary-school kid with a dirty mind.

Of course, Eddie did have a primary-school kid's dirty mind. It was one of his greatest personality traits.

It was dark, but demon sight pierced the darkness easily, showed me the coats and boots from Gabe's hall closet scattered in careless lumps, each pocket sliced. They were coming back for another search, looking for the four vials I had given away.

I smelled *kyphii* and Gabe's particular scent, the tang of Eddie's dirt-drenched aura. Then I felt the other psion's shock as I dropped the outer layer of my shielding and blazed through the Power-soaked house like a star.

I pressed down on the trigger, and had the satisfying experience of hearing the locks on each window and door click shut. Maglocks, to turn the house into a fortress. The front door whooshed on automatic hinges, thudding closed and locking too.

I'm sorry, Gabe. I walked through the foyer, my boots absolutely silent. I could *feel* them both, the sloppy wash of the normal man tainted with fear and thudding heart, copper adrenaline. And the healer's deep well of violet-scented calm, underlain with a slight nasty wet-fur smell of panic fighting with her training and genetic disposition to tranquility.

The kitchen. I gave them plenty of time, walking slowly, the rage rising until my aura flushed red, almost in the visible range. A low punky crimson stain spread through the trademark swirling glitter of a Necromance's aura, mixing with the black diamond flames of an almost-demon. Strength flowed hot down my left arm, poured through the mark on my shoulder. I wondered if Japhrimel could feel me drawing on the mark, could feel my anger.

I didn't care.

The sword whispered out of its sheath as I stepped into the hall. Nothing had changed—the place still looked like a tornado had hit it. It hadn't even been dusted or scanned for prints; it hadn't even been touched by a Reader or another Necromance.

I would have thought they would go through the motions of investigating, for a cop as good as Gabe. Or had this case been given to Pontside too? Of course, if the Chill cure was still here, they couldn't run the risk of anyone else finding it. Not after they tossed the house with a psion to clean up the traces of normals trooping through.

If the cops didn't care or were unable to investigate, Gabe would never be avenged, and her daughter would remain in danger.

Not while I'm alive. Not while I have a single breath in me.

Tension, screaming in my shoulders; the cuff blazed with dappled, fluid green light. Light like Japhrimel's eyes, blazing while he looked up from the floor. I drew in a long sweet breath scented with *kyphii* and the old delicious smell of Gabe's house, the scent-landscape of a place lived in and loved by generation after generation of Necromances.

I stepped around the corner and into the kitchen.

A ricocheting blaze of loud pops, pain tearing into my chest. Black blood rose to seal the bullet wounds away even as I blurred, moving with inhuman speed. The bullets from a Glockstryke 983 projectile repeater would have killed a human psion—but I was no longer human. My sword was a solid arc of silver, white flame singing in its heart, as I carved Pontside's hand off at the wrist.

He was blond, but his muddy hazel eyes were the same as hers. He wore a crumpled gray suit and a damp tan trenchcoat, a gleaming badge clipped to the front pocket of his blue cotton button-down shirt. I could see the resemblance—they shared a parent, at least. Did Pontside hate psions because his half-sister was one and he wasn't, or did he simply hate all of us except her because he was a cop? Did he even hate his sister? Or was the rumor about him hating us just coffee-break fodder?

Blood sprayed. He howled and I kicked him, heard ribs snap under the force of the blow. He fell backward, grinding into broken dishes, before Mercy even had time to scream. The gun, with his hand still clutching it, thumped wetly on Gabe's kitchen floor.

Revenge filled my mouth, sweet and hot. I let out a chilling little giggle that shivered glass from the cabinet doors and made the windows squeal as they bowed out in their frames. Then I stamped down hard into his fair blond face.

It was like kicking a watermelon with fragile glass bones. Mercy let out a short, violent cry, I looked up as Pontside's body jerked and twitched, flopping. I saw the light as the soul fled, one sharp burst of brilliance fading into the foxfire glow of false life, the nerves beginning to die in increments.

I wanted to stuff his soul back into his body and kill him again. But I'd settle for *her,* the bigger traitor.

Mercy's eyes were wide and dark. Sweat stood out on her pale skin, darkening her plain blue T-shirt. The smile stretched my lips, a grimace that made her flinch and cower against the kitchen island, her hip smacking a piece of broken plate and pushing it down to shatter on the floor.

I studied her for a long moment, my sword flicking. Blood smoked off the blade. The smell of violets and white mallow mixed with the reek of blood and stink of released bowels.

I lifted the blade. "Why?" Again the windows squealed, as my voice throbbed at the lowest registers of what could be defined as "human." "You're a psion! A *healer! Why?*"

Her hands curled into fists as she stared at me, her proud spiked hair beginning to droop. Spots of fevered color blossomed on her cheeks and her lower lip trembled.

I can kill her. I can kill her right now. Right fucking now.

I shook with the urge to do just that.

But I wanted to make it *last.* And I wanted to know *why.*

"We were poor," she choked out, her eyes falling past me to linger on the mess of meat that was her brother. "Herborne paid for my Academy schooling, I was in debt up to my eyeballs and Gil...he never made enough." Her chin quivered. "Eddie was going to *give it away,* Valentine! Give away the cure! The stupid motherfucking Skinlin was going to ruin everything." She sucked in a deep painful breath. "You don't know," she whispered. "He was *rich,* he had his little rich-girl Necromance and—"

So she had hatched this plan, bombed her own clinic, arranged Eddie's death, arranged Gabe's death, collaborated in the murder of how many? "For *money.*" My contempt smoked, shattered more glass, made the walls tremble. "How many have you killed? And how many have fucking *died* of Chill while you tried to cover everything up?"

Noise, cutting through the syrupy tension and crackling static of my fury. Sirens in the distance. I heard them, and maybe she did too. Pontside probably had time to trigger a call for help on his HDOC. The Saint City PD was on their way.

Doesn't matter. If they had a hand in this I'll kill them too. The ease and naturalness of the thought should have disturbed me.

My hand twitched, the tip of my blade making a precise little circle, painting blue flame on the air from the runes running along the keen edge. The steel's heart flamed white, and the sword sang to itself, a low echoing song of bloodlust and chill certainty.

"You've never been poor," she whispered. "You don't—"

What the fuck? "I've been *poor.*" My voice sliced through hers. "I've eaten heatseal—and sometimes not even that. I was poor and hungry for *years,* you stupid bitch. I did espionage and bounty hunting. But I never assassinated anyone." It wasn't strictly true—I'd killed in self-defense, and I'd killed Santino.

But that was different. Wasn't it?

I don't kill without cause. My own words rose up to taunt me. But by the gods, this was cause.

This was vengeance.

"Congratulations." She jerked her chin in the direction of the still-twitching body. "That makes him your first."

How dare you, you piece of shit? The fury rose in me again and blue fire answered, crawling up my sword to caress my hand. I stopped, my jaw dropping as I stared at the shivering *sedayeen*. The sirens whooped and brayed, getting closer.

No. It *couldn't* be.

The world slowed down. Time stopped. Blue fire closed over my vision, and I felt the touch of my god, slipping through the stubborn, torn-raw layers of my mind. The feeling was weightless, like leaving the meat of the body behind and rising into the clear rational light of What Comes Next, the great secret Death whispers into the ears of the departing. My left shoulder squeezed with sudden pain so sharp and fierce I gasped, falling back into the low guard, the blade slanting up and singing a high thin keening note as my steel recognized the presence of the only Power I bowed my head to, Death Himself.

This? This little bitch, this *traitor,* was who Death wanted me to spare? This was the geas laid on me by my god, who I had always trusted with everything, my life, my fears, my vulnerability itself?

The choice is yours, He said, His deep infinity-starred eyes resting against mine. *It is always yours.*

"No," I whispered. "*No.*"

I wanted to kill her. I ached, I *hungered* to strike, to carve, to watch the blood flow, to end her miserable life. I'd *sworn.* Was I required to break the oath I had sworn to my best friend, my only friend?

The sirens dipped closer, and I heard the whine of police hovers. I heard my voice, shaking, freighted with a fury so intense it shivered more glass into breaking. *"Anubis et'her ka...."*

The prayer died on my lips. My vision cleared. I saw her teeth pulled back in a grimace of effort as she cowered against the counter. She was *sedayeen,* a healer, incapable of defending herself.

But she was perfectly fucking capable of betraying Eddie, of tossing Gabe's house while looking for the cure, capable of lying to me. Lying like Japhrimel, lying like a stone-faced demon. Lying worse than a demon, even; Japh hid things from me for a reason!

"Cameron," I croaked. "Your bodyguard. Pico-Phize."

Mercy shook her head, sadly. "She suspected. We were going to eliminate her at the clinic, but.... She was Pico-Phize corporate too, she was going to meet Massadie yesterday, when he called from

Tanner's, gabbling something about seeing you. It was...we had to...
well." Her eyes flicked down to Pontside's body again. "He did it."

Realization, detonating like a reaction fire in my head. The team
waiting to assassinate near the clinic hadn't been Tanner Family
troops. They'd been off-duty Saint City police normals, crooked cops,
to get rid of an inconvenient bodyguard who had maybe started to ask
too many questions. Then I'd shown up, and Mercy had lied with a
cool ease that would have put even Lucifer to shame.

Cam had been going to meet her death yesterday, while I'd been
in a demon house. If they hadn't taken me I might have saved her too.
"Herborne supplied the staff for the hit on Eddie, it was routine given
the amount of profit you were talking about. But for Gabe, you needed
more. You needed crooked cops with your *brother* in the lead."

Her teeth chattered. She said nothing. There was nothing she
could say. I was right.

"I should kill you." A strained, unhealthy whisper. She shivered
and cowered even more, sliding down the side of the island until she
crouched, making a small screaming sound like a rabbit caught in a
trap. "I should kill you slowly. I should send you to Hell in the flesh. *I
should kill you.*"

"Go ahead!" she screamed, lifting her contorted face. She didn't
look young now. *"Go ahead, you goddamn fucking freak!"*

The next few seconds are hazy. My sword chimed as I dropped it,
my boots ground in shattered dishes and broken glass, and I had her
by the throat, lifted up so her feet dangled, my fingers iron in her
soft, fragile human flesh. The cuff pulsed coldly; green light painted
the inside of the kitchen in a flash of aqueous light. She choked, a
large dark stain spreading at the crotch of her jeans. Pissed herself
with fear.

My lips pulled back. Rage, boiling in every single blood vessel.
Heat poured from me, the air groaning and steaming, glass fogging,
the wood cabinet-facings popping and pinging as they expanded with
the sudden temperature shift, the floor shaking and juddering. The
entire house trembled on its foundations, more tinkling crashes as
whatever Pontside and Mercy and their merry crew of dirty fucking
Saint City cops hadn't broken as they searched the house shattered.

It is your choice. It is always your choice. Death's voice was kind,
the infinite kindness of the god I had sworn my life to. If I denied
Him, He would still accept me, still love me.

But He should not have asked this of me.

She was helpless and unarmed, incapable of fighting back. But she was guilty, and she had lied and murdered as surely as any bounty I'd ever chased.

Anubis et'her ka…Kill. Kill her kill her KILL HER!

I could not tell if the reply was Anubis, or some deep voice from the heart of me. *But she can't fight back. This is murder, Dante.*

There was only one prayer I could utter as I shook, trembling, on the verge of grateful insanity.

"Japhrimel," I breathed, and the mark on my shoulder twisted again. I *reached* for him, for help, for strength, for anything. "*Japhrimel*…oh gods help me…."

Strength flooded through the demon mark on my left shoulder. No answer, except the soft velvet heat of Power sliding through his name scarred into my skin, dappling my entire body with heat.

A piece of his power, given without reserve or hesitation. Did he feel it when I drew on the mark? Did he care?

Did it matter?

I dropped her. She thudded onto the floor and lay there moaning. My hands shook. Hot tears splashed onto the sweater Eve had given me. The house groaned again, complaining, and settled on its foundations.

The god waited, his presence filling the room, invisible but heavy. I smelled *kyphii* and the odor of stone, felt the invisible wind of the blue-crystal hall of Death touch my cheeks, ruffle my hair. My god waited to see what I would do, if I would spare this traitor at his request…or if I would *strike.*

If I killed her, like this, would I be any better than her and her brother? Was I any better right now?

Oh, gods. Who am I?

I no longer knew.

"Thy will be done," I grated out, and backed away. She groaned again, scrabbling against the floor as terror robbed her of everything but the urge to get *away*. I sobbed, once, hoarsely. Sirens rattled the air, and I heard shouts. Someone was pounding on the magsealed front doors.

My sword made a low metallic sound as I picked it up from the debris-littered floor. Mercy gurgled. I slid the blade home in its sheath slowly, every muscle in my body protesting. My hands and legs shook with the urge to rip the metal free, pace back to the helpless cringing animal on the floor, and finish her off as bloodily and painfully as I could.

The sense of the god's presence faded, bit by bit. I felt it go, swirling away from me.

Kill her. Rage swirled through my skull, tender bruised places on my psyche cracking under the strain. *She betrayed Gabe. Kill her.*

I walked heavily out of the kitchen. Paused for a moment in the middle of the dark hallway, my head down, hair curtaining my face. I heard the whine of lasecutters at the front door.

Blood slicked down my skin, warm and wet. My feet moved, carrying me into the front hall. I lowered myself down on the steps, watching the bright points of light as the lasecutters began slicing through the magshielded door to let the Saint City PD back into Gabe's house.

As I sat there, I rocked back and forth, both hands wrapped around my sword, softly repeating in the deepest recesses of my brain the only prayer I had left since my god had betrayed me too.

Japhrimel. Japhrimel, I need you. Japhrimel.

CHAPTER 29

Horman hunched his shoulders like a turtle, pulling his bald head down and back. "Asa Tanner's confirmed everything. The lab's sent out the formula to the West Coast Chill clinics, for real this time." Fog crept up to the sides of the house, moisture breathed in the air, the storm had moved inland and left a foggy dark five A.M. in its wake. Gabe's house rose above us, lights blazing. Finally, her death was being investigated by the cops for real.

"I should have checked," I said dully. "All Mercy had to do was send it to a dropfax number." My throat ached. I'd been hoodwinked by a *sedayeen.* If I'd been able to care, I might have blushed with embarrassment. "I never guessed you were Internal Affairs, Lew." *I wonder if that was what Gabe meant when she called you incorruptible.*

"I never guessed you was a fucking moron." His beady eyes sparked for a moment. The shoulders of his tan trench were damp, his breath plumed in the air. "You didn't even check for a tran number on a fucking datafax."

I shrugged. Dried blood crackled on my clothes—Pontside had

shot me six times, probably counting on volume of lead to kill me as it had killed Eddie and Gabe. Most of the bullets had gone right through me, black demon blood closing the holes and inhuman flesh twitching to expel any chunks that hadn't escaped. The twitches were only now fading as demon adrenaline leached out of my tissues. My heart beat thin and sour in my throat.

We watched, the night exhaling fog between streetlamps, as the lights went out and the last of the techs filed out of Gabe's house. The entire place had been dusted and scanned finally, and a Reader would be sent in tomorrow morning. Not that it was necessary—there was more than enough proof to indict Mercy, and she was so terrified she would probably testify against both Herborne and the circle of dirty cops—whoever was left after I'd attacked them at the clinic and escaped them in the Rathole. There were going to be a lot of empty desks in the Saint City South Precinct house. And a lot of freelance bounty hunters would be very busy tracking down whoever fled from justice. It would take a long time to get it all sorted out.

I was no longer suspected of killing my best friend. The police hovers I'd destroyed and cops I'd killed in self-defense wouldn't be mentioned—after all, the department wouldn't like to admit to a conspiracy this big, funded by Chill money, in its own hallowed halls. It was bad for their image.

Horman, leaning against a police hover, shifted his bulk from one foot to the other. The hover's landing-springs sighed as he settled his ample ass more firmly against the plasteel hull. "The kid," he said finally.

"She's safe. I know where she is." *I can't believe I was so stupid as to miss that even for a moment. I'm slipping in my old age.* Guilt pinched me. I should have been planning to hunt down the rest of them. I should personally dispatch everyone who had *anything* to do with the whole sordid plot. I owed it to Gabe.

It was a debt I wasn't going to be able to pay. I had broken my word twice now, once to Lucifer and once to my best and only friend.

"Don't suppose you're gonna tell." Horman sighed.

"Not with half the precinct implicated in a murder plot against her mother, no." My tone was just as flat and ironic. The simmering smell of decaying fruit and spice from my blood was damped by the fog, beginning to thicken in earnest, wrapping the world in cotton wool.

"It ain't half the precinct, deadhead. Just some dirty-ass cops." His neck flushed beet-red, he reeked of Chivas soy whiskey. His tie was askew, and there was a stain on his shirt that looked suspiciously like mustard.

I'm still alive. I let out a long soft breath. Herborne Corp was already disassociating itself, claiming Mercy hadn't been acting under its directives. That told both Horman and me that they had supplied the team for Eddie's death. It would come out in court and the corporation would be dissolved. The publicity was going to be *hell*.

Gil Pontside's pockets held, among other things, a handheld EMP pulse generator that should have been sitting in a techlocker at the precinct house. Annette Cameron had been found in the Tank, her body riddled with bullets and her datband blinking, flushed red. I wondered if the bullets would match up to the ones used to kill Eddie or Gabe, and if her death was to have been blamed on me or the Tanner Family as well.

I wondered how Asa Tanner had survived the demon attack on his house to capture me and bring me to Eve. Wondered if we were even now, the werecain Mob boss and me. Wondered where Lucas and Leander were.

I wondered if Japhrimel was free yet.

Time to get back to work. My shoulders ached with tension. I rolled them back in their sockets, my sword thrust through the loop on my rig. I still didn't trust myself. "I've got other business to handle," I said finally, when the silence had grown too uncomfortable even for me. "I trust I won't have any more problems with you brave boys and girls in blue?"

"Go fuck yourself." Horman looked miserable. I didn't blame him.

"Thanks to you too." I turned, ice on the slick pavement crunching underfoot as my new boots scraped. Night air was chill through the bullet holes in my clothes. Eve's clothes. I was getting hard on my laundry.

Three long strides later, Horman spoke again. "Hey, Valentine."

I stopped but didn't turn, my neck steel-taut, my shoulders as hard as hover mooring cables. The sensation of being watched returned, stronger than ever, scraping against my nerves. The Gauntlet was silver again, and so very cold.

As cold as the inside of my chest, perhaps. "What?" *Be careful what you say to me right now, sunshine. I'm in a very bad mood.*

It was the goddamn understatement of the year. I was ready to explode, and I wasn't sure anyone in my path would be safe once I did—guilty *or* innocent.

"You a good friend." For once he wasn't sneering. I suppose he had to wait until my back was turned to say it. "Gabe'd be proud."

I didn't do what I promised. I left her killer—Eddie's killer— alive. I turned my back on the man I love and I'm about to break my word once more and turn against the Devil, who is going to be very unhappy with me if he isn't already. "Thanks." My voice cracked.

He said nothing else as I walked away, heading for Gabe's front gate and the rest of all my problems.

Coda

In the depths of the Tank, I found a callbox that hadn't been gutted. Picked up the phone and dialed a number still scored into my Magi-trained memory. It rang seven times—it was dark, and everyone there was likely to be busy with the night's games.

Finally, the phone picked up. "House of Love," a honey-scented voice purred in my ear, strangely androgynous for a sexwitch's soft submissive tone.

I cleared my throat, staring out through the plasglass of the booth's sides, scanning the street. *I look like hell. Can I please go for a few days without getting shot, or blown up, or having my goddamn clothes shredded?* "Dante Valentine, for Polyamour."

There was an undignified squeak at the other end, a gabbled apology, and I was put on hold. No music, just a crackling silence.

I watched a hooker pace her piece of cracked concrete across the street. She wore blue pleather pants and a white synthfur coat, her clear plasilica platform heels twinkling in the foggy light from the streetlamp. The faint clacks of her heels hitting the pavement beat slower than my heart, she cocked a hip as a hover drifted by. Her shoulders slumped as it passed out of sight. She went back to pacing. Dried blood made little sounds, crackling on my clothes and skin as I breathed.

"Dante?" Polyamour's voice, even caramel. My shoulders tightened a little more.

"Poly." The words cracked yet again. I said her other name, the name she'd been born with. "Steve."

She sucked in a breath. "It's all over the news. Don't worry, everything's taken care of."

"I've got some business," I whispered. Why was my throat so full? "Will you take care of…"

"I said it's taken care of. Dante, you sound..." Her voice deepened, a young boy's instead of a woman's. I could almost see her, leaning against a chair with a sleek white ceramo phone pressed to her ear, her exquisite transvestite face ever-so-slightly creased with worry.

The effort to speak louder almost tore my throat in half. "I'll be back, but I don't know when." *I'm lying. I'm sorry, Poly. I don't think I'm coming back. I promised Gabe I'd look after her daughter, but if I've got demons after me, what else can I do? She's safer with you.*

"It's in good hands, Dante. Come back soon." She paused. "If you wanted to come tonight, I would be happy to see you."

"I can't." *It's too dangerous, especially with demons in town.* "But I'll be back as soon as I can. I p-promised." *I promised Gabe, and I'm about to break that promise. Break my word. Again.*

"Be careful." Her voice changed again. "Dante, we had a... a visitor. A green-eyed thing, he said he was from you. I didn't give him anything."

My heart froze in my chest. "Blond?" If Lucifer knew about Gabe's daughter....

"What?"

"Was. He. Blond?"

"Nope. Tall, dark and grim. Long black coat, nice boots."

"When?"

"Three hours ago."

I closed my eyes. Japhrimel was out, and probably looking for me. "I'll be back when I can. Do you need—" *What? Money? An armed guard? What can I possibly give her now that I'm about to be hunted by something more than a few dirty cops?*

"It's taken care of." Her tone became again the even restful purr of a sexwitch. "When you come back, you're free to stay here. I haven't forgotten."

"Neither have I." One of the curses of a Magi-trained memory: I couldn't forget even if I wanted to. I didn't bother saying good-bye, just hung up and rested my forehead against the plasglass. One problem temporarily shelved.

The cold crept up my arm and finally slid past Japhrimel's mark on my shoulder. A fishhook, settling into flesh and twitching. After a few moments of tranced, exhausted wondering, I finally placed the sensation.

It wasn't a sense of being watched, now. It was the knowledge that I was being *pulled.*

The premonition rose in front of me. Now that I was too exhausted to move, it had a chance to rise through dark water and unreel in front of me, the inner eye blind except for the vision of my boot-toes moving against cracked pavement.

I lifted my head, shaking free of the vision with an effort.

When I could look out at the world again, everything had changed. Not much, just ... a little of the color had gone, my demon-sharp sight blurring. A layer of gray covered every surface, from the cracked street to the uneven paving and the tired skin of the hooker still pacing across the street. The old wounds—Lucifer's kick, hellhound claws, and now bullet holes—all twitched as if they were about to reopen. I'd wondered what the limit was to my body's regeneration. Maybe I would find out now.

Dante, that's a spectacularly pessimistic thought even for you.

There was a faint green gleam at the edges of my eyesight, reflected off the plasglass of the booth's walls. The cuff glowed, and as my eyes locked onto it I suddenly *knew,* with an instinctive jolt, what I had to do next. The compulsion settled home, humming in the metal of the demon artifact, and the sensation of numb cold Japhrimel's mark had been fighting off closed around me like walls of diamond ice.

Time to throw all the dice down and see where it lands, Danny. If you can't do something right, do what you have to.

I sucked in my cheeks, biting gently. Trailed my fingers over my swordhilt.

What I was contemplating was madness. It was sheer *suicide.* The compulsion tapped at my brain, whispered in my ears, pulled at my fingers and toes.

Come on, it cajoled. *Come with me. Someone wants to see you, Dante.*

I lowered my head and banged out of the callbox, my bootheels clicking against the pavement. I knew where I needed to go. Compulsion married to premonition—instinct and logic rising and twining together—spoke in an undeniable whisper, like the voice of a star sapphire on its platinum chain.

Like the chill lipless voice of the wristcuff, glowing on my wrist and finally tugging me in the right direction. Gently, but with increasing urgency.

I caught a cab on the corner of Fiske and Averly, tapping my swordhilt as the driver kept up a steady string of invective at other hoverpilots. A cab can run on an AI deck for everything other than takeoff and landing. But the hovercab drivers won exemption status under the AI Job Loss Prevention Act and so were mostly fanatically determined to prove that a human was better than an AI for the cab-riding experience. I suppose it was nostalgia or nervousness that made my driver keep cursing.

When he let me out, I smelled the heavy wet blind scent of the sea. Fog was rolling in. I could catch a transport out to Paradisse or hovertrain to North New York Jersey or another hub. Would Japhrimel and Hellesvront be watching the transports for me? I would have to figure something out, I didn't want to lead him to Eve.

Dante, you know it doesn't matter.

When I got to the low slumped building, I found the demonic shields on the dilapidated place that had once been a school were now earthed. There was no sign of anyone — demon, human, or other — as I pushed through the broken-down fencing and paced over the cracked concrete of the outside gravball court.

I shivered, right hand clamped around my swordhilt. The place was silent. Too silent, and it reeked of spice and Power, the smell of demon. Gravel crunched underneath me, the sounds of tiny breaking bones. I flinched as soon as I thought that, drew my sword. Blue flame dripped along its keen edge, glad to be free. The cuff on my wrist thrummed, pulling me forward as if a fine chain was attached to it, pulling me along. Just like a leash bringing a bloodhound in.

If I couldn't spill the traitor's blood I would settle for trying to kill a demon. I would die, of course — I couldn't kill a demon, no matter how minor.

Could I? I'd killed a hellhound. The memory of claws tangled in my ribs made a small sound escape my lips. I'd also killed an imp, with the help of a lot of reactive paint.

A hellhound's not the same thing, Dante. Neither is an imp. What you're about to try is suicide.

It was. What else did I have left? Even the most faithless of traitors could redeem themselves by choosing the moment of their death.

"Just going to have a chat with an old friend," I whispered. The chilling little giggle that rose in my throat didn't comfort me. There was no amusement in it.

I let myself into the building I'd left just this afternoon. It felt like a lifetime ago. Eve wasn't here, and Japhrimel in all likelihood wasn't here . . . but I thought someone might be here. Someone I'd met before.

Premonition blurred under my skin, pushed me forward, impelled as surely by my own minor talent for seeing the future as by the cold glow of the Gauntlet leading me on.

The mark on my shoulder was a glove of soft heat, curiously distant, trying to reach through the shell of ice. The wristcuff dulled. Green light stretched forward, easing me along. Seducing me through the labyrinth, luring me just as my own voice could lure a human.

Gods help me. Head held high, sword ready, I walked into the open jaws of the building.

The school resembled a stage set now, its walls bare and white, no furniture left. Everything was gone except the faint echo of musk and thrumming in the air, the sound of cackling, little whispers just out of human auditory range. Nasty little voices that jeered and whimpered even as they screamed and begged for release.

I *extended* a little past the borders of my shields. Power swirled, uneasy, my own fragrance of spice and musk rising to twine with a darker scent. I knew that smell. Phantom goosebumps crawled up my spine, ruffled my upper arms, and spilled down my forearms. My teeth chattered until I clenched my jaw, pain blooming down my neck. But my stance was good, and I checked the halls and empty rooms, working closer to an almost-familiar part of the building.

The gymnasia.

The layout of the school was clear in my mind. In the end, I simply stopped checking the rooms and walked slowly through the halls. Fog creeping up from the bay wrapped the entire building in a cotton blanket of silence. It might have been the last night of the world.

For all I know, it might be. The cuff on my wrist pulled me on, I didn't resist. It was useless to resist.

The voice of self-preservation shrieked at me. I paid it no mind. There was only one thing I could do now, one action that was mine alone.

Lucifer wanted to kill me.

Fine. But *I'd* choose the place and the time.

The door to the gymnasia reared up in front of me. I didn't even have to touch it, because it opened at my approach. A slice of ruddy light showed, and I could see leatherbound books, a rich patterned-red rug. I smelled woodsmoke, heard the crackle of flames.

The door was wrong. It pulsed, its lintels swaying like seaweed. I blinked, hoping my eyes were deceiving me for the first time in my long angry life. Power fumed in the air.

There were no books here before. Goosebumps—*real* goosebumps—turned hard and prickling on my arms, little finger-tips trying to claw free of my skin. I had never had goosebumps before, not in this demon's body.

My blade began to sing, blue flame dripping wetly from its point to smoke on the floor, scorching the hardwood. My shields shivered, on the verge of locking down to protect me. The blood cracking and simmering on my clothes heated up, rough dried edges brushing my shivering, shrinking skin.

There was only one demon who would go to these absurd lengths of theater.

The door swung open all the way, its hinges uttering a small pro-testing squeak. I peered through a door torn in the fabric of the world and into a room I was unhappily almost-familiar with. A neoVictorian study done in crimson and heavy wood, carpeted in plush crimson. Leather-clad books lined up on bookcases against the dark-paneled wooden walls, three red velvet chairs in front of a roaring fireplace, red tasseled drapes drawn over what might have been a window. A large mahogany desk sat obediently to one side. Next to one red velvet chair by the fireplace stood a slim figure clad in black. His mane of golden hair blazed in the firelit richness of the room, a second sun.

The cuff on my wrist glowed, frosty green light swirling around me like colored oil on water. The Gauntlet was from Lucifer; I'd been warned several times not to take anything from the Prince. Yet Japhrimel had put it back on my wrist again while I slept, hadn't he?

Hadn't he? *I* hadn't done it. Then again, if I'd been asleep so deeply I didn't know Japhrimel was leaving me during the day to hunt down Eve, would I know Lucifer was sneaking into the room? McKinley was a Hellesvront agent—and anyway, would he be able to stop the Prince of Hell from opening up reality and walking right into a room?

The thought of lying asleep, dead to the world while the Devil was in the room, sent a sharp spike of terror through me.

Everything else was gray, covered with a leaden film. But through that door, in Hell, color sprang to life, sparked by his hair. The shad-ows of bullet holes, twinging fiercely, melded shut in the warm bath of Power that curled along my skin and stifled the sob trying to escape my throat. My left wrist yanked forward, the Gauntlet thrumming, pulling me behind it. Japhrimel's mark on my shoulder was warm and forgiving, humming with taut alertness.

Lucifer looked back over his silk-clad shoulder, presenting me with a quarter profile of a face more sheerly beautiful than any demon's. The emerald glowed mellow in his forehead, and the wrist-cuff sparked with light. *His eyes.* The thought was almost delirious in its fevered panic. *It echoes his eyes, it's exactly the same color as —*

It was a door into Hell, and the Devil had his back to me.

"Come in, Dante," Lucifer said. "Sit down. Let us better understand each other."

to be continued...

Book 5

To Hell and Back

For Nicholas Deangelo. Peace.
Another charm's wound up.

Tempt not a desperate man.
   —Shakespeare, *Romeo & Juliet*

I was a-trembling because I'd got to decide forever
   betwixt two things, and I knowed it. I studied for
   a minute, sort of holding my breath, and then says
   to myself. "All right, then, I'll go to hell."
   —Mark Twain, *Huckleberry Finn*

Prologue

*T*here is more than one way to break a human," he said, softly. "Especially a human woman."

I hung between sky and ground, the constellations of Hell over-head and sterile rock underneath, the icy inhuman heat of a place far removed from my own world lapping at my skin. I had come looking for my own clean death in battle, and found this instead. This indignity.

The Devil doesn't believe in killing you, if you can be made to serve.

I will not scream. *The world narrowed, became a single point of light as the writhing claws slipped below my flesh and the wet sounds of the* thing *that would break me to his will echoed against stone walls.* I will not scream. I will not give in.

I did scream. I screamed until my voice broke itself again as the scar on my shoulder woke with frigid hot pain, my body healing even as he tore at me. I fought as hard as I could. I am no stranger to fighting, I have fought all my life.

None of it mattered.

Nothing mattered.

I died there. In Hell.

It was the only way to escape something worse.

CHAPTER 1

Darkness closed velvet over me, broken only by the flame of a scar burning, burning, against my shoulder. I do not know how I wrenched myself free, I only know that I *did,* before the last and worst could be done to me.

But not soon enough.

I heard myself scream, one last cry that shattered into pieces before I escaped to the only place left to me, welcome unconsciousness.

As I *fell.*

Cold. Wherever I was, it was *cold.* Hardness underneath me. I heard a low buzzing sound and passed out again, sliding away from consciousness like a marble on a reactive-greased slope. The buzzing followed, became a horde of angry bees inside my head, a deep and awful rattling whirr shaking my teeth loose, splitting my bones with hot lead.

I moaned.

The buzzing faded, receding bit by bit like waves sliding away from a rocky shore. I moaned again, rolled over. My cheek pressed chill hardness. Tears trickled hot out of my eyes. My shields shivered, rent and useless, a flooding tide of sensation and thought from the outside world roaring through my brain as I convulsed, instinct pulling my tissue-thin defenses together, drowning in the current. Where was I?

I had no prayers left.

Even if I'd had one, there would be no answer. The ultimate lesson of a life spent on the edge of Power and violence—*when the chips are down, sunshine, you're on your own.*

Slowly, so slowly, I regained my balance. A flood of human thought smashed rank and foul against my broken shields, roaring through my head, and I pushed it away with a supreme effort, trying to *think*. I made my eyes open. Dark shapes swirled, coalesced. I heard more, a low noise of crowds and hovertraffic, formless, splashing like the sea. Felt a tingle and trickle of Power against my skin.

Oh, gods. Remind me not to do that again. Whatever it was. The thought sounded like me, the tough, rational, practical me, over a deep screaming well of panic. *What happened to me?*

Am I hungover?

That made me laugh. It was unsteady, hitching, tired hilarity edged with broken glass, but I welcomed it. If I was laughing, I was okay.

Not really. I would never be *okay* again. My mind shuddered, flinching away from...something. Something terrible. Something I could not think about if I wanted to keep the fragile barrier between myself and a screaming tide of insanity.

I pushed it away. Wrestled it into a dark corner and closed the door.

That made it possible to think a little more clearly.

I blinked. Shapes became recognizable, the stink of dying human cells filling my nose again. Wet warmth trickled down my cheeks, painted my upper lip. I tasted spoiled fruit and sweetness when I licked my lips.

Blood. I had a face covered in blood, and my clothes were no better than rags, if I retained them at all. My bag clinked as I shifted, its broken strap reknotted and rasping between my breasts. I blinked more blood out of my eyes, stared up at a brick wall. It was night, and the wall loomed at a crazy angle because I lay twisted like a rag doll, pretty-much-naked against the floor of an alley.

Alley. I'm in an alley. From the way it smells, it's not a nice one either. Trust me to end up like this.

It was a sane thought, one I clung to even as I shivered and jolted, my entire body rebelling against the psychic assault of so many minds shoving against me, a surfroar of screaming voices. Not just my body but my *mind* mutinied, bucking like a runaway horse as the *something* returned, huge and foul, boiling up through layers of shock. Beating at the door I had locked against it.

Oh gods, please. Someone please. Anyone. Help me.

I moaned, the sound bouncing off bricks, and the mark on my

shoulder suddenly blazed with soft heat, welling out through my aching body. I hurt everywhere, as if I'd been torn apart and put back together wrong. The worst hurt was a deep drilling ache low in the bowl of my pelvis, like the world's worst menstrual cramp.

I could not think about that. My entire soul rose in rebellion. I could not *remember* what had been done to me.

The rips in my shields bound themselves together, tissue-thin, but still able to keep me sane. The scar pulsed, crying out like a beacon, a flaming black-diamond fountain tearing into the ambient Power of the cityscape. The first flare knocked me flat against the ground again, stunned and dazed. Successive pulses arrived, each working in a little deeper than the last, but not so jolting.

Breathe. Just breathe. I clung to the thought, shutting my eyes as the world reeled under me. I made it up to hands and knees, my palms against slick greasy concrete as I retched. I don't usually throw up unless poisoned, but I felt awful close.

Too bad there was nothing in my stomach. I curled over on myself, retched some more, and decided I felt better.

The mark kept pulsing, like a slow heartbeat. Japhrimel's pulse is slower than mine, one beat to every three my own heart performs, like a strong silt-laden river through a broad channel. It felt uncomfortably like his heartbeat had settled in the scar on my shoulder, as if I was resting my head on his chest and hearing his old, slow, strong heart against my cheek and fingertips.

Japhrimel. I remembered him, at least. Even if I couldn't remember myself.

I cursed, in my head and aloud as I found the other brick wall confining this alley. Drove my claws into the wall, my arm quivering under the strain as I hauled myself to my feet. I couldn't afford to call on him. He was an enemy.

They were all my enemies. Everyone. Every single fucking thing that breathed, or walked, or even touched me. Even the air.

Even my own mind.

Safe place. Got to find a safe place. I could have laughed at the thought. I didn't even know where I was.

Not only that, but where on earth was safe for me now? I could barely even remember *who* I was.

Valentine.

A name returned to me. My name. My fingers crept up and touched a familiar wire of heat at my collarbone — the necklace, silver-dipped raccoon baculum and blood-marked bloodstones, its potent force spent and at low ebb. I knew who wore this jewelry.

I am Valentine. Danny Valentine. I'm me. I am Dante Valentine.

Relief scalded me all over, gushed in hot streams from my eyes. I knew who I was now: I could remember my name.

Everything else would follow.

I hauled myself up to my feet. My legs shook and I stumbled, and I was for once in no condition to fight. I hoped I wasn't in a bad part of town.

Whatever town this is. What happened? I staggered, ripped my claws free of the brick wall, and leaned against its cold rough surface, for once blessing the stink of humanity. It meant I was safe.

Safe from what? I had no answer for that question, either. A hideous thing beat like a diseased heart behind the door I'd slammed to keep it *away.* I didn't want to know right now.

Safe place, Danny girl. I flinched, but the words were familiar, whispered into my right ear. A man's voice, pitched low and tender with an undertone of urgency. Just the way he used to wake me up, back in the old days.

Back when I was human and Jace Monroe was alive, and Hell was only a place I read about in classic literature and required History of Magi classes.

That thought sent a scree of panic through me. I almost buckled under the lash of fear, my knees softening.

Get up, clear your head, and move. There's a temple down the street, and nobody's around to see you. You've got to move now. Jace's voice whispered, cajoled.

I did not stop to question it. Whether my dead lover or my own small precognitive talent was speaking didn't matter.

The only thing that mattered was if it was right. I was naked and covered in blood, with only my bag. I had to find somewhere to hide.

I stumbled to the mouth of the alley, peering out on a dim-lit city street, the undersides of hovers glittering like fireflies above. The ambient Power tasted of synth-hash smoke, wet mold, and old silty spilled blood, with a spiked dash of Chill-laced bile over the top.

Smells like Jersey. I shook my head, blood dripping from my nose in a fresh trickle of heat, and staggered out into the night.

CHAPTER 2

The street was indeed deserted, mostly warehouses and hover-freight transport stations that don't see a lot of human traffic at night. There *was* a temple, and its doors creaked as I made it up the shallow steps. It could have been any temple in any city in the world, but I was rapidly becoming convinced it *was* North New York Jersey. It smelled like it.

Not that it mattered right at the moment.

The doors, heavy black-painted iron worked with the Hegemony sundisc, groaned as I leaned on one of them, shoving it open. My right leg dragged as I hauled myself inside, the shielding on the temple's walls snapping closed behind me like an airlock, pushing away the noise of the city outside. The damage to my leg was an old injury from the hunt for Kellerman Lourdes; I wondered if all the old scars were going to open up—the whip scars on my back and the brand along the crease of my lower left buttock.

If they did open up, would I bleed? Would the bleeding ever stop?

Take out all the old wounds, see which one's deepest. The voice of panic inside my head let out a terrified giggle; my chattering teeth chopped into bits. The door in my head stayed strong, stayed closed. It took most of my failing energy to keep that memory—whatever it was—wrestled down.

Every Hegemony temple is built on a node of intersecting ley lines, the shields humming, fed by the bulge of Power underneath. This temple, like most Hegemony places of worship, had two wings leading from the narrow central chamber—one for the gods of Old Graecia, and one for Egyptianica. There were other gods, but these were the two most common pantheons, and it was a stroke of luck.

If I still believed in luck.

Jace's voice in my ear had gone silent. I still could not remember what had been done to me.

Whatever it was, it was bad. I'm in bad shape.

I almost laughed at the absurdity of thinking so. As if it wasn't self-evident.

The main chamber was dedicated to a standard Hegemony sundisc, rocking a little on the altar. It was as tall as two of me, and I breathed out through my mouth because my nose was full of blood. I worried vaguely about that—usually the black blood rose and sealed away any wound, healing my perfect poreless golden skin without a trace. But here I was, bleeding. I could barely tell if the rest of me was bleeding too, especially the deep well of pain at the juncture of my legs, hot blood slicking the insides of my thighs.

I tried not to think about it. My right hand kept making little grasping motions, searching for a swordhilt.

Where's my sword? More panic drifted through me. I set my jaw and lowered my head, stubbornly. It didn't matter. I'd figure it out soon enough.

When I held my blade again, it would be time to kill.

I just couldn't think of who to kill first.

My bag shifted and clinked as I wove up the middle of the great hall, aiming for the left-hand wing, where the arch was decorated with dancing hieroglyphs carved into old wood. This entire place was dark, candles lit before the sundisc reflecting in its mellow depths. The flickering light made it even harder to walk.

My shoulder pulsed. Every throb was met with a fresh flood of Power along my battered shields, sealing me away but also causing a hot new trickle of blood from my nose. My cheeks were wet and slick too, because my eyes were bleeding—either that, or I had some kind of scalp wound. Thin hot little fingers of blood patted the inside of my knees, tickled down to my ankles.

I'm dripping like a public faucet. Gods. I made it to the door and clung to one side, blinking away salt wetness.

There they sat in the dusk, the air alive with whispers and mutters. Power sparked, swirling in dust-laden air. The gods regarded me, each in their own way.

Isis stood behind Her throned son, Horus's hawk-head and cruel curved beak shifting under Her spread hand of blessing. Thoth stood to one side, His long ibis head held still but His hands—holding scroll and pen—looking startled, as if He had been writing and now froze, staring down at me. The statues were of polished basalt, carved in post-Awakening neoclassic; Nuit stretched above on the vault of the roof, painted instead of sculpted.

There, next to Ptah the Worker, was Anubis. The strength threatened to leave my legs again. I let out a sob that fractured against the temple's surfaces, its echoes coming back to eat me.

The god of Death regarded me, candles on the altar before Him blazing with sudden light. My eyes met His, and more flames bloomed on dark spent wicks, our gazes flint and steel sparking to light them.

I let out another painful sob, agony twisting fresh inside my heart. Blood spattered, steaming against chill stone. This might be a new building, but they had scoured the floor down to rock, and it showed. My ribs ached as if I'd just taken a hard shot with a *jo* staff. Everywhere on me ached, especially —

I shut that thought away. Let go of the edge of the doorway and tacked out like a ship, zigzagging because my right leg wouldn't work quite properly. I veered away into the gloom, bypassing Anubis though every cell in my body cried out for me to sink to the floor before His altar and let Him take me, if He would.

I had given my life to Him, and been glad to do it — but He had betrayed me twice, once in taking Jason Monroe from me and again in asking me to spare the killer of my best and only friend.

I could not lay down before Him now. Not like this.

There was something I had to do first.

I kept going, each step a scream. Past Ptah, and Thoth, and Isis and Horus, to where no candles danced on the altars. The dark pressed close, still whispering. It took forever, but I finally reached them, and looked up. My right hand had clamped itself against my other arm, just under the scar on my left shoulder, each beat of Power thudding against my palm as my arm dangled.

Nepthys's eyes were sad, arms crossed over Her midriff. Beside Her Set glowered, the jackal head twitching in quick little jerks as candlelight failed to reach it completely. The powers of Destruction, at the left hand of Creation. Propitiated, because there is no creation without the clearing-away of the old. Propitiated as well in the hope that they will avoid your life, pass you by.

What had been done to me? I barely even remembered my own name. *Something* had happened.

Some*one* had done this to me.

Someone I had to kill.

Burn it all down, a new voice whispered in my head. **Come to Me, and let it burn away. Make something new, if you like — but first, there is the burning.**

There is vengeance.

Between Isis and Nepthys, the other goddess lingered. Her altar was swept bare, which meant it was probably the end of the month wherever I'd landed. Offerings to Her and to Set were cleared away at the dark of the moon.

Unless they were *taken*. Which happens more often than you'd think.

I folded down to my knees, each fresh jab of agony in my belly echoed by my dragging right leg and a thousand other weals of smoking pain. My fingers were slippery with blood, and I kept swiping at my face. I tipped my chin up.

My eyes rested on Her carved breasts, the stone knot between them. The shadows whispered and chuckled again, soft little feathery touches against my skin and ruined, flapping blood-crusted clothes.

Her face was a male lion's, serene in its awfulness, the disc above Her head most likely bronze but still lit with a random reflection of candlelight, turning to gold. My eyes met Hers.

"Sekhmet." My aching lips shaped the word.

The prayer rose out of my Magi-trained memory, from a page of text read long ago in a Comparative Religions class at the Academy. Psions are trained to almost-perfect memory, a blessing when you want to remember an incantation or a rune; deadly misery when you want to forget the sheer maddening injustice of being among the living.

Or when you *have* to forget, to stay sane. When you must push away something so monstrous your mind shivers like a slicboard over water as violation strains to replay itself in the corridors of your brain, the place that should be the most private of all.

I did not whisper. My ruined voice crept along the walls, flooding the air with husky seduction. "*Sekhmet sa'es.* Sekhmet, lady of the sun, destructive eye of Ra. Sekhmet, Power of Battle, You who the gods made drunk; o my Lady, *n't be'at.* I evoke You. I *invoke* You. I *summon* You, and I will not be denied."

No answer. Silence ate the end of the prayer. The ultimate silence.

I tipped my head back.

A scream welled out of me, out of some deep numb place that was still fully human. However wrecked and shattered that place was, it was still mine, the only territory I had left. Everything had been taken from me—but by every god that ever lived, I would take it *back*.

Just as soon as I could figure out who to kill first.

The prayer beat inside my head, an invocation as old as rage itself. *I invoke You. I summon You, I demand You, I call You forth and into me.*

Sound careened and bounced against stone, echoes like brass guns tearing the air itself, the walls of the temple creaking and groaning as I howled. My lips were numb and my body finally failed me. I slumped over to the side, my head striking the floor with a dim note of pain, my fingers clutching empty air. Blood smeared between my cheek and the stone, and as my vision wavered Her lips pulled back, teeth gleaming ivory-white as the rushing of flame surrounded me. I spiraled again into oblivion. This time it wasn't dark, and there was no blue glow of Death's far country.

No. This time I descended into blood-red, the sound of an old slow heartbeat and the running liquid crackle of flame. I fell, again, and this time I felt no pain.

I don't know how long I was out. It seemed a very long time. I would surface, hazily, and something would push me back down. Two things never varied—the feel of softness under me, and a low rasping voice, even and quiet. And the third thing: fever, sinking through my flesh like venom. Each time it rose, the cool cloth on my forehead and the voice would drive it back.

The voice was familiar and unfamiliar at the same time. Male, a low whispering tone, produced by a human throat. Or was it only that the ragged pleading in it sounded so human?

"Don't you dare give up on me, Valentine." Hoarse and harsh, a throat-cut voice, suffering through the syllables. "Don't you *dare.*"

My eyelids fluttered, shutterclicks of light pouring into my head, scouring. The light was from a candle on a bare, sticky wooden table, glimmering in a ceramic holder. The candleflame cast a perfect golden sphere of light, and my naked skin shrank under the weight of a sheet. The room was warm.

"Hey." Lucas Villalobos's lank hair was mussed and dirty; flecks of dried blood marked his sallow face. The river of scarring down his left cheek twitched as an odd expression filled his yellow eyes and exposed his strong, square white teeth.

He was grinning. With *relief.*

Now I've officially seen everything.

I let out a sharp breath, my right hand feeling around slick sheets. The thin mattress was getting harder by the second. I felt every individual slat of the low cot.

I flinched and blinked. Stared up at Lucas. Managed a single, pertinent question.

"What the *fuck?*"

"That's more like it. You're one slippery bitch, Valentine."

Another question surfaced. "How..." I coughed. My throat was a dust-slick river of stone. I hurt all over, heavy and slow. But everything on me was working. My belly ached, way down low, as if I carried a hot stone.

Another hot rill of bile worked up my throat.

"I got ways of trailin' my clients." He shrugged, picking something up from the nightstand. He slid one wiry-strong arm under my shoulders and tipped tepid chlorinated water down my throat.

It was the sweetest taste I'd had in ages. He took the cup away despite my sound of protest, stopping me from getting sick on it. I didn't think I'd retch, but I wouldn't put it past me.

"You disappeared six months ago." He shook his lank hair back, rolling his shoulders in their sockets as if they hurt. He wore a threadbare Trade Bargains microfiber shirt, but his bandoliers were freshly oiled, resting on reinforced patches. "I been knockin' around tryin' to find you, keep one step ahead o' everyone else. Two nights ago I found you in Jersey, of all fuckin' places." He paused, as if he wanted to say more. "Care to tell me how the fuck you managed to vanish like that?"

I sank back onto the thin mattress. Shut my eyes. Darkness returned, wrapped me in a blanket. "Six months?" My voice was just as ruined as his, but where Lucas's harsh croak was a raven's, mine was cracked velvet honey, strained and soft. "I...I don't know."

"You was in pretty bad shape. I didn't think you'd make it."

Relief rose up, fighting with pure terror as I strained to remember what I could, tiptoeing around the huge black hole in my head...

My sword chimed as I dropped it, my boots ground in shattered dishes and broken glass, and I had her by the throat, lifted up so her feet dangled, my fingers iron in her soft, fragile human flesh. The cuff pulsed coldly; green light painted the inside of the kitchen in a flash of aqueous light. She choked, a large dark stain spreading at the crotch of her jeans. Pissed herself with fear.

My lips pulled back. Rage, boiling in every single blood vessel. Heat poured from me, the air groaning and steaming, glass fogging, the wood cabinet-facings popping and pinging as they expanded with the sudden temperature shift, the floor shaking and juddering. The entire house trembled on its foundations, more tinkling crashes as whatever Pontside and Mercy and their merry crew of dirty fucking Saint City cops hadn't broken as they searched the house shattered.

It is your choice. It is always your choice. *Death's voice was kind, the infinite kindness of the god I had sworn my life to. If I denied Him, He would still accept me, still love me.*

But He should not have asked this of me.

She was helpless and unarmed, incapable of fighting back. But she was guilty, and she had lied and murdered as surely as any bounty I'd ever chased.

Anubis et'her ka...Kill. Kill her kill her KILL HER!

I could not tell if the reply was Anubis, or some deep voice from the heart of me. But she can't fight back. This is murder, Dante.

I didn't care. And yet...

"I didn't kill her," I whispered. "The healer. I didn't...I walked away. I went to a phone booth, and I called Polyamour."

"She told me so. She was the last person to talk to you, near as I could figure. Nobody else knows. I had a hard enough time gettin' her to give *me* anything."

I could see why. Lucas Villalobos was every psion's worst nightmare. We knew what he charged for his help. Only the desperate bargained with him, and I hadn't had time to tell Poly he was on my side.

"Valentine?" Lucas restrained himself from shaking me, thank the gods. "Care to tell me where you was?"

I thought about it. Where *had* I gone?

My heart thudded, a sharp strike of pain inside my chest. Clawed fingers, digging in —

Lucas grabbed my wrist, locked it, and half-tore me out of the bed as he backpedaled to avoid my punch. We went down in a tangle of arms and legs, my claws springing free and slashing at empty air as he evaded the strike. *"Stop it!"* he yelled, producing an amazing amount of noise through the gravel in his throat. *"Calm the fuck down!"*

The sheet tangled around my hips. One of Lucas's skinny, strong arms locked across my throat, his knee in my back. "Calm down," he repeated, in my ear. "I ain't your enemy, Valentine! Quit it!"

I froze. My heart thundered in my ears. I felt my pulse in my wrists, my ankles, my throat, in the back of my head. Even my hair throbbed frantically.

It was true. He wasn't my enemy.

Who was? What had *happened?* "I don't know," I whispered. "I don't know what happened. The last thing I remember is being in that phone booth."

It wasn't strictly true. I knew I'd left the phone booth and gone... somewhere.

Pretty damn far, a sneering little voice spoke up inside my head. *You went right over the moon. Right over the goddamn moon and into the black, sunshine.*

Lucas was out of breath. "You calm?"

I'm not anywhere near calm, Lucas. But it'll have to do. I stared at the floor—filthy boards, dirt squirming in cracks, my narrow golden hand spread in front of my face to keep me from being mashed into the ground. I still had my rings, but each stone was dull and empty, no spells sunk into their depths. I had used them all.

When?

I coughed, racking. Wanted to spit. Didn't. "Let me up."

He complied. I made it up to sitting, my back braced against the cot, the sheet wrapped around me. Lucas squatted, easily, his yellow eyes on my face. Just like a cat will stare at a mousehole, patient and silent.

I shut my eyes. Breathed in. My shields were in bad shape, ragged patches bleeding energy into the air, heat simmering over my skin as my demon metabolism ran high. The surfroar of human minds outside this small room was just as loud as ever, but it wasn't crashing through my head. The discipline of almost forty years as a psion stood me in good stead, trained reflex patching together holes in the shimmering cloak of energy over me, little threads spinning out to protect me from the psychic whirlpool of a city.

Almost forty years, last time I checked. I didn't even know what year it was.

The absurdity of the situation walloped me right between the eyes. Danny Valentine, part-demon bounty hunter and tough-ass Necromance, and I didn't even know what goddamn decade I was in.

I bent over, wheezing. Lucas rose to his feet and shuffled away. I laughed until black spots crowded my vision from lack of oxygen, fit to choke as the candleflame trembled and the bare white-painted walls ran with shadows.

Lucas came back. He settled down cross-legged, and when I could look at him again, swabbing hot salt water from my cheeks, he offered me the bottle. It was rice wine, fuming colorlessly in my mouth. I took a healthy draft and passed the green plasglass bottle back to him. He took a swig, didn't grimace, and tossed it far back. His throat worked as he swallowed.

I wondered who the blood on his face was from. Discovered I didn't want to know. There was only one thing I needed to know from him.

"What the fuck's going on?"

He shrugged, took another hit off the bottle. "You disappeared and all hell broke loose. Your green-eyed boyfriend's tearin' up whole cities looking for you, and he's not too choosy where he looks or how hard. Your blue-eyed girl was scrambling to keep away from him at first, but she pulled a vanishing trick too, about a month ago. Everyone wants a piece of Danny Valentine, and I nearly got my head taken off a few times lookin' for you myself. I never been so happy to see a datband trace go live in my *life*."

So that's how he'd tracked me, with a datband trace. I was glad nobody else had been close enough to me to slip that code in. "Six months." I stared down at my hands. The battered black molecule-drip polish on my fingernails was almost gone, the fingernails themselves translucent gold.

Claw-tips. I could extend them, if I had to, and rip the sheet to shreds.

A year in Hell is not the same as a year in your world. Eve's voice floated through my head.

Why would I think of that now? I'd been out of action for six months, six months I couldn't remember. Six months I would probably, if I was lucky, never get back. I didn't *want* to remember them.

What do you do now, Danny? Japhrimel's looking for me, and Eve... Has he done something to her? Where have I been?

It didn't matter.

"What do you think we should do?" I whispered. I was fresh out of ideas.

Lucas took another mouthful, handed the bottle to me. "I think we should contact your boyfriend. There's other shit goin' down too, Valentine. Magi casting circles and invoking, and things coming through."

"Isn't having something come through the *point* of Magi casting circles?" I took a hit of rice wine, let it burn all the way down into my chest. It wouldn't do a damn thing for me—my part-demon metabolism mostly shunted alcohol aside now.

But the idea of getting drunk was so fucking tempting I wondered if I should find a vat of beer or something stronger.

"Not when Magi keep getting torn apart, even when they're just casting regular sorceries. The Hegemony's issued a joint directive with the Putchkin Alliance. No Magi are allowed to practice for the foreseeable future."

I stared at him, my jaw suspiciously loose. *"Sekhmet sa'es,"* I breathed, a thrill of fear running along my skin. "A joint directive?"

No Magi practicing meant the corporate shields of gods-alone-knew how many companies weren't being worked on. The glut of work could be ameliorated by some Shamans, but the finer industrial thieves were probably having the time of their lives. All sorts of other effects would ripple out through the economy—the potential loss in tax revenue was enormous. The setback in research labs would cost a hefty chunk, too.

"I ain't no coward." Lucas gave me a straight yellow-eyed glare. "But I can't see keepin' you alive much past sundown if we break cover. There's just too much fuckin' flak up there. Your green-eyed boy will keep you alive, and I confess I'd like a little backup m'self."

Now I have *officially heard everything.* For the man they called "the Deathless" to admit to wanting backup was thought-provoking, to say the least.

Thought-provoking *isn't the word you want here, Danny. The word you want is* terrifying. I sighed, swallowed another slug of clear fiery liquor. Even if I couldn't get drunk it was a calming ritual. My stomach rumbled a bit, subsided. I should have felt ravenous.

I only felt slightly unsteady. Nauseous. And *heavy,* my limbs filled with sand. "I need clothes. And weapons." *Where is my sword?* I badly wanted to close my hand on a hilt, hear the deadly whistle as a keen blade clove air. I wanted *my* sword, the sword my teacher had gifted to me.

I came back to myself as the bottle groaned sharply in my clenched hand, thick green plasilica singing with stress. Lucas eyed me.

I had to force my fingers to relax. I breathed deeply, in through the nose, out through the mouth. Just like the first and last meditation instruction every psion has hammered into her head—*breathe, and the mind grows still.*

I wish that was true. My datband gleamed on my wrist, which looked suddenly naked without the thick cuff of silvery metal.

The Gauntlet, the demon artifact that marked me as Lucifer's little errand girl. Where was it?

That was another thought I didn't want. I pushed it away.

"You got it." Lucas levered himself to his feet. "You got any idea how we're gonna find your boyfriend?"

My fingers tingled, and the scar on my shoulder burned, shifting. I could *feel* the ropes of scarring writhing against the surface of my skin. "We won't have to." My voice sounded very far away. "Sooner or later he always finds me. One way or another."

When he did, I would at least be safe for a little while. Everything else was just noise.

"Good thing, too. You get in *more* fuckin' trouble." He shuffled away, past the table with the dancing candleflame. Halted, his shoulders coming up and tensing. "Valentine? You okay?"

Do I look okay to you? "Yeah." I set the bottle down and scrubbed my hands together, as if they were dirty. I *felt* dirty. Filthy, in fact. Maybe it was the room. I dearly wanted a shower. "Is there a bathroom around here? Any hot water?"

"There's a bathroom. Knock yourself out." He started moving again, a fast light shuffle barely audible even to my heightened senses. "Spect you might want to get cleaned up." He vanished through the door.

I wanted to scrub myself raw under some hot water. Still, I had more important work to do. I'd left Japhrimel trapped in a circle of Eve's devising, and told him it was war between us. He probably wasn't going to be happy with me in the slightest.

It didn't matter. My fingers crept up to the mark on my shoulder, its frantic dance against my skin oddly comforting.

Japhrimel. The word stuck in my throat. *Even if you are angry at me. Even if you're furious. I* need *you.*

My fingers hovered, a scant half-inch from touching the moving scar. I pinched my eyes shut, my skin crawling, and curled over, my arm coming down to bar across my midriff. I *squeezed* myself, earning a huff of air from my lungs in the process. I was tired, and however good hot water sounded I suddenly didn't want to visit the bathroom.

There might be a mirror in there, and I didn't want to see myself.

Why not, Danny? The soft, mocking voice of my conscience came back on little cat feet as darkness swirled against the candle's glow. My cheek hit the floor, and I pulled my knees up. Lying down seemed like a good idea. A *really* good idea.

What are you so afraid of, Danny? Huh? Answer me that.

I didn't want to. So I just lay on the dirty floor and nailed my eyes shut, waiting for Lucas to come back.

CHAPTER 3

I jolted up out of a deathly doze when I heard the footsteps. Lay, my eyes closed, every inch of my skin suddenly alive with listening.

I'd scooted back under the rickety cot, seeking blind darkness. It just seemed like a good idea, especially with so many people looking for me. I was too exhausted to fight much, especially with my shields so fragile.

The fact that hiding under the bed wouldn't necessarily keep me safe never occurred to me. If it had, I'm not sure I would have cared.

Under the bed the floor was even filthier, but the wall next to the cot felt cold and solid against my back. I pulled my knees up, twitching the sheet under me and dispelling the urge to sneeze at the dust suddenly filling my nose. With that done, I *listened,* my sensitive ears dilating.

There. Four sets of footsteps. One very light, brushing the earth, one shuffling equally lightly—Lucas—and the third, a tread of heavy boots.

The last set I would have known anywhere. It was a noiseless step, quiet as Death Himself, but the mark on my shoulder woke with renewed soft fire spilling all the way down my arm.

My eyes squeezed shut. Shame woke, hot and rank, pressed against my throat and watering eyes. I didn't want him to see me like this.

Like what, Danny?

I couldn't name it even to myself.

The door opened. The footsteps had gone silent.

I *felt* him come into the room like a storm front over a city, his attention sweeping the walls once and focusing, unerringly, on the small dark space where I huddled on my side, curled up as tightly as I could without breaking my own bones.

The door closed, and he filled up the room like dark wine in a cup. The black-diamond fire of a demon's aura almost blinded me, with my shields so fragile and torn. OtherSight blurred through the veil of the physical world, showing me the thick cable of my link to him, a bond cemented by blood. His blood, and mine.

He'd *changed* me, given up Hell for me, and bargained to regain a full demon's Power as well. Lied to me. *Hurt* me, held me up against a wall and shaken me, left me sleeping alone while he hunted Doreen's daughter as I'd begged him not to.

Every time the water got deeper, I found out he'd known the game from the beginning, and was playing against me.

And yet, he always came for me. My heart swelled, sticking in my throat like a clot of stone.

There was a slight sound as he reached the cot. I managed to open my eyes.

A pair of boots, well-worn, placed just so against the dirty floorboards. I saw the edge of his coat, too, liquid darkness stirring a little. He must have been agitated for his wings to move so much.

I saw something else, too.

The tip of a familiar lacquered indigo scabbard.

He eased himself down to sit cross-legged facing the bed, his coat flaring away along the floor. Set my sword down with a precise little click, just out of reach.

His silence was so absolute the candleflame's hiss became loud. I saw his knees—a pair of worn jeans ragged at the hems, and the scarred leather of his boots tinged with darkness. He'd been wading through something liquid, up to the ankles.

I didn't want to know *what.*

I stared at the sweet curve of my sword, lying quiescent and tempting. Hot water boiled out of my eyes, tracked down to touch the dirty, blood-crusted hair at my temple. My vision blurred.

Japhrimel said nothing.

It took every remaining erg of courage I possessed to make my right hand unclench. I eased forward, bit by bit, silent as an adder under a rock.

The mark on my shoulder flared again, Power spilling from it and coalescing, a cloak of black-diamond fire closing around my battered shields. It was the equivalent of a borrowed coat, the weight of so many psyches shunted aside from my shivering mental walls. Along with the soft caress of Power against my skin came something else — my rings beginning to swirl with deep light again.

Japhrimel's strength. Given without reserve or hesitation, as simply as he might have poured water into a cup. I let out an involuntary sigh, my arm falling limp to the floor. The relief was overwhelming. No more shouting of messy normal minds trying to get *in,* trying to drown me. The blessed silence was almost enough to make me weep with relief.

He *still* said nothing. His silence was sometimes like speaking, a complex patterned thing. But not now. Now his silence was simply the absence of every sound, a breathless feeling of waiting.

I realized, as if I'd known it all along, that he'd wait there for as long as it took for me to gather myself. He would let me make the first move.

He'd wait forever, if that was what it took.

Two sides of a coin, the betrayal and the waiting. I wished he'd just choose one and get it over with, so I could fight for him or against him.

I inhaled sharply, catching the last half of the sigh in my teeth. When I spoke it took me by surprise, my voice rusty and disused for all its velvety half-demon roughness.

"I guess I don't look so good." The words trembled.

Great, Danny. Can you sound any more fucking stupid? The darkness behind my eyelids had knives in it. Every one of them was pointed at me, and quivering with readiness. The black hole in my memory yawned.

Japhrimel didn't stir. When he spoke it was soft, even, and soothing, the most careful of his voices. "I care little for how you *look,* Dante."

More sharp relief, tinged with deep unhealthy shame and a dose of panic, made my heart thud frantically inside my chest. "Something happened to me." *I sound about five years old and scared of the dark.*

I'm really going to have to work on my vidpoker face.

"Indeed." Still very quiet. "I am still your Fallen, you are still my *hedaira.* Nothing else is of any importance." He paused. "It is... enough that you are still alive."

I flinched. *You don't get it.* Something boiled below my breastbone, something sharp. Claws, sinking into my chest, something wriggling and squirming against violated flesh. "Something *happened* to me."

"Your sword was delivered to me two days ago, by the Prince of Hell's messenger." His shielding didn't quiver, but I knew enough of the faint shadings in his voice to read terrible, rigidly controlled fury in him.

Japhrimel was a hairsbreadth away from rage. The thought, for once, didn't frighten me. Instead, it filled me with a sick unsteady glee.

I *wanted* him to be angry.

"I left you," I whispered. "In Eve's circle." *Trapped. I told you it was war between us.*

"That is of no account." He didn't shift his weight, but I got the idea he would have waved the idea away with one golden hand. Just gone, *poof,* like so much smoke.

"You're mad at me." *I sound like a stupid girl on a holovid soap.* I opened my eyes, stared at the light of sanity and the beautiful curve of my sword, its scabbard a mellow indigo glow. "I *left* you there."

"I did not expect you to release me. In fact, I demanded that you do so in order to make you more valuable in the escaped Androgyne's eyes, so she would keep you alive as a bargaining chip and not slaughter you to revenge herself on me." Japhrimel sighed, a slight colorless sound. "I expected to collect you soon enough. I broke free of the Androgyne's trap and searched for you, but you had disappeared. I found no trace of you in the city but your perfume, and the knowledge that a door had recently been opened into Hell. Then I knew Lucifer had taken you, and the game had changed."

"Oh." I began to feel slightly ridiculous, hiding under the bed. He sounded so calm, so rational. I didn't feel ridiculous enough to risk leaving this safety, no matter how flimsy it was. "I don't remember." *I'm beginning to get a bad feeling about what I don't remember.* I felt so *heavy,* every particle of flesh weighed down by gravity. Had it always been this hard, this tiring to draw breath?

"I suspect that is a mercy of short duration. Events are afoot, *hedaira.* I think it best we do not linger here." He didn't shift his weight.

"What's going on?" I didn't think for a minute he'd tell me anything. Keeping things from me seemed to be a real hobby with him. I wondered if he got any satisfaction from it.

Then I had to swallow that thought, because he opened his mouth again.

"I have not only declared war on Vardimal's Androgyne, but on the Prince of Hell himself. I intend to kill my Maker, *hedaira,* and to do so I will need your help."

My help? Killing Lucifer? I shut my mouth, opened it to speak, and shut it again. I felt like a fish tossed onto shore, and probably looked just as ridiculous. If anyone could see me under the bed, that is.

Is that who I have to kill to get myself back?

Somehow the idea didn't seem laughable at all.

"Do you hear me, Dante?" The fury was back, circling just under the surface. I had sometimes thought I *knew* him, the demon who had Fallen and bound himself to me. This rage was something new, and the only thing scarier than its icy crackle was how good he was at keeping it tightly reined and controlled. "I have not only Fallen but *rebelled.* Yet I will not yoke myself to Vardimal's Androgyne in the Prince's place. I shall make you a bargain, my curious one. If you wish me to lay aside my claim on the rebel Androgyne, I ask that you help me defeat my Prince."

My heart squeezed itself down to a concrete lump in my chest. Blackness rose from the hole in the floor of my mind, threatening to choke me or tip me into howling insanity. I struggled, my rings popping and snarling with sparks—no spells in them, but pure Power fluxing and trembling through metal and stones. Moonstone, amber, bloodstone, and silver, each ring bought and charged and worn continuously. The rings had seen me through countless bounties, never leaving my skin even while Japhrimel murmured in my ear in a Nuevo Rio bedroom, the taste of his blood in my mouth and the feel of his body imprinted on mine, my bones crackling as he *changed* me into something else. Something more than human, or less, depending on how you looked at it.

"Why?" I whispered.

"Is it not enough that I will?" Tension crackled below the surface of his familiar voice. I should have been terrified.

What's enough, Japh? My right hand crept out. My wrist looked fragile, too thin; my fingers slid out into the flickering candlelight along the dirty floor. My sword was a little too far away, so I edged forward, moving my heavy recalcitrant body like a sled on reactive-greased runners. My hip bumped the cot above me, my head barked itself on a metal support.

The lacquer of the reinforced scabbard was cool and slick under my fingers. My left hand slid out from under the bed too, and I groped empty air for a terrifying moment, thinking maybe he'd changed his mind or I was hallucinating.

Japhrimel's fingers threaded through mine. I found myself dragged out of my sheet and from under the cot like a stuffed toy, almost limp. He flowed upright, carrying me with him and ignoring my sudden panicked flinch, every inch of my body shivering as terror rose with a blinding snap like the sound of a hammer on a projectile gun.

Air flirted and swirled unsteadily as he pulled me against him, his coat separating in front as his wings spread, wrapping around me and pulling me into the shelter of his body. The musk-cinnamon smell boiling from his skin closed around me, a heavy drenching scent, and my knees buckled.

Damn him. He still smelled like *home.* Like safety. Except something trembling under the surface of my skin told me safety was just a word. I doubted I would ever feel safe again.

He dropped his face to my tangled, filthy, blood-caked hair and inhaled, shuddering, his bare chest feverishly warm with the heat of one of Hell's children. And I surprised myself again by starting to scream—but the screams were muffled by wrenching sobs as I pressed my face into the exposed hollow between his collarbone and his shoulder, his arms and wings around me and the only haven I had left safely reached at last.

That's the problem with being a tough girl. The crying fits never get to last long enough.

The bathroom door yawned like an open mouth. I stared at it like a rabbit stares at a snake. I'd wrapped the sheet around myself again, clutched my sword's slim hard length, and perched guiltily in the one chair. Japhrimel settled himself on the edge of the cot, his eyes burning green and half-shuttered.

I couldn't look at his eyes. I glared at the open door, daring it to come get me, if it wanted me.

Outside the room, I heard a muttered question. Lucas's answer reassured me.

Since when did I find Lucas Villalobos reassuring? The world had indeed gone mad.

Tall, saturnine, gold-skinned demon, sitting motionless on the edge of the rucked bed. Japhrimel's coat fell away from his knees, clasped his throat with a high Chinese collar, and trembled just a little under the gold of the candle's uncertain light. His face was familiar, winged eyebrows and sharp nose, the architecture of his cheekbones unfamiliar to anyone used to human faces, his lips thinned and held in a straight line, betraying nothing. His hair had grown out, a fall of darkness softening the harsh lines of his face. The length was new— he'd always kept it trimmed, before.

I wondered again how I could have ever thought of him as ugly, long ago in the dim time of our first meeting.

He finally stirred slightly. "We should go, Dante. It isn't wise to linger."

My legs trembled, but I hauled myself to my feet. Pulled the sheet up, tucking it under my arm to keep it wrapped around me, and cast around for my bag. "Fine. Where are we going?"

"Don't you want a shower?" He very carefully didn't look at me, but the edges of his coat ruffled again. Light ran wetly over its surface. "I seem to recall you have a fondness for hot water."

I spotted my bag, lying on the floor. It looked very small and very sad, its knotted strap and stained canvas a reminder of...what? Something terrible.

Panic trembled under my skin until I took a deep breath, just like I would calm a rattling slicboard. *One thing at a time, Danny. You've got your sword and Japh's here. Just take it one step at a time.*

"There's a mirror in there." The queer flatness of my tone surprised me. For a completely ridiculous objection to the idea of a shower, it stood up pretty well the more I thought about it.

Japhrimel rose, slow and fluid. He ghosted over the floor, his coat now making no sound as it moved with him.

I searched for some way to ask the question I needed most answered, and failed miserably. "Lucas said you were looking for me."

He shrugged as he pushed the bathroom door open and flicked the switch inside. Electric light stung my eyes, flooding a slice of none-too-clean tile. "I seem to spend a distressing amount of time doing so."

I opened my mouth, but a wall-shattering sound smashed through whatever I would have said. Japhrimel stepped out of the bathroom, his fingers flicking. He stopped, his coat rippling and settling and his eyes not quite meeting mine. "There is no mirror." The words turned sharp and curt. "Be quick, and careful of glass on the floor." His stride lengthened, and my Fallen brushed past me on his way to the door.

My pulse slowed down a bit. I caught my breath, my knuckles white around the scabbard. Lacquered wood groaned as my fingers flexed, battle between my will and my unruly body joined again.

Japhrimel halted, between me and the door. His head dropped, and if I hadn't been shaking so hard myself I might have sworn he was trembling. His hair whispered as it brushed his shoulders, strings of darkness. "I would counsel you also to be careful of me," he said, softly. "I do not think I am quite... safe."

You know, of all the things you could have said, that's one of the least comforting. My mouth had turned dry and glassy, a tide of terror rising up against my breastbone. "Are you saying you'll hurt me?" *Because, you know, I wouldn't put it past you. Even if I am* really *glad to see you.*

Go figure. Ten minutes with him and I was already feeling more like myself. Except I felt so goddamn heavy, my body weighed down with lead.

And I had no real clue who "myself" really was anymore. Details, details.

His shoulders hunched as if I'd screamed at him. "I would not," he said, clearly and softly, "hurt *you*. But I am not quite in control of my temper. You could cause an injury to someone else, by way of me."

Great. That's really reassuring. The familiar bite of irritation under my breastbone spurred and soothed at the same time. "Oh." My fingers relaxed, a millimeter at a time. "Japh?"

He said nothing, and he didn't move. The shaking in him communicated itself to the air.

"Thank you." *I'm going to have to rethink any plan that includes cutting loose of you.*

My Fallen's black-clad shoulders dropped. The sense of breathless fury in the air waned, swirling uneasily, ruffling the candleflame and touching the creaking walls.

"I told you I would always come for you." As calmly as he might have told me what was for lunch. "Be quick, Dante."

I hitched the sheet up on my chest and edged for the bathroom. There was nothing to be scared of in there, now.

CHAPTER 4

We were still in North New York Jersey, deep in the festering wasteland of the Core. Japhrimel brought me clothes—a Trade Bargains microfiber shirt, a pair of jeans too new to be comfortable, and a pair of boots in my size that would need hard use before they were anything close to broken-in. With Fudoshin's comforting weight in my left hand, I almost felt like myself again.

I came out of the bathroom rubbing at my hair with a towel that had seen much better days. Once I scrubbed the crusted blood and filth away, I felt scraped-raw and naked, but at least I'd stopped bleeding. The city dozed outside my borrowed mental walls, a pressure I didn't have to directly feel to be wary of.

If a psion's shields broke, the mind inside those shields could fuse together in meltdown, just like any delicate instrument after a power surge. I was lucky my brain hadn't been turned to oatmeal.

Lucky. Yeah. I was lucky all over, lately.

My heart slammed into my throat.

Japhrimel stood by the door, his eyes half-closed and burning green. "How do you feel?"

I took stock. I felt like I'd eaten too much and now had to lie in the sun to digest, like a lizard. A slow heavy cramp wended its way through my belly, and I sighed, testing my arms and legs. I could still make a fist, and my toes wiggled when I told them to. "Fine." *I don't feel quite like myself, but after the week I've had, I don't blame me.* A half-hysterical sound caught me off-guard, and I clapped my right hand over my mouth to trap it.

Stop it. I struggled for control, peeled my hand away from my mouth. I locked my fingers around the hilt instead. A simple motion clicked the blade free and it leapt up, three inches of steel shining, oiled and perfect. My voice turned into something else, cut off savagely midstream.

Blue fire tingled in the steel. Fudoshin hummed, ready for blood to be spilt. "Just fine," I repeated, my eyes locked to the blue shine. "Where are we going?"

"We must leave here." Did he sound uneasy? "There is much to be done."

Does it involve killing someone? If it does, I'm all for it. I slid the blade back home with an effort. *Not now. Soon.* "What's first?"

"First we must have a small discussion." He had gone utterly still. "There are some things we must say to each other, and they are not comfortable."

Great. Why don't we just get a sedayeen *arbitration specialist? I hear they're cheap this year.* "Like what?" *He's going to ask me why I left him trapped in that circle and let Eve get away. He's going to ask me where I was, what happened to me.*

Japhrimel paused. Electric light slid lovingly over the planes of his face, touched the wet blackness of his coat. The edges ruffled, his wings responding to agitation. When he spoke, it was the gentlest of his voices, and he held himself very still. "You were taken to Hell." The question ran under the surface of the words.

I closed my eyes.

How much did Japhrimel know or guess? "It hurt," I heard myself say, in the flat odd voice that only showed up when I was talking about the past. That was a relief—it was over and done, now. The worst had happened.

I winced as soon as I thought it. Thinking the worst has happened is a sure way to invite Fate to serve up another heaping helping of gruesome.

"Did you take anything from the Prince? Accept any gift, eat anything? Even a single mouthful of water, a single bite of food?" Gentle, but tense, the words straining from a dry throat.

Tierce Japhrimel sounded worried.

"No." *I don't think you'd call it a gift.* Black unhealthy humor rose in my throat, I pushed it down and away. *Don't think about that, Danny. You'll go mad.*

"Are you certain?"

I nodded, my jaw set so hard I could feel my teeth groaning. If they hadn't been demon-strong, those teeth, would I have shattered my own jaw?

It was an unpleasant thought.

"You accepted *nothing* from the Prince or his minions?"

There wasn't any accepting involved. "Nothing." My jaw eased up a little. I could speak, now. The darkness behind my lids was more comforting. "He dragged me through a door and into Hell."

"What happened?"

A delicate touch—the brush of his callused fingers against my cheekbone. Gently brushing the line of my jaw, turning and sliding down the hollow of my throat.

Back when I was fully human my neck was bigger, a slope running down to my shoulders, the cord of the sternocleidomastoid muscle well-developed. Now, the cervical curve was better designed, demon bones capable of taking a greater hit and the muscles running just slightly differently to provide more leverage and flexibility.

Japhrimel's palm met my throat. His warm fingers curled, his thumb stroking just where the tension had settled. When I swallowed, harshly, my skin moved against his.

My eyes flew open, his face filling my vision, familiar and oddly, terrifyingly different for a split second before I recognized him.

What could I tell him? How could I possibly put it into words?

"He hurt me," I whispered. "Then I fell out of Hell and Lucas found me."

"He hurt you?" Calm and quiet, as if I couldn't feel the fine explosive quiver running through his bones. His eyes burned green, lightening two awful shades until they looked...

Like *his*. Like Lucifer's. Like they could strip me down to bone and burn until not even ash remained. I tensed, muscle by muscle, staring into his eyes. My breath drew itself in, held against the back of my throat. My chin jerked down in a facsimile of a nod.

Very softly, the most human of his voices turned into the brush of cat's fur. "Tell me, beloved. Tell me what was done to you."

The words refused to come. They sat in my chest like a stone egg, like the heaviness in my belly, like the betraying weakness of my treacherous body. I smelled cinnamon, and musk—the darker smell of Japhrimel's pheromones, the lighter overlay of mine, blending together to make a bubble of safety and climate control. The walls creaked and groaned sharply as Japhrimel's aura cycled up into the visible, streaks of blackness painting the air like colored oil on water.

I held his gaze, only capable of doing so because at the back of the green light, at the very center of the hot darkness that was his pupils—not round like a human's or slit like a cat's, but somewhere between the two—a different darkness moved.

Before he'd bargained with Lucifer to regain a demon's Power, his eyes had been humanly dark, and it was that I saw in them now. The darkness hadn't been eaten by the green light spilled over his irises.

It was there, *under* the light. How had I never seen it before?

"He hurt me." The little-girl whisper wasn't me. It *couldn't* be me. "I don't want to talk about it."

His hand fell away from my throat, leaving cold bareness behind. His eyes held mine. "Then you do not have to." Japhrimel's tone was still killing-soft, but its edge was not directed at me. "When you wish to, I will listen. But first, answer me this. Did you accept anything from the Prince or his minions, anything at *all?*"

Of course not. Nobody in their right mind takes a gift from a demon. Except me, of course. I'd taken gifts from Japhrimel too many times to count.

"No," I whispered. "There was no accepting involved, Japhrimel." *And if you ask me that one more time, I'm going to scream.*

"He merely...hurt you?" His voice scraped and burned along the edges of my numbness.

"He hurt me enough. I *said* I don't want to talk about it." I turned on my heel and took two steps away toward the bathroom door again, stopped restlessly. Despite the shower, I suddenly felt *filthy.*

"We are not finished."

I stopped. My hair brushed my shoulders, the mark pulsing with soft velvet heat. My rings swirled with light, my aura settling down under the healing weight of Japhrimel's.

He was holding me together, the cloak of a demon's Power easing around me like a caress. Each successive wave from the scar on my shoulder worked in a little deeper, thin filaments spinning across the ragged gaps in my shielding, patching them. My wrists and knees felt naked and vulnerable, but the slim heavy length of my sword in my left hand more than made up for it.

My skin crawled. I wanted to scrub myself again, with a wire brush if I had to. Shock had kept me numb before, but I wasn't numb now.

Not even close.

"What else?" My brittle tone would have been a warning to anyone else.

His footfalls were silent, but I felt each one against my back, my skin roughening instinctively under its tough golden perfection.

Warm hands touched my shoulders, and he turned me to face him, with gentle inexorable pressure.

His skin used to be so hot, before. When I was human, and my flesh was humanly cold.

What am I now?

I didn't know.

He held my shoulders and examined my face, his gaze a physical pressure over my cheekbones, my mouth, my forehead. His eyes didn't frighten me now, despite their green glow.

His mouth was a thin line, his hair falling over and shading his burning eyes. The air in the room jolted once, as if hit by a projectile cannon. I flinched, but Japhrimel held me still and deathly silence fell again, wrapping around both of us.

When he spoke, it was quiet and level, each word evenly spaced. "I will repay the Prince tenfold for any harm done to you." His inhaled breath was a slow hiss as his eyes locked with mine.

I wonder if that's supposed to make me feel better. Shame rose, hot and vicious, and I tasted copper. He held me for a few more moments, and whatever he saw on my face must have satisfied him, because he let go of me. "We have little time, and must leave now."

"Where are we going?" I suppose I sounded normal — if by *normal* you mean *like a ten-credit-per-minute vidphone sex queen.* Something in my throat was permanently broken, thanks to the Prince of Hell's habit of strangling me.

It was a favor I longed to return, and with Japhrimel firmly on my side it might just be possible.

Maybe.

If Japh really was on my side.

Oh, gods above, Danny, don't start doubting him again.

"We have an appointment to keep." His shoulders straightened as he stepped away from me. "Come."

I shivered, a reflexive movement. Any other time, I would have flinched under the plasgun charge of Power and cold fury in Japhrimel's voice. "Japhrimel."

He paused, his coat coming to rest with a slight betraying flutter.

"Where are we going?" *Don't just order me around, dammit. I've had all I can take of being ordered around.*

Five seconds of absolute silence ticked by before he replied. "Konstans-Stamboul."

My shoulders dropped. *Great. Wonderful. Making progress. Why are we going there?*

He strode out of the room as if he expected me to follow.

So I did. What else could I do?

CHAPTER 5

Ten hours later, on a hover bristling with demonic shielding, we were in Konstans-Stamboul. I spent most of the journey on a narrow shelf of a bed in one of the hover's three cabins, grateful for a chance to simply rest. There were sounds under the well-tuned hum of hover transport—Lucas, other voices. I didn't care; Japh had brought me on through the cargo bay so I didn't have to see anyone.

I was grateful for that. I didn't *want* to be seen. I wanted to be alone.

I'd like to get a good few hours of meditation in. Even praying wouldn't hurt if we're going near a temple. It was a reflexive internal movement, a reaching for the faith that had always sustained me. The space where that faith had been was an ocean of bitterness, and I shivered like a child with a mouthful of sour candy as I buckled the rig on. It was new and custom-made, oiled leather holding two 9 mm projectile guns in low holsters, a 40-watt and a 20-watt plasgun (60-watts have a habit of blowing up in the hand), and a collection of knives, from two main-gauches long as my forearms from wrist to elbow to a thin flexible stiletto on the inside of one strap. The steel had faint dappled marks in the metal, as had all the knives Japhrimel had produced for me.

He understood good gear, the Devil's assassin. At least we always agreed about that.

The rig was going to chafe. The leather hadn't been broken in yet, despite its oiled softness. My other rig was gone.

Don't think about that.

I rolled my shoulders back in their sockets, breathed in, and felt the familiar weight of weaponry settle into shoulders and hips. My hand tightened around the scabbard, and I let the breath out in a soft hiss.

Armed and dangerous again, Danny. I dropped, with a jolt, fully into my skin, and opened my eyes.

Japhrimel stood just inside the door, watching me arm myself. "Are they acceptable?"

"I've never had a problem with any of the gear you get me." My voice was flat and weary, my face frozen into a mask. "You have a good eye for steel."

If I hadn't glanced up at him, I might have missed the faint smile touching his thin lips. "A compliment indeed, coming from you."

I checked the guns. They cleared easily, the projectiles clicking as I spun them, reholstering. The plasguns whined as I drew them, and I finished by testing the knives. The smallest stiletto was a bit sticky in its glove-tight sheath, but that was only to be expected, and if I had to draw it I probably wouldn't need it quickly anyhow. No, it would be a quiet draw, quiet as slipping the blade between ribs, as quiet as a prison cell with a lock that needs picking.

Japhrimel had even remembered the type of projectiles I usually carried ammo for, Smithwesson 9 mms with interchangeable cartridges. I had ammo in my bag, but I wasn't sure if my bag could take much more abuse.

Just as I thought it, Japhrimel raised his arm. I heard faint voices outside—Lucas's painful whisper, mostly; the others were just murmurs.

My bag, its strap no longer knotted, dangled from Japh's hand. He held it like it weighed nothing. "I repaired some small damage to this. I thought you would want it." He paused. "Even though it does still smell of Hell. I could not mend that."

A lump rose in my throat. I crossed the room, the new boots stiff and making each step oddly clumsy. I took the bag, ducked my head, and settled the strap diagonally across my body. When I looked up, Japhrimel was still staring down at me.

We stood like that, my head tilted back, his shoulders no longer ruler-straight but slightly slumped. His eyes were fixed on my mouth, their green glare hooded and alert.

I searched for something to say that would lead me on to the next thing that had to be done. *Roll with it, Danny. Get with the holovid.* "Thank you." I would have licked my dry lips, but the way he was staring at them stopped me. A flush of heat went down my body, followed by a wave of panic nailing me in place. "Don't look at me like that."

His eyes swung up to meet mine. Tension sparked in the air between us, a circuit closed or broken. Either way, it snapped once, then twice, as his hands came up to touch my shoulders. Leather creaked; the rig wasn't anywhere close to broken-in.

Great. If I have to sneak around it's not going to be very quietly. I swallowed several times. The funny coppery taste in my mouth didn't need an introduction.

It was fear. I was afraid of my own Fallen.

How was I going to work around that?

Work all you want, I told myself. *But there's someone who needs killing first. Then you can take your sweet time and figure out everything you've ever wanted to know.*

My voice surprised me. "I have to kill him." I searched Japhrimel's face, looking for the hidden human darkness in his glowing eyes. It was there, if I could just look deep enough. "I *have* to kill him. You have to help me."

He nodded, a short sharp movement. His coat ruffled along its edges, a rustling sound.

He did not ask who I meant.

"No more tricks. No more lies or plans I don't know about. No more hiding."

Another short nod. He looked as if he would say something, stopped.

"Promise me, Tierce Japhrimel." I could not sound any more deadly serious. My belly twitched, the skin flinching as if I expected a suckerpunch. "*Promise* me."

"What could I promise you that I have not already? I am in rebellion for your sake, is that not enough?" His quick motion arrested my protest, he laid one finger against my lips. "Come with me."

I flinched, covered it well enough. "Where now?" As if it mattered.

"We have an appointment. One I never thought I would keep." His mouth twisted bitterly at one corner, a swift snarl. It should have chilled my blood.

It didn't. For some reason, I felt a jagged burst of relief inside my chest. He'd promised.

It would have to be enough.

CHAPTER 6

Konstans-Stamboul is an amazingly low-built city. Zoning laws are tight and archaic here, and the traffic is mostly wheel or air-bikes, with a generous helping of slicboards. There aren't many hovers, and the freight lanes over the city are full of slow silvery beetles marching against a sky often starving-deep blue, old pollution and new citybreath laying a bowl of refraction over dreaming blocks of stone buildings mixed with concrete and weathered plasteel.

In the midst of this, the white walls and piercing towers of Hajia Sofya rise like a flawless tooth in otherwise-shattered gums. Graceful and pristine, the temple thrums with agonized centuries of worship and belief—Old Christer, Islum, Gilead Evangelical, and finally the multicolored, multilayered hum of Power collected consciously by psions coming to pray to their personal gods and normals coming to propitiate those same gods. Belief like sweat dews the white, white walls, and everywhere in the city you can *feel* the temple looming, a heart pumping slowly but surely.

There are other temples in Konstans-Stamboul, but none of them feel like Sofya. That's how psions refer to her—*Sofya*. And even more familiarly, as *She*. There are only two temples referred to in the feminine singular—Hajia Sofya, and Notra Dama in Paradisse.

Vann crouched easily on the grated plasteel floor of the hover, tossing what looked like brown knucklebones onto a square of dark leather painted with three concentric rings. He didn't *look* like a psion, but I supposed a Hellesvront agent working for Japhrimel might pick up a little divination here and there.

McKinley slumped in a chair, his head tipped back and a pale slice of throat showing. He wore all black, as usual, and his left hand lay cupped on his knee, more metallic than ever, glowing in mellow Stamboul light falling through the portholes. He looked tired, dark bruised circles graven under his closed eyes.

Lucas leaned against the hull, peering out a porthole, his yellow eyes slitted and the river of scarring down his face red and angry-looking. He rested one hand on the butt of a 60-watt plasgun, stroking it meditatively. Leander Beaudry, his cheeks scruffy with stubble over his accreditation tat, very pointedly didn't look at Japhrimel. He sat in another chair bolted to the floor, his knees drawn up and his sword across them. His emerald glowed, a spark popping from it as I stared at his familiar, suddenly-strange face. He looked so...human. He even smelled human, the odor of mortality a spice against the scent of *other* everyone else in the hover carried.

Even me. My thumb rested against the katana's guard.

"We're exposed here." Lucas didn't acknowledge my presence with anything else. "How long we staying?"

"We shall be leaving shortly." Japhrimel's heat against my back was comforting. He stood close, shadowing me in a way he never had before. "As soon as we have collected what we require."

McKinley's eyes showed a faint gleam under the heavy lids. They rested on me, those little gleams. I didn't like it. The sandpaper-on-skin distaste I always felt for him rasped at me. The little clicks as Vann threw the bones irritated me too.

I wondered if I could kill either or both of them before Japhrimel intervened. I actually even started planning how to do it, a thin unhealthy joy rising behind my heartbeat when I imagined slipping my katana free of its sheath and letting the rage take me.

The first few steps would be forward, gathering momentum and leaping, committing myself while McKinley was still in the chair. The sword would clear sheath with a musical ring, and the strike would be an upward diagonal, so that even if he tried to leap to his feet he would walk into it. He wouldn't take the easiest way out, kicking the chair over backward, because it was bolted to the floor. The second stroke would be a reverse, wrist twisting and hilt floating as the blade sped back down, and it would finish him and position me for a crouch to launch myself at Vann—

McKinley's dark eyes unlidded themselves halfway, his lashes rising with agonizing slowness. He looked at me like he could read my mind.

I'm sure my face reflected what I was thinking. I could feel it, a chilling little smile pulling the corners of my lips back, showing strong white demon-altered teeth.

McKinley didn't move. His Adam's-apple bobbed as he swallowed, but there was no stink of fear from him. Instead, he examined me from under half-closed eyelids, wearing the same set expression he might use to watch a poisonous but not terribly bright animal, one to be cautious of despite its inherent stupidity.

The friction on my nerves got worse. Vann said something I didn't quite catch, his stance changing just a fraction as he crouched fluidly over whatever he was doing.

Japhrimel's hand descended on my left shoulder, his fingers curling around and tightening over his mark in the sensitive hollow under the wing of my collarbone. "There is no cause for alarm," he said quietly. I had no trouble hearing *his* voice through the sudden rushing noise in my ears. "It is, after all, natural."

McKinley shrugged, a lazy movement. "Doesn't look like she agrees, m'Lord."

Japhrimel's thumb stroked the wing of my shoulderblade, brushing one of the rig's leather straps. The touch burned through me, clearing away the sick unsteady feeling of violence.

He irritates me, but that's not a reason to kill him. What am I thinking?

I didn't know. And that was dangerous in and of itself.

Silence stretched out until McKinley closed his eyes again. Vann scooped up the bones and the leather square, rolling them into a neat packet he tied off with a leather thong. The resultant little thing disappeared into his clothes and he rose with swift economical grace. "Will we be accompanying you, my Lord?"

The way the two agents spoke to Japh—with careful deference but absolute trust—rubbed me the wrong way too. It wasn't that they were so respectful. I of all people understood the need to be cautious where demons were concerned, especially if you work for them. But the lack of unease told me these two had known Japh longer than I had, and that I didn't like at all.

Sekhmet sa'es, Danny, are you jealous? *Of a couple of Hellesvront agents?* I slid away from Japhrimel's hand. He let me, but I didn't miss the sudden tension in the air as I crossed the hover in swift strides, my new boots and rig creaking, to stare out the porthole next to Lucas's.

"You will be accompanying me, but not in the usual manner." Japhrimel said it carefully, giving each word particular weight. "Your task will be to protect what is most precious to me."

Silence spread out in ripples again. I peered out the porthole, seeing the edge of a landing pad, a bare weedy empty lot, and the unmistakable slumped tenements of Konstans-Stamboul's poorer section. This wasn't quite where I would have picked to park—a shiny hover sitting around in this neighborhood would draw attention. Thick, golden late-afternoon sunlight dipped every surface in honey.

My fingers tightened on the sheath as the silence grew more intense. I felt eyes on me, didn't turn around. What was I supposed to do?

"Very well." Japhrimel sounded like something had been decided.

Lucas let out a soft breath, a tuneless hum. I glanced over, meeting his yellow gaze. A thought froze me, seeing the river of scarring running down his face.

They called Lucas the Deathless, and the rumor was that he'd done something so awful even Death had turned His back on the man. I'd always assumed Lucas had been a Necromance.

What if I was wrong?

"Lucas." The word was out of my mouth before I was aware of speaking. "Can I ask you something?"

He shrugged, turning his gaze out his own porthole. "We stick out like a hooker in a Luddite convention, parked here." Under the threadbare yellowing shirt, his wiry shoulders were hunched. Call me sensitive, but I got the idea he didn't want to answer any questions just now.

"I thought the same thing." Thin amusement rode the edge of my voice. I rolled my shoulders back in their sockets, settling the rig. "I just wish I could stop getting my clothes blown off me and bloodied."

"Quit gettin' yourself into trouble with demons." He jerked his chin toward his right shoulder, a movement I belatedly realized took in the silent and visibly unhappy Leander. "Boy's learned his lesson."

"You don't have to call me a coward, Villalobos." Leander's voice was soft, the professional whispering tone of a Necromance. We who enforce our will on the world with our voices learn to speak softly. It's also kind of an affectation—a whisper is better than a shout when it comes to scaring the hell out of someone.

I don't usually feel like scaring the hell out of someone. People—at least, *normal* headblind people—are simply scared of psions as a whole. It's xenophobia and fear of the unknown all wrapped up in one economical package, with lingering hatred left over from the Evangelicals of Gilead and their theocratic North Merican empire making a festive bow. The Seventy Days War and the fall of the Republic were years and years ago, but people have long memories when it comes to hating the different.

"Not callin' you a coward, Beaudry. Think it's your smartest move." Lucas gave the whistling gurgle that was his laugh.

I turned away from the porthole, looking at Leander directly. A scintilla of light from the emerald embedded in his cheekbone sent a swift bolt of something too hot and nasty to be pain through me. "What's going on?"

The Necromance shrugged, an economical movement. His katana rattled unhappily inside its sheath, and his shielding shivered as the charged atmosphere stroked at it. His eyes were shadowed, and the inked lines of his accreditation tat shifted under scruffy dark stubble. "Your friend doesn't like me, Valentine." He didn't have to point for me to know it was Japhrimel he was talking about. "But if I strike out on my own, I'm looking at trouble. I'm associated with you now. So do I stick around and wait for your pet demon to take more of a dislike to me, or do I find a hole to hide in until this blows over?" A short bitter laugh, and he palmed his face wearily. "Except things like this don't blow over. I'm just unhappy. I'm not a goddamn coward."

"Nobody's saying you are." My eyes fastened on the emerald, alive with green light. He still had his connection with his psychopomp, with whatever face of Death had revealed itself at his Trial.

He was a Necromance. His god hadn't forced him to spare a traitor's life.

Except my god hadn't forced me, had He? No, He had simply *asked*. I could not blame Him. Who did that leave to blame?

Anubis — The prayer started inside my head, I shoved it away. I would not call on Him.

Not now. Not like this. The determination was raw and painful, heavy sunlight on already burned skin.

"So I'm in." Leander's tone said plainly, *That's that. Don't push me.*

I considered him for a long moment. He was right. I'd stepped in over my head this time, worse than usual. The hideous beating secret inside my brain was almost as black as the traitorous tingling on my cheekbone where my own emerald flashed.

After all my worship, all my love, and all my service, my god had let me down just when I needed Him most, by even *asking* the sacrifice of me. How could I reconcile my faith to that? I had been *forced* to spare a killer's life. I had been used by the god I loved.

Would another Necromance understand my pain?

Why don't you ask him over coffee, Danny? Whenever you can take a moment out of your busy schedule of being dragged into Hell and strangled to death by demons.

I scraped together the most tactful thing I could think of to say. "Fine. You're in." *Just stay out of trouble.* I half-turned again, meeting Japhrimel's eyes.

My Fallen stood with his hands loose at his sides. It was the closest to bored I'd ever seen him, but he also had a look I didn't like at all. A look of listening to some sound I would never be able to hear, no matter how hard I strained my better-than-human senses. It was only a millimeter's worth of difference in the set of his mouth, a slight tension in his winged eyebrows, but it was as loud as a shout to me. I'd spent long enough looking at him to know.

He'd worn that look a lot in Toscano, before our life together had gone merrily to Hell.

Icy spider-feet walked up my spine. "You have a problem with that, Japh?"

He considered me, his eyes burning incandescent green. The raggedness of dark hair falling over those eyes helped make his gaze a little less awful, as did the thin oval of human darkness behind the glow.

He ended up saying nothing. It might have seemed like the wisest course, considering the way my right hand itched for my swordhilt. I wasn't used to this kind of simmering rage.

Still, I didn't *dislike* it. It felt clean. Cleaner than the dark thing pulsing in my head, at least.

"See?" I swung back round to face Leander. "You're in." Another thought stopped me, so fast I snapped off the end of the last word. A sudden inspiration. "My very own Necromance to hang around. Just like getting a puppy for my birthday."

The sharp intake of breath, for once, wasn't mine. It was McKinley's. His eyes flew open, and I could swear Vann went white under the copper tone of his skin.

Wow. Maybe I just said something right for a change. Either that or I've just made a huge mistake. Guess which way my luck's running lately.

Japhrimel nodded. "As you like, my curious." No more than that. No color to his voice except simple acceptance.

I wished I could figure out whether he was giving in because it didn't matter in the long run *what* I did. It was pretty damn likely.

There you go, Danny old girl. You're thinking like yourself again.

The trouble was, I wasn't sure I really was thinking like myself. It's hard to tell when you're not sure who you are anymore.

"My Lord." Vann clasped his arms behind his back, standing poker-straight. It looked ridiculous on him, especially with the fringe hanging off his leather coat. "I would remind you—"

"Not necessary, Vann." Japhrimel said over the top of him. Not dismissively, and not with any real heat. But his face settled and set, a demon's essential oddity closer to the surface than ever before, and my heart turned over inside my chest.

He wasn't human. It should have bothered me. It should have reminded me of the thing beating like a diseased heart inside my skull, the memory sleeping uneasily behind the strongest door I could make to shut it away.

It didn't. Instead, I saw the thin line of his lips, the fineness of his eyelashes, and the raggedness of his hair. I saw the oval of darkness behind his burning eyes.

I saw the man—no matter if he was a demon—who always came for me.

Whatever was on my face might not have been pleasant, but it seemed fine by my Fallen. His mouth relaxed into a half-smile, one corner quirking up in that sardonic expression that meant he was enjoying himself. As if I'd made an unexpected move in a game of battlechess, or done something that pleasantly surprised him.

I liked that look.

But what I liked even more was the thought that I might have some sort of control over my relationship with him. A little bit of control might sound like a small thing, but it was the difference between screaming insanity and some kind of rational shape to the inside of my head.

I actually felt happier than I had in a long time. Maybe I shouldn't have, but there it was. But still, my arms and legs were heavy, and deep in my belly a stone sat, dragging me down.

"So." I actually sounded perky. *Chalk up a winning gravball goal for Danny Valentine. It's about time.* "What's this about an appointment?"

CHAPTER 7

I hadn't thought it would affect me like this.

Sofya's outer beauty was nothing compared to the magnificence inside. I'd seen holostills and travelogues, but they...nothing could do her justice. The blue, white, yellow mosaics had been carefully restored, domes soaring with mathematical precision above the standard Hegemony sundisc, its burnished glory little match for the piercing shafts of dying russet and gold sunlight falling through space harmonized, sanctified, and made agonizingly sweet by centuries of Power, praise, prayer, and above all, sheer undiluted *belief.*

Belief is what magick works on, after all. And so *much* of it is bound to give anyone who works the highest art humanity's capable of a high cleaner and sweeter than Clormen-13.

The temple was also heavy with demonspice and a tang of mortality's decay—a heady stew when added to the *kyphii* incense swirling hazily through the interior and the sweet blue-black resin they use in temples in this part of the world. The time to find any temple deserted is dusk, when incense grows heavy and shadows skitter with a life of their own. Normal humans instinctively avoid places of Power after dark, and psions are just waking up as the sun goes down. It's like a psychic shift-change for the entire world.

The gods, in this slice of the world, were mostly Old Graecian. Hermes with winged sandals and helmet, Héra in Her place of primacy, Apolo's small statue next to the more massive Artemisa Hekat holding a bow and touching the head of a sleek marble greyhound. Hades was there, shadowed by Persephonica, with Her basket of flowers echoing Demetre's horn of plenty. Âres crouched behind His shield, shortsword thrusting belligerently up. Aphroditas swooned on a long couch, Her naked body glowing triumphantly.

There was another long gallery of gods, mostly Old Perasiano, along with a round shield of calligraphy for the remnants of old Islum, enduring its last death here in a part of the world it once ruled, just like Novo Christianity. The Religions of Submission had a good run, but once the Awakening had happened and people could speak directly and reliably with gods...well, they just didn't make sense anymore.

At least, to most reasonable people.

I'm not really up on my Old Perasiano, but I recognized Ahra Mzda, as well as Ah'rman, His destructive shadow-twin. There was a rough carved stone for Allat, who hadn't been Perasiano but who made sense, given the once-popularity of Islum in this part of the world.

It was beautiful in a way only sacred space can be. For just a moment the spell of beauty and belief closed around me like a warm bath, almost dispelling the twitching heaviness in my belly. But the emptiness of my naked face, my emerald still twinkling unnecessarily from its grafted roots on my cheekbone, hit me like a slap.

What was I doing in a house of the gods, now that my own god had asked me for more than I could give? I had always been so certain, so sure of being cradled in Death's hands. Now I couldn't even look at Hades's dour shadowed features under his anachronistic crescent-peaked helm. He was just another of Death's faces, not the slender canine head of my own personal psychopomp, but my eyes skittered away from Him all the same.

I couldn't look Death in the face anymore.

I tore my eyes away and paced into the temple, Japhrimel's step soundless behind me. He was alert and wary, the cloak of his Power against my skin drawing together more and more tightly, covering me with a mantle of warmth.

I was grateful for that, even as I shamefully averted my eyes from one of Death's faces. Our little group made next to no noise except for the creaking of the blasted new rig, announcing to the world that I was wandering around even more loudly than the light-filled scar of my aura on the ambient landscape of Power.

Kyphii filled my nose. Gabe Spocarelli had always been burning the stuff, its fragrant bite filling her house. Except now her house was empty, everything inside it searched and possibly broken, and Gabe was dead.

Another reason not to look Death in the face. If I went into the blue land where my god resided now, would I meet my oldest friend? Would she ask if I was protecting her daughter, like I'd sworn to? Would she ask me if I had avenged her death?

Would her soul believe me if I told her I'd tried?

The temple spun around me, a spiked wheel of sanctity and belief. I took a deep breath of *kyphii-laden* air, the Power contained in those thrumming walls bleeding out in organ-tones of deep red and deeper violet just at the edge of hearing, rattling my bones. The floor clicked underfoot, permaplas mosaic tiles distressed to look like old chips of silica glass, and in the middle of the vast empty bell of the deserted temple a monstrous cramp gripped the lowest regions of my belly, sinking its rusty teeth right through me.

Japhrimel's arm circled my shoulders. "Dante?"

Vann swore. There were little clicks as he and McKinley moved up to what I recognized as cover positions—and I would have cared about that, really, if the pain hadn't been eating me alive, a blowtorch in my guts. Lucas swore too, but more quietly, and I heard the whine of an unholstered plasgun.

The temple shivered like a parabolic mirror swiveling on jeweled bearings. The Power in the walls turned to streaks of oil on a wet surface as I collapsed, only Japhrimel's sudden clutching hand keeping me from spilling writhing to the ground.

What the hell it hurts oh no now what?

I *felt* it, the thrumming in this building even older than the Republic of Gilead. A darkness lived at its very roots, and as fresh pain gripped me I bent over without even the breath to scream. My emerald sparked once, twice, green glimmers in the gloom.

Pain eased, in dribs and drabs. I hung from Japhrimel's hands, limp and wrung-wet, sweat standing out in great clear drops on my skin. "—ohgods—" I managed, in a very small voice. "I think I'm going to..." *Throw up. Pass out. Something.*

"Do what you must. I thought we had more time." Japhrimel's hands were gentle. Too gentle. I would have preferred him to use the iron-under-velvet strength he was capable of, because if he was being this exquisitely careful, something was *most definitely wrong.*

"More time for *what?*" I gasped, my legs shaking. The only other time I'd felt this unsteady was when I had my worst bout of reaction fever after landing in a slagheap on a bounty in Hegemony Suisse. I'd thrown up so hard I'd been weak and shaky for days and almost burst a few blood vessels.

Back when Doreen was still alive.

I didn't need that thought. I had enough keeping me occupied. "I think I'm all right." I shook Japh's hands away—or would have, if I could have stood up on my own. My legs refused to obey me. They'd turned into wet noodles.

Is it me? Am I not allowed in temples anymore? Anubis, my Lord, my god, why? What have I done? I spared the traitor You wanted me to spare.

But I'd cursed Him, hadn't I? I had cursed my god bitterly, down in the very roots of my being. I'd thought it could not matter. I had been *sure* it would not matter. I had also lied, broken my sorcerous Word, and betrayed everything I held dear.

No wonder sacred space did not want me.

The voice came from nowhere, skittering through the temple's shadows like thousands of pairs of decorative insectile feet, pricking hard and hurtful against shivering skin. "Kinslayer." It spoke Merican, but the accent was pure demon, twisted and wrong. "How dare you enter this place?"

I managed to raise my head. Shadows gathered between the swords of dying sunlight, and the house of the gods rustled with currents of uneasy Power.

Japhrimel's sure steady grip on me didn't change. "Sephrimel. I greet you."

"You greet me. How courteous. How *dare* you enter here?" The insect feet turned to pinpricks of fire, and Sofya's entire interior shuddered. It was a demon's voice, but somehow wrong. It was a voice of casual power, full of a demon's terrible alienness. There was something else in that voice, something that twisted hard against my bones. It was as if a murderous forgotten artifact, old and blind in a corner, had suddenly risen up to demand attention — and blood.

Japhrimel sounded just as he usually did. Calm, quiet as a knife slipped between ribs. "I have come for what you stole. It is time."

The owner of the skittering voice stepped out of shadows that shouldn't have held him as casually as a human might step from one room into another.

He was tall and gaunt, as starved-looking as I've ever seen a demon. Golden skin drew tight over bones as architecturally beautiful as Sofya's own grace. His hair was an amazing shock of clotted ice, twisted into dreadlocks pulled back and looped several times with hanks of red silk. The hair looked like it had drained the life from him, and his baggy black robe, belted with a length of frayed rope, didn't help. Narrow golden feet, callused and battered into claws, rutched against the mosaic floor. His hands were skeletal, the claw structure built into fingertips and wrist musculature clearly visible with no extraneous flesh to disguise it.

His eyes. Dear gods, his eyes.

They were dark, not incandescent with awful power. Black from lid to lid, but not empty. No, his eyes were grieving holes in a face that had drawn itself tight around a sorrow like a burning stone in the throat.

Like the burning stone in my belly.

I met his gaze, and the gripping pain in my belly coalesced around a hot hard fist buried in my flesh. I knew that grief.

I'd lost people too. Their names were a litany of pain, each one a different scar on my still-beating heart. My social worker Lewis, killed by a Chill junkie. Doreen, slaughtered by a demon intent on breaking Lucifer's hold on Hell. Jace, throwing himself past me to take on a Feeder's *ka*. Eddie, dead in his lab, betrayed by his *sedayeen* research partner. And Gabe, my best friend, lying tangled in her garden, dead protecting a traitor my god had asked me to spare.

Each anguish rose up to choke me as I stared into those black, black eyes. Whoever this demon was, he had lost something.

No. Not something. Some*one.*

Another cramp unzipped me. I spilled against Japhrimel, the agony drawing a curtain of redblack over my vision. I lost sight of the white-haired demon. Japh murmured something to me as I inhaled sharply, wondering who was making that soft mewling sound of pain.

It was me.

"You have lost whatever wit you once possessed." The demon's voice was now a bath of terrible icy numbness. "So it is true. You have Fallen, committed the sin you punished others for."

"What talk is this of sin, between us? You have spent too long with humans." Japhrimel braced me, the scar on my shoulder spilling warmth into my racked body, fighting with the hideous clawing in my belly.

It hurts it hurts oh Anubis — I dragged in another breath. "*Anubis et'her ka;* oh my Lord my god, *please* —"

Again the pain retreated. It left no relief in its wake. How could I call on Him? Why would He answer me? I was a traitor to myself, and this was my punishment.

But it *hurt.*

"I have spent my penance with mortals. *You* still reek of Hell and murder, Kinslayer." His voice was rising, and the entire temple throbbed. I had a sudden uneasy vision, between flashes of pain so immense it was like drowning, of Sofya's white walls weeping blood like an injured tooth.

Breathe, Danny. Breathe.

But I couldn't. Not until the swell retreated and I found myself sweating and shaking, wrung out, hanging in Japhrimel's hands. *Fine time to have an attack of nerves, sunshine. What the hell? I was feeling fine.*

But I hadn't been feeling fine for a long while, had I? Stumbling from one terror to the next, staggering from one suckerpunch in the gut to the next, spilling from horror into agony and ending up at numb grief each time.

My eyes cleared. I didn't look up at the demon's face again. "I think I should wait outside," I whispered. The urge to retch rose and passed through me, so immense it felt like all my insides were trying to crawl out the hard way.

Nobody paid any damn attention. Lucas had gone silent and still as an adder under a rock. Leander's pulse thrummed audibly, the only human heartbeat I'd heard for a while. Vann and McKinley had their laserifles trained on the dreadlocked demon.

That hair's amazing. I wonder if he smokes synth hash and rides a slic in his spare time. He looks like a sk8 in Domenhaiti. All he needs is permaspray stains on his fingers and a few circuit wires in his hair.

The thought sparked a jagged laugh. Why was I always *laughing* at times like this?

"I do not dispute that," Japhrimel said, still calmly. A steady bath of Power flushed from his aura to mine, working in to meet thin wires of flame running through the core of my bones. "I have merely come to claim a certain article from you. It should please you to hear that I am ready to use it for its intended purpose. McKinley."

I snapped a glance at the black-haired Hellesvront agent, who slung his laserifle's strap over his shoulder and stepped forward. Japhrimel, without so much as a glance down, transferred my weight to the agent by the simple expedient of pushing me. I spilled against McKinley like a newborn kitten, my legs useless and the rest of me not far behind.

What the hell? Another cramp was gathering, my belly quivering with anticipated pain, something trying to climb up through the space caged in my ribs, twisting and clawing.

"Japh? *Japhrimel?*" I'll admit it. There was no room for pride. My voice was the thin piping squeak of a child caught in a nightmare.

Maybe he can make it stop. Oh please, please make it stop.

No wonder my god didn't want me. I was praying to a demon, the only intercession I had left.

"It's all right." McKinley closed his right hand over my arm, bracing me so I didn't go straight down to the floor. "Just relax, Valentine. It's okay."

This is not anywhere near okay.

A new quality crept into the stillness. It was the unsettled boiling of air about to erupt with violence, and Japhrimel moved out in front of us as Vann stepped in, laserifle socked to his shoulder. Even Leander had a plasgun out, though he was chalk-white and visibly shaking, his eyes flicking between me and the pair of demons who faced each other on Sofya's pebbled floor.

Seen so close, the difference was startling. The white-haired demon was more than human, true. It screamed from every pore and angle of his frame.

But Japhrimel was more, too. If the other demon was a candle compared to the weak shimmer of a human's aura, Japh was a halogen lasebulb, burning hot enough to scorch plasteel.

He hadn't looked like that compared to Lucifer, had he?

My brain shivered away from the idea. *Eve. What is she doing now? Where is she?*

The thought enraged the tearing thing living in my vitals. Pain swelled, blackness bulged under the surface of my mind, and whatever Japh and the other one said was lost in the fact that I was pretty sure I was dying here in Hajia Sofya.

The blackness swelled, pulsing obscenely as something *alien* fought for control of my brain and agony-wracked body. Out. I had to get *out* of the temple and away from whatever divine anger was punishing me.

Unfortunately, McKinley thought otherwise. My sword dropped to the floor with a clatter as I feebly tried to fight his hands off me. Then the most amazing cramp-bolt lanced my belly and I went down to the floor, scrabbling for my sword to cut out whatever monstrous thing was growing in me.

I convulsed.

Sudden coolness ran from the crown of my head down through my flesh, a river of balm. I gasped, mouth working like a fish's, and was aware of a slick pattering sound and Leander's muffled curse. The pain in my belly turned back into inert heaviness, as if I'd swallowed something indigestible, lodged in the bowl of my pelvis.

My hands searched fruitlessly for my sword. Warm bony fingers caught my wrist. *"Avayin, hedaira."* Weary kindness in each syllable. "Peace, beautiful one. Be at peace. You will not die of this."

Are you sure? Because I really think I might. I collapsed against the unforgiving floor, pebbles of mosaic digging into hip and cheek. They felt cool and good against my fevered skin, as the darkness struggled to birth itself inside my head and the thing in my belly twisted. I heard my own breath, a panicked whistling I wasn't sure I liked.

The kind voice wasn't familiar, and it turned unkind again. "She carries *a'zharak*." Each word laden with disgust and some other, less definable emotion. "This is how you treasure your prize?"

"I made no claim to be the best of my kind. I make no claim to be the best of *yours* either. The Prince seeks to control my link to her world. She has suffered for it — and suffers now." Japhrimel sounded just as tired, and just as sharp. "I did not come here for my sake, but for hers."

"Then it is *her* I will help, Kinslayer. Draw your minions away."

The heavy spiked agony in my belly crested again, and the bony hands of a starving demon clamped down with inhuman strength. A hissing breath of effort filled my ears, and I screamed as the weight was suddenly torn from me in a rush of blood and battered viscera.

Leander yelled. Lucas let out a shout of surprise, and the sounds smashed the calm of the temple's interior. I curled around myself, endlessly grateful for the cessation of pain, and passed out for one brief starry moment as chaos erupted around me.

CHAPTER 8

*T*he water was full of knives, and as I thrashed it drained away, liquid weightlessness replaced by the agony of cutting.

No. You can't go yet. *A familiar voice, the words laid directly inside my consciousness, as I struggled to escape, flesh a prison and my soul the struggling captive, digging her way out with broken fingernails as sharp edges pressed into numb flesh, invading.*

Blue flame rose, the entrance to the land of Death, and not even the fact that my god might well deny me the comfort and rational clear light of What Comes Next could deter me. I strained toward that blue glow.

There are times when Death is not an adventure, but an escape from a life descended too far into Hell. Any hell.

Not yet. *Maddeningly, the voice barred my way. The knives retreated, my skin still numb. I couldn't tell if I was bleeding or just cold, if I was standing or lying down, if I was alive or something else.*

Then the light came, a sharp living light, not the glow of What Comes Next that lifts the soul up and away on a streak of brilliance. This was a human light, and as I blinked I heard the sound of dragging footsteps on wet stone and felt arms around me, stick-thin but very strong.

I blinked again. A dizzying moment of vertigo, and the world came into focus, into clear heartstopping detail. The light was coming through the window.

Along the edge of each window ran a thin line of gold. It poured through each pane of glass, a curtain of sunshine dancing with infinite dust-motes.

It should not have surprised me to see sunshine when I dreamed of Jason Monroe.

He sat cross-legged on the floor, looking up with mild interest, blue eyes catching fire under the flood of light. It glowed in his hair, a human furnace of gold, and he was again the young Jace of the first violent flush of our affair. The Bolgari chronograph glittered on his wrist, and he wore a white T-shirt, muscle flickering underneath as he lifted the sword a little, balancing it on his palms.

The room was a surprise. It was Jado's room, the room at the top of the stairs where my sensei *gave out his prized swords, one at a time, to his most trusted students. Only here, the wooden racks along the wall were empty, and the mellow hardwood floor was scratched and scarred, white paint on the walls chipped. The window was bare, and the hall beyond the open doorway stood empty as a soymalt 40 can rolling down the street.*

"Nice." Jace was barefoot, in jeans, and the fine golden hairs on his forearms glistened in the light. "I like this venue, too."

He actually spoke, *instead of the words being laid in my head like a gift. And no wonder the voice that called me away from Death was familiar, for it was his.*

Breath left me in a walloping rush. I sank down to the floor, finding myself in a tattered blue sweater, ripped jeans showing pale human skin underneath. In these dreams, I was human again. My nails were painted red with molecule-drip, and my hair was tangled, dull with black dye, and full of split ends. "I'm not dead." Three words, through the lump of misery in my throat, forced out despite myself.

It dawned on me, through the fog of light and the good smell of dust and paint and fresh air, as if the room breathed summer wind through every crack. "And I don't think I'm really dreaming," I whispered.

His grin widened, the smile that had brought no shortage of female attention his way. "Got it in one, sunshine. We have a little time, here. A little space."

"I miss you." The simple truth of it frightened me, took shape in the air, looming invisibly behind thick syrupy golden light. "Why are you doing this? Why didn't you let me die?"

"You're being dense. What else would I do for you?" A shrug, his face turning solemn. The sword eased back down, into his lap, across his knees.

It was his dotanuki, *the sword broken by the shock of his death. Not precisely broken, just twisted into a corkscrew and leaking agony into the air, the agony of a soul ripped from its moorings by a Feeder's* ka. *My eyes traced the familiar scabbard, and every question I had never asked him rose in my throat and stung my eyes.*

"Gabe," I whispered. "Eddie."

"You did the right thing." His hand twitched, as if he would reach forward to touch me. Then it relaxed, and his fingers trailed over the familiar wrapped hilt. "It isn't like you to kill a defenseless woman, Danny. You would have hated yourself for it. Later, that is. When you calmed down."

I shook my head. "That's not what I meant." And he still hadn't answered me. Why would he call me back, of all people? He was *dead too.*

I'd failed him just as surely as I'd failed everyone else.

"You wanted to ask if I see them. I can't tell you that, you know that. Go into Death and ask for yourself, that's your question." He sighed. "You're always asking the wrong fucking questions, baby."

"When did you get so goddamn shallow?" I flung back at him. It was easy, the reflex of a fight. Always better to fight him—I have always been more afraid of the damage a soft word could do.

I suppose he might have even understood that he was the only person I had ever fought so hard.

The question was, had he understood it while he was alive?

"You're a lousy Shaman. Loa work better when they're cajoled."

"You're not a loa.*" I was fairly certain of that, at least. Had he been one of the spirits the vaudun Shamans of the world traffic with, he wouldn't have bothered to wear someone else's face. I've only caught glimpses of them, since they have little use for Necromances. But no* loa *would appear in another skin here, in whatever dreamspace this was.*

They do not dress, while they are at home.

"Other people get loa. *You get me."*

It dawned on me in slow stages. I stared at him, at the bump on his nose, where a break from a bounty he'd run with me as apprentice and backup had gone horribly wrong in Freetown Hongkong. We had just barely made it out of there alive, and he had never bothered to get the break in his nose bonescrubbed. No, I'd set it with a healcharm, and he'd left the tiny imperfection there, saying it would teach him to be more careful when facing a bounty with a laserifle in close quarters.

"Like a familiar?" I hazarded, prickles spilling down my back. Lucifer had given me Japhrimel as a familiar, long ago. I knew most of the rules where a demon familiar was involved, except for maybe the one about letting the demon fall in love with you.

But what are the rules when your dead boyfriend shows up as a meddling spirit?

"Like, and unlike." He nodded approvingly, his fingers smoothing the hilt. It was a familiar movement. Whenever he rode transport or discussed the finer points of hunting bounties, his fingers would move, slightly. On a swordhilt, on the butt of a gun . . . or on my hip, gently, as we shared a bed late at night.

Long, long ago. Before Japhrimel. Before everything.

I couldn't help myself. I had to. "Japhrimel."

Jace's eyes flicked down to his lap, rested on the sword. "I can't see a lot about demons from here, Danny."

"That's not what I asked."

"It's the only answer I'm giving. I'm not going to stop watching your back because of him, Danny girl. You're heading into deep waters, and you'll need all the help you can get."

Sekhmet sa'es, can the water get any deeper? *The thought must have shown on my face, because he laughed. It was the short, bitter bark he used while hunting, a sound that brought back memory upon memory until they crowded in the sunlight, shadows passing the windows like giant silent fish.*

"I'm here if you need me, Danny. But you know what to do."

Why didn't you let me die, Jace? *I opened my mouth to ask again, but a soft sound cut me off. It was the whispering drag of oiled metal leaving the sheath, and I jolted up to my feet, realizing in one horrified second that I was unarmed, I wore only rags, and I was human again, my pulse pounding thinly in my throat and wrists. The sunlight dimmed, clouds drifting over the sun—or something huge settling over the house, perhaps.*

Jace cocked his head. His sword was still in his lap, but I heard a soft creak. A footstep, bare flesh against wooden floor. Was it in the hall, or was I hallucinating?

"You're not finished yet. Better go, Danny girl."

The sunlight dimmed even further, and I heard something else: a rushing crackle, flame devouring something. The smell of burned paper and another deeper stench turned the air orange, and I whirled, my hair fanning out as I—

—was underground. The lack of psychic "static" told me I was underground. It was dark until I opened my eyes, and candlelight flowed like gelid gold into my brain. The spurred, twisting heaviness was gone, but I felt tender and savagely stretched all over.

"You will live." The white-haired demon bent over me, claws pricking my wrist as he felt for my pulse.

What the hell?

A rock wall rose up to my right. I lay on something unforgivingly hard, cold seeping into my skin. The weight of my rig was gone, and my clothes were stiff with the decaying-fruit stench of my own blood. My shoulder pulsed reassuringly, another bath of Power sliding down my skin.

I wet my lips. The demon's face was inches from mine. Long thin nose, long thin mouth, cheeks scraped down parchment-thin over high cheekbones, and those suffering, suffering eyes like shots to the gut. A fat white snake of his hair slid over his shoulder, dropping down to brush my cheek and slide off the edge of whatever hard surface I rested on.

Okay, I'll admit it. I screamed like an unregistered hooker caught holding out on her pimp. I also surged up and tried to hit him in the face.

He avoided the strike gracefully, dropping my wrist and stepping aside. I scrambled away along the platform, my back hitting a hard pebbled wall. I clutched the ragged edges of my shirt together and realized my jeans were unbuttoned and stiff with dried blood all the way down to my ankles. The scream died on a sucked-in gasp as my head cleared.

"I had forgotten how fragile they are," the white-haired demon said, meditatively. "*Avayin, hedaira.* You are well and whole."

He was right. Thin traceries of scar crisscrossed the bowl of my belly, golden skin marred with threadlike white. It looked like my guts had been run through a badly set laseslicer. I flattened my hand over warm flesh and realized my breasts were hanging out, clutched. the shirt closed over my front, and stared gape-mouthed at him.

What the hell? One second my innards are falling out, and now... what?

"Do you know who I am?" He didn't retreat, pitched forward at the edge of the rough stone rectangle I braced myself on. The walls crawled with color — little bits and chips of stone, plasteel, plasilica, and other hard shattered things, in every conceivable shade. Figures whirled and swam in the mosaic, a wash of screaming art covering the dome above dark wooden bookshelves stacked with scrolls that smelled like rotting animal skins, stuffed in no apparent order. The only space not taken up by the shelves was broken by a low wooden door and the stone I perched on.

The dome itself was no slouch, a ribbed chamber easily thirty feet high. At its apex, a mellow sphere of something that looked like gold glowed, flickering. It had the breath of alienness that meant something demon-made, as did the arches of the vaulting.

My breath hitched in again. I searched for something to say. What ended up coming out of my mouth was almost as mortifying as it was comforting, because it sounded just like me.

"I'm pretty sure you're not Father Egyptos, sunshine. You look like a sk8 with a bad hair fetish." The words hit the mosaics, my voice a thin husk of its former throaty self, and I glanced frantically around for Japhrimel. He was nowhere in sight.

I was alone, underground, with a dreadlocked demon.

You should have known you'd end up like this, Danny. I mean, you really should have known. This is par for the course.

My sword was nowhere in sight either. But my bag, faithful companion that it was, lay at the end of the stone rectangle. It was open, and my rings spat an angry shower of gold sparks. Someone *else* had been going through my goddamn messenger bag. Would it ever end?

As if he'd read my mind, the demon held up a book-shaped object.

I knew what it was as soon as my eyes lighted on it. *Hedairae Occasus Demonae,* the ancient demon-written book given to me by Selene, consort of the Prime of Saint City. I hadn't had a quiet moment to look at the goddamn thing since she'd handed it over, being busy hunting down a conspiracy that killed my best friend.

Funny how that works out.

"You are too young to understand this." His mouth turned down for a moment, as if he tasted something so bitter his entire body revolted against it. "You are too young to even begin. I will explain to you, in detail, what it means. If you will do me a service."

Just like a demon. Quid pro quo. My right hand curled into a knot, looking for a vanished swordhilt. No rig, no weapons, no Japhrimel.

Great. Just when I could really use him.

"I don't bargain with demons." I felt faintly ridiculous saying that, with my shirt torn open and my weapons gone. "I'm not a Magi."

"You are *hedaira,* beloved of a Lord of Hell, and under sentence of death wherever you roam." The demon's gaunt face twisted in on itself, then smoothed. "I am Sephrimel." Of all things, he held out his skinny hand, like we were at a dinner party.

I eyed his fingers like they might bite me. You never know, with demons.

After a few long moments he dropped his hand back to his side. His frayed robe whispered. "I am also called accursed, Fallen, *A'nankhimel.* I did what no demon dares to do."

My mouth had no trouble keeping up, even while the rest of me frantically tried to figure out what the hell was going on. "There's a lot of that going around these days." I began to feel even more ridiculous, which was a stretch. What was I doing with my clothes all opened up?

That question sent a bolt of sheer panicked nausea through my abused stomach. "What did you do to me?" *And where's my sword?*

His mouth compressed itself even thinner, his scraped-down face pulling itself into a parody of distaste. "I rid you of an unwelcome guest."

It is so easy to break a human—Memory rose inside my head, was pushed away, retreated snarling. I grabbed for the only thing I could. "Where's Japh?"

"Your Fallen is above, holding the temple against any intrusion." Sephrimel's eyes flicked down my body, once, and away. The book dangled in his other hand, tempting. Everyone seemed so damn interested in the thing. "I could, possibly, stay you here until the Prince's dogs—or some other of my kind, with a grudge—arrive. The Kinslayer will fight to his last breath, but the Prince's minions are numberless even when weakened, and even a killer such as yours may eventually fall. When he does, you may find yourself without protection."

A thin thread of panic wormed its way through me. He looked like he meant it. My sense of direction didn't work so well underground. Where the hell *was* I?

I decided to start with the most important questions first. "Who are you really? And what the *fuck* do you want?"

His shoulders dropped, and he opened the book with spidery dry-claw hands. The paper rustled thickly against cavernous silence broken otherwise only by my increasingly harsh breathing. Finding the page he wanted, he offered it to me with both hands and a slight bow, as if presenting a gift to royalty.

"You cannot read this, of course. But the picture is clear enough."

I glanced down, meaning only to take a tiny sip of the pages. But my eyes locked themselves to an illustration, as finely colored as a holostill, with snakelike demonic glyphs on the page facing.

In the picture, a slim golden-skinned woman with a glory of long blood-colored hair held her hands up in supplication, her white robes cut like a holomag film star's to show a twisting mark painted into the right side of her belly. She wasn't screaming, but the lines of her face expressed horror and pleading, mixed with terrible resignation. She had no weapons, and her back was to a white wall.

Filling a third of the page in front of her was a demon with a long narrow nose and thin lips, winged eyebrows, and laser-green eyes under short military-cut dark hair lying like ink against his skull. His clothing was a long cassock-coat with a high collar, feathered as it flared behind him and dripping with something dark. The glyph over his head was familiar, because it was scored into my own skin. His hand was raised, a slim curved blade rising in a wicked slash that had just finished, because the arc of the blade's passing was shown with a swipe of bloodspray.

The lower right quadrant of the picture held a demon curled into a ball and flying backward from a terrific blow, fat white snakes of his hair writhing in agony no less than his face. The glyph over his head, announcing his name, was the same as the symbol on the hapless woman's belly.

Just the three of them in this picture, and the white wall behind the woman. The breath left me in a rush. My gaze stuttered back up to Sephrimel.

He nodded, the dark grieving holes of his eyes gathering the soft luminescence and turning it into pain. His hair slithered against itself as he moved. "Her name was Inhana." All the insectile rage had left his voice, and it held the same weary kindness I'd heard before. His lips shaped the name lingeringly. "She was my *hedaira,* and the Kinslayer slew her in the White-Walled City on a day of blood and lamentation. I have been bleeding from the wound ever since, diminished and alone." The book shut with a convulsive snap, dust puffing from the pages. "I have spent longer than you can imagine wishing for his screaming death, with all the torments Hell could possibly offer. And yet, he brings his beloved to me, and he asks for my help."

Boy, bad luck for you, sunshine. Only a sheer effort of will stopped the words in my throat. His eyes met mine, like a knife to the gut. I couldn't shrink back against the wall any harder, chips of color pressing into my back and touching my tangled hair.

"I will grant you what I can of the means to kill Lucifer, *hedaira.* But in return you will perform me a service, and if you do not I will strike you down to revenge myself on your lover." His thin lips stretched in a death's-head grin, showing old, strong, discolored teeth getting longer by the second. "That is our bargain. I suggest you accede."

I was fairly sure we were still below Sofya, since the Power throbbing in the stone was soaked with belief and pain. I hadn't known the temple was built on a honeycomb of passages in dank crumbling stone, somehow kept free of the water table but musty all the same. It smelled of demon. No—it *reeked* of demon, the fragrance of one of Hell's children rising through tunnels with curved roofs, their walls decked with mosaic. Repeating geometric patterns wove borders between scenes of gardens and blue skies; the sun repeated over and over in a strange golden metal giving out a pulsing of spiced musk, lighting the passageways.

The style of the art was odd, an echo of Egyptianica in the way figures were stylized, a touch of the Byzantin in the placement of the chips. Fantastical birds straight from Sudro Merican folk art mixed uneasily with Renascence lions and Assyriano griffins, gamboling on sealike lawns of green plasilica.

The woman with blood-colored hair was everywhere. She peered from behind trees in the gardens, stood with her face lifted to the sun, gazed inscrutably at the tunnels with sad dark eyes lovingly made of obsidian chips. It must have taken unimaginable years to cover all these walls with such tiny little pieces, each arranged for maximum effect.

It was obsessive, and just a bit frightening.

I'd buttoned up my jeans and edged behind Sephrimel, wincing each time my eyes found the woman again. She was *everywhere,* in the same white robe. It was like being stalked by a ghost, and after a while I began to feel dizzy as he led me down, and down, through a tangle of tunnels that messed up my internal navigation even more.

How long had he been here? Because it just didn't seem likely that anyone *else* had done all this.

No time like the present to ask. "How long have you been down here?" *Since I might as well get some information out of you.*

His shoulders hunched, but his even tread didn't falter. "A short while. Before that was a city they called eternal, but no city of mortals is. I was in Babylon once, too." He paused, before choosing a right-hand fork that led us even further down. The woman— Inhana—peered from behind a fig tree with a shy smile, the twisting mark I'd bet was her Fallen's name worked in lapis down the sweet curve of her hip.

Japhrimel killed her. I'm looking at pictures of a woman he killed. Sekhmet sa'es, *how many people has he killed? Do the other demons count?*

I'd never thought of it quite this way before. But her smile, replicated endlessly through these tangled passages, was like a padded sledgehammer blow each time. "So you...she died. And you survived." *Great, Danny. Remind him of what has to be the happiest event in his widdle demon life.*

"You call this survival?" Sephrimel's sarcasm bounced off tiled walls, fractured like the small pieces clinging to stone. "I bleed out through the wound left by her death, *hedaira.* I wander through a darkening world, falling toward a mortal death. Lucifer left me alive as a warning, and to punish me all the more."

"I thought there hadn't been any Fallen for—"

"I was the third." Sephrimel reached out one thin hand, brushed the wall the same way he'd touch a lover's breast. I had to look down, heat rising abruptly in my cheeks. "Certainly not the last, and I was counted not the least among us. I helped in the making of the Knife, and thought my theft had gone unnoticed. How much has the Kinslayer told you?"

Knife? I shifted the strap of my messenger bag uncomfortably on my shoulder. I'd finally settled on pulling up the shreds of my shirt and tying them like Gypsy Roen's midriff-baring hoochie costume. Every few steps I'd start and nervously rub at my belly, feeling the thin white raised scars. *Told me? He's told me damn near nothing, and right now I'm starting to think I should thank him for it. I'm starting to think I should buy him a holocard.*

As idiotic as it sounds, I was feeling better. The sick pulsing in the middle of my head had faded a bit, locked behind iron doors and safely held at arm's length. I had more important things to concentrate on. I could almost forget the aching nakedness of my left cheek, where my emerald should have been spitting and sizzling, alive with the double gift of my god's presence and my faith—instead of merely glowing numbly. I *should* have been two steps away from screaming and beating my head against the walls until my skull split and released me.

Instead, I felt lighter. Cleansed. As if something unholy had been ripped out of me, and I was no longer tainted.

The scars on my belly twinged, a heatless reminder. I almost faltered, but the demon in front of me stopped, his dreadlocks dragging on the worn stone floor. I wondered if there were parts of this labyrinth where the floor wasn't scraped smooth.

How long had he been recreating her in little bits of broken things? If something happened to me, what would Japhrimel do? The thought of him reduced to something like this gaunt shuffling creature was...

Terrifying. That's the word you're looking for, Danny. You've spent all this time doubting him, accusing him at every goddamn turn. My heart lodged in my throat, bitter and pulsing.

Sephrimel put his wasted hand up. His claws clicked as he trailed them lightly, lovingly, over a door made of old, dark stained wood. The metal holding it together was corroded bright green, and the wood was scored with angular crosshatch strokes that looked intentional, though I couldn't for the life of me figure out if I'd ever seen them before.

"Child. I asked you a question." He sounded like my old *sensei,* Jado, whenever I was being particularly dense. "What has your cursed *A'nankhimel* told you?"

My right hand curled into a fist, aching for a swordhilt. "Nothing. I mean, very little. What's this about a knife?" *It would really help if you gave me a clue here. Just one, that's all I'm asking for.*

"I do not blame him." Thin fingers tightened on the door's creaking wood, glassine claws easing free of his fingertips. I watched, fascinated, as they made fresh scars in the door's surface. "I would not tell you either."

Well, that's a vote of confidence, isn't it. I kept sarcasm back by sheer force of will. Huzzah for me.

"Let me teach you a few things, before we open this door." His claws slid free, and he turned to face me. I backed up four nervous steps, ending up bumping into a wall made of shattered edges, pressing myself back as if it could hide me.

The Fallen demon advanced, step by slow step, his horror-stricken eyes great holes above his starved cheekbones and twisting mouth. He looked like a vox sniffer approaching his next high, face contorting as the nerves fired randomly, twisting and bunching muscles in ways no face should. I had no weapon but the blessed items in my bag, and they weren't clinking and shifting.

Of course, I was no longer sacred, was I? My faith had broken. There was no longer a god living in my bones and breath. I was wholly a demon's creature now.

Should I have been so grateful that Japhrimel's mark on my shoulder turned tense and hot, Power straining against the surface of my skin and shields? And why, when I felt so utterly alone, did the emerald on my cheek spit a white-hot spark of defiance?

Sephrimel stopped. His hand shot over my shoulder, claws sinking into solid rock with a screech like a hover slamming through a fiberoptic relay tower. For all the lunacy of his dark-burning eyes, his tone was cool and pedantic.

"Why does a demon Fall, beautiful one? Answer me." Hot cinnamon breath touched my cheek. The prickle of my accreditation tat writhing under the skin intensified.

I braced myself, weight settling into the balls of my feet. He could rip my throat out in a millisecond, and his teeth looked just strong and yellow enough to do it.

"I d-don't really know." For someone with a possibly insane Fallen demon breathing right in her face, I sounded almost calm.

Sephrimal gave a short galling laugh. His eyes didn't blink. They just *stared,* and each moment his gaze threaded itself though mine was another fresh burst of grief so intense I wanted to crawl away from it.

"For only the simplest of reasons, child. In Hell there is power, and primacy, and glory. There is pain and vassalage and exacting obedience. But when humanity crawled up out of the mire—and despite what Lucifer says, he did *not* extend a helping hand—we found there was one thing we did not have, a thing mortal creatures are blessed with." His eyes narrowed, their force undiluted, pinning me to the wall. The scar on my shoulder writhed against my skin, turning hot, a mass of warning spikes spreading from its twisting black-diamond fire marring my aura.

I never thought I'd be *happy* about that. I knew I could pull Power through the mark. Could I pull enough to strike at Sephrimel before he opened me up like a sodaflo can?

"The first of us to Fall knew it would not be long before the Prince moved to strike us down. In secrecy, with his *hedaira,* he created a weapon."

This part I could help out with. Just call me a mentaflo genius. "The Knife." The words eased past my lips. I couldn't stand looking in his eyes anymore. I dropped my eyelids, every fiber of my body screaming at me to *look at him look at him how will you know what he's going to do if you don't LOOK at him?*

"Exactly. The Knife of Sorrow." Tension bled out of the air like heat. Stone creaked, and I realized something fantastic, something utterly wonderful.

I could calculate this demon down to the last erg of Power he possessed. And it was conceivable, with a whole lot of luck and some fast thinking, that I could somehow hurt him.

Which led me inexorably, logically, on to a different thought. *Bleeding out through the wound. He's been slowly losing bits of himself, or his Power, since... when? Before Stamboul was built? That's a long time. Since Japh killed his* hedaira.

Just how long ago was that? Is he even "demon" anymore?

The only thing worse than having to ask a question like that is the possibility of having it answered for you.

"The Knife rests in two parts," Sephrimel whispered. He leaned so close the wiry snakes of his dreadlocked hair swung forward to touch me, and a fainting horror swam up through my head, rising like bad gas from the memory locked behind its reinforced door. Backed up against the wall. Again. "The Kinslayer took one half from the body of the first Fallen's *hedaira*. The other half, kept in the great temple in the White-Walled City, *I* stole, and have been glad of it ever since. I thought the Kinslayer did not know, since my portion would be swift death, no matter how much Lucifer wishes to keep me as an example."

Two parts? What the hell? "Wait a second." I forgot myself and looked up, just as quickly averted my gaze as it glanced across the edge of his. "Two parts?"

"The Knife is twain as the *A'nankhimel* are." Sephrimel's claws squeaked against stone and plasilica dust as his hand flexed. "Either shard will wound beyond measure a demon, even one of the Greater Flight. Together, there is no demon they cannot kill." He paused. Repeated it slowly, insistently. "No demon they cannot kill, no matter how powerful."

A shock went through me like lightning striking, and the thunder behind it was a familiar feeling. It was the first arc of intuition that told me a hunt was underway, the same feeling I got working bounties for Hegemony law enforcement. The first click of instinct always takes the longest.

After that, everything speeds up.

It's just a hunt like any other, Danny. Only now you're hunting the thing that can kill Lucifer. That's what you're doing here. So quit flinching and do what you have to.

I raised my eyes again. Stared at his almost-lipless mouth, drawn tight over those strong yellow teeth. He'd probably been beautiful, once. To *her*.

The same way Japh was beautiful to me.

"Where's the other half?" I whispered. *And what do you want from me in return?*

"It was given to our cousins the Anhelikos to hide, for they brought more than one *hedaira* to grief. Sneaks and spies, with their gardens and pretty faces." His lips curled in a bitter sneer. "The Kinslayer probably knows its route, and will collect it. If Lucifer does not do so first."

A shiver slid from my crown to my soles. I remembered the Anhelikos in DMZ Sarajevo, with its pretty sexless face and sticky, clinging web of euphoria. I wouldn't put it past that thing to eat someone whole, if they wandered into its nest. "But he figured he had a better chance of getting one half from you, rather than chasing after something Lucifer already knew about. Because Lucifer thinks the

Anhelikos have both halves." *And so does Eve, I guess, or why was she in Sarajevo? Or did she even know there were parts to the thing? Does Lucifer?*

Sephrimel stepped back, freeing his claws from the wall. I stayed where I was, shaking despite setting my jaw and internally reciting every filthy term I knew in Merican, Putchkin trade-pidgin, and any other language I've heard the blue words in. His hair dragged on the floor. I wondered if it had done its part to scrape the stone so smooth, the tunnel bottoms worn concave by repeated dragging footsteps. He paced back to the door and opened it with a simple push. Dappled light touched the ceiling, golden radiance reflecting off water making crazy patterns against the mosaic.

I glanced back over my shoulder. The woman's sad face peered back at me, the mark of Sephrimel's claws cradling it tenderly, as if he had been trying to feel her skin again.

I was shivering from more than the cold. But when the Fallen demon stepped down through the low door, ducking a little, I followed. Cold water lapped at my boots, ankle-deep and smelling of salt. I blinked against sudden dazzlement and found myself in a long low oval chamber, its walls blessedly free of mosaic. I didn't think I could stand to see Inhana's face one more time.

CHAPTER 9

In the middle of the chamber stood a low wet obsidian plinth, and a plain wooden box lay open on its top. The water wasn't more than a few inches deep anywhere in the room, over a floor of rough blocks. It was clammy-cold, and steam lifted in lazy curls from my skin and his, demon metabolisms working overtime.

"Take it," Sephrimel said, and moved aside. He glided silently through the water, but I made wet noises every time I stepped. I hoped the boots were up for this kind of abuse. I *hate* wet shoeleather.

Great beads of sweat dewed the walls. I stepped forward cautiously, feeling gingerly each time I set my foot down, not committing my weight until I was sure I was on safe ground. When I finally reached the pedestal, the lid of the box quivered like one of those plants that eats unwary flies.

It moved because the box was rotting to bits, crumbling into a pile of slime. Velvet that had probably once been blue filled its interior. The cloth's decay sent a sharpish-sweet note through clean salt and a thread of demon scent. And there, on the bed of soft swelling corruption, the Knife lay.

It looked complete within itself, its geometry just slightly off like all items of demon make. The hilt was flattened and curved first toward me, then away, and the blade was the same. The guard was oddly shaped, finials reaching out for something but clasping only air. It hummed with malignant force, and now that I was close enough I saw a taint of black-diamond flame in the glow of Power it gave off. The world warped and shimmered around it, announcing *here's something that doesn't belong.*

I stared at the thing for a long ten seconds, water lapping at my boots.

"It's made of *wood.*" I finally announced, hearing the same tone I'd use to announce it was fucking raining during a slicboard match. It was made of an old, dark wood, oiled and pristine. Its edge looked too sharp to be a tree's flesh.

"You are unnaturally observant," Sephrimel piped up, dryly. "Take it in your hand, *hedaira.*"

"Why is it made of wood?" I persisted. I'd cut Lucifer once — with good old-fashioned steel. This thing didn't look like it could trim a demon's claws, let alone kill the Devil.

That is what we're talking about here, isn't it? Killing Lucifer. If it's possible.

"Ask your Fallen." The demon stirred restlessly, and water lapped against the walls. "For now, simply take what is yours by right."

By right? I don't think I want this thing, but thanks ever so much.

I stared at the thing. Wood or not, it looked deadly wicked. Did it throb with its own dark glee, or was I just shell-shocked and ready to believe it after all this drama of tunnels and a dead woman's dusky eyes? My bag clinked and rattled against my side.

Just pick it up, Danny. You touch that thing, and you're committed. You'll have to kill Lucifer. There's no way around it.

Still...I hesitated. I reached out, and saw the shape of my forearm, my fragile-looking wrist, tough golden calluses on my fingertips from almost-daily fighting or training. If I was going to kill the Devil, this was the hand I'd do it with.

My other hand rested on the thin raised scars crisscrossing my belly. I was suddenly, mortally certain Sephrimel had pulled *some-thing* out of my cramping midriff.

I had a good idea of what that *something* was, too. If I'd had anything in my stomach I might have heaved until I was dry.

If I kill Lucifer, I can feel clean again. It was really that simple. Everything else, even protecting Eve, was taking a backseat to that one imperative. How shallow was that? I should have been more worried about protecting my daughter.

If she really was my daughter. It bothered me. Would Santino have worked with a contaminated sample? Doubt circled my brain again.

But still, her face. The little half-smile she wore, so like mine it could have been my twin.

I was doubting everything now. The world was a collage of lies and half-truths, everyone with their own agenda. Even Japhrimel.

Even me.

My hand hovered in midair. Who was I fooling? It had been too late the moment Japhrimel had knocked at my front door.

Do you believe in Fate, Dante?

My standard reply was ringing ever more hollow. *No more than the next Magi-trained Necromance.*

Pretty soon I was going to have to start saying *yes.*

I picked up the Knife. It was obscenely warm. Or was I just chilled by the idea of what I was about to do? The wood was silken, like warm skin. The black fire of its aura socked home against mine, for all the world as if it recognized the taint of demon in my personal cloak of energy. My shields, battered and broken, blazed with a river of wine-dark Power.

Instinct born of bounty hunting for most of my life warned me, a prickle against my nape and the sound of water splashing suddenly married to chill certainty as the scar on my shoulder flamed into hot agonized life.

I stepped back from the pedestal, a cry wrenching itself from my throat, and spun in time to see Sephrimel extended in the air, claws outstretched, his face contorted as he leapt for me.

How can I say what it was like?

The Knife rammed home in his chest, his arms flung wide at the last possible moment, claws whistling as they clove sickly, salt-filled air. We hit the pedestal with a sickening crack, and slivers of glassy obsidian exploded from the physical and psychic force of that sound.

Flying shards of obsidian whickered through the air, peppering stone walls and pocking into thrashed salty water. I skidded, lost my footing, and went down hard, screaming until my voice broke. Sephrimel collapsed on top of me, twitching heavily, thick snakes of white hair spilling down to brush my face with woolen fingers.

I choked on a mouthful of salt water and *shoved*. Black demon blood bubbled between his lips, foaming. The Knife twitched in my hands like a live thing and made a greedy keening noise. Between the thin high moans was another sound, one I didn't understand until the first wave of energy spilled through me.

The Knife was gulping. It slurped like a toothless man inhaling a bowl of wet noodles.

Sephrimel made a low choked sound. "Inhana," he whispered, black blood dripping down and dewing my left cheek. He was close as a lover, and the weight of his body against mine was enough to touch off panic in the darkest corners of my head. *"A'tai, hetairae A'nankimel'iin. Diriin."*

My back, against cold hard stone, ran with prickles. It was a phrase Japhrimel had spoken to me, one I recognized even though I couldn't translate it. Something about a *hedaira* and an *A'nankhimel*.

But in return you will perform me a service, and if you do not I will strike you down to revenge myself on your lover.

He hadn't wanted to kill. I realized it only now, too late to pull back. He'd attacked me so I would kill *him*. Tit for tat. Japhrimel had killed his *hedaira,* and here I was, finishing up the job.

Ogods I've killed him. Oh gods.

Sephrimel's eyelids fell. His gaunt, starving face relaxed. I heard a sobbing noise, realized it was mine, repeating the only prayer I had left.

"Japh...*Japhrimel* ohgods *help*..."

The gulping sound ceased. Ash trickled through veins of darkness running through the demon's golden flesh. Like porcelain, his skin cracked and broke, larger shards crumbling into fine cinnamon-scented dust. The veins of dryness even spread to his hair, threading through the clotted white.

The Fallen demon exploded into ash that ground itself finer and finer as a heavy silken tide of pleasure slammed through me. My heart drummed against my rib cage like a hummingbird's wings, the space where something had been ripped from my belly throbbing in response. My hips jerked up as I tasted the remainder of ash, vanishing until no trace of spice or musk remained on the air.

I gasped, got another mouthful of salt water, and scrambled to my feet. I wasn't losing my balance, the dome trembled. A chunk of stone fell from the vault, landing with an ominous splash. *Ohgods. Oh, dear gods.*

My knees almost gave out on me. I backed away from the spreading fine film of ash on the water's chopped surface. *Is the whole place shaking, or just here? Great. I'm underground and I just killed my only guide. Just wonderful, Danny.* I backed up, hardly caring where I stepped at this point, and my shoulders hit the wall with a thump. I stared up, only dimly aware of pleading. "Please don't fall, don't fall, *don't fall*—"

The dome shuddered once. Water trembled. Two things became apparent to me at once. The first was that something else was causing it to shake, some event communicating itself through stone like the squeal of overstressed hover dynos cuts through concrete like jelly.

The second thing was that the water was rising, lapping at my knees instead of my shins.

Move, Danny. Move now.

I bolted for the door as another huge chunk of stone tore free of the dome, falling with a whistle and sending up a sheet of foaming, ash-laced seawater. My fingers clamped around the Knife's satin-smooth, warm wooden hilt, and even in my adrenaline-laced terror I didn't want to drop the goddamn thing. If it could kill Lucifer—or even *wound* him—the last place I wanted it to end up was buried under tons of rubble.

Though it just might end up there anyway. Run, Danny. Run.

I ran.

CHAPTER 10

M y sense of direction underground isn't the greatest. Fortunately, my Magi-trained memory had been busy taking in the mosaics, and Inhana's sad, lovely face pointed me the right way.

I hoped like hell that Sephrimel hadn't repeated the patterns over and over again down every passage.

That's a thought you don't need, sunshine. Just keep moving.

I did, because the air was moving with me, a cold exhalation of salt brushing my hair as I pounded down stone worn concave by a demon's dragging, grieving feet. I hit the door to the room I'd awakened in at full tilt, smashing it back against the wall, and shoved it shut with hysterical speed. Then I halted, my ribs flaring and flickering as I gasped, looking around for some clue of how to get *out* of here. The bookshelves looked too flimsy for anything, and the scrolls stacked on them were no help either, their smell a blind weight in my nostrils.

Up. Got to get up. When my breathing evened out, the low groaning coming through the stone became audible again. I turned in a full circle, searching for another door, and realized my folly almost immediately. Just because I'd woken up here didn't mean this room had an escape hatch.

Think, Danny. Quit fucking around and think!

I cast around again, trying desperately to force my brain to gear up and get me out of *this* one. Then the thing I was afraid of most happened.

Water trickled under the door, a few innocent little streamlets sending thin questing fingers over the dry stone.

"Shit," I hissed between my teeth. *Trust you to end up like this. Going to drown like a rat in a sewer if you don't—*"Shut up. Shut *up.* Think, damn you! *Think!*"

I would never have seen it if I hadn't hunched down, clapping my hands to either side of my head and thwacking myself a good one with the Knife's hilt against my temple. I'd almost forgotten I was carrying the damn thing.

When my eyes cleared, smarting and stinging furiously, my attention snagged on the wall directly over the chunk of stone Sephrimel had laid me out on. The mosaic there was blues and greens, and it stretched up in a passable imitation of a door, a round wheel of yellow right where the knob should be.

The edges of the pattern shimmered, just like a psion's glamour once you've slowed down to take a really good look at it. Illusion rippled, and my heart leapt up into my throat, pounding there like it intended to tear free of my ribs and dance.

I didn't stop to think. I scrambled across the room, wet feet skidding in the rivulet of water coming under the door, leapt up—

—and smashed into the wall full-tilt, knocking myself half-senseless back down onto the rectangle of stone.

I shook the stunning impact out of my head. *Dante, you idiot.* And with the utter lunacy of the desperate, shell-shocked, and insane, I reached up, my claw-tips scraping against polished bits of stone, and touched the yellow circle.

It felt round, firm, and real, under the screen of demon illusion. I used it to pull myself to my knees, hearing the soft insidious lap of water against the base of the stone chunk. It was rising fast.

I twisted my wrist. The shell of illusion on the door—a perfect piece of demon magick, either a cruel mockery or an aesthetic utterly divorced from practicality—folded aside as the door swung open, the golden orb at the apex of the dome beginning to dim as its light spilled through...

And touched stairs. Going *up.*

I let out a relieved sob and began to scramble on hands and knees, the worn edges of the risers biting into my flesh. The Knife made a little clicking sound against each step until I managed to get my legs under me. I ran, heart exploding with pain inside my ribs and the fear of the caverns behind me, filling with cold stone water mixed with Sephrimel's ashes, in my mouth like bitter wine.

The stairs were narrow and dark, golden light from below fading as water mouthed and lapped behind me. If I could have stopped, I probably would have lain down despite the hard stone edges and tried to at least catch my breath. As it was, I had a hard enough time trying to keep myself upright, slipping on slick stone.

I ran, my fingers cramping around the Knife's warm pulsing hilt. Sick fever-warmth spilled up my arm with each pulse. Whatever it had taken from Sephrimel it was feeding into me, in controlled bursts like an immuno-hypo's time-release function. I'd been hurt bad enough, once or twice as a human bounty hunter, to slam painkiller-cocktails from a first-aid kit. This was the same feeling—knowing the pain was there, that I was functioning on borrowed time, that soon I was going to push my body past its limits, muscles tearing free of their moorings and my brainpan filling with blood from burst vessels—

Danny, you're running blind. Slow down.

I couldn't. Darkness was rising with the water, soft squelching sounds behind me that I *knew* was just the water sucking at the steps but my imagination had no trouble making into soft padded feet. Before the last glimmer faded and the dark wrapped close and soft as cotton wool over my eyes, the clutching of claustrophobia began in my chest. There wasn't enough air. If I didn't drown in the flood I would in the darkness, the weight of how many tons of earth and rock pressing down to crush the life out of me.

Focus. You have to focus. You have *to.*

I knew I had to. I tripped, barked both knees, and fell, my head hitting the wall with a sickening crack that made phantom stars swirl in front of my starving eyes.

Dammit, Danny, quit rabbiting! Get hold of yourself!

I lay on the stairs, panting, my shallow gasps echoing against the narrow stone hall. I sounded like an animal, exhausted from struggling in a trap. Just waiting for death from shock or blood loss, or for the hunter to come and put a plasbolt in me.

Claustrophobia descended on me, sheer terror wringing out what little sanity I had left. This was like Rigger Hall again, like the Faraday cage in the basement, where I had learned to fear dark closed spaces. It was ever so much worse than an elevator, because there was no escape.

My left shoulder flared with soft heat. It was so warm I expected it to glow as I stared up at the ceiling, stone edges digging into my hip and the back of my head.

Wait a second. I can see.

I shifted, and the light moved too, dappling the stone as soft wet sounds drew closer.

Just like a demon to die and leave his house to flood. The hideous, panicked amusement in the thought was a thin shield against rising hysteria. The light moved again as I tilted my head.

It was my emerald, glowing fiercely. Green light danced as I moved my head, slowly, watching the play of color against the stone. Spectral illumination—far too much to come from the one tiny gem in my cheek—bathed the steps. My tat writhed madly on my cheek, an itching so familiar and so comforting tears pressed hot against my eyes. I blinked them away. With the light came a little air past the clutching in my chest.

Get up, Danny.

I didn't want to. I wanted to lie there and rest.

If you stop moving you'll drown. Get up. Move.

I couldn't. I just wanted to rest. Just for a moment, until I could find enough breath to move. Until the terror went away.

Then Lucifer's already won. The deep voice was pitiless. Merciless. It wasn't someone else's voice used to prod me into action, unconsciously using a familiar tone so I could pretend someone was here with me, that I wasn't alone. *Are you going to let him win?*

"Shut up," I whispered. "Shut the fuck *up.*"

You might as well admit it, Danny. You've only got so much left in you. You're only human. There's no shame in admitting you're beaten. He's the Devil. He'll win. All you have to do is lie here and wheeze. There's plenty of air. Get up.

The soft lapping drew closer. How far below the water table were the mosaics, Inhana's dark eyes now watching blackness instead of the slow dragging passage of time and the shuffling of her *A'nankhimel?*

The thin moaning sound, I realized, was mine. I was lying on the steps groaning while the water rose. Like a beaten animal cowering in a corner.

Just stay there. The deep voice sounded disgusted. *I* sounded disgusted at myself.

The Knife hummed in my hand. Squelching, lapping sounds moved closer, teasingly.

"Get up," I whispered. "Get *up,* you bitch." *If I can talk I can breathe.*

I tried. My legs refused to move. The muscles were shaking, quivering as nerves rebelled, drunk on terror.

Just lie there, sunshine. Choke a little bit when the water reaches you. It will all be over soon, and you can rest.

Here in the dark. Forever.

It was amazing. Laughter rose inside me, from the wrecked place where I used to be human. It bubbled up past my lips, a dark rancid howl, and my eyes rolled up inside my head as I *strained,* the chilling little giggles broken by a long *hunnnnngh!* of effort.

I twitched.

Just lie there, sunshine. The voice was so reasonable, so calm, and so fucking disgusted with me. *It's all over.*

"Like...*hell*...it...is!" The pauses between the words filled up with howling, insane laughter.

Something cold touched my boots. Moved up, slowly, along the outside edge of my shins, my soaked jeans turning colder as fresh fingers of water caressed them.

I jerked away from those caressing fingers. Scrambled, finding fresh strength as the Knife hummed in my hand like a high-voltage cable. The world turned gray, light from the emerald set in my cheek bleaching stone. Strings of damp hair fell in my face. I was sweating, great drops of unhealthy water standing out on my skin. Salt stung my eyes as I gasped, heaving for air against the constriction around my ribs.

I made it up to my knees.

Well, look at that, the disgusted voice remarked. *You can move after all.*

"Shut up." Then I saved my breath for moving. The mark on my shoulder spilled a wave of strength down my skin, working in, barely enough to keep me upright. I choked on something hot rising from my abused, empty stomach, and stumbled along.

Each step was torture, working against the weight of childhood fear like a lead blanket. My knees felt shattered, my thighs on fire, my neck steel-strung cables drawn tight by a demented dwarf. I climbed up, swearing at myself with each step, curses that spilled past my lips the longer I moved, until I was gasping both for breath to move and to keep up the string of obscenities.

The sound of water faded. I kept going, until the stairs vanished and I emerged into a long, low corridor lit by orange orandflu strips, long-burning firesafe illumination. My breath returned with a whoosh, claustrophobia easing. I stared at the shapes on either side of the hall, not believing what I saw.

What the hell?

Stacked on either side of the hall were bones. Great pyramids of skulls over neatly piled femurs, pelvic bowls stacked like bread bowls, the arched shapes of what I realized were ribs arranged aesthetically, fingerbones mortared into the wall, smaller bones sticking into crumbling concrete.

Sekhmet sa'es. Catacombs. The word swam up through layers of shock and exhaustion, and I let out a short bark of relief. My lips were cracked and stinging with salt. My clothes were ruined, blood and seawater drying as they plastered against my fevered skin. I itched all over. Skulls leered at me, their empty eyes holes of madness.

They're dead, Danny. They can't hurt you. Going to stand there and gawk all day?

"Anubis—" The prayer began, but I stopped it short. *On my own again.*

But the emerald, and my tat—

Don't think about that now. You have other credits to fry right now.

The walls trembled. I put out a hand to steady myself, touched a stack of bones that spilled from their careful teetering and puffed into dust on the way to the floor. The splinters that reached the stone broke with a dry whispering sound. How long had they been down here?

What was that? I braced myself against more crumbling bones.

The scar on my shoulder rippled with heat. And not just that—a sudden certainty bloomed just below the smoking surface of my mind, losing any conscious semblance of thought. It felt like a grass-fire inside my skull, like I'd once seen on the rolling savannah of Hegemony Afrike. Smoke and crimson and dull gray dust, as far as the eye could see, the air too thick and hot to breathe, chunks of charred stuff visible even from a hover's-eye view—animals too slow to escape the burning.

I blundered down the aisle of bones as Hajia Sofya tolled in distress overhead, her walls singing a long sustained note, like a real crystal wineglass stroked by the lightest of touches.

Japhrimel. His name rose from the smoke in my head. *He's in trouble. He needs me.*

I didn't argue with the certainty. I just stumbled forward, wearily, with all the speed my exhausted, aching body would allow.

CHAPTER 11

The long hall gave onto another bigger chamber, an ossuary with old stains showing against patched crumbling mortar where bones had dissolved into mineral streaks. There were more strips of orandflu lighting and a few dim bulbs burning out overhead, hanging from long cords. I got the idea nobody had come down here for a while except a mad dreadlocked demon.

The temple kept crying out as I stumbled through other passages, following a faint indefinable pulling against my bones. I no longer questioned it, I knew Japh was nearby and he needed me. I had the Knife now. I was going to save the day.

Well, at least half the Knife. Better than nothing, wouldn't you say, Danny?

I told that voice inside my head to shut up and almost ran into a dead end, a blank wall barring my path. I turned back, retraced my steps, and found a long sloping corridor going up, with decent lighting and—thank the gods—signs in Merican, Pharsi, and Graeci.

I'd somehow found my way into the part of the temple set aside for tourists. I could have laughed at the irony, decided to save my breath.

The letters blurred and ran together, but I glimpsed enough to tell me the main part of the temple was down this hall and to the right, behind a massive blue-painted door that loomed up, quivering in its socket.

I started down the hall, dragging my right leg a little. It didn't matter. Nothing mattered except the fact that Japhrimel was on the other side of that door.

Unholy screechings and thuddings resounded as the door shook again. The entire temple flinched.

The Kinslayer will fight to his last breath, but the Prince's minions are numberless, and even a killer such as yours may eventually fall.

Had Sephrimel done what he had threatened?

The door rocked as something hit it from the other side, a long bloodchilling howl shivering it against its maghinges. They let out a distressing squeal, and the door sagged, no longer looking quite right. The massive sheet of blue plasteel, decorated with the Hegemony sunwheel, looked like someone had slammed it with a plascannon bolt on the other side.

I kept moving, finally within touching distance. *Last thing I need now is the damn door to fall on me. Hurry up, Valentine.*

I reached out with both hands, intending to shove. If the maghinges were damaged they might not open, and I'd have to think of something else.

Doesn't matter. The cold disgusted voice spoke up, the one that only showed itself when simple endurance was the only thing left. *Japh's in there and he needs me.*

The Knife let out a shuddering, bloodchilling howl, one that burst out of my own lips as I coiled myself, compressing demon-elastic muscles until I exploded forward, hitting the doors with tired flesh and unhealthy, feverish Power both. My heart stuttered under the strain, a blinding flash of pain searing between my temples as mental muscles stretched, straining.

I landed on both feet, the door flung away like a ball of trash. It soared in a graceful arc across interior space, and I was driven down to one knee as my legs almost failed me. The Knife vibrated in my hand, force pouring into me, beating back exhaustion.

The inside of the dome was soaked with bloody light. McKinley, his face a mask of effort, drove a winged hellhound down to the floor, his left hand clamped in its throat as Vann unloaded plasbolt after plasbolt at it, missing by a hairsbreadth each time as it twisted, cartilaginous spine crackling. Lucas skipped to the side and fired on an imp, its greasy sick white skin stretching as it chattered, its bald, hairless babyface twisted around the syllables of Hell's mother-tongue. Other imps writhed on the floor as rotting fluid gushed from mortal wounds.

Japhrimel stood before the high altar, his hands clasped behind his back as he regarded the demon in front of him. The left side of his face was black with mottled bruising, something I had never seen before. Behind his slim dark shape, Leander crouched, his katana an arc of brightness held in the guard position, spitting blue sparks as runes twisted in the steel's heart.

My arrival halted everything except the hellhound's gurgle as it died under the lash of plasbolts. The demon crouched in front of Japh was mantled in darkness like feathered wings, a shadow of black flame and diamond spangles. Corpses littered the inside of the temple, stinking and running with brackish fluid as demon flesh decayed. Hellhounds with and without wings rotted as I glanced at them, my attention centering on the feathered demon as it turned fluidly to face me, drawing itself up, and up, and *up*. It had to be at least nine feet tall.

I'd interrupted a hell of a fight. Twisted shapes of dead demon-flesh were everywhere — some with a mass of hideous legs and others vaguely human-shaped, but with a grace and alienness even in death that humans couldn't match. There were also imps, their claws blackened and their faces grotesquely puffed.

I stayed on one knee, trying to get in enough breath as the demon in front of Japh turned its piercing silvery eyes on me. Feathers ruffled, each one edged with a dark steel gleam.

It had a slim, ageless face, built like Japhrimel's — lean and saturnine, long nose and thin mouth, winged dark eyebrows. The hair feathered into wisps so fine they lifted on uneasy air as everyone froze.

All eyes on you, Danny.

Or maybe they weren't looking at me. Maybe they were looking at the Knife, its finials stretching out and clasping empty air, my hand fitting against its hilt as if it was made for me.

The wooden weapon keened, a low hungry sound.

Get up, I told myself. *Get up, you stupid bitch. That thing is threatening Japhrimel.*

It worked. Fury poured through me, a rage red and deep like hot blood from a ragged hole. My legs straightened. I gained my feet in a stumbling rush and threw myself forward, the Knife held in the way my *sensei* taught me, flat against my forearm for slashing, the pommel reversed with its claws digging into my wrist.

Burn, a half-familiar voice whispered inside my head. **Burn them. Make them pay.**

Shapeless shouts rose, Lucas yelling my name, Leander screaming, McKinley letting out a cry that shivered the air. Everything vanished but the enemy in front of me and the need to make him — whoever he was — *pay.*

In blood.

My left shoulder woke with a crunch of agony, Power flushing along my aura and hardening. Japhrimel's strength filled me like a river in a burning bed; the demon and I collided with a sound like all the jars of the universe smashing at once. The Knife rammed through muscle and bone, shrieking with satisfaction as the entire world stopped, crackling flame filling my ears and running through my veins. I was made of it, this fire, and if it escaped me the world would burn.

The only thing scarier than not caring was how *good* it felt.

I held the silver-eyed demon on the Knife, ignoring the sudden blooming of pain as it clipped me a stunning blow on the head with one taloned fist. A soft breath of satisfaction slid past my lips, ruffling the pin-fine black feathers along its high cheekbones. We were close enough to kiss, its teeth champing as it writhed, held away from me by the humming force of the demon-made weapon in my aching, bruised, battered hand.

I found I didn't mind. Not with the flame pounding behind my heartbeat, thumping in time to a song of fury and destruction.

I had called upon Sekhmet, the Fierce One, and She had answered.

Burn, I thought, and the heat passed through me as the Knife gulped. The demon writhed, its mouth contorting in a scream of pure agony. But still, it reached for me, its claws flexing as it prepared to kill, even with the blade buried in its ribs.

I knew I couldn't kill a demon, I thought, and braced myself.

Japhrimel arrived.

He tore the demon off me, the Knife pulling free of my fist with an unholy screech. The world snapped back into its normal pace, chaos descending out of the stillness of concentration. I went flying back, the heavy shield of Japhrimel's aura over mine blunting the force of my fall as I collided with Vann. McKinley skidded to a stop while Vann and I went down in a tangle of arms and legs, I struck out with fists and feet, screaming.

The sound was incredible, howls of anguish and agony meshed with thudding booms and tearing like limbs pulled from their sockets. Vann had an arm around my throat and McKinley descended on us, trying to hold me down as I thrashed. The noise reached an amazing crescendo, felt more through the body than heard. My own scream was lost in that wall of clamor.

Sudden silence, sharp as a sword, sliced through blood-drenched light. I sagged in Vann's hands, smelling the dry demon-and-*other* reek of Hellesvront agents. McKinley was repeating something over and over again, and it took a while for the echoes to shake out of my head so I could hear what he was saying.

"Christos," he kept saying. "Jesu Christos. Mater Magna, Jesu Christos. Is she all right? Tell me she's all right."

I'm fine, I wanted to say, *get off me.* But my mouth wouldn't work.

"Get over here." Lucas's throat-cut rasp was as hoarse as ever. "He's bleeding, *bad.*"

"Leave me be." Japhrimel sounded as dangerous as I'd ever heard him, the edge of his voice sharp enough to cut steel. "I am well enough. *Dante?*"

Vann's grip on me fell away. McKinley settled back on his heels, his dark eyes not leaving my face. "She looks okay." Every line of his body screamed weariness. His hair was wet with sweat, hung dripping in his eyes. "Valentine? Are you all right?"

"Get the fuck away from me." I erupted to my feet, or tried to. My limbs failed me, heavy and leaden, and I spilled back onto Vann, driving my elbow into his ribs. He let out a curse and Japhrimel appeared, leaning on Lucas.

That bothered me.

What bothered me more was the terrific bruising blotching Japh's face. He slumped wearily, black demon blood dripping from his right arm, which hung useless and limp at his side, his long elegant golden fingers clasped gingerly around the Knife's hilt, almost flinching away from its touch. His hair was wildly mussed, and his eyes burned almost wholly green, spitting and snapping with laser intensity.

Lucas looked like hell too, shirt torn and bandoliers missing, his pants ripped and bloody, garish streaks of gore painting his face and torso. He was wet to both knees with fluids I decided I didn't want to think about. McKinley was oddly pristine, but his fishbelly paleness was marked by dark bruised circles under his aching eyes.

I stared. I didn't like McKinley, I had *never* liked him, but the unguarded pain on his face was enough to make me pause.

He wore the same expression Sephrimel had, only diluted by his essential humanity. His silvery hand twitched, falling back down to his side, and the Hellesvront agent and I shared a moment of profound communication.

You don't know what I've lost, his eyes said, and I knew it was true.

Japhrimel went down heavily to one knee, with little of his usual economical grace. "Dante. Are you hurt?"

Am I *hurt? Look at you!* I struggled to hold back a rusty scream. What ended up coming out was a mangled sob as I reached up. His left hand came down, and he pulled me up, hugging me as best he could one-armed. I shuddered into his shoulder, burying my face in the warmth of him.

"Are you hurt?" He moved, probably trying to get a better look at me, but I clung to him.

Am I *hurt? Sekhmet sa'es. Let's see. I was dragged through Hell, betrayed by my god, left in Jersey, and finished up nearly being drowned by a demon with a bad haircut and a hobby that makes freight-jumping seem sane.* A high squeaking sound quickly melted into muffled giggles. I laughed as if I'd been told the world's funniest joke.

Laughed, in fact, fit to die, while the steady pounding of rage inside my veins retreated under Japhrimel's touch.

CHAPTER 12

Hades." Leander was pale, his shirt soaked dark with sweat and various types of blood. He slumped against the hover's hull, the dusky glow of Konstans-Stamboul falling under night's wing receding over his shoulder through the porthole. "*Hades.* I never want to do that again."

We'd just managed to escape the temple before the aid hovers arrived, drawn by the noise and ready to dump plurifreeze to put out the fire.

Our hover was still at its landing pad under a carapace of demon shielding, and as soon as we approached it a tall shape with a mop of dirty-blond hair had melded out of the shadows, greeting me with a wink and a grin that exposed the tips of his long canines.

Tiens, the Nichtvren Hellesvront agent with the face of a holovid angel, was in the control booth, piloting us like a vast silent fish. "We do not appear to have been followed." His calm flat tone was shaped by the song of an ancient accent. I wondered where he came from and how old he was, but not nearly enough to ask him.

Go figure, I'm getting almost used to demons, but a suckhead scares me silly. Everything seemed hilarious right now, in a darkly morbid sort of way. I had my sword and my new creaking rig back, Fudoshin shoved through a stiff loop on the rig's side. I couldn't settle enough to sit down, so I stood restlessly near the hatch, turning the heavy wooden weight of the Knife over and over in my hands. It hummed happily to itself, a low moan sending steady pulses of unhealthy warmth up my arm.

If using the thing makes me feel like this, I'm not sure I want to. I considered this, staring at the gleam of oil against its carved grain, too close and fine to be of any tree growing in the real world.

What kind of trees grew in Hell? Or was it from somewhere else?

"God's wounds." McKinley finished bandaging Leander's arm, rattling an empty disposable hypo of glucose into a wastebasket bolted to the floor. "Winged hounds out of Hell. And one of the Greater Flight. Christos. We would have been toast, if you hadn't been there."

"Then it is well I was." Japh sounded tightly amused. His eyes glowed fiercely.

"Yeah, well, I don't want to die *just* yet. Vann owes me for our last round of vidpoker." McKinley's gaze skittered across the room toward me before he looked back at Leander's arm. "But what does it *mean?* Is it *him?*"

"I do not know if we can blame the Prince for this event." Japhrimel's hand was still clamped over his bleeding shoulder. I had tried to bandage it, but he'd simply, gently pushed my hands away and pointed me toward the largest cabin for fresh clothes.

I was hard on laundry nowadays.

"Who else?" Vann lay flung on a plasteel-and-canvas couch, one arm over his eyes. He seemed none the worse for wear, even if he wasn't nearly as neat and unmarked as McKinley.

"He is not our only concern. The Prince has lost his hold on egress from Hell, and the Greater Flight are settling scores. The one now dead had a grievance with me, and rather a large one." Japhrimel peeled his fingers away from the bloody mess of his shoulder and peered at it. His coat was shredded, and the bleeding wouldn't stop.

Why won't it stop? My hands ached, clenched so tightly claw-points prickled into my palms.

"So which one was that?" McKinley fished another hypo out of the aid kit. "Immuno," he told Leander, who nodded, his jaw tight and his eyes dark with pain.

Japhrimel's eyes half-lidded. It looked like his shoulder hurt. "He is dead and it matters little. Suffice to say I spoiled one of his toys some time ago, and he sought to return the favor. Our task now is to reach the Roof of the World."

"Why won't the bleeding stop?" My voice dropped like a stone into a placid pond.

McKinley pressed the hypo against Leander's arm, and the human Necromance sucked in a breath as the airpac discharged, forcing happy immunity-bolsters and a jolt of plasma into his veins. Vann shifted restlessly, a plasgun's butt clicking against a knifehilt. Lucas had settled himself on the floor, weaponry spread on a ratty blanket in front of him as he cleaned, oiled, and checked his gear. It was the closest to a nervous tic I'd ever seen in him.

Japhrimel merely considered his shoulder, his sensitive fingers probing at the shredded material of his coat. To see the bloody mess made me feel unsteady in a whole new way. He had always seemed so invulnerable, before. "It will stop soon enough." He visibly caught himself, glanced up at me again. "Some of us have poison teeth as well as claws, and I had those more fragile than myself to defend."

I choked back my irritation. After complaining so often that he didn't tell me anything, it was nice to see him trying.

The Knife's humming slid into a lower register. I lifted it up and stared at it. The finials were still writhing like a live thing, frozen in time. It was heavier than it had been, too. "I need a sheath for this," I muttered, and my eyes stuttered back to Japhrimel's face. "Are you all right?" *I should have asked before, shouldn't I.* Sekhmet sa'es, *Dante, you selfish bitch.*

Yep. Feeling more and more like myself all the time. Whoever "myself" was.

"I will be well enough. See?" The seeping had finally stopped, thick black blood sealing away the wound. But so slowly, far more slowly than usual. "There is no need for concern."

What if I'm concerned anyway? I looked back down at the Knife. My belly twinged, the mass of thread-thin scarring on the surface of my skin responding to the plucked-string hum of the wooden weapon.

I hardly recognized my own voice. "He tore that thing out of me, didn't he."

It wasn't a question.

Silence turned thick and dangerous. The hover rattled a bit, wallowed, and began to climb, probably to avoid traffic streams. I didn't want to know how we were avoiding the notice of federal patrols. Traffic to this sector was probably under heavy watch, since Sofya's interior now looked like something thermonuclear had hit it.

I raised my head again. Japhrimel looked at the floor of the hover as if it was the most interesting thing he'd ever seen in his life. His hair shielded his eyes, falling forward in soft ragged darkness. It looked like bits of it had been charred away.

"It is customary for a Fallen to care for any *hedaira* in distress." His fingers tightened on his shoulder, digging in, tendons standing out on their back. If it hurt, his voice gave no sign. "Especially in... such distress as yours."

I realized my left hand was rubbing at my fresh shirt over the scarred tenderness of my belly. Revulsion swept through me, followed by a swift bite of nausea that faded as I took a deep breath. The rage running through my bones rose, flushing my cheeks with heat, and the inside of the hover rattled.

"Just what distress would that be? I'm only curious, Japh. What did...what was in me?" I tried hard to sound disinterested, failed miserably. The burning in my throat turned the words even hoarser than usual.

"Something to bind you—and your Fallen—to Lucifer's will." Each word delivered with care and finicky precision. "Sephrimel was adept at treating *hedaira* who suffered from..."

I shut my eyes, opened them again. *Well, everyone here saw it except Tiens. I suppose it can't hurt to say it out loud. Get it out in the open.* "You can say it," I whispered.

He did, the word cutting off the end of my sentence like a slamming door shutting away the sound of an argument. "Miscarriage. Only in this case, it was somewhat different. It was *a'zharak.* The word means *worm.*"

Worms. I've been dewormed. The black, yawning hole in my memory expanded, ran up against the wall of my will. Retreated, snarling, back down into its hole.

What did I have matched against that void? Just my sorcerous Will, holding up fine despite my betrayal of my sworn word. My Fallen, who seemed to be holding up fine as well, despite my betrayal of *him.* And the fire in my blood, the song of destruction that was a goddess answering my prayers—but not my god.

My god had asked me to betray myself, and I had acceded. I'd had no *choice.* Yet His gem on my cheek had lit me out of darkness.

Had He abandoned me, or could I just simply not bring myself to go to Him?

I stared at the fall of hair curtaining Japh's eyes from mine. He studied the floor, his shoulders down but tense, waiting. The inside of the hover was as quiet as the rare texts room in a federal library.

A'zharak. The word means worm, *but he treated me for miscarriage.* I shivered.

I was an adult. I was tough. Right? One of the top ten deadliest bounty hunters in the Hegemony, a combat-trained Necromance, an all-around ass-kicking wonder.

So why were my knees shaking?

Japhrimel continued, each word deliberately placed. "Had your body not rejected the...rejected it, Lucifer would have a means of controlling you. You would become a vessel for his will as well as one of his...least-attractive progeny. The separation, when it bursts free of incubation, is...energetic."

Nausea slammed hard and fast against my breastbone, burrowed in and finished with acid at the back of my throat. I forced it down, swallowing sourness. "So that's why he did it." The queer flatness of my tone was surprising. I sounded like I was discussing the latest Saint City Matchheads gravball game. "To control me, use me for bait. Use me against Eve, and probably against you."

I heard the faintest of sounds, like feathers ruffling in the wind.

"Yes." The hem of Japhrimel's coat moved restlessly. Under the whine of hover transport, it was the only sound. Was everyone holding their breath?

If I turned just a little, I had a clear shot to the bedroom door. My boots moved independently of me, squeaking ridiculously as I tacked out across industrial flooring for that harbor.

"Dante." Japhrimel's voice was raw, the bleeding edge of something smoking and terrible.

"I'm all right," I lied, still in that colorless flat voice. "I just want to be alone for a little bit. Call me when we get where we're going."

He said nothing more, but I could feel his eyes plucking at me. My shoulder ached with velvet flame, his name on my skin crying out to him.

My sword's scabbard creaked slightly as my fingers clenched around its safe, slim sanity. I didn't want the goddamn Knife. Just thinking of that satiny wood touching my palm again was enough to make the nausea triple.

I made it to the bedroom door. Pushed at it blindly. The sound of it shutting away the rest of them was not as satisfying as it could have been.

Lucifer wanted to use me as bait. I hadn't been fulfilling my purpose fast enough—in Sarajevo, Eve had left before the Devil showed up, and he hadn't really wanted me to kill any of the escaped demons. I was just a pawn, dangled out in shark-filled waters to see who bit, and if the bait isn't drawing your prey fast enough, you reel it in, readjust it, and throw it back out there.

He had put something *in* me. A worm in my body. In *my* body. *Eve.*

My brain shivered, turning aside from what had been done to me and fastening on Doreen's daughter, like a shipwreck survivor latching onto a piece of driftwood. She'd been taken to Hell as a little girl. What had Lucifer done to her, to make her so determined to rebel?

Had it hurt? Had it scraped her insides out and made a black hole inside *her* head?

It bothered me. It bothered me a *lot*.

If I thought about what he had probably done to Eve—the closest thing to a child I might ever have—then maybe, just maybe, I could get away with *not* thinking about the violation of my own body.

My body.

Kill him. For Eve. For yourself. It whispered in my ears, tapped at the walls of my mind. Sweet hot flame, the undoing of the world.

"Make him pay," I whispered to the empty bedroom, as the hover ascended sharply. My stomach flipped one more time, and I slid down with my back to the door, my legs sprawled out in front of me, repeating it to myself. I could, if Japh was on my side. I could do this.

There was no way out now. The funny thing was, when I thought about it, there didn't seem like there had *ever* been any way out.

CHAPTER 13

There's an old psion joke taken from a Zenmo koan. It goes like this: *Before they discovered Chomo Lungma, what was the highest mountain in the world?*

The answer, of course, is another Zenmo joke. *The one inside your head still is.*

Normals don't get it. But pretty much every psion who hears it cracks up. The laughter is bright and unaffected if you're a child, somewhat cynical and world-weary by the time you hit eighteen, and turns knowing when you're older. When you get to the combat-trained psions, the bounty hunters, cops, and government agents—we don't just laugh. We laugh as if our mouths are full of too much bitterness to be contained, because we know it's true. There aren't any geographical features that can stop you. It's the faults, fissures, and peaks inside your own skull that bring you up hard and short.

Chomo Lungma is the mountain's name—Great Mother Mountain. She rises in pleats and tooth-shapes from the rest of the Himalayas, a low thundering bass-note of Power throbbing from her rock and ice. She is more than a mountain. Generations of belief and thought have made her a symbol of endurance and the unconquerable, no matter *how* many climbers have climbed to her top unaided by hover technology. It's still an act of faith to scale her.

Our hover drifted through a night sky starred with hard points of brilliance, unwashed by any cityglow. The mountains around the Mother are a historical zone in the Freetown Tibet territory, no cities allowed, precious few hovers, the infrequent temples lit by torchlight, oil lamp, and candleflame.

I stared out the porthole, resting my forehead on chill slick plasglass. Hoverwhine boiled through my skull, rattled my back teeth, slid into my bones. Pleated gaps and gullies of stacked stone vibrated like plucked strings under the hover's metal belly. Starlight danced on snow and knife-edged crags. The air was so thin up here it sparkled.

A slim slice of waning moon drifted in the cold uncaring sky, shedding no light.

Japhrimel stepped into the room. I hadn't moved for a long time, watching the shapes of mountains as we circled the Mother of them all.

He shut the door and said nothing, but the mark on my shoulder hadn't stopped its distress-beacon pulsing. I searched the edged gullies and piles of rock below, my eyes not fooled by thin starshine. The mountains were hooded with snow, but it didn't soften their contours. Instead, it laid bare every grasping, razor edge.

My voice surprised me again. "I'm all right."

Another lie. They were coming fast and thick these days. I had always been so proud of keeping my word; I wondered if that pride was about to turn on me, cutting my hands as I tried to use my sorcerous Will. A Necromance uses her voice to bring back the dead; it's why we whisper most of the time.

We know what the spoken word can do.

He was silent for so long I closed my eyes, the darkness behind my lids comfortless. When he finally spoke, it was a bare thread of sound. "I do not think so, my curious."

The bitterness of my reply surprised even me. "I should think up a cute little nickname for you, too, you know."

It was something I might have said in Toscano, back when the world had still been on its course, not descended into insanity. I'd thought I was fucked-up then but beginning to heal. I hadn't had any idea of how fucked-up it could get.

A nasty little voice inside my head whispered that maybe I didn't have any idea now, either.

"You could," he finally said. "I would answer."

"You always do." The darkness behind my closed lids made it easier to say. "Somehow."

"I have not been kind to you." The words came out in a rush, as if he'd been sitting on them for a while and just now set them free. "What I have done, I have done with the best of intent. You must believe me."

"Sure." *Who the hell else do I have to believe?* "Look, Japh, it's okay. You don't have to."

Meaning, *I'm not in any position to throw stones when it comes to good intent.* Meaning, *you came for me, even when you didn't have to.* Meaning, *someone else hurt me, not you.* Meaning other things, too, things I couldn't say. There might have been a time when I could have opened up my mouth and spilled everything, but that time was long gone.

Besides, he probably wouldn't understand anyway even if I could say it. I had been reduced more than once to incoherence by his inability to comprehend the simplest things about me.

I didn't hear him cross the room, but his breath touched my hair. The warmth of him radiated against my back. "We do only what we must." Each word touched my hair like a lover's fingers, raised prickles on my nape. Precious few people got this close to me. "You more than most, I think. May I ask you something?"

Oh, gods. "If you want." The stone lodged in my throat coated itself with ice, froze the words halfway.

He paused. His fingers touched my left shoulder, skating over the fabric of my shirt. My chin dipped, shoulders unstringing, losing their tension.

Maybe I could relax for just a few seconds. I needed it. I was on the knife-edge of psychosis—too much violence, too high an emotional pitch for too long. It was a wonder I hadn't had a psychotic break yet. I just wanted to curl up somewhere and rest, close my eyes and shut out the world.

Trouble was, the world doesn't take too kindly to being shut out.

The hover lifted, gravity turning over underneath my stomach. We were in a holding pattern, drifting quietly over the tallest mountain in the world.

Except the one inside my head, that was. The one standing

between me and any semblance of reasonable humanity. I heard Lucas mutter something outside the door, the sound of metal clinking—ammo, probably. Leander's muffled reply was short and terse.

Japhrimel sighed. It was a very human sound, stirring my hair as a soft rustling began. When his arms came around me I didn't pull away, but neither did I lean back into him. His wings unfolded, rippling as they closed around me, heavy and silken. Spice and demon musk freighted the air, carrying the indefinable smell of maleness and the faint tinge of leather and gunpowder that was his, unique.

His wings draped bonelessly, the slice of starshine coming through the porthole closed off as they cocooned us, liquid heat painting my skin. He was always so warm.

A very long time ago I'd read a treatise on Greater Flight demons and their wings. It is a tremendous show of vulnerability, almost submission, for a demon of Japhrimel's class to close his wings around another being. The writer of the treatise—a post-Awakening Magi whose shadowjournal had been more difficult than most to decipher—hadn't used the word *trust,* but I'd inferred it anyway, fully aware of imputing human emotions to something...not human.

I just couldn't stop doing it. Not when I made a short broken sound, all my air leaving me in a half-sob, and relaxed, abruptly, all at once against him.

The darkness behind my eyelids turned kind and comforting. He held me carefully, resting his chin atop my head and occasionally shifting his weight as the hover banked. His pulse came strong and sure, one beat to every three of mine.

"I thought to ask your forgiveness," he murmured, his voice a thin thread of gold in the stillness. "I thought to ask if you regretted our meeting. I also thought to ask..."

I waited, but he said nothing more. *How am I supposed to answer either of those questions, Japhrimel? You hurt me, manipulated me...but you always show up just when I'm about to get strangled by yet another demon. And if I never met you Santino would still be alive, Doreen would be unavenged—but maybe Jace and Gabe and Eddie would still be alive, too.*

If I'd never met you the Lourdes hunt would have killed me. A thin shiver walked up my spine with tiny, icy claws. Taking on a Feeder's ka birthed from the ruins of Rigger Hall would have been chancy at best for even a fully-trained Necromance. Maybe I would have been strong enough, maybe not.

Probably not. I would have been only human, after all. If I hadn't met him.

If he hadn't *changed* me in so many ways. The physical changes were only the least of them.

How could I even *begin* to untangle it all? Lies and truth and hate and need, all twisted together into a rope. Even as it burned my hands and dragged me down, at least that rope could be counted on to yank me back out of the abyss. Every other safety net I'd ever had was gone.

Tell him the truth, Danny, if you can admit it. Tell him you wish you'd never seen his face. Tell him you wish he and Lucifer had just left you alone instead of fucking you up so bad you can't even think straight, so bad you can't even talk to your god anymore.

Go ahead, sunshine. Deliver the bad news. It might even hurt him.

My fingers relaxed, my katana dangling from my left hand. The rig was heavy, straps cutting into my shoulders, weapons poking at odd places. In a while the leather and hilts would conform to me, would be unfelt until I needed them.

Tell him, Dante. You're always so proud of telling the truth and keeping your Word. Look where it's gotten you. Tell him.

"I'm glad I met you." The lie sounded natural. For once, I delivered an untruth, and I meant it while I said it, too. "Don't be ridiculous."

Japhrimel's weight pitched forward, resting fully on me for one heavy second. He straightened, a small sound escaping his lips as if I'd hit him. "Forgive me?" he whispered. It sounded less like a question, more like a plea.

What am I supposed to say to that? The answer came, and I was grateful for it. "If you forgive me." *We can be even, this once. Can't we?*

"There is nothing to forgive." He sounded more like himself, contained and even. His arms tightened, and for a moment his wings pulled even closer, warm scented air touching my wet cheeks.

I didn't know I was crying. I hadn't cried since Gabe's death. Not so long ago, really, but it felt like a lifetime.

The hover banked into a curve, Japh's weight shifting. He inhaled, his breath moving against my hair, and his body tightened the merest fraction. I knew that tension in him, had shared it so many times. It was a subtle invitation to have a conversation in the most intimate way, skin-on-skin, the only language we ever truly shared.

I flinched.

Japhrimel froze.

I struggled to contain the urge to flinch again. He had never hurt me in the private space of our shared bed. It was ridiculous to think he ever would.

Still, my body turned cold, the tears changing to ice on my cheeks, a black hole where something had been torn out by the roots opening in my head, my body robbed of its integrity. My own voice, breaking as I screamed, echoed up from that well of darkness.

Don't think about that. Don't.

When he moved again, it was to reach up, smoothing my hair. His fingertips were unerringly gentle, not even a prickle to remind me of his claws. I remembered to breathe again, took a deep steadying gulp of warm air full of his goddamn safe-smelling pheromones.

"I'm sorry." Memory curved, overlapped—how many times had I said the same thing to Doreen, to other lovers? How many times had I apologized for my inability to respond, my coldness, the echoes of trauma lingering in my head blocking me from accepting even the smallest gift of touch? "Japh, I—"

"No." At least he didn't sound angry. "Leave it be, *hedaira.*"

"What if..." *What if I can't ever go there with you again? What if I can't ever stand to have anyone touch me again?*

He inhaled again, smelling me, his ribs expanding to make his chest brush my back. It was a relief to find out I didn't want to cower away from that touch. "It doesn't matter."

"But—"

"It *does not matter.* You will heal. When you're ready, we shall see." His fingers combed through my hair, infinitely soothing.

I had to ask. "What if I'm never ready?" *What if I don't own my own body, ever again?*

"Then we will find another way." The darkness changed as his wings unfurled, slowly, flowing back down to armor him even as his arms remained around me. He let out a short, soft sigh. "But first, we have a Prince to kill and our freedom to accomplish."

Just those two little things? Sure, we can get that done in an afternoon. An unhealthy, sniggering laugh rose up in my throat, was mercilessly strangled, and died away. "Japh?"

"Hm?" He sounded just as he always did. Except for the banked rage under the surface of his tone.

"I feel...dirty." *Unclean. Filthy, as a matter of fact.* I couldn't frame the question I needed answered most.

Does that *matter to you?*

He was silent for a long, long moment. Finally, he spoke into my hair, a mere thread of sound. "I did too, my beloved, when Lucifer broke me to his will. I healed. In time, you will."

His arm uncoiled from my waist and he stepped away, quickly. His retreat to the door was killing-silent, but I felt every step in my own body. I kept my eyes tightly shut. *Oh, gods.* "You mean he—"

"It is one of his preferred methods." The door opened, a slight click as he turned the handle. "We shall be landing soon. Bring your weapons, and especially the Knife. I regret there is not more time for rest, but we must move."

CHAPTER 14

Wind moaned against antennae and landing-struts. The buffeting increased as Tiens held the hover steady. McKinley tapped a knifehilt, his metallic left hand clenching and releasing as he stared over the Nichtvren's shoulder at a wilderness of rock and snow. The air was thinner up here, so the hover had more bounce; even inside the pressurized seals the weight against eardrums made Leander and Lucas yawn in synchrony, their faces contorting. I could have found that amusing, but I was busy going through my rig one last time, making sure each projectile gun, plasgun, knife, and stiletto was in place. Vann had produced a sheath that fit the half-Knife, a nice bit of leatherwork with two straps for attaching it to a rig. The Knife's humming, malignant force was uncomfortable against my left hip, but better there than in my bag where I couldn't get to it if another demon showed up.

I'm not sure I like it. My skin chilled as Sephrimel's dying screech echoed in my memory, over the hideous sucking sound the Knife made. *Still, if it'll get the job done… but are we sure it will? It's only made of wood, for fuck's sake.*

I ducked through the strap of my bag and settled it on my hip, scooping up Fudoshin from the bolted-down table. *Add it to the list of things to think about later, sunshine. Right now there's a job to be done.*

Story of my life. Push it away so you can get it done, whatever *it* is. Worry about the cost later.

After a certain point, it's useless to worry about the debt you've built up. Just put your head down and go straight through, and hope it doesn't hurt too much. Just like a slicboard run through Suicide Alley back home.

"This is as close as I can bring us, *m'sieu.*" The Nichtvren's face was bathed in eerie blue from reflected starlight, the tips of his canines showing as his upper lip pulled back and he finessed the hover down to land. Leafsprings creaked and the hover kissed down as sweetly as a sheet settling over a tethered hoverbed, despite the tilt to the soft landing surface that had gyros whining as the craft stabilized.

It really takes a human touch to land a hover right, especially on a deep snowpack likely to shift and settle in unexpected ways. AIs just can't do it. Though how far I would go toward calling a bloodsucking predator *human* I don't know.

"Close enough." Japhrimel leaned down slightly, peering out the observation bubble. There was nothing out there but snow, rock, and a sheer cliff face going straight up. It looked damn cold.

"Someone is certain to be watching." McKinley couldn't contain himself any longer. "At the very least, let us come with you. Or leave her here with us. If they—"

"Nobody's *leaving* me anywhere," I immediately objected. "I've had enough of being left with you to fill me to the back teeth." *And then some.* Fudoshin rattled in his scabbard, sensing my readiness, I steadied myself with an effort.

"If the Prince catches her here, he'll kill her. Especially now that she's free of the..." Vann caught himself, leaning against the hull on the other side of the control bubble. Tiens's fingers flicked, going through procedural cooldowns to keep the hover landed but ready to take off again at the slightest notice.

He's already had his chance to kill me, kid. I shuddered. *Besides, he still needs me as bait, whether I've got that thing in me or not.*

Japh clasped his hands behind his back again. "She is *hedaira*. The Knife was made for a *hedaira*'s hand; demonkin cannot tolerate the thing. Even a Fallen cannot, for long. It is best she accompanies me for that reason alone." His tone was quiet and reasonable. "All is well, Vann."

McKinley spoke up again, running his hand back through his hair so it stood up in messy spikes. "My Lord? Who knew about Sephrimel?"

"As far as I am aware, I am the only one who suspected. The Prince left the matter in my hands." Japhrimel did not even glance in my direction. The wind screeched and fell off, stinging particles of snow rattling against the bubble. "That was of the time when he was certain of my loyalty."

"When did that stop?" I laid a hand against the chill plasglass of the nearest porthole. The hull vibrated, not with the whine of antigrav but with the force of the wind.

It looked *damn* cold out there.

"When I Fell." Japh's coat fluttered once in the stillness. "I shall need the item I left in your care, McKinley."

"Yes, my Lord." McKinley quit fidgeting and strode away, disappearing at the far end of the main cabin, heading for the cargo bay.

"M'sieu?" Tiens half-turned in the pilot's chair. "I may accompany you?"

"Thank you, Tiens. I require only my *hedaira.*" Japhrimel half-turned, his gaze sweeping across the cabin and fetching up against Leander, who hunched in a chair, staring out a low porthole at a waste of ice and rock falling away from the narrow sloped shelf we were precariously perched on. The Necromance glanced up, and the flash of fear in his dark eyes was enough to make my breath catch.

I knew what it was like to feel that frightened of a demon. How could I ever forget?

Distract him, Danny. Let's get this show on the road. "It looks goddamn cold out there. Where are we going?"

Japhrimel's reply came after a long moment of considering silence, the color draining from Leander's face and his emerald spitting a single nervous spark.

"The entrance is very close." My Fallen still didn't turn to look at me. "The cold will not touch you."

Entrance to where? "There's nothing up here." I wanted his attention on me. "This is a Freetown Tibet historical zone. It's Chomo Lungma, for fuck's sake. They wouldn't let anyone build—"

"It is older than your kind, my curious." He turned away from Leander on one heel, a precise economical movement. "Come. If 'tis to be done, best it were done quickly."

I didn't know you were a student of the classics, Japh. "If Lucifer doesn't know—"

"It is," he said, "always better not to underestimate *him.*"

*   *   *

The cargo bay was dark, lit only by orandflu and stacked with crates of supplies. I caught sight of a pile of ammo boxes while I shrugged into the coat Vann had handed me—an explorer's canvas number with plenty of pockets, slightly too big for me, and smelling too new to remind me of Jace's old coat with its Kevlar panels and the hole in one pocket. I'd lost that one, with everything else except my bag and jewelry, in Hell.

Strange that I should suddenly want, with surprising fierceness, a battered, sweat-stained old jacket. I'd worn Jace's coat at the end of the Lourdes hunt and for a long time afterward, while the ghost of his scent wore out of the tough fabric. I wanted it back.

It was only one thing in a long list that I wanted *back*. I stuffed two fresh ammo clips into the biggest right-side pocket, thought about it, and added another in the left. You never can tell.

McKinley handed over a small cylindrical iron container, darkly stained and reeking of demon. "Are you sure you want to use this?"

"What better time?" Japhrimel's tone was just amused enough to put me on edge. "Dante?"

"Right here." I flipped my bag closed, caught a whiff of Hell drifting up from its material. The strap was seamless, as if it had never been broken, the webbing reknitted. *It's a good thing he's so great at sewing, with the amount of laundry I bleed all over.* I caught McKinley's nervous glance at me and the reply died well short of my throat.

Feeling better, Danny? You're wisecracking again. Means you're okay, right?

Right?

"Thank you, McKinley. Inform Tiens and Vann that we shall only be a short time, and to keep our transport ready." It was a dismissal, Japhrimel's back was to me as he triggered the side-hatch from the cargo bay. The lens of the hatch opened, climate-control seals shimmering into life, and the sound of the wind got a lot closer. The seals bowed a little, stabilizing, and I clenched my jaw to equalize the pressure in my ear canals.

"Yes, my Lord." McKinley gave me one last dark look and hurried toward the ladder leading up to the main hall.

Japhrimel stared out through the seals for a moment, his face set as if he was contemplating a complex but not particularly challenging riddle. I'd never seen that expression on him before, equal parts demonic concentration and almost-human amusement, with a soupçon of seriousness thrown in to give it flavor and make his lambent eyes narrow slightly.

"It looks cold out there." I rolled my shoulders in their sockets, settling my rig a little more securely. "What's in the box?"

He shrugged, and just as I was about to take offense, thinking it was a dismissal, he spoke again. "Only a demon artifact. It will draw attention, but for a short time it is the best protection we can use. Do you trust me, Dante?"

My jaw threatened to drop. *You're asking me that* now*?*

Then again, what better time to ask? Did he need to know, the way I needed to know so many things?

"Of course I trust you." I tried not to sound irritable. Took a deep breath, smelled oil and the burnt-dust scorch of a difficult hoverlanding, the flat scent of climate control and the iron tang of snow. The wind howled, the seals bowing a little as they coped with the sudden change in pressure. "Why? Are you planning something that might change that?" I didn't add the *again* only through sheer strength of will.

"Perhaps. I must warn you, it is likely the escaped Androgyne will show her hand." He kept staring out the climate seals, where the windscream reached a fresh pitch and the darkness thickened as the hover's landing-lights switched off. Now there was only starshine and the orandflu strips inside the cargo bay. He melded with the thick uncertain shadows, only his eyes firing to break the effect. "I may have to act without regard for your conscience."

You mean, you might have to kill Doreen's daughter, or take her back to Hell no matter what I have to say about it? Don't make me choose between you and Eve, Japhrimel. I can't. "Is Lucifer going to show up too?" I didn't expect myself to sound so calm at the thought. I *also* didn't expect the thick choking flare of panic that went through me, breath catching and pulse hiking, copper coating the back of my palate.

"I most sincerely hope not." He turned slightly, his eyes coming to rest on me, the light sliding over half his saturnine face, picking out the hollows and planes. He looked about to say more but stopped, his mouth thinning into a line that turned down at the corners even as his eyes paled, their glow less awful than Lucifer's but still...

My heart lodged in my throat, beating thick and quiet. *Focus, Danny. Just get through this. You only have to do this once.*

Even if it was a lie, I was grateful for it.

"Me too." I hefted my sword, its slim weight reassuring as it vibrated in the sheath, steel feeling my tension. "Let's get this over with. The sooner we have the other half of this goddamn thing, the sooner we can kill that bastard. That's the agreement, right?"

He nodded. "Then come. Stay close, and fear nothing."

I can do about half of that, Japh. I think. If Eve doesn't show up, and if the Devil doesn't know we plan to kill him. I didn't say it. I just shut my mouth and followed him.

CHAPTER 15

The cold was immense, titanic, walloping all the breath out of me in one shocked second before Japhrimel's aura closed harder over mine, flushing me with heat. I shivered once, a short cry caught in my throat, and my body quivered, ice congealing in my lungs before I blew out a cloud that immediately flashed into ice and fell with a tinkle on the packed snow. I sank in powder-dry snow to my knees, stepping off the cargo hatch's open metal stairs, glad I hadn't touched the half-railing. In this kind of weather, skin could freeze to metal instantly.

A terrific spike of glassy pain sank through my head before my body adapted to the lower oxygen load in the air, a hazy stain of Power spreading out in the ambient atmosphere. Steam drifted away from the egg-shaped field covering us both, Japhrimel steadying me as I almost toppled, sinking in the snow. Iron-hard fingers closed around my upper arm, hauling me up, and I found myself balanced on the thin top crust just like Japhrimel, whose boots rested feather-light, leaving no impression.

It was a nice trick, but it dried my mouth out and gave my heart an all-new reason to start hammering.

I knew he was a demon. But such a casual use of so much Power was terrifying in an all-new way. *Just how many ways can a Necro-mance be scared to death?* It sounded like a stupid riddle.

I found I could breathe again, and looked up to find Japh studying me. The wind, pawing at the hover's corners and struts, hurling itself around rock edges with a sound like silk endlessly tearing, covered any sound I might have made. The scar in the hollow of my left shoulder flared with soft heat, stroking down my body just like a caress—one that didn't remind me of the blank black space inside my head, and the hideousness it contained.

Japh tilted his head slightly, and I took an experimental step when he did. My feet crunched in the snow and his fingers tightened, my boots leaving an impression a quarter-inch deep.

I took another step. Panic bubbled up, I set my teeth against it. Anyone coming behind us would look at my tracks and think I was alone, stepping lightly over powdery snow deep enough to swallow me even if it had afforded a soft landing to the hover.

Japh's hand on my arm gentled, slid up to circle my shoulders. He pulled me into his side, Power cloaking us both, and I had the sudden startling feeling of being invisible. The psychic static of a *demon,* spreading through the ether with black-diamond-spangled haze, cloaked and outshone me completely. It was the equivalent of not being able to smell my own pheromones, disturbing and comforting in equal measure.

He set off, shortening his long strides to mine, and we moved over the snow together, not bothering to talk. The sound of the wind would have overpowered anything I could shout, anyway. Steam turned to ice, cracking and tinkling as it shredded away from the small space of warmth he carried us in.

Could he have done this when he'd just been Fallen, not Fallen with a demon's Power restored? Add that to the list of questions I wasn't sure I was ever going to get answered.

We headed straight for the cliff face. I wondered what was about to happen—was he going to take us right up the sheer, ice-laden wall? *Could* he? What about spreading his wings and catching the wind? They were built more for gliding than actual flight, but he'd carried me before. Was he going to do it again?

There were people I might have wanted to share this with, tell them what it was like if I could find the words.

Unfortunately, they were all dead.

The cliff loomed, a trick of angularity making it wavelike, as if rock and stone might crest over and crush us. Japhrimel aimed us for a sharp spear digging itself into the side of the mountain, a slender black stone the wind had scoured clean, wet and glassy in the eerie snow-reflected light. I shivered, though I was nowhere near cold, and his arm tightened.

That type of rock doesn't belong here.

We drew closer, step by slow step. The wind stilled for a moment, howling elsewhere while a freak of drift deadened its force around us. My nape prickled, uneasy, and I tried to glance back to see the hover. Japh drew me on, either not noticing or not caring.

Next to the sharp black stone, a deeper darkness beckoned. *Is that what I think it is?*

It was a slim crevice in the stone, festooned with clear sharp icicles. One of the ice-spears had broken and lay in shattered crystalline fragments on a rough-carved rock step. The aperture exhaled a low moan as the wind changed again, veering, and my ears protested at the pressure shift.

Japh kept going. The crevice looked smaller than it was, dwarfed by the massive bulk of the mountain. It was actually large enough for both of us to slide in, despite the sharp teeth. His stride didn't alter; he walked right up to the vertical mouth and maneuvered us in, one of the ice-daggers touching my shoulder and crackling as the heat of the shield touched it. I flinched, but nothing else happened, and with two more steps into darkness the wind fell off as if cut by climate seals.

The blackness thickened. *Japh, what are you doing?* I tried to hang back, slow down, but he pulled me forward, his arm gently irresistible. Another soft caress of warmth down my skin, a flush of Power against my nerve endings, and the skin of darkness lay against my eyes like a wet bandage.

"Japhrimel—" Claustrophobia filled my throat. *No. Not into the dark, it's too dark—*

"One more step." His aura hardened, slashing the blackness with diamond claws, and the night slid aside, crimson light spiking through its torn coat. Light struck across my adapted eyes. I flinched, and Japh steadied me as the shielding I hadn't even seen from outside snapped back out behind us, a wall of glaucous rippling black. Displaced air ruffled my hair, fingered my coat, and finally swirled away.

"Holy *shit*," I whispered when my eyes cleared.

"It is a sight, is it not?" Japhrimel sounded tightly amused, but the bitterness in his tone robbed it of warmth. "No mere human has seen this, and precious few demons. Welcome to the Roof of the World, my curious."

We stood on a platform of smooth, glassy red rock. The cavern was so immense even the great bloody light couldn't fill its corners or its true height. A thin arching bridge of the same glassy redness poured away from our perch, its geometry just a fraction *off,* and that fraction hammered into my midriff, turning my stomach over hard. It was unquestionably demon work. Three other bridges slung inward from the circuit of the cavern, and their goal and apex was a massive crag of floating rock. Its bulk hung down like a shark's fin, and as I stared, trying to figure out the physics of something so vastly unreal, it drifted a little bit. It actually *moved,* like a whale will move slightly in the ocean's embrace, and when it did the bridge nearest us made a low sound that threatened to turn my bones to jelly.

The air was full of heat, sudden and shocking after the frigid waste outside. But this heat wasn't human. It mouthed my exposed skin with fierce chill, and my throat closed as I tried to backpedal, my body wiser than I was. Panic rose, beating in my head with jagged-edge wings.

Japhrimel's voice was lost in the terror filling my skull. I struggled to get free of his arms, because it was hot in here, so hot it *burned,* and I had felt a close cousin to that heat before.

In Hell.

"Stop!"

Down to my knees, teeth clicking together painfully as I jolted, Japhrimel's hands still at my shoulders. He shook me. "Dante. Stop. You will harm yourself."

I blinked up at him. For one horrifying second his face was a stranger's, only the green eyes searing and his lips drawn back as he said more, words lost in the roaring of memory.

I remembered. Claws snicking against my ribs, cradling the living beat of my heart, a sword of fire in my vitals. And a voice, deadly soft and oh-so-amused. *There are so many ways to break a human. Especially a human woman.*

I screamed, but it died halfway when Japhrimel clapped his hand over my mouth, the scar on my shoulder suddenly red-hot wire, digging into vulnerable flesh. The human darkness behind the green flame of his eyes returned, drowning me, and I struggled to *think,* to climb out of the sucking whirlpool of fear.

"You know me," he repeated. "You *know* me, *hedaira.* Come back."

I shuddered, teeth locking together and muscles turned to bridge cables, straining against his hold. Still, there was a curious comfort. I did know him. How many times had he repeated the same thing, over and over, while I shook and sobbed with the echo of psychic rape tearing through my head? The hunt for Kellerman Lourdes had left me with nightmares and reaction-flashbacks, none as intense as this but frightening enough.

I *did* know him. All the way down to my bones.

I broke the surface with a convulsive movement, almost tearing free of his hands. Even now, he was so careful not to hurt me.

I bent over, fingers locked around the slim comforting length of my sword, clenching around the terrible fist in my middle, lower than any nausea I'd ever felt before. "Anubis," I whispered, the reflex of a lifetime hard to break. My lips moved against his palm. *"Anubis et'her ka. Se ta'uk' fhet sa te vapu kuraph."*

The prayer died on my lips. Hot water scorched my eyes, and I looked up to find Japhrimel still there, still holding me. His coat rippled, a small sound like feathers shifting as his hand fell away.

Tears trickled hotly down both my cheeks. "I'm okay." It felt like a lie. I was getting good at lying, finally.

Maybe not. Japh's silence was eloquent enough to pass for speech, and it was a relief to find I could understand, at least, this one little silence of his. It meant he didn't believe me in the politest of ways, and wasn't going to press the point.

His face was set, that human darkness very close to the surface of his glowing eyes. His mouth was a thin line, one corner slightly quirked, one of his winged eyebrows elevated too. My heart leapt, banging against my ribs and pulling the rest of my chest with it.

Gods above. I just had a panic attack and I think I'm having a cardiac arrest now.

"We should be quick." Half-apologetic, his mouth drawing down again and becoming solemn. "I would not ask it of you, but—"

"I'm *all right*." To prove it, I tried to make my legs work. I failed miserably, and was suddenly very aware of a hollowness inside me. I was *starving*.

Fine time to get the munchies, sunshine.

Japh pulled me up, held me steady, and indicated the floating rock. It shifted again, and another bridge sang as it took the stress. The vibration passed through me, from scalp to soles, the same way a badly tuned slicboard will thrum right before it dumps you. "Up there." The pulsation stopped as he spoke. "This is a place between your world and Hell, not fully of either. Tread carefully."

How careful can I be? I've got a head full of C19 and vaston, and someone's got their finger on the detonator circuit. Problem is, I can't tell who. I don't think it matters. I contented myself with nodding, my hair falling forward into my eyes. I blew it back, irritably, and Japhrimel smiled. It was a small, strained expression, but a smile nonetheless.

"Let's get this over with." I eyed the bridges and the chunk of floating rock, my brain struggling with the sheer *scale*. There was nothing to compare it to, so it seemed absurdly in proportion, but my eyes would snag on the delicacy of the glass bridges and recoil in self-defense. "Are you sure it's here?"

He didn't answer, just set off for where the closest bridge met with our platform, his arm settling over my shoulders again as if it was designed to. The bridges looked absurdly frail compared to what they held—were they really supporting that chunk of stone?—but they were wide as two hoverlanes and twice as thick.

Oh dear gods, do I have to? I've never been afraid of heights, but this—there were no handrails.

The bloody glow painting the cavern flared, a wash of crimson light like a silent explosion. Japh's steps quickened, soundless. My bootheels made small dry sounds against the rock as he led me onto the bridge.

It was a steep slope, and slippery. The surface was grainy, with a slightly oily-grit feel like granite steps after a hard rain. I blinked several times, furiously, because we didn't so much *walk* as almost... I don't know, *blink* along the curve, Japhrimel's arm steady and warm over my shoulders but everything else shaking and juddering, especially when the hunk of rock would shift and one of the bridges would cry out in pained stress.

It didn't seem to take very long to reach the sharpest curve of the bridge, and from there it was a matter of seconds before Japhrimel exhaled, a sound of effort, and we stepped from the glass onto something soft.

The surface of the central rock was matted with dark dryness, crumbling off the edges as the bridges sang. Awful icy heat touched my cheeks and my knuckles, white-clenched around Fudoshin's hilt and scabbard.

Screw the wooden Knife, if Lucifer showed up we were going to see how much steel he could eat.

The bravado made me feel better until I looked up from the maroon dirt disintegrating under my boots.

It was a ruined city. Jagged broken towers pierced the red sky, a cobbled road rising from the dirt in front of us, shattered walls scattered like broken teeth, glowing sickly-pale in the bloody light. They had probably once been beautiful, luminous white stones interlocked with care and precision, but now they leered and toppled like a drunken man.

Even broken as it was, the city held an echo of something lovely. The ruins sang, each with its own slow silent voice, a chorus of sorrow. *"Sekhmet sa'es."* I could barely breathe the words. "What the hell is this?"

"This?" Japhrimel's tone was so bitter it scorched my own mouth. "This is the White-Walled City, where the *A'nankhimel* would bring their brides. I was here once, long ago. I do not think the stones have forgotten."

CHAPTER 16

I've been in plenty of places and seen lots of urban decay. It was still eerie to walk on a road with missing cobbles and see broken buildings with just a breath of demon oddity to their shape, dry blasted places that might have once been gardens, fluid piles of white stone that might have been fountains but were now only dry bones. Every building leaned hopelessly on its foundations, crying out for something lost. Every missing cobble was a hole in my own heart.

Japhrimel was silent, only removing his arm from my shoulders to help me scramble over piles of rubble. We were heading, near as I could figure, for the city's heart. He seemed to know his way, only pausing every now and again to look at a particular building as if taking his bearings.

Sephrimel's half of the Knife hummed in its sheath, the sound working through leather and into my hip each time the city shifted. I eyed each building nervously, every stone worked fluidly into its fellows except where some unimaginable force had torn them apart.

I kept glancing up at Japhrimel's face, set and quiet, and I began to wonder.

What was it like for him, to walk through here again? Were scenes of murder and screaming replaying in his head? Were all of them like the illustration in the book I carried even now in my battered, Hell-smelling messenger bag?

The strangest thing in the world happened. I began to feel *sorry* for him. I never had, before.

It took a while. The place ran with subaudible song, a long slow moan of stress that alternated between nostalgia like a sharp knife and memory like a fist to the gut. The psychic imprint of something horrible trembled in the air, and I was glad of Japhrimel's aura over mine. This physical space was *haunted;* had never been drained by a cadre of Hegemony-trained psions; and even though we've come a long way in the science of using Power and sorcerous Will I didn't know if there were psions alive capable of dealing with this kind of carnivorous reverberation in the ether. It could eat a Reader alive or tip a Skinlin dirtwitch into berserker rage. It might even drive a *sedayeen* healer mad. And a Magi? Forget it, the spice of demons hanging in the air would tempt them and the devouring grief singing from the stones would creep into their heads, replicating like a virus.

Like a Feeder's *ka,* devouring everyone in its path in its mad scramble to spread, a psychic cancer.

My battered shields, mending only because of the steady flushes of Power from Japhrimel's mark on my shoulder, quivered like the raw wounds they were. I was aware now of the extent of the damage soaking down through my psyche, huge gaping holes and fault lines, the terrain of my mind bombed-out like a city after the Seventy Days War. Like this city, in fact, still keening after an unimaginable tragedy.

We paused for a few moments by a waist-high wall. On the other side a blasted space that might have once been a garden lay, dead trees crumbling to dust. Japhrimel stared across it for a moment, his face settling deeper against its bones.

I put out my hand, blindly. Closed my fingers around his arm. "Don't."

His expression didn't change, but the hurtful tension in it eased a fraction. "It was so long ago," he said quietly. "Long and long. I still remember each of them."

"The *hedaira?*" The minute it was out of my mouth I regretted it.

"All of them. Each life the Prince ordered me to take. I keep them here." One elegant golden finger tapped at his temple. "We're very close now."

There was nothing to say. Still, I pulled on his arm. "Japh. Hey."

He didn't look at me. His eyes narrowed as they swept the crumbling garden. "We should hurry."

"Hey." I tugged on his arm until his gaze swung down, touched mine. "Come here."

"I'm here." His expression didn't change.

I pulled him close and slid my arm around his waist, a moment of awkwardness as my sword got briefly tangled up. I hugged him as hard as I could, squeezing until rewarded by his brief exhale.

He hugged me back, a slight careful pressure, before freeing himself with exquisite gentleness. His face had eased a little.

We set off through the ruined city again. I was beginning to get almost used to the sound the bridges made when the city shifted, and almost used to the vibration underfoot, sliding through the echo chamber of my body. I mean, as much as you *can* get used to being shaken like a bad sodaflo can every few minutes in a place that wasn't quite the regular world, drenched with a cousin to Hell's chillfire air.

The streets smoothed out, widening into an avenue that dumped us into a huge plaza floored with more red-glass stone. Here the light was brighter, but deeper in shade, heart's-blood instead of arterial flow.

In the middle of the plaza a massive building lifted, bone-white marble glowing along its pillared front. Its walls rumbled with grief and Power, and I stared, forgetting to move forward until Japhrimel, not unkindly, pulled me along.

"It's a Temple." The plaza threw the words back at me. Surely I didn't sound that horrified? The idea of a Temple here, in this twisted sorrowing place, filled me with unsteady loathing.

He waited four steps before he answered me. "It wasn't built for one of your gods."

The sound of my lonely footsteps echoed too, magnified by weird acoustics. I tried to imagine this place full of people and failed miserably. "A demon god?" *Call me a coward, but I don't want to know what kind of god a demon would worship.*

"No. This was a place to celebrate what we could become." He paused, thoughtfully, and the echo of my footsteps trickled away like running water. "The *A'nankhimel* spoke blasphemy, to the rest of us. This was where that blasphemy bloomed. When I came here, it was as a fire comes to cleanse." The words began to tumble out. "This was not just a place for *hedaira* and Fallen. Others were brought here, humans who showed promise, and taught. They were given many gifts, which they took outside to the world. Lucifer flatters himself that he *allowed* it, to bring humans up from the mud. *Shavarak'itzan beliak.*" It was obviously an obscenity; the air cringed away when he said it. "The first products of the unions between your kind and mine were born here. Later, an *A'nankhimel* would take a *hedaira* away to give birth in secret. They had good reason."

I knew about this. There was a chance that a *hedaira* could give birth to an Androgyne—a demon capable of reproducing. Which would pretty much destroy Lucifer's monopoly on reproduction in Hell. It was a big deal to demons—after all, the Devil had wound me up and sent me after Santino, who had merrily absconded with the means to experiment genetically until he performed the biggest hat-trick of all, making Eve.

Eve. The child I hadn't been able to save. Little girl all grown up and making trouble.

"Were all of them women?" I was curious, you see. This was the most information about *hedaira* he'd ever given me.

"There were stories about males—*hedairos.* I saw none."

You'd be in a position to know, wouldn't you. I was suddenly glad I hadn't eaten anything. "Okay. So why only women?"

The bloody light exploded again, soft crimson lapping at the air. I flinched.

"The human female breeds, my curious."

That's why Lucifer killed them, you idiot. "Oh." *You know, I'd give just about anything to go back to the hover now.* I tried to speed up, but Japh kept us to the same even pace. For a demon in such a hurry, he wasn't moving very quickly. Just steadily, our steps like clockwork measuring off eternity.

How long had it been since someone walked here? Did I want to know? There was no dust but plenty of the dry sterile red dirt, and the way the place shook every few minutes probably wasn't conducive to dust settling.

Another thought came hard on the heels of that one. *Where are all the bodies?*

Add that to the list of questions I could live without answering. The longer I lived, the more of those there seemed to be.

The Temple's steps sloped up, some of them broken and cracked. Another shudder and bridge-scream left the air shaking, icy hell-heat flapping at my new coat, reminding me of things I needed to forget if

I was supposed to stay sane. I kept my sword in a white-knuckle grip, tried to ignore the way my hands were shaking. Maybe an onlooker wouldn't have noticed it, but I could feel the tremors, like an over-stressed dynamo.

What if Lucifer shows up?

I told myself it was ridiculous. Japh wouldn't bring me here if he seriously thought the Devil would appear. He was just being cautious.

Yeah, right, sunshine. Tell me another one. I stole a look at Japh's face, its set lines, the perfection of his golden skin drawn tight against the bones. He didn't look as starved as he had. His hair fell over his eyes, feathering out in ragged bits.

"Up the stairs," he said, but he didn't look at me. The expression crept into his face, a look of *listening*. No matter how hard I strained, I suspected I wouldn't be able to hear whatever he was hearing — or *trying* to hear.

It was the same look he'd worn in Toscano, keeping to himself the fact that the Devil was asking for me, playing for time to let me heal.

Something's about to happen. I only have a touch of precognition; it's nowhere near my strongest Talent. Still, it's just enough to warn me when something awful is about to go down.

I wish it wasn't so well-exercised. I have just enough precog to warn me right before I step into quicksand up to my neck, not nearly enough to stop me from sinking.

Closer to the top, the steps were deep and riven. It looked like someone had taken a plashammer to them in several places, marble crushed and ground to pebbles by resonance-harmonics. I had enough to do in scrambling over broken stone, Japh's arm somehow never leaving my shoulders. He was impossibly graceful even now, as I slipped and slid.

We reached the top, and I hopped onto the porch. The pillars were chipped but otherwise whole, marching along the front of a building big enough to house a whole fleet of freight transports.

Typical demon. Build everything so huge it's unbelievable. Wonder what they were compensating for? The snigger caught me off-guard, echoes booming and shattering between the pillars, touching the doors. There were five of them, the central one largest and holding two shattered slabs of marble that once had been able to close. The last door on the left *was* closed, marble writhing with carving I didn't want to look at. The other three smaller doors were in varying stages of brokenness.

Knock knock. Who's there? Just me. Just me who?

Just your favorite demon assassin, that's who. I waved away Japhrimel's quizzical look. "Nothing. I'm okay."

"Keep the Knife ready." His voice fell flat, didn't bounce up from the hard edges like mine did.

No worries about that. The panic died. My left thumb caressed the sword's guard, ready to click the blade free. I could draw, drop my scabbard, and yank the wooden Knife free of its sheath if I was given half a chance.

There was no way I was facing a demon without good honest steel in my hand, no matter how powerful the demon-wrought thing at my hip was.

Sharp repressed anger stained the world for a moment, as if the bloody light had crept inside my eyes. I took a deep breath, shoved it down, and found the trembling in my hands had receded just a little bit. Just enough. "Which door?" *Sounds like a goddamn holovid game show. "I'll take the demon behind Door Number Three, Martin."*

"It matters little." He indicated the largest with an economical gesture. "If we were here before the City was broken, this would be the door I brought you to, at least the first time. There would be a celebration, and sacrifices to mark the occasion."

How the hell do you know? "You were here?"

"*Know thine enemy* is not only a human proverb, my curious." The listening look deepened, and he cocked his head. The city moved again, a huge restless stone animal accompanied by screams. "Some few demons came here to learn, and to watch."

"Learn what?" What could a demon possibly learn from humanity? Hadn't they been the ones to teach *us?* Or at least, that was the suspicion enshrined in academia.

"How to Fall. Come." He stepped over a rivulet of broken stone and dust, his arm leaving my shoulders. His hands flicked and two silver guns appeared, held low and ready as he edged forward. That's when I finally realized what I should have known all along.

Japh wasn't hoping trouble would pass us by. He knew trouble was about to happen, and had tried to keep me from worrying about it as long as possible.

Great.

CHAPTER 17

The Temple's roof had either been nonexistent in the first place or destroyed so completely it didn't matter. The inside was such a mess either was a fair guess. Great chunks of masonry were gouged up and scattered around, and unlike the outside, dust lay in a carpet up to my shins, whispering against my jeans as I waded in. The massive rectangular space focused on the far end, where a bank of glowing nacreous steps crouched under a long winged shape I had to blink at before recognizing as an altar.

The walls ran with a riot of color unsmirched by damage, and I had to swallow hard when I saw it was mosaic. Fantastical creatures with wings and fins leapt and cavorted against jungle green, and everywhere there were slender graceful golden women, all with glyphs worked into their flesh, white robes cut aside to reveal the marks proudly. After the desertion of the city outside, it was an assault, and the echo of Inhana's dark sad gaze was enough to make me wish I'd never seen this place.

"Anubis." I sounded choked. "The mosaics."

"It was traditional." Japhrimel lowered his guns slightly. "Hurry."

Hurry? There's nobody here. Still, I wasn't about to argue. "Where?"

"Where do you think?" He tipped his head toward the altar, red light bringing out odd highlights in his shaggy hair. "Up the steps, while I make certain no other intrudes."

"It's up there?"

"If the Anhelikos brought it, the casket is there. Please, *hedaira,* as you love life, hurry." He backed away from the doors, covering them in standard position, something I might have learned at the Academy. Still, he did it far more gracefully than a human could. His coat rustled, its long edges rippling and settling.

He must be nervous. His wings wouldn't do that otherwise.

I waded through the dust, picking my way around beached hunks of stone. When I glanced up, there was nothing but the red light. I couldn't see the roof of the cavern, and it was probably a good thing. I didn't want to see what was glowing fiercely enough to drench this entire place with light. I *also* didn't want to be reminded of how far we'd fall if the bridges quit screaming and started breaking. It would be just my luck to have centuries-old demon glasswork fail just as I got here.

My boots slid on a hard pebbled surface under the shed skin of centuries. More mosaics? Probably. The thought made me feverish, the icy heat tearing at the edges of Japhrimel's borrowed Power over my aura.

I'm in a temple. What if I start feeling like my insides are being ripped out again?

I told myself not to worry. There was nothing sacred left here. The gods had fled, if they'd ever been invited in the first place. My cheek sizzled as my accreditation tat shifted under my skin, inked lines twisting.

Besides, I've been dewormed. The black humor in the thought almost helped.

Almost.

There was a long unbroken sea of dust, the stairs rearing out of it like spines. Oddly, no grime had settled on those white, white planes. The altar crouched, its shape less rectangular and more sinuous now, carved with deep scored lines I recognized as angular demon writing, their peculiar rune-alphabet. My shoulder twinged, the mark settling deeper into my flesh, nestling in the hollow of my shoulder like a bird with its own heartbeat.

I wanted to fix each rune in my Magi-trained memory, but settled for swimming my boots through the dust and struggling cautiously up onto the steps, testing the first one with my boot before trusting my weight to it. OtherSight was almost useless here, between Japhrimel and the haze of grief in the air it was even difficult to see my own aura. It was like being blind, being unable to see the interplay of forces under the skin of the world.

The altar's main portion had a curved back, and something I stared at for a long moment before making sense of it.

Manacles made of silvery metal lay tangled across each end of the main part. On the winged sub-altars on either side were deep lines — *blood-grooves,* a long-ago memory of an illustration in a textbook rose to supply the term. The chains looked thin, strands almost hair-fine twisted together in complex patterned knots, but I would have bet every credit I ever earned doing bounties and quite a few I never laid hands on they would have held just about anything down.

In the middle of the tangled mess of metal, a rectangle of darkness sat. I recognized it immediately.

It was the twin to Sephrimel's wooden box. Only this one looked oiled, well cared for, and was closed, with a dainty little silver padlock shaped like wings.

For now, simply take what is yours by right, Sephrimel whispered inside my head.

I reached out for it, stopped halfway. What about those chains? Who had they chained here?

Hedaira? Or demons?

"Dante?" Japhrimel, his voice falling oddly away. He didn't echo here like I did.

"There's chains." I couldn't get enough air in. "What were they for?"

"For a *hedaira*'s safety. Is it there?" Impatience snapped the end of each word off.

"There's a wooden box. It looks like —"

"Pick it up. For the sake of every god of your kind *and* mine, *hurry.*"

The premonition hit so hard my chin snapped aside, as if I'd been punched. If I could relax, it would swim up through dark water and swallow me, and I would see a bit of the future. Not much, never enough, but maybe something useful.

The trouble was, *relaxing* wasn't anywhere close to what I wanted to do. I stared at the box, my eyes unfocusing as the premonition circled, drew closer...and passed me by, close enough that I felt a brush like thousands of tiny feathers through the air around me.

"Dante." Japhrimel's tone brooked no disobedience. "Take it from the altar."

Just as I leaned forward to do so, another voice slid through the Temple's shocked quiet. It was clear, and low, and definitely a demon's.

"Yes. Take up the Knife, Dante Valentine. Let us see what you can cut with it."

CHAPTER 18

jerked around in a tight half circle, Fudoshin clearing the scabbard with a low rasp of oiled steel. Blue fire woke along its edge, runes from the Nine Canons twisting on its curve, the heart of the blade burning white. Rage woke in a blinding red spray and I took two steps, my body coiling, compressing elastic demon muscle preparatory to explosive action.

The breath left me in a sharp sigh. I stopped, my rings spitting a cascade of golden sparks—no spells left in them, just pure Power accumulating in the sensitized stones and metal.

Eve stepped out of the shadows of wreckage at the far left side of the altar, her pale hair catching fire and lifting a little, framing her sweet face. She was beautiful in the way only demons can be, wearing her exotic golden skin like a silk glove, her wide dark-blue eyes—*Doreen's* eyes—meeting mine with the force of a hover collision. Above and between those eyes, an emerald glowed, set into the smoothness of her forehead. Just like Lucifer's.

I flinched at the thought.

She had Doreen's triangular face, Doreen's mouth, and a wary little half-smile that was all mine, under the supple carapace of demon beauty.

On Lucifer, beauty looked deadly. On Japh it was purely functional. On Eve, it was...magick. And under it, I saw the shadow of the child I had rescued from Santino's lair, the child Lucifer had taken as I watched helplessly under the bright hammerblow of Nuevo Rio sunlight.

The only child I might ever have.

Behind her, resolving around a pair of bright blue gasflame eyes, was Velokel the Hunter, broad and powerful as a bull, his large square teeth closed away behind lips that thinned as they took me in.

I twitched. But Eve's eyes met mine, and she smiled. It was a genuine smile, not the little half-grimace we shared, the armored expression I faced the world with. "You've come so very far." Her voice was soft and restful, and the smell of her—bread baking and demon musk, a powerfully comforting scent—boiled out from behind a screen of dust and age.

"How..." I had to clear my throat. "How did you get here?"

"Kel has tracked more tricksome beasts than the Anhelikos, Dante. It was not quite child's play to follow the Knife, but it was close—and still, so much depends on you." Her smile widened. "Now here we are, and we have little time. Stay where you are, Kinslayer."

Japhrimel halted midway across the sea of dust. Both his guns were trained on Eve. "If you touch her—"

Eve shrugged. She wore black, a merino sweater and loose elegant slacks, a pair of what looked like handmade Taliano boots. Kel made do with buff-colored canvas slacks and a blouse under a leather doublet, something like a Renascence illustration of a woodsman, complete with a pouch and a curved horn hanging from his broad leather belt.

They called Velokel *the Hunter,* and I wondered if he'd seen this city before. When he was hunting *hedaira.*

That's exactly the least comforting thought in the world.

"There is no need for threats, Eldest." Eve took a step toward me, measured Japhrimel with a single glance, and took another. "We are not at cross-purposes here."

There were two slight clicks—Japh, pulling the hammers back on both silver guns. It was an absurd bit of theater, since I wasn't sure what they fired, but it was at least effective. The city screeched again as it wobbled in its setting, but his voice sliced through the low basso grumbling. "I will not serve *you.*"

"I have not asked for your service." Eve's voice, soft and restful, stroked the air. I stared at her face, transfixed. She looked so much like Doreen. "I have offered myself to my mother." Her smile was wide, white, and so forgiving I could have bathed in it.

My mother. She said it like it meant nothing, like she was talking about the weather. My heart leapt inside its cage of ribs, pounding high and hard until it settled in my throat. A worm of unease turned inside my battered brain.

Danny, something's very wrong here. Grab the box and let's go.

I hesitated, my sword dipping just a little. If Japhrimel moved on Eve, I would have to try to protect her. He was too damnably quick, and I was tired, starving, my head full of broken connections and even my shields incapable of protecting me from a direct hit. Maybe I could slow him down enough for her to escape.

Why was she here? I was supposed to meet her in Hegemony Franje, in Paradisse. Uneasiness bloomed into full-blown suspicion. What game was being played now?

I didn't care. She was safe, Lucifer hadn't caught her yet. Relief scored through my chest. At least I hadn't betrayed her. I'd taken the worst the Devil had to dish out, but she was safe.

Thank you, gods. If there are still gods who want to hear my prayers. Thank you.

"What nonsense you speak, even for one so young," Japhrimel replied. "Stay *back*. Dante, move away."

It wasn't a request. It was an order. I swallowed, my dry throat clicking in the charged silence. Fury turned sharp and cold in my veins, rising with the low keening of a swordblade cleaving air. "No."

I didn't have a free hand to pick the box up with. My eyes flicked to Velokel. His lip lifted as he caught me looking at him. He wasn't as powerful as Japhrimel; I could calculate him down to the last erg of energy.

I was getting good at doing that to demons. They could all kick *my* ass, but Japh was another thing entirely. Still, Kel might be able to buy Eve enough time to escape if my Fallen moved on her. Which left me with getting the other half of the Knife and helping hold Japh, if I could.

Once I had the whole Knife I had a chance. If it could injure *any* demon…

I felt sick at even thinking it. I didn't want to hear its disgusting little gulping noise ever again. And how could I even think of using the thing on Japh, now that I'd seen what it could do?

Eve. Think about her. You promised you'd save her, you couldn't before and Lucifer took her. Now you have a second chance. You'd better use it, Dante.

It took every scrap of courage I possessed to slide my sword back into its sheath and clutch it tight, a practiced, almost-silent movement I didn't need my eyes for. I edged back two steps, put down my other hand, and touched the altar.

The stone was warm, resonating under my fingertips like a plucked string. I snatched my hand back, and found all three pairs of demon eyes on me.

The city held its breath. Its low thrum of grief and agonized shuddering stilled. The dust around Japhrimel's boots stirred, little vortices rising as if tiny dancing feet dimpled its top layers.

"We should go." Velokel's voice, low and full of restrained thunder, broke the hush. I caught a breath of his scent—musk and torn-open oranges, demon spice and blood.

I felt behind me to my right again, searching for the box without touching the altar's stone. *Please. Sekhmet sa'es, please. This is beginning to get ridiculous.* My emerald spat a green spark, my accreditation tat running under my skin with sharp little insectile feet.

Eve folded her arms. Her emerald shot a dart of bright green, and looking at it made me feel sick all over again. "The next move is yours, Dante. When you take up the Knife, you will become the Key to the throne of Hell. *He* will have to come to terms with you, and so will the Eldest."

I'm the Key. Great. That makes so much sense now. Thanks for telling me. "When did you guess it was me?" *And why didn't you say something before?* I kept feeling for the box. *She doesn't know the Knife is in pieces. So maybe Lucifer doesn't know either. That's either very good or very bad, depending.*

"Your coming was foretold." She indicated the altar with a sketch of a polite gesture, stopping when Japhrimel moved forward another two steps, his boots suddenly making soft shushing sounds in the dust.

"Nice of someone to tell me." My questing fingers touched oiled wood. I hooked them down and pulled the box toward me, cautiously. My hip brushed the altar.

A thrill like fire shot through my bones, blooming from my hip like an unfolding flower. The altar let out a piercing note, like plas-glass right before a harmonic shatters it. I scooped up the box and whirled, faced now with carrying it and getting the hell out of here somehow.

Japhrimel stood, his guns vanished. I blinked. The long slim iron cylinder McKinley had given him was in his narrow golden hands, and his attention was fixed on Eve. I snapped a glance in her direction, but she'd already seen my eyes widen, and her gaze flicked to my Fallen, the color draining from her face, leaving an unhealthy pallor under the even goldenness.

"No—" she began, panic roiling under the smoothness of her voice, cutting the city's expectant silence like a lasedrill. *"No!"*

"Veritas in omni re." Japhrimel pronounced each syllable distinctly, his fingers curving over the iron box's lid. "Now we shall see your true face."

What the bloody blue hell? "Japhrimel—" I didn't have any idea what I was going to say to stop him.

He tore the lid off, tossing the contents of the cylinder from him with a convulsive movement. It *roared,* shattering the stillness, and my body reacted without thought, crouching and bringing the box to my chest, almost braining myself with my swordhilt in the process. It was a good thing, too, or I might have been knocked across the altar instead of into it.

The entire city woke in a cacophony so immense it was almost soundless, felt in the bones instead of heard, and hot blood gushed painlessly from my nose, rivulets of warmth sliding down my neck from my violated ears. I must have screamed, because my mouth was open, and I damn near dropped my sword.

Combat instinct pitched me to the side, rolling, and I bumped down the stairs in a flurry of arms and legs, gaining my balance in a crouch at their foot. I lurched to my feet unsteadily, just before Japh collided with me, rib-snapping force pulled just at the last second, and both of us went sprawling as a flare of black-diamond Power tore the air apart and left it bleeding.

Eve! I was struggling against Japh's hands almost before we landed, a chance twist of my torso breaking me halfway free. He caught me again, fingers digging into my nape just as a mama cat will hold an unruly kitten, and somehow he was kneeling next to me, his fingers irresistible as he forced my head up.

Eve had gone down, but Velokel was still standing. The Hunter's flesh blackened, running on his bones as he screamed, the cry tearing more stone loose and kicking up great gouts of choking dust. His shape *changed,* like ink on wet paper, and horns lifted searing-black from his forehead, curling back around his ears. He was even more squat now, corded with muscle, his legs sprouting fur and ending in massive hooves that cracked the stone steps as he leapt back to avoid whatever Japh had thrown. It was a smear of hurtful golden brilliance, rolling like an apple, with odd bounces as it leapt up the stairs in merry defiance of physics.

Only Velokel's eyes were the same, bright blue above a blackened ruin of a face that mutated even as I watched. I had to gasp in a scorched breath, having wasted all my air screaming.

Eve leapt to her feet. Her shape was still the same, slender and female, but a shell of Power clung to her in tattered streamers, painting streaks of green on the air as her emerald spat spark after spark, each a point of hurtful brilliance. Her eyes lightened, a blue to match Velokel's, and her haggard face was no longer a copy of my dead lover's.

I stared. Japhrimel hauled me up as the massive sound drained away into the subsonic, and the ground underfoot began to vibrate like a freight hover's deck.

"—go!" Japhrimel shouted. But I couldn't tear my eyes away from Eve.

Her shape changed like clay under running water, shards of illusion plainly visible to OtherSight now that it was broken. It was a glamour, a sorcery meant to feed the eyes a lie.

She was beautiful, still, as only a demon could be. Her eyes were blue and her hair ran with snow-white flame. But there was no echo of Doreen in her face.

And no echo of me.

Then who the hell is she? It can't be, she has to be Doreen's, she has to be!

Japhrimel hauled me up, his fingers biting into my neck. My ears twinged with pain as they healed, twin nails driven into the sides of my head. The noise was still massive, but not enough to burst tender membranes. The wooden box almost squirted out from under my arm. I clutched at it, and my bag banged against my hip as Japh dragged me aside just in time, a chunk of stone nailing the floor right where we'd been standing. He whirled aside, yanking me into a lunatic spin like a dance move, ending with us both somehow facing the door. *"Run!"* he yelled through the noise.

I'd lost all my air again, screaming, adding my thin voice to the crashing and rending. *Think about it later. Now* run, *run like hell and hope you get out of this alive.*

I got my feet under me and pelted for the door, leaping a pile of rubble and almost slipping as I landed on unsteady ground, my unruly body once again going too fast for me. Disturbed dust rose choking-thick, and behind me, Velokel roared something in the demons' unlovely tongue that I didn't need a dictionary to translate. The other piercing cry was from the demon who had claimed to be Doreen's daughter, *my* daughter.

The demon I was going to kill Lucifer to defend.

Japh's fingers closed around my left arm instead of my nape. He pulled me aside, the doorway we'd entered through crumbling. Its massive marble slabs teetered and swung before crashing down. I flinched, and the entire city shuddered again, a gigantic cracking noise like the world's hugest egg broken against the side of a red-hot city-sized skillet echoing through both physical and psychic space.

What the goddamn motherfucking hell is going on?

We made it through one of the smaller doors just in time. The ground quaked, and I had nasty, uncomfortable ideas about what exactly *was* going on. If one of those bridges had failed and we were even now falling—

Then, between one moment and the next, it stopped. The sudden cessation of noise was shocking in and of itself, but even more shocking was Japhrimel skidding to a halt, his fingers turning to iron and digging in mercilessly. He plucked the wooden box from me as easily as taking candy from a child.

I'll admit it. I screamed again. I was doing a lot of that lately. A complicated flurry of motion, his fingers lacing with mine, ended with me shoved behind him just as the one voice I never wanted to hear again broke the newborn stillness with its awful dulcet music.

"This is unlike you, my Eldest."

My ribs flared with starved heaving breaths. I blinked at Japhrimel's back, one of his hands behind his back holding *my* right hand with bone-crunching force, his knuckles pale under their goldenness.

He inclined his head, and I sagged. This was it. It was over.

Because in front of us, his very presence staining the air with black fury, was the Prince of Hell. Again. My entire body turned into a bar of tension, Japh's fingers squeezing pitilessly at mine, small bones creaking. Pain bolted up my arm, exploded in my shoulder as I backpedaled, trying to rip my hand free and escape. The scar writhed madly against my skin, and my Fallen's aura clamped down over me like a frozen kerri jar over an unlucky silkworm.

I *knew* it was Lucifer. I didn't have to see him and I didn't want to. Japhrimel held me in place, my arm stretched awkwardly as I twisted, my boots scraping against stone.

Japhrimel laughed. It wasn't the gentle, almost-human sound of amusement I'd heard from him so many times, or even the slight ironic *hm* he gave when I beat him at battlechess or otherwise surprised him.

No, this was a swelling demonic laugh, a harsh caw marrying delight to disdain, with a generous helping of pure hatred. He laughed like murder in a cold alley at midnight.

The sudden idea that I could probably tear my own arm off and escape didn't sound as laughable as it might otherwise have. There was a black hole in my head, dilating with terrible force, and at any moment I would *remember*—

"And this is unlike you, *Prince*." Japhrimel's tone was terribly, utterly cold. I had never heard him speak so. "I thank you for your care of my *hedaira*. Your hospitality remains ever the same."

The silence changed, pressure shifting and sliding as I struggled to free myself from Japh's iron fingers. When Lucifer spoke again, the coldness in his voice matched my Fallen's, and everything inside my skull trembled on the edge of insanity.

"I used her as I saw fit. What else is a Right Hand for?"

"We are all toys for your pleasure, my Lord." Accusation boiled under the words. Japhrimel made a small movement, and something clattered. Wood, striking the ruined stone. In the terrible hush that small noise punctured my heart.

"Of course you are." The Devil didn't even give it a second thought.

Ogods Japh let go what are you doing let GO of me—I swayed. It hurt, Japh's hand grinding mine into powder. The pain was a silver spike nailing me to earth even as the hole in my head widened, my psyche cracking under the strain like microtears in silk hovernets.

"*That* is what the rebellion was after, Prince. You should take more care with such trinkets."

Anubis, someone, help me. I bent back, my entire body a stretched-taut bow of longing, aching for escape; I could leave the arm behind if I had to, I just wanted *away*.

I have never, before or since, understood so completely an animal's struggle to free itself from the trap that bleeds it.

Lucifer said nothing, but the pressure of his rage was a storm front moving in, an eyepopping strain. Even the icy heat of this place between earth and Hell felt warm and fuzzy by comparison. Japhrimel drew himself up. He was a good bit taller than me, but he seemed even bigger now, and I was suddenly deeply grateful he was between me and the Devil.

Shame boiled up hot and vicious under my breastbone. I'd always fought my own battles before, hadn't I?

Not against that. Not that again. I can't.

My aura trembled under Japhrimel's, on the verge of locking down hard and crystalline. If that happened, if I went nova, I'd implode right before I did something stupid. I would die.

But we'd see just what my half of the Knife would do to any demon in my way first.

I heard the Devil take in a long breath, as if he was about to speak. The air hissed past his teeth, and I felt those teeth in my own flesh again, tearing at whatever remained of my sanity. They speared deep as I screamed, the world turning into shutterclicks as my eyelids fluttered, and Japhrimel's fingers gave one last terrible squeeze, the scar on my shoulder burning, *burning*.

Whatever Lucifer would have said was lost in a blur of hoofbeats and a cry rising from a demon's throat.

I slammed back home in my body, my head whipping to the side just in time to see Velokel the Hunter pound out of the Temple and across the dead plaza. He stuttered through space with the eerie graceful quickness of demons, his aura blazing. Blue fire veined his hooves and crackled between the points of his horns, and as he ran time stopped, slowed, and crystallized into a lattice of action, reaction, and sudden explosive motion.

Japh *moved*.

Kel collided with Lucifer.

The shock of that impact would have knocked us both sprawling if Japh wasn't already down, his body folded over mine, my scream lost in the noise and his own tearing more blood from my ear as we tumbled, the world turning upside down and inside out. Streaks of rancid light tumbled past, and a warm wall of displaced air shoved us even further.

Crunch. Japh let out another short cry, a flying needle of debris stinging my cheek. The breath knocked out of me but I struggled up, my left hand still weighed down with my sword, singing a thin note of distress inside its sheath. Dust scorched the back of my throat, a fume like the kick of hoverscorch while slicboarding through fast traffic, and the most amazing thing happened.

I realized I'd survived seeing the Devil again.

So far.

Japhrimel gained his feet in a leap that might have surprised me once. His eyes blazed, casting shadows down his gaunt cheeks, and his hair was caked with dust. His mouth moved, but I couldn't hear whatever he might have said. I was deaf from the noise of the world ending. He grabbed my arm again, the prickle of his claws sinking in through tough fabric, and *pulled*.

I went willingly. He didn't bother to slow down, just dragged me over a pile of broken house-sized stones jittering in place like marbles tossed by an angry giant. It was a good thing, too, because the snarling mass that was two demons in combat hit the pile right behind us, stone grinding into powder and flying aside, another shockwave hitting me in the back with an impact so massive it was almost painless. Japh's boots touched down and he leapt, his wings coming free with a convulsive fluid tearing, and the world turned over again because he'd tossed me, my arm almost pulling free of the socket, tendons screaming savagely as they stretched and I had to gasp in air flavored with heat, dust, and the sweet rotten-fruit smell of demon blood.

I tumbled weightless for what seemed like eternity. He'd flung me free of the blast zone, just like tossing a gravball for the hoop. Awful nice of him.

This is going to hurt. Body twisting on instinct, my legs might shatter if I landed on them, there was not time to look for a landing no *time* and I hit, hard, shoulder driving into stone and my head hitting something that might have cracked it like a melon if the hard shell of Power over me hadn't deflected most of the force. It still rang my chimes pretty good. I blinked, laying dazed and pinned to the floor of a nightmare, before being jerked to my feet once more.

A new vibration poured through the overstressed fabric of reality. I reached up, trying to smear the blood out of my eyes, and my hand hit Japh's shoulder. He pulled me down a narrow alley floored with quaking white stones, earth shifting below our feet as the city moved again. Not like an animal turning over in its sleep—no, this time it shook itself like someone had just poked that animal with a big sharp stick.

Danny, how do you get yourself into these things?

Don't answer that, Jace's voice whispered in my ear. I was too busy to care, for once. **Just run. You're running for your life, sunshine.**

As if I didn't know.

The alley twisted like it wanted to throw us off its back. I caught flashes of gates made of sculpted rosy metal, crimson light gouting from stab wounds in the walls, courts behind screens of carved stone full of blasted trees slowly turning to dust.

The dead tree gave no shelter. Panicked hilarity ran through my head in time with our blurring footsteps. *And no bird sang.*

I still could not stop screaming, though I needed all my air. My lips moved, soundless because I was still temporarily deafened. Light ran and blurred because my eyes watered, trying to cope with the caustic dust blowing everywhere.

Japhrimel dragged me aside, and we ran down a long avenue receding into infinity, rows of fantastical statues marching down either side. The shapes were hybrid—cats with wings, serpents with paws and manes—and each one was faceless, the features clawed off. It was like running in a bad dream, feeling the monster's hot breath on your back, the air turning to quicksand.

One of the statues uncoiled, streaking across the avenue and leaping for us. It was a long black sinuous shape, its eyes glowing green, and I was still screaming breathlessly when Japhrimel struck the hellhound down, the heat of its obsidian hide exploding around us. He shot it twice without breaking stride, shouting something sharp and heated in the demons' unlovely language, and runnels of decay poured through its body before it finished its leap. He yanked me past so quickly my head snapped back, and the bloody dust-choke light filled my streaming eyes.

We burst out onto the fringes of a long field of dry black crumbling dirt, and my hearing began to come back. Echoes ran and dripped like water, running feet, screeches, howls, and the great glassy snarls of more hellhounds. There was a streak of flame lifting to our right—one of the bridges, twisting like taffy and bouncing in ways nothing that looked so fragile should.

I stumbled and might have sprawled headlong if Japh hadn't given my arm another terrific yank, and my shoulder gave way with a crunch of agony. The field flashed underfoot and I let out a small hurt cry. My lungs burned, a live nuclear core dropped into my stomach, my dislocated shoulder crunching with furious agony each time Japh pulled, and he ran right off the edge of the world, carrying me with him. We fell, and the last thing I heard before a brief moment of merciful unconsciousness was the liquid sound his wings made as he spread them, his fingers slipping through mine as my abused shoulder suddenly gave way again. I fell free, cartwheeling through space, and a brief starry moment of darkness flashed over my eyes.

CHAPTER 19

He was cursing. At least, it sounded like cursing, between steady thudding sounds, like a heartbeat. Gravity returned, and with it, the live fire in my shoulder.

I opened my eyes.

For a moment I thought I was flying. The vast cavern wheeled away underneath me, lit with bloody light.

Then there was a bump, fiery pain spilling through several parts of my body, and I saw with a great scalding wash of relief that my numb left hand was locked around Fudoshin. My right arm flopped uselessly, and I swallowed something hot and acidic as I jolted again, staring down past my dangling sword into a sea of waxy, directionless crimson.

The cavern went down for what looked like *miles*. But rising up underneath us was a thin thread of shadow. We hit the bridge hard and almost tumbled off, Japhrimel making a low sound of lung-tearing effort, and I found myself clinging to him, one of his hands tangled in my rig, my messenger bag's strap cutting into my shoulder, caught in his claws. His other hand flashed down, driving a silver-bladed knife — one of the short, slightly curved blades he sometimes used for sparring — into the bridge's surface. The sudden deceleration brought up a painless retch, and I started to feel a little pale. My legs hung out into space, the hard stony edge of the bridge right at my hips, and I would have thrashed if I could have moved, trying to get back up onto solidity.

Japh's eyes closed. His lips moved, still shaping words in his native tongue that hurt to hear. If I'd had a free hand I would have tried to stop my ringing, aching ears so I didn't have to hear that language spoken again.

He *pulled*, my dead weight sliding back from the abyss.

How the hell did he do that? We ran off the edge.

We lay there for a moment, tangled together, and I was mildly surprised to find myself still alive. Heart beating. Lungs mostly working. All original appendages mostly still there.

Hallelujah. I'd've shared my joy, but I was still shuddering with great gouts of unholy, uncontrollable panic. *I've gone mad. Wonderful. Marvelous. Great.*

The most horrible thing was that it didn't feel abnormal anymore. Insanity seemed the order of the day.

The bridge flexed underneath us. Japhrimel's eyes snapped open, their greenness a sudden relief in all that red. He pulled me into his chest, his other hand still on the knife, driven hilt-deep into stone. His lips pressed my forehead, once, so hard I felt the shape of his teeth behind them.

I'm happy we're alive too. Now can we go home and forget about all this?

His ribs heaved. He was gasping for air, too. I suddenly didn't feel too happy about that. *Get up, we have to get up. Come on, sunshine. Move your ass.*

I twitched.

He seemed to understand, because his entire body tensed and he rolled to his feet. I struggled up to my knees, my dislocated arm flapping bonelessly, and he pulled on my rig. I barely managed, even with that help, and when I was finally set on my boots, I leaned against him, burying my face in his coat.

My ears buzzed. I realized it wasn't because I was deaf. It was an actual sound. The bridge flexed again, and if Japh hadn't moved we would have been pitched overboard.

"Can you walk?" He didn't quite shout, but his voice cut through the chaos. I heard hellhound snarls, their low coughing roars, and shuddered. Kel had sent hellhounds to chase me, and so had Lucifer. Maybe they were busy fighting each other now, and they would forget all about me.

Yeah. And wild hoverbunnies will fly out your ass. Get moving!

I tilted my head back. Tilted my chin back down to approximate a nod.

He wasted no more time, but set off down the snaking gallop of the bridge. It was hard going, trying to negotiate a road that either dropped out from under us or slammed up to shake us off with no discernable rhyme or reason. My head dropped forward, chin resting almost on my chest, and I concentrated on one foot in front of the other.

Lucifer. That was Lucifer back there.

I *should* have been screaming in utter panic. Instead, I felt only weary amazement to still be actually breathing, however short the time remaining for that miracle was.

Go figure. I must be stronger than I thought. Then I wondered if that would be a challenge to the gods to prove it.

When we finally reached a broad shelf of rock anchored to the cavern wall, the sudden cessation of movement was shocking. Just as my feet landed on relatively solid ground, there was a cry unlike any of the previous hellish noise. It was a high keening ending on a throat-cut gurgle, and ice filled my veins.

That sounds like someone's dead. I hope it's him. If there's any justice in the world—

"Not much time." Japhrimel pulled me into his side. "Only a little farther, *hedaira*. Stay with me."

Not going anywhere. Sticking like glue. I wanted to nod, to tell him so, to make some sort of response. All that came out was a half-choked garble cut short by a longing gasp for air that wasn't full of dust. I sounded like I'd lost my mind.

Maybe I have. I hope I have. This would be so much easier to handle if I did.

"Not so far," he whispered. "Just stay with me, beloved. Only a little farther, I swear. I have not brought you this far to lose you now."

I would like to say I remember how we got out of the cavern, but I don't. Patches of darkness and the immense shock of the cold, the mark on my shoulder sending pulses of warm oil down my skin that couldn't touch the frozen inner core of me. I do remember the hover looming up out of the crystalline air and thinking, *How did he manage to get us back here?* I remember snow drifting up against the leafsprings holding the landing legs, icicles blooming on the moorings. The stairs were too much for me; Japh had to drag me up one by one, and he pushed me through the seals and into the blessed smells of humanity, oil, metal, and hover. I fetched up against a stack of ammo crates, my skin twitching with exhaustion and my dislocated shoulder settling into a deep unhappy throb.

I do not ever want to do that again.

The cargo hatch closed. A faint whine filled the stillness. I knew that sound, and it filled me with fuzzy alarm.

I looked up.

Leander Beaudry stood in the low orange glow of orandflu strips, the plasrifle socked to his shoulder and pointed right at me. A little in front of him and out of his fire angle stood a tall, slim demon with ice for hair and burning blue eyes.

The demon I'd known as Eve was still smiling, a rather gentle, childlike expression.

Japhrimel stood by the hatch control, dust ground into his hair and his eyes volcanoes of green. Metal popped and pinged, responding to the sudden flush of heat as his aura flared.

"Your agents have been overpowered, and the Prince will not long be delayed." The Androgyne's voice stroked soothingly, calming. The emerald in her forehead glowed, casting triangular shadows under her pretty, inhuman eyes. "I think it best we parley quickly, Eldest."

CHAPTER 20

Japhrimel stared at her for a few long seconds, as if a new and interesting insect had crawled out of the drain. The laserifle whined, unholstered and primed. Even if Japh went for Leander, he'd still have to deal with Eve, or whoever the hell she was. Demons couldn't outrun a plasbolt.

I sure as hell didn't feel up to outrunning one either. The laserifle was pointed right at me, and I wasn't sure what a plasbolt would do to me if it was set to kill instead of stun.

I was Japhrimel's weak point. If I ended up dead, would he turn into another Sephrimel, bleeding away through centuries and obsessively recreating me in whatever he could get his hands on? Which brought up an interesting, chilling little question—just how would he go crazy? Did he ever think about it while I was sleeping? When he looked at me?

How did it make him feel?

I found my voice. Amazingly, I even sounded halfway coherent. "Beaudry. What the *fuck?*"

"Sorry, Valentine." Even, neutral, his dark eyes never leaving my chest. If I twitched, he'd put a bolt through me. His accreditation tat twitched on his left cheek. "I've got orders."

You bastard. Laying on the "I'm so scared" act. And I fell for it, just like a green kid. Loathing coated my tongue. "Working for demons now?"

He didn't shrug, but the way his eyebrow lifted was just as

eloquent. "Hegemony federal, actually. Field agent. Running across you in New Prague sure made my life interesting."

"Charming." The blue-eyed demon's tone shouted she found our chattering anything but. "I am ready to bargain, Eldest. Or we can let *him* find us here."

"Speak." Japhrimel's lips barely moved. The single word coated the air with ice, made it tremble. I slumped against the ammo crates, trying hard to come up with something brilliant.

Nothing happened.

The blue-eyed Androgyne folded her arms. "Where is the Knife?"

He threw the other half at Lucifer. We're fucked. I kept my mouth shut. So did Japhrimel.

"Come now. I saw you. You would not have handed over the one weapon that could set you free of his games so easily. Ergo, there is something amiss." One ice-pale eyebrow lifted, and the grin she wore turned wolfish, a trick of a few centimeters changing in the landscape of her face. I couldn't stop staring, searching for echoes of Doreen, of the child Lucifer had taken so long ago.

It has to be Eve. It has to be. She just looks different because of whatever Japh threw at her.

Japhrimel's eyes flicked to me, his attention never wavering. "It is elsewhere. The box was a decoy. I did not think it wise to trust such a weapon to the Anhelikos."

What? "What?" I wanted to screech the word, but the only thing that came out was a pale whisper. "What did you say?"

"The box on the altar was one of three decoys. Meant to force both the rebellion and the Prince to show their hands."

Disbelief curdled in my throat, but I spit it up anyway. "A *decoy?* You... we... *I* ..." *You mean I went through all that for a* decoy? I leaned against the crates, my right shoulder burning with deep drilling pain as it twitched. I hoped it was healing.

"The moment the Prince opens the box, he will know I am playing a new game. He may know now. When he does, he will be angry." He acknowledged the understatement with a slight lift of one eyebrow. "But it will also alter the playing field. He cannot afford to let me reach the Knife, but he also cannot afford to strike me down without knowing where it rests and holding it in his hands, to assure himself he is safe. This one—" His tone changed as he regarded Eve, or not-Eve, or whoever the hell she was, "he will slay on sight."

The demon shrugged. "I am his favored one, and the thing he longs to possess. He has sought to capture me, because he will not let me die unbroken."

"He may change his mind," Japhrimel observed.

I sagged against the crates. I was so tired. Even my hair hurt. Even my *teeth* ached, and burning dust still scorched my throat and lungs. *Let's just go. Can we just please leave?* The thought of Lucifer maybe still alive back in that city full of red light, smashed things, and Hell's cold fire was enough to make the black hole inside my head shiver like a cat shaking off unwelcome rain. The pain of my dislocated shoulder was beginning to seem very far away, and that was a bad sign.

"Such pretty things." The blue-eyed demon didn't look away from Japhrimel, and her stance was just a little bit too tense. "They are so very fragile. How is her health, Eldest?"

I'd be a lot better if people would stop dragging me around. Oh, and if demons would stop trying to kill me. I'd have a much *better time. It would be a vacation.*

"How does Velokel the Hunter fare, Androgyne?" Japh flung it at her like a challenge.

"Sometimes a piece must be sacrificed. You have played such games."

"I hate to interrupt," Leander cut in, "but we're exposed here. If there's a pissed-off demon heading this way, we'd best conclude our business quickly."

"Cease your yapping, little human." Japh's tone could not have held more contempt.

Where's Lucas? And the agents? Not to mention the goddamn Nichtvren. "Japh?" My scabbard rattled against the ammo crates as I shifted. "He's right. We should get the fuck out of here."

"I am waiting to hear something of consequence." His eyes glowed, and one corner of his mouth curled up, slowly, dangerously. "I will not wait much longer."

"The Prince wants me." The blue-eyed demon's expression matched his, an eerily perfect mimicry. "I have become the bait that will lead him to the killing field. You are the hand that will strike. And *she* is the Key. We should not linger here."

That's three votes for getting the fuck out of here now. I consider the motion carried. "Japh." My knees almost gave way. I propped myself against the crates. Prickles raced up my arms, the cold in my bones spreading out. Soon I would be made of ice. It seemed a wonderful thing. "We need to go now."

"Very soon, beloved." How could he sound so coldly murderous one moment, and so tender the next? I blinked, trying to figure it out, and the scar on my shoulder sent a hot torrent of Power through me, driving back the cold.

Still, even pure Power wasn't enough. I was too tired, too hurt, and the broken places in my head were too raw. I'd seen Lucifer again. Well, not *seen* him, because Japh had kept himself between us. But I had heard the bastard's voice again. I had survived.

I heard a noise that didn't belong. A slight, definite click. I froze.

Everything happened at once. The hover woke into humming life, acceleration pressing down on everything in the hold as Japhrimel *moved*. He did not so much blink through space as reappear, knocking aside the other demon's hands as she spat at him, his fingers sinking into her throat. The laserifle crackled, and McKinley's arm was across Leander's throat, dragging him backward. The Hellesvront agent's black hair was wildly mussed, his clothing singed and torn, and his aura flared with violet light that fumed like homicidal rage.

I spilled over, my muscles suddenly unable to cope with the task of keeping me upright. My sword clattered against the metal grating, my bag clinking and clacking as I curled over it, my wounded right arm twisting uselessly.

Chaos. My eyelids were terrifically heavy. As soon as I got one to peel up a little bit the other one would fall down.

Japhrimel? Will you please explain what's going on?

I got no answer, just the feeling of gravity pressing along my body as the hover pressed up, my consciousness lifting away, disconnected. Gone.

CHAPTER 21

There was a sickening crunch, and I let out a short, half-chopped yell. My eyes flew open, and Japhrimel caught my fist, the punch stopped as if by a brick wall. My right shoulder was back in its socket, throbbing with a high note of yellow pain before another warm bath of Power slid down my weary flesh.

He slid his arm under my shoulders and lifted me just a bit, held something to my lips. "Drink."

It was a sign of how confused and miserably tired I was that I didn't even think to question it. I simply filled my mouth with whatever was in the cup and swallowed. It was warm, thick, and gelid, and the spice of it coated the back of my throat, touching off a chain of memory like flashbulbs inside my aching head.

For a moment I thought I was back in Nuevo Rio, golden sunlight striping the bed as a demon held me in his arms, Power burning inside the channels of my bones just as his blood burned in my throat, reshaping me from the inside out while barb-wire pleasure slammed through each changing atom of my flesh. Since I'd awakened with a new body and a seriously screwed-up life, he had been the only constant.

Even dead and ground to cinnamon dust in a black lacquer urn, he had been my guiding star. The taste of his blood in my mouth brought it all back, memory strong as a lasecannon ricocheting through my aching head.

I gagged, but it was already down. *"Avayin, hedaira,"* he murmured. "Peace. All is well."

The lunacy of his assurance hit me sideways, and I almost choked again. He tipped the cup, and I had to swallow. I took it down in three long gulps. Japhrimel made a small sound of approval and set the cup aside. He sat next to me on the bed, his solidity comforting. His eyes were still glowing green, casting small shadows under his high gaunt cheekbones. He didn't look half-starved anymore, but he didn't look happy. The dust was still in his hair, stiffening the silk of it. A smear of something dark traced one high cheekbone, his mouth was set and thin. Still, I felt ridiculously relieved to see him. The relief was as deep and unquestioning as my trust in whatever he wanted to make me drink.

I was spending a distressing amount of time knocked-out lately. Did half-demons get brain trauma?

Would I live long enough to find out?

Warmth exploded in the pit of my stomach, a comfortably full feeling as if I'd just eaten my way through one of our old Taliano meals. I was able to sit up, finding myself still fully clothed. I was probably still able to wear my clothes again, despite them being dusty and dirty. At least they weren't torn to shreds and soaked with blood.

Not much blood, anyway.

My right shoulder throbbed before the pain vanished. The only question I could ask, the one I'd been trying to ask all along, bubbled up. "Eve?"

He was quiet for a long few moments as the hover began a long slow descent. "That is not her Name."

I don't care. "But she...is she Doreen's? *Is* she?" *I have to know. I don't care about anything else.*

"She is Vardimal's Androgyne." The words were heavy. "You do not understand."

I wanted to set my jaw and shove down the sudden flare of anger. It flared anyway, the shout bursting past my lips. "Whose fault is it if I don't understand? You won't *tell* me anything!"

He actually flinched. I don't blame him. My voice rattled everything not bolted down and the hover shook like a nervous cat. The injustice boiled over, and I lashed out at the closest thing, the thing I could be sure of providing a good target.

"You keep lying to me! All of it, *lies!* You won't tell me what I am, you won't tell me what's going on, you just keep lying, lying, *lying!*"

"Yes." His voice sliced through mine.

Whatever I'd expected, it hadn't been simple agreement. It managed to shut me up so he could get a word in edgewise.

His eyes slid away from me, stared across the small cabin. Outside the porthole, faint dappled gray danced—clouds. Wherever we were, it was now cloudy, and still night. "I will lie to keep you safe. I will lie to save you pain. I will lie to ease your mind, and I will lie so you may be certain of me. Answer me this, my curious—if I, even *I* will lie to you, what might another demon who does not cherish you do?"

I think I have an idea. More than an idea, in fact. My new rig lay tangled at the end of the bed. My sword was propped against the nightstand, but Japhrimel was between me and its comforting slender length.

"Is she still alive?" The last thing I remembered was Japh's fingers in its throat. *Her* throat. Which was the true face—the echo of Doreen with my faint iron-clad smile, or the demon with her clotted-ice hair and blue, blue eyes? I wanted, *needed* to know.

"She is more useful to us alive. She is chained, and watched. The human is also alive, a gift for my *hedaira.* Does that please you?"

I'm all aglow, Japh. Why, that's just marvy. Sarcasm smoked inside my head and I restrained myself with an effort that left me shaking, my hands clasping together and biting down. "What did you do?" I barely recognized the raw, shocked whisper as my own.

"What have I not done? I set my trap and baited it, I played the Prince of Hell for a fool and lured him into showing his hand too soon. Today I have cost him a great deal, in pride, in Power, and in peace. The knowledge that he no longer has possession of the one weapon that could kill him has reached Hell, for I made certain of it when I invited him to meet me in the White-Walled City."

"You did *what?*" Open-mouthed shock was apparently the order of the day. The hover's nose tilted down a little more sharply. We were descending, and quickly.

"One of the Prince's marks of favor for his assassin was a certain item. When used, it strips the disguise from a demon, forcing him to take his true form. We are a tricksome species, and sometimes the veil of seeming must be torn. We have different weaknesses. If you know the form of a demon, you may fight him." A single, elegant shrug. "Using the Glaive, unfortunately, creates a disturbance that can be felt in Hell, especially in a place where the walls between our world and yours are so thin. All of Hell knows the Glaive was triggered in the city. The Prince could not afford to stay away, as that is the agreed-upon resting place for one of the decoys."

"Decoys." *Keep talking, Japh. This is the most you've ever given me, and what do you know? It's too goddamn late.* I was ashamed as soon as I thought it.

He rose like a dark wave, the mattress creaking slightly as he did. I tasted dust and bitterness, added to the thick spice of his blood. The room was narrow and curved, squeezed under the hull and bare of anything that might be considered a personal possession—that is, if I didn't count my new rig. My sword. And my bag, now suddenly visible on a table bolted to the wall near the porthole.

Japhrimel crossed to the porthole and looked out. His back was perfectly straight, his shoulders drawn up. Dust streaked along the curves of his coat, revealing subtle dips and creases of musculature hidden in the liquid black. "You must understand, Dante. I have served the Prince for so long. Obedience became its own kind of trap, and I buried the rebellion in my heart. I was not free to act until *you* freed me. But still...I had dreams."

"Dreams?" I didn't mean to sound like an idiot. I just couldn't seem to say anything applicable or even intelligent.

"The Prince was younger then, too; I was able to hide the fact that I had only recovered *half* the Knife. He told me what he wished—that the Anhelikos would hold the Knife, for they care little who rules Hell as long as their nests are not tampered with. That if a demon without the proper signs and signals came to fetch it, they would send it along a route known only to Lucifer and myself, each Anhelikos theoretically knowing only the next stage of the route. I was to create two decoy routes as well. It was my only disobedience in longer than you can imagine, to make all three routes empty games and hide the half of the Knife we possessed...elsewhere. Even today I do not know why I did so."

"So you.... Is that why you helped Santino escape Hell, with the Egg? Because you were being disobedient?" *Don't interrupt him, Danny. Maybe he'll keep talking.*

"No. I was ordered to do so, by Lucifer himself." Each word was clipped and short. "I bless the day he did, Dante. It brought me to you." He turned away from the window, approached the table with two long steps, and opened my stained canvas messenger bag. The tough cloth made a whispering sound against his fingers.

I scrambled up out of bed, my legs finally obeying me, a hot knot of liquid warmth behind my breastbone. "Leave that alone!"

It was too late. He held up the book, its cover with leather too fine-grained to be animal skin shocking against the goldenness of his fingers. "What price did you pay for this, *hedaira?* What lies came with its presentation to you? I did not tell you of the *A'nankhimel* and their doom for a *reason*. To know that you would be hunted, sooner or later, reviled, suffering endless fear because of a crime you were innocent of—I tried to save you that! I have *tried* to save you from the knowledge of what you have been drawn into, what has been done to you. You hate me, and well you should."

I came to a halt less than five steps away from him, my hands curled into fists and shaking. "You should have told me." Quiet venom dripped from each word. "I don't care what you thought you were saving me from."

"Told you what? How could I have explained what I feared, to you? How could I burden you with *this?*" He tossed the book at me. It was a passionlessly accurate throw, and it landed on my feet with a tiny thud before it slid off to the side, spine-up and open, its pages pressed into the flooring.

We faced each other over a small space of crackling, pulled-tense air. I struggled to contain the rising tide of anguish and red fire inside me.

"Look at what I have done to you." It was his turn to whisper. "No wonder you hate me."

Sheer maddening frustration rivaled the bitterness of dust in my mouth. "I don't hate you." The words felt foreign against my lips. "I can't hate you. That's my goddamn problem." *Or at least one of them. I've got so many others now this one seems like a walk in the holopark.*

It was hard work to bend down, keeping my eyes on him, and pick the book up. The feel of the cover against my fingers was enough to make my gorge rise. I was getting so used to nauseated disgust, I wondered if I'd ever eat again. "Nobody gave me any information with this at all. Selene only knew it was a book on the Fallen. Eve never told me what was in it. Sephrimel showed me *one* picture and...gods, Japhrimel, if you're so fucking worried what I'll think of it, why didn't you just tell me yourself? I could have tried understanding, you know."

He actually *shrugged,* a complex eloquent movement. I *hate* demons shrugging at me. They do it so much, like the only thing humans are worthy of is a shrug. Or maybe we perplex them. I'd like to think it's the latter.

Call me an optimist.

"Fine." I gave up. My shoulders slumped. I was too tired to fight with him over this. I had other questions, other problems, and other things I needed to figure out before Lucifer got another crack at me. "Let's move on to something productive, at least. Where's the Knife?"

"Close." Silence stretched like taffy. "I have some other things to tell you, but not yet."

Great. More secrets. "I don't want to hear it." My fingers tensed, pressing into the leather. I struggled with the beast of pain tearing inside my chest. Tearing like glass-clawed fingers around my beating heart.

It took every scrap of self-control I possessed to hold the book out to him. "If it means that much to you, you can have it, and all your goddamn secrets too."

The hover evened out. We'd descended a long way. He didn't move, staring at my hand holding the book the way a mongoose stares at a cobra.

"Just take it," I persisted. "Just fucking take the thing, Japhrimel."

He slid it from my hand gently, as if afraid I'd change my mind. The hover bounced a bit, atmospheric pressure rippling around it. His hand fell back to his side, carrying its cargo. Whatever the goddamn book said, I no longer wanted to know. He couldn't tell me what I was.

Nobody could.

I was broken, I knew that much. I was a wreck in the shape of a woman, and I had something to get done. But most importantly, I was who I decided to be. Hadn't my life taught me at least that much?

I am Danny Valentine. Everything else was just noise.

"Now." I drew myself up in my dusty, bloodspotted clothes. "You're going to answer a couple questions, and then we're going to get this goddamn thing done. I'm tired of Lucifer fucking around with my life. Fucking around with *me*." *You can't even comprehend how tired I am of that.* The black hole in my head shivered and retreated under the sound of rushing flame. I pushed both things away, bottled the rage and covered over the horror. "Where's Eve?" I almost said, *where's my daughter?*

I couldn't let the words past my lips. I was keeping my own secrets from him. I couldn't throw any stones on that account, could I.

But oh, how I wanted to.

He actually answered me directly, for once. "Chained, and watched. In the hold."

"Great." I turned on my booted heel and stalked back to the bed, scooped up my rig, and began buckling it on. "Where are we flying to now?"

"Sudro Merica. Caracaz." In Japhrimel's voice was something new — a hoarseness, as if there was something in his throat.

The rig was none the worse for wear, and it creaked much less than it had. I guess that kind of hard use will take the starch out of any gear. It was all to the good as far as I was concerned.

I scooped up my sword. The sound of fire in my head abated, a thin red thread at the bottom of my consciousness. Waiting.

What do we do next, sunshine?

"All right." I rolled my shoulders habitually, settling the rig. "Let's get this run started."

I left him standing there and stamped for the door.

CHAPTER 22

I was getting pretty sick of the cargo hold.

McKinley leaned against a stack of plasteel crates, his aura flushed a weird violet, matching the purplish light running over his metallic left hand. My eyes wanted to slide right over him, helped by the smooth shell of *seeming* that wasn't quite a glamour, since it didn't carry any stamp of personality like sorcery or psionic camouflage would. He was like a chameleon, blending motionlessly into his surroundings. His dark eyes met mine and flicked away, and I recognized the hair-trigger tension in him.

Past him, in a space cleared of all gear and boxes, sat a small, slender shape with a flame of pale hair. Her arms locked around her knees, and it became apparent she'd had a hell of a fight. Her sweater was torn, her slacks singed, and she was missing a boot.

I stepped forward. Eve's face was buried in her knees, that pale sleek cap now subtly wrong, ropes instead of the silk of Doreen's hair. I couldn't even *smell* her, and that was wrong too.

"Valentine." McKinley's voice, oddly respectful. "Don't get too close."

Don't tell me what to do. I took another step. I'd shoved my sword into the loop provided on my rig, not trusting myself with edged metal right now. "Eve." All the things I might have said boiled through my head, and I settled for just one. "I know you're not asleep."

Her face came up slowly, a pale dish on jeweled bearings. Doreen's daughter looked at me, and there was nothing human in that blue-fire gaze.

My eyesight was keen even before Japh changed me; thanks to genesplicing it's hard to find anyone with bad sight anymore, except Ludders. I can't see like a Nichtvren, in total darkness—even demon eyes need a few photons to work with. So I stared at Eve, searching the demon's face for any shadow of what she'd looked like before.

Running along the floor between us was a thin silver strip, humming with malignant force as it circled her. It matched the brutally thick cuffs around her ankles and wrists. The silver seemed a part of the metal grating, despite its fluid movement. It was a piece of demon sorcery I'd never seen before and should have been surprised at.

Nothing seemed surprising anymore.

"Why?" I barely had the breath for the word. "Why lie to me?"

One corner of her perfect lips tilted up. She acknowledged the question with a slight, wry smile. "Would you have believed me, if I looked like this?"

"But when you were small—"

"That was humanity. It burned away from me. In Hell." One shoulder lifted a little, dropped. The silver circle responded with a change in pitch, its low evil hum stepping up a half-note and dropping back down.

Damn demons, always shrugging at me. But something else crossed her face—a swift flash of vulnerability, gone in less than a moment. The look of a child caught with her hand in a jar full of candy, incongruous on a demon's face.

I kept forgetting how young she had to be, even if time moved differently in Hell than it did here.

I felt Japhrimel arrive, though he was soundless as Death Himself. His hand closed gently over my shoulder, and I didn't know whether it was to offer support or because he wasn't sure if I'd pitch myself at the circle to free her.

Eve's gaze flickered up past me. She studied Japhrimel intently for fifteen long seconds, the color draining under her golden skin, and dropped her face back into her knees. The air subtly changed, and I got the idea she was ignoring us, very loudly and pointedly.

And very desperately.

Good for you, kid. I couldn't find it in me to blame her. I turned and headed for the end of the cargo bay, brushing past Japh. His hand fell away from my shoulder.

The ladder leading up to the main deck was solid cold plasteel. I rested my hands on a crossbar, staring at my wrists. It occurred to me that they were like Eve's, seemingly frail and made of demon bone. We'd both started out human, hadn't we? Partly human?

Was I still? I felt human where it counted, inside the aching ruin of my heart. "Japh?"

He made no sound, but I felt his attention. He was listening.

"Is that...what she really looks like?"

Why was I even asking? I had seen the glamour shred away from her with my own eyes, I saw her now. I *knew*. But I still wanted to hear it. I needed to hear someone say it.

"We are shapeshifters, my curious." His breath touched my ear; he was leaning in close, the heat of him comforting against my back. I hadn't been this aware of his closeness in a while.

My breath caught in my throat. I leaned forward, rested my forehead on the plasteel. "So what do you look like?" *If you're wearing a glamour, I might as well just get it over with now. Horns? Fangs? Hooves? Let's take a peek. It can't hurt.*

After all, I've shared a bed with you. Does a demon glamour fool the skin as well as the eyes?

Japhrimel considered for a long moment. "What would you like?"

I swallowed so hard I was surprised my throat didn't click. I turned to face him. "No, I mean it. What do you really look like?"

The dimness of orandflu lighting painted the hollows of his face. The hover started to descend again, pressure pushing against my eardrums.

"What would you have me look like, *hedaira?* If it would please you, I can wear almost any shape you can imagine."

You know, before I met you, I might have had trouble believing that statement. Now I don't have enough trouble believing it. I wonder which is worse. "But what are you underneath it? What's the real you?"

A shadow of perplexity crossed his face. "This is the form I have worn most often," he said slowly. "It does not please you?"

Just when I thought I had a handle on this, something new managed to wallop me. "Never mind." I swung back toward the ladder and put my boot on the first rung. "We've got work to do." *I can't believe I'm even having this conversation.* "When are you going to let her out of that circle?"

"When I am certain she is more a help than a threat." His hand came up, touched my shoulder. "Dante—"

I shook him off and began to climb.

CHAPTER 23

We entered Caracaz as morning rose steaming over the city, the hover dropping down into a haze turned rosy. Tiens had given the controls up to Lucas, who guided us down through freight lanes and streams of regular commuter traffic. The Nichtvren had vanished, and I wondered—not for the first time—where he spent his days. If there was a spot for him to sleep during daylight on the hover, it was well hidden.

Vann pushed a battered, bruised, and bandaged Leander out into the main cabin, not very roughly. The Necromance half-stumbled, but the Hellesvront agent made no move to help. From where I sat, straight-backed in a chair magsealed to the flooring with my sword over my knees, I could clearly see the damage done to Leander's face. It turned my stomach.

"Bring him." Japh stood, staring out a porthole dewed with condensation. We'd been flying through high clouds, and the drop into Caracaz's muggy breathlessness would make the hover's exterior stream with water before long.

Vann escorted Leander across the hover's length. I hoped we were going to shift to a smaller craft. Flying around in this barge was enough to paint a big target on us.

Lucas glanced over his shoulder, turned back to the controls with a shrug. The message was clear. Leander was on his own.

Japhrimel let the Necromance stew for a bit. I kept staring at Leander's accreditation tat, his emerald sparkling and singing with the presence of his god. Was he praying?

Would it do him any good? Even I had no idea what Japh was likely to do next. I wasn't complaining much—I was hoping Lucifer couldn't predict him either—but still.

Finally, his profile harsh and clear in the returning light of dawn, Japhrimel moved slightly, clasping his hands behind his back. "Do you know why you are still alive?"

Leander couldn't help it. He shot me a glance, his dark eyes widening. He looked almost naked without his katana and weapons rig, his broad shoulders uneasy without their cargo of leather straps.

"Exactly," Japhrimel said, as if Leander had spoken. "You are alive because it pleases my *hedaira* to see you so, and because it does not matter. There is no compelling reason to remove you. Still, it is a marvelous turn of events, that one such as you would help a demon in rebellion against the Prince."

My ears perked. *Does Japh just mean that he's human and helping out a demon, or does he mean something else? Hegemony federal, which means Leander's domestic internal affairs. Field agent, which means his Matheson score was over the moon to tip him into the domestic-defense program as an active instead of an analyst.*

I sat up a little straighter, and watched the Necromance turn pale. The sharp smell of human decay under the screen of healthy male pheromones hiked in response to the fact that he was sweating, now.

I didn't blame him. Japhrimel turned away from the porthole and let the full force of his glowing eyes rest on Leander. Vann stepped back, a move calculated to make the Necromance subconsciously aware he was alone.

He handled it well, shrugging and folding his bruised arms. He wasn't cuffed or magtaped; the habit of years of bounty hunting rose under my skin. That was *wrong,* he was a combat-trained psion, a Hegemony field agent, and if I'd been hauling him somewhere I would have made *damn* sure he was trussed up tighter than a Putchkin Yule turkey.

But really, what could he do?

"I'm a sucker for bright-eyed girls with cute smiles." The Necromance actually flashed Japhrimel a cocky grin. His pulse thundered audibly, and a chemical tang of fear spilled through the air.

I had to give him points for sheer brass. I couldn't help myself. A laugh jolted out of me, the soft husky sound broken by the permanent damage done to my throat by the Devil's fingers.

Japhrimel's eyes flickered toward me.

I regained control of myself with an effort that made my hands shake just the tiniest bit.

"You are an agent of the human government." Japhrimel's tone hadn't changed. "You are Lucifer's tool just as surely as a Hellesvront vassal. Why would you, a human, aid a demon in rebellion against the Prince?"

I blinked, replayed my mental footage. Yes, he'd just said that.

"Wait a second." I took a step forward, my boots making a slight creaking sound. "The Hegemony—"

Japh's tone was kind but utterly weary, as if I'd overlooked something so stupid-simple even a child could see it. "Do you really think Lucifer would allow it to remain in power if it was not thoroughly subject to his will?"

"The Alliance—" It occurred to me that surely, if the Hegemony was controlled, the Putchkin Alliance would be as well. And they were the only games in town as far as governments went, unless you were a Freetown with an independent charter—and sometimes, even then. The Hegemony and Putchkin often function as one world government with two major departments rather than rivals. With thermonuclear capability and the freedom of information traffic nowadays, rivalry doesn't make sense. "Oh."

I'd never bothered to think about just how deep the net of financial and other assets demons held on earth was. *Hellesvront,* Japhrimel called it, and he'd used it before while hunting Eve. But to think that those resources reached up into the government itself, that the Hegemony might be infested with Lucifer's influence...

Is there anything around that demons don't control?

"Hades." Leander stared at me. "I never thought you were such an optimist, Valentine."

Oh, shut up. The trembling went out of my hands as I took a deep breath. "You're working for Lucifer?"

"I work for my division. We get orders from higher up." Leander rubbed gingerly at his bruised face, stubble rasping against his blunt callused fingers. "You came to New Prague while I was following an arms-trafficking ring. I'd almost gotten in, too. Eight months of work down the drain as soon as I got word you were in town and I was to try and make contact if I could. Seventeen agents in the city got that message, but I was the only one unlucky enough to stumble across you. I was supposed to ID, keep a lock on you, and call in a strike. Orders from high up—they didn't want you dead, just something noisy enough to draw attention to you. I was waiting for the teams to get into position when a hover falls out of the sky and some idiot lets off a plascannon."

I shuddered. The reactive paint on the bottom of hovers and a plas field—*that* had been uncomfortable. Only a moron mixes reactive and plas; the resultant molecular-bond-weakening explosion is enough to give even the most hardened criminals pause.

Plot and counterplot, everyone having an agenda, and me blundering through the middle of it all, trying to keep my head above water.

Bait intended to draw Eve out so Lucifer could close his filthy paws on her. All my struggling and striving had been next to useless.

And instead of treading water, I'd finally drowned. "So who dropped the hover on me?" Go figure, everything happening and me fixating on the one unimportant detail.

"You were not the target." Japhrimel hadn't moved his attention; it was still on Leander. His tone wasn't combative, merely flat. "Though the strike was aimed at you, it was me they intended to kill. I have other enemies, *hedaira,* and your death would be a prize to any of them. Lucifer cannot control the avenues from Hell to your world any longer. We are on the brink of chaos."

Tell me something I don't know. The steady hissing whisper of fire under the surface of my thoughts surged; I fought to keep it back. Now was not the time to explode in homicidal rage. *Save it for the next fight, Danny. There's bound to be another one, after all.*

"I got a directive after that, while we were in Saint City." Leander dropped his hands. The hover dropped, water streaming down the porthole. Lucas whistled, a low tuneless sound of concentration as we banked, a wide shallow turn that meant he'd probably spotted our landing area. Vann leaned over his shoulder, murmuring something. "I was supposed to hook up with Omega—that's what we call her, Project Omega—and liaise to neutralize *him.*" A quick sketch of a movement, his chin jerked toward Japh.

"Project Omega?" *Hello? The Hegemony knows about Eve? Did they know about Santino too?*

I had the answer to that one, a cynic's answer. Of course. Trying to hunt Santino down after he'd killed Doreen was just one closed door after another, no help from law enforcement ostensibly because the murdering bastard had incorporated under the Mob laws and those files were sealed, unable to be opened for a simple homicide no matter how hard Gabe and I tried to link him to the other serial murders. You'd think they would have cooperated.

Now I was beginning to see why they hadn't.

The memory of Gabe and me working together, frustration and grief making us both walking time bombs, finally giving up but never really stopping to pick at the scab of Doreen's death, sent a pang right through me. The mess inside my skull twinged, turning over. I owed Gabe; I'd promised to look after her daughter.

Broken promises, a trail of deceit and manipulation. Just throw Danny Valentine into the snakepit and watch her jump.

"She was supposed to be the Hegemony's way of slipping loose of Lucifer. If we had access to her, we could have experimented. There was a whole division ready to do testing. A real live cooperative demon to study? It's the fucking Holy Grail. The scientists went gaga. Then something happened, she vanished, and the goddamn demons had her." Leander made a slight restless movement, an abortive shrug. "And we couldn't figure out what *you* had to do with it, and how you'd ended up involved with *him*." Another jerk of his chin toward Japh, standing motionless and unblinking. "It was decided to just keep you under surveillance and see if the demons would bite again. They did, and I got sent in."

"Gods." I swallowed. "So that's why you were so intent on sticking around." *And I let you. I even tried to protect you.* Bile rose in my throat, was repressed, retreated. If I threw up now, the only thing that would come up was demon blood, and the thought made me feel even sicker.

"Got a job to do. You know how it is, Valentine."

The worst thing was, I did.

Behind him, the water began to lift off in globular droplets as the temperature equalized. Our descent evened out. Lucas muttered something, and Vann murmured right back.

They're Hellesvront agents too, Vann and McKinley. Why does Japhrimel trust them? Did he lie when he told me they were agents?

I didn't know what to believe anymore. "So what's your job now?"

"Right now I'll settle for staying alive. I've missed four call-ins. They probably think I'm dead. No big loss, just another agent down in the crossfire." His shoulders hunched, the crossed arms more of a defense now. "We're expendable, even the psions. You get to knowing that for a while and it does funny things to your head."

Was he fishing for sympathy? I didn't have a whole hell of a lot left over for anyone but myself, and even that was in short supply.

The hover juddered a bit as landing gear unfolded. Japh's glowing eyes met mine, and I could have sworn he was asking me for something. I couldn't understand what. I simply stared, my brain shivering between past and present, a monstrous design coming clear. The Hegemony, Lucifer, Japhrimel, Eve…

Was there anyone still alive who *hadn't* wanted to use me? When had I become such a game piece? Just pick me up, put me down, shove me from one place to the other. Even what Lucifer did wasn't directed at me—it was a way to hurt Japhrimel, catch Eve. I wasn't even worth personalized violence. No, it was all about who he could hurt *through* me.

Even my god, my safety in times of trouble, my refuge, had used my obedience to His will to spare a murdering *sedayeen* who had killed my best friend. Slaying a defenseless healer was a violation of who I was, but still...there was no way, standing over her with my sword in my hand, that I could have kept every vow I'd made, to my god, to my friend, or to myself.

And now this. Gods, demons, the government, everyone had their finger in the pie.

Even Japhrimel, who probably wasn't telling the whole truth either. He was conducting his own war against Lucifer, a war that sounded like it had started before I had ever been born. I might just be a convenient excuse, no matter what affection he felt for me.

Affection? Call it what it is, Danny. He loves you, but he won't tell you the whole truth. Nobody will.

By every god there ever was, I hate being *used*.

My left hand tightened on Fudoshin's scabbard. Were there any more lies waiting to be discovered?

I'll bet there are. You'd better start thinking how you're going to get out of this one alive, Danny. And once you do, where in the world will you be safe? Nowhere. There's going to be game after game as long as Lucifer's alive. The Devil doesn't give up easily.

That left just one option. Playing *back*.

I'd lied too. My sorcerous Will was still strong, despite my betrayal of my sworn word in circumstances beyond my control—but still inexcusable. It was an article of my faith that my word was my bond. That I used my words, my voice, to control and shape the Power necessary to bring a soul back from the dry land of Death, so it was best to speak softly and do what I said I would. Wasn't that who I was, who I had *decided* to be?

How far could I lie and still keep my own soul?

It was another article of faith that Japhrimel loved me, would always come for me, and would do his best to see me through this alive. Was that enough to excuse the lies? How much could I weigh each part of that equation?

Yet another article of faith: that my god would never abandon me by asking me for more than I could give. My right hand crept up, touched my naked right cheek. On my left cheek, the emerald sang a thin piercing note before it spat a single spark, my cheek prickling as the tat moved, a thorny caduceus twisting under my skin.

Not Anubis. Sekhmet. You should swear by Her, now. Who answered when you lay bleeding? Who has not broken faith with you?

Who have you *not broken faith with, Necromance?*

"Dante." Japhrimel, softly, as if he didn't want to disturb me. "It is your decision. I will spare him, as a gift to you. Still, he is a liability. This dog's loyalty is to his masters."

The color drained from Leander's face. It would have been funny, if I'd been in a humorous mood. Why anyone was scared of me while Japh was around was beyond me.

Still, I considered Leander, holding his dark eyes with mine, my left thumb caressing the lacquer of the scabbard. The sword rang softly inside his sheath, just aching to be drawn.

Compassion is not your strongest virtue, Danyo-chan. My teacher's voice when he handed the sword to me, a warning I hadn't known the depths of.

Compassion. It kept fucking me up every time. Staying my hand when I should strike. Being honorable. Submitting to my god, or my ethics. Doing the right thing.

What the hell was the *right thing* now? Had there ever been one right thing?

I used to be so certain. Didn't I used to know what to do, no matter what?

"Leave him alone," I said, finally. "Give him back his weapons. If he needs killing, I'll do it." I held Leander's gaze with mine, and whatever he saw on my face could not have been pleasant. "If they've given you up for dead, Beaudry, I suggest you start rethinking where your loyalty lies."

With that, I turned on my heel and stalked for the cabin, just as the hoverwhine crested and we touched down on Sudro Merican soil.

CHAPTER 24

Caracaz was a center of resistance during the last third of the Merican Era, digging in its heels as the Evangelicals of Gilead rose and the Vatican Bank scandal began to unfold. When the Republic reached its height of power, Caracaz and Old Venezela were a major clearinghouse for supplies to be sent to Centro Merica, where Shamans and others fought the desperate guerilla battles against the Republic's tide. Psions flooded over the borders during the Awakening, joining in the fight against the Gilead fanatics who considered us subhuman, worthy only of extermination—just like anyone else who got in their way.

In pretty much every language now, *Gilead* is a dirty word. *Republic* isn't far behind. You can only fight the whole world for so long before the world starts fighting back, a lesson the Evangelicals didn't learn while they choked on their own blood after the Seventy Days War. But then, fundamentalists aren't bright thinkers. Fanaticism tends to blind people.

Caracaz is built with plasteel and sandy-colored preformed concrete. The ambient Power tastes like coconut oil, hot spicy food, and sweat, with the bite of petroleo underneath it. The crash of petroleo as an energy source had hit here hard, but the War and its buildup provided the city with the chance to become a major trade hub, which the entire country grabbed with both hands. Or it should be said, which the anarcho-syndicalist collectives who had taken over day-to-day running of the country after the crash seized with all hands. The Venezela territory is still administered by those collectives, which make it the nearest thing to a Freetown in the Hegemony.

The old proverb is, *In Caracaz you can make ten fortunes in a week—and lose fifteen.* Just about anything can be bought or sold here, and head on its way in less than an hour to another port. Only in Shanghai is turnover quicker.

In short, it's so busy it's easy to hide a hover. Which was great, since we weren't inconspicuous, in a freight transport the size of a small building.

We landed in a deep transport well, the hover powering down. It was an anonymous berthing, at least until someone started running registry traces. How many people were looking for me now? How many were looking for Eve?

There was a knock on the door, very polite. I turned away from the porthole, where I had been staring blankly at strips of reactive and double-synaptic relays, feeling the familiar urban wash, the surf-roar of many minds squeezed into square miles. Japhrimel's borrowed Power kept the screaming chaos away. If he withdrew it, my shields were in no shape to cope, even with the repair work going on. And forget about taking a direct hit, sorcerous or psionic.

I was as vulnerable as it was possible to be, without him. It was a wonder the connections inside my head hadn't fused, turning me into a mumbling idiot.

Should I call that good luck, or bad?

Vann opened the door, his face set and composed, shades of brown overlapping and the whites of his eyes startling. A brief glance, then he stared at the floor. "Jaf wants you." A pause, letting me absorb the fact that they used the shortest version of his name, when they weren't calling him *my Lord.* Just like I had when I'd first met him. "If you would like to come, that is." So excessively polite.

I wonder what new parade of heartstopping excitement he's got planned next. Another decoy? I rolled my shoulders back, settling the rig more securely, and gave Vann my best *fuck you, sunshine* glare. "Am I really all that necessary?"

The Hellesvront agent didn't even blink. He moved into the cabin, smoothly, freeing himself from the door. "To *him.* So, to us." Another pause, letting me digest an all-new cryptic comment. "Hellesvront is the Prince's toy, but McKinley and I—and some others—were recruited by Jaf. We're his shadow organization, his vassals inside. Something happens to him, we're left without protection. Sometimes the only thing keeping a demon from unzipping your guts is fear of the other demon—the one you belong to. So we'd like to keep you breathing. For *his* sake."

Well, that's a nice bit of news. "Glad to hear it."

"You should be." Vann's thin mouth stretched into a mirthless grin. "If we didn't, there'd be no place on earth you could hide."

I stared past him, at the slice of the main chamber, the shape of the hull giving it an odd distortion. "You know, that sounds an awful lot like a threat." My throaty whisper, a Necromance's voice with an overlay of demon seduction, turned cold. The small flaming thread running through the bottom of my head paused, swelling slightly.

It would be so easy, even if he was armed to his shiny bright teeth. Even if his stance shifted slightly, shoulders coming up a fraction and his weight pitching a little forward, ready to move in any direction if I exploded.

I didn't blame him.

"Not a threat. The truth." He stepped back, aiming for the door, and edged out, not looking directly at me. It was the way he might ease out of the cage of a not particularly tamed or predictable animal. His soft shoes made no noise against the grated flooring. He didn't even *breathe* loud enough.

Go away. Just go away. I unfocused my eyes and stared at his moccasins, the way his feet moved inside supple thick leather.

He vanished. I let my vision stay hazy for a few moments, breathing deep and soft until the rage retreated, folding back down into its bright ribbon.

"I don't like it," Lucas muttered darkly, glancing back over his shoulder at me. "Leavin' him there is just an invitation for ol' Blue-Eyes to get loose."

"It matters little." Japhrimel walked with his hands clasped behind his back, his long dark coat moving fluidly. The heat painted every surface, a wet Sudro Merican heat smelling of tamales, rice, beef cooked in spices, and the ever-present coconut oil. I'd gone from Chomo Lungma's deep-freeze to this, and I wasn't unhappy. This weather was purely, blessedly human.

Vann and McKinley flanked me, McKinley hanging back on my right, Vann close enough to touch me on my left. Between them, Japhrimel, and Lucas, I was beginning to feel hemmed-in. They surrounded me like Mob bodyguards around a Family Head.

I shot a look back myself at the hover, drifting gently in its berthing. Leander was locked in the cabin I'd just vacated, and Eve was in the hold, surrounded by a thin silver line.

Japhrimel pressed the button for the cargo lift. "If the Necromance sets her free, where will she go? Lucifer will not care what prey is snared in his nets, and will not treat her kindly now. I am her only chance, and my *hedaira* is her only chance for mercy. No, I think the Androgyne will remain our guest for some time."

I eyed the metal grating. There was an elevator not thirty steps away, along the curve of the platform. A hot wind blew steadily up from the depths of the well, air buffeted by reactive and antigrav.

Thank the gods we're not taking the lift. I couldn't stand it. The thought of being trapped in such a small space made prickles race up my back, spreading down my arms. The claustrophobia was getting worse. I wondered if it was stress.

In fact, I wondered so hard I didn't hear the conversation, slapping myself back into awareness as the cargo lift shuddered to a halt. *Pay attention, Danny. Don't wander.*

I'd been doing more and more of that, lately. All through the hunt for Gabe and Eddie's killer. Staring off into the distance, thinking about the past.

As a coping mechanism, it sucked.

The cargo lift was open plasteel meshwork, no walls to close the air out. I was grateful for that, at least, even though the agents pressed closer and Lucas eyed me speculatively.

We spilled out onto a Caracaz street, all hot sunshine and bright colors. They paint the sandy concrete in primary colors, outside. Under that sun it's an assault, the head reeling and the breath suddenly stopped by a riot of color. The crowd wasn't bad, but we were still outside a transport well. Hovers lifted off every few moments, their rattling whine cycling up as they rose to take their places in the complicated pattern overhead, run by an AI in realtime and watched over by failsafes. Others landed, a stream of blunt reactive-painted undersides feeding into the well.

Japhrimel looked up, taking his bearings. He looked suddenly out of place, a tall golden-skinned man in a long black coat under the oppressive yellow weight of sunlight. The world spun underfoot. I blinked against the assault of light, the unfamiliar weight of Japhrimel's shielding over mine restrictive, bearing down and squeezing me into my skin.

Japh finally tilted his head back down. He reached back with one hand, his fingers open, and I didn't think twice, just stepped forward and laced mine into them.

"Walk with me," he said, as if there was nobody else around. It was suddenly like every other time I'd ever been beside him, close to the not-human heat from his skin.

Even my rage retreated from him.

"Where are we going?" I finally thought to ask.

"To see a Magi. It's not far."

CHAPTER 25

I t's not hard to hide in cities. That is, in the right *parts* of cities. As a bounty hunter, you get the feel for a place where nobody asks questions—the red light districts, the bordellos and hash dens, the places where a drink makes you friends and another drink makes you liable to get killed one way or another. Places where the air is thick with sex and violence, psychic static to hide even the stain of a demon on the ether.

Unfortunately, we were in the wrong part of Caracaz. It was a quiet, upscale neighborhood, and we walked down a sidewalk in the shade of giant genespliced palms, broad fronds fluttering and drenching the sidewalk with relative coolness. There were no crowds and precious little cover.

So we walked along, two Hellesvront agents, Lucas in his worn boots and bandoliers strapped across his chest, his shoulders hunched, and one tall demon with eyes that glowed even through Caracaz's hot sunlight.

And me. I was beginning to feel more and more conspicuous. Almost naked.

The houses were large, high sand-colored walls surrounding gardens that peeped through iron gates. Several had shimmers of shielding over them, each with its particular tang—a Shaman's spiked honey-smell, another with the earth-taste of a Skinlin. At least Japh's shielding didn't stop me from Seeing here.

Welcome to the psionic district. I wonder who's peering out the curtains, seeing us coming for dinner. The thought of psions running to their windows, peeking at us like old grannies, drew a sharp bitter humor up in my throat.

"Do you think he's home?" Vann stepped carefully, amazingly quiet for someone with so much metal strapped to him.

"He'd better be," McKinley replied, shortly.

Japhrimel didn't even slow down, though his steps were shorter to compensate for mine. He strode right up to a low, pretty villa behind a scrolled-iron fence, the walls blocked in red and yellow, harlequin paint screaming in the heat of the day and covered with a nervous, shifting mass of energy. I catalogued it before I could stop myself—Magi, with the subtle spice-tang that meant both *active* and *demon-dealing.*

Japh broke stride only once, to wait for the gates. They were already opening on silent maghinges, the curtain of energy parting to let us through.

Someone's expecting us. Knock knock, demon calling. I kept a straight face with difficulty. The front of the house, pillared to within an inch of its life and covered with yellow and blue mosaic—I suppressed a shudder—yawned sleepily and regarded us with falsely closed eyes, each window blind with polarized glass.

The door was a concrete monstrosity hung on mag-hinges and reinforced with shielding so strong it sent a weak glimmer even through the vicious sunshine. *Someone's paranoid,* was my first thought. And, *I wish I'd had shielding like that when Japh came to my door the first time.*

Too late, sunshine.

Japh didn't even knock. He simply stepped close to the door and stopped, regarding it with a narrow green gaze.

He didn't have to wait long. The door creaked, the shielding's shimmer pulsing. A slice of cool darkness grew as someone pulled it open, frictionless hinges working slowly with the mass.

A breath of cooler air slid out, fragrant with musk, spice, and the thick sweetness of *kyphii.* The Magi in the door was well over six lanky feet tall, with large paddlefish hands and skin shaded a rich dark cocoa. His chiseled lips set themselves in something less than a grimace, despite the laugh lines bracketing his mouth and fanning from his chocolate eyes. He wore a loose indigo tunic and a pair of blue canvas pants with enough pockets and loops to make any plas-teel worker proud. Bare feet resting gently against the floor, placed just so, told me he was combat trained. The scimitar riding his back, its hilt topped with a star sapphire, told me so as well, quietly and with no fuss.

He watched Japhrimel the way I might watch a poisonous snake hanging on a tree branch right before it's hurled at me.

"Anton." Japh got right to the point. "Your services are required."

The ripple of fear spiking through the smell of dying human cells plucked at my control. My lips parted, the fear scraping against raw edges on my shielding, taunting. My Magi-trained memory gave a twitch, sending a hook through dark waters, fishing for a name to match the familiarity of his face. His tat, fluorescing with Power and inked with dullglow to make it visible against his skin, was a Krupsev, its spurs and claws fitting nicely on his cheek.

Then I had him. I'd seen the newspapers and holostills, not to mention the retrospectives. "Anton Kgembe." I was too shocked to whisper. "But you're *dead!*"

The Magi's eyes flicked to me, their irises so dark the pupil was almost indistinguishable. "So they tell me." His voice had the crispness of Hegemony Albion, each syllable precisely weighted. "My Lord. You are welcome in my house, and your companion as well." He stepped aside, and Japhrimel moved forward, taking me with him.

"You have not lost your courtesy." Japh's tone veered from politeness toward amusement, settled somewhere between. A cool draft folded around us, and Lucas made a slight tuneless whistling sound as his worn boots touched the floor.

Inside, it was dark before my eyes adapted. The floor was bare stone, the interior walls mellow wood hung with loose linen hangings and a few priceless, restrained pieces—mostly masks, none prickling with life or awareness but still gorgeous and worth a great deal to any Shaman for their aesthetics alone.

The Magi padded in front of us, his back very straight and the sandpaper perfume of fear roiling off his aura. He didn't *look* like the most powerful Magi in the world, and he further didn't look like a man who had died years ago in an industrial accident. He looked healthy and unassuming, just like any other combat-trained psion wandering around. He didn't even seem all that twitchy.

He also didn't look like the most dangerous Left Hand theorist around, the one who had single-handedly revised the entire canon of those who worship the Unspeakable. Kgembe's Laws, four principles of dealing with Left Hand magick, had been standardized only because they were so effective the Hegemony and Putchkin Alliance needed some way of dealing with practitioners who used them for purposes outside the law. In other words, he was responsible for one of the biggest cover-your-ass moments in Hegemony psionic-affairs history.

All things considered, I figured he had a legitimate reason for wanting to be dead.

He's a Left Hander. That means dangerous *and* not particularly careful about casualties *all in one pretty package.* I suppressed a shiver. Japh's arm tightened around my shoulders. The scar sent another warm oil-bath down my skin.

"Might I inquire what I'll be doing for you, my Lord?" Kgembe's tone hadn't altered its crisp politeness. The Hegemony Albion stiff upper lip at its finest. The doors closed with a click, sealing us in coolness and quiet, the walls thrumming with shielding that felt familiar because it was demon-laid.

I was beginning to suspect I knew which demon.

Japhrimel glanced down at me, his face unreadable. "You will be opening a door into Hell, and keeping it open long enough for one demon to pass through."

I slammed the Knife down on the tabletop. Glass cracked with a sound like projectile fire, a single well-placed shot. I didn't even feel bad for killing someone else's furniture. *"No."* My voice cracked too, like a young boy's.

The small room was lined with bookshelves, its polarized windows looking onto a central courtyard teeming with lush green. A bird feeder stood on a graceful curve of iron just outside, and a fountain plashed musically, audible even through the glass.

"There is no other way." Japhrimel's face was set and drawn, his eyes veiled as he stared at the Knife. "Creating a scene does not help."

I folded my arms, mostly to disguise how my hands were shaking. The Knife hummed inside its new sheath. "You hid the other half of this thing in *Hell?*"

"It seemed a fine idea at the time. Lucifer is not at home—he is traveling the wide world, dispensing his own justice and hunting for both us and his wayward Androgyne. I may very well go unnoticed."

"Lucifer's looking to finish me off. What am I going to do if he finds me and you're stuck in Hell?" When I got right down to it, *that* was what worried me most.

Lo, how the mighty have fallen. And I used to be so tough.

Japhrimel clasped his hands behind his back and inclined his chin, slightly. "Vann and McKinley will protect you. If need be, they will sacrifice themselves for your safety."

"Oh, that just makes me feel *so much* better." Sarcasm. The last refuge of the doomed. Not to mention that I didn't trust either of them. I was getting to the point where I didn't trust *anyone.*

"We have little time. At any moment, Lucifer may find the other two decoys are merely that—empty boxes. Then he will know how far my betrayal extends. When that happens, it will be war. He will scour the earth with his minions, those he can afford to trust. They should be few, but they are powerful. And he has an endless supply of the Low Flight to work his will."

The rock in my throat swelled. The Knife's finials writhed silently. It was a hideous feeling, staring at the inhuman geometry of the thing and feeling that it had *just* moved, and that I wouldn't necessarily notice or remember if it moved again. "This isn't helping."

"I would take you with me, were it possible."

The thought of going back into Hell dried my mouth. So much for hiding my shaking hands—my fingers bit into my arms and my rig creaked slightly. What could I say? *Gee, thanks, but the last two times I've been I haven't enjoyed it a bit.* I shook my head, actually feeling all the blood drain from my face. Something occurred to me, then. "That's why you went back into Hell while we were in Toscano. You went to see if you could get a chance to get your hands on the other half."

His mouth tilted up at the corners, a rueful expression. "All the hosts of Hell save me from your ideas, my curious. Yes, I thought it might be possible to retrieve it. The Prince kept too close a watch on me."

"Which meant you suspected something."

"I suspected a time would come when my potential value to Lucifer was outweighed by my status as *A'nankhimel*. After all, Lucifer left you alive." A single, short nod. "When I returned to myself after dormancy, I thought it very likely, so I waited. When he called for us again, I knew half the Knife of Sorrow would perhaps afford me an edge, and you some protection. Then I could collect Sephrimel's half at leisure before anyone discovered my plan."

"When were you going to get around to telling me *this?*"

"We have had little time, of late, and we have even less now." He reached down, touched the oiled wooden hilt with one golden finger. Pulled his hand away, as if it had pricked him. "I need your help, my curious."

Funny, you seem to be doing all right on your own. Why don't you, Eve, and Lucifer fight this out, and leave me alone? The Knife hummed, a low dangerous sound. "Nobody in this thing needs my help," I muttered.

"I do. You freed me from Lucifer, you mourned my dormancy, you brought me back. If anyone can be said to own one of my kind, I am yours. Give me the freedom to act in this matter."

Give you? "You're going to act whether I *give* you anything or not. You always have."

"Give me some credit for seeking to change, even at this late hour." It was his turn for a sardonic tone.

Why is it that as soon as I think you're a complete bastard you say something like that? "Credit given, Japh. Fine. If this is what we have to do, let's do it." I turned on my heel and stalked away from the table, leaving the Knife in its spiderweb of broken glass.

"Dante."

I stopped.

He approached me silently. "This is yours."

I turned my head a bit. He gingerly proffered the Knife, hilt-first. In his hands it actually looked normal, the alienness of its geometry matched by the subtle difference of his bone structure.

It would be idiotic not to take it and use it, especially if Japh was going to make a suicide run into Hell.

Story of your life, sunshine. You're on your own.

I took it, its unholy satin warmth sliding into my palm, rattling the bones of my fingers with its low hum.

Either shard will wound beyond measure a demon, even one of the Greater Flight. Sephrimel's voice. He'd proved it, too. So had the bird-feathered demon.

Japh shook his hand, a quick short movement, as if ridding his skin of the feel of the thing. "I will return." He made it sound like a fact instead of a promise. "As quickly as I may. Time moves differently in Hell."

Don't I know it. "If you're going to do it, do it." For once I sounded steady, and strong. "Let's not wait around."

CHAPTER 26

The walk back to the hover was too short for serious brooding and far too long for me to feel anything other than horribly exposed and completely vulnerable. I wanted to stay and watch, but Magi don't practice in front of other psions... and as Japh had pointed out, a doorway to Hell was not anything I wanted to be around.

Because if something can go in, something might be able to come *out.* So we all stepped merrily out Kgembe's front door.

Without Japhrimel.

Ten minutes later the scar in the hollow of my left shoulder went numb, a varocained prickling that probably meant he was nowhere in the normal world. I'd felt that before, and it was miserable to have confirmation of what it meant.

Vann spoke once. "Don't worry. He'll be back before you know it."

When I said nothing, he shut up. The rest of the walk was accomplished in complete silence, except for Lucas swearing under his breath, a steady monotony of obscenities mixed in different languages, a song of nervousness. That certainly didn't help my mood. Wet heat lay thick and clotted against every surface, the shadows knife-edged and drenched with color. I carried my sword, wanting it to hand.

Just in case.

Sirens boiled through the air as we drew closer to the transport well.

That doesn't sound good. Precognition tickled my nape under tangled hair. Still, why assume that every disturbance in Caracaz had to do with me?

We rounded the corner. *Because it probably does, Danny.*

There was a snarl of hover traffic in holding patterns and a column of black smoke lifting from the depths of the well. I stared, Vann cursed, and McKinley pushed me back around the corner. "Stay back. Lucas?"

"On it." The yellow-eyed man unholstered a plasgun and set off down the street, moving quickly but smoothly. He looked bleached, surrounded by blocks of primary color.

Who the hell put McKinley in charge? I swallowed my protest and tried to peer around the corner. McKinley pushed me back, his metallic left hand glittering. A fine sheen of sweat covered the Hellesvront agent's forehead. "Just a minute, Valentine. Let's not be hasty."

"Leander. And *her.*" Eve. *Or whoever she is.*

"Lucas'll see what's going on. We don't want to risk you." He exchanged a worried look with Vann, one I could decipher all too easily. This changed things a little. It was faintly possible the column of smoke had nothing to do with us.

Faintly.

The semi-industrial district butting up against Kgembe's quiet neighborhood provided no cover at all. I felt like a huge neon-lit sign. *Tasty demon treat, just come and take a bite.*

"Mac." There was a long, low, sibilant hiss—Vann had drawn a knife.

"I know." McKinley let out a short sharp breath, and I smelled sudden peppery adrenaline from both of them under the dry stasis-cabinet smell of Hellesvront. "Valentine?"

"What?" My right hand almost-cramped, and I squeezed my swordhilt and felt every nervestring pull itself taut. This suddenly began to feel normal. There was violence approaching.

I didn't mind a bit.

"If this gets ugly, you'd better run. As fast and as far as you can. We'll take care of the rest."

We'll see about that. "What is it?" *A demon, all right. Which one, and where, and what the hell are you two going to be—*

I didn't even get to finish the thought. They boiled out of the daylight, low unhealthy shapes with skittering legs, and I swallowed a scream before McKinley shoved me so hard I stumbled. *"Run!"* McKinley screamed.

My sword cleared its sheath, and the rage woke in a blinding red screen.

Oh, no. I have had enough of running. I rocketed forward past Vann, who had gone into a crouch as one of the things leapt, an unco-ordinated fluid movement twisting its flexible two-part body. It looked like a nightmare of a spider, with the off-kilter grace of something demonic. It was also sickly-hot, a feverish icy heat cutting through the sunshine and raising my hackles. A coughing roar exploded, either from my throat or from someone's projectile gun.

No. It was me. It was the cry of a hunting cat.

I ducked into a crouch, sword whipping in an arc, blue flame painting the air behind it in a sweet natural curve as the scabbard clattered to the concrete and my left hand closed around the hilt of the Knife, ripping it free.

Tchuk. Fudoshin split demonic flesh, and the spider thing made a screeching hurtful sound. I rose from the crouch, the long muscles in my legs providing impetus, and leapt, twisting with the follow-through of the slash. The Knife whipped out, following the arc, and the hell-thing screamed again.

I hit the ground before I'd finished my yell, my throat scorching with the sound.

And *fire* bloomed. Red-yellow flames coughed into existence, running wetly over the thing's bristling, glassy black hide. The scar hummed with Power, flushing along my skin and armoring me in liquid heat.

Had it always been this simple? The world was no longer a garden of threat and fear. Instead, it was a clear, shimmering web of action and reaction, violence and death. All I had to do was *look* to see the shining path of killing that would free me from this.

It had never felt so right to destroy everything in my path.

"Valentine!" McKinley, screaming. I pivoted on the ball of my left foot, bringing the sword around again, and engaged the second spider. Plasfire crackled around me, the air seared with a stinging smell of something dry and bristled, its mouth stuffed with silk, flicked into a candleflame and shriveling.

Something ripped along my calf, but I paid it no heed. Short thrust, pivoting again, boots scraping the concrete, and the Knife let out a high keening as I plunged it into the spider's back. The horrid gulping noise cut short, a flood of hot sickening Power jolting up my arm before I pulled the blade free and ducked, venomous black blood flying.

More whining plasbolts. There were so many of them, the spiders clicking and hissing, moving to flank me. Rage smoked and strained as the reflex of a lifetime spent bounty hunting calculated the odds and came up with something I didn't quite like.

They were about to surround me.

Don't care, the rage whispered. *Kill them. Kill them all.*

Make them pay.

It hit me hard and low, driving me down as a laserifle whined. I landed hard, twisting, and almost drove the Knife into McKinley's throat before I realized he wasn't one of *them.*

It was harder than it should have been to stop myself.

The spiders screeched and writhed, black rotting blood steaming on the concrete. The aftermath of a repeating laserifle isn't a pretty sight, and these creatures seemed even more vulnerable to lasefire than the hellhounds. The smell was incredible, but even more incredible was the sound of little bristled demon feet scratching, scratching, *scratching.*

More of them, and they're massing. I gulped at stale, fetid air. The heat was incredible.

"Get *up!*" McKinley hauled on me, I scrambled to my feet. "Now *run, goddamn you!*"

I didn't wait to be told twice. Still, every muscle in me resisted for the first few steps, wanting to turn back and kill until there was nothing left. He shoved me again, right between the shoulderblades, and it took every vanishing thread of control I had left not to spin and plunge bright steel into the man's body.

I ran.

His footsteps followed mine as we flashed through wet sunlight and sharp-edged shade, harsh heaving breaths echoing in my straining ears. I heard more lasefire, and the chattering of projectile fire. On the far end, another explosion rocked the transport well.

They're certainly going all-out, aren't they. Whoever they are. I wonder if I'll ever find out. Does it matter?

I can move very quickly, especially since Japhrimel taught me to use the demon-born strength he'd given me. McKinley kept pace, having enough breath to yell when I instinctively bolted left at the next intersection, impelled by the idea that I had to find some cover. The city thrummed, a deep well of ambient power at its core beckoning. There was enough static in those depths to hide me, maybe.

Except for the sudden ravine cutting across our path, a waist-high railing and hover traffic whizzing by. A major traffic lane, an artery feeding the city's throbbing heart.

Oh, shit. I was moving too fast, dug my heels in, and skidded to a stop.

McKinley almost ran into me, gasping for breath. He snapped a quick glance down into the hovertraffic. "Do you trust me?"

What? "What?" I looked over my shoulder. The street seemed clear, but the shadows warped in a way I suddenly didn't like. As I looked, one of the shadows developed legs and skittered out into the hot sun, sending up a high piercing cry.

"Do you *trust* me?" McKinley repeated. He still held a knife, the blade reversed along his right forearm, his metallic left hand limned with pale violet.

I had no time to lie. "No." *I don't trust you. I don't even* like *you.*

"Fine." He grabbed, his left hand tangling in my rig's straps, and *hauled.* The railing hit me at hip level, he yanked again, and we tumbled over the edge.

Instinct pulled my arms and legs close, I twisted like a cat in mid-air and almost crunched into the side of a freight hover, its wash of warm air stinging my eyes. Gravity eased for a heart-clenching moment, McKinley fell free, and we landed *hard* on a moving surface, the breath driven from my lungs in a *hungh!* of effort that might have been funny if it hadn't hurt so goddamn much.

"—ow—" My voice was very small in the rushing wind.

He'd aimed us for a hovertrain, bulleting along at the bottom of the trough. If I'd been human, the fall would have killed me. As it was, I shook the stun out of my head and made it to my feet, sword in one hand and Knife in the other, miraculously mostly unharmed. Wet warmth dripped into my eyes before black blood sealed the hurt away. The top of the train was dimpled from my landing, lines of force clearly showing in the plasteel.

Hope we didn't scare anyone inside.

McKinley was on all fours, coughing up bright crimson blood. He looked terrible, and his ribs on one side were malformed, hammered in by the force of our landing.

Oh, lovely. This is ever *so much better.* I opened my mouth to say it, but a motion further down the flexible snake of the hovertrain caught my eye.

Shit. I spared another glance at McKinley, whose eyes had rolled back into his head. The violet glow around his left hand flashed, getting brighter, and crackling noises punctured the wind-sound as his ribs snapped out, mending.

He'll live, the voice of experience inside my head whispered. *But not for long, if they get to him in this state.*

Loping on all fours up the hovertrain's bouncing back, their bald heads glistening in the golden light and their eyes firing when they passed through brief shutterclicks of shadow, were imps. Their long, waxen-white flexible limbs bent in ways no human's would, and they snarled and chattered through the roaring wind as the train took a sharp bend, my knees flexing to keep me upright. My sword came up, blue flame streaming and dripping from its keen edge, its heart burning white-hot, visible even through daylight.

I could just leave him here. I really could.

I launched myself over McKinley, who blurted out something through his coughing and choking for breath, and ran headlong for the imps, not realizing I was screaming in defiance until I ran out of breath and slammed into the first imp with a sound like hovers colliding. The Knife rammed into the thing's chest, and its screech was sweet music as rage took me again, the inside of my skull turning into a grassfire, smudges of charcoal and dull stained crimson taking the place of thought.

Front foot planted, yank the Knife free and swing back foot around, whirling to extend in a lunge as effortless as it was deadly, a roar of speed-laced wind stinging my eyes, my hair rising and obscuring my vision. It didn't matter, I wasn't using my eyes to track them anyway. They were smears of black-diamond fire on the landscape of Power, interlocking cascades of intent and threat. I lost track of myself in the clear light of what Jado called *mind-no-mind,* moving with a speed and clarity I had rarely achieved in my human life and never since — until now.

The enemy vanishes, Danyo-chan, and all you face is yourself.

The leap uncoiled, my knees coming up, and I *kicked,* my boot meeting another imp's face. The sound of a watermelon with glass bones dropped on scorching pavement was satisfying, to say the least, but not as satisfying as carving the thing's arm off on my way down, landing splay-footed and bouncing again, the train's rollicking passage suddenly a rhythm I had no trouble catching.

Just like riding a slicboard, eh, Danny?

The flood of feverish Power up my arm from the Knife was almost natural. Gritty ash exploded, demonic flesh sucked clean of vitality, and the sound I heard — a falsetto giggle, high and clear as ringing glass in an empty room after midnight — was my own insane laughter. I was *laughing* as they swarmed me, jaws champing and sharp teeth clicking through foam, maddened by daylight or by my presence, I couldn't tell.

I was still making that sound when McKinley grabbed the back of my rig again. The train halted for one vertiginous second, and I realized what was happening as it fell away from underfoot and we launched out into space again. The hovertrain was heading down a sharp almost-vertical slope to plunge underground, probably a commuter line, and we were in freefall again as one imp leapt the sudden distance, slavering and champing, for my throat.

Landed, *hard,* breath driven from my lungs again and something snapping in my right leg, a sudden sickening sheet of pain bolting through the clarity I'd just achieved. McKinley was cursing, low and steady in a hoarse broken tone. My hair stung my eyes, whipped into a tangled mass by the wind. I fetched up on my side, trying to get in enough breath to scream as the freight hover we'd landed on bounced, a sudden application of force controlled by its whining gyros. The imp vanished into the slipstream, not lucky enough to catch our trajectory.

Oh, ow. Ouch. Agony rolled through the rage, sharpening it like a shot of vox sharpens a sniffer's senses. Pulling everything into a different kind of clarity. *"Sekhmet sa'es,"* I moaned, the words filling my mouth like hot copper blood. *Why does it take getting the shit beat out of me before I feel human again?*

"Don't *ever* do that again!" McKinley yelled. "Goddammit! I'm trying to *protect* you!"

You didn't look in any shape to take on those guys, buddy boy. My right femur crunched with pain as the bone swiftly healed itself, demon metabolism running fiercely, heat blurring out from my skin. It actually felt *cold* with the wind howling as us, the freight hover moving at a good clip away from the trainline.

Caracaz wheeled above and below, skyscraper spires piercing hot hazy sky, stretching down to pavement crawling with crowds below. Ambient Power stroked my skin, interference rising like steam to cloak my aura. *This is better.*

This, I can work with. I coughed, swallowed a mouthful of something too warm and nauseatingly slick to be spit, and tested my right leg. It hurt like hell, but it was better. I made it up to hands and knees, the hilts jarring against my palms as the hover bounced again. The Knife hummed, a low satisfied sound that suddenly made me feel like emptying my stomach.

Quit it, Danny. Puking won't get you anywhere. I snapped a glance over my shoulder—the hovertrain had vanished. I wondered if the imps had survived.

I got my feet underneath me, made it up. My right leg ached fiercely, the bone assaulted and unhappy. The scar sent another warm pulse of Power down my skin, and I was suddenly glad Japhrimel's repair work on my shields had held up.

And glad that neither imp nor spider-thing had been able to use Power against me.

McKinley grabbed at my shoulder, and I controlled the twitch that could have buried the Knife in his guts. *Twitchy, twitchy, Necromance. Mellow down easy.* I came back fully into myself and felt suddenly...what was it?

Whole. Cleansed, the fire of rage having burned something sticky and viscous away from me. I'd fought them off. I'd *won*.

I liked the feeling. I wanted it to last.

I tore myself out from under McKinley's hand. "Watch it."

"We've got to get off this thing." He checked the sky, his black hair lifting on the wind of our passage, cut now because the freight hover was in a downtown holding pattern.

My eyes followed the loops and curves, hovers delicately woven into streams of unsnarled traffic. *This one's remote from the realtime AI controller, probably, since it didn't change course when we thumped into it. At least, let's hope so.* My eyes stung, whipped by wind and hair. I should have tied it back, but how was I to know I'd go jumping off hovers?

You should have guessed, Danny. Isn't that how these things always go?

"There." McKinley pointed. A residential high-rise, with the hoverlane going directly over it. The fall was bad but not immense, and there was plenty of room for error.

"You want me to break my leg again?" I sounded delighted, the remainder of the chilling little giggles spilling through my voice.

"Better than the alternative," he snapped. Dark circles had bloomed under his eyes, and he was chalk-pale. The violet glow around his left hand had subsided.

"Guess so." The Knife slid back into its sheath. "What about Vann and Lucas?"

"They can take care of themselves. They'll provide a distraction, it's part of the plan."

"Plan? What *plan?*" *There was a plan?*

"Standard for bodyguard duty. If we get separated, Vann goes low and fast and loud, drawing everyone away. I get the package and we rendezvous." He coughed, a racking sound, and winced. His ribs didn't look staved-in, as they had before. I wondered just how fast a Hellesvront agent healed.

"Where?" *I would have liked to know this, you know.*

"Where else? Hegemony Europa. Paradisse, actually. We've got a safe place there. That is, if it hasn't been blown. That town's always crawling with demons." His lips pulled back from his teeth, a sharp delighted grin. "Don't worry, Valentine. We're going to keep you in one piece for our lord, whether you like it or not."

CHAPTER 27

Paradisse started out as a Roma Taliano colony, back in the mists of time. During the era of the Religions of Submission Franje became a country, and the city grew like a pearl around the muddy banks of a river now running deep underground. Layer upon layer of history added itself to each street, each house, each tower.

During the Awakening the Old Franje government—still not folded into the nascent Hegemony—threw open the city as a sanctuary for the emerging psionic community, sheltering them from the ravages of the Evangelicals of Gilead. Kochba bar Gilead had pronounced psions abominations, and the beginning years of the Awakening were marked by death camps and persecutions, rising to a fever-pitch during the bloodbath that led to the only tactical nuclear strike of the Seventy Days War, the bombing of the Vegas Territory. Paradisse, however, was shelter for any psion who could reach it, and the Awakening accelerated even as the Evangelicals choked to death on their own fanaticism, their vestigial gift to the social fabric the Ludder party and their xenophobic hatred of psions and paranormals— not to mention the lingering distaste of normals for anything psionic or paranormal.

While her daughter Kebec is pearl and shimmer, Paradisse *shines*. The city throbs with light, glowing spires crisscrossed with moving walkways, hanging gardens, open-air cafés with climate control, each zipping hover gilded and each slicboard leaving a glittering trail in the effervescent air. Paradisse has been built on for centuries, and even though everything is Hegemony Europa now still the Old Franje shines through, in all its aesthetic and chauvinistic splendor. Aboveground, on the Brightside, Paradisse is often used in holovid representations of nirvana, and artists have wandered its upper byways for centuries, sketching and immortalizing.

Underground, under the centuries of accumulated human habitation, is something else.

The Darkside of Paradisse isn't like the Jersey Core. It isn't even like the Tank in Saint City. It's Chill-fed urban blight, true, but down in the Darkside the rule is assassination, stealth, and debauchery.

Some parts of the Darkside are mostly safe for regular citizens to go slumming; in those slices the bordellos and hash dens are strictly policed by Hegemony police regulars, Hegemony federal marshals, and a contingent of freelancers known as the Garde Parisen.

The rest of the Darkside isn't somewhere you want to go, even on a bounty. I wondered if the running sore of urban decay would begin to heal now that there was a cure for Clormen-13—Chill, the drug that caused so much death and destruction. It would have been nice, but if history has taught us one thing, it's that people *want* to get high. The pharma companies would come up with more drugs to be abused, and the Mob would sell them. As Old Franje says it, *plus ce change...*

That's the problem with studying history. It will make even the sunniest optimist a cynic. For someone with my pessimistic bent, it gets downright fucking depressing.

Two days after escaping Caracaz during a bloody sunset—as stowaways on a trans-ocean freight hover, no less—I sat very still on a chair in the middle of a dark little hole of a room, my sword across my knees. There hadn't even been a chance to find a scabbard for the blade, despite the fact that wandering around with naked steel was likely to draw notice.

Outside the curtained window, the Darkside seethed.

McKinley twitched the curtain aside, slowly, and peered out into a narrow street lit only by sodium-arc lamps. Down here under the rest of the city, it was always night. The immense press of centuries and dirt overhead threatened to trigger claustrophobia with every breath I took.

I closed my eyes and breathed. The wards I'd put on the walls and window—subtle, gentle wards, meant only to warn me if someone was looking at the room—shivered uneasily. I wished I could shield the room like Japhrimel did, but that would have been like advertising my presence on the local holoboards.

My shoulder was still numb. Now I knew that feeling. It meant Japh was in Hell, somewhere far away from the normal world. If anything could be said to be *normal* nowadays. The ban on Magi practicing hadn't slowed down the ferment one bit, psions being notoriously edgy when denied the chance to practice their gifts. Magi were still showing up dead or going missing, and the Hegemony had its hands full with the confusion *that* was causing. Industrial espionage and theft was at an all-time high. The holonews was full of chaos and destruction.

There were other whispers too—of *things* glimpsed on the street in broad daylight. Things not seen since the Awakening, when psionic and sorcerous talent flowered and the world was turned on its ear again, taking a collective jump into the future and struggling free of the Era of Submission.

The underworld of bounty hunters and mercenaries was alive with the news that I was out there somewhere, and worth a fantastical sum dead or alive, if you could just figure out who to deliver me to. Information on my movements would fetch a fine price too.

Since I hadn't moved from this room since we got to Paradisse, I could only imagine what was going on. McKinley had made one run for supplies, not bringing back a scabbard, and returning pale and shaking just a little, smelling of demon and adrenaline. He brought back food, several bottles of distilled water, and two medikits. And he didn't hold it against me when I met him at the door with a projectile gun, my finger tight on the trigger—and the Knife in my other hand.

I was liking him more than I had, which still wasn't much. Still, I slipped the sheathed Knife inside my bag. The throbbing whisper of the thing set me on edge, and I didn't need more of a reason to lose my temper.

I had plenty of reasons anyway, and a naked sword as well.

I held on to the armrests. The room was in a rundown little boarding-house deep in one of the worst sections of the Darkside, enough pain and despair—not to mention illicit sex, spikes and eddies of violence, and just plain psychic noise—to almost cover up the stain of my aura on the landscape of ambient Power. It was barely furnished, just a cot and this chair, and a ramshackle table made of splinters and glue. McKinley had taken to sleeping on the floor, his hand on the hilt of a knife and his eyelids lifting whenever there was the slightest noise.

I didn't sleep.

Instead, I closed my eyes and breathed, the red ribbon of flame sliding at the bottom of my conscious mind comforting. It was the same comfort I used to associate with the blue glow of Death, the rising crystal traceries of my god's attention. My sword rang softly, and the Knife hummed in its sheath, responding to each twist and curve of rage. My fingers sometimes lifted and touched the back arc of the katana, warm metal responding to me like a purring cat.

Waiting is the hardest part of anything, bounty hunt or combat run. The circular mental motion can be maddening. Add to that

McKinley pacing, peering out the windows, or dozing lightly with one eye open, and you had a recipe for wearing my nerves down to bare threads.

Not that there was much thread to wear off.

I slid out of the chair, settling down cross-legged on the floor. My bag was flung near the chairlegs, a forlorn little canvas pile. I opened the top flap, laying my sword aside but within easy reach, and dug for a familiar hank of blue silk, knotted tightly.

The fabric smelled of *kyphii,* gun oil, and faint nose-tingling human sweat, as well as the ever-present taint of demon spice. I had to pick at the knots for a while before they finally gave way, and my worn deck of tarot cards with their blue-and-black crosshatch backs lay in a nest of silk.

I scooped them up, smoothing the silk out, and shuffled them with quick gunning snaps. McKinley tensed, turned his head to watch. His profile was almost ugly, a narrow nose and the bruising of exhaustion under his eyes, his mouth set like he tasted something bitter.

I hadn't touched my cards in a long time. When I'd been living with Japh in Toscano, there didn't seem much need. And since he'd broken the news that Lucifer wanted my services, I hadn't had time for any quiet reflection, let alone divination.

I snap-shuffled them again, the sound very loud in the empty room. Echoes whispered off the walls. McKinley said nothing.

The cards almost laid themselves out. *Two of Blades. Death,* with a skull's grimace looking pained instead of its usual saucy smile. *The Tower,* screaming faces and shattered stones. The *Devil* card fluttered as I laid it down, despite the absolute stillness.

The next card was blank.

Well, that's useless, Danny. It only tells you something you already know. My rings sparked, snapping as Power swirled in the charged air, something about to happen.

"What is it?" McKinley's soft whisper almost hid the low sound of a knife sliding from its sheath.

I've seen these cards before. My eyes flicked toward the door just as it resounded with three hard knocks, shivering in its frame.

I froze. Memory curled over inside my skull, past sliding seamlessly into the present. McKinley ghosted between me and the door, his left hand suddenly aglow with violet light. My right hand curled around the sword's hilt, yet I didn't try to push myself up from the floor.

I smelled musk and baking bread, and I thought I knew who it was. I didn't reach for my bag and the Knife's almost-audible pulsing.

Another cascade of knocking, fast light polite raps. McKinley glanced back at me, black eyes narrowed.

Suddenly I heard a rapping, as of someone gently tapping, tapping at my chamber door. I swallowed, hard. The Knife's humming rattled against my hip. "You might as well answer that." *If they're knocking, they haven't attacked yet.*

He eased forward, weight balanced catlike. "Be ready."

For what? But I only nodded. My hair fell forward into my eyes, I blew it irritably away with a sharp exhale.

McKinley edged toward the door. He was four steps from it when the knob turned, the locks groaning sharply before they flipped, one by one. It creaked theatrically as it opened, slowly, revealing the dirty hallway outside and a slice of weak golden light from one unshattered bulb.

There, in the doorway, stood a demon.

CHAPTER 28

Y ou'd better come in." Wonder of wonders, I even sounded steady.

Eve stepped over the lintel delicately, like a stray cat. Her pale hair caught all the available light, a torch in darkness. Behind her, a strange-familiar face swam out of the darkness of the hall. Anton Kgembe's hair was damp, beads of water clinging to it, and the star sapphire in the hilt of his scimitar winked. My cheek burned—his tat moved under his skin, the faintly fluorescing dye adding a highlight to the gleam of his eyes.

McKinley lifted his left hand, the violet light streaming in weird geometric patterns from his fingertips. His knees loosened, and if Eve had come for me—or so much as pitched her weight forward at the wrong moment—I think he might have actually tried to kill her.

I never liked you much before, sunshine. But I'm beginning to change my mind.

They came fully into the room, step by step, and I almost wasn't surprised. "McKinley. Close the door." Who was the person using my voice? She sounded almost prim. She *also* sounded like someone you didn't want to fuck with.

He gave me a look that suggested I was a few bananas short of a full sundae. "Valentine—"

"Shut the *door.*" I made my hand unloose with an effort of will. He moved, the geometrics streaming from his fingers, and the door swung slowly closed. "Kgembe."

He bowed slightly. The knives strapped to his rig looked well-oiled and loved, and he eschewed plasguns for a pair of serviceable 9 mm projectile Smithwessons. Just my type of gun.

I braced myself. "Eve."

"Dante." She tilted her head a little, and I got the idea she would have curtsied. Her hair rubbed against itself, much rougher than the silk of Japhrimel's. She was cool, calm, and clean, in a long deep-indigo Chinese-collared shirt and tailored khakis. Low blue Verano heels clicked slightly as she took another two steps forward, seemingly not noticing McKinley's immediate move to put himself between us. "Mother."

The word itself was salt in the wound. I shook it away and rose, not quite as gracefully as a demon, but at least I didn't fall over. "How did you find me?"

"We share a bond." Eve's smile broadened, just a little. It was difficult to look at her.

I couldn't look away. *And I suppose having that Magi right there, the one that opened a door for Japh, didn't hurt.* "Let's just get to the point. What do you want?" *And do you know I have the Knife? Or half of it, anyway?*

A shrug, her shoulder lifting and dipping gracefully. "What I have always wanted. To survive. And not so incidentally, my freedom. Surely you can understand."

"Even if you have to lie to me to get it." I tasted bitterness with the words. The room rattled a bit under the lash of my tone. Her smell wrapped around me, cajoling, teasing, and I found with a burst of relief that I didn't respond to it. The black hole in my head stirred uneasily.

Her bright-blue eyes actually dropped. She looked, of all things, *ashamed.* Like a kid caught cheating on a mentaflo test.

Was it another trick?

"Would you have believed me if I looked like this?" Eve spread her hands, long supple fingers hiding her claws. "What could I have done? Tell me."

Guess we'll never find out, will we. I didn't say it. Instead, I studied her face, searching for some echo of myself in the lines of demon bones, the suppleness of her skin, the gaunt beauty.

There was no human left in Eve. Had there ever been?

It was burned away. In Hell.

I could have hated her for it, except I knew what it felt like. I'd felt that burning myself. Did she ever regret it?

Was she capable of regretting it, now?

How long would it be before I was incapable of regretting the same thing?

No. Stubbornness rose up inside me. *I decide. I'm human. Wherever it counts, wherever I have enough of me left to make it, I'm human.*

Hollow words or not, at least it sounded good. "Where's Leander?" I didn't shift my weight, but I might as well have. The words were ready for war, my tone a lot less than conciliatory.

"I don't know. I had enough to do rescuing *this* human." Eve took a half-step back, avoiding McKinley and keeping an avenue of escape open. Her gasflame-blue gaze flicked toward the darkened window, the Darkside pressing against dusty plasglass. Kgembe didn't look in the least discouraged, or even afraid. The smell of his fear was muted under the screen of Eve's perfume. Still, his gaze settled on McKinley, and I could have sworn the Magi was daring the Hellesvront agent to look at him.

Did you abandon Leander, Eve? Did you even stop to think before you did? What about Velokel? I discarded the questions as useless. Wherever the Necromance was now, I couldn't help him. I had my hands full.

I'd feel guilty about it later. Later, later, later. "You're here, you must want something. What do you want me to do?"

"The Eldest?" Her tongue darted out, smoothed her shapely lips. If I'd still been dazzled by her resemblance to Doreen, I might have been distracted.

That's what you're actually after, I bet. My shoulders dropped a trifle. "You can find me, but not him? Oh, that's right. You've got a pet Magi there. Which side of the street is *he* working?"

The Magi tensed, but still didn't speak, his liquid dark eyes on the hand clasping my swordhilt. Why was he looking at *me* like that? He was hanging around with demons far more dangerous than I ever would be.

Then again, he was a Left Hander. The thought that maybe I'd
end up worshiping the Unspeakable myself if I kept breaking my
Word was chilling, to say the least. Could he tell?

"We share a link, Dante. I did not lie about that." Eve almost
seemed to shrink, a little girl in a demon's body. McKinley moved
restlessly, straining against a leash. Dust shifted against the room's
plain, dirty surfaces, reminding me of the choking grit in a city full
of shattered white walls.

I'm not even going to dignify that with a response. "Get to the
point, Eve. What do you *want?*"

I didn't think it would make any difference. But she opened her
mouth, and she told me.

Silence like dark wine filled the room. McKinley's eyes widened,
a ring of white around the dark irises like a spooked horse's. I didn't
blame him.

"You want me to *what?*" If we'd had any neighbors in the adjoin-
ing rooms, they might have heard my shriek.

So much for dignity. Fudoshin rang gently, the steel responding to
my voice. It hadn't lit with blue fire yet, but the quiver in my wrist
spoke volumes.

Kgembe folded his arms, one eyebrow lifting. Like he didn't
believe I was making such a big deal about it.

Eve still looked very small, and very young. And very much like
a demon, her eyes the brightest thing in the drab, dull room. "I need
time, both to gather my allies and plan. You can provide me with that
time, and enough confusion to distract anyone we need to. No Magi
has your power, by virtue of what you are—enough Power to do
what must be done. I *need* your help, Dante."

Oh, ouch. The way into my psyche, the key precious few of my
human friends had known about. *I need.*

Not *want. Need.*

I am a sucker for being needed. Jace had known that. Doreen had
too. And so had Gabe.

Did Japhrimel know? It was unlikely. He didn't have the first clue
about what made me tick. Maybe that was why he loved me.

Maybe that's why I loved him.

The realization hit me between the eyes like a projectile bullet.
Eve needed my help, certainly. But I could help Japhrimel, maybe,
too. By *doing something,* not just waiting like a lost suitcase, yearning to be picked up and rescued.

Play their games back at them, Dante. See how well you can.

Besides, no human Magi could do what Eve needed. It would take plenty of sheer Power—the same Power that thundered through the mark on my shoulder. Maybe it was time to use it instead of moaning about how different it made me.

I took a deep breath, filling my nose with the musk-sweet spice of Androgyne and the dry demon-tang of Hellesvront agent. Eve might need me, or she might be using me as a distraction—just as Lucifer had.

But Japhrimel definitely needed me right now, for once. If this would create a little chaos to cover his path, I was all for it. I was all for taking back some control in this mess.

"All right." My swordblade dipped, my wrist relaxing. "Tell me how. Use small words so I can understand."

McKinley actually choked, his pale cheeks turning crimson; I glared at him and he shut his mouth over a protest I didn't want to hear.

"Anton can explain much of it, I can fill in any gaps in his knowledge." A flash of something hard and delighted bolted through Eve's eyes, almost too quickly for me to identify. "It is not so difficult, once one knows *how*." Her hands relaxed, and she smiled, a thin small cruel curve of her sculpted lips.

She still looked nothing like Doreen, and just a little like Lucifer. But that tiny smile, fleeting as it was, was still so familiar a chill touched my spine.

Maybe she was my daughter after all.

McKinley stared at the empty hall for a few moments, then swept the door closed. The hinges squealed in protest before he locked it. He stayed where he was for a moment, his left hand braced against the knob. "Are you insane?" His shoulders dropped, shaking under his torn shirt.

Do you really want to know? I looked down at the tarot cards scattered around my booted feet. My heel rested on the Devil card, my weight pitched forward in combat-readiness. I sank back down from the balls of my feet, my boots creaking as I shifted, and my heel ground sharply into the floor. "McKinley." *Dear gods. I sound like Japhrimel.*

"I'd really like to know what the *hell* you're thinking, Valentine. Jaf should have been back by now. He's gone and we're fucked, and you just made it worse by agreeing to openly throw down the gauntlet." He leaned into the door, wood groaning sharply. Outside our bolt-hole, the Darkside inhaled, catching its breath before the plunge.

The gauntlet? Like the cuff I used to wear, saying I was Lucifer's errand-girl? I ground my heel down even more sharply as the thought made my stomach twinge, the darkness inside my head revolving on oiled bearings, silent and deadly. *Okay, Danny. Think your way out of this one.* My brain began to work again. "Please tell me you have a way to get in touch with Vann."

CHAPTER 29

The Il deCit is now underground, and the spires of Notra Dama melt into the landfill top of the cavern of Plásse Cathedral. Unlike most of the Darkside, the Il deCit runs with crimson light—from low-heat sublamps during the night and the sublamps plus incandescents during the "day," or whenever the city's central AI tells the lamps it's between dawn and dusk on the surface. The Il is also one of the bigger thoroughfares, so mini-airbikes and slicboards are popular, the air unsteady and trembling with antigrav wash from reactive paint on the boards and bikes.

The sk8s in the Darkside are different than slictribes in most other parts of the world, being lethal and filthy instead of just clannish and unhygienic. A gang of Darkside slictribers can strip a corpse in seconds or a live victim in under a minute; citizens are just lucky the organ trade isn't on fire in Hegemony Europa like it is in, say, Nuevo Rio.

We crouched in the shadows of a refuse-strewn alley. There's really no smell like a main street in the Darkside. Maintenance 'bots come through at regular intervals, but the constant ambient temperature and the volatile hoverwash make it a breeding ground for all *sorts* of smells, including the effluvia of humanity.

We melded out of the shadows and crossed the street, McKinley flanking me. The crowd was thick but not overly so, and nobody went up the steps of the Notra Dama without having serious business. As soon as it became obvious we were heading for the old temple, the milling pedestrians—Darksiders and regular Paradissians out for a night of slumming fun—suddenly avoided contact with us, a path opening without comment.

I wished it didn't feel so depressingly normal.

Notra Dama rose broken-toothed and slump-shouldered but still beautiful, vibrating with uneasy energy. If Paradisse had a heart, it was probably the Floating Arc Triomphe, retrofitted with hovercushions and a popular tourist destination.

But if the Darkside had a pulsing heart, it was the Lady, as the Notra Dama was known, an ancient Christer temple slumped into the rubble and wreckage, waiting for the next turn of the great wheel. She'd seen pagan sacrifices and the rise and fall of the Religions of Submission; she was where a small group of psions had barricaded themselves during one of the last battles of the Seventy Days War. Old Franje had tried desperately to shield paranormals and psions, granting them sanctuary and parrying both the diplomatic and the military maneuvers of the Evangelicals of Gilead, who demanded the return of any escaped North Merican citizens for internment in the death camps.

I shivered. Hegemony Albion and Old Franje had both been horrifically bombed during the War. The first and last nuclear strike, resulting in the Vegas Waste, had been in North Merica...but in Hegemony Europa, people had long memories. Notra Dama had taken a direct hit, and sometimes, it was said, you could hear the screams of the dying.

I didn't doubt it. An old temple built at the juncture of five ley lines feeding energy into the city's gravitational center was a prime place for ghostflits. She really deserved her own collegia of Ceremonials to drain her charge and restore her, but down here in the dark it wasn't a good idea.

Psions tend to go a little nuts underground.

My boots clicked gently on the steps. At the top the great doors hung, creaking slightly on their ancient hinges as currents of Power threaded through the physical structure of the building. The Lady was restless tonight, maybe reading my intentions—or perhaps just restless because the presence of demons made the entire city shiver like a hooker watching a knife in a pimp's hand.

Like a Knife made out of wood, Danny? The voice of strained hilarity had a particularly jolly tone tonight. *The Knife in your bag? Not going to do you much good in there.*

I pushed the doors open, scanning the interior of the temple through a haze of Power. To OtherSight, white-hot snakes crawled and writhed over the floor, crackling up the columns and walls, dripping from the ruined choirloft and the magnificent chipped stonework and fading frescoes.

It was even better than I'd hoped, the magickal equivalent of a fallout zone. It would keep me hidden in the first stage of the work I intended to perform, and when I drained the ambient Power to fuel the spell it would make a huge stinking noise—a noise noticed by every psion and probably every demon in a good three-hundred-mile radius.

"It just doesn't get any better than this," I muttered, shoving my sword into the loop on my rig. My voice rang off stone, fell back at me, given fresh echoes by the buzzing vibration of Power.

Small shuffling noises edged around us as pale transparencies of ghostflits rode the currents of Power, some of them silently screaming, others just drifting, wearing out their chains until they found by accident the way into the clear rational light of What Comes Next. The flits were a good sign, gathering here where there was enough Power to bathe them in something approximating borrowed flesh, even though my skin chilled to See them, cold breath on my back and wariness rising to my nape.

Necromances don't like flits much. They congregate in nightclubs, some old uncared-for temples, anywhere there's enough Power, instability, and heat to give them a simulacrum of life. Back in the days before the Awakening, those gifted with the ability to see the dead were often pursued by flits, and battered into insane asylums and suicide by the harassment. It technically isn't *harassment,* since flits are just confused and can't understand why normals can't see them...but it's still pretty damn uncomfortable, and before the Awakening the training to keep mental and emotional borders clear and firm to ward off the confused dead wasn't available in any systematic way.

I had to breathe through my mouth, trying not to smell the ripe fresh odor, hitting the back of my throat like a kick of Crostine rum back when I was human, spilling through my bloodstream in a hot wave. Power stroked along my ragged shields, almost matching the soft numbness in my left shoulder. I pushed the door closed, scanning the entire place. Not a soul except the rats in the walls and the flits, a few of them taking notice of the glittering sparkle in my aura that meant Necromance.

Do you know what you're doing, Danny?

I ignored the voice of reason and made a slow circuit of the whole place.

I checked the door in the east quadrant, behind a screening pile of rubble and garbage that smelled unwholesome in the extreme. It opened up into a narrow alley excavated between Notra Dama and the sloping tenement next door. At the end of that alley, at the bottom of a well that went up to the third level—that is, three discrete levels down from the surface, if the Darkside could be said to have actual official *levels*—the slim shape of an airbike was a thin metal gleam. It hadn't been touched, the thread-thin warding I'd laid on it undisturbed.

"All right," I whispered. Turned to McKinley. "It's still there. *Now* are you happy?"

He nodded. "Ecstatic."

I had to suppress the urge to snort. "I wish we'd been able to find Vann and Lucas." *Not to mention Leander. I hope he's still alive, federal agent or not.*

He pulled his lips in, his shoulders tensing. "They can take care of themselves. You're who I'm worried about."

Maybe you should be. I'm about to do something insane. "You might want to take notes. You're going to see a Greater Work of magick performed tonight." *And if it doesn't work, maybe we'll both die in here.*

"Are you really going to do this?" He took up his position by the door, his hands shaken out and loose. The violet glow around his left hand brightened, maybe in response to the ambient Power. I wondered just what exactly that metallic coating on his flesh meant, decided I didn't want to know.

"I said I would. Eve's right—this will buy us some time and create enough confusion to keep us in the game a bit longer. Not only that, but Japhrimel needs some cover." My throat went dry, my heart picking up its pace against my ribs. "If it doesn't work, at the very least it'll make a lot of noise and distract a bunch of demons."

"Or the Prince will find you." His pupils had swollen in the dim light, crimson-tinted from the sublamps outside. He sounded like I'd just informed him of my intention to put on petticoats and sing the entire score of *Magi: The Musical.* With sound effects. A rancid giggle rose up in my throat, was strangled, and fell back down.

Thanks, McKinley. You know, I might have forgotten about that if you hadn't reminded me. "Which is why Eve can't do this. If Lucifer or one of his stooges grabs her..." I swallowed the rest of the sentence. I wasn't about to let that happen.

"If he shows up we might both die. I'm supposed to look after you."

I know. But we're both out of our depth here. It's only a matter of time before someone other than Eve finds me. I shrugged. "I'm going to help Japh and Eve at the same time, McKinley. You want to try to stop me, all you'll get is a bellyful of steel. You want to test me on this?"

His pause was gratifying, at least. "Jaf can take care of himself. And *she—*"

Quit stalling, Danny. "This isn't under discussion, sunshine. You want to leave, there's the door." I turned away, my bootheel scraping the ancient stone of the floor. There was a clear space in front of the altar, and I flipped open my bag as I strode away, around the mound of rubbish that would give us some cover if we had to retreat firing. My fingers rooted through the chaos — spare ammo, leather-wrapped wood pulsing with its own obscene life, a plasglass container of cornmeal still miraculously unhurt, and the small jar of salt.

What I really needed was the chunk of consecrated chalk. My pulse began to hammer, my mouth tasting sour, and I inhaled a long deep breath as I stepped back out into the soaring space of the ruined temple and surveyed the mounds of garbage.

It isn't the location that matters, Danny. Magick is a state of mind. Get moving.

"Fuck," I whispered in lieu of a prayer, as my fingers closed on the chalk.

The sorcerer's circle is an invention of seventeenth-century magick, but it's still a useful innovation. A psion has to be ready to deal with nasty things outside the charmed border of a circle, but as a *container* for magickal force, the circle is without equal.

I didn't precisely hurry, but I didn't take my time either. I'd bought a bottle of Crostine rum at a tiny Darkside shop run by an anemic-looking normal woman, and the pack of synth-hash cigarettes sat with it at the north point of the circle. I made it double, runes from the Nine Canons sketched between the outer and inner rings, each drawn from Magi-trained memory sharp and crisp against cracked stone. Between them, the twisted fluid glyph scored into my flesh writhed, doodled so many times I could have traced it in my sleep.

I should have had incense, and divination to pick the proper time, and a ritual robe. I should have had a consecrated cup, expensive wine instead of cheap liquor, and a week or so to pattern and prepare myself. I should have meditated for an hour or so to clear my head.

Instead, I finished the circle and stood inside it, then dropped the chalk back into my bag with a faint uneasy click. Ever since the climax of the hunt for Kellerman Lourdes, the thought of consecrated chalk raises my hackles just a little.

The leather straps of my rig creaked. I'd fastened my sword to the backcarry, hilt standing up over my shoulder; I'd need both hands for this and possibly for piloting the airbike in a hurry if this worked the way I wanted it to. I settled my bag against my side, breathing deeply, cinnamon musk rising to combat the odor of garbage and the sour sharp smell of stagnant Power.

Danny, what are you doing?

I pushed the voice of reason away one more time. I was trying to stay alive, same as usual. The game was rigged, sure—but I was going to make it a little more difficult to rig. Hopefully.

The hollow place under my ribs, pulsing with my heartbeat, whittled itself deeper as I stood in the middle of the circle, checking its confines. The salt, the rum, the cigarettes…all present and accounted for.

If I pull this off it's going to be one of the finest Greater Works I've ever seen performed. And I'm not even a Magi.

Most Magi would kill to have a demon tell them even half of what Eve had told me. Kgembe had handed over his shadowjournal, something Magi *never* did, with the steps to break open the walls of the world clearly delineated. I wondered what kind of hold she had over him, or if he was one of Japh's people, playing along with her for an unspecified reason. Games within games, plot and counterplot, and me with the benefit of a successful Magi's magickal diagrams and explanations. "Yeah," I muttered, my right hand caressing a knife-hilt. "Lucky me."

I was still stalling.

I sank to my knees, facing the north. Shut my eyes and tried to breathe calmly.

Rage bubbled and boiled under my breastbone. It was never far from the surface these days, and it was good fuel.

I uncapped the rum, took a swallow, and let it burn the velvet cavern of my mouth. I tore the package open and arranged the synth-hash cigarettes in a wheel, all pointing outward. The salt made a fine thin noise as I tossed it straight up, letting it sift down, kissing my hair and face.

I let Power bleed out, fueled by my rage. It slid free with a slight subliminal hiss, filling the chalk marks and turning them silvery. Power soaked into the runes marked between the rings, each one named as I drew it, a sudden subsonic note beginning to thrum as I chanted silently, my lips moving, burning with rum. Alcohol has no effect on me anymore, but the fume of it still brought back memories. Bounties, drinking sessions, celebrations, the ceremonial sharing before a fast dirty suicide run or a slicboard duel...

Jace. Was he watching me? Were all my dead watching?

Enjoy the show, everyone. I'm about to make my mark.

McKinley shifted nervously behind me, his aura a drawing-in, a point of tension in the sea of Power. Notra Dama shivered again, like a sleeper rolling over in bed, struggling toward waking.

If this doesn't work right a whole hell of a lot of people in Paradisse are going to have a very bad day. For a moment my conscience pricked at me. What was I *doing*?

But needs must when the Devil drives, and the Devil was driving this engine. Besides, the damage would be contained—I hoped.

You're playing roulette with other people's lives, Danny.

I knew it. But if Lucifer caught Japhrimel *or* Eve, how many other people would suffer? All of Japh's agents, however many he had salted away. All of Eve's rebellion—demons, sure, but still. Was the enemy of my enemy worth what I was about to do?

If Lucifer keeps playing these games, more people are going to suffer. Here's your chance to end it, Danny.

I shut all the arguments away. I needed all my concentration now.

The last rune shimmered. *Uruthusz,* the Piercer of Veils, with its two downward-spiking teeth. I let the Power slip through my mental fingers, filling the rune like a cup. The circle clicked into completeness, a sound felt more in the solar plexus and teeth than heard.

Moving air mouthed my tangled hair, pushing it back. The ghost-flits rode closer, drawn to the circle's humming tautness. None of them approached me yet, but they shimmered, taking on false substance. Eyes glittered, hands of tinted smoke reaching out and curling away, their mouths opening. If I listened, I could hear them chittering, pleading, squealing.

Touch me. Feed me. Give me life.

Not tonight.

Heat bloomed in the center of the circle, in a space behind the physical. It was a good sign, the walls of reality thinning here under an onslaught of centuries of Power. The point of heat became a flame, wavered, and held.

The cigarettes trembled like spokes of a wheel about to roll into motion. All it needed was a little push.

"Valentine..." McKinley didn't sound too happy. Maybe he was having second thoughts.

Too late. I centered myself, the pattern of what I was about to attempt rising through the surface of the world.

Then I jacked into Notra Dama's ambient Power and sent everything I could reach pouring into that small, nonphysical flame.

The cigarettes lit, fuming, synth-hash smoke rising in angular shapes. The runes froze, sparking with blue and crimson light, then settled into a golden glow and began writhing against the floor, running between the two circles in a smeared streak. The temperature rose. My voice was suddenly audible even to me, chanting.

It wasn't a Necromance's power-chant, to bring a soul over the bridge and allow it a voice in the world of the living.

This was something else, a harsh sliding tongue that bloodied my lips even as I spoke it. It roiled the air and tore into the circle, the words taking weight and form, streaming into a vortex of *absence* blooming like a camera lens away from the flame, now visible as a pale colorless twisting.

I had no idea where the words came from but I went with it. Once you start a Greater Work like this, the magick takes its own shape. It rides you, for good or for ill, and you are a passenger on its tidal wave. If the Work miscarries you can get backlash sickness, or drained down dangerously far as it tries to complete itself even through its flaws. Which is why preparation, planning, divination, and good old-fashioned luck are key to surviving your own Greater Works.

Ghostflits began to peel away, their smoky forms shredding. Their mouths opened in silent crystal screams and the Power rode me, a riverbed in its channel. I was actually draining Notra Dama, the floodtide of energy directed at weakening the walls of the world, already tissue-thin but made of strong, resilient stuff.

The Knife vibrated in my bag, harmonic resonance aching in my teeth and bones. Fudoshin answered with his own scabbarded hum, echoing the runes in the circle, now moving so fast they were a golden ring, a hoop of fire, a thin thread of crimson running through the warp and weft of the spell, drawing it tight, tighter, tightest.

McKinley shouted something, but I didn't care. I was too far gone in the spell. There was more and more Power, forcing itself through my shredded shielding, tender scarred patches in my psyche smoking under the strain. I was a glove too small for the hand forcing its way in, the magick uncaring of my human limits, the fabric of my mind bending and ripping under the strain—

—just as the cloth of reality tore, a vertical slit opening with the sound of parachute silk tearing under too much stress.

McKinley yelled again, a shapeless noise. The second half of the spell locked down, anchors driven deep into the temple's floor, stone groaning and the entire city ramming through my unprotected skull for one endless, horrific moment. The anchors held, reality warping and skewing at the edges of the hole I'd just torn in the world.

Through that long tunnel, a weird directionless red-orange glow bloomed. The icy heat of Hell boiled through, cracking the floor and straining against mortal chill. But it *held*, the circle shuddering and pulling Power through the temple—and from the city's deep, sonorous heart with its acres of pain, fear, and the psychic sludge of a whole population jammed together, living cheek-by-jowl and boiling for centuries.

The door was open.

I'm not even a Magi, I thought in stunned wonder. *Any Magi worth their salt would pay to have me do this; I've done what it takes them years to do.*

Damn. I'm good.

I fell backward as they boiled through, the temple groaning in distress, and McKinley grabbed me. Consciousness narrowed to a thread as the rushing tide of darkness took on lambent eyes and horns, feathers and long arms, chuckling and chittering in their unlovely language as the denizens of Hell grabbed their opportunity and *escaped.* Chaos smashed against the temple's walls, and Notra Dama woke in a blinding sheet of Power and thundered against the violation.

McKinley dragged me. Psychic darkness washed against the temple's walls, coated its refuse-strewn floor, and no few of the demons paused in their headlong rush to eye me as my bootheels scraped against the floor. The Hellesvront agent swore, pulling me behind a pile of garbage, cutting off my view of the circle and the escaping Lesser Flight demons. "What the *hell* is wrong with you?" he screamed in my ear, just as the temple shivered again. The snap of connection breaking between me and the circle was blessed relief, my mind contracting behind the borrowed weight of Japhrimel's shielding.

Yet another time my brain should have turned to oatmeal. Lucky lucky me.

The door would stay open as long as the taplines feeding it Power could handle the strain before slamming shut, the fabric of reality reasserting its structure. Demons would flood through, and since Lucifer's big thing was controlling which demon went where, he'd have his hands full.

I'd just altered the playing field and hopefully created enough chaos to cover McKinley and me for a little bit, until Japh could get back—he would also, hopefully, find it a little easier to sneak around Hell now that I'd thrown the dice again. I'd given Eve the time she asked for.

For my first toss of the dice in the game, it was a doozy.

I'd also just unleashed who-knew-how-many demons on the world. *Gods forgive me.*

The Hegemony would also have its hands full dealing with this eruption, and that meant they wouldn't be sending any more field agents after me.

Welcome to the game, Danny.

The temple's side door yawed, and McKinley hauled me through, greasy crud scraping against our boots. He swore, filthily, in every language I had the blue words in and quite a few I didn't.

We made it to the airbike, Notra Dama tolling in distress. Little scrabbling sounds behind us didn't sound human *or* animal, and McKinley thumbed the starter. Antigrav whined. I threw my leg over the bike's saddle and looked back to see imps boiling over the trash-heap, their bald heads gleaming and their naked limbs moving in ways nothing of this world should move. Nausea rose, I almost pitched off the bike and retched—but McKinley bent over the handlebars and kicked the maglock off. I grabbed at his waist, the antigrav woke with a rattling whine, and we rocketed away even as the imps ignored us and scattered like quicksilver.

Notra Dama surged behind us, psychic stress becoming physical, masonry creaking and squealing as the first surfroar of crowd noise began. I clutched at both McKinley and consciousness, hanging onto each by the thinnest of threads. My cheek ached, the tattoo shifting madly under the skin. We raced for the surface of Paradisse on the expanding edge of a circle of chaos I had just unleashed on an unsuspecting world.

CHAPTER 30

The rooms were beautiful, singing arches pierced with shafts of golden light that wasn't daylight but well-placed full-spectrum bulbs. It was a nice touch, even if the air swirled and trembled with the tang of spice and musk that said *demon*.

Priceless antiques, mostly vases, sat on fluted plasglass tables, each one humming with magickal force. Demon warding was anchored to the walls, but straining bits of demon magick were also set in each knickknack and curio, sending up waves of interference into the atmosphere. Someone was taking a great deal of trouble to make this place invisible, protections woven over every inch of wallspace, triplines and protective wards showered over the flooring and furniture.

It was uncomfortably close to the way things looked in Hell, and the shivers juddering just under my skin didn't help. I kept expecting to glance in a corner and see a pair of level burning-green eyes in a lean golden face, a straight mouth and the long black Chinese-collared coat of my Fallen. Or a pair of green eyes and a shock of golden hair, burning like an aureole.

I sat in Eve's hideout, the air buzzing and blurring with demon musk, McKinley by the door to the suite she'd shown us to. This tower rose among hundreds of others, a forest of glowing spires watching as dawn rose over the world.

The city trembled. Up here on the Brightside it wasn't too bad, but the ambient Power tasted like burning cinnamon. The holonews was full of weird occurrences—a street on one of the Darkside's lowest levels turned to a sheet of glass, a wave of fights breaking out in taverns, a "paranormal incident" at Notra Dama calling Hegemony containment teams from around the globe. People were uneasy.

Even the normals feel it when the ambient Power of a city is drained or altered.

I was hungry.

McKinley sighed, leaning his head back against the wall. "You okay?"

He kept asking me, about once an hour. Normally it would have dragged irritation against my bare nerves, my shoulder still prickle-numb, my eyes sandy and aching.

But right now I was glad of the company. "Peachy." I shifted, and the chair squeaked. Little sounds came through the walls — footsteps and faroff voices too strange to be human.

"Tell me again why we're trusting her. Jaf won't like this."

"He said himself that she has a reason to keep me alive and him happy. We need more backup, McKinley. This is safer than being on our own." *In any case, it's too late now.*

"It's not like Vann. He's never been late before."

And he has Lucas with him. "I'm not happy about it either. I bought us some breathing room, at least." The hollowness of my belly taunted me. I needed food. What I wouldn't give to be able to walk down the street to a noodle shop, or even grab a heatseal packet of protein mush.

Too bad, Danny. You've worked hungry before.

"Guess so." The electric light ran over his hair, glittered in his black eyes. The windows were polarized; we would be invisible from outside — if anything but empty air was this high up, sandwiched between hoverlanes. Nobody would think to look for me in a tower in the poshest slice of Paradisse.

I found myself rubbing at my left shoulder, pushing cloth over the twisted, numb scar. *How long is this going to take, Japh? I've about run out of delaying tactics.* "What do you think is going to happen?"

The agent shrugged. "Jaf will come back. He always does, sooner or later."

Now there was an opening. "How long have you been ... working ... for him?"

"Long enough to trust him." He shifted his weight, peeled himself away from the wall. "You don't have to like me, Valentine. I just do my job."

Sekhmet sa'es. "I was just *asking*." I pushed myself up to my booted feet. My hair felt filthy, tangled with dust and dirt, reeking of Notra Dama, spent magick, and demons. At least I hadn't had my clothes blown off me this time. "He never tells me anything."

"Not known for explaining himself."

Could you sound any more dismissive? "What *is* he known for? Or is that classified information, too?"

McKinley sighed. "He's a demon. He's the Prince's Eldest and the assassin."

The city glowed, fingers of gold reaching through the streets as the sun lifted itself up over the rim of the world. The Senne glittered in the distance, a river of molten stuff coming up from underground amid the sprawl of the suburbs, and I could just see the column of light that was the plasglow beam atop the Toure Effel fading as the sky flushed with rose instead of gray. I could feel the plucked string of the Toure vibrating as it channeled the city's distress. "Fine. I get it."

"What can I tell you that you don't already know?" McKinley moved behind me, not quite silently, and my back prickled. "Jesu Christos. He's risked *everything* for you."

I didn't ask McKinley what he thought *I'd* risked for Japh.

It would take a few days for Paradisse to get back to itself, its population feeding back into the ambient well of Power. The psions around here were probably having headaches and nausea, their bodies getting accustomed to a lower level in the energy flux.

Congratulations, Danny. Making friends everywhere you go, aren't you?

My psychic fingerprints were all over the work at Notra Dama. That was the trouble with the use of Power, it was so highly personal. I was going to be very famous once everyone figured out what had happened.

If, of course, word got out. The Hegemony had a reason to keep this under wraps, if they were Lucifer's toy. Plot and counterplot; nobody was what they seemed.

Not even Japhrimel. Not even me, playing the Devil's game now. My breath fogged the glass, a circle of condensation. "You know, I'm getting a little tired of everyone assuming I made Japh Fall."

"What exactly *did* you do?"

What did I do? "I was just trying to stay alive. All of a sudden the Devil wanted me to kill someone, and I had a reason to do it. Then things just got out of hand, and before I knew it I had a demon all over me and a serious case of genesplicing. Then he up and dies on me and..." The circle of breath-fog spread. I rested my forehead on the cold, reinforced plasglass. It was thick enough to be projectile-proof, humming slightly with the shielding applied to it and the everpresent sound of a river of high-altitude air shifting around the tower's walls. The words curdled in my throat. Why was I trying to explain myself to *him,* of all people? "It wasn't my fault." *There's enough that* is *my fault.* "Forget it. I was just trying to find a few things out."

"Why don't you ask *him?*"

The stupid man. As if I hadn't been trying to do just that for so long now. "He won't answer me. Or he lies. Look, McKinley, I'm sorry I fucking well asked you. Just shut up."

Mercifully, he did. I rested my forehead on the glass and bumped Fudoshin's hilt on the window. Once. Twice. Three times. For luck. Eve had even come up with a scabbard, a lovely black-lacquered curve of reinforced wood. "I don't like this," I muttered. "Don't like it at all."

McKinley held his peace. I swung away from the window, my rig creaking, and cast a sharp glance over the room. Bed fit for a princess, choked in blue velvet. Fainting-couches in the same blue velvet, lyrate tables holding knickknacks humming with sleepy demon magick. The pale cream carpet was thick enough to lose credit discs in. Electric light grew paler, compensating for day rising in the east.

Fine hairs on my nape rose. Premonition ruffled past me, icy fingernails touching my cheeks. Whatever was going to happen was coming soon, rolling toward me like ball bearings on a reactive-greased slope.

The black hole inside my brain shivered. The same sounds chuckling up from its depths were coming through the walls—the muffled evidence of things not human walking around, making themselves at home, doing whatever it was demons did.

Keep moving, Danny. If you stop you'll drown.

That was rabbit-talk. Right now I was safest with my head down, staying in a protected location. The more I moved around, the more people would see me, the more chance someone would get word of where I was.

I had just acted on my own, for once since this whole thing started not just being pushed from place to place. I was pretty sure nobody would have expected this from me. The thing to do now was wait for the countermove, just like in battlechess.

I let out another long, soft breath. My stomach twisted unhappily. Finally, I peeled myself away from the window. "You hungry?"

McKinley had picked another wall to lean against, where he could see both me and the door. He glanced up, the bruised circles under his eyes harshly evident in the new light. "I could eat," he said, as if it had just occurred to him.

"There's bound to be a kitchen in this pile. We'll find something."

If I can't move around out in the city I'll settle for poking around here. If I have to stay in one room for very long I'm going to go insane. I wished I was exaggerating.

We didn't have to go very far—at the end of the short curving hall outside the suite's door, there was the hoverlift we'd come up in and a small kitchen, stocked with the usual Paradisse hotelier fare— cheese, bread, fruit, coffee, a wide array of gourmet freeze-reheat stuff like individual pizzas and packets of beef pho with noodles like brain wrinkles pressing against plaswrap. Human food, which made me wonder about this place. I knew demons *could* eat—sometimes Japh ate with me, for example, and seemed to enjoy it—but I wasn't entirely sure if they had to. Was this just Eve planning for me, or did it come with the tower? Who was paying for all this?

Then again, demons have no problem with money.

McKinley settled down with a hunk of yellow cheese and a baguette, taking bites off an apple in between. I popped one of the individual pizzas into the microwave and hit the button. Everything was new, top of the line, and unused.

This is weird. Then again, sunshine, weird is your middle name these days. "Why would she have human food?"

"They like it. It's not nourishment to them, it's an accessory." McKinley cracked a bottle of mineral water open with a practiced twist of his wrist. "Plus, any demon is going to have human retainers. It's how it works. They like to stay behind the scenes unless there's killing to be done."

Just a fount of useful information, aren't you? When you're not sneering at me, that is. "Oh." I watched through the plasglass door as the pizza heated, cheese melting and bubbling, the smell of marinara and cheese, not to mention crust, suddenly filling my mouth with water. "Retainers. This is so very feudal."

"Guess so. Like the Mob, only not so nice." He was perking up, eating in great starving bites, barely stopping to chew. His eyes never stopped roving the room, and he'd picked the seat between me and the door.

Exactly where I'd sit, if I was doing bodyguard duty on someone. My nape prickled again. The microwave dinged, and I retrieved my little pizza. I settled myself in the safest spot, my back to the blind corner holding a mini-fridge and the disposal unit. McKinley shifted a little in his seat, his metallic left hand lying discarded on the blondwood tabletop.

"How did you end up working for Japh?" I didn't think he'd tell me, but it was a way to pass the time. I waited for the pizza to cool down, eyeing the gobbets of melted cheese. It smelled like real cheese too, and I was suddenly reminded of the first meal I'd ever eaten with my Fallen.

My, how the world turns.

"I was almost dead but I'd put up a hell of a fight. He was impressed, and offered me either a quick passing or service." McKinley shrugged. "I wasn't ready to die yet."

I peeled a precut slice out of the golden wheel. Blew across the piece to cool it. "You know, you could give a demon lessons in not really answering the goddamn question."

"My former lord wanted to kill the Eldest. We tried like hell, but we were only human, even with... modifications." He lifted his left hand slightly, laid it back to rest on the tabletop.

I held the pizza, my mouth hanging open, for what seemed an eternity. Then I took a bite. *Huh.* "We meaning you and Vann?"

"And a few others." His face changed, and he laid down the hunk of cheese. "They should be looking for you too. That's another reason why I'm worried."

"Looking for me?"

"Just like guardian angels, Valentine." He took a long pull of mineral water, washing some taste out of his mouth. "We had a perimeter set up in Toscano, keeping you under wraps."

I was getting tired of my mouth hanging open in astonishment, so I took another bite. Hot tomato sauce, melted cheese, a little heavy on the oregano. The food helped, made me feel more solid. "I never knew."

"That was the *idea,*" he replied in a stunningly good *you are an idiot* tone.

I'd suspected something, of course. But I'd never had a whisper of anyone watching Japhrimel and me while I did my best to settle into a boring regular life, shopping for shadowjournals and antique furnishings, going for walks in the afternoon sun... and waking up screaming with Mirovitch's *ka* whispering inside my head, ripping and tearing as fingers of burning ectoplasm tried to claw down my throat and rape my mind.

I shivered, dropped my pizza back down to its nest of plaswrap. The black hole in my head widened, echoes spilling through my skull.

The scar in the hollow of my left shoulder twinged, warningly.

"You okay?" McKinley eyed me.

My shoulder twinged again, like a fishhook in flesh, plucking as it twitched. "Fine." I scooped up the pizza again and began wolfing without tasting it. I'd need fuel, no matter what happened next. "You know," I said between bites, wiping tomato sauce away from my lips, "I don't think I should stay up here like a princess in a pea, or whatever. I think we should wander around this place and peek at what the demons are doing."

McKinley choked on a bite of baguette. His black eyes got very wide. "Why not just get the hell out of here?"

I settled down to the rest of my pizza. "Because without Japhrimel, you and I are *both* dead out there. This isn't just a papercut to Lucifer. I threw down a challenge big-time. I'm sure the Hegemony would love to get their hands on me too. I'm too hot to handle now — but I don't trust demons either, even if they have good reasons to protect me. I'm getting to where I don't trust anyone, not even myself. So I want to look around where I've landed." *Besides, I can't take being cooped up in this tower.*

I felt horribly naked, even with all the demon shielding on the walls. I also felt filthy, messy, ugly, and the slightest bit shaky. I itched for some kind of action — sparring, or a hard clean fight. Something to get rid of the bright red ribbon of rage under the surface of my thoughts, growing in increments, pressing against the confines of my temper.

A shadow fell over the kitchen door, and I knew who it was even before she appeared. I *smelled* her, a smell that was quickly growing unique, impressing itself on my sensitive nose.

McKinley's chair scraped as he bolted to his feet, the color draining from his cheeks and turning him whey-pale as the scorch of a demon filled the air. I finished the last two bites of crust, and Eve folded her arms, smiling that imperturbable smile. Her clotted-ice hair touched her shoulders, almost writhing with life, and her gas-flame eyes passed over me in a long arc.

"I see you found your provisions. I thought it best not to ask you to dinner with our other guests."

I licked my fingers. "Charmed. I could probably eat my way through here in an hour or so. But I was thinking of looking around, seeing what your setup is here."

A slim shoulder lifted, dropped. She wore blue, again, an indigo cable-knit sweater and slacks that had to be designer, the same pair of low Verano heels. Nothing but the best for this demon.

I found myself searching her face again for any echo of Doreen, comparing her to what she had looked like, the glamour that had fooled me into...what? Going up against the Devil? I'd've done it anyway. It wasn't like Lucifer was going to leave me alone.

"If there is time," she finally answered.

I deliberately didn't reach for Fudoshin's hilt. The Knife hummed against my hip. "What's going on? Where's Kgembe?" The scar twined again, and began to tingle—not the numb prickle of Japhrimel *elsewhere,* but a waking-up feeling.

I hoped it was what I thought it was.

"The Magi has disappeared—wise of him, I think. We have planned a council of war, and I thought to request your presence. Several of my allies have found themselves recently freed from Hell." A slight tilt of her head, like a servomotor on jeweled bearings, a graceful oiled inhuman movement.

"Fancy that. War, huh?" *Well, what else would you call this, Danny?* "When?"

"Tonight. At dusk. It's traditional. May I count on your presence?"

I nodded, my hair moving uneasily on my scalp. I was suddenly aware of how I must look—dirty, bled on and air-dried, and probably just two short steps away from crazed. "You can."

"Very well." She turned on her heel, sharply, without even deigning to look in McKinley's direction.

"Eve." *If that's even your name.*

She halted, her narrow back to me.

"You can put that face back on. If you want. The one that looks like Doreen." *I might even find it easier.*

She paused for just the barest of seconds. "Why? This is what I am, Dante."

I might find it a little easier to look at you. Or then again, I might not. "You were human. At least partly." Not just human. She'd been a little girl.

A child I had been unable to save.

"Nothing of humanity survives Hell's fires." No shrug, just a simple statement of fact. Fresh dawning light ran along the snakes of her hair, touched the supple curve of her hip under the sweater's hem, and cringed away from something that didn't belong in this world.

I let her kiss my cheek, once. I got so close to her I could smell her, feel her heat. The thought sent a shiver through me. Had it just been that she looked like Doreen? Was there any truth to her claim that I was part of the genetic mix used to make her?

How else had she found me? "What about what you got from me? Doesn't that count?"

"It matters as little or as much as you want to make it matter. You're still the only mother I have."

McKinley made a restless movement. Maybe he wanted to argue.

"I can't hold a gun to your head and make you human." *I can't even do that to myself.*

"If you could, would you?" She still didn't turn around, and her tone was excessively gentle.

"No." It came out immediately, without thought. "I wouldn't."

"Why?"

Because that's not the way I play, goddammit. "Just because. It wouldn't change anything."

She turned back, slowly, letting the light play over each feature, each hill and valley geometrically just a little *off,* altered. "I cannot afford to be *too* human. Not with *him* to slay, and all of us to save— and your lover, ally or not, to reckon with." As usual, her face twisted slightly when she referred to Lucifer, her lip lifting and nose wrinkling. I watched, fascinated. It was a curiously immature movement, like a teen sucking on bitter algae candy.

My right hand fell limp at my side, no longer aching for the feel of a hilt and a blade cutting flesh. The ribbon of rage shrank, just a little bit.

"But as human as I can be, I will be in your honor, my mother." A slight little bow, her icy hair falling forward over slim shoulders, and then she was gone, the sunlight falling through where she'd stood as the sound of her footsteps—too light and quick to be human, and faintly wrong in the gait as well—retreated down the hall.

The scar began to burn, faintly at first, heat working through its numbness. A candleflame moving closer and closer to the flesh, a spot of warmth.

I found my right hand hovering over my dirty shoulder, fingertips aching for the feel of the ropy scar twisting and bumping under my touch.

"Valentine—" McKinley began.

"Shut up." I sounded strained and unnatural even to myself. "Just eat. I'm going to get cleaned up."

CHAPTER 31

Dying sunlight turned bloody in the west, and the room was long and wide, windowless, and full of movement that stopped the moment I stepped over the threshold. Plain white walls vibrated with demon warding, and the long, slim, highly polished table running down the center was full of demons.

I froze.

At the head of the table Eve straightened, pushing back her pale ropes of hair. The plunging inside my stomach turned into a full-fledged barrel roll with dynos straining.

The room full of demons turned still and trembling as a pool of quicksilver on a level surface, twitching with Power as each of them turned their lambent eyes on me.

Tall or short, most slender and golden-skinned, but each with that aura of *difference* demons carry. They are not beautiful or ugly, though some of them are bizarre in the extreme. It's that breath of alienness that makes the human mind shiver when looking at them.

They were all of the Greater Flight. There was no mistaking it. To my left, dozing in a corner, two hellhounds slumped together, sleeping, their obsidian limbs splayed in a caricature of relaxation. From under one eyelid, a sliver of orange peeked—not sleeping, then.

A prickling shiver ran through my entire body, and I was suddenly very sure that I wanted to see Japhrimel again.

Right fucking now.

"Dante." Eve's voice stroked each exposed edge, from the table to the ceiling, and a breath of baking bread and fresh musk reached me. The smell of an Androgyne.

Like Lucifer.

My stomach heaved, the black hole in my head pulsing and

straining until I could push it down, lock it away. I swallowed with difficulty and met her eyes again.

I found myself relieved she hadn't taken on Doreen's face again after all. There was no denying the demon in her. Even the way she held herself, completely still, as if liquid grace had frozen itself at one particular point in a dance.

"Gentlemen," she continued, "I present to you Dante Valentine, the Eldest's *hedaira,* and the Key to the throne of Hell."

I wondered if I should take a bow.

"What nonsense are you speaking?" This voice, from a demon with dappled, mottled skin like the side of a painted pony, was a knife against the skin after the soft restfulness of Eve's. "This is the Eldest's whore, and our hostage."

A ripple ran through the assembled demons. One at my end of the table, a tall sharp-faced male with a shock of black thistledown hair, tensed as if to rise to his feet. He wore white, rags fluttering as his fingers curled around the edge of the table, and my awareness centered on him, my hand itching for the swordhilt again.

When Eve spoke I almost twitched.

"Zaj." The single word was loaded with gunpowder threading through the softness of her tone. The shortening of a demon's name sounded like a weapon in her mouth. "Our plan requires the Key. Without the Key, we could not retrieve the Knife. Without the Knife, there is no challenge we can make to Lucifer that will not end in our death or capture. With Dante's help, we can rob Lucifer of the greatest support of his regime—the Eldest's loyalty. And *with* the Knife, there is hope for us to topple Lucifer, or simply reach a treaty with him that he dares not break."

"You are a fool. No demon can wield the Knife." The mottled demon's chair grated along parquet as he rose slowly to his feet, his bright blue burning eyes fixed on me. My skin chilled, my throat going dry, and I was vaguely aware of McKinley moving closer to me, his peculiar null aura contracting.

"She is *not* demon. What does the riddle say? *The hand that can hold the Knife has faced fire and not been consumed, has walked in death and returned, a hand given strength beyond its ken.* So spoke Ilvarimel's *hedaira,* in the Temple of the White-Walled City, before she died at the hands of the Kinslayer." Eve turned away from the table, passing the high-backed chair, pacing to the wall and staring at its smooth white gleam. The warding sunk into the walls trembled under her attention, my knees echoing that tremor.

Well, that's bad poetry. Why didn't anyone ever tell me about this before?

"Who fits this description, Zaj?" Eve's voice was soft. "Who has escaped fire, walked in Death, and been given strength beyond a mortal's ken by the first Fallen in millennia? If you have another candidate who fits the bill, feel free to produce them for our study and illumination."

Zaj dropped back into his chair, still staring at me. I didn't like the look on his broad face. Neither did I like the increasing sense of motion threading through the other demons present. Their faces ran like ink on wet paper, because I couldn't make my eyes focus on one of them — too busy trying to watch them all.

You'd think this sort of thing would seem almost normal to me by now. Dark hilarity welled up in my throat, was shoved down with hysterical strength.

"You think she can wield the Knife." This demon, halfway down the table, was dressed all in fluttering red, long sleeves and a minstrel's dreamy face marred by the thin crimson lines of what looked like tribal tattoos swirling across his cheeks. His eyes were scarlet drops with black teardrops painted over them, I stared at the sharpness of his white teeth against golden skin and scarlet markings. He looked oddly familiar.

I am not thinking clearly. I am not even close to thinking clearly.

Increasing heat mounted through the lines of the scar on my left shoulder. I touched the Knife, buzzing in its hilt strapped to my rig, and the demons went still, each pair of lambent eyes fixed on me.

Maybe taking it out of my bag hadn't been such a great idea, after all. On the other hand, if any of them came at me . . .

Another demon, with a veil of gold tissue over its head and the shadow of something under it I had no desire to see, let out a slow hiss, like an adder swelling with poison. "I applaud our leader for her show of strength." Its voice loaded the sibilants with toxic strength. "What precisely are we discussing?"

"Rebellion, and the death of the Prince of Hell." This, from the crimson-painted demon. Its voice was strangely sexless, a high clear tone like glass under moonlight. "That *is* what we are speaking of, is it not?"

With a whole bunch of you guys for backup, it might even be possible. My entire body was a block of numb ice. My stomach filled with uneasy, unsteady loathing.

I hoped my eyes weren't the size of plates. "Sounds great." I spoke before Eve could, my mouth bolting the way it always does. "I'm all for it. When do we start?"

"You see?" Eve whirled away from the wall, her hair swinging in a heavy pale wave of ropes. "A *hedaira* does not fear him. Why should we of the Greater Flight fear him, when we have the means to make the Eldest behave—or at least remain neutral? If we are allied with the holder of the Knife of Sorrow, we have the upper hand."

"None have ever successfully challenged the Prince." A demon with fat yellow tentacled dreadlocks leaned slightly aside in his chair, his fingertips drumming the tabletop in one smooth arc. He had eight fingers on his right hand, and I stared at the muscle working in his slim forearm. "Still, we have come this far. It is logical for us to pursue our course." He paused, his fingers drumming down again, eight beats marking off time. "After all, *he* will not forgive us. Are we resigned to death?"

"He will suspect our intentions, and send someone to collect the Knife." This from a tall, thin demon whose face was hidden under the hood of a gray cloak, the material shifting oddly as it twitched.

Eve's eyes met mine. "He did. But we had our own viper in the heart of that mission. Any other demon he sends will meet a harsh fate."

"Our own viper?" Zaj's eyebrow didn't lift, but he sounded skeptical. "This little thing?"

I could not look away from Eve's face. My heart thudded thinly, and I was suddenly aware of sweat prickling under my arms and at the small of my back. It took a lot of effort to make me sweat, a half-hour of hard sparring at least—or a room full of demons.

Go figure.

"She has been far more successful than any of you, has she not? And as long as we hold the allegiance of this Necromance, we hold the allegiance of her Fallen. If you do not respect her might, I should hope you are not stupid enough to disregard his." Eve's voice was very soft. "We do have your allegiance, do we not, Dante?"

Silence. Every eye in the place on me. McKinley shuffled slightly, near the door. I wondered if the coppery smell of fear riding the air was from him—or from me.

It came from that black place in me, the thing I didn't want to remember. The rush and crackle of flame filled my veins, a lioness's head lifting behind my eyes, Her face full of bloody light.

The world turned over, ramming me back into myself with a concussive internal blast. I almost staggered, caught myself. Air scorched my lungs as I let out the breath I'd been holding, returning to my skin with a rush of certainty. "You told me you wanted me to set myself up against the Prince of Hell. Here I am. That son of a bitch has messed with me for the last time."

"And your Fallen?" Eve persisted, but she looked pleased. A slight cruel smile lifted the corners of her mouth, and my face felt so numb I couldn't tell if I was copying the expression—or if she'd stolen it from my face.

"He's with me." My throat was dry, but the words were soft, husky, laden with promise.

"You are certain?"

Don't ask me that. I'm pretty certain, but he's pulled fast ones on me before. I searched her face, finding only the taint of demon overlaying her skin with a high gloss, covered with the dark hood of my own guilt at not being able to save her from Lucifer in the first place. There were so many I had failed to save—Lewis, Doreen, Jace, Eddie, Gabe...the list stretched on. My arms and legs were frozen, my face a stiff mask.

All that remained was to say the words. "I'm sure," I husked. "What do you have in mind?"

She opened her mouth, but my scar turned molten, sending a soft wave of Power down my skin. I shivered, my right hand empty without a swordhilt. A susurrus ran through the assembled demons.

The sun turned into a bloody eye, low in the sky. Paradisse glimmered, slim plasteel towers each vetted by an aesthetic committee before the first hoverload of dirt was lifted. They pierced the gathering twilight, shimmers resolving near their tops, lights blurring along each graceful arch.

"Ah." Eve lowered herself into the iron chair at the head of the table, its high spiked back spearing the air. The demons all turned still as statues, waiting.

Usually when demons are this still, they're conserving their energy, compressing the elasticity of their bodies so they can unleash that spooky blurring speed of theirs when the time comes. This was a different immobility, almost tranquil except for the razor-edge of nervousness under it, like hounds scenting blood and waiting tensely for the leash to slip.

Crimson painted the windows, and if I hadn't been so nervous and just plain exhausted I might have enjoyed the once-in-a-lifetime view of Paradisse stretching out beneath us, the buildings beginning their nightly dance of illumination, streams of hovertraffic winking with reactive paint, the towers also beginning to let loose scarves of synth-perfume that glittered crystalline as the lowering sun shone through them. Walking in Paradisse is an olfactory experience as well as visual.

I should have been having the time of my life.

Darkness gathered along the floor, and I felt the quivering that ran through the building. It felt like a padded hammer tapping at my left shoulder, and I let out a small sound between my lips. Every demon in the room turned his gaze to me, except Eve, who settled down languorous into the chair.

"It begins," she murmured. "Semma?"

A demon at the far end of the table—the one with a long shock of blue hair woven with glittering gold charms that tinkled as he moved—rose and padded to the hoverlift door. I heard the lift machinery beginning, the whine of hover transport and a swoosh of displaced air. I didn't look, staring down the table and off to the left, where the windows framed a cityscape just falling under night's cloak.

Steady now, Dante. I edged along the table, passing behind demons so still they might have been statues, and finally paused, almost to Eve's chair. To get there I had to pass the mottled demon, and I didn't want to. The mood of the room turned dark, Power spilling against my nervestrings like warm oil, a sizzling bath.

The lift arrived, and the doors opened with a soft chime. Silence, three soft steps I knew as well as my own heartbeat, and he came into the room.

Dear gods. Thank you. He's out of Hell. The scar on my shoulder turned live, singing against my skin, a burst of Power working its way down through flesh and racing through my bones.

Another silence, this one managing to convey shock and growing apprehension. He tipped a room full of scary-ass demons into fear just by walking in.

Japhrimel. My Fallen.

My very own demon. *I am so happy to see you right now, Japh.*

I let my eyes swing over to him. He'd come alone, and stood in front of the hoverlift doors, his eyes burning green under winged dark eyebrows. His hair was longer, too; he hadn't cut it. It fell in his eyes and shadowed the first shock: the gauntness of his face.

He looked *starved,* perfect skin drawn tight over bones that revealed demon architecture as surely as my own. There were hollows under his cheekbones, and dark smudges under his eyes, just as piercing and laserlike as Lucifer's, but just a shade less inherently awful.

It was still too close for comfort. Little whispering fingers chuckled nasty things inside my head, taunting me. McKinley let out a sigh that didn't bother to conceal his relief.

The second shock was the threads of paleness in Japh's hair, silvery gray strands in the rough dark silk. I took all this in with a glance, met his eyes again. A burning prickle started in the scar, like a limb waking up. Like my entire body, a swift pulse slamming through me and shouting his name even as remembered screams boiled up, as the Devil chuckled and whispered in my ear.

Oh, gods. There was a lump in my throat. It was my heart. *I am so glad to see you. You have no idea.*

Eve spoke first. "Welcome, Kinslayer." The softness and conciliation had dropped from her voice. It was almost as sheerly, nakedly powerful as Lucifer's. The only thing saving me from flinching was the mounting discomfort as the scar turned hot on my shoulder, molten liquid spreading out from it in intricate pathways.

Japhrimel's eyes didn't leave mine.

He didn't even acknowledge Eve's opening salvo. Instead, he spoke to me, as if we had just met on the street. "You are well?" Just the three words, but the air cringed away from them.

He was *furious.* His rage circled the room lazily, gathering itself, and the bottom of my stomach dropped out. I had never seen this in him before. I'd seen him calm and I'd seen him lethal, I had seen him languid and I'd seen him tense with danger, but I had never seen him look so much like he was going to start killing and he wasn't particularly picky about who he began with.

My shirt fluttered a little, though the air was still. His aura crackled, and the other demons shifted uneasily in their chairs, darting bright nervous glances at Eve.

Who looked completely unaffected. She tilted her head slightly, as if giving me permission to respond.

"Never better," I lied, my mouth moving independently of my

brain again. I closed it with an effort—the words *you look like hell* were just dying to come out.

And right after them, *why do I get the feeling you're not happy to see me?*

Japhrimel studied me for a long few moments. Immovable, a sword of darkness against the glow of Paradisse leaking through the plasilica behind him. The sun died, sinking below the earth's rim, and the city suddenly blazed.

"Make your offer," he said finally, tossing the words like a challenge. His eyes didn't leave mine, and his hands tensed slightly at his sides. Fudoshin hummed inside his sheath, a single low tone of dissatisfaction. The Knife's hum slid up another notch, rattling my bones.

Before I could ask him what the hell he meant, Eve spoke in the harsh, consonant-laden language of demons, a long string of rolling words that tore the tattered air even further. The mood of the room was beginning to tip again, the fine hairs on my nape rising. It felt like a riot was going to break out, or a thunderstorm.

It *also* felt like I was standing right in its path. Normally I'd have been looking for a wall to put my back to.

There's no easy way out of this one. Little invisible tremors twitched through my muscles. *Fine time to start coming down with the shakes, Valentine. Focus!*

Japhrimel spoke briefly, pointedly keeping his eyes locked with mine. Eve responded, her tone softening—if anything can ever be *soft* in the language of Lucifer's children. Even her voice couldn't make the hard sounds any prettier, and Japhrimel's short reply shivered the plasilica windows in their mounts.

"Let's ask her, shall we?" Eve spoke Merican, but the shadow of demon language lay behind it. I shivered. "Who do you prefer, Dante? Him, or me?"

Prefer? Both of you are pretty goddamn scary right now. I peeled myself away from the chair, my legs suddenly weak and shaking. Some kind of letdown from all the adrenaline I'd been soaking in, at the worst possible time, as Japh's mark on my shoulder pulsed, burning away the veil of numbness.

I took two steps back from the table. The demon Zaj tensed, and so did McKinley, twin movements I could feel like a storm-front against a sensitive membrane. "Japh. We're all on the same side here, and Eve—"

"I did not come here for *her*." He answered so quickly the words bit off the tail of my sentence. "The Prince has pronounced doom on every *Ifrijiin* in this room." His eyes still didn't flicker away from mine. "You are all under sentence of death, for treason to the throne of Hell. I am here to execute that sentence."

The way he said it, it sounded like a done deal.

What? The reality of what he'd just said hit me square in the chest. *Hey. Wait a second. When did this happen?*

Betrayal, sharp and pointed, hit me just afterward. *Sure, Danny. Let me go into Hell and get the Knife. You* idiot. *He probably went to have another little tête-à-tête with Lucifer, and you let him! You fell for it!*

It was the last straw, the last betrayal. A small, quiet part of me was asking why I was jumping to conclusions, but the rest of me shouted that little voice of doubt down. How many times would Japh have to pull a mickey on me before I got the idea?

I was *justified* in thinking he'd turn on me. How could I not be?

Sentence of death. That meant he wanted to kill Eve.

Not while I'm breathing, bucko. "Japhrimel." My right hand closed around Fudoshin's hilt. The blade left the scabbard with a short singing note, and I settled into second guard, a movement so habitual and natural it seemed easier than standing upright and feeling the shaking work its way into my bones. Light ran like oil over honed steel, blue flame waking along its sharp sweet curve, and I tossed the words at him. "You can start with me."

Are you kidding, Dante? You know how fast he is. You don't have a chance.

It didn't matter. Nothing mattered now. And if nothing mattered, everything was permissible.

Everything was *possible*. So it was glancingly possible that I might hit him if he came at Eve.

Reality made one last stab at my consciousness. *Sekhmet sa'es, Danny. You at least could have drawn a gun.*

Eve's laughter rattled the table, blew through the assembled demons like a hard wind through a field of wheat. "You see, Kinslayer? Come for me, and she will do what she must. If I am a traitor, so is she. Will you kill your own leman?"

That brought his eyes to her for the first time, and I felt faintly ridiculous, standing there dressed in air-dried wrinkles with drawn steel and nobody paying any goddamn attention to the fact.

"It matters little," Japhrimel returned equably. "Neither you, nor Death, nor even the Prince may have her, and I have time to teach her manners. Which is none of your concern. Yield and return to your nest, Androgyne, and you may yet be forgiven."

I sensed Eve's chin lifting. When she spoke, it was the soft finality of a declaration of war. "Come and take me, if you dare."

The trembling air was riven again, demon Power spiking and tearing. A low glassy growl started.

I knew that sound. *Hellhounds. Oh, gods.* This was rapidly getting out of hand — if it had ever been manageable in the first place. The growling was coming from right behind me, and McKinley let out a short low curse he must have picked up in Putchkin Near Asia.

"Game," Zaj said. He rose slowly, his chair scraping, and I was suddenly conscious he was far too close to me. "And set."

Japhrimel actually smiled. It was one of those slow murderous grins I'd seen him use during the hunt for Santino, only it was dialed up to ten instead of two on the scary scale.

The urge to dive for cover collided with the need to back up, both fighting with the sudden desire to turn around and see what was behind me.

Right behind me, breathing heat into my hair. My mouth went dry, and the strength left my legs in a liquid rush. Only the locking of my muscles kept me standing, the scar suddenly blazing with spiked iron wire, driving into my flesh. Burrowing in.

Japhrimel's right hand came out from behind his back. Gold glittered in his palm.

It was a wide round golden medallion, demon runes scored deeply into its soft surface and writhing madly, beginning to burn with clear crimson radiance. Chairs scraped as the assembled demons scrambled to their feet, a collective growl raising itself, plasilica cracking as the windows finally gave up under the onslaught.

"Game. Set." Japhrimel's tone did not alter. "Match."

His hand came forward with a sweet economy of motion, and he tossed the gold medallion toward the table. An extension of the motion brought him into an effortless lunge, and I threw myself down and past Zaj, colliding with the iron chair bruising-hard, tipping it over and going down in a tangle of arms and legs with Eve as Japh met the hellhound with a sound like freight transports crashing together.

The beast was low and sinuous, heat smoking off its glassy obsidian pelt, its eyes a flaming carnivorous orange. It wasn't like the other hellhounds I'd seen, those smooth basalt creatures with fiery snouts. This one had a longer, pointed muzzle with viciously curved teeth made of volcanic glass, and wings with sharp daggered feathers half-spread as Japhrimel struck it down, gunfire blooming in the sudden screaming chaos. He had both silvery guns out, and *twisted* in midair, somehow landing lightly as a cat on the table as I made it to my feet, McKinley's hand sinking into the skein of my hair and doing more than anything else to pull me up. The agent's fingers slid free as he yelled, the noise swallowing whatever he wanted to say.

The world turned sideways. The medallion flared with a thundercrack of sound, demon protections laid in the room shattering. It tore through the careful layers of warding like the whine of hoverfreight thrums in the bones, a deep undeniable sound.

I made it to hands and knees and launched myself, rolling. Fudoshin's hilt socked into my hand as I struggled up. The blade sliced air, a small sound lost in the swelling chaos.

Eve rose like a wave from the wreck of the iron chair, spun on her toes, and bolted for the stairs. I whirled and sprinted after her, hysterical strength filling unruly limbs suddenly weighted with scrap plasteel. I heard McKinley yell something else short and sharp behind me.

Sorry, sunshine, but you work for the demon that just threw a wrench in the works. My priority now was getting Eve *out* of the fire zone. The past had looped over and touched the present again — Doreen in front of me, pale hair swinging as she ran; my heart in my mouth, tasting of copper and bile — and the sound behind us of demons, and a hell of a fight breaking out. My katana blurred down in a half-circle, ending up with the blade tucked behind my arm; it would do no good to spit myself on my own sword if I fell.

It felt goddamn good to have the hilt in my hand again, to have a fight in front of me, everything becoming clear and sharp as only the last desperate battles are. It felt so stupidly good my breath caught on a half-sob I couldn't afford, I needed all my lung-strength for running.

The stairs spiraled up, and Eve outdistanced me. I lagged under the weight of effort, my breath coming harsh and tearing, and saw the door just as she neatly nipped through it.

Roof access. Good plan. Hope she has a hover stashed, or this could get real ugly. McKinley's footsteps pounded on the stairs behind me — at least, I hoped it was McKinley.

I was fairly sure I could outrun *him.*

I tumbled out of the door into the moaning wind of a high-altitude platform. I almost ran into Eve, whose golden hand shot out and caught my upper arm, digging in with fingers like steel claws. The sudden stop almost tore my arm out of my socket and my stomach from its moorings, and I was suddenly very sorry I'd eaten.

The landing-platform spread out like the petal of a flower, glowing a pale amber to match the rest of the tower. My hair lifted on a wave of sweet synth-perfume. I caught my balance just as McKinley plowed through the door behind us, and I brought my sword around in an easy semicircle, blade cutting air with a low whispering sound into the ready position. My scabbard was in my left hand, and I turned my wrist to brace it, using it as a shield and potential weapon. My sleeves flapped, pulled by the freshening breeze.

"Eve." My voice cut through the whine of the wind. "You go. I'll take care of this."

Because there on the platform, with a laserifle and two plasguns pointed at us, were Vann and Lucas Villalobos. Of course they hadn't come to meet up with me. They were on Japhrimel's side.

CHAPTER 32

Eve's fingers fell from my upper arm as I moved forward, blocking their firing angle. Vann was on one knee, laserifle against his shoulder and his other weapons glinting. A bruise spread up his neck, mottling the left side of his face, dried blood clinging in his hair.

Lucas stood, disheveled and threadbare and dangerous, his yellow eyes focused past me on Eve. His guns glittered too — SW Remington 60-watt plasguns. Not even a demon can outrun *that.*

Lucas, on the job and working overtime. Only he'd forgotten he was working for me.

Which made him an enemy.

Great. It's me against the world now. Why am I not surprised? I felt almost like myself again, with the unholy urge to laugh rising under my breastbone.

"Eve. I mean it. Go." I took another step forward, and Vann twitched.

"Give it up, Valentine." The wind flirted with his hair, his eyes were narrowed and professional, cool and distant in the bruised mask of his face. "Don't make us hurt someone."

He sounded like it would be so *easy*. And Lucas's finger tightened on the trigger, his entire body tensing. There could be no question about it. He'd betrayed me too.

I. Have. Had. Enough.

My temper snapped behind my breastbone, and welcome wine-dark rage flooded me. It scorched through tender burned channels where psychic scars still smoked, courtesy of whatever Lucifer had done to me and the strain I'd put on myself since then. A roar filled my throat, flame springing up from a deep burning well of rage. I dropped my scabbard, both hands closing around the hilt and bringing the swordblade high.

Fucked with me for the last time, it whispered in the sudden silence of utter berserk rage. *Kill them. Kill them all.*

I flung myself across the intervening space, a sound I barely recognized bursting from my throat. It was a cat's scream, fury and terror rolled into a pretty package wrapped with barbed wire and ignited with nuclear force. Eve ran for the edge of the bare empty platform as I brought the sword down, blue-white flame streaking along the arc of the strike, light stuttering because I was moving with berserker speed, the crackle and hiss of flame filling my ears.

Time slowed down. The streak of red down low was Vann, firing at Eve. I crashed into him first, the katana making a high shivering note as I followed through with the strike, a perfect downsweep. The laserifle split asunder, a burst of plas splashing out and underlighting the scene with bloody glow. I pivoted on my front foot, hearing faintly my *sensei*'s habitual admonition from the soup of memory inside my imploding head.

Move, no think! Fight, no think!

My knee met Vann's face with the sound of a melon dropped on a hot sidewalk. He flew back like a rag doll, and my leg paused, cocked now for the strike back, which pitched the top half of my body forward under Lucas's fire. He was shooting over my head, aiming at Eve.

At *my daughter,* at the only piece left of my dead demon-murdered lover. Human or not, she was mine.

She was all I had left.

I snapped my leg back, my heel hitting something soft and crunching. It snapped like a flag in a high breeze. Another pivot, heel sliding out, and my katana blurred as my wrist turned, everything gaining momentum by the spin, and I struck not to injure but to kill.

If Lucas hadn't flown backward from the kick, I would have cut him in half. As it was I completed the movement, stamping down with what was now my lead foot, the blade kissing only air.

The building swayed like a plucked harpstring, and I heard the whine of a hover engine, close. Very close.

"Valentine!" McKinley screamed, his voice breaking. *"Stop it!"*

Oh, no. I am not nearly finished here. They're still breathing— and so are you. A hover rose up to the landing pad, sleek and black, and I saw a hatch in its side dilating as a pilot or AI held it steady. I also saw Lucas dragging himself up to his feet, blood painting his face into a mask of yellow-eyed rage as Eve paused at the edge of the platform, her pale hair whipped by the wind.

She leapt.

I forgot all about Vann, who lay gasping and choking some ten feet away, his ribs battered in. I forgot about Lucas, painfully hauling himself upright. All I could think of was that pale head, vanishing straight down. *Eve!*

I flung myself after her, my boots grinding in broken bits of laser- ifle, and was just gaining momentum when the entire side of the tower shattered and the hellhound landed with a thud on the plat- form, which was swaying in earnest now. Demon warding sparked and fizzed, fluorescing into the visible range as *something* huge and powerful as a magickal tornado exploded below somewhere in the tower, like a freight hover looming up out of nowhere under a slic- board. It was that explosion that saved me, the tower bucking at the precise moment the winged hellhound leapt for me; the heaving of the entire edifice knocking me off my feet and sending me rolling toward the edge, my sword hammered from my hand and skittering along the platform's floor.

Sword get your sword that thing's coming for you, it's coming for you, get up and kill it and go after her— My fingers closed on the hilt as I scrabbled, and chaos boiled behind me. The whine of plasbolts mixed with a high squealing roar told me the hellhound had been hit; I rolled to my feet, body moving with inhumanly precise coordina- tion as my mind struggled to keep up, to control the motion. I skid- ded, gained my feet, snapped one glance back, and saw the hellhound crouching as plasgun bolts peppered the platform around it. It leapt again, this time thankfully not aiming for me, and Lucas rolled aside as the thing crashed into where he had been standing a moment before. There was too much plasfire in the air to be accounted for, but I didn't care.

I turned back to the edge.

The air became molten and my scar turned to clawed fire, nailing my feet in place. I almost overbalanced, wind screaming up and pouring over the platform in a wash of burned plas, hoverscorch, and the musky fume of demons. My shirt flapped in the wind, my whipping hair stinging my eyes.

"Stop." Japhrimel's voice sliced through chaos.

Poised on the brink, I looked back over my shoulder again. He halted, too far away, and his wings settled, the edges of his coat ruffling. His eyes burned, and behind him the hellhound snarled. More plasgun bolts whined. The streaks of silvery gray in his hair, new and shocking, threw back Paradisse's light.

Japhrimel took another step forward, his hands out, palms cupped. Demon blood smoked along his sleeves and the hem of his coat, and there was a spatter of it high on one gaunt cheek. "Dante," he mouthed, and the world stopped its rolling inevitable course.

His boots were wet, and he'd left dark bloody prints on the shattered floor of the platform. The tower heaved again and I heard a massive belling note of rage from below, a howl that chilled my blood and lifted every fine hair on my body. I could even feel the individual hairs on my scalp trying to rise.

Demon. That's a dying demon. Which one? I exhaled, the breath lasting forever.

I no longer cared.

"Dante." Again, Japhrimel did not precisely speak, but mouthed the word. Or was there so much noise I couldn't hear him, though a great silence had settled over the world?

His voice bypassed my ears, smashing directly into my brain like carbolic flung across reactive. *Come with me. You must come. Now.* Sheer naked command in the words, wrapping around me and yanking.

Demanding. Controlling me.

Forcing me.

Gods above and below, how I hate to be forced.

My fingers loosened, and my sword chimed on the platform, Japhrimel's will wresting it from my hand as easily as an adult might wrench a toy away from a small child.

It is so easy to break a human. Especially a human woman. Claws buried in my chest, and the sound of my own screams as someone hurt me, invaded me, *hurt* me—

I had thought nothing else inside me could break. But something deep-buried in my mind snapped and rose up like a shattered cable suddenly free of weight, a sheet of flame blinding me. My lips shaped one single word, the only thing I could say.

No.

The alpha and omega of my epitaph, what they would lasecarve on my urn when I finally was forced kicking and screaming into the dry land of Death.

But not yet. I wasn't finished yet. The hardest, most stubborn deep-buried core of me ignited even as my body betrayed me, already starting to shift its weight to obey him, to accept the inevitable and *submit.*

To give in.

No. The word boiled through me. I am not sure if I screamed, or if the roar was merely psychic, locked behind my rictus-grin of a face. The curtain between me and a black hole of something too terrible to be spoken or thought of pulled aside for a single heartstopping moment, and I remembered what had been done to me.

Who had done it.

And how much it had *hurt.*

No. The single word filled me. I would *not* give in. I would not endure another rape of my body or my mind. I would not go gently into any dark night of submission. I would not be *forced* any further.

I would die first.

I tore myself free, and hurled my traitorous body out into empty space.

The roar of the wind cradled me as I fell, arms and legs pulled close. A streak painted the air—my rings, boiling with golden light, their gems and silver screaming in defiant rage as I narrowed my welling eyes against the stinging hurricane.

Looking for that pale head, the spot of brilliance I could aim for. What did I think I was going to do? I couldn't survive a fall like this, and Eve had vanished. Paradisse wheeled crazily under me, hover-traffic reaching up to swallow my falling body, the buildings turning to streaks of amber, silver, and anemic gold.

I couldn't see her anywhere. Eve was gone, disappeared.

A curious comfort spilled through me. I was going to die. None of it mattered anymore. I was done, and once in Death's arms the Devil couldn't harm me or involve me in any more games.

A swift, piercing pain lanced through my heart. *Japhrimel.*

He can't save you, Danny. Nobody can. The truth whispered in my ears, in my fingers, in my heartbeat, which stupidly kept plowing ahead, not understanding or stubbornly ignoring the fact that I was *dead,* finally dead, that I was falling and it was over.

Finally, blessedly over. My left cheek burned as the emerald embedded atop my accreditation tat spat a glowing-green spark, a high sudden fracture-pain as if I'd been punched hard enough to crack my cheekbone. The flash of green dyed the entire world for a timeless second before it was swallowed by the rip of torn air.

Flying, a bubble of something hot behind my lips, my clothes fluttering and snapping as my body relaxed, tumbling through space and time, synth-perfume filling my nose — apples, musk, peaches, fresh-mown grass.

If you have to die, Paradisse is a good place to do it. Why is this taking so long?

Then, the impossible. Tumbling in freefall, completely free for the first time in my whole miserable existence —

Fingers closed around my wrist and a jolt of arrested motion popped my shoulder from its socket with a sickening crunch.

I screamed. Wings beat, filling the air with crazy mixtures of synth-perfume tainted with the dark musk of demon, familiar to me as breath. I hung pinned between the point of no return and the absolute freedom of death, the world spinning frantically as the sound of straining wings and a long howl of effort smashed through my head. My arm stretched like elastic, tendons creaking and popping as the rooftop loomed below us, flowing nacreous pearl. It was another tower, and I flinched away from the impending shock, screaming again until the bubble behind my lips broke and sweet spicy black demon blood filled my mouth.

Impact. A crunching, hideous shock drove me out of myself, ribs snapping, the force of the fall broken just enough to keep me from dying on impact. Something in my other arm snapped too, and I was flung across the rooftop like a doll, rolling limp as a rag. Plasteel buckled and bent, an invisible layer of force closing around me, cushioning, a flexible shield stopping me just short of a climate-control housing shaped like a whipped confection of spun plasteel and plasglass.

Warm wetness dripped into my eyes. I lay against the housing, blinking, my breath stuttering out in an abused howl.

I saw him rolling too, shedding momentum as his wings gracefully bled the force away from his body, rising in a perfectly coordinated movement and whirling, a familiar curve of steel in his hands. He drove my sword into the rooftop with one economic movement, shaking his hand out as blue sparks popped and snarled between him and the hilt. He turned, his wings beginning to flow back down to armor him, a flash of his narrow golden chest heaving as he filled his lungs—

—and the winged hellhound streaked down from the sky and hit him with a bone-shattering crunch.

Japhrimel! Agony roared through me, preternatural flesh stretched to its limits, bones struggling to reknit themselves, a tide of black demon blood smashing through my lips as I coughed, creaking sounds spearing through my chest as my ribs snapped out, mending themselves. The scar turned into a red-hot drill, and if I could have breathed through the convulsions I would have screamed again, pointlessly, as the flurry of motion disappeared, driven past my line of sight by the collision.

My arms boiled red-hot with pain as I made it up to elbows-and-knees, realizing I wasn't healing fast enough. Black blood should have been welling up and closing the wounds, sealing them away—but more blood pattered on the rooftop as I scrabbled, my fingers slipping in slick hot wetness as the air closed around me, suffocatingly heavy. Material ripped as my claws extended, shearing through plasteel and fabric alike. Gunfire echoed behind me, and the snarls of the hellhound made the whole building shake like a flower on a slender stem.

Get up! Get up and fight! Stark terror boiled up through my mouth as I coughed more blood.

Every cell in my body rebelled. I forgot his betrayal, I forgot my own, I forgot everything but the need to get to my feet and fling myself at the thing that was going to kill him.

I don't know why. It was an instinctive response, like jerking your hand back from a red-hot stove.

Power smashed through the scar, flaring down my skin and sparking into the visible range, black-diamond flames twisting through the trademark sparkles of a Necro-mance's aura. My shielding, smashed and rent, cracked open, and for one dizzying eternal moment the entire city of Paradisse shattered through my skull again, as if I had once more opened the taplines in Notra Dama and ripped a hole in the world.

The assault smashed me flat onto the floor of the roof, blood sizzling with the heavy odor of decaying fruit. My shields closed, mended by the thunderbolt of pure Power spilling through me. I heard my own voice from very far away, an animal's howl, breaking in the higher registers as it spiraled into a deathscream.

Still I tried to get up, to *make* my body respond. Beating darkness closed over my vision—whether my eyes were shut or I was just blind with effort was anyone's guess. A great glass bell of silence closed over me as my body twitched, little moans escaping my mouth between sips of air.

"Be still." The voice was hoarse but utterly familiar. "*Shavarak'-itzan beliak,* woman, be *still.* Calm yourself. Stop. *Stop.*"

Hands on me, familiar hands. I lay limp as clingfilm as he pulled me into his arms, my ribs still crackling as flexible demon bones tried to heal themselves. Yet more Power roared into me through the scar, coating my skin and working in, filling the hollow channels of my nerves and skeleton, I coughed one last time and convulsed, my heels slapping the rooftop.

I collapsed.

Something against my forehead—I realized it was his mouth just as he began kissing my cheeks, my temple, my hair, anywhere he could reach. He almost crushed me, his arms like steel bars, holding me to earth as my dislocated shoulder howled with pain.

I didn't care.

They had to be obscenities, whatever he was saying in his native tongue. Curls of steam threaded away from us both, heat bleeding off through his aura as his shielding closed over me, a touch almost as intimate as his wings pulled close, enfolding me in a double layer of protection.

Sobs came fast and hard, breaking me open. I wept against his chest, his skin against mine again, as he kissed every part of me he could and cracked his voice saying, over and over again in a language that I for once needed no translation for, that I was safe. That he had plucked me from the sky, because not even Death would take me from him.

CHAPTER 33

I lay on my side, in a bath of delicious heat and softness. It was like sleeping on clouds, and the heat burrowed into me, all the way out through my fingers and toes. Flushing away the last remaining traces of pain and injury. Soothing.

The entire world was a gray smear. I wanted it to stay that way.

Along with the warmth and the softness was Japhrimel's hoarse voice, another constant. He spoke, sometimes calmly, sometimes not, but I didn't listen to the words. Other voices intruded, but I paid no attention. I simply curled in on myself, shutting them away as best I could. My mind shivered, psychic wounds raw and smoking, all careful work to heal them undone. Quivering on the edge of insanity, not even the blue crystalline glow of Death's country to break the darkness.

I came back in bits and pieces, drifting for a while. Then I lunged into consciousness, jolting off the table, my hands around a hilt and the blade making a low whooshing sound as air split.

Warm irresistible fingers closed around my wrist. Hoverwhine drilled through my back teeth. I opened my eyes, and Japhrimel twisted my wrist — not hard, but enough to lock it and keep the blade down and to the side.

I still had my boots on. They scraped grated metal flooring as I shifted my weight, left hand coming up in a flat strike, meaning to break the nasal promontory and drive it up into the brain. It was a reflex action, snake-quick, and Japhrimel avoided it gracefully, his streaked hair ruffling as he ducked aside and caught my left wrist. The room was narrow, very small, and smelled of hoverwash and oil.

He drove me back, pinned me to the wall, I brought my knee up and he avoided that too. My breath caught in my throat, my shoulders suddenly against the hull. It was a hover, we were traveling, and the entire ship shuddered as I struggled with flesh and Power both. His aura clamped down over mine, the pressure excruciating for a long infinite moment.

"Calm," he said, softly. "I am here. Calm, my curious."

He looked just the same, except for the streaks in his hair and the shadows under his burning eyes. His face had hollowed out, but it was still essentially his, and the same essentially human darkness lay under the green fire of his irises.

"Let go." I didn't recognize my own voice, low and flat, with the terrible weight of fury behind it. "Let go *now*."

"No." He didn't even bother to dress up the refusal, his fingers clamping home. Leather creaked, the rig responding to pressure. I tried shifting and sliding away, struggled until sweat broke out along the curve of my lower back, pressed into the metal hull. My hair fell in my eyes. "You do not understand."

"I don't *want* to. You *lie*." Still quiet, as if every shade of inflection had been washed out of my throat.

"I have the other half of the Knife, Dante. We are so very close to being free." He sounded so reasonable. Over his shoulder I could see the rest of the narrow room, a shelflike bed and plasglass-fronted cabinets. "I have returned from the very depths of Hell, and I have—"

I know what you did. You sold me out. "Shut up." I didn't know if it was possible to care less. "Where's Eve?" *If you've hurt her I'll—*

"Vardimal's Androgyne is safely confined. Lucas and McKinley restrained her." His fingers softened, but not nearly enough for me to slip free. The hover settled into a rhythm, short choppy bounces as if we were just above rough water, gyros straining as antigrav slipped and slithered against waves. "Her supporters are scattered. It was *necessary*. I had to, Dante."

I finally slumped against the wall, leather and hilts digging into me as Japhrimel leaned in. His eyes were inches from mine, filling the world until I closed my eyelids, shutting out that green fire. Fudoshin's bladetip clattered, my shaking hand pushing forward against a vise-grip. "You were going to kill her," I whispered.

"If it would serve my plans, I would."

Great. I suppose that's one statement I can unequivocally believe. The deep, sarcastic voice inside my head showed up again, right on time. "Your *plans*. Do I serve your plans?"

If the words had carried any steel they could have cut. They could have shattered the hull and left me free. I would have tried to struggle free, but it would do no good. Instead, I gathered myself, harsh hurtful tension building in my muscles.

"You do not serve my plans. You are what I engage in planning to keep safe. Look at me."

"No." Other people might have a witty saying or a pretty epitaph.

Not me. I will have only sheer, stubborn refusal. He was still forcing me, still demanding.

"*Look* at me." The softest of his voices, the most careful. The most human. "Dante. Please."

My eyes flew open.

He leaned in close, lashes veiling the green burn of his gaze. His hair fell, thick choppy streaks of silvery contrasting sharply with wet blackness. Fine lines bracketed his mouth, fanned out from the corners of his eyes.

After so long unchanging, he seemed to have aged. But demons don't age. Was it another mask?

"What happened to you?" My traitorous heart pounded inside my chest.

"I made a fresh bargain with the Prince." He overrode my sudden surging struggle. "Our salvation is so very close, do not doubt me now."

"Eve—"

"That is *not her Name*. She is Lucifer's Consort, not a human child. You *fool*. Did you open a door into Hell at her bidding? Do you have the least comprehension of what that means? A large portion of her allies, her precious resistance, escaped into the free air. Lucifer will make war upon them himself, he cannot afford to do otherwise— but she was my bait in a trap I laid with care, a trap you almost made unusable. I *had* to kill her gathering once you broke the walls between your world and Hell."

How could I even begin to explain? "I was giving you time," I whispered. "And staying alive. It was the only way I could—" *Do something, instead of waiting for you!* I was going to finish, but he didn't let me.

"McKinley was more than capable of hiding you."

"Not from *her* he wasn't." *She's mine, Japhrimel.* The words trembled on my lips, the secret I had not opened my mouth to tell him directly. My own small private deceit in this snakepit of lies and clashing agendas. I couldn't tell him now. "I had to, Japh." I sagged against the wall, going limp in his hands, but my fingers were tight on Fudoshin's hilt. If he let go of me now—

He sighed, a sharp dissatisfied sound. "It matters little now. We are on our way to a meeting with Lucifer. I will deliver the wayward Androgyne and—"

I brought my knee up, sharply, he countered the movement, and we almost spilled to the floor. He regained his balance, fingers biting in cruelly. *"Stop."* Did he sound breathless? The scar turned to molten metal on my shoulder, another warm pulse of Power filling my nerves and veins.

My skin crawled. I opened my mouth to scream at him, but he overrode me.

"Once she is delivered to him, she has agreed to distract his attention. I will strike him down even as he gloats over her. *Will you stop?*"

I went utterly still, a clockwork spinning inside my head pausing for just a moment. *Don't trust him. Don't listen. Plot and counterplot, Danny.*

When I did speak, it was a low, gravelly whisper. "How can I trust anything you say to me?"

"I have gone into Hell for you, not once but several times." He let go of me in a sudden convulsive movement. "That should be enough. Even for you."

"You think I've been on a fucking holiday cruise? Where do you think *I've* gone?" My arm fell to my side, Fudoshin avoiding a stack of crates strapped to the floor.

"As far as necessary. As I would for you." His hands dropped. His coat was just as black as ever, but that shock of silver-threaded hair... he was different. Too different.

We had both changed out of all recognition. What was left?

"Let me get this straight." I swallowed, my dry throat clicking. "You expect me to stand there and trust you while you hand Eve over to Lucifer—the very thing he's *always* wanted out of this game." *He wanted me to tell him where she was, and when I wouldn't I was a Judas goat, meant to lure her in. He used me, you used me—what's the goddamn difference?*

His left hand came up. In it, satiny wood gleamed, and the sheathed Knife at my hip gave a slow sonorous ringing, like crystal stroked just right. The finials of its other half cradled Japh's hand, moving slightly, yearning out of his grip and toward me. His fingers trembled as he held it, as if he wanted to drop it.

He took two slow steps forward as the hover's gyros stabilized, the bounce telling me we were ashore now. We'd just made landfall.

Where the hell were we?

Off the map, sunshine. You've just gone off the fucking edge of the world.

Japhrimel offered me the Knife. "Take it."

My heart thumped against my ribs. I eyed his hand, eyed the other half of the Knife. So he *had* retrieved it. Where had he hidden it in Hell?

Would I ever have the time or the courage to ask him?

He cupped the blade in his right hand and released the hilt, offering it like a goblet of wine to thirsty gods. If it hurt him, his face showed no sign. Time ticked by as the hover began to climb, the ear-popping of altitude a heavy auditory weight.

If you take that, Danny, you'll be able to kill him. He's fast and strong, but you saw what it did to Sephrimel. You'll have some power in this relationship. You'll have a little control.

And if he pulls a mickey on you one more time, you can bury the thing in his guts.

My tat shifted on my cheek, diamond pinpricks under skin. My emerald lit, a spark popping in the gloom. Japhrimel waited, half of the Knife trembling in his hands, aching to clasp its twin and be whole again.

"It's yours." Very softly, his mouth its usual straight line after it had given the words to the air. Still, he didn't look at me, his eyes hidden behind that fringe of hair. A muscle in his cheek flickered. "It was made for a *hedaira*'s hand."

Go ahead, Danny. Take it. You've got to finish this game anyway. You dealt yourself in at Notra Dama. Time to pick another card.

I didn't realize I'd moved until I closed my fingers over the hilt. It hummed in my hand, happily, and the memory of the sick gulping noise turned my stomach over hard.

Japhrimel raised his eyes, shaking his hair back. He shook both his hands free, flicking his fingers. "Will you trust me?"

Four little words. I weighed half the Knife in my hand, its mate vibrating against my hip like a slicboard rattling before it dumps you. *I don't know if I should. I don't know if I want to.* "I don't know if I can."

His shoulders dropped. My stomach rattled and flipped, as if I was tumbling in freefall again. Roaring wind in my ears, prepared to leave all this struggling and striving behind. The look on his face was like being stabbed, and all the broken places inside my head gave a flare of devouring pain.

Why was I such an idiot for him? Just when I thought I had no reason to trust him, he went and did something like this. Like giving me a weapon.

My mouth opened. "But I can try."

We stared at each other. The hover groaned and rocked as the angle of ascent sharpened. I stood there gripping half the Knife with white-knuckle fingers, my head suddenly full of the rushing noise of Paradisse wind sliding past as I prepared to splatter myself over the pavement below. I'd been so ready just to give up.

Again.

Japhrimel nodded, a short sharp movement. The silver in his hair glittered. "Thank you." Gravely, as if he hadn't just handed me the only weapon in the world that could possibly kill him.

The scar flamed with soft heat, and his aura over mine settled, thin fine strands of gossamer energy binding together rips and tears, healing the rent tatters of my shielding with infinite care. Was he doing it consciously?

Did it matter?

I searched for something else to say, another question to keep him standing here and talking to me. "What happened to you? In Hell?"

One shoulder lifted, dropped. Goddamn shrugging demons.

"Nothing of any account." Dismissive.

The sharp bite of frustration whipsawed through me, drained away. "Come on, Japh. Your hair."

"It doesn't please you?" He tilted his head slightly, letting the dim orandflu light play over its shagginess.

Goddammit. "That's not the point. I just wondered what happened." *You're not going to tell me a damn thing, are you? Especially not now. You just want me to trust you blindly. You want to control everything about this.*

But the weight of half the Knife in my hand said differently.

"Tell me why you almost killed yourself fleeing me." His hands spread slightly, expressive. I glimpsed dark shadows across his palms—from the touch of the Knife?

I wondered.

The edges of his coat ruffled as the hover shifted, settling at a new altitude.

You really want to know? "I…" How could I put it into words? Because he'd tried to force me. Because Eve was the last shred of Doreen left walking the earth, and I had to believe there was some humanity left in her—because if there wasn't, there was none left in me either. Because I could no longer pray, because the Devil had robbed me of myself, because Eve was sticking it to Lucifer where it hurt—for any number of reasons, none of which I could explain without a half-hour, absolute silence on his part, and a whole lot of luck. Or maybe a demon-Merican dictionary, if such a thing existed.

"Exactly." He clasped his hands behind his back, his feet placed just precisely so. "There are some things that cannot be explained, even between us. Whether we founder on them or learn to leave them unsaid, I leave to you." He turned on one heel, his long black coat flaring with a sound like feathers rippling. "You should gain some rest. We will be there sooner than you think."

"Where?"

"Where else would Lucifer meet us? Where he can see us coming." With that, he was gone through a hatch door, a brief slice of daylight outside stinging my eyes.

I let out a sharp breath. The shaking in my arms and legs circled like a beast waiting to pounce.

I drew the first half of the Knife from its sheath. It was awkward, but I hitched one hip against the shelflike medbay bed and compared the two wooden weapons. They both looked complete, but after a few moments my brain started to work and I saw how they could be fitted together, by tangling the finials and twisting just so. They hummed, my hands drawing together as if I held two powerful electromagnets, thrumming their attraction almost audibly.

I slid them together with infinite care, my almost-translucent fingernails still bearing chips and flecks of black molecule-drip polish. They matched the mellow glow of the wood, and the humming intensified until I gave the final twist, locking both halves of the Knife into place.

Power drew heavy and close in the confined space. The hover bounced, and the Knife's hum dropped below the audible. The world warped around it, the same kind of seaweed drifting I remembered around the edges of a door torn in the fabric of the world. The geometry of the Knife was slightly off, for all its grace, yet it looked at home in my grasp, the finials caging and protecting my slim golden hand. The blade, now leaf-shaped and slightly curved, looked wicked enough to do some damage just sitting there, and I suddenly had no trouble believing this thing could kill any demon it chose.

Still, it didn't do the other women any good. Don't get cocky, Danny.

Had Sephrimel's *hedaira* ever held this thing? If I tried, could I find any traces of the women who might have thought they could wield it locked under its glossy surface? Psychometry wasn't a skill of mine; I was no Reader.

And it was only made of wood, from some unspeakable tree I couldn't imagine.

The Knife hummed. It was power, and control, and a way to end this madness so I could breathe again. So I could think again, without the black hole in my head threatening to drive me insane, without the hole in my heart that kept crying Japhrimel's name. Without the weight of sick grief and guilt I couldn't let myself feel if I was to function.

"It doesn't matter," I whispered to the empty air.

Because it didn't. It didn't make a damn bit of difference whether I could trust Japhrimel or not. We were locked into this course, like an AI locking in a freight hover. Like a Greater Work of magick completing itself, snapping home and driving a change into the fabric of the world, reshaping reality according to its own laws.

He would either hold up his end of the deal or he wouldn't. Either way, a demon or two—or more—was going to die. I was going to see this thing finished.

Nothing else mattered.

CHAPTER 34

There's no pretty way to describe the Vegas Waste.

The nucleus is an immense slag-crater full of radiation and thin glass where silica sand fused together, broken by twisted screaming shapes of ferrous metal. On the outside edges, the Ghost City slumps and crawls. Even from the air bones are visible, buried in drifts of sand that ride up and fall away so the entire place shifts. Moaning wind is the only sound left.

Once, the city stretched into the desert, full of gambling, liquor, and the peculiar Merican Era duo of fleshly urges and frantic penance for those urges. The Gilead government was like every other totalitarian regime—the ones in power wanted a playground, and Vegas was nothing if not accommodating.

Maybe the hard-line Republic thought it was being tricky by moving its StratComm into the city once it was pushed out of DeeSee by opposition forces after Kochba bar Gilead's assassination. Maybe they had nowhere else to go, having been blown out of the Coloradin Bunkers in massive firefights. Maybe it was just sheer disorganization.

Whatever it was, their threat of nuclear strike was met by an *actual* nuclear strike. Nobody after the Seventy Days War took responsibility for actually giving the codes to drop the bomb. Whoever did it saved plenty of lives—the hard-liners weren't going to go out quietly, and they had enough fanatics and material to wage war for a while, especially in the mountainous regions.

But whoever did it also slaughtered a million civilians if not more, not just in the first bomb-blast but also in radiation sickness and pure misery in camps afterward as the provisional government struggled to figure out who was a Gilead guerilla and who was a civilian.

McKinley was in the cockpit, guiding the hover over the shallow dips and crests of desert. Acres of broken ruins stretched in every direction, old crumbling concrete and real steel too twisted and heavy to be salvaged, crusted with rust. Glaring light reflected from sand in shimmering dapples wherever there was a porthole, casting weird shadows into the interior. The hover was slim, much smaller than our previous version, with no extraneous chambers. The cargo bay was open, a deep narrow well bare except for one pale-haired demon trapped again in a silver-writhing circle, her face tilted back to look at me above her.

I had my scabbarded sword in my left hand and the Knife in my right, its hum rivaling hoverwhine. Behind the cockpit, Vann leaned against the hull, occasionally exchanging soft words with McKinley. Japhrimel loomed behind them, his hands clasped behind his back, his hair gleaming. And, wonder of wonders, Anton Kgembe, his springy hair wildly mussed, shot an indecipherable glance at me before leaning toward Japh to whisper, very fucking familiar, into Japh's ear.

Plot and counterplot, double agents and deception. Where was Leander? Had he survived whatever had happened to the last hover?

Lucas, arms folded and a scowl settled over his thin sallow face, stood at the railing at my right shoulder. "You shouldna done that."

You shouldn't have pointed a gun at me. You're working for me. Or at least, you said you were. "I already said I was sorry." I sounded unhelpful even to myself. "I'm having kind of a bad week, Lucas."

"Not used to my clients tryin' to kill me. I've put rabid bounty hunters down for less." He shifted his weight as the hover tilted, wind pressure moving against its skin.

My back prickled. I swallowed my temper with an almost sweat-inducing effort. "You were firing on her." *And on me, come to think of it.*

"Orders. Your boyfriend's got better sense than you." The sneer loading his whisper was almost visible.

"So you're working for him now?" I stared at Eve's pale head, the ropes of her hair stirring as she crouched immobile in the empty cargo bay. The humming line of silver tautened as her shoulders came up, as if she felt my gaze. "Just so I'm clear on this, because I thought *I* hired you." When he didn't respond, I considered the point carried. "Fuck you, Lucas."

"No way, *chica*. You too high-maintenance."

"Now is not a good time to bait me." *I just might do something silly.*

He was unimpressed. "Not a good time to try to kill me, either."

"You *welshed* on me!" I rounded on him. "I'm *warning* you, Lucas. Don't ride me. I'm not in the mood."

"I been watchin' this whole thing play out." His yellow eyes narrowed, and despite his slumped shoulders and crossed arms Lucas was on a hair trigger. If he twitched for a knife or a plasgun, what was I going to do?

The engine of chance and consequence inside my head returned the only answer possible. If he moved on me, we were going to find out if he was as deathless as everyone claimed.

Once, before Japh changed me, I stood in a Nuevo Rio deadhead bar with a demon in my shadow, facing down Villalobos, almost too terrified to talk. And now there was only the calm, almost-rational consideration of how I'd kill him before he could return the favor.

My, how times change.

He continued, and I forced myself to pay attention. "I gotta admit, you were smart when it started. But you gettin' dumber and dumber. Wind you up and watch you knock down everything in your way's kind of fun, but it don't get the job done."

"Where's Leander?" I didn't want to hear how stupid Villalobos thought I was. I didn't care if I was stupid or not. All I wanted right now was a chance to kill a demon, and I was getting to the point where I wasn't too picky which one.

Lucas stared through me. His lean sallow face was the picture of contempt. "You just gettin' around to wondering? Glad you didn't get a crush on me, or I might be in even more trouble."

That was uncalled-for. I couldn't drop my eyes, trained reflex resisting the urge to look away. "Keep your goddamn commentary to yourself, Villalobos." If Leander hadn't been able to keep up, would Kgembe be any different?

Was it horrible that I didn't care? The thought was a pinch in a numb place. He was *human.*

But he'd taken his chances.

You sound just like a demon, Dante. He took his chances, so sorry, too bad. I shifted, restlessly.

"What if you need to hear it? You've fucked this up six ways from Sunday and it's only goin' to get worse. I always see a job through, but —"

"Lucas." Japhrimel's quiet word sliced through our rising voices. The hover rattled. "Enough."

As if we needed any reminding who was actually in control of this situation. We stared at each other, Lucas Villalobos and I, and my sudden desire to smash his fucking face in made the Knife quiver in my hand. It was a weapon meant for demons, but I wondered just how much damage it could do to the man Death had denied.

"Are you thinking about it, Valentine?" Very softly. If Lucas had ever had a lover, he might have whispered to her in just this deadly quiet tone, almost-tenderness over razor-sharp rage. "Come on and try me. It'd be a fight worth having. Before you do, though, you'd better think about who was on that hover with Leander. D'ya think *she* stopped to cover his retreat? You think she gave a rat's ass about him? You bein' *used,* and if it wasn't so pathetic it'd be goddamn hilarious to see you barkin' up whatever tree ol' Blue-Eyes there points you at —"

I pitched forward, but Japhrimel arrived, his fingers locked around my wrist. I had started to bring the Knife up, its humming in my hand a sudden siren call. *Strike. Kill. Make someone bleed.*

"Lucas." Japhrimel matched his quietness. "You have a contract with me."

"I lived up to it so far, ain't I?" Villalobos's teeth-baring grimace wasn't a smile. "You an idiot too, demon. You shoulda done what had to be done when you had the chance."

"I did not ask for your opinion of my methods." Japhrimel's hand tensed and released, his coat ruffling slightly along its wet lacquered edges. "I asked for your skill in killing Hell's citizens. Any more is not your concern."

"Your funeral." Lucas wheeled and stalked away, the effect of his retreat ruined by the close quarters. He ended up near the cockpit, reflected desert light stippling his lean face. I wondered if the flesh between his shoulderblades was prickling because of *my* nearness, now.

Japhrimel did not look at me. Instead, he clasped his hands behind his back and stood very still, gazing down into the well of the cargo hold. Eve still crouched, motionless, and my heart gave a sudden pang. She was trapped down there without even anyone to talk to, alone in a bare hold.

Not a very human way to treat someone, is it, Danny? "Can I go down there?"

Japhrimel appeared not to have heard, staring fixedly at the demon's pale head. I drew in breath to ask again, but he stirred. "Why?"

Sekhmet sa'es. "Do I have to get a permit?"

"You hold the Knife, my curious. I can hardly stop you." A single shrug, his shoulder lifting, dropping.

It hung heavy in my hand, curved, obscenely warm wood. My rings sparked and sizzled in the uncertain air. Out here in the radiation wastes, static would build up, discharging in blue-white sparks. I could almost feel the silent killer against my skin, lethal power unleashed by the splitting of an infinitely small piece of the universe.

Should I be worried? I'm part-demon; will I get radiation sickness? Will I care if I do? "When were you going to tell me about this prophecy thing?"

"Meaningless gibberish." No shrug this time, but a slight tension in the straight line of his shoulders. "I suppose the Androgyne made it sound tailored to you."

The hand that can hold the Knife has faced fire and not been consumed, has walked in Death and returned, a hand given strength beyond its ken. "It sounds pretty specific."

"Ilvarimel's *hedaira* did speak before her death. She spoke her *A'nankhimel*'s name, and cursed me. The prophecy is simply noise." Each word was so bitter it was a wonder it didn't dye the air blue. "I suppose you will not believe me."

I don't know what to believe. My eyes snagged on the Knife's finials, clasping my hand. *Revenge. Kill the bastard and stop him playing around with me.*

But what then? Could I even imagine anything past that? If the gods smiled on me and I was lucky enough to kill Lucifer—by no means certain, even with Japh's help—what the hell would happen *then?*

There was Gabe's little girl in Saint City, playing in a House run by a sexwitch transvestite. I'd promised to raise her, to look after her and protect her.

I'd also promised to protect the demon crouched in the cargo hold, the child-demon who held bits of both me and Doreen in her genetic matrix. Who set me barking at trees in a way Lucas found so fucking amusing.

Who I would have killed for—or died for—atop that Paradisse tower. If Lucas or Vann had been human still, would I have slaughtered them in the name of keeping Eve safe?

Who was I really trying to save? Eve, or myself?

My teacher's voice drifted out of a cracked memory vault. *Compassion is not your strongest virtue, Danyo-chan.*

I could not keep every promise I made. I'd broken my vow of vengeance on Gabe and Eddie's killers; I had left that faithless murdering *sedayeen* bitch alive. Because Anubis, my god, my patron, had asked.

More than that, though. Because she was incapable of fighting back, because she was a healer. Because I could not murder an unarmed woman and retain any tattered shard of my honor. Because I had lived my life with no shortage of killing and violence—but always directed at someone who *deserved* to die, by any standard. Someone who had chosen to fight without honor, broken the law, or attacked me first. It was who I was.

Or who I used to be. Who was I now? A Necromance who couldn't stand to face her god. A half-demon with a head full of reactive fumes, liquid fury in place of blood, and a weapon that could hopefully kill the Devil in my fist.

Nobody's ever tried this Knife on Lucifer. You don't know if it works or not.

Still, I had Japhrimel, didn't I? He had declared war on Lucifer. If I could believe him. If I could trust him to hand Eve over to Lucifer in one breath and rescue her with the next.

What then, Danny? What comes after this?

More lies and games? What would happen in Hell with Lucifer gone?

Kind of late to be thinking this over now, sunshine.

The hover jolted a bit, steadied. Silence crackled, and when I blinked, returning to myself, I found Japhrimel had half-turned. He looked at me now, the silver threading his hair dappled with reflected light and his eyes burning holes in the artificial dusk left by the sealed portholes.

The human darkness behind a screen of green fire sent another sharp bolt through me. Had he even paused before throwing himself off a high-rise after me?

Of course not. You know he didn't. Sounding disgusted with myself was turning into a full-time career by now.

I set my jaw and lifted my chin. I also lifted the Knife slightly, but he didn't look at it. "I need a sheath for this. The old one won't fit."

He nodded. My heart ached. There was nothing else to say; I couldn't tell him a quarter of what I wanted to, and he wouldn't do a quarter of what I needed him to do. Go figure, the love of my life, and I couldn't trust a goddamn word he said. I *had* to trust what he would do.

I turned away, breaking eye contact with a small sharp pain, a needle going into whatever heart I had left. There was a ladder leading down to the cargo bay, and I slid my sword into the loop on my rig, needing at least one hand free for climbing.

"Dante." Why did he sound so ragged, as if he'd just finished some huge task? "May I ask you one thing?"

I studied the blank hull on the other side of the open cargo well. Deathly silence even managed to quiet the whine of hover travel. Vann and McKinley had stopped their murmuring. "Ask away." *All I can do is lie to you, you know. All I can do is betray you, keep things from you, manipulate you. Like you've done to me. Is turnabout fair play?*

"When Lucifer lies dying at your feet, what will you do?"

Good question. I swallowed dryly, closed my left hand over the railing, and prepared to climb down. Let out the breath I'd been holding. "I'll find out when I get there, Japhrimel."

I just hope that's the destination you really have in mind.

Sand swirled. The cargo hatch opened, a thin gleam bowing out as the airseals took on the load of oven-hot, evening desert wind. A flat glass field shimmered under a pall of fierce sunny heat, and even though I knew it was invisible I shivered, thinking of the radiation soaking that reflective waste. The hover would need decontamination and a plurifreeze wash on the way back, if there *was* a way back.

Eve still hadn't opened her eyes. She crouched in the very center of the thin silver circle, its taut drone an octave or so lower than the Knife's buzzing against my hip. Vann had produced yet another leather sheath, fitting the ancient weapon as if custom-made.

Airseals bowed again as the wind picked up, moaning between struts and sending fine sand hissing against the static containment field. I imagined radiation creeping into my flesh and shuddered again. Long shadows stretched away from the hover, made tall by the westering sun. We'd spent the whole day circling the city, wastes of twisted metal and old shattered buildings heaving under the hover's metal belly.

Vann tried again. "At least let us accompany you. For *her* protection."

Japhrimel shook his head. He checked a silvery gun, sighting down its barrel, and made it disappear. "I am all the protection she will require, and if I fail you could hardly succeed. No, Vann. It ends here."

"My Lord." McKinley this time, even paler than usual. "It'll be dusk soon. Tiens—"

"No." Japh's tone brooked no further argument.

Lucas slung a bandolier over his shoulder, buckled it. "Goddamn sun," he muttered. "Goddamn Vegas. Goddamn everything."

I heartily agreed. At least my clothes were still mostly in one piece and not too filthy. My hair tangled wildly, and I ran my fingers back through it, wincing as I encountered matted knots. My heart thumped, skipped, and settled into a fast high walloping run. Inside my head, the thin red ribbon of rage smoked. My shields crackled, another flush of Power reinforcing the tissue-thin energetic scabs. I was in no shape to take *anyone* on, let alone the Devil himself.

My knuckles drifted against the Knife's smooth warm hilt, the remainder of my left hand closed firmly around Fudoshin's hilt. A hot burnished smell of cooking glass and oven-warm sand filtered in through the seals, distant wet mirage-shimmers on the curved, receding horizon.

The sword kills nothing, my teacher whispered inside my head. *It is* will, *kills your enemy.*

I hoped it was true. Old Jado had given me this sword, and it had already tasted Lucifer's flesh once without breaking.

Sekhmet sa'es. *Lady, I invoke You. You answered me once. Be with me, I pray.* The reflex of faith was too deeply ingrained for me to escape. I'd spent forty-odd years or more praying to the god of Death, my own personal shield against the vastness of whatever lies beyond human understanding.

Now I was praying to someone else, and I hoped She was listening. My right hand rose to my throat and touched the knobbed end of a silver-dipped baculum, Jace's necklace quietly resting against my collarbone, its weight a comfort. All the voices in my head were silent, for once.

Waiting.

Japhrimel stepped to the edge of the silver double circle. The glyphs between the inner and outer layers responded, their dance becoming a single solid streak of light, running through the grated metal flooring without a single hitch. "It is time."

Eve's gasflame eyes opened. She rose to her feet in a single fluid movement. She tilted her head back, the pale supple cervical curve gleaming. Demon-acute sight picked out the pulse throbbing in its secret hollow, vulnerable and strong.

"Consort. You are a piece in this game." Japhrimel's tone was flat. He stood in his habitual manner, hands clasped behind his back, head slightly cocked as if the demon he regarded was an interesting specimen in a kerri jar, nothing more.

Eve stared over his shoulder, her blue gaze finding mine. The Knife buzzed against my hip. "Merely a pawn, Eldest?" Her voice was familiar, and a thread of her scent escaped the circle. Baking bread, heavy musk, and the edge of some spice, purely demon. "Who is the queen?"

"None of us may move as we will." Japhrimel shrugged at someone other than me for once.

"Are you so sure?" She indicated the circle holding her captive. "I am to play the prisoner, very well. Will I be shackled?"

"I see no need for such theatrics." Japhrimel didn't move, but the circle's hum slowed, deepening. "Though were I to return your recent hospitality, we might learn the look of your blood."

I made a small restless movement. McKinley's shoulders came up, his metallic left hand flexing into a fist as he stared at me. No, not at me.

At the Knife at my hip, and at Japhrimel's unprotected back, turned to me. At Eve, looking over Japh's shoulder.

Did he think I was going to stab my Fallen in the back?

Wouldn't put it past me right now, would you. Can't blame you. Instead, I looked out the hatch, the airseals shimmering as sand rasped them. The vast bowl of the blast zone shed heat like liquid, the hover's climate control working overtime. Puffs of cool air touched my cheeks.

"It was necessary." Eve didn't sound regretful in the least. "Even your *hedaira* knows as much."

"I am not here to bandy words of what might have been. I am here for what is to be done now. *Should* I shackle you?"

"You say yourself there's no need." Eve's relaxed amusement filled the air with softness.

Impatience boiled under my breastbone. "I realize this is the usual roundabout demon way of doing things." The scabbard creaked as my fingers clenched, lacquered wood protesting. "But can we pretty please with sugar on top get *on* with this?"

"You're so anxious to see *him* again?" Eve spread her hands, a graceful movement expressing resignation. "I am ready, Eldest. We may as well accede to your *hedaira*."

Japhrimel was silent for such a long moment I almost thought we were going to have trouble. The world slowed down, hissing sand caressing the hover's plasteel skin, a thin film of sweat covering my forehead.

The circle's hum spiraled up and winked out of existence. Silver drained away, fading under the assault of actual daylight. The thought of radiation sickness returned again, circling my brain, and I shifted my weight back as Lucas holstered his last plasgun and sighed.

"I'm pretty sure I got somethin' more pleasant I could be doin'," Villalobos said. "We're not meetin' *el Diablo* until dark."

"I would prefer some necessary reconnaissance of the terrain, which will allow you the time to hide yourself should you so choose." Japhrimel turned away from Eve, who stood smiling at me, the tips of her white, white teeth showing. My Fallen's boots were soundless as he took three long strides away from my daughter.

I tensed. Premonition tickled my nape, swam through dark water, flowered in the space behind my eyes—and sank away, showing me nothing. Nothing except the dread of *something* unpleasant about to happen.

"I ain't gonna hide," Lucas said. "I want him to know I'm standin'
with you. That was the deal."

What the hell? "What deal?"

Lucas coughed, rolled his shoulders back, and settled his bandoliers. "The one I made with your boyfriend, *chica*. The one that kept
me in this game. What, you thought I was workin' for you?"

"That was my understanding, yes." *But Eve hired you before I
did, and Japh paid you. So I suppose you were working for me until a
better offer came along.*

"If I was still workin' for you I'd've killed you. After you tried to
unzip my guts, that is." Lucas brushed past me. McKinley and Vann,
wearing identical expressions of worry, stood like statues. Eve still
didn't move, watching me with that unsettling smile.

You lying sack of shit. "I said I was sorry," I repeated, despite
Japhrimel halting less than two feet from me, his head slightly bowed.
The scar, softly burning against my shoulder, pulsed once. Another
warm, soft coat of Power eased down my skin. Caress or last-minute
bolstering, it cleared my head a bit.

The thin red ribbon of rage smoking in the bottom of my mind
shivered, uneasy. Eve finally eased forward, stepping cautiously over
the now-defunct borders of the circle. My nape prickled, the skin of
the world suddenly too thin and full of whispers just beyond my auditory range.

I braced myself. Eve's smile widened, and her hands came up,
elegant fingers spread. The thermagrenade bounced as she flung it,
one deadly accurate throw, straight into the middle of the ammo
crates Lucas had been digging in, stacked alongside the wall.

"Oh, *shi—*" McKinley never got time to finish the word.

The world turned over. Japhrimel spun aside and I dove for cover,
oxygen hissing as fire bloomed, a hungry flower. I hit hard, rolling to
the side, searching for something, anything, in the vast naked space
of the cargo bay to hide myself behind.

Eve landed next to me, catlike, one hand tented against the floor
for balance as the other curled around my upper arm and hauled. The
scar gave a flare of spiked heat, Japhrimel's aura compressing over
mine, and the desert invaded the hover as an explosion so huge it was
soundless tore plasteel like paper.

*What the he—*This time it was me who didn't get to finish a word
as my body left the grating, the shockwave and Eve's application of
force conspiring to drag me through air turned hot and viscous. I

went limp as a rag doll, the slim iron bar of Eve's arm now around my waist as she compressed herself, then let loose, flinging through space, my head jolting as we cleared the huge starfish hole torn in the side of the hover.

Bleeding. Nose and ears. Sand grinding underfoot as Eve landed hard, physics taking revenge as we both skidded. A cloud of grit rose, Power screaming, and I realized debris was raking the ground around us.

Eve leapt again, my sword almost jolting free before my fingers clamped shut, and I searched for a way, any way, to help her instead of just bouncing along for the ride.

Nothing came to mind. There was a brief starry moment of unconsciousness, desert heat mouthing my skin, and Eve dragged us both down a rocky incline scarred with detritus. We reached the cover of the edge of the blast zone, but even then she didn't stop, fleeing not just for escape but also for her life.

There was no water. We sheltered in the twisted ruins of what might have once been a tallish building, one side of it black and flash-fried from the blast centuries ago. Eve propped her back against the wall, gasping, and peered out onto the wasteland of Vegas. "Are...you...hurt?"

I shook my head, struggling to bring my own lungs under control. When I could talk, I still kept breathing, savoring the feel of air in my lungs. It was hellishly hot even in the shade, and something about this heat wasn't as nice as, say, the sun I'd basked in outside the boarding house in Hegemony Afrike. I'd always hated sweating before Japhrimel changed me; afterward I'd had much more tolerance of temperature variance. But this heat was something else — an oppression, helped along by the thought that thousands had died and crumbled to dust in these very buildings.

"You're bleeding," Eve finally said. Fine thin stripes of black demon blood on her own strange face glistened before they soaked back into golden skin. "My apologies."

"So were you." I braced my back against the wall and cast around, calculating fire angles. "Didn't know you had a grenade."

"Necessity being the mother of invention." She shook her head, the icy ropes of her hair providing no relief from the heat. "I could not warn you, either."

"Understood." And it was.

"I couldn't afford to let the Eldest chain me, or take the chance he might—"

I wouldn't trust him either, if I was you. "Understood, Eve." I sounded weary even to myself. The scar on my shoulder throbbed angrily, another bolt of pure Power flushing down to my bones and spreading outward. "Really. So what's the plan?"

"The best I can come up with is not very good." She slid down to sit cross-legged, scooching herself between a shattered chunk of concrete and something that might have once been a couch covered in faded tattered plaid. Shards of silica glass littered the building, sand-laden wind whistling on the other side of the wall. In this wilderness of cracked and dead buildings, cover was cheap and sight-lines a dime a dozen. If I'd had six or seven bounty hunters and was up against a human adversary, it might have been a good locale. "*He* is due to arrive at dusk." Her face twisted, blue eyes rivaling the heaving light outside. Every time she mentioned Lucifer, her expression held such pure loathing it almost covered up the fear. "We can either run and search for another opportunity to kill *him,* or take our chance now. Without allies—unless your Fallen decides, as I hope he will, that covering your attempt is the best way to keep you alive."

I tipped my chin down toward the scar. "I'm not exactly inconspicuous. He's going to come looking for me."

She nodded. "Dusk approaches. It won't be long, and we are not the only danger here. Listen."

I did, tilting my head in a parody of her graceful motion. My entire body ached.

Wind, moaning. The ever-present hiss of sand, and the sound of roaring distance without hovers or crowds.

And little, skittering noises. Too light or too heavy, too fast or too slow to be mortal. Noises that hit the ear wrong and raised my hackles.

I breathed in softly, tasting the air. Dust, dry rotting things, decay and the faint odor of long-ago violence. Threading under that, a faint well-traveled hint of burning cinnamon and musk.

"This is not a human place," Eve whispered. "Even when it was a city, it wasn't a human place. Since the catastrophe here, a door to Hell has remained open. *He* will use it, if *he* has not already, either to issue forth from Hell or to return once *he* has won. At least, that is what *he* thinks." Her eyes glittered, her mouth twisting. She seemed not to notice her sweater was torn to rags, the firm golden slopes of her breasts peeping out.

Nausea rose hot and acid. I swallowed it, my rig creaking as I shifted. I had all my weapons and a serious case of sand-in-the-crevices; it's why I never go to the beach. "Okay." *You and me against the Devil? We're dead.*

"We know where *he* will be," she persisted. "And despite the Eldest, I am not without allies. Hell is in revolt. We have challenged *him,* you and I."

Exhaustion crested, washed over me. *Just shut up and show me where I can die, all right?* "Eve, there's no need for the speeches. Just tell me what you want me to do." My muscles trembled on the edge of cramping; I slumped against the wall and shook the ringing out of my ears.

She paused for a few of the longest seconds of my life. I watched the knife-sharp shadows, sunlight spearing through the temporary shelter of a building older than the Hegemony and still clinging, wrecked and broken, to the edges of life.

"Will you kill *him?*" She sounded very small, and very young. But that smile was neither small nor young. It was the smile of a vid-poker shark holding a full hand of wonderful about to call your bet and take your firstborn.

Or maybe just your soul. Were demons even interested in souls anymore, now that they had all the government, sex, Power, and favors humanity could come up with?

"Sekhmet sa'es," I whispered back. "Why do you keep asking me? I'm sure as hell going to try."

CHAPTER 35

It wasn't that long until sundown, and I spent most of that time not-thinking as Eve and I flitted from shadow to shadow, working along the edge of the bomb crater and the huge reflective glass pan. Purple veils of shade grew longer and longer, and once I crouched next to her in the lee of a huge pile of scrap preserved by dry desert air while a hellhound slid in plain view through a golden column of fading sunlight, its green eyes catching fire and heat shimmering from its pelt. The Knife vibrated against my hip so hard I expected the beast to pause and look for whatever was buzzing like a wasp, but the slitherings and skitterings of demons in the ruins must have drowned it out.

Or at least, so I hoped. My eyes, dry and heavy from the flying sand, kept welling with hot water. My shoulder pulsed with soft velvet heat.

This is a bad idea. You know this is a bad, bad idea, right? Even if Japh was planning to hand Eve over to him, he would have kept you alive. This is a bad idea.

I dismissed the thought as not even worthy of the craven bastard I was turning into. There was no shame in being afraid, but there *was* shame in hiding from it. So I was afraid. So what? I've been afraid most of my life, of one thing or another.

But I've never let that fear drive me. Spur me, maybe. But not drive me.

Eve circled our destination a few times before we worked our way closer, picking our way through piles of junk and broken concrete. The sun lowered itself into the west like an old man sinking into a bathtub, slow and aching. I tried not to feel the insistent tugging in my shoulder, a pulling against the ropes of the scar. Where was he? Had he intended to turn Eve over to Lucifer? He'd promised not to, asked me to trust him. Still, I could see how Eve might not want to take that chance.

It didn't matter. Nothing mattered now.

The sun turned to blood, and I thought I could see the haze of radiation crawling over every sand-scoured surface. Or maybe it was just the blurring in my eyes.

As the sun sank, Power rose.

It was coming from somewhere close, a diseased heart in the ruins thumping irregularly but gathering strength. One huge broken building, a massive structure that looked like it had once been a pyramid, loomed over a twisted unrecognizable statue. I guess humanity's never lost its taste for making things huger than they need to be.

A slight rise of rubble made a natural amphitheater, the mountains in the background and the edges of the blast zone spilling away, the glass fractured in crazy spiderweb patterns that reminded me of the deep angular scorings on the altar in the city under Chomo Lungma. I shivered as the baking wind, redolent of sand and demon spice, breathed up into my face.

I lay on my stomach and peered down into the bowl of rubble giving out onto the wastes. Eve crouched below the lip of the hill, dust grimed into her hair turning it the color of clotted cream instead of pale platinum ice. Both of us were tattered almost beyond recognition. I pushed matted, filthy hair out of my face and shivered again. My nervous system was rebelling like a Chill junkie's, out on the edge of control, ready to jolt away from under me.

Breathe, Danny. Just breathe.

There, in the middle of the wreckage, something that should not be . . . was. The dying sun gathered itself and plunged fully below the horizon, desert stars striking sparks as the wind veered again, the ground thrumming below. The paint of dusk bled down the vault of heaven, and as true night dropped like a curtain—because it does fall fast out here in the desert, with no streetlamps to hold it back—a slim figure with a shock of golden hair melded out of nothing and took his place at the focal point.

The ruined city cringed.

Other shadows gave birth. The spiderlike things clicked and scuttled, straining at leashes held by graceful, inhuman forms with burning eyes in shades of blue, green, and molten gold. Hellhounds, winged and flightless, snarled and jostled. Imps lolled, some chittering in the strange unlovely tongue of Hell, and the deeper shadows held eyes that had to be higher-ranking demons, not deigning to show themselves.

"Anubis," I breathed, then clapped my hand over my mouth.

Eve said nothing, but crouched tense as a violin string next to me. "Not so many of the Lesser Flight, and none at all of the Greater." The words mouthed my ear as if she'd placed her mouth next to it.

So what? They're still fucking demons. I spotted a way down through the rubble, an easy path.

A primrose path, Danny? Get it? Howling hysterical laughter rose up under my skin, was mercilessly choked, and died without even a gurgle. "I don't suppose we have a plan," I whispered back.

"Do you believe in Fate, Dante?"

Past turned into present again, looped and stuck tight, a gear-wheel sliding into place. Nothing to do but finish this, now.

"No." I wasn't sure whether it was a lie or the truth, but I said it.

Lucifer turned in a circle, the flame of his hair not replacing the sun. My hands shook. My entire body shook. The gaping hole in my mind struggled to open like a cancerous flower, the reality of what had been done to me fighting to break free and douse my sanity with black water. My shields shivered, one powerful burst of fear tinting them purple-red before I controlled myself again. Fudoshin sang as it cleared the sheath and I found myself on my feet at the top of the slope, clearly visible in the backwash of starlight.

Pebbles clicked and shifted, and I knew without looking that Eve had risen too, her lambent eyes glowing over my shoulder. For a moment my heart paused. It should have been Japhrimel standing there, watching my back as I faced down the Devil.

It doesn't matter. It won't matter in a few red-hot minutes.

My sword woke. Blue flame twisted along its edge, runes of the Nine Canons spilling through the steel, its white-hot core singing its own silent song of destruction. I took three steps forward, and my fingers loosed themselves from the scabbard. It clattered to the ground, and my left hand closed around the Knife's warm, wooden hilt.

Lucifer slowly turned. The movement was exquisitely leisurely, light sliding down the line of his body. Gold lived, scorching, in his hair, casting a glimmer around him. He tilted his head back slightly, and the dish of his face rose to catch my gaze.

His face was a holovid angel's, sheerly beautiful and just as completely male. The emerald set above and between his flawless, burning-green eyes snapped a spark. The marvel of his mouth was set and unyielding. There were shadows under his flaming eyes, and his beauty was somehow worn but not diminished.

The Devil looked very tired.

My left cheek itched, the twisted-caduceus accreditation tattoo straining inked lines under my skin. My own emerald burned like a lase bonedrill, spitting a tearing-green spark fat as a teardrop.

His eyes met mine and I recoiled without moving, a scream tearing through the blank spot in my head, the one space where my Magi-trained memory mercifully failed.

Lucifer paused, the silk of his simple black tunic and trousers fluttering. A hood of darkness slid over his perfect features, a psychic miasma of hate made visible. His eyes slid past me as if I was a piece of furniture, coming to rest on Eve.

When he spoke, it was with the utter finality of a being who expects immediate obedience. The voice of the Prince of Hell lashed every exposed surface of the wreckage and made it groan and tremble.

"Aldarimel, the Morning Star, most beloved of my consorts."

Lucifer's mouth twisted down at one corner, rose again in a sneer. The thin white scars on my belly twitched as if something still lived in the bowl of my pelvis, a heavy heated stone.

The wall inside my head quivered, stretched—and *held,* my stubbornness sticking fast. I lifted the Knife and stepped forward again. The demons had frozen, hellhounds, spiders, and imps all alike crouched and staring like statues.

Lucifer took no notice. He *ignored* me, speaking past me to Eve. "I shall offer you one chance, and only one, to return to your nest and await your penance."

I'm not sure what she would have said. She never got the chance. I opened my big fat stupid mouth.

"Hey." My voice, cracked and husky, echoed all along the bowl of rubble. "Blondie. You two-faced lying sack of demon *shit.*" My face froze, lips stretched in a facsimile of a smile. "You've got business with me first."

"Indeed I do." He nodded, and I almost had no time to duck before the first hellhound leapt for me.

The Knife jerked in my hand. Fudoshin sang, and wood met demon flesh as I pitched forward, blade stuck to the hilt in the roasting hide of a hellhound I had barely even seen.

The sucking sound hit a high keening note, and Power slammed up my arm, exploding in my left shoulder and fluorescing in the visible range. Black-diamond fire burst in a perfect sphere around me, the edges of my ragged aura clearly visible under the smooth carapace of Japhrimel's borrowed Power.

A quick twist of my wrist, muscles flexing in my forearm, breaking the suction of muscle against the blade. The finials scraped against my skin, caging my hand and protecting it as a writhe of the hellhound's flexible body almost tore the Knife free.

I kicked the body, fine ash already spreading in capillary-patterns through the glassy shifting heat of its hide. I rose from the half-crouch its attack had driven me down into, Fudoshin sweeping down in a curve painted with blue fire, slicing across an imp's face.

Clarity spilled through me, rage sharp and bright as a new-pressed credit disc. They descended on me, the lowest of the scions of Hell, and the Knife screamed in my hand as the world unrolled, strings of energy under its surface showing me the path through. Step-kick, demon bones crunching and the Knife sending another shock of feverish Power up my arm, the sword halting in midair and slicing down, the Knife's finials crunching against a hellspider's face. They moved in on me, skittering and chittering in their demonic language, or snarling and clicking.

This is what I was born to do.

All thought vanished. My grip on Fudoshin's hilt was gentle, like clasping a lover's hand. The sword responded, steel flexing as it bent, whipping through forms coded into the very lowest levels of my brain.

Turn. Flex the wrist, back foot stamping down, front foot turning out, bring the knee up, quickly, don't think don't think, kill it, drive the Knife in, pull it free.

It was a string of fire tied to my wrist, the Knife humming as it settled into jerking my body like a marionette's, burning all the way down to the bone, the finials clasping tighter and tighter as the weapon took over.

And I didn't care.

The last hellhound fell at my feet with a thud, whimpering as veins of ash threaded its flesh. It convulsed, and hissing whimpers sounded as the rest of them drew back, a circle of glowing eyes and heatshimmer in the darkness. The temperature had dropped, steaming sands losing the day's baking. My boots crunched on silica glass at the bottom of the hill, and I faced Lucifer over a rubble-strewn plain. Raised my eyes, the ribbon of rage widening. It flushed my body, this clear clean fury, sweet in its single-mindedness.

I knew what he had done to me. I didn't quite remember it, but I knew as if it had happened to someone else, some brutalized girl crouching in the corner of a bedroom, whimpering as she beat her head against the wall, the borders of her body violated, her mind no longer quite her own.

The Prince of Hell's green eyes narrowed. That was all. The emerald in his forehead ran with light as sterile as the radiation crawling through the ruins.

It occurred to me that I hadn't seen a single plant or animal since touching down. Just sand, shattered buildings, and trash. Pure destruction, so intense that after centuries nothing grew here.

Lucifer's hands were loose at his sides, elegant fingers relaxed.

I filled my lungs. Grit-laden wind touched my cheeks, fingered my filthy hair. My ribs heaved with deep gasping breaths, but I didn't care. My heartbeat mounted behind my eyes, so quick and hard it threatened to burst out through my veins.

"Here I stand, Lucifer." My throat cracked with dry heat, but my voice was steady. "And not all the hosts of Hell shall move me."

In other words, you want Eve? Come and get her—but you're going to go through me first. And I have some payback for you.

The voices in my head stilled. My left shoulder ran with velvet fire, and the heat was building in my arms, my legs. It pressed against the thin film of my psyche, stretched over some unknowable bulge.

More lamps lit in the dark behind him. Demonic eyes, shadows resolving around slim graceful shapes. The air crawled and ran with Power, whispers, little tittering gasps of laughter. Those of the Greater Flight that still called the Devil "Master" gathered, just in time for the show.

I didn't care.

Lucifer stirred. "Not all the hosts of Hell are necessary, Necromance." His hair lifted, gold running along its edges. His Chinese-collared tunic ran with wet light as he lifted one graceful arm and pointed at me, the claw-tip at the end of his index finger lengthening. "Just one."

Fudoshin's tip described a precise little circle in the air before the hilt floated to the side, a natural movement settling in second guard, the Knife along my left forearm singing its high-voltage song of gathering murder. Stars ran overhead, their crystalline fires not choked by cityshine. Eve was still behind me at the top of the hill; I felt her attention, spark after spark crackling from the emerald in her forehead echoing Lucifer's. The gem on my cheekbone sparked too, my tat running wildly under the skin, a high sweet itching pain.

The world narrowed, shrank to a single point. Neither of us could back out now. Gauntlet thrown down, challenge accepted, and I was about to die.

I wondered if my god would take me in His arms, or if I would slide unnoticed into the well of souls I had crossed over so often.

Did it matter?

"Come on," I whispered. *Come and get me. If you can. If you dare.*

I had no warning. Before the words died he was on me.

The shock was like worlds colliding. My left arm was thrown aside, his bladed fingers striking my solar plexus, robbing me of breath as shocked lungs and heart struggled to function. Fudoshin jabbed in, hilt used like a battering ram to strike the Prince of Hell's fair golden face, now twisted with rage and horribly, inescapably still beautiful. It snapped his head back and he was flung down as I stumbled back, digging in my left heel to regain my balance, nausea rising and my bruised torso seizing up, cramping.

Nausea retreated as he flowed to his feet. A single dot of black blood welled at the corner of his mouth and I dropped into position as he lifted the back of one golden hand to touch his lips. Fudoshin described a bigger circle this time, the blessed blue flame along its edge adder-hissing.

I heard myself speak. "I remember."

I remember how I screamed when you put that thing in me, how you sliced me open like I was a sodaflo can—and how you laughed when I screamed. I remember what you said, and how you really seemed to enjoy yourself. I remember how you sent me out to betray my daughter and my lover.

"What do you think you remember?" Contempt loaded Lucifer's voice, smoking land glittering like carbolic tossed over reactive paint. "Where were *you* when I made your kind? Where were you when I made your *world?*" He drew himself up and pointed again, the holocaust glow of his eyes so intense teardrop trails shimmered horizontally from their corners. "You have interfered for the *last time!*"

Oh, will you just shut up and kill me? I raised the Knife slightly, its clawlike finials prickling against my forearm, and felt the points slide into my skin. The sweet rotting-fruit smell of demon blood hung cloying in the air. Was I bleeding?

I didn't care. I brought my sword down and around, a swordsman's move, hilt rotating in my hand as the blade spun like a propeller, before he leapt for me again.

Impact. Bones snapping in my side, the agony immense and useless, like everything else. Stars of pain shattering across the surface of my mind, I brought the Knife up in a sweep and felt the blade *bite,* a feedback squeal grinding the rubble around us into dancing cascading dust—

—and the Knife, wrenched from my grasp, clawed my hand desperately before flying in a high impossible arc, up and *away,* the Power feeding up my arm jolting to a stop as Lucifer backhanded me, smashing me to the ground.

CHAPTER 36

Rolling.

Get up get up get up—Before the words faded I was on my feet, every ounce of demon speed I could use in one last desperate lunge, swordblade screaming as it split air and twisted, driving home in the Devil's chest. A spike of fire jabbed through my left lung, blood dribbling down my chin, muscles pulled out of alignment by smashed bones, I swayed on my numb feet and saw what I had done.

We stood like that, Lucifer pinned like a butterfly, the scream dying on my lips as the Devil, black blood griming his ivory teeth and his eyes inches from mine, *smiled*.

The world halted. Sick realization thumped home in the wasteland my shattered mind had become, smoking with fury. *That's not going to kill him.*

There seemed no shortage of time as I watched his hand come up, claws springing free. *This is going to hurt.* I shifted my weight to pull Fudoshin free, knowing I would never be able to cut him a second time.

The Knife I dropped the Knife ohgods I'm dead I'm dead—

It was hopeless. But I tore my blade free, metal howling under the abuse, Power raying out from the event we had just created in spiderwebs of force and reaction, rubble grinding to smaller bits and dust pluming, shaping into mushroom clouds.

Everything inside me rose and halted, hanging in the air above my skin. My left shoulder burned, a prickling mass of hot ice and barbed wire flooding me with a desperate burst of Power, straining through me, trying to shield me against the inevitable. Flexible demon-altered bones crackled, and the relief and weightlessness I had felt falling through the roof of Paradisse wrapped around me again.

It's over.

Lucifer's hand began its descent, claws sparkling with emerald flame to match the gem in his forehead. His face was a mask of unholy rage, psychic darkness flooding under its beauty, and my heart stuttered as the essential inhumanity of the thing I saw beneath that screen of loveliness was revealed.

And I *recognized* it. I recognized the twisted teeth and burning eyes. I heard its echo in my own brain. It was my own hatred.

How much more *like* the Devil was I going to have to become to kill him?

No.

Time paused again.

No. I will not be like you. No. The only word I could say repeated, gathering force in my eyes and arms and lips, filling me. It was the only prayer I could utter.

Dante, you have been so blind.

And I *struck*.

Not with my sword. If I tried to cut with Fudoshin again, it would be in rage, in anger. I already knew how useless that would be, fury turning back on itself, destruction for its own sake.

Compassion is not your strongest virtue, Danyo-chan.

How had my teacher known?

The red ribbon of rage in my head paled. It shrank to a thread-thin line. I did not want it to go. It was my only defense. I could not help what had been done to me, but I could fight. I could *kill*.

Couldn't I?

I can't hold a gun to your head and make you more human.

The dead rose about me, each of them a distinct shape of silver lattice and crystalline intent holding an imprint of the flesh they wore in my life. Lewis, with his smile and his steadfast love. Doreen with her gentleness; Jace with his stubborn refusal to give in. Gabe, who had known me better than I knew myself—and Eddie, always on the periphery but still necessary, who would have done for me what I did for him and not counted the cost.

All of them rose in me, a tide of love and obligation, the nets of duty and the lines of promises made, kept, broken, and kept again. The dead keened in my bones, spilled through my blood, and blazed through me as the red thread inside my head opened its jaws and *roared*.

Has a god ever used you to complete a circle? Have you ever been ridden by a *loa?* A vaudun Shaman will understand. The god or spirit spills into you, stretching you like a too-small glove on a hand, and the thin ecstasy of a bursting, too-ripe fruit shatters whatever you thought you were. Infinity recognizes you, and how can you help but recognize the infinity in your own soul?

My god woke in me, His slim canine head turning to look with its terrible eyes that became *my* eyes. For a dizzying moment Death filled me.

Compassion is not your strongest virtue.

Lucifer screamed. The force boiled out of me, my hand spread instead of locked in a fist. I touched the Devil's face, cupping his cheek as if he was a lover, my fingers gentle and delicate, the silk of an impermeable, invulnerable skin sending a heatless pang through my cracking ribs and bleeding meat.

Yes, it is, I replied. *Gods grant I do not forget it.*

They did not.

Married to Anubis's still quiet, Sekhmet woke. She took a single step, the stamping dance that would unmake the world moving on, creation flooding in its wake. It was and was not me who did the striking, at the last. It was *them.*

No, it was me too. I swear it was.

The scream was the world stopping. It was a death-cry, or the cry of love like a knife to the heart. The god I thought had abandoned me gathered me to His chest, comfort singing through my sobbing, broken body.

It was not Anubis who had turned away. It was me. He had never left me for a moment.

You may not take this, Anubis-Sekhmet said. ***This is Mine, and you may not have her.***

Ash threaded through Lucifer's skin, the even gold and bright light dimmed by spreading veins of dusty dirty gray. The sound was a crackling. My other hand came up, met his face. His emerald cracked, sending out one vicious caustic flash. The gulping sound was very loud in the stillness. A dripping point speared free of Lucifer's ribs, and over the Devil's shoulders, a pair of yellow eyes dawned, meeting mine with a blow no less critical than the one I had just meted out.

Lucas twisted the Knife, and Lucifer screamed again. My breath jagged out of me, the gods receding like a tide full of wreckage, foaming and split.

The flesh under my fingers collapsed, runnels of dry decay replicating furiously. The twin pieces of Lucifer's emerald ground themselves into dust. The Knife keened, satisfaction in its chill, curling voice.

The explosion of dusty diamond grit blew my hair back, scouring my eyes and filling my mouth with dry sand. I coughed, choked, and stumbled back, my legs failing me.

Someone caught me, breaking the force of my fall. My sword clattered on the ground, my fingers spasming open. Power slid through the mark on my shoulder, detonated inside my bones, and Japhrimel folded himself over me, saying something I could not quite hear. It might have been my name. It could have been anything.

I convulsed. Footsteps sounded through the deafness of pain in my ears. My head tilted back, stars scoring the sky through veils of dust.

The ground tilted, desert shaking like liquid brushed with hover-wash. The pain was a diamond nail, driven through me from crown to soles. My body struggled against it, a fish on a hook.

Lucas said something, in a deadly-quiet whisper. Footsteps brushed a slope of wreckage, picking their way delicately down.

Japhrimel's arms tightened. He pulled me, once more, into the shelter of his body. My cheek burned, the emerald grafted into the bone red-hot. "The Prince is dead," he said quietly. "Long live the Prince."

Eve laughed, the sweet carefree giggle of a little girl. "It is the way of our kind, is it not?"

Demons drew close. I felt them against the raw edges of my broken shielding, Japhrimel's aura over mine smooth and seamless. Whispers and chittering, their voices tearing at the night. The smell of burning cinnamon turned cloying, dust-decay threading its sweet muskiness. Eve's smell—baking bread, vulnerability, pure sweetness—rose in my nose, slid down the back of my throat.

I gagged.

"Come any closer and I'll make you eat this thing." Lucas's tone was flat and utterly serious.

"Give me the Knife." Eve sounded like she was smiling. "It's what you were contracted for."

"Funny thing about that." Dust squealed under booted feet and a clicking sounded before the whine of an unholstered plasgun drilled the air. "I ain't never welshed on a contract before. All three of you tryin' to hire me away from each other, and all for a simple goddamn assassination."

I was just trying to stay alive, Lucas. The thought was clean, the shock of a god's touch falling away from my mind. The blank spot in my memory receded, Japhrimel murmured something into my hair.

"Lucas." Eve's voice held a warning now. "Give me the Knife."

"It ain't yours. Neither am I." The footsteps paused. Something nudged my shoulder. "Here, *chica*. You'd best hold this." Cold fingers touching mine. Something obscenely warm touched my palm, fever-ish energy jolting up my wrist, slamming into my elbow, and socking into my shoulder before spreading down through my healing bones. I tried to open my eyes. They obeyed, slowly. A slice of blurry light danced in front of me. *What the hell just happened?* Echoes of a god's touch drained away, swirling. Leaving me alone again inside my mind, the red ribbon of rage turned to ash, blowing away. Fine, cinnamon-scented ash, lifting on the confused wind.

My vision cleared. Lucas stood, threadbare and slump-shouldered, an unholstered 60-watt plasgun pointed at the ice-haired demon who stood, her emerald glowing. Dust danced as if the amphitheater was a hot griddle.

The Knife buzzed in my hand. Japhrimel kissed my forehead. "Merely breathe, *hedaira*. All is well."

"I hired you first," Eve said, silkily. "Don't make an enemy out of me, Deathless. You won't like the results."

He leveled the plasgun, yellow eyes narrowed. "I think you'd bet-ter get the fuck out of here, Blue Eyes. I already killed one demon today, and I might take it in mind to kill another. Besides, ain't you got some trouble back home to take care of?"

She shrugged. The movement was so uncannily like Lucifer's my heart jolted in my chest. "It makes little difference, anyway."

"J-J-Japh—" My voice wouldn't work properly. I finally managed to wrap my lips around a single syllable. "Eve—"

Her eyes slid away from Lucas, traveled over acres of burning air to look at me. Around the rim of the rubble-bowl, the paired lamps of demon eyes were winking out, stealthy scrapes and clawings retreat-ing. *Show's over, folks. Nothing left to see here. Move along.*

"Goodbye, Dante. Thank you for your help." Her smile was the plastic grimace of a child's doll. "Though you were wrong."

About what? My throat was stoppered with dry dust. I could only stare, accusingly, from the shelter of Japhrimel's arms. His fingers closed around mine, sliding under the Knife's finials, his lips against my filthy hair. Still murmuring something, over and over.

"Any Key will do in a lock, with enough coaxing." Eve's gaze lingered on the Knife for a few moments. A calculation crossed her face, and another.

I almost cringed. Was she thinking how easy it might be to set me barking up another tree?

I had been so *blind*.

Japhrimel raised his face from my hair. When he spoke, the entire pan of rubble rattled, little bits shifting and sliding. "This stays with me, Androgyne."

"One day, I might come to reclaim it." The gasflame glow of her eyes dimmed slightly, a new color blooming underneath the screen of light.

Green. Like sunlight through new leaves. Like a laser.

Like Lucifer's gaze.

I shuddered. Japhrimel's hand was warm and steady, holding my fingers against a silken hilt of wood and grief.

"On that day, you will meet *his* fate. Rule Hell if you will; I care little. But us you will leave in peace." He sounded absolutely certain.

I found I could breathe again. *Eve.* I struggled to sit up, to shake free of Japhrimel's arms. What was happening to her?

My daughter tilted her head slightly as the last shades of blue died out of her eyes. She was unmistakably female, the sheerness of her beauty maturing in breathtaking leaps, her face thinning a little and the gold of her skin flushing warmly. Had it been another glamour?

No, this change was something else. Something deeper. Any pretense she might have made at humanity was now laid aside, and I found myself lying under the hard brilliant sky of the Vegas Waste and watching something inhuman settle into its newest form.

The Prince is dead. Long live the Prince.

She turned away, her supple back under the torn dust-smeared sweater shining with its own grace. "My thanks for your aid, my friends. But now I have a whole world to conquer."

"May it give you joy," Japhrimel said softly, like a curse. But she was already gone, vanishing between one breath and the next. A sound like ripping silk assaulted the air, died away.

My Fallen let out a long, shaking breath. For a few moments, he held me, while the dust settled, silence returning and filling the amphitheater like liquid in a cup.

It was over.

I was still alive. But I had failed in every way that ever counted.

CHAPTER 37

There was another hover, a long sleek new craft with a battery of mag-and-deepscan shielding that resolved out of the desert sky, landing with a bump and opening its side hatch like a flower. I didn't question it, even when Tiens greeted us all with a cheery smile that showed the tips of his abnormally long canines. Anton Kgembe, his head bandaged, didn't even look up from strapping down cargo containers. Vann looked a little worse for wear, bruised and battered and moving slowly as he brought a blanket that Japh wrapped around me before handing me and the Knife over to McKinley.

I felt nothing except a numb wonder that they had all survived.

All except Leander, that is. Was he dead? The numbness even covered that with a sheet of plasticine wrap, insulating me from the bite of guilt.

It was McKinley, oddly enough, who brought me up to speed on the long twilight journey back from the Waste. Him, and the holonews, because Japhrimel wouldn't speak to me and neither would Lucas.

The incidences of Magi dying had tapered off a little. The Hegemony directive was rescinded and everyone got back to work. There were still...problems, of course. Plenty of demons had escaped Hell and would have to be dragged back kicking and screaming. But that was a job for the new head honcho, the brand new Prince of Hell, the leader of the successful rebellion.

Eve. Or more properly, Aldarimel, the Morning Star, Lucifer's youngest and most favored consort. The new toy he'd brought back to Hell, reverse-engineered from Doreen—a human descendant of the Fallen—and his own genetic material. Was it narcissism, or was the Devil just like a human with a new love affair?

In any case, she'd gotten just what she wanted. The Prince of Hell was dead.

Long live the Prince.

Hello? I said to the silence inside myself. *Hello?*

The holonews was salt in the wound. Picture after picture of shattered houses, Magi gone missing, weird occurrences all over the world as the jostling factions from Hell fought it out. I watched the flickering pictures through a heavy blanket of water-clear exhaustion, refusing to close my eyes, refusing to look away. They were comparing it to the chaos at the time of the Great Awakening, and expert holo-heads weighed in with utterly useless analyses.

"Here." McKinley handed me a thick china mug. It smelled like coffee, and I slumped in an ergonomic chair bolted to the floor with the blanket pulled tight around me, staring fixedly at the dark liquid. "You should drink." He even managed to sound kind.

"Why?" Shell-shocked, numb, and exhausted, I pushed away a curtain of weariness and tried to take a drink. My stomach closed, tighter than a fist.

He shrugged, rubbing at his metallic left hand. His fingers left no smudge behind on the smooth, gleaming almost-skin. "It's over. At least, for now."

What, you're expecting more? I set the cup down on a slice of table snugged into the chair's side. "What happens now?" I sounded like a kid again, breathy and scared.

"Now we pick up the pieces." He tilted his head slightly, indicating the front of the hover, Japhrimel in whispered conference with Vann and Tiens, Kgembe slumped asleep in a foldout chair bolted to the hull, Lucas leaning on the hull at the periphery of that conversation, his yellow eyes trained on me.

I swallowed hard. The hover bounced a little, the AI piloting since Tiens was now leaning closer to Japh, making some earnest point. The Nichtvren's gaze flicked to me and away, and he brought one fist softly into the palm of his other hand for emphasis.

My sword lay across my knees, the metal quiescent and shining only as much as ordinary steel. It had rammed through Lucifer's chest, and still remained intact. The Knife lay on the table, its slow song of grief and rage sounding more and more foreign.

My eyes drifted closed. The coffee sloshed. I drifted, my fingers and toes gone cold and rubbery. The broken places inside my head shivered, too tired to even try knitting together.

For a long time I rocked like that, my head lolling against the back of the seat, the bumps and jostles of the hover a cradle's soft movement. I heard raised voices, and Japhrimel's tone suddenly cutting through the cotton wool surrounding me. He said something short and sharp, and all discussion ceased.

Not too long afterward, someone touched my dirty, dust-caked

hair. The fingers were gentle, and I opened my eyes to see Japh standing over me, his face drawn and thoughtful. My left shoulder
twitched, as if a fishhook in the flesh had been pulled.

"Can you stand?"

He might as well have asked if I could fly.

I grabbed the arms of the chair. Braced myself, tensed, and managed to push myself up with a low sound of effort, my right hand
scooping up Fudoshin's hilt.

Japhrimel steadied me with one hand, picked up the Knife with
the other, using only his fingertips and wincing slightly. "I shall have
Vann make another sheath for this."

I shook my head, the entire hover tilting as I did. "You keep it. I
don't want it." *I'd say give it to Lucas, but I don't know if he wants it
either.*

Japhrimel paused. He glanced over his shoulder. Lucas had closed
his eyes, leaning against the hull and listening while McKinley said
something to Tiens, the Nichtvren casting a dubious look at me.

I didn't care anymore.

His hand fell away from my arm.

I swayed. "Where are we going?"

"I thought you might prefer a bed. Such as it is." His eyes caught
fire, but his face was merely set and thoughtful. "Dante."

I set my jaw. *A bed. Just one more thing, and I can sleep for a
week. That'd be nice.* "Japhrimel."

*Then I can start untangling the rest of this mess. All those things I
swore I'd do once I finished. All those promises I made.*

The pain wouldn't go away. It was right under my ribs, my heart
caught in a nest of splinters. All my friends were dead, and so was
the Devil.

Why didn't I feel any better?

The hover bounced. McKinley finished what he was saying, and
silence folded through the interior.

All eyes on you, Danny. Do something.

I took an experimental step. Swayed. Japhrimel moved restlessly,
but I waved his hand away. I'd make it to the bed on my own, goddammit. One thing at a time.

Why don't I feel better? Tears rose in my throat, prickled behind
my eyes. *Why?*

"Valentine." Lucas, his whisper half-strangled.

I stopped, tensed, and waited. *The hand that can hold the Knife has faced fire and not been consumed, has walked in death and returned, a hand given strength beyond its ken.*

Had there truly been a prophecy? Or was it just absurdity? He was the Deathless, but Eve had thought I was the Key.

Had I been? Would I ever know?

What he said next bordered on the absurd. "We even?"

Even? How the hell could we be even? I tried to kill you; you were working for everyone except me—but you killed Lucifer. And you gave me back the Knife. Even doesn't happen in this kind of situation.

An exotic thought stopped me. I considered it, in my exhaustion-fogged state. Thought about it for a long while, as the hover rose and fell, its gyros coping with various stresses.

"Valentine? Are we *even?*" Tension under his throat-cut whisper, I could almost feel his entire body tightening.

Amazing. Was Lucas Villalobos asking if we were still friends?

I never thought I'd live to see the day.

It didn't matter. Nothing mattered, now. If I could live without knowing some things, I could live with calling Lucas Villalobos something other than an enemy. "We're still friends, Lucas. If that's what you're asking."

Nobody moved. I barely even breathed.

"Good 'nough." Villalobos sounded relieved, and my heart eased, a sudden convulsive movement. "Get some rest."

Not all my friends are dead. I followed the hem of Japhrimel's coat, stumbling with exhaustion and clutching Fudoshin's hilt. When the door closed behind us and he took me in his arms, I found tears running hot and thick down my cheeks.

For once that didn't matter, either.

"Where are we going?"

"Santiago City, Dante. Your home. Ours, now."

Epilogue

*T*he city lies under its pall of orange light and fog, sheets of white coming up from the bay. It pulses, from the depths of the Tank to the spires of downtown, the financial district to the suburbs. Against the skyline, lines of hovertraffic slide between buildings in patterns almost random enough to practice divination with. You can spend a whole night up here, the curtains pulled back and the bulletproof plasglass dialed to maximum transparency, the entire room dark except for the red eye of the nursery monitor. Each night the sound of human breathing soothes me, a child's deep trustful sleep in a room guarded by two agents.

They take turns at her door.

In our house, a little human girl sleeps. She does not ask, anymore, when her mother is coming back. I know better than to think she's forgotten the question.

She has Eddie's golden curls and Gabe's wide dark eyes, and dimples when she smiles. Oddly enough, it's the demon she likes best; he is endlessly patient with her, willing to spend hours reading brightly colored primary books or playing small games designed to teach her how to control her gifts. Of course, she is a child of psions, and testing at birth returned a Matheson score almost as high as mine.

Her mother's will is explicit; I'm named as guardian and trustee. Gabe, with her inherent precision, reaching from beyond the grave to hold me to my promise. Love and obligation, the net that holds me here, all boiled down to a child's laugh and scattered toys.

Did I break the other promises so I could keep this one?

Do I want to know, if I did?

Tell me what you want, *he says,* and each time I shake my head. I take my sword into the long dimly lit practice room, its wooden floor smelling of workouts and its mirrored wall reflecting a body I no longer have to strain to control. The katas my teacher first taught me unfold, each movement precise and restrained.

Sometimes that control breaks, and the blackness infecting my mind leaks out. It is most often at night, and I will resurface to find myself in his arms, my throat aching with unshed screams and my body tense, stiff and wooden with the strain of holding it back.

If I can't, if it escapes me and I struggle, there is another net to hold me above the abyss. It is the net of a demon's arms, his hand cupping my skull to keep me from battering it to pieces, the grip he keeps on my wrists so I cannot claw my own eyes out.

We do not speak, those nights. I cannot stand the sound of another voice.

There are whispers.

The net of human and financial assets available to demons on earth is strangling in its own blood. The only ones safe from vengeance and chaos are vassals of another demon, one the new Prince does not control. They hear the whispers, and pass them on, safe in their scrupulous neutrality. Kgembe visits each month with a report, and each time he studies me as if I am the answer to a question never asked.

Hell has never been quiet. Lucifer ruled with fear and iron discipline, torture and trickery. Ousting him from his throne was the easy part; now the new Prince must solidify her grip on power. She is young, and there are older and mightier among the Greater Flight. There are also those who might not believe Lucifer is quite dead.

He was, after all, the Prime. The alpha of demonkind, if not the omega.

The whispers are mounting. Magi have never found it so easy to break the walls between our world and Hell. It's a Renascence in their branch of magick, and precious few are looking for a sting in the tail of the gift. Those who question its provenance are told they don't have to participate. Psions are uneasy, and violent attacks on those with Power are at an all-time high.

If it's a chemical reaction, it's nowhere near finished yet. Even the cure for Clormen-13, that great drug blight of our time, hasn't helped. There are new drugs, and rumors of a high better than any drug—a high available, for a price, from new sources. Inhuman sources.

There's one more thing.

The urn sits on the mantelpiece, over the nivron fire I never turn on, in the bedroom where I sit at night and watch the city glow. It's black and wetly lacquered, a beautiful restrained demon artifact. It is full of cinnamon-scented ash.

Japhrimel and I do not speak of it.

The broken places inside my head are healing, slowly. I have not spoken to a god since the moment of spillskin ecstasy when they filled me, denying me, body and soul, from a demon's grasp. I can't call my faith lost, precisely. It's just…quiet.

Dormant. If it ever wakes, I'll light my candles and speak to my god again. I think He, of all creatures, understands.

On the other end of the mantel, set on a twisting stand of glass, a Knife of silken wood and grief hums sleepily to itself. Its point spears toward the urn, and sometimes it quivers a bit, as if sensing…

But that's impossible, isn't it? Lucifer was not Fallen. A Fallen's dormancy doesn't apply to him, does it?

It matters little. The Knife was made to kill demons, no matter how powerful. While we hold it, the weapon guarantees us some safety.

If the new Prince manages to hold Hell, we're safe.

Or are we? Plot, counterplot, lies, and agendas.

If the new Prince doesn't hold Hell in check, what might happen? The walls between their world and ours grow thinner every day. And sometimes, when he thinks I'm not looking, my Fallen's face holds a familiar expression. Listening for a sound I can't hear, ready for a threat I can't imagine.

A Knife, and an urn full of ash. Right now the Knife is insurance, and the urn is…what? A token? A memento?

Tomorrow they might be bargaining chips in a new game. And I have a daughter to keep safe now. A promise I will keep, even if it means playing their games again. I'll be better at it next time.

Much better.

I wait, and watch, and raise my best friend's daughter. Already there's an idea growing in the back of my mind, a little tickle of precognition, a plan I might have to put in play. Whoever occupies the throne of Hell, I hope they have sense enough to leave us alone.

Because if they don't…

…all Hell will break loose.

That's a promise I'll have no trouble keeping.

Glossary

Androgyne: 1. A transsexual, cross-dressing, or androgynous human. 2. (*demon term*) A Greater Flight demon capable of reproduction.

Animone: An accredited psion with the ability to telepathically connect with and heal animals, generally employed as veterinarians.

Anubis et'her ka: Egyptianica term, sometimes used as an expletive; loosely translated, "Anubis protect me/us."

A'nankhimel: (*demon term*) 1. A Fallen demon. 2. A demon who has tied himself to a human mate. *Note: As with all demon words, there are several layers of meaning to this term, depending on context and pronunciation. The meanings, from most common to least, are as follows: descended from a great height, chained, shield, a guttering flame, a fallen statue.*

Awakening, the: The exponential increase in psionic and sorcerous ability, academically defined as from just before the fall of the Republic of Gilead to the culmination of the Parapsychic and Paranormal Species Acts proposed and brokered by the alternately vilified and worshipped Senator Adrien Ferrimen. *Note: After the culmination of the Parapsychic Act, the Awakening was said to have finished and the proportion of psionics to normals in the human population stabilized, though fluctuations occur in seventy-year cycles to this day.*

A'zharak: (*demon term*) 1. Worm. 2. Lasso or noose. 3. A hand fitted into a glove.

Ceremonial: 1. An accredited psion whose talent lies in working with traditional sorcery, accumulating Power and "spending" it in controlled bursts. 2. Ceremonial magick, otherwise known as sorcery instead of the more organic witchery. 3. (*slang*) Any Greater Work of magick.

Clormen-13: (*Slang: Chill, ice, rock, smack, dust*) Addictive alkaloid drug. *Note: Chill is high-profit for the big pharmaceutical companies as well as the Mob, being instantly addictive. Rumors of a cure have surfaced.*

Deadhead: 1. Necromance. 2. Normal human without psionic abilities.

Demon: 1. Any sentient, alien intelligence, either corporeal or noncorporeal, that interacts with humans. 2. Denizen of Hell, of a type often mistaken for gods or Novo Christer evil spirits; actually a sentient nonhuman species with technology, psionic, and magickal ability much exceeding humanity's. 3. (*slang*) A particularly bad physiological addiction.

Evangelicals of Gilead: 1. Messianic Old Christer and Judic cult started by Kochba bar Gilead and led by him until the signing of the Gilead Charter, when power was seized by a cabal of military brass just prior to bar Gilead's assassination. 2. Members of said cult. 3. (*academic*) The followers of bar Gilead before the signing of the Gilead Charter. *See **Republic of Gilead.***

Feeder: 1. A psion who has lost the ability to process ambient Power and depends on "jolts" of vital energy stolen from other human beings, psions, or normals. 2. (*psion slang*) A fair-weather friend.

Flight: A class or social rank of demons. *Note: There are, strictly speaking, three classes of demons: the Low, Lesser, and Greater. Magi most often deal with the higher echelons of the Low Flight and the lower echelons of the Lesser Flight. Greater Flight demons are almost impossible to control and very dangerous.*

Freetown: An autonomous enclave under a charter, neither Hegemony nor Putchkin but often allied to one or the other for economic reasons.

Hedaira: (*demon term, borrowed from Old Graecia*) 1. An endearment. 2. A human woman tied to a Fallen (*A'nankhimel*) demon. *Note: There are several layers of meaning, depending on context and pronunciation. The meanings, from most common to least, are as follows: beloved, companion, vessel, starlight, sweet fruit, small precious trinket, an easily crushed bauble. The most uncommon and complex meaning can be roughly translated as "slave (thing of pleasure) who rules the master."*

Hegemony: One of the two world superpowers, comprising North and South America, Australia and New Zealand, most of Western

Europe, Japan, some of Central Asia, and scattered diplomatic enclaves in China. *Note: After the Seventy Days War, the two superpowers settled into peace and are often said to be one world government with two divisions. Afrike is technically a Hegemony protectorate, but that seems mostly diplomatic convention more than anything else.*

Ka: 1. (*archaic*) Soul or mirrorspirit, separate from the *ba* and the physical soul in Egyptianica. 2. Fate, especially tragic fate that cannot be avoided, destiny. 3. A link between two souls, where each feeds the other's destiny. 4. (*technical*) Terminus stage for Feeder pathology, an externalized hungry consciousness capable of draining vital energy from a normal human in seconds and a psion in less than two minutes.

Kobolding: (*also:* **kobold**) 1. Paranormal species characterized by a troll-like appearance, thick skin, and an affinity to elemental earth magick. 2. A member of the kobolding species.

Left-Hand: Sorcerous discipline utilizing Power derived from "sinister" means, as in bloodletting, animal or human sacrifice, or certain types of drug use (*Left-Hander:* a follower of a Left-Hand path).

Ludder: 1. Member of the conservative Ludder Party. 2. A person opposed to genetic manipulation or the use of psionic talent, or both. 3. (*slang*) Technophobe. 4. (*slang*) hypocrite.

Magi: 1. A psion who has undergone basic training. 2. The class of occult practitioners before the Awakening who held and transmitted basic knowledge about psionic abilities and training techniques. 3. An accredited psion with the training to call demons or harness etheric force from the disturbance created by the magickal methods used to call demons; usually working in Circles or loose affiliations. *Note: The term "Magus" is archaic and hardly ever used. "Magi" has become singular or plural, and neuter gender.*

Master Nichtvren: 1. A Nichtvren who is free of obligation to his or her Maker. 2. A Nichtvren who holds territory.

Mentaflo genius: 1. An individual with a registered intelligence level above "exceptional," generally channeled into Hegemony or Putchkin high-level civil service. 2. A highly intelligent individual. 3. (*slang*) An individual who, while being "book-smart," lacks common sense.

Merican: The trade lingua of the globe and official language of the Hegemony, though other dialects are in common use. 2. (*archaic*)

A Hegemony citizen. 3. (*archaic*) A citizen of the Old Merican region before the Seventy Days War.

Necromance: (*slang:* deadhead) An accredited psion with the ability to bring a soul back from Death to answer questions. *Note: Can also, in certain instances, heal mortal wounds and keep a soul from escaping into Death.*

Nichtvren:(*slang:* suckhead) Altered human dependent on human blood for nourishment. *Note: Older Nichtvren may possibly live off strong emotions, especially those produced by psions. Since they are altered humans, Nichtvren occupy a space between humanity and "other species"; they are defined as members of a Paranormal Species and given citizen's rights under Adrien Ferrimen's groundbreaking legislation after the Awakening.*

Nine Canons: A nine-part alphabet of runes drawn from around the globe and codified during the Awakening to manage psionic and sorcerous power, often used as shortcuts in magickal circles or as quick charms. *Note: The Canons are separate from other branches of magick in that they are accessible sometimes even to normal humans, by virtue of their long use and highly charged nature.*

Novo Christianity: An outgrowth of a Religion of Submission popular from the twelfth century to the latter half of the twenty-first century, before the meteoric rise of the Republic of Gilead and the Seventy Days War. *Note: The death knell of Old Christianity is thought to have been the great Vatican Bank scandal that touched off the revolt leading to the meteoric rise of Kochba bar Gilead, the charismatic leader of the Republic before the Charter. Note: The state religion of the Republic was technically fundamentalist Old Christianity with Judic messianic overtones. Nowadays, NC is declining in popularity and mostly fashionable among a small slice of the Putchkin middle-upper class.*

Power: 1. Vital energy produced by living things: prana, mana, orgone, etc. 2. Sorcerous power accumulated by celibacy, bloodletting, fasting, pain, or meditation. 3. Ambient energy produced by ley lines and geocurrents, a field of energy surrounding the planet. 4. The discipline of raising and channeling vital energy, sorcerous power, or ambient energy. 5. Any form of energy that fuels sorcerous or psionic ability. 6. A paranormal community or paranormal individual who holds territory.

Prime Power: 1. The highest-ranked paranormal Power in a city or territory, capable of negotiating treaties and enforcing order. *Note: usually Nichtvren in most cities and werecain in rural areas.* 2. (*technical*) The source from which all Power derives. 3. (*archaic*) Any nonhuman paranormal being with more than two vassals in the feudal structure of pre-Awakening paranormal society.

Psion: 1. An accredited, trained, or apprentice human with psionic abilities. 2. Any human with psionic abilities.

Putchkin: 1. The official language of the Putchkin Alliance, though other dialects are in common use. 2. A Putchkin Alliance citizen.

Putchkin Alliance: One of the two world superpowers, comprising Russia, most of China (except Freetown Tibet and Singapore), some of Central Asia, Eastern Europe, and the Middle East. *Note: After the Seventy Days War, the two superpowers settled into peace and are often said to be one world government with two divisions.*

Republic of Gilead: Theocratic Old Merican empire based on fundamentalist Novo Christer and Judic messianic principles, lasting from the latter half of the twenty-first century (after the Vatican Bank scandal) to the end of the Seventy Days War. *Note: In the early days, before Kochba bar Gilead's practical assumption of power in the Western Hemisphere, the Evangelicals of Gilead were defined as a cult, not as a Republic. Political infighting in the Republic — and the signing of the Charter with its implicit acceptance of the High Council's sovereignty — brought about both the War and the only tactical nuclear strike of the War (in the Vegas Waste).*

Revised Matheson Score: The index for quantifying an individual's level of psionic ability. *Note: Like the Richter scale, it is exponential; five is the lowest score necessary for a psionic child to receive Hegemony funding and schooling. Forty is the terminus of the scale; anything above forty is defined as "superlative" and the psion is tipped into special Hegemony or Putchkin secret-services training.*

Runewitch: A psion whose secondary or primary talent includes the ability to handle the runes of the Nine Canons with special ease.

Sedayeen: 1. An accredited psion whose talent is healing. 2. (*archaic*)

An old Nichtvren word meaning "blue hand." *Note:* Sedayeen *are incapable of aggression even in self-defense, being allergic to violence and prone to feeling the pain they inflict. This makes them incredible healers, but also incredibly vulnerable.*

Sekhmet sa'es: Egyptianica term, often used as profanity; translated: "Sekhmet stamp it," a request for the Egyptos goddess of destruction to strike some object or thing, much like the antique *"God damn it."*

Seventy Days War: The conflict that brought about the end of the Republic of Gilead and the rise of the Hegemony and Putchkin Alliance.

Sexwitch: (*archaic: tantraiiken*) An accredited psion who works with Power raised from the act of sex; pain also produces an endorphin and energy rush for sexwitches.

Shaman: 1. The most common and catch-all term for a psion who has psionic ability but does not fall into any other specialty, ranging from vaudun Shamans (who traffic with *loa* or *etrigandi*) to generic psions. 2. (*archaic*) A normal human with borderline psionic ability.

Shavarak'itzan beliak: (*demon term*) A demon obscenity, exact meaning obscure.

Sk8: Member of a slicboard tribe.

Skinlin: (*slang:* dirtwitch) An accredited psion whose talent has to do with plants and plant DNA. *Note: Skinlin use their voices, holding sustained tones, wedded to Power to alter plant DNA and structure. Their training makes them susceptible to berserker rages.*

Slagfever: Sickness caused by exposure to chemical-waste cocktails commonly occurring near hover transport depots in less urban areas.

Swanhild: Paranormal species characterized by hollow bones, feathery body hair, poisonous flesh, and passive and pacifistic behavior.

Synth-hash: Legal nonaddictive stimulant and relaxant synthesized from real hash (derivative of opium) and kennabis. *Note: Synth-hash replaced nicotiana leaves (beloved of the Evangelicals of Gilead for the profits reaped by tax on its use) as the smoke of choice in the late twenty-second century.*

Talent: 1. Psionic ability. 2. Magickal ability.

Werecain: (*slang:* 'cain, furboy) Altered human capable of changing to a furred animal form at will. *Note: There are several different subsets, including Lupercal and magewolfen. Normal
humans and even psionic outsiders are generally incapable of
distinguishing between different subsets of 'cain.*

A Few Notes on
Danny Valentine's World

Hopefully, after five books I have earned enough indulgence to provide a few notes. I am at least confident that those uninterested will flip past these pages. After all, who reads these things? *Besides* grammar junkies like me, that is.

I have often been asked about Danny and how she occurred to me. I've answered that question elsewhere. Another source of constant comment and query is Japhrimel and where he came from.

To be honest, he wasn't supposed to be more than a one-book character. Really, in the book I set out to write, he double-crossed Dante and left her holding the bag, infected with a demonic virus. The rest of the series he was pretty much a foil to her humanity, sort of a Mephistopheles.

Then he had to go and fall in love with her, and develop wings. Which just goes to show you can't trust a demon.

I realize now with twenty-twenty hindsight that Japhrimel was actually informed by the legends of the Nephilim, angels who fell in love with human women and fell (supposedly) from grace as a result, fathering huge progeny while also teaching humanity "forbidden" arts such as sorcery, city-building, and medicine. I had heard this legend for years, although my only clear memory of it is in Madeline L'Engle's *Many Waters*. I suppose when you study metaphysics and the occult you can hardly get away from all sorts of odd stuff. I'm only glad Japh didn't take after Cthulu or Aiwass. Or, say, old-school vampires—the type that suck your blood out through your toenails or nostrils.

And people say mythology is *boring*.

I have always been of two minds about legends and myths. One part of me looks for the psychological truth hidden inside. The other—the ravening storyteller, no doubt—likes to play the *what if* game, with lots of sauce. *How can I invert this legend? How can I play with this story? What makes it work? How can I tinker with the engine?*

So Japhrimel dug around in a vast mass of scholarship, research, half-forgotten legends, and references from books devoured since my high school days, and came up with a coat made of whole cloth—demons instead of angels falling, and the consequences of those unions. Many Gnostic and occult traditions hold that nonhuman intelligences taught humanity "forbidden" arts against the will of a God who wanted only slaves, an act of compassion and defiance both sides paid dearly for.

I remember calling Japh a Promethean figure once, and it amused him so much I had trouble getting any actual work out of him for weeks.

Then I killed him, and that might have taught him a lesson if he hadn't known I would be bringing him back. Damn demon.

So Tierce Japhrimel, like every good character, rummaged through the dustheap at the back of my mind and came up with something wonderful, something I took as a writer takes these sorts of things—a gift not to be examined too closely in the heat of creation, for fear of the magic draining away.

Danny's world was another fish entirely. She was very definite about what had happened historically and what was going on now in her world, and had very strong opinions about both. Some things I had often thought about—what would happen if individual spiritual experience was no longer co-opted by "organized" religion, what a relatively clean hover technology would mean for transport of goods and people, what might be the likely ending point of fundamentalism in the twenty-first century—were about what I'd expected. Other things, like the fear of psions and the pop culture and day-to-day government administration of a world six hundred years in the future, were a surprise.

Please note, dear Reader, than I am in no way implying Danny's world is a utopia, dystopia, prognostication, or social commentary. I am fully aware that any imagining of the future says more about the imaginer than the imagined, so to speak. I strove for logic and a historical tone where I could, and had fun where I couldn't. Like, with slicboards. I mean, come on. Flying skateboards? Even after *Back to the Future*'s many reruns, flying skateboards are still *cool*.

However, I like to think that I've read enough history, both for schooling and for fun, to say with some certainty that people throughout the ages are largely the same. The issues that resonate with a regular-Joe type of person in my own time are largely the same issues that would resonate with a regular-Flavius Roman, or a regular Han Chinese. We all worry about those damn kids today and food and shelter, and the approbation of our social set, and where the world is going. We survive, and when we have room left over from survival we create, and we raise our kids and laugh and cry and grieve.

Not too long ago I was in a pediatrician's waiting room. There was a Ukrainian family (at least, I think they were Ukrainian) and a Hispanic family, each chattering away in their respective languages, the kids either playing or sticking close to Mum or Dad or Grandma if they were feeling poorly. I remember a glance of total accord exchanged between two mothers from different continents — a glance I had no trouble deciphering — when one child ran around in a circle making an airplane noise. The slight smile, lifted eyebrows, and rueful love in the expression was universal.

It is that moment I think of when I say the word "history." Often we forget, when studying other cultures or even our own, that people are pretty much the same the world over, with the same basic needs for food, shelter, love, and art. The diversity of cultures does not detract from that one glance shared between mothers — a glance no mommy, from the earliest furry human to whatever cyberpunk age comes next, would ever have trouble translating.

But I digress. Hey, it's an appendix. I suppose I'm allowed.

Danny's world probably says more about me and my own position as a reasonably literate middle-class citizen of America at the turn of the twenty-first century than it does about whatever future will be slouching along toward infinity six hundred years from now. The influences feeding into the world of psions and the Hegemony are many and varied — from a long list of music I've listened to, like Rob Dougan, the Cure, the Eagles, and Beethoven; movies like *Blade Runner* and *Brazil,* not to mention *The Matrix* and *Life of Brian,* and *Kill Bill* where Danny got her katana; books like *From the Ashes of Angels* and *The Devil in Love,* not to mention *The Club Dumas* and LJ Smith's *The Forbidden Game* series; and the history books that are my touchstone and, to some degree, Dante's as well. Her love of the classics springs from my own unrepentant and unabashed love for the same works, books that survive because they touch something deep in the soul. Livy and Shakespeare and Milton and Dumas and Gibbon and Sophocles and...

You realize I couldn't begin to list all the different influences that shaped Danny's world, any more than I could list every influence that shapes my own. Still, I am conscious of them, an underground river feeding whatever well I dredge up stories from. I am neverendingly grateful that I live in an age and a cultural-social position where I have access to a truly stunning array of human knowledge and the leisure time (however harried by deadlines and children and cats) to sample this great buffet largely at my own discretion. I am even more grateful that I am in a position to do the thing I love and was made for, telling stories.

Danny and Japhrimel's story is finished now. I don't know if I'll ever go back to their world. I don't know if I told their story the best way possible, but I told it as best as I know how. I enjoyed every goddamn minute of it. (Even revisions.) I am glad I did it.

Even if Japhrimel pulled a doublecross on me, and even if Dante is a difficult and unlikeable person sometimes, and even if I imagined a world that says more about me and my time than it ever will about the future. I had a Hell of a time.

I can't wait to do it again.

When I do, dear Reader, you're invited to come along. The story is in the sharing, after all. It would be right bloody useless if it wasn't.

The only thing that remains to be said is, thank you for reading. I hope you had a good time.

And flying skateboards are *still* cool.

Acknowledgments

Thanks are due first to Maddy and Nicholas, my darlings. And to the usual suspects: to Miriam Kriss, who never gives up; to Devi Pillai, who won't stop until it's good enough; to the long-suffering Jennifer Flax; to Mel Sterling, the best writing partner ever; to Sixten Zeiss, for love and coffee; to Christa Hickey, with simple love. Last but not least, I thank you, dear Reader. Without you, this would not be.

extras

orbit

meet the author

Amanda Hupp

LILITH SAINTCROW was born in New Mexico, bounced around the world as an Air Force brat, and fell in love with writing when she was ten years old. She currently lives in Vancouver, Washington. Find out more about the author at www.lilithsaintcrow.com.

introducing

If you enjoyed
DANTE VALENTINE,
look out for

NIGHT SHIFT

Book 1 of the Jill Kismet series

by Lilith Saintcrow

Sit. There."

A wooden chair in the middle of a flat expanse of hardwood floor, lonely under cold fluorescent light.

I lowered myself gingerly, curled my fingers over the ends of the armrests, and commended my soul to God.

Well, maybe not actually commended. Maybe I was just praying really, really hard.

He circled the chair, every step just heavy enough to make a noise against bare floorboards. My weapons and my coat were piled by the door, and even the single knife I'd kept, safe in its sheath strapped to my thigh, was no insurance. I was locked in a room with a hungry tiger who stepped, stepped, turning just a little each time.

I didn't shift my weight.

Instead, I stared across the room, letting my eyes unfocus. Not enough to wall myself up inside my head—that was a death sentence. A hunter is always alert, Mikhail says. Always. Any inattention is an invitation to Death.

And Death loves invitations.

The hellbreed became a shadow each time he passed in front of me, counterclockwise, and I was beginning to wonder if he was going to back out of the bargain or welsh on the deal. Which was, of course, what he wanted me to wonder.

Careful, Jill. Don't let him throw you. I swallowed, wished I hadn't; the briefest pause in his even tread gave me the idea that he'd seen the betraying little movement in my throat.

I do not like the idea of hellbreed staring at my neck.

Silver charms tied in my hair clinked as blessed metal reacted to the sludge of hellbreed filling the ether. This one was bland, not beautiful like the other damned. He was unassuming, slim and weak-looking.

But he scared my teacher. Terrified him, in fact.

Only an idiot isn't scared of hellbreed. There's no shame in it. You've got to get over being ashamed of being scared, because it will slow you down. You can't afford that.

"*So.*"

I almost jumped when his breath caressed my ear. Hot, meaty breath, far too humid to be human. He was breathing on me, and my flesh crawled in concentric waves of revulsion. Gooseflesh rose up hard and pebbled, scales of fear spreading over my skin.

"*Here's the deal.*" *The words pressed obscenely warm against my naked skin. Something brushed my hair, delicately, and silver crackled with blue sparks. A hiss touched my ear, the skin suddenly far too damp.*

I wasn't sweating. It was his breath condensing on me.

Oh, God. I almost choked on bile. Swallowed it and held still, every muscle in my body screaming at me to move, to get away.

"*I'm going to mark you, my dear. While you carry that mark, you'll have a gateway embedded in your flesh. Through that conduit, you're going to draw sorcerous energy, and lots of it. It will make you strong, and fast—stronger and faster than any of your fellow hunters. You'll have an edge in raw power when it comes to sorcery, even that weak-kneed trash you monkeys flatter yourself by calling magic."*

The hellbreed paused. Cold air hit my wet ear. A single drop of condensation trickled down the outer shell of cartilage, grew fat, and tickled unbearably as it traced a dead flabby finger down to the hollow where ear meets neck, a tender, vulnerable spot.

"I'll also go so far as to help you keep this city free of those who might interfere with the general peace. Peace is good for profit, you know."

A soft, rumbling chuckle brushed against my cheek, with its cargo of sponge-rotten breath.

I kept my fucking mouth shut. "Stay silent until he offers all he's going to offer, milaya." Mikhail's advice, good advice. I was trained, wasn't I? At least, mostly trained. A hunter in my own right, and this was my chance to become . . . what?

Even better. It was a golden opportunity, and if he thought I should take it, I would. And I wouldn't screw it up.

I would not let my teacher down.

So stay quiet, Jill. Stay calm.

I kept breathing softly through my mouth; the air reeked of hellbreed and corruption. Tasting that scent was bad, as bad as breathing it through my nose.

I just couldn't figure out which was worse.

Something hard, rasping like a cat's tongue, flicked forward and touched the hollow behind my ear, pressing past a few stray strands of hair. If I hadn't been so fucking determined to stay still, muscles locked up tighter than Val's old cashbox, I might have flinched.

Then I probably would have died.

But the touch retreated so quickly I wasn't sure I'd felt it. Except that little drop of condensation was gone, wasn't it?

Shit. I was now sweating too bad to tell.

The hellbreed laughed again. "Very good, little hunter. The bargain goes thus: you bear my mark and use the power it provides as you see fit. Once a month you'll come visit, and you'll spend time with me. That's all—a little bit of time each month. For superlative use of the power I grant you, you might have to spend a little more time. Say, five or six hours?"

Now it was negotiation time. I wet my lips with my tongue, wished I hadn't because I suddenly knew his eyes had fastened on my mouth. "Half an hour. Maximum."

Bargaining on streetcorners taught me that much, at least— you never take the john's first offer, and you never, ever, ever start out with more than half of what you're willing to give.

Sometimes you can pick who buys you, and for how much.

That's what power really is.

"You wound me." The hellbreed didn't sound wounded. He sounded delighted, his bland tenor probing at my ear. "Three hours. See how generous I am, for you?"

This is too easy. Be careful. *"An hour a month, maximum of two, and your help on my cases. Final offer, hellbreed, or I walk. I didn't come here to be jacked around."*

Why had I come here? Because Mikhail said I should.

I wondered if it was another test I'd failed, or passed. I wondered if I'd just overstepped and was looking at a nasty death. Bargaining with hellbreed is tricky; hunters usually just kill them. But this wasn't so simple. This was either a really good idea or a really bad way to die.

A long thunderous moment of quiet, and the room trembled

like a soap bubble. Something like masses of gigantic flies on a mound of corpses buzzed, rattling.

Helletöng. The language of the damned. It lay under the skin of the visible like fat under skin, dimpling the surface tension of what we try to call the real world.

"Done, little hunter. We have a bargain. If you agree."

My throat was like the Sahara, dry and scratchy. A cough caught out in the open turned into a painful, ratcheting laugh. "What do you get out of this, Perry?"

That scaly, dry, probing thing flicked along my skin again, rasped for the briefest second against the side of my throat, just a fraction of an inch away from where the pulse beat frantically. I sucked at keeping my heartrate down, Mikhail warned and warned me about it—

"Sometimes we like being on the side of the angels." The hellbreed's voice dropped to a whisper that would have been intimate if the rumbling of Hell hadn't been scraping along underneath. "It makes the ending sweeter. Besides, peace is good for profit. Do we have a deal, little hunter?"

Christ. Mikhail, I hope you're right. *I didn't agree to it because of the hellbreed or even because the thought of that much power was tempting.*

I agreed because Mikhail told me I should, even though it was my decision. It wasn't really a Trader's bargain if I was doing it for my teacher, was it?

Was it?

"We have a deal." Four little words. They came out naturally, smoothly, without a hitch.

Hot iron-hard fingers clamped over my right wrist. "Oh, good." A slight wet smacking sound, like a hungry toddler at the breakfast table, and he wrenched my hand off the arm of the chair, the pale tender underside of my wrist turned up to face cold fluorescent light. My heart jackhammered away, adrenaline soaking copper into the dry roof of my mouth, and I bit back a cry.

It was too late. Four tiny words, and I'd just signed a contract.

Now we'd see if Mikhail was right, and I still had my soul.

CHAPTER 1

Every city has a pulse. It's just a matter of knowing where to rest your finger to find it, throbbing away as the sun bleeds out of the sky and night rises to cloak every sin.

I crouched on the edge of a rooftop, the counterweight of my heavy leather coat hanging behind me. Settled into absolute stillness, waiting. The baking wind off the cooling desert mouthed the edges of my body. The scar on my right wrist was hot and hard under a wide hinged copper bracelet molded to my skin.

The copper was corroding, blooming green and wearing thin.

I was going to have to find a different way to cover the scar up soon. Trouble is, I suck at making jewelry, and Galina was out of blessed copper cuffs until her next shipment from Nepal.

Below me the alley wandered, thick and rank. Here at the edge of the barrio there were plenty of hiding places for the dark things that crawl once dusk falls. The Weres don't patrol out this far, having plenty to keep them occupied inside their own crazy-quilt of streets and alleys around the Plaza Centro and its spreading tenements. Here on the fringes, between a new hunter's territory and the streets the Weres kept from boiling over, a few hellbreed thought they could break the rules.

extras

Not in my town, buckos. If you think Kismet's a pushover because she's only been on her own for six months, you've got another think coming.

My right leg cramped, a sudden vicious swipe of pain. I ignored it. My electrolyte balance was all messed up from going for three days without rest, from one deadly night-battle to the next with the fun of exorcisms in between. I wondered if Mikhail had ever felt this exhaustion, this ache so deep even bones felt tired.

It hurt to think of Mikhail. My hand tightened on the bull-whip's handle, leather creaking under my fingers. The scar tingled again, a knot of corruption on the inside of my wrist.

Easy, milaya. *No use in making noise, eh? It is soft and quiet that catches mouse.* As if he was right next to me, barely mouthing the words, his gray eyes glittering winter-sharp under a shock of white hair. Hunters don't live to get too old, but Mikhail Ilych Tolstoi had been an exception in so many ways. I could almost see his ghost crouching silent next to me, peering at the alley over the bridge of his patrician nose.

Of course he wasn't there. He'd been cremated, just like he wanted. I'd held the torch myself, and the Weres had let me touch it to the wood before singing their own fire into being. A warrior's spirit rose in smoke, and wherever my teacher was, it wasn't here.

Which I found more comforting than you'd think, since if he'd come back I'd have to kill him. Just part of the job.

My fingers eased. I waited.

The smell of hellbreed and the brackish contamination of an *arkeus* lay over this alley. Some nasty things had been sidling out of this section of the city lately, nasty enough to give even a Hell-tainted hunter a run for her money. We have firepower and sorcery, we who police the nightside, but Traders and hellbreed are spooky-quick and capable of taking a hell of a lot of damage.

Get it? A Hell of a lot of damage? Arf arf.

Not to mention the scurf with their contagion, the adepts of the Middle Way with their goddamn Chaos, and the Sorrows worshipping the Elder Gods.

The thought of the Sorrows made rage rise under my breast-bone, fresh and wine-dark. I inhaled smoothly, dispelling it. Clear, calm, and cold was the way to go about this.

Movement below. Quick and scuttling, like a rat skittering from one pile of garbage to the next. I didn't move, I didn't blink, I barely even *breathed*.

The *arkeus* took shape, rising like a fume from dry-scorched pavement, trash riffling as the wind of its coalescing touched ragged edges and putrid rotting things. Tall, hooded, translucent where moonlight struck it and smoky-solid elsewhere, one of Hell's roaming corruptors stretched its long clawed arms and slid fully into the world. It drew in a deep satisfied sigh, and I heard something else.

Footsteps.

Someone was coming to keep an appointment.

Isn't that a coincidence. So am I.

My heartbeat didn't quicken; it stayed soft, even, as almost-nonexistent as my breathing. It had taken me a long time to get my pulse mostly under control.

The next few moments were critical. You can't jump too soon on something like this. *Arkeus* aren't your garden-variety hellbreed. You have to wait until they solidify enough to talk to their victims—otherwise you'll be fighting empty air with sorcery, and that's no fun—and you have to know what a Trader is bargaining for before you go barging in to distribute justice or whup-ass. Usually both, liberally.

The carved chunk of ruby on its silver chain warmed, my tiger's-eye rosary warming too, the blessing on both items reacting with contamination rising from the *arkeus* and its lair.

A man edged down the alley, clutching something to his chest. The *arkeus* made a thin greedy sound, and my smart left eye — the blue one, the one that can look *below* the surface of the world — saw a sudden tensing of the strings of contamination following it. It was a hunched, thin figure that would have been taller than me except for the hump on its back; its spectral robes brushing dirt and refuse, taking strength from filth.

Bingo. The *arkeus* was now solid enough to hit.

The man halted. I couldn't see much beyond the fact that he was obviously human, his aura slightly tainted from his traffic with an escaped denizen of Hell.

It was official. The man was a Trader, bargaining with Hell. Whatever he was bargaining *for,* it wasn't going to do him any good.

Not with me around.

The *arkeus* spoke. *"You have brought it?"* A lipless cold voice, eager and thin, like a dying cricket. A razorblade pressed against the wrist, a thin line of red on pale skin, the frozen-blue face of a suicide.

I moved. Boots soundless against the parapet, the carved chunk of ruby resting against the hollow of my throat, even my coat silent. The silver charms braided into my long dark hair didn't tinkle. The first thing a hunter's apprentice learns is to move quietly, to draw silence in tight like a cloak.

That is, if the apprentice wants to survive.

"I b-brought it." The man's speech was the slow slur of a dreamer who senses a cold-current nightmare. He was in deep, having already given the *arkeus* a foothold by making some agreement or another with it. "You'd better not —"

"Peace." The *arkeus*'s hiss froze me in place for a moment as the hump on its back twitched. *"You will have your desire, never fear. Give it to me."*

The man's arms relaxed, and a small sound lifted from the bundle he carried. My heart slammed into overtime against my ribs.

Every human being knows the sound of a baby's cry.

Bile filled my throat. My boots ground against the edge of the parapet as I launched out into space, the *arkeus* flinching and hissing as my aura suddenly flamed, tearing through the ether like a star. The silver in my hair shot sparks, and the ruby at my throat turned hot. The scar on my right wrist turned to lava, burrowing in toward the bone, my whip uncoiled and struck forward, its metal flechettes snapping at the speed of sound, cracking as I pulled on etheric force to add a psychic strike to the physical.

My boots hit slick refuse-grimed concrete and I pitched forward, the whip striking again across the *arkeus*'s face. The hell-thing howled, and my other hand was full of the Glock, the sharp stink of cordite blooming as silver-coated bullets chewed through the thing's physical shell. Hollowpoints do a lot of damage once a hellbreed's initial shell is breached.

It's a pity 'breed heal so quickly.

We don't know why silver works—something to do with the Moon, and how she controls the tides of sorcery and water. No hunter cares, either. It's enough that it levels the playing field a little.

The *arkeus* moved, scuttling to the side as the man screamed, a high whitenoise-burst of fear. The whip coiled, my hip moving first as usual—the hip leads with whip-work as well as stave fighting. My whip-work had suffered until Mikhail made me take bellydancing classes.

Don't think, Jill. Move. I flung out my arm, etheric force spilling through my fingers, and the whip slashed again, each flechette tearing through already-lacerated flesh. It howled again, and the copper bracelet broke, tinkled sweetly on the concrete as I pivoted, firing down into the hell-thing's face. It twitched, and I heard my own voice chanting in gutter Latin, a version of Saint Anthony's prayer Mikhail had made me learn.

Protect me from the hordes of Hell, O Lord, for I am pure of heart and trust Your mercy—and the bullets don't hurt, either.

The *arkeus* screamed, writhing, and cold air hit the scar. I was too drenched with adrenaline to feel the usual curl of fire low in my belly, but the sudden sensitivity of my skin and hearing slammed into me. I dropped the whip and fired again with the gun in my left, then fell to my knees, driving down with psychic and physical force.

My fist met the hell-thing's lean malformed face, which exploded. It shredded, runnels of foulness bursting through its skin, and the sudden cloying reek would have torn my dinner loose from my stomach moorings if I'd eaten anything.

Christ, I wish it didn't stink so bad. But stink means dead, and if this thing's dead it's one less fucking problem for me to deal with.

No time. I gained my feet, shaking my right fist. Gobbets of preternatural flesh whipped loose, splatting dully against the brick walls. I uncoiled, leaping for the front of the alley.

The Trader was only human, and he hadn't made his big deal yet. He was tainted by the *arkeus*'s will, but he wasn't given superstrength or near-invulnerability yet.

The only enhanced human being left in the alley was me. Thank God.

I dug my fingers into his shoulder and set my feet, yanking him back. The baby howled, emptying its tiny lungs, and I caught it on its way down, my arm tightening maybe a little too much to yank it against my chest. I tried to avoid smacking it with a knife-hilt.

extras

I backhanded the man with my hellbreed-strong right fist. *Goddamn it. What am I going to do now?*

The baby was too small, wrapped in a bulky blue blanket that smelled of cigarette smoke and grease. I held it awkwardly in one arm while I contemplated the sobbing heap of sorry manflesh crumpled against a pile of garbage.

I've cuffed plenty of Traders one-handed, but never while holding a squirming, bellowing bundle of little human that smelled not-too-fresh. Still, it was a cleaner reek than the *arkeus's* rot. I tested the cuffs, yanked the man over, and checked his eyes. Yep. The flat shine of the dust glittered in his irises. He was a thin, dark-haired man with the ghost of childhood acne still hanging on his cheeks, saliva glittering wetly on his chin.

I found his ID in his wallet, awkwardly holding the tiny yelling thing in the crook of my arm. *Jesus. Mikhail never trained me for this.* "Andy Hughes. You are *under arrest.* You have the right to be exorcised. Anything you say will, of course, be ignored, since you've forfeited your rights to a trial of your peers by trafficking with Hell." I took a deep breath. "And you should thank your lucky stars I'm not in a mood to kill anyone else tonight. Who does the baby belong to?"

He was still gibbering with fear, and the baby howled. I could get nothing coherent out of either of them.

Then, to complete the deal, the pager went off against my hip, vibrating silently in its padded pocket.

Great.